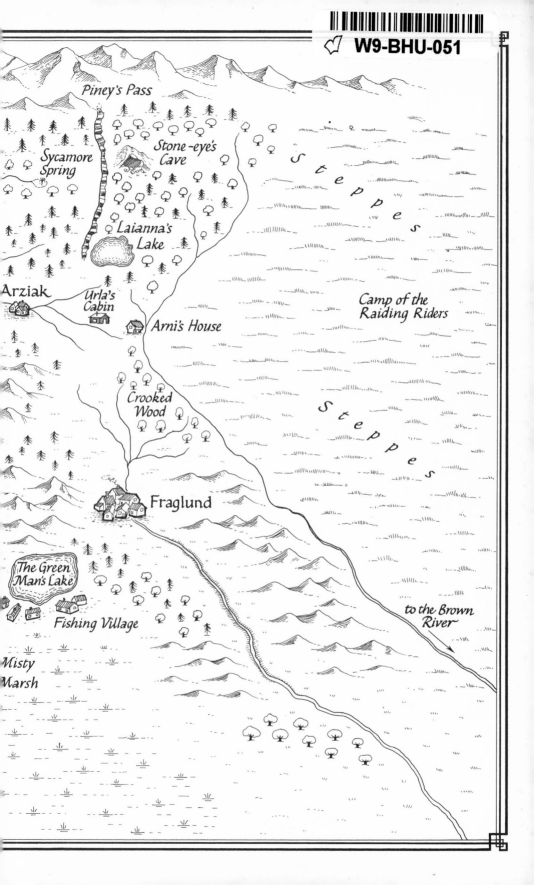

Hans Bemmann

The Stone and the Flute

TRANSLATED FROM GERMAN BY
ANTHEA BELL

VIKING

VIKING
Penguin Books Ltd, Harmondsworth,
Middlesex, England
Viking Penguin Inc., 40 West 23rd Street,
New York, New York 10010, U.S.A.
Penguin Books Australia Ltd, Ringwood,
Victoria, Australia
Penguin Books Canada Limited, 2801 John Street,
Markham, Ontario, Canada L3R 1B4
Penguin Books (N.Z.) Ltd, 182–190 Wairau Road,
Auckland 10, New Zealand

The Stone and the Flute was first published in
German under the title *Stein und Floete* by
K. Thienemanns Verlag, Stuttgart

This translation first published by Viking, 1986

Copyright © Edition Weitbrecht in
K. Thienemanns Verlag, Stuttgart, 1983
Translation copyright © Anthea Bell, 1986

Typeset in Monophoto Baskerville
Printed in the United States of America by
R. R. Donnelley & Sons Company, Harrisonburg, Virginia

British Library Cataloguing in Publication Data
Bemmann, Hans
The stone and the flute.
I. Title
823'.914[F]   PR6052.E44
ISBN 0 670 80186 0

*Library of Congress Catalog Card Number
86-040190*

(Library of Congress CIP data available)

Contents

Book One

which tells
how Listener comes by a strange stone,
and in looking for its secret
falls into the power of lovely, blue-eyed Gisa.
Here he is led astray, and commits a crime
that can never be undone
even by his penance of three years' hard journeying
as servant to a wandering minstrel.
Yet as he travels
he hears many tales
and learns the art
of listening.

Once upon a time a boy was born in Fraglund, and this is his strange story. His father was a mighty man whom folk called the Great Roarer: he was tall and burly, and liked to wear his shirt open on his hairy chest. His was a tempestuous nature. One moment he would fly into a terrible rage, the next he would be shaking with loud laughter. Yet he was known for a just man, and so the people of Fraglund had asked him to come from far away and be judge over them in that part of the country.

Now when the Great Roarer came to Fraglund to take up his duties, he brought his wife with him, a quiet woman who kept so much out of the public eye that at first many thought she was not wedded to him. She was said to be the daughter of the Gentle Fluter, of whose arts they had heard in Fraglund, although he lived very far away, beyond the great forests of Barlebogue. Folk said his fluting was so sweet that even the birds would fall still to hear him, and so soothing to the spirit that many a man's quarrel had been settled by the notes of his flute alone.

When the Great Roarer had been judge in Fraglund for a year, his wife bore him that son whose tale is told here. She had been in labour all night, and it was nearly morning before the midwife called her husband into her room and showed him the baby, naked as it was.

'Anyone can see he's your son,' said she, for the child's whole body was covered with a furry down.

'Hm,' said the Great Roarer in his booming voice, and he took his son in his arms. 'Can they, indeed? Why isn't he roaring, then?'

'That's strange,' said the midwife. 'I kept thinking there was something missing, and now you mention it, I know what. He doesn't roar! Why, just look at him – you'd say he was listening!'

'A baby ought to roar,' said the child's father, baffled.

'Ah, let him be!' said the midwife. 'A roaring infant can't hear so well – let the child listen!'

'So be it,' said the Great Roarer. 'And we'll call him Listener.' He handed the baby back to the midwife, seeming a little disappointed in a son who might be hairy, like himself, but wouldn't roar in his own fashion.

'That's a quiet baby you've had,' said the Great Roarer to his wife, when he had thanked her for bearing him his son.

'I dare say he takes after my father,' said she.

However, the Great Roarer was a just man, and over the next few years he always spoke gently to his son, even learning, in time, how to lower his mighty voice, for it turned out that Listener could not understand words unless they were spoken softly, and roaring confused him. This was particularly noticeable when he witnessed any quarrel or argument, and there were plenty of those in his father's house, since the Great Roarer was judge in Fraglund. The louder the speakers raised their voices in dispute, the more helplessly Listener looked at them, and when they started shouting at each other he would run away in alarm. As a small child, he probably took his father for a powerful magician, able to outroar the contestants with his great voice and make them fall silent.

So Listener grew up in his father's house, and nothing of note happened until he was seventeen years old. But then the Raiding Riders came out of the east, and fell upon the countryside, plundering and burning. The Great Roarer summoned all the men in Fraglund able to bear arms to march out against the Riders. That same day, he took Listener into his armoury and told him to choose a sword.

'But I don't want a sword,' said Listener, in his quiet voice.

'What, would you rather stay at home with the women and toothless old men?' asked the Great Roarer, unable to hide his contempt for such cowardice.

'No,' said Listener. 'I'll come with the rest of you. But wounding folk isn't in my line. Let me care for the wounded instead.'

The Great Roarer thought poorly of this proposal, coming from a healthy young man, but as nothing would induce Listener to carry arms, he let the boy have his way in the end.

So Listener set out with the other men of Fraglund to meet the Raiding Riders. When they had been on the march for three days, their scouts brought back news of an advance party of the enemy. The Great Roarer decided to lie in wait for the horde of Riders in a wooded ravine, through which they must pass if they meant to advance on Fraglund. He placed archers in an ambush, and when the Riders were well in among them the men of Fraglund shot several out of their saddles. But the Raiding Riders were good archers too, so that some of the Fraglunders had fallen when the Riders galloped headlong away and the Great Roarer gave the signal for his troops to rally.

'Very well, your turn now,' he told Listener. 'Search the bushes for our wounded!'

Listener went into the undergrowth, and found three dead Fraglund men lying among the brushwood. Then he came upon a wounded Rider, lying at the foot of an oak tree with an arrow in his breast. He was an old man. His lank grey hair was plaited into two braids that hung over his shoulders, and he had thin, sparse whiskers on his chin and upper lip. When Listener tried to pull the arrow out of the wound, the old man opened his eyes, shaking his head.

Listener himself could see there was no helping the man now. He took his water bottle from his belt and put it to the old man's lips. When he had drunk from it, the old man looked him in the face. 'Why, you are one of the Great Roarer's folk,' said he.

'I'm his son,' said Listener.

'Then why are you tending a dying Rider shot from his horse by your own friends?' asked the man.

'I came along to care for the wounded,' said Listener. 'It makes no difference to me which side they're on.'

'A strange sort of son for the Great Roarer,' said the old man.

'I'm supposed to be more like my grandfather,' said Listener.

'And who is he?' asked the old man.

'You wouldn't know him. He is called the Gentle Fluter.'

'Ah, but I did hear the sound of his flute, many years ago,' said the man. 'I am old, and have seen and heard much, but that is no good to me now. Perhaps I should have stayed beside him. Tell him I said so, when next you see him.'

'I've never met him myself,' said Listener, 'but if ever I do, I'll tell him. Who shall I say you are?'

'Give him greetings from Arni of the Stone,' said the old man. He began rummaging in a leather bag that hung at his belt, and brought out a smooth, round stone. For a while he held it in his hand, and as he gazed at it, the deep folds around his mouth smoothed out as if he were suddenly free of pain, his features began to relax, and Listener saw, to his amazement, that the dying man seemed cheerful, even merry. His eyes were a young man's eyes when he looked up at Listener again, offering him the stone.

'Take this,' he said, 'by way of thanks, because you did not leave me to die alone in the bushes.'

Listener took the stone, and examined it. It was worn smooth as a pebble in a brook, almost translucent, shimmering with dark shades of green and blue and violet. When he held it up to the light, he saw that the colours in the stone formed a ring of rays, like the iris of an eye.

The old man was dying now. He opened his eyes once more, and murmured something. Bending down, Listener heard the dying man whisper:

> *Seek the light*
> *where the glow may fall;*
> *you have not sought aright,*
> *if you don't find it all.*

'Seek what, exactly?' asked Listener. 'What am I to find?'

'You'll see, you will see,' murmured the old man. 'Keep the eye-stone well. But never forget that that is far from all.'

And then he died.

What happened next is of no significance to this story, and not worth the telling for its own sake. Matters are always much the same when men go killing each other. Suffice it to say that the Great Roarer succeeded in beating off the Raiding Riders, and he and his men – rather fewer of them than before, to be sure – returned to Fraglund and were soon going about their usual business again, in so far as missing limbs did not hinder them.

But since the day when the dying Rider gave him the eye-stone, Listener had lived in a state of dreamlike confusion, and even when he got home he could not wake from that dream properly. He wandered aimlessly around the roads, or sat on the chopping block outside his father's house, staring into space. Now and then he took the stone out of his pocket and looked at it. He felt as if some kind of comfort flowed from that smooth, cool stone. And then he would remember what the old man had said to him before he died.

One day Listener went to his father, and said, 'Give me a horse, and some food for the journey. I am going to ride to the land beyond the forests of Barlebogue to look for my grandfather.'

'I was rather thinking of training you to succeed me here,' said the Great Roarer, lowering his voice as he now habitually did when speaking to his son.

'I don't know that I'd be much good as a judge,' said Listener. 'I am no roarer, I can't stand quarrels, and I'd have to listen to a great many of them before I could bring myself to raise my voice.'

'Ah, well, I see you really do take after the Gentle Fluter,' said his father. 'Very well, go and look for him. I'll give you a horse and whatever you need for the journey.'

So next morning Listener saddled his horse and packed food in his coat pockets. He had made a little leather bag to hold the eye-stone, and wore it on a string around his neck. When he said goodbye to his parents, his mother told him, 'Keep riding westwards through the forests of Barlebogue, and let nothing detain you there. Many a man has gone into those woods and never come back again. And listen for the sound of the flute. When you hear a tune that brings tears to your eyes, the Gentle Fluter is not far off. Tell him his daughter sends her love.' Then she kissed her son, and Listener rode away, going west and making straight for the forests of Barlebogue.

On the first day he came to the edge of the forest. He tied his horse to a tree, lit a fire, and ate some of his food. Then he took the eye-stone out of its bag and let its colours play in the light of the setting sun. A blackbird, sitting in the tree above him, was singing its evening song. It sounded so sweet that Listener wondered if the Gentle Fluter himself were nearby. But no, that could not be: for one thing, the vast forests of Barlebogue still lay between him and his grandfather, and for another his eyes were dry. He looked up into the tree, and saw the blackbird sitting on a branch directly overhead. It had fallen silent, and was eyeing the stone, which Listener still had in his hand.

'You like this sparkling thing, do you?' said he. As if it had understood him, the blackbird flew down from its branch and perched on Listener's shoulder. He crumbled a piece of bread with his other hand and offered the blackbird the crumbs. It hopped down on his hand and pecked up the food.

'I seem to have found a friend,' said Listener. The bird looked at him with its shiny black eyes and whistled three notes, as if confirming what he said. Then it flew back to its branch and settled there to sleep. Listener himself took his blanket off the horse and lay down by the embers of his fire.

Next morning he rode into the forest. He had found a narrow path that seemed to lead westwards, and he followed it for seven days. It was a good path at first. He rode through ancient beech woods. The smooth, silvery grey trunks of the trees rose like gigantic columns, bearing a thick canopy of foliage that let only a green twilight through. The forest floor here was covered with old brown leaves, and clear of any undergrowth.

Later, the trunks of the trees grew closer together, branches reached across the path, and Listener had to take care he did not get knocked off his horse unawares. The path grew narrower and narrower, and finally became an almost invisible track winding its way through thick brushwood. In the end Listener had to dismount and lead his horse by the bridle. Brambles kept tearing at his clothes; he had to clamber over fallen tree trunks and avoid quagmires where bulrushes and horsetail grass grew as tall as a man.

On the evening of the seventh day, shabby and travel-stained, he stumbled upon a clearing that opened out unexpectedly beyond a barrier of brushwood. He decided to spend the night there. When he had seen to his horse, he lit a fire and ate the last of his food. Then he took the eye-stone out of its bag again and looked at it. But whether it was that the sun stood too low in the sky, or that the shadow of the forest cast a shade over it, the colours of the stone remained hidden beneath its smooth surface. All he saw was an ordinary kind of round pebble such as you might pick out of a brook.

'That's a pretty toy you have there,' said a voice behind him.

Listener turned quickly, and saw a woman leaning against a tree. He thought the woman wonderfully beautiful. She was gazing at him with a pair of dark blue eyes which had such power over him that he found it hard to look away from them.

'Your eyes are lovelier,' he said, and when he looked back at his stone it did indeed seem dull and lifeless, compared to this woman's eyes.

'Did the stone bring you here?' the woman asked.

Listener looked at her in surprise. Could it be so? Why had he come here, anyway? He could no longer tell. What was it the old Rider had whispered? *Seek the light where the glow may fall* . . . was this what he was meant to seek and find?

'I don't know,' he said. 'Perhaps this stone did lead me here.'

'Do you prospect for stones?' asked the woman. 'If so, you've come to the right place. I will show you stones more beautiful than any you ever saw in your life. What is your name?'

'I am called Listener, and I'm the son of the Great Roarer.'

'The judge in Fraglund? Then you have a mighty man for your father.'

'I have indeed,' said Listener. 'And who are you?'

'I am Gisa, the mistress of Barlebogue,' said the woman. 'And if your horse is not too tired to carry you a little way farther, you need not sleep on dead leaves and moss tonight.'

Listener put out his fire, loaded up his horse and led it by the halter as he crossed the clearing beside Gisa. They rounded a wooded thicket jutting out over their way, and then Listener saw the mistress of Barlebogue's castle lying ahead. The clearing opened out here into a deep valley with a hill in the middle of it, and the castle rose upon this hill. It was crowned with turrets and battlements, its dark walls were made of blocks of black basalt, and its mighty shape dominated the countryside around. Gisa had tied her horse to a tree here on the edge of the forest. She unhitched it and swung herself into the saddle without allowing Listener to help her. He mounted too, and rode through the valley and up the steep path to the castle beside her. When she came to the gateway, a drawbridge was let down on rattling chains. They rode over the drawbridge and through a dark entrance that led to the inner courtyard. Servants came hurrying up, took Listener's horse and baggage from him, and Gisa told them to prepare a bath and fresh clothes for her guest.

Soon Listener was sitting opposite Gisa at a table in the great hall, while servants brought in a meal of freshly caught fish, game, and heavy, golden wine to drink.

'You lack for nothing here!' said Listener, leaning back when he had eaten and drunk his fill.

'No,' said Gisa. 'I am mistress of this castle, and all around it is mine as far as the eye can see.'

'Yours alone?' asked Listener.

'Mine alone – but that could change.' And as she spoke she looked at Listener again, turning on him those compelling eyes that made him forget all that had gone before.

'What do you mean?' he asked.

'I mean I might share the rule of this domain with you, if you show yourself fit for it. Would you care for that?'

Listener looked into her eyes, and now he knew that she must have been what he was seeking when he set out on his way.

'I'll try,' said he, 'for it seems to me well worth the effort.'

'Then tell the servants to take the dishes away.'

Listener hesitated. 'Will they obey me?' he said.

'That's no question to ask if you mean to give orders!' replied Gisa impatiently. 'Go on, tell them!'

Listener looked at the servants who stood waiting by the wall. 'Come and clear the dishes away,' he said, in his soft voice. The servants looked uncertainly at their mistress, and Gisa laughed. 'You must

speak a little louder!' she said. Then she turned to the servants, and
told them brusquely, 'Didn't you hear your orders? Do as he said!
From now on you are to obey his orders as if they were mine.'

At this the servants came hurrying up and made haste to clear the
table. 'Now, come with me,' said Gisa, rising to her feet. 'You have a
lot to learn yet. I will show you what pleasure there is in being lord of
Barlebogue!' She led him into a bedchamber, and without delay took
off her clothes. When Listener saw her there, naked before him, he
thought he had never seen anything so alluring in his life. He gazed at
her, spellbound, until Gisa's own laughter brought him back to his
senses. 'Am I the first woman you've seen like this?' she asked. 'Or are
you ashamed to stand naked before me?'

Listener knew that both were true, but he was not going to admit it.
Hands flying, he undid the hooks and buttons of his clothing, and soon
was wearing nothing but the little leather bag with the eye-stone in it.

'Take that off too,' said Gisa. 'We want nothing but our skin between
us.'

So Listener pulled the string over his head and dropped the bag on
the floor where his clothes lay.

'Well, you're hairy as a real man,' said Gisa, laughing, 'so come here
and let me make a man of you.'

So on the first night he spent in the castle, Listener lay in the arms of
the lady of Barlebogue, and slept with her till morning.

When he was getting dressed next day, he could not find the bag
with the eye-stone.

'Are you looking for something?' asked Gisa.

'Yes,' said Listener. 'Do you know where that little bag is? The one I
was wearing round my neck?'

'That worthless thing? Oh, the servants will have cleared it away,'
said Gisa, carelessly. 'Come with me, and I'll show you much finer
stones.'

Listener was sorry to have lost his stone, but he forgot his regret
when he looked into Gisa's eyes. Was this the light and the glow he had
been seeking? Or had the colours of the eye-stone been different after
all?

'Stop dreaming and come with me!' said Gisa, impatiently. So he
shook off his thoughts and followed her out to the courtyard where the
horses stood.

They rode to the river that broke out of a rocky ravine at the far end
of the valley. It shot along between steep banks, a headlong torrent

like a mountain stream, until it reached the middle of the valley, and then poured out, below the castle, into an almost circular pool where the foaming water whirled and eddied. Gisa reined in her horse here. A group of sunburnt, naked men were busy diving into the strong current to fetch something up from the bottom.

'What are they doing?' asked Listener.

'You will soon see,' said Gisa. She dismounted and went over to a man who was obviously the divers' overseer. He wore a shaggy wolfskin, and he looked at his mistress with devotion that reminded Listener of a dog's in his yellowish eyes.

'How is the yield?' Gisa asked him. Without a word, he picked up a linen bag from the ground and tipped its contents on to a cloth. Out rolled blood-red rubies, deep blue sapphires, golden yellow topazes; washed smooth by the water and still wet, they sparkled in the morning sun.

'Take what you like,' Gisa told Listener, 'and forget that worthless thing you've lost.'

At that moment a cry rang out from the bank. The naked men ran down the slope and jumped into the water. Soon afterwards, they pulled a lifeless body up on land. Gisa went over to them. 'What's the matter with him?' she asked.

'He stayed down too long, lady,' said the overseer.

'Then his death is his own fault, the fool!' said Gisa. 'Get back to work! Don't stand around here!'

The men left the corpse lying in the grass and began diving again. Listener looked at the drowned man's pale face. He was young, with curly black hair. His sunburnt skin had turned a sallow colour.

'He sacrificed his life for your stones,' said Listener. 'Why do you speak of him so scornfully?'

'His life belonged to me,' said Gisa brusquely, 'and he was careless in risking it.'

'You're a hard woman,' said Listener.

'If you mean to be master here, you must learn to be hard too,' replied Gisa. 'And don't you want to be lord of Barlebogue, and share my bed? Be hard by day and gentle by night. You can't have one without the other. Don't you want it all?'

Listener looked into her eyes. Was what he had found here really *all*? He tried to recollect the last words the old Rider had said to him, but he could not remember them.

'You haven't picked a stone yet,' said Gisa.

Listener chose a dark blue sapphire. 'The colour of your eyes,' he said, and felt the stone lie hard and cold in his hand.

The overseer in the wolfskin was not the only one of his kind that Listener encountered over the next few weeks. Such men might be met with all over the valley. They saw to it that Gisa's instructions were carried out. They drove the peasants to work, they supervised the craftsmen in the villages, and the oldest of them, a grey-haired giant whose stony countenance never betrayed the least emotion, was steward of Gisa's castle and ruled the household.

These men looked remarkably like one another: they all had the same bristling grey-brown hair, the same yellowish eyes, and they never took off their wolfskin coats, however hot the weather might be. It also struck Listener as strange that these servants of Gisa wore, as their only ornament, a blue sapphire on a leather thong around their necks. As time went on, it occurred to him that he had never seen one of them laugh. Their expressions were usually surly, and sometimes a sudden ferocity would flash across their faces. They seemed to feel a positively dog-like devotion to their mistress. They carried out her orders in silence, without questioning, and scarcely dared to look her in the eye.

Listener had never seen one of the yellow-eyed men lend a hand with any work himself. They seemed to be constantly on the move, going at an intent kind of trotting pace, stealing down the corridors on their soft-soled shoes, stepping soundlessly into rooms, so that Listener felt the watchful gaze of their yellow eyes was observing him all the time. But at evening, and not until then, they vanished as if the earth had swallowed them up. Or at least, Listener had never met with one of the wolfskin-clad men after sunset, either out of doors or within the castle walls.

At first he felt uncomfortable whenever one of these men was near. Day by day, however, he saw how much at ease Gisa was with her retainers, and in the end he told himself that you probably couldn't manage without men of that kind when you had so wide a domain as the valley of Barlebogue to rule. And there was no denying that Gisa's men kept the place well in order. They knew how to command respect, as anyone could see from the way the servants in the castle or the peasants in the fields cowered in alarm when one of the yellow-eyed men passed by.

Listener often rode down the valley with Gisa. They hunted in the forest together, and Listener practised his archery, not wishing to lag behind Gisa in any way, for she could shoot an arrow from a hundred paces and pin a mouse to the ground with it. When they were riding home from the hunt one day, Listener realized that his horse had gone lame. He dismounted and examined its hooves, but he could not find anything wrong. Gisa had reined in her own mount, and was waiting impatiently beside him. 'Oh, get up again and spur the nag on!' she said. 'That will soon teach it not to limp!' But Listener shook his head. 'I don't want to ride the horse to death,' he said. Gisa only laughed. 'What does a horse matter?' she replied. 'I have plenty of steeds in my stable.'

To Listener, however, this was not just any horse. He had been riding the bay mare since he came to Gisa's castle, and he was fond of the animal. So he took her by the bridle and began slowly leading her on. Angrily, Gisa whipped up her own horse and raced away on her own towards the castle, over the fields and meadows.

Listener did not hurry on the way home. He was aware that Gisa had expected him to display harshness again, but he could not bring himself to cause a defenceless animal unnecessary pain. He hoped that by the time he got back to the castle Gisa's anger would have blown itself out. As for his behaviour to the servants, Gisa might well be content with that. To be sure, he could not yet manage to raise his voice to the volume of sound she required, but he had become very well used to giving orders, and leaving people in no doubt that he meant to have his will obeyed. You need not roar for that. He was even beginning to take a certain pleasure in knowing that everyone would do as he said without question, whatever he asked.

Thinking such thoughts, he climbed the hill to the castle, led his horse in through the gateway and took it to the stables. The groom, a tall, strong fellow, was busy rubbing down Gisa's mount, which was wet with sweat. Listener beckoned him over, and told him to take a good look at the mare's hooves. The man nodded, in silence, and took the horse from him. Then Listener went into the castle.

Gisa curled her lip mockingly when she saw him. 'Well, did you bring your mare safe home, then?' she asked. 'You had better be careful, or I'll turn jealous!'

'What, jealous of a horse?' said Listener, laughing, and he looked into her sapphire-blue eyes. 'You don't seem very confident of your beauty, Gisa!' That dispersed the very last of Gisa's anger, and she ordered the servants to bring wine, and serve their supper. Listener was relieved to find that her fit of temper had passed over so quickly. He let the servants set all kinds of delicacies in front of him, ate with relish, and thought the wine tasted particularly good tonight.

When the servants had cleared the table, however, he remembered his mare again. 'I'll just go and take a look at the horse,' he told Gisa.

'Shall I have a bed made up in the stables for you?' she asked, and Listener was not sure whether to take this as a joke or a threat. He decided to assume it was a joke, and said, 'Only if you want to sleep with the horses yourself.'

The reply pleased Gisa. 'No, I think I prefer my bedroom,' she said. 'And I hope you don't stink of horse dung when you come back!' Then she dismissed him with an imperious wave of her hand.

It was already dark when Listener crossed the courtyard to the stables. He stopped for a moment and looked up at the mountainside to the east, where the moon was rising, a great silvery disc. The dark tops of the pine trees stood out against it like teeth in a pair of black jaws that held the valley in its grip. Listener shivered when he heard wolves howling in the forest, and it was not just the chilly night air that made him shudder. He felt suddenly afraid of being trapped in those gaping jaws. They might rise up slowly over the dark sky, until at last they snapped greedily shut. But then the moon rose clear of the horizon, lifting above the borders of the forest below. Listener shook off his fears, and went on, to the open doorway of the stable. The warm light of a lantern spilled out of it, falling on the paving stones of the yard.

The groom was busy examining the right forefoot of Listener's mare. 'Have you found anything?' he asked.

'Yes,' said the groom, without looking up. 'She's trodden on a long thorn – I got it out, but the place is inflamed.'

By now, Listener was accustomed to being treated by the servants with more respect than this man showed him. He seemed to think the horse more important than the masters of the castle! Or perhaps, in the groom's eyes, Listener was not one of those entitled to give orders here? The attitude of this underling, who seemed only a few years older than Listener himself, shook his confidence. But then he told himself that it was a groom's job to tend the horses, after all. 'Can you do anything about the inflammation?' he asked.

'I could,' said the groom, 'but I haven't the right herbs for a poultice to hand.'

'Do you know where to find them?' asked Listener.

'I do,' said the groom.

'Then go and get them in the morning!' said Listener, impatiently.

The groom set the horse's hoof carefully down on the ground, and slowly straightened up. He looked Listener in the face, without any trace of servility, and said, 'I can't do that.'

'Why not?' asked Listener.

'Because I'm not allowed to leave the castle,' said the groom.

'Oh. I didn't know,' said Listener, realizing as he spoke that he was admitting to the man he did not know everything that went on in the castle. 'I'll have a word with the steward, and then he'll let you go,' he said, and seeing scepticism in the other man's face, added, 'Yes, that's what I'll do, straight away!'

At that the groom smiled, and it struck Listener as the indulgent smile of an adult at the impulses of a child who still knows nothing about the world around it. Then the smile vanished abruptly from the groom's face. 'You won't find the steward,' he said.

'You leave that to me!' said Listener, brusquely, and he turned and left the stable.

He went straight back to the castle, and asked the first servant he met where to find the steward. The man looked at him in alarm. 'Oh, you won't find him now,' said he. Listener had heard this once already, and he thought it was about time to clear the matter up. 'Show me his room!' he ordered. But the servant did not move from the spot, though he began to tremble. 'I don't know where it is,' he stammered.

Listener felt as if he were running his head against a wall. 'Then tell me who *can* show me!' he snapped angrily. The servant only shook his head, dumbly. Listener turned his back on the man and stormed into the great hall to ask Gisa. But she was gone from the hall.

He found her in the bedchamber. Gisa was standing naked by the window, in the cold light of the moon, looking out at the night, a spotless marble statue whose beauty took Listener's breath away. He gazed at her motionless figure for some time, not daring to move, as if he feared to put the vision to flight. But it was no vision, for suddenly, and without turning to look at him, Gisa said, 'So you've finally managed to tear yourself away from your mare?'

'She's injured,' said Listener, and he told her what the groom had told him. Then he asked, 'Where can I find the steward?'

Gisa whirled around. 'You can't, at this hour,' she said sharply. Listener looked at her in alarm, baffled. Then she came towards him. 'Never mind that now!' she said. 'It will keep till morning. Do you mean to waste the whole night worrying about your horse?' Listener shook his head, and when he looked into her eyes he forgot everything he had been going to ask her. 'Come here,' said Gisa, 'and let me run my fingers through your soft pelt!'

Next morning Listener spoke to the steward. 'Ah, you should never trust these folk,' said the old man, surly as ever. 'The groom's only looking for a chance to run away.' But Listener was thinking of his mare, and he remembered how carefully the groom had treated her. 'He knows the right herbs to use, so we must let him go and look for them,' he said.

'If you say so,' growled the steward, 'but I'll send one of my own men with him, to keep him from any foolishness.'

The steward might be in the right of it there, thought Listener. For the groom did not seem a particularly obedient servant. Listener saw himself standing in front of the man again, and felt belated anger when he remembered how he had been made to feel aware of the groom's superiority. Gisa's men would know how to deal with such folk! Not long afterwards, he saw the groom leaving the castle with one of the yellow-eyed men. When Listener went to see his mare that evening, she was already on the mend, and he was able to ride her again in a few days' time.

Listener did not forget the violence of Gisa's reaction to his question about the steward, and he did not mention the subject again. In future, he took it for granted that Gisa's retainers would not be around in the evening, and he thought no more of it. He still felt uneasy in the company of those yellow-eyed men: they still seemed uncanny to him, but he made use of them when it appeared necessary, for he had soon seen that you could do anything you liked in Barlebogue if you had them on your side. As Gisa trusted her men, he saw no good reason not to do the same himself, as indeed he must if he was to be one of those who gave the orders here. He thought he was getting better at giving orders daily, and he felt full of satisfaction when the servants obeyed his least gesture. He also noticed that Gisa observed this with pleasure, and he was becoming used to thinking of everything in the valley of Barlebogue as his own, just as she did.

One morning she said, 'The court sits today. And as you have so famous a judge for your father, you shall deliver judgement in Barlebogue in future.'

Listener felt greatly honoured by this proposal. 'My father did mean to train me to succeed him,' he said, 'though nothing came of it. And now my own efforts have raised me to be judge!'

'Then show me how well you can maintain our laws,' said Gisa. 'I will stand aside, so that everyone can see you are lord of this place now.'

The judge's seat had been set up in the middle of the great hall. There was a table beside it, with an unsheathed sword lying on the table, in token that the court was sitting. Gisa remained in her usual place by the hearth, while Listener sat on the judge's seat and told the servants to let in the petitioners.

The first was a man who accused his neighbour of stealing three chickens from his poultry yard at night. He brought two witnesses who had been present, and saw the thief roasting and eating the chickens with his family next day.

'Is the thief here?' asked Listener.

'Yes, my lord, he's over there,' said the petitioner, and he pointed to a man being held fast by two others.

'Let go of him, and let him step forward,' said Listener.

Rubbing his wrists, the man took a couple of steps forward.

'Do you confess to this crime?' asked Listener.

The man nodded.

'I want to ask you a question,' said Listener. 'Is there anything at all on my land that is *not* mine?'

'No, lord,' said the man.

'Then who did you steal those chickens from?' asked Listener. 'From that man there, who didn't own them?'

The thief looked at him, baffled. 'Well, if he didn't own them, I can't have stolen them from him,' he stammered.

'Correct,' said Listener. 'As they were mine, you stole them from me. And as a punishment, you shall work for me without pay, one week for each chicken. I will set you to cleaning out the henhouses – you seem to be fit for that job.' And he told the servants to take him to the workers' quarters.

'But who's going to replace my stolen chickens?' asked the petitioner.

Listener looked thoughtfully at him for a while, and then said, '*Were* they stolen from you?'

The man thought for a moment. 'No, my lord,' he said, and stepped back into the crowd.

The next man was carried into court on a stretcher. The men with him, all woodcutters, judging by their clothing, were dragging another man along, bound, and they set him before the judge.

'What has this man done?' asked Listener.

'Went for my cousin's leg with his axe while they were quarrelling,' said one of the men. 'This is my cousin on the stretcher here.'

'You will have to pay me for that,' Listener told the man in bonds.

'You?' he asked. 'What did I do to *you*, then?'

'Don't you know?' said Listener. 'Why, you did harm to my property!'

He turned to the spokesman of the group. 'How long before your cousin can work for me again?' he asked.

'Looks like a nasty wound,' said the man. 'Right through to the bone, it went. He'll be able to walk again in three months' time, if he's lucky.'

'How many hours a day do you woodcutters work?' asked Listener.

'Ten,' said the man.

'Then the guilty man shall work for me fifteen hours a day until he has made up for the loss I've suffered,' said Listener. 'Very well, you can go!'

As he spoke, the door of the hall was flung open. Glancing up, all Listener saw at first was the groom who had tended his mare standing in the doorway. Yet again, it struck him how little this man's bearing resembled the humble demeanour of the servants. He came in without knocking, as if he were in his own home. Listener was about to reprove him when he realized that the groom had not come into the hall of his own free will. The steward stood behind him, grasping the tall fellow's arm, and he hauled the groom before the judge's seat. 'Here's another case to be tried,' said he.

The groom wrenched his arm away from the yellow-eyed giant's grasp, and looked right past Listener and out of the window, as if none of this had anything to do with him. Listener had to look up at the man from the chair where he sat, which irked him. 'What do you accuse him of?' he asked the steward.

'He has robbed you,' said the old man, taking a leather bag out of his pocket. Listener immediately recognized it as the bag in which he used to keep the eye-stone.

'Is there a stone in that bag?' he asked.

'There is,' said the steward.

'Take it out, and put it and the bag on the table,' said Listener.

The steward opened the bag, let the stone roll out on the table, and placed the bag beside it. There was a dull glow about the stone, but its colours remained hidden beneath the smooth surface.

'Why did you take it?' Listener asked the groom, who looked down at him quite calmly, as if he had nothing to fear.

'I never stole the bag,' he said. 'My lady there gave it to me.'

Listener looked at Gisa, and saw her eyes grow dark with anger. 'A stable lad's idle chatter!' she said. She rose and came over to him, stopped by the table and looked at the stone. 'There's been too much fuss altogether over this worthless thing,' she said scornfully.

'Worthless or not,' said Listener, 'it was mine. Did he steal it, or did he get it from you?'

'Why should I take your pebble, when I can give you stones a thousand times more valuable?' said Gisa. 'A bold liar – may he fare the same as this cheap rubbish!' And so saying, she snatched the stone up from the table, took aim, and flung it far out of the open window. It glinted in the sunlight for a moment, and then it was gone.

'Why do you call me a liar, Gisa, when you know what really happened?' asked the groom angrily.

'I will call you what I like,' said Gisa, 'for you belong to me.'

'Yes,' said the groom. 'I belong to you, like everything else here as far as the eye can see. This man in the judge's seat belongs to you too, and is only doing your will. You have taken the only thing he owned away from him, and then heaped gifts upon him so that all he has comes from you. You bought him so that he would do your bidding and play your game with you.' He turned away from her, and looked at Listener. 'Listener, can't you see that you have no more say here than any of the rest of us? Or do you enjoy your enslavement?'

At that Listener leaped to his feet, overturning the chair behind him, and cried, in blind rage, 'Cut his tongue out and drive him into the forest!'

The steward signed to two of his men to drag the condemned man out of the hall. As for Gisa, she went up to Listener, saying, 'That is the way to do justice in Barlebogue!' And she took him in her arms and kissed his mouth.

Listener clung to her until he could see clearly again. Then he freed himself from her embrace, and looked thoughtfully into her eyes.

'Was what I did justice?' he asked.

'A man who deals out justice must not doubt himself, or he is lost!' said Gisa. 'Come, let's go hunting! That will calm your anger.'

Before they left the hall, Listener picked the empty bag up from the table and put it in his pocket. Out in the yard, they had their horses saddled, took their hunting bows and arrows, and galloped out over the drawbridge and down into the valley, followed by the pack of hounds.

The hounds put up a stag on the edge of the forest and chased it, yapping, through the undergrowth. Listener went after them. Branches whipped at his face, thorny shoots tore at his clothes, but he spurred his horse on, riding it far into the forest, where he could hear the barking of the hounds. They had brought the stag to bay in a small clearing. He stood there, antlers lowered, in front of an ancient oak tree, tossing one of the hounds to death. Listener put an arrow to his bowstring, bent his bow, and shot. Leaping from the bow, the arrow struck the stag in the shoulder. The beast flung his head back, the death rattle in his throat, and collapsed. As Listener whipped the hounds away from the dead game, getting them back on the leash, Gisa trotted into the clearing. She dismounted and cast an expert eye at Listener's shot.

'You did well,' she said. 'This is a pleasant place; we'll rest and eat here.'

Listener spread his saddle-cloth in the shade of the oak tree, and Gisa took bread, meat and wine out of her saddle-bag. As they ate, a blackbird began to whistle high in the tree-top. Listener listened, and thought it was a long time since he had heard so sweet a song. The melody reminded him of something, but he could not think what. Curiously, he looked up into the leaves, trying to see the bird.

'Up there,' said Gisa, showing him the place. 'You're a pretty good marksman now, but I'll wager you can't bring down that bird with an arrow.'

'Why should I kill him?' asked Listener. 'He sings so beautifully!'

'Only a blackbird, like a thousand others,' said Gisa. 'Why, are you afraid you'll miss and lose the wager?'

'Let him go on singing,' said Listener.

'I'll show you how to shoot a blackbird,' said Gisa, and she rose to her feet and picked up her bow.

Then Listener took the sapphire he always carried with him out of his pocket, held it out to Gisa and said, 'Please – for the sake of the stone you gave me, let the bird live.'

Gisa laughed. 'What would I do with the stone? I have thousands of them! Are you too feeble to watch a blackbird die?' She took an arrow and set it to her bowstring. At that, Listener leaped up and knocked the bow from her hand. Gisa turned to face him, pale with rage. 'You fool!' she cried. 'Is a bird worth more to you than my pleasure? Or is your wretched eye-stone worth more than my sapphire? You will never be a man, you dreamer!'

She jumped on her horse, raced across the clearing and sent the horse leaping into the bushes, which closed behind her, rustling. Listener looked down once more at the sapphire, gleaming blue as ice in his hand. Then he flung it into the thicket where Gisa had disappeared. 'There, take your stone, you witch!' he shouted after her.

The stone flew high above the clearing, like a shooting star sparkling with blue light, and fell in the shade of the trees. Listener thought he caught the sound of a muffled cry, and then he heard nothing but the crack of snapping twigs and the hollow thud of hooves on the forest floor, rapidly dying away in the distance. He let the hounds go, chasing them after Gisa. Then he sat down under the oak again, leaning against its trunk. Suddenly he felt as if he were free of a burden, though just what burden he could not have said. The blackbird began to whistle again above his head. Its song sounded much closer now. Listener looked up, and saw the bird sitting in the lowest branches of the oak, directly above him. The sight seemed familiar – where had he seen it before? He could not remember.

Now the blackbird fell silent, eyeing him. It fluttered down to a hollow place in the trunk, clung tight to the fissured bark with its claws, and pecked busily away at the decaying spot in the branch. Pieces of bark and splinters of wood fell on Listener's hair.

'Hungry, are you?' he asked, and as he spoke he remembered where he had seen the blackbird before. 'My little friend from the first day of my journey!' he said, offering the bird a few breadcrumbs on the palm of his hand. At that moment something shining rolled out of the hollow in the tree and fell into his lap. He picked it up, and found he was holding his eye-stone.

'Did you keep it safe for me?' he asked the blackbird. 'You're a friend indeed, and a true one!'

He held his stone up to the sun. Caught in the ring of rays, the light brought out all its shining colours, lovelier than he had ever remembered them, a thousand times lovelier than all the rubies and sapphires and topazes of Barlebogue.

Meanwhile, the blackbird had hopped down to the ground and was pecking up the crumbs that had fallen from Listener's hand when he reached for the stone. And as he gazed at the stone, Listener remembered why he had ridden into the forest in the first place. How could he have forgotten he was on his way to the Gentle Fluter? He had not thought of his grandfather since the moment he lost the eye-stone. Or since he had been carrying the sapphire about in his pocket. Let nothing detain you, his mother had told him when she said goodbye. But he *had* let himself be detained, had played the great lord at Barlebogue, and let them set him on the judge's seat. He could have laughed at all the rest, but now he thought of the way he had delivered judgement that very morning, he was nothing like so light at heart as he had been a moment ago. I must have been bewitched, he thought. She bewitched me from the first. He thought, with horror, of the groom whose tongue he had had cut out because the man told the truth. The groom himself must be wandering somewhere in the forest now.

Suddenly he felt panic terror at the idea of meeting him. He leaped up in such haste that the blackbird, alarmed, fluttered up into the tree. It perched on a branch above him for a moment, whistling its three notes. Then it flew out into the open, circled the clearing once, and flew away over the tree-tops, going west.

Listener took the leather bag out of his pocket, put the stone in it, and hung it around his neck. Then he quickly gathered up the remains of the meal, stowed them in his saddle-bag, saddled his horse and mounted. He glanced once more at the spot where Gisa had disappeared. Then he turned the horse and rode into the forest as fast as he could go, riding westwards and away from Barlebogue.

Listener made slow progress that day. He kept riding on west, without any path, but going uphill through the forest; he guided his horse through thick undergrowth tangled with tough honeysuckle bines, and often had to dismount to find a way through. As he struggled painfully with branches that lashed back at him and unyielding creepers, he thought he heard twigs cracking in the thickets over to one side, as if some large animal were making its way through. But as soon as he halted his horse, there was nothing to be heard.

The higher he climbed, the darker did the forest become. Instead of the oaks and beeches, which let in a greenish light through their foliage, he was now riding uphill among the trunks of towering firs and pines. There was hardly any undergrowth in this dark shade, and so he could stay in the saddle. Although the soft carpet of needles muffled the sound of his horse's hooves, there was scarcely anything to be heard here: no birdsong, no sudden rustling. Then the trees thinned out, and Listener saw the crest of a mountain range ahead. Only a few pines grew on it, contorted into curious shapes by wind and weather. He urged his mare on, feeling as if the influence of Barlebogue must cease beyond that high range.

When he was up among the weather-beaten pines he looked back once more, down over the wooded slope that fell away in long ripples to the green valley, in whose midst the castle cast its shadow over the surrounding meadows. Then he turned his horse, and rode down into the forest on the other side of the ridge.

Towards evening he came to a stream running sluggishly along between the gnarled roots of trees, and decided to stop here for the night. He unsaddled his horse, let her drink from the stream, and sat down on a mossy stone. As he sat there in silence, eating some of the remains of the food they had taken out hunting, the sounds of the forest gradually penetrated his consciousness: quiet birdsong, a sudden rustling in the dead leaves on the ground, the crack of dry twigs under some animal's footsteps, the distant cry of a wild cat – there was secret life moving everywhere, and Listener felt that a thousand eyes were watching him.

He tied his few provisions up in a bundle, to keep them from being eaten by some nocturnal creature, and hung the bundle from a branch with his halter strap. Then he rolled himself up in his saddle-cloth and closed his eyes. But as darkness came on, the noises grew louder, and seemed to come closer and closer. The stream flowed gurgling along its stony bed; an owl hooted in the branches above him. Then he heard something splashing in the water, right beside his head. He opened his eyes in alarm, and saw a fat toad quite close to his face, looking at him out of unblinking, golden-brown eyes.

'What beautiful eyes you have,' said Listener.

The toad came a little closer, and a purple shimmer tinged her warty skin. It was evidently her way of blushing.

'There aren't all that many people notice,' she said, flattered. 'I can see that the lady of Barlebogue hasn't quite ruined you yet.'

'What I did while I was with her was bad enough,' said Listener, his voice troubled.

'Bad enough, yes, bad enough,' agreed the toad. 'It was lucky for you that you threw the blue stone after her, or you would never have got out of her toils.'

She stretched her mouth even wider than it was already, and smacked her lips wetly, which is the way toads chuckle. 'It hit her in the middle of the forehead, and now she has a bump there as big as a hen's egg and as blue as her own sapphire pendant.'

'How do you know?' asked Listener.

'Such news gets around fast in the forest,' said the toad. 'Particularly when it's the good news that someone has got away from her. Doesn't happen often enough. It'll encourage people.'

'What people?' asked Listener.

'All the people she thinks belong to her. You marked her proud brow and so damaged her power a little. She'll never forgive you for it.'

Listener felt alarmed. 'Can she still harm me here?' he asked.

'Not she,' said the toad. 'You are outside the limits of her power now. But she could still set her servants on your trail. You'd better ride on again first thing tomorrow. Where are you going, anyway?'

'I'm looking for the Gentle Fluter,' said Listener. 'Can you tell me where to find him?'

The toad looked thoughtfully at him with her beautiful eyes. 'Far away to the west,' she said at last. 'But it all depends whether he wants to be found. Why are you looking for him?'

'I'm his grandson,' said Listener. 'And I am to give him greetings from Arni of the Stone.'

'You mix with great folk,' said the toad. 'They say Arni's dead. Is that right?'

'Yes,' said Listener. 'I was with him when he died. And before he died he gave me his stone.' He got the eye-stone out of its bag and showed it to the toad.

Although it was dark, the stone shone in Listener's hand, showing the play of its colours, which were mirrored in the toad's eyes. The toad gazed at the shining eye-stone for a long time, marvelling. At last she said, 'And you'd exchange this for the lady of Barlebogue's cold blue stone, you fool?'

'I thought I'd found what I was looking for,' said Listener, subdued.

'Well, what an impatient fellow you are!' said the toad. 'Don't you know that that's far from all?'

'I'd forgotten,' Listener said.

'Don't you ever forget again!' said the toad. 'Tomorrow you must ride on. Keep going downstream. On the seventh day you will come to the end of the forest, and that's where you can find the Gentle Fluter – always supposing he wants to see you. But take care! There is something stealing through the forest. You must find out for yourself whether it means you good or ill; I tell you this only by way of thanks for showing

me the stone. You will never be quite without comfort while you carry
it with you. Good luck for your journey.'

Listener put the stone back in its bag, and watched the toad crawl
clumsily away into the bushes. Then his eyes closed, and he did not
wake up until a sunbeam fell on his nose, tickling it. He opened his
eyes, and the first thing he saw was the empty halter strap dangling
from a branch above him. His provisions had vanished. He leaped to
his feet and looked at the straps. It couldn't have been an animal. The
straps had not been bitten or gnawed; somebody had neatly undone the
buckle. The thief was a human being.

Listener remembered the toad's warning. So it was some other person
who was stealing through the forest, and had stolen his breakfast. He
listened, but there was no sound to be heard around him except for
birdsong and the murmur of the brook. He felt uneasy, all the same.
Hastily, he saddled his horse, mounted, and rode downstream as fast as
he could.

That, however, was not much faster than a walking pace. Thick
undergrowth grew beside the stream, there were patches of swamp
that he had to avoid, and finally the watercourse began to sink down
between steep banks. Listener had to dismount again, for his horse
kept missing its footing on the slippery slope.

He journeyed on like this for three days, picking a few berries as he
went along, frying mushrooms found underneath the bushes for his
supper. He was sorry now that he had left his hunting bow beside the
slaughtered stag, because his stumbling horse put up a hare or a deer
from time to time. The horse ate better than he did, for there was
plenty of grass growing beside the stream.

On the third evening, he felt so tired and exhausted that he let
himself fall on the moss beside the brook and went to sleep at once,
without eating anything or tending the horse he had been dragging
along after him by its halter all day. He was woken by a hoarse cry
that made him start up. All around him, ancient trees reached their
gnarled branches into the morning mist, in the pale light of dawn. As
he rose to his feet, with difficulty, a second cry made him start again.
And then, far up the slope, he heard the clatter of hooves. Only then
did he realize that his horse was gone. Whoever had uttered those
mysterious cries must have stolen it, and had probably been the person
who took his provisions too.

Listener felt too weak to follow the thief. He stared up at the spectral,
giant trees and felt fear rise within him. All he possessed now were the

clothes on his back, rent by thorns on his long journey, and the eye-stone he wore on his breast. He took the bag out and let the stone fall into the hollow of his hand. The colours glowed warm beneath the smooth surface. Listener looked into the stone eye, and felt his fear recede. It was as if the eye were telling him to go on and not lose heart. He put the stone back into its bag, drank a little water from the stream, and set off once more.

He had not gone far when the sound of hoofbeats approached again, from the forest above. He could see nothing; thick foliage hid the rider from sight. However, he could hear the thief urging his horse on down the slope, until he brought it to a halt in the bushes, just above Listener. Then he uttered that hoarse cry of his again: a vengeful and malignant cry that filled Listener with horror. He began to run on, he leaped from rock to rock along the stream-bed, he slipped, fell into the water, struggled to his feet again, and ran and ran until he thought he must have escaped whoever made those sounds. But no sooner had he slowed down to a comfortable pace than the horseman broke through the bushes above him yet again, driving him on with his cry.

This chase lasted four days. Listener hardly dared to sleep a wink at night. He would start up at the least sound and drag himself a little farther. Gathering berries or looking for mushrooms was out of the question. Hungry and tired, he staggered along the bank of the stream, which was growing broader and broader now, rushing in foaming cascades over mighty smooth-washed boulders.

On the evening of the fourth day the forest began to get thinner, the trees grew farther apart, and at last Listener looked out between their trunks and saw rolling hills covered with green grass. Once he had stumbled out of the forest he was unable to go a step farther. He dropped to the grass and fell asleep at once.

He must have slept for a long time when he was woken by a hollow thudding sound that made the ground shake. It was like the hoofbeats of a galloping horse! Whoever gave those cries is back, thought Listener, jumping up. And there came his pursuer, racing down from the top of the nearest hill, making straight for him. He was uttering his hoarse cry again, and swinging a stout cudgel in his right hand.

Now that he could see the man for the first time, Listener instantly recognized him. It was the groom whose tongue he had had cut out. The groom must have followed him through the forest for seven days, and now he was going to take his revenge. He was upon Listener already, circling him on horseback, making his cudgel whistle through the air. His circles closed in and in, and then he struck. Listener sprang aside, and took a blow that might have shattered his skull on his shoulder. With difficulty, the rider kept his balance, wrenched his horse round, and made for him again. His cudgel was raised for a second blow, but he did not strike it, for at that moment a sweet melody arose from the bushes on the edge of the forest, lovelier than anything Listener had ever heard in his life. He forgot the rider, forgot the danger he was in, wished only to listen to the music, and felt water come into his eyes.

Through a mist of tears, he saw the frail figure of a man playing on a silver flute emerge from the bushes. He came closer, slowly and with swaying tread; it looked almost as if he were dancing to his own music, head slightly to one side, utterly absorbed in his playing. He played and played, and the song of his flute made Listener both happy and sad at once. Sad, because he became aware of all he had done wrong, and realized at the same time how far removed he was from the likeness of the man he might have been; happy because of the mere existence of something as lovely as the melody of that flute, in which the conflicting discords of life were resolved, in the playing, into a well-ordered whole.

He saw the Gentle Fluter's fingers covering and uncovering the holes of the instrument with tiny movements, easily, effortlessly, yet not at random or without rules. This music obeyed laws that set no restrictions, used no force, but freed the hearer from constraint and resolved all contradictions.

If he had pictured his grandfather as an impressive, awe-inspiring figure he was in for a disillusionment: before him stood a rather small old man, face wrinkled with a thousand laughter lines, with rosy apple cheeks and a wreath of silver-grey curls above his high forehead. A pair of gold-rimmed eye-glasses trembled on his nose, slightly askew and apt to slip whenever the fluter played a trill. Finally the Gentle Fluter lowered his instrument. 'So here you are at last, Listener,' said he. 'It took you a long time to ride through the forests of Barlebogue.'

'I was delayed,' said Listener.

'I know,' said the Gentle Fluter. 'Perhaps it would be more accurate to say you let yourself be delayed, for delaying always takes two, and I don't suppose the lady of Barlebogue used force.'

'You are quite right, Grandfather,' said Listener. 'I let myself be delayed, and fell into her trap, and no good came of it.'

'You may well say that, my boy,' said the Gentle Fluter, shaking his head sadly, so that his eye-glasses wobbled again. 'And we may see what did come of it in, for instance, the person of this unfortunate man still sitting his horse here, cudgel threateningly raised, like a monument to the stupidity of other-folk.'

Listener had completely forgotten his pursuer, who gave those hoarse cries. Now he turned to look at him. The man was still sitting in his saddle as if turned to stone, cudgel raised aloft like a sword, staring bemused at the inconspicuous old man who had prevented him from taking his revenge. The Gentle Fluter went over to him, patted the horse's neck, and said, 'What are you doing, sitting up there on your steed like a statue? Put that club down, do, and get off the horse, so that I can talk to you man to man!'

Only now did the horseman lower his arm and drop the cudgel. Then he dismounted, and looked down at the Gentle Fluter, who was shorter than himself by almost two heads. However, the Gentle Fluter did not appear to mind that. He took the dumb man's hand and led him over to Listener. 'By the way, what's your name?' he asked the man as they went, then struck his forehead with the flat of his hand, saying, 'I'm sorry; of course, you can't speak. I'd quite forgotten. But I think we can put that right again. In my own way, if you see what I mean.'

The dumb man shook his head.

'You don't?' continued the old man cheerfully, as if he were conducting a conversation about some trivial matter with a friend. 'Never mind, you soon will. And don't cast such dark glances at my grandson there. I know he used you ill, but he's young, and rather stupid still. You saw how that power-hungry woman tried her wiles on him.'

As the Gentle Fluter spoke to him in his equally gentle voice, the dumb man's expression grew calmer too. Then the old man asked Listener if he knew the groom's name. Listener merely shook his head.

'I might have known it,' said the Gentle Fluter, and his voice was not quite so gentle this time. 'Having folk to serve you, dealing out justice to them – if one may so call it, and I do assure you that one may not! – and never so much as asking a man's name, for all that! Well, we must find out some other way.'

He raised his flute to his mouth, and blew three ringing notes like a call. It was answered directly from the bushes nearby. Then a blackbird fluttered out of the leaves, came flying low across the grass, and settled on the Gentle Fluter's shoulder. Listener thought he recognized his old friend – yes, he was sure it was the same bird.

'Now then, you tell me this man's name,' said the Gentle Fluter.

The blackbird whistled a rapid sequence of notes into his ear. Then it put its head on one side, and its little black eyes looked at Listener, as much as to say: So here you are at last, are you?

'Well, at least one can rely on you,' said the Gentle Fluter. 'So his name is Barlo. That was once a famous name in Barlebogue.'

The dumb man nodded, and attempted a smile, although it looked more like a contorted grin, which was hardly surprising, considering his injury.

'Still hurts, I suppose?' asked the old man. 'Then the first thing we'll do is go home and see to it.' He turned and strode away along a path trodden over the meadows, without looking to see if the other two were following him. Listener still felt disinclined to be alone with the dumb man, and hurried after his grandfather. Barlo took the horse by its halter and came slowly along behind.

The path led along the stream, through the green hills, and when they had rounded three or four bends they saw a group of three ancient lime trees, with a comfortable little house nestling against the slope in the shelter of their thick leaves. The reed thatch of its roof came almost down to the ground, and there were window-boxes full of red pinks and yellow begonias under the green-painted shutters.

The Gentle Fluter took the blackbird from his shoulder with his right hand and threw it into the air. 'Go and say we're coming,' said he, and the bird shot away like an arrow. 'Your grandmother doesn't much care for surprises,' he told Listener, who had caught up with him by now.

This was an understatement, for even before they had reached the shade of the lime trees the door of the house was flung open and a stout old woman stepped out, glaring at the new arrivals with some ferocity. On top of her round head she wore a bun of white hair, of considerable circumference and with a mighty pin stuck through it, like a skewer through a baked apple. Powerful arms akimbo, she called in booming tones, with an old woman's deep voice, 'So who have you gone and picked up this time? Don't you go bringing those ragged vagabonds into *my* house! And a horse too! Dear heavens above, what have I done to deserve it?' This whole speech sounded like a mother trying to prevent her offspring from inviting a horde of grubby street urchins into her freshly scrubbed home.

Listener was taken aback. How could anyone speak in such a way to so important a man? Why, even the Raiding Riders in the distant east had heard of him! He looked at his grandfather, who was indeed standing there like a guilty little boy. But then he winked at Listener and said, under his breath, 'Don't worry. She does shout a bit, but only to hide her kind heart.'

He put his hand on Listener's shoulder and guided him towards his grandmother, who was examining his torn clothes with obvious disapproval. 'And I suppose you'll be wanting me to mend this dirty fellow's things too?' she inquired, crossly.

'Always supposing you wish to do your own grandson that service,' said the Gentle Fluter, in his gentlest voice, but this remark only let loose a new torrent of words.

'My grandson?' cried his mighty wife. 'What, the son of the Great Roarer? Now *there's* a man! Tall and broad and hairy as a man should be! Why didn't you say so before?' She clasped Listener to her ample bosom while she went on scolding her mild husband. 'That's him all over, you see!' said she. 'Doesn't say a word, lets me talk on and on, looks as if butter wouldn't melt in his mouth. Dear heaven, what a dreamer I went and married! Wanders around the place, whistling a quiet little tune here and there, bothering about all sorts of things that are none of his business and paying no attention to his own home. You come along in, Listener, and I'll put you straight into a hot bath. You stink like a flock of goats. You can bring that other fellow in too if you like. He looks as if he could do with some breakfast. But I'm warning you, that horse stays outside!'

And so in this way everything was set in order. First of all, the Gentle Fluter tended Barlo, brewing him a decoction of herbs that took away his pain. 'You'll hardly feel it at all in a few days' time,' he said, and sent the dumb man into the kitchen. By now Listener's grandmother had scrubbed her grandson from head to foot, and refilled the bath tub for her second guest. In a little while, all four of them were sitting at a table lavishly laid with all you could desire for a good breakfast: a big, squat pot of steaming, freshly made tea, fragrant cakes of bread, a pat of butter as round and golden as the full moon, a pot of honey and a whole goat's milk cheese. Listener and Barlo were red as lobsters from the hot bath, and clad only in the merest essentials, for Grandmother had not given them back their clothes yet; she wanted to mend all the holes and rents in them. 'And I've nothing else to give you,' she said. 'What made me marry such a midget? You'll have to manage like that meanwhile. Doesn't worry me, I've seen more men in their underwear than I could wish. And in my own husband's case, I can tell you, it's not a very edifying sight.'

This remark made even Barlo grin. 'Aha, that's better,' said the Gentle Fluter. 'There's nothing like a good woman's hearty humour.'

'Never mind your little jokes,' said his wife. 'You put those two lads to bed. Listener can hardly keep his eyes open, and the dumb one doesn't seem much livelier.'

'Come along,' said the Gentle Fluter. 'I'll stable your horse while you two are sleeping. I know a good place to keep it, not far away.' He took them upstairs, to a room with two freshly made-up beds in it, the covers already turned down. Listener and Barlo were scarcely able to crawl between the sheets before their eyelids closed.

Many hours later, Listener was woken by the call of a blackbird sitting in the lime tree just outside the window. It was whistling its song in the evening twilight, and another bird answered from below, outside the house. It must be sitting on the fence. Listener got up, and saw his own and Barlo's clothes, mended and neatly folded, lying on the chairs beside their beds. He dressed, and that woke Barlo too.

Listener went to the window to look for the second blackbird, whose song he could still hear. But there was no blackbird down by the fence, only his grandfather playing a little wooden flute. When he saw Listener standing at the window, he took the instrument from his mouth and called, 'Come down, and bring Barlo with you.'

'There, you see,' said the Gentle Fluter, when they were both leaning on the fence beside him, 'this is the way you can talk to blackbirds.' He blew a sequence of notes, and the blackbird instantly took it up and whistled variations on it. At that moment Grandmother came out of the house.

'Thought as much!' said she, sarcastically. 'Sitting on the fence like Tom Thumb, playing a tune to his blackbird! Come in, do, you idlers, it's time for supper!'

You can say what you like about my grandmother, thought Listener, washing down the last of his supper with a sip of her home-made bilberry wine, but there's no one to match her at keeping house. However, he was still rather surprised by the way she spoke to her husband. His fame did not seem worth much here at home. Listener found it hard to think of his quiet mother as this talkative woman's daughter. He supposed that, like himself, she took more after the Gentle Fluter. While he was musing on the matter, he remembered the greetings his mother had charged him with, and delivered them. 'And I have another greeting for you too, Grandfather,' he went on. 'From an old

man who once met you, some time or other. He said his name was Arni
of the Stone.'

'I heard of his death,' said the Gentle Fluter, 'and I know he gave
you his stone. Indeed, I had hoped that jewel would protect you from
the cold eyes of the mistress of Barlebogue, but I suppose you don't
really know what it is you have there yet.'

'Do you?' asked Listener.

'I don't entirely know either,' said the Gentle Fluter, 'but I know a
little more than you. Did Arni tell you anything about it?'

'Well, yes,' said Listener. 'Before he died, he murmured a verse. It
went like this:

> *Seek the light*
> *where the glow may fall;*
> *you have not sought aright,*
> *if you don't find it all.*

Can you tell me what I'm supposed to be seeking?'

'No, I can't,' said the Gentle Fluter. 'All I can say is that you won't
know until you have found it.'

'Didn't Arni know either?' asked Listener.

'Who can tell?' replied the Gentle Fluter. 'Perhaps he did know at
the moment when he gave you the stone. Or perhaps he had stopped
seeking, and was content with the comfort he got from looking at the
stone.'

'Where did you meet Arni?' asked Listener. 'Before he died, he said
perhaps he ought to have stayed beside you.'

'Did he say that? Then his life was not an easy one with the Raiding
Riders,' said the Gentle Fluter. And then he told:

The Tale of Arni of the Stone

This story happened many years ago. At the time, Arni was not
much older than you are now, Listener. And I was wandering about
far to the east, going from village to village on my mule, learning
the power of my flute. One day, as I was sitting in the steppes somewhere, making myself some soup, two riders appeared on the horizon
and came galloping up at breakneck speed on their shaggy little
horses, making straight for the place I had chosen for my camp. One
seemed to be in pursuit of the other, and caught up with him just
where I was sitting. Then the other turned his horse, they both drew

daggers from the sheaths at their belts, and they began to fight to the death.

This disturbed my mid-day rest considerably, so I took my flute out of my pocket and played them a little tune. At that they lowered their daggers, dismounted, and came over to me. I could see at once that they were twins, for you could hardly tell them apart: the same bold, flat-nosed faces, the same dark brown eyes, the same straggling dark hair worn in braids at their temples, the same broad shoulders and rather short legs; even their clothing was the same, and they had been trying to stab each other with identical daggers.

'Would you like to share my meal?' I asked. 'I've made some good hearty soup, so be my guests!'

Now in those parts it is a deadly insult to refuse such an invitation, so the two of them nodded and sat down by my fire. We ate my soup, and they enjoyed it, for I had seasoned it with fresh herbs. Then they wiped their mouths on the backs of their hands and looked expectantly at me, because, in the eastern steppes, it is usual for the host to start a conversation, and it is thought rude to mention anything of importance while you are actually eating.

So I said, 'Thank you for sharing my modest meal with me. And now I would very much like to know what brings two brothers to draw knives on one another.'

The two of them exchanged dark looks, stared at nothing for a while, and then they both began to talk at once.

'Wait,' said I. 'One at a time, please. And if you can't agree upon it, let's throw to see who speaks first.'

I found the knuckle-bone of a goat in my pocket, and told the one sitting on my right, 'Yours is the side with the hollow in it.' I told the one sitting on my left, 'Yours is the smooth side.' Then I threw the bone, and it decided for the one on my right.

'You know our customs well, stranger,' said he.

'A little,' said I. 'But I never heard of its being customary for brothers to try killing each other before. Who are you, anyway?'

'We are the two sons of the Khan of the Raiding Riders,' said the man on my right. 'I am Hunli, and he is Arni. As you see, we are twins, and no one can tell us which came out of our mother's womb first. Nobody noticed at the time. So now we are quarrelling over which of us is to be regarded as the Khan's heir. Only one of us can rule, and the other one must serve. I am the better rider, and since we live on horseback, I demand the succession as my right.'

'But I am the better marksman,' Arni interrupted, 'and since we live by hunting prey, I demand the succession as *my* right.'

'I am the better dancer,' said Hunli. 'I am the better chess player,' replied Arni.

'And as for quarrelling, there's nothing to choose between you,' I said. 'You will never agree like this. And I'm not old or wise enough to advise you.' For I was only some twenty years old at the time.

'Why are we talking, then?' said Arni, and they both reached for their daggers again.

'Just a moment,' said I. 'I have heard of a wise woman called Urla, who is said to live in the mountains on the edge of the steppes, and to be able to decide such questions. I suggest we ride there and lay the case before her.'

'We have heard of the wise woman Urla ourselves,' said Hunli. 'But only the Khan himself may consult her.'

'Then let's ride to your father and ask him to take the matter in hand,' I proposed. The pair of them nodded, rose and caught their horses, I saddled my mule, and we rode off together to the Raiding Riders' camp.

To tell you the truth, my suggestion was not entirely unselfish. Not only had I heard of wise Urla, I was extraordinarily anxious to meet her myself. It's worth going far out of your way to find wisdom. The people of the steppes told marvellous tales of her, and many actually believed she was a powerful enchantress.

The Khan received me kindly, and when we had eaten a tender young kid together, the Khan placing the choicest titbits in my mouth with his own hand, the brothers explained their difficulty. The Khan listened attentively, and when they had finished he said, 'I cannot and will not settle this quarrel myself. For only one can rule, and the one I decide must serve will hate me. I will not take that upon myself. So I will ride to Urla with you, and this stranger shall come with us, because he has given you good advice. He who listens to wisdom shall be wise.'

So next day the four of us rode through the steppes towards the distant mountains, blue outlines standing on the horizon. Every day they came a little closer, and after a week we reached the woods at the foot of the range. We left our mounts on the edge of the woods and climbed for a long time, going uphill on foot along a narrow, stony path through low-growing brushwood, until the path led us out into the open again, and we were in an upland meadow. A small flock of sheep was grazing on the hillside, and farther up, between two huge rocks, there stood a log cabin made of roughly hewn tree trunks.

'Wait here,' said the Khan. 'I will go and ask Urla if she will see you.' Then he climbed up to the log cabin by himself, and disappeared through the doorway. He soon came out again, signing to us to follow him.

Urla was standing in the middle of the low-ceilinged room when we came in, looking our way. She was a slender, white-haired woman of medium height. Despite her age, her face was still as smooth and lovely as a young girl's. I shall never forget her eyes, although I couldn't describe the colour of them. When they looked at you, you knew that little could be hidden from them.

'Welcome to my home, Hunli and Arni,' she said. 'And you too, stranger. They say you can play the flute well. You must all be hungry after coming so far, so be my guests.'

She made us sit down at a round table, offered us bread and milk and sheep's milk cheese, and pressed food and drink upon us until we were satisfied. Then she asked the Khan to tell her why we had come. He explained the case of the twins, saying that they had been upon the point of murdering each other. 'You decide between them,' he finished. 'I can't do it without wounding one, for I love them both equally, but only one of them can have power.'

'And what will the other one get?' asked Urla.

'What will he get?' asked the Khan, at a loss. 'Why, nothing. He'll have to serve his brother.'

'Are you surprised they quarrel over it, then?' asked Urla. 'You put this decision the wrong way. Each must be given an aim in life, so that they will not point the arrows of their desires the same way.'

'I know only one aim in life,' said the Khan, 'and that is power over the tribe of the Raiding Riders.'

'You know no other aim because that has always been your own,' replied Urla. 'Do you think there's nothing apart from what you can imagine? Ah no, that's far from all.'

'So you're prepared to decide between them?' asked the Khan.

'No,' she said. 'Hunli and Arni shall decide for themselves.' She rose, opened a chest, and took out two objects which she laid on the table before the twins. One was a round stone worn to smoothness, with a ring of coloured rays shimmering beneath its translucent surface. You know the stone, Listener; you wear it on your breast. The other was a golden brooch made in the shape of a Rider brandishing a curved sword above his head.

'Now choose, twin brothers,' she said. 'Choose the Rider or the Stone. Either is a good choice, but only one will bring you power. Take your time and consider well. First, however, you must swear to accept the decision you take now for ever, and make up your quarrel. Shake hands on that.'

The brothers did as she said, and then they spent a long time gazing at the two objects lying there before them. 'I have chosen,' Hunli said, at last.

'Then come here and whisper in my ear which you want,' she said. Hunli did so, and then Arni rose too, and whispered his own decision in her ear. When he was sitting down again Urla looked at the two brothers, smiling, and she said, 'Well, now the decision is made. Why did you choose the Rider, Hunli?'

Hunli thought for a moment, and then said, 'For three reasons. First, he sits his horse like all the men of my people. Second, he is brandishing a curved sword in the manner of a leader. And third, he is made of gold, which is kept for the ruler's ornaments.'

Urla nodded, and then she asked Arni what had made him choose the Stone. 'I have three reasons too,' he said. 'First, it is clear and without blemish, as a man should be. Second, it warms my heart to look at it. And third, it hides a mystery that I should like to fathom.'

'And now do you see that your sons are not really the same?' Urla asked the Khan. 'They look alike, that's all, and what does it prove? They themselves have shown which is meant to rule.'

'So which of them is my heir?' asked the Khan.

'Don't you know? Why, Hunli, of course. First, he loves the ways of his people who ride on horseback; second, he will not hesitate to draw his sword for his people when he thinks it necessary; and third, he is ready to make use of the power that gold gives him. He is a born ruler.'

'And I am not?' asked Arni, disappointed, but without taking his eyes off the stone that lay before him on the table.

'No,' said Urla, 'you are not. You have chosen something that, for you, is better. As a ruler, you could not remain clear and without blemish like this stone, for you would have to do things that go against your nature. You would not be able to follow your heart, and you could never fathom the mystery hidden in this stone. For in reality the ruler is a servant, and must act according to the dictates of his power. But you will be free to seek the mystery. It is up to you how far you get. As long as you keep that freedom, however, men of power will ask your advice as your father has asked mine.'

'Have you discovered the mystery?' asked Arni, looking expectantly at Urla. For a while, they looked into each other's eyes. At the time, I could not help thinking they were like a pair of lovers, although she could have been his grandmother. And then she spoke those lines of verse, Listener, the verse Arni told you before he died.

That was how Arni came by his stone. He still held it in his hand, gazing at it, while Hunli proudly fastened his golden brooch to his jerkin. Urla rose to her feet, which was the sign for us to leave. The Khan bowed and thanked her for her wise words. But as the others were going out, Urla stopped me and said, 'Wait a moment, Fluter. I must speak to you.'

So I stayed behind, alone in the room with her, waiting and curious to know what this wise woman might have to say to a young vagabond.

'The Khan told me,' she began, 'that your flute-playing prevented the brothers from fighting one another. Is that so?'

'Yes,' I said. 'My modest art can sometimes bring men to better thoughts.'

'Play me something,' she said directly.

So I took out my flute, and as I played Urla looked at me in such a way that I could not tear my gaze from her eyes. I plunged into those eyes as into a well becoming ever wider and lighter as I went deeper down, and a nimbus of colours embraced me, green and blue and violet, dissolving into shapes and pictures. I saw beggars become kings and kings become beggars, I saw human beings in their blindness doing harm and entangling themselves in guilt, and I saw those folk being cured of their blindness by the love of others, so that they recognized their guilt, and grew and grew until that guilt dropped away from them like a worn-out shirt. And I played all that I saw upon my flute, played until I was out of breath, and I saw Urla there in front of me again. Then she took me in her arms and kissed me as a girl kisses her lover, saying, 'Thank you, Fluter, for playing me your music. And now I have one more thing to ask you: stay in the Khan's camp as long as you can, and give Arni your friendship. He will need it. Now go.'

The Khan and his sons were waiting at the place where the path led down into the woods at the foot of the mountains again. 'Urla seems to think a lot of your art, Fluter,' said he, as we began the downward climb together. 'Will you give me the pleasure of staying as a guest in my camp?' I thought of Urla's words, and accepted his invitation.

We rode back through the steppes for seven days, and the mountains sank away behind us until they were resting just above the horizon again, like a distant bank of blue cloud. The Khan gave me a tent of my own in his camp, and after that I lived with the Raiding Riders for a whole year.

The brothers kept the promise they had made to Urla. But during this time they began to go their separate ways. Hunli could generally be found by his father's side, taking part in the councils in his tent, accompanying him when he went riding over the steppes to visit neighbouring princes. Arni, on the other hand, kept very much to himself, so that it was not hard for me to win his friendship.

When I entered his tent he would often be sitting by the fire with the stone in his hand, staring at it as if that could tear its mystery from it. 'It won't speak to me,' he said once, when I had been sitting beside him in silence for some time, spellbound by the play of colours that the firelight brought to life within the stone. I reminded Arni of Urla's words: the stone by itself was not all.

'It's all very well for you to talk,' said Arni. 'Your flute speaks to you when you play it. But my stone is dumb, even if the sight of it warms my heart.'

'It's not exactly as you think,' I told him. 'At first I tried to play my flute for myself alone. But all I produced was a sequence of notes that meant nothing much to me. Later, I discovered that I must play the flute for others if it was to speak to me as well. And so I would guess that you're not likely to discover the secret of your stone inside your own tent, either.'

'You may be right,' he said. 'Come, let's ride out on the steppes.'

After that we spent a great deal of time riding together, Arni on his shaggy horse and I upon my mule. Now and then Arni took us for a longer ride than usual. If we came to a spring in the steppes, or a solitary tree whose shade invited us to rest there, he would stop only briefly, saying, 'I've been here before.' Then he would spur his horse on, as if the goal he was seeking lay only beyond the borders of those lands he knew.

So we came to the farthest-flung parts of that country, right down to the great Brown River that divides the steppes from the mountain ranges of the south. And there, one evening, we rode into a village of the Carpheads. They were given this name because of their facial resemblance to the head of a carp, with receding chin, pale blue eyes, and the moustaches hanging down over the corners of the mouth that the menfolk wear. They dwell on the banks of the Brown River, make their living by fishing, and are peaceful people, little used to battle. This has earned them the scorn of the Raiding Riders, who call them contemptuously, 'Mud-biters'.

The Carpheads had hidden in their huts as soon as they saw a Raiding Rider trotting towards their village. They had good reason to hide, for the Khan's men descended upon their villages from time to time to carry off a few of the girls for slaves. I had met these light-eyed, pale-skinned women here and there about the camp, when they went out to the herds to collect dried dung and take it back to the tents, where it was used as fuel. They were also considered knowledgeable about herbs, and it says much for their peaceable natures that they did not refuse to heal the wounds of those men who had dragged them off to slavery.

'The Mud-biters have crawled away into their holes,' said Arni, laughing, as we rode through the village.

'Shall we spend the night here?' I asked, for by now twilight lay over the river, and mist was beginning to rise from the reeds.

'What, with the Mud-biters?' said Arni, amused. 'A Raiding Rider would never so much as imagine doing such a thing!'

'Do you suppose,' said I, 'there's nothing apart from what you can imagine?'

Taken aback, Arni said, 'I've heard that before.'

'Yes,' said I, 'you've heard it before, and maybe you ought to reflect upon it if you mean to fathom the mystery of your stone. Those are the words Urla spoke to your father.'

Arni brought his horse to an abrupt halt, and dismounted. 'Very well,' said he, 'let's spend the night with the Mud-biters.'

'The Carpheads,' I said. That term was not considered insulting, for the folk who lived by the river venerated the carp as the ancestor of their people, which was not so surprising when you took their appearance into account.

We tied our mounts up to a fence behind which lay a low-built hut, made of rough-hewn logs. Arni knocked on the door with the pommel of his dagger. We heard a stifled scream inside, and then all was still again. Arni knocked for the second time. Now footsteps approached us, a wooden bolt was pushed back, and the door opened. In the doorway stood a stocky, broad-shouldered man with grey hair cut short, and the drooping moustache of the Carpheads. There was naked fear in his watery eyes. 'Lord,' said he in the language of the Raiding Riders, 'lord, spare my house.'

Arni laughed. 'Don't worry, old man,' said he, 'I have no designs on your daughters. Can we sleep in your home tonight?'

'Lord, what would you do here?' stammered the old man, amazed. 'Mine is a poor house.'

'Never mind if it's poor or not,' Arni interrupted him. 'Will you refuse us hospitality?'

'No, lord,' said the man. 'How could I dare do that?' And he straightened his humbly bent back, looked us both in the face, one after the other, and said, almost with solemnity, 'Krushka's house stands open to you. Come in and be my guests.'

Whatever the Raiding Riders might have done to this man, once he had spoken those words we were as safe in his house as in our own tents.

Stepping aside to let us in, Krushka called a boy to him and told him something in the soft, lilting language of the river folk. The boy went out to our mounts, untied them from the fence, and led them to a stable behind the house. Arni watched his horse go off with some concern, but our host said, 'Have no fear; the lad understands animals.' Then he led us into the living-room. Smoke from the wood-fire hung in the air under the low beams of the ceiling. The fire burned on an open hearth by the side wall, its flickering flames lighting up the room. The rest of the household were standing at the far end of the place, pressed close together, looking at us in alarm. There were two elderly women and three young ones, two young men, and several children. Krushka said a few words to them in his own language, and at that their faces relaxed. They examined us with curiosity as Krushka came back to us, saying to Arni, 'Lord, it is our custom here to address a guest by his name, but I do not know what to call you.'

'You are right to ask,' said Arni. 'I ought to have told you at once who was requesting your hospitality. This stranger here, my friend, is known as the Fluter, and my name is Arni.'

'Then you are Arni of the Stone, the Khan's son,' said Krushka. 'You do me great honour.' This was the first time that I heard Arni given that title. So the tale of the brothers' quarrel and Urla's wise advice had reached the Carphead people by the Brown River.

Krushka led us to a low settle by the opposite and narrower wall of the room. As we sat down on this wooden settle, ornately carved and covered with woven rushes, one of the younger women spread a brightly coloured, woven cloth in front of us, and laid salt and dark bread on it, along with some wooden platters and earthenware cups. Meanwhile one of the older women, probably Krushka's wife, was busy about the fire. She put dry wood on it, and brought a huge pike in from outside. She stuffed the fish with herbs and laid it in the kettle that hung over the hearth. Soon the room was full of the fragrance of the fish. Now the other members of the family came to sit around the cloth, and Krushka filled the cups with liquor clear as water that had a sharp aroma, pouring it from a squat jug. Then the fish was served, and Krushka himself gave us the best portions.

Let me tell you, I had never eaten so deliciously cooked a fish in my life before! Arni relished it too, and praised the cook. Apart from that, hardly a word was spoken during the meal.

When we had all eaten our fill, Krushka turned to me and said, 'We have heard of you too, Fluter. Will you do us the favour of playing something on your silver pipe?'

'A host's request is not to be denied,' I said, and I got my flute out of my pocket. Putting it to my lips, I began with the call of the water ouzel, which I had heard as we rode along by the riverside. As I played on, I saw Arni with his stone in his hand, gazing at the soft shimmering of its rounded form. In the light of the flickering fire on the hearth, separate colours began to glow: green, blue and violet melted into one another, parted again, and formed a glimmering ring, into whose dark centre I plunged as into a pool. A great blue carp came swimming towards me through the swaying greenness, looking at me with his round eyes, pale as water. He wore a shining, silvery armour of mirror scales on his back. Opening his bearded mouth, he sang a song that is hard to put into words. I heard the rushing of the Brown River, the cry of the water-birds, the sound of the wind in the reeds, the splash of fish leaping, the snap of the pike's jaws closing, for that too is part of the watery world the regal carp was praising in his song, and I loved the mighty creature for his beauty and his singing, and played what his song of praise put into my mind. I played until the carp closed his round mouth and shot off into the green waters with a mighty flick of his tail, until the colours merged together, and at last were closed again within the smooth, round stone that Arni held in his hand. Then I took my flute from my lips and put it back into my pocket.

Krushka was silent for a while, and I saw that he too had been looking at Arni's stone. Finally he looked up, thanked me, and said, 'You know a good deal about the river folk, Fluter.'

'I didn't know much when I came here,' said I, 'but I know a little more now.'

'Your flute speaks to you,' said the old man. He did not seem surprised.

'And my stone speaks to me,' said Arni. From the way he said it, I knew he must have seen much the same as I did.

'It is a great gift Urla gave you,' said Krushka to Arni. 'I thank you, too, for showing your stone in my poor house.'

'I am glad that you give me hospitality,' said Arni, 'and sorry I alarmed your people before.'

At the time I was surprised to hear a Raiding Rider say such things, but as yet I knew little about the properties of the stone, and I was only just learning the power of my own flute. In Urla's cabin, I had realized for the first time that it was more than a game. And now, in Krushka's house, I had learned a little more.

Soon afterwards, his wife made us a bed beside the fire, and I slept deep and dreamlessly that night.

Next morning we were woken by Riders galloping into the village. Soon their high-pitched cries and the crack of their whips mingled with the girls' screams of fear. Arni leaped up and ran to the doorway. Following him, I saw, when he flung the door open, Hunli and a troop of his Riders outside, rounding up the girls who had gone down to the river in the morning to fetch water. Their overturned buckets were rolling about the village street, in among the horses' hooves.

Arni rushed out and caught his brother's horse by the bridle. 'Hunli!' he shouted. 'Let the girls be!'

Hunli looked at him in surprise. 'What are you doing here, Arni?' he asked. 'Why shouldn't we get ourselves a few girls from the Mud-biters? That's always been our custom!'

'And a bad custom too,' said Arni. 'Must one do ill just because it's the custom? Ride home again!'

'What's come over you?' said Hunli, looking down contemptuously from his horse's back. 'Since when has a Raiding Rider ranged himself beside the Mud-biters?'

'Beside the Carpheads,' said Arni. 'I am a guest in Krushka's house.'

'Krushka?' said Hunli. 'Who may Krushka be?'

'The owner of this house,' said Arni, 'and I'm his guest.'

'Urla was right to think you'd never make a leader,' said Hunli scornfully.

'She was right to think you wouldn't remain clear and without blemish like my stone, too,' said Arni. 'And for my stone's sake I claim the right to order you out of this village. Or would you rather strike down your own brother before you drag those girls away?'

Hunli stared at him grimly for a while, chewing the moustache he was just growing at that time. Then he snatched his reins out of Arni's hand, whistled up his men, and galloped out of the village with them.

From that day on, Hunli avoided his twin brother. I was never quite sure whether he did so merely because he was angry with him, or whether he felt uncomfortable with this strange brother of his. For it can happen that one ceases to feel as much at ease with a person as before, if that person begins to seem different from other folk, through some peculiarity of character, and takes no account of their way of life. And Krushka too betrayed a certain surprise, almost perplexity, at the behaviour of this high-ranking Raiding Rider when we were saying goodbye, and he thanked Arni most effusively for his intervention: rather as if Arni had been trying to forbid a pike to hunt young carp in future.

And after that the two of us became even closer, for I was an outsider in the camp too, being a stranger. Arni continued to go for his long rides with me, and usually would not rest until he could say, 'I haven't been here before.' At this time we saw various strange regions and met with strange people out on the edge of the steppes, but they are of no significance to this story.

Almost a year passed by in this way. I came to know the cruel winter of the steppes, when snowstorms sweep across the dead, white plain, and the fires in the felt tents never go out. Then spring came, and I rode out with Arni towards the distant horizon again. In the camp, they had become used to our going our own way. No doubt the Khan said to himself that this was not likely to bring the two brothers together, and no doubt he also thought of the mysterious link forged by the stone between wise Urla and his son Arni. All his experience told him that people of their kind do keep aloof, and perhaps he hoped, secretly, that Arni would become much sought after, possibly even a man versed in magic arts, and would thus increase the fame of his tribe.

As we took very little notice of the affairs of the others, we had no idea whether the Khan was planning to ride out raiding, as was usual in the spring, let alone what way he was thinking of going with his horde. We had ridden out in the first light of dawn, but Arni did not choose the way leading to the Brown River this time; instead, he turned farther northwards, because he had 'already been to the Carpheads'.

Here to the north the land was hilly. The Bear Folk had laid out their fields in the shallow hollows of the valley, and beyond the fields, in the valley itself, the handsome wooden gables of their houses stood among plum trees in blossom. Wherever you looked, you saw the men ploughing the untilled fields with teams of horses: tall, strong men with thick brown beards and hairy arms and legs. They were considered rich, for the soil was dark and fertile here, so that they could not only live well on their produce but trade with the surplus too. It was said that they knew where their advantage lay, and you couldn't easily take anything from those strong, bear-like fellows by force.

They paid little attention to us as we came trotting along, for they had nothing to fear from two horsemen on their own. But then, suddenly, I felt a hollow thunder that made the ground shake, and directly afterwards a horde of Riders came up over the summit of the nearest hill, galloping at speed towards the village. The Bear Folk who were ploughing had looked up at the hill at the same time as we did, and then there was a great yell: the men drew knives and cut their horses loose from the harness, mounted them, and each was grasping a mighty spear that had been ready to hand, stuck in the ground on the edge of the field. They rode towards each other from all directions, and before the horde was half-way down the hillside, they had united to form a troop galloping to meet their attackers.

'The Khan!' cried Arni, spurring his horse so hard that it reared up before setting off at a gallop. Whatever unusual qualities Arni might have, he belonged to the horde and must ride with the horde when the long-drawn-out cries of the Raiding Riders called to the attack. I trotted after him on my mule, and reached the battlefield just as the opposing troops clashed. The Bear Folk were far outnumbered, but luckily for them the Raiding Riders had hardly had the time to shoot any arrows, and it was not easy to do much with their curved swords against the Bear Folk's long spears. However, I didn't feel inclined to wait and see who was going to kill whom, particularly as Arni was already at the Khan's side, in the middle of the fray. Well, you know what I think of such proceedings. So I took my flute out of my pocket, and began playing a little tune to the men on horseback and locked in battle.

I had never before had a chance of trying out my art on an entire horde of warriors hewing wildly away at each other, and I was surprised, myself, to see the horses slow to a walking pace as soon as they heard the first notes, and then stop, while the men stopped fighting too and lowered their weapons. They sat their horses, bemused, gazing at their enemies, who did not want to fight. Meanwhile, more and more men came riding up from the village in troops, to join their own people, until anyone could see that the attackers no longer had any chance of breaking through that barrier, all bristling with spears. Then I thought the time had come to stop playing my flute.

When I had finished my tune, it was so quiet for some time that you could hear nothing but the snorting of the horses. All the men were looking at me, and seemed to expect me to make some further move in this affair, while I sat on my mule, feeling awkward, not sure what to do with my hands. Finally Arni, who had stayed near his father, came trotting over to me. 'What happens now?' he asked.

This confused me even more. 'I don't know,' I said. 'That's your business.'

'You began it,' he replied, 'and now you must see it through. Come along, the Khan wants to speak to you.'

I rode along the Raiding Riders' front line with Arni, and I saw nothing but rejection in their faces, even fear in the faces of some. The Khan looked at me with ill humour.

'And what was the idea of that?' he asked. 'Are you aware that only my duty as your host prevents me from knocking you off your mule?'

I summoned up all my courage, and said, 'I can't claim to be sorry for the way I acted, Khan. The fact is, I'm so made that I cannot stand a fight.'

'So what's supposed to happen now?' asked the Khan.

'You'll have to come to terms with the Bear Folk,' said I.

'Yes,' said the Khan, grimly, 'I suppose I will. And you are the first man who has ever brought me to do something I don't wish to do.'

He turned abruptly away from me, unfastened a heavy, golden, decorative brooch from his jerkin and held it raised in his right hand as he rode his horse towards the Bear Folk. At that a mighty horseman rode out of their own ranks, a man whose brown beard, streaked with grey, hung down to his belt. He came towards the Khan, taking a chain of golden amber from his neck as he rode. Not a muscle of their faces moved as they met between the two front lines and exchanged gifts. Then the Khan turned his horse and trotted back to his men. 'You, Arni, and you, Fluter, will come back to the camp with us,' he said as he rode past. He shouted an order, and galloped out of the valley at the head of his horde.

As soon as we were back at the camp the Khan summoned Arni and myself to his tent. When we came in I saw that he had called the full assembly of his Council. He sat on high on his throne of cushions, Hunli sat on a lower cushion beside him, and the chieftains of the various clans were squatting in a semicircle on the thick carpet on either side of them.

'Now, what do you say of the thing the Fluter did today?' asked the Khan, opening the debate.

'He has done the horde harm,' said one of the elders, and the others nodded in agreement.

'Did you hear that, Fluter?' asked the Khan. 'They say you have done the horde harm. Is it so?'

'I do not agree,' said I. 'It is not so. I prevented the horde from doing others harm.'

'Hair-splitting,' said the Khan, with a dismissive gesture. 'It comes to the same thing. Do you know whose guest you are?'

'The guest of the Raiding Riders,' said I.

'Exactly,' said the Khan. 'And now, tell me how we are to be Raiding Riders if you prevent us from going on raids? You will not change our nature, any more than you can change your own, which forces you to intervene in any fight. Or can you promise never to do it again in future?'

'No, I can't,' I said. 'If I could, I wouldn't be the Fluter.'

'I expected as much,' said the Khan. 'Fluter, you are my guest, but now I require you to leave the horde.'

Arni had kept silent up to this point, but now he came before his father, crying, 'Would you chase my friend from the tents like a dog?'

'Not like a dog,' said the Khan. 'I will give him a spare horse and provisions enough for him to ride anywhere he likes.'

'And as far away as possible!' said Hunli scornfully. 'Don't you want to go too, Arni? Or would you rather go to your host and friend that Mud-biter?'

'Silence!' snapped the Khan. 'You are not to despise your brother because he is different from you. Don't forget the oath you swore to Urla! However, Arni, I will not hinder you if you want to accompany the Fluter. I don't know the way you are going; you must find it for yourself. Do you wish to stay with the Fluter?'

Arni thought for a long time. Then he said, 'No. I belong to the horde, for I am a Raiding Rider, even if I desire to search for the secret of my stone. I have at least come to understand that it is not a matter concerning myself alone.' Then he smiled suddenly, and added, 'Perhaps it will be a good idea for me to stay near you, Hunli.'

That was the time when Arni made his decision, and he remained a Raiding Rider until the day of his death, a Rider's death. 'It was good to go riding over the steppes with you,' he told me as we parted. 'But as you have seen, I cannot break free of the cry of the horde.'

'What about Krushka?' I asked.

'A man must protect the friend who gives him hospitality,' he said. 'That's one of the Raiding Riders' customs too, or you wouldn't be alive now yourself.'

'You will not have an easy time of it if you make many more such friends,' said I.

'I don't suppose that Urla gave me the stone so that I would have an easier time than others. But I am sure she didn't mean it to bring me misfortune.'

He rode to the borders of the steppes with me, and then went back to his horde, and I never saw him again.

* * *

It had become quite dark outside while the Gentle Fluter was telling the tale of Arni of the Stone. Listener's grandmother had brought a taper from the kitchen and lit a pair of candles. Then she sat down with the others again, looking almost in surprise at her husband as he told of these wonderful things. He had taken off his gold-rimmed eyeglasses when he began his tale, and they lay on the table before him, sparkling in the candlelight. And the longer he went on talking, the more clearly did another face appear behind his apple cheeks and laughter lines: a face marked by strange experiences, and not without a touch of daring in it. This man, anyone could see, had ridden the steppes with the Raiding Riders.

Grandmother had cleared her throat loudly now and then, when the story struck her as really too peculiar, but she had not interrupted the storyteller, though she had sometimes seemed on the point of doing so. 'Such a lot of fuss about a stone,' she said now. 'May I have a look at it, Listener?'

Listener brought the bag out from under his shirt, took out the stone and let it fall into her open hand. 'Looks like any old pebble from the brook,' she said, disappointed. 'Bit more colour in it, maybe. I wish I

knew what you menfolk see in a thing like this.' She held the stone up
to the candlelight. 'Hm, very pretty,' she said, as the flame brought the
ring of coloured rays to life. 'Almost like an eye looking at you. Well,
like I said, this is a man's toy; you never can resist a pair of pretty eyes,
eh, any of you? Not you, Listener, nor this vagrant fellow I married, as
we've just heard. Didn't even stop at that old woman, looked into her
eyes and dreamed up something, dreamed and dreamed, and when he
tells the tale you could almost believe he saw the whole of life in that
one moment, the way we never can see it else, not with our poor little
minds. Well, no wonder, if her eyes were as fair as this stone – ah, look
how the colours flow together, you'd almost think the stone eye was
alive. Your heart grows warm when you look into those eyes in that
lovely face. Yes, a young face, as you said, Fluter, but her hair's not
white, it's a young woman looking at me. Come over here, Listener,
look at that face and don't forget it – you have far to go yet, and many
a long way round – ah, my boy, you will roam the woods like a wild
beast before she runs her fingers through your shaggy pelt at last . . .'

While she uttered this speech her voice had grown steadily softer
and more monotonous, as if she were not speaking to any of the people
in the room with her, but only to herself, talking to no one else, until
her voice broke off. Listener had risen and come to stand behind her,
but all he had, just for a moment, was the fleeting vision of a face,
guessed at rather than seen. And perhaps it had been nothing but an
illusion induced by the unsteady light of the candle, whose flame
flickered in the draughts of air. But can an illusion so pluck at one's
heart? He felt an indescribable longing for that face he had not actually
seen, longing for someone beloved, familiar to him, and yet her face
was buried in memory and not to be found. He put a hand on his grandmother's shoulder. 'What are you talking about?' he said. 'Where is
there a face?'

The old woman slowly raised her head and looked at him, empty-
eyed. 'Face?' she murmured. 'Did I say anything about a face?'
Gradually, she came back to herself again. 'Oh, there you are, Listener,'
she said, and such a soft and gentle expression came over her features
that Listener suddenly saw his own quiet mother in them. As he was still
gazing at this transformation in surprise, she suddenly took him in her
arms and pressed him to her capacious bosom. Before Listener could
recover from his amazement, she pushed him away again, saying, 'Oh,
boy, I don't know what it was. You men can turn a person's wits with
such things! Here, there's your stone. Look after it well. But don't

forget: that's not all. Wearing such a stone on your breast is not all. Why, you've scarcely poked your nose into life at all yet!'

'And even so he's done a good deal of mischief,' finished the Gentle Fluter. 'But we will concern ourselves with that tomorrow.'

Next morning's breakfast is of no importance to this story, but in Grandmother's honour we should mention that it was just as delicious as breakfast the day before. When the Gentle Fluter had drunk the last of his tea, he put on his gold-rimmed eye-glasses, which he always took off at mealtimes, rose and went out. Directly afterwards the sound of his flute was heard once more, by the fence outside the window. At first Listener thought he was talking to his blackbird again, but then he realized that the sound was different this time, like a kind of language consisting of nothing but musical tones, and yet you could tell its meaning. He saw Barlo raise his own head to listen. The flute fell silent for a moment, and then began again on the same alluring sequence of notes that seemed to be telling him to go out, out to the place where the music came from. He could not have said just how he got this message, yet he was sure he had understood it. And then he saw the dumb man push his chair back, rise quickly and go to the door, as if someone had called to him. So he too had understood the tune the Fluter was playing outside. Listener jumped up and went after him.

The Gentle Fluter was sitting on the garden fence, as he had sat the evening before, playing on the same wooden flute. When he saw the two of them come through the doorway he lowered the instrument from his lips, saying, 'Ah, there you are at last. Come here, Barlo, and we will begin your language lesson.'

'So that's the idea of it,' said Listener, slightly disappointed. 'I thought you'd only have to play a few notes on your silver flute and he'd be able to speak again.'

His grandfather jumped off the fence, shaking his head so vigorously that his eye-glasses wobbled alarmingly. 'What on earth do you take me for?' he said furiously. 'Do you suppose I can simply make his tongue grow again? Am I a magician, eh? What you did can't be done away with so easily. Now, you be quiet, but listen well, because you'll need to.'

Then the Gentle Fluter began to teach the dumb man his art. He had his own method of doing it: all the first week he taught him only a single note, the one played by the instrument with all the fingerholes uncovered. 'Just blow into it and think of something!' he told Barlo.

'Imagine you are afraid, for instance. How does it sound? Like that? No, you must imagine it a little more precisely. Yes, that's better! Now think of something that gives you pleasure. Forget all the sadness I can still hear in the note! Be happy, not just with your head, with your heart too! Good, we're getting somewhere now.' And so he tried out all possible imaginary situations and states of mind with Barlo, until the dumb man could express the most diverse ideas and moods in the sound of that one tone.

During the second week he added a second note, and during the third a third note, until after seven weeks Barlo could not only play the seven fundamental notes of his flute, but in their tones he could express much of what he was feeling. 'You must play from the heart,' the Gentle Fluter never tired of repeating. 'That is the only way the notes will get colour and clarity, just as people used to be able to tell, from the tone of your voice, whether you were afraid, or asking a question, or about to laugh.'

It was winter by now; the lime trees around the house had lost their leaves, and there was snow lying on the hills. Lessons had been held in the living-room for some time. Listener was present at these practice sessions, but his grandfather would not let him play the flute himself. 'You must learn to listen to the music first,' he said, 'but if you seriously mean to be a fluter then I'll show you, to begin with, how to make a flute.'

After the lesson, he took Listener to a room at the back of the house which looked like a carpenter's workshop. Hatchets, saws, drills, chisels, and all kinds of knives hung in rows on the walls, there was a turning-lathe under the window, and pieces of wood cut square and of different lengths were stacked in one corner. 'It all begins with the choice of the right wood,' said Grandfather. 'Find yourself a piece.'

Listener looked at the pieces of wood, roughly trimmed with hatchet and saw. Some of the wood was light, some dark brown, some reddish. Some of it had a smooth, close grain, other pieces had mottled or wavy graining. He chose a piece with an intricate grain that stood out in attractive patterns on the red-brown wood.

'That's cherry-wood,' said his grandfather, who had come up behind him. 'Looks pretty, but that's not all that matters. Restless wood has too much tension.' He took the rough wood in his hand, tapped the surface where it had been cut with his knuckle, and shook his head. 'Try this piece of maple,' he said, picking up a light-coloured, plain piece of squared wood with a grain of lines running parallel. This time

Listener tapped the wood to test it, and lo and behold, it resounded with a clear, vibrating note.

'We'll take this,' said Grandfather. He fixed the wood in place on the workbench, got a long, narrow drill down from the wall, and showed Listener how to begin by drilling the bore of the flute. 'Not too much force,' he said, 'or the wood will split.' Listener felt the drill go deeper into the wood, as if of its own accord, with every turn it was given, scraping out the centre, and when that job was done the outside had to be shaped. His grandfather rounded off the angular edges of the wood with a knife and put it on the lathe. As soon as he worked the treadle with his foot the rough wood began moving so fast that it looked as if it were round and regular already, although the slender body of the instrument took shape only gradually, as thin shavings curled away under the sharp steel.

And thus, day by day, Listener was initiated further into the art of flute-making; he learned to cut the notch for the sound-hole cleanly, how to prepare the block for the mouthpiece, and finally how to bore the fingerholes at carefully calculated intervals from one another, adjusting his work until every note sounded at its correct pitch.

Meanwhile, winter passed by, the snow melted, and when new leaves appeared on the lime trees Listener asked his grandfather if he could begin playing the flute at last.

'Didn't I tell you you must learn to listen first, and earn your name?' said the Gentle Fluter.

'How many more days, then?' asked Listener.

'Days?' cried the Gentle Fluter, shaking with laughter. 'He actually asks how many more days he must listen! Why, it'll be years before you can really listen properly, impatient as you are!'

Listener did not think this prospect at all amusing. 'Suppose I really take very great pains?' he asked.

'Take pains?' said the Gentle Fluter, scornfully. 'I can see you don't understand anything yet. What's the use of taking pains? You must *want* to listen: listen not just to get it over with, but because the listening itself gives you pleasure. Do you know how long Barlo was forced to do nothing but listen? Three whole years. For he was a servant for three years in Barlebogue castle. And at the proper time you will find out how hard it must have been for him to hear and obey orders in that place. Tell him what it was like, Barlo!'

Barlo put his flute to his lips, and began to play distorted tones in a wild rhythm; then the music changed to a low, monotonous singsong, and finally it became a clear and almost dancing melody that Listener would have liked to continue singing.

'Well,' asked the Gentle Fluter, 'what did he tell you?'

'How am I to know?' asked Listener. 'All I heard was music.'

'All you heard was music?' said the Gentle Fluter. 'Isn't that enough? You are rather slow in the uptake! Listen carefully, and pay attention to what you're feeling as you listen. Tell him again, Barlo, and exaggerate a bit. His heart's not ready for subtlety yet.'

Barlo played the same tunes again, and Listener tried to let the sounds and rhythms work upon him. As the shrill sequences of notes in the first part leaped and plunged wildly, disturbing him, he suddenly said, 'I feel anger.' The Gentle Fluter nodded, and when the theme of the second part began, confined to a few notes circling each other, he asked, 'Now what do you feel?'

'It makes me sad,' said Listener, and waited tensely until the melody rose to its last part and danced towards its end. 'I feel excitement, and interest, and I recognize the principle of order,' he said, when Barlo had finished.

'There, now do you see how to understand Barlo's new language?' asked the Gentle Fluter, pleased. 'He's not dumb any more. You have given an exact translation of what he wanted to tell you: first he was angry at having to serve in that castle, under the witch; then he sank into dull grief, and hardly noticed what was going on around him; but at last he learned to listen, began to understand what was happening, and played the game too in his own way. You know only too well what that cost him.'

And seeing Barlo's face darken again, he told him, 'You mustn't grieve for what has happened any longer. Don't you yet understand that, through it, you will find a new way?' Then he took the flute from Barlo's hand and raised it to his own lips. He played the last part of Barlo's tale again, but this time he did not let the music die away as his pupil had; he spun it out farther, linking the themes into new figures, into a web of sound swinging up and down, unfolding freely from its first beginnings, and still following distinct rules that Listener understood more clearly the longer he listened. And as he listened to that music he also understood, at least for this brief time, that everything that had happened so far conformed to an underlying pattern, although he could not have grasped or described the pattern's nature. But it was there, and he could still feel it long after the sound of the flute had faded.

'That was a good theme you made up, Barlo,' said the Gentle Fluter. 'You've learned a great deal this winter. It is time the two of you set out on your travels.'

Listener looked at him, bewildered. On what travels was he supposed to set out? His grandfather spoke in as matter-of-fact a way as if the whole thing had been settled long ago. 'I was really planning to stay with you rather longer,' he said, disappointed. 'Where else could I learn to listen as well?'

'Oh, don't worry,' said his grandfather. 'There are far more effective methods. If you hadn't let yourself be detained in Barlebogue, we might perhaps have discussed the matter, but even so I wouldn't have kept you here so very long. What can you learn with two old folk like us? In any case, you incurred certain obligations in Barlebogue, and you can't wriggle out of them now.'

'What kind of obligations?' asked Listener. 'I'm glad I got away from that witch!'

'You may have done,' said the Gentle Fluter, 'although the last word's not been said on that subject either. But you can't run away from what you did there.'

'Well, where am I to go, then?' asked Listener.

'That depends where Barlo is going,' said the Gentle Fluter. 'I think you should go with him, and as his servant. He has learned a little flute-playing from me, but it will be some time before he is such a master of his art that everyone can understand his language. First and foremost, you'll be his interpreter when he wants to talk to people. But you should also obey all other orders he gives you.'

'And how long am I supposed to serve a man who was once a groom?' asked Listener, sullenly.

The Gentle Fluter looked thoughtfully at his grandson. 'If that's the way you think,' he said at last, 'it will probably be quite a long time. You will be Barlo's servant until the day comes when he no longer needs you, and dismisses you from his service of his own accord.'

On hearing this, Listener hung his head. The outlook seemed gloomy if the very man who had good reasons to be revenged on him was to decide his freedom. He glanced at Barlo, but he was leaning calmly on the fence, looking gravely ahead of him, betraying nothing of the way he would regard this servant of his.

'You don't particularly seem to like my suggestion, Listener,' the Gentle Fluter continued. 'Of course, I can't force you to accept it – you must decide what you want to do for yourself. You can always go home again, although I don't know that I'd advise it. By now your father has probably heard of your remarkable exercise of jurisdiction in Barlebogue, and I'm afraid it will not have made his mighty voice any softer. For he is a just man, if a little too loud for my liking.'

Listener could well imagine the kind of welcome he would get from the Great Roarer. Dear heaven, he would most certainly live up to his name! He sat down on the grass, leaned back against one of the posts of the fence, and thought. As he was thinking, he felt the bag containing his stone lying on his breast. He took the stone out and let its colours play in the sun. For a long while, he gazed at the iris ring of rays beneath its smooth, cool surface. He was glad of the beauty of the glimmering colours, as always when he looked at the stone, and he felt his fear of the future fade away. But still he did not know how he should decide.

'No one can take the decision for you,' said his grandfather, smiling. 'Not even your stone.'

'No, of course not,' said Listener. 'But I can stick it out with Barlo, so long as I have the stone with me.'

'Then that's all settled,' said the Gentle Fluter, relieved. 'You will ride away tomorrow morning.'

'Both on the same horse?' asked Listener. 'Or can you whistle another one up with your flute, the way you call to your blackbird?'

'No, I can't do that,' said his grandfather. 'But I think we can get hold of a mount, even if it won't be a horse.'

'For Barlo?' asked Listener hopefully.

'No, for you,' said his grandfather, unrelenting. 'You must let Barlo have the horse; it is his due, since he will be your master. Come along, we'll set off at once.'

As they were leaving the garden by way of the gate in the fence, Grandmother came to the door, calling, 'Where are you all going? Dinner will be ready in two hours' time!'

'Never fear, we'll be back on the dot,' said Grandfather. 'Just a little visit to mine host who keeps the donkeys!'

'Idlers, the lot of you!' scolded Grandmother, watching them go. 'I suppose my dinner's not good enough for you without a drink first! If you're not sitting at my table in good time, I'll send that blackbird after you!'

The three of them could not hear any more of what she said, because the house had disappeared from sight as they rounded the first bend in the path. In spite of his frail build, Listener's grandfather walked fast

on his nimble little feet, but where he took two of his dancing steps, tall
Barlo need take only one. Listener went along beside them, wondering
what kind of man it was they were going to see. Mine host who kept
the donkeys? Did he keep an inn called The Donkeys, or did he have
donkeys for sale? Listener could already picture himself trotting along
on a tiny grey beast behind Barlo's tall horse, his feet dangling, and he
almost regretted his decision.

They had passed two more of the bends in the path which wound its
way through the grassy slopes of the hills. Now the little valley widened
out, the stream flowed down into a lowland plain, and farther on,
where alders grew beside it, it joined a river. Half-way there, a large
tract of land had been divided off by low board fencing and there was a
sizeable property in the middle of this enclosure, obviously a kind of
inn, with a wide gateway and stables behind the main building. As they
came closer, Listener could make out the inn sign hanging from a
wrought-iron arm above the entrance, and showing a bright blue donkey
leaping a fence. So it *is* an inn called The Donkeys, thought Listener
with relief as they went through the gateway.

They entered the main room of the inn through a side door. The
small windows did not let in much light, so that it was difficult to
make much out in the dimness at first. There were settles running
along the walls, and three tables in front of them, their thick wooden
tops so well scoured that dark knots stood out from the pale wood like
brown bumps. A huge tiled stove filled the far corner of the room, on
the wall away from the windows.

The Gentle Fluter tapped one of the tables with his knuckles, and
immediately a door opened on the opposite side of the room and a
thick-set, elderly man came in. He was wearing a workmanlike blue
apron, and had a round felt cap of indeterminate colour on his shorn
and almost square head.

'Morning, Fluter,' he said, in a surprisingly high, almost whinnying
voice. 'What can I do for you?'

Listener's grandfather returned his greeting, and went on, 'I need a
good mount for my grandson. Can you ask one of your friends if he
would be kind enough to carry the young man for a while?'

'You mean that tall fellow there?' asked the innkeeper, pointing to
Barlo. 'Don't know that any of 'em will take *him* on.'

'No,' said Listener's grandfather. 'This is Barlo, and he has come to
fetch the horse I stabled here.' He took Listener's shoulder and propelled him to a place in front of the window where the innkeeper could

see him better. 'This one's my grandson. Take a good look at him. He's still young, and not very heavily built.'

The innkeeper examined Listener from head to foot, as if he were up for sale. All we need is for him to look at my teeth, thought Listener. The man had now walked round to inspect him from behind as well. Then he nodded, satisfied, and said, 'Nice lean sort of lad. Yes, I know who to ask. Come outside the door, will you, and you can see my friend galloping up.'

They followed him out of the gateway. The innkeeper stopped by the side of the path, shaded his eyes with his hand and peered up at the distant hills on the far side of the stream. Then he cupped his hands round his mouth like a speaking trumpet and uttered a long, high-pitched, whinnying cry, so loud and shrill that Listener, who was sensitive to noise, started in alarm. For a while nothing happened at all. Then a grey speck moved out of the bushes on top of one of the hills and came gliding swiftly down the green slope. As it came closer it grew larger, and turned out to be a four-legged animal racing up over the meadows full tilt. Its long ears flew out behind its raised and slender head. It was a donkey galloping along, but what a donkey! It was almost as big as a wild horse, with a dark stripe running over the back of its mouse-grey coat. Its hooves drummed powerfully over the ground, flinging up pieces of turf. It took a great jump over the board fence, galloped across the last of the meadowland, jumped the stream, and came to a halt only when it reached the waiting men, so suddenly that stones flew up from the path and Listener, alarmed, swerved aside.

'Don't you worry,' said the innkeeper. 'He acts a bit wild, but that's all. Saddle him up and he's quiet as a lamb.' He laid a hand on the donkey's neck, and the animal rubbed its muzzle against his cheek, as if it were trying to kiss him. 'Thank you for coming so quickly, Yalf,' said the innkeeper. 'Say hullo to my friends too.' The donkey trotted over to the others, let them pat his neck, and then stopped beside Listener as if he knew already why he had been summoned.

The innkeeper looked at Listener, smiling. 'Well, how do you like him?' he asked.

'He's a wonderful donkey,' said Listener, and meant it. 'I should like to ride him very much indeed.'

'Then you'll have to ask him,' said the innkeeper. 'That's our custom here. And call him by his name when you're asking.'

Listener thought all this ceremony rather unusual, but when he looked into the animal's large, moist eyes it did not seem at all strange to say, 'Yalf, will you carry me for a while?'

The donkey rubbed his soft muzzle against Listener's cheek too, by way of answer.

'He's accepted you all right,' said the innkeeper, as though it all depended on the donkey. 'Up to you to keep things that way now!'

'How ought I to handle him?' asked Listener.

'*Handle* him?' repeated the innkeeper, as if the word were quite uncalled for. 'Oh, not at all, that's best — just treat him like a brother. And never tie him up; he won't run away from you. If you want him to do something, just ask him, nice and friendly. And don't forget, whatever you do don't beat him.'

'I'll remember,' said Listener.

'That's all right, then,' said the innkeeper. 'Well, you can all go back indoors now. I'll just find him a saddle and bridle. Come along, Yalf, and we'll get you fitted out.' And he gave the donkey an affectionate pat on the crupper, whereupon it trotted after him through the gateway to the stables, while the other three went back into the inn and sat down at one of the tables. In a little while the innkeeper came back too, saying, 'You'll drink to this new friendship with me, I hope?' Since no one had any objection to that, he put four tankards on the table and then went to the next room to fetch a jug, misty with the cool moisture of its contents, from which he poured out a foaming, white liquid. Then he drew up a stool and sat down with them. 'May they hold one another dear!' he said, raising his tankard. The others did so too, and all drank the toast.

Listener had regarded the strange brew with suspicion at first, but had not dared to ask what their host was pouring out. He tasted it, rather cautiously, and was surprised by its pleasantly sharp and slightly tingling flavour. 'Delicious!' he said. 'What is it?'

'Speciality of the house,' said his grandfather. 'Fermented ass's milk.'

'Do you like it too, Barlo?' asked the innkeeper.

Barlo gave him a friendly grin, nodded silently, and drank some more.

'Not particularly talkative, that young giant!' said the innkeeper. 'Hasn't spoken a word all this time. Dumb, is he?'

'Not now,' said Listener's grandfather. 'Tell him about yourself, Barlo. You must begin getting used to talking to people.'

Barlo brought out his flute and began to play. Listener could follow him better this time, and besides, he knew roughly what his future master had to say. Barlo made use of the same themes he had thought of that morning, but then went on, in a dramatic crescendo, to describe the court of justice, and after that he broke the angry music off short in the middle of a shrill passage. Listener had an almost physical impression of what it must have felt like when Barlo had his tongue cut out. Miserably, he glanced at him, but Barlo was calmly putting away his flute as if he himself were not at all concerned with the tale he had just told.

The innkeeper had been listening attentively. No doubt his acquaintance with the Gentle Fluter had accustomed him to interpreting such information.

'So you're from Barlebogue,' he said. 'Yes, well, might have known it! That's the way they treat people there. Not just people, either. You and my donkeys, you're companions in misfortune, so to speak.'

'What have your donkeys got to do with Barlebogue?' asked Listener. 'The donkeys I saw there were poor jaded creatures that could hardly put one foot in front of another, and were always being beaten.'

'That's the point,' said Grandfather. 'Tell him your story, landlord, it'll interest him.'

'Aye, well, you and Barlo, you're not the only ones have got away from the wicked mistress of Barlebogue,' said the innkeeper. 'For from what you say, I fancy you were there too, young fellow.' He drank some more of the ass's milk, and then told them that a few years ago he had been a donkey driver on the Barlebogue estates. 'I had a dozen donkeys to look after,' said he. 'They were mostly used to carry corn from the barns to the mill, and sacks of flour back to the storehouses. That's the kind of work donkeys are used to; they don't mind it a bit, not if they get fed properly, and kindly treated too.

Well, but all that changed when Gisa's prospectors found gold in the mountains above the upper part of the valley. She told her men to get fifty day labourers together, and had them dig out galleries up there and mine the ore. And I was ordered to take the heavy lumps of ore down to the valley with my donkeys. Now, there's no donkey can stand up to that kind of work for any length of time. Soon they had patches of their coats rubbed bare on their backs, and there wasn't the right sort of food to be found up in the mountains either. So I gave my donkeys lighter loads to carry, and let 'em trot along no faster than their strength allowed them. That wasn't fast enough for Gisa, though. She wanted to see the gold in her coffers. So she sent a couple of her yellow-eyed men up the mountains to drive the donkeys in future. Those fellows had cut themselves stout cudgels of hazel-wood on their way up, and used 'em to beat my donkeys when they turned stubborn and wouldn't go on.

First of all I tried reasoning with the men, for they didn't know a thing about donkeys. But all they wanted was to content their mistress – "Let us be," said they. "You and your donkeys! There's plenty of donkeys around, and if a few of 'em die we can get more up from the valley." So I decided I wasn't going to stand around and watch this any more. I loved my beasts, you see. That night I slipped out of the cabin where the men slept, knocked together in a hurry up by the mines, and went to my donkeys, tethered out on the stony land there chewing at the tough weeds they'd been thrown for fodder. I untied them and set off into the forest with them. That wasn't difficult, seeing that my donkeys knew me and would trot along after me like puppy-dogs.

I knew there were pastures to the west, beyond the forest, so that's the way I went. We were on our travels for two weeks, up hill and down dale. The donkeys could find enough to eat in the forest, but I was more dead than alive myself when I staggered out on the green hills at last. What'd have become of me I don't know, if your grand-father hadn't found me on the edge of the forest, Listener, where I lay senseless in the middle of a herd of donkeys snuffling at me. I fancy his blackbird whistled him the news. Anyway, he took me home with him, and your grandmother coddled and cosseted me, once she'd searched me all over to make sure I wasn't bringing any vermin into her house!

Well, so your grandfather told me this inn was standing empty a little way on down the valley. The last landlord had left it a while back, seeing almost nobody ever comes this way, now that folk avoid the path to Barlebogue. So I settled in here, and my twelve donkeys were my first guests. I kept them in the stables at first, till their wounds were healed and you couldn't see the ribs sticking through their skin. Then I let them out into the meadow.

When I had to take my donkeys to the mines, I'd left all my be-longings back in my own hut. Wasn't much, to be sure, but there were a few things there I valued, because they came from my father: a heavy, finely wrought knife, for instance, and an old bronze brooch made in the shape of a donkey jumping, since my father was a donkey driver before me. Well, seeing I was all right again, and my donkeys didn't need me so badly, I went back through the forest to Barlebogue, but by a shorter way this time, one your grandfather told me. And I slipped into my hut in the village below the castle by night.

While I was getting my things together, the door creaked. I'd only latched it, and I was frightened to death. But it was only a friend of mine come in to see who might be fumbling around in my hut at night. And this friend told me Gisa had been furious when she heard I'd gone, taking the herd of donkeys. She'd sworn out loud in front of everyone, he said, to be revenged on all the donkeys there were, and she'd had their beasts taken away from all the donkey drivers and given them to her retainers, to be treated as badly as the men had treated my own donkeys at the gold mine. That's why what you said about the donkeys in Barlebogue didn't surprise me, Listener.

When he heard where I was living now my friend decided to come with me, for he was sick of life in Barlebogue. He was a smith, and he could ply his trade anywhere. First we went to the out-buildings below the castle and cut the halters of all the donkeys we could lay our hands on. We drove this second herd to my friend's house. He woke his wife and had her pack the essentials they would need for flight. He took his tools too, since we had plenty of animals to carry things. Then we set off back through the forest, and my place here was full of new guests in need of nursing. And somehow or other news of our escape must have got around among the donkeys of Barlebogue, for there's always another of 'em coming out of the forest, exhausted, asking for a place to stay. So now do you see why I'm known as mine host who keeps the donkeys?'

'Are your donkeys all up on the hills now?' asked Listener.

'No,' said the innkeeper. 'Some of 'em are still here in the stables. For instance, the mares always come here to have their foals, and then they stay a while. That's how I generally come to have ass's milk in the place, so there's something to offer my other guests. And besides Barlo's horse, there's two new runaways here that need feeding up.'

'And what about your friend the smith?' Listener inquired. 'Is he still here?'

'Oh, he only stayed a little while,' said the innkeeper. 'Life here was too lonely for him, and he didn't want to forget his trade either. He and his wife live in a village two days' journey down the river now. But he sometimes comes back to visit. He brought me the wrought-iron arm for my sign one day.'

As he was uttering these last words, there was a pecking at the window pane from outside, and then they heard the shrill whistle of a scolding blackbird, a sound usually heard only when a cat comes prowling through the bushes.

'Oh, dear heaven!' cried Listener's grandfather. 'Our dinner!'

All three hastily thanked the innkeeper for his hospitality, and took their leave of him. Yalf and Barlo's horse were already waiting in the yard, both of them ready saddled and bridled.

'Let me get up behind you, Barlo,' said Grandfather, 'and then we'll soon be home.' And so the three of them – or the two of them, depending which way you look at it – trotted back along the path through the hills and arrived just in time, as Grandmother was putting steaming soup plates on the table.

Next morning Listener rode downstream again with his new master. Up to the very last minute, his grandmother had been giving him good advice, telling him to mind he always washed properly ('My word, boy, how you did stink when you arrived!'), and have nothing to do with light women, and further exhortations of this kind. Not until he was about to swing himself up into the saddle of his donkey did she clasp him in her arms once more and press a damp kiss on his cheek, snuffling slightly. What with all this, the Gentle Fluter could hardly get a word in. All he said, now and then, was, 'Stick by Barlo; he'll know what he means to do.'

But did he really know? Listener was not so sure. Barlo had not asked the Gentle Fluter for any advice at all, hadn't even asked about conditions on the path they would be taking, and it was unlikely he had received any unsolicited information. He had shaken hands with his hosts, and then mounted his horse and rode away. Nor, apparently, had he any intention of telling Listener his plans, always supposing he had any. And considering the circumstances governing his new method of speaking, he was probably going to remain silent too. For the time being, at least, his few communications were confined to brief gestures.

Thus, when the inn of mine host who kept the donkeys came in sight beyond the slope of the last hill, he merely pointed, to let Listener know that he wanted to stop there again. The innkeeper must have seen them riding up, and came to the entrance as they reined their mounts in outside his house. When they had dismounted and greeted him, Barlo began a strange pantomime: first he led the innkeeper to his horse, then to Listener's donkey, pointing at their hooves. Then he pointed downstream along the river, and raised first one and then a second finger, counting.

'I understand,' said the innkeeper. 'You want to get your beasts shod, and you're asking after my friend the smith. Well, you won't find a better man for the job; he can shoe donkeys too. Ride on downstream for two days, then, till you get to the next village, and once you reach it ask for Furro. Give him greetings from me, and tell him to come and visit me again someday.'

Barlo nodded his thanks, shook hands, and mounted his horse again. Listener said goodbye too, swung himself up on his donkey and trotted after Barlo, who had set off along the path down to the river.

They rode along beside the river all day. It was swollen with melted snow from the mountains, and rushed on past poplars and alders. To the right of them lay the hilly country, covered with the young green of spring, and on the horizon the range of hills was bordered by the dark woods, behind which Barlebogue lay.

At mid-day, Barlo gave the signal for them to stop and rest. They sat down on the trunk of a fallen poplar and ate some of the provisions Grandmother had packed in their saddle-bags. Then Barlo took out his flute and played a little music to himself. At first it sounded like the pieces the Gentle Fluter had made him play for practice, but then a melody arose from the musical figures and developed in broad phrases, calmly and surely linked. Listener paid attention, letting the playing of the flute work upon him, and the more he gave himself up to the music, the more clearly did Barlebogue castle take shape in his mind, rising up upon its hill, fairer than he remembered it. He saw the gate standing wide open and people going freely in and out, seeming to fear no coercion. Listener wondered how Barlo could remember the castle as such a fine place. Looking into his face, he was surprised to see that Barlo obviously loved that castle, in spite of all the cruel things that had happened to him there. Barlo himself was deeply rapt in his playing, but at last he seemed to notice Listener observing him. He looked up and into Listener's eyes as he played his melody to its end. When he had put his flute down, a fleeting smile seemed to flash over his face, just for the fraction of a second, as if to say: You'll soon see . . .

Then he was grave again, as he had been before, and gave the signal to ride on.

They spent that night under a haystack, and on the afternoon of the second day they saw farmers ploughing the arable fields whose brown expanses now interspersed the meadows more and more frequently. Towards evening, as dark began to fall, the village came in sight. It consisted mainly of poor cottages laid out rather at random, their roofs thatched with straw, and apple trees blossoming above them.

Listener asked a farmer coming home from working in the fields with his team of horses the way to Furro's house, and was directed to a fairly large building at the other end of the village. Long before they got there, they could hear the clang of his hammer, and as they came closer they saw the blacksmith standing by the anvil with a journeyman, in a smithy that stood open to the street. Both of them were naked to the waist under their stiff leather aprons. The smith was a powerful man, tall, with broad and muscular shoulders. He looked about the same age as mine host who kept the donkeys, for his curly hair was grey, lying tangled on his forehead, which gleamed with sweat.

When Barlo and Listener dismounted, tying their beasts up to the post outside the smithy, Furro looked up, laid his hammer down on the anvil, and told his journeyman to put the piece of metal he was working in the fire, which glowed under a hood in the workshop behind them. Then he came over to the two newcomers. 'You have work for me?' he asked.

Listener glanced at his master, but Barlo remained where he was, standing a little to one side in the dusk, and signed to him to speak. 'Yes,' said Listener. 'But first, we bring you greetings from mine host who keeps the donkeys.'

'Ah – I thought as much when I saw that mount of yours,' said Furro. 'Well, that's a good recommendation. Come in and be my guests! You'll stay the night, I hope?'

Once again, Listener waited for Barlo to nod his consent. Then he thanked Furro for the invitation. 'And as for the work,' he added, 'my master's horse needs new shoes, and my donkey needs shoeing too.'

'You've come to the right smithy. I can deal with donkeys,' said Furro. 'But it's too late to fit eight shoes today. Not in a hurry, are you?'

Listener had no idea whether Barlo was in a hurry, but when his master shook his head, he said, 'No, it can wait till tomorrow.'

By now the journeyman had taken the metal out of the fire with a long pair of pincers and laid it back on the anvil. 'Finish that off yourself, and then come in to supper,' Furro told him. He patted the horse's neck and examined its hooves. 'And this is Yalf, unless I'm much mistaken,' he said to Listener. 'He was one of the donkeys I and my friend drove back through the forest. My wife rode him part of the time.' The donkey obviously recognized him too, and greeted him in its own way.

'Where can I stable our beasts for the night?' asked Listener.

'Come with me,' said the smith, 'and I'll show you.'

The journeyman had begun hammering again, and you could tell he was beginning to shape the flat piece of metal into a shoe. Barlo watched with interest.

'Like to stay here while the two of us see to your mounts?' the blacksmith asked. Barlo merely nodded, without looking at him, and went on watching the red-hot iron as it changed shape under the blows of the hammer.

Listener took their mounts by the halter and followed Furro round behind the house with them. There was a roomy stable built on to it here, with three horses in it already. While Listener led the animals to an empty stall, Furro filled their mangers with oats. 'Is your master dumb?' he asked, abruptly.

'Yes,' said Listener. 'Or at least, he can't speak with words.'

'What do you mean?' asked Furro.

'Well, he speaks a language the Gentle Fluter taught him,' said Listener.

'So you've been at the Fluter's too?' asked Furro.

'Yes,' said Listener. 'I'm his grandson, called Listener.'

The blacksmith's brows shot up. He was obviously surprised to find such a man's grandson riding the country on a donkey in the position of a serving man. But he left it at that, merely asking, 'What's your master's name?'

'Barlo,' said Listener.

When he heard that, the smith stopped short in what he was doing and straightened up. 'Barlo?' he asked. 'Does he come from Barlebogue too?'

'Yes,' said Listener.

'So there's a Barlo riding the land again,' said the smith, as if it were something remarkable. Listener did not know what to make of his words, but he dared not ask what the smith meant. When they were back in the workshop, he noticed that the smith treated Barlo with what was almost a kind of awe. 'Forgive me for keeping you waiting, lord,' he said. 'If I'd known . . .' But Barlo cut him short with a brief, imperious gesture, and shook his head. Listener could not make head or tail of all this, particularly as he could feel that the smith now regarded him too with different eyes. Plainly it was far from demeaning to be the servant of this man whose name had so impressed Furro.

Barlo and Listener washed off the dust of their journey at the well beside the workshop, and then the smith washed too and put on a linen shirt before asking them to follow him into the house. He led them into a spacious room, where a woman was busy laying the table for supper.

'We have guests, Rikka,' said Furro. 'You'll need to make them up two beds for the night as well.'

When the woman turned round, Listener saw that she must be considerably younger than her husband, although there were already a few grey strands in her smooth brown hair. She looked at them, and her eyes immediately brought Listener under their spell. They reminded him of something, though he could not have said just what.

The smith introduced her to their guests, and when he mentioned Barlo's name she, in her turn, began to ask a question, but her husband waved it aside. 'And don't wonder at his silence,' was all he said. 'He knows another way to say what he wants. Oh, and his servant is a grandson of the Gentle Fluter.'

'Then you too are doubly welcome to me, Listener,' said Rikka. 'My father was a friend of your grandfather's, and loved him dearly.'

She looked at Listener as she spoke, and once again her eyes seemed strangely familiar to him. But the Gentle Fluter had certainly made many friends in his long life.

The hammering out in the smithy had stopped some while ago, and now the journeyman joined them indoors, and they all sat down at the table. During the meal the smith asked after his friend, and was pleased to hear that his inn was still sought out by donkeys escaping from Barlebogue.

After supper he poured his guests dry cider. 'I hope it's not too sour for your liking,' he said. 'I prefer it to the wine the lady of Barlebogue gives her guests.'

'And well you may,' said Listener. 'Her wine is apt to leave a bitter aftertaste.'

'Oh, so you've been in her castle, have you?' said the smith, surprised. 'I suppose the two of you came to the Gentle Fluter together?'

'In a way,' said Listener, thinking uneasily of his headlong flight through the forest, and the dumb man's terrifying cries. He glanced at Barlo, but Barlo was looking straight ahead of him and did not move a muscle.

'They say that lady is even worse than before,' the smith went on.

'And there's another tale too, that someone threw one of her sparkling stones in her face because he liked a stone of his own better. And the mark can be seen on her forehead to this day. They sing mocking songs about it in secret.'

Listener brought out the bag he wore under his shirt, and took the eye-stone out. 'It will have been this stone they meant,' he said.

The smith's wife gazed at the stone in Listener's hand as if spellbound. 'Urla's stone,' she whispered, as if she could hardly grasp it.

'What do you know about the stone?' asked Listener, wonderingly. 'Where have you seen it?'

'It belonged to my father,' said Rikka. 'I had news last year that he had died on a raid, but no one could tell what had become of the stone.'

'If your father's name was Arni, then he was the man who gave me the stone before he died,' said Listener, and he told her briefly how Arni had met his death.

'He died like a Raiding Rider,' said Rikka, 'although he spent his life arguing with his brother as to whether it was right to live like a Raiding Rider.'

'Yet he stayed with them,' said Listener.

'Yes,' said Rikka, 'he always kept in the neighbourhood of their camp, and went with the horde on their raids. But he was still a thorn in his people's flesh.'

'Why did you say: in the neighbourhood of their camp?' asked Listener. 'Didn't he live in his tent any more, the one my grandfather told me of?'

'No,' Rikka said. 'When I was a child we lived in a log cabin on the edge of the steppes. It stood on the spot where the path up the mountain to Urla's hut begins. For you must know that Urla was my great-grandmother.'

Listener looked at her in surprise. Her eyes were turned on him again, and now he knew what they reminded him of: the coloured rays of their irises were like those in the stone he held in his hand.

'You have Urla's eyes,' he said.

'Yes,' said she, 'all of us who are descended from Urla have her eyes.'

'Did you know Urla?' asked Listener.

Rikka nodded. 'She died when I was five,' she said. 'She must have been well over ninety years old at the time, but her eyes were still clear, and you couldn't avoid them.'

'Did your father leave the camp when his brother Hunli became Khan?' asked Listener, thinking of the estrangement Urla's advice had caused between the brothers.

'No,' said Rikka. 'It was probably to do with his marriage. To the Raiding Riders, my mother was a foreigner, and she would not have been recognized as Arni's wife in the camp, but treated as a slave. This is the Raiding Riders' way: foreigners are usually tolerated in their camp only as slaves. And my mother couldn't have endured their nomadic life either, for she came of settled folk.'

'I guessed that Urla did not come from the tents of the Raiding Riders,' said Listener.

'No; the Riders think little of their own women,' said Rikka. 'I imagine it would never have occurred to them to ask one for her advice.' And then she told:

The Tale of Urla

Urla lived among the ore miners on the other side of the mountains, in the first place. Other folk also call them the Mountain Badgers, because they dig deep tunnels into the mountain slopes as badgers do; not to live there, however, but to dig for ore, or hack stones out of the clefts in the rock. They are also famous for the skill of their smiths, who can make fine jewellery as well as forging tools and weapons.

Urla's father was such a smith. They say that even when she was an infant she had a particular liking for the bright stones her father got from the miners, to set them in gold or silver. And they say that one day, when Urla was seven, a strange old man came into her father's workshop. He wore the clothing of a prospector, and had one of the narrow, pointed hammers that prospectors use in their work at his side. Urla happened to be in the workshop, playing with the stones her father kept in a wooden box until he needed them for a piece of jewellery.

'Do you want to sell my father pretty stones?' Urla asked the old man, but he shook his head and said he had only one stone, and that was not for sale.

'Show me!' said the child.

Then the man took a stone out of his pocket, a translucent stone, worn smooth and with many colours playing in it, and put it in her hand. And he placed his own hand under her chin and raised her head, so that he could see her face better.

'You have the eyes,' he said, 'so the stone is for you too.' And then, so the tale runs, he spoke some lines of verse, but I don't know how they went.

Urla's father was standing at his work-bench, not sure what to make of this man, whom he had never seen before. However, before he could speak to him, the old man kissed the child, and went away so quickly that the smith could not find him again.

And that, I have heard, is how Urla came by her stone. She always carried it with her, and when she was twenty she married a young smith called Russo, who had learnt his trade from her father and was especially skilled in goldsmith's work. She gave him the stone on their wedding day. He enclosed it in a net of silver wire, put it on a thong, and wore it next to his heart.

They lived childless for ten years, until at last Urla had a daughter. That year a trader came to her husband's workshop and bought all manner of jewellery. When they had finished their business, the man asked how he could get over the mountains.

'What do you want over on the other side?' asked Russo. 'That's where the steppes begin, and only the Raiding Riders travel those wild lands.'

'I know,' said the trader. 'I want to journey on to the Raiding Riders, because they love fine jewellery above all things.'

'Aren't you afraid they will take all you have and kill you?' asked Russo.

But the trader only laughed. 'I can see you don't know much about them,' said he. 'They regard traders as sacrosanct when they come into that country, and they know very well why they do so, too. If they laid hands on one of us, it wouldn't be long before no one came to visit their tents any more.' So Russo told him how to find the path over the mountain pass, and the trader rode away. The Raiding Riders in their tents admired the skilfully made brooches, rings and chains, and bought his whole stock. They also asked him what master goldsmith could make such precious things. So the trader praised the skill of Russo, whose workshop was on the other side of the mountains where the Mountain Badgers lived, and he said he would visit him again on his way back and order more jewellery.

The Raiding Riders paid him well and let him go. So he rode back over the mountains again, and he did not forget to visit Urla's husband. He told Russo about the good business he had done, and asked him to put his very best work aside for him to fetch when he rode over the mountains again next year.

However, the Raiding Riders had sent a scout after him to find out where the path over the pass lay, for they were greedy for gold, and thought that there must be more of it to be had where such jewellery was made.

When the scout returned to camp, the Khan summoned his Council and got the man to tell his tale. What he had to describe sounded so tempting that they decided to make a raid, although it was rather late in the year. Fifty Riders from the horde rode over the mountain pass, without encountering any difficulties, and towards evening of the next day they attacked Russo's house, which stood a little way from the ore miners' settlement. The goldsmith drew a weapon and fought them, and was killed at once. Then the Raiding Riders plundered his workshop, laying hands on all they could find in the way of precious stones, either set or uncut, metal bars, and pieces of jewellery, and they also took Urla, who was a very beautiful woman, as their prisoner. There was no one else in the house, not even Urla's daughter, who was six months old at the time. A few days earlier Urla had taken her to her own mother, a skilled healer, because the child had a high fever.

When there was nothing left to rob, the Raiding Riders set fire to the house, and went in search of further hoards of gold. But the miners were coming home from work in the galleries of their mine at this time of day, and the smoke alerted them to the attack. They raised the alarm, and when the Riders eventually found their way to the miners' houses they met an adversary well able to stand up to them, for the Mountain Badgers also knew how to forge good weapons, and the horses they stabled in their smithies were considerably larger and stronger than the Riders' little steppe ponies. When half a dozen Riders had been struck from their saddles in the very first onslaught, the rest turned and disappeared into the woods, so swiftly that pursuit seemed pointless.

Later, Urla described what happened next. While the Riders were looking for the Mountain Badgers' houses, their plunder and their prisoner had been left in a secluded place in the woods, guarded by a couple of men. After the failure of their attack, the other Riders came back to this spot and spent the night there. Next morning they decided to ride back over the mountains, for the plunder they had taken from Russo's house was rich enough by itself.

Urla had wept all night for the death of her husband, murdered before her eyes. Next day she saw the Riders preparing to return, and she knew that they would have to go by way of the pass over the mountains. She glanced involuntarily at the sky, and saw from its colour and the formation of the clouds that there was a sudden change in the weather coming, as often happens at the end of autumn in the mountains. But she did not warn the Riders, for her wrath at her husband's death was great, and as for herself, she did not mind what happened to her now.

The storm broke when they were just over the highest point of the pass. Black clouds raced up so fast that the sky was darkened all in a moment, and then such snow fell that it was impossible to go any further. Men and horses braced themselves against the dazzling white flakes that drove almost horizontally towards them, and lost their way. Many plunged over precipices and steep rockfaces, and were smashed to pieces down below. Others huddled together, and soon froze, for the Riders were not familiar with the weather in the mountains, and wore only their light summer clothing.

Urla had fallen off the pack pony over whose back she had been slung like a bag of flour, and as she fell her bonds had come undone. She crawled on all fours towards a rock that loomed up before her in the driving snow like a dark shadow. Underneath an overhanging ledge, she found a cave, and let herself roll into it. She was safe here from the worst fury of the snowstorm.

When she had been lying there a while, she heard a whimpering noise, quite close, in between two howling gusts of wind. It sounded almost like a child crying. Peering out, she saw a figure lying only a few paces away, already almost covered with drifting snow. Without stopping to think about it, she crawled out and saw that this Rider was a boy, not much more than fourteen years old. She seized him by the feet and dragged him into her shelter. The boy was weeping to himself, and hardly seemed aware of what was happening to him. When she had laid him down inside her cave, she took him in her arms and warmed him with her body until he stopped crying and fell asleep against her shoulder, his arms round her neck like a child's.

She did not know how long she had been lying there when the snowstorm stopped, as suddenly as it had begun. The wind drove the clouds away over the mountain heights, and a moment later the icy blue sky was swept clear, while the newly fallen snow sparkled in the sun so brightly that it hurt the eyes. Urla shook the boy awake and dragged him out of the cave. Staggering, he rose to his feet and put a hand over his dazzled eyes. Narrowing her own eyelids, Urla looked around her. Here and there, a small mound stood out in the rocky terrain, but far fewer of them than the troop of Raiding Riders had numbered. A little way downhill, three horses were getting to their feet, with difficulty, and shaking the snow from their coats. There were two Riders with them; they had sheltered from the snowstorm under the warm bellies of their mounts. They were the only members of the troop of Riders left alive.

For a moment or so, Urla had thought of making her escape back over the high pass, but it would have meant certain death in the great drifts of snow after such a storm. So she and the boy waded down to the men with the horses. She recognized one of them: the man who had killed her husband. And she noticed that the Riders hailed the boy with a certain deference. They seemed to be relieved he was still alive. When they were going to bind Urla again the boy intervened and said something to them, and then they left her alone. After that, they treated her with as much respect as a Raiding Rider is able to show a woman.

Being the lightest of the three survivors, the boy took Urla up on his horse, and so they rode down to the plain, and on over the steppes for a week, until they came to the Raiding Riders' camp. Their arrival occasioned much mourning, and Urla said later that she had heard the wailing of the dead Riders' widows for nights on end as she lay awake, thinking of her murdered husband.

At first she was surprised that she had not been taken straight to the slaves' huts, being a prisoner, but was allowed to sleep with the Khan's women, and she was even more surprised by their friendliness towards her. One middle-aged woman even took her in her arms and kissed her, but Urla could not understand what she was saying.

Next day she was taken before the Khan. He had sent her a slave that morning, a woman who came from the mountainous country of the ore miners and was to act as her interpreter. There were several other chieftains of the Riders gathered in his tent, and the boy Urla had kept warm in the snowstorm was sitting beside the Khan. He smiled at her when she came in.

First the Khan asked her name: Urla told him, and added, 'The widow of Russo the goldsmith, whom your men killed.'

The Khan raised his eyebrows in surprise when this remark was translated, for women were not used to speak in such a way in the Raiding Riders' tents. Then he said, 'My son Kurgi has told me that you saved his life. I cannot understand why you did it, to be sure, since you had every reason to leave him to freeze like the others, but now I am in your debt.'

'Yes,' said Urla, 'you are indeed in my debt, but not on your son's account. Among my people we consider it nothing remarkable when someone is unable to stand by and watch a child perish. However, I see that you Riders think differently.'

'I cannot dispute with you over the matter of your husband's life,' said the Khan, 'for then I would be in debt to far too many more besides. You are among the Raiding Riders here; did you not know? But I will give you your freedom for my son's sake. You may live in my wives' tent until the paths are open again and you can go home. And I will also permit you to express one wish.'

Urla had been looking around the Khan's tent, and among the chieftains she had recognized the man who killed Russo, and was now openly wearing on his bare chest the stone in its setting of silver wire that she had given her husband on their wedding day. She went up to the chieftain, pointed to him, and said, 'I would like to have back the stone this man has taken.'

'That will not be easy,' said the Khan. 'The stone does not belong to me, so I cannot give it to you. But we Raiding Riders love a contest, and I will let you play against this man for the stone. I will even go so far as to let you choose the rules of the game yourself, since you don't know our own games.'

Urla looked hard at the man, and then turned back to the Khan and said, 'I have chosen my weapons.'

'And what are they?' asked the Khan.

'My eyes,' said Urla.

The Khan smiled. 'Well, you have chosen the sharpest weapons at a woman's command,' said he. 'And how do the rules of the game go?'

'He must look into my eyes,' said Urla. 'And whichever of us is first to shrink from the other's gaze has lost the stone.'

When the slave woman had translated Urla's words the Khan asked the man if he agreed. He nodded, laughing, and seemed very sure of victory. Then he rose to his feet and stood opposite Urla. The rest of them, sitting in a circle, watched the two adversaries tensely; you could tell from their faces that this was a contest after their own hearts.

The two stood there in the middle of the tent for a long time, looking into one another's eyes. Gradually the smile vanished from the man's features. His expression grew grave; then he began to press his lips together, and his eyes flickered. Drops of sweat stood out on his forehead, and there was no sound to be heard in the tent but his panting breath, which came ever louder and faster. The stone shone in its silver setting and began to sparkle and glow with many colours. Suddenly the man uttered a loud cry, as if he felt unbearable pain. His hand went to his breast, he tore the stone from its thong and flung it at Urla's feet, and at the same moment he turned his face away and looked down. They could all see a red mark burning on his bare chest, just at the place where the stone had touched his skin.

So Urla had her stone back, and after that she spent the winter in the Raiding Riders' camp, until the way over the mountains was passable again in spring. From that time, she was able to speak the Riders' language. The Khan gave her a horse and enough provisions for her long journey home. Before she rode away, he summoned her to his tent once more and said, 'I send you back with a message for your people. The Raiding Riders will never venture into the mountains again, for the mountains are your friends and give you their riches. And I have learnt that they can avenge their friends too, for I have lost nearly fifty Riders to them. Moreover, I saw what your stone could do to the man who took it. It would be rash to try fighting such adversaries.' And with that the Khan let her go.

But Kurgi went with her as far as the foot of the mountains. Before he turned back, he said, 'We killed your husband, and in return you took me in your arms like your own child. Why did you do it?'

Urla looked long into his eyes, and then said, '*You* did not kill my husband. No one is responsible for anything but what he does himself.'

'I might have killed him, though, for I was there when it happened,' Kurgi persisted. 'I shall wonder all my life why you acted as you did.'

'Do so, Kurgi,' said Urla. 'And I shall watch to see what you make of the life I saved.' Then she stroked his beardless cheek with her hand, turned her horse, and rode up the mountain path.

*   *   *

Listener had hung on every word of Rikka's tale. 'Was that Kurgi your grandfather?' he asked when she had finished. 'The father of Hunli and Arni?'

'Yes,' said Rikka. 'His own father perished on a raid ten years later. During this time Urla and her daughter had been living in her father's house. When she heard that Kurgi had become Khan, she had a cabin built for her in the mountains, just where the path leads down to the steppes. She left her daughter behind with her parents, and lived alone in the mountains with her flock of sheep. A member of her family would come over the pass from time to time, to see that she had what provisions she needed. And Kurgi heard where Urla was living now, and often came to visit her and ask her advice.'

'Yes, so my grandfather told me,' said Listener. 'It was on one such occasion that she gave your father her stone.'

'And now it is yours,' said Rikka, 'which means that in a way you are one of our family. All who own the stone by right belong to Urla's kin, but if a man takes it by any other means it will bring him misfortune.'

Barlo nodded at these words of hers, as if he could confirm them. Rikka looked inquiringly at him, and he brought out his flute and began to play. He started with the desolate theme in which he expressed the misery of his days as a servant in Barlebogue castle. Listener recognized the sequence of notes, and was so enthralled by what Barlo played next that he felt the course of the story the music was now telling almost present before him, the more so as he had lived through part of it himself. Gisa came into the stables, gave Barlo the bag, and told him to throw this rubbish away. But Barlo guessed the owner of· the bag. He opened it, and as soon as he saw what it contained he felt that some mystery surrounded the shimmering stone. Perhaps Gisa had taken it from her guest to rob him of his power? Power! Yes, that must be what the stone hid beneath its smooth surface. For a moment Barlo toyed with the thought of giving the bag back to its rightful owner, and thus strengthening him against Gisa. But then he succumbed to the temptation to keep the power for himself. It seemed to him the only way he could free himself from his wretched existence as a groom. His hatred of the lady of Barlebogue, which he had almost overcome, flared up again, like a flame consuming his reason. Barlo carried the stone with him, and waited for something to happen; but nothing happened, nothing changed. And then the steward of the castle found him gazing fervently at the stone yet again, willing it to show its power at last. Barlo was dragged before Listener, sitting in judgement, the stone lay on the table, out of reach, yet Barlo made one last, desperate attempt to bring his judge round to his side. He was as powerless as before, however, and was condemned to be dumb. Once again, the melody of the flute broke off at this point so abruptly that everyone in the room could feel the knife that put an end to the man's speech for ever.

The smith and his wife had been able to tell that this was a tale of secret triumph, the temptation of power, and a terrible punishment, but they could not understand the details, so Listener did his duty as an interpreter for the first time, telling them what he had seen while the flute was playing. When he had finished, Barlo indicated that this was exactly what he meant to say.

'I can understand your actions very well, Barlo,' said Furro. 'But you would both have been spared much grief if you had given Listener back the stone.'

Barlo nodded. Then he put his flute to his lips and played his desolate theme of servitude once more, but linking it, this time, to an easy melody that freed itself from the fetters of those few notes.

'I think I understand you,' said the smith. 'Yes, you would still be able to speak, but you would have remained a groom with your evil mistress, and could not ride the land a free man, as you do now.'

Smiling, Barlo confirmed his interpretation.

'Well, it's good that you are riding the land,' the smith repeated. 'It will give hope to many in Barlebogue when that comes to their ears.'

But Barlo did not seem to take any notice of this remark, and soon afterwards they all went to bed. Listener lay awake for a long time, however, wondering exactly what the smith might have meant.

Next day Barlo and Listener were woken by ringing hammer blows from the smithy. When they went into the living-room, Rikka brought them milk, bread, cheese, and smoked freshwater fish. She sat down at the table with them and pressed them to eat. When they had had enough, she asked, 'Are you riding on today?'

Barlo nodded.

'Then I hope you reach your goal,' she said. Oh, thought Listener, have we got one, then? Obviously everyone here knew more about Barlo's intentions than he did. Rikka seemed to sense what he was thinking, and looked at him, smiling, with Urla's eyes. 'You have plenty of time yet, Listener,' she said. 'One must be patient with Urla's stone. I am glad you carry it now, even though you may think it's brought you nothing but difficulty so far. My father was just the same, until he realized that you always *do* get into difficulty when you try to discover its secret. However, he found it was worth the trouble in the end. When you eased his death for him, I am sure he knew he had found the heir to Urla's stone.'

Listener felt like a child unable to understand the grown-ups' talk. However, he could tell she meant it kindly, and he thanked her for her hospitality. Then he went out to the smithy with Barlo.

*

Furro had already shoed the horse, and was just leading the donkey into his workshop. 'I must make two pairs of shoes for him first,' said he. 'I don't usually keep such things in stock.' He got a bar of iron, laid it in the fire, and blew up the flames with his bellows. 'Donkey's shoes are special,' he said. 'They must be light and delicate, so as not to weigh down the donkey's little hooves. I learned to make them from the Mountain Badgers.'

'Do you come from Urla's native place too?' asked Listener.

'No,' said Furro, taking the iron out of the fire and knocking part of it off with a hammer. 'I was born in Barlebogue village. I'd been blacksmith there for a while when I heard there were things you could learn from the master smiths up in the mountains. So I set off and apprenticed myself to Rikka's grandfather, who worked iron. He must have been about seventy then, but he stood at his anvil every day. He was married to Urla's daughter; Rikka told you about her yesterday.'

Furro began beating the piece of iron out flat and bending it, until the metal stopped glowing and formed a grey skin that flaked away under the hammer blows. Then he put it back in the fire, and went on talking as he used his bellows. 'The smith's name was Hefas, and his two grandchildren lived with him too: Rikka and Akka, the daughters of Arni of the Stone. Their mother, the smith's only child, had met Arni in Urla's house. I sometimes think Urla had a hand in that marriage, for she loved Arni dearly, and knew he needed someone he could talk to. But his happiness did not last long. His wife died when the twin girls were only ten. So he took the twins to live with his mother and father-in-law, knowing he couldn't care for them properly with the unsettled life he led.'

Listener felt personally involved in the tale the smith was telling. In a way that he could not understand yet himself, he too was part of these events, events spanning more than a century, and yet they seemed to him as real and present as if the course of time had ceased to be. Did Urla seem so close, close enough to be touched, because she had looked at him through Rikka's eyes? He could not tell. He was still wondering about it as the smith finished shaping the first shoe and laid it aside to begin on the second. 'And I learned to make shoes like this from Hefas,' he added. 'Prospectors and ore miners like to use mules up in the mountains because their little hooves are better at climbing. Rikka had a mule too, and used to ride it over the mountain pass to visit her father in his house on the edge of the steppes.'

'Did you ever meet Arni?' asked Listener.

Furro knocked holes for the nails in the second shoe, and said, 'Yes. He came to Hefas's smithy now and then to see his daughter. And he came to the wedding when I married Rikka. I liked him. He was a good man to talk to.'

Then Furro turned back to his work, and said no more until Yalf's four hooves were shod. 'They'll hold a good while,' was all he said then, and a little later Barlo and Listener had left the village behind them and were riding along the riverside again.

They went on like this for four days, sleeping in barns by night, and at first Listener got the impression that Barlo kept going in this direction merely because there was a path to follow, never mind where it might lead. On the fourth day, however, it struck him that Barlo was glancing up at the grassy slopes on either side of the river valley from time to time. Was he looking for something? Listener asked him, but Barlo just shook his head and rode on.

Towards evening of that day, Listener saw a flock of sheep grazing far up the hillside, a dense throng of little white specks with a dog like a restless black dot circling them. Barlo saw the flock at the same moment, and reined in his horse. Was this what he was looking for? Listener could make no sense of it. What would Barlo want with sheep? And obviously they were indeed what he was after. He turned his horse aside from the path and trotted over the pasture towards the flock of sheep. Listener followed on his donkey, wondering what next.

He soon found out. When they had ridden up the hill and were close to the flock, Barlo dismounted so as not to alarm the sheep. He tied his horse up to a hazel bush, and indicated to Listener that he was to leave the donkey there too. The shepherd, standing on top of the hill above his flock, had noticed them by now and came to meet them as they walked on towards the sheep. He whistled up his dog, who was rushing towards the intruders, yelping, and greeted them. 'Looking for me, were you?' he asked.

Barlo nodded.

'And what can I do for you?' asked the shepherd, looking from one to the other, but with the best will in the world Listener could not tell him what his master had in mind. Then Barlo took out his flute and began to play. The tune that he drew from his flute this time sounded like a herdsman's song, such as a shepherd might play on his pipe on a spring day such as this, when he had nothing else to do. Listener paid careful attention, for he had realized that he would be called upon to act as interpreter again. And the farther Barlo spun out his tune, the more clearly did Listener see that his master wanted to keep sheep himself. After all the mysterious hints Listener had heard in the smith's house, without being able to understand them fully, this was not exactly what he might have imagined Barlo's aim to be. He had begun to think of his master as setting out on some heroic enterprise in which he himself would bear a certain part. And now he wanted to keep sheep – yes, no doubt about it.

'A pretty tune,' said the shepherd, when Barlo's music died away. 'If you hadn't come riding up on horseback I'd say you were a shepherd yourself.'

'If I've understood my master correctly,' Listener said, 'he would like to be a shepherd. And no doubt he would like me with him, as a herd-boy.'

Barlo nodded, and looked at the shepherd with a question in his eyes.

'Doesn't seem very talkative, your master,' said the shepherd to Listener. 'Though that's no bad thing for a shepherd, seeing you don't get much company. As a matter of fact, you've come along at just the right time. I have a second flock grazing the valley on the other side of this hill. Their shepherd's hurt his leg, won't be able to get about again in a hurry. Meanwhile I have to look after both flocks. I spend all day chasing from one side of the hill to the other to make sure I don't lose a sheep. So you can start right away as far as I'm concerned.'

Listener was not particularly thrilled by this prospect. He had hoped to be, as Furro put it, riding the land with Barlo, and possibly having a few interesting adventures in the process. And now it looked as if he was going to spend the whole summer stuck on this grassy hill, keeping sheep. How was he supposed to learn to listen here, an exercise the Gentle Fluter had thought so well worth while? Would the sheep teach him, maybe? They were slowly grazing the grass before him, bleating now and then as they avoided the dog who drove them together whenever they strayed too far from the rest of the flock.

'Where are we to sleep?' he asked, clinging to a hope that Barlo would tire of a shepherd's draughty quarters in the long run.

'Get your mounts and come with me,' said the shepherd. 'I'll show you.'

He led them to the other side of the hill. There was a shepherd's hut a little way down from the hill-top, standing among hazels and alders, its outer walls and roof reinforced with peeled spruce bark. It was an airy dwelling, but no one had to live in it in winter. 'We cook our meals and sleep here,' said the shepherd. 'Provisions are brought up from the village every other week, and we get paid in late autumn when we've driven the sheep home. Well, what about it? Will you stay?'

Barlo nodded, and shook hands with the shepherd to confirm the bargain. So Listener could only do the same. Then they unsaddled their beasts and brought the saddles and bags indoors. The hut consisted of only one room, with four truckle-beds to the right of the door covered with straw mattresses and coarse woollen blankets. To the left, in the corner, there was a roughly constructed hearth made of boulders, and there was a table, and drum-shaped blocks of wood to sit on. Pots and pans hung on the wall, along with four hunting bows and quivers full of arrows.

'What are the bows for?' asked Listener.

'Wolves sometimes come down from the forest in winter,' said the shepherd. 'But you don't need to worry about them now, not in spring. Can you use a bow?'

'A bit,' said Listener, and Barlo nodded. When Listener turned to go out of the hut again, he saw the sun-drenched landscape outside like a picture painted in glowing colours, surrounded by the dark frame of the doorway: the hillside pasture rising again on the other side of the valley, with a few bushes growing on the slope, and a graceful rowan tree here and there. The second flock was grazing the lower part of the hillside, with a powerful, long-haired sheepdog circling them. Farther up the slope, the bushes grew closer together, and beyond them was a dense, dark green stand of spruce trees. Wooded scene after wooded scene opened out along the gentle indentations of an adjacent valley, stretching into the blue of the distance. Somewhere over there, Barlebogue must lie.

They had settled in by the end of the first week. The shepherd had taught them the rudiments of his craft, and if there was something they did not know Listener had only to go over to the other side of the hill and ask him. They let the horse and the donkey graze at will, and the sheep were soon used to the two animals, although the dog still looked at them suspiciously if they came too close to his charges, and would chase through their legs, yapping. Barlo spent most of the day sitting under a hazel bush, playing his flute.

And gradually Listener came to understand why Barlo had sought out this lonely occupation. Obviously he wanted peace in which to perfect his flute-playing, and a chance to try out all his instrument could express undisturbed. In time, Listener felt that the runs of notes he played were so much a part of the landscape, he noticed them only if they fell silent.

Sometimes, however, he listened, and not only because he knew he was meant to be learning to listen, but because some theme or other Barlo had made up would hold him spellbound. He was getting better and better at following Barlo's thoughts and feelings; in his own imagination, they took shape like the images of events which almost always seemed to centre upon the tall castle of Barlebogue, towering up in the middle of the broad valley with its surrounding forest. But this was not the gloomy Barlebogue he knew, silent under the witch's evil power, but a merry world in which men went about their work singing, in which folk danced and laughed, a castle full of cheerfulness and love.

'You think about Barlebogue a lot,' he said to Barlo one evening, as the two of them sat outside the hut with the shepherd after supper.

Barlo nodded. The shepherd had pricked up his ears when Listener mentioned the name of the castle. 'So that's where you're from,' said he. 'Well, I'm not surprised you came away. They say that since Gisa took the valley for her own, all joy has gone from that place.'

'What do you know about it?' asked Listener.

'Nothing much for certain,' said the shepherd. 'It's not often anyone gets out of her power. But they do tell a grim tale down in the villages by the river on long winter evenings, a tale they call "Gisa and the Wolves". Do you know it?'

'No,' said Listener, 'but I should like to hear it. I was in Gisa's castle myself, and found out just what she can do to a man.'

'I'll see if I can put together those fragments of it I've picked up,' said the shepherd.

And he began to tell:

The Tale of Gisa and the Wolves

In the mountainous country of the upper reaches of Barlebogue river, there lived a prospector who had a daughter called Gisa. This girl was known as the most beautiful woman for miles around. Many young men came to woo Gisa, but she was proud and sent them all away. She said she would marry none but the man who brought her a sapphire as large and flawless as the one her father owned. He kept this stone as his most precious treasure, and would not show it to a living soul except his daughter. He had it in a casket that stood in his room, beside his bed, and he always carried the key on him, and put it under his pillow at night. Whenever a young man came to Gisa and showed her a stone he had found after long searching, she would say, 'Worthless rubbish! You don't know what my father's sapphire is like.' Wooers who had heard of Gisa's beauty even came up to the mountains from the rich valley of Barlebogue, but none of them brought her a stone that could compare with the sapphire her father possessed.

So it went on until a stranger turned up one day, a man who pleased Gisa very well. He had a strong yet lean figure, and curly black hair, and the way he looked into her eyes made Gisa's heart beat faster. But once again, his stone would not pass muster. She was sorry to have to reject the stranger, but as usual she said, 'Worthless rubbish! You don't know what my father's sapphire is like.'

'Then show me!' said the stranger. 'How can I find a stone as good if I don't know what to look for?'

'Impossible,' said Gisa. 'My father won't show his stone to any living soul but me.'

'Then you know where he hides it,' said the stranger. 'Let me in when your father is asleep, and then he'll never know that you showed me the stone.'

'It isn't as simple as that,' said Gisa, 'for he keeps the stone locked in a casket and puts the key under his pillow at night. He will wake if I try to pull it out.'

'Don't worry,' said the stranger. 'I'll give you a herb that will make your father sleep if you mix it into his evening drink. Then he won't wake up even if you should drop the key.'

Gisa looked into the stranger's brown eyes, and she could no longer deny him. 'I do not like doing this,' she said, but in the end she agreed. The stranger brought her the herb, and she mixed it into the drink her father took in the evening. It seemed effective, too, for soon afterwards he felt tired and went to bed.

That night Gisa opened the door to the stranger, when he gave a signal they had agreed on, and led him to her father's room. Once there, she cautiously removed the key from under her father's pillow, and he never even stirred in his sleep, and then she opened the casket.

When the stranger saw the stone his eyes began to gleam with greed, for that sapphire was the size of a pigeon's egg, and as clear and deep blue as the water of a mountain lake. He put his hand into the casket and took out the stone. 'You were right,' said he. 'A second such stone can never be found.'

'Hush!' whispered Gisa. 'You'll wake my father!'

The stranger laughed, and his laugh froze Gisa to the marrow. 'Your father?' said he. 'No one will ever wake him now. As for the stone, I'll take it, and without taking you into the bargain.' So saying, he leaped out of the door, and was never seen again in those parts.

Gisa had always been proud, but that night she became wicked too. She had been in love with the stranger, and now she hated not only him but everyone who had ever come asking for her hand, and she swore revenge on men. 'I will not rest,' she cried into the night, 'until I'm rich enough to buy any man I want!'

And she too disappeared from the valley that night. As for what happened to her afterwards, this is the tale they tell: she left the house where her father lay, murdered by her connivance, and went out into the woods. That same night she met with a huge wolf who stared at her with yellow eyes, and then sprang at her to bite out her throat. But before he reached her Gisa cried, 'Wait, wolf! I will get you and your pack better food.'

'How will you do that, Gisa?' asked the wolf.

'I shall take you to the rich valley of Barlebogue,' said Gisa. 'The folk there live a carefree life and are not on their guard. It will be child's play for you to attack them. And then you will rule the place along with me. I give you my word.'

The wolf looked at her with his yellow eyes, and said, 'You are a wicked woman, Gisa. I like that. But I will make three conditions before I go along with your proposal.'

'Make your conditions,' said Gisa, unhesitatingly. 'I will fulfil them.'

'Listen, then!' said the wolf. 'Are you still a maid?'

'I am,' said Gisa. 'I have never slept with any man, for none of them were good enough.'

'Excellent,' said the wolf. 'They say that if a maiden willingly gives a wolf her blood to drink he will take on man's shape as long as the sun is in the sky. Will you do as much for me and my pack?'

'Yes,' said Gisa. 'I will give you my blood to drink.'

'Then listen to the second condition,' said the wolf. 'While we are still in these woods you shall lie beside me every night and run your fingers through my coat.'

'Very well, if that is all,' said Gisa. 'Come here, wolf, and I'll do as you ask.' And the wolf came and laid his head in her lap, and as she ran her fingers through his coat Gisa asked what the third condition was.

'This is the hardest one,' said the wolf. 'If you ever love a man with all your heart, you shall become a she-wolf yourself. Do you agree to that?' Gisa uttered so shrill a laugh that even the wolf lying in her lap started. 'That's the easiest one!' said Gisa. 'Indeed I agree, for I shall never have to make good *that* promise.'

'Good,' said the wolf, 'for if that should happen, we too must be wolves again for ever.' Then he rose and howled into the darkness to call his pack together. Soon Gisa heard the wolves trotting through the forest, but the night was so dark that all she could see was their glowing eyes in a circle around her.

'Now give us your blood to drink, Gisa,' said the old wolf. Then Gisa took a knife and cut her left arm until the blood dropped down. One by one the wolves came up and licked the blood from the wound. Then the pack lay down where they were to sleep, and Gisa took the old wolf in her arms and ran her fingers through his coat.

When she woke up next morning she was lying in the arms of a man whose hair and beard were as thick as a wolf's coat, and her fingers were buried in the fur jacket that he wore. Gisa looked around, and saw fifty men lying in a circle, all with greyish brown hair and wearing wolfskin clothing. She rose to her feet, crying, 'Wake up, my wolves, and let's be off to Barlebogue!'

They trotted on through the forest for twelve days, and every night Gisa lay beside the old wolf to run her fingers through his coat. On the evening of the twelfth day they came to the end of the forest, looked down into the broad valley of Barlebogue, and saw the castle on its hill, towering up among the fields and meadows. Sheep were grazing the slopes of the hills below the forest.

'You shall eat your fill tonight,' Gisa told her companions, pointing to the flocks. The men stared at their prey with yellow eyes and waited for night to fall. As soon as the sun had set they turned into wolves, gathered together in a pack, and fell upon the sheep.

It was late that night before the old wolf came to Gisa to feel her hand in his coat. Gisa herself did not sleep that night, but waited impatiently for morning to come.

As soon as the sun had risen, and the wolves had changed back into men, Gisa went down into the valley with them. They met farmers and shepherds in the sheep pastures bemoaning their loss. Gisa stopped and asked them what had happened.

'Wolves came out of the forest last night and slaughtered over a hundred sheep,' someone told her. 'How can we defend ourselves from such a pack of wolves as that?'

'We are well met,' said Gisa. 'My men here hunt wolves, as you can see from the coats they wear. Take us to your lord and they will enter his service. Then we'll send the thieving wolves about their business.'

The owner of the sheep was glad to hear that, and he took Gisa and her companions to see his lord the Count. The Count was holding a feast in the castle, with people in fine clothes going in and out, good food being served, and laughter and dancing everywhere.

When Gisa came in with her wolf-men the music died away, the dancers stopped, and everyone stared at those sombre figures in their greyish-brown wolfskins. The Count went up to them and asked what all this meant. The farmer who had come with Gisa told him about last night's disaster, and asked him to enlist these men's aid. The Count listened to what the farmer had to say, and then asked Gisa who she was and where she came from.

'My name is Gisa,' she said, 'and my men hunt wolves up in the mountain woods. We have heard that a pack ravaged your flocks last night, and we offer you our services.'

'Which I am happy to accept,' said the Count, 'for I haven't enough huntsmen to drive such a pack away. Be my guests here today and join our feast, and we will go hunting tomorrow. You shall sit at my own table, Gisa, because you have brought me aid.'

The wolf-men mingled with the guests, and Gisa sat at the Count's table. It struck her that he addressed no one sitting there like a member of his family. 'Have you no wife or children?' she asked.

'My wife died a few years ago,' said the Count, 'and my only son rode away last week to buy horses down in the lowlands. For my part, I'm surprised to see that you go through the forest alone with these men of yours; it doesn't strike me as any life for a woman. Why not stay and live here at the castle?'

Gisa looked at him and said, 'Perhaps I may.'

'I'll take your men into my service too,' said the Count, 'and they'll be well paid, for I am rich. You must know that precious stones can be found in the bend of the river down below the castle.' He put his hand in his pocket and brought out a sapphire as large and flawless as the stone her father had owned. 'I'll give you this for that half-consent of yours,' said the Count, who was close to falling under the spell of Gisa's beauty. Gisa could hardly manage to hide the greed in her eyes, and she waited impatiently for the sun to sink to the horizon.

As soon as the last rays of sunlight had vanished behind the mountains, Gisa's men turned back into wolves and fell upon the guests. First of all the old wolf bit out the Count's throat, and soon there wasn't a living soul left in the castle.

From that day on Gisa was mistress of Barlebogue. Her men were known by the local people as 'Gisa's shaggy retainers', and the household servants soon began whispering that none of them was ever to be seen after sunset. Gisa made them bailiffs and overseers, with authority over the farmers, craftsmen and castle servants, whom they considered their own property, together with all they owned and all they earned. There was only one thing she failed to do: they say she is still waiting for the Count's son to come back so that she can kill him as well. She intercepts and questions every young man who enters her domain, but she hasn't found him yet; all she gets is a playmate now and then to while her nights away, until she turns him out again and leaves him to her wolves. But there has been no joy in Barlebogue since she came there.

* * *

'And that is all I've heard of Gisa and her wolves,' said the shepherd. 'I don't know what to make of it, myself; folk tell a good many tales when winter nights are long. *You* may know more, Listener, if you've been there yourself.'

'Who knows what may lie behind the things he sees?' said Listener. 'It may be that I escaped a danger I never knew about. I've never seen wolves turn into men, but I know from my own experience that Gisa can turn men into wolves.'

Barlo had listened attentively to the shepherd's tale, but with a reserved expression on his face, which gave away nothing of what he was thinking. Over the next few days, however, all merriment was gone from the music of his flute, and when Listener heard it he saw wolves trotting through the valley of Barlebogue.

There is hardly anything else worth mentioning to tell of that summer on the grazing grounds. Barlo made good use of his rights as master of a servant, in that he generally left it to Listener to look after the flock, while he sat under a tree somewhere or other himself and played his flute. And since the shepherd too put himself on a level with Barlo, rather than with the servant of that semi-skilled shepherd, he exercised similar rights. So Listener was kept busy: he had to sweep the hut, do the washing, bring water up from the stream at the bottom of the valley, cook, do all kinds of tasks which, in his longing for unusual experiences, he found far from satisfying; to which we may add that cooking can certainly be an art and indeed an adventure, but not very easily when all you have to hand is water, flour, fat, and with luck a little sheep's milk cheese. Above all, you need to want to cook, and that Listener most certainly did not.

His one comfort at this period was his donkey Yalf. He had only to call the beast by his name and he would come galloping up across the meadow to rub his soft muzzle against Listener's cheek. Listener got used to riding him bareback, and they trotted over the hills if there was nothing else to do and Barlo was prepared to look after the flock. Listener jumped his donkey over low hedges, and if he fell off, Yalf would come back to him and nuzzle him until he got to his feet again. But this happened only at the start, and it was not long before Listener went racing through the valley on his donkey like a grey-skinned centaur.

Meanwhile the summer passed, the rowan berries turned a brilliant red, and the sharp mountain wind blew nuts off the hazel bushes. It was getting quite cold in the shepherd's hut at night.

One of these nights Listener was woken by Yalf, kicking the door of the hut and braying aloud, a wild donkey's bray, re-echoing from the other side of the valley. Barlo and the shepherd had woken abruptly too, and Listener got up to see what had disturbed his donkey. Even before he reached the door he heard the howling of wolves from the borders of the forest above them. Both the others leaped from their truckle beds too, each man snatched up a bow and arrows, and they ran out into the night. Listener swung himself up on his donkey and galloped over to the sheep, which were huddled together and bleating with alarm.

As he rode around the flock, he heard the heavy beat of Barlo's horse's hooves behind him. But the howling was fast coming closer too, and in a moment Listener saw shadowy figures flitting down through the bushes on the borders of the forest. He put an arrow to his bowstring and waited for the first wolves to come close enough. His first shot hit the leader of the pack. It leaped into the air and then lay on the ground, kicking. Next moment Barlo was beside Listener, shooting arrow after arrow into the pack as the wolves raced up.

Almost every shot killed one of them, but the rest came swiftly closer. One huge beast leaped at Listener, but Yalf reared up and smashed in the wolf's skull with his front hooves, uttering his terrifying bray. It was the sound of that bray that halted the attacking pack. The wolves stopped running, as if at the lash of a whip, turned, and careered wildly back towards the forest.

Now the shepherd too came up, breathless, and sent a few last arrows after them. A minute or so later the nightmare was over.

'We'd have been too late but for your donkey, Listener,' said the shepherd, once he had his breath back. 'What a pack that was! I've never seen so many of the brutes all together before. Lucky for me I wasn't alone.'

They stayed out for the rest of the night, keeping watch over the flock, in case the wolves came back again. But all was calm, and when the first light of dawn came up over the hilltops they dragged the dead wolves together. There were nine of them. And as it became lighter, they made an eerie discovery: each wolf wore a leather collar with a sapphire sparkling in it. The shepherd, terrified, made the sign to ward off evil spirits and muttered, 'Gisa's shaggy retainers!'

But whatever these wolves might be, they showed no sign of turning into men as the sun rose. Whether that was because they were dead, or whether folk had made up those tales about Gisa's wolves, at least the fact that they wore those collars showed clearly enough where they had come from. The longer Listener thought about it, the more he felt fear rise within him. Had Gisa found out where he and Barlo were, and set her wolves on their track? It seemed to him high time to leave this part of the country.

When the shepherd tried to break one of the blue stones out of its setting Barlo uttered a warning growl, almost like a wolf's, and pulled his hand away. Listener understood all too well. 'I wouldn't touch one of those pretty things myself for the world,' said he, 'and I can only advise you to leave them alone.'

Then they dug a pit on the edge of the forest, threw the dead wolves into it, collars and all, and covered them up. The shepherd piled a few heavy stones on top, as if he feared the uncanny creatures might rise from their grave by night.

They grazed the flock on the other side of the valley that day, down below the hut, and the shepherd said, 'I'm not staying here a day longer. We'll drive the sheep to their winter quarters tomorrow.'

It took them a week to drive the flock along the river valley to the village where its owner lived. The farmer came out of his house to count his sheep, and praised the shepherd for losing none of the older animals as well as rearing so many lambs.

'Not my doing alone,' said the shepherd. 'But for the help of Listener and Barlo here, the wolves might have got half the flock last week.' However, he did not mention the collars. Perhaps he was afraid of being laughed at – or then again, perhaps he feared to speak of those eerie beasts aloud.

The farmer thanked Barlo and Listener, and gave them a part of the agreed wage. He also invited them to spend the winter as guests on his farm. Once again, Barlo consented with a nod, and had Listener express their thanks for the invitation.

A few days later there was a festival at the farm, for it had been a good harvest, and the cattle had done well that year too, not to speak of the sheep Barlo and Listener had been keeping. The farmer had invited all his neighbours, and there was such roasting and baking in the kitchen that the serving maids were kept standing by the fire from morning till night, while the farmer broached a cask of his best cider.

First they all ate until the sweat stood out on their foreheads, then they drank to cool their inward heat again, and then they danced, lest they become too cool, until the sweat broke out and had to be cooled once more. Listener liked this better than their frugal shepherd's life up on the hills. He enjoyed the feasting, and whirled the peasant girls about the dancing floor so that their skirts flew.

Barlo sat to one side, in a corner of the living-room, drinking a little now and then and watching the merry throng. If anyone spoke to him, he answered only with a few gestures, so soon they left him to himself. However, when the fiddler who was playing music for the dancers stopped for a rest, Barlo took out his flute and went to the middle of the dancing floor. Now he attracted everyone's attention, the more so as he was a head taller than almost anyone there. He put his instrument to his lips, and the dancers' legs started to twitch at the very first notes he played. They began to dance, whirling around him. Listener was caught up in the current, seized a girl and stamped out the rhythm the fluter was playing. Barlo stood there in the midst of them like a rock with the water swirling around it, and played as Listener had never heard him play before. Faces flew past, laughing mouths, eyes that met Listener's for a split second and then were gone again in the wild turbulence of the dance, bright scarves floated by, jewels sparkled, and all merged into a glimmering mist that turned swiftly, driven by the sweet power of the flute music that rose and fell and swayed, until there was nothing in the world but that music, and eyes formed out of that surging mist, eyes of a shade difficult to describe, they took shape and looked at him out of a face he knew and yet did not know, and he let himself plunge into those eyes, fell into them, sank down, did not know where he was and yet knew, at the same time, that he wanted to be nowhere but in the unfathomable depths of the eyes, young as a child's yet still as old as if they were looking at him over the centuries, and the gaze of them promised an answer to all he did not understand, and as he sank and sank there came a sound like a bell ringing within his head, saying, 'Wait, Listener, wait, for that's not all.'

Then the tune of the flute stopped, and the eyes vanished away, like a vision. The figures of the dancers came out of the mist, and Listener, confused, looked at the girl he had swept into the dance, a peasant lass with flushed cheeks, whose bright blue eyes were looking at him in wonder. 'Well, you can dance so that it fair takes the breath away,' said she, 'but Heaven knows what you're thinking of the while!'

Everyone clamoured for Barlo to play again, but he would not, and went back to his corner. Listener dropped into his chair, exhausted, and poured himself a glass of cider. The farmer sat down beside him. 'I guessed your master was no shepherd when I saw his horse,' said he, 'for it's a horse of noble breeding. What is he really, then? A minstrel?'

Listener shrugged his shoulders, and said, 'Maybe. Yes, perhaps he's a minstrel.' He had less and less idea what to think of Barlo. Who *was* he, in fact? A runaway groom? A minstrel? That could be it. Minstrels were in the way of riding through the land to play at fairs and festivals. But then he remembered that Barlo had learnt his art from the Gentle Fluter and not before. Although he had proved a very apt pupil. Perhaps he once used to play some other instrument which he no longer owned. Or perhaps he had been one of those singers who performed old ballads at the fairs. He could find no answer, and if he knew Barlo, Barlo would not be giving him one in any hurry.

'You're a strange couple, you are,' said the farmer. 'Riding the land together, keeping my sheep, fighting off a pack of wolves, and then your master turns out to be a flute-player such as I never heard in all my life before, barring one man, but you wouldn't know him. All this, and you can't even tell who your master really is!'

'Whom did you mean by the one you've heard play the flute as well before?' asked Listener, already guessing the answer.

'He must be old by now – that is, if he's still alive,' said the farmer. 'The Gentle Fluter, folk call him.'

'We spent last winter with him,' said Listener. He did not mention that he was the Gentle Fluter's grandson; he had had enough of re-flected glory, the more so as he himself had little to his credit to make him worthy of such a relationship.

'Ah, then he *is* alive still,' said the farmer, 'and if your master learned the flute from him, I'm not surprised he can play like that.'

'When did you hear the Gentle Fluter?' asked Listener.

'Oh, many years ago,' said the farmer. 'I wasn't married then, but there was a girl I liked. We'd been courting for a while, as they say, but then we had a quarrel. You'll think the cause of it ridiculous enough. That's the way it often is, such quarrels do begin for ridiculous causes. She would keep calling me "my little farmer", that's what it was. Her father was a huntsman, you see, and since the huntsmen in these parts pride themselves a lot on the freedom of their lives, I thought she was mocking me. And my friends started laughing at me when she called me by that name in front of them. "So you belong to her, eh? The proud huntress!" they would say. "Shot you down already, has she?"

At all events, it annoyed me, and I snapped at her one day when she used her pet name for me. Then she was angry and said, "Well, if you don't want to be mine, I might as well be off!" After that we would pass each other by with scarcely a greeting. But I still liked her, and I wasn't just angry with her but with myself too, for losing her on account of such a little thing. However, the longer matters went on like this, the harder it seemed to me to go to her and make the quarrel up.

That was how things stood when harvest festival was to be held, just as we're holding it now. The crops were brought in, the cattle driven home from the pastures, and that's why we have such a festival every year. It was being held in this very room, too, for this is the biggest farm in the village, and it's the duty of its owner to hold the festival. My father was the owner at that time.

So we ate and drank and danced. But my father had a guest staying with him – I hadn't seen much of him yet, because I'd been busy from morning to night carting sheaves home to the barn. I'd not taken much notice of the man, either, for he was small, with gold-rimmed eye-glasses on his nose, like a clerk, and there didn't seem anything remarkable about him. This man was sitting at the table by my father's side, not talking much. However, when the dancing began, my father asked if he'd play something for the company.

"With all my heart," said the man. "I can thank you for your hospitality in that way." He rose to his feet, took a silver flute out of his pocket, and went out on the dancing-floor. I remember thinking it strange the way people made room for him, looking at him expectantly, insignificant as he seemed. Then he began to play, and his music sounded quite different from anything I'd ever heard before. That tune carried the dancers along with it from the very first beat, and I couldn't stay sitting at the table myself, so I got up to look for a partner. Then I saw my own girl standing at the far end of the room, my proud huntress, and she was looking at me too, and we walked towards one another through the dancers as if we'd never quarrelled at all. I took her in my arms, and as we danced we forgot everything going on around us. "My little farmer," she said to me, and it didn't annoy me a bit any more, because I knew she said it in love, not pride, and she wanted me just the way I was, exactly as I wanted her, my proud huntress. I realized it had been my own pride standing in my way, and my fear of being laughed at by my friends. But the music made me grow. I danced and danced, and what had looked like a wall I couldn't scale now lay far below me, like gravel you can kick aside without more ado. It seemed so comical to have been afraid of all this that I began to laugh. I laughed and laughed, and I was still laughing when the fluter had finished his tune. My proud huntress was laughing too. She flung her arms around my neck and gave me a kiss. We were married that winter, and I've never regretted it! Some folk think it's remarkable there were so many weddings that winter, but if anyone's surprised, well, he can't have been at that festival!'

Listener smiled. He did not think it at all surprising himself. A man who could quell a whole horde of Raiding Riders was certainly capable of getting a couple of quarrelling lovers into their marriage bed, particularly when that was what they themselves really had in mind. 'I'd like to see the man who could withstand his flute,' said he.

'Yes,' said the farmer. 'I tell you what, sometimes you get so obstinate you have to be gently forced to see where your happiness lies.'

Barlo and Listener lived quietly on the farm all that winter. Sometimes they joined in the work when there was a job requiring it, but there was not very much to be done at this time of year, and once the farmer and his household had learnt that their guests came from the Gentle Fluter they would hardly allow them to soil their hands. However, Barlo and his servant tended their own beasts. Listener would not have allowed any strangers to look after Yalf while he was with him. He took him out riding as well, to give him exercise, and keep in practice at riding a donkey himself. Sometimes he turned Yalf towards the hills, behind which the forests of Barlebogue lay on the horizon like a dark border of lace, now sprinkled with winter white; sometimes he took his donkey trotting along the causeway beside the river.

He chose this path one windy morning, late in winter. There had been a thaw over the past few days, leaving the river swollen with melted snow, and then it had frozen again, and snow had fallen, and the water had gone down a little. Listener rode his donkey through the lowland meadows and up on the causeway, where he gave him his head to run as he liked, and let Yalf carry him along under the grey sky, streaked with clouds.

After he had been riding like this for a while he suddenly felt like going a little way on foot. He dismounted and gave Yalf a pat, which told the donkey that he wasn't needed just now, so Yalf turned off into the meadows to see if he could find a few blades of juicy grass left among the withered, greyish-brown tufts.

Listener walked slowly on along the causeway. To his left, flat sheets of ice like ragged washing hung among the bare, rough bushes along the bank of the river, left there when the water at its highest washed through their branches. The muddy ground was frozen, and the puddles were covered with milky ice that splintered underfoot. Stones lay along the path, with borders of crystal rime: red stones, grey stones, black stones. He walked on past them, accompanied by the rushing of the river, treading a path leading out of time, running from somewhere or other to somewhere or other, and he heard the ice crunch under his feet. Or were those someone else's feet he heard? He dared not raise his eyes from the ground, where the pattern of ice and stones blurred as if the ground itself were dissolving underfoot. He heard the other person's footsteps, and a voice, a woman's voice. It sounded as if it came from very far away, and yet was near, like the chiming of a bell carried across the fields to him, though it felt as close as if it were sounding within his own brain. 'Oh, Listener,' said the voice, 'do you think this way has no end?' And he heard laughter that sounded like the cooing of a dove. 'He who carries the stone,' the voice went on, 'has an end in view, even if he doesn't know it yet. Keep your eyes open, Listener, because what you know is far from being all. Keep your eyes open, so that you don't pass me by when I stand at the wayside waiting for you.' And as the sound of the voice still echoed in his head, he felt the brief touch of a hand on his face. Or was it only the strong, biting wind blowing his hair over his face instead? He looked up, and into two eyes that were familiar to him. Urla's eyes? Or Rikka's? Or the eyes of a child? He could not tell, for they were already drifting away on the wind, merging with the grey clouds, and all he saw was the flat horizon, broken by the poplars that grew along the banks of the river. But he could feel the stone he wore on his breast warming his heart. He stood there by the river for a while, staring down at the fast-running water. Then he called Yalf up, and rode slowly home along the causeway.

A few weeks later winter was over at last. The farmer went out to walk over his fields, and many people were already beginning their spring ploughing. When the farmer came back from the fields, Listener was standing outside the stables, cleaning saddles and tack. Barlo was sitting beside him on a pile of wood, and the tune he was playing on his flute sounded like a song of travel. The farmer came across the yard and stopped beside them. 'Getting ready to leave, are you?' said he. 'Or would you like to keep my sheep again this year?' Listener had no idea what his master's plans were, and shrugged his shoulders. 'You'll have to ask Barlo,' he said.

Barlo had heard this conversation, and gave his answer in his own fashion: his flute-playing changed immediately to a tune that everyone knew, for it was played by professional minstrels to announce the beginning of a performance.

'Ah, I knew you were a minstrel!' said the farmer. 'Are you off again now with Listener?'

Barlo nodded.

'Then I know a good place where you can go for a start,' said the farmer. 'The big fair begins in Draglope four days from now. If you ride away tomorrow you'll be there just at the right time.'

Listener thought the step up from being a shepherd's boy to acting as servant to a travelling minstrel was not much in the way of promotion. He supposed he would have to get a hat and collect money from the audience. Still, at least there'd be more variety in such a life than in another summer on the pastures with the sheep.

Next morning they rode on again, going downstream along the causeway. Their saddle-bags swung heavily against the flanks of their mounts, for the farmer's wife had given them generous provisions for the journey. Listener had even managed to get hold of an old hat. He had stuck a cockerel's feather through its felt, and set it jauntily upon his head.

As they rode past, Listener looked for the place where he had dismounted when he went out riding in the winter and had gone along the causeway on foot. But everything looked different now. The stones of the path were trodden deep into the wet mud, the bushes on the banks were putting out their first leaves, and the bright green of the low-lying meadows shone in the morning sun, already high in the blue springtime sky among puffy white clouds. He tried to summon up the presence he had encountered here again, longing for the sound of that voice, the glance of those eyes he thought he had seen in that place, for the hand that had touched his face, unless it had been the same wind that was now tugging out his hair from under his hat. But nothing of the kind appeared this time, and soon he realized that they must have ridden past the spot long ago without his knowing it again, for by now they were trotting along under the poplars he had seen on the horizon in winter. The green hills where they had kept sheep lay behind them now, sinking beneath the horizon as they rode out across the plain, on and on along the river that wound its way in great curves, the brushwood on its banks parting the flat country before them.

On the morning of the third day, they saw Draglope lying on the river ahead of them: a market town of low-built houses pressing close around a few larger buildings. The place lay on a tongue of land, between the river down which they had ridden, and another stream that flowed down from the distant mountains on their right and into the river below Draglope. It was some time since the two riders had had the road to themselves. They caught up with farmers driving cattle before them, women carrying things in baskets and cloths, and traders in horse-drawn carts. The alleys through which they now rode were crowded with people, and merchants and craftsmen were putting up their stalls in the market place.

Barlo and Listener stabled their mounts at an inn, got a room there for themselves once they had shown the colour of the money they had earned keeping sheep, and drank a bowl of soup. Then they made their way through the crowd to the market place, where business had now begun. Potters were crying their wares; farmers' wives singing the praises of their poultry; cattle and horse dealers bargaining at the tops of their voices for calves and foals; there was woollen cloth for sale, and

linen, leather belts and shoes, hoes and axes, knives and scissors, ropes
and cords, and all kinds of trinkets, necklaces or brooches, to give your
sweetheart. There was such a noise you could hardly hear yourself
speak: cows were mooing, horses neighing, geese cackling, and the
louder the noise rose the more vigorously people shouted into one
another's ears to make themselves understood. Indeed, Listener could
scarcely hear the old man standing by the corner of a house, singing a
ballad. He was surprised to see that a few people had gathered in a
circle around the singer, all the same, and he went closer out of curiosity. The old man seemed to be taking no notice at all of the babble of
voices, and was singing quite quietly to himself. Yet his voice had so
penetrating a sound that you could hear every word if you came close
enough. Listener stopped, for there seemed something familiar about
the song the old man was singing.

> *... and she slept with him*
> *the evil, the old one,*
> *scratching his shaggy pelt*
>
> *twelve nights in the woods*
> *in a hairy embrace*
> *with fifty companions around*
>
> *twelve days in the woods*
> *on fast padding paws*
> *with fifty shaggy retainers*
>
> *they came to the valley*
> *they slaughtered the sheep*
> *they mangled a hundred by night*
>
> *and they came to the castle*
> *and there they drank wine*
> *and waited for night to fall ...*

But at this point the singer was interrupted by a harsh voice. 'What
sort of a wretched, lying song is that you're droning out?' Listener
turned, and saw a bearded man wearing a grey fur jerkin standing
close to him. 'Well, I'm right, aren't I?' this man continued, addressing
the people who had been listening to the old singer. 'Hardly able to
utter a true note, yet still he can't leave off frightening children with

his grisly ballads. He should be chased away, don't you think? All he does is disturb the peace of the market place!'

Several people agreed with him. Another man said, 'Ah, leave him alone! He doesn't bother me. There's many folk like such stories, and who knows, maybe there's something in this one.'

'Old wives' tales!' said the bearded man. 'Is this stuff for men to listen to? I can offer you something better! I'm looking for a few strong young men who are after more than fairy tales. Men who can wield a hammer and a pick. Any such men here?'

'Why, I can do that!' said a young man standing near Listener. A few others were intrigued as well, and asked the bearded man what was to be hewn and hammered.

'Come very close,' said the man. 'We don't want everyone to hear, or they'll all be clamouring to come, and I can't use that many.' He gathered the men around him and whispered. 'What is there to be hewn? Gold! Gold, I say, in lumps as big as your fist, any amount of it, all the gold you want. Don't any of you want to take a look at it?'

As he waited for their answer, the old singer struck up another verse of his ballad:

> *For they toil by day*
> *and they toil by night*
> *and die with the gold in their hands.*

At this the bearded man thrust the inquirers aside and shouted, 'Must I stop your mouth for you, you poisonous toad?' And he made for the singer, but before he could reach him, tall Barlo appeared before him as if out of nowhere. He placed himself in front of the singer and began to play his flute, taking up the melody of the ballad, and everyone could understand what he was playing:

> *She sends them out*
> *her shaggy retainers*
> *to capture and bring her more slaves*
>
> *they lure men with gold*
> *not a word of death waiting*
> *in their evil mistress's mines*
>
> *so take my advice:*
> *drive the wolves from your town*
> *and stay with your darling at home.*

As he played, he danced back and forth in front of the bearded man's nose, confusing him so that he could not get at either the flute-player or the singer. The bystanders began laughing at the helplessness of the man in the fur jerkin, and when at last he was about to fall on Barlo, blind with fury, they prevented him, and someone said he'd better make sure he cleared out of there, because anyone who disturbed the peace of Draglope market place got short shrift. At this the bearded man slipped away into the crowd.

'Thank you for your help,' said the old man to Barlo. 'You play the flute well. I've never seen you before; where d'you come from?'

Barlo shrugged his shoulders and looked around in search of aid. Listener was there, and answered for him. 'My master cannot speak to you except on his flute. His name is Barlo, and we've come down from the villages on the river. I am called Listener.'

'Well, well,' said the old man, 'and so his name is Barlo!' He sounded as if he meant more by that than Listener could understand. 'A Barlo who's a master of the flute!' the old man went on. 'Good, good. Do you mean to play here in the market place, Barlo?'

Barlo nodded.

'Well, you'll find a ready audience,' said the old man. 'I'd advise that place by the pillar over there.' The pillar was at the far side of the market place, and Listener was not sure whether the singer suggested it to Barlo because it really was an advantageous spot, or because, if he took it, Barlo would not be enticing any of his own audience away. At all events, it seemed sensible not to encroach upon another man's pitch in this profession.

'And in your place, I'd watch out for that bearded fellow in future,' the old man added. 'Come to the Silver Harp this evening, and I'll introduce you to a few members of our guild. Ask for me there – I'm known as Rauli the singer.'

Barlo and Listener made their way through the bustle of the market and over to the pillar towering above the stalls and booths on the opposite side of the square. The stone image of a dragon, the emblem of Draglope, stood on top of it, and it was let into a stone pedestal the height of a man's knee. Barlo jumped up on this platform and took his flute out of his pocket. First he played a wild dance tune which rang out so shrilly through the hubbub of the market that people stood still, and then gathered around the pillar. Without a pause, he went on to a simple melody, playing a ballad of which Listener thought he could understand every word. It ran like this:

A dragon in the valley sat,
the dragon of Draglope,
he sat upon his rock erect
his town and people to protect,
the people of Draglope.

The dragon looked towards the woods,
the woods of Barlebogue,
he looked to see his brother there,
but he showed neither hide nor hair,
the bear of Barlebogue.

The bear sat in his castle tower,
the tower of Barlebogue,
feasting his guests to make them glad,
and one-and-fifty guests he had,
the bear of Barlebogue.

He asked them all within his halls,
the bear of Barlebogue;
the woman who his heart beguiled,
fifty retainers rough and wild,
came into Barlebogue.

Then night fell on the castle tower,
the tower of Barlebogue,
and fifty wolves howled loud in scorn,
devouring, before the morn,
the bear of Barlebogue.

The dragon in the valley sits,
the dragon of Draglope.
Does he not hear his brother's cries?
The wolves draw near, beware, be wise,
ye people of Draglope!

By the time he reached the third verse people had begun to hum the tune, and when Listener began to sing the words out loud others joined in too, and they ended up repeating the last two lines.

The wolves draw near, beware, be wise,
ye people of Draglope!

As they were still singing, a knife came hissing out of the crowd,
thrown to hit the flute-player, and struck a splinter of stone from the
pillar close beside him. Listener looked in the direction from which the
knife must have been flung, and was just in time to see a grey fur jerkin
slipping away as hubbub broke out. Everyone was shouting in confusion, some seizing their nearest neighbours at random by the scruff of
the neck, believing that they had caught the thrower of the knife, and
Barlo's first performance as a minstrel was very near to ending in a full-
scale brawl.

Before things could reach that pass, however, Barlo uttered one of
those penetrating cries that Listener remembered only too well, and
calmed the crowd with a gesture. He put his flute to his lips again, and
played a dance with an enticing melody that instantly went to everyone's feet. They began stamping in time to the flute, they put their
arms on one another's shoulders and moved in a circle around the
pillar and the flute-player. Listener went along the line, holding out
his hat, and it was by no means only small change that the dancers
threw into it. The faster the stamping echoed, the more dancers joined
in. One of the market stalls toppled over – and once again the bearded
man in the grey fur jerkin obviously had a hand in things, for Listener
saw him vaulting over the fallen counter. In so doing, he knocked
down a stack of earthenware pots, which smashed to pieces with a
clatter on the paving stones. But before the irate trader could grab
him, the man in grey fur was gone again.

Now the market warden made his way through the chain of dancers
and scrambled up on the pedestal beside Barlo. 'You can't go on
playing here,' he said. 'There's disorder wherever you go.'

Barlo stopped in the middle of his dance tune and tried to assure the
warden, by means of gestures, that it wasn't his fault, but the man only
said, 'Your fault or not, you're sending the people crazy with your
flute-playing. Play anywhere else you like, but not in my market.'

Although the people murmured discontentedly, Barlo put his flute
away and jumped down to join Listener on the paving stones. They
spent the rest of the afternoon wandering around the market, going
from stall to stall and looking at the wares for sale. Towards
evening, Listener asked one of the traders the way to the Silver Harp,
and was directed to a tavern building standing all askew in a narrow

side street. The landlord, a stout little man with merry eyes, was standing in the doorway, and spoke to them as they came up. 'You'll be the fluter,' said he to Barlo, 'the one who had everyone in the market place dancing to his tune, right?' When Barlo nodded, the landlord took them both into the main room of the inn, saying, 'Rauli's waiting for you.'

The old singer was sitting in the far corner of the room with two other men. When he saw Barlo and Listener come in, he rose to his feet, beckoned them over to his table, and introduced them to his companions. 'This is Gurlo the storyteller,' he said, indicating the elder of the two, a tall and incredibly thin man, his lean face furrowed by a thousand wrinkles, so that it looked like a crumpled piece of parchment. Next Rauli pointed to the other man, a chubby-cheeked young fellow with red hair and a sizeable hump on his left shoulder. 'And this monstrosity here's called Trill, and is known as a jester, though there are many who fear him, rather, on account of his sharp tongue.'

The hunchback seemed to take no offence at all these remarks. 'Seeing Nature allowed herself her little joke with me,' said he, 'I try to outdo her with jokes of my own.'

'A natural jester, as you can see,' said Rauli. 'One more question before you sit down: have you found lodgings?'

'Yes,' said Listener, 'at the Red Ox in the market place.'

Rauli laughed. 'I fancy mine host wanted to see the colour of your money first?' said he. 'That's no place for you two; only the rich merchants put up there. Minstrels and players usually spend the night here at the Silver Harp. You'd better be off to fetch your things.'

Barlo indicated consent, so Listener went back to the Red Ox to fetch their mounts and their baggage. When the horse and the donkey were stabled at the Silver Harp, and the landlord had shown him a room for two, Listener rejoined the others in the main room of the inn, and found them in the middle of a conversation about the confusion Barlo had set going in the market place.

'And that won't do,' Rauli was just saying as Listener sat down, pouring himself, at a gesture from Barlo, a cup of red wine from the pitcher that stood on the table. 'Tackle the matter head on like that, and you'll keep finding that bearded fellow in your way,' Rauli continued. 'And then there'll be trouble with the market warden. If what we hear is true, the lady of Barlebogue has a whole troop of such

shaggy fellows, and you'll be no match for them if you try force, Barlo.
We must think of something else.'

'Why, make fun of this Gisa,' said the hunchback, and he sang:

> *Lady Gisa was handsome to see,*
> *and proud as a peacock was she.*
> *A playmate she had*
> *but that daring young lad*
> *marked her forehead before he did flee.*

'Sing that about her, and she'll be setting her shaggy retainers on *you*,'
said Listener.

All this time Gurlo had been sitting in silence, listening. Now he
shook his head, and said, 'Trill has a point there, all the same. Reminds
me of an old story I'll tell you. It's called:

The Tale of the Merry King

Once upon a time there was a merry king. He lived with his queen and
his beautiful daughter in a wonderful palace which stood in the middle
of a great garden. There were delightful beds of bright flowers in the
garden, and yew and box trees along the paths, clipped into all kinds
of pretty shapes. And there was a fountain in the middle of the garden
too, with stone dwarves in its basin; they looked very funny. It was
called the Fountain of Merriment, for when the water played down on
the stone figures it sounded as if there were someone laughing in every
corner of the garden.

The merry king lived a happy and contented life in his palace, until
a troop of wicked giants came striding down from the forest one day
and broke into the garden. You could tell, just by looking at those
giants, that they had never laughed in all their lives. They looked so
fierce that everyone in the castle ran away from them, full tilt, including
the king and his queen and their beautiful daughter. They ran as fast as
they could go to the other side of the valley, where they were taken in
by a farmer whose farm lay up in the hills.

So there was the king, not at all merry any more, sitting all day long
on the farmyard wall, looking down at his palace, where the giants
now lived. They marched all over the beautiful garden, trampling on
the pretty flower beds and tearing up the nicely clipped bushes as they
passed, so as to scratch their heads with them. One of them even took a
bath in the Fountain of Merriment, and broke the pipe from which the

water sprayed, so that the fountain dried up and couldn't play any more. The king saw all this, and he felt very sad indeed.

When he realized that the giants were not going to go away, but were making themselves quite at home in the palace, by the simple means of throwing chairs out of the windows, the chairs being too small for their fat bottoms, the king decided to do something about it. He sent out messengers, and summoned the knights of his kingdom to do battle with the giants.

In a few days' time the knights in armour came riding up on their steeds: grim-faced fellows they were, iron-clad, rattling their swords in their sheaths. 'Thank you all for coming to my aid,' said the king. 'Now, I'd like you to drive those hulking great giants out for me, and whoever kills the strongest of them shall have my daughter's hand in marriage.'

So off galloped the knights, all the way across the valley and up to the palace, waving their swords, with a view to attacking the giants. But the strongest giant simply put his stout arm out of the window, plucked the knights in armour out of their saddles one by one, just as if they had been hazel nuts, and tossed them down into the stream that flowed through the valley, out of which they eventually and with some difficulty made their way. They limped back to the farm, and their king, to tell him that it was no use attacking those giants with the sword.

'If the sword won't work, let's try magic,' said the king, and he sent his messengers out again to summon all the magicians of his land. In another few days' time, along came a lengthy train of pairs of mules, each pair carrying a litter between them, and a magician sat in each litter. When the magicians came before the king they climbed out of their litters, they re-arranged their long robes, their faces assumed grave and portentous expressions, and they asked the king what he wanted.

'I want you to drive the giants out of my palace,' said the king. 'My knights aren't up to the job. And whoever can do it shall have my daughter's hand in marriage.'

So the magicians went up to the palace, and the first of them stepped forward. He traced a magic circle on the ground, stood inside it, and began to recite his magic spells. However, the strongest of the giants stood at the palace window, blew out his cheeks, and puffed the magician up in the air, so far that he flew away like a broken-winged raven, borne up on his long robes, until he was caught in the top of a tree. And the same thing happened to every one of the magicians who traced magic circles on the ground in front of the palace.

Finally the last magician clambered down from the tree in which he had landed. The others had been politely waiting for him. Then they all went back to the king. Their faces still wore grave and portentous expressions as they confessed that their arts had not availed against the giants.

The king grew sadder than ever, for now he had no hope left at all of winning back his palace and the Fountain of Merriment. So there he was one day, sitting on the farmyard wall again, tears in his eyes as he looked down at the palace, where the giants were just throwing golden balls at each other, when a young man came along the road and asked him why he was weeping.

'Look over there,' said the king, 'and then you'll know. The giants have taken my beautiful palace away from me and stopped up the Fountain of Merriment, and nobody can drive them out again.'

'What, nobody?' said the young man. 'You must be joking!' And he laughed so loud that the giants over on the other side of the valley stopped their game, and looked that way.

'How can you laugh when I have such good cause to be sad?' asked the king, bitterly. 'If my knights and my magicians can't get rid of them, you wouldn't be able to do it either.'

'Well, I might as well try,' said the young man. 'What will you give me if I drive the giants away?'

'I've promised my daughter's hand in marriage to anyone who can do the job,' said the king. 'But I can't imagine how you are planning to set about it.'

'You'll soon see,' said the young man. 'However, I must ask you and your people to do whatever I tell you.'

'Well, anything you say,' said the king, not very hopefully. 'Just what do you want us to do, then?'

'Be merry!' said the young man. 'Be as merry as ever you can. Laugh and dance and sing, and make enough noise about it to be heard all over the valley.'

'You're asking rather a lot,' said the king. But he didn't want to leave anything untried, so he ordered his queen and his daughter and all the courtiers who used to live in the palace, and even the farmer and his household, to laugh and dance and sing. He showed them the way himself: he laughed louder than anyone, sang more merrily, and danced most vigorously of all. He had to force himself to do it at first, but gradually he felt the sadness lifting from his heart, and in the end he was enjoying being as merry as he used to be in the days when he still lived in his palace. And when they had laughed and sung and danced all day, the young man told the king, 'Now, look down at your palace again.'

So the king stopped laughing and singing and dancing for a moment, and looked across to the other side of the valley. The giants were still trampling all over the garden, but it struck him that they looked considerably smaller now.

'Here, let's take a closer look at this!' said the king. Laughing and singing, he and all his companions danced down to the stream in the valley. Before he leaped across it, he glanced up at the palace once again, and this time the giants looked yet a little smaller – why, they seemed almost the same size as ordinary people! Then the king jumped over the stream, and everyone else followed him. Still laughing and singing, they danced up the slope leading to the palace grounds. Once there, they peered cautiously over the wall, and all they could see were some tiny little giants running about the garden, looking almost like the funny dwarves in the basin of the fountain.

'You stop where you are!' the king bellowed, in between two great gusts of laughter, and then he told his daughter to go and get a dustpan and brush from the palace, and sweep that riffraff up. So she went indoors, and by the time she came back those furious little dwarves were so tiny, you could hardly tell them from the ladybirds on the rose leaves. It was such a funny sight that no one could help laughing more than ever. And when the king's daughter had swept them all up, there was nothing to be seen of them but a little bit of dust, which blew away in the wind.

Then the king had his palace and his garden set to rights, and as soon as the Fountain of Merriment was playing again, there was a fine wedding, for the young man had earned the hand of the king's daughter fair and square. And ever after that, if the king saw anyone in the palace looking glum, he would say, 'Cheer up – laugh a little and be merry! For it may be that there's one of those nasty giants caught under your fingernail, and just beginning to grow again.'

* * *

'A good tale,' said Trill. 'That's the way to deal with such folk. What's more, Barlo, no market warden will drive you from the market place if you can make people laugh. I can tell you that from experience.'

'What do you really have it in mind to do, Barlo?' asked Rauli. 'Your name did seem familiar to me, but I don't know much else about you. And when I think what you did in the market place today, it strikes me you didn't pick up the theme of my ballad just by chance.' Barlo confirmed this remark, and Rauli went on, 'If I understand you correctly, you would like to do something against the evil mistress of Barlebogue. Am I right?'

Barlo nodded. 'Good,' said Rauli. 'Then we're all of one mind there. However, the five of us can't march out on our own against her troop of shaggy retainers. They would hunt us down like hares.'

'That may well be,' said Gurlo. 'But there are others of our kind. I have a suggestion to make: we will part here, we will travel the country separately for a year, performing at fairs and weddings and harvest festivals and anywhere else folk need amusement. And we will invite all the members of our guild whose paths cross ours to meet us here a year from this day: in the Silver Harp at the time of Draglope fair. Will you all do that?'

Everyone agreed to it, and Trill added, 'And don't forget to collect merry tales as you travel along. We shall be needing them.'

They spent the rest of that evening drinking wine together and talking of this and that, but we need not go into it here, for it is of no importance to our story.

So now Barlo really had become a minstrel, and Listener travelled with him from place to place, collecting money in his hat and tending their beasts. Barlo practised the music for comic songs and merry dances, and whenever they met with another minstrel, or a storyteller or some other member of the strolling players' guild, Listener told him of the plan and finished, 'So don't forget: next spring, the Silver Harp in Draglope market place.'

At first they went through the lowland villages, riding in a wide arc through the countryside. Then, when summer came, and it was hot and oppressive in the plains, they turned towards the mountains. Soon they were trotting through narrow valleys and cool highland woods, and Barlo played for the woodcutters at their festivals. They were masters of the art of mocking one another in satirical songs. Barlo would often sit late by their fires of an evening, for this was a craft that would come in handy for him.

One day, Barlo and Listener had been riding in these parts since morning, going through the forest along narrow mountain paths beneath towering fir trees, without meeting a soul. As evening came on, Barlo smelled the smoke of a fire, and urged his horse on, for it was getting dark. Soon they saw firelight between the trunks of the trees, and heard the laughter of the woodcutters sitting around their fire.

They gave Barlo and Listener a friendly welcome, and the foreman of the gang gave them a place by the fire, saying, 'Be our guests tonight. You'll be hungry, and once you've eaten your fill we'll talk, and have a bit of singing. So out with your spoons.' For in these parts it was wise to carry your own spoon about with you wherever you went, as Barlo and his servant knew by now.

So the foreman gave one of his men a sign, and the man put an iron pan on the fire and made a porridge of milk, butter and flour, so stiff you could eat it out of the pan with your spoon. Barlo and Listener fell to, for this was their first hot meal that day, and when they had had enough they wiped their spoons on their trousers and put them away again. They thanked their hosts for the porridge, and then the foreman asked who they were and what brought them to these woods.

'My master's name is Barlo, and he's a minstrel,' said Listener. 'You mustn't take his silence amiss, for he can't speak; he has other ways of expressing himself. I'm his servant, and I am called Listener. We are riding through the land to collect merry tales and songs, and they say that you are not unversed in such matters.'

The woodcutters roared with laughter when they heard that. 'Not unversed?' cried one of them. 'That's a nice, mild way of putting it! Like a taste of one of our verses, donkey-rider?' And he sang:

> *For listening, I fancy,*
> *your ears are too small.*
> *You donkey, your donkey*
> *we'll Listener call.*

The woodcutters slapped their thighs and bellowed with laughter. At first Listener thought the joke a rather crude one, but when he saw Yalf proudly pricking up his ears, he couldn't help laughing too. 'You're not so wide of the mark there,' he said. 'I was given the task of serving this minstrel so that I'd learn to listen properly.'

He had meant what he said in good earnest, but the remark let loose further gales of laughter. 'Hear that?' spluttered one of the woodcutters. 'He's to learn how to listen from a dumb man! Well, you're a curious couple, I must say!' And he went straight into singing another verse:

> *Now why does a minstrel*
> *a-wandering come,*
> *when he can't sing a song,*
> *for the minstrel is dumb?*

Listener was horrified when he heard this one, and looked at his master to see how Barlo took the joke. But Barlo only smiled, took out his flute, and played:

> *Don't you hear my flute playing?*
> *Then go back to school.*
> *If you can't understand me,*
> *why, you are a fool!*

And now the laugh was on his side. The foreman clapped him on the shoulder so heartily that even the powerful Barlo flinched, and said, 'You're the kind of folk a man can trust. Stay with us as long as you like.' Barlo played another tune, a dance that soon had the woodcutters on their feet. The heavily built men stamped around the fire, making the ground echo to their tread, and sparks flew up when one of them trod in the glowing embers. Then they all rolled up in their blankets and lay down to sleep, their feet to the warmth of the dying fire.

Listener woke in the night; his donkey was uneasy. He could hear the beast snorting and pawing the ground. Then Yalf came over to him and pushed at his shoulder with his muzzle. Listener got up and strained his ears for anything in the darkness that could have made the donkey restless. The woodcutters were snoring around the fire, which had burned down, the night wind was whispering in the tree tops, but there was nothing else to be heard. Yalf had his ears pricked in the direction of a mossy rock that lay among the tree trunks beyond the camping place, like a log cabin standing askew. Listener went to fetch a wooden club, and then slipped quietly uphill over the stony forest floor. Yalf followed him, but gave a snort of warning as they approached the rock. Then, suddenly, the donkey leaped forward and struck out with his hooves at a bush which grew at its foot. Howling, a wolf leaped out of the shadows, ran a little way off, then stopped and growled at its attacker, fangs bared. Listener had already picked up a stone the size of his fist from among the boulders, and now he flung it at the wolf's shaggy head. The beast turned, yowling, raced away through the fir trees, and disappeared into the night.

Listener put an arm around his donkey's neck, praised his watchfulness, and got a kiss on the cheek from Yalf's soft muzzle in return. Then they went back to the camping place. By now the foreman was awake, and came to meet them. 'Sounded like a wolf,' he said.

'It was,' said Listener. 'Yalf hunted it out of the bushes.'

The foreman whistled appreciatively through his teeth. 'Shouldn't ever underestimate anyone,' said he, 'not even a donkey.' And he patted Yalf's neck. Then they lay down to sleep again, and Listener did not wake until the woodcutters were putting their iron pans on the fire to cook their porridge for breakfast.

As they ate, and the foreman was telling the others about last night's incident, making much of Yalf's merits, the donkey got wind of something, and pricked up his long ears, snorting. Immediately afterwards they heard footsteps, and a man in a wolfskin coat appeared on the edge of the clearing.

Barlo and Listener exchanged glances, and went on eating porridge.

The foreman rose to greet the bearded stranger, who asked if he could join them by their fire and warm himself. He had eaten already, he added, when he was invited to share the woodcutters' breakfast. From the look he gave the contents of their iron pans, however, it was plain that their porridge was not much to his liking. 'Used to better, I dare say?' asked one of the woodcutters, with irony. 'Wearing a fine fur even in summer and all, like a gentleman!'

'What's that to you?' growled the bearded man, looking for a place where he could get warm. But as he was just about to sit down, Yalf came racing up behind him with a shrill bray, and rammed his head into the man's back so hard that he turned a somersault and landed in the fire. Cursing, he got up and beat the embers out of his singed wolfskin coat, while everyone around the fire roared with laughter. The bearded man lost his temper. He whipped his knife out of its sheath and was about to fall on the donkey, but even before Listener could get to his feet the foreman had grabbed the stranger, twisting the knife out of his hand. 'Can't you take a joke, Wolfskin?' said he. And one of yesterday evening's singers instantly made up a verse for the occasion:

> *Our Yalf will hunt wolves*
> *run they never so fast,*
> *and into the fire*
> *the Wolfskin has cast.*

And another man added a second verse:

Wolfskin doesn't like porridge –
alas, what a waste!
Now he's cooking himself,
for he's more to his taste.

By now Listener was used to the rather peculiar humour of the woodcutters, but he was not surprised that this utterly infuriated the bearded man. He howled with rage, twisted and turned in the foreman's powerful arms, and when he found there was no way he could free himself from their grasp, he bit his hand. The foreman yelled, and let go of him. For a moment, he was free, but now all the others had jumped up too, and closed in around him so that he could not break through their ranks. He stood there in the midst of them, watchful, like a beast brought to bay, and his restless, yellowish eyes were seeking some way out.

'You're a funny sort,' said the foreman, wiping the blood off the back of his hand on his trousers. 'Don't you ever laugh at all?' The bearded man made no answer, but only growled furiously at him. The foreman shook his head sorrowfully. 'You listen to me, Wolfskin,' said he. 'We don't want folk here that can't laugh. Now, we're going to open up our circle, and you'll get out of here just as fast as your legs will carry you. And I advise you not to come back, or you might get a good hiding.'

Before they let the bearded man go, however, the two previous singers each had another verse ready. The first of them sang:

If you can't take our jokes,
you are haughty and proud.
Bite us, you bite wood,
and you'll howl out aloud.

And the second man sang:

With soot from our fire
your face is stained black,
and we'll tan your hide well
if you ever come back.

Then the woodcutters drew apart again, and the bearded man broke through the first gap in the circle that he saw, and disappeared into the woods faster than you would have thought a human being could go.

The woodcutters started gathering up their tools to set to work, and

the foreman came over to Barlo and Listener again. 'That fellow was
no good,' said he. 'I didn't like him from the first – nor did your
donkey, Listener. I fancy he's got a good nose for such things.'

'That may well be so,' said Listener, thinking of the wolves' nocturnal
attack on the sheep pasture. 'But you and your friends were pretty
rough with the man.'

'Ah, you don't understand,' said the foreman. 'We're a friendly lot,
we are, but we've no time for folk that can't take a joke, nor laugh
neither. It's like this, you see: ours is dangerous work, every man must
be able to depend upon his mates, and our axes aren't just tools, they
can be deadly weapons too. Now if we have men among us that are
going to take every joke or accidental shove ill, we'd soon be in real
trouble, none of us sure his life was safe. We don't want anything to do
with such as them. That's how it's always been with us, and we've
done all right that way. I know that elsewhere they think the most of
the man who can strike hardest, and stands very much on his dignity.
But here it's the man who can make up the funniest verses and takes a
joke best who's the most admired. We've a power of stories about that,
but there's no time to tell 'em now. We've lingered long enough. If you
two are still here come this evening, you shall hear one. You said you
were after that kind of tale, didn't you?'

Barlo indicated that he wouldn't miss such a tale for the world.

'And don't leave your beasts alone,' the foreman added. 'That
bearded fellow may still be prowling around here somewhere. Yes, and
keep your distance when you hear our axes ring, or you might get a
tree falling on your heads, enough to strike even our minstrel here
dumb.' He looked searchingly at Barlo, and when Barlo laughed, he
laughed too, and followed his men.

Barlo and Listener saddled their beasts and rode uphill through the
woods. The higher they went, the more huge rocks they saw lying
among the lichen-covered tree trunks. Then the woods began to thin
out, and they came to a highland meadow rising gently to a parapet of
rock that was the mountain peak. As they rode across the springy grass
and flowers of the sun-warmed hillside, the scent of wild thyme and
sage wafted up. They dismounted when they came to the rocky parapet,
and let their beasts graze. Barlo began climbing the rock, with Listener
after him. They reached the peak at last, and had a wide view all
around them. To the north, they could see down over the waves of the
forest falling away to the plain. The curve of a river shone far away in
the distance, and village after village stood along its banks. And some-

where beyond the mountains to the south-west, the valley of Barlebogue must lie hidden.

That was the way Barlo looked, as he sat down on a ledge of rock, took out his flute, and began to play. Yet again the notes of his melody called up the castle of Barlebogue, and Barlo's tune said clearly that he could hardly wait to get back there. And yet again Listener was surprised to find scarcely a trace of anger, let alone vengefulness, in the melody of the flute.

While Barlo was still playing, Listener heard stones falling farther down the mountainside. He glanced down at the ravine in the rock up which they had come themselves, and saw an old man climbing it. Soon the white-bearded old man heaved himself up over the last ledge of rock and sat down on a boulder, exhausted. He wore the clothes of a prospector, and had a leather bag and his sharp hammer slung around him. As soon as he had got his breath back, he greeted Barlo and Listener. 'Lauro the prospector I'm called,' said he. 'I just wanted to see who was playing the flute so beautifully up here.' Then he looked out towards the mountains at which Barlo himself was gazing, and said, 'Aye, Barlebogue's over there. And if it's there you long to go, you obviously haven't been to Barlebogue for some time. If you'll take my advice, you'll master your longing and stay put here, for you wouldn't be running around free for long in Barlebogue.'

'What do you know about Barlebogue?' asked Listener. 'Have you been there?'

'I have,' said Lauro, 'and not so long ago either.' Barlo put his flute down and turned to him. 'Interested, are you?' the old man continued. 'Then listen to me, and you won't want to go there any more. I only just got away myself.' He chuckled quietly. 'I still know the mountain paths better than that wicked woman's shaggy retainers. Prospectors are in demand there just now, you see. Though only if they're not working on their own account.'

'Hasn't Gisa got enough of her blue stones yet?' asked Listener.

The old man cast him a sharp glance. 'You seem to know quite a lot about it,' he said. 'But not the latest news, apparently. It's some while since she had any time for those blue stones – she can't stand them now. She's after another stone, but no one's been able to find it for her yet.'

'What kind of a stone?' asked Listener, holding his breath.

'I wish I knew,' said Lauro. 'Plainly she can't describe it exactly herself. Folk tell a strange story about it. They say she got a young man into her clutches who had such a stone. A magic stone, they say. But at the time she didn't yet know the virtue of the stone, and the lad himself didn't really know either, or else he wouldn't have fallen for her lures so easily. They say she cast aside his magic stone, threw it carelessly away, to tame the young man with her fine sapphires. But as the way is with such magical things, you can't do as you like with them, and least of all can you throw them away. Folk say the stone took on a life of its own and kept coming back to its owner, whatever Gisa did to stop it. And so she lost her power over the young man. One day she rode out with him, and she came galloping back on an exhausted horse, with a blue mark on her forehead. Rumour has it that the lad worked magic to set one of her blue stones in her head, and now it's lodged there like an incurable ulcer, poisoning her brain. And since then she hasn't set foot outside the castle gates, and lets no one but her shaggy retainers see her. And that's why she is seeking out all the prospectors she can, to find her such a magic stone, for she thinks only such a stone will cure her. She has word spread all over the countryside that there's plenty of gold to be found in Barlebogue. But the truth of it is that her men drive the poor souls up into the mountains and make them dig for the magic stone day and night, until they fall down dead. Do you still want to go to Barlebogue, fluter?'

Barlo nodded, and before the old man could say any more, Listener brought out his bag, and took the stone out of it. 'I hope she won't be able to harm me as long as I carry this stone,' he said. 'For now I know a little more than I did at the time.'

The prospector raised his head in surprise, and looked Listener in the face. 'So you're the man,' he said. Then he looked at the stone, and added, after a while, 'Well, now I believe this stone has more power in it than all Gisa's sapphires put together. Whenever I look at those blue things I feel cold, but your stone warms my heart.'

'Mine too,' said Listener.

'Be on your guard!' said Lauro. 'You are still very young, and I'm afraid you don't know it all yet, nothing like all. What do you mean to do in Barlebogue?'

'My master wants to see if an end can't be put to Gisa's mastery there,' said Listener, 'and there are folk who will help him.'

'If that's so, you can count on me too,' said the old man. 'You may need someone who knows his way around the mountains where her shaggy retainers drive the prospectors to work.'

Barlo gladly accepted this offer, and Listener said, 'We are all to meet at the Silver Harp in Draglope, at the time of the spring fair.'

'I'll be there on time,' said Lauro. 'But I have a few things to do first.' And so saying he took his leave of them, clambered down the rock, and soon afterwards disappeared into the woods on the far side of the highland meadow, waving back at them once more.

Barlo and Listener returned to the camping place that evening aware that they had gained a useful ally. The woodcutters were already cooking their supper, and set another pan full of food before their guests again. After supper, the foreman said, 'I promised you a story this morning, and now you shall hear it. Hey, Tubby, tell them the tale of Wurzel and how he wanted to be a miller's man. They'll like that one.'

The man thus addressed was one of the two woodcutters who had distinguished themselves as singers, an elderly fellow of considerable girth. It was not that his stomach was flabby; everything about him was solid and robust, and he had a belt around his belly like the hoop a cooper has knocked well into place around the staves of a barrel. He did indeed look like a great, tall tub, and no better nickname could have been found for him. Tubby settled himself comfortably, wiped the last of his porridge from the corners of his mouth with the back of his hand, and asked, 'Did you ever hear of Wurzel, then?' Barlo and Listener had to confess that they had never heard a thing about this Wurzel, however famous he might be in these parts. 'Then it's high time you did,' said Tubby, and he began to tell:

The Tale of Wurzel and the Magic Miller

Wurzel was a woodcutter, a huge great fellow, tall as a tree and with muscles like an ox. Folk called him Wurzel because he had a face like a mangold-wurzel, round and ruddy, and he had a thick shock of hair on top of it. Wurzel was a great one for getting strange notions, and you never knew for certain if he meant them in good earnest or if he was joking. It's to be supposed he knew himself, but he could put other folk well and truly out of countenance, the more so if they weren't woodcutters. And there was one thing Wurzel couldn't understand a bit, and that was if he couldn't make someone laugh. For he himself could laugh so loud it made the trees in the forest shake.

Well, the beginning of this tale is that one day Wurzel had had enough of cutting wood. He made a hearty breakfast, but then he drove his axe into a tree-stump and simply walked off, along beside the stream and down into the valley until he came to a mill. He knocked up the miller, and asked him what kind of work it was, grinding corn, and if he could use a man to help him.

Now the miller, a thin little fellow without a single laughter line upon his face, was a man well skilled in magic. He looked Wurzel up and down, and he thought to himself that he could get this fool working for him for nothing if he went about it the right way. 'Ah, it's hard work,' said he. 'Much too hard for a man as frail as you.'

Wurzel took this for a joke, and laughed so hard he rattled the window panes. Then he said, 'Why, little fellow, if you can do the work then so can I.'

'And I say you're too weak,' said the miller. 'Want to bet on it?' For he knew that a woodcutter could never resist a bet, and that was just what he was after.

'Done, little fellow,' said Wurzel. 'What are we betting, then?'

'If you lose, you must serve me for three years,' said the miller. 'Without pay, mind you.'

'And if I win, you must give me that pretty knife hanging from your belt,' said Wurzel, laughing again. The miller didn't like that much, for his knife had a fine, ornate silver handle, and a precious blade that had been forged by dwarves and never rusted. But since he had suggested the bet, he couldn't withdraw now. However, he was so sure of himself he didn't much fear to lose his knife.

'Yes, if you win you shall have the knife,' he said. 'I'll set you three tasks to perform – though weak as you are, I fancy you'll fail at the first of them. I want you to carry these sacks up to the grinding floor in one journey.'

Now there were five sacks of corn standing by the door, and the miller thought not even a man as strong as Wurzel could carry them all at once. But Wurzel only laughed. 'Is that all?' he said. He laid the sacks over his shoulders one by one, and began climbing the steps to the grinding floor. When the miller saw that Wurzel really could carry all those sacks at once, he went to his magic arts for aid. Standing close behind Wurzel, he touched the top sack with a hazel wand, for by doing that he could double the weight of the sacks. At that moment Wurzel broke wind good and loud, which made him laugh so heartily the sacks on his back jumped up and down, and the miller couldn't keep his hazel wand touching them. Three more steps, and there was Wurzel on the grinding floor, where he put the sacks down. ' 'Scuse me breaking wind so rudely, little fellow,' said he. 'All of a sudden those sacks weighed so heavy, I couldn't keep it in. Maybe you didn't ought to walk so close behind a man who's had a good breakfast when he carries a heavy load.'

'You'll soon be laughing the other side of your face,' said the miller, for Wurzel's laughter fairly enraged him. 'If you found that first task hard, you'll never do the second.'

'What's to be done now?' asked Wurzel.

'Tip the corn into the mill,' said the miller.

'Is that all?' said Wurzel again, and he untied the first sack and began tipping the corn into the hopper. But as he was bending over the hopper, the miller, standing behind him, put his cat on Wurzel's back, and by his magic arts he made the cat heavy as lead. He hoped this uncouth fellow would lose his balance and fall into the hopper himself. The millstones will smooth the rough edges off his manners, he thought. But no sooner was the cat upon his back than Wurzel gave so deeply resonant a belch that the cat leaped into the air in fright and fell into the hopper itself. The way it struggled about there in the corn struck Wurzel as so comical that he burst into roars of laughter again. He didn't calm down until the miller had fished his cat out of the hopper, and then he said, ''Scuse me, little fellow, I really must have breakfasted too well. And you want to take care your cat doesn't get in the way of a man at his work, you know.'

'Well, if even the cat bothers you, you'll never perform the third task,' said the miller. 'Want to give up?'

'A woodcutter never gives up, not with a good breakfast in his belly,' said Wurzel. 'What do I do now?'

'Now you must set the mill wheel turning,' said the miller.

'Is that all?' said Wurzel, wondering what could be so difficult about that. He went down the steps and out of the door, to turn the water out of the millstream to drive the mill wheel. But the wheel wouldn't turn, for the miller was secretly holding it in place with his little finger, and that magic was so strong no one could have moved the wheel a hand's breadth.

'Weather's been pretty dry, I guess, if the millstream runs so slow,' said Wurzel. 'Looks as if I'd better help it along a bit.' And he climbed out on the channel through which the millstream ran, stood there straddling it, unbuttoned the flies of his trousers and pissed on the mill wheel. As he pissed he laughed so heartily the whole mill shook. The miller involuntarily snatched his hand away, and the wheel began turning faster than it had ever turned before. 'You don't puzzle a man that's had a good breakfast so easily,' said Wurzel, clambering down from the channel at his leisure. 'And you don't want to keep your hand on the mill wheel when the water's running over the paddles. Might do yourself an injury. Well, now do you reckon I'd make a miller's man?'

'Maybe,' said the miller, angry because he had lost his bet. 'I don't like your manners, though.'

'It's mutual,' said Wurzel, 'for you didn't laugh once, though there was plenty to laugh at. I don't want to work for a master like you. So give me the knife, and we're quits.'

The miller had to give him the knife, for he saw his magic was no match for this man's merriment. And when Wurzel was home again he used the good knife to cut the bacon he ate with his porridge in the morning. 'A good breakfast is half your day's work done,' he used to say as he cut it, and then he would laugh so loud that the cones fell off the pine trees.

* * *

The woodcutters nudged one another and laughed long and heartily, although all of them had heard this story many times before. Barlo and Listener joined in their laughter, though Listener feared this rather dubious type of humour might not be to everyone's taste. But he said, 'That fellow Wurzel would be the kind of man we could use.'

'What for?' asked the foreman.

So Listener told them briefly what Barlo had in mind, and what kind of plan they had agreed upon in the Silver Harp. 'And unless I'm much mistaken,' he added, 'the bearded fellow with the wolfskin coat who came to your fire this morning and wouldn't laugh was one of Gisa's shaggy retainers. It may be that he was spying on us, or maybe he wanted to lure some of you to Barlebogue to prospect for gold. But you never let him get a word in edgeways, and now I see why you set such store by a man's ability to laugh. What we've learnt from you may come in useful in Barlebogue, and I'd like to have Wurzel along with us.'

Tubby laughed. 'Got to disappoint you, I'm afraid,' said he. 'Wurzel doesn't exist except in the tales that are told of him, and that's more than can be said of many a man. But if you'll make do with me, I'm willing: it's the kind of thing I'd enjoy. Never let it be said Tubby missed a spot of good fun!'

Listener thanked him for his offer, and said, 'Why, that'll be almost the same as having Wurzel himself with us. You know the meeting place.'

'To be sure,' said Tubby. 'In the Silver Harp at the time of Draglope spring fair.'

Barlo and Listener wandered around the mountains for a while longer, and when the nights began to get cooler they rode down through the woods again. The trees came to an end where the lowlands began, opening on to a view of a great lake, beside which the road ran. The blue-green water of the lake was so clear that you could see the fishes lying still above its stony bed. The shimmering, silvery surface of the water reached almost to the far horizon, where it was bordered by low hills. The reed-thatched roofs of a village on the banks of the lake appeared before the two riders, and farther off they saw a few fishing boats lying motionless on the water. Barlo pointed to the houses, indicating to Listener that he meant to spend the night here.

He turned aside from the road as they came into the village, and Listener on his donkey followed him down to the bank of the lake. A landing stage was built out into the water on wooden posts here, and some boats were made fast to it. Barlo and Listener dismounted, watered their beasts, sat on the planks of the landing stage and let their legs dangle over the still water. There were shoals of tiny fish swarming in the shade beneath the planks. A fish jumped now and then out in the lake, leaving a circle on the surface, a ring that spread slowly outwards, intersecting other circles. Once, a flight of ducks came over the lowlands against the pale evening sky, flew low over the lake, and then settled on the water near the fishing boats.

Barlo took out his flute and began to play: a tune that sounded like water and that had the rustle of the reeds in it. After a while Listener felt the padding of bare feet on the planks, and when he turned he saw some children come from the village to listen to the fluter. When Listener nodded to them they stood there looking awkward, but then they slowly came closer, magically drawn towards the sound of Barlo's flute.

After a while Barlo brought the tune to an end with a long trill which sounded like the splash of waves, put his flute down, and smiled at the children.

'You play lovely music,' said one of the girls.

Barlo made a dismissive gesture, as if there were nothing special about it, and pointed to the pan-pipes one boy was holding. They were made of seven reeds cut to different lengths and tied together with rushes.

'You're a piper too,' said Listener. 'Will you play us something?'

'I only know simple songs, the kind we sing here,' said the boy.

Barlo beckoned him over to come and sit beside him, and without more ado the boy sat down on the planks and began to play. Listener was immediately enthralled by the simple melody he drew from his instrument. It sounded both sad and merry, and seemed to be telling a tale. After the first verse, indeed, the girl who had spoken to them first began to sing the words of the song:

> *To the lake a girl did go*
> *every year,*
> *to the lake a girl did go*
> *with her cheeks as white as snow.*
>
> *Oh the Green Man he came out*
> *every year,*
> *oh the Green Man he came out*
> *and he kissed her on the mouth.*
>
> *The poor girl she wept sore*
> *every year,*
> *the poor girl she wept sore*
> *and she never came back more.*
>
> *To the lake did Agla go*
> *in that year,*
> *to the lake did Agla go*
> *in a dress as white as snow.*
>
> *Oh the Green Man he came out*
> *in that year,*
> *oh the Green Man he came out*
> *and she kissed him on the mouth.*
>
> *Oh fair Agla's laugh was light*
> *in that year,*
> *oh fair Agla's laugh was light*
> *and the Green Man sang all night.*

'What song is that?' asked Listener, when the girl had come to the end of it. 'I've never heard it before.'

'Oh, we all know it here,' said the singer. 'It's sung by the girls.'

'And who is this Green Man?' asked Listener.

'That's a long story,' said the girl, shaking her head. 'I can't tell it.'

In the meantime, the fishermen out on the lake had pulled in their nets and were now rowing towards the moorings. When they reached the landing stage, they made their boats fast and climbed out. An elderly man with a wide, grey, shovel-shaped beard greeted the strangers.

'We heard there was a fluter had come to the lakeside,' he said. 'We seldom get travelling players in these parts, and we'd be glad if you would stay a while.'

Listener waited for Barlo's nod of consent, and then said, 'We'll be happy to accept your invitation. We already know you play and sing here, and my master is eager to learn new songs. His name is Barlo, and I am his servant Listener.'

'My name is Valosh,' said the bearded fisherman, 'and you shall be guests in my house as long as you please. The girl who sang you the song of Fair Agla is my granddaughter Marla. But now we must get our fish ashore.'

Listener and Barlo helped the fishermen take the nets out of the boats. The fish they had caught were struggling in them. The catch was sorted out at once, on the landing stage. The men threw any fish that were too small back in the water, and the fish they could use – tench, grayling and carp – were killed with a blow on the head from the back of a knife, gutted, and put in baskets which a couple of boys had brought along. Then two men took each basket and went back to the village. But Valosh stayed behind, and asked his guests to come home with him. 'You run ahead,' he told Marla, who was still standing on the bank with the other children. 'Go and tell your grandmother we have guests.'

Barlo and Listener took their mounts by the reins and walked along the road with Valosh, past low-built, whitewashed fishermen's cottages, until they reached his house at the far end of the village. A tall, grey-haired woman was standing in the doorway waiting for them. Her face was thin and wrinkled, but her eyes looked young and merry, as if she liked to laugh, and often did. She welcomed the guests and asked them into the house. Valosh took their mounts and led them to a low stable

beside the house. 'I know about horses as well as fish,' he said. 'My son
will see to your beasts in a moment, when he feeds our own.'

Barlo and Listener entered a large living-room with woven rush
matting on the floor. There was a fireplace by the inner wall, where a
younger woman, who might be Marla's mother, was busy roasting two
fat carp from that day's catch on a grid. Smelling the aroma of the fish,
Listener felt hungry.

He did not have long to wait, for Valosh came straight back from
the stable and invited his guests to sit down and eat. The other members
of the family came and sat down too; besides the two old people, there
was a young man, so like Valosh's wife that anyone could see at once
he was her son, and Marla and the two smaller children, boys. The
children's mother, who had cooked the meal, served the guests with
the best pieces of roast carp laid on freshly baked flat cakes of bread.
The only seasoning was coarse-grained salt, which stood on the table
in a wooden dish.

After they had eaten, Valosh fetched a pitcher of reddish-yellow
perry, and poured the perry into goblets made of wood turned on the
lathe. 'Not too sharp for you, I hope,' said he. 'I dare say you've drunk
better along your way.' But Barlo and Listener thought the perry was
just right after the roast carp, and took a second goblet of it.

'You played well while we were out on the lake, Barlo,' said Valosh.
Barlo thanked him for the compliment with a smile, took out his flute
and played the Song of Fair Agla that Marla had sung to them. He
played the first three verses slowly and sadly, but when he came to the
last three he changed the melody a little here and there, making it
sound like a merry dance.

'You're a quick learner too,' said Valosh, when Barlo came to the
end. 'We often sing that song here.'

'Marla said that there's a story goes with the song,' said Listener,
'but she couldn't tell it to us. Do you know the tale?'

'I do,' said Valosh, 'but I'm no storyteller myself. My son's better at
that. You must know that he's descended from that same Agla through
his mother, or so it's said. And they say that she had the same merry
eyes. Will you tell them the tale, Lagosh?'

Lagosh looked at the guests with his merry brown eyes, took another
draught of his perry, and began to tell:

The Tale of Fair Agla and the Green Man

Long, long ago, our people already lived here by the lake. In those days, there was a young fisherman called Yelosh. He was a man always inclined to keep himself to himself, and he had a liking for strange things. One morning in spring, he went far out on the lake, all the way to the reeds on the opposite bank, because he thought he would get a particularly good catch there. And when he came back in the evening there was a girl sitting in his boat. No one in the village had ever seen her before. This girl was strangely beautiful: her skin had a glow like the shimmering inside of a shell, her brown hair was long and smooth, and her dark brown eyes looked as if she would begin to laugh any minute. She wore nothing at all but the old linen smock Yelosh kept in his boat in case he needed a dry garment to put on. Even at the time, this struck everyone who saw Yelosh come home that day as very remarkable, for one had to suppose that he had found the girl naked.

Yelosh, who lived alone in his house, his parents having died early, took this girl for his wife, and nobody in the village was really surprised that he refused to say anything about her origins. He called her Aglaia, and the people thought this an extremely odd name for a fisherman's wife. However, Aglaia was always cheerful, so that they soon got used to her, and the men came to think that Yelosh really had made a remarkably good catch when he brought his wife home, for not only was she so beautiful that many a man's eyes followed her in secret when she walked through the village, she also kept Yelosh's house in good order, and could embroider coloured patterns on his shirts such as no one here had ever seen before. The only thing that did still strike the villagers as strange was that the hem of her long skirt always seemed a little damp, but that might be because you had to cross the stream by way of a low-lying bridge to get from Yelosh's house to the village. And these days Yelosh was merrier than he had ever been before, and sang almost all day long.

Not a year had gone by when Yelosh had to fetch the midwife from the village because Aglaia was about to bear a child. Her labour was a hard one, and went on for hours. In the end, Aglaia gave birth to a girl, and had scarcely seen the child before she herself died. All she had time to say was, 'Call her Agla.'

Yelosh wept all night long for grief, so loud that the whole village could hear him. Next day, when people came to his house to see the dead woman for the last time, he was quiet again, and dry-eyed, but it is said that he never laughed or sang again in his life. His one comfort was the child. He found a nurse who lived nearby to come to the house and look after Agla while he went out fishing on the lake. And in the evenings he would sit by Agla's cradle for hours, looking into her eyes, which were already as merry and brown as her mother's.

Exactly a year to the day after Yelosh had brought Aglaia home to his house, a storm arose in the middle of the night, although it had been clear, cloudless spring weather all day long. Waves splashed on the bank, and a strange howling and crying could be heard through the whistling of the wind. A few stout-hearted men got up and went down to the lake, to pull the boats moored by the landing stage up on land.

Out of doors, the howling and crying could be heard more clearly than ever, and when the men looked out at the turbulent water they saw a huge, round head rise above the surface in the foam of a wave close to the bank. In spite of the darkness, it shone green above the boiling black water. At first it looked like an old man's head, but then like the head of a water creature such as none of the fishermen had ever seen before. A greenish beard hung around the broad, frog-like lips, and the huge eyes above the flat nose were round and fixed like the eyes of a carp. Then the fish-man's body rose slowly from the waves, water running from his scaly arms as he raised them aloft, still howling and crying. And now the men could make out his words. 'Aglaia! Aglaia!' he was crying.

Terrified, they all ran back to their houses, barred the doors behind them, and stayed awake all night long. Not until nearly morning did the storm slacken, and the crying and howling became quieter and at last died away in the distance. When it was light, the fishermen went off to Yelosh's house, knocked on the door, and told him to come out. After a while Yelosh came out of doors, and asked what they wanted.

'Didn't you hear the storm last night?' one of them said.

'Just a little bit of wind,' said Yelosh, 'it didn't disturb me. I turned over on my other side and went back to sleep.'

'Then I suppose you didn't hear the green fish-man howling either?' asked another man.

'What fish-man?' asked Yelosh, turning pale.

'The one who was crying out for your dead wife all night long,' said a third fisherman. 'And now you must tell us where you found Aglaia, so that we know what this matter is all about.'

At first Yelosh refused to say where Aglaia had come from, but in the end, when they threatened him, and one man said they would throw Aglaia's child into the water if he still said nothing, he gave in, and told them how he had come by his wife.

That day, he said, he had found a little island among the reeds by the opposite bank, an island you couldn't see from the lake. He had climbed out of his boat there to look for duck's eggs; he had collected a whole basket of eggs, and then he sat down on the sandy soil and sang himself a little song. While he was still singing, a girl arose from the water by the shore of the island and listened to him. 'You sing beautifully,' she said, and he asked her to come up on the island with him. And then, naked as she was, she had climbed out of the water, sat down beside him and asked him to go on singing. As he sang, he looked into her eyes, and he could think of nothing but that he must win this girl for his own. When his song was over, he had asked the girl if she would live in his house with him. 'If I do, will you always sing for me?' she asked, and when he assured her that he would, she climbed into his boat without a moment's hesitation. As for the rest of the story, they knew it already, said Yelosh, and he just left the fishermen standing there and went back into his house.

Now the men realized that Aglaia had been a water-spirit. 'When he brought her home, it did seem to me as if she had webbing between her toes,' said one of the men. 'Afterwards, she always wore shoes, so that you couldn't see her feet.' If Aglaia had been alive, the fishermen might have dragged her out of the house and thrown her into the lake, but she was dead and buried, and by daylight the turmoil of the night did not seem to matter so much that they need trouble themselves about it any more.

That year, however, they soon noticed that their catches were getting poorer and poorer. It was as if the fish were gradually disappearing from the lake, or keeping well away from the places where the fishermen threw out their nets. Their stocks of dried and smoked fish were not nearly large enough, and towards the end of the winter the people began scratching for waterweeds under the ice and digging up roots to satisfy their hunger.

When the ice melted at last, and spring came, nothing would go right with the fishing, and so it went on until that day when the Green Man had come up from the lake howling the year before. The fishermen had already begun to wonder if it might not be he who kept the fish from their nets and creels, and they had decided that if the Green Man came up again, the village elder should speak to him.

This time, the men were not surprised when a storm arose in the night. They gathered on the shore, and after a while they heard the Green Man's howling and crying again. 'Aglaia!' his voice echoed over the dark and swirling waters. 'Aglaia!' And then the water-spirit's mighty head broke through the waves again, and drove closer to the shore, swaying, until the Green Man rose from the water and could be seen to his waist. He turned his streaming face to Yelosh's house and howled again, 'Aglaia! Aglaia!'

'Is it you that's keeping the fish from our nets?' the village elder cried.

The Green Man turned his head, which had no neck, and stared at the elder with his round and lidless eyes. Then he opened his broad mouth and cried, 'You shall catch no more of my fish now that you have caught my Aglaia. Give her back to me!'

'We cannot,' said the elder. 'Aglaia is dead.'

'Dead?' howled the Green Man. 'What does dead mean? I don't know the word.'

The fishermen looked at each other, dismayed. Then the elder called back, 'A dead person can't go anywhere. We can't give her back to you now even if we wanted to.'

'Have you eaten her as you eat my fish? Then you shall never catch a single one of them again!' roared the Green Man through the storm, and he began to sink back into the waves.

'Wait!' cried the village elder. 'You will kill us all. What must we do to calm your anger?'

'Aglaia!' howled the Green Man. 'Give me Aglaia back!'

'We can't,' repeated the elder. 'Shall we give you Yelosh, who took her from you?'

Yelosh, who was standing among the men, turned pale when he heard this offer, but he did not try to escape, for he had realized that the life of the whole village was at stake.

'What would I do with this Yelosh?' cried the Green Man. 'Have him remind me daily that he took Aglaia from me? Will he deliver me from my grief? No, send me a girl to gladden my heart, tonight and every year upon this day. If she is with me before the sun rises from the lake, you shall catch plenty of fish in your nets.' As he spoke these words, the Green Man went down into the water until it was over his shoulders again, and then he disappeared in a swirl of foam.

The fishermen stood on the bank, so horrified they scarcely dared to look at one another. Then the village elder said, 'Go and wake everyone, and call them together in the village square. We must discuss this before the first light of dawn rises over the lake.'

When the people heard what the Green Man demanded, horror seized them in its grip. 'Are we to let the monster have our daughters?' cried one woman. But the village elder said calmly, 'Do you all want to starve to death?' And then the people realized there was no other way out. They all fell silent, looking at the ground before them. In the silence, one man asked, 'So who is to sacrifice a daughter?'

'We'll cast lots to see which girl must go,' said the village elder. He put a handful of sticks on the ground in front of him, took one from the pile for every girl who had reached the age of seventeen during the last year, and scratched the sign of her family's house on it. Then he threw a blanket over the sticks he had marked, and told the fisherman standing nearest him to take one out from under it. But the man refused, and no one else was willing to draw the lot of the girl to be delivered to the Green Man either. 'If none of you will do it,' said the elder at last, 'then you must draw the lot, Yelosh. You cannot refuse, for you have brought us to this pass.'

So then Yelosh went to him, drew out the lot from under the blanket, and gave it to the village elder, who looked at the sign he had scratched on the stick, spoke the girl's name, and added, 'We haven't much time left, for the sky is already growing light in the east.'

As the women held back the girl's screaming mother, the men went to the house where she lived with her father. In a little while they came back, two of them leading the girl between them. She wore a black dress, and her snow-white cheeks were wet with tears. Followed by the other villagers, the men took the girl down to the lake and led her in until all three of them were up to their breasts in the water. It began to eddy and to foam in front of them. The girl uttered a shrill scream, and was pushed forward by the men. Then she sank in the swirling water as if the ground had been pulled from under her feet.

That year the fishermen were content with their catches, and the people had enough smoked fish to eat in winter, and need not go hungry. And so they kept their bargain with the Green Man over the years that followed. Every spring, on the day Yelosh had brought Aglaia to the village, he had to draw the lot, and he did it without protesting. If he had once kept himself to himself by his own choice, now the villagers avoided him like the plague. Even the nurse left his house as soon as the child could do without her, and after that Yelosh looked after his daughter himself. He loved her with all the love that was left to him, but he turned grey early, his face wore a morose and withdrawn expression, and he went his own way and cast his nets in remote places where the other men did not fish.

In the circumstances, it seemed strange to the villagers that despite her father's nature, Agla grew into a happy girl who loved to laugh and sing. There were reasons enough why the people of the village might not have wanted anything to do with her, any more than they did with her father, but when she looked at you with her merry brown eyes, you couldn't resist her cheerfulness. Everyone liked her, and would say a friendly word to her when she walked through the village. But people avoided mentioning her father when they spoke to her. When the village lads started casting glances at her, she began to be called Fair Agla, for not only had she inherited her mother's eyes, she was as like her as a twin sister in every respect. It may have been a comfort or it may have been a torment to Yelosh that in this way, his memory of Aglaia could never fade.

The spring when Fair Agla was seventeen years old, Yelosh had to draw the lot on the fateful night again, and he knew that the sign of his own house was scratched on one of the sticks. This time his hand trembled as he put it beneath the blanket, and he tried to feel the scratched signs, but his fingers seemed numb. He drew out a stick, and gave it to the village elder. When the elder read the sign, everyone standing around him in silence could clearly see how he swallowed as if his voice had failed him. Then he said, loud and clear, 'Agla.'

Yelosh turned and went away without a word, as if he had always known it. Slowly, the people followed him. They took their time, and tonight there was no wailing mother to be held back. They did not have long to wait outside Yelosh's house before he came out of it again. But no weeping girl clad in black mourning garments followed him. Agla had put on a festive, snow-white dress, and she smiled at the villagers as if she were going to her wedding. 'You don't need to lead me,' she told the two men who stepped forward to take her arms and lead her down to the lake. 'I know the way.' She kissed her father on both cheeks, and then went down to the bank ahead of all the people. And as she walked unhesitatingly into the water she began to sing, a melody of three tones such as children use in their games:

> *Green Man*
> *grant our wish,*

from your deep lake give us fish.
Lie not in the water
sorrowing for your daughter;
lord of fish to north and south,
kiss Fair Agla on the mouth.

She walked into the lake until the water was over her hips. Then she stopped, for the waves were beginning to boil in front of her, and the Green Man's round head came up from the foaming eddies. Dripping with water, his mighty trunk emerged, and around him the lapping, spraying water glittered in the moonlight like a thousand precious stones. The Green Man looked at Agla with his round eyes. 'Have you come back at last, Aglaia?' he asked.

When she heard that, Fair Agla laughed and said, 'Are you still waiting for Aglaia, then, Green Man? Look at me! I am Aglaia's daughter, grown up now, and as merry as my mother once was.'

'Yes,' said the Green Man, 'you are merry. But all the other girls they sent me were sad, and none of them could gladden my heart.'

'Come here, Green Man,' said Agla, 'and let me kiss you.'

So the Green Man made his way to her through the water, and when he had reached her she put her arms around his shoulders and kissed his broad mouth. 'Are you still sad now, Green Man?' asked Fair Agla.

'No,' said the Green Man. 'My grief is gone, like a duck flying over the water. Will you come down and live with me?'

'I can't do that,' said Fair Agla, 'for I have a human father. I must live among human beings, and I cannot be happy without them. But I will sing for you whenever you like.'

'Then I will not be sad any more,' said the Green Man. 'And tell your people that I have had enough of their weeping girls. They shall have plenty of fish as long as people with Aglaia's merry brown eyes live among them and sing their happy songs. Goodbye, Fair Agla. The Green Man will not forget that you kissed him.'

Then he threw himself back in the water, but he did not sink down into the depths; instead, he swam out over the lake, singing so that his voice rang through the night like a bell. The people stood there on the bank a long while, listening to his song, until it died away in the distant reeds by the far bank.

* * *

When Lagosh had come to the end of his tale, his father said, 'So now you know why travelling players are so welcome to us here. The Green Man loves merry songs above all else, and whenever we've had a singer or minstrel here as our guest who was skilled at his trade, the fish has been particularly plentiful that year. So if you'd like to stay for the winter, we should be very glad.'

Barlo indicated his assent, and Listener thanked the fisherman for his hospitality. Then he asked, 'And what had really happened to the other girls?'

'Well, that's a strange thing,' said Lagosh. 'The story goes that they came back out of the lake at sunrise on the morning after the night when Fair Agla kissed the Green Man. Nobody saw it happen, but there they were standing on the bank in the morning, so it's said, and their black dresses were as dry as if they'd never been in the water. But the strangest thing of all was that none of them had aged. There they stood beside the lake, just as young as the day they'd been pushed into it, and not one among them could remember what had happened in the meantime.' Lagosh laughed. 'And that year, they say, there were so many marriageable girls here in the village that many a confirmed old bachelor thought of taking a wife.'

Barlo and Listener spent a peaceful time in the lakeside village. Before winter began, they would go out with the fishermen, helping them to haul in their nets or set their basket traps in the water, and while they were still on the lake Barlo often brought out his flute to play it. If the Green Man heard the music, surely he took pleasure in it, for Barlo soon knew the tunes of all the songs that were sung in the village, and there were a great many of them.

One sunny day in late autumn, Barlo and Listener came to Aglaia's Island, as the little sandbank among the reeds where Yelosh had found his wife was called. They had rowed over alone. They got out of their boat in the shallows, pulled it up on land, and sat down in the sand, which was warmed by the sun. For a while they watched the ducks that came flying across the lake in arrow-shaped formation and settled close to them. The birds paddled around in the rustling reeds, dabbling in the water with their tails in the air and quacking softly. Among the drakes with their shimmering blue-green plumage and the brown ducks one white bird swam. Perhaps it had flown away from a farmer, and now preferred a life of freedom to a future in the roasting-pan. Or then again, thought Listener, perhaps it was some enchanted creature.

Anything seemed possible, here on this island hidden in the reeds with the water lapping around it.

Barlo took his flute out of his pocket and played the Song of Fair Agla, decorating the tune with all the runs and trills that this strange watery world put into his head. He had new and unexpected variations for each verse, and he let the last note linger in the air for a long while as it died away, like a call awaiting an answer.

And the answer came. No sooner had he taken the instrument from his lips than they heard a sudden rustle in the reeds to one side of them. A round object gleamed in the sun, flew up in the air and over their way, and rolled to a halt in the sand before their feet. It was a large and beautifully coiled sea-shell, something you would never have expected to find in the country here. But Listener had once heard tell of such shells, and knew what it was. 'A triton's horn!' he said, amazed.

He had hardly spoken the word when they heard a gurgling in the reeds, like the sound of suppressed laughter. 'Then you know it!' called a girl's voice. 'Our Green Lord sends the fluter this, to thank him for his beautiful song. If ever he needs help upon the water, let him blow this horn. He knows how to blow an instrument well enough!' Yet another clear laugh, a splashing in the water, and then all was quiet again, except for the gentle quacking of the ducks still searching the bottom of the lake around the island. But the white duck was no longer to be seen.

Next morning the fine autumn weather was at an end. Black clouds had come up overnight, and an icy wind blew from the north, sweeping the last yellowed leaves off the trees. The broad surface of the lake looked dull and grey, and the boats tugged at their mooring ropes in the choppy water by the landing stage. Fishing was over for this year. The men brought in their nets and creels, to repair them during the winter months, pulled the boats up on land and laid them keel upwards on the slope of the bank. A little while later the first snow fell, and a thin skin of ice formed on the surface of the shallows, reaching out farther into the lake every day. People sat together in their living-rooms in the long evenings, singing songs, telling stories, or dancing to the music of Barlo's flute.

When Barlo and Listener came out of the house, one morning that was ringing with frost, they saw Valosh hauling a long sleigh out of the stable and making it ready for a journey. 'Are you going out in such cold weather?' Listener asked.

'We're bidden to a wedding at my sister-in-law's, in the next village,' said Valosh. 'Her daughter Valya is marrying a fisherman there. Valya's another of Agla's kin, and they say she's as lovely as her ancestress was. Ride with us if you like! A minstrel's always welcome at such times.'

Valosh lent his guests a couple of heavy fur coats, and then they fetched the horse and the donkey from their stable, while Valosh harnessed two shaggy little horses to the sleigh. His whole family got into it, children and all, and he cracked his whip and set the horses trotting along the broad, untouched stretch of snow that ran along the bank of the lake. Barlo and Listener rode beside them.

To the right of their track, the snow-covered surface of the frozen lake reached to the distant, wooded mountain slopes on the opposite bank. A stiff pattern of dry reeds marked the lake's edge. Once, as they crossed a narrow inlet, the ice sang beneath the runners of the sleigh.

After about two hours, Listener saw smoke rising from the snow-drifts ahead of them, and only then did he realize that the drifts were really the snow-covered roofs of the next village, just appearing above the top of a dip in the ground. Valosh urged his horses on, yelling, and let the sleigh shoot down the gentle slope so fast that the snow flew. He brought it to a halt outside the fisherman's house in the middle of the village, and at that same moment the door was opened. An elderly man came out first, and after him a grey-haired woman with the merry brown eyes of Agla's kin, and then some younger people. By now Barlo and Listener had arrived as well. They dismounted and stood aside, waiting, while the two families greeted one another.

Then Valosh led his brother-in-law over to them, telling him, 'And I've brought a couple of friends, Kurlosh; they're staying the winter in my house. The tall one is Barlo the minstrel, and the one with the donkey is called Listener and is his servant. I hope they'll both be welcome at the wedding.'

'A minstrel?' said Kurlosh, surprised, looking at the two strangers suspiciously. 'What does he play, then?'

'The flute,' said Valosh.

'The flute, eh?' said Kurlosh, looking even warier than before.

'Why, yes, he's a fluter!' said Valosh. 'How long have you had anything against folk who play the flute?'

'I must have a word with you before I welcome them as guests,' said

Kurlosh, and he drew his brother-in-law aside and spoke quietly to him. Listener saw how Kurlosh kept glancing at Barlo, while Valosh shook his head and seemed to be trying to soothe his brother-in-law. Finally he said out loud, 'I'll vouch for both my guests! Now, let us come in and get warm.'

Kurlosh still seemed undecided, but at this he came over to the strangers, saying, 'Well, come into my house and warm yourselves, then, for you've had a long ride through the cold.' Listener could not help noticing that he was not actually welcoming them as guests, and he wondered what the man could have against them.

He was soon to find out. First, a boy took their mounts away and led them to the stable behind the house. Lagosh, who had been un-harnessing the horses from the sleigh, followed him. Then Barlo and Listener entered a hallway, took off their fur coats, dusted now with snow, and the master of the house led them into the living-room, which smelled of the smoke of the wood fire burning on the hearth to one side of the room.

As soon as they had sat down on the settle by the fireside, Valosh said, 'You'll have wondered about my brother-in-law's strange greet-ing. I must explain why he's suspicious. He tells me a man was here a few days ago and told him there was a fluter wandering in these parts, a fellow who wasn't to be trusted, and was really a runaway groom whose tongue had been cut out because he stole from his mas-ters and talked rebellion. And he had a sly and cunning young man along with him. I must admit there's a good deal in this that fits you two, but I've known you long enough now, and I can't believe the rest of it.'

By way of answer, Barlo put his flute to his lips, and played a short sequence of notes that instantly put a picture of wolves trotting through the forest into Listener's mind. As the same idea had already occurred to him, too, he said to Kurlosh, 'Will you let me ask you a couple of questions?'

'You've a curious way of making yourselves understood, you two,' said Kurlosh. 'But ask away, and if I know the answers to your questions you shall have them.'

'Did the man who told you all this wear a wolfskin coat?' asked Listener.

'Why yes,' said Kurlosh, 'but there's nothing unusual about that at this season of the year.'

'Were his eyes a yellowish colour?' Listener went on.

Kurlosh glanced up in surprise. 'Yes, that they were, too,' he said. 'In fact we wondered how a man can come to have such eyes.'

'Then I've a third question to ask,' said Listener. 'Did he spend the night with you?'

'No,' said Kurlosh. 'He wanted to be on his way again, although I did offer him a bed as evening came on. It struck me he was in a great hurry all of a sudden, and I wondered where he was bound that night, for the sun was already low on the horizon when he left.'

Listener looked at Barlo, and when Barlo nodded, he said, 'Then I know who your guest was, and you should be glad he didn't stay overnight.'

'That's as may be,' said Kurlosh. 'But now I'd like to know if it was you two he meant, and if all he told me was right.'

'Yes, he meant us,' said Listener. 'And what he told you about my master was not all invention either. Only I think you'll see it differently once you've heard the whole story.'

'Well, I listened to the yellow-eyed man, so now I'll listen to you,' said Kurlosh. 'I know well enough there are two sides to everything. Whether yours is the better side or not we'll see.'

Briefly, then, Listener told the tale of Gisa and her shaggy retainers, and he also, without sparing himself, told how it was he who had passed judgement on Barlo, and how it came about that he was now riding through the land with Barlo as his servant.

Kurlosh thought for a while when he had heard the story, and then said, 'You frankly admit your part in Barlo's misfortune, which makes your tale the more credible. And if what you have told me about that yellow-eyed man's origins is true, such frankness is beyond him. He thought it more likely you'd accuse Barlo, as he did, for he and his wolfish kind can't imagine a man repenting of his deed. There's one more thing I'd like to know: you mentioned a stone that Barlo took. Do you still carry that stone with you?'

'I do,' said Listener.

'Will you show me?' asked Kurlosh.

'Willingly,' said Listener, bringing out his little bag and taking the stone out of it.

Kurlosh looked at the shimmering eye-stone in Listener's hand, and nodded, as if some guess of his had been confirmed. 'I thought so,' he said. 'Arni's stone.'

'What do you know about Arni?' asked Listener, surprised. 'Did you ever meet him?'

'Yes,' said Kurlosh. 'Many years ago. But there's no time for that tale now. We've a wedding to be celebrated first! This evening, however, I'll tell you where and when I saw the stone for the first time.'

'Do you believe me now?' asked Listener.

'I do,' said Kurlosh, 'and I welcome you both to my house as guests.'

Just then everyone rose, for the bride came into the room. The first thing Listener noticed was the look of her merry brown eyes, in a delicate and clear-skinned face. Aglaia must have looked like that, he thought. This girl, too, seemed like a stranger among the broadly built, big-boned fishing folk. She wore a long robe shaped like a shift, embroidered all over with intricate coloured patterns, and a bridal crown of silver ornamented with mother-of-pearl shone in her hair. Kurlosh took the girl's hand and turned to the door, which had been closed behind Valya again. Immediately, there was a knocking outside, and Kurlosh called, 'Who asks for entrance?'

'A fisherman,' said a man's voice outside.

'What is your name?' asked Kurlosh.

'Daglosh,' said the voice.

'What do you want?' Kurlosh asked.

'I want your daughter Valya for my wife,' replied the man outside the door.

'Come in then, so that I can see you,' said Kurlosh.

Then the door was opened, and a young man came in, wearing a wide, blue, embroidered shirt over the coarse trousers of a fisherman. An elderly couple followed him; Listener supposed they must be Daglosh's parents.

Kurlosh scrutinized the young man as if he had never seen him before, and then said, 'You seem to me like a man who can look after a wife. Here is my daughter Valya standing beside me. Look at her well, if you want her for your wife.'

Daglosh smiled, and said, 'I have looked at her before.'

Then Kurlosh summoned his wife, who had kept in the background up to this point, took her hand too, and said to Daglosh, 'Now look at Valya's mother Gurla, for this is what Valya will be like when she grows older. Do you see her grey hair, her wrinkled cheeks and sunken lips? Do you still want her?'

'I do,' said Daglosh, 'for it will be good to live with a wife who has such merry brown eyes.'

'Then make sure they are not saddened,' said Kurlosh, 'for now I give you Valya.'

'Wait,' said Daglosh's mother. 'We haven't got to that point yet! For now, Valya, I ask you if you will have this young man. Do you know he is light-minded, quick-tempered, and a terrible braggart? Do you really want this windbag for a husband?'

'I do,' said Valya. 'I want him just as he is.'

'And will you still want him when he grows to be as old as his father?' asked Daglosh's mother. 'Look well at my husband here, with his wrinkled neck and knotted hands. See how his trousers hang about his skinny loins! Will you still love your husband then?'

By way of answer, Valya let go of Kurlosh's hand, went to Daglosh's father and kissed him on the mouth. Then she looked at Daglosh's mother with her merry eyes and said, 'You need say no more ill of your menfolk! Will you give me your son now?'

Then Daglosh's mother smiled, and said, 'Well, you will bring the boy to see sense! I entrust him to you.'

Listener got the impression that these rather curious remarks had been exchanged according to some well-established tradition, and that its demands had now been met, for as soon as Daglosh's mother had spoken these last words it was as if a spell had been broken. Everyone laughed aloud, and all present began talking at once, until Gurla asked the guests to sit down at the table and begin the wedding feast.

There is no need to describe the whole array of dishes here; it is enough to say that fish was not the only food served. Gurla had plainly wished to show her daughter's mother and father-in-law that they were familiar with boiling and roasting and all the arts of cookery in this house.

When the guests had all eaten their fill, the girls began to sing. They sang the same songs Listener had already heard in Valosh's village, but now he saw that you could dance to those songs as well. Tables and benches were pushed aside to give the young people room, and then the boys and girls stamped and jumped in a circle, so that the room echoed to their tread, and dust floated in the sunbeams that shone in through the window.

At the end of one of these wild fishermen's dances, the dancers all collapsed on the settles by the walls, exhausted. Then Barlo took out his flute and played all the songs he had heard among Valosh's people, and many that were unknown in these parts too. The company marvelled at the way he could manage to convey the content of those songs when nobody was singing the words. 'Why, you speak more clearly without your tongue than many a man who still has his, but can't get it to utter anything sensible,' said Kurlosh. 'You should have played that flute of yours when I took you for a runaway thief, and I'd have asked you to be my guest directly.'

So the afternoon passed, and when another and no less lavish meal was served for supper, and nobody felt much like rising from his seat any more, Kurlosh said to Barlo and Listener, 'And now the time has come for you to learn how it was that I first set eyes on Arni's stone.'

And with that he began to tell:

The Tale of Arni and the Lake Dwellers

I hadn't long been married when these things happened. One spring morning we had gone out on the lake to fish before the break of day. It was good fishing weather, and no one who could pull an oar or help with the nets had stayed at home. We fished all day long, and when we rowed back as evening came on we sang the Green Man a song or so, for we had had a good catch.

Darkness was falling as we approached the landing stage. But the closer we rowed, the stranger everything seemed: there was nobody waiting on the bank, no children, no women. And then one of us spotted horses from the steppes behind a house. 'Raiding Riders!' he shouted. And at that very moment they came striding down to the bank: ten, twenty, thirty men and more. There they stood at last in a long row by the waterside, legs spread, clad in worn leather jerkins, and laughing so hard that their braids of hair danced. 'Have a good catch, did you?' one of them who knew our language shouted. 'Here, come in to the shore, do! We're hungry! We've got your wives, and all sorts of other things besides. All we need now is a little fresh fish!' And then they laughed again, slapping their thighs with satisfaction.

By now we had heaved to. We didn't know what to do next. Many of the men wanted to go straight on land and join their families, but they had to admit that we couldn't deal with this horde of Raiding Riders if we must wade from our boats to the bank, unarmed as we were. Finally we decided that the first thing to do was row away from the bank again and think calmly of the next step to take. For as long as we were out on the water, the Raiding Riders could do nothing to harm us.

That was a long night, I can tell you. First of all we rowed to the next village, moored there and knocked the villagers up from their beds. But we couldn't stay there either, for the Raiding Riders might arrive next morning. So all the people of that village got into their own boats too, taking with them everything that wasn't nailed down. They took the women and children and all their portable property over to Aglaia's Island; the Raiding Riders wouldn't find them in that great thicket of reeds. For you must know that nimbly as they ride around the steppes, and anywhere else on firm ground, they are very reluctant indeed to venture on the water. Then we rowed out into the middle of the lake again, and waited within sight of our village to see what would happen next.

As long as it was dark, all was quiet. At least, I remember thinking, they haven't set fire to our houses yet. But that was small comfort when I thought of what might have happened to my wife and all the other people still in the village. Then it grew slowly lighter, and in the morning twilight we saw a single man come down to the landing stage, untie a boat and row out to us. We soon saw that he was a Rider, for you couldn't miss the braids hanging to right and left of his temples.

'I'll kill the man when he gets here,' someone said. But Rulosh, who was village elder at that time, said, 'You will not, for that would do us no good. If this man is coming out to us alone, he must want something, and he knows he is putting himself in our hands. So let's hear what he has in mind first, and at any rate he will provide us with a hostage, which could come in useful.'

That made sense to everyone, so we watched calmly as the man laboriously rowed out to us. You could tell he wasn't used to handling oars, and many of us laughed to see what heavy weather he was making of it, frequently going off course. When he reached us, he let his oars trail in the water and raised his hands palms upwards, to show us he had no weapon and came with friendly intentions. 'My name is Arni,' he said. 'With which of you can I treat?'

'With me,' said Rulosh, bringing his boat up beside the Rider's with a few strokes of his oars. 'What have you got to say to us?'

'I give myself into your hands of my own free will,' said Arni. That was clear enough to us by now, but we were still surprised to hear him say such a thing, for it was not at all like the Raiding Riders.

'If you are planning some trick or other,' said Rulosh, 'you're out of luck. You must know that the lake's pretty deep here, and our heavy oars are good for other things besides rowing.'

'There's no need to threaten me,' said Arni, 'though I can understand that you don't trust me. But think: what could I do against so many of you?'

'It's as well you understand that,' said Rulosh. 'Well, what do you want?'

'It may seem strange to you,' said Arni, 'but I want to show you a way to get back your wives and children, along with your property too.'

This fairly took Rulosh's breath away. He looked Arni up and down, and then said, 'That is certainly a very odd proposition, coming from a Raiding Rider. Are you only a prisoner yourself, and not one of the horde, or what makes you suggest such a thing?'

'I can't explain it to you in a hurry,' said Arni, 'but I do belong to the horde. I am the Khan's twin brother.'

'Then at least you're a good catch for us,' said Rulosh. 'I'll take you hostage, and your brother will have to give us back our people and our goods to redeem you.'

Arni did not take this at all ill, but nodded impatiently, as if Rulosh were a little slow in the uptake. 'Exactly what I had in mind,' he said. 'But it won't be quite as easy as that, for the Raiding Riders have their own laws in such matters, and so far as the redemption of hostages is concerned it's men for men, but never men for goods. However, I want you to get all your property back as well.'

Rulosh had less and less idea what to make of this remarkable man. 'Well, I may not understand why you're doing this,' he said, shaking his head, 'but you'd better tell me how we're to set about it.'

'Yes, that's what I'm here for,' said Arni, as if it were the most natural thing in the world. 'You must challenge my brother Hunli to a game.'

'A game?' asked Rulosh in surprise. 'What sort of a game?'

'Chess, for example,' said Arni. 'We consider chess the right thing in such circumstances. You must know that it's thought shameful among the Riders to refuse a challenge to a game, however high the stakes may be. Only your opponent must be in a comparable position, and so you will be if you have me as a hostage. That's the real reason I came out to you: so that my brother would agree to play a game.'

'And what stakes do you suggest?' asked Rulosh.

'Everything the horde has taken from you,' said Arni. 'It will be a great honour for the Khan to play for such high stakes.'

'And what do *we* stake?' asked Rulosh.

'Yourselves, as you sit here in your boats,' said Arni, as if this were hardly worth mentioning.

'That's all very well,' said Rulosh, 'but I can't play chess, and nor can any of the rest of us. So what use is your generous offer if we're sure to lose the game and fall into your brother's hands? It seems to me your whole idea is just a cunning attempt to make us prisoners of the Riders without putting up any resistance.'

'I see it's hard to convince you of my good intentions,' said Arni, 'but the fact is, you're not familiar with our customs. A man who proposes a game doesn't have to play it himself; he can name a deputy instead to take his place. And I will be your deputy.'

'Ah, so there is a trick behind it after all!' said Rulosh. 'For one thing, I won't have you in my power as a hostage if you're facing your brother over a chessboard, and for another, you can easily let him win.'

For the first time, Arni showed some indignation. 'Haven't you any regard at all for the rules of a game?' he asked. 'How on earth do you manage to maintain order in your village? Once a game has been agreed upon, all enmity between the opposing parties must be left aside, and outside the game, neither must do anything to harm his opponent. What's more, it is thought one of the most shameful of misdemeanours not to exercise your skill to its utmost in the game. You may think Raiding Riders untrustworthy, but you can be sure that they keep their own rules.'

'Who's to tell me you're not lying?' asked Rulosh.

'Nobody,' said Arni. 'You'll just have to believe me.'

'I can see that,' said Rulosh, 'and you might tell me, too, why I should believe a Raiding Rider whose horde has just attacked my village.'

'You're a suspicious man indeed,' said Arni, 'but you've a right to be suspicious if you speak for your people. I will give you a pledge from which I wouldn't part in any other circumstances.' He reached for a leather bag hanging from his belt, and took out a stone. When he held it in his fingers there was a ring of colours shining in the middle of the stone, like the iris of an eye. 'I will give you this now, as a pledge that I will play for you honourably.'

Rulosh took the stone and looked at it. Later, he told us that those few moments swept all thought of distrust from his mind. He looked into the stone as you might look into an eye, and then, suddenly, he thought he was looking at the face of an old woman whose eyes were like the stone, and this woman brought him to trust Arni without ever speaking a word. At the time, anyway, he looked up again after a while and said to Arni, 'Well, now I know you mean honourably by us. I put the life of my village in your hands.' He tied the stone up in his neckerchief and put it in his pocket.

After that, Rulosh took counsel with Arni as if he were one of ourselves. On Arni's advice, Rulosh rowed towards the village with two of his men and Arni himself, who had got into his boat. He rowed until he was just out of bowshot range, and then hove to, stood up in the boat and called for Hunli. After a while, the Khan came out of the houses and asked Rulosh what he wanted.

'Khan Hunli,' called Rulosh, 'did you know I've taken your brother Arni hostage?'

'You must show me your hostage if you're going to make such claims,' said Hunli.

So Arni stood up in the boat and showed himself to his brother.

'What possessed you to put yourself into the hands of these fish-eaters, Arni?' shouted Hunli, furious.

'You know my mind,' called Arni, 'but now you'd better talk to Rulosh here if you don't want to bring shame upon yourself for leaving your brother in the power of the fish-eaters, as you call them.'

'I can see you've got me into a difficult position, Arni,' Hunli called back. 'Very well, Rulosh, tell me how I can redeem my brother.'

'I could offer him in exchange for our wives and children,' called Rulosh.

'Don't you want to do that?' called Hunli. 'I'd let you have them.'

'I believe you,' called Rulosh. 'But does your brother mean so little to you that you'd exchange him for a few women and children of us fish-eating folk? It seems to me your brother's worth a higher price.'

'Impudence!' bellowed Hunli. 'Out with it, Rulosh, tell me what you want!'

'I challenge you to a game,' called Rulosh.

'What sort of a game?' asked Hunli.

'Chess,' Rulosh called back.

At that Hunli roared with laughter. 'Fisherman, you amuse me!' he called. 'Do you think you'll beat me at chess, then?'

'We'll see,' said Rulosh.

'And what are the stakes to be?' asked Hunli. You could tell he was pleased with this turn of events.

'My men in the boats out there against all you've taken from us,' called Rulosh.

'I like your game,' called Hunli. 'I accept your challenge.'

'You can call your men now and go ashore with them,' Arni told Rulosh. 'You will be safe from all hostility until the game is over.'

While the fishermen tied up by the landing stage, the Khan had a place made ready for the game. A valuable carpet was laid on the shore, and one of Hunli's retinue placed a chessboard in the middle of the carpet. It had beautiful carved chessmen of ivory and dark green jade. Riders marked off a square on either side of the board with their lances, surrounding it with a leather strap. Then they told the fishermen and Arni to step inside one of these enclosures, and Hunli had the village women and children driven into the other. The Riders occupied the two free sides of the carpet. When the arrangements had reached this point, Hunli stepped forward and invited Rulosh to take his place at the chessboard.

'I name a deputy to play for me,' said Rulosh.

'That is your right,' replied Hunli. 'Who is to represent you?'

'I imagine you would prefer a chess-player more skilful than myself,' said Rulosh. 'My deputy is Arni.'

'Ah, now I understand your boldness in challenging me!' said Hunli bitterly. 'A ruse of your devising, eh, Arni?'

Arni stepped out of the fishermen's enclosure, saying peaceably, 'Is there anything against the rules in Rulosh's proposal?'

Hunli looked angrily at him and said, 'You know very well that this isn't against the rules, Arni. But do you think it right to play against me here?'

'Isn't it usual for Riders to play against one another?' asked Arni. 'Haven't we two played chess often enough? Or is it that you're afraid of losing the game, and that's why you are making such excuses?'

Hunli swept the flat of his hand through the air as if to sweep all Arni's questions aside. 'There's no arguing with you, Arni,' he said. 'Come here, will you, and let's begin.'

So then Arni stepped on to the carpet and sat down at the chessboard on the side turned towards the fishermen, while Hunli sat down on the other side. 'Let's draw lots to decide who has the first move,' said Arni. And Hunli beckoned one of his Riders over and told him to make the decision according to the rules. The Rider took one white and one green chessman off the board, hid them both behind his back, and then held out his two closed fists. 'The choice is yours, Hunli,' said Arni, 'since I'm playing for the challenger.'

'No need to remind me of that,' snapped Hunli, tapping the man's right hand. He opened his fist, and there lay the white chessman.

'You move first,' said Arni casually, picking the chessboard up from the carpet and turning it round, for the white pieces had been on his side.

'Is it a bad thing for Arni if his brother moves first?' one of us asked.

'I don't know,' said Rulosh. 'I watched another game once that was played with pieces on a board, and it was a bad thing not to have the first move then.' Although we couldn't understand the game, we all watched in suspense as the two brothers began moving their chessmen about the board. They played in silence for a while, pushing the pieces from square to square, and nothing very remarkable happened. We held our breath when Hunli took one of Arni's little chessmen, but then Arni took one of Hunli's men with his next move, so they were all square again. When the same thing happened again we didn't get so agitated. But then Hunli took one of Arni's beautiful green jade castles off the board, and put one of his white knights in its place. We thought this was not very good, for Hunli uttered a curt laugh and said, 'How do you like that, Arni?' All Arni said, however, was, 'Ah, you've often fallen for that move of mine, Hunli,' and he moved another piece right across the chessboard. 'Now see how you can get out of that, Hunli,' he said.

Hunli frowned, and looked at the board for a long time. Then he raised his head. 'Why are you playing for these fish-eaters, Arni?' he asked. 'And don't tell me again that we've always played against one another, because that's not your reason.'

'Oh, but it is,' said Arni. 'It is my reason. We've always played against one another, and not only at chess.'

'Yes, this is not the first time you have crossed me,' said Hunli. 'Do you owe debts of hospitality to anyone here, as you did to the Mud-biters?'

'Perhaps I may yet,' said Arni, and he turned to Rulosh and asked, 'Will you offer me the hospitality of your house this evening?'

Rulosh looked at him in surprise, and said, 'Supposing I still have a house, you shall be the first guest I welcome into it, Arni.'

Arni nodded to him and said, 'Thank you, Rulosh.' Then he turned back to his brother. 'Your move, Hunli,' he said.

Hunli moved a piece wearing a crown aside, and with his next move Arni took a chessman of Hunli's that wore a circlet. 'You may have taken my queen,' said Hunli angrily, 'but you haven't won yet, not by a long way. There's no relying on women, in any case.'

'I disagree with you there too, Hunli,' said Arni. 'But show me now how you'll manage without your queen.'

'Manage I will!' said Hunli, and with that the real battle began. Anger made a vein on his forehead swell, and he played like a man striking out around him in blind fury. Move by move, the jade-green pieces fell victim to his onslaughts, but Arni gave as good as he got in the combat, for the white pieces disappeared from the board one by one as well. Finally there were only six or seven chessmen left in the game, and Hunli, whose turn it was, moved his remaining castle aside and said, 'Check! Now let's see if you can save your king, Arni!'

I was dismayed by these words, picturing us all as slaves of the Khan already, but Arni smiled and said, 'Rash of you, Hunli! Have you forgotten my queen? She can protect her king. I'd take that move back if I were you.'

'There's always a woman looking after you, Arni,' said Hunli bitterly. 'And not just on the chessboard. Aren't you ashamed to let a woman protect you?'

'No,' said Arni. 'Were you ashamed when Urla judged you worthy to be Khan?'

'I was worthy to be Khan without her saying so,' said Hunli. 'But I understood Urla's cunning only when that stone of yours brought you to set yourself against me again and again. And not just against me, but against the horde too. That was her long-delayed revenge for her husband's death. Did you never see that?'

'All I see is that you will never understand Urla's mind,' said Arni. 'The stone in no way loosened my links with the horde, or would I ride with you? But since I have carried it, I have taken to asking myself if one cannot live except by raiding and killing. And I have made friends with people of whom you think no more than you do of a hare you shoot down in the steppes with an arrow, to roast it over your fire.'

'You even talk like an old woman,' said Hunli, 'and that cunning enchantress has made you one.'

'Have you forgotten that she saved our father's life when he was a boy, even though the horde had just killed her own husband?' said Arni.

Then Hunli roared, 'I wish she had let him freeze! Someone else would have become Khan then. It wouldn't have changed the lives of the Raiding Riders. But what she did so softened our father's heart that he used to go to her for counsel – and now she has chosen you to destroy us!'

'You speak in anger,' said Arni, 'for you know I mean to do no such thing. I love the horde as much as you do.'

'Then tell me how we're to live if you keep us from going raiding!' said Hunli.

'I don't yet know,' said Arni, 'for the secret of my stone can't be fathomed in so short a time. Even a whole lifetime may not be long enough. But I shall never cease searching for that secret. Now, do you want to take back that move of yours?'

'No!' cried Hunli. 'Am I too to enslave myself to Urla's accursed meekness?' And in a rage he swept the remaining chessmen off the board, and shouted a command at his men. They all ran to their horses, mounted, and in a moment the horde had ridden out of the village.

Later, Arni told us who this Urla was, and how he had chosen her stone, but at the time we didn't understand much of what the brothers were saying. We still stood there in our enclosure, and the women and children opposite us in theirs, staring at Arni as he sat there on the carpet, picking up the chessmen from the ground. He seemed to be distressed at this outcome, although he had obviously won the game. Then he got to his feet and said, 'Go home to your houses. The horde has ridden on, and they never descend upon the same place twice in one year.' Then, at last, we broke out of our enclosure and hurried to our families. All except for Rulosh, who went to Arni, took his neckerchief out of his pocket, untied it, and gave Arni back his stone. 'You kept your word, Arni,' he said, 'and now I ask you to come to my house and be my guest.'

Arni stayed with him for three days, and then he rode after the horde.

* * *

'And so now you know, Listener, how I come to be acquainted with your stone,' said Kurlosh. 'However, I suppose you know more about it than I've been able to tell you.'

'I don't know all yet, far from all,' said Listener, 'and I have learnt a great deal about the stone from your story. When Arni gave it to me, he hadn't much time left to tell me about it.'

Soon after that the newly married couple took their leave, and everyone went to bed.

When Barlo and Listener were riding back beside the sleigh next morning, Lagosh, who held the reins today, beckoned Listener over to him. 'Why did Gisa set her yellow-eyed retainers on your track?' he asked. 'Is she so vengeful that she won't leave you in peace even outside her lands?'

'Very likely,' said Listener, 'but now she has other reasons as well to keep an eye on us, and make people think Barlo is not to be trusted.' And he told Lagosh what had been agreed upon in the Silver Harp at the time of the Draglope spring fair. 'And the friends we met there are travelling the country now too, looking for allies among the minstrels and jesters and storytellers, to go to Barlebogue with us.'

'This will be the strangest war I ever heard of,' said Lagosh. 'If I can be of any use to you, I'll happily ride to Draglope with you in the spring, for I can tell a great many stories, and one can always learn a few more on such a journey.'

'We can't have too many friends to help us against Gisa's shaggy retainers,' said Listener. 'And it will be good to have someone with Agla's merry eyes among us, for this is to be a merry war. At least, it seemed to us that we had little chance of success if we tried to attack that evil rabble with their own weapons.'

So it was that Lagosh rode to Draglope with Barlo and Listener in the spring, mounted on his stocky little horse. First they rode along narrow paths through desolate marshes, past stunted birch trees and pools of oily water, in which marsh gas gurgled when they trotted past on the soft, unsteady ground. Lagosh led the way, for he knew this country inside out.

'They call these swamps the Misty Marsh,' said Lagosh, 'but the air is usually clear here in spring.' Towards evening, he led them to a low rise in the ground in the middle of the marshes, where a mighty oak tree stood, and said they would spend the night here. Listener had been surprised to see Lagosh pick up a dry twig here and there while they were riding, and put it under the straps of his saddle-bags. But when he and the other two were searching the ground under the oak for dry wood to make a fire, he was glad of Lagosh's foresight; there was not much to be found here, apart from a few bits of rotten branch that had broken off and fallen under the weight of the snow in winter. Lagosh finally managed to kindle a flame and set fire to some dried stalks of last year's reeds, but it was a poor, smouldering sort of fire, for the wood that had fallen on the damp ground was more inclined to rot than dry out. However, at least the smoke drove away the midges that were beginning to swarm.

After they had fed their beasts and eaten some of their own provisions, they rolled up in their blankets under the branches of the oak, which were still bare, and soon fell asleep after their long ride.

Yet again it was Yalf who woke Listener in the middle of the night, nuzzling him with his soft nose. The donkey was snorting in agitation and twitching his long ears. Listener sat up. The fire had burnt low, and was now no more than a glimmer under the grey ashes. Listener poked it with a half-burnt branch, and got it to flare up again with a handful of dry grass. Then he strained his ears to hear the noises of the night.

For a while he heard nothing but the rushing of the wind in the branches of the oak. Then there was a rustle, farther away on the marshes, as if something were passing through the dry stems of the reeds. And Listener thought he heard the soft padding of paws. He woke his two companions, and as all three of them gazed out into the darkness they saw little yellowish, twinkling points of light, by two and by two, coming closer to their camping place from all sides. Now the two horses grew restless too, snorting and pawing the peaty ground. Lagosh snatched a burning branch from the fire and flung it towards the little sparkling lights. In the light of this torch, they saw two wolves leap aside from one another, howling.

The three riders realized that they were surrounded. First of all, each of them picked up a few of the remaining pieces of wood, set light to them, and flung them at the wolves. They managed to keep the pack off like this for a short time, but their small supply of wood was soon exhausted.

'We shall have to climb the oak,' said Lagosh.

'And what about our mounts?' asked Listener. 'Are the wolves to get my Yalf?'

'Better Yalf and the horses than us,' said Lagosh. 'When the wolves have eaten their fill, they'll go on as morning approaches.'

By now the circle had closed in again. Barlo looked around, and let out a long, hoarse cry, which made the wolves retreat again. Then he ran to his horse, and snatched the triton's horn from his saddle-bag. Putting it to his lips, he blew a deep and resonant note that echoed out into the night, making the dark sky shake. Yalf and the two horses stood quite still by the oak tree's gnarled trunk, and nor did the wolves move. Then a gurgling and a bubbling started up in the marshes all around, as if hundreds of springs were suddenly rising from below. Splashing, water poured around the clumps of reeds; the rushing streams flowed together, and the water began to rise up the slope of the hill on which the three men stood. And out of the night, everywhere around them, rang the sound of clear and girlish laughter, as if it came from very far away and yet was quite close, mingling with the splashing of the swirling water – laughter so infectious that the three men joined in, laughing at the pack of wolves as they raced away in frantic flight, howling, through the spraying water.

'Thank you for your help, Green Man!' Listener shouted into the night, and immediately a deep and rising note was heard, far away, similar to the note of Barlo's horn. Then they heard the silvery laughter once more, but in the distance now, and then silence fell over the marshes again. Listener gave Yalf a hug, by way of thanks for his timely warning, before he lay down again with the others to sleep.

When Listener woke next morning, the water had gone down again. The sun already stood high above the horizon, sparkling on the countless pools of water. The air was full of the whistling and quacking of the marshland birds. For a while, Listener gazed at this unfamiliar landscape, so full of secret life. Some wild ducks were dabbling in a sizeable pool a little way aside from the path, and he thought he saw a white bird swimming among them again. Had the water spirit sent them a guardian to watch over their journey? After last night's events, Listener did not find this notion at all eerie, but rather reassuring. Eventually he woke his two companions, and soon afterwards they were riding on along the narrow, quaking path.

By about noon they had crossed the marshes. They came to grassland, and towards evening their path joined a cart-track. They went on along this track, and rode through the countryside for three days, by which time the cart-track had become a good road, sometimes passing through a hamlet where they could shelter for the night. They met a cart or carriage now and then, or overtook a farmer going out to work in the fields with his team of oxen.

On the third day, they saw a remarkable figure ahead of them. At first it looked like a boy riding a mule, trotting along the road in the same direction as themselves. The little rider was hanging on his mount rather than actually sitting it, and seemed to be carrying a shapeless bundle on his back, which he would have done better to strap to the saddle behind him. When they came closer, Listener recognized the man riding the mule by his shock of fiery red hair. 'Trill!' he cried, and spurred on his donkey until he was level with the jester.

Trill reined in his mule, stared at Listener with assumed dismay, and said, 'So that bearded fellow was right after all!'

'What bearded fellow?' asked Listener, baffled. 'And what was he right about?'

'Why, he said there was a dumb minstrel of evil disposition some-where around these parts, riding about the country with an idle young vagrant. I'd never have thought one of those Wolfskins could be believed!' And then he roared with laughter at the foolish expression on Listener's face. 'Looking at you, no one would think it worth Gisa's while to set her shaggy retainers after you, pursuing you through the land. I chanced to meet one of them only yesterday, and he warned me about you. Didn't you know you're famous?'

'All very well for you to laugh,' said Listener, 'but our fame nearly cost us our lives three days ago.'

By now Barlo and Lagosh had joined them, and when they brought their horses to a halt, Trill wrinkled up his nose, sniffing, and said,

> *'To Draglope a dumb man would ride,*
> *with a fool of an ass by his side,*
> *and the last of the three*
> *is no better, I see,*
> *for he smells of dead fish at low tide!*

Is this the entire fighting force you've drummed up?'

'By no means, my witty friend,' said Lagosh. 'But the rest travel by water: a whole troop of merry water nymphs who laugh all day long, led by their lord, the mighty Green Man, the spirit of the lake. How-ever, I ought to warn you, Trill: it is said that he once fed a red-headed, hunchbacked dwarf to the crayfish, because the fellow held his nose at the smell of fish that always clings to a water-sprite. So watch your step!'

Trill laughed, and said, 'I can tell you two have found the right man for us, even if anyone can smell where he comes from a mile away!'

'He's not the only man we've found,' said Listener, and as they rode on he told of all the folk they hoped to meet in the Silver Harp. The journey took them four more days, and then they saw Draglope lying before them again. They had to make their way on their mounts through the crowd of people going to the fair, just as they had done the year before, but this time they rode straight to the Silver Harp. When they came in, they found the main room of the inn full to bursting point with the most remarkable of figures. There were clowns in motley there; jugglers and contortionists were practising their tricks; fiddlers, flute-players and harpists and all kinds of other musicians were trying out their instruments, and there was such a droning and scraping and strumming that you could hardly hear yourself speak. Tall Barlo stopped in the doorway and looked inquiringly around. Then he pointed to the corner where they had sat a year ago, and made his way through the throng. The other three followed him to the table where Rauli the singer and Gurlo the storyteller were sitting. Tubby the woodcutter and Lauro the prospector were with them. 'So there you are at last,' said Rauli. 'We're just making a plan. Sit you down and wash the dust of the road from your throats!' He poured red wine into the goblets standing ready for them, and Listener introduced Lagosh.

'A fisherman, as I can smell,' said Rauli. 'That's convenient, for most of us will be going along the river to Barlebogue, and we can use a man who knows how to handle boats.' He had obviously been on the point of discussing the taking of Barlebogue, and would not let the others speak now. 'Look here,' he said, putting the wine jug in the middle of the table, 'this is the castle of Barlebogue.' He dipped his forefinger in the wine, and drew a wet line from the jug to his goblet on the cracked table top. 'Here's the course of the Barlebogue river, running into the other river here in Draglope, where my goblet stands.' Finally, he moved the bread basket, supposed to represent the mountain range, to a position behind the jug. 'Lauro will lead the first group through the woods to the left of the river and into the mountains. They will go around the valley of Barlebogue, trying to bring a little cheer to the slave labourers who must dig gold and precious stones for Gisa in those hills.'

'I wouldn't mind going along,' said Tubby, 'for I know my way around in a wood.'

'Why, if you'll go with that group, I've nothing to worry about!' said Rauli. 'Jokes like yours will put even Gisa's shaggy retainers out of countenance. And then you will all come down from the mountains to Barlebogue. We and the rest of the players' troupe will go by the direct route, taking our time. There are plenty of villages and farmsteads along the river where we can ply our merry trade, and we'll all meet again at the castle.'

As Listener heard Rauli's plans for this remarkable campaign, he wondered how Gisa would oppose such a motley army. Rauli seemed to have little fear of her wolfish servants. Was he overestimating the power of the singers and jesters? Was he an old man in his second childhood, with nothing in the world but his songs to love, and no notion of the dangers into which he was venturing? What could these merry, light-hearted players do against Gisa's shaggy retainers, deadly serious as they were? Listener realized that he had got himself into a game whose rules he did not understand. He looked into the old singer's thin face as Rauli played with the drinking vessels, unperturbed, as if the whole matter would be decided on the worn surface of this table. Everyone here seemed to think so. Including Barlo. The dumb man sat at the table, scarcely stirring, making no move to indicate his part in this game, and yet he seemed to be at the centre of it, the man for whose sake it was all being arranged. And it was no runaway groom who sat there, no poor shepherd, nor a wandering minstrel who must be grateful to the farmer who let him sleep in his straw by night. He sat there like a king, like a lord weighing up his counsellors' proposals. Now he was nodding to Rauli, as much as to say: yes, that is how we will do it. And Listener wondered: who is this man Barlo? This was the third year he had been riding through the land with Barlo, and still he didn't know.

They set off next morning. Crowded as the town was, people stopped in the streets to stare at the procession of adventurers, for no one had ever seen the like of it. Barlo rode at its head, playing a tune that brought all who were still at their breakfast out of doors. The other musicians took up the melody, and soon many were singing the words, for by now Barlo was such a master of his own language that everyone could understand the sense of the tunes he played. The song ran like this:

> *Good fools, awake!*
> *Your pleasure take*
> *in jests and laughter.*
> *Come following after,*
> *and join our merry band,*
> *for Barlo is riding through the land.*

> *Play the fiddle and fife,*
> *dance for your life!*
> *Charm every mouse*
> *from hole or house.*
> *Squeak, mouse, and see*
> *the big, bad wolves turn tail and flee!*

And in among the singers and minstrels, acrobats turned somersaults and walked on their hands, and jugglers played with balls and hoops.

The clowns made forays into the ranks of the interested citizens standing at the roadside, and joked with them. And wherever the laughter was loudest, there you saw the untidy head of Tubby the woodcutter rising above the crowd.

Listener trotted along beside Barlo at the head of the procession, on his donkey, trying to imagine himself in the part of a paladin riding into battle at the side of his lord the duke. This notion, however, was hard to sustain in the face of the very unheroic demeanour of the strolling players, who were obviously bent on making this departure into a curious kind of popular entertainment. No one in the town seemed to realize the serious nature of the undertaking – neither the participants, who were making themselves appear fools in every possible way, nor the spectators, who probably took the whole thing for a masquerade, such as mummers often performed in the streets at the beginning of spring.

More and more people kept coming out of the houses to the right and left of the street, many of them grotesquely disguised and wearing masks over their faces. Witches, capering wildly, danced at the head of the procession, waving noisy wooden rattles and alarming the spectators, who scattered, squealing, when their warty faces loomed up close. Other mummers wore spangled costumes with bits of shiny mirror-glass sewn all over them. They gazed at the crowd through the empty eye-holes of their masks, and drove the witches before them with staves bearing little bells. Jesters mingled with the procession, shaking the bells on their pointed caps to make them ring, and carrying long slapsticks with which they struck anyone who still looked grave, or who wouldn't join in Barlo's song. Its tune rose above the rattling, ringing, shouting and whistling, playing ever wilder, ever louder.

The crush ahead of Listener became so great that he had to bring his donkey to a halt. One of the witches dived under Yalf's neck, straightened up again very close to Listener, and grinned in his face. The witch's lips curled back, baring sharp fangs, and a pair of yellowish eyes flickered behind the holes cut in the mask. 'Why aren't you laughing, Listener?' hissed the witch. 'Do you dread this ride? Then you're wiser than all these fools!'

Listener flinched away from the grotesque horror of the mask, and before he could pull himself together, one of the white-faced figures in mirror costumes came leaping up and beat the witch about the head with his staff, ringing its bells. Immediately, a way opened up for

Listener to ride on through the crowd of mummers. Barlo had never stopped playing all through this brief delay. He was looking out into the distance, over the heads of the masked figures, and his thoughts seemed very far away.

When they had left the last houses of Draglope behind them, most of the mummers stayed behind too. However, a few of them accompanied the procession on its way, obviously wishing to be there when an end was put to the present state of affairs in Barlebogue.

Without hesitation, Barlo took a turning that led to a track running along the banks of the Barlebogue river. The farther they went, the more thickly did the grass grow over the old ruts made by cartwheels in the muddy ground. It looked as if few vehicles passed this way. Here and there they met a farmer, who stood by the side of the track shaking his head as he gazed, astonished, at the strange procession. They made slow progress, for very few of the travellers were mounted. Towards evening of the third day, they reached a village where they meant to stay the night, for only an hour's journey beyond the last houses the gloomy forests of Barlebogue began, reaching right down to both banks of the river.

Even in the hamlets where they had stopped to rest this last day or so, Listener had thought the local people seemed increasingly monosyllabic and unforthcoming, and there was no mistaking it here in this village on the borders of the forest. When Barlo and Listener rode into the village street at the head of the procession, a few women and children ran into their cottages and slammed the doors behind them. Listener was struck by the desolate look of the place: plaster was crumbling from the dirty grey walls of the houses, patches of straw had slipped off the thatch on the crooked roofs, and the sky looked in through their bare rafters. Many of the cottages seemed to have stood unoccupied for a long time; broken shutters hung askew at their empty windows.

When they reached the green in the middle of the village, Barlo gave the signal to halt, and dismounted. Gradually, all the rest of the company came up. Those who had mounts unsaddled their beasts, led them to the village pond to drink, and then let them graze on the green. Those who were travelling on foot sat down on the grass, took off their shoes and stretched their weary legs. A fiddler tuned up his instrument and began to play Barlo's song, as if he could entice the people out of their houses with it here as well as in Draglope.

Soon many of the travellers had taken up the song, and before they reached the end of the second verse, the door of a tumbledown house opened and an old man came out. He stopped and listened attentively as they sang the song once more. Then he came slowly over to their camping place, looked at the strange company resting there, and asked, without addressing anyone in particular, 'Why does your song say Barlo is riding through the land? It's a long time since any Barlo rode to this village. Are you dreaming of the old days, or what does your song mean?'

Rauli rose to his feet, greeted the old man, and said, 'The song means Barlo is travelling with us to put things to rights in Barlebogue.'

'With you?' said the old man in surprise. 'I can't remember that Barlo ever rode about the country with a troupe of acrobats and street musicians.'

'I don't know what Barlo you mean,' said Rauli, 'but the man I'm talking about is a minstrel himself.'

'Ah, then I mean another one,' said the old man. He seemed to lose interest in the people sitting here on the village green, turned and made as if to go back to his house.

'Wait a minute,' said Rauli. 'Barlos come and Barlos go; you'd better have a look at ours. He's sitting over there playing the flute.'

'A Barlo who plays the flute!' said the old man, shrugging his shoulders. 'He'd find a wolf-spear come in more useful.' But he seemed curious to see the man, all the same, and walked past the people resting on the grass towards the sound of the flute tune that came from the other end of the green. The moment he caught sight of the flute-player, he stopped dead in surprise, and looked closely at him. Barlo went on playing his song to the end, then put the flute down, and nodded to the man, as if to an old acquaintance. The old man bowed, and said, 'Greetings, Barlo. We have waited a long time for you. We'd hoped, however, that you would come back someday with a host of warriors to drive Gisa and her shaggy retainers out. Under Gisa's rule, folk nowadays have other matters on their minds than listening to minstrels and laughing at the jests of fools. There's no joy in Barlebogue any more, didn't you know?'

Instead of answering, Barlo raised his flute to his lips again and played. Listener paid close attention, for he guessed that he would have to act as interpreter once more. 'Greetings, Dagelor,' Barlo piped. 'You should think less slightingly of my companions. Didn't you say yourself, just now, that all joy was gone from Barlebogue? Perhaps the folk there should be made to laugh again instead of waging violent war. That's why I have brought with me the best jesters, storytellers and minstrels to be found in the land. Will you welcome us to your village as guests?'

Listener was about to translate what Barlo said, but Dagelor waved him aside, saying, 'No need to help me. We heard your speech had been taken from you, Barlo, but now you speak so clearly that the heart as well as the mind can understand your words. I thank you for coming, and bid you all welcome to our cottages as guests.'

It struck Listener that Dagelor uttered all this with a certain solemnity, as if greeting some very eminent person. Barlo did not seem to be in the least unknown here, nor was he regarded as a man of small consequence. But before Listener could ask Dagelor a question, the old man turned to his house and shouted something, obviously a name, which Listener did not catch. Immediately afterwards a boy of about nine came out of the door, and Dagelor beckoned him over. The old man told him to fetch the villagers from their cottages, and tell them guests had come: guests who deserved a friendly welcome. The boy looked curiously at Barlo and his companions, but at an impatient gesture from the old man he hurried off, running from house to house and shouting out his news in a shrill voice. And now all the doors were opened, but only some women and small children and a few old men came out, looking at the strangers. Not until Dagelor stepped forward and called out a few words to them did they come hesitantly closer. Listener thought these people were like timid animals, ready to flee back to their dens at any moment. Dagelor had to encourage them to come closer several more times, with words and gestures, before they were finally gathered around him, a wretched little company of frightened people, pressing close to each other as if some mortal danger threatened them.

'Where are your younger men?' asked Listener.

'Gisa's retainers have taken them away,' said Dagelor. 'Anyone who could still do the work they think so needful. We don't even know where they have been taken, and we have hardly any hope of ever seeing them again. You are late in coming, Barlo.'

At these words, Barlo rose and began to play his flute again, but not his song of the fools, for that might well have rung like mockery in these people's ears. He told them, in his own language, that he was going to Barlebogue to break Gisa's power. 'Your sorry grief has come upon you like an illness, depriving you of all courage. We cannot fight such black magic with swords and spears, only with the merriment of players and storytellers.' And then he said no more, but began to paint pictures with the notes of his flute. Listener saw the broad valley of Barlebogue, among its boundless forests, he saw the castle rise in the middle of the valley, dark and gloomy in the shadow of Gisa's evil power, and the gloom spread over fields and meadows to the very limits of the valley like cold, slimy mud, it lapped out beyond them, and the people of the village moaned with horror as they saw it. But then the tune changed, happiness began to spread from the edges of the picture, the gloomy torrent boiled up, seething and swirling, and gradually dissolved into pale mist that the wind blew away across the valley, until its vapours were lost in the tree-tops on the far horizon. Then bright colours shone out, green willows, sea-green lakes; poppies flowered scarlet in furrows beside the fields, and the dark gloom peeled away from the castle walls, crumbled off and revealed pale stone, the gates opened wide and people came streaming out, laughing and dancing, flung their arms around one another and kissed. Listener was there with them, he heard their voices, he saw their merry faces, and another face too, a face looking at him, that face he knew and yet did not know, those eyes of a colour he could not describe which he had seen before, and was seeking, and for a moment he held a girl in his arms, a girl looking at him out of those eyes, very close and yet seeming infinitely far away. Then Barlo's flute broke off.

Listener tried to hold fast to the picture, but it faded, and he saw the villagers again. They were standing around Barlo in a circle, but now the expression of hopelessness that had dulled their gaze was gone from their faces. Many had tears in their eyes, and they embraced each other as if to keep the picture Barlo had shown them alive. 'Come, be our guests!' Dagelor repeated, and now, at last, the villagers ventured into the ranks of Barlo's army encamped on the green. They all took some of the travelling folk home to their cottages.

Dagelor welcomed Barlo and Listener into his own house. His son's wife, who lived there with her two children, offered their guests flat cakes of dry bran bread, and goat cheese, and there was a mug of goat's milk for everyone. 'You must make do with what we have,' said Dagelor. 'When old Barlo used to ride the land, he got better fare here, but now that Gisa's retainers have taken all the young men away the women have all the work to do, and we old folk can't do much to help.'

It was not the first time Listener had heard tell of this Barlo who used to ride the land; everyone but himself seemed to know all about the man. He had often wondered just what the name meant to the people he met. 'Who was old Barlo, and why was he always riding through the land?' he said aloud, and then was alarmed to find he had uttered a question which he meant only to ask himself.

Dagelor looked at him in surprise. 'Do you mean that seriously?' he asked, and when Listener nodded, Dagelor suddenly began to laugh; he slapped his thigh and laughed as loud and long as if to make up, all at once, for the many times he hadn't laughed since joy departed from the village. Finally he sobered down, and asked Listener, 'How long have you been with your master?'

'About three years,' said Listener, who had begun to wonder just what kind of hilarious joke he had cracked.

'And you still don't know who he is?' said Dagelor, starting to laugh again. 'Didn't you tell him anything about yourself, Barlo?' he added. 'Not even with your flute?'

Barlo shook his head, smiling, and then nodded when Dagelor asked him if he might satisfy Listener's curiosity.

'Then mark my words well, Listener,' said Dagelor, and he began to tell:

The Tale of Old Barlo and His Son Fredebar

I often saw him riding through the village when I was a young man. He sometimes stopped his horse outside our house, dismounted and gave me the reins to hold, while my father came out to welcome him. My father didn't bow low, or anything of that kind, for old Barlo couldn't stand that sort of thing. My father only shook his hand and then led him into the house, where they would both sit down on the settle at the table in the corner, drink a jug of wine, and talk of this and that: of whether it looked like being a good harvest that year, maybe, or of some legal dispute or other. My father was village elder, as I am now myself, and old Barlo knew his way about the law better than anyone, for he was the judge, and lord of Barlebogue castle.

Though you mustn't think he was such a tyrant as Gisa is today, considering everything her property, even the people. The folk of the valley were free then, and could do as they pleased so long as they lived at peace with their neighbours. Barlo would listen to anyone who thought he had suffered an injustice, and he very quickly saw who was trying to deceive him. Soon nobody had the nerve even to attempt such a thing. Justice was done in Barlebogue at that time – it wasn't like these days, when Gisa lets any chance-met fellow deliver judgement, or so they say.

Barlo was by no means an old man when people began telling stories about him, such as the tale of the farmer who came to him accusing a neighbour of stealing some of his land, by means of moving the boundaries of his fields a little farther forward every year when he was ploughing. Barlo invited both men to a meal and talked to them. 'How is your farm doing?' he asked the plaintiff. 'Oh, very well, except for the land this man here has stolen,' said the farmer. 'My cows give more milk than any other man's in the village. And now I own the pasture up by the outskirts of the forest, and since I had it I've more than doubled the number of my sheep.'

'And how long have you had this pasture?' asked Barlo.

'My son brought it into the family two years ago, when he married,' said the complainant. 'Not just the pasture, either, but a couple of yokes of arable land too, and thirty head of cattle that are now mine. Yes, I know how to increase my property – and I know how to look after it when anyone tries to take it from me, too.'

'I can see that,' said Barlo, and then he asked the defendant how he was doing.

'I'm content,' said he. 'The harvest was so good that I could give my daughter's husband some when his own fields were damaged by hail.'

'They say it was a merry winter on your farm,' said Barlo.

'Why, yes,' said the defendant, a little embarrassed. 'When the first snowflakes fell, a couple of minstrels drifted into my house along with them, and I gave them board and lodging through the cold season. By way of thanks, they made us a bit of music to while the long evenings away, and some of the neighbours came to listen too.'

'Did you give them hospitality?' asked Barlo.

'Well, you can't let folk sit around without a mug of cider and a bite to eat,' said the man. 'A little hospitality never beggared anyone yet.'

By now the three of them – Barlo, the plaintiff and the defendant – had finished their meal, and the plaintiff was getting impatient. 'Listen, I want you to give me my rights!' he said. 'You haven't questioned my neighbour about my accusation yet.'

'Ah, but I have,' said Barlo. 'And in my opinion you accuse him unjustly. But if you like we can go out to your fields, for I know the boundaries of both your properties.'

At that the plaintiff turned pale and said, 'I suppose I might have made a mistake, so I think I'll withdraw my charge, although you haven't even mentioned the subject of it yet.'

'There was no need,' said Barlo, 'for it was enough to listen to the pair of you. You both spoke of what gives you pleasure. You yourself take pleasure in getting and owning goods, and so you talked of nothing but what you possess. Your neighbour, however, takes pleasure in giving to others, and so that is what he talked about. And I watched you both as you ate: you served yourself first, with the biggest slice off the joint, while your neighbour waited to take what he was offered. It seems to me very unlikely that he has designs on your land, for that isn't his nature at all. However, perhaps we ought to mark out the boundaries of your fields all the same, for it could be that you yourself have done what you accuse him of doing.'

That was indeed the case, and the plaintiff not only had to give back the stolen land, but pay the other man a fine too. Bite off too much and you may choke on it, folk said when they heard of this affair, and so the plaintiff had to bear ridicule as well as his loss. This judgement of Barlo's was not an isolated case, and as such stories are good to tell, word soon went around the whole countryside of how Barlo used to settle such legal disputes. And so it was that not only the farmers from the valley of Barlebogue went to him for justice, but other folk came from the plains, or the hills beyond the forest, to ask his advice as well.

It was at this time that Barlo began riding the land. He had always believed that you cannot be a good judge of anyone or anything you haven't seen for yourself, and besides, he was a curious man who always wanted to know the precise nature of everything. So he rode all around the countryside, and would sit for hours in a smithy to watch as the red-hot iron was shaped into a scythe under the hammer. He would talk to traders and to shepherds, and would listen to the ballads sung by minstrels in the market place. He was a very good listener, in fact, not like those know-alls who are shaking their heads or looking around them, bored, before you've really begun to tell them anything. When folk said in those days, 'Barlo is riding the land,' it was like saying, 'Fine weather today,' or 'The corn's looking good,' and a man with anything on his conscience did well to put it right before Barlo found him out.

Even folk who didn't know Barlo regarded him with respect from the moment they met, although he was always simply dressed. He was tall and strong, but when he sat in some village inn talking to the farmers, you might have taken him for one of themselves, drinking his beer with his neighbours of an evening.

His son Fredebar, however, was different. The boy had always had a liking for showy, expensive clothing, and richly ornamented harness for his horse. Very probably he got this taste from his mother, who came of a rich family in Draglope. Barlo had brought her home to the valley. Life in the castle then was much the same as life on any large farmstead, and may well have seemed to her frugal. At all events, she began providing the rooms with valuable furniture and carpets, and holding festivals to which she invited her friends from home. So the grand ladies and gentlemen came riding through the valley in their magnificent clothes, and the children ran after them, thinking this fine show was some peculiar kind of buffoonery, as it well may have been too. But Barlo let his wife have her way, for he loved her dearly, and could deny her nothing, particularly when she had borne him his son.

Fredebar grew up in the midst of all this stir and bustle, and as a child he probably thought life consisted mainly of such festivities. When he had his first horse, and rode it through the villages, he looked to the people like a prince of royal blood in his silken doublet, with all his golden ornaments. He was a pretty boy, rather thin and fine-boned, and everyone liked him, for he was always fond of a joke and a good laugh.

Later, when he was fully grown, Barlo often took him out on his rides and let him listen when he dealt justice, for he meant to train him as his successor. Fredebar was quick to grasp all he saw and heard, and soon he could speak as cleverly as his father. But when I think back to that now, I see it was a kind of game to him, a game whose meaning mattered less than showing the audience that you knew the rules. I don't know if his father realized at the time; if he did, he may have thought it was enough to learn those rules for a start, and the boy would take it all as seriously as he should later. In any case, Barlo used to listen, smiling, when Fredebar gave his views on a case at his request, and now and then he would praise the elegance of his train of thought.

Now it happened that Barlo had a message from a friend of his called Kratos, who acted as judge up in the mountain range. Kratos said he had a difficult legal case on his hands which he would like to put to Barlo. So at dawn next day Barlo had his horse saddled, and he took Fredebar with him. They rode all day long, and in the evening they came to the mountain village where Kratos had his house. The judge came to his door to meet them, told a groom to see to their horses, and then led the visitors indoors. 'You are welcome guests,' he said. 'You'll be hungry after coming so far. We can talk later.'

He offered them seats, and then a girl came through the doorway, laid the table, and brought in bread, smoked gammon, and a pitcher of red wine. 'This is my daughter Raudis,' said Kratos. 'She's been running my household since my wife died.' He told Raudis to sit down with them, and so his guests were able to look at her at their leisure. And I think that Fredebar at least did so, thoroughly, for Raudis was worth looking at. She wore her long, dark blonde hair in a thick plait, and the first thing you noticed in her fine-boned face was a pair of large, dark brown eyes, with which she gazed at you thoughtfully when you spoke to her.

When the guests had eaten their fill, Kratos said to Barlo, 'I have asked the persons concerned in the case on which I want your advice to come to my house tomorrow. However, I'd like to tell you about the affair this evening, if you're not too tired.' Barlo told him to go ahead, adding, 'In any event, I'd have asked you to acquaint me with the facts of the matter. Since you wish to consult with me, it seems to be a difficult case, and one ought always to sleep on such decisions.'

Meanwhile, Raudis had cleared the table, leaving only the pitcher of wine and the goblets. Then she sat down with the others again.

'It's a case of murder,' Kratos began, 'and the first difficulty is the fact that there are no witnesses. The murdered man's name was Vargos, and he was a hill farmer with a considerable herd of cattle. His men found him dead in his pasture in the morning, and there is no doubt that he was stabbed with a knife.'

'Is anyone suspected of the murder?' asked Barlo.

'Yes, indeed,' said Kratos, 'and that is just what makes this case so hard for me. The suspect, whom I have had to take into custody, is my son Terlos. He was courting Vargos's daughter Varya, but he hadn't found much favour with her father, for I may fill the office of judge here, but to Vargos's way of thinking I was a poor man.'

'Is that the only reason why your son is suspected?' asked Barlo.

'No,' said Kratos. 'Vargos's foreman says he heard my son arrange a meeting with Vargos in the pasture the evening before the murder. Moreover, he says he can produce another witness to that. And then, he states, his master left the house at nightfall, and nobody saw him alive afterwards.'

'Have you questioned your son?' inquired Barlo.

'I have,' said Kratos, 'and he admits to arranging the meeting.

However, he doesn't want to say why until the trial. In any case, he assures me, Vargos was alive and well when they parted. But of course there are no witnesses to that either.'

'I can understand that you can't come to a decision on your own, in a case involving your son,' said Barlo. 'Still, I should like to know if you believe him, and whether you have any other suspicions.'

'Two questions at once,' said Kratos, 'and I'll try to answer them both. Yes, I do believe my son, for I've known him since his birth. It's possible to imagine him killing a man in anger, but he wouldn't stab him in the back, which is what happened to Vargos. You may think that it's a father's love makes me say that, and so I'll give you another and reasonable argument for believing him: I know he loved Varya, and would do anything to get her for his wife. And I know Varya favours his courtship. Whatever Vargos might have done to him, Terlos saw him as the father of the girl he loved, and he must have known that murdering the man would destroy his hopes of happiness, whether he was convicted of the crime or not. Tell me: how could he ever have looked Varya in the eye again?'

'That sounds sensible,' said Barlo, 'even if it's still the father in you speaking. And what about your suspicion?'

'The suspicion is one that I find hard to express, as a judge, since it concerns my son's affairs yet again. So I tell you only as a friend of my family. The fact is that Terlos has a rival for Varya's hand, that very foreman who heard the meeting being arranged. Thus, the man's evidence also brings him personal advantage, and I always find such witnesses suspect. Vargos thought a lot of his foreman; many people in the village think he trusted him too much, but that's just idle talk and a judge should take no notice of it. However, you'll understand that I have my doubts of him all the same.'

'I understand it very well, having a son myself,' said Barlo. 'So it will not be easy for me to keep my feelings out of it either, particularly as you're my friend. Will you let me ask my son Fredebar what he thinks of this matter?'

'I'd be glad to hear what he has to say about the case myself,' said Kratos. 'Folk say he is very sharp-witted, and can speak well.'

Barlo nodded to Fredebar, who thought for a while, and then said, 'It strikes me as necessary to separate the proven facts carefully from the suppositions and opinions in this suspected murder. For where suppositions and opinions are concerned, one is only too easily inclined to believe what one would like to believe. We may regard it as proven that Terlos did arrange to meet Vargos, and that this meeting actually did take place. Further, it is clear that Terlos had good reason to be angry with Vargos, since his love for Varya, and what her father thought of his courtship, seem to be generally known. Everything else Kratos has said about the case may be explained by his love for his son, and won't be worth much in court.'

Fredebar had spoken with the enthusiasm of a man presented with a problem, in solving which he is to show his own mettle, and at this point Barlo laid a hand on his arm, to let him know he was now going too far. However, Kratos shook his head, saying, 'Let him speak. After all, he's right, and he's only stating facts that I wouldn't admit to myself. What else were you going to say, Fredebar?'

'Much will depend upon what Terlos has to tell you about the reason for the meeting,' said Fredebar. 'But things don't look good for him unless he can prove what he says.'

Raudis had been listening to him attentively, and the longer he spoke, the angrier her dark eyes became. Now she couldn't control herself any longer. 'You talk about my brother as if this were some stranger's case and nothing to do with you, Fredebar,' she said.

'Raudis!' her father interrupted her. 'You're not to meddle with this.'

'If his son may speak, then I suppose your daughter may do so too,' said she. 'And I say again that I don't think it right for my brother to be discussed in this manner.'

'I can't agree,' said Fredebar. 'Please believe me when I say I have nothing against your brother. But how can you judge rightly if you let your feelings confuse you?'

'I don't let my feelings confuse me,' said Raudis, 'and it would be a poor thing for justice if a judge had to forget he has a heart. I know very well what my brother might be capable of doing. Yes, I do love my brother, but that just means I know him better than you do. And so I also know that he didn't stab Vargos.'

'That won't be much use if you can't prove it,' said Fredebar, but one could tell that he was impressed by Raudis's whole-hearted championing of her brother. Raudis flushed as his admiring gaze rested on her, and she said, 'If there's any proof to be found, I believe I can find it.'

Barlo had followed this conversation closely. He gave Raudis a nod, and then said, 'I have a suggestion to make, Kratos. Our children have just shown us how the trial should be conducted tomorrow. My son shall be the accuser, since he will let none but proven facts influence him, but your daughter shall defend her brother, for if there's anything that shows him innocent she will discover it. I will be the judge, hear all the evidence, and then deliver my verdict.'

After a little thought, Kratos agreed to this, and soon afterwards they all went to bed.

When they had breakfasted next morning, Barlo asked, 'Where is the trial to take place?'

'Outside my house,' said Kratos. 'I have already had a table and chairs carried out. The people will want to see whether this case concerning my son is justly tried.'

They went outside, and saw that a number of people had already assembled and were standing around in groups, discussing the murder in low voices. When Barlo came out with Kratos and the two young people, the waiting crowd fell silent, and formed a large semi-circle before the table. Barlo took the judge's seat, and asked Raudis and Fredebar to sit to right and left of him. Kratos remained standing, and told one of his servants, 'Bring my son Terlos before the judge.' Then he turned to the spectators, and cried, 'Let Lujos, foreman on the murdered man's farm, come before the court to bear witness!'

At this a tall, sturdy man of about thirty stepped forward and said, 'I am here, and I have brought the cowman Rullos, who can confirm what I say.' With these words he propelled a slight, grey-haired man before the judge's table.

'Then let Rullos stand here too,' said Kratos. 'I have also summoned Varya, the daughter of Vargos.'

'Here I am,' said a girl with a black mourning veil flung over her head and draped like a voluminous cloak around her shoulders. Thus enveloped, nothing of Varya could be seen but a small part of her tear-stained face. She looked past Barlo at the door through which Terlos was just being brought out, and Terlos looked back at her and smiled briefly, before he was led around the table and placed opposite the judge. Kratos had had his son's hands tied behind his back; he might have little fear that Terlos would escape justice by flight, but he wanted to show that he was being particularly scrupulous in the conduct of this case. As soon as Terlos came before him, Barlo told the servant who had brought him in, 'Untie his hands,' and you could see the man was glad to do it. Terlos nodded to him, and then said, 'Thank you, Barlo. I would have appeared before this court come what may, if I'd had to run day and night to get here.'

'Don't thank me too soon,' replied Barlo, but not in an unfriendly tone.

'Which witness will you hear first?' asked Kratos.

'The foreman Lujos,' said Barlo. 'Have the other two witnesses taken into the house, so that none of them can influence what another says.' As soon as Varya and Rullos had been led in, Barlo told the foreman to say what he had heard about the meeting.

Lujos glanced briefly at Terlos, and then began his evidence. 'While Rullos and I were feeding the beasts in the cowshed,' he said, 'I looked through the open door and saw Vargos go past outside. He seemed to be angry, and next moment I heard him ask out loud, "What are you doing here, Terlos?" Terlos told him he had been looking for him, to speak to him. "Speak away, but keep it short," said Vargos. Then Terlos lowered his voice, but I could still hear him quite well, because they were both standing near the door of the shed. He said what he had to tell Vargos was not for anyone else's ears, and asked if Vargos would meet him in the pasture where the cattle grazed at nightfall. "Why all this mystery?" said Vargos, but Terlos was very pressing and said it was important. "To whom?" asked Vargos, and Terlos said, "To you." Then Vargos agreed, and they arranged to meet at the place where the path from the forest leads to the pasture. And that's exactly where Vargos was found next morning.'

'Is that all you heard?' asked Barlo.

'Yes, and enough to convict Terlos, I think,' said the foreman.

'That we shall see,' said Barlo. 'Now stand aside and keep quiet when the others give evidence.' Then he asked the servant to fetch Rullos from the house. The cowman was brought out, and when he was told to speak, he glanced uncertainly at Lujos.

'You must look at me when you speak,' said Barlo. 'There is no need for you to trouble yourself about Lujos now. Tell me what you heard when you and he were feeding the cattle.'

'Well, I didn't take much notice of what was going on outside,' said Rullos, 'not until I noticed Lujos pricking up his ears. Then I heard Vargos talking to Terlos out there. Terlos was just saying he wanted to meet Vargos out in the pasture at nightfall. And not only did he want to talk to him, he had something to show him too.'

'Something to show him?' Barlo repeated. 'No one has mentioned that before. Did he say what it might be?'

'No,' said Rullos. 'He only said it was important, because it had to do with Vargos's property.'

'Did you hear this quite clearly?' asked Barlo.

'Yes,' said Rullos, 'those were his words. And then they agreed to meet at the place where Vargos was found in the morning.'

'Lujos, did you hear what Rullos said?' asked Barlo, and when Lujos nodded, he asked him if he could confirm what the cowman's evidence had added to his own. Lujos looked morosely at the ground and said he could not, and he couldn't be expected to have noticed every single word: he'd only picked up a bit of it by chance, really. 'What's the idea of all this splitting of hairs?' he added. 'The whole thing was only an excuse to lure Vargos to that lonely place in the dark, after all.'

'I just want to know what you heard, Lujos,' said Barlo, 'and I want to know in as much detail as possible. I shall then form my own opinion.' He asked Rullos to step aside in his turn, and had Varya brought out to be questioned.

'Before I hear what evidence you have to give in this matter,' said Barlo, 'I must ask you one question: what are your feelings for Terlos, who stands here accused of stabbing your father?'

Varya raised her head so abruptly that her veil fell back, revealing her face. Her wide mouth with its full lips showed that she had always liked to laugh, but just now her eyes were flashing angrily. 'He never murdered my father!' she said, with decision.

'That is for this trial to discover,' said Barlo. 'But you haven't answered my question yet.'

'If it had been left to me to decide,' said Varya, 'I would be the wife of Terlos today.'

'Then you will try to make sure your evidence does him no harm,' remarked Barlo. 'From what you say, Lujos stood little chance in courting you.'

'He never had any chance, none at all,' said Varya firmly. 'And I gave him no reason to think he did, but my father was always encouraging him, for he thought a great deal of Lujos.'

'And you did not?'

'No, I did not,' said Varya. 'But it was hard to convince my father.'

During this exchange, Lujos was looking away, as if indifferent, but you could tell that he was having difficulty in controlling himself. Barlo seemed to notice this too, for he said, 'We will leave these personal matters out of it. Tell me, did you know anything about the arrangement Terlos and your father are said to have made to meet?'

'Not much,' said Varya. 'The day before all this happened, Terlos did tell me that now he knew how to convince my father Lujos was not the right man for me, and I might be confident that he would do away with the obstacles my father was putting in the way of his own courtship. He struck me as being very sure of himself, and I trusted him, as I still trust him today.'

'He told you no more?' asked Barlo.

'No,' said Varya. 'There was no need.'

'Then you may step aside too,' said Barlo, 'for now I want to hear what Terlos has to say about that meeting.'

Varya went over to the place where the other two witnesses were standing, but she stopped some distance away from Lujos, turned her back to him, and looked at Terlos, who had not taken his eyes off her all this time. Even if she had not spoken so frankly of her relationship with him, none of the spectators could now have failed to see what the two felt for one another.

'You must look at me for a moment, Terlos,' said Barlo. 'Will you tell us now what you wanted of Vargos?'

'I will,' said Terlos, 'but I must go a little farther back in the story. Two days before the murder, when I was walking through the woods above Vargos's pasture in the evening, I saw a stranger among the bushes. It looked to me as if he were hiding there, waiting for someone, and I remembered that twenty cows had been stolen from Vargos's pasture a couple of weeks earlier. The man who kept watch over the cattle by night had been found dead drunk in the bushes, and afterwards he swore by all that's holy he didn't know how the brandy got into his flask, because he'd filled it with water himself, but after the first sip he couldn't stop drinking. I thought the stranger might have something to do with the theft of the cattle. So I hid behind a tree and waited too. And after a while, somebody did come uphill across the pasture. The stranger came out of the bushes, and when the other man met him and stopped, I recognized Lujos. You'll understand, Barlo, that I felt all the more interested in the matter now. I was close enough to hear what the two men were saying. Lujos asked the stranger if he had the money. Not yet, said he; it was too dangerous to sell the cattle in this neighbourhood. He could dispose of four cows in two days' time; a friend of his was driving the rest over the mountains, and he expected him back with the money in ten days' time, but not before. Lujos told the stranger to leave the money for the first four cows in the hollow tree the day after next, and he would come and get it. And he was to do the same with the rest of it in ten days' time.'

'What hollow tree is that?' asked Barlo.

'An old beech standing up there on the edge of the forest,' said Terlos. 'Everyone here knows it by that name. And Lujos also told the stranger to be punctual if he wanted to do any more such deals. Then he went down to the village again, and the stranger disappeared into the woods. So now I knew how Vargos had lost his cows: Lujos had made the cowherd drunk, so that the stranger could come and drive the cattle away whenever he liked.'

'He's lying!' shouted Lujos, who had been listening to Terlos with mounting fury. 'Don't believe a word he says!'

'It's for me to decide whether he is lying or not,' said Barlo sharply, and then he told Terlos to continue his evidence.

'You know now what I had to tell Vargos, and what I wanted to show him,' said Terlos. 'But he wouldn't believe what I said. "If you think you'll discredit your rival in my eyes, then you're out of luck," said he. So I led him to the hollow tree and asked him to see if the money was hidden there. Vargos reached into the hollow and brought out a purse of gold pieces. He shook them out on his palm and counted them. "A poor price for four cows," he said. Then he put them back in the purse, pocketed it, and laughed. "Cleverly planned!" he said. "I'll wager you hid the purse yourself so that I'd believe your lying tale – and as you say this money doesn't belong to you, then I can keep it!" Then he laughed again as if the whole thing were a great joke. It made me so angry that I left him there and went away downhill, over the pasture and home. But I can well imagine what happened next.'

'You'd better leave the imagining to me,' said Barlo. 'Was that all you had to say?'

'Yes,' said Terlos.

'Why haven't you told anyone about it before?' asked Barlo.

'Because the stranger is to bring the rest of the money this evening,' said Terlos, 'and I thought that the fewer people who knew about it the better. And now Lujos must be kept from warning his accomplice. Perhaps I'll be believed if the stranger is caught with the money.'

'Perhaps,' said Barlo. 'But now my son Fredebar is to speak for the prosecution in this case.'

Fredebar rose to his feet, and you could tell he enjoyed playing so important a part in the trial. He took up his position and glanced at the spectators before turning to his father. 'It looks,' said he, 'as if this is a matter of one man's word against another. It is my task to find the arguments for Terlos's guilt. I have listened very closely, and it seems to me that several witnesses have said more than they intended. Let us suppose Terlos really did want to lure Vargos to the borders of the forest in the dark. He asks for a private talk, out of earshot of anyone else, but Vargos refuses. Then Terlos says he doesn't just want to talk to him, he wants to show him something too. And as he knows that Vargos sets great store by his property, he adds that it has to do with that. Could he have gone about it more cunningly? But what exactly does he mean to do? He didn't even tell Varya, although he could trust her. And yet he gives himself away out of his own mouth: he told her he was going to do away with the obstacles her father was putting in the way of his courtship. Is that the way a man with peaceable intentions speaks? Doesn't it smack of violence? So what really happens on the edge of the forest? Even if we believe the tale of the purse of gold, how are we to know that Terlos did not in fact hide it there himself, and is trying to get rid of his rival in this way? But Vargos doesn't believe him, for he trusts his foreman. He laughs, and what's more, he takes the money for which Terlos has scraped and saved. Then Terlos loses his temper, as he has told us himself. But he doesn't walk away; he stabs Vargos. It is my opinion, from all that we have heard, that Terlos committed the crime.'

Fredebar had spoken expressively and with conviction, lending a certain drama to his account of the case. The people put their heads together, whispering, and were obviously impressed. Lujos seemed relieved by this turn of events, and said, 'Yes, that's how it must have been. Well, it's obvious! You'd better pass judgement now, Barlo.'

'I'll wait till the right time comes for that, Lujos,' said Barlo. 'And now we will hear what Raudis has to say in her brother's defence.'

In the meantime, Fredebar had sat down again, and now Raudis stood up, smiled at her brother, and placed herself where she could see both Barlo and Lujos. 'I too have listened closely,' she began, 'but I have drawn other conclusions from what I have heard. First I want to ask you something, Rullos: which of you two was closer to the cowshed door when you overheard the conversation arranging the meeting – Lujos or yourself?'

'Lujos,' said Rullos. 'He was right behind the doorpost, while I was over with the calves.'

'Then how is it, Lujos,' Raudis continued, 'that Rullos heard more of the conversation than you did? Or is it not the case that you failed to mention anything which might betray what really happened up on the pasture? You never said that my brother was going to show Vargos something – and so there must have been something for him to show;

you never said that it concerned Vargos's property, for that might have led us too close to the idea of a possible connection with the theft of the cows. What one fails to say can be revealing too, Lujos! Let us suppose things happened as Terlos said. You overhear his conversation with Vargos, and when you hear the meeting place Terlos suggests, you suspect my brother has found you out. When your master goes up to the edge of the forest at nightfall, you steal after him. You see the two men talking, but you are not close enough to hear what they say. However, you watch Terlos leading your master to the hollow tree, and you see your master take out the purse and then pocket it. Now you think your treachery has been discovered. You have only one way out: you must murder your master and lay the blame on Terlos. As soon as my brother has gone, you creep up to Vargos from behind, perhaps as he's counting the money again, and stab him. Then you take the purse and go. Was that not the truth of it?'

'No!' said Lujos, hoarse-voiced. 'It wasn't!' Then he turned to the spectators, and said, 'Don't believe the tale Raudis is telling to save her brother! He's the murderer.'

'Silence,' said Barlo, motioning him back to his place with a vigorous gesture. 'This case is still a matter of one man's word against another, one opinion against another opinion.'

'Not entirely,' said Raudis. 'What Fredebar said was cleverly thought out, but he was speaking of people he doesn't know, moving them around like chessmen on a board. I, however, know who I am talking about, and my heart tells me that Terlos is not guilty.'

'Your heart!' cried Lujos. 'Who's asking what your heart says?'

'Not you, for certain,' said Raudis, 'having no heart yourself. I wonder that you dare court Varya.'

'Oh, you do, do you?' said the furious Lujos. 'Well, you'll see – I shall get her as soon as your brother's proved guilty.'

'Are you so sure Varya will have you?' asked Raudis.

'As sure as if she'd already given me her word,' said Lujos.

'If you were so certain of getting her father's property, along with Varya herself, why did you need the money?' asked Raudis.

'A man wants to give presents –' retorted Lujos, and then he realized he shouldn't have said that.

'His guilt is proven,' said Raudis, turning her back on Lujos. He stood there perfectly still for a moment, as if he had not quite grasped it. Then he uttered a bellow of rage, drew his knife and lunged at Raudis. Before anyone could come between them, she swung round and looked him in the face. Lujos froze in the middle of his movement, and Raudis said, her voice expressionless, 'And that is just how you killed your master, Lujos. It's in your nature to stab people in the back.'

Barlo told the servants to seize Lujos and bind him, and then he asked, 'Do you confess to the crime, Lujos?'

Lujos looked at him defiantly, saying, 'Do I need to, now?' But then he nodded.

At that Barlo rose and said in a loud voice, so that everyone could hear, 'Now I will pass judgement. This man, Lujos, shall forfeit all his property, and be sent into the forest weaponless. He may take nothing with him but a loaf of bread and a bottle of water. He shall have one day's grace, and after that anyone who meets him here in the valley of Barlebogue may strike him down with impunity, for Lujos is now outlawed.'

As for Terlos, he was present when they caught the stranger about to hide the rest of the money in the hollow tree that evening.

You must forgive me for telling the tale of this murder at such length. Old Barlo told me the story himself, with all its details. I am particularly interested in legal cases, and easily forget what I meant to say. I was really just going to tell you how Fredebar met his bride. At the trial, it didn't look as if there could be any understanding between those two, but as soon as Lujos had been taken away, Fredebar went up to Raudis and said, 'I'm glad you won, Raudis.'

'Don't you mind?' Raudis asked.

'Why should I?' said Fredebar in surprise. 'I tried to play my part as well as I could, but I'd have been sorry if judgement had gone against Terlos, who seems a pleasant fellow.'

Raudis couldn't help laughing at that. 'So he is,' she said, 'and you may be sure he won't hold anything against you.'

'Why should he?' asked Fredebar.

Raudis looked at him, shaking her head, and then said, 'You have less guile in you than anyone I ever met! Are there any things you take seriously?'

'Not things, no,' said Fredebar, 'but it may be that I'm beginning to take *you* seriously.'

'And so you should,' said Raudis, when she heard that.

Barlo was glad to see that his son liked this girl, for he had admired her cleverness during the trial and the courage with which she had challenged Lujos. After that, he kept finding reasons to ride into the

mountains with Fredebar and take the opportunity of visiting Kratos.
A few weeks after the trial, his wife died. She had invited some of her
grand friends from the town to go hunting, and when their motley
train put up a stag, hunting it over a hedge, she had such a bad fall
from her horse that she broke her neck. There was no more merriment
at Barlebogue for some time. Barlo mourned long for his wife; he had
loved her dearly, for all her frivolity. A year later, however, the wedding
of Fredebar and Raudis was held, and bright banners flew from the
castle to welcome the guests, while a magnificent cavalcade of noble
ladies and gentlemen came trotting back through the valley they had
left so sadly last time they came here.

Barlo got on well with his daughter-in-law, for he realized that
she understood his view of a judge's duties better than his own son
did. He hoped, I suppose, that Fredebar's playful nature would find
its proper counterweight in her. While Fredebar rode out hunting,
or listened to a wandering minstrel playing the latest dances on his
fiddle, Raudis would often sit with Barlo, discussing legal cases with
him. And when, after a while, she bore a son, it was by her own
wish that he was called after his grandfather, who was known henceforth
as old Barlo.

Raudis had had a difficult labour, and never recovered from it. She
spent most of her time indoors now. Old Barlo had become used to
discussing all his decisions with her, and his grandson was with them
from the first. To begin with, no doubt, he sat in a corner playing while
the two of them talked, but soon he joined them and paid close attention
to what they said, as he himself told me later. 'I will try to tell you all
the tales of remarkable legal cases I know,' the old man once said to
Raudis. 'And in so far as the boy doesn't understand them now, you
must tell them to him in his turn when I'm gone. For I can see that my
son's mind is on other matters.'

When his grandson was seven, old Barlo died, and Fredebar became
lord of the castle, and judge. But he did not ride the land like his
father; what justice had to be done in the valley of Barlebogue was
enough for him. He would rather go hunting with his friends from the
town, and when the year's mourning was over, he began to hold feasts
in the castle again, as his mother used to do. You could hear the music
of those festivities right down in the village.

They say it quite often happened that folk from the valley would go
to Raudis before they brought their cases to Fredebar. He was happy
to take her advice, for all things considered he wasn't a bad man, and

had not forgotten how Raudis showed her sense of what was right in her defence of Terlos.

Raudis grew weaker and weaker, and died when young Barlo was fifteen. It was a great blow to Fredebar, for in spite of her illness she had been a good wife to him. He withdrew from all his friends, hardly showed his face, and if he had to hear a case at law, the parties to it often thought he hardly seemed to be attending. Folk sometimes found his judgements very strange, I'm told. Well, this went on for over a year, and then his friends came back to cheer him, so they said, and persuaded him to lay his grief aside, ride out with them again and hear music played in the evenings. However, he was never as merry and cheerful as he had been before; he began to drink more and faster than had been his custom, and devoted himself less to the law than to the deposits of precious stones that were found in the curve of the river below the castle at about that time.

It was then that disaster fell upon Barlebogue. Here in the village, we heard about it from a servant who had escaped. He came out of the woods next day, exhausted, with his clothes in tatters. He couldn't utter a word at first, and it was only gradually that we discovered what he had been forced to watch. It had almost deprived him of his reason. Two days later, young Barlo came riding into the village, leading three unmounted horses by their halters, and as soon as I saw him I ran out of my house and asked where he had come from.

'Why, from market,' said he. 'I've been there to buy horses. Why are you so agitated?'

'Don't you know what's happened at Barlebogue castle?' I asked, and when he shook his head I told him what we'd learnt from the servant. At that Barlo dismounted. 'Where is this servant?' he asked.

'In my house,' said I, for my wife had been looking after him.

Barlo was horrified when he saw the man's condition. He too questioned him, and had to hear the terrible tale a second time. 'Be careful, Barlo,' the servant said, when he had finished. 'Gisa means to set her wolves on you as well, and then there'll be no one left alive with a right to be lord of Barlebogue. And she knows you are on the road with some horses.'

The servant's story had made Barlo so angry that he strode out and swung himself up on his horse to ride straight to Barlebogue. I ran after him, clung to his bridle and begged him not to ride to certain death. In the end, he saw that he wouldn't be able to do anything on his own, so he stayed in my house for the time being, waiting for more news. But all we heard was worse, if anything, than what we had learnt before. With the help of her retainers, Gisa had got control of the whole valley, and she left no one who tried to oppose her alive.

So a few weeks passed by, until one morning Barlo said, 'I can't sit about here doing nothing any longer. Give me some old clothes; I know a farmer in the valley I can trust. I'll take service with him as a labourer, and find out what can be done against that pack of wolves.' I tried to dissuade him from this dangerous venture, but he had made up his mind. So I gave him some cast-off clothing, and he set off that evening to make his way back to the valley of Barlebogue by secret paths. And that was the last time I set eyes on Barlo before he came riding into the village with all these strange companions.

* * *

When Dagelor had come to the end of his story, Listener looked at Barlo. So this was the rightful lord of Barlebogue, sitting there calmly chewing a crust of bread! 'Why didn't you tell me who you really are, Barlo?' he asked. But Barlo simply smiled and shrugged his shoulders, shaking his head as if it were of no importance.

'I hope I didn't speak too ill of your father, Barlo,' Dagelor said. 'From all I've heard, and all I know, I can see things no other than the way I told them, and I'm too old to beat about the bush.' Barlo laid a hand on his shoulder, letting the old man understand that he bore him no grudge for his honest opinion.

'There was a great deal about justice and the law in your story,' said Listener. 'Do you take so much interest in them?'

'How could I not?' said Dagelor. 'Since my father died, I've dealt out justice here in the village, and paid careful attention whenever I heard tell of such things. All we can know about legal decisions comes from old tales of the cases that have been handed down to us. My father knew a great many, I heard more from old Barlo, and I've had experience of some myself. For new things are always being added to the law; that's how justice lives. If we should ever stop passing on such tales, the law would die. Men can't find justice within themselves alone. We need the help of everyone who ever thought about right and wrong, and even so we can never do anything but what we believe to be right, taking all this knowledge into account. And the good judge is the judge who knows he has only a faint idea of what he is doing. We live in a house that is constantly threatening to collapse, and we can't do much more than prop up a beam here, and mend the roof there, so that the rain won't come in. And when you walk across the room next day you put your foot through the floorboards again. That's the truth of it, Listener. But I reckon you'll have to be a little older before you can understand.'

They went on again next day. The villagers accompanied Barlo's merry company to the edge of the forest. Their faces now were different from the way they had looked the day before, when the travelling companions arrived: their eyes were no longer dull, but full of hope and interest. Some were still laughing at the jokes their guests had cracked, and there was talk of the tales that had been told and the songs that had been sung in many a cottage until late the night before.

Their ways parted when they came to the forest: the villagers went back to their cottages; Lauro the prospector and Tubby the woodcutter, with their group, took the path going left into the forest and up the hills to the mountain range; and Barlo and Listener rode at the head of the others along the old road leading straight to Barlebogue along the banks of the river. Not that much of the road could now be seen, only two rutted tracks made by cartwheels, the space between them long since overgrown by brambles. Birch saplings the size of a man's arm had grown up in the middle of the road, and the branches of beech, oak and alder trees hung down over it, so low that you could hardly make your way through them. Listener, in the saddle of his donkey, had an easier time than Barlo on his tall steed, but soon they both had to dismount, or they would have been swept off the backs of their mounts. The procession made only slow progress, accompanied all the time by the rushing of the river flowing towards them through the narrow, wooded ravine to the right of the path.

Towards evening, they reached a small, deep basin in the valley, which was closed at its far end by a barrier of rocks as high as a house. The river had made itself a way through the rocks, and came tumbling in turbulent cascades down from its narrow channel, to flow more quietly once again when it reached the meadow at the bottom of the basin, until it disappeared into the forest, going down the valley. There was room for the company to camp here. 'Stay close together, and keep well away from the woods,' said Rauli. 'You can never tell what may be slinking around under those trees by night.'

When the sun had set, one of the players came over the meadow to Barlo and showed him a bundle of clothes with a witch's mask attached to it. 'I found this in the bushes over there,' he said. 'I could swear the fellow who wore it has been walking along with us through the forest all day, but he's gone now.'

Listener picked up the mask and looked at it. He had seen those sharp fangs between the twisted lips before, and there had been yellow eyes shining behind the eye-holes then. 'I know that mask,' he said. 'I am afraid I know who wore it, too. It could be that he is running through the forest on four legs now, summoning the pack. We had better take care tonight.'

Nobody now needed warning not to stray from the camp. A fire was kindled in the middle of the meadow, and they lay around it in a ring to sleep. Those who owned weapons made sure they lay ready to hand.

Rauli, who liked making plans and arrangements, had seen to it that a watch was set, and Listener had undertaken to be on duty in the hour after midnight. When he was woken, the sky was covered by a thin veil of cloud, and a pallid moon with a broad, shimmering halo was shining. Listener crawled out of his blanket and went slowly over to the place where Yalf lay with the horses. Pale clusters of lady's-smock swam above the dark grass in the moonlight. The rushing of the river was a like a wall, rising above all other sounds in the cool, damp air. If anyone here could sense the approach of danger, it was the donkey with his keen nose. He had always been the first to scent wolves. Listener sat down beside him, leaned against his soft belly and stroked the short hair of his coat.

When he had been sitting there for a while, gazing at the black wall of the trees, he felt Yalf becoming restless under his hand. A shiver ran over the donkey's hide, he snorted softly, and then raised his head and looked in the direction of the forest. Listener could not make anything out, but he knew from experience that it was time to wake the others. He had hardly risen to his feet when Yalf woke them for him: he leaped up, uttering a hoarse and piercing bray that could be heard even above the rushing of the waterfall. 'The wolves are coming!' Listener shouted, and immediately the whole company were on their feet. The horses rose too, crowding close together and pawing the ground. And then the pack came out of the forest, howling, their dark backs sliding through the grass, their yellow eyes flitting above the ground like will-o'-the-wisps.

Barlo had his triton's horn to hand this time, for Listener heard its deep and echoing note rise above the sound of the rushing river, making the air shake. The wolves stood still, frozen, and before they could move into the attack again, the roaring and splashing of the rapids suddenly seemed to swell, and then turned to cascading laughter, as if of a thousand clear and silvery girlish voices. The laughter sprayed up to the sky and fell again, like the shower of sparks from a falling star; it filled the valley from end to end, as if there were nothing in the world but that laughing. And above the rapids there was a flash and gleam as if of naked bodies leaping over the cascades, carried up and down, at one with the foaming water that shot through the narrow channel in the rock.

It was the laughter that drove the wolves away. They put their tails between their legs, afraid, and pressed close to the ground in the tall grass. Then they leaped up, one by one, and raced back to the forest. It must have been the laughter that took their courage and belligerence from them, Listener was sure of it, for no water had come bursting up out of the ground this time, there had been no flooding, the laughter alone had been enough. Its many echoes were still breaking on the slopes and rising to the topmost ridges of the wooded mountains, and it was so infectious that all the company who had been standing around the dying fire just now, alarmed and ready to defend themselves, joined in the laughter too, so that deep and clear voices mingled.

A boundless merriment took possession of them all. The minstrels fetched their instruments and began to play a wild dance, led by Barlo, whose flute rose clear above the drone of bagpipes and the scraping of strings. The travelling folk gathered around the place where the river came bursting out of the cleft in the rock. Those who had no instruments danced and leaped boldly on the gravel of the river bank, vying with the water nymphs who shot up out of the swirling water like shimmering fishes, still laughing, and teasing the men who tried to seize them, until the Green Man came up out of the cascading water and put his great horn to his lips. Its note rose, deep and shaking, until you could hear nothing but the booming roar of it, and in that sound the wild dance came to its end. When the note of the horn had died away, the waterfall lay there alone in the moonlight again.

'Thank you for your aid, Green Man!' cried Listener, and from far above, like the sound of the strings of a bass fiddle, came the voice of the water spirit. 'Thank you for your dance, and do not forget to laugh.' And then there was nothing but the constant rushing of the river in the night air.

The men went back to their fire, and put dry wood on the embers until it flared up again. Then Barlo picked up the witch's mask and the ragged robe, and threw them on the flames. There was a gleam of yellow and red through the empty eye-holes again, and the grinning

mask twisted, as if the frightful face were alive. Finally it burst apart
with a bang and a shower of sparks, and was devoured by the flames.

By now they had all come back to lie by the fire, and were talking in
low voices of what they had just seen. 'It's like your fairy tale, Gurlo,'
said Rauli. 'Even the wolves cannot bear laughter. We should remember that.'

'Then how was it possible for them to get such power?' Listener
asked.

'Does that surprise you?' said Rauli. 'Do you think anyone thought
of laughing when Gisa's retainers fell upon Fredebar and his guests?
Gisa made sure that there was no cause for laughter then, and today
there's not a man or woman in the valley but lives in fear and terror.
The power of the wolves increases where all joy is gone.'

'We'd better stick together,' said one of the minstrels, 'or our lives
won't be safe in the valley of Barlebogue.'

Hearing this, Barlo shook his head and picked up his flute. 'Don't
you yet know what's at stake?' he asked, in his musical language. 'We
didn't set out only to drive that evil woman away. It's more important,
or so it seems to me, to bring joy back to everyone in the valley, for
human beings cannot live without it. Your suggestion of sticking together may sound like sense, but for what we plan, nonsense is the only
answer. As soon as we have the forest behind us, we shall part company,
and go off in groups of two or three. There must be no farmstead in the
whole valley, no cottage in any of the villages, where one of us isn't
cracking a joke. And we must at least try to find out how Gisa acts
when someone laughs in the faces of her shaggy retainers. Only when
matters have reached that point do we meet again at the castle.'

Next day, about noon, they came to the place where their path led
out of the forest and down to the wide valley floor. The trees on
either side of the river retreated to half-way up the slope, growing in
a rim around the valley itself and up into the towering mountains
that rose behind them. Down below lay fields and meadows; the red
rooftops of farmsteads and little villages were bright among the white
clouds of blossom in the apple orchards, and far away, beyond the
river that wound in gentle curves through the valley, the towers of
Barlebogue castle rose against the blue-green wall of the woods,
delicate as a child's toy. Listener looked at this peaceful scene, which
betrayed nothing of the evil magic that was cast over the countryside
like an invisible cobweb.

'To work, friends!' cried Rauli, and he fell to playing master of ceremonies again. He told each group the name of the place where its members were to ply their trade, and he made sure that a storyteller always had a minstrel or jester with him to cheer the audience if the tale should seem too long. Barlo laid his hand on Listener's shoulder, indicating an isolated farm lying on the left-hand slope of the valley, in between the place where they stood and the castle. Then he urged on his horse and rode away.

Now they had come to the valley of Barlebogue, Barlo did not seem to be in any great hurry. He let his horse trot down the grass-grown path at an easy pace, took his flute out and began to play again: a rambling and cheerful tune, outlining the shape of this peaceful landscape, and the last line of his jester's song kept coming in as the refrain. *For Barlo is riding through the land* . . . And wherever the minstrels went their way down the valley, answering music could soon be heard from bagpipes and fiddles, shawms and flutes. The tune echoed back from slope to slope, a torrent of music running down that wide green river basin to fill it to the brim, and anyone could hear, from the wooded ravine up to the mountain range, that Barlo was riding on his way.

Listener rode beside his master on his donkey, thinking of the days when he had galloped over these fields at Gisa's side. The peasants used to do their work in silence then, and he could not remember that there had ever been any singing, let alone dancing in the villages of an evening. The ploughmen had trudged doggedly behind their beasts, hardly daring even to stop for a moment's rest when their mistress was riding anywhere near – not like the farmer ahead of them on their road, who had been just about to turn his plough when the music came surging from all sides. Now he stood there by the furrow at the side of the field, arm around his horse's neck, watching the two riders as they came up.

Barlo reined in his horse and nodded when they reached him, and Listener, wishing to be friendly too, said, 'It's a fine day.'

'Yes, a fine day,' growled the farmer, his tone cool. He turned to the flute-player again. 'You're young Barlo,' he said. 'I know you from the days when your father was alive. But this fellow here on the donkey, wasn't he the one who . . .' And he mimed the cutting out of a man's tongue. However, Barlo laid one hand on Listener's shoulder, and made a dismissive gesture with the other, as much as to say: never mind, that's all old history.

'Only thinking,' said the farmer. 'Well, he found out later what he'd let himself in for with Gisa. Been riding with you long, has he?'

Barlo nodded.

'What are you about, then?' asked the farmer.

'Teaching you to laugh again,' said Listener.

'You think a little bit of music will drive Gisa and her retainers away?' asked the farmer. 'Well, I just hope you're not mistaken.'

'We can always try,' said Listener, and at that very moment the farmer seemed to see something behind him. Alarmed, he immediately tried to drive his horse back into the field. Listener looked round, and Barlo too glanced down the road along which they had come. They saw one of the shaggy retainers, galloping up on horseback.

Barlo took the farmer's arm, with a reassuring smile. Then the yellow-eyed man drew level with them and reined in his horse.

'Why aren't you at work?' he shouted at the farmer.

'Because he is talking to us,' said Listener, in friendly tones.

The man looked at him in surprise, obviously unused to such answers. Meanwhile, Barlo had put his flute to his lips again, and was beginning to play his merry song. This time, he played the verse that ended with the words, 'Squeak, mouse, and see the big, bad wolves turn tail and flee!' It infuriated Gisa's retainer. 'Stop that damned piping!' he roared, and tried to bring his horse up beside the fluter, but Barlo made his own steed rear so that the other animal had to back away.

'Don't you like the music?' asked Listener. 'Listen to it! There's music playing all over the valley!'

A hunted expression came into the shaggy man's yellow eyes. 'Just you wait!' he shouted. 'We'll show you!'

'The way you showed us last night by the waterfall?' asked Listener, beginning to laugh, and Barlo stopped playing his flute too, and laughed so loud and heartily that the farmer joined in as well, although he had no idea what they were laughing at. The shaggy retainer stared at the three laughing men for a moment, and you could see his rough hair bristling. Then he turned his horse abruptly and raced away across the ploughed field, jumping hedges and ditches, but the laughter was close on his heels, following him until it drove him over the meadows far down the valley, like a dead leaf blowing in the wind.

'He was afraid!' said the astonished farmer.

'If you will all learn to laugh once more,' said Listener, 'Gisa's shaggy retainers will never be free of fear again.'

'We've had little enough cause to laugh these last years whenever we met with one of them,' said the farmer. 'But it looks as if things could change. Where are you going?'

Barlo pointed to the farmyard by the roadside a little way ahead of them.

'To Eldar's place?' asked the farmer. 'Then you're going to the right man. He's one of the few that have never quite given up hope. And now I shall let my ploughing be, and go home to tell my own folk what's afoot.'

'Just what I was going to suggest,' said Listener. 'And it may be that by now you have guests who can tell you more.'

'You make me curious,' said the farmer, and he said goodbye to the two riders. Then he unharnessed his horse from the plough, swung himself up on it, and trotted off down the road, the way the other men had come.

When Barlo and Listener rode into Eldar's yard, they saw that the people there had come out of doors and were looking down the valley, where the minstrel's tunes were still ringing out, as if there were a fair somewhere. There were three women, some children, and a stout, short-legged man, whose rosy cheeks were in striking contrast to his bristly grey hair. Barlo smiled when he saw him, and played a couple of notes on his flute that sounded like a signal. The stout man heard them, and looked down the road. 'Barlo!' he cried. 'I might have guessed you were behind these strange goings-on!'

Barlo leaped off his horse, and embraced the stout man like an old friend met after a long absence. Listener got off his donkey too, and waited for someone to take notice of him. At last the stout man turned to him, saying, 'I think I know you too.'

'I am afraid so,' said Listener. 'You probably used to see me riding over the fields with Gisa.'

The stout man drew in his breath with a whistle. 'Well, well. Gisa's playmate,' he said, looking Listener up and down in no very friendly way. But then his face cleared, and he said, 'Ah, then you're the fellow who gave her that blue mark on her brow before he ran away from her. That makes up for a lot. From that day on, my hopes began to rise again, for you were the first to raise his hand against her. And what are you doing here now?'

'I've been Barlo's servant these last three years,' said Listener.

'Then you're as welcome to me as your master,' said the stout man. 'My name's Eldar. Come into my house and be my guests.' And he shook Listener's hand so vigorously that all the joints in it hurt. Then he introduced him to his family. Eldar's wife was considerably taller than her husband, but neither of them seemed the sort of folk to let themselves be bothered by such unimportant matters. Eldar's daughter-in-law Gildis was there too, with her three children. Eldar told them that Gisa's men had taken his son away one day. 'And this is my daughter Eldrade,' he continued, but the girl did not even notice he was speaking of her. She had eyes for no one but Barlo, who was wordlessly playing a cheerful game with the children. 'Ah, well, don't take it ill of her!' said Eldar. 'She hasn't talked of anyone but Barlo since he left my house.'

Eldrade was slender and tall, like her mother, but her full, strong face showed her father's features, though finer-grained and less gnome-like than in Eldar himself. In the end, Eldar laid a hand on her shoulder, saying, 'No doubt you'll be seeing plenty of Barlo now. You must welcome our other guest as well.' His words did not cast her into much confusion; indeed, she seemed to take it as quite natural to have her name linked with Barlo's. 'I envy you, Listener,' she said. 'I envy you, allowed to ride the land with Barlo all these years.'

'You put me to shame,' said Listener. 'There was no question of being *allowed* to ride with him at first; I did it only because the task was laid upon me. But later I was glad to go with him, and now I know that I shall never forget that time.'

Then Eldrade shook hands with him, as if with a comrade, and said, 'You must be our guest,' and they all went into the house.

The meal set before the guests was a frugal one here too, for Gisa left her people only the barest necessities of life. 'How I still come to be so stout I've no notion,' said Eldar. 'Maybe it's with all my pent-up rage at seeing those yellow-eyed fellows call the tune here so long.'

'They won't be calling the tune much longer,' said Listener, and he told them of their encounter on their way to Eldar's house. Eldar and his household, sitting at table with them, listened intently. When Listener described the shaggy retainer's flight, they began to laugh, and you could tell they had not done that for a long time. Eldar laughed so hard that his double chin shook. Then he smote the table with the flat of his hand and said, 'There's a change coming, and the best of it is that there's cause for good cheer! Barlo is riding the land once more.'

'Are you going to help me feed the horses again?' Eldar's grandson asked. He had been sitting beside Barlo, never taking his eyes off him.

Barlo laughed and nodded, rose to his feet, perched the boy on his shoulders, and went out with him.

'Ah, he fed the horses every evening while he was here,' said Eldar. 'Best groom I ever had!'

'Why didn't he stay?' asked Listener.

'Ask Eldrade,' said Eldar. 'Nobody can tell you about Barlo better than she.'

'Will you do so, then, Eldrade, if I ask you?' said Listener.

'Willingly,' said the girl, and she began to tell:

The Tale of Young Barlo

Barlo often came to our house, even as a boy. From the first, he didn't have much time for the feasts his father held for his town-bred friends. You mustn't think he didn't like to laugh, but his merriment was of a different kind. And another reason why he always came to see us when there were parties of visitors from town, making merry at the castle, may have been the way they would ride their horses hard when they went out hunting, setting them at every hedge and fence, for Barlo loves horses, just like my father, who always has a couple of good brood mares in his stables. So the talk was generally of horses when Barlo was with my father, and they soon came to trust each other. And no doubt, too, that was why he came to our farm when Gisa and her shaggy retainers had seized power in the valley. I was scared to death when he tapped at my window by night, for we expected nothing but harm in those days. But then I heard the whistle we had always used as a signal between us, and I let Barlo into the house.

That night he took me in his arms for the first time, and wept like a child while I held him fast. I don't know how long we stood in the dark hall like that. Some time or other my father came in, we sat down in the living-room, and Barlo asked us to tell him all we knew. His face was like a stranger's in the candlelight; I had never seen it so full of hatred before. He asked about some of the people from the castle, but they were all dead. And as we sat at the table talking, wolves began to howl outside. Such a thing had never been known in the old days. 'Nobody in the valley dares venture out of doors after dark,' said my father, blowing out the candle.

'Are you all turned cowards?' asked Barlo angrily. 'Why, you used to go out hunting wolves!'

My father shrugged his shoulders. 'You expect us to attack them with our bare hands?' he asked. 'Gisa's retainers have searched every house in the valley for weapons, leaving us nothing but a few kitchen knives and a hatchet to chop wood. What's more, these wolves always stay in a pack, and they hunt down anyone they meet outside at night.'

'I shall go into the forest tomorrow to cut myself wood for a hunting bow,' said Barlo. He did not wait to see if my father had anything more to say, but rose and went to the bedroom where he always used to sleep when he didn't want to go home.

Next morning Barlo asked my brother Bragar if he would like to come, or if he too had grown accustomed to the wolves' tyranny. So Bragar went with him, and each of them cut himself a stout piece of yew as tall as a man for a bow, and shafts for arrows.

By day Barlo worked as our groom, because my father thought it too dangerous to give him shelter in our house merely as a guest. But a man standing in the yard grooming horses was nothing to wonder at here. In the evenings, Barlo and Bragar went to work on the making of their bows. I can still see Barlo sitting there, every evening for a week, whittling away at the hard wood, and finally fitting the string to the bow. And when he pulled the bowstring taut and let it snap back, there was murder in his eyes. He kept out of my way at this time, as if I might distract him from what he meant to do.

The one person he would talk to was Bragar, and when their bows were ready, he told him, 'We must make ourselves a hide in a tree where the wolves can't get at us.' It took them some time to find a place which the pack frequently passed, but then they made their hide in an old oak on the edge of the forest, and left their bows there, for it would have been unwise to keep them in the house. By that time, five weeks had passed since Barlo came to our house.

I was there when the two of them were discussing their first hunt. 'We will aim only at wolves who have strayed a little way from the pack,' said Barlo. 'And when we shoot, we must kill, for a wounded wolf might set the others on our track. We should try to retrieve our arrows too.'

Towards evening, they set off in the last of the sunlight, and did not come back till the sun was up next day. We had risen early and were waiting for them. My father looked inquiringly at Barlo, but got no answer. However, before Barlo went into the house, he drew his knife from its sheath and cut two notches in the doorpost. Then he lay down in his room to sleep, for my father had already fed the horses. All Bragar said was, 'They wear collars with blue stones in them.'

So it went on for some days. Sometimes Barlo cut a notch in the doorpost, sometimes he didn't, but never more than two such notches for one night. You could tell from looking at him and my brother how tired they were; there was too much work on the farm for them to be able to sleep all day. And Gisa's retainers were beginning to search houses again, too. You would see them everywhere, riding through the valley in groups of three or four, and our farm was one of the first places they visited. They came galloping over the paddock and jumped the fence, scattering the chickens. Outside the house they dismounted, flinging their reins to Barlo, who was just coming out of the door. Then they burst into the house, making their way into every room, flinging open cupboards and chests, rummaging through everything that came into their hands. At last, after ravaging the place like robbers, they gave it up and left the house in a fury. One of them stopped in the doorway, looking thoughtfully at the freshly cut notches, which stood out clearly in the weatherbeaten wood of the doorpost. Then they took their horses and rode on to the next farm.

That evening Barlo and Bragar went hunting again. When they came back in the morning, I could tell at once that something had gone wrong. 'A wounded wolf got away from us,' said Bragar. And that same morning Gisa's retainers came riding into our yard again. One of them had his arm in a sling and was carrying an arrow. He sniffed at it like a bloodhound. They didn't go into the house this time, they called for my father instead.

'Who works on this farm besides yourself?' one of them asked.

'My son Bragar and a groom,' said my father.

'Call them out!' said the shaggy man.

When Barlo and Bragar came out of the house, the wounded retainer looked at them hard and went close to them, as if to pick up their scent. There was cold rage in his yellow eyes. 'You have too many young men on this farm,' he said. 'We shall employ them in other ways, to keep them from getting any stupid notions. Your son is small but strong; he'll work well in the mines. And we can use that tall groom there up at the castle.'

'And who's to look after my horses?' asked my father.

'No need to trouble about that,' said the shaggy man. 'We have a use for your horses as well. We'll leave you a couple of nags for working in the fields, and that should do.' And they set about leading the horses out of the stables straight away. Luckily they didn't know the first thing about horses, so that my father managed to keep back his two best brood mares. Meanwhile, Barlo and Bragar had fetched their things, and now they came out of the house with their bundles. Bragar had said goodbye to his wife and children indoors, not wanting Gildis to weep before the shaggy retainers' yellow eyes.

All this time I had been standing outside, and when Barlo had said goodbye to my father, he was about to give me his hand as well. Then I took him in my arms for the second time, and I did not care a bit if Gisa's men were watching me and grinning. 'I'm leaving you my knife,' Barlo whispered in my ear. 'It's in your chest. Keep it sharp, for I'll be needing it again.' Then he kissed me, and went to the horses he was to take to the castle.

There was reason to fear one of the servants who had been brought to work there might recognize him, but I couldn't imagine anyone betraying Barlo, who was as generally liked as his grandfather. All the same, I couldn't bear to stay at home for as much as three days; I went down the valley and wandered around the village just below the castle, hoping to see Barlo, or hear news of my brother. When I failed to do either, I went to Furro the smith, who used to shoe the castle horses and would be the first to know anything. 'They took your brother off to the mountains, with some other young men,' said Furro. 'I saw Gisa's retainers driving them past myself. All I know about Barlo is that he's working as a groom up at the castle, but you needn't fear any of our folk will tell Gisa who is tending her horses.' And he added that he'd send me word when Barlo was going to bring the horses to the smith for shoeing. He had realized that it was important to me to see and speak to Barlo.

A few days later a neighbour called, and said Furro sent word that he couldn't shoe our horses tomorrow, because he had to work for the great folk at the castle. 'Have we got a horse that needs shoeing?' my father asked in surprise. 'Yes, of course,' said I, 'don't you remember?' And I secretly gave him a sign to ask no more questions. So he thanked our neighbour for bringing the message, and when we were alone again he took me into the living-room and told me this was no time to have secrets from one another. So I told him what I and the smith had agreed, and I said I must see Barlo even if it cost me my life.

'Barlo has other things on his mind than secret meetings with a girl just now,' said my father. I'd known he would say that, and it made me furious to think that men can hate so bitterly, they'll forget everything else. 'Yes, I'm sorry to say he has nothing but those other things on his mind,' said I, 'and full of hatred as he is, he will turn to evil himself in that accursed castle.' My father looked at me blankly. 'Do you want that witch and her shaggy retainers to go on doing us violence for all time?' he asked. And at that moment he looked just as hard and grim as Barlo when he was carving his bow. 'You know I don't want that,' said I. 'But anyone who means to get the better of this nightmare must get the better of his own hatred first, and I won't allow Barlo to forget how human beings ought to live. Perhaps he will remember if I take him in my arms again, and you won't stop me.' My father looked thoughtfully at me for a while. Then he smiled, and said, 'I won't set anything in the way of your going to the smithy tomorrow, but don't put yourself and Barlo in danger.' Then I kissed him and said, 'The only danger I can see is that this wolfish crew may devour our hearts.'

Next day I was there in the smithy when Barlo came with the horses. Two of the shaggy retainers were with him. One of them was going to send me away, but the other one just grinned when he saw me, for he had been there when Barlo was taken from the farm and had watched our parting. 'Let 'em go to it and breed like rabbits,' said he. 'Our mistress can always do with more workers.'

I saw Barlo turn pale with rage, and I stepped quickly up to him and embraced him. 'They talk like that because they think like animals,' I said. 'It can't hurt me.'

'It sickens me, though,' he said, and I felt him quivering with fury. 'I've been sick with hatred ever since I saw that rabble prowling the rooms where my grandfather and my parents used to live.'

'I know,' I said, 'that's why I'm here. To remind you that hatred isn't everything.'

'I'm glad you are here,' said he. 'But up in the castle, it's like wading through poisonous mire. I'm so close to the witch now that I shall soon find a way to put an end to her, and I'll send you news by way of Furro when I need help.'

We didn't say much else, and then the horses were shod, and Barlo had to go back up to the castle stables with Gisa's men.

But no more news came from Furro. He disappeared from the village a week later with his wife, taking most of the tools of his trade with him. It was said he had fled with that donkey driver who went off into the woods with a whole herd of pack animals about then. Gisa had a blacksmith installed at the castle, and so it was that I never saw Barlo again in all the three years he worked there.

But I saw you towards the end of that time, Listener, when you came riding over the meadows with Gisa. Once you passed quite close, and I heard Gisa tell you, 'You must learn to raise your voice, or nobody will obey you.' I liked your voice when you answered her as quietly as before, and I am glad you still speak no louder today.

We heard what happened to Barlo afterwards from a servant, and for a while I hated you for that as much as Barlo had hated the evil lady of the castle. But then I thought of what I myself had said about such hatred, and I began to pity you, for it was Gisa who had brought you to do it, even if not entirely without your consent. There was no trace of Barlo, but I didn't give up hope that he might still be alive. They say a knife turns dull and rusty when its owner dies, but Barlo's knife was still as sharp and bright as the day he left it in my chest. And now you are neither of you to be pitied, for it's a long time since I saw two men as merry.

*　*　*

Eldrade was just coming to the end of her tale when Barlo came back from the stables with Eldar's grandson. He put the boy down, and laughed when he heard her last words. Then he reached for her, picked her up from the settle where she had been sitting, and danced through the room with her, making her skirts fly. 'Put me down! You stink of horse dung!' squealed Eldrade, laughing as she tried to struggle free, but Barlo wouldn't let go of her, and whirled her round and round until he was breathless. Swaying a little, the two of them stood there in the middle of the room for a while, clasped in each other's arms. Then Barlo let the girl go at last, and sat down on the settle by the wall. He took out his flute, and played his jester's song again, but this time he added a third verse:

> *Hunt the wolves away*
> *from my house today,*
> *sing and dance by night*
> *and in broad daylight.*
> *In merriment ride,*
> *for Barlo is bringing home his bride.*

'Well, after all this, I suppose you don't actually need to ask for her hand,' said Eldar. 'Once my daughter has taken something into her head, there's no stopping her. And she talks so fast, her tongue will more than make up for the loss of yours.'

Then Barlo put his flute to his lips once more, to show them all he was very well able to speak. But Eldrade took it out of his hand, saying, 'I can understand you even without your flute, and I will be your mouth as long as I live.'

That night there were no wolves to be heard, either near the house or up in the forest. Listener lay awake for a long time, wondering what Gisa would do when she heard about Barlo and the coming of the players. And the longer he thought about it, the eerier the silence seemed.

Next morning, while Barlo was breakfasting on a mug of milk together with Eldar and Listener, he picked up his flute and said, 'We had better go into the woods and cut a yew sapling each. It may be that the wolves will still defend themselves if they are all assembled in a pack.'

'You could be right,' said Eldar, 'and I for one will be happier if I have a hunting bow in my hand, and needn't rely entirely on our laughter.'

As they climbed up the hillside meadows to the edge of the forest, Listener told his host the tale of Wurzel, and Eldar was still laughing when they reached the shade of the trees. Up here, they could hear that other men had had the same idea. There was snapping in the undergrowth all around them, and the blows of axes echoed through the woods.

'Have you got merry guests too, Eldar?' another farmer called to him. 'They're light-minded folk, to be sure, but they know how to encourage a man with their jesting. It's said that Barlo came with them. Do you know where he is?'

'Here with me,' said Eldar, 'and he was betrothed to my daughter yesterday evening.'

At that the other man laughed and said, 'Well, he's in a hurry all of a sudden! And if there's a wedding being planned, the nightmare can't last much longer.'

Barlo had been standing in the bushes with Listener, listening to this exchange. Now he stepped out of the woods and into the meadow, so that they could all see him, and he played all three verses of his song. Everyone could understand how the words ran, and they joined in too when he played it for the second time.

'And when do we hunt that rabble out of your castle?' one man asked, when the song was over.

'Make ready your bows and wait until I send word,' played Barlo.

'In the meantime, you can practise laughing, should you have forgotten how. My friends will show you the way to do it.'

When they went back down to Eldar's farm, Listener saw that Barlo had cut wood for two bows.

Barlo and Listener stayed on the farm for a week. Eldar had increased his stock of horses considerably with the help of his two brood mares, even if the women and children had had to lend a hand with all the work. Counting Barlo's horse and Listener's donkey, there were now twelve animals in the stables, and Eldar was glad to have his groom back. Whistling contentedly to himself, Barlo did his familiar job, and instructed his servant in the finer points of the craft.

Listener was impatient. Gisa still held sway in the castle with her retainers, and here was his master acting as if he had come merely to devote himself to working in the stables and grooming horses. Had they ridden through the land so long for no other reason than to become grooms instead of shepherds? It didn't seem much in the way of progress.

Even in the evenings, when they sat together in the living-room, making their bows, Barlo gave the impression of whittling at some unimportant toy. Eldrade noticed, too. 'Your face looked very different when you were making your last bow, Barlo,' she said.

Barlo looked at her, eyebrows raised inquiringly.

'No,' said Eldrade, 'I like you better the way you look now.'

Then he laughed a little, and turned to his piece of yew again.

The wolves kept quiet all that week. Listener waited every evening to hear their long-drawn-out howling, but there was no sound but the wind blowing around the reed thatch of the roof. As they sat in the living-room once more on the seventh evening, he asked, 'Do you think we've driven them away already?' Barlo shook his head, and pointed in the direction of the castle. Then he took his flute and played the Song of Fair Agla, for it was a particular favourite of Eldrade's.

While he was still playing, there came a knock on the window from outside. They all sat perfectly still for a moment. The knocking came again, and then they heard somebody whistling, a brief run of notes like a signal. 'Bragar!' cried Gildis, leaping up and running out of the room to the door of the house. By the time the others got there, she had already pushed back the bolt and opened the door. Listener saw a man standing outside in the dark, a man with rather short legs and noticeably broad shoulders. 'Bragar!' said Gildis again, and in two strides he was beside her and took her in his arms.

'I thought you'd be here in our house, Barlo,' said Bragar, when they were back in the living-room. 'I have some news for you. Three days ago Lauro the prospector and that huge great fellow known as Tubby turned up in the mountains, with a number of jesters, and set up such a torrent of laughter that Gisa's shaggy retainers almost went out of their minds. There was naked terror in their yellow eyes as they ran to their horses and galloped down into the valley, as if a devil were after them. Then Tubby told us what had turned their wits like that, and he made sure we had something to laugh at ourselves. By now all our men from the mines are on their way through the valley, together with your merry companions, and I've come ahead to tell you the news.'

When he had heard it, Barlo nodded, put his flute to his lips and said, 'We'll ride to the castle at the first light of dawn. Fetch your donkey from the stables, Listener, and go and tell them on the neighbouring farms. And Eldar, will you take word to the men on the other side of the river? Tell them not to forget their bows. I have a bow ready for you too, Bragar.'

Eldar saddled a tall brown mare. Listener was surprised to see how large the farmer suddenly looked on horseback. When they had ridden out of the farmyard, Eldar brought his horse to a halt again, and told Listener how to find the farms he was to visit. 'Can't I go the longer way instead of you?' asked Listener, for he was sorry Eldar would have to ride over half the valley tonight instead of talking to his son. However, the farmer shook his head. 'You wouldn't find the ford across the river by night,' said he, urging his horse on, and he galloped down the road into the valley as if it were broad daylight.

Listener had to leave it to his donkey to find the way up into the higher part of the valley in the dark. At first he could not even see the grassy verges by the roadside, but gradually the darkness seemed to lift, the shadowy shapes of trees and bushes stood out from the slope of the meadows, and then, suddenly, he could make out the delicately jagged outline of the forest against the clouded sky. Listener rode faster now, for the path along which he was going was clearly visible. Ahead of him, a light seemed to be hovering over the floor of the valley below. Listener reined in the donkey and looked that way. The castle of Barlebogue must stand on its hill where that faint glimmer hung in the night. They were still awake there, too. Listener wondered what might be going on now in those lofty rooms, and a shiver ran down his spine. But then he shook off his mounting dread, and let the donkey trot on.

An orchard loomed up to the right of the path. The branches of apple trees in blossom stood above the dark grass like a light cloud. As Listener rode past, smelling the fragrance of the blossom, he heard bagpipes playing. Then, beyond the trees, he saw the lighted windows of the next farmstead. Here, too, the household was still awake, with people dancing and stamping their feet to the music of the minstrel who was their guest.

Listener dismounted from his donkey, opened the gate in the fence and went up to the house. He stood outside the door for a moment, listening to the nasal melody above the droning bass and hearing the laughter of the dancers. Then he knocked. The music instantly stopped short, the laughter died away, the dancers stood still. He heard whispering. Then footsteps came to the door, and a man asked who was there.

'A messenger from Barlo,' said Listener, as loud as he could. At that the bolt was drawn back and the door opened. All Listener could see was the shape of a man standing there against the light. 'Come in,' said the man, but Listener had no time for that; he said he must take the news to other farms as well. 'We are all to ride to the castle at first light of dawn,' said he, 'and don't forget your hunting bows.'

'Well, that's the best news I've heard in years,' said the man. 'Tell Barlo we'll be there on time. And you can turn back yourself – I'll tell them on the other farms, for I know the paths hereabouts better than you do.'

It was said, later, that no one in the valley slept that night. People sat together in every house, listening to the storytellers, joining in the minstrels' songs, laughing at the players' jokes. But it was shrill and hectic laughter, as if to cover up the suspense with which they all awaited the dawn. Again and again, someone would stand up and go out of doors to see if the sky was brightening yet above the eastern woods.

Listener had ridden back to Eldar's farm, led Yalf back to his stable, and then sat with the others in the living-room for a while. But he scarcely heard what Bragar was telling them of the time he had spent in the mines. Now and then Listener glanced at the young man, whose pale, bearded face was marked by hard labour in the darkness of the shafts and galleries, and who spoke of it as if of some dangerous adventure long ago, interesting only for the unusual nature of its incidents, which could now be told in a voice that need not falter with the onset of fear.

But Listener still saw the distant light of the castle of Barlebogue flickering above the valley floor. He stared out at the darkness, where there was nothing to hold the gaze but that evil spark, that nucleus of howling terror, hovering lost in empty space, and his heart froze, while his awareness shrank into that one wavering point of dread towards which he must soon go. He put his hand to the icy lump whose deadly cold filled his breast, and felt Arni's stone beneath his fingers. Then he brought out the bag, took the stone out of it, and gazed at the ring of colours, its warm tones shimmering in the candlelight. The stone eye looked at him; blue, green and violet rings spread out in pulsating waves and filled the black emptiness, pushed back fear to the farthest horizon, until there was nothing left but the living light shining radiantly out of the eye, or out of the face looking at him from that eye, and he could not tell if it was the face of a very old woman or of a child at whose gaze his heart began to beat once more, and then he heard that voice again, the voice that sounded like bells ringing very far away, or the cooing of wild doves, and the voice said: Listener, make use of your stone.

'Is that the stone that Gisa wants?' asked Eldrade.

Listener raised his head, and saw the girl standing before him, looking at the stone he held in his hand.

'Yes,' said Listener, 'this is Arni's stone. But she shall not have it.'

'Will you let me hold it?' asked Eldrade.

'Gladly,' said Listener, handing her the stone. Eldrade took it, and looked at it for a long while. 'It's warm,' she said.

'Yes, of course,' said Listener. 'I wear it on my breast.'

'I don't mean that,' said Eldrade. 'It warms my heart.'

'I know,' said Listener.

'Is that why you brought it out?' asked the girl.

'Yes,' said Listener. 'I was afraid.'

'It warms the heart,' Eldrade repeated. 'Until this moment, I have hated Gisa for all she did to the valley, and to Barlo. But now I'm sorry for her, for this stone will show her what she lost when she went with the wolves.'

She gave Listener back the stone, and as he put it away in its bag, Bragar came in from outside and said, 'It's getting light over the forest. Time we set out.'

A little later they were riding down the slope of the meadows. The valley still lay in darkness, but to the east the wooded mountain range stood out sharply against the pale sky. Listener looked at the broad shapes of Eldar and Bragar trotting along before him, longbows held in their left hands: two centaurs on the track of wolves. Then other riders emerged from the darkness, among them some of the strolling players, who had been lent horses if they had none of their own. When they had reached the floor of the valley, and were riding towards the dark castle that now loomed up before them, flutes and bagpipes began playing Barlo's song, more and more of the men joined in, and the singing and laughter spread all over the valley, for now, in the pale light of dawn, Listener saw the miners coming down from the far end of it as well. The procession divided, and began to surround the castle hill on both sides. And then the mounted men rode up and leaped off their horses to greet sons who had been driven away to the mountains by Gisa's retainers years ago, and while they were all still shouting and exclaiming and hugging each other, Tubby, who towered above the throng like a ship's mast, struck up one of his verses in a great, booming voice:

> *Awaken, fair Gisa,*
> *you've slept enough now,*
> *let's see the mark Listener*
> *left on your brow!*

Then Listener heard Gisa's voice, shrill above the laughter that rose and broke against the walls. 'Silence them!' she screamed. 'Hunt them down, my wolves, rend them!' And when the laughter died away you could hear the wolves whining. 'Are you all turned cowards?' screeched Gisa. 'Off with you, off and away! Tear out their throats, and there'll be no more laughter then!' Her voice was still echoing back from the sides of the valley when the drawbridge came crashing down. Pressed close together, the pack came racing out of the gateway, and fanned out on the steep slope. But the men had bent their bows, and shot arrow after arrow into the attacking wolves. One by one they fell, howling, rolled down the slope to the foot of the hill and lay there in the bushes. Within a few moments, the hillside had been swept clear.

Up above, the open gateway yawned darkly. Listener gazed up at it, expecting Gisa to appear, but nothing moved. Then the first ray of sunlight touched the top of the tower, glinting off the golden weather-cock. At that Barlo swung himself up on his horse, signing to Listener to follow him. The other men mounted again too, and joined Barlo as he rode up the path that led to the castle gates.

When they came to the drawbridge, Listener saw the sky above the mountains glow in bands of red, and then the sun rose over the tree-tops, dazzling his eyes. Next moment, hooves were clattering over the wooden bridge, and the riders passed through the narrow gateway. Now they were cut off from that blazing flood of light, and a chill wafted towards them from the paved entrance where their hoofbeats echoed deafeningly back at them. Listener shivered. Yet again, he felt fear rise within him, but then the path curved, he saw the bright outline of the courtyard gateway itself, and the dread receded once more.

The courtyard was empty, apart from a few doves sitting in the windows of the stables and cooing. No sound came from the castle, but the door at the head of the flight of steps up to it stood open wide. Barlo waited until all the riders were assembled in the courtyard. Then he gave the signal to dismount, leaped down from his own horse, and walked slowly up the steps. Listener and the other men came after him, in silence; they walked down empty corridors, past pictures dark with age, and the pungent smell of wolves lingering in every corner rose to their nostrils. Listener felt as if he were wading through a swamp. Every step he took cost him an effort, and when Barlo pushed open the heavy double doors of the great hall and went in, dread of that place, only too familiar to him, made him falter. But the other men behind him felt no such fears, and thrust him over the threshold before them.

The windows of the hall still lay in darkness. The whole place was bathed in a dim twilight, in strange contrast to the sun-drenched countryside beyond these walls. Listener gazed out at the green slopes of meadows beneath the blue-green forests, as if his desperate gaze could pluck him from the deadening atmosphere of this room and wake him from a nightmare, and he would find himself lying amidst fragrant grass and flowers. But at the same time he knew it was no dream, for in this very hall he had sat at table with Gisa, in this hall he had tried to give orders in his quiet voice, in this hall he had delivered judgement. And now he heard Gisa's voice too, the voice he had heard so often in this hall.

'Listener,' said Gisa, 'have you brought me your stone?'

He turned his gaze from the window, and saw her standing at the far end of the hall. Her blue eyes were icy, and the swollen mark on her snow-white forehead was like a third and evil eye, whose fixed gaze he could no longer avoid. He could see nothing but that blue-black mark, swelling and swelling until it filled his being with boundless, howling terror that sucked up every other thought, leaving nothing behind but a black void that squeezed the breath out of him. In a spasm of choking, he tore open his shirt, and clutched the bag containing Arni's stone. And then, in the midst of that nameless dread, he suddenly found a firm handhold again. Warmth flowed into his fingers, and he could feel the ground steady beneath his feet.

He saw Gisa's drawn face once more, and now he could also see the fear flickering in her cold eyes. 'The stone!' she cried. 'Give me the stone!' Then he took the stone out of its bag and crossed the hall to Gisa. It seemed an endless way, and he had to summon up all his strength to raise his feet from the floor, but he went over, step by step, until he stood before her. She was staring at the stone he held.

'What do you want with my stone?' he asked.

Then Gisa seized his hand and pressed it to her forehead, stone and all. She stood there for a moment, rigid, and then she uttered so piercing a scream that it froze everyone in the hall to the marrow. Listener dared not move. And then Gisa's grip loosened, and she thrust his hand away.

The mark had gone. But that was not the only change that had come over Gisa. Looking at her, Listener wondered who this woman was, standing here before him. She could not be the evil mistress of the wolves, who had gone prowling through the forest with them, for all signs of lust for blood and power had vanished from her face. Was this the girl who once had so many suitors coming up the valley to court her? In those days, Gisa's face might well have looked as it did now. She was gazing at him as if he had just returned to her after a long journey.

'Are you back at last, Listener?' she asked softly.

'Yes,' said Listener, 'I'm back.'

'I have had bad dreams,' she said, 'ever since you went away. But now I am awake.'

At that moment Listener noticed something moving by the far wall of the great room, and only now did he see the gigantic figure of the castle steward, standing in the shadows of a niche in the wall. So the eldest of her shaggy retainers had not gone running with the wolves, but had stayed with his mistress instead. Hatred and fear stood in his yellow eyes, and he had raised one hand as if to keep his lady from taking a dangerous step. Gisa, however, paid no heed.

'Do you remember how we rode through the valley together, Listener?' she asked. 'Those were good times.'

'Gisa!' said the steward, but Gisa did not seem to hear him.

'There's still some of the wine we drank then down in the cellar,' she said. 'Shall I send for it?'

Then her grey-bearded retainer strode up to her and seized her by the arm, saying, 'Gisa, do not forget your promise!' But Gisa shook off his hand, as if it were some troublesome creature, and said, 'Won't you sleep beside me tonight, my hairy Listener? Let me stroke your soft pelt, and then you'll stay with me.'

She stretched out her arms to Listener, but she could not reach him any more. 'Gisa!' cried the steward, but it was no longer a warning; it was a cry of horror from a man falling into an abyss, who has lost his last foothold, and the cry changed suddenly into a wolf's howl. The onlookers had been gazing in dismay at the yellow-eyed old man, but all at once he was gone, and so was Gisa. Two great grey wolves raced through the hall, gathered themselves to leap, and shot out of the window with a crash of breaking glass.

Listener had scarcely taken in Gisa's first transformation when the second occurred. Dazed, he looked at the bare wall before which he had seen Gisa's face a moment ago: a soft and girlish face, free of greed, ready to give. But now there was nothing but the empty wall, and he asked himself if Gisa had been here at all, or if he had dreamed the whole thing. Only the acrid reek of wolves that filled the whole hall made him aware of what had just taken place before his eyes. He went over to the shattered window and looked out. Beneath the castle hill, the meadows of the valley shone emerald green in the morning sunlight, stretching up to the dark forests on the mountainsides, and two grey beasts, far away now, were running through the waving grass of the pastures towards the shade of the trees.

So now the war of the strolling players and the wolves was at an end, and you can imagine the rest of that story for yourselves. The travelling folk stayed at Barlebogue, of course, until the wedding of Barlo and Eldrade was held. And there was fiddling and flute-playing and singing and dancing in the castle from morning to night. Listener could hear it when he sat up at the window of the tower, looking across the valley to the forest. Somewhere over there, two grey wolves were running. All his companions were rejoicing in the wedding, and the war they had won, but somehow he could not enter into the spirit of it. Whenever he closed his eyes, he saw Gisa's face before him once again, looking at him as it had in those few seconds after the stone touched her brow. Could he have prevented what happened next? He could not believe that the fate of a human being might be unalterably pre-ordained. His stone had extinguished all that Gisa had become since she made her pact with the wolves. In that moment she had loved him, and she had not stopped to count the cost – for she must have known what the consequences would be. Would the evil spell have been broken if he had taken her in his arms? That seemed to him too simple a solution, unless it had meant his taking her terrible transformation on himself. Would his heart have felt lighter now if he too were running through the forest on four legs? It seemed pointless to wonder, for he had done nothing, he had been incapable of moving so much as a finger while she spoke to him. Yet he felt paralysed by a dull sense of having left something vital undone, by the vague awareness of a guilt which he could not define. Gisa's face had been so close, and now he longed to touch it. Had whatever it was he sought vanished into the woods for ever with her grey shadow? He would never be able to free himself of that image while he sat here at the window of the tower, looking at the forest. He must ride on, away from this all too lovely valley, into the shadowy thickets on the far side of the gently sloping meadows.

Barlo had freed him on the day of his wedding. When Listener was about to wish him joy, Barlo had embraced him as a friend, making it clear that his servitude was over now. Eldrade said, 'Stay friends with us, and be our guest here as long as you like.' So Listener had moved into the room in the tower, and went riding the land with Barlo again as if nothing had changed. But that inexplicable trace of uneasiness remained with him, a vague sense of oppression that came over him whenever he set eyes on the woods.

He rose now, went down the narrow spiral staircase, and crossed the courtyard to the stables. Yalf looked at him with his big, shining eyes. Listener stopped beside the donkey, put an arm around his neck, and scratched his rough hide. 'We must ride on again, Yalf,' he said, 'we must ride on.' Yalf snorted, and rubbed his soft muzzle against Listener's hand. And while Listener still stood there, leaning on his donkey and feeling the animal's warmth on his skin, the bright rectangle of the stable door darkened and Barlo walked in. He came over to Listener, with a question in his eyes.

'Yes,' said Listener. 'I'm riding on tomorrow.'

At that Barlo took his flute out of his pocket, but he did not set it to his lips; instead, he pointed to the western woods with it.

'You're right,' Listener said. 'I had better go and see the Gentle Fluter. Do you think I've learned to listen well enough yet?'

Barlo looked thoughtfully at him. Then he shrugged his shoulders, which might mean, 'I don't know,' or 'Perhaps,' or, 'You'll have to ask your grandfather.' So then Listener knew what way he must ride when he set out next day.

Book Two

which tells
how Listener gets his second gift,
a silver flute,
and hopes to win great power with it
among Arni's Folk.
During this time he has many dreams,
yet what he dreams of having always escapes him,
not least the green-eyed falcon maiden Narzia.
The three adventures
he undertakes for her sake
bring him a reward he did not expect.

The first time Listener rode westward through the forest and away from Barlebogue, he had just marked Gisa on her lovely brow. He did not, to be sure, know it at the time, but as a general rule it is only later that we learn the real results of our actions. This time, it seemed, he had put an end to Gisa. He could think of nothing else as he rode up the wooded slope, just as he had done three years before, although he did not need to make his way through brushwood and undergrowth now, for Barlo had told him of a path along which he could ride and stay in the saddle of his donkey. Listener was leading a horse as well, given him by the rightful lord of Barlebogue in thanks for his services: a bay mare, called Snowfoot because of the white hairs around her hooves, and the offspring of that other bay mare Listener had so liked to ride when he first came to Barlebogue. 'You will have to part from Yalf when you reach mine host who keeps the donkeys,' Barlo had piped on his flute. 'And you are no longer the skinny boy for whom your mount was chosen.'

No, he was no boy now. What was he, then? A man? Had Gisa made a man of him after all, for good or ill? As he rode on and on up the path, which ran diagonally across the slope of the high ridge, beneath a few weathered firs, Listener thought it over, and could find no answer to that question. He had ridden the land with Barlo for three years, and it had always been Barlo who decided where they were to go and what they were to do. Listener realized that his decision to leave Barlebogue did not of itself yet give him that independence which he thought befitted a man. All he knew was that he was alone now, by no means the same thing as being independent. I must find an aim, he thought, an aim I have chosen for myself. Then and only then shall I be free and independent.

That other time, too, he had ridden through the mountain woods alone, fast, driven on by the fear of meeting the groom he had condemned to speechlessness in his rage. He wondered whether he was being followed this time as well. Somewhere or other, two grey wolves were running through this forest. Had they yet picked up his scent? When they parted, Barlo had pressed a hunting bow into his hand and given him a quiver of arrows with sharp steel heads, such as are used to shoot big game. Barlo had not meant them for the shooting of a rabbit for Listener's supper, or he would have chosen other arrows. But Listener was not at all sure he would use the bow if he met a grey she-wolf in the forest. Would he not see Gisa's face behind the wolf's hairy one, looking at him as it had looked before she jumped out of the window like a grey shadow? He felt less dread of the danger of wolves than of having to make such a decision.

But for the time being there was no need for any such fears. Up here on the crest of the high ridge, the windblown firs grew sparsely, a considerable distance apart, and the low undergrowth on the stony ground offered little cover for an animal of any size. When Listener had reached the top he did not look back at the valley of Barle-bogue this time, but urged his donkey on along the path leading westward down the other side of the heights. Wherever his goal might lie, he had not found it in Barlebogue; indeed, it seemed to him rather as if that three years' journey with Barlo had been no more than a long way round, leading him back at last to his point of departure.

That day he rode a good way farther on, down into the woods, until his path crossed the stream he had followed earlier in his flight from Barlo. He watered his two beasts here, and found a place to camp for the night. He sat by the stream for a while, hearing the water gurgling past the mossy stones, and listening to the rustling of the forest. However, there was nothing unusual to be heard, no un-expected crack of twigs, no startled bird chattering shrilly. And when Yalf lay down to sleep, Listener felt sure no danger threatened here. He rolled himself up in his blanket beside the donkey and soon dropped off to sleep.

Some time or other during the night, Listener woke as Yalf raised his head. However, the donkey did not seem ill at ease; he was merely looking past his rider at the stream tumbling over the pebbles of its bed behind Listener's back. Turning his head, Listener saw a plump toad sitting on the bank, gazing attentively at him with her beautiful golden eyes. As he was wondering if this was the same toad he had met before she chuckled in her moist, lip-smacking way and remarked, 'So here you are again, Listener. I hear you've been around quite a bit since last we met.'

'That may well be, Golden-eye,' said Listener. 'Yet I feel almost as if I hadn't gone a step farther forward.' 'Oh, do you, though?' said the toad, swelling up slightly, so that Listener got the impression she was mildly annoyed. 'Well, am I not right?' said he. 'Here I sit again, beside the very same stream, on my way back to my grandfather, after I've been obliged to ride around the country as a servant these three years, and never a soul has asked me where I really want to go.'

'Well, do you know where you want to go?' asked the toad, scrutinizing him ironically. 'Haven't learnt much, then, have you? Still as impatient as ever! As if getting anywhere mattered.'

'Doesn't it?' asked Listener, beginning to feel annoyed by the condescending manner in which the toad addressed him. And now, bloated, wobbling, warty creature that she was, she actually began to laugh. If you have ever seen a toad laugh, you will agree that it is a disconcerting sight: the toad's mouth, big enough to start with, gapes so wide that you fear the flattened head could fall in half, and in its gaping midst the toad's long and mobile tongue flutters about like a ballad singer's when he has pitched his song too high. Listener watched in some alarm, disconcerted to find the toad thought his question so ludicrous. Finally she calmed down, and said, 'You remind me of an uncle of mine. Just like you, he was, always gadding about, forever wanting to get somewhere, reach his goal, as he used to put it. He chased about so much he'd grown quite lean. Thinnest toad I ever saw. And he hardly ever caught a fly, on account of his head being full of the wonderful flies he'd catch tomorrow. "You just wait," my uncle told me one day, "I'll rise in the world yet." And no sooner had he said those words than a stork caught him, swung him up in the air in its long beak and swallowed him.'

'Poor thing!' said Listener, not without sympathy for the ambitious uncle, and thinking the toad rather heartless for seeing it all as such a joke; she was laughing again in her alarming fashion. However, the toad was not at all put out by the coolness of Listener's tone, and said, 'Oh, my uncle was all right. The stork brought him up again next minute. Spat him out on the grass. I expect he was so bony, he got stuck in the stork's throat. Anyway, there was my uncle, sitting just where he'd been before, and once he had his breath back he said, "Didn't mean I wanted to rise quite *that* far." And afterwards he took things the way they were, and not the way they just might be tomorrow. He'd arrive where he was going soon enough, he always used to say after he had that accident, and he generally added that it was a moot point whether you really wanted to be in the place you had taken such trouble to reach. That's what he said, and he led a long and happy life, and grew nice and fat again, the way a self-respecting toad ought to be.'

Listener did not care for this tale. 'You want me to live like a toad?' said he. 'Hearing you talk, I'm inclined to believe you think it would be best for me just to sit here and wait to see what happens next.'

'You really are slow in the uptake,' said the toad, shaking her head in reproof: another very strange sight, since a toad has no neck. 'I never said a word about sitting and waiting. I was talking about people not being content with what they have.'

'Doesn't it come to the same thing?' said Listener. 'Yours may be the way toads think, but I am a man, not a toad. Other folk have decided what I was to do and where I was to go long enough, and I let them decide for me too, but now, at long last, I mean to travel where I want to go myself.'

This last remark drew another chuckle from the toad, causing her wobbling skin to shake. 'Somehow or other, I got the impression you didn't know where you do want to go yet,' said she.

'Well, I'll soon find out,' said Listener, all the more annoyed because he had to admit that the toad was right.

'Why don't you ask your stone?' said the toad. 'Didn't you want to discover its secret?'

'I've tried doing that long enough,' said Listener, 'and all it has shown me are dreams and illusions. Now I mean to seek something I can grasp and hold.'

'You've changed since last we met,' said the toad. 'Don't you value your stone any more?'

'I am afraid it's only been leading me astray,' said Listener. 'Arni followed it until he came to die with an arrow in his breast. Perhaps he did nothing but dream, all his life long. Now, however, I will see if I can't do something standing on my own two feet!'

'A very manly sentiment!' said the toad, sarcastically. 'Just mind you don't fare as my uncle very nearly did!' So saying, she shook her head once more and hopped away into the bushes. Listener heard her rustling among the dead leaves for a while, and then he fell asleep. But it was not a peaceful sleep, for he unexpectedly found himself dreaming:

The Dream of the Toad

He wore a bright, silken robe, and was riding a horse with costly harness through the forest, playing on a golden flute, and whenever he took the flute from his lips he heard the birds singing the same tune he had just played. It sounded like an echoing chorus, cast back all at once from every side: from the bushes all around, and from up in the tree-tops, and down from the sky that could be glimpsed between the leaves and branches. Birds soared and circled aloft there too, repeating his tune. It was as if all the birds of the air had forgotten their own song, and heard nothing but his flute.

So he rode on, playing, until he came to a stream and saw the toad sitting on its banks. 'Do you see how far I've risen in the world?' said he. 'Even the birds of the air imitate my flute. You must sing too!' But the toad just croaked, 'Bosh!' and swelled up considerably. 'Wait,' he said, 'wait, and I'll teach you the notes of the flute!' And setting the instrument to his lips again, he played the most alluring melodies he knew. Yet the longer he played, the bigger the toad grew, until her golden eyes were level with his own face, looking like two gigantic garnets. He played and played, as if nothing in the world mattered but to bring the toad under the spell of his music too, but the toad opened her wide mouth and began to laugh her dreadful, gaping, toad's laughter, and the dark cavern of her jaws opened wider and wider until it hid the forest and seemed as if it would touch the vault of the sky. Then the toad repeated, 'Bosh!' and next moment she had swallowed him. There was nothing left around him but darkness and emptiness, no horse, no flute, no costly robe. Blind and naked, he hovered in what he could not grasp, with no handhold anywhere, and he was inexorably drawn into the howling horror of nothingness. He tried to scream, but as he screamed he felt his cry stifled within his own breast, unable to get out into the never-ending empty dread around him. 'Let me out of your mouth, toad!' he cried soundlessly in his heart, and no sooner had he thought those words than he was spat out of the blackness of that monstrous mouth again, and lay naked and hairy as he was on the dead leaves of the forest floor. 'So now you know how high you can rise by your own efforts,' he heard the toad say. And she chuckled again, but this time her chuckle sent a shiver of horror down his back.

* * *

He started up when a splashing in the stream awoke him, but there was no sign of the toad. The reflection of the thin, sharp outline of the crescent moon, standing in the dark sky among the tips of the fir trees, broke into thousands of sparks of light on the swirling surface of the current. Yalf had laid his head back on the moss long since, and was asleep. Listener shivered, although by now he realized that he was not after all lying naked and uncovered on a bed of leaves. He pulled the blanket closer around his shoulders, put out his left hand to touch Yalf's skin, and felt the donkey's comforting warmth. So he fell asleep again, and did not awaken until he was roused by the morning song of a blackbird sitting on a branch of a hazel bush just above him.

As soon as he had opened his eyes, the bird flew off its branch and down to the ground, whistling three notes that Listener had heard before. 'Good morning, messenger of the Gentle Fluter!' said he. 'So you have found me again.'

The blackbird put its head on one side, gazed at him with bright black eyes, and whistled a short sequence of notes with a slightly impatient sound to them. 'High time I got up, you mean?' said Listener, and by way of reply the blackbird whistled those three notes once more, flew a little way westward along the path, and then came back. 'Well, you're in a hurry and no mistake!' said Listener. 'Surely you'll share my breakfast with me before we set off?'

The blackbird apparently thought this an acceptable suggestion, for it flew back to the hazel bush and watched expectantly as Listener brought his provisions out of his saddlebag. When he crumbled a piece of bread and held out the crumbs, the bird hopped down on to his hand and pecked them all up. Then Listener ate his own breakfast, gave the donkey and the horse water again, and rode on west. The blackbird kept flying ahead, and then waited until he had caught up.

The path led down the gently sloping side of a mountain ridge and on into the valley. Down below and to his left, Listener heard the rushing of the stream along whose banks he had once been hunted through the brushwood. Progress was easier up here above it, although he was not out of the forest even by the third day of his journey.

When the sun stood low in the sky, shining through the trunks of the trees, the path brought them to a little clearing overgrown with soft, straggling woodland grass, with the brown stems of dead foxglove flowers standing tall among it. Finding a spring at the side of the clearing, Listener decided to spend the night here. He let the horse and the donkey drink and then graze freely. As darkness fell they came back to him of their own accord and lay down to sleep. No doubt the blackbird had found a place among the bushes, for Listener could see no sign of it.

In the night, however, he was awoken by its shrill chattering. 'What, time to go on again, is it?' he asked drowsily, sitting up. It must be nearly morning, for the sky was pale, and thin wisps of mist floated above the grass. 'You won't get me moving as early as this!' said Listener crossly, and was about to wrap himself in his blanket again, when the blackbird began scolding once more. Now Yalf pricked up his ears too, and immediately leaped to his feet. Listener peered into the forest, where he heard the blackbird's shrill cries, and there he saw two grey wolves standing in the mist.

He stared into the animals' eyes for a while as if spellbound. Well, he thought, now we shall find out if I can use my bow! And he began cautiously groping in the grass for its smooth curve of yew. But before he could snatch up the bow and put an arrow to its string, the larger of the two wolves had sprung at him without a sound. Listener would have had very little chance of fending him off, but the old wolf did not get far. The smaller beast, a she-wolf, sprang sideways at him, growling, and sank her teeth into the skin of his neck. The old wolf was forced around, and stopped. Listener forgot his bow, waiting with bated breath to see what would happen next. The wolf shook off his attacker and turned his head again to look at the place where Listener sat. But as soon as he took a step in that direction, the she-wolf uttered her throaty growl and sprang at him. She had bitten harder this time, for the wolf howled and almost fell. He managed to shake her off, but before he could attack again, the she-wolf had moved around him, describing a semi-circle, and now she was in the clearing, standing between him and Listener, her legs braced firmly on the ground, the hairs on the back of her neck bristling, as if she were determined at all costs to defend the man sitting there. The old wolf tried one last time, but all he got for his pains was another bite that halted him in his tracks. Listener was surprised that he did not turn to fight the she-wolf, a weaker animal, but each time he merely shook her off, without biting back. And now he gave up his attempts entirely. He raised his mighty head, sent a great howl up to the sky, and with a few bounds he had disappeared into the forest.

The she-wolf turned and looked at Listener. She stood there for a while, motionless; her hair was lying flat again, and all expression of wolfish ferocity was gone from her raised head. Listener looked into her sapphire-blue eyes and thought he had never seen so lovely an

animal. 'Gisa!' he said. Then the she-wolf flung back her head, howling, and turned to run. Three leaps, and the mists had swallowed
her up.

All this time, Yalf had not stirred. Now he trotted over to his friend
and rider, snorting softly, as much as to say: no need to fear that she-
wolf. Listener scratched his neck, and then made himself breakfast, for
he would sleep no more tonight. They set out early, which seemed to
suit the blackbird too. No sooner had it pecked up its crumbs than it
began flying ahead down the path again. Listener began to wonder if
it had been sent to fetch him as fast as possible. He urged Yalf on to a
faster pace, as far as the path would allow, for it was narrower now,
winding its way in sinuous curves down a steep and rocky slope. That
evening, Listener reached more level ground, but he had another night
to spend in the forest before he reached its borders, about noon of the
next day, and then rode out into the green and hilly countryside
beyond.

Here he came once again upon the stream he had followed three
years ago, and so it was not difficult for him to find his way to his
grandfather's house. The blackbird had flown on ahead of him as soon
as he came out of the forest. Off to let the Gentle Fluter know I'm
coming, thought Listener, and so it was: when the house under the
three lime trees came in sight between the grassy hills, his grandfather
was standing in the doorway, looking out for him.

As he rode closer, Listener saw that his grandfather had changed.
He seemed very much older than when Listener last set eyes on him.
His white hair was thinner, and hung in shaggy tangles around his
emaciated face. There was no trace of rosy chubbiness about it now:
pale skin like parchment stretched over his bony cheeks, and his gold-
rimmed eye-glasses wobbled precariously on the bridge of his nose,
which was thinner too. Only the laughter lines around his eyes had
outlasted the passage of time. The Gentle Fluter was supporting himself
with a hand laid on the doorpost, as if it were hard for him to stand
upright. 'You've been away a long time,' said he, as Listener dismounted from his donkey outside the house. 'If I hadn't had to wait for
you, I dare say I'd be gone by now.'

Listener went up to him and embraced him, feeling as he did so how
light and fragile the old man, whose thin hands now clung to his
shoulder, had become. 'Why, where would you have gone if you hadn't
waited for me?' asked Listener. He could not imagine what kind of
journey this frail old man might have thought of taking.

'Where your grandmother is already,' said the Gentle Fluter, smiling, as if it were a very foolish question.

'Isn't she here, then?' asked Listener, dismayed, for he had loved that sturdy woman, despite her forthright manner, and not only for her culinary skills.

'No,' said the Gentle Fluter, 'she has gone on a little way ahead of me, but never mind that now. I am glad to see you, for it's time for you to enter upon your inheritance. Come indoors. I can't hold a candle to your grandmother as a cook, but I picked up a few tips from her all the same.'

Listener wanted to tend his two beasts first, but his grandfather said, 'You can just unsaddle them and let them loose. There's plenty of grazing here, and they'll find water in the brook. And tomorrow you can take them and stable them with the innkeeper.'

So Listener carried the harness and saddlebags indoors, and then sat down in the living-room. Soon the Gentle Fluter served up a deliciously aromatic rabbit stew, and new white bread. There was a pitcher of red wine on the table, and Listener felt he had come home again. When he praised the meal, his grandfather said, 'Ah, well, you mustn't think I still go hunting in my old age. Mine host comes by every few days or so and makes sure I have what I need.' They did not talk much while they ate, for the Gentle Fluter still observed the custom of leaving matters of importance to be discussed after a meal.

Finally the dish was empty, and Listener cleaned it out with a piece of bread, for the stew had been excellent. Meanwhile, the Gentle Fluter poured wine, and then said, 'So Barlo's given you your freedom, then.'

'Yes,' said Listener. 'He has mastered your language so well now that anyone can understand him, and he's found a wife to stand at his side too. He doesn't need me any more.'

'Ah, you shouldn't say that,' replied the Gentle Fluter. 'A man always needs his friends. And aren't you his friend?'

Listener thought for a moment. 'I don't know,' he said. 'I was his servant for three years, and at first I had no idea what might be in his mind. He didn't even try to tell me what he meant to do. Later, I came to understand him better, but to the very end we did only what he wanted. Yes, he embraced me like a friend when he gave me my freedom, but I don't know if one can really call it friendship. He was more like an elder brother.'

'Does that trouble you?' asked the Gentle Fluter.

'Well, I think it's time I decided for myself what I do and where I go,' said Listener.

The Gentle Fluter smiled. 'But you chose the way you would go yourself, before,' said he. 'Don't you remember? And judging by all that has come to my ears about your journey, you've had opportunity enough to learn to listen. However, it seems to me that you still listen to yourself too much.'

'Must I not find out who I am?' asked Listener.

'Yes, indeed you must,' said the Gentle Fluter. 'But that won't be done as fast as you think in your impatience. You will not find the answer in yourself, but if you are able to listen, you will gradually come to hear it from others.'

'So I still haven't learnt to listen well enough,' said Listener, feeling like a schoolboy who has made a mistake in solving a problem.

His grandfather made a pacifying gesture, and said, 'Ah, what does *enough* mean? You will never come to the end of learning how to listen all your life. I can only hope that you have learnt enough in these three years to take on my inheritance now. For I cannot wait another three.'

'What inheritance?' asked Listener, although he already guessed the answer.

'My flute,' said his grandfather. 'Now that you have helped to set things right in Barlebogue, so far as that was possible, it seems to me time for you to learn the flute. I hear that your voice has grown no louder in these three years, and that at any rate bodes well for your ability to learn my art.'

Listener's heart leaped. Now he too would be a fluter, perhaps even a famous man like his grandfather, of whom they told tales even in the tents of the Raiding Riders. Barlo's wooden flute was only a kind of makeshift, to help him to express himself. The silver flute was a very different matter, for the sound of it gave one power over others, as he himself knew. 'When do we start the lessons?' he asked eagerly.

The Gentle Fluter laughed softly to himself, and said, 'I suppose you can't wait, impatient as you are!' And there he was right: Listener felt every moment between now and the beginning of his lessons was a waste of time. 'Will it take me long to learn to play the flute?' he asked, and thought anxiously of the many weeks it had taken Barlo to master his instrument.

'It depends what you mean by playing,' said the Gentle Fluter. 'All I can show you is which fingers to put on which holes to produce a certain note, and that's soon done. But then you must learn to play for yourself, and that will take you much more time than I can spare you.'

'Will it be anything like Barlo's flute lessons?' asked Listener.

'No,' said his grandfather. 'My silver flute is not of the same kind as Barlo's wooden instrument. Once you know the notes, the flute will express your thoughts of its own accord, and it will compel those who hear you to do what you have in mind as you play. Never forget that! For you must know that there is a condition to the handing on of the flute: the inheritor of it must be taught nothing but the fingering, and he himself must decide what he plays upon the flute. So my lessons will not take long.'

So saying, the Gentle Fluter rose, took his silver flute from a shelf on the wall, and handed it to his grandson. Now Listener had a chance to examine it closely at his leisure. It was all in one piece, and looked as smooth and perfect as if no human hand had made it, but it had grown of itself like the stem of a flower. The one ornament on the silver pipe was a finely chiselled fivefold ring at its lower end. Listener saw that this ring was really a pattern of tiny letters, and that a verse was engraved on the flute. It ran:

> *Follow my song,*
> *whither you will,*
> *yet force is wrong;*
> *use none, or the song*
> *will bring you ill.*

When he had deciphered this text, Listener asked, 'What does it mean by telling the player of the flute that force is wrong? You told me yourself that the sound of it compels all hearers to do what the player has in mind.'

'Yes, I asked myself the same question at first,' said the Gentle Fluter. 'But that is one of the things you must find out for yourself. Now, pay attention, and I will show you the fingering.' So Listener had his first lesson. He was surprised at the ease with which he could find the separate notes; indeed, it almost seemed as if his fingers went to the right holes of their own accord. That very first afternoon he was easily able to master the seven fundamental tones of the instrument. However, when he began to play a tune that had just come into his mind, the Gentle Fluter took the instrument out of his hand, saying, 'No, let that be. You must wait until I'm gone. That's enough for today. I must go and lie down for a little while, for I am very tired.'

Listener went to bed early that day, too. He was glad to be lying in a proper bed again, after so many nights in the open. As he fell asleep, he pictured himself returning to Fraglund, a fluter. His father would have to admit he had made good after all, and the Great Roarer would soon find out how useful it was to have such a fluter in the house, particularly if the Raiding Riders should fall upon that part of the countryside again. Listener saw himself riding at the head of the Great Roarer's fighting men, playing his flute in the face of the enemy. The men of Fraglund would be amazed to see the fierce Riders suddenly rein in their shaggy steeds and lower their weapons. But before he could add any more to this picture, Listener fell asleep, and did not wake until the sun shone in through his window next morning.

All was still quiet in the house. He went down to the kitchen, blew up the fire on the hearth, and put water to boil for tea. His grandfather was obviously not so frail that he couldn't keep the kitchen in order. Everything was in its place: bread, butter, honey, cheese, cups and plates, just as it had been in the days when his grandmother was mistress of the house. Listener laid the table, and the clatter of crockery woke his grandfather, who came in just as Listener was pouring the tea, brewed from dried herbs.

'Ah, I've missed that lately,' said the Gentle Fluter, 'the sound of pots and pans of a morning, the clink of cups and the fragrance of that tea spreading all through the house! Makes me feel more like getting up.' He glanced at the breakfast table, and added, 'I see you made a pretty useful servant.'

'And I hope to be a useful fluter too,' said Listener.

'Useful?' repeated his grandfather, as if that were quite the wrong word. 'I hope not, myself! You will not be required to make yourself useful – but you'll find that out soon enough. You can take your two mounts off to our friend at the inn after breakfast.'

An hour later, Listener was riding downstream through the green hills. He had saddled his donkey once more, for this would probably be the last time he ever felt his grey-coated friend beneath him, and he had Snowfoot on a leading rein. Yalf snorted and quickened his pace when they saw the inn appear beyond the last of the grass-grown slopes. A moment later, he broke into a gallop, and raced in through the gateway as if he couldn't wait to greet his foster-father. Listener brought him to a halt with some difficulty, and noticed, as he dismounted, that there were two horses and three mules tied up in the yard. The horses were harnessed after the fashion of the Raiding Riders, the mules wore pack saddles, and there were sacks and bales stacked up beside them by the stable wall. While he was still wondering what two solitary Riders could be after, so far from their horde, the door was opened, and the innkeeper came out into the yard. Before he could say a word, Yalf trotted up to him, pushed his head into his ribs so vigorously that the powerful man nearly lost his balance, and then pranced around him like a dog greeting his master after long absence.

'I thought it was you,' said the innkeeper, when Yalf had finished lavishing wet kisses upon him. 'I know only one donkey that comes galloping into my yard and sends the stones flying like that! Well, you hunter of wolves, we've heard fine tales of your brave deeds!' And he scratched Yalf's neck and then greeted Listener, who had been standing by, unheeded, thinking not for the first time that a donkey was valued at least as much as a man at this inn.

'And have you two been friends?' asked the innkeeper.

Listener nodded. 'You couldn't have found me a better travelling companion,' said he. 'Though I'm afraid that I am too heavy for him now, and it's time for us to part.'

'Just as well you see that for yourself,' said the innkeeper. 'But Yalf will be your friend as long as he lives, and I see you have a horse to ride now.'

'Barlo gave her to me at our parting,' said Listener. 'Her name is Snowfoot. Will you tend her for me while my grandfather teaches me to play the flute?'

'With all my heart,' said the innkeeper. 'It was about time you came back.'

Listener had thought he would be telling the innkeeper a startling piece of news when he mentioned the playing of the flute, but obviously it was no more than the man expected. He took both beasts by their bridles and led them to the stable. Listener went with him, and as they passed the other five animals tied up in the yard, he asked, 'What are Raiding Riders doing at your inn?'

'Raiding Riders?' asked the innkeeper, surprised. Then he said, 'Ah, you mean those two men of Arni's Folk stopping here.'

'What's the difference?' asked Listener. 'Aren't Arni's folk Raiding Riders these days?'

'They can tell you about that for themselves,' said the innkeeper. He unharnessed the two animals, and put fodder in front of them. 'A good feed of oats will do you no harm, after coming all this way,' said he. 'You'll stay the night here, Yalf. You can go up to your friends in the hills tomorrow.'

Listener embraced his donkey once again, and got Yalf's soft nose
pushed into his face in return. As he was turning to go, the innkeeper
said, 'Come into the house – I fancy you won't say no to a mug of
fermented ass's milk, eh?'

Listener certainly would not, and he was interested, too, to see what
kind of guests they were that called themselves Arni's Folk. He could
tell at first glance, as he stepped into the room, that the two men sitting
there over a jug of ass's milk were indeed Raiding Riders: there was no
mistaking their olive complexions, flat noses, and straggling black
hair. However, there was one difference: they did not plait their hair
into braids, but wore it cut so short that it only just covered their ears,
and they left it hanging straight.

'Here's a guest that'll be welcome to you,' said the innkeeper. 'His
name is Listener, and he's the Gentle Fluter's grandson.'

As soon as the two men heard who the newcomer was, they rose
from their seats and bowed to Listener, although they were both at
least ten years older than he was. 'Any member of the family of that
honourable man the Gentle Fluter is always welcome to us,' said one of
them. 'Will you do us the favour of sitting at our table? My name is
Gunli, and my friend here is called Orri. We belong to Arni's Folk.
You must forgive Orri if he does not talk much; he has yet to learn
your language, and means to do it on this journey.'

Listener was surprised to be greeted so deferentially by the two men,
and his curiosity about these Raiding Riders who wore no braids
increased. 'Thank you for your friendly invitation,' he said, 'and I will
be happy to join you, if I may.' The innkeeper brought him a tankard,
poured foaming ass's milk from the jug, and then drew up a stool for
himself as well.

'We are very glad to meet you,' said Gunli, having waited politely
for Listener to take the first sip from his tankard. 'For we mean to pay
your honourable grandfather a visit and assure him of our deep regard.
Do you think he will be inclined to receive us?'

Listener thought Gunli's manner of speech very strange. His foreign
accent, which showed that the speaker was used to expressing himself
in another language, increased the oddity of his courteous compliments.
'I'm sure my grandfather will be very pleased to see you,' said Listener.
'You can talk to him in the language of the Raiding Riders, too, for he
spent some time living in your tents.'

'We are not Raiding Riders, we are Arni's Folk,' said Gunli,
some coolness in his tone. 'We know, however, that the honour-

able Gentle Fluter rode with Arni – may his name be praised!'

Listener could restrain his curiosity no longer. 'Well, you must forgive my mistake in supposing you were Raiding Riders,' he said, 'but will you be kind enough to tell me just who Arni's Folk are?'

'You do a simple merchant great honour in asking him for instruction,' said Gunli. 'And it will be advantageous to us if you can tell the honourable Gentle Fluter about the humble people of Arni's Folk before we venture to come before his face. I take it, from what you say, that you know something of that incomparable man called Arni of the Stone.'

'My grandfather, and others too, have told me about him,' said Listener. 'He was the twin brother of your Khan Hunli.'

'Yes,' said Gunli, 'he was the brother of Hunli, whom the evil spirits have struck blind.'

'Blind?' asked Listener. 'Has he lost the sight of his eyes?'

Gunli smiled. 'There is a worse blindness than loss of one's eyesight,' said he. 'Hunli suffers from a blindness of the spirit that keeps him from understanding the wise words of Arni. He is not our Khan now, for we who call ourselves Arni's Folk have parted from him, and have cut off our braids as a sign that we are Raiding Riders no longer.'

'I have heard that Arni often went against his brother's will,' said Listener, 'but until now I thought he stood alone in the tents of the Raiding Riders.'

'So he did, for a long while,' said Gunli. 'No one could understand what Arni – honoured be his name! – had in mind when he sought hospitality from strange folk, or thwarted the Riders' raids. Some even thought him mad, and said Hunli should cast him out of the horde.'

'And why didn't he?' asked Listener.

'He could not,' said Gunli, 'for he had sworn an oath to do his brother no harm.'

'Yes,' said Listener, 'he swore it in Urla's presence.'

'So you know that too, O knowledgeable grandson of the honourable Gentle Fluter!' said Gunli. 'Yes, the great Urla – long may her wisdom last! – had bound him with an oath, for she had the gift of foresight. So Arni – may his name be praised! – still rode with the horde, but the meaning of his enlightened deeds remained hidden from our poor eyes until his death. He was shot from his saddle in an ambush, and died the death of a Raiding Rider, with an arrow in his breast. Hunli and many others in the horde seemed more relieved than otherwise when the dead man was found, but they gave Arni – may his name live for ever! – an honourable burial in the steppes, and raised a tall mound over his body.

Soon after his death, it so happened that strangers began coming to the land of the Raiding Riders to lay gifts on Arni's grave, folk from the Brown River among them, and people from the mountains, and from the wooded country to the west. Hunli let them have their way, for he would have brought shame upon himself if he had prevented the bringing of death offerings to his brother. Many of the Riders rode from their tents to the grave mound – may all men show it honour! – to see the strange gifts that had been laid there: finely made fishing nets, for instance, or a richly carved chair of honour such as one offers to a guest of great repute, or a bronze cauldron, its sides adorned with cunningly wrought pictures of the deeds of Arni. And those who visited Arni's grave mound said they had also found offerings there such as only Raiding Riders are accustomed to give their great leaders: harness decked with silver, say, or a precious tent of finest sheep's wool with a gilded tent-pole.'

'So there were men in the horde who honoured Arni's memory, after all,' said Listener.

'Yes,' said Gunli, 'and not a few, as one might see from their gifts. When Hunli heard of it, he said that after all it was the Khan's brother who was thus honoured, but one could tell he was angry from the way he chewed his moustache. He might have been expected to be the first to bring his brother such a gift, but he had not done so publicly, and there was no call for him to do it in secret.

Until now, no one knew which Riders of the horde had brought those gifts, but if Hunli had hoped that it would soon stop, he deceived himself, for once a beginning was made, such gifts were soon heaped so thickly on Arni's grave mound that they covered it to the very top.

At this time, some of the chieftains who had always been among the enemies of Arni – may their eyes at last be opened! – urged the calling of a great council. It was necessary for the unity of the horde, they said, to discover once and for all which men from the Riders' tents had an interest in thus keeping alive the memory of Arni – may it never be forgotten! And so that assembly which we now call the Parting of the Ways, or the Great Parting, was held. It took place in the open air, no tent being large enough to take all the men. When they were all sitting on the ground in a circle, Hunli stood up and made a speech. He said that in former times, to his own certain knowledge, all men had agreed that Arni's strange behaviour did the horde harm, and he reminded his hearers of all kinds of incidents that had given rise to this opinion. If anyone now thought otherwise, he went on, let him stand up and tell the council his reasons.

For a while everyone remained sitting there in silence, staring at the ground. Hunli looked around him, and his face grew visibly more content. But as he was just about to proceed, up stood Honi, one of the most important chieftains, and said it was he who had taken Arni the tent with the gilded pole as a death offering, and he could give excellent reasons why Arni deserved all possible honour.

'You are late in coming round to this view, Honi,' said Hunli, bitterly. 'I remember very well how you, like many others, condemned what Arni did.'

'I must admit you are right there,' said Honi, 'for at the time I did not understand what was in Arni's mind. His words, like his deeds, were of such a kind that you might hold them in your memory, but their meaning often could not be understood until later. I have now discovered that there is more pleasure in friendship with other peoples than in killing them for the sake of booty.'

Hunli laughed scornfully. 'So that's why you sent your slave women back to the huts of the Mud-biters!' said he. 'And I thought it was because you couldn't stand the fishy smell of them any more!'

'Some people smell of fish, some smell of the smoke of their smelting furnaces, and we smell of horses,' said Honi. 'And I have also learned from Arni's words that it is foolish to mock the way in which other folk differ from us. Don't you know that many people beyond the steppes think our braids ridiculous, because among them only the women wear their hair braided?'

'You address your Khan with little respect!' said Hunli, furiously. 'And what is more, your words show that you despise the ways of the horde. If this is supposed to be Arni's wisdom I don't want to hear any more of it, and you are offending my ears.'

But Honi was not to be deterred. 'I speak like this,' said he, 'because you asked us to say what we thought. And I don't despise the ways of the horde. But what seems familiar to us is far from all, as Arni used to say. I suppose he meant that there are other ways of living your life which are no worse. Perhaps there are even better ways, ways that we don't know yet. And he was looking for them all his life long.'

'Don't you see how you condemn yourself out of your own mouth?' cried Hunli. 'Is it not shameful for a grown man to begin changing his mind?' And so saying, he looked around the circle of his hearers for approval. Some of the men sitting there nodded agreement, but there were a good many who went on staring ahead of them, and did not move. Honi was not giving in, either. He looked Hunli in the face and said, 'If you can say that, I'm not surprised you don't understand Arni's wisdom. Isn't it yet more shameful not to change your mind when you know you have been wrong? I will tell you, Hunli, why I think Arni the greatest man the horde has ever known: he had the courage to set himself against all the Riders for the sake of what he thought was the truth, even at the risk of being despised for it by many.'

'Many?' said Hunli, scornfully. 'Almost all! Am I not right?'

At these words of Hunli's, Honi turned to the assembly and said, 'If there are any more men here who have found matter for thought in Arni's words and deeds, then let them stand up now.'

So far, everyone had been following the argument between Hunli and Honi intently, but upon being thus challenged the men looked at one another in dismay. For by now it was clear to them all that a decision was at hand which could not but affect the existence of the horde itself. After the death of Arni – may his memory live on! – I had often discussed these matters with Honi, and with others, and so learned to understand many of his words better, but even I stayed put at first, for it seemed to me an audacious thing to set oneself against the Khan. But then men began to stand up, one by one, some of my friends among them, and I knew that now was the time to bear witness to Arni's noble wisdom. So I stood up as well, and many more men rose to their feet with me. About one third of the horde went over to Honi at that assembly.

Hunli turned pale when he looked around him. 'So now you see what Arni has brought us to, Honi,' he said grimly. 'He has destroyed the unity of the horde. What else do you mean to do? Are we to fall upon one another like enemies?'

Honi shook his head. 'Don't you yet realize, Hunli,' he said, 'that it is pointless to settle differences of opinion with a dagger? It appears to me that you wasted your time in Urla's cabin. I will leave your camp today, and let every man who will follow Arni's way strike his tents and go with me.'

Hunli laughed mockingly. 'I thought as much,' said he. 'I thought you'd back out of a fight, since we outnumber you. And can you tell me what you're going to live on if there are to be no more raids?'

'Our own council will decide that, once we've pitched camp somewhere else,' said Honi. 'That's our business, and none of anyone else's.'

And so the Great Parting of the horde came about. Honi led us
away, seven days' ride, to the foot of the mountains and the spot where
Arni's house stands. Then we pitched camp. Honi thought the fact that
Arni had settled there – may his House never fall into ruin! – was a
kind of omen.'

'That's where the path up to Urla's hut in the mountains starts,' said
Listener eagerly.

'So it is,' said Gunli, surprised. 'Have you been there, then?'

'No,' said Listener, 'but one of Urla's family once told me about the
place.'

'If Urla's kin themselves have told you of these mysteries,' said
Gunli, in some awe, 'then you are truly a worthy grandson of that
honourable man the Gentle Fluter, may his flute never fall silent! Well,
so we pitched our tents at that spot, and next day Honi gathered
together all the men who had ridden with him, and we discussed the
future course of our lives. 'Arni, in his wisdom, built a cabin here,' said
Honi, 'and so I think that we too should build cottages for ourselves
and our families. Tents are the dwellings of Raiding Riders who go
from place to place in search of plunder. But as we don't intend to live
in that manner any more, it seems best if we take to other dwellings too,
and lay aside the name of Raiding Riders. All who are gathered here
shall be known as Arni's Folk in future. And so that everyone may see
we are no longer bent upon taking plunder by the sword, I suggest that
our menfolk cut off their braids and wear their hair smooth, like those
who used to fear us.'

We all thought this a good speech, but then one of the men stood up
and asked Honi what we were going to live on. 'I have thought of that,
and had thought of it, indeed, before Hunli asked me that same question,' said Honi. 'However, I believed it wrong to mention the matter
before those who were not coming with us. On our last few raids,
however, I kept my eyes well open, and saw how other folk got their
living. And I found two ways in which we can get our food, or even
make money. One of them is the breeding of livestock, a craft we have
always practised. Not only can we keep our horses here on the edge of
the steppes, we can pasture sheep on the grassy mountain slopes, as
Urla the wise did in her own day, may her spirit stand by us! And as
we are used to travelling through the lands of other peoples, we can go
trading too, nor need we confine our trade to the extra livestock we

raise. I have often found that many things are considered of less value
where they are made, or where they are found in abundance, than in
those places where there is a lack of them, or nobody knows how to
make them. A man travelling the countryside with a couple of packhorses can make a profit by this means without robbing anyone.'

When I heard these words I was very much relieved, for I had been
racking my brains, wondering what was to become of us. The others
praised Honi's wise foresight too, and urged him to become our Khan.
But Honi firmly refused. 'We will have no one man whose word is law,
not among Arni's Folk,' said he. 'We will consult together in all we do,
and remember Arni's words and deeds.' When he had said that, another
man rose and said, 'No one here remembers Arni's words better than
you do, Honi. If you will not be named Khan, then we will call you
Arni's Deputy, and after your death we will choose as your successor
whoever can interpret Arni's words the best.' As everyone agreed to
this proposal, Honi accepted the honour, and since then he has been
the leader of Arni's Folk.'

'My grandfather will be pleased to hear that you hold Arni's memory
in such honour,' said Listener.

'We do indeed,' agreed Gunli. 'His house is the centre of our settlement, and our elders meet to take counsel in the room where Arni used
to live. We keep all that remains to us of Arni there too – his dagger,
for instance, and his saddle. But the stone which he said led him along
his way disappeared at the time of his death, and we traders are
charged to look for it wherever we go.'

'You need look no longer,' said Listener. He opened his shirt, brought
out the little bag, and took the eye-stone out of it. The two traders
leaped up from their seats, staring at it as it lay in Listener's hand.
'Arni's stone!' they cried, both at once, and Gunli added, 'May it shine
for ever!'

Listener was surprised at the effect the mere sight of the stone had on
both men. 'If you had not met me here,' he said, 'my grandfather
could have told you where to find it.'

'How did it come into your possession?' asked Gunli.

'Arni gave it to me before he died,' said Listener, and he told them
how he had come by the stone. When he had finished his story, the two
men bowed low to him, and Gunli said, 'In you we venerate the
rightful inheritor of Arni's stone. I think it was not by chance we three
met here. He who follows in great Arni's footsteps will find his journey's
end. When we go home, we will tell them who now bears the stone,

and you will be no less honoured among Arni's Folk than Arni's Deputy himself. Should you ever feel inclined to visit our poor houses, you shall sit at Honi's side.'

'Do sit down again, please!' said Listener. 'You show me too much honour.' But all the same, he was impressed by the standing his stone gave him among Arni's Folk. Was this what Arni had been trying to tell him as he died? Was he to seek the light of fame, the glow of veneration? He would find both among Arni's Folk; had the dying man foreseen it? These traders seemed to think the dead man perfectly capable of seeing into the future. 'I must stay with my grandfather for the time being,' he said, 'since he is teaching me the art of playing the flute, but after that I'll be happy to accept your invitation.'

'You will be doubly welcome to us,' said Gunli, 'as bearer of the stone, and as grandson and pupil of the honourable Gentle Fluter.'

Soon afterwards Listener set off again, for it was nearly noon. Gunli and Orri bowed many times as they said goodbye, and Gunli punctiliously repeated his invitation to the houses of Arni's Folk, asking Listener once again to prepare his grandfather for their visit.

The innkeeper saw Listener on his way. 'What do you think of those two, then?' he asked as they went out through the gate. 'There used to be a saying: never trust a Raiding Rider within bowshot range! And no sooner do they cut their braids off than they're brimming over with good manners and pious remarks.'

Listener shrugged his shoulders. 'They changed their ways when they parted from the horde, that's all,' he said. 'And traders need good manners if they're going to do any business.'

The innkeeper laughed. 'You're right there,' said he. 'I dare say I'll have more such guests in future. Now that Barlo's driven the wolves away, the old trading road leading through the woods and mountains, from the river to Barlebogue, will be coming back into use. At least, Gunli told me he and his silent travelling companion are on their way to it. Well, I must turn back now. Give your grandfather my regards, and keep an eye on him, will you? He's not been looking too strong recently. And let me know if the pair of you need anything.'

After their mid-day meal, Listener told his grandfather about the two strange men at the inn. The Gentle Fluter listened attentively, cleaning his gold-rimmed eye-glasses with a little piece of leather. 'So obviously Arni didn't live in vain,' Listener finished.

'You may well be right,' said the Gentle Fluter, putting his eye-glasses on his nose again. 'Yet it's a strange thing that his own people won't

listen to such a man until he's dead. I expect he was an awkward kind
of fellow to have around when he was alive.'

'But they obey his words now, and isn't that the main thing?' asked
Listener.

The Gentle Fluter shook his head so vigorously that his eye-glasses
danced, and said, 'Who knows if they're really obeying his words or
not? Arni's not here now to contradict them if they interpret his sayings
as they themselves think right.'

'Is what Arni's Folk have done wrong, then?' asked Listener,
dismayed, for he had been quite carried away by what Gunli told him.

'I didn't say that,' said the Gentle Fluter, 'and I shan't say anything
of the sort to your two trader friends either. We won't be able to tell
until later. It's always easier to honour the dead than the living, though.
There are many who've laid a dead man's name around their shoulders,
to cloak themselves in its fame.'

'I'm sure you are doing Arni's Folk an injustice,' said Listener. 'And
they don't just honour the dead. They call you "the honourable Gentle
Fluter" yourself.'

Upon hearing this the Gentle Fluter laughed so much that his
shoulders shook and his eye-glasses slid down to the end of his nose. He
looked at Listener over the glasses and said, 'How surprised they'll be
to see what a doddering little old man I am now!' Then he straightened
his eye-glasses again, and added, 'It may be that there's still talk among
their people of a young vagabond who was Arni's friend for a while.
Their storytellers will have polished up the tale until he became a
figure worthy of honour, perhaps a kind of magician who did marvellous things, but what has that to do with me? Well, we've talked
enough now. Hand me the flute so that I can begin your next lesson.'

And so another afternoon passed with practising the fingering. 'Your
fingers must find the right holes on the flute so naturally that you don't
have to think how to play the note you need next,' said the Gentle
Fluter. And under his keen eye, Listener practised separate notes,
intervals and scales until evening. He was not allowed to play a con-
secutive melody that day either. At last the Gentle Fluter was tired,
and said, 'That'll do for today. I'm going to bed now. You know where
to find things in the kitchen if you want a bite to eat. I'm not hungry.
Sleep well, and don't dream too much!'

In the kitchen, Listener cut himself a slice of bread, spread it thickly
with butter and honey, followed it with an apple, and then went up to
the room which he had once shared with Barlo. He lay down on his

bed, but he was not sleepy yet, and lay wondering what he would do when he had finished learning the flute. So far, his ideas of the future had not gone much beyond his grandfather's house. Today, however, Gunli had shown him a goal to aim for. He thought it was no chance they met, he had said. And Listener was more and more inclined to believe him. Was it his stone that had led him to the meeting? It seemed to him, suddenly, as if he saw all that had happened in the past and all that would happen in the future in a new light, and he tried to imagine what way his life would take through this change in the course of events. And as he lay there on his bed, he closed his eyes, and his thoughts drifted into:

The Dream of Listener's Visit to Arni's Folk

He was riding his horse Snowfoot along the frontier between the mountainous forest and the steppes, for he knew that he would be sure to come upon the settlement of Arni's Folk somewhere in those parts. He had been travelling for many weeks through this inhospitable countryside, and he could no longer remember how many days ago it was that he ate his last piece of bread. He could keep in the saddle only with difficulty, and he desperately searched the horizon for the smoke from the houses of Arni's Folk. The sun was already sinking in the west behind the wooded slopes of the mountain range. In his desperation he took out his silver flute, put it to his lips, and called for help:

> *Come hither, come hither,*
> *wherever you be,*
> *from steppes, wood or river*
> *come hither to me.*
> *Blackbird or toad*
> *or donkey grey,*
> *turn from your road*
> *and come my way,*
> *for the stone I bear, and the flute I play.*

When he took the flute from his mouth, he heard three familiar notes in answer, right above his head. Looking up, he saw the blackbird sitting on the lowest branch of a birch tree. 'Lost your way again?' said the bird. 'I can't help you, here in this strange land. I always knew what way to go to find your grandfather's house, but you don't want to go there now, for you have other things in mind.'

'Won't you help me, then?' asked Listener.

'I can't,' said the blackbird. 'It will soon be dark, and I'm afraid of the night. I'm off to look for a place to sleep up on a high branch. You just ride on, and you're sure to get somewhere.' And whistling those three notes again, the bird flew away to the woods, and disappeared in the darkness of the tree-tops.

So Listener urged his horse on, and rode down the path between the steppes and the mountain slopes until the last of the red sunset glow faded above the trees. Darkness covered the sky, and he did not know if it was night falling, or if his weakness made all black before his eyes. He reined in his horse again, and called for help a second time:

> *Come hither, come hither,*
> *wherever you be,*
> *from steppes, wood or river*
> *come hither to me,*
> *No bird, but the toad*
> *or donkey grey,*
> *turn from your road*
> *and come my way,*
> *for the stone I bear, and the flute I play.*

No sooner had he finished playing than he heard a rustling in the bushes near Snowfoot's hooves, and the toad came crawling out. 'At your wits' end, are you, Listener?' said she, chuckling. 'Calling for help in so pitiful a way! I thought you were going to do something standing on your own two feet. Does a little hunger discourage you, then? You'll have to endure much worse than that if you wish to find what you are looking for.'

'Won't you help me, then?' asked Listener.

'I can't,' said the toad. 'How should I know what you're after? Anyway, I crawl much too slowly to fetch you any help. You'll have to rely on that horse of yours. Ride on! You're sure to get somewhere.' And the toad looked at him once more with her beautiful golden eyes, and then shook her head and crawled slowly away.

Listener watched until she had disappeared among the broad coltsfoot leaves by the wayside.

When he let his horse move on at a walking pace, he could scarcely make out the path before them. To the east reached the boundless steppes, merging with the black night sky. Listener stared into the darkness, trying to make out a light somewhere, or the flickering of a fire, but everything swam before his eyes. Were those stars shooting across the sky or circling in his brain? Dizziness came over him, and he swayed and slipped out of his saddle. Snowfoot stopped and stood beside him, her soft-breathing nostrils nuzzling his face. With the last of his strength, Listener put his flute to his lips once again, and called for help a third time:

> *Come hither, come hither,*
> *wherever you be,*
> *from steppes, wood or river*
> *come hither to me.*
> *No bird, no toad,*
> *but my donkey grey,*
> *turn from your road*
> *and come my way,*
> *for the stone I bear, and the flute I play.*

And then he heard the sound of hoofbeats mingling with the last notes of the flute, hoofbeats coming towards him from the steppes. Listener opened his eyes, and saw his donkey racing up at the gallop. He took a great leap and jumped the last few bushes, and then stopped short so abruptly that Snowfoot shied sideways in alarm.

'So there you are at last, Yalf,' said Listener. 'Will you refuse to help me too?'

Yalf uttered a piercing bray, and sang:

> *I come, I come*
> *to bring you aid,*
> *before the sun*
> *drives out night's shade.*
> *When he hears your plea*
> *your donkey grey,*
> *wherever he be,*
> *will come your way,*
> *for the stone you bear, and the flute you play.*

'Good,' said Listener. 'Then run to find Arni's Folk, or I shall die of starvation here.'

Yalf nodded three times, to show he understood, and raced away as fast as he had come. The sound of his hoofbeats rapidly receded, dying away in the distance. Listener let himself sink into the grass, closed his eyes, and listened to the sounds of the night. He heard the wind that whistled through the dry grass of the steppes, and then rustled in the leaves of trees on the outskirts of the forest: a high singing, sighing sound, and then a deep rushing and a roaring. It was like a conversation between men's and women's voices. The longer he listened, indeed, the more clearly he thought he heard voices, and gradually it seemed he could make out the words too. 'Here lies a man who rode the wrong way and became bemused,' sang the voices from the steppes. 'Do you know who he is?' And the voices from the forest answered, 'He was impatient to be on his way, but he will never endure it out there, where trees roar in the storm tonight.' And the high voices of the wind on the steppes came again, 'Will he find help before the stars vanish from the sky?' To which the forest answered, 'Men are on their way, men of Arni's Folk. They are catching horses, filling their saddle-bags, racing, racing through the land.'

When Listener heard that, he took heart. He sat up, but there was still no sound to be heard but the roaring and the singing of the wind, and again the steppe wind sang, 'Will this lost traveller know that it is no use to bear the stone if he forgets the way to use it?' And the leaves of the forest roared back, 'If he listens to what is outside him, and looks into the eyes, the magic will fail, but the terrible wolves are after him.'

As he was still wondering what these strange words might mean, he saw swaying lights appear along the steppes, coming closer to him. And then he heard the hollow beat of hooves, headed by Yalf's as he galloped on ahead, sweeping over the steppes like a grey shadow and uttering his hoarse bray to let the riders following him know they were nearly at the place. Yalf stopped at Listener's side and nudged him with his nose, as if to see if his friend were still alive. When Listener scratched the donkey's forehead Yalf snorted, satisfied. Next moment the riders came galloping up too. They leaped off their horses and strode over to Listener, storm lanterns held aloft. There were three of them: men dressed like Raiding Riders, but their hair was not worn in braids.

'Arni's Folk,' said Listener, relieved.

'Yes, we are Arni's Folk,' said the eldest of the three, a lean, grey-haired man, with a thin moustache whose long ends drooped over the corners of his mouth. 'Were you looking for us?'

'I have been looking for you so long that I almost perished on the way,' said Listener.

The old man signed to one of his companions, who handed him a round flask about the size of an apple. 'Take a drink of this,' the old man told Listener. 'It will revive your strength.'

Listener set the flask to his lips and tasted its contents. The liquor had a sour-sweet flavour, tingled slightly in his mouth, and flowed thick as honey down his throat. He took a good gulp of it, and immediately felt wonderfully refreshed; his hunger and thirst were both satisfied, and new strength came back into his limbs.

'Will you be able to ride?' asked the old man. 'It isn't far.'

Listener tried to stand up, and to his surprise he felt perfectly recovered. 'After drinking that, I could ride anywhere,' he said.

The old man smiled. 'You may feel you can,' said he, 'but in an hour's time weariness will suddenly overcome you again, and then you will sleep for a long while. However, we shall be home well before then.'

'Thank you for coming to my aid,' said Listener. 'You will want to know who I am, and what brings me to you.'

'Not now,' said the old man. 'There'll be plenty of time for that later, when you have slept. It is our custom not to speak with a guest until he has eaten and slept his fill. So mount your horse and come with us, or the weariness may overcome you before we are home.'

Feeling as much refreshed as he now did, Listener thought poorly of this custom. He would have liked to see his host's surprise on learning that the bearer of the stone stood before him. But he consoled himself with the thought that he would surely be able to enjoy that moment at some other time, and he swung himself up on his horse.

As they rode slowly along between the steppes and the forest, Listener heard the wind whispering in the tall, dry grass again. 'Soon he will be at his journey's end,' cried its voice, and the wind moving in the foliage of the tall trees on the left-hand side of the path rustled back, 'So he thinks, too, but the wolves are close on his trail.'

Then the wind died down, and they rode on through the night. The rounded shapes of bushes stood out in the light of the storm lanterns, looming up out of the darkness like shapeless beasts and sinking back again beyond the limits of the flickering circle of light. Then, farther on along the path, the square outlines of houses appeared, brightly lit windows welcomed the riders home, and the smoke of wood fires hung in the cool night air. The old man reined in his horse outside a house of some size, and said, 'We are home. Dismount, come in, and be my guest!'

Listener let himself slip from his horse. As he went to the door, he felt a pleasant weariness in his limbs. Once he was inside, a woman took his arm and led him straight to a bed. Already half asleep, Listener allowed her to help him undress. Then she told him to lie down and spread a woollen blanket over him. What strange eyes this woman has, thought Listener, as his own lids closed. And he felt as if he were plunging into a bottomless pit, down into ever deeper darkness, but those eyes stood high above him, two infinitely distant stars in the night sky, and his headlong fall held no terrors beneath that double star.

When he woke, the evening sun was low in the sky above the forest, casting a slanting beam of light into the room. Listener sat up, and at the same moment the woman who had put him to bed rose from a cushion near the door and hurried out. Had she been watching over him all the time? In a little while she came back, put a bowl of steaming soup on an intricately woven mat on the floor, and placed some freshly baked little rolls of wheaten bread beside it. Then she looked at him, saying, 'Get up now, and eat!'

Once again Listener noticed her eyes. He felt as if he had seen them somewhere else. However, before he could ask if they had ever met, the woman hurried out of the room again. He rose, dressed, and sat on one of the leather cushions that surrounded the mat. The bowl contained a good hearty meat broth with all kinds of vegetables in it. Listener breathed in its delicious aroma, and slowly began to eat. Warmth spread through his body at every spoonful, filling him with a sense of well-being. At last the bowl was empty, and Listener cleaned it out with a piece of bread. Then he rose to his feet and looked out of the window. To his left, the wooded range of foothills reached to the horizon, and to his right the wide steppes shone in the evening sunlight like a carpet of golden silk. A little way off, grazing horses walked slowly through the tall grass. Listener saw them bending their necks and whisking flies away with their tails. Then the door behind him opened. He turned and looked at the man who came through it, an unusually tall man, and strong in spite of his white hair. He was followed by the old man who had found Listener in the night.

'I am Honi, Arni's Deputy,' said the white-haired man. 'Vanli here has told me you were on the way to our settlement when your strength failed you. I hope you feel rested now, and are not hungry any more.'

'Your people have looked after me very well,' said Listener. 'I must have slept a whole day.'

The hint of a smile touched the corners of Honi's mouth. 'A day?' he said. 'Almost three! But that was only to be expected after the drink Vanli gave you to get you on your feet again. Do you feel strong enough for conversation now?'

'I feel so strong that I could ride on again directly, if I had not reached my journey's end!' said Listener.

'Then sit down, and let us talk,' said Honi. He waited until his guest was sitting on one of the cushions, then chose another for himself, and signed to Vanli to sit down with them. 'You say you have reached your journey's end,' he began, careful to ask no discourteously direct questions.

'Yes,' said Listener. 'I was on my way to the houses of Arni's Folk.' And as if to explain his intention, he added, 'My name is Listener.'

When he heard that name, Honi raised his head and said, 'My premonition, then, has come about. You are the grandson of the honourable Gentle Fluter, son of the Great Roarer and, as we are told, the man chosen to bear the stone by Arni – may his name be praised until the end of time!'

Instead of answering, Listener opened the bag he wore on his breast and showed the stone. The two old men rose from their cushions and bowed deeply, without taking their gaze off the eye-stone.

'We bow in veneration of the secret of Arni, which we were so late to recognize,' said Honi. 'But we also bow to you, for Arni – may his wisdom never be doubted! – has chosen you to be his heir.'

Listener was enjoying the situation. After all, this was Arni's Deputy in person bowing to him, not any chance-met traveller like Gunli, in whom such behaviour could have been taken for the humble courtesy of a trader. Here, among Arni's Folk, he would not be just anyone – servant of a wandering minstrel, for instance, or a young man mocked even by toads for not knowing what he wanted. He counted for something here, and not just because he had a famous grandfather either. He feasted his eyes a little longer on those two bent heads, the white and the grey, and then said, 'I would be glad if you'd sit down again. It is easier to talk sitting.'

'Not while we see Arni's secret unveiled before our eyes,' said Honi. 'The sight of it commands respect.'

So Listener put his stone back in its bag and then asked the two men to sit down. 'Now I know,' he said, 'that I have truly reached my journey's end, for I mean to stay with you.'

'This is a joyful day for all of us,' said Honi, and his face showed that he meant what he said. 'We have hoped for your coming ever since Gunli told us about you, and when your donkey raced braying into our settlement three days ago, struck the door of Arni's cabin with his hooves and tugged at the halters of the riding horses with his mouth, I guessed whom we were to fetch, for Gunli had said you were friendly with a donkey named Yalf.' When he had said that, he whispered something to Vanli, and Vanli rose and went out.

'Do you know where Yalf is now?' asked Listener.

'No,' said Honi. 'Vanli said he galloped off into the night as soon as you were found, and did not come back. However, your horse has been well tended and is now in my own stable. You will have to stay with me until we have built you a house of your own.'

As he was speaking, they heard sounds outside, a murmur of voices becoming louder and louder, as if a great crowd of people were gathering. Listener saw men hurrying past the window, singly and in groups, and many of them glanced at the house where he was sitting with Honi. Noticing the direction of Listener's gaze, Honi said, 'I have called an assembly outside Arni's House for this evening, so that everyone may know who has come to us.'

'Must I speak to the people?' asked Listener, not much liking this idea. Once again the corners of Honi's mouth twitched, as if to suppress a smile. 'It will be enough if you let them see you, to begin with,' he said, and stood up. 'Come, let us go out.' He stood aside for Listener to precede him, and as soon as they came out of the door the people all stopped talking and stared in silence. Listener looked around. He was in a circular space surrounded by sturdily built log cabins, and one cabin, grey with age, made of roughly hewn tree trunks, stood in the middle. More than a hundred men had gathered here, men wearing the leather clothing of Raiding Riders, but with smooth, unbraided hair.

Honi laid his right hand on Listener's shoulder and led him down the alley formed as the men stepped respectfully aside. They went to the door of Arni's House. Here, Honi turned to the assembly, still holding Listener's shoulder in a firm grip, so that he was standing on Honi's right. Listener had never had so many eyes directed on him before, and if he had been required to say anything now he could not have uttered a word. He was glad when this moment of silence was over, and Honi began to speak. 'For three days,' he said, 'we have had a guest among us. He rode here from far away, and has suffered great privations to come and live with us. He seems like a stranger, and yet is one of Arni's Folk. He is Listener, the Bearer of Arni's Stone.'

Now the murmur of voices rose like the rushing in the tree-tops as a sudden gust of wind blows through them. Listener felt Honi's hand propelling him forward, and looked over the heads of the assembled men to the house where he had slept for three days. The woman who had watched over him was just coming out of the door. She looked back at him. Despite the distance between them, he felt her eyes on him as if they were directly before his face, those eyes which seemed to be trying to rouse some memory within him, a memory which still remained buried.

As he was staring at the woman, feeling incapable of taking his eyes off her, he heard Honi behind him, whispering, 'Show them the stone!' As if compelled, Listener reached for the bag, took out the stone and held it aloft so that it caught the last rays of the setting sun, which made the circle of its own rays shine in glowing hues. All at once the men fell silent, staring spellbound at the sparkling play of colour. Their eyes were full of admiration, indeed veneration for the stone, and for its bearer, chosen to keep the jewel. Listener thought he could read all this quite clearly in the men's faces. Possession of the stone raised him high above the people of Arni's Folk, and this was the gift Arni had meant to give him. His time of service and aimless wandering was over for ever. He looked over the crowd to the woman, to see that veneration in her eyes too, but all he saw was that she had turned her back on him, and was slowly walking away past the houses. For a moment he was tempted to run after her, but then he realized how unseemly it would be to disturb so solemn an assembly on account of a woman, who had nothing to do with such matters. After all, this was men's business. And a moment later, in any case, he could not have moved from the spot, for Arni's Folk came crowding up from all sides, and began calling out his name, louder and louder: Listener, Listener, Listener!

* * *

Those loud cries were still ringing in his ears when he opened his eyes and found himself back in his bed. It must have been the rustling of the trees outside his window that had woken him. Great gusts of wind were tossing the leaves of the old lime trees, and in the distance, flashes of lightning lit up the sky, casting the shadows of lashing branches on the whitewashed wall of the room. Or were they the men still raising their arms in greeting, swaying shadows with gnarled fingers that seemed to be reaching for him? He closed his eyes, and once again felt uplifted by the veneration Arni's Folk accorded him. Yet there had been something or other that marred the sublimity of that moment, some lurking uncertainty, some unfulfilled expectation, although he could not remember just what had cast a shadow over the glory of the dream. The longer he thought about it, the vaguer became the images he was trying to hold fast. Finally none of the dream was left but the rushing noise of trees in the wind that lulled him back to sleep.

It was raining next morning. Water dripped off the leaves of the lime trees, and the branches were black with moisture. After breakfast Listener reminded his grandfather of the visit that the traders who called themselves Arni's Folk were going to pay him.

'Fetch a flagon of rowanberry spirits from the cellar,' said the Gentle Fluter. 'One should offer travellers something warming to fortify them in such weather.' He told Listener where to find the flagon, and Listener went through the trapdoor in the kitchen floor with a lighted candle, and climbed down the ladder leading to the cellar beneath the house. The uncertain candlelight flickered over shelves holding rows of earthenware pots, and all manner of flasks and flagons both great and small. Each jar or flask had a parchment label describing its contents, some of them written in a clumsy, wandering hand that was probably Grandmother's, for those labels indicated things to eat – blackberry jam, quince jelly, honey, lard – or things to drink, bottles of perry or cider.

Farther back on the shelves stood some little flasks whose labels were written in delicate, spidery letters, which Listener took to be his grandfather's handwriting. 'Spirits of masterwort, bitter to the tongue but kind to the stomach,' read one, and the flagon next to it was labelled, 'Spirits of rowanberry, reviving to the mind and warming to the limbs.' This was the one he was looking for. But before he took the flagon from its shelf, he fell to wondering what other fortifying liquors his grandfather kept here. He found an extract of arnica flowers, labelled, 'Cools contusions and heals wounds,' and the next flagon bore the legend:

> *Gentian root,*
> *Centaury too,*
> *Drink it down fast –*
> *Bitter the brew.*

Listener was about to turn back again when the light of his candle fell on three small flasks the size of apples, which were hidden behind the others. He pushed the flagon of gentian and centaury bitters aside, and raised his light. The writing on the labels of these three flasks was faded, and the letters were strangely formed. Listener took one of them off the shelf, held it close to his candle, and read:

> *One drop:*
> *sweet dreams for a night*
> *and never again.*
> *Two drops:*
> *fall into the depths,*
> *again and again.*
> *Three drops:*
> *death and forgetting*
> *for ever.*

He shuddered, and quickly put the flask back in its place. This was no liquor to offer one's guests. But although he had a feeling he was doing something not permitted, he could not resist reading the writing on the next little flask as well. It ran:

> *Strength for an hour,*
> *sleep for three days.*
> *Be sure, be sure,*
> *to come home fast.*

Listener was puzzled. Had he not heard something of the sort before? There was a voice still ringing in his ears, telling him, 'Come with us, or the weariness may overcome you before we are home.' It was a man who had spoken those words. But when, and where? His memory of it was vague, and would not be grasped. As he still stood there, wondering about it, he heard the Gentle Fluter calling from above, 'Can't you see the flagon?'

Listener jumped. 'Yes, I've just found it,' he called back, hastily returning the little flask to its place and putting the larger one, containing gentian and centaury bitters, back in front of it, though not without casting a glance at the label on the third of those mysterious little bottles. But the writing on that one was so faded that he could not make it out at all. He took the flagon of rowanberry spirits from the shelf and climbed up to the kitchen again.

'That took you a long time,' remarked the Gentle Fluter.

Listener shrugged his shoulders. 'There's a lot of stuff down there . . .' he said vaguely.

His grandfather gave him a sharp look. 'Poked around a bit, did you?' he asked.

Listener flushed. 'Well, I had to read the labels to find the right one,' he said defensively.

'And a number of them are hard to decipher,' said the Gentle Fluter, smiling. Then, becoming grave again, he added, 'I fear there are some things down there which should stay hidden in the darkness of a cellar.'

Before Listener could think of any answer to that, the blackbird came flying in through the window, settled on the Gentle Fluter's shoulder and whistled something in his ear. He bent his head to hear the bird better, and said, 'Thank you for your news, little friend. Our guests are on their way,' he added, when Listener looked inquiringly at him. 'Fetch four of the little tin beakers from the dresser, will you? And put them and the flagon on the living-room table.'

In a moment they heard hoofbeats and the jingle of harness outside. The Gentle Fluter went to the door of his house and opened it, to welcome his guests on the threshold. As soon as the two traders set eyes on him, they jumped off their horses, stood just where they were in the rain, although they were still a dozen paces from the house, swept their fur caps off their heads and bowed so low that their unbraided hair hid their faces.

The Gentle Fluter observed them with some surprise, and the laughter lines at the corners of his eyes began to crinkle up slightly. 'If you mean to visit an old man, then don't just stand there! Come into my house and be my guests,' he called. At that both men stood up, led their horses to the house, and tied them to one of the lime trees. Then they came back to the Gentle Fluter, and when they had bowed again, Gunli spoke. 'You show great favour to two humble traders of Arni's Folk, most honourable one, by inviting them into your house as guests,' he said.

'Oh, never mind that!' said the Gentle Fluter. 'Don't make such a fuss about it – come in! You're wet enough already.'

In spite of this second invitation, however, the courteous visitors stood very much on ceremony, and handed the Gentle Fluter their presents as soon as they were inside his door, with many more bows and tokens of respect. The presents were a silken rug, most exquisitely worked, and a set of chessmen made of milky white mountain crystal and smoky quartz of a deep honey colour. 'May it ever remind you of the wisdom of Arni, who foresaw the ways of mankind as a good chess-player foresees the moves of the chessmen,' said Gunli.

'Did he, though?' remarked the Gentle Fluter. 'Well, he was a good chess-player, at any rate, and fooled many an opponent!'

The traders seemed rather taken aback by their host's comment, which obviously struck them as disrespectful, but when he asked them to come in for the third time, they were at last persuaded to enter the house, go into the living-room, and when pressed, to sit down at the table, although not until the Gentle Fluter had taken a seat himself. He filled the four tin beakers with rowanberry spirits, saying, 'Take a sip of this to warm yourselves up!'

Without turning a hair, Gunli and Orri drank down the strong liquor as if it were water. Thus encouraged, Listener took a good gulp from his own beaker. The spirits went down his throat like molten lead, and instantly exploded fierily in his stomach. For a moment he felt as if someone had stabbed him with a red-hot knife, but then the fierce heat abated, spreading through his whole body in pleasurable waves. Listener breathed deeply and tried to follow the others' conversation; their first few sentences had reached his ears only as a distant rushing sound. Gunli and Orri were perched on the edges of their chairs, as if ready to leap up at any moment and offer the Gentle Fluter further proof of their respect. 'O honourable one,' Gunli was saying, bowing again as he addressed his host, 'many tales are told in our poor houses of your friendship with Arni, may he ever be the friend of us all.'

The Gentle Fluter chuckled quietly. 'I can well imagine what kind of tales your storytellers have made up!' said he. But Gunli was not to be discouraged, and continued, 'Your modesty shows your noble nature, O honourable one. However, our storytellers invent nothing. They faithfully preserve the words of Arni, so that they shall never be forgotten, for the life of our community is founded on them. Moreover, they are constantly at work collecting tales of Arni's noble deeds, and Arni's Deputy has given us traders the task of inquiring for such tales on our travels.'

'Ah! It sounds as if we're coming to the point now,' said the Gentle Fluter. 'I must say, all these respectful compliments were starting to make me feel uncomfortable! But I see you trade in stories too, and would like to get some from me.'

Gunli shook his head, seeming embarrassed and upset by this interpretation of his carefully chosen words. 'You misunderstand me, honourable one!' said he. 'I will admit that I entered your well-built house in the hope of hearing from your lips an account of events from

Arni's life as yet unknown to us. This wish, however, has nothing to do with my business, but springs from my desire to probe ever deeper into the wisdom of Arni, which our little minds can never quite encompass. Consider us your pupils, humbly requesting instruction!' With which words he half rose from the edge of his chair, and bowed. Orri, who was trying to follow the conversation without actually grasping much of it, started up too, carefully imitating every move his companion made.

'Oh, do sit down, for goodness' sake, and have another drink!' said the Gentle Fluter, filling the beakers again. 'Drink up, and meanwhile I may think of some suitable story worth passing on to your people.'

The two traders sat down again, picked up their beakers, and emptied them at a single draught, like obedient children told to drink up their milk. The Gentle Fluter only sipped at his. Listener, more cautious now, did the same. He felt the rowanberry spirits warming the cavity of his mouth, and this time he liked the flavour of the strong liquor better. By now the Gentle Fluter seemed to have thought of a tale, for he cleared his throat and said, 'Well, here's a story which I don't expect you know, for it happened when the horde was in winter quarters and Arni had ridden up into the mountains alone to visit his daughters, who, as you'll remember, were living in their grandfather's house with the folk known as the Mountain Badgers. One of them, Rikka, is now married to Furro the blacksmith, and stayed for a while with mine host who keeps the donkeys, and she told me this tale.

She was twelve years old at the time, she said, and in those days the Bloodaxe People were making the mountains perilous. I don't know if you've ever heard of them – a rapacious lot, they are, very ready to make use of their narrow axes, except for chopping wood. They live farther to the north, but at that period they would come over the passes and down into the valleys from time to time, attacking small villages or robbing tradesmen. The Mountain Badgers, Rikka said, could always keep their children at home by warning them not to go into the woods alone or the Bloodaxe People would get them. She was told the same, too, when she wanted to go to the next village by herself. It was a good hour's walk farther down the valley, and a fair was being held there that week. On hearing that all manner of jugglers were to perform among the stalls at this fair, and there was even going to be a conjuror who could do the most wonderful things, she begged her grandfather to take her, but he had no time for such tomfoolery, as he put it. 'Then let me go alone,' she asked him. However, her grandfather repeated that saying about the Bloodaxe People, and turned back to hammering the red-hot metal on his anvil. Rikka, however, wasn't to be so easily deterred, and she ran off without his permission, for she felt as if she would be missing the most wonderful thing in her life if she couldn't see those jugglers perform. It was still early in the morning when she set out, and she told herself she could be back home before anyone started looking for her, in time for the mid-day meal.

At this point in her story Rikka paused, and when I looked into her eyes I saw horror come into them, horror of that far distant memory. 'So the Bloodaxe People did come,' I said. 'Yes,' she said, staring past me into space as if she saw it all again, and then she told me what had happened. There was a place about half-way between the two villages where the path leads through the bushes that run down to the stream at that point, and a great red-headed fellow jumped out from behind a tree, seized her by the hair and covered her mouth with his other hand. 'I can still remember the feel of his fingers on my tongue,' said Rikka. 'They tasted of sweat and smoked bacon.' He dragged Rikka into the shade of the trees, where five other men stood, all wearing fur-lined leather jackets like his own. Their red hair was knotted up above their ears, and each of them carried an axe with a narrow blade at his belt. So then Rikka knew into whose hands she had fallen.

One of them looked at her as if she were a beetle he was just about to crush, and he drew the side of his hand across his throat. They're going to cut my throat, thought Rikka, but the other man, the one who had seized her and still had his hand over her mouth, shook his head, said a couple of quiet words, and pointed to her clothes. Hoping to go to the fair, she had dressed in her best skirt that morning, and was wearing a silver chain with an amethyst pendant which her great-grandfather had made. It probably saved her life, for as it later turned out, the men took her for a girl from a prosperous family, who would bring them a good ransom. However, she didn't know that at the time, since she couldn't understand their language, and she was trembling all over in mortal terror. The man holding her now took a dirty cloth out of his pocket and gagged her with it. Then he pushed Rikka down on the ground and tied her hands and feet with a leather strap. So they don't mean to kill me at once, she thought, as she lay among the bracken, with the harsh pine needles pricking her arms and legs. From this vantage point, she could see all that happened next.

The men took no more notice of her. They were loosening the axes at their belts and looking down the path. Three of them crossed it and hid in the bushes on the other side. For a while there was nothing to be heard but the murmur of the stream, flowing down below. Then she heard footsteps, and caught the occasional sound of men's voices coming along the path from Arziak. They must be a party of prospectors on their way to the fair to sell uncut gems to the traders there, and now she knew what the Bloodaxe People had in mind. I must warn the prospectors, thought Rikka, trying to get the stinking gag out of her mouth or wriggle her feet free. But the man who had tied her up knew what he was about, so she had to watch helplessly as the prospectors came laughing and chattering down the path, guessing nothing of the danger ahead. As they came in among the trunks of the trees, Rikka could count them. There were eight men, each carrying a well-filled leather bag.

Now the men lying in wait took their axes from their belts, and when the prospectors on their way to the fair were level with them, one of the red-haired fellows let out a piercing cry. Then they all leaped out of hiding at the same moment, on both sides of the path, and Rikka had to watch as they showed how they got their name. The prospectors were all butchered before they realized what was happening to them. Their red-headed murderers wasted no time, but cut the leather bags from the dead men's belts and hurried back into the woods again. The huge fellow who had caught Rikka picked her up with one hand and threw her over his shoulder like an empty sack. Then he strode off through the thickets with her, branches whipping about her ears. They had left their horses deeper in the wood, and now they mounted them and galloped up a narrow pathway into the mountains. Rikka just had time to feel the Bloodaxe man laying her across his saddlebow and galloping off, and then she fainted away with fear and pain.

Rikka could tell me the tale thus far from her own memory. Later, she learned what had been happening at home. Her father Arni, she said, had unexpectedly arrived at her grandfather's smithy to visit his daughters that very morning, just after she ran away. Her sister Akka had come running as soon as she heard their father's voice, but nobody had been able to find Rikka. Then her grandfather began to suspect that she might have gone to the fair in spite of him. When Arni heard that, he got on his horse and rode down the valley to look for her. He came upon the murdered prospectors, and knew at once who had done the deed. He also found the trail of the Bloodaxe People leading back into the wood, and following it, he picked up the silver chain with the amethyst. It had been torn from Rikka's neck accidentally as her kidnapper hastily rode away. Now Arni knew that the Bloodaxe People had his daughter, and he went after them. Later, when folk wondered at his courage in following six armed men all alone, he said only that at the time he could think of nothing but his child in the hands of those murderous men.

He did not catch up with them, for they had been riding fast, and he had to keep dismounting and examining the ground so as not to lose their trail. That was probably lucky for him; no doubt the men would have killed him out of hand if he had tried to stop them. So he went on, higher and higher into the mountains, until he had left the trees behind him. Snow was lying on the upland meadows, clearly showing the tracks of the horses' hooves. Arni could tell that the kidnappers had crossed the pass, and he had to abandon any hope of catching up with them before they reached their homes. As his horse made its weary way up the steep slope, his quarry might well be riding fast down the other side of the mountain. At this point, as he later told the tale, he began to make his plan. On his long rides through the countryside beyond the steppes he had learned something about the customs of the Bloodaxe People. Cruel and rapacious as they were when they fell upon the valley folk, they too observed the laws of hospitality in their own log cabins. A stranger asking shelter for the night need not fear for his life, though he was safe only for a day, and even then only if there was no danger that he had come to take revenge for some violent act on the part of his hosts. You may well imagine that, in these circumstances, the Bloodaxe People did not often get the chance to entertain guests. But Arni was ready to take the risks involved. He also knew that they were said to be passionately fond of games and contests, outdoing even the Raiding Riders in that respect. He based his plan on this fact.

When he approached their cabins, the sun was already sinking to the horizon. The village of the Bloodaxe People lay in a little upland valley, beside a lake fed by the water of the torrential mountain stream along which Arni had ridden on his way over the high pass. He was seen before he came within hailing distance of the cabins. One of the gigantic red-haired men came out of his door, looked up at Arni, and then called something back into the log cabin. Immediately afterwards two other men came out, and the three of them began walking towards Arni together. He had brought his horse to a halt, and dismounted. The three men stopped a few paces away from him, looking at him suspiciously. Then the one who had first seen him spoke up, saying, in

the language of the Raiding Riders, 'What's your business with us here
in the mountains, wolf of the steppes?'

'I've a fancy to try what the air is like, so high above those steppes,'
said Arni. 'Will you give me shelter for the night?'

'Maybe, if you don't find our air too thin for you,' said the red-
haired man. 'But you must know that you can be our guest for one
day, and no more.'

'I didn't intend to be a burden upon you any longer,' said Arni.

The red-haired man grinned broadly. 'Very well advised of you!'
said he. 'But I must ask you another question too: have we ever killed
any of your kin?'

'Not that I know of,' said Arni. 'Or have you been fighting the
Raiding Riders lately?'

'We hunt in the mountains, and you hunt on the steppes,' said the
red-haired man. 'It would be foolish for us to fight each other. Be our
guest! I will take you to Skullcleaver's house. He is our chieftain, and
will give you shelter, as the custom is.'

One of the men took Arni's horse by the bridle, led it into the
village, and took it to a stable, while the other two went with their
guest to a large log cabin built on a platform of stone slabs almost as
high as a man and standing in the middle of the village. The man who
had done the talking was the first to go in, telling Arni to follow. The
other man stayed outside.

Arni had to grope his way along a dark, narrow corridor built of
stone, turning two corners. Only when he was round the second corner
did any light come through the door his companion had opened at the
far end of the passage and fall on the rough masonry. It wouldn't be easy
for an uninvited guest to make his way into such a house, said Arni,
when he was telling his part of the story. The Bloodaxe People were
cautious folk, and no doubt had very good reason for their caution.

The room into which Arni walked was a large one. A fire of huge
logs crackled on an open hearth, lighting up the room, for not much
daylight fell in through the narrow windows. There was a mighty
wooden table by the opposite wall, and at it sat the biggest man Arni
had ever seen, cutting himself a slice of smoked bacon with a long
knife. He took no notice at all of his visitor at first, but cut the bacon
into small pieces, speared one of them on the point of his knife, and
stuck it into his mouth. As he chewed his jaws worked away like the jaws
of an ox. Only when he had eaten the bacon did he look up and ask,
'Who's this you've brought me, Legsmiter?'

'A Raiding Rider crossing the mountains alone,' said Arni's companion. 'He wants shelter for the night.'

'Did you ask him the question?' said Skullcleaver.

'I did,' said Legsmiter, 'and there's no reason to refuse him hospitality.'

Skullcleaver nodded, dismissing the man, who was obviously on some kind of guard duty. 'Right, you can go,' he said. He beckoned Arni over to the table with an imperious wave of his hand, saying, 'Sit down and cut yourself a slice of bacon, then. I suppose you've got a knife.'

Arni thanked him for the invitation, sat down on one of the wooden benches standing around the table, and drew his knife from its sheath. There was a flat cake of hard bread on the table too, and he broke himself a piece off that. The bacon had been well hung, and was easy to slice. It tasted of the juniper twigs over which it had been smoked. Arni ate, Skullcleaver the chieftain ate, and they both sat there opposite one another in silence for a while, chewing deliberately. Finally Arni wiped his knife on his trousers and put it away. The chieftain had finished his own meal, and now scrutinized his guest closely. 'I never knew a Raiding Rider travel alone before,' said he. 'Least of all in the mountains! Is the horde nearby?'

'No,' said Arni. 'I rode out alone.' And as if by way of explanation he added, 'My name is Arni.'

'Is it, indeed?' said Skullcleaver. 'Then I suppose you're the Khan's brother, known as Arni of the Stone?'

'I am,' said Arni, 'and if you've heard of me, you will not be surprised that I ride alone.'

'Quite right, I'm not,' said Skullcleaver, 'not now. Your own folk, I believe, are not particularly fond of you.' Then he leaned back and began to laugh heartily, now and then uttering the words, 'Arni the Meek!' When he had finished laughing, he added, 'I always wondered what you might be like – a Raiding Rider who can't bring himself to hurt a living soul! Legsmiter needn't have stood on ceremony. There's no call for us to guard against the likes of you!'

'You are probably right,' said Arni, undisturbed, 'at least so far as killing is concerned.'

'But apart from that, you're a highly dangerous man!' said Skullcleaver mockingly, and he began to laugh again. 'I dare say you think I'm afraid of your magic stone, do you? I'm not. I put my trust in my axe.'

'It will not always help you, however,' said Arni.

'Oh?' said the chieftain. 'When won't it?'

'In a game, for instance,' said Arni.

Skullcleaver stopped laughing and looked at Arni, his interest aroused. 'So that's what you're getting at!' said he. 'I hear you're good at board games. But you may meet your match in playing games here too.'

'I may indeed,' said Arni, unconcerned, as if he did not particularly mind whether he put his prowess to the test. But that only aroused the chieftain's desire for a game all the more. 'Sorry you brought the conversation round to it now, are you?' he said. 'Well, you must stand by what you say! It's too dark for a game today, unfortunately, but be ready tomorrow morning. I'll have you called, and then we'll see which of us is the better player. You can go now. Legsmiter's waiting for you outside, to show you where you can sleep. And you'd better decide what stakes we're playing for overnight. I hope the thought of the game won't keep you awake.' And Skullcleaver laughed once more, briefly, and waved Arni away.

When Arni stepped out of the doorway, the sun had set. The sharp outlines of the mountain crests around the valley stood out against the pale evening sky, and a cold wind was blowing down from the pass. Legsmiter, who had been leaning against the wall of the house, straightened up and said, 'I'll show you the place where strangers sleep.' He led Arni on through the village, and thus he found his daughter Rikka. She was sitting outside the door of a house, tied to the door-posts, eating a piece of bread. Her clothes were tattered, and there were weals suffused with blood on her arms, legs and face, left there by her fast ride through the undergrowth. She looked up when Arni passed her.

Rikka told me that she was frightened to death to see her father in the village of the Bloodaxe People. At first all she could think was that he too had fallen into their hands. She stared at him in horror, but her father smiled at her and quickly put a finger to his lips. That made her hope that he would try to free her, and she hastily bent her head, so that her gaze would not give him away, since nobody here yet knew that she was Arni's daughter. Her kidnapper had tried talking to her, but she could not understand his language, and would not answer even when he asked laborious questions about her parents in the language of the Mountain Badgers. She realized it was her own fault that she was in this situation, and she had meant to wait and see if she couldn't find some opportunity to escape. That night, after Arni came, she did not sleep a wink, and listened intently to every sound, hoping her father would slip into the house while everyone was asleep. But he did not come. They tied her up outside the door again next morning, so she was able to see all that happened then, which I shall try to tell you just as she told it to me.

Some time after Rikka had been brought out, Arni came out of the log cabin where he had spent the night, stretched like a man who has slept well and long, and then strolled through the village without once looking at Rikka. A little later Legsmiter emerged from the chieftain's house and spoke to Arni. Arni listened, nodding once or twice, as if he were agreeing to whatever proposal was being put to him. Legsmiter went back into the chieftain's house, and came out again with a table and two stools, which he placed in the middle of the village square. While he was doing this, he called out something to the people who had stepped outside the doors of their cabins, and were watching curiously. Whatever was about to take place seemed to be of the utmost interest to them all, for more and more people came out of their houses. The men clustered close around the table, while the women and children hung back, and sat down on their doorsteps. Rikka was jostled by her kidnapper's children; she had to stand up to avoid falling on the dirty ground outside the door.

By now Legsmiter had placed a board on the table, with a set of stones on either side of it, one set black and the other white. Then the chieftain came out of his house, signed to Arni to sit at the table, and he himself sat down opposite. When she saw this, Rikka felt angry with her father. He must know these people had kidnapped her, but instead of doing anything about it, he was sitting down to play a game with their chieftain as if he were an old friend. At that moment she almost gave him away, for she was upon the point of shouting out and telling him what she thought of him. But luckily she didn't, and now she discovered what her father had in mind.

The chieftain had asked him a question, and Arni said, in reply, 'I will play for that girl over there by the door.' He pointed to Rikka, and now they all looked at her. Her kidnapper's wife, who was standing on the steps behind her, nudged her, and when Rikka turned around the woman said, 'You're the stake!' Rikka had difficulty in hiding the triumph in her eyes, for she knew that her father was unbeatable at board games.

On hearing that Arni wished to play for a girl whom he said he had happened to see in passing, Skullcleaver laughed mockingly and said, 'Does it upset your tender heart to see the girl our prisoner, then, or do you just fancy little children?' Rikka saw her father grind his teeth so hard that his cheek muscles bulged, but all he said was, 'Will you give her to me if I win?'

'You shall have her,' said Skullcleaver, 'but what will you set against her? Or don't you think you can lose?'

Arni shrugged his shoulders. 'I have nothing of value with me to set at stake,' he said.

'That's not true,' said Skullcleaver. 'Set your stone against the child. They say you always carry it with you so that you can consult it.'

Arni thought for a while, and then he put his hand into the bag at his belt, took out the eye-stone, and laid it on the table before him. 'Very well, if you don't mind playing with this eye looking at you,' he said.

'I'm not afraid of such a man as you,' said Skullcleaver contemptuously, 'and I am certainly not afraid of a stone. I'll even let you have first move in the game. Come on, then, show me what you can do!'

So the game began. First the two players, moving each stone in turn, set out their pieces on the board, which was much like a chessboard but with considerably more squares. When all the stones were on the board they could be moved again, and the object of the game was obviously for each player to form certain patterns which his opponent would try to counter. Skullcleaver and Arni sat bent over the board, often thinking for some time before moving a stone from one square to another, and they looked to Rikka like two wrestlers cautiously trying one another's strength.

Mid-day came and went, but none of the watchers thought of going home for a meal, and in any case there would have been nothing to eat, since the women stayed outside their doors too. They were all watching the players intently, and a murmur of approval would run through the crowd at a particularly good move. Rikka could tell that these people's passion for play drove everything else out of their minds.

The sun was low in the sky once again when Arni moved a stone that closed the last gap in a square his pieces had formed, enclosing the whole centre of the board. He leaned back, and said, 'Own yourself beaten, Skullcleaver.'

'You're better than I thought,' said the chieftain. 'The girl is yours.'

'Then I will take the child and ride on,' said Arni, rising. Rikka felt her kidnapper's wife undo her bonds, and she was going to run to her father, but the chieftain held him back, saying, 'Not so fast to leave this table! We've only just begun! You must play me again now.'

'I don't see what for, or why,' said Arni.

'Then let me show you,' said Skullcleaver, pointing to the sky, where the sun was now just two hands' breadths above the jagged crest of the mountains. Arni looked up, then nodded, and settled on his stool again.

'I see you understand,' said Skullcleaver, with a pleased grin. 'The sun stood just there when you came to our village yesterday. Your day's grace is up, and now you must play for your life.'

Rikka was terrified when she saw the danger her father was in, and all because of her. She was sure, of course, that he would win this game too, but she went over and stood beside him. The stakes for which they were now playing increased the spectators' tension. The men crowded around the two players, waiting for the first move, which was Skull-cleaver's this time. But Arni soon had the game in hand again. He tried to finish it faster than the first, and soon everyone could see that he planned to arrange his stones in a triangle. And whatever the chieftain did to prevent him, Arni managed to close the ranks of his stones, move by move. The veins stood out on Skullcleaver's broad, pock-marked brow, and a feverish light came into his eyes. The fascination of the game had him firmly in its grip, and it may have impaired the clarity of his mind. At all events, he could not frustrate his opponent's plan, and just as the sun rested on the mountain range, Arni moved his last stone into place and completed his triangle.

'Am I free now?' he asked, looking his opponent in the eye. But still the chieftain was not prepared to let him and Rikka go. He was furious to have been defeated twice, and at the same time he longed to go on playing and even the score. 'Now that you've won twice, Arni,' he said, hoarsely, 'you can't refuse me a third game.'

'I don't want to play any more,' said Arni, beginning to rise to his feet.

'Wait!' said Skullcleaver quickly. 'I will offer you stakes you can't refuse. If you win a third time, you shall be chieftain of my people, and I promise you that from that time on every one of them will do whatever you think right. Doesn't that tempt you, Arni the Meek? Don't you want to tame the Bloodaxe People?'

Arni stared at the chieftain as if he had not understood the proposal. Then he shook his head, and said, 'No. I play for no such stakes!'

A red flush of rage rose to Skullcleaver's face. He leaped up, shouting,

'How dare you refuse my stakes? Do you mean to insult me? I'll force you to play this game. You've won your life, but not your freedom. If you won't accept my challenge, I will make you my slave, and your task shall be wiping the blood from my axe!'

So Arni sat down again, saying, 'Very well. I accept your challenge. But we must make haste, for it will soon be dark.'

'Night never yet kept me from playing a game to its end,' said Skullcleaver, and he sent for torches.

Arni looked at Rikka, and smiled, before he placed his first stone on the board with a steady hand. She was glad to see the chieftain's hand trembling as he picked up his own stone. He's much too agitated to win, thought Rikka, feeling sure her father would defeat his opponent this time as well. Soon it could be seen that he meant to place a long line of stones diagonally from corner to corner across the board, and Skullcleaver was pursuing the same plan. The diagonal cross formed ever more distinctly, and both players' chances of winning would have looked almost the same if Arni had not always been one step ahead. So it went on until he needed only to place his last stone on the central square of the board in order to complete the line. Everyone could see that he had won. The stone was already in his hand when his glance fell on the eye-stone that still lay on the table before him. Its rings of colour glowed in the flickering light of the torches, and seemed to pulsate as though some secret life were contained within the smooth curve of its surface. Arni looked long into those shining hues of blue, green and violet, and Rikka thought he had quite forgotten he was sitting here, about to gain power over the Bloodaxe People with the winning of this game. His lips moved as if he were speaking to someone nobody else could see. Or it may be that he spoke to the eye in the stone, or to someone looking at him out of that eye. He nodded, almost imperceptibly, and put his last stone down to one side, so that Skull-cleaver could close his own line of pieces with his next move. Everyone saw what had happened. The triumph that flared up in the chieftain's eyes was extinguished a moment later, when he too realized what Arni had done. He swept the board violently off the table, shouting, 'You let me win!'

'Yes,' said Arni quietly. 'Aren't you glad you're still chieftain of the Bloodaxe People?'

Skullcleaver was white in the face with fury. 'Don't you know it's a shameful insult to let your opponent win?' he shouted. 'And even greater shame to the man who does such a thing?'

'I know,' said Arni, picking up his eye-stone and putting it away, as if that concluded the matter. 'I won the child in the first game, I won my life in the second, and I won my freedom by playing the third. Can I go now?'

'Go?' repeated Skullcleaver, in a toneless voice. Then he bellowed, 'I'll hunt you out of this valley in disgrace!' And he told his men, 'Put him on the steed of shame!'

Rikka said she remembered what followed as a nightmare. The men brought a mangy old donkey out of its stable, seized Arni and bound him facing backwards on the bucking animal. Then they hit the donkey a couple of times with a stick to make it go, and chased it along the way up to the pass, shouting and swinging torches at it. Women and children ran along behind, screeching, and threw stones and mud at the man on the donkey, while they shouted, 'Shame on you, Arni the Cheat!' And so they drove him out of the village. Rikka herself ran along after him, not even feeling the stony ground beneath her bare feet, half blinded with tears as she saw her father's face swaying up and down before her in the torchlight. It was smeared with dirt, and blood was running down over his cheek from a cut under his right eye, but he was smiling as if he were well content with this outcome.

The Bloodaxe People pursued them all the way up to the pass, and only then did they drop behind. After a while the donkey slowed to a walking pace, and Rikka was able to untie her father. Then he put her on the beast, saying, 'Do you mind riding a steed of shame?' He did not wait for any answer. And so he brought her home. That', the Gentle Fluter finished, 'is the story Rikka told me, many years later, and I think it is a tale worth passing on to Arni's Folk.'

Gunli and Orri looked awkwardly at the floor. It was obvious that they did not care for the story, and Listener couldn't understand Arni's behaviour either. 'Why in the world did he let Skullcleaver win?' he asked. 'Can you explain it, Grandfather?'

'Well, yes, I could,' said the Gentle Fluter, 'but I'm afraid it still wouldn't mean much to you, and even less to these two good traders, who cannot imagine Arni cheating in a game.'

Gunli nodded his agreement to this, and remarked, 'One shouldn't put too much faith in tales told by women. It may all have been quite different.'

'Would you doubt the word of Arni's daughter?' asked the Gentle Fluter sternly, and Gunli shook his head in silence, shrugging his shoulders. But Listener still was not happy. 'It's not that little bit of cheating I can't understand,' he said. 'What I wonder is, why didn't he take his chance to make the Bloodaxe People men of peace? It was in his power. I don't mind his cheating. But why did he do it?'

'That's what Rikka asked him, too,' said the Gentle Fluter.

'And what did he say?' asked Listener.

'Just one thing,' said the Gentle Fluter, 'and I don't know if you'll be able to make much of it. She says he said: May one force a wolf to eat grass when he has no appetite for it?'

Listener shook his head, baffled. 'I wish you old men didn't always have to talk in riddles!' he said.

'Do we?' asked the Gentle Fluter. 'I think it only seems so to you because you are looking at the outside of things too hard. You can't tell what the truth is if you are only describing its visible surface that everyone can see. The truth stands behind things, and you can speak of it only in images, you cannot seize it as you can seize a cat by the tail. If such a saying as Arni's seems puzzling to you, then you haven't understood much of the truth yet.'

'Then perhaps the story Rikka said she remembered was just one of those images?' asked Gunli, obviously ready to grasp at any straw that would save him from the confusion into which the tale of Arni's peculiar conduct had cast him.

'You may be right,' said the Gentle Fluter, but when he saw the relief on Gunli's face, he added, 'though I don't mean that those things didn't really happen. I am sure everything was just as Rikka told it, and yet the whole story is also an image of the truth that made Arni smile while he was being so humiliated.'

'It will be hard to find ears ready to hear this story,' said Gunli. 'But I will have to keep it in my mind, for I can't forget it now.'

Soon afterwards, the two traders left, with much bowing and copious expressions of gratitude. They bowed low to Listener too, and Gunli said, 'I can safely speak in the name of Arni's Deputy and all of Arni's Folk, O chosen bearer of the stone, in expressing the hope that you may do our humble houses the honour of paying us the visit for which we now long.'

Listener stood in the doorway with his grandfather, watching the two men ride away. It had stopped raining, and a few patches of blue sky could be seen again among the ragged clouds. When the two traders turned off on the road to Barlebogue, they took their fur caps off once more to wave them in a last respectful farewell.

*

Listener had his next lesson in playing the flute that afternoon. This time he learned how to play the various notes loud or soft. 'If your playing is to be strong,' said the Gentle Fluter, 'you must wish for it truly, with all your heart, otherwise you'll just be making a noise that's good for nothing but scaring birds. However, it is even harder to play so softly that you can only just be heard, and yet give each separate note the expression it needs to make the hearer hold his breath.'

Listener practised both kinds of playing, until his grandfather nodded, satisfied, and soon afterwards went to bed.

The next few days were spent in similar practising. One day the Gentle Fluter taught him trills, and then how to play a note fast, with the tongue fluttering, to make a sound like the nightingale's song. His teacher thought his tone in the lower register was not yet full and rounded enough, while his high notes still seemed to sound a little too shrill. So Listener had plenty to do to get through the exercises he was set, and still he had no chance of using his newly acquired skills to make melodies of his own. If he tried it, the Gentle Fluter would interrupt his lesson at once and put the flute away.

On the morning of the seventh day, Listener had to go over everything his grandfather had taught him again. He played long notes, he played rapid sequences, he made the instrument sound loud and strong or quiet and gentle, going through the whole register of the flute from the very deepest to the very highest notes. 'That will do,' said the Gentle Fluter at last. 'Now you have learned all you need to know to play the flute. We must take a walk this afternoon, but I think I'll go and lie down for a little now.'

Listener went into the kitchen to prepare their mid-day meal, and noticed that their provisions were almost gone. He would have to go and see mine host who kept the donkeys tomorrow, to stock up their larder. However, there was just enough for today. He found some eggs, a little flour, and the jug of milk that was left outside the door every morning. They still had some butter, so he put a pan over the fire and made pancakes. Then he opened the trapdoor and went down to the cellar to find a pot of plum jam for the filling. Once again he saw the shapes of the jars and flagons emerge from the gloom in the unsteady light of the candle. He soon found the plum jam, for such items of food were right at the front of the shelves, where it was easy to lay your hand on them. But he could not resist taking one more look at the three mysterious little bottles standing in the farther part of the cellar,

behind his grandfather's strong and medicinal liquors. He pushed aside
the flask of gentian bitters, and raised his candle. There they stood,
side by side, those dusty little bottles with their curious inscriptions. He
knew about the first two already, and now he was going to find out
what the third contained. He took it carefully off its shelf and held it in
the candlelight. At first all he could see of the eight lines of writing on
the label were a few faded brown letters, but when he held the candle
yet closer, the writing became clearer, resolved into words and sentences, and Listener read:

> *When you stand at last*
> *by yourself dismayed,*
> *bitter though it taste,*
> *this will bring you aid.*
> *In the stone be bound,*
> *held there by this token;*
> *if you are not found,*
> *you shall not be woken.*

Strange potions his grandfather kept in this cellar, thought Listener.
He certainly wasn't going to try this one, whatever the advice on the
label, for in any case it was sure to be bitter. Obviously you were to
take it only when 'dismayed' by yourself, and he had no reason at all to
feel any such dismay. Indeed, just now he was rather pleased with
himself and the way things were turning out. Who had written those
labels? He decided to ask his grandfather when he had a chance. For
the time being, he put the little flask in its place again, hiding it behind
the larger flagon. Then he took the pot of plum jam and climbed back
up to the kitchen.

After their meal, the Gentle Fluter said, 'Come – let's go for a walk.
You can wash these few dishes just as well later.' He seemed to be in a
cheerful mood, and his cheeks even showed a trace of that rosy
plumpness they had lost of late years. Nor did he seem as frail as he
had been a week ago. He picked up a little walking stick that stood by
the doorway, and almost danced out of doors with his usual quick step.
When Listener asked where they were going, the Gentle Fluter said
only, 'To visit someone,' but he did not say whom. Listener was all the
more surprised when his grandfather did not turn towards the inn
where the donkeys were kept, and started off in the opposite direction
instead. Who in the world was he going to visit that way?

When they had walked through the green hills for a while, the Gentle Fluter stopped, cast a searching glance around, and laughed a little. 'This is where it was,' he said.

'Where what was?' asked Listener.

'The place where we first met,' said the Gentle Fluter. 'Don't you remember?'

Then Listener did recognize the place again, and his memories of his situation at the time were not at all comfortable. He saw himself once more, standing exhausted on these grassy slopes, a hunted man, staring at the speechless avenger who was making for him, cudgel raised aloft.

'You were pretty frightened at the time, eh?' said his grandfather, laughing merrily, as if the whole episode had been extremely funny.

'I didn't think it was as amusing as all that,' said Listener, a trace of annoyance in his voice.

'Still, you'd well and truly earned it,' said the Gentle Fluter cheerfully. 'Don't you agree?'

Reluctantly, Listener nodded. Why was his grandfather digging up old history? 'Yes, but I rode the land with Barlo for three years as his servant, to put everything in order again,' he said.

'And you now suppose everything *is* in order?' inquired the Gentle Fluter, much amused.

'Well, isn't it?' asked Listener.

The Gentle Fluter laughed as one laughs at a child's foolish saying. 'What do you understand by order?' he said. 'Upon the whole, we're no good at creating anything but disorder in the world. If you've turned the course of events in a new direction, you can't undo what you have done, and the consequences of your deed will be seen to all eternity. Sometimes all the wrong turnings we take do come together in a new order, but no thanks to us.' He looked thoughtfully at Listener, and added, 'I don't know that I am doing you any favour by leaving you my flute. I am afraid you still haven't got the right idea of the power it will give you. But I suppose I must rely on sense coming out of the nonsense you'll make of it, some time or other.'

Listener liked neither his grandfather's remarks, nor the place where they stood, bound up as it was with such uncomfortable memories. 'Weren't you going to pay someone a visit?' he asked, hoping to bring the scene to an end.

'A visit?' asked his grandfather, and then struck his forehead with the flat of his hand, crying, 'Why, yes! Of course. A good thing you reminded me. You must forgive an old man his tendency to start chattering on and forget what he really meant to do.' Putting his hand on Listener's shoulder, he added, 'Come along, we have to climb up there.' And he pointed to a few trees standing alone, like outposts of the forest of Barlebogue, as they rose above the last of the hilltops.

They climbed the slope side by side. The short, harsh grass was dry again after that morning's rain. There were still a few purple knapweed flowers on their tough stems, along with the silvery calyxes from which the seedheads had dropped, but otherwise only the pale mauve clusters of autumn gentian lent a touch of colour to the greyish turf. Up on the hill stood three ancient rowan trees, heavily laden with bright red bunches of berries. Listener stopped and looked at the beautiful trees, their leaves already beginning to turn colour. Then he saw the grave mound standing among the trees. He looked inquiringly at his grandfather, who said, 'Yes, here we are.'

They walked the last few paces to the trees and stopped beside the grave. The only ornaments on the mound of earth were fallen red and yellow rowan leaves. 'Grandmother?' asked Listener, and the Gentle Fluter nodded, but he did not seem sad; indeed, he was in a merry mood, and nodded to the grave mound as if his stalwart wife stood there in person to greet him. 'There, you see,' he addressed her, 'Listener's back, and we needn't wait for him any longer.' Then he sat down on the grass, and signed to Listener to sit beside him.

For a while they gazed silently down at the hills. From up here, you could look down on the river that wound its curving way, alders and poplars growing on its banks, through the grassy hills and out into the far-flung plain that faded into a haze on the horizon. When they had been sitting there side by side for a while, Listener's grandfather said, 'Well, so this time you're the flute-player about to ride out into the world.'

'Like Barlo?' asked Listener.

'Yes,' said his grandfather, 'yet not quite like him. He had a task to perform, and you have yet to find yours.'

'But his flute was only wood, and mine . . .' Listener hesitated, for it occurred to him that his grandfather's flute did not belong to him yet. But the Gentle Fluter smiled, and completed his sentence. 'And yours is made of silver.'

'Where did you actually get it?' asked Listener.

'I'm glad you ask,' said the Gentle Fluter, 'or I might have forgotten to tell you, and that story is one of the things that must be passed on to whoever inherits it.

As a child, I used to keep sheep. My father was a shepherd too, just like his father before him, and no doubt *his* father and grandfather herded sheep as well. You know how it is by now: a shepherd must be able to stand solitude, and if you've been used to it from childhood, you don't want anything else. And I dare say that's why shepherds' sons so often become shepherds themselves. But that's not what I was going to tell you.

At that time I lived farther north, where my father drove his flocks out to pasture on the grassy slopes at the foot of the mountains, often going far down into the valleys. I had just finished learning my trade, and my father had entrusted a flock of my own to me for the first time, while he himself pastured his sheep in a valley nearby. He had sent me off to the far end of the main valley, where the grass grows right up to the scree slopes below the glaciers. I was sitting there on a large boulder one day, looking down on my flock below and playing a willow pipe I had made myself. Most shepherds play the pipe; indeed, if you should ever meet one who doesn't, he is probably in the wrong job. Sitting there all alone under the great arch of the sky, you see, you feel a need to fill that endless space between one horizon and another with something. Talking's no good. For one thing, you go crazy once you start talking to yourself, and for another, the spoken word will crack that blue bell of air and vapour stretching its vault above you. What you need is something that will ring out far and wide, something whose sound will fit itself to the rounded vault and make the sky sound too. So you whittle yourself a pipe and you begin to play.

Well, I was playing to myself at the time, feeling the sound of my pipe make the horizon tremble slightly. The bell of the sky began to hum, and the humming grew louder, and rose to the height of the heavens, until its echoing chord filled all my mind. Just then, someone behind me said, "You play the pipe well, young fellow."

At first I was angry, because the interruption had shattered my carefully built structure of sounds. I turned around, and saw an old prospector who had obviously come down from the mountains and was attracted by the music of my pipe. His leather bag was slung around him, and he had the sharp little hammer of his trade in his belt. His brown, leathery face was wrinkled with countless little laughter lines, and he was looking at me in so friendly a way that I forgot my anger and asked him to sit down with me.

Groaning a little, he sat down at my side, looked at me for a while, and then said, "Do you like keeping sheep, young fellow?"

"Like it?" said I. "My father's a shepherd, and I suppose all my forefathers were shepherds too, so I keep sheep. What else would I do?"

"What about the piping?" he said. "What about that?"

Well, I've told you how I felt when I sat in the open air, playing my pipe. "It's the finest thing I know," I said. "When you came, the whole wide sky was ringing in my ears."

"I know," said the old man. "I heard you. You have the sound of it." Then he took a silver flute out of his leather bag and laid it in my hands. "This is for you," he said.

I looked at the flute. I thought it was perfection. When I noticed the ornamentation at the end of it, I said, "It's smooth except for the fivefold ring. What does that mean?"

"Can you read, young fellow?" asked the old man.

I shook my head, for at that time no one had yet taught me my letters.

"Then I will tell you what is written there," said the old man.

> *"Follow my song,*
> *whither you will,*
> *yet force is wrong;*
> *use none, or the song*
> *will bring you ill.*

Will you keep to that?"

I just nodded, although as yet I had no idea what meaning lay behind those words. I wanted the flute so much that I wouldn't have let it go now for anything in the world. As we sat there, the old man also told me on what conditions the flute should be handed on when I tired of playing it, but I told you about that before, when you began to learn it. "And you'll have to find out all the rest for yourself," the old man added. Then he laid his hand on my shoulder for a moment, rose, and went away. I went on gazing at the silver flute for a while; it shone in my hands, and now it was mine. When I turned at last to wave goodbye to the old man, he was nowhere to be seen. And that is how I came by my flute.'

'Did you ever see that prospector again?' asked Listener.

The Gentle Fluter shook his head. 'No, never, although I was often up in the mountains, and I even went looking for him there,' he said. 'There were a great many more things I would have liked to ask him, but there you are: we have to find such answers for ourselves, though it may take us our whole lives long, and still we don't know them all.' He shivered, and added, 'Come along, it's getting cold. Let's go home.'

He leaned on Listener's shoulder as he rose to his feet and nodded once more to the grave mound, saying, 'I'll see you soon, my dearest. The trees will guard you until I come.'

'The trees?' asked Listener, looking up into their graceful crowns, hung with clusters of red berries.

'Don't you know the power of the mountain ash?' asked the Gentle Fluter. 'Rowan trees are friendly to every living creature that seeks their aid, not just to birds. All evil things shun the shade of those trees.' He put his hand on one of the trunks, which were overgrown with lichen, as if he were saying goodbye to an old friend, and then he turned to go. They did not talk much on the way back, and the Gentle Fluter went to bed soon after they reached home.

Listener went into the kitchen to see what provisions he must get from the inn next day. He found a last piece of bread and a few apples for his supper, and then went up to his room. At first, however, he could not sleep, not for a long while. Lying in bed, he looked out of the window at the branches of the old lime tree that rose black against the moonlit sky. Now and then a gust of wind shook the withering leaves, drove a few of them against the panes, and swept them into a rustling heap on the window sill. The full moon shone through a gap in the branches, casting a broad beam of light on the floor of the room, and the shadows of the driving leaves kept tumbling over it. And suddenly, among these swaying shadows, Listener thought he saw something that was not a chance movement, but came slowly and steadily on along the shimmering beam of light. At first it was only a shadow like the others, but then a figure stood out, more and more clearly, and the farther the figure climbed along its path of light the clearer it became, gaining in substance, moving with a strangely familiar, dancing step, surrounded by the light of the moon as it went its way. As it raised its arm, something gleamed in its hand, and then Listener heard the Gentle Fluter playing his silver instrument.

Afterwards, he could not have given any adequate description of what he heard that night. He only knew that the melody of the flute contained all that had filled his grandfather's life: incidents which he himself had heard of, and others of which he knew nothing. He saw the young flute-player riding the steppes at Arni's side, saw him stand in Urla's house and play the tune that sent him sinking deep into that beautiful old woman's eyes, heard the rushing of the Brown River, the cry of the fish eagle and the whistling of the water ouzel, and all these things, all this multifarious world of rocks and plants, beasts and men, moved in swirling colours, gradually revealing an order that lay beneath its movement, a great and living ornament that was constantly changing shape, bringing forth new things that grew in all their diversity, and yet the order still remained whole. Listener was no longer a spectator of the process, but felt that he was taking part in that mighty game; he was drawn into it, yet not despite himself, for he made his own decision and knew that new moves in the game might proceed from every movement of his body, every thought that formed in his brain, and while this living, pulsing structure grew and grew, spreading like rings of ripples on water, Listener still saw his grandfather walking towards the light, his figure brighter and brighter, until it melted into the brilliance.

He could still feel that brightness warming him when he woke next morning, and it made him very cheerful. Had he been dreaming, or had his grandfather really gone back into the living-room to play his flute last night? Its sound was still so clear and real in Listener's memory that he decided to ask the Gentle Fluter about the tune which he felt he could not describe in words. He rose, dressed, and went down to his grandfather's bedroom. The door was open, so he went in, and saw the Gentle Fluter lying on his bed. He lay resting on his back, the flute still in his hands, and the wrinkles of old age had been smoothed away from his face, leaving only an expression of unclouded cheerfulness. But Listener knew at once that his grandfather had died in the night.

A day later Listener packed up his things. When he had gone to mine host who kept the donkeys, the day before, to tell him that the Gentle Fluter was dead, he had also fetched his horse from the stable, to take it with him. He and the innkeeper had buried his grandfather under the three rowan trees, beside his grandmother. 'I helped him dig the grave when his wife died, too,' said the innkeeper, firming the mound of soil. 'And your grandfather stood beside it, looking a little impatient. "It's about time Listener came back," said he. Did he teach you to play the flute, then?'

Listener had nodded, although he was not at all sure that he had had enough teaching. When he first tried the flute, he had been surprised to discover how easily he found the right notes, and he could hardly wait to play all the tunes lying hoarded in his mind. But now, as he decided what to take with him, he hardly dared touch the instrument. He wrapped it in a soft woollen cloth that he had found among his grandmother's belongings, and put it at the very bottom of one of his saddle-bags.

As he was thinking what else he might take on his journey, he remembered the rowanberry spirits. A warming drink would do no harm at this time of year, he thought, and he went down to the cellar. He took the flagon from its shelf, and then it occurred to him that there were other bottles here which might be worth taking. The three little flasks with the strange inscriptions wouldn't weigh his baggage down very much. He took them from their hiding place, and read the faded writing on the labels once more. He could never ask his grandfather who had written those puzzling words now. But anyway, I mustn't let them fall into the wrong hands, he thought, and took the flasks back up to the kitchen with him. He buried them in the depths of one of his two saddle-bags, putting some stockings and shirts over them. He packed the rowanberry spirits at the top; better have that bottle ready to hand.

It was still early in the morning when he locked up the house and set off on his way. He went to the inn first, to leave the key, for the innkeeper had promised to go and see that all was well with the Gentle Fluter's house now and then. Listener also wanted to stock up with provisions for his journey, and the innkeeper provided them lavishly, so that he had difficulty getting everything into his saddle-bags.

'Where are you off to, then?' asked the innkeeper, when Listener said goodbye to him at the gate.

'To Fraglund first, to see my parents,' said Listener. 'It's nearly four years since I left home.'

'Then you'd better go by way of Barlebogue,' said the innkeeper. 'That's the shortest ride.'

Listener had thought of that himself, but he did not want to ride again through those forests where the two grey wolves roamed, nor was he especially anxious to be welcomed as a little brother by the great Barlo. Before he faced Barlo again, he at least wanted to be sure he had mastered his flute. 'I'm in no great hurry,' he said. 'And I don't much want to ride over the mountains so late in the year. I'll go by way of Draglope. Goodbye, and give Yalf my love!'

Once again he turned in at Furro's smithy, and not just because Snowfoot's left fore shoe was loose. To be honest, the shoe was not as loose as all that. It was the memory of Rikka's eyes that made him stop at the smithy, and he told Rikka so too, a little later, although he was not sure where he got the courage to say it.

Listener had ridden fast, so that he reached Furro's house early in the afternoon. The smith recognized him at once, looked rather doubtfully at the supposed damage, and said, 'Well, if you think the shoe's loose, I'll see to it. But I'd have given you shelter without the job, and I fancy Rikka would have been angry if she'd heard that you just rode by! Take your saddle-bags, then, and go indoors. You know your way around. I've a few more things to do here.'

Listener entered the house through the side door from the smithy, and went into the living-room. Rikka was standing at the window, and turned to look at him. 'I saw you coming,' she said, smiling. Listener could not reply. All he could see were Rikka's eyes, those dark eyes of a colour that was difficult to describe, in between blue, green and violet: Urla's eyes, into which the Gentle Fluter had fallen as one might fall into a well. 'Yes, I've come,' he said at last, awkwardly. 'I came to see your eyes.'

Rikka laughed quietly, but there was no mockery nor even a trace of condescension in her laughter. She just likes me, that's what it is, thought Listener in surprise. She's glad to see me.

'Come over here to the window and let me look at you,' said Rikka. He put down his saddle-bags and went over to her, and she took him by the shoulders and looked in his face. Her eyes were close before him now, and he could not have avoided them. Not that he wanted to. 'You've seen a great deal in the years since last you were here,' said Rikka.

'Your eyes were the only real things I saw in all that time,' said Listener. And then he took her in his arms and kissed her. To his surprise, she returned his kiss, but then she pushed him away, saying, 'Oh, Listener, I'm not the one you seek! We all have the same eyes, you know we do.'

Listener looked at her in confusion. Now he saw that her hair had turned almost white since his previous visit, although her face still seemed smooth and young. Rikka laughed again, and said, 'Now, tell me what you have been doing. Where did you come from today?'

'From my grandfather's,' said Listener, and he told her about the death of the Gentle Fluter.

'I know he was only waiting for you,' said Rikka. 'Did he teach you to play the flute?'

'Yes,' said Listener, 'but he never let me play anything of my own.'

'Then do it now!' said Rikka. 'Play something for me!'

With alarm, Listener realized that he was afraid of making his own music on the flute. 'I've never tried before, not alone,' he said.

'You aren't alone,' said Rikka, 'and I am asking you to play.'

So Listener went to his saddle-bags and found the flute. He carefully unwrapped the soft cloth and showed Rikka the instrument. She looked at it for a while, and then looked Listener in the face again. 'The flute is perfection,' she said, 'but now I would like to hear it.'

Then Listener put the flute to his lips and began to play. Although a moment ago he had had no idea what sequences of notes, let alone what tune he would play, his fingers moved over the holes as if of their own accord, and he could not have said, later, what kind of music it was he played as he stood in that room before Rikka. He saw nothing but her eyes, plunged into them, was enclosed in that play of colour, blue, green and violet, from which images detached themselves, images he was to find again long afterwards, stored in his memory.

All around there was foliage, leaves tinged with shades of blue and violet, and among them shimmering green where a few sunbeams broke through the tops of the tall trees, and this foliage washed about him like waves of water round a rock; red-tinged sycamore leaves moved, swaying, on their long and flexible stems, the little lancets of the privet shone bluish green, and among the deeper green of oval beech leaves danced the light green heart-shaped leaves of the birches, flickering on their thin, black twigs. He looked into that moving sea of leaves, and heard the rushing of the wind and the splash of water. A blackbird was whistling in the branches above him. Then he heard the flap of wings close beside his ear. It was only when he tried to turn his head aside that he realized it would not move, and yet he saw the blackbird sitting on his shoulder although his eyes were not looking at it. It was as if, in a way that was difficult to describe, he could see out from inside himself without using his eyes at all. The blackbird put its head on one side, inspecting his ear with its black and gleaming eyes, as if to ask whether he had learnt to listen at last. He was surprised not to feel the bird's claws on his bare skin, and then he saw that his shoulder was overgrown with thick green moss. This moss also covered the upper part of the arm that hung by his side, and the curly ripples of the shaggy animal skin that covered him from the hips down to the spot where his smooth-haired legs bent backwards at a curious angle, before ending in a pair of cloven hooves. He stared at those clumsy, goat's feet. They were embedded in moss and stood on a rocky ledge below which a spring gushed out, its waters gathering into a small, clear pool with smooth pebbles lying at the bottom. So he stood there motionless in the wood, stone overgrown with moss, a perch for birds, hearing every sound: the rustle of the leaves, the clear splashing of the spring, the whistling of the birds, the crack of dry twigs under the tread of unseen animals. And farther away he heard the wind whispering through the dry grass of the steppes that reached from somewhere beyond the wood as far as the distant mountains, whence the tumbling burns came foaming down, carrying clattering stones along with them, while golden eagles soared, crying, high above the crags. He listened to this multifarious harmony, and amidst all those sounds and noises, he heard the song of a child. He could not tell if it came from near or far away, a song sung by a childish voice that was yet deep and full as the voice of a woman, or the lower register of a flute, and the words of it ran:

He lives in the wood,
don't know who.
He lives in the wood,
his skin is of stone,
his mouth hard as bone,
cold as death, you would
say if you knew
don't know who.

He stands in the moss,
don't know where.
He stands in the moss,
never shifts from that place,
and his motionless face
shows no pain, no loss,
no joy and no care;
don't know where.

He waits by the spring,
don't know when.
He waits by the spring,
for the spell to be broken;
he waits to be woken
by one who will bring

new life to him then.
Don't know when.

The song was still in his ears as he came up again out of the green branches of the vision, and took his flute from his lips. Rikka was still looking at him, and smiling.

'What kind of wood was that?' asked Listener, as if he could be sure that Rikka had seen and heard the same as himself. 'Who sang that song, and what does it mean?'

'That doesn't matter at the moment,' said Rikka. 'You will forget it, as you will forget much else. But you'll remember it when the right time comes. What you forget is never lost. It is only sleeping, to wake again one day.'

'But I do know what I saw and heard!' said Listener, and he tried to remember. However, there was nothing left but a flickering of dappled light, green and blue and violet, that gradually faded, and the sound of a song dying away in the distance. 'No, I don't know now,' he said sadly, for he still knew enough to remember how lovely the song had been, and how comforting.

'It will come back to you when you're not trying to remember it any more,' said Rikka. 'However, I see that you have indeed learned to play the flute.'

Furro had come into the room. 'Yes,' said he, 'anyone can tell where you went to school, Listener. It's good to know that the Gentle Fluter found an heir. I had to leave off hammering when I heard the music, strange as it seemed to my ears. But I don't suppose it was meant for me.'

'No,' said Rikka, 'it was meant for himself.'

'And you taught it to him, did you?' said Furro, smiling. 'Cast a little spell on him with those magic eyes of yours?'

Listener blushed at this, and wondered whether the smith would still be smiling if he knew he had kissed Rikka. But Furro did not seem to be taking the matter very seriously. He gave Listener a friendly clap on the shoulder, saying, 'Don't stand there looking so sheepish! You've always got to expect that sort of thing with Urla's granddaughters. Well, the shoe sits firm again, supposing it was ever loose, and as for me, I'm ready for my supper.'

When they had eaten their fill, Furro fetched a pitcher of wine from the cellar, and Listener told of his meeting with the traders Gunli and Orri. 'Yes, that pair were here too,' said the blacksmith. 'Glad to find a man who could shoe mules, they were. Here, see what they paid me with!' He took a couple of coins out of his purse and laid them on the table. Listener picked one up and examined it. It was made of silver: one side was stamped with a woman's head and the other with the figure of a galloping horseman. 'Do you know who the pictures show?' Listener asked.

'Yes, Gunli told me,' said Furro. 'The woman is meant to be Urla, who has always been much venerated by Arni's Folk, and the horseman is Arni himself. Raiding Riders though they once were, those folk seem to think no end of Arni these days.'

'I know,' said Listener. 'They asked me to visit them. They call me Bearer of the Stone.' He spoke with some pride. Rikka looked at him searchingly, and he could not quite interpret the expression of her eyes. 'Are you on your way to Arni's Folk, then?' she asked.

'I'm going to Fraglund first, to see my parents,' said Listener. 'But after that I'll probably ride to Arni's Folk.'

'Then no doubt you'll be a great man there,' said the smith.

'Maybe,' said Listener, 'and indeed I think Arni had such a thing in mind when he gave me the stone. He had the gift of foresight, so they say.'

'So who say?' asked Rikka.

'Well, Gunli, for instance,' said Listener. 'Arni's word is law to his followers, and they think he knew what would happen after his death.'

'And so now they take Arni's word, and out of it they build themselves houses where they may live in comfort,' said Rikka. 'If they're so sure what he meant now, why need they have waited until his death to understand him?'

'Well, I dare say it took them some time to grasp the sense of his words,' said Listener. 'You don't always understand what happens to you at once.'

'No,' said Rikka, 'understanding takes time: you must always remember that, Bearer of the Stone.'

When Listener set out from the door of the smithy next morning, Rikka took him in her arms and kissed him as if it were the most natural thing in the world, and Furro did not seem to mind at all. 'You're one of Urla's family now you wear the stone on your breast, as anyone can see,' said he, wishing Listener a good journey.

There is nothing of note to tell of Listener's ride along the river this time. He was in no hurry. He let his horse go at its own pace, and found himself a place to spend the night as evening came on, usually in a haystack, since there were not many villages so far upstream. The pastures on the hillside below the forest were deserted at this late season of the year, and Listener saw no reason to revive memories of his time spent in service to Barlo, when they herded sheep. He rode fast through the village where the farmer who owned the sheep lived, although the sun was already low. Indeed, it was dark by the time he eventually came to another farmhouse, and he had to rouse the people from their beds to get shelter for the night. And so at last he came to Draglope, and put up at the Silver Harp.

The landlord knew him at once, but Listener was not very forthcoming in answer to the man's questions about Barlo and the events leading to the driving out of Gisa. The autumn fair was over, and the tumblers and minstrels who used to stay at the Silver Harp at such times had gone away. Instead, all kinds of riffraff were making themselves at home in the big room of the inn. Listener's company today was none of the best. Most of these folk looked like vagabonds or drunkards, and not wishing to leave his possessions unguarded, he put his saddle-bags under the table where he sat down to drink a bowl of hot soup before going to bed.

He did not like the noise in the room. Loud sounds, in particular loud voices, had always troubled him, and these dubious characters lounging at the tables in their tattered clothes were bellowing as if every man jack of them was hard of hearing. Nothing could be distinguished in such a babble of voices. Looking around, all Listener seemed to see were mouths in flushed, unshaven faces, mouths gaping wide in raucous laughter.

He was on the point of rising and going hungry to bed when the landlord at last made his way through the shouting, gesticulating guests, steaming soup bowl in hand, and came over to Listener's table. He sat down there too, but conversation was impossible. In answer to whatever remark it was the innkeeper addressed to him, Listener could only shrug his shoulders. The man leaned over and shouted in his ear, 'I've got to live when there's no fair too! Can't pick and choose my customers!'

Listener gave no sign of having understood these words. Wrapped in his own reserve, he hastily spooned up his soup, meaning to get out of this appalling noise as soon as possible; it seemed to be constantly increasing, and was swamping his brain until he could feel nothing but a cold rage with everyone in the room. And as he sat there with his rage, the voices at the next table rose to a clamour of dispute, a quarrel was audibly under way, filthy insults flew like broken shards of earthenware, men were already picking up stools and knocking them together, knives flashed out. The landlord took Listener by the sleeve and jerked his head towards the door. Fear flickered in his eyes. By now Listener was almost deafened. He stared at the distorted faces of the quarrelling men. His rage concentrated into an icy point in the middle of his brain, and then he knew what he would do. Tearing his arm out of the innkeeper's grasp, he drew his saddle-bags towards him and felt at the bottom of one of them for his flute. Now he would see what power he had as a fluter! He leaped up on the table, sending the soup bowl clattering across its surface, put his instrument to his lips and began to play. At the very first note the brawling men fell back from one another, and stood there quite still for a moment. Then they threw up their arms and began to dance, stamping their feet. The shouting had died down instantly at the other tables too. Soon they were all on their feet, including the landlord, moving in time to the angry tune that shrilled above their heads. Tables and benches were kicked aside to make room for the dancers, who moved like marionettes to the sound of Listener's flute. Now that he saw he had them in his power, Listener began to feel a wild pleasure in forcing them to do his will. He made them form two lines facing one another as they stamped and swayed, then drove them apart, sending both lines back to the barriers of fallen chairs, benches and tables, drove them together again until the dancers were glaring into each other's eyes in sullen fury, and so he made them go back and forth, back and forth, in the dim light of those few oil lamps which had not been put out and were still smouldering among the rising clouds of dust, back and forth he drove them, back and forth, until he brought them heavily charging towards each other one last time, and their heads crashed violently together.

When he lowered his flute, nothing moved. He put it away again, picked up his bags and left the room without a glance at the haphazard pile of bodies. That night he slept the deep and dreamless sleep of utter exhaustion, and did not wake until late.

The main room of the inn had been tidied up again, cleaned and aired when he came down in the morning to break his fast. The landlord himself served him, approaching him with fawning servility. 'I didn't know I had such a master in my house, I'm sure,' said he, busily wiping down the table with a rag before setting it with bread, milk, ham and cheese. There was a huge red bump on his forehead,

going blue around the edges. Now and then he cooled this evidence of
Listener's musical talent with a wet cloth. 'The great Barlo could play
pretty well,' he remarked, 'but I'll be bound he could never have done
the likes of what you did last night.'

This observation gave Listener great satisfaction. 'Well, high time
you had a little law and order here,' he said, as casually as if bringing
that state of affairs about had been no great matter. 'I hope your guests
are feeling better now,' he added, for form's sake.

'Why, the moment they had their wits about them again they crept
away like so many rats,' said the landlord. 'One of 'em muttering that
next time I had a great magician putting up here who fancied leading
folk a dance, he hoped I'd let them know beforehand. Oh, I can tell
you, my lord, they're all in great awe of you!'

Listener was impressed. So this was how the power of his flute tasted!
He tried it, and found it sweet. No sooner did he start to play than
people did his bidding and called him 'my lord'.

'Will you do my poor house the honour of staying longer, my lord?'
inquired the innkeeper, bowing low.

Listener shook his head. He was almost sorry now that he hadn't
come by way of Barlebogue. He felt sure he could have given Barlo
quite a surprise with his music. Well, at least he'd show his father that
he amounted to something after all, and then he'd be off to Arni's Folk
without further delay. 'No,' he said. 'I ride on today.'

If Listener's arrival in Draglope had passed unnoticed, his departure
made a great stir. News of his performance in the Silver Harp last
night had plainly spread like wildfire, and no doubt many a man
who took part in that dance had exaggerated slightly when required to
explain how he came by such a great bump on his forehead. At any
rate, Listener thought there was an unusually large crowd in the vicinity of the Silver Harp that morning, and the people all looked curiously
at him as soon as he rode out through the inn gates. Some of them
bowed low, as if to a great lord, when he trotted past. Others made the
sign against evil spirits and shrank into alleyways as soon as they set
eyes on him; these were very likely some of the brawlers who had been
at the inn yesterday. They wouldn't want to dance again in a hurry.
Women stood by the roadside, pointing out the great magician to the
infants in their arms. 'Look, that's the Mighty Fluter!' he heard one
woman say. So it sounded as if he already had a name among the
common folk! Listener reined in his horse and gave the woman a
friendly nod. Encouraged, she stepped forward, asking, 'Are you

leaving Draglope so soon, my lord?' She seemed sorry, and when Listener nodded, she said, 'Oh, what a pity, my lord! You could have taught our menfolk a few good manners with that flute of yours.'

Listener laughed. 'Well, tell your menfolk I'll be back if they step too far out of line!' he said. 'I've something more important on my mind just now.' He pinched the cheek of the woman's child in a friendly way, and let his horse move on. That boy will be telling his grandchildren how the Mighty Fluter pinched his cheek, he thought with satisfaction as he rode through the streets, whistling. A few children tore themselves away from their mothers and began running after him. First there were three of them, then five, and soon a whole troop. The fastest ran along beside him, and there must have been about a hundred trotting along behind, all shouting and laughing at once. Then one of the children raised a clear voice and began to sing:

> *Fluter*
> *be not mute,*
> *play upon your silver flute.*
> *Let us dance, let us spring,*
> *to your music let us sing,*
> *through the gate let's set foot,*
> *play upon your magic flute.*

And more and more children joined in the simple, three-note melody, and soon the whole throng of them were repeating the sing-song chant over and over again. So Listener took his flute out of his saddle-bag and began to play. 'Come with me!' he played. 'Run after me! It's better out there in the meadows than here within walls! Come with me, and you can dance and laugh and spring! Dance, then, my little friends, dance out through the gate!' And the children danced as they had never danced before, leaping higher than they had ever leapt in their lives, uttering laughter shriller than any they had ever laughed, and they ran past the last of the houses, following the fluter, and out through the town gates into the open country.

Listener reined his horse in to a slow pace and went on playing, letting the children dance on ahead of him. He saw them moving like marionettes to the notes of his tune, doing his will, he saw them jump in the air with arms raised, as if to seize something that they couldn't reach, yet they would keep on and on trying; he heard their shrill shouts and laughter, he coaxed ever wilder leaps and runs from his flute, intoxicated by the shouts of the children and his own playing, and he made his puppets dance. Every movement of their little bodies was what he had willed, he had hundreds of arms and legs at his command, he was master of every move made by their fingers and toes, he felt the cool grass under his countless bare feet, and the autumn wind blowing through his countless fingers.

When he turned in his saddle to look for the little dancers who had lagged behind, he was surprised to see how far they had come from the town. He also saw a troop of horsemen just galloping out through the town gates. They are coming for their children, he thought, they want to take away my dancers, all my little hands and feet. He urged the children on, making them run faster, but the horsemen were quickly approaching, coming to spoil his game. Couldn't these dismal, narrow-minded folk bear to see their children dancing happily over the meadows? He lowered his flute, crying, 'What, won't you let the children have their fun?'

He got no answer; perhaps the horsemen were still too far off to catch his words. But at the same time he saw that as soon as he stopped playing, the children went staggering helplessly over the turf. Many collapsed and lay there, quite still, and now he could see their pale, exhausted faces, while the fevered gleam in their eyes died away. Those few children who could still keep on their feet, if unsteadily, stared dully at him, and Listener thought he saw revulsion and fear in their glance. Then he turned his horse, spurred it on and galloped away, pursued by the men's angry cries; they were close enough now for him to hear their voices. But they'll never dare lay hands on the Mighty Fluter, thought Listener, looking back over his shoulder. The horsemen, however, had dismounted and were picking up the children who lay on the grass in their bright clothes, like fallen autumn leaves after a storm.

Listener did not let his horse slow to a trot until he was out of sight of the horsemen from Draglope, and could be sure that none of them were after him. Only now did he realize that he had fled like a man afraid of being outnumbered, instead of teaching those men to dance too. Or had it been the fear in the children's eyes that put him to flight? As long as he played his flute they had run along with him, laughing up at him, and he had felt at one with those dancing children who looked to him as their lord and master. He tried to recall that sense of elation, all the pleasure of the shared game, but he couldn't. As he rode slowly on he felt a stale taste in his mouth; it was as if he had suffered some deep humiliation that darkened his mood, although he could not have named the cause of it.

On the morning of the third day after he rode from Draglope, he came to the Misty Marsh. He had crossed it once before, going from north to south, while he rode the land with Barlo, but they had had Lagosh to guide them then, and Lagosh knew these parts like the back of his hand. This time he must find his own way, going east towards Fraglund.

It was a hazy day of late autumn. The narrow path, seldom used, ran over scanty greyish-brown grassland, and then the ground began to slope downhill. He was able to follow the path a little way farther, between sedge and heather, and then it disappeared into the rolling mists that covered the marsh at this time of the year.

Only a man who's lost his reason
walks the Misty Marsh in the autumn season

the landlord of the Silver Harp had muttered, when Listener asked him for directions. 'Wouldn't set foot near the place myself, not so late in the year, but of course a fluter such as you may venture there,' he had added, describing a few landmarks by which Listener might find his way. After about half a day's journey, he had said, he would reach the dead stump of a willow tree, and here the path divided. If you went left you came to the lake at the foot of the mountains, but he must turn right if he wanted to go to Fraglund.

Listener had imagined the marshes as he remembered them: wet, of course, full of pools and muddy waterholes, which were better avoided, but at least visible. Now he saw what he had really let himself in for. A sea of milky grey mist stretched out before him as far as the eye could reach, and he must ride through that mist if he wanted to get to Fraglund. At that moment he came close to turning back, but then he thought of the angry men of Draglope, and the innkeeper who had been sure he was capable of such a journey. His reputation as a Mighty Fluter would be gone even sooner than it had come if he turned back.

Slowly and cautiously, he walked his horse down the path towards the marsh. Snowfoot snorted uneasily, but did her master's bidding. After a few paces, her hooves stepped into the edge of the drifting mist, and the farther Listener rode, the higher that slowly surging tide of vapour rose, soon lapping above his knees, climbing higher and higher, until only his horse's head could be seen above the dim mists before him, and then that too disappeared from sight, and Listener went under himself, breathing in the damp, cold vapours that wrapped him round, hiding everything from view. There was no firm point of reference left, no horizon, no landmark, no solid ground under the horse's hooves, as Snowfoot put them down with a dull thud on the invisible quaking marsh somewhere and lifted them again with a sucking noise. Quite soon Listener had lost all sense of direction, and left it to the horse to find the way. He gave up staring into the formless grey mists, closed his eyes, let the horse carry him on, and only started up in alarm now and then when her hooves splashed into a waterhole. Gradually he lost any sense of going anywhere at all. It was as if the mist made its way into his mind with every breath he drew, dissolving his thoughts into a shapeless mass. Perhaps his horse was going round and round in circles with him, or simply marking time on the spot, but the idea scarcely interested him, and anyway there was nothing he could have done about it.

He did not know how long he had been riding on like this when Snowfoot suddenly stopped dead. Listener looked up, and he thought the mist to his right was a little darker than before. He urged his horse in that direction until the shadow took shape, and could be recognized as the willow stump the innkeeper had mentioned. So this was where the path divided. Listener dismounted, got down on his knees and investigated the ground. There was scarcely a thing to be seen, but his hands felt the place where the trodden path forked. He led Snowfoot a few paces along the path that went right, and then mounted again, leaving everything else to the horse.

The mist seemed to be getting even thicker now, weighing on Listener's chest as if to choke the breath out of him. Evening was probably coming on as well, since the monotonous grey all around him was gradually assuming a darker tone. Listener was just beginning to wonder where he could spend the night when a horseman unexpectedly emerged from the mists, quite close to him, and rode on at his side. Listener wished the newcomer a polite good day, but got no answer. Perhaps the man had nodded to him, but a nod would hardly have been perceptible in the gathering gloom. Listener tried to make out the appearance of his silent companion, so far as the thick, milky mist would allow him, but he could perceive little more than a grey figure on a grey horse. Even the stranger's face looked grey as the face of a corpse. For a while this grey man rode along beside him in silence, and then he suddenly swerved aside from the path. Unhesitatingly, Snowfoot remained at his side.

'Where are we going?' asked Listener. Instead of replying, his companion pointed forward, as if anyone could see where the path they were now following led. And a moment later they actually could see, too; a dark shape appeared in the formless mist before Listener's eyes, and became a brown wall. The horseman dismounted, tied his horse up to a stake in the ground, and opened a door in the wall. He turned in the doorway, looked at Listener with empty, expressionless eyes, and said, 'Dismount and come in!' His voice was flat and unexpectedly high, and there was no telling if this remark was meant as a friendly invitation or an order given to a prisoner.

Listener dismounted and went to the door. He could now see that the brown wall was the front of a house; the outline of its roof loomed vaguely in the rolling mist. As he entered, he touched the wall with his hand, and thought it curiously spongy, saturated with moisture. It was made of blocks of peat cut to a regular size and set together like masonry.

The stranger went first, leading him into a room where pale twilight prevailed; casting no shadows, this dim light seemed to proceed from the damp walls. The room's furnishings, a couple of benches and a kind of table, were made of stacked peat blocks too. There was no fireplace. The stranger sat down on one of the peat benches and told Listener to sit opposite him. 'Welcome to my house, Listener,' he said as soon as his guest was seated. Listener was surprised to be addressed thus by name. He could scrutinize the stranger at his leisure now, but he could not have said much if anyone had asked him to describe the man. Even here indoors, everything about him looked grey: his hair, eyes and face were of so indeterminate a colour that you forgot them again the moment you turned your gaze away. His clothing was grey too, although he seemed to take the greatest pains with it; his grey neckcloth was perfectly tied, his coat and breeches fitted without so much as a wrinkle, and in spite of the long ride his grey boots were spotless and shining.

Listener raised his eyes and looked the man in the face again. 'How do you know my name?' he asked. 'Who are you, anyway?'

'I am known as the Grey One,' said the man, 'and you needn't wonder at my knowing you, considering all the attention you attracted in Draglope.'

'Shouldn't I have done so?' asked Listener.

The Grey One shrugged his shoulders, indifferently. 'That's your own business,' said he, 'but you'll hardly make many friends that way.'

'What do you mean?' asked Listener. 'Weren't those children my friends when they came out of the town with me?'

'Maybe,' said the Grey One. 'But when your game was over they feared you. You always will overdo things, won't you? Using your flute like a club or a whip. You play it because you're angry, or just because the spirit moves you to play. And as long as you play the flute, you can bend others to your will, but your power is gone as soon as you stop. Nobody likes to act under duress.'

'Well, that's the nature of my flute,' said Listener. 'No one can withstand its music.'

'Scarcely anyone,' the Grey One corrected him. 'I know. But as yet your power goes no farther than the sound of the flute. Does that satisfy you? You could learn to use it in such a manner that, afterwards, everyone would think he had acted entirely of his own free will. Only then will your power be boundless. Do you want to learn the trick of it?'

Listener had heard the Grey One's remarks with interest. Here, at long last, was someone who could tell him how to use the magic powers of such a flute as his. His grandfather had always avoided answering the question. He nodded eagerly, and expected to hear a speech of some length. But the Grey One only said, 'Then watch carefully!'

Listener was about to ask what he was supposed to watch when the wall of peat blocks before his eyes brightened, as if it had unexpectedly turned transparent. Looking through it, however, he saw no misty marsh, but a bright, green landscape with grassy slopes, bushes and little woods stretching to the distant blue horizon. And while he looked out through this window that was no real window, he dreamed:

The Dream of the (Almost) Perfect Flute

He was riding through that countryside, trotting along through fragrant summer meadows, enjoying the beauty of the landscape. I would like to live here, he thought, and as his mind entertained this wish he heard horns blowing on the borders of the forest. Looking up, he saw a hunting party riding out of the trees: ladies and gentlemen in fine clothes, and a number of huntsmen with a pack of hounds. They stopped when they came to the edge of the woods. One of the gentlemen, who wore a golden circlet around his hat and seemed to be the chief among them, gave an order, and instantly the huntsmen jumped off their horses, pitched a tent and began to prepare a meal. Meanwhile the hunting party sat down on the grass. Listener heard the sound of joking and laughter, and wished he were among those merry gentlemen and ladies. 'Then go and join them!' he heard a voice say, so he turned his horse aside from the path and rode towards the hunting party.

When he reached the hunters' horses he dismounted, and was making for the merry company when a servant, one of the huntsmen, barred his way and asked in no very friendly tone what his business was. Listener did not know what to say, for he could hardly reply that he felt like dining with the fine ladies and gentlemen. 'Off with you,' said the huntsman, 'or I'll set the hounds on you!'

'Try it!' Listener heard himself say, and was instantly much alarmed by his own words. I must be out of my mind, he thought. As he stood there, undecided, watching the huntsman go over to the hounds, he heard that voice again. 'Take out your flute,' it said, 'and bend the hounds to your will.' By the time Listener's flute was out of his pocket, the huntsmen had reached the hounds and was letting them off their leashes. Yapping, the pack raced towards Listener, but he raised his flute to his lips and began to play. 'Come here, little dogs, come to me!' he played. 'Show me how prettily you can jump! Come and let me stroke you and pat you! Come and lick the dust from my boots and wag your tails!' And immediately the yapping turned to a cheerful barking and the whole pack fawned around the fluter, some of the hounds even lying down with paws in the air so that Listener could bend down and tickle their stomachs between trills.

The huntsman stood watching in amazement, left quite at a loss. The sound of the flute had attracted the attention of the ladies and gentlemen too. Some of them rose to their feet and came strolling over, among them the nobleman with the golden circlet on his hat. 'What's all this racket?' he asked the huntsman, who could only stammer, 'Well, my lord, I was setting the hounds on this stranger, you see . . .'

At that the fine ladies and gentlemen began to laugh. 'Setting the hounds on him!' they repeated again and again, scarcely able to contain their mirth.

'But obviously without much success!' said the man with the golden circlet. Then he turned to Listener, and said, 'If you've quite finished playing with the hounds there, I should like to know who you are.' He spoke in an offhand manner, yet there was a note in his voice that made it seem advisable to comply with his wishes at once.

'Run back to your places and lie down, little dogs!' played Listener, and as the pack ran off to lie quietly down in the grass where they had been before, Listener went over to the nobleman, bowed, and said, 'My lord, my name is Listener.'

'Do you know in whose presence you are?' asked the nobleman.

'No, my lord,' said Listener. 'I saw your party and rode this way.'

'Tell him, then, my brave setter-on of hounds!' said the nobleman. It was plain to see how the importance of this task shook the huntsman out of his confusion and straightened his back. 'Hear this, young fellow!' he told Listener. 'You are standing before Duke Gelimund, lord of the Towering Castle and all the country round about as far as the eye can see.' He bowed deeply to his master, and Listener bowed again too, saying, 'Greetings, Duke Gelimund.'

'And what do you do when you're not playing the flute?' asked the Duke.

'Nothing,' said Listener, 'for I am only a fluter.'

'I see,' said the Duke. 'I suppose you're after a position in my retinue, eh? You'll need to be capable of more than piping to a pack of hounds, Listener. I have the best minstrels in the land at my court, and you look rather young to me.'

'Age doesn't make a man a good fluter,' said Listener. 'You haven't heard me play to men and women yet.'

The Duke frowned. 'Not particularly modest, are you?' said he. 'I warn you, if we don't care for your playing, I shall find means of setting my hounds on you after all. Will you still venture to play?'

'I trust to my art,' said Listener.

'Then come and show us what you can do,' said the Duke, commanding Listener to follow him back to his party. As they walked over to the group of ladies and gentlemen, Listener keeping a little way behind the Duke, who strolled on ahead, he heard the voice again. 'Bend them to your will,' it said. 'Play so that they never want the music of your flute to stop!'

The Duke indicated to Listener that he was to stand in the middle of the circle of ladies and gentlemen, and asked his friends to listen carefully to this fluter, a fellow with rather a high opinion of himself. 'In any case, we'll have some amusement,' he said. 'Either the lad's as good as he says, in which case we'll enjoy some excellent music, or he's not worth anything, and then we'll have our jest with him!' He sat down on the grass beside a beautiful dark-haired woman, laid his head in her lap, and made a sign to Listener to begin.

Listener bowed to his audience, who were laughing as they made remarks about his rustic clothing, and then he looked around and let his eyes dwell on the sparkling, mocking gaze of the dark beauty who had won Duke Gelimund's favour. Only then did he raise the flute to his lips and begin to play. He piped a wheedling little tune that sounded like a question. 'What would you like to hear, fair one?' he thought as he played, and as if in answer the lady patted her hair with delicately spread fingers, and straightened the string of pearls whose muted light was entwined in her piled braids. 'So you want praise of your beauty,' thought Listener, and his flute sang, 'You are the loveliest woman here, most noble lady, there is none to compare with you. Your hair is glossy as the raven's wing, and when you laugh your teeth are a row of shining pearls more regular than the pearls in your hair. And being the loveliest of all, you have won the Duke's heart.' He saw the lady's slender fingers running through the Duke's curly fair hair. 'The great Duke is in your hands, as well you know,' Listener played on. 'He will do whatever you wish, for you are truly the mistress here.'

As he played, Listener watched the mockery vanish from the dark beauty's face, at first giving way to an expression of surprise. Then that face began to glow with pride, and she listened spellbound to the flute's song in praise of the power of her beauty.

When Listener had finished playing, the lady bent her head to the Duke's ear and whispered something into it. The Duke nodded, as if granting a wish, took a gold piece from the purse at his belt and threw it to Listener, who caught it neatly. 'Well, you can play sweet music for pretty ladies, I'll admit,' said he. 'I obviously underestimated you. Now let's see if you can play music fit for men!'

Listener bowed again, and this time he looked the Duke himself in the eye. Once more he began his tune with a question, keeping close watch on the man to whom he was playing, who was now sitting upright beside his lady. The Duke's head was raised high, so that his strong, cleft chin jutted, and his eyes ranged haughtily beyond the hunting party. His right hand lay on the dark beauty's knee. 'You pride yourself on your strength, Duke,' thought Listener. 'Well, I can oblige you there.' And he let his flute speak to the Duke. 'By right you wear the golden circlet, Duke Gelimund, for you are the best and strongest man here or anywhere within the borders of your land. With your curling tawny hair, you resemble the mighty lion, and when you frown your courtiers tremble. No woman could withstand you if you desired her.' Listener saw the Duke's hand take the beauty's knee in a firm grasp. 'Go on, then, Duke!' played Listener. 'She is the loveliest of all the ladies here, so she is yours. Take what you desire! There's no one here who could refuse you anything, and the lady herself can hardly wait to take great Duke Gelimund in her arms.'

With that, Listener ended his second tune. The Duke leaped up, went over to him and embraced him. 'You are the best fluter that ever I heard!' said he. 'Ask for whatever you want! I must have you at my court.'

Now that the courtiers saw their lord's enthusiasm, they too joined in the applause, praising Listener's art to the skies. When the Duke again urged him to say what he wanted, Listener thought for a moment, and then said, 'Let me have lodging at your castle, and a new suit of clothes so that you need not blush for me, and then I'll gladly serve you.'

'You are too modest,' said Gelimund. 'But at least that leaves me the satisfaction of rewarding you as I think fit.' He took a precious ruby ring from his finger, gave it to Listener, and said, 'Take this as the first proof of my favour, and wear it always, so that everyone can see you are Duke Gelimund's fluter!'

When the food was brought, Listener was given a place at Gelimund's left hand; the huntsmen spread linen cloths on the grass before the company, served poached fish and roast game and all kinds of salads, with sharp relishes, and poured golden wine into chased silver goblets. And as they lounged there drinking, Listener played a tune for anyone who asked, so that by the time they finally set off again, he had made most of the hunting party his friends.

They rode cheerfully on through the valley, first over meadows and pastures, then past cornfields and through villages, until at last the Towering Castle came in sight. Its countless towers and turrets crowned a steep rock with a threefold wall around it. The evening sun was reflected a thousand times over in the castle windows, which shone and sparkled as if the place were covered in liquid gold. As they rode closer Listener heard a trumpet signal from the topmost tower announce their arrival. Drawbridges were let down with a rattle of chains, portcullises drawn up, so that the Duke and his companions could ride in unhindered. They went up the steep path within the threefold encircling walls, and rode into the castle courtyard, and Listener was amazed at the magnificence of the walls and towers and oriels, works of the stonemason's finest art. Beside this building, Barlebogue Castle would have seemed a humble farmhouse.

That same evening the Duke held a banquet, and all his minstrels were to compete in singing and playing. The whole hunting party and a number of other courtiers gathered in a great hall whose furnishings were more magnificent than anything Listener had ever seen. The long tables were laid with solid gold plate, and the food served was so choice that much of the time Listener hardly knew just what he was eating.

At the banquet, Listener was seated at the lower end of the table, among the minstrels. When the dishes were cleared away, the Duke beckoned Listener over to him and said, 'Wait until the others have all performed. I want to keep you to the end, as a surprise.' And then he signed to his minstrels to begin the contest.

Listener could soon tell that the musicians assembled here were masters of their art. First a fiddler played; the agility of his fingers verged on the incredible. His bow leaped singing over the strings, coaxing such bold runs and trills from his instrument that it took the hearers' breath away. But Listener soon realized that his music was mere virtuosity, and expressed nothing but, perhaps, the vanity of the fiddler, for he revealed himself in his playing.

Next came the harpist, who plucked the strings of his sturdy instrument with the greatest of delicacy. His music sparkled and foamed like a waterfall, but like the fiddler, he could not deceive Listener, who saw that he was in love only with the exquisite ornamentation which so overloaded his tunes, you could hardly hear the melody. And so one man played after another, and Listener could tell that they were all masters of their craft indeed, but none of them was able to draw such music from his instrument as to be any threat to himself.

Last of all a grey-haired singer rose. Listener had seen him among the hunting party; he was one of the few who had not asked him for a tune. He was obviously in high favour at court, for as soon as he came before the Duke the conversation died away, and all present waited with bated breath for his song. But the singer disappointed them. 'I have sung for you so often, Duke Gelimund,' said he, 'that it seems to me unnecessary to put my art to the test. So if I may, I will tell you a fable instead.'

The Duke frowned, and seemed displeased that he was not to have his way. 'Well, I'm used to your foolery, Sparrow,' he said at last, 'and your wit has seldom disappointed me. So do as you please today.'

The singer thanked him with an exaggerated bow, and then went over to the wall of the great hall and sat sideways in a window embrasure. His eyes on the Duke, he leaned back and began his story.

'Once the lion lay in the shade of a tree, resting from his duties as king of the beasts. While he was thinking of the effort it was, to be forever ruling his kingdom, he heard the birds singing in the branches above his head. "Can't you think of anything better to do than whistle and sing all day?" he asked. "How are you going to help the king of the beasts rule his kingdom, pray?"

Then the nightingale raised her voice and carolled, "I sing to let everyone hear the beauty of my voice and the pretty trills I can perform. Doesn't it do your heart good to hear such lovely songs, O king of the beasts?"

"You may boast of your voice, but what use is that to the king?" said the thrush. "You're just indulging your own vanity. Listen, O king of the beasts! Mine is a voice that can change, suiting itself to any of your desires. If you wish to be assured of your strength, then I will praise it. If you desire love, I will coo in the voice of your beloved. If you are angry, I will stir up your rage with my shrill whistling until it bursts into bright flame. And so I can always make you content."

But the chirping sparrow interrupted the thrush, saying, "You may praise all his moods, but what use is that to the king? It seems to me you just want to win power over him through your flattery, and bend his strength to your service. I'll tell you what I can do for you, O king. If you boast of your strength, I'll mock it: you may be strong, my lord, I'll say, but you can't catch a little sparrow that flutters past your nose. If you rejoice in the favours of your beloved, I will ask: are you sure it's not just a share in your power that she wants? And if you roar in anger, I will twitter: roar away, O king, let everyone hear that even you are not all-powerful. And that, to my mind, is the way to help a king."'

The singer fell silent. When he said no more, the Duke looked at him, first in surprise and then with gathering annoyance, and asked, 'But what's the moral? A fable always has a moral!'

'Oh, has mine no moral, then?' asked Sparrow, pretending surprise. 'I believe that if you look for one you'll find it there, O wise Duke Gelimund!' And he laughed, briefly, sketched a bow, and returned to his seat at the table.

Listener saw very well that the singer's challenge was meant for him. He felt as if exposed to the ladies and gentlemen, all of whom were looking at him now. Was it merely in anticipation of his playing, or was there mockery or even scorn in their eyes? For the fable had impressed him too, and he wondered whether the singer had perhaps been right to attack him. 'Right or wrong – what does it matter?' said the voice. 'He is your opponent, so you must fight him. Take the Duke's trust from him! Or do you want to be thrown out of here when you've only just arrived?'

No, Listener did not want that, not by any means. He must go on playing his game, that was quite clear, and the Duke was already making impatient signs, indicating that at last it was time for him to display his art. He stood where he could see the Duke as well as his court, bowed low to the lord of the castle and his beloved, and then, not quite so low, to the other ladies and gentlemen. After that he raised his flute to his lips and began to play.

The magic of the music brought the Towering Castle before his audience's eyes, even taller and more magnificent than it really was, and the image established in everyone who heard Listener's tune the certainty that there could be no greater honour than to be permitted to go in and out of that castle, whether as lord and master of it all or as the least of his servants. 'For you yourselves are the castle,' he played, 'and the castle being perfect, you are parts of its perfection. You are lovely, because the castle has no equal in loveliness; you are strong while these walls stand; you are mighty while this castle rules the land. You yourself, O Duke, are the rock that bears it; you are the wall that surrounds it; you are the tower that rises in its midst. Your magnanimity is like that of the tower which indulgently bears the scolding of the sparrows nesting in the vines upon its walls, spattering it with their dirt, thinking to harm its grandeur and strength and beauty. I praise your generous heart, O Duke, but I ask too: should you show such generosity? Ought you to let doubt poison the hearts of your people, or even your own, as the sparrows' dirt eats away at the masonry bit by bit? Do you not see that they cannot endure your greatness, and will not rest until the castle falls upon you?' And here he showed the castle crumbling away piecemeal before all their eyes: towers falling, the great walls caving in, the outer fortifications blown up, until nothing but a smoking heap of rubble crowned the rock.

His hearers groaned with horror, many buried their faces in their hands, and the Duke clenched his teeth so that the muscles of his cheeks stood out, and he stared at that dreadful picture. 'Is that what you desire, O Duke?' Listener played again. And then he lowered the flute from his lips, and let the picture of the ruined castle disappear.

All was deathly still in the room. The Duke passed his hand over his eyes, as if he were waking from a nightmare. His gaze sought out the old singer, and found him at the other end of the banqueting hall. Sparrow was there alone, leaning back against the wall; everyone else had retreated from him as if he had the plague and his skin were just breaking out in the first signs of it. 'I think you had better leave this castle, Sparrow, and very quickly too,' said the Duke. 'The farther you go, the better for you, for from tomorrow any man in my land may strike you down with impunity.' Gelimund scarcely raised his voice as he spoke these words, but they sounded more terrible than if he had shouted them.

'And won't you have all looking glasses banished from your castle too, Duke Gelimund?' inquired Sparrow. 'For it could be that one day you will see your own face, and take fright.' Instead of answering, the Duke turned his back on Sparrow, who shrugged his shoulders and left the banqueting hall, without any haste. Only when he had closed the door behind him did the Duke turn round again. He went to Listener, laid an arm around his shoulders, and said, 'Thank you, Listener. I thank you for opening my eyes. From now on your flute shall be my counsellor.'

Gelimund would not allow Listener to go back to his place at the lower end of the table, with the minstrels, but made him sit between himself and his beloved. 'Bring wine for the victor!' he cried, and now the ladies and gentlemen all applauded, not in the casual way in which they might applaud any chance-come minstrel, but as courtiers show honour to a new lord. The dark beauty laid her hand on the Duke's arm and said, 'Sir, will you allow me to reward the fluter for his music?' And when the Duke nodded, she leaned over to Listener and kissed him on the mouth. As he felt her warm lips, he thought he saw not just liking in them, but desire too, but at that very moment another pair of eyes came between them. 'Your wine, sir!' said a serving girl, and as she placed the goblet on the table she looked at Listener in such a way that the whole image of the festive scene seemed to quiver. Her eyes were of a colour difficult to describe, and they seemed to Listener not only strangely familiar, but very much more real than everything else that was going on around him. The beauty's dark eyes lost all expression, they were merely black holes punched out of a flat mask, and behind the mask the rest of the courtly company paled to a collection of foolishly grinning puppets, while the walls of the hall lost all their magnificence and began to flap in a soundless wind, until the entire image of the banqueting hall and the people in it crumbled. Another image was superimposed on it, as if the normal course of time were suspended. Listener suddenly found himself standing in the castle courtyard, with the courtiers dancing to his flute, headed by the Duke with his beloved, a twitching troop of marionettes, their jerky steps following the same grotesque pattern. He could produce only meaningless, unmelodious sequences of notes; he played and played as if compelled to do so, and could not stop, although he felt horror of those lifeless creatures that were kept in motion only by his flute. One figure alone had independent life, and was not drawn into the stupefying rhythm of the dance, a woman who had appeared in the background and now slowly approached Listener. She walked straight through the shapes of the dancers as if they were water, she was the only living creature in a world of shadows, and Listener recognized the serving girl again, saw her eyes bent upon him, a flickering play of colour, blue and green and violet, and before the depth and reality of those eyes the phantom movement of the dancers vanished like smoke, until the face of the serving girl was close to his, filling all his field of vision, the face of a strangely ageless woman who asked him, 'And do you think a tune or so upon the flute is all?'

*   *   *

That question was still ringing in Listener's ears when he opened his eyes, and found himself looking at the wall of greenish brown peat again. 'Where's the castle?' he asked, bewildered.

'Just what I'm wondering myself,' said the Grey One, looking at him with suspicion. 'What's that you have in your hand?'

Only now did Listener realize that he was clutching something, something soft, but with a hard object beneath its surface. When he looked down, he saw what it was. His shirt was open, and his hand had grasped the leather bag containing the eye-stone.

'What's in the bag?' asked the Grey One sharply.

'Only a stone,' said Listener.

'Give it to me!' the Grey One demanded, stretching out an imperious hand.

'No,' said Listener. He leaned back, and looked the Grey One in the face. 'Why do you want my stone?' he asked.

'It does you harm,' said the Grey One. 'I must free you of it.'

'And what will happen if I don't give it to you?' asked Listener.

'Then you will never find your way out of the Misty Marsh,' said the Grey One, 'for I alone know that way.'

Listener thought for a little while. Then he laughed briefly, and said, 'But I will make you show me the way.' And he took out his flute and began to play. 'No one can withstand my art,' he played, 'not even you, Grey One. Get up and go to the door, take your horse and ride before me until we are out of the Misty Marsh!'

He tried to put all the power at his command into this order, but the Grey One did not so much as raise his head, let alone get up or go to the door. While Listener was still playing he said, in his colourless voice, 'Don't bother, Listener. Your magic doesn't work on me. I'm not particularly musical.'

So Listener stopped playing, and lowered his flute. 'Well, now do I get your stone?' the Grey One asked. But Listener shook his head. 'I can't let you have it,' he said. 'How could I play my part as Bearer of the Stone among Arni's Folk if I have no stone to bear? It's the only currency I have to buy myself power, and I must keep it for myself.'

The Grey One had been listening attentively. 'What you say sounds not uninteresting,' he remarked, after a while. 'If that's how you see the matter, then it may turn out to be just as well if I leave you your stone. On the other hand, inanimate as the thing is, it sometimes seems to develop a kind of life of its own, so that one can't count on it. I don't like that. Won't you let me have it after all?'

'By no means,' said Listener firmly. 'If I lose my stone I might as well perish here in the Misty Marsh anyway.'

'You are obstinate,' said the Grey One. 'But you seem to have a very good idea of what you want – or at least, of what you don't want – and I won't stand in your way.'

'Then you'll show me how to get out of the marsh?' asked Listener.

The Grey One shook his head. 'We will leave your fate to chance,' said he. 'And you may think yourself lucky that I don't lead you astray. Find your own way out!'

His voice had grown softer and softer as he spoke these words, until finally it was like the rustle of paper, or dry reeds, a dull whisper of a sound that seemed to reach Listener's ears from far away. And now exhaustion from his hard journey through the marsh came over him so suddenly that he could not fight against it; numbing weariness rose around him like a black flood, submerging his brain, and extinguishing his consciousness.

* * *

He woke amidst milky brightness, and found himself lying in an old pit that had partly fallen in. Quite close to him a stack of peat blocks, cut from this pit at some time or other and then forgotten, stood mouldering, already overgrown with green again. Beyond it, nothing could be seen but the thick white mists. Hadn't there been a house or a hut here? Listener tried to remember what had happened, but he could recapture only a few confused and dreamlike scraps, which eluded him again as soon as he tried to put them in any kind of order.

He heard his horse snort somewhere nearby. When he called, Snowfoot came splashing through the marsh and stood by him, hanging her head. Not until he rose to his feet did Listener realize how damp and clammy his clothing was. He got the flagon of rowanberry spirits out of his saddle-bag and took a gulp of it. The liquor burned as it ran down his throat, but it did not seem to warm his body. Instead, he felt as if the mist were swirling wildly around him in a circle. Before the dizziness took control of him completely, he hauled himself laboriously into the saddle, and let Snowfoot have her head to go where she liked. Once her front hooves had stepped into boggy patches a couple of times, she went forward with great caution, and at last found a relatively firm path along which she could trot.

Listener had no idea in what direction he was riding, and after a while, indeed, he began to wonder if there was such a thing as direction here at all. The whole world had dissolved into a shapeless, opaque sludge which absorbed all sound. Listener felt lonelier than he had ever been in his life, and fear of having fallen out of the steady structure of time and space into an empty vacuum attacked him like a wild beast leaping on him: a numbing fear that he too might be sucked into this insubstantial greyness.

Later, he could not have said why he took his flute out of his pocket and began to play. Perhaps it was a desire to give some kind of structure back to time again, perhaps it was just that he could no longer endure the silence, or wanted to reassure himself, like a child striking up a song at night to banish its fear of the dark. And that was the likeliest reason, for he played no new tunes, but songs he had known from childhood, or picked up later somewhere, at some time, songs in which his memory took shape and painted him pictures of a world in which there were scents and colours, shapes and sounds, and a sense of warmth and security in the presence of other people. So he rode on, playing his flute, setting the songs of his childhood

against the dreadful insubstantiality of the mist, playing this tune
and that, and finally the Song of Fair Agla that the girl children of
the Lake Dwellers liked to sing.

When he had played the tune to its end, he heard a deep and
echoing note in the distance. It was quiet at first and then grew stronger
and stronger, until Listener could feel it making the air vibrate against
his skin. At once the mists in front of him began to drift apart, as if
divided by that vibrating note. To the right and left of his way, the
rolling vapours towered up like high walls, but the path through the
marsh lay clear before him, a narrow, trodden track that ran between
reeds, moss and brown pools of water. In places where the quaking
ground did not offer a firm enough footing it was reinforced with logs.
The grasses and clumps of moss were wet with dew, and as the sunlight
flooded into the pathway thus opened up, millions of little waterdrops
sparkled with every colour of the rainbow.

Listener urged his horse on, for now there was no danger of straying
off the path and into a bog. Some wild ducks came flying up on his left,
into the strip of pale blue autumnal sky above the path; they came
down between the walls of mist and settled on a stretch of marshy
water to one side of the track. Listener saw that among the brown
birds there was one white duck, which looked hard at him as he rode
by. The Green Man has sent me help, he thought, and now he was
sure he would find his way out of the Misty Marsh. This was the
domain of the water spirits, and if they were on his side, nothing could
harm him.

The ducks flew after him from time to time, passing him and settling
again on a ditch or pool a little way ahead. They accompanied him
until the path became firmer underfoot and began to slope upwards.
Listener rode on until he had left the banks of mist behind him. Then
he reined in his horse, dismounted, and sat down on a granite rock
overgrown with heather. The great expanse of mist, shimmering in the
pale sunlight, now lay below him, and had closed together again. He
looked back at the drifting mists, and played the song the Green Man
loved so much once more, by way of thanks.

> *. . . fair Agla's laugh was light*
> *and the Green Man sang all night.*

And when he came to the end of the tune, he thought he heard the
song of the Green Man back in the marshes, rising and falling with a

deep, soft swell. But it may have been only the wind blowing through the bare branches of the birch trees up there on the hills.

Listener's journey took him another week. First he rode over rolling moorland, then through woods of oak trees under whose gnarled branches wild boar rooted, grunting, for the acorns fallen among the dead leaves, and finally he rode downhill again into a broad valley of meadowland, and then he knew where he was: Fraglund lay a little farther up the valley, where five streams flowed into the little river along which he was riding.

Listener slowed his horse to a walking pace, and gave himself up to the memories aroused by the sight of this familiar countryside. Over there, on that bend in the river, he had caught his first trout, and here, where the wood came right down to the path, his horse had thrown him when it was startled by a stag suddenly leaping out of the bushes. Listener greeted every stone along his way, and when, towards evening, he saw houses appear beyond a dip in the valley, his heart leaped, even though he knew very well that that was where he would see them. He reined his horse in for a moment, as if to check that everything still stood in its old place, and then let Snowfoot trot on. Half an hour later he was riding through the gateway of his parents' house.

Even as he dismounted from his horse in the yard, he heard his father's mighty voice resounding through the open window of the hall of justice. 'Raiding Riders, that's what you are and always will be!' bellowed the Great Roarer. 'First you try plundering this valley by force, and when you fail to do that, you cut off your braids and disguise yourselves as respectable traders, hoping to get what you want in that way. Well, if that's your game, you thieving lot, I'll soon put an end to it!'

Listener was dismayed. His father was obviously shouting at one of Arni's Folk. Much as he disliked the sound of raised voices, he left Snowfoot standing where she was and strode into the house to find out what was going on in the hall of justice.

His father sat there at the judge's table, tall and broad, and anyone could tell that he relished the resonant boom of his great voice as he scrutinized the three thin and slightly bow-legged men who stood before him, looking subdued, between a couple of Fraglund farmers. 'Cut-throats you've always been, one way or another,' he continued bellowing, 'and like as not you're spies too! But we all know your sort, all of us here in Fraglund – or can you name me a single man who'll vouch for you?'

Such aid was scarcely to be expected from the farmers of Fraglund; they were probably the very men who had dragged these traders before the judge. At any rate, the three prisoners merely bent their heads and made no reply. Arriving in the doorway, Listener said, 'I will vouch for these three men of Arni's Folk.' Although he had spoken quietly, as was his way, everyone in the hall of justice turned to look at him in surprise.

The Great Roarer rose from his table, and asked, according to the custom of the law, 'And who are you, that you offer to stand surety in this case?' But even as he spoke, delighted recognition abruptly swept over his grim countenance. 'Listener!' he cried, striding to the doorway with an agility one would hardly have expected in so heavy a man, and he embraced his son.

Moved by his father's outburst of affection, Listener returned the embrace, although the breath was almost squeezed out of him by so powerful a display of tenderness. Eventually his father held him away at arm's length and scrutinized him. 'Why, you look almost a man now!' he said in his thundering bass, and noticing Listener flinch slightly under his hands, moderated his voice as he added, rather more softly, 'And very glad I am to see you back at last!'

'I'm glad to be back too,' said Listener, slightly breathless, 'and it looks as if I've arrived at just the right moment.'

'Right moment?' asked the Great Roarer, and seeing Listener glance at the traders, he continued, raising his voice again, 'Well, I suppose you were joking when you said you'd vouch for these Raiding Riders, eh?'

'No, Father,' said Listener, quietly but firmly. 'I mean what I say. In any case, they're not Raiding Riders, as far as I can see.' He freed himself from his father's arms and went over to the three men. 'You do belong to Arni's Folk, don't you?' he asked. One of the three bowed to him, and replied, 'Yes, we are traders from that settlement. My name is Tangli, and my two companions are called Lungi and Flangi.' As he named them, the other two bowed as well.

'Why were you brought before the judge?' asked Listener.

Tangli shrugged his shoulders. 'A misunderstanding, I suppose,' he said. 'We tried to trade with an honourable farmer of this pleasant village, and perhaps some lack of skill in us made the man feel he had been defrauded. He called his neighbours, among them one who bore on his face the scars of a good fighter, a man who had plainly proved his courage in battle against the Raiding Riders, for he took us to be men of the horde in disguise, on account of our appearance, and he and his friends brought us before the Great Roarer, may Arni grant him wisdom.'

'It's all right, I'll stand surety for you,' said Listener. 'I met another of your traders, far away in the west, who told me about the Great Parting of the Raiding Riders and Arni's Folk.'

'Will you tell me what that man was called?' asked Tangli.

'Yes, his name was Gunli,' said Listener.

Tangli seemed visibly moved to hear the name, and his two companions were now following the conversation intently too. 'Gunli came back from his journey before we ourselves set out,' said Tangli. 'He told us that he had found the Bearer of the Stone on his travels. Did the Great Roarer call you Listener just now?'

'That's my name,' said Listener, 'and the Great Roarer is my father.'

At this the three traders almost prostrated themselves, and Tangli said, 'We pay our respects, O Bearer of the Stone, and we give ourselves into your hands.'

Much surprised to observe the deference paid to his son by the three traders, the Great Roarer came closer and asked Listener what on earth he had had to do with these people.

'It's a long story, and I can't tell you all the details just now,' said Listener. 'But I can at least assure you of one thing: these men are neither Raiding Riders nor spies for them, but peaceful traders. Haven't you heard of Arni's Folk?'

'Arni's Folk?' asked the Great Roarer. 'What Arni? Do you mean that brother of Khan Hunli's who was called Arni of the Stone? I heard of him in his time, sure enough. A strange kind of man for a Raiding Rider! They say he was a very peace-loving fellow.' And the Great Roarer laughed his booming laugh. 'Think of that, then: a peaceful Raiding Rider! It's beyond me! Oh, and they say this Arni was killed at the time the horde tried raiding Fraglund. You were there yourself when we drove them off.'

'Yes, so I was,' said Listener. 'And I found Arni dying in the bushes, and gave him a last sip of water. He gave me this stone in return.' He brought out the bag from inside his shirt, took the stone out of it, and showed it to his father. As soon as they saw the stone shining in Listener's hand, Tangli and his two companions bowed low and said, in solemn, singsong accents, 'May Arni's Stone enlighten the hearts of men!'

The Great Roarer noted this with some astonishment. 'Why all this fuss over a little stone?' he inquired, baffled. 'You never told me anything about it at the time.'

'No; I didn't know then what the stone was,' said Listener. 'But this will have been the stone that made Arni different from his brother Hunli and all the rest of the horde, a peaceful Raiding Rider, strange as that may seem to you. And now there are others among that people who want to follow his example, and so they call themselves Arni's Folk.'

'Arni's dead,' said the Great Roarer, as if there were something wrong about following the example of a dead man.

'Yes,' said Listener, 'Arni is dead, but his stone, the stone here in my hand, doesn't die, and now I bear it.'

He realized that his father was suddenly seeing him in a new light. 'Hm, well, these people seem to think a lot of you,' remarked the Great Roarer, not without surprise at finding his son regarded with such respect. As if in confirmation, the three traders struck up their singsong chant again. 'Arni has chosen you, O noble Bearer of the Stone, Arni's wisdom is within you!'

The Great Roarer raised his bushy eyebrows in astonishment, having hitherto been quite unaware of any notable wisdom in his son. Also, he did not feel much at ease with the solemnity which had entered into this scene, and decided it was time to get back to the subject of the judicial hearing. 'Well, I can tell that you're entitled to vouch for these men,' he said, 'and it looks as if we were wrong in taking them for Raiding Riders or spies. But we still have to decide whether one of my people has been defrauded.' He turned to the farmer who had laid the charge, asking him to describe exactly what had happened, but the man cast down his eyes and muttered that maybe he'd been too hasty; he did not make it clear whether this was his own better judgement speaking, or whether, in view of the altered situation, he saw no likely prospect of winning his case against the strange traders who had unexpectedly turned out to owe some kind of allegiance to Listener.

'Then you had better hurry off home, all of you!' thundered the Great Roarer, 'or I myself will teach you what may happen to a man who brings a case before the judge when he can't sustain it!' And indeed he looked as if he were about to fall upon the alarmed farmers, in what Listener thought a sudden burst of rage hardly justified by its cause. He found himself observing his father as if he were a stranger. What had made that normally imperturbable man lose control in such a way? The fact that there had turned out to be no legal foundation for the farmer's case? But such things happened often enough. Or was he angry because the unexpected turn events had taken shook his confidence? Did it anger him that his son's arrival had suddenly removed him from the centre of the stage? In Listener's memory, the Great Roarer had always appeared an unassailable figure, an invulnerable example of overwhelming might, whom there could be no possibility of emulating, a judge standing aloof from all else and always, indubitably, in the right. The Great Roarer still seemed to him very great and powerful; the mighty thunder of his father's voice still made him tremble; but he also saw, for the first time, the imperfections in that rough-mannered man, and realized that his fit of rage was meant only to hide a moment's weakness. And having uttered his threat, the Great Roarer let it rest at that, calmed down again, and said, 'You may thank my son for it that you're getting off so lightly. I won't cast a shadow over his return by punishing anyone.'

The farmers did as they were told and made haste to leave the hall of justice. Then Tangli went up to the Great Roarer, bowed, and said, 'We thank you for your just ruling, O mighty-voiced guardian of the law. Will you permit us to continue on our journey?'

'Yes, yes, you're free and can go where you like,' said the Great Roarer; it was obvious that he would be glad to see the back of these curious Raiding Riders who were not Raiding Riders at all. Before they left the room, the three traders took their leave of Listener too, with a low bow. 'Will you grant our humble houses the honour of a visit, as Gunli said you might?' asked Tangli.

'That's what I have in mind,' said Listener. 'I'll set out once the winter's over.'

'Then joy will visit our dwellings in spring,' said Tangli. 'Do you know the way to our settlement?'

'Not precisely,' said Listener. 'But I know that it's on the borders of the steppes, at the spot where Arni built himself a cabin.'

'So it is,' said Tangli. 'Allow a simple trader, I beg you, to venture to tell you the way.'

'Yes, by all means please do,' said Listener.

'You show me great honour,' Tangli assured him. 'Listen, then: here in Fraglund, five streams meet like the fingers of a hand. Choose the midmost of these watercourses and follow it to its source. There the

Crooked Wood begins, and the shortest way to Arni's House would be through that wood. Yet you had better not set foot in it; the stunted tree trolls of that place hate men for their straight and upright bearing. So beware of them, and choose instead the longer way, up the pass and northward, until you come to a narrow path leading over the mountain summits and then down to the edge of the steppes. If you turn north there, you will reach Arni's House after some two days' riding.'

Listener thanked him for these directions, and asked him to deliver greetings to Arni's Deputy. Tangli accepted this errand with another deep obeisance, and then he and his two companions left the hall of justice.

The Great Roarer heaved a sigh of relief when, after a good deal of bowing, they were out of the room at last. 'Gets on my nerves, all that politeness,' said he. 'The way those traders were fawning on me, right from the start, I didn't know if they were just afraid, or trying to make a fool of me! What way is that for a man to behave? At least you knew where you were with the Raiding Riders. I can't imagine what you see in such folk, Listener.'

'They obviously see something in me,' remarked Listener, putting his stone away again.

'They seem to think a great deal of that stone of yours,' said the Great Roarer, as if to make it quite clear that no cause for the showing of such respect to his son could be sought in that son's person. Or at least, that was how Listener understood the remark, and he said more brusquely than was usually his way, 'They trust me because Arni chose me Bearer of the Stone. Anyway, I'm going to accept their invitation.'

'Well, plenty of time to discuss all that between now and spring,' said the Great Roarer. 'Don't speak of going away again when you've only just arrived! Now let's go and find your mother. She's waited long enough to see you again.' And he took his son's arm and led him out of the hall of justice and into the living-room of the house. Even as they came in, he was calling in his great voice, 'Look who I have here!'

Listener's mother was sitting by the window, looking out at the garden behind the house. She turned quickly in alarm, like someone caught idling, and then recognized her son. The sewing things that had been lying in her lap fell to the floor as she jumped up and ran to Listener. She took him in her arms, and only now did he feel he was truly home again. He felt her tears in his throat; much moved, he cautiously hugged his mother's frail shoulders. 'Now, now, there's nothing to cry about!" growled the Great Roarer, but rather as if to hide the emotion that threatened to overcome him too.

'It's only happiness,' said Listener's mother, hugging her son once more. Then she let him go, and looked at him. 'You've grown taller!' she said, and added, with a smile, 'Or it may be that I've shrunk a little! Come, sit down beside me and tell me what you have been doing! When did you last see my mother and father?'

Listener had been fearing this question since the moment he entered the room. He sat down opposite his mother at the window and looked into her face. To his surprise, he could tell from the expression in her eyes that she was prepared for the news he had to give her, and he could not quite see why she had put her question in such a way. So he told her the full story: how he had first met his grandparents, and about his second visit, and how at last he had buried the Gentle Fluter next to his wife on the green hill under the three rowan trees. His mother listened as if she already knew it all, and only wanted to make sure of what had happened. 'I am glad that you were with them,' she said at last, 'and particularly in those last days when my father was alone in his house. What became of his flute? Did he take it to the grave with him?'

'No,' said Listener. 'When I was with him the second time, he taught me how to play it, and made me his heir the day before he died. I am a fluter now.'

'I hoped for that,' said his mother. And the look she cast her husband as she spoke showed that this was not the first time the two of them had discussed the matter, and Listener could well imagine why. Very likely, he thought, his father had not yet given up the idea of training him to take over the office of judge in Fraglund. The Great Roarer was not a man who could hide such feelings, and disappointment could clearly be read on his face now. 'Well, satisfied, are you?' he asked his wife. She looked at him with her calm grey eyes, and said, 'Do you really think all I cared for in this matter was being right? Don't you yet see that you cannot force your own ways on Listener?'

'Ah, well, I suppose I'll have to get used to it, if he's got other things in mind,' said the Great Roarer, with resignation. 'No sooner had he come than he was talking of going away again!'

Listener's mother looked at him in alarm. 'Won't you stay, then?' she asked, and Listener saw her making an effort not to burst into tears again. He nodded, and said, soothingly, 'Well, until spring, at least.' Seeing the trouble disappear from her face, he told her how he had come by the stone, and of his invitation to visit Arni's Folk. His mother listened intently, and when he came to the end of the tale, she said in surprise, 'So you have Arni's stone as well as the flute!'

'Is it so special?' asked the Great Roarer.

'What, Arni's stone?' said Listener's mother. 'My father often told me of that precious jewel when I was still a child. He said it was probably due to the mystery of that stone that Arni wished to live at peace with all men, but that was not by any means all the stone hid beneath its smooth surface.'

'Then it's a fitting companion for your gentle father's flute,' said the Great Roarer. 'But how can anyone who cherishes such dreams live a man's life?'

'Ah, my dear,' said his wife, laying her hand on his arm, 'can't you see that there may be other ways of living well besides your own?'

'Better ways, I suppose you mean,' said the Great Roarer, gruffly.

'No,' replied his wife, firmly. 'I mean other ways. For I like your own way very well too.'

Listening to this conversation, Listener realized, to his surprise, that for all her fragility, his mother had more strength in her than the strong, hairy man to whom her words had just returned his confidence. The Great Roarer suddenly began to laugh. 'Just like your father!' he said. 'There was no real quarrelling with him either.'

One morning not long afterwards, Listener went out into the garden. He strolled along the gravel path surrounding the large circular flower bed, already covered with branches of pine for winter protection. In spring, fat, round paeony buds would come up here, opening as if by magic into deep red flowers the size of cabbages. As he thought of it, he could almost smell their sharp scent.

When he was half-way round the dormant flower bed, he stopped at the archway into the orchard. The thin, thorny branches of the climbing rose that grew over the weathered framework of the arch had already lost their leaves, and only quantities of wrinkled, dark red hips still clung to the ends of the shoots. Listener went through the archway and into the farther part of the garden. This place, under the gnarled, spreading branches of the apple trees and the tall pears, had been a favourite of his as a child. Then, the garden had seemed to him enormous, a wood among whose trees you could get lost, and when you had finally gone through it and were approaching the fence you reached a wild thicket of vigorous stinging nettles, huge heads of hogweed, and the divided leaves of ground elder, which had a curiously aromatic taste if you chewed them. Sometimes he used to lie down in the middle of that rank green wilderness, so that the rough stems of the weeds towered high above his head, and he was sure no one would find him here.

The orchard seemed much smaller now than he remembered it: a place kept well within bounds, visible in its entirety at a glance, and one he could cross with only a few strides. He looked up at the branches where a few leaves still hung against the blue autumnal sky, those of the apple trees brownish yellow and wrinkling as they withered, the smooth pear leaves tinged with red. Most of the leaves had already fallen, and their acrid fragrance rose at every step that stirred them. Listener leaned against the rough trunk of an apple tree, closed his eyes, and gave himself up to those thoughts suggested by the pungent odour of autumn. That odour seemed to him more real than anything that had happened since he left Fraglund: more real than his nights with Gisa in Barlebogue, his long journey with Barlo, his time of study with the Gentle Fluter. Were all these things, perhaps, only stories that someone had invented, dreams that would dissolve into nothing if you tried to touch them? The only reality was what he felt here and now: the fissured bark of the apple tree beneath his hand, the dead leaves he heard rustling underfoot, their bitter, acrid scent bringing him back a reality he thought he had lost. He was still a child, safe beneath the trees of his garden where no one could find him, and here he would stay, for there were no difficulties and no confusions here. Was it really so? Was there any tangible proof that he had not been dreaming after all? He felt the little bag on his breast, the slight yet perceptible weight of the stone on his bare skin. 'Leave me in peace, stone!' he said, but the stone was there, gentle yet heavy around his neck, a weight he could not shake off. Listener put his hand inside his shirt, brought out the stone and looked at it. The branches of the apple tree were mirrored in its surface, shrunk to the size of a tiny decorative motif, but underneath the colours shimmered, going deep, deep down, blue and green and violet, a living, throbbing eye that looked at him, or out of which someone was looking at him. 'Do you think you can still escape into your childhood, Listener?' asked the woman with the lovely, ageless face. 'You are no longer the little boy who hid here among the grass and weeds so that nobody could find him. You were found long ago, Listener, didn't you know?'

'You always used to hide here as a child, too!' said his mother.

Listener looked up and saw her standing in front of him. 'Is that Arni's stone?' she asked, looking at the shimmering eye-stone in Listener's hand.

'Yes,' he said. 'I was just talking to it.'

'And what did it say?' asked his mother, smiling.

'It said I couldn't hide here like a child any more,' said Listener, 'and it was right: you found me.'

'A clever stone,' said his mother. 'May I hold it for a moment?'

'Of course,' said Listener. His mother made a cup of her two hands, and he put the stone in it. It lay there like a mysterious egg, nesting in the warmth of her palms. She looked at it closely, as if to discover what was hidden under its smooth and shimmering surface. 'It's very beautiful,' she said, after a while. 'You go deeper and deeper down into the play of those colours. It's as if all the eyes that were ever reflected in the stone were looking at you: your eyes first, Listener, and my father's too, and then there's a blue gleam caught in the stone like the blue of sapphires, a lost blue fleeing through the green woods, forever hiding like a wolf in the bushes, and that dark, almost violet glow must be Arni's eyes, the dark eyes of a Raiding Rider who trusted this stone so much that he found the strength to set himself against all his people until the day he died, leaving only his eyes to live on in the stone; and shining far down below, all colours in one, the eyes of Urla, that old and beautiful woman with whom the story of the stone began. Or is it a little girl looking at me, a child who knows nothing of all this, and yet is ready for anything because she sees the world with Urla's eyes? Oh, Listener, you cannot hide from these eyes; you have been found, though you will yet lose your way.'

'Shall I?' asked Listener, disbelievingly, for he thought his mother was getting the sequence of events confused. Surely the time in which he had gone the wrong way was well behind him now? 'I know what the stone will bring me,' he said, but the glance his mother gave him made him less sure of that after all.

'Do you really know?' she asked. 'I am afraid it is far from being all that you hope for.'

'Well, I'll be content for the present with knowing my next step,' said Listener.

His mother nodded. 'I think it is the quality of the stone that it will show you no more than what you seek to know yourself,' she said. 'At least, that was how Urla once explained it to my father.'

'When?' asked Listener. 'On the day that Arni got the stone?'

'No,' said his mother. 'It was later, when he had left the Raiding Riders' camp. Didn't you know he visited Urla once more?' And when Listener shook his head, she said, 'Come, let's walk in the garden for a while, and I will tell you what I know about it.'

She gave Listener back the stone, and he put it in the bag around his neck again. 'You keep it in the right place,' said his mother, smiling. 'If it hasn't yet reached your mind, at least it lies over your heart.'

And what was that supposed to mean, Listener wondered, as he walked beside his mother, shuffling through the rustling leaves under the fruit trees. 'You always liked to do that as a child,' she said. 'Sometimes I feel as if you'd hardly been away at all.'

'That's how I felt just now when I was standing under the apple tree,' said Listener. 'The fallen leaves smelled bitter, exactly as they did all those years ago. Nothing's changed here. But I'm not the same person I used to be when I hid in this orchard. Perhaps I was only hiding from myself. However, since Arni gave me his stone I've been trying to find out who I really am. I thought for a while that the stone was going to bring me nothing but misfortune.'

By now they had reached the fence. The rank weeds had died down, leaving a tangle of stiff brown stems and withered tufts of grass. As they walked along by the fence, Listener's mother said, 'Arni may have felt the same too, at first. That was why my father rode straight to the place from which the path led up to Urla's hut, after saying goodbye to Arni on the edge of the steppes. He left his mule and the packhorse the Khan had given him at that spot and climbed up into the mountains.

He found Urla with her sheep in their pasture. She welcomed him, took him into her cabin and urged him to sit at her table. When my father asked if he could talk to her she shook her head and said not yet, but she was glad she need not eat alone today. She put bread on the table, and a piece of her goat's milk cheese, and all kinds of other things that I have forgotten, although my father could have told you every detail. Food was a matter of some importance to him, but you probably know that. When she had laid the table, she sat down too, saying, "Be my guest, Fluter!"

They did not talk much during the meal, according to the custom of those parts; my father praised the good cheese, and Urla remarked that he had become a little like the Raiding Riders in his movements. She will have said this when he had ·eaten enough and firmly refused anything else she could offer him, for she went on, "Anyone can see you have lived in the Riders' tents for a year, Fluter. And now you have left the horde's camp." She simply stated this as a fact; my father hadn't mentioned it at all.

He took that as an invitation to bring the conversation round to the reason for his coming, and he told her what had happened to cause him to leave. "You see," he said at last, "as a fluter, I couldn't have lived with the Raiding Riders for any length of time, even though Arni and I have indeed become very good friends. And it seems to me that he is not much better off now than he was before: whenever he tries to fathom the secret of his stone, he comes into conflict with the customs of his people, and yet he can't withdraw from the cry of the horde. When you gave him your gift, did you mean that he must always live in such conflict?"

When my father told me this story, he added that he did not know where he got the courage to ask this question at the time, but he had to put it for the sake of his friendship with Arni. However, Urla only smiled and then asked him if he would have preferred Arni to help his brother carry off the girls of the Carpheads down by the Brown River.

"He would never do a thing like that!" said my father at once. Urla nodded. "I know," she said. "It goes against his nature. He is not one of those who enjoy using force on others. Even without the stone, he would have been reluctant to take part in robbery, looting and murder, but he would have despised himself for being unable to live like the other men of the horde. I gave him the stone so that he would know he has the right to tread another path. His own path. It is one of the stone's qualities that it helps one to become what one would like to be."

My father listened intently. Then he asked, slightly disappointed, "Is that the whole secret? Wouldn't it be enough to inquire of oneself and so reach the same conclusion? And if so, what's the point of the stone?"

Then Urla began to laugh in earnest. "Oh, Fluter," she said, "you are still very young if you can say such a thing. Haven't you yet discovered how easy it is to deceive yourself? Even with the stone, it will take him his whole life to get any notion of who he is and what's expected of him. The stone will never show him more than his next step, and that only if he is ready to take it and not ask what the consequences to himself will be. The bearer of the stone does not know all, Fluter, he is very far from knowing all!"

Then my father asked Urla how she could laugh when she was telling him what a hard life Arni was going to lead. He did not think the prospect of it at all amusing. At that Urla shook her head and said, "A hard life? He will learn more of the beauty of life than most, for that's a thing you generally learn only if you don't shut yourself off from whatever seems strange to you.''

I was deeply impressed by these words when I first heard the story. It may be that my father intended it to have that effect on me, since at the time I was hopelessly afraid of anything strange, so much so that many visitors to our house thought I must be deaf. If I had met your father then, I should probably have run away from him in terror.' She laughed, and Listener joined in her laughter. 'No need to be particularly timid for that!' he said. 'I've sometimes wondered how you came to marry such a loud-voiced, forceful man.'

At this his mother stopped laughing. 'You speak of your father as if he were a stranger,' she said. 'You shouldn't. I married him because I love him just as he is. When I met him, of course, it was a few years after my father had told me the tale of his visit to Urla, and by then I wasn't so shy, and had learned to listen to what other people said.' Now she was smiling again, and she added, 'And where your father's concerned, it is very necessary to have learned that, if one's to find out what the Great Roarer is really trying to say.'

By this time they had gone all along the fence and back to the archway with the climbing rose, through the arch and down the gravel path leading to the house again. Listener's mother stopped on the doorstep, looked at the grey bank of cloud lying over the forest of Barlebogue to the north-west, and said, 'A good thing I've covered my flower beds. It will snow tomorrow.'

And snow it did. Winter came down from the mountains, covering all Fraglund and the land around it with a thick blanket of white. Listener stayed indoors most of the time; he was not particularly fond of stamping knee-deep through the snow in icy winds and cold weather. Here, too, he was unlike his father. The Great Roarer was out and about a great deal in the next few weeks; he would often harness the horses to his sleigh in the morning and drive out to the villages, to talk legal disputes over with the farmers, matters they had had no time to settle in autumn because of all the work on the land. At first he had told Listener he should come too and 'get a bit of fresh air into his lungs', as he put it, but when he realized that his son did not much care for driving out in the sleigh he dropped the idea. When he came home in the evening, he marched into the living-room in his thick fur coat, powdered with snow, like a hulking great bear, snatched the fur cap off his head, blew out his cheeks, reddened with the frost, and bellowed something such as, 'So cold today, the snow fairly sings under the sleigh's runners! I hope you've some hot soup on the stove, wife!' And then he would peel off his coat, grunting, and add, 'Ah, you two have no idea how fine it is to let the horses race over the fields till the snow flies about your ears!'

Such hearty pleasures were not to Listener's taste. He would sit for hours by the fire on the hearth, looking into the flames, and in his thoughts he was already riding east to the settlement of Arni's Folk. Sometimes he took out his flute, and tried all the tunes that came into his head, but he could do nothing much with them. The silver flute obeyed his fingers, certainly, but just as any ordinary flute might do. 'Those are pretty tunes you're playing,' said his mother once, and it sounded as if she were a little surprised to hear anyone play such trifling music on her father's flute. Listener soon stopped playing it when his mother came into the room. She would often sit down by the fire with him, and he asked her about the days when she still lived with her parents. Curiously, it seemed she had never heard her father play his silver flute. She had certainly been aware that he was no ordinary man, but all she knew of his playing as Gentle Fluter had been told her by other people, though he did play one of his wooden flutes at home, to talk to his blackbird or for some such reason. Listener's mother also said that he always brought her home new tunes from his long journeys, and played them on a wooden flute until she could sing the melodies for herself.

A new closeness arose between Listener and his mother during these winter days. The Great Roarer noticed it too, and now and then remarked upon it. He was obviously not best pleased that the two of them need only look at one another to communicate, or might suddenly both begin to laugh for some reason that he didn't understand. He may have thought that they were laughing at him, which was certainly not the case. 'You and your secrets!' he would growl. 'Can't the pair of you talk out loud, like normal people?'

And so the winter passed by. The snow melted from the garden beds, icicles dripped day and night from the slope of the roof, and the Great Roarer left his sleigh in its shed and rode out on his big-boned horse. One evening he came back from such a ride in a rather bad humour. 'The people are beginning to talk about you, Listener,' he said, on seeing his son sitting by the fire again and staring into the flames. 'A farmer asked me today if you were sick, or maybe disturbed in your mind, because you never go out and about among them. You must start to do something sensible with yourself, you know. If you don't want to be a judge, then why not play the people some dance tunes on your wonderful flute?'

'I wouldn't wish for that, not if I were them,' said Listener, thinking of the dancing in the Silver Harp at Draglope. His father, naturally enough, had no idea what he meant, and roared, 'Then what in the world is that flute of yours good for?'

'Well, not for amusing your peasants here, at any rate,' said Listener. 'But you're right, it's time I was doing something. As soon as the last of the snow on the mountains has melted, I shall ride to Arni's Folk, where they know how to appreciate a fluter's art.'

This plan was not exactly what his father had meant by 'something sensible', but he had given up all hope of ever seeing his son come round to that way of life which seemed to him the only reasonable one. 'Well, if you like the way those folk who used to be Raiding Riders dance attendance on you . . .' he said, with some scorn. 'Though I for one think they did away with their courage along with their braided hair.'

'Did you like them better when they were attacking our valley to take plunder and burn our houses?' asked Listener.

'I liked them just as little then,' said the Great Roarer, grimly, 'but at least you knew where you were with them, and you could strike back fair and square. But all this courteous to-do of theirs – it's as if they were always putting you in the wrong.' Here he suddenly stopped, as if he had noticed just in time that he was about to betray his own lack of confidence, or that at least was how Listener took his father's sudden silence, and all at once he was sorry he had entered into this argument. 'Let me ride to see them,' he said, soothingly. 'I must find out the qualities of the stone, and I'm most likely to do that among Arni's Folk.'

'Do as you please,' said the Great Roarer, more gently than was usually his way. 'I suppose I should be glad you've got any purpose in mind at all, even if I can't see what you hope to discover. Tell me when you want to set out, so that I can equip you for the journey.'

A week later Listener found his mother uncovering her flower beds in the garden again. The low-growing rose bushes were putting out deep red shoots, the green spikes of crocus leaves were coming up out of the ground, and in the middle of the round bed, still shrivelled and curled, the first pale purple paeony shoots were showing through the fallen brown pine needles. 'Spring is here,' said his mother, and Listener understood the unspoken question behind this remark. 'Yes,' he said. 'I'm setting off for Arni's Folk tomorrow.'

'From all you say,' observed his mother, 'they will receive you with great honour.'

The thoughtful way she looked at him with her grey eyes as she said this made Listener feel uncertain. 'Do you mind?' he asked. His mother shook her head, smiling. 'No, of course not,' she said. 'Why should I mind anyone showing my son such respect? I am only wondering how you will like the position they offer you there.'

'What do you mean?' asked Listener. 'I shall be received as the Gentle Fluter's heir, and Bearer of the Stone. Either of those on its own would be reason enough for Arni's Folk to give me a position of high rank in their community.'

'An heir you will be, anyway, and an inheritance too,' said his mother. 'I would just like to know what Arni's Folk expect to make of that.'

'If I understand Gunli correctly,' said Listener, 'they will see in me the affirmation of those men who left me the stone and the flute.'

'Affirmation?' said his mother. 'Affirmation of what?'

'Well, of the path they're taking,' said Listener. 'Since the Parting of the Ways, many of Arni's Folk must find it isn't always easy to change the customs they've known from childhood. Anyone who still isn't sure needs the kind of confirmation that shows in tangible things – like my stone, or the flute.'

'That may be so,' said his mother. 'But it was not Arni's way, or my father's either, to confirm others in what they said and did. You mustn't forget that no one can be sure of the way he is going, and that includes you, in spite of all that has been laid upon you.'

Listener wondered why she said 'laid upon you'. It sounded as if the gifts of Arni and the Gentle Fluter were a burden placed on his shoulders, one he would find it hard to carry. Well, he supposed that his mother didn't see these things quite straight. It was just that mothers are often unnecessarily concerned when their sons go their own way. So he said, 'Don't worry. I'll do my best to live up to the expectations Arni's Folk have of me.'

'I don't doubt that,' said his mother, but he saw in her eyes that she still harboured other, deeper doubts. He took her in his arms and said, 'Oh, Mother, do you think me capable of so little?'

He felt his mother hugging him close, and heard her say, 'I think you capable of anything, Listener. And don't forget that I shall love

you whatever you do.' Then she freed herself from his arms and cleared
the last of the pine branches off the flower beds, saying, 'Look, everything's coming up out of the ground! It's hard to imagine that that
poor crumpled little shoot will ever be a magnificent paeony, but one
day it will open in all its glory, just as it does every year.'

Listener rode a good distance on the morning of the next day. His
father had given him a packhorse, so that he could take enough provisions for the long journey: a gentle dun who trotted patiently along
beside Snowfoot. The air smelled of spring. Coltsfoot flowers like bright
yellow sunbursts stood among the bushes to right and left of the way,
and the catkins on the pussy willows were fat as bumble bees. Here and
there, a farmer could be seen in the fields, busy with his spring
ploughing. The freshly turned earth gleamed brown and rich, steaming
slightly in the sun.

Listener spent the first three nights in farmhouses, where he was
welcomed in and well entertained as the judge's son. On the fourth day
he stopped in a village at noon and asked a farmer's wife for a mug of
milk. He would not accept her invitation to come into the living-room,
but sat on the wooden bench outside the door to warm himself in the
spring sun.

Standing by him, the woman remarked, 'Looks as if you've a long
way to go, from the stuff your packhorse is carrying.'

'Yes, it is a long way,' said Listener. 'I'm going to the steppes.'

The farmer's wife looked at him in alarm. 'The steppes?' she cried.
'Aren't you afraid of the terrible Raiding Riders who roam those
parts?'

'No,' said Listener. 'I ride with a safeguard that the Khan himself
would not refuse to honour.' He had the stone that lay on his breast in
mind, for he thought that the oath Hunli had sworn to Urla must hold
good for the inheritor of the stone too.

The face of the farmer's wife betrayed her doubts. 'I never heard of
any way at all that'd keep those Raiding Riders from robbery and
murder,' she said. 'Better not feel too sure of yourself! It's downright
dangerous, that's what it is, not to be afraid when you're going into
danger.'

Listener smiled at the woman's concern. 'Thank you for the warning,' he said, 'for I know you mean well. But I've learned that there's a
change coming in the steppes.' Then he thanked her again for the
milk, mounted his horse and rode out of the village.

The farther he left the houses behind him, the narrower his path became. When the last fields ended, so did the cartwheel ruts deeply embedded in the soft ground. The path, seldom used here, ran along beside the midmost of the five streams, only occasionally taking a short cut over one of the wide bends in which it wound its way through the flat grasslands on the floor of the valley. The green slopes of the hillsides, sprinkled with white and purple crocuses, became gradually steeper; the still bare branches of low-growing bushes on the hilltops reached up to the blue spring sky. Listener went happily on his way, enjoying the gentle and pleasant countryside.

Towards evening the ground became stony. The grass grew sparsely here, and the stream, its bed deeply carved, rushed in foaming cascades over large pebbles. The path began to climb the left-hand slope of the valley, and was marked from time to time with cairns of stones, so that a traveller would not lose his way here, where nothing much grew. Finally the valley narrowed. The stream ran sparkling down a steep channel, at whose far end the bushes that had previously grown only on the hilltops closed in to form a wood of crooked, low-growing trees. The path reached the hilltop and the end of the valley, and came to the source of the stream which sprang out, bubbling, into a basin edged with mossy stones under a broad-branched rowan on the outskirts of the wood. Branches of dogwood and spindle arched over the small, almost circular pool of water, making so thick a roof that although there were no leaves on them yet, it felt like entering a cave.

Listener let his two horses drink, and scooped up some of the ice-cold, crystal clear water of the spring for himself. As he drank from his cupped hands, he saw the smooth pebbles lying at the bottom of the basin: white pebbles, translucent at the edges, pebbles with brownish veins, pebbles flecked with green, and others that were a mosaic of many colours. Tiny air bubbles had formed on them all, so that they looked as if they were framed in pearls. Listener picked an egg-shaped pebble out of the spring and looked at it. Its wet surface shone as if polished, and underneath it had a sprinkling of many shimmering colours that seemed to be alive when he turned the stone this way and that in the light of the setting sun.

All of this together – the bubbling spring, the network of branches over it and the pebble that shimmered with colour – gave Listener a sense of familiarity, as if he had come back to a safe harbour that would shield him from all the troubles of the confusing world far below in that hazy distance that stretched beyond the valley. He lay back, and decided to spend the night here.

He saw his two horses grazing on the edge of the wood, went over to them, unsaddled them and hitched them to the trunk of the rowan with long halters. He carried his saddle-bags into the cave where the spring rose. When he had eaten a little, he wrapped himself in his blanket and curled up to sleep on a soft, rustling bed of dry leaves.

By now the sun was below the horizon, and it soon grew dark. Listener saw the pebble lying on the moss, close to his eyes. He took it in his hand and felt its smooth, cool curve between his fingers. The stone had lost its depth of shimmering colour, and looked grey and dull, but when Listener dipped it back in the spring water by his side the surface turned bright and translucent again, and showed sparks of green and violet in the fading light. Listener looked at the play of colour in it, and as he did so his eyes closed and he began to dream:

The Dream of the Woman at the Spring

His shoulders lay nestling on something soft and warm and rounded. Could moss and dry leaves be so soft, he wondered, so warm and full of life? He felt as if gentle arms were holding him, and when he opened his eyes he saw a woman's face above his own. She bent over him and looked at him. Her face was strange to him, and yet curiously familiar, and the starlight shone in her dark eyes in thousands of little coloured sparks. He felt her lap beneath his head, and breathed in a fragrance like wine or aromatic woods. 'Are you the water spirit of this spring?' he asked, quietly and without moving, for he felt that any movement might destroy the image, and this delicious sense of being held with loving care. Instead of answering, the woman put a finger to her lips, and then caressed his face with her hand. 'Ah, Listener,' she said, in that voice which resembled the lower register of a flute, 'you chose the right place to sleep. Here, at the spring, I could find you and take you in my arms. Perhaps you won't entirely forget where you are really going, once you have seen my eyes above you and felt my lap beneath you.' She bent down and kissed him on the mouth, and as he looked into her eyes the image melted away, and he saw the stars sparkling above him through the gaps in the web of branches. 'Don't go!' he murmured, half asleep, and put out a hand, but he felt nothing there but rustling leaves. Disappointed, he lay back again, wondering if it had all been real or only a vision. But her fragrance was still in his nostrils.

* * *

Next morning he was woken by the singing of the birds that nested here in the bushes by the spring. Listener opened his eyes. The first thing he saw was the pebble he had picked out of the basin of the spring the evening before, lying on the moss near his face. He recognized it by its oval shape, although the surface was dry again and would let none of the colour shine through. 'What, hiding again?' he said. 'Then you'd better stay here.' He threw the stone into the water, and it lay there among its fellows, shining and glowing with colour once more. Listener lay on his front, put his face so close to the surface of the water that he felt the fine spray of the rising air bubbles on his skin, and gazed at the strange play of colours. 'What a curious stone you are!' he said. 'Beautiful and alluring when you lie in your pool, but if I take you out to put you in my pocket and carry you away, you soon look like any ordinary stone such as one might throw at a dog. Stay here and wait for me! I may be back.' Then he rose, made a hearty breakfast, saddled and packed up his horses, and then rode on.

According to Tangli's directions, he should ride along the top of the pass northward from here, but the trader had also said that the way through the Crooked Wood was shorter. Listener glanced at the low-growing copse before him; yes, the place deserved its name. It consisted mainly of grotesquely distorted beech trees, with a few hawthorn and barberry bushes among them, and an occasional birch. The ground was still wet and slippery with the snow that had melted only in the last few days. It was probably due to the snow, as well, that the trees could not grow to their proper height on a slope exposed to the worst of the weather.

So it all had natural causes, thought Listener, failing to see what there was to fear in this piece of scrubby woodland. 'Hey there, you ugly tree trolls!' he called. 'Here comes the Bearer of the Stone! So bend your shaggy heads a little lower yet!' And laughing, he urged his horse through the bushes and into the Crooked Wood, thinking up all kinds of mocking names for the wizened objects growing at the wayside, and calling them out as he trotted by. But the farther he rode, the stranger the gnarled, distorted trunks of the beech trees seemed, and they did indeed look rather like a crowd of trolls frozen motionless by daylight, and as if they would wake at night to grisly life. Now and then Listener had the sensation that they were looking at him with hollow eyes that were the knots in their wood, and he had some difficulty in withstanding the temptation to look around. But it was too late to turn back now, and he hoped to have this eerie wood behind him before evening came on: a hope, however, which proved deceptive. When the path reached the top of the next range of heights, Listener saw hilly ground broken by shallow valleys stretching before him as far as the eye could see, and it was covered with the sparse growth of the Crooked Wood to the far horizon.

He urged his horse on as fast as the path would allow; they were still going north-east through valleys and over heights, yet Listener felt as if he were not moving from the spot at all, for the Crooked Wood to the right and left of his path always looked the same. When he came to a stream in one of the valleys where he could water his horses, the sun was already low in the west over a hillside thickly overgrown with bushes. A little farther on there was a rowan tree, its own growth stunted, but with broad branches, and a few clusters of withered, dark red berries still clinging to them. Well, at least this tree had a straight trunk, thought Listener, and he made himself a place to spend the night under the roof formed by its hanging boughs.

When darkness fell a light breeze got up, blowing through the bushes in irregular gusts, and making the few dead leaves still hanging on their branches rustle. A whispering sound arose here and there on the slope, depending where the wind blew, and was continued, came closer and retreated again, as if passing on some secret message, or so it seemed to Listener when, tired from his long ride and already half asleep, he came wide awake again at the sound of that hissing whisper. Whether the wind was getting stronger, or whatever the cause might be, the sound seemed louder with every new ripple of it that reached him, and in the end he thought he could make out separate, distinct voices.

'Is Listener asleep yet?' one voice asked.

'No, he's still awake,' whispered another.

And then came a chorus of enticing voices. 'Come out, Listener, come out!'

Listener did not move, and thought of the countless stunted tree trolls past whom he had been riding all day long. He strained his eyes, looking out into the dark, and by the faint starlight he thought he saw that the trunks of the beech trees around him had moved closer, but it might be his eyes deceiving him. No sooner did he lie back than the whispering began again.

'Won't he?' asked a voice.

'I know what to do,' said another. And next moment the horses became restless, stamping and snorting as if they were afraid of something. Listener threw off his blanket, rose to his feet and peered out at the place where he had tied them up to a dead tree trunk. His mare threw up her head and pranced on the spot, and the packhorse pressed close to the mare. Something was wrong. Listener broke off one of the dipping branches of the rowan, so that at least he would have some kind of weapon in his hand, and started to go over to his horse, but he had only gone a pace or so when his foot caught in the tough snare of a root, and he fell to the ground.

'Now he's ours!' whispered the chorus of voices. Listener felt gnarled fingers reaching for him, but as soon as he hit out with his rowan branch he was free again. He stood up, and now he saw them quite clearly: a circle of hunchbacked trolls pressing close around him. The only gap in the circle was where the rowan stood, as if that stunted rabble feared to be near it. With three great strides, he reached the safety of the roof the tree made over him, and leaned against its trunk, breathing a sigh of relief, while the rustling and whispering outside grew to an angry hiss. 'You let him go!' one voice said angrily, and another whispered, 'He knows that he's safe under the rowan now.'

Listener wondered if this was what had drawn him to the tree. Evidently what the Gentle Fluter had told him by his grandmother's grave was true. 'Thank you for your protection, rowan tree!' he said. 'And please forgive me for breaking one of your branches.' The rowan shook its remaining branches in a gust of wind, as if to show that one more or less scarcely mattered. At the same time the whispering voices outside rose again, growing louder, and now they sounded as if they were quarrelling. 'Take revenge on his horses, then!' screeched a thin voice, and a deeper one, howling like the wind blowing into a hollow tree trunk, replied, 'No, let them be! Don't you know we have no power over them? Animals are innocent; we may only seize upon men.' And then the whispering and rustling died away once more.

Listener sat at the foot of the tree trunk, wrapped himself in his blanket, and waited. But all was still. He felt reasonably safe with the rough bark of the rowan at his back, and it seemed as if nothing would happen to harm his horses. 'Animals are innocent,' the voice had said, and it sounded as if the speaker were one who had authority over those grisly folk. The phantoms of the night had no power over the innocent, but their gnarled claws had grabbed at him the moment he ventured out of the shelter of the rowan. What fault of his, then, had delivered him up to the crooked trolls? Had he not yet atoned for what he did to Barlo? Or was there something else, some deeper guilt, lurking hidden far within him, like a worm secretly gnawing his entrails, a hungry maggot eating and eating until the smooth skin of his consciousness surrounded nothing but an empty cavity? 'We may only seize upon men –' it sounded as if no man was free from guilt, and thus all were vulnerable to any kind of nocturnal haunting.

Listener spent most of the night deep in such thoughts, and did not fall into a restless sleep until it was nearly morning. When the cry of a magpie flying away woke him, it was full daylight. Painfully, Listener straightened up from the uncomfortable position in which he had been leaning against the sheltering trunk all night. His back hurt. His blanket was wet with dew, and the ground was covered with beads of moisture. His two horses stood quietly in the morning sun a little way off, grazing. The gnarled beech trees were all back in their proper places, their crooked roots dug into the ground as if they had never stirred from the spot.

Listener wondered if he had merely dreamed the whole thing, but when he went over to the horses to untie them and get them ready, he saw that the grass around the rowan looked as if countless feet had been trampling it down. He scarcely took time for any breakfast, and he had another sip of his grandfather's rowanberry spirits to warm his stiff limbs. Then he watered his horses and rode on as fast as possible. He had no desire whatsoever to spend a second night in the Crooked Wood.

The path was now following the gently falling slope of the valley downstream, but at first the look of the landscape scarcely changed at all: the shallow slopes on either side were thickly overgrown with those weirdly stunted trees and bushes. Afternoon came, and Listener began to look around in some concern for another rowan, but then he was relieved to discover that the valley suddenly and steeply fell away not far ahead. The tops of tall trees growing down below rose above the horizon: pines, larches, and among them the broad crowns of oaks and maples. At that point in the valley where the high plateau of the Crooked Wood came to an end, the stream rushed down in a torrential waterfall over a rocky cliff to the depths beneath. Here the path turned off to one side, winding its way past the last of the stunted trees, down the steep slope, and so to the timber forest beyond.

Listener rode in under the shade of the tall trees with a sigh of relief.

He felt safe again at last under the roof of that great vault, borne up on the pillars of its trunks. Only now did he realize that since that night by the spring, he had not heard any bird sing in the Crooked Wood except for the magpie that woke him in the morning. Here among the tall trees, the air was full of the whistling and twittering of countless tits and finches, and a jay chattered, and now and then he could hear the tapping of a woodpecker.

Listener rode on for three days past the tall tree trunks, sleeping by night in a mossy bed among the roots of the ancient trees, and letting the dawn chorus of the birds wake him. On the morning of the fourth day the forest began to grow lighter, there were fewer and fewer coniferous trees, and finally none at all. Instead he saw birches growing among the vigorous shoots of young grass, well spaced apart, the fine web of their pendulous branches thickly covered with plump green cones. And ahead of him, through the birch tree trunks, shimmering white and streaked with black fissures, Listener looked out at the wide grey-green plain of the steppes.

The path came to an end here, on the borders of the birch wood and the endless expanse of the grassy steppes, as if it were now up to any traveller to find his own way. But that did not worry Listener. The settlement of Arni's Folk must lie to the north, on the edge of the steppes. He turned his horse left and let her trot briskly over the open ground. This was better than stumbling along the narrow, stony mountain track! From time to time he let Snowfoot fall into a gallop, so that the silver birches flew past on his left, and the poor packhorse could hardly keep up.

He had gone a good way like this when, about noon, he saw five horsemen appear behind a bush and gallop towards him. Judging by their clothing and harness, they were men of Arni's Folk, and Listener spurred on his horse; he could hardly wait to meet these people, who regarded him with such respect. Only when he was quite close to them did he see, to his dismay, that they wore their hair in braids. Next moment they had surrounded him; one man took the reins of the packhorse, another brought his own mount up close to Listener's side, snatched the knife from his belt, and before he knew it, Listener's hands were tied behind his back. Then the Raiding Rider took Snowfoot's bridle, and they set off at a gallop, straight into the steppes. They raced on for a long time over the whispering grass. Once, Listener looked back, and the graceful shapes of the silver birches had already merged into the haze; the mountains upon which the Crooked Wood grew lay like a bank of blue cloud on the horizon. The Raiding Riders urged their horses forward, never once hesitating, and Listener wondered how they could be sure of their way on this monotonous plain, where there was nothing upon which the eye might rest. Nor, hard as he looked, could he see any place where they might be going on that boundless expanse of grass, over which the wind sent silvery, shining ripples from time to time.

It was nearly evening when a black dot emerged from the grey-green shimmer of the steppes, coming rapidly closer. It soon resolved into a troop of some forty Riders, racing towards them at a gallop. Listener felt as if the two unequal groups were going to attack each other, for his companions as well as the men galloping towards them seemed to be spurring on their horses rather than holding them back, and they were now uttering long-drawn-out, piercing yells. Only at the very last moment, when it seemed that they could not avoid crashing into each other, did they rein in their mounts and stop abruptly. One of the warriors with braids who had captured Listener rode over to the leader of the larger troop, a tall, thin old man with a wrinkled face, whose own snow-white braids dangled over his temples, and said something in the language of the Raiding Riders. At this, the old man looked at Listener and beckoned him over. Listener's companion let go of the mare's bridle and pushed him in the back, to make sure he obeyed the old man's command at once. All Listener could understand of the remark accompanying this action were the two words 'Khan Hunli'.

When Listener brought his horse to a halt in front of Hunli, and looked into the Khan's face, he thought he saw Arni himself before him. The similarity between the twin brothers was striking, and yet there was a difference, lying in more than the fact that when Listener saw him for the first and last time, Arni had been wounded to death. Listener saw Arni's eyes on him again, dark, thoughtful eyes with a look of merriment in them. He still remembered how the dying man's merriment had surprised him. But Hunli's eyes were different: of the same colour, yes, but their gaze was hard, as if they were cut out of dark bloodstone. Hunli's leather garments bore no ornaments but the golden brooch that held his jerkin together at his chest. Urla's gift, thought Listener, but then the Khan's sharp voice brought him back to the present. 'You come from Fraglund,' said the Khan, and when Listener looked at him in surprise, for he had no idea how Hunli could know that, the Khan added, 'I didn't

say that you live there. It may equally well be that you stole your
packhorse in Fraglund. Did you?'

Listener shook his head. As he now realized, the Khan had obviously
drawn his conclusions from the harness of the packhorse, which was
out of the Great Roarer's stable.

'A pity,' said the Khan. 'Anyone who robs the Great Roarer's folk
could hope for my sympathy. Well, who are you, then?'

Listener's thoughts were in confusion. Should he divulge his name,
and thus his origins? This did not seem a particularly advisable move,
after what the Khan had just said about the Great Roarer. On the
other hand, here was an opportunity to stake all on the power of his
stone. However, Listener was not so sure now that Hunli would observe
the terms of his oath towards an inheritor of the stone who was not one
of his own people.

Indeed, he might seize the stone, and then how was Listener himself
to prove his identity to Arni's Folk? He had no time to think about that
any more, for the Khan was now saying impatiently, 'Haven't you got
a name, or are you dumb?'

'I'm a wandering minstrel,' said Listener. 'They gave me the
packhorse in Fraglund as my fee.'

'Then you must be a master of your art, not that you look it to me,'
said the Khan. 'If it should turn out that you don't play as well as a
man who makes his living by it ought to, you must have something to
hide. However, I shall discover what it is. Plenty of time for that. So
now show us what kind of a minstrel you are.'

While the Khan was speaking, a vague memory had come into
Listener's head, a memory of having tried the power of his flute on
animals once before. The animals had been dogs that time, only he
could not remember where and when it was. He knew now what he
was going to do, though he was not at all sure that it would have the
desired result. 'You will be satisfied, Khan Hunli,' he said, with a
rather forced smile. 'But you will have to have my hands untied.'

The Khan signed to one of his men, who rode up to Listener's side
and freed his hands from their bonds.

'Now prove that you are a minstrel,' said the Khan.

'I hope I shan't disappoint you,' said Listener. He bent over his
horse's neck, and as he took the silver flute from his saddle-bag with his
right hand, he whispered to Snowfoot, 'Close your ears, and don't
move from the spot!' Then he sat upright, and put the instrument to
his lips.

An expression of incredulous surprise appeared on the Khan's face.
He gazed at the silver flute, and must have known at once whose
instrument he was to hear. But it was too late now for him to raise his
hand to halt proceedings, for at that very moment Listener began to
play.

'Run, horses!' he played. 'Turn and run south, race over the steppes
so fast that the grass whips about your fetlocks, and never stop until
you have no strength left!'

At the first few notes, the Raiding Riders' shaggy little horses reared,
turned, and were off so fast that the turf they kicked up shot into the
air around Listener's ears. Their riders tried to get the animals under
control, but in vain. Some of the men had let themselves fall from their
saddles as soon as they realized that their horses were obeying another
man's will, but only a few of them landed safely on their feet. Even a
Raiding Rider took a risk in jumping out of the saddle at full gallop.
The horses were already far away, Listener's packhorse among them.
As they raced towards the horizon with the main body of the troop,
Listener saw a couple of the men who had jumped to the ground
running through the grass towards him and unslinging the bows from
their shoulders. At that he stopped playing, turned his horse and rode
away fast, going north. Soon the men's cries of rage died away behind
him, but he still spurred his horse on, galloping over the steppes until
the sun sank close to the horizon.

When he realized that night was about to fall, he reined in his horse
and looked around him. There was nothing to be seen but the endless
plain, glowing red in the west with the light of the setting sun: for miles
upon miles, nothing but grey-green, rippling grass, not a tree anywhere,
or even a bush under which to shelter. Listener had no idea how long
the Raiding Riders' horses would obey his flute. Perhaps they really
were still racing southwards and would go on until they collapsed; or
perhaps they had come under their riders' control again quite soon.
However that might be, some time or other the horde would be after
him, for Hunli had not looked like a man who would think his performance much of a joke. Upon realizing that, Listener decided to stay
in the saddle all night.

He tried to take his bearings by the position of the sun that was just
dipping below the horizon. He must ride that way if he wanted to get
back to the woods on the edge of the steppes. As long as the shallow
bank of clouds to the west still glowed dull red, that was not so difficult,
but the crimson glow soon dimmed to streaks of violet, and was gradu-

ally extinguished by the darkness of night coming up from the east. For a while Listener could still make out a trace of light ahead to follow, but then that guiding mark disappeared too. The sky was overcast. A star shone out now and then among the broad bands of cloud, but not enough of them to show the whole of any constellation, which might have enabled one to determine the points of the compass, quite apart from the fact that Listener had only vague notions of how to set about that. He wondered whether he ought not to stop for the night after all, and ride on again in the morning, but the thought of lying alone and unprotected on this plain filled him with fear. Moreover, he had lost his blanket and all his provisions along with the packhorse. He might just as well ride on as lie cold and hungry in the grass of the steppes. So he gave his mare her head, in the hope that she would find the right way.

Snowfoot trotted sturdily on through the dark, and Listener dozed in his saddle. He was not making fast progress now, but he hoped that at least every step his horse took brought him closer to his goal, always provided he was not going the wrong way.

Perhaps the stiff wind blowing over the steppes from his right, where he thought the north must lie, would help the mare.

Can one fall asleep on horseback? The Raiding Riders had to master that useful skill, but Listener had never tried it before. When he started up in his saddle, roused by his horse's sudden stumbling, he realized that you only had to be tired enough to let the regular movement of a horse lull you to sleep. And he was tired to death after spending last night in the company of the malevolent tree trolls. He felt that the wind had died down. His eyes were heavy as lead in their sockets, and he was scarcely able to keep them open, but before his lids closed again he saw something moving far ahead of him on the dark steppes. He tried to keep his eyes fixed on whatever it was, but found he could not. The image kept flickering and moving out of his field of vision again. And yet he saw that the thing was coming closer all the time. He was surprised that he could make out anything at all on this moonless night, but now he saw it more and more clearly: a Rider coming at a leisurely pace towards him. The man sat on a shaggy steppe horse, shoulders hunched forward, and braids dangled at his temples, braids of snow-white hair. So Hunli has caught me after all, thought Listener. But it was not Hunli who came riding out of the dark and reined in his horse quite close to Listener. This Raiding Rider's eyes were unlike the Khan's, not hard and chilly, but kind, almost merry.

'Where are you riding, Listener?' asked Arni.

'To your own folk,' said Listener, though he was not at all sure Arni
would know what he meant.

'Are you going the right way?' asked Arni.

'I hope so,' said Listener. 'I don't know for sure. I may be lost. Will
you show me the way?'

Arni shook his head. 'No, you must find it for yourself,' he said. 'I'm
needed out in the steppes.'

'What for?' asked Listener.

'You ought to know that,' said Arni. 'I must help my brother gather
his men together again.'

'What do Hunli's men matter to you?' asked Listener. 'I'm glad
they're not after me yet.'

'And haven't they every reason to be after you?' said Arni. 'You
should have shown Hunli the stone. Why didn't you?'

Listener bowed his head. 'I was afraid of relying on just the stone,'
he said.

'A man who gives way to his fear will make mistakes,' said Arni.
'You must have more faith, or the stone won't help you much. Even
among those people you call my folk, whoever they may be.' He gave
Listener a friendly nod, urged his horse on again, almost touching
Listener as he rode by, and next moment he had disappeared into the
night without a sound. Only then did Listener realize that he had not
heard him riding up either: there had been no hoofbeats, no clink of
harness, as if Arni's horse were moving in a different world. And then,
with a chill of fear, it struck him that he had just been talking to a man
who had been dead for years. Where was this place? Was he riding
over the steppes at all, or had the world shifted without any warning?
There was not a star to be seen in the sky now. Perhaps the clouds had
covered it. But were they really clouds, or had a black lid come down,
cutting him off from the sky and the stars and the clouds, from the
world of the living? Perhaps he had been riding for hours through a
world of phantoms come to haunt him.

And suddenly the wind got up again. Listener felt its impact as if he
had just ridden through a gateway into the open air. All at once his
sense of oppression was gone. When he turned in the saddle, he saw the
black lid of the sky beginning to lift. Far to the east, a chink of brightness
appeared on the horizon, casting pale light over the steppes. Listener
urged his horse on faster, for now he could see where he was going
again. Gradually the wide plain became lighter, and then, far ahead,

he saw the shape of a mountain range standing out, dark purple against the grey of the sky. The border of the steppes, where he was bound. Although he was now hanging on his horse rather than riding it, Listener decided to go on until he had reached the first of the trees.

It was morning, and bright daylight, when he felt their shade. He had been lying over his horse's neck most of the time, eyes closed, letting her carry him. At some point he had noticed, half asleep, that Snowfoot was trotting faster. Perhaps she can smell water, he thought, but he was too tired to look. Now he heard the splashing of a stream, and realized at the same moment how thirsty he was himself. Laboriously, he straightened in his saddle and looked around. Snowfoot was trotting through a light copse of alders. Her head was stretched forward as her distended nostrils scented the stream flowing through a grassy hollow a little way ahead. The willows on its banks were in full bloom: fluffy yellow catkins ranged thickly on every branch. Listener let his horse go down to the stream, and waited until she had drunk her fill. Only then did he dismount, dip his hands into the fast-flowing water, wash his face to cool his burning eyes, and then drink himself.

The icy water dispelled his weariness, but it could not satisfy his hunger. Listener searched his saddle-bags, and found nothing to eat in them. However, he did come upon the flagon of rowanberry spirits. He took a sip from it, but realized immediately that it was better to avoid such liquor on an empty stomach. The strong spirits rose to his head at once, the scene began to go round and round, and the ground seemed to sway. Listener clung to his saddle until the dizzy fit was over, and then put the flagon away again. As he did so, his fingers touched the curved outlines of the three little flasks he had brought from his grandfather's cellar. 'Strength for an hour, sleep for three days' – that elixir might be useful now, and he wondered whether to try it. But he thought he had better not, since he couldn't be sure of reaching his journey's end within the next hour. 'Be sure to come home fast' – yes, well, easily said, if you knew how much farther you had to ride.

He began by trying to take his bearings. He thought he recognized the slopes of the Crooked Wood to the south. So the long way round he had taken had brought him a little closer to where he was going. Now he must ride on northwards as fast as possible. He might be in luck and come to the settlement of Arni's Folk before evening. At any rate, he must not linger here too long. The Raiding Riders would have no difficulty in following his track to this stream; it stood out as a dark line through the grass of the steppes.

As he let Snowfoot graze for a while, so that his mount at least would not faint from weakness, he wondered what to do to keep the Riders from knowing which way he had gone from here. His horse's hoofprints would be visible for days in this soft, grassy ground, and he thought it would be a poor sort of present to his hosts to draw the enmity of the Raiding Riders down upon Arni's Folk. Then he remembered Barlo's once telling him how he covered his tracks from Gisa's retainers when he was serving as a groom in Eldar's house by day and hunting wolves by night. He and Eldar's son had gone down a watercourse from their hide in the trees to the valley, and only then turned home. He could do something of the same sort now. The stream flowed from the north along the foot of the mountain range as far as the eye could see. He could use it as a path, for a while at any rate.

As he hauled himself into the saddle, he felt the effects of having had scarcely any food and even less sleep for two days. He urged his horse into the water and let her walk upstream. The mare did not seem to like it much. She kept slipping on the smooth stones, but Listener was pleased to see that she left hardly any tracks at all on the stony bed of the stream, and the little that could be seen would soon be smoothed away by the current. He made only slow progress in this way, but with every hour that passed his certainty of having covered up his tracks grew. At the same time his need for sleep and his hunger were increasing to an alarming extent. More than once, he almost slid out of the saddle when Snowfoot stumbled on a particularly slippery stone.

When his horse's stumbling startled him into consciousness once again, he saw he had reached his journey's end. The stream flowed out of the bushes to cross meadowland; to the left, these meadows filled a semi-circular bay set back into the mountain range. A fine herd of horses was grazing in this hollow, and on the far side of it, where bushes came down to the stream again, stood a row of log cabins and sheds, half hidden by alder and birch trees.

There was no more need for caution now. The light pressure of his thighs was enough to guide Snowfoot out of the bed of the stream. Listener stopped when he came to the last of the alders and looked at the houses. He was not in very good shape, but he could ride the short distance to the horses' paddocks. And yet he hesitated. He tried to think what it would be like facing Honi, Arni's Deputy, over there. He would scarcely be able to keep on his feet, dizzy with exhaustion and weakened by hunger as he was. Ought that to be the first impression Arni's Folk had of the Gentle Fluter's heir, Bearer of the Stone? Who was going to take him seriously if he made his first appearance like that? This anxiety took such hold upon him that he ended up feeling his future depended entirely upon the way in which he appeared to Arni's Folk at their first meeting. And then he knew how he could make an entrance of a suitably impressive nature. Hands flying, he opened his saddle-bag and took out the flask of that mysterious liquor that gave strength for an hour. Anyone would understand a traveller's wishing to sleep after the greetings were over. He opened the stout little apple-sized flask, and sniffed it. A deliciously refreshing fragrance rose to his nostrils, one that aroused a dim memory in him. He must have smelled this fragrance some time or other before. Without stopping to think any more of it, he put the narrow neck of the flask to his mouth and took a small sip. Tasting the sour-sweet flavour of the tingling liquid, he was sure, again, that he had drunk it before, but he could not think when and where.

Even as he closed the flask and put it away, he began to feel its effects. All of a sudden his weariness was gone, and he felt refreshed and strong as if he had only just begun his ride. But I must make haste, he told himself. Be sure you come home fast! He spurred Snowfoot on.

He was spotted as he rode fast through the paddocks. A few children who had been playing in the bushes by the stream heard the sound of hoofbeats and looked to see who was coming. Then they ran into the settlement, shouting out loud.

Reaching the first house, Listener let his horse slow to a walk, so as not to give any impression of being in a particular hurry. When the village street lay before him, he saw that his entrance would not go unremarked. People had come out of their houses everywhere on hearing the children's shouts, and were now standing in their doorways looking at him curiously. As he was not quite sure how to behave, he rode past them to the middle of the settlement, where he supposed he would find Honi. Listener was looking for a house whose size and appearance showed that it belonged to a man of the Deputy's importance. But the first thing he saw in the middle of the village square was a small building made of logs now grey with age, so that one could guess it had been here longer than the other houses, whose timbers were still so new that resin oozed in places from the white surfaces where the axe had cut them. This modest log cabin must be Arni's House, and the fine building behind it, distinguished from the others by a kind of veranda on its front, must be where Arni's Deputy lived.

As Listener rode on, he had a splendid idea: he would pay his first respects to the old log cabin. That would be sure to impress these people, and it would save him the awkwardness of having to address some stranger. Everything else would follow naturally. So he rode his horse to the door of the cabin, taking no more notice of Honi's house, although as he rode by he noticed a man coming out of its doorway too. He halted Snowfoot outside Arni's House, dismounted, walked up to the rough-hewn door and bowed low.

He stayed in that position for some time, looking at the worn threshold. Obviously the place had been left in the state in which these people had discovered it when they founded their settlement. After all, Arni's feet, among others, had trodden those worn places on the wooden planks.

Something ought to happen now, thought Listener, beginning to feel uncomfortable in his bent position. He heard the people whispering behind him. Then footsteps approached, and stopped at his side. Without straightening up, Listener glanced aside, and saw a pair of man's shoes made of the finest deerskin. The sturdy legs above them were clad in leather breeches such as the Raiding Riders and Arni's Folk wore. Straightening up slightly so that he could see the man's upper half, Listener noticed that he too had bowed low, and was now raising his trunk to exactly the same height as his, Listener's. It seemed that courtesy did not allow him to stand upright beside a guest who was still bending over, and this obviously caused him some difficulty, for he was a man of considerable girth and was breathing heavily. Was this Honi? Listener had not really thought of Arni's Deputy as such a man, imagining him tall and lean, a fine figure of a leader. Well, whether he was Honi or not, at least the stout man must be a person of importance, and so Listener decided not to subject him to his painfully respectful position any longer. He straightened up entirely, and was pleased to see that the other man copied him, heaving a sigh of relief. Then they turned to each other.

The stout man said something Listener could not understand. I hope I'll be able to talk to these people, thought Listener, and he asked, 'Do you know the language of Fraglund?'

'Yes,' said the stout man, 'and you'll find others here who can speak your language too.'

'Good,' said Listener. 'Forgive me for paying my due respects to Arni's House first. I've made a long journey to get here, and now I should very much like to speak to Honi, Arni's Deputy.'

'You have acted like one of ourselves,' said the stout man. 'May every stranger show such honour to wise Arni, whose name be praised! And if you are looking for Honi, you've found him, for he stands before you.'

So then Listener bowed to Honi, who for his part instantly replied with another bow, and when they were both upright again, Listener said, 'I greet you, Arni's Deputy! My name is Listener, and your men called me Bearer of the Stone.'

When Honi heard this, the tears came to his eyes. He spread his arms and took the long-awaited newcomer to his extremely broad breast. Then he held him away at arm's length, saying, 'Welcome to Arni's Folk, Bearer of the Stone! I will not greet you as a guest, for you are one of us indeed. May the power of Arni's Stone and the art of the Gentle Fluter, whose heir you are, bring wisdom and joy to our humble houses!' Then he turned to the people who had gathered in the village square and cried, 'Listener, Bearer of the Stone, has come at last! May his name be great among Arni's Folk!'

According to Listener's expectations, the people of the village ought now to have shouted for joy, but nothing of the sort happened. All who had followed him to Arni's House bowed low, so that Listener felt obliged to bow again himself, and they said, more or less in chorus, something that Honi immediately translated. 'May Arni be with you, Bearer of the Stone!' They did not even say it particularly loud; it was more like an ordinary kind of greeting. And that was all, for then the people went back to their own houses, talking in undertones.

Listener watched them go, feeling slightly disappointed. He knew from the experience of more than one occasion that Arni's Folk were extremely courteous, but still, he had expected a little more enthusiasm. However, it then occurred to him that a considerable part of the hour for which his potion would keep him going was now over, so he decided he was quite glad not to be detained here any longer. As if reading his thoughts, Honi said, 'One must not weary a man who has travelled far with lengthy greetings. Come into my house, not as my guest, but as one of my family.'

He led him over the square to the house with the veranda. A young woman, or a girl, stood under its jutting roof, which was held up by carved pillars. She was looking at him. When Listener and Honi came up she bowed, though not as low as the people in the square. Listener returned her greeting in the same way, and as the thought passed through his mind that you might well end up with backache in this place, what with all the politeness, Honi said, 'This is my daughter Narzia.'

Listener stood up again, and the girl's bold beauty struck him like a knife. Narzia did not resemble her father at all. Beside Honi's broad if not fat face, Narzia's features looked even finer than in fact they were. It was her green eyes that Listener noticed first: they were the colour of damp moss, and looked at him so keenly that he almost lowered his gaze. Nor did the rest of her fair-skinned face show any kinship with the flat-nosed people of the settlement. She is like a proud falcon who knows her noble ancestry, thought Listener. Narzia began to smile at his admiring gaze, and said, 'We have been waiting a long time for you, Listener. Come into your house!'

She led Listener to a living-room of good size, showed him to the place of honour at the table, and she and Honi did not take their own places until he was seated. Instantly, maidservants began scurrying busily back and forth, bringing dishes more delicious than any Listener had been served since he ate with Gisa in Barlebogue: all kinds of fish, large and small, many different varieties of game, preserved sweet and sour fruits, which Listener could not identify even from their appearance, soft white bread, and tasty morsels such as nuts and honeycakes. Listener could not conceal his surprise at finding such delicacies set before him here in the wilderness. 'A trader gets plenty of choice,' said Honi, with some pride, when he noticed Listener's surprise, and he poured deep red wine into his silver goblet.

As they ate, Listener had leisure to look around the room, for these people evidently retained the custom of leaving serious conversation until after meals. The ceiling was made of richly carved beams of some aromatic wood, and silver vessels stood on shelves around the walls. 'Didn't look much like this when we first settled here,' said Honi, contentedly. 'But we've done pretty well these last few years, thanks be to Arni!'

Since entering Honi's house, Listener had forgotten that the time in which he had fresh reserves of strength at his disposal was limited. That glance into Narzia's green eyes had driven a great many things out of his mind, as it was to turn out later. And so the end of his allotted hour took him quite unprepared. The mouthful he had been about to swallow almost stuck in his throat. He just managed to swallow it, but when he tried washing it down with a sip of wine his hand shook so much that he knocked the goblet over. 'Apologies!' he babbled, thick-tongued, and stared with glazed eyes at the blood-red patch spreading fast over the white linen cloth. 'The long ride ...' He felt himself begin to slip off his chair, he fell and fell, tumbling fast down a bottomless well, and in its depths there awaited him:

The Dream of the Falcon

He felt soft, fragrant grass beneath his hands and the back of his neck. Sunlight warmed his limbs and made its way through his closed eyelids, a faint red shimmer. For a while he enjoyed simply lying there motionless, feeling the warmth of the sunbeams on his skin. He must have slept a long while, for his limbs were still heavy as if after deep exhaustion. When he had lain there for a time, he decided to open his eyes.

He looked straight up into the blue sky, and saw a falcon hovering high above him among the white spring clouds. The slender bird with its fine plumage seemed to him wonderfully beautiful in its freedom of movement, with nothing to weigh it down, and when he had been watching it for a while he felt sorry he could make out nothing but its dark outline against the bright sky, and wished the falcon would come down and let him see it close.

No sooner had he formed this wish in his mind than the falcon did come dropping down, swift as an arrow, as if to sink its talons into his flesh. But at the last moment it slowed up, spreading its wings, and settled on a rotting tree-trunk near Listener. Now he could see the bird at close quarters, its slim body and brown feathers, its proudly arched neck, the bold head with the noble curve of its beak.

'You are beautiful, falcon,' said Listener. 'I wish I could be like you; I would like to hover in the sky, free and weightless.'

Then the falcon looked at him with its moss-green eyes and said, 'I could help you to soar in the air too, and feel the wind carrying you above the tree-tops.'

'I'd give anything for that kind of freedom,' said Listener.

'If you really mean it, then you shall be as I am,' said the falcon. 'Give me the stone you bear. You'll never be able to fly with that stone weighing you down.'

Listener brought out his stone and looked at it, and the longer he watched its play of colours, the less ready he felt to give the jewel away. 'You want to keep it, do you? Then stay as you are!' said the falcon, spreading its wings and soaring upwards. Listener followed it with his eyes, and the wish to soar as freely himself overwhelmed him once again. 'Come down!' he called. 'I will give you the stone!' Then the falcon came down to the tree stump again, and Listener laid his stone in front of its talons. As soon as the cool curve of the stone was no longer touching him, he felt a strange itch in his hands and arms, and saw brown quills begin to sprout all over his skin. They grew, and became thick wing feathers. 'I have wings!' he cried. 'Now I'll fly!'

'Try, then!' said the falcon. But was it still a falcon sitting on that tree stump? For it too had undergone a transformation. Instead of the beaked bird's head, a smooth and slender neck rose from the brown plumage of its shoulders, with the head of a boldly beautiful girl upon it, and it had been the green-eyed girl's smiling mouth that spoke those last two words. 'Come!' said the falcon maiden. 'Let your wings carry you up!' And so saying, she rose into the air herself and began circling above Listener's head.

He tried to imitate her, but he could hardly manage to rise from the ground at all. He flapped just above the meadow for a couple of wing-beats, and then his strength failed him and he fell heavily to the grass.

Disappointed, he went back to his place by the tree stump and looked up at the falcon maiden, who was now sailing high in the clouds above him. 'Come up! Come up!' he heard her distant voice call down. He put his head back and cried up to her, 'You promised me I could fly! Now keep your word!'

The falcon maiden immediately sank down again and settled on the tree stump. 'You're still too heavy, Listener,' she said. 'Give me your silver flute. It's the flute that keeps you from soaring on high.'

'You ask a great deal,' said Listener, for he dearly loved the flute.

'Didn't you say you would give anything to be able to fly?' asked the falcon maiden. 'And anyway, what are you going to do with that flute now? You won't be able to play it with feathers instead of fingers.' So then Listener realized that his flute was no use to him any more, and he didn't mind what happened to it. He thrust it out of his pocket with one of his wings, sending it rolling over the grass, and then pushed it towards the tree stump with his foot, saying, 'The flute won't be much use to you either.'

'We'll see,' said the falcon maiden, and next moment Listener knew what she meant. The quills and down fell away from her wings, giving way to a girl's smooth, slender arms. At the same time, Listener thought the falcon maiden was now much larger than she had seemed before. Or was it that he had grown smaller? Looking down at himself, he saw that his clothes had disappeared. His body was covered with brown feathers instead, and talons clung to the grassy ground where his feet had rested just now.

'Now fly, Listener!' said the girl with the falcon's body, and she picked up the flute in her slim fingers and began to play it.

Once more Listener spread his wings, and this time his first few wingbeats bore him up to the height of the young tree-tops on one side of the meadow. Now he saw that he had been lying in the middle of a clearing surrounded by the slender trunks of young oak, beech and birch trees. As he flew above this clearing, he saw the falcon maiden sitting on the tree stump below, and he heard the enticing melody she played on her flute.

He wanted to fly higher, right up to the clouds, but he soon realized that the heavy beat of his wings was far removed from the smooth flight of the falcon. And when a gust of wind hit him he felt dizzy, and had to make a great effort not to fall. So he contented himself with circling low above the clearing, and as he did so he felt a stronger and stronger attraction to the music the falcon maiden was playing on the flute. 'Come to me, Listener, my falcon!' she played. 'I will show you how to hover light and free below the clouds.'

Listener could not withstand that compelling melody; he circled lower and lower, and finally settled on the hand that the girl with the falcon's plumage reached out to him. 'You aren't light enough yet to rise to the sky like a falcon,' she said. 'You must give me another thing that is weighing you down.'

'What else can I give you?' said Listener. 'I have nothing left.'

'You have more than you think,' said the falcon maiden. 'Give me a third gift, give me the thoughts that make you dizzy up in the air and draw you down to earth again!'

'How can I give you my thoughts?' said Listener. 'They dwell inside my head, and I can't take them out even if I wanted to.'

Then the falcon maiden looked at him with her green eyes and said, 'But I can take them from you.' She crooked her arm and brought the falcon, whose name was still Listener, close to her face. 'Kiss me!' she said. 'Kiss me on the mouth, Listener!'

So Listener kissed the falcon maiden on the mouth, and for a while he saw nothing but the moss-green light of her eyes; he lost himself in that green and glowing world, his thoughts vanished away, and with them the memory of what he once had been. And as he kissed her the green-eyed girl's brown plumage fell away; she stood in the grass on slender legs, and the fair skin of her body shone like a moonstone.

The falcon on her fist opened his sharp beak and uttered a falcon's cry. 'You are my falcon now,' said the girl, stroking his feathers. Then she threw him up into the air, crying, 'Fly, my falcon, fly up to the clouds. And when I want you to hunt for me, my flute will call you back.'

The falcon spread his wings and rose up and up, until his feathers touched the edge of the clouds. He looked down at the curling tree-tops of the green woods, where the little clearing was now barely visible. But what does a falcon want with a clearing? He wallowed in the wind, he rose again and hovered above the forest, which meant no more to him now than the possibility of perching on a branch.

* * *

When he woke, he could still see those green eyes. He was lying under soft woollen blankets on the cool sheets of a wide bed, and Honi's daughter was sitting by the bedside looking at him. 'Falcon maiden!' said Listener, still half asleep.

Narzia smiled. 'No sooner do you open your eyes than you think of a pretty name to call me!' she said. 'And we feared you might never open them again. Do you know how long you've been sleeping?'

Listener tried to put his thoughts in order, and then he remembered how he had managed to keep on his feet when he arrived. 'Exactly three days,' he said, laughing.

At that, Narzia looked at him thoughtfully. 'Yes, you seem to have a very good notion of it,' she said. 'One might almost think it was on purpose you gave us such a fright when you suddenly fell off your chair as if you'd suffered a stroke.'

'I'm sorry I frightened you,' said Listener, reluctant to say more. He did not want to mention the mysterious little flask before he knew rather better where he stood with this girl. Moreover, the fact that he had used the powerful potion without real necessity, as she could easily work out for herself, might seem to shame him. So all he said was that he had hardly eaten or slept for two days, and then he told her how he fell into Hunli's hands.

'You must be very cunning if you managed to escape him,' said Narzia. Listener smiled. 'He didn't know he had the Gentle Fluter's heir before him,' he said, and told her how he had sent the horde chasing out into the steppes. But if he had hoped to make Narzia laugh, he had gone about it the wrong way. A deep line appeared between her brows. 'Were you absolutely bent on making an enemy of the Khan, then?' she said angrily. 'From all I know of your flute, you could have used it to free yourself without doing Hunli harm. But now he'll look for you until he finds you, and next time you meet he'll be on his guard, for he'll know who he's dealing with then.'

'He won't be able to follow my trail very easily,' said Listener, describing the way he had reached the village.

'Well, at least you showed a bit of sense there,' said Narzia. 'But still, you might have refrained from insulting Hunli.'

Listener looked at her in surprise. 'I didn't expect Arni's Folk to feel such concern for Hunli's welfare,' said he. 'The Great Parting doesn't seem to have been as great a one as I was told.'

'You speak like a child who thinks he knows everything when he's once been told a story,' said Narzia. 'I can see you still have a great deal to learn. The matter stands thus: the Parting of the Ways was final, and divided us from the horde for ever. But Hunli let us go without any opposition, nor will he do anything to harm us in the future. He would bring shame on himself if he fought his brother's followers. Arni, may his name never be forgotten, protects us even in death. And we need that protection. How could we rear cattle and go trading if Hunli's men were always after us? Now do you see the danger you've brought upon us?'

Listener saw it clearly enough – now, at any rate. 'Do you want me to leave your village again?' he asked, repentantly.

Narzia smiled at his readiness to atone, and shook her head. 'No, Listener, I don't,' she said. 'This is and always will be your home. What happened out in the steppes doesn't matter so much, set against the fact that you bear Arni's stone, for surely Arni knew best why he gave it to you. We shall find some way to placate Hunli. All kinds of things, evidently, may be done with your flute. You must just learn to handle it a little more gently.'

'I'll try,' said Listener. 'You could help me learn, falcon maiden.' And he saw, from the way her green eyes lit up, that she liked that name.

'Do you have so much faith in me?' she asked, laying her hand on his arm.

'Yes,' said Listener, for looking at her eyes, he could not say otherwise.

Over the next few days, Listener realized that he was not the only one to feel such faith in Narzia. He frequently found Honi consulting his daughter on the affairs of Arni's Folk: what new trade routes they might venture upon, for instance, or what advice should be given to men setting off to trade in foreign parts concerning their conduct there.

When Listener first found the two of them deep in such a conversation, he turned to leave the room again, but Honi asked him to join them at the table, saying, 'Arni in his wisdom – may it be granted to us all! – put his faith in you, so naturally your place is here with us.'

After this, Listener took part in their councils, though he only listened at first; he had not forgotten Narzia's reprimand when she said he still had much to learn. And so he had, if he was to understand the way that Arni's Folk thought. Weighty decisions were indeed taken by an assembly of all the elders of the various families, but as these former Raiding Riders had always been used to obeying their Khan's orders, they tended, even after the Parting of the Ways, to wait and see what proposals would be made by their chieftain, as they regarded Arni's Deputy. And so whether Honi liked it or no, he had been allotted the part of a leader whose commands were obeyed more or less unquestioningly. Perhaps that was why he had become accustomed to discussing his ideas with his daughter, for Narzia was perfectly ready to contradict him or even make suggestions of her own, and as time went on Listener in fact got the impression that she was the one who really held the reins. Honi would usually begin such conversations with a question which might show what matter was on his mind, but did not indicate how far he had formed any opinion on it. Listener could never be quite sure whether he made her views his own; all he saw was that things generally went the way Narzia had suggested.

'Your father has a great deal of faith in you,' he told Narzia after one such council, when Honi had left the room.

'He loved my mother dearly, and often listened to her advice,' said Narzia. 'When she died, not long before the Great Parting, he put his faith in me instead.'

'I suppose you look very like your mother?' said Listener, captivated once again by her green eyes.

Narzia looked at him, smiling. 'That may be so,' she said. 'One can't exactly say I'm like my father.'

'Nor like any of the other women I've seen here,' said Listener. 'Your mother must have been very beautiful.'

'She was not from the tents of the Raiding Riders,' said Narzia. 'My father found her when he was on a long ride that took him far down south to the plains of the Brown River, where the Falcon People live in their stone houses.'

'Did he capture her in a raid?' asked Listener, fascinated by this adventurous possibility.

Narzia uttered a peal of laughter. 'I can see you still don't know much of the ways of the steppes,' she said. 'I can't recollect that a man of the horde ever married a slave girl he had captured. He would have slept with her, yes, but he'd never have given her the rights of a wife. No, my father was riding with an embassy from the Khan to the Great Magician of the Falcon People, to conclude a treaty with him. Hunli thought it would be useful not to have that man for an enemy, skilled as he was in many mysteries, and my father's errand was to negotiate a frontier which neither side would cross.

He has often told me how he and a dozen of his Riders went downstream along the Brown River until he reached the lands of the Falcon People. Down in those lowlands it's all green, rich pasture; the grass is fresh, not harsh and grey like the grass of the steppes through which they had been riding for many days. And you see herds of cattle with great horns grazing everywhere, and tall, slender horses with narrow heads.

Then they met a troop of armed horsemen. My father held out his empty hands to show he came in peace, and rode over to them alone. The men were out hunting, some of them with tamed falcons on their wrists. They looked scornfully at my father's shaggy little horse from the steppes, but as he had messages from the Khan to deliver he pretended not to have noticed their glances, and told them he was on his way to the Great Magician as an envoy from Khan Hunli. After that the falconers treated him with more courtesy, broke off their hunt, and offered to accompany the party of Raiding Riders on their way to the capital city, which they call Falkinor. Two of them rode on ahead to announce the arrival of the Khan's envoys.

They rode on for three more days through the lush pastures by the Brown River, which is so broad at that point that horses grazing on the opposite bank look as small as ants. Towards evening of the third day, a strange mountain appeared out of the haze, looking as if it had been cut with a knife from a great mound of earth, in the shape of a flight of steps. When my father asked what kind of mountain that might be, the falconers laughed, and one of them said it was the house of the Great Magician of Falkinor.

The closer they rode, the higher this mountain that was said to be a house rose from the plain, and all around it they saw the rectangular stone houses of the Falcon People behind the pentagonal wall that surrounds Falkinor. When they were so close that the house of the Great Magician seemed to tower right up to the sky, a trumpet signal sounded on its topmost terrace, and next moment out came hundreds of horsemen from a gate in the wall, galloping to meet them. The falconers asked my father and his Riders to stop and dismount. Next moment the other horsemen came up, with a black-bearded man in blood-red silk at their head, carrying a magnificent falcon on his fist. My father asked his companions this man's name, and was told he was Vendikar, Keeper of the Falcons.

When my father told me about this meeting, he said he had wondered at the time if they intended an insult when they sent a man to meet him whose office was only the care of hawks for hunting. He was surprised, to be sure, to see how magnificently such a servant was clothed in this country, and he could take no exception to the conduct of the Keeper of the Falcons, for the man had dismounted from his own horse at once, greeted him with great courtesy, and given him the falcon he had been carrying on his fist as a gift for the Khan. And then they rode into the city together through the gate in the wall.

The street led straight from the city gate to the house of the Great Magician. Those people they met stepped aside and bowed so low that my father was surprised at the honour they showed an ambassador from the Khan here. After a while, however, he began to doubt whether their obeisances were meant for him, and indeed it seemed rather as if everyone were looking at the Keeper of the Falcons riding beside him. As for Vendikar, he took no notice of the people, but looked straight ahead, as behoves a servant accompanying an honoured guest.

Like the city, the mighty house of the Great Magician was surrounded by a pentagonal wall. Later, my father had a chance to take a good look at the building, and he said that the walls had a gate in each of their five sides, and a street ran from each of these gates to one of the five gates in the city wall. They were now riding towards one of the inner gates, and when they came close to it, it opened. So they came into an inner courtyard surrounding the house itself. There were servants ready to take their horses, but when my father was going to hand the falcon to one of these retainers Vendikar raised his brows, and indicated that he should keep the bird on his fist. And it was Vendikar who led the party into the house. My father's retinue stayed in the lower rooms and were very well entertained, while Vendikar asked my father to follow him.

He had never thought a path so long as the way they went now through the Great Magician's house, said my father. It led through great halls and richly carpeted apartments, up flights of stairs and down more corridors, extensive rooms and galleries, and so ever upward, climbing yet more stairs. At first daylight came in through doors or skylights, but soon the rooms were lit only by lamps that burned deliciously scented oil, and the farther they went the deeper the darkness became. There were only a few lamps lit in the upper storeys, and here and there a golden vessel shone in their dim light, or the colours of some precious tapestry stood out blue and purple in the darkness.

Finally Vendikar stopped at the last door. The bronze head of a falcon shone on the middle of the door, lit by two oil lamps hanging from chains on the doorposts at either side. Vendikar took hold of the falcon's head, lifted it lightly and let it fall again. The curved beak dropped into an opening, and immediately a deep, throbbing hum like the note of vast metal cymbals filled the room. As long as this vibrating hum lasted, nothing happened, but when it died away the door slid aside, and so bright a light flooded out through the doorway that my father was dazzled and had to close his eyes. He felt Vendikar's hand on his elbow, and the Keeper of the Falcons led him into the room that lay beyond the door. Once he was accustomed to the bright light, and could use his eyes again, he saw that he was on the topmost terrace of the building. You could look down on the city through great windows on all five sides of the room, and see the design to which it was built: a regular pentagon divided into equal parts by five streets. Beyond the outer wall, you saw the green countryside and the Brown River, and the evening sun, shining in the west, cast a broad beam of light straight towards the doorway through which my father and his companion had passed.

My father was so enchanted by the view that at first he paid no attention to anything else, until someone asked if he liked it. Only then did he notice the thin and almost insignificant man dressed in black who was leaning in one of the window bays, and had put this question to him. Vendikar was standing beside the man, and they were both smiling at my father's amazement.

'I never looked down on the countryside from such a height before,' said my father. 'I feel like a bird hovering in the sky.'

'Like a falcon,' said the man in black, 'and such is the idea of it. I am glad you like my house, as the Khan will like the bird you bear on your fist, for it resembles him in three things: first, it loves a clear view of the

plain; second, it sweeps down when it sees its prey; and third, it avoids
territorial disputes with a neighbour.'

Then my father realized he was in the presence of the Great Magician. And Vendikar, whom the Great Magician treated as a friend,
was far from being a simple servant, if one disregards those services he
did his master, for my father discovered that the title of Keeper of the
Falcons denoted the highest of all offices among the Falcon People,
after that of the Great Magician himself.

I won't weary you with the tale of my father's negotiations with the
Great Magician. Let it suffice to say that they came to an agreement,
and afterwards Vendikar invited my father to be his guest for a week.
He and his family lived on the second highest storey of the great house,
so that my father could enjoy the immense view daily, if not from quite
such a great height as on his first day. And it was here that he met my
mother. Her name was Belenika, and she was Vendikar's daughter.

The night after my mother died, my father told me a great deal
about her, and said she had enchanted him from the very first. She had
green eyes like mine, and you are right to say I resemble her in many
other ways as well.

The women and girls of the Falcon People have much more freedom
than the women of the Raiding Riders, and my father told me that he
had been cast into some confusion when this beautiful girl simply came
up to him, greeted him, and then asked directly if he would like to go
out hawking with her next day. I almost think he'd have declined the
invitation, as being unseemly, if he had not already been spellbound
by her beauty.

Next morning, Belenika led him down to the mews in the courtyard.
It stands in that corner of the inner wall facing east. My father was
surprised to see so splendid a place built just to house birds. Halfway
up the outer wall, which was the shape of a pentagon, a frieze of
falcons' heads was carved in the stone, and the bronze doors were
ornamented with representations of falcons spreading their wings, as if
to forbid entry to anyone who had no right to pass through them.

Belenika very clearly had that right, for she opened the doors without
hesitating and led my father into the mews. Each of the birds had its
own little room, no less richly furnished than the rooms in the Great
Magician's house. The birds sat on golden perches, and were given
their food in silver bowls. Great windows covered with curiously
wrought gratings let in the light and air. There were servants whose
constant task was to keep the rooms clean. As soon as these men saw

Belenika, they bowed, and a keeper who was obviously in charge came over and asked what she desired.

"Give me Whitefeather," said Belenika, "and my guest shall hunt with Arrow."

The falcons that the keeper brought wore red leather hoods decked with heron's plumes on their heads, covering their eyes. When the keeper put the falcon on my father's glove, and in so doing realized that this Raiding Rider was not used to hunting with hawks, he was about to give him some advice, but Belenika said, 'Leave it to me; I will teach him how to do it.'

Two servants were waiting with their horses outside the mews, and soon Belenika and my father were trotting through the gate, down the straight street between the houses, and then out of the city and into the open country.

Even on this first ride, my father decided he was going to win this girl for his wife, although he was aware that it would present him with problems at home. The women of the Raiding Riders scarcely ever left their tents, and he was sure that Belenika would not take kindly to that way of life. But it was her free and self-assured nature that impressed him as well as her beauty. He had never seen any but men ride so daringly before.

Belenika reined in her horse in a low-lying wood of widely spaced trees down by the Brown River. A few broad-branched balsam poplars grew here, and herons used to rest in them. "Here we are," said Belenika, showing my father the birds with their silvery plumage perching in the branches, almost hidden among the leaves.

"Will the falcon obey me?" asked my father.

Belenika laughed. "Chiefly, he will obey his own nature," she said. "The art of hawking lies in making use of the falcon's lust for prey. While he is hungry he will bring down any prey he sees. Don't let him eat too much, and he'll hunt well for you."

My father understood this well enough. "Yes, I'm sure he will kill his prey," he said, "but not so sure he'll bring it back to me."

Belenika took a small piece of meat from her saddle-bag and gave it to my father. "Let him eat from your hand, and then he'll return to you," she said. "He'll spurn his prey for the sake of the morsel you give him."

So my father offered his falcon the piece of meat, and the bird ate it greedily. Belenika nodded, satisfied, and then said, "Now for some sport!" She clapped her hands, sending the herons in the poplars flying

up, and then took off her falcon's leather hood and threw him into
the air. My father imitated her, and watched his own falcon rise into
the sky. The bird rapidly gained height, and my father marvelled at the
lightness and elegance of the flight that bore him above the fleeing
herons with only a few wingbeats. The falcon had earned his name
well, for he shot down like an arrow on one of the herons, sinking his
talons into the bird's neck and making the gleaming silvery feathers
fly. Belenika's falcon had taken its heron too, and both birds came
down to the ground with their prey at almost the same time.

For today, they contented themselves with the two herons, hooded
their falcons again and galloped over the green meadows along the
Brown River. Once, when they stopped, Belenika said she was never
happier than out here where the view reached from horizon to horizon.
"I sometimes feel like a prisoner in the narrow streets within the walls
of Falkinor," she said. My father liked these words, which expressed his
own feelings. He looked into her green eyes and thought he saw something to encourage him there. "If you love a wide view, you would like
the steppes," he told her.

Belenika held his gaze for a while, and said, "That may well be."
Then she turned her horse and sent it racing back to the Great House
whose terraced outline dominated the plain below.

My father rode out with Belenika on the following days as well, and
it seemed to him that Vendikar was not unwilling to see his daughter
help their guest to pass the time. They visited the horses' paddocks,
and my father admired the noble animals bred there. With their narrow
pasterns they looked almost fragile beside his sturdy stallion from the
steppes, but when he was allowed to ride one of them he thought he
was flying over the meadows like a bird. Belenika raced beside him,
her hair fluttering in the wind. "I like to ride with you, Honi!" she cried,
which sounded to my father like a pledge, and he was on the point of
asking if she would not ride home to the steppes with him, but he
couldn't quite pluck up the courage to do it.

The day before he was to leave, he rode out hawking with Belenika
once again. As they trotted towards the wood on the banks of the
Brown River, my father said, "This way of hunting pleases me. It's a
pity, though, that one can only stand by and watch! I wish I could soar
up in the sky myself, like my falcon, and swoop on my own prey."

Belenika looked at him, smiling, and said, "If that is what you'd care
to do, then it can be arranged."

My father found these words so extraordinary that at first he thought she was mocking him. He reined in his horse, saying, "I may seem to you an ignorant Raiding Rider, but you needn't think I'll believe that!"

Then Belenika grew serious, and said, "If I thought so little of you I would never have made the suggestion. I promise you, you shall fly like a falcon, over there by the trees where the herons perch."

They rode to the water meadows, and dismounted. "Get your falcon ready, but don't fly him yet!" said Belenika. When my father had taken the hood from his falcon's head, she stepped in front of him and laid the palm of her ringed hand on his forehead. He gazed into her eyes for a long time, felt himself sinking into their green depths, and heard her clap her hands and cry, "Now fly, my falcon!" And then he was rising in the air, he felt the wind beneath his wings, and soared up into the sky. It seemed as if all weight had fallen from him, everything that bound him to the earth was gone, and he was hovering free above the black branches of the poplar trees. Soon he saw the herons fly out of the dark green leaves and over the meadow, at their head a great white heron, a noble bird. Then he let himself fall and swooped on his prey, the air rushing through his wings. The heron's feathers shimmered like mother-of-pearl before his eyes as he took it in his talons. The sweet sensation of seizing prey flooded his being, he spun through the sky, clinging to his victim, colours swirled, there was no above and no below, only the intoxicating union of hunter and hunted.

When he came back to his senses, he was lying in the grass holding Belenika in his arms. "Did you like the hunt, my falcon?" she asked, and kissed him on the mouth. The falcon Arrow was sitting on the great white heron beside her, withdrawing his talons from its bloody plumage.

That evening, my father asked the Keeper of the Falcons for his daughter's hand. He told me he had been prepared for a refusal, but to his surprise Vendikar had agreed at once, as if he had been expecting some such thing. And he had obviously discussed the matter with the lord of Falkinor already, since he said, "The Great Magician will miss Belenika, for he loves her like a daughter. But he thinks, too, that such a marriage will seal the friendship between Raiding Riders and Falcon People better than any treaty."

Next day my father rode home to the steppes, with only his men, but he returned to Falkinor three months later, this time at the side of Khan Hunli, who wished to be present at the wedding celebrations in the Great Magician's house. And now, Listener, you know where I get my green eyes.'

Listener had been looking at those eyes, and nothing else, all the time Narzia was telling her tale, and at times he had felt as if she were speaking not of the past but of the present, and he too was involved in it. When she told of the hunting of the white heron, he thought he was soaring in the sky, a falcon too, and the sensation seemed as familiar as if he had already felt the air rush through the plumage of his wings, and tasted the freedom of weightlessness. Even if he had only known these things in a dream, then it had been one of those dreams, he felt sure, that anticipate the future. 'I've already flown with you once already, as a falcon,' he said. 'It was in a dream I had, falcon maiden.'

'Ah, so that was why you gave me that name before you knew my parentage,' said Narzia. 'Tell me the dream.'

Listener tried to remember it, but the images blurred together in his mind, and he could not recapture them. All that was left was that wonderful sensation of flying. 'I can only remember that it was very pleasant,' he said. 'And I think, now, that the dream was trying to show me something.'

'What?' asked Narzia.

'Yourself,' said Listener. 'I've had several such dreams since I first bore Arni's stone. They have always had to do with eyes looking at me when I look at the stone, and now I believe I know whose eyes they are.'

'Show me the stone!' said Narzia.

Listener brought the leather bag out from inside his shirt, and took out the stone. He felt momentarily disappointed as he looked at it. The surface seemed dull and lustreless, but that might have been because of the failing light in the room; it had become almost dark outside while Narzia told her tale.

'Wait!' said Narzia. 'I'll make your stone shine again.' She went out, and came back in a moment with a silver candleholder that had three wax candles burning in it. As soon as the stone caught the light of the candles it began to shimmer: green sparks glowed in its depths and came together to make a shining circle like the iris of an eye. But were there no other colours in it? Listener leaned over the stone and let himself sink into the play of colours. Yes, now he saw blue lights mingling with the green, a violet glow came up from the depths, the eye was alive and looking at him. Listener forgot where he was; he lay under the bushes by the source of the midmost stream once more, looking at the face of that woman in whose eyes the stars danced.

'Are you dreaming again?' asked Narzia.

Listener started, and looked at her. The deep line had reappeared between her brows, and he thought her green eyes looked cold and hard. Had he angered her? 'Was it you who came to me that night by the spring, at the source of the stream?' he asked, still caught up in the image that the stone had recalled to his mind.

'I don't know anything about a spring,' said Narzia. 'But I have often thought of you since our traders met you and brought home their tales. It may be that my thoughts reached into your dreams. However, the time for dreaming is over, Listener, for you are now, in sober fact, where Arni's stone was guiding you. Don't you understand that yet?'

As she spoke, the anger vanished from her face, and her eyes seemed to promise Listener all he had ever longed for these last few years.

'It has brought me to you,' he said.

'But chiefly to Arni's Folk,' said Narzia. 'Have you so little pride that you would woo me when you can boast no notable deeds of your own, only those things that other men have left you?'

And Listener saw that he must indeed prove his worth: he could not do otherwise without demeaning himself, and perhaps Narzia too. 'I will do what I can for Arni's Folk,' he said. 'You and your people must tell me what's expected of me. You must know that I would do anything to win you.'

'I don't doubt it,' said Narzia, smiling, and pleased. 'You will learn at the appointed time what hopes we have of you.'

Some weeks later, Honi asked Listener to attend one of those discussions between himself and his daughter which always preceded the elders' assemblies. By now Listener had learnt enough of the language of the Raiding Riders, which Arni's Folk still used, to be able to follow conversations in it.

'I am concerned about the mountain folk,' said Honi, when Listener was sitting with him and Narzia at the table in the big living-room. 'Even though we've lived peacefully in our settlement at Arni's House for some years now, the Mountain Badgers still regard us as part of that same horde whose Khan promised, long ago, never to enter their land again. It is not good to live at odds with one's neighbours, never mind the fact that trading with their goldsmiths could bring us in much profit.'

'I don't understand,' said Listener. 'Wasn't Arni related by marriage to Urla's family, who were people of the Mountain Badgers?'

'He was,' said Honi. 'But his daughters never lived in the Raiding

Riders' tents, and he himself is the only man of the horde who was ever allowed into the Mountain Badgers' villages. The fact is that the violent deeds of many live longer in people's minds than the friendship of a single man. I have long wondered how we can convince the mountain folk that we are peaceably inclined, and whether there isn't a way to strike up some friendly arrangement with them.'

Narzia looked at Listener, and said, 'Might this not be a task fit for you? Looking as you do, nobody would take you for a man of the Raiding Riders' stock, not even if you let your hair grow and braided it. And with the aid of your flute, it should be easy for you to get the Mountain Badgers into a friendly frame of mind.'

'Why, yes, I believe I could do that,' said Listener. 'And my stone will help me to refresh their memory of Arni too.'

'I wouldn't rely on that if I were you,' said Honi. 'The Mountain Badgers are down-to-earth folk in general, and it's said of Promezzo, who is their Ore Master and head man of all the mountain villages, that he will believe in nothing but what his hands can touch. He trusts only those things his keen mind can explain, and you may be sure that your stone isn't among them. Promezzo thinks very little, I hear, of mysteries and dreams.'

Narzia nodded, and told her father, 'You say just what I was thinking myself. And in any case, wouldn't it be better if Arni's stone were kept in Arni's House?' She added, seeing Listener's hand go involuntarily to the little bag inside his shirt, as if to protect it from anyone else, 'Don't misunderstand me, Listener. No one grudges you the stone, for Arni chose you to bear it. And you should wear it openly around your neck, at the assemblies of the elders, as a sign of your dignity. But is it sensible to take it with you when you go on such a ride? Some accident might happen – you might lose it, or it might be stolen from you. The stone is too precious to Arni's Folk for us to expose it to such dangers. Moreover, I've seen how easily the sight of the stone sets you dreaming, and in the task you have now undertaken it could be dangerous for you to be lost in a dream. You must set your mind on what's real now. And remember what you hope to win by it.'

Listener thought of nothing else, and he could find no other reasonable objection to what Narzia suggested, even if he was sorry to think of parting with his stone. He agreed that it had indeed served its purpose in leading him here, and yes, he said, it was time he showed what he could do on his own now.

Such was the decision taken next day at the assembly of the elders in

Arni's House, amidst much solemn ceremony and many speeches, particularly concerning Listener's laying down of the stone. During the assembly, Listener wore the leather bag on his breast, where everyone could see it, as a sign that his office as Bearer of the Stone gave him the right to sit among the elders, even though he was a young man without a family of his own here. Following Narzia's advice, he waited until Honi began to speak of the Mountain Badgers, saying how desirable it would be to strike up friendly relations with them. Only then did Listener speak, offering to undertake this errand for the good of the village. 'Allow me to go and remind them of the wisdom and goodness of Arni, for which we all strive,' he finished his speech. 'With his help, I hope I shall succeed in winning their friendship, for myself and for all Arni's Folk.'

These remarks were loudly applauded, and one of the elders said that now they could see Arni kept them in mind even in death, for the Bearer of his Stone would turn things to their advantage. Perhaps he sounded rather as if he really wanted to say it was about time the young man went out and did something, but Honi ignored that undertone, and said, 'Yes, so he will, for Arni, who meant his gift for all of us, knew what he was about when he chose the man who was to bring it here. This young man Listener, son of the Great Roarer and grandson of the Gentle Fluter, shall be named Bearer of the Stone henceforth, since Arni, in his wise foresight, gave him the task of keeping the jewel until his Folk could lay the foundations of their community after the Great Parting, and he shall also be the only man allowed the right of wearing the stone on high days and holidays. But this great heirloom shall now have its permanent resting-place in Arni's House, so that its secret power may bring us all enlightenment.'

This was not really the way Listener had envisaged things. Unexpectedly, the stone had passed out of his own hands and into the possession of the community of Arni's Folk, who regarded him merely as the man who had brought it to them. He was sure that when Arni gave him the stone he had not said anything of the kind, but Honi delivered himself of his remarks with as much certainty as if he had been present at the time himself. His broad face looked as if it had been hewn from a block of wood, and showed no feeling at all as he made his speech in a kind of chant, as if repeating a long-established form of words. And before Listener could make any objection, Honi asked all present to rise from their places and show the stone due honour as its Bearer now revealed it. They all did as he said at once, and bowed again, so that there was nothing Listener could do but take the stone out of its bag and show it to them, if he was not to disturb the solemnity of the occasion. 'Thanks be to Arni for his gift!' murmured the elders, trying to get a glimpse of the jewel from their bowed position.

Listener did not feel at all happy standing there, and was not sure what to do next, but Honi had it all planned out. When Listener looked at him inquiringly, he indicated the back wall of the room with a barely perceptible nod of his head. There was a table standing there; judging by its simplicity, it must have been one of Arni's possessions, and a golden dish had been set on it. So this was destined to be the permanent resting-place of Arni's stone. Listener hesitated for a moment, but another and rather more marked nod of Honi's head stifled the last remnants of his resistance. It also occurred to him that Narzia would not like it at all if he refused to go along with this ceremony, which merely put her own suggestions into practice. So he walked over to the table with measured steps and let the stone drop into the dish. The ringing bell-like tone of the golden vessel filled the room. Listener looked at his stone, lying there shining dully in the curve of the dish, showing no colour but the greenish-gold reflection of the metal. He waited until the note had died away, and it seemed to him as if it were ringing in a new phase of his life.

A week later Listener was ready to leave. When he said goodbye to Narzia, the evening before he set off, he told her, 'You know what I hope to win by this journey, Narzia.'

She looked at him with her green eyes, and then laid her cool hand briefly against his cheek, saying, 'First and foremost, I know that you will return to me, Listener. Bring me back the finest piece of jewellery you can find in the workshops of the Mountain Badgers!'

Listener had really hoped for more than this fleeting touch of her hand, but he told himself that such things must be earned first.

Next morning he led his horse up the steep slope behind the settlement and into the mountains. If he had not known, from the tales told by his mother and the Gentle Fluter, that there had once been a path here, he would hardly have ventured to set off with a horse over this precipitous and rock-strewn terrain. After some searching, however, he did find the beginning of the path, a narrow track long overgrown with thick tufts of grass, and leading diagonally up across the slope, past boulders and weatherbeaten bushes. As he followed the winding track, leading Snowfoot by her bridle, he was surprised to find how closely it all corresponded to his imaginary picture of the path to Urla's hut. It was almost as if he had been here before.

After a long and difficult climb, he finally reached the top of a rocky cliff, and seeing that he could ride on from here over gently sloping mountain pastures, he decided to allow himself and his horse a rest first. He sat on a rock and looked down at the steppes, stretching silver-grey to the far horizon. Somewhere in that trackless plain stood the tents of the Raiding Riders, somewhere there the horde was racing through the singing grass, and some time or other they would come upon his trail. This thought made him so uneasy that he ended his rest as abruptly as if Khan Hunli could actually see him here on this ledge of rock.

The old track could still be made out, crossing the scanty grass of the pasture over which he rode. He followed it until he came to a rise, and when he had reached the top of it, he looked down at a shallow valley, with a hut standing at the foot of some gigantic boulders at its far side. Urla's cabin. She must have kept her sheep in this sheltered hollow, but the pasture was deserted now, and there was no living creature in sight except for a falcon hovering high up in the sky above the meadows. As he rode over the upland pasture, Listener felt he was being watched, and not just because the falcon was directly over his head. The log cabin itself, nestling among the rocks, seemed to be looking at him through the eyes of its little square windows. He had expected a building falling into ruin, but as he rode closer he saw that the roof and walls were intact, and it looked as if the space outside the door had been swept quite recently.

Whether Urla's cabin was inhabited now or not, Listener could not have ridden by without at least glancing through a window, for it was here, in her living-room, that it had all begun on the day Arni chose his stone. Listener did not need to leave the path, for it led straight past the door. He stopped his horse there, dismounted, put up a hand to shade one of the windows and tried to look inside, but all he could make out were the shapes of a round table and a couple of stools with woven straw seats. Too little light fell into the room for him to see anything else. His desire to go into the room and touch those objects upon which Urla's hand had once rested grew all the stronger. As he went to the door, he noticed that the falcon had followed him, and was now hovering over the hut, much lower than before. The latch closing the door itself on the outside was a simple device, worked by a wooden peg that swivelled in a circle. Listener turned the worn peg to a vertical position, and opened the door. At that moment the falcon swooped down, uttering a shrill cry and brushing past Listener's head so close that its pinions touched his hair. He was so startled by this sudden attack that he hurried into the cabin for safety, closing the door behind him. But he had just had time to see that it led into a small entrance hall, which was not quite dark. He stood there for a while, breathing in the fragrance of herbs and pinewood. Then his eyes became used to the darkness, and he made out another door, which must lead into the living-room.

He felt as if he were doing something illicit, not so much because of the falcon, whose behaviour might almost have suggested that it did not want him to enter the hut, but because there was nobody here to say: Come in and be my guest. Even the old Khan, the father of Hunli and Arni, would not have dared to cross the threshold without such an invitation, all those years ago. However, as Listener stood in the entrance hall, hesitating, he felt his misgivings suddenly wiped away all at once; it was as if someone had actually invited him into the room after all. He could not have said exactly what changed his mind in this way, he only felt that he was welcome. Opening the door, he crossed the worn floorboards to the round table in the corner, and sat down on one of the stools. There was no one here to speak to him, but the fragrance in the room, even stronger here than in the hall, spoke of the woman who had once lived in it; there was an odour of thyme and sage, arnica and yarrow, dried apple rings, honey and wool. The pine panelling of the room, itself fragrant with resin, had absorbed these scents and preserved them through the years. As he breathed them in, the old woman who used to dry her herbs and spin her sheep's wool in this room came closer. He saw her before him; although he kept his eyes closed, the better to give himself up to the fragrance of the air, he saw her beautiful face and her eyes looking at him, eyes of a shade that was hard to describe, those eyes that he knew so well. And he understood what she was saying, although there was no sound to be heard but the chirping of the grasshoppers in the meadow outside. 'Ride on over the mountains,' she said, 'go to the Mountain Badgers and do what you have said you will do! You will have to carry out your errand now, although a time will come when you will wish you had never done so. Ride on, my boy, but don't expect too much to come of it.'

Listener wondered what he did expect of his journey. Some good to Arni's Folk? Or was he solely concerned with winning Narzia? And which of the two did Urla mean when she warned him not to expect too much to come of it? He tried to think of Honi's daughter, but he could not conjure up her image from his memory. The old woman's presence was stronger, enveloping him in a flood of goodwill that warmed his heart, and the longer he sat in the room the more he wanted to stay here, and never leave a place where he felt so safe. He could sense the old woman's smile as she said, 'You're nowhere near your journey's end yet, Listener. Ride on now, and don't entirely forget the stone that lies in its cold golden dish in Arni's House, instead of on your heart where it belongs.'

Listener opened his eyes and looked at the scoured table top upon which Arni's stone had once lain, long ago. He stroked the rough wood with his hand, rose, and went to the door. He drew in one last deep breath of the fragrance of Urla's house, as if he could take it with him on his journey. Then he went out, carefully closing the door with the wooden peg behind him.

When he went to his horse, the falcon was still hovering above the hut. It looked almost as if the bird had been waiting for him, for as soon as Listener mounted, the falcon sailed eastwards over the pasture, and dropped down to the steppes on the far side of the rising ground.

The path led away from Urla's cabin through a mass of jumbled rocks, and then up across a steep slope overgrown with short grass. This part of the track had had much more use, and was easier to see; here and there the prints of narrow hooves were visible in the greyish earth, shot through with silvery scales of mica. They could be the hoofprints of a mule that had passed this way not too long ago. Listener was no longer surprised to have found Urla's cabin in such good condition; obviously the people on this side of the mountains visited it regularly and kept it in good order.

Listener soon had to dismount again and lead Snowfoot, for the climb was getting more and more difficult. The path wound steeply upwards over a precipitous scree slope, with jagged pinnacles of rock rearing up on its flanks. The rock underfoot, which had splintered into slaty sheets, gave at every footstep, and Snowfoot had to take several sudden jumps to save herself from being swept away downhill with a fall of shale.

At last, about mid-day, Listener reached the top of the slope. A high plateau stretched before him, strewn with rocks and with strangely shaped mountain peaks towering above it. It fell away into a deep gully on his right. The path seemed to slope only slightly to the top of the pass, so that Listener could get back into the saddle again. However, the ground was so full of crevices that he walked Snowfoot on at a slow pace, for he could see he would have to ride past some steep precipices.

After a while he saw a tall pyramid of stones with a staff on top of it, set up on the stony ground between himself and the top of the pass. He thought at first that this cairn, which could be seen from afar, was a waymark, but he soon noticed that the path passed it by on the right, at some distance from it. As he rode closer he saw that the curious construction was considerably larger than he had thought at first. It must be at least four or five times the height of a man, and a plume of some kind was fastened to the staff, waving in the keen wind from the pass. There was a strangely shaped object on top of the staff too. All this excited Listener's curiosity, and he decided to take a closer look at the thing. Someone seemed to have gone to a great deal of trouble to set it up, so that it would be visible from afar. As soon as he reached a place from which he could get to the monument without difficulty, he dismounted and clambered over the rocks. When he finally stood before the tall pyramid, which now seemed to tower even above the peaks around it, he realized what it was. The staff jammed into its top was the spear of a Raiding Rider, with a horse's tail fixed to it, and a horse's skull was stuck on the steel point, its empty eye sockets looking eastward towards the steppes. This must certainly be the grave of those Raiding Riders who had perished here in the snowstorm, after they had robbed and murdered Urla's husband and dragged her away as their prisoner. And it was also plain to see who must have erected the monument: only the Mountain Badger people could have set up the horse's skull in such a way that it would grin at an oncoming Raiding Rider, serving as a warning to any who ventured to cross the pass again. Turn back, said the skull, if you value your life! Such was its message to the Raiding Riders. Or was it intended for others besides the Riders? Unexpectedly, Listener found himself facing the question of whether or not to ride on at all. Did he know how the Mountain Badgers might treat people who came climbing down the mountains from the east? But then he thought of Narzia, and going back to her with nothing achieved. No, he must ride on; he had no choice. However, he decided to keep quiet in the first instance about the identity of those who had sent him.

Amidst such thoughts, he turned back to his horse, feeling quite glad now that Arni's stone was lying safe on its golden dish far away. These inhospitable mountain dwellers had certainly heard of Arni's Folk – how else could they have placed an embargo on any traffic with them?

– and as, judging by what was said of their Ore Master, they were pretty quick thinkers, it was not out of the question that they might connect him, the Bearer of the Stone, with those former Raiding Riders, always supposing they got a sight of the stone itself somehow or other, a thing which might well have happened through some carelessness of his own, or perhaps if he had an accident, and was unable to prevent some helpful soul from opening his jerkin and shirt to bring him relief, and thus finding the bag with the stone in it . . . He was aware of the tortuous nature of his thoughts as he rode slowly on over the bleak and stony ground, but he could not manage to get free of the maze into which his mind was making its way; indeed, it sometimes seemed to him as if he were only looking for some justification for giving up the stone without any resistance to speak of. On the other hand, there was always the possibility that the stone could have been useful to him with Arni's relations among the Mountain Badgers. But what did he know of these people? Anyway, what was done was done. The stone lay where it did, and the bag on his breast was empty.

Meanwhile, Listener had reached the top of the pass, after a last short climb, and now he looked down into the valley where the Mountain Badgers lived. He gazed over the tops of the spruce trees growing on the slopes, and saw a plain nestling between wooded hills, where there were villages, and a few houses standing by themselves. Smoke rose everywhere from the chimneys of the many smithies, and Listener also saw smoke in the narrow valleys running off the plain, which were closer to him, cutting deep into the mountain range. No doubt it was in these smaller valleys that the Mountain Badgers smelted the ore they mined.

Listener did not stand viewing the scene before him too long, for the sun was already low in the west, and he wanted to reach the first houses before night fell. He had no need to search long for a path down which man and beast could go on this side of the pass. There was a cart track with a good surface here, winding down the slope, which was partly overgrown with knee-high timber, to plunge into the shade of the spruce trunks farther below.

When he finally reached the bottom of the valley it was dark. Listener heard a brook running through the trees and bushes to one side of him, and the path followed its course for a while. Then he came out of the woods and had a clear view of a small hollow. Ahead of him he could see the shape of a dark building, its tall, broad chimney standing out against the night sky. There was a low-built house beside it, with lights in the windows. Hoping to find shelter for the night here, Listener turned his horse towards the house, and when he had ridden so close that Snowfoot's hoofbeats could be heard within, a man came out of the door, looking to see who might be here so late. Listener dismounted and asked if he could spend the night there.

'Plenty of room,' said the man, 'so long as you don't mind sleeping a bit rough. We're simple iron smelters, can't offer you any soft feather-beds.' Work at his furnace had left its mark on this man: the right side of his face was disfigured by the wide, pocked scar of a burn, reaching from his empty eye socket to his lips, and causing him to draw his mouth down to the left as he spoke, which gave his face an expression of malice. But his remaining eye gave the lie to this impression, for there was a friendly look in it. When Listener expressed his willingness to sleep in any kind of shelter, he led him to a shed built on to the house, showed him where he could stable his horse, helped to unsaddle Snow-foot, and carried one of his saddle-bags as they went back to the door of the house. 'It's not often a stranger loses his way around here,' said he. 'Where did you come from, then?'

'The mountains,' said Listener vaguely, hoping there were other ways across them besides the pass that led by the Raiding Riders' grave. The iron smelter seemed satisfied with this, and said, 'Come along in. We were just sitting down to supper, and you're welcome to join us.'

Six men were sitting at a table in the house, and a dish of some kind of brown mush stood steaming on the table. It did not look very appetizing, but smelled deliciously of fried bacon.

Listener was relieved not to be obliged to tell his tale at once, whether the true story or an invented one. He was familiar enough with the customs of hospitality, but this was the first time he himself had had occasion to note the advantages of not being asked where he came from and where he was going before he had eaten. The men moved up on the settle by the wall, to make room for Listener, one of them set a spoon in front of him, and then they all fell to. The mush in the dish consisted of crushed grain, boiled in water and then fried in a pan with some smoked bacon. It didn't taste bad at all, particularly when one had hardly had a thing to eat all day. Listener spooned it up in silence, listening to the talk around the table. The conversation turned mainly on a great fair to be held in a village called Arziak within the next few days. Obviously this fair was also an opportunity for all manner of merriment, and all the people of the valley went. The men talked of the dancing and drinking they were going to enjoy. From what they said, Arziak couldn't be far away. Listener also gathered, from several remarks, that matters of public interest were to be discussed there. 'They do say,' said one of the men, 'that traders from the west have been to see the Ore Master, asking leave to buy wrought iron and goldsmiths' work from our craftsmen, and Promezzo is going to put their request to the Valley Council.'

'Why didn't he send them packing straight away, then?' asked another. 'Forgotten it was a trader like that brought the Raiding Riders into the valley that time Urla's husband was killed, has he?'

'And have *you* forgotten how long ago that was?' asked the man who had come out to speak to Listener, and whom the others called Wry-mouth. But most of them said the first speaker's remark was none the less true for that, and the traders would soon see what the valley dwellers thought of them. By this time Listener had realized it was not going to be easy to win the Mountain Badgers over to the idea of taking Arni's Folk as their partners in trade, and it now looked as if he was going to have competition from the west as well.

As the men talked, they had emptied the dish, and now they wiped their spoons clean and Listener thanked them for their hospitality.

'Don't mention it,' said Wry-mouth. 'You look as if you're used to better, you do. What are you after in this out-of-the-way spot, anyway?'

Listener had made up his mind about that by now. 'I play the flute, and I'm on my way to the fair at Arziak,' he said, with the nonchalance of a man who has often given such information about himself; anyway, that really was where he now meant to go.

This was startling news to the simple iron smelters, as Listener realized at once from their expressions of surprise. Evidently minstrels seldom strayed into this remote valley, and still less did they ask for shelter here. He soon found himself pressed to give his hosts a tune or so, and he didn't refuse; after all, this was why he had ridden over the pass to the Mountain Badgers. So that he could see what effect his flute had on them, he sat himself sideways on the table top, and began to play, first some of the tunes he had picked up on his long ride with Barlo, and now and then a rustic dance such as might please these sturdy fellows. Right from the start, they sang along with him at times, and then they began to slap their thighs and beat time with their stout wooden clogs. Listener soon discovered what rhythm set their feet moving. He got them up from the settle, and had them dancing, stamping around in a circle until they were staggering like drunken men. When they sank back on the settle again, he played them a ballad of the rough, popular sort he had heard at fairs himself. It was only considerably later that the iron smelters realized they had understood the words, although nobody was singing, and indeed they understood them so well that the ballad was sung in the valley for many years afterwards. It ran like this:

> *Little Rikka wanted the conjurors to see.*
> *They wouldn't let her go, so away ran she*
> *to the fair that morn*
> *in the light of dawn –*
> *and now will you hark to the rest of my tale?*

> *To the wood she went, through the wood she ran.*
> *She was taken captive by the red-haired man.*
> *Eight good men and true,*
> *the Bloodaxe People slew –*
> *and what do you think is the rest of my tale?*

> *Rikka's father came, after them he went,*
> *angry as he was, on the Bloodaxe scent,*
> *down dale, up hill,*
> *by paths good or ill –*
> *and what would you say is the end of my tale?*

> *To the chieftain's house up he goes and cries,*
> *'Skullcleaver, come out, do battle for your prize!'*
> *Before the day is done,*
> *his daughter he has won –*
> *and who do you think was the man in my tale?*

> *Arni was his name, he carried Urla's stone,*
> *he rode with the horde but he rode alone.*
> *Welcome as a guest,*
> *wherever he would rest –*
> *aye, here in this valley, the scene of my tale!*

When Listener had finished playing the ballad, he put his flute down at last. By now the men had their breath back, and they applauded him loudly. 'You'll find a ready audience in Arziak with that song, sure enough!' said Wry-mouth. 'There's plenty of folk with kind memories of Arni there, most of all the Ore Master's wife, for she's Arni's own daughter!'

Listener was pleased to hear this. Things could hardly have looked better for him. If Arni's daughter was married to the most powerful man in the valley, it ought not to be hard for him to win the Mountain Badgers over to the cause of Arni's Folk. 'I had hoped to meet Akka here in the valley,' he said. Wry-mouth looked at him in astonishment when he spoke that name. 'You seem to know a lot about us,' said he. 'Ever been in Arziak before, then?'

'No,' said Listener, 'but I've been the guest of Akka's sister Rikka, and I once met Arni himself.'

'Well, you certainly seem to have got around a bit, even as a boy,' said Wry-mouth. 'There was a tale went about in these parts, a few years back, that Arni was dead.'

'Yes, he is,' said Listener. 'He died four years ago.'

'That's a shame, that is!' said one of the other men. 'He was the only one could've kept those Raiding Riders within bounds. But Khan Hunli doesn't seem the man to take his brother's advice.'

'Not Khan Hunli, no,' said Listener. 'However, they say Arni found followers among the Raiding Riders all the same, though not until after his death.'

Wry-mouth laughed. 'Yes, I've heard some such tale before,' said he. 'They're cunning, though, those Raiding Riders, you see? Spread rumours about the place, so's to be let into the valley, and once they're in, why, they'll come up behind you and cut your throat!'

One of the other men, however, was afraid of missing a good story. 'Let him tell what he knows!' he protested. 'Minstrels pick up a lot of news, riding the land the way they do.'

This was a tempting request, but Listener declined it all the same. 'I'm not much of a storyteller,' he said. 'The only language I under-stand is the language of my flute.' Not surprisingly, they all then clamoured to hear him play again, exactly as he had intended. He let them plead a bit longer, and then, with a show of slight reluctance, picked up his flute and began to play. This time he played neither a song nor a dance, nor a ballad with words they could repeat later. Listener painted pictures with the music of his flute: pictures of a village with a log cabin in the middle of it, grey with age, and when he led the men inside and showed them the stone lying on its golden dish, each of them knew that this was Arni's House, and the people who had settled at that spot meant to follow Arni's peaceful ways. Then Listener took them out of the cabin again and showed them the men of the settlement, wearing their hair loose instead of braided, men who wanted to go raiding no more, but trade instead, if they could, for they had to make a living somehow. What better shield can we wish for than Arni's Folk between us and the steppes, thought the listening iron smelters, spellbound by the pictures that passed before their eyes, as if in a waking dream, and they understood that they would be protecting their own valley if they made common cause with Arni's Folk. Listener watched the men's faces, wearing the enraptured expressions of dreamers, and it was easy to see the feelings his music had aroused in them. When he was sure he had convinced them all, he passed straight into the tune of one of those country dances which had set their feet tapping a little while before, and then he stopped playing.

There were no shouts of applause this time, but it was plain that the men's silence only conveyed a higher degree of admiration. Such wonderful flute-playing left them without any words. It was quite a while before Wry-mouth said, 'You know, fluter, there's a lot of things go through a man's head when you play, and he begins to see 'em different-like. Thinking of what I've heard now and then about those people, Arni's Folk or whatever they're called, seems to me we might think of making friends with 'em after all.'

Listener was careful not to pursue the subject, saying only, 'Well, it can never hurt to think hard about such things.' And soon afterwards they all lay down to sleep, Wry-mouth apologizing profusely for their inability to offer 'a master fluter who's travelled so far' any bed more comfortable than an old straw mattress and a couple of coarse woollen blankets.

Next day Listener rode on down the valley, with a good hearty breakfast of porridge inside him. The slopes to right and left of the stream were thickly grown with tall spruce trees, and drew close together now and then, but the path was broad and firm, for the smelted pig iron had to be carted this way, down to the smithies of Arziak.

While the stream finally turned right to go cascading down a steep and stony channel to the main valley, the path continued over the slope, about half-way up, and dipping only gradually towards the valley floor. When it came out of the last trees, leading the traveller towards a gently sloping meadow, he could see the smoke from the chimneys of the Arziak smithies farther down the valley, and in another hour's time he was riding down the village street, looking for an inn where he could stay. A green bush fastened to a long pole and sticking out of an attic window showed him the way to go, and as he came closer he saw that the freshly plucked boughs surrounded a wooden replica of an anvil, painted yellow. Obviously the innkeeper had once been a smith and changed his trade; or it might be that in this valley, where so many of the people were ironworkers, an anvil was the first thing you thought of when you wanted a symbol that folk would remember. Listener did not spend any more time wondering how the inn came by its name of the Golden Anvil, but asked the landlord, who came to meet him in the doorway, if he could have a room until the fair. The innkeeper, a heavy man grown rather stout with age, and obviously once a smith, looked him up and down appraisingly, and asked, 'What d'you sell?' It seemed as if he judged his guests by their trade at the time of the fair.

'I'm a minstrel,' said Listener, an answer of which the landlord did not seem to approve. 'Minstrel?' he repeated, in a tone which implied that this was a highly disreputable occupation, and added, 'What do you play, then?' in a manner suggesting that he expected there was even worse to come.

Listener was not to be shaken by this unfriendly reception. 'I play the flute,' he said, smiling, feeling a certain curiosity as to the nature of this stout fellow's next question. It followed promptly, and was just what he might have expected. 'Got any money?' The innkeeper spat out this remark like a splinter of bone which had accidentally stuck between his teeth. Instead of replying, Listener put his hand into the pouch at his belt and brought out a handful of the silver coins Honi had given him for his journey. The sight of them instantly transformed the look on the landlord's face. He raised his bushy brows, and drew in his breath quite audibly. Obviously events had taken an unusual turn, and it threw him slightly off balance. 'May I?' he said, took one of the coins from Listener's hand without waiting for an answer, examined it, shaking his head, put it between his teeth and bit it. Then he inspected it again, and said, 'Good silver, but I don't know the stamp of it. Where'd you get those coins?'

'I'd be glad to tell you indoors, over a goblet of wine,' said Listener.

'Well, no objection to that, not now,' said the innkeeper, in a very much friendlier tone. 'Come along in, and we'll find you a room.'

As they sat over their wine in the taproom, the landlord brought the conversation back to the silver coins. 'Who gave you that money, then?' he asked.

'Remarkable fellows, they were,' said Listener. 'I took them for Raiding Riders at first, but then I saw they wore no braids. They call themselves Arni's Folk, and seem to be peaceful traders, paying good money for what they want.'

'Arni's Folk?' said the innkeeper. 'Sounds like it's true, then, what people say.'

'What do they say?' asked Listener.

'Why, they say a part of the horde's settled down and turned all peaceful, same as that Arni of the Stone I used to see here in Arziak, times he came visiting his daughter.'

'Yes, that's how it looks,' said Listener. 'The horseman on the coin represents Arni, and the woman on the other side is supposed to be Urla, who gave Arni his stone.'

'If that's the way of it,' said the innkeeper, 'then I reckon this silver of theirs is good money in Arziak, for Urla was from this valley, you know, and one of Arni's daughters is our Ore Master's wife.'

'So I've heard before,' said Listener. And later, when he had paid in advance for his room, he saw the innkeeper going from table to table, showing people the silver coinage of Arni's Folk.

Over the next two days, Listener found his way around the place, took Snowfoot to a smithy and got the blacksmith to make sure her shoes were not loose, looked at the jewellery the goldsmiths were getting ready for the fair, listened carefully to what the people were saying and said little himself. The fair opened on the third day. The inn had suddenly seemed very full the evening before. New guests kept arriving, and Listener observed, with amusement, that the innkeeper put new arrivals through the same catechism as himself, unless he knew them from previous years.

After breakfast Listener took his flute and went out to the market place. There was a hurry and bustle such as he remembered from the Draglope spring fair, except that most of the wares offered for sale here were the work of blacksmiths and goldsmiths. However, in among the stalls of tools and weapons, or gold and silver jewellery set with precious stones, the farmers had cattle to sell, and there were wandering pedlars selling leatherwork, earthenware pots and all kinds of other wares. There was even a drawer of teeth, praising his own skill at the top of his voice, with much dramatic gesturing, and an old minstrel sat by the corner of a house, scraping away on a scratched fiddle, and nodding his head to passers-by in thanks for the coins they threw into his hat.

Following the custom of the minstrels' guild, with which he was well acquainted by now, Listener looked for a good place at the other side of the market place, where he wouldn't be luring an audience away from the old fiddler who had been there first. He found a wooden frame to which people used to tie up their horses outside a smithy. It consisted of two posts rammed vertically into the ground and connected by two crossbeams. Listener clambered up on this frame, from which he could see just above the heads of the fair-goers, and began to play.

He brought out his stock of songs and ballads and dances, just as he had that evening with the iron smelters, and joined the various tunes together, as minstrels sometimes do, with short transitional passages, so as to change from one key to another, or to avoid setting a gentle love song too close to the stamping rhythm of a woodcutter's dance. His hearers probably noticed nothing but the more or less familiar tunes, for people like best to hear something they have heard before, a tune they can whistle themselves. To Listener, however, the transitional passages were the important part of his playing. Although the people who had gathered around him did not fully realize what was happening, the little runs and themes he played left them with fleeting, momentary impressions of Arni's gentle ways, and the peaceful life of Arni's Folk in their settlement. One of the listening traders, for instance, might see in his mind the image of a hand offering a wealth of silver coins stamped with the picture of Arni in payment for his goods; another might unexpectedly think how pleasant it would be if he needn't carry heavy metalwork from place to place himself when he wanted to sell it, and he would immediately see an image of leather-clad traders who were ready to take on that laborious task for him. So Listener quietly smuggled his contraband into the people's hearts, and after a while everyone listening would, if asked, have stated unhesitatingly that he had always been in favour of a trading agreement with Arni's Folk on the other side of the mountains.

Finally, after another such transitional passage, Listener played the Ballad of Little Rikka, and to his surprise he heard somebody singing the words to his tune from the very beginning. When he looked around him for the singer, he saw the scarred iron smelter in the crowd, raising a remarkably fine tenor voice in song. The people liked the ballad so much that they even threw silver into Listener's hat, and wanted to hear the whole thing again directly. Naturally, Listener did not deny them. Meanwhile Wry-mouth had made his way through the crowd to him, and greeted him heartily as an old friend. Then he struck up the attitude of a singer, and gave of his best as soon as Listener began the tune again.

As Listener played, watching the faces of his hearers the while, his glance fell on a woman whose eyes immediately held him spellbound: eyes of a colour that was hard to describe, eyes that he knew very well. He could not tear his glance from those eyes all the time he played, nor when he had taken his flute from his lips either. The hearers thought the performance was over, and began to disperse. However, the woman came up to him, saying, 'I'm glad to hear Arni's memory kept green. How do you know that story?'

'My grandfather told it to me,' said Listener, 'and he heard it from your sister Rikka. Or aren't you Akka, the Ore Master's wife?'

The woman looked at him in surprise, and said, 'How do you know me, fluter? I don't know your name, and I never saw you before.'

'Nor I you,' said Listener, and then he told her his name and added, 'I've been Rikka's guest twice, and anyone can see you're her sister.'

The two of them were indeed as like as only twins can be. Akka's hair, too, was beginning to go grey early, but her face was still as young and smooth as Rikka's. She turned to thank the iron smelter for his singing as well, and then asked Listener, 'Will you give me the pleasure of being my guest? I haven't heard anything of my sister for a long time. You must tell me your news of her!'

Listener thanked her for the invitation, put his flute away, and followed her through the busy alleyways of the fair to a large stone house, which he had suspected to be the Ore Master's dwelling as soon as he arrived. They were just going up to the door, which was ornamented with cunningly wrought ironwork, when it was pushed open, and a girl of about twelve came running out. She went straight to Akka, crying, 'Have you brought me a fairing?'

Akka stopped. 'Why, Arnilukka, you act as if I'd been away for weeks!' she said, laughing. 'Look what I found you, my little water sprite!'

Putting her hand in the pocket of her full, red woollen skirt, she brought out a little silver chain with a tiny shell hanging from it, the colour of mother-of-pearl. Arnilukka carefully took the chain in her fingertips, and was at once utterly absorbed in watching the play of colours that the sunlight conjured up within the curving shell. Or were the iridescent blue, green and violet lights in the shimmering hollow only the reflection of her eyes, which were like her mother's eyes: Urla's eyes, into which he had looked in the hut on the other side of the pass? Listener stood there spellbound, looking at the child in whom her great-grandmother's inheritance lived on through the generations.

Akka watched her daughter for a while, too, but then she said, 'You must welcome our guest now, Arnilukka!' So captivated was the girl by the sight of the shell, however, that her mother had to lay a hand on her shoulder before she at last looked up, and glanced at Listener. 'Who's that?' she asked.

'His name is Listener, and he's a fluter who knows many good tunes,' said Akka. 'He has been a guest in your aunt Rikka's house, too, and will tell us about her.'

Arnilukka looked Listener in the eye, and then suddenly smiled and said, 'I like you, Listener. Will you play me something on your flute?'

This forthright declaration made Listener feel awkward. 'Of course,' he said, not sure what to do with his hands.

'Then come into our house and be our guest!' said Arnilukka, with as much self-assurance as if she were mistress of the place herself. She put the silver chain over her head, and cast one more quick glance at the shell now hanging on her breast. Then she took Listener's hand and said, 'Come on!'

A little later Listener was sitting with Akka and her daughter in the living-room. Akka had offered her guest a goblet of wine 'to help pass the time until dinner', as she said. Listener told them how he had last seen Rikka and her husband at the smithy, and mentioned his first visit to them too. 'Your sister asked me to tell her about Arni that time,' said he.

'Why, did you meet my father as well?' asked Akka, surprised.

'Yes,' said Listener. 'I saw him once.' But at the same moment he realized that he could not tell the tale of Arni's death without mentioning the stone, or being asked about it by Akka. And how was he to explain why he no longer wore it? So he went back to the subject of Furro's smithy, telling the tale of the smith's flight from Barlebogue with the donkey driver, and Rikka's own part in that adventure. Akka was diverted by the story, and Arnilukka laughed once or twice too when he told them about the inn where donkeys went in and out as if they were guests paying their way. But the girl kept casting him thoughtful glances, and when he had finished his story she said, 'You looked so sad just now, as if you had lost something.'

Listener felt as if the girl had caught him out, and he found he could not manage to look her in the face and lie to her. 'That may well be,' he said, evasively. 'Minstrels are always travelling about, and it's easy to lose things then.'

'I'll help you look for it if you want,' said Arnilukka eagerly. 'I don't like to see your eyes so empty.'

Even if Listener could have thought of an answer to that, he was relieved of the necessity of doing so by the entrance of the Ore Master himself: a powerful man of middle height, about forty years old. 'I see we have a guest,' he said, greeting Listener, and when his wife had told him more about the young fluter, he added, 'Well, you've been around quite a bit for your age! Akka will be glad if you'll stay here as our guest for a while. You must know she loves mysterious tales, and they say minstrels always have a good stock of those!'

From his tone of voice, it was easy to see that he didn't think much of 'mysterious tales' himself, but wouldn't grudge his wife her pleasures. Then he greeted his daughter too, gave her a kiss, and saw the chain with the shell on it. 'So your mother's bought you another pretty piece of magic from the fair, I see!' he teased her, but Arnilukka wouldn't go along with that. 'It's not magic,' she said seriously. 'It's a real shell out of the water. I like it because it's so beautiful.'

'Quite right,' said Promezzo with a nod, pleased. 'No point in veiling a thing in mystery if reason will explain it! And there's always a reasonable explanation for everything if you just put your mind to it long enough.'

One could tell, from Akka's face, that she did not agree with this remark; Promezzo observed it too, and it was obviously nothing new to him. 'I know, I know!' said he. 'You can always see something else behind all natural things, something that reason alone won't grasp. But then you're a woman of Urla's kin, and your father wasn't any different, always after the secret of his stone.' However, seeing his wife's eyes cloud over, he laid a hand on her shoulder and added, 'I didn't mean to hurt you. Your father was one of the most likable men I ever met. I only mean reasonable argument might have got him farther with his own people than his obscure dreams.'

Listener, who had been interested by this discussion, now said, 'But it seems as if he did get somewhere with them, if only after his death. They say a part of the horde decided to follow his ways.'

'Yes, I've heard that myself,' said Promezzo. 'A man called Honi, he's the one said to have taken the matter in hand, and a clever fellow he seems to be. From what little I know of it, he sought out Arni's most reasonable notions and put them into practice. He obviously realized a peaceful life is advantageous to those who lead it, and comfortable too! Though some do say the whole thing's no more than a cunning trick on the part of the horde, to lull their neighbours into a sense of security. And I must say I've never yet known folk to change their ways so quickly.'

At this point the conversation was interrupted by the serving maids bringing in dinner, and Listener discovered that they lived pretty well in Arziak too. As he enjoyed a dish of tender ham baked in a crisp bread crust, he thought of what Promezzo had said about Honi and Arni's Folk. He could not share the Ore Master's doubts of the sincerity of their change of heart, but he thought the rest of his remarks very illuminating. First and foremost, Honi had recognized the practical advantages of the life he now led, and he had very likely made such a to-do about Arni just because simple minds need an example to which they can aspire; if possible an example who is dead and thus can't disappoint them. Probably Honi thought as little of Arni's stone as did this sober-minded Ore Master, and had laid hands on it because he wanted something tangible to set before the people, something which would, so to speak, embody the spirit of their community. Listener felt as if he had been caught up in dreams himself, but at last saw clearly. What he must now do was convince Promezzo of the advantages of concluding a trading agreement with Arni's Folk. Very likely his flute, which he had been employing for that purpose, was not such a mysterious instrument as he had hitherto supposed after all. People were affected by music, everyone knew that; it was something you could calculate, like the trading value of goods. The minstrel just had to play the tunes that would guide his hearers' thoughts in the desired direction, that was all.

As all this went through Listener's head, he felt new confidence, and he could not help smiling to think how he had always had a lurking, guilty feeling that he was misusing the flute when he played it to change his hearers' minds. After all, he did so in a good cause, which was what mattered most. And Narzia would be pleased with him. For there could be no doubt now that he would achieve his ends. He was just imagining what it would be like when his falcon maiden took him in her arms and kissed him on their next meeting, when Arnilukka said, 'You look happy again now, Listener!'

'And so I am,' said Listener, but as soon as he looked at her he wondered: am I really? For under her gaze, everything he had just been thinking seemed less sure again. Was the stone which was the likeness (or the original model?) of those eyes really just a dead piece of quartz? Arnilukka laughed, and said, 'A silver penny for your thoughts!'

'They're not for sale,' said Listener, feeling ridiculous for letting a little girl cast him into such confusion.

'Then I'll give you the silver penny for a tune on your flute this afternoon,' said Arnilukka. Listener smiled and said she could have that free, for it wouldn't be right to take money from such kind hosts.

And so it was that after their meal, when Promezzo went out about his own business again, Listener stayed behind with Akka and her daughter. First Akka asked him more about her sister's way of life, and he had to describe Rikka's house in detail, so far as he could remember it: her living-room, even the food she set on her table, for Akka wanted to know everything he could tell her.

Arnilukka did not find this particularly interesting, and kept asking when they were going to hear the flute again, so that at last her mother gave way, laughing, and asked Listener if he would keep his promise.

The child's appetite for music proved insatiable. Listener played all the songs he knew, both sad and merry, searched his memory for grisly ballads and catchy dance tunes, but Arnilukka never tired of listening, drinking in the music with all her being, jumping up from her chair to dance across the room, between tears and laughter. Once, when Listener stopped playing to ask the reason for her tears, she said, 'Because it is so beautiful.' She liked the Song of Fair Agla best of all, and Listener remembered that her mother had called her a 'little water sprite'. He felt as if there really were something magical about this child, something that he could not fathom, yet he dared not ask why her mother called her by such a name, being afraid to disturb the girl's innocent pleasure in the music.

When Promezzo joined them again, later that afternoon, Listener played his ballad of Arni and Little Rikka, and Akka sang the words. He had not been playing any linking passages, stopping instead to tell Arnilukka where and in what circumstances he had first heard this song or that. Now, however, he added a clever little variation between each verse of the ballad, once again conveying all manner of pleasing pictures of the world of Arni's Folk.

It was plain that even the sober Ore Master could not withstand the magic of such playing. He sat leaning forward intently in his chair, as if he were watching a gripping game of chess that utterly absorbed him. Even when Listener had taken his flute from his lips for the last time, Promezzo remained thus for some while longer, silent and thoughtful as he stared into space. Then he said, 'You know how to give a man new ideas with your playing. I owe you thanks.'

After supper Promezzo said so again, repeating that he was indebted to Listener, and adding, 'So since you won't take money in my house, as is only any minstrel's right, I have thought of a way to keep my gratitude in your mind. Will you lend me your flute overnight?'

Listener hardly knew what to make of this. He was most unwilling to let the flute out of his hands, but he could not very well refuse his host such a request, and after all, it wasn't to be supposed that Promezzo meant any harm to himself or his instrument.

Soon afterwards he went to bed. He had already brought his horse and his bags from the Golden Anvil inn, when Promezzo repeated his invitation. The Ore Master himself had seen to it that Snowfoot had a good place in his stables, and had told his groom to care for the fluter's horse well. Now he called his daughter and told her to show their guest his room.

Arnilukka lit a candle, put it in a bronze holder, and led Listener to the upper floor. As he followed her down a broad corridor, he saw finely wrought weapons gleaming on the walls in the candlelight. At last the girl opened a heavy oak door on the right, and let Listener in. He felt soft carpets underfoot, and saw their twining patterns of red and blue glowing as Arnilukka followed him in and set the candlestick down on a table. Then she scurried over like a little household brownie to fold back his covers. Watching her, Listener felt it was very pleasant to be seen to bed like this.

'Is there anything else you need?' she asked, turning to him.

'No,' said Listener. 'You have seen to everything.'

'Sleep well, then!' she said. The candlelight set a thousand stars dancing in her dark eyes as she looked at him, smiling. Then she dropped a polite little curtsey – or was it, perhaps, a mocking one? – and was out of the door again.

When he woke next morning, he did not know where he was at first. The remains of a dream mingled with the image of a strange room, through whose window the sun shone in on the carpet with the red and blue pattern. Hadn't there been a falcon here just now? All he remembered of his dream was that he had been trying to catch a falcon, a beautiful bird with brown and white plumage that flew ahead of him, settling from time to time on a tree stump or a fence post, looking at him out of moss-green eyes, until he was very close and tried to seize it. But before his fingers could touch it, the bird spread its wings again and flew on. Then, at some point, a child came out of the darkness, laughing at him, and said, 'Let the bird go, it will only scratch your hands!' Or was it his heart that said so? He no longer knew. At any rate, he had run past the child, still following the falcon, but he never reached it. He tried to remember the child, but that image had sunk beneath the horizon of his consciousness now, and would not be dredged up again.

However, now he remembered how he came to be in this room, which seemed to him much smaller in the daylight than by candlelight the evening before: a room with whitewashed walls, upon which ibex horns and deer's antlers hung. There was a bronze bowl of water standing on a carved chest by the opposite wall, and in the middle of the room stood a table and two stools. Beside the candlestick on the table lay a flute that shone golden in the morning sunlight. Listener flung back his covers, got into his trousers and walked barefoot over the soft carpet to look at this flute. Yes, it was indeed golden, although otherwise like his own instrument in every respect. He picked it up and examined it closely. It was his own flute, he was sure of that now, for the five-fold ring at the far end was there too. However, the letters of the inscription that had been engraved upon it were no longer visible; it was as if the metal of the grooves had been smoothed out. He tried to remember how the words that once stood there ran, but they would not come back to him.

Listener wondered how a silver flute could be turned to gold. Or had Promezzo made an exact replica overnight? He raised the flute to his lips to see if the instrument obeyed him, as before. He thought the sound of it was stronger, and bewitchingly sweet. His fingers, as if of themselves, picked out a tune telling of the friendship of Arni's Folk with the Mountain Badgers.

As he played, the door opened and Arnilukka came in. She was carrying a water jug, and waited for him to put the flute down before she said, 'Good morning, Listener! How do you like your flute? I brought it back while you were asleep.' Her eyes were sparkling, as if she were enjoying a joke, and Listener could well imagine how she had crept into the room on tiptoe to surprise him with the transformation of his flute.

'But what's happened to it?' he asked. 'It looks as if it were made of gold.'

Arnilukka laughed. 'It isn't made of gold,' she said. 'It's your own flute. But my father had it gilded last night, by a man who is a master of the goldsmith's art, to give you pleasure. It hasn't harmed the flute, has it?'

'No, indeed,' said Listener. 'You heard it just now – why, it sounds better than ever before. I'll play it at the fair again today!'

'No,' said Arnilukka, 'you can't do that.'

'Why not?' asked Listener.

'Look out,' she said, going to the window. Listener followed her, and looked out at the market place. The stalls had been cleared away, and there was not a trader in sight. Instead, groups of men stood together, talking, and more and more came from the side streets to join them: master blacksmiths with their leather aprons, miners and prospectors with hammers at their belts, and the iron smelters too, of course, in their wooden clogs. 'What are all these people here for?' asked Listener.

'The Valley Council meets today,' said Arnilukka. 'We can watch from this window – but you'll have to hurry with your breakfast, if you don't want to miss any of it.' She looked him up and down, and added, laughing, 'But I think you'd better wash a little first, and comb your untidy hair, and maybe put your shoes on.' She poured water from her jug into the basin on the chest, and said, 'Don't be long!' before she went out.

A little later Listener had completed all these morning tasks, and was leaning out of the window of his room with the girl beside him. By now the market place was full of people again, arranging themselves in what was obviously due order, according to their trades. Arnilukka pointed out various prominent characters to Listener, mentioning a number of names which he forgot again directly. All he remembered was that Wry-mouth, who stood in the first rank of the iron smelters, as their spokesman, was really called Sparro. 'But nobody calls him Sparro any more since the day his furnace burst and splashed his face with the red-hot iron,' said Arnilukka. The square was buzzing with the conversation of so many men, but as soon as the Ore Master came out of his house, all was suddenly still. Promezzo wore a broad chain of office over his red woollen jerkin, its links forged alternately of iron, bronze, silver and gold, as a sign that he knew every metalworking trade in the valley.

Matters of justice were discussed first, questions of prospecting rights,

and such things, all of them no doubt of importance to the valley folk,
but they did not mean much to Listener, who had very little idea what
they were talking about except in a general sense. However, he pricked
up his ears when Promezzo announced that he was now going to put a
question of trading rights to the assembly. 'The traders from the western
towns,' he continued, 'have asked me whether we will let them buy
gold and silver jewellery and wrought iron wholesale here in the valley
of Arziak, to take it away and trade with it themselves. I believe that
the whole assembly should decide upon the answer. Who has an opinion
to give?'

The first to speak up was a white-haired master goldsmith, who said,
'I'm against it. A trader from the west once brought misfortune to this
valley. It could happen again.' His fellow goldsmiths nodded in
agreement, and there were several other men who called out that they
wanted nothing to do with the western traders. A blacksmith, a man of
considerable girth, did object that it was all very well for the goldsmiths
to talk; they didn't have so heavy a weight to carry when they went
about from place to place selling their own wares, but smiths were not
so lucky. However, another called out, 'And wouldn't it do your belly
a power of good if you had to carry your iron about the country yourself!'
and the objection was drowned in general laughter.

Promezzo waited until the assembly had quietened down again, and
then asked, 'So you want nothing to do with traders?'

'Not with the westerners, anyway!' somebody cried. Listener recognized the speaker: it was Sparro. The iron smelter had stepped a
couple of paces forward, as if he had more to say.

'Why, are there any other traders?' asked Promezzo.

'Yes, to be sure,' said Sparro, and Listener was glad once more to
hear so loud and clear a voice proceed from the twisted mouth. Sparro
turned to the assembly and continued, 'I reckon we've mostly heard of
those people called Arni's Folk, that have built their houses to the east,
beyond the mountains, and don't go out raiding any more, but are
peaceful traders instead. I say we ought to help them by letting 'em
buy from us.'

'And why should we do that?' asked the old goldsmith.

'Because it'd be a good thing for us, that's why,' said Sparro. 'You
laughed at our stout friend just now, but he's not so wrong neither. If
craftsmen don't need to go about the country selling their own wares,
then they have more time for their real work, and can make more than
they did. So they make more money too. That's one thing, but that's

not all, or we might just as well do business with the folk from the west. But what I reckon is, we'll be better off dealing with Arni's Folk. If we strengthen their new community, see, they'll stand like a bulwark between us and the Raiding Riders, and from all I hear of 'em, they'll be the very last to show that thieving gang the way into our valley. I'm for Arni's Folk!'

At that, everyone took up the cry. 'We're for Arni's Folk!' they shouted. Promezzo took this in, and Listener had the impression that such a turn of events did not come amiss to the Ore Master. After a while he raised his hand to silence the crowd, and then said, 'I myself have been weighing up such a proposition in my mind. If that is your opinion, then I will send a messenger to Arni's Folk, and invite their traders to come to Arziak.'

His last words were drowned in a roar of acclamation from the assembly. The men slapped each other on the back, and many even embraced, as if their dearest wish had been granted.

Listener watched, wondering if this was his flute's doing. 'Aren't you pleased too?' Arnilukka asked him. He looked into her face, into those eyes of a colour that was so hard to describe, and that were looking at him with a question in them. Why did she ask? Did she mean only that she didn't want to see anyone left out, when all others present were in such ecstasies? Or did she guess, with a child's intuition, that he had something to do with the enthusiasm for Arni's Folk that had come over the people of the valley like an epidemic breaking out? He shrugged his shoulders, and then looked back at the tumultuous crowd, and the longer he watched them milling about, the stranger it all seemed to him.

This sudden outbreak of rejoicing brought the assembly to its end. After a while the people dispersed, and Listener went down into the living-room with Arnilukka. Here they met the Ore Master, still wearing his chain of office, and drinking a goblet of wine as he stood. 'All that talk has dried my throat,' said he, offering Listener wine too. Listener saw this as his opportunity to thank his host for that morning's surprise, but Promezzo would hear no thanks, as if it were a very small matter, and said he hoped the embellishment of his flute had pleased him. Then they both sat down at the table, and Arnilukka stayed with them.

Meanwhile, Listener had been thinking of what the messenger whom Promezzo had suggested sending would learn from Arni's Folk concerning the 'Bearer of the Stone' who could play the flute so well. So far, no one in Arziak knew that he had actually ridden to the valley on Honi's behalf, and it would probably be better if no one did know until trade had been established. He had also thought of a way to avert such revelations. 'I have a suggestion to make, Promezzo,' he said. 'You told the assembly just now that you were going to send a messenger over the mountains to Arni's Folk. Now, it so happens that after the fair here in Arziak, I'm planning to ride on to Arni's Folk myself. Will you make me your messenger? I would be happy to do your errand.'

Promezzo thought for a while, and then said, 'Well, you relieve me of a difficult decision, Listener. It's not so easy to find a suitable man for such a task here in the valley. Our folk are sparing with their words, but a minstrel like you knows how to talk, and there's no one can withstand the sound of your flute either. So I'll thank you for your offer, and happy I am to accept it.'

Here Arnilukka spoke up too. 'Can I ride over the mountains with Listener? I'd so much like to see Grandfather's house on the steppes again.'

Promezzo laughed, and said, 'Not this time! Listener has a difficult job to do, and can't be looking after a little girl as well! There'll be time enough for that later, when trading's established with Arni's Folk.'

'Have you been to Arni's House before, then?' Listener asked the girl.

Arnilukka nodded eagerly. 'When he was alive, he often used to put me in front of him on his horse, and we rode over the pass to his house,' she said. 'I liked it better than anywhere there! You can see so far, over all the grass!'

'Arni had a great fancy for his little granddaughter,' said Promezzo, 'and not only because we called her after him. Ever since he first took her to his house, she's been wanting to go back again.'

'Were you ever in the steppes yourself, Listener?' asked Arnilukka.

'Yes,' said Listener. 'Yes, I rode through the steppes once.'

'Why do you make such a funny face when you think of it?' asked the girl. 'Didn't you like it there?'

'I don't know,' said Listener. 'So wide a view, from end to end of the sky, and nowhere for the eye to rest in between – I was a little afraid.'

Arnilukka uttered a clear peal of laughter. 'How can anyone be afraid of something so beautiful?' she cried. 'Just wait till you're there with me – you'll like it then, and you won't be afraid any more.'

At that both men laughed too. 'You sound very sure of yourself!' said Promezzo. 'But Listener must ride alone this time.'

'Tomorrow?' asked Arnilukka.

'There's not such a hurry as all that,' said Promezzo, and added, turning to Listener, 'For I hope you'll be our guest a few days longer.'

At first Listener was going to refuse this invitation. Didn't he intend to ride back to Narzia as fast as he could and lay Promezzo's message at her feet as a wedding gift? He was surprised to find himself hesitating, and wondered what could keep him here. And then, when Arnilukka too began begging him to stay, he found it very hard to make his mind up. Suddenly, Narzia seemed very far away, nor could he manage to conjure up her face. He looked at Arnilukka, and he could not withstand her eyes. 'Why, yes,' he said. 'Yes, I'll stay.'

One morning a day or so later Promezzo told Listener he was going to ride into the next valley, where the horses were at pasture, and asked if his guest would like to come. By now Listener knew his way all around Arziak, and felt he would be glad of a change. As soon as Arnilukka heard of the plan, she began pestering her father to take her too. 'You know how I love the Shallow Valley,' she begged. 'It's almost as good as the steppes.'

Finally Promezzo let his 'little Raiding Rider', as he called her, win him over, and he said to Listener, 'We'll take a hunting bow each. We may find game somewhere up in the Weird Wood.'

'Are you going to ride across the mountains, then?' asked Arnilukka, and Listener could see she didn't care for the notion. But Promezzo said he hadn't the time to go the long way round through the valley. 'If you're afraid of the Weird Wood, you'll have to stay at home,' he told her.

Arnilukka gulped, as if to swallow her fear. Then she said firmly, 'I don't mind which way you go so long as I get to the Shallow Valley.' They could tell that she did mind, but she stuck to her determination to go.

'Right, then be off and saddle your pony,' said her father, 'and we'll be with you directly.' Asking Listener to wait a moment, he went out of the room and soon came back with two hunting bows and quivers of arrows. 'Which do you fancy?' he asked. Listener tried both bows, stretched the bowstrings and let them spring back. The second bow seemed to lie better in his hand, and he asked for that one.

'Looks as if you know how to use a bow,' said Promezzo. 'What did you hunt last, then?'

'Wolves,' said Listener.

The Ore Master whistled appreciatively through his teeth. 'We don't get many wolves here,' he said. Then they went out to their horses, which the groom had saddled and led out of the stables. Arnilukka was already sitting her pony, a sturdy, black and white piebald, and could hardly wait to get to her beloved Shallow Valley.

They went a little way downhill along the road first, and then Promezzo turned off to the right along a track leading into a side valley, and running for a while beside a stream and through meadows over which the morning mist still lay. Wooded hilltops rose on either side, closing gradually in on the valley floor. The path began to rise perceptibly, and at every bend more mountain ranges came in sight, seeming to shift and intersect with every change of view, until at last the eye rested on a tall and distant range lost in a blue haze. 'We have to cross that range, and then come straight down to the Shallow Valley the other side,' said Promezzo.

'But we have to go through the Weird Wood first,' said Arnilukka.

'Why is the wood called weird?' asked Listener.

'I don't know,' said the girl, 'but it's frightening. The trees there are very old and twisted, and they have beards like old men.'

'Nonsense!' said Promezzo. 'It's a perfectly ordinary wood with some old pines in it, hung with lichen that's been blown about by stormy winds. As for its name, I don't know the reason. Maybe there was once a weir set in the stream to catch fish, and in time folk turned a plain Weir Wood into an uncanny Weird Wood.'

The farther they rode, the narrower became the strip of meadowland through which the stream wound its way. The wooded slopes came closer and closer, and soon they reached the outposts of the wood itself: hazel bushes stood beside the path, and now and then they rode in under the shade of a gnarled sycamore. Soon they reached groups of half a dozen trees or more, their branches shading the stream, and a little later they found they had come right into the wood without actually noticing the point at which it began. The path now left the stream, leading up and across the slope. For a while they could still hear the babble of the water down below, but then the sound mingled with the rushing of the wind in the tops of towering beech trees, and soon it could not be distinguished.

Down below in the meadows, Arnilukka had sometimes let her pony gallop on until she was well ahead of the two men. But now she kept as close to her father's or Listener's horse as the narrow bridle path would allow, although there was nothing at all weird about the wood just here, or not so far as Listener could tell. Indeed, he liked the place: the silvery grey trunks of the beeches rose high above luxuriant bracken, their branches spreading far overhead into a vault of young spring leaves, shimmering in every shade of light green in the sunlight.

The hoarse cry of a jay made Arnilukka jump. Listener laid a hand on her shoulder, saying, 'There's nothing to fear. We've not come to the Weird Wood itself yet, have we?'

'No,' said the girl, 'but I don't like woods anyway. You can't see as much as ten paces ahead, and you never know what may be hiding in the shadows among the trees.'

'Well, nothing can harm you while we're here,' said Listener, but he felt that the girl's uneasiness lay too deep for him to reach it with any cheering words. It was not that she was afraid of any particular harm. Her fear had no immediate object; it was simply with her, and would stay with her until she had a clear view to the horizon again. Arnilukka did not like woods; that was all. A pity, thought Listener. I like them myself.

He took care to keep Snowfoot beside the piebald pony after that, and told Arnilukka all kinds of amusing stories to keep her mind occupied. Once he even made her laugh, and felt quite proud of his success. So they made good progress, and the appearance of the wood began to change. Slender pines, their trunks dangling dead twigs, started to mingle with the paler trunks of the beeches. The dark needles of their crowns shut out more and more light, and finally the little party was riding almost soundlessly over the springy floor of the wood, softly covered with fallen needles. There was nothing to be heard but the rush of the wind whistling through the tree-tops. The track climbed steeply here, and if one of the horses slipped on the pine needles, the hollow clatter of its hooves was swallowed up again directly by the silence. And with every step farther up the slope that they went, the look of the trees was changing. Stringy beards of lichen hung from their branches here and there, their trunks no longer rose like the masts of ships but were stocky, often dividing into two or three main branches not far from the ground, these branches then curving upwards again and ending in the splintered stumps left after stormy winds had broken off their tips.

'This is the Weird Wood now,' whispered Arnilukka, and Listener saw that her eyes were wide with fear. Even his funny stories were no more use. He did try to dredge some more up from his memory, though rejecting such broad humour as the Tale of Wurzel and the Magic Miller, but there was no distracting Arnilukka any more. 'Never mind,' she said, in a curiously composed voice, 'I'm scared now, and I will be till we get into the open again. I know there's no sense in it, but that's not much help.'

It was indeed a strange wood that grew on the undulating ground, its slope now very slight as it approached the pass. Since it was higher than the other hills and mountain ridges round about, it had been left defenceless against the force of winds and storms, and there was scarcely a tree that had not at some time had a branch snapped off, or lost its crown, or been split by lightning. Many of them had suffered more than once, and yet, with that tough obstinacy peculiar to trees, they had always found a side shoot with sap enough in it to grow upwards and form a new if curiously distorted crown. And each of these weirdly distorted branches was thickly hung with long grey lichen that drifted in the air as it hung down. Yet the wood did not have anything like the same effect on Listener as those twisted trees in the Crooked Wood, which had seemed to be pinned down to the ground by evil magic. Whatever force had been brought to bear upon these trees, they still had not forgotten that their branches must grow up towards the light, and nothing in the world would keep them from it. Listener could not help respecting them, and even tried to convey to Arnilukka the idea that the wood was a good place, though its trees might be deformed by the weather, but even if she took in what he was trying to say, there was no way for his words to cross the barrier beyond which her fear began. He might as well have tried snatching a handful of air to show her.

The wood came to an end just before they reached the top of the slope. The summit of the pass itself was swept clean; not a tree had been able to withstand the force of the storms up here. The ground was covered with thick, short grass, in which countless herbs and flowers bloomed: yellow and orange hawkweed, velvety blue gentians, red dianthus, the pink and white flower clusters of milfoil, and delicate purple-flowered thyme, its scent rising from the mountainside where it lay exposed to the mid-day sun.

As soon as Arnilukka rode out of the shade of the last pines and into this sunny mountain meadow, she urged her pony into a gallop, so as to reach the top of the pass first. Her hair blew in the wind; she shouted aloud with pleasure now that she had a clear view again, and obviously her fears had all been forgotten in a moment. Up on the height of the pass, she waited for the two men, who were riding slowly after her. 'You can see the whole world from here!' she cried down to them, and when they reached her she asked if they could stop here for their midday rest, which was due now in any case. Promezzo had no objection, and so they all three dismounted and let their horses graze the fragrant meadow.

It was indeed an impressive view, and even if one could not quite see the whole world, at least it was Arnilukka's world that was visible from this high place. To the south, the winding stream they had followed made its way between the wooded heights and hills until it reached the valley of Arziak, cutting into the undulating landscape in the haze far below. Beyond and to the south-east rose the steep mountain range, crowned with jagged peaks. To the north, the land opened out into a wide and shallow valley of meadows, surrounded by woods, but one could see farther, to the north-east beyond that belt of woods, where the boundless plain of the steppes shimmered, merging with the pale blue sky on the horizon. Listener could understand Arnilukka's liking for the place, and was glad to stay here for a while.

When they had eaten some of their provisions, Arnilukka ran off into the meadow to pick flowers. Meanwhile, Promezzo showed Listener landmarks in the country at their feet, naming the mountains and valleys and telling him where the settlements hidden by the woods lay. 'You can see the whole of the Shallow Valley from here,' said he. 'We've used it as pasture since time immemorial, for the valley of Arziak is too narrow to graze herds of any size. But the Shallow Valley has another advantage too: you see that stream running through it? If you follow its course east to the source, you pass through more woods at first, but where the woods come to an end, the ground falls steeply away the whole breadth of the valley, in a rocky precipice that can hardly be climbed from the steppes at all, certainly not by horses. And so our herds are safe from the Raiding Riders.'

Listener had been looking at the spots to which the Ore Master pointed, and now glanced out again at the distant steppes. Hunli and his horde must be riding somewhere in the shimmering, silvery expanses of that plain, perhaps on a trail that would lead them to the village of Arni's Folk at last.

He was brusquely wrenched away from such thoughts by a scream rising from the outskirts of the wood. He and Promezzo jumped to their feet at the same moment, looking down. Arnilukka came racing wildly along the woodside, screaming something again and again: a word that Listener could not make out at such a distance. 'What's the matter with her?' he asked the Ore Master. Promezzo looked down at the wood, and then pointed abruptly at a spot where the girl had been only a moment before. And then Listener saw them as well: grey shadows running fast through the twisted trees of the wood. 'Wolves!' cried Promezzo, snatching up his bow and quiver and running down the slope. Listener seized his own weapon too, and followed him.

Arnilukka was making for a tree that stood alone in the meadow, a little way from the wood, but as she reached it she stumbled over a stone or a projecting root, and fell on the grass. By now the two men were almost within bowshot, but the wolves, two great grey beasts, came racing out of the wood and towards the fallen girl. Perhaps Arnilukka had hurt herself, or was paralysed by fear; at any rate, she made no attempt to rise. It was obvious that the wolves would reach the girl before the men could get there. 'We must shoot!' Promezzo shouted to Listener as he ran. 'I'll take the bigger one!' He stopped, snatched an arrow from his quiver and bent his bow. Next moment Listener was beside him, putting an arrow to his own bowstring. But when the wolves were only a little way from Arnilukka, they suddenly stopped in their tracks, as if held back by some invisible force. They stood there for a moment, the hair bristling on the backs of their necks, raised their heads and uttered a howl that echoed far and wide. 'Shoot!' cried Promezzo. The arrows whirred from their bows at almost the same instant, and each hit its mark. The wolves leaped into the air and then fell, twitching.

Next moment the two men had reached the girl. 'You see to those brutes!' Promezzo told Listener, snatching his daughter up from the grass and holding her tight. Listener drew his knife and cautiously approached the two wolves where they lay in the grass, not far off. The larger wolf was dead, but the smaller one was still alive, drawing gasping breaths from time to time. Listener was kneeling beside the animal to give it the death blow when he made a discovery that stabbed his own heart like a knife: this wolf had eyes as blue as sapphires! And as he gazed into the wolf's blue eyes, the creature began to change. It looked as if its shaggy grey hairs were gradually melting into the skin, its shape altered, it stretched its limbs, the gaping wolf's jaws drew back and smoothed out into a face, the face of a beautiful woman. 'Gisa!' said Listener, dropping his knife.

'You have finished me now, Listener,' said Gisa, groping for the arrow that projected from her naked body, just under the left breast. She was breathing with difficulty, but her face was calm, as if she were content with the way things had turned out.

'Why were you going to kill the girl?' asked Listener.

'Wolves must take prey,' said Gisa harshly. But then she suddenly smiled, and added, 'Ah, Listener, there is still so much you don't know. Perhaps I thought I could win you back if that child were out of the way. Not a good idea, as it turned out.'

'What has Arnilukka to do with it?' asked Listener.

'You can't expect me to tell you that,' said Gisa. 'But I ought to have known she had protection.'

'Didn't you see us then – Promezzo and myself?' asked Listener, puzzled.

'You two aren't much protection,' said Gisa. 'We have been following you for hours. I'd have let the girl go if I had not seen her with you, Listener. No, you couldn't have saved her. The tree was better protection.'

'What tree?' asked Listener.

'The one that took her under its shade,' said Gisa. 'Didn't you see what kind of tree it is?'

Listener looked around, and saw Promezzo, his back turned, standing under the spreading branches of a blossoming rowan with his daughter in his arms. Now he knew why the wolves had hesitated, and only that hesitation had saved Arnilukka. Gisa was breathing with difficulty. 'Will you do one thing for me, Listener?' she asked, and when Listener nodded, wordlessly, she said, 'Bury my body up here beside the wood, and plant a young rowan on my grave. In death at least, I will not run with the wolves.' Then she stretched out, and died.

Listener sat beside her in the grass, looking at her face. Its expression was calm and peaceful, as it had been long ago when he touched her with his stone.

'Are the wolves dead?' called Promezzo.

'Yes,' said Listener. 'Both dead. I am going to bury one of them here on the edge of the wood.'

'What for?' asked Promezzo. 'Leave them for the eagles to eat!'

'No,' said Listener. 'I have known this wolf a long time, and I owe it that service. Go back to the pass with Arnilukka while I do it; she ought not to see the dead beasts again.' He waited until the Ore Master and his daughter had gone far enough not to be able to see just what was being buried. As they rode up the pass, Listener had noticed a place on the outskirts of the wood where an old pine had been blown over and uprooted by a storm. The hole left by its roots would do for a grave. He carried Gisa's corpse to this spot, laid her in the hole, and covered her with stones and loose soil. Then he found a young rowan sapling nearby, dug it up with his knife and planted it on the grave. When he had trodden the earth down, he stayed there for a while, wondering what ways Gisa might have gone since he last saw her. He could not understand her. Once she had come between him and the old wolf whose body now lay in the meadow for the eagles to eat. And now she had tried to kill Arnilukka. Why? He could not answer that question. Then he heard Promezzo calling; yes, it must be time to ride on. He cast one more glance at the young rowan, hoping it would grow and protect the dead lying beneath its roots. Then, slowly, he went back to the others.

Arnilukka was still feeling the shock. She was white in the face, and clung to her father, trembling. 'There's nothing to fear now,' Listener told her. 'The wolves are dead. They can't hurt you any more.'

'I know,' said Arnilukka. 'But we'll have to go down through the wood again.'

'You can ride on my horse in front of me, and Listener will lead your pony,' said Promezzo. 'We can't stay here any longer if we want to reach the herdsmen's huts before nightfall.'

The climb down into the Shallow Valley was considerably steeper than the path up which they had ridden from Arziak. They could go no faster than a walking pace, and had to dismount in many places. Arnilukka did not say a word the whole time, and held her father's hand when they went on foot. They reached the bottom of the valley at last, just before sunset. Arnilukka mounted her own pony again, and a fast ride brought them to the herdsmen's huts as the sun was dipping behind the woods in the west.

Next morning, Promezzo rode out to the herds alone, and said he would not be back till nearly noon. Listener was still sitting at breakfast with Arnilukka. He had slept badly. Again and again he saw himself standing on the slope, his bow bent, his arrow pointing at the howling grey she-wolf; again and again the arrow flew from the bow and over the mountain meadow as if in slow motion. 'Swerve aside!' he cried, but the she-wolf stayed where she was, spellbound by the rowan tree, and the arrow reached its mark and buried itself in her hairy grey flank. Again and again Listener wondered if he could have broken that chain of cause and effect at any point, but it was not in his power to alter what had happened. Why did it have to be his arrow that struck Gisa? And what was Arnilukka's part in the linking together of these events, whose finality there was no gainsaying now? He felt he was caught in a web of connections anchored deep in the unknown.

'Will you come to my favourite place with me?' asked Arnilukka.

Listener shook off the thoughts that had troubled him all night. 'Of course,' he said. 'Did you sleep well?'

'Wonderfully well,' said Arnilukka, and indeed, she seemed as happy as ever, and had obviously overcome her shock now.

'Do we need the horses?' asked Listener.

'No,' said Arnilukka. 'It's not far, and I'd like to walk along the stream.'

She ran ahead of him through the dark green grass, where shiny, yellow, fat marsh marigolds bloomed, and followed every bend in the course of the meandering stream. When she reached an old pollard willow she stopped, lay flat on her stomach on the grassy bank, and looked down into the flowing water. As Listener came closer, he saw that she had dipped her hand in the current and was playing with the foaming little waves that formed around her fingers. Then she began groping about beneath the slope of the bank, suddenly snatched something, and lifted a crayfish out of the water, its pincers waving helplessly in the air. Laughing, she held the crayfish up to show Listener, and then put it carefully back in the water and watched it scuttle off to its place beneath the bank.

They walked on together now, but Arnilukka would not take a short cut over a single loop in the course of the stream, and there were a great many of them. The meadows spread flat as a pancake to the wooded slopes on either side of the valley, and the stream had gone its own sweet way over the valley floor, curving now to the left, then to the right again, almost describing a circle so that it was suddenly flowing in the opposite direction, and did not swerve aside until it had nearly met its own bed, so that when they had been walking for almost an hour, the distance might have been covered in a quarter of that time if they had gone straight ahead. But Arnilukka liked to hear the quiet babble of the water. She kept leaning down as she walked to dip her fingertips in the stream, as if she were caressing a living creature.

So they came to a place where a slight rise in the ground partly dammed the stream, and it formed a round pool before flowing on through a narrow channel. Pollard willows stood on the banks of this pool, their upright branches of fresh green leaves like huge brushes pointing to the blue sky. Some stood in the water which reflected them;

their branches seemed to point downwards, as if the ground were transparent here so that you could see their roots.

'This is my favourite place,' said Arnilukka, sitting on the gnarled roots of one of the willows growing by the water. Listener sat beside her and looked at the pool; a trout jumped in the middle of it, starting a circle of ripples that slowly spread. 'There are fish here,' he said.

'I know,' said Arnilukka. 'Would you like to meet my friends?' And without waiting for an answer, she took a piece of bread from her pocket and began to sing a strange little song, whose words meant nothing, or at least Listener could make no sense of the soft twittering, cooing noises the girl was chanting. However, there seemed to be creatures in the pool who understood that language, for suddenly the water at their feet began to crinkle and bubble, small shadows shot across the gravel at the bottom, and then the fish began to jump, leaping out of the water in their dozens, describing shining arcs through the air and plunging back into their own element again, the splashing eddy of drops they left sparkling with every colour of the rainbow.

Arnilukka crumbled the bread and held it above the surface of the water on the palm of her hand. Instantly the eddying of the fishes' silver-scaled bodies calmed down and they swam up, not fast and shyly, but with slow calm. Then Arnilukka dipped her hand beneath the surface, and her friends took their morsels carefully, lips pursed, nestling into the curve of the girl's hand and letting her touch and stroke them. Arnilukka spoke a word now and then, as if talking to her friends; Listener even felt as if she were calling some of them by their names.

'Now I know why your mother called you a little water sprite,' said Listener. 'Your fish do whatever you say.'

By now Arnilukka had fed the fish all her bread, and she leaned back against the trunk of the willow tree. She thought for a while, and then said, 'My father says it's perfectly natural. After the first time I sprinkled crumbs for the fish to eat, their greed will drive them to the bank as soon as they see me leaning over the side with my hand above the water.'

'But didn't you talk to your friends too?' said Listener. 'That's what it sounded like.'

Arnilukka shrugged her shoulders. 'Perhaps it's only a game I made up,' she said.

'Did your father say that too?' asked Listener.

Arnilukka admitted it, and went on, 'He says nobody can talk to the birds and beasts and fishes.' Listener could tell that she herself was not so sure, although obviously she was reluctant to doubt her father's word.

'My grandfather knew a blackbird and always used to talk to it,' he said.

'And you talk to wolves, though I don't think it was really a wolf you buried up there beside the wood,' said Arnilukka, looking at Listener with her dark eyes, in which the reflection of the rippling surface of the water shone.

'You mustn't think of that dreadful meeting any more,' said Listener.

'But you are still thinking of it,' said Arnilukka, shivering as if she suddenly felt cold.

'That's nothing you need to fear,' said Listener. 'It was a part of my own story that's over now. Come along, let's walk on, or you'll catch cold sitting here by the water.'

As they went on along the stream, Listener wondered if what he had just said was true. Was the story of Gisa really over? Did the stories of human beings ever come to an end at all? If so, Gisa would not have minded what tree grew on her grave. And he, for one, would never be able to blot her story out of his mind; it was a thread in the web of his own life, and could not be removed without destroying the whole pattern of the weaving. The longer he thought about it, the more deeply he feared that he would never be able to free himself from the tangle in which he was caught.

'Don't think of it any more!' Arnilukka's words brought him out of his thoughts. She was looking at him sideways, and had probably been watching him for some while. It did him good to be with this child whose eyes were like his stone. They warmed his heart as if he still wore it on his breast.

Arnilukka utterly refused to ride back over the pass next morning, and after all that had happened on the edge of the Weird Wood, no one could blame her. Listener also suspected that she wanted to spare him a return to that strange wolf's grave, and thankfully he took her side, saying he would like to go home a different way, to acquaint himself better with the low-lying part of Arziak. So Promezzo, as a courteous host, could only give in. 'However, the way through the valley is rather longer, and not without its own dangers,' he said. 'We shall have to ride through a narrow gorge, where stones may easily fall on our heads. Still, if you prefer that to the way through the Weird Wood, I've no objection.'

Listener said he would risk it, the more so as he noticed that Arnilukka did not seem to mind. She was probably glad she could stay near the stream, through whatever rocky places it might flow. And Listener was almost inclined to believe it impossible for any harm to come to her there.

So they rode on down the valley and through the meadows, until they came to woods that way too. At this point the stream began to cut its way deep into the stony ground, tumbling down a ravine in a series of foaming cascades. From up above, a narrow path could be seen winding tortuously down into the gorge at a more or less negotiable place on the slope. If Listener had been alone he would probably have abandoned any plan of leading a horse down that path. But Promezzo, who had certainly been this way before, dismounted and began the downward climb without a word. Arnilukka unhesitatingly followed him with her pony, and so Listener had to clamber down after them, willy-nilly. Apart from some exposed places where the rock fell steeply away, the path was safer than it looked from above, and he was not very long in reaching the bottom of the ravine.

Once down, Listener could not at first see any way of going on. Cliffs of a reddish hue towered up on all sides, leaving only a narrow strip of the blue sky visible above them. The tumbling water roared so loudly through its hollow bed that you could hardly hear yourself speak. Arnilukka seemed fearful again, and the horses did not appear to like this confined and noisy place either; they pranced nervously, showing the whites of their rolling eyes. Promezzo tried to soothe his horse, and led it along a strip of sand beside the stream. Next moment he had disappeared beyond an overhanging spur of rock. Listener let the girl go ahead again, and brought up the rear. Quite soon he was deafened by the rushing of the water and the clatter of the stones in the riverbed. The gorge seemed to be cutting deeper and deeper into the mountains, and sometimes its walls came so close together that scarcely any light from above filtered down. At such places Listener's horse almost panicked, and he had to hold on to the bridle to keep it from breaking loose. So they went on for about an hour, sometimes on the narrow bank, sometimes through shallow water. Listener had the oppressive sensation of going farther and farther into a cave, a dim and twilit cave with no way out of it. Promezzo did not seem very much at ease here either, and glanced up now and then as if expecting a rockfall any moment. Arnilukka gazed at the rushing water most of the time. Down here, where the steep walls of rock cut off any view of the open, it was probably her one comfort.

At last the rocks drew farther apart, giving way, after a final bend of the little river, to a view of wooded heights and meadows of emerald green on the hillsides. 'The valley of Arziak!' cried Promezzo, pointing ahead. His voice told how glad he was to come out of the ravine unscathed. They stopped to eat in a village inn at noon, but they had to ride on up the valley until after dark before reaching home.

That night the green-eyed falcon soared through Listener's dreams again. This time, however, the bird let him catch it. Listener stroked its neck and back, and the cool, smooth feathers turned to warm skin beneath his fingers. 'When are you coming back, Listener?' asked Narzia, putting her arms around his neck. 'Don't you know I'm waiting for you?' And he was going to kiss her mouth, but before he could touch it the falcon's hard wing feathers struck him in the face, it escaped his hands and flew away. He saw it circling overhead for a while, and then the bird flew off eastwards, growing smaller and smaller, a dark dot in the sky; next moment it was gone from his view, and he could not find it again.

This vision was still clear in his mind's eye when he woke, and he decided to set off that very day. It was early in the morning. Dim twilight fell into the room through the window, spreading like pale mist over the carpet. Listener jumped out of bed, dressed hastily, and went downstairs. On the staircase, he remembered that he had something still to do; he had not yet found the piece of jewellery for which Narzia had asked. But he was soon to be relieved of any anxiety about that.

Down in the living-room he met Promezzo, obviously an early riser and already sitting at his breakfast. Listener told him he meant to ride over the pass to Arni's Folk today.

'A day more or less won't matter, will it?' said Promezzo. 'And if you are to be my messenger, you must take something with you. The goldsmiths of Arziak have suggested that you seek out a piece of jewellery from every workshop, so that you will have something to show Arni's Folk. Let their traders see what we can sell! And we'll need the whole of today for that task, for there are many goldsmiths here, and they've all been hard at work through the winter.'

Listener had often heard praise of the skills of the master craftsmen who lived in these mountains, and had seen and admired specimens of their work at the fair, but what he saw that day surpassed all his expectations. As he went with Promezzo from workshop to workshop, he began to see why he was to take an example of every master's work, for each of them practised a separate branch of his trade. One man made golden chains whose delicate links, fine as hairs, were so skilfully interwoven that you thought you were looking at a massive golden collar until you took the thing in your hand, and could feel it settle, snake-like, into every fold of your skin. Another made silver buckles for belts, set with filigree patterns of fine gold wire. A third made decorative golden studs and clasps for horses' harness. Then there was another who made rings: rings broad and narrow, smooth and chased, many of them ornamented with precious stones in superb settings. Wherever he went, Listener chose a piece which he thought would win the approval of Arni's Folk, and if he hesitated at first to ask for a particularly valuable specimen, he soon realized that the goldsmiths were proud if he chose what they themselves thought their best work.

So at last they came to a master who made brooches ornamented with figures of animals and birds of every kind: stags with branching antlers, mountain goats whose horns curved right back from their heads to their stumpy tails, eagles with great wings, and other birds of prey. Among them there was a falcon in flight, its eye a sparkling emerald of considerable size, and green as moss. As soon as Listener saw this brooch he knew what to take Narzia. When he picked up the bird, which was about the length of a finger, the goldsmith said, 'You've chosen well! That falcon's the best piece I've made in years. May it bring you and all of us luck.'

'You say just what I was thinking,' said Listener, wondering if the master goldsmith could have read in his eyes for whom he intended the brooch. Now that he had it, he would have liked to ride straight off, to see Narzia's eyes when she took the golden falcon out of its deerskin wrapping, but it was too late to set out that day unless he wanted to be overtaken by night in the mountains, for the whole morning and part of the afternoon had been occupied by the choosing of his treasures.

That evening, Listener thanked the Ore Master's wife for all her hospitality, and was going to take his leave of her there and then, not knowing if he would have a chance to do so when he left early next day. 'Oh, no need to say goodbye yet!' said Akka. 'If you will let me, I'll go part of the way with you tomorrow. I have to ride up to Urla's house with a couple of men to see that all's well there. Nobody lives in the cabin any more, not since Urla died, but it must remain in good repair to keep her memory green.'

So Listener did not ride up the valley alone in the morning mist next day. Akka trotted along beside him on a sturdy mule, and her two menservants were similarly mounted, for mules, with their narrow hooves, could climb the mountains with greater ease than the more heavily built horses kept by the Mountain Badgers. Arnilukka stood in the doorway of the house with her father as the little procession rode across the market place, calling after Listener, 'Come back soon! If you don't, I'll ride to Arni's Folk myself to find you!'

'You gave her great pleasure with your music,' said Akka, as they rode past the last houses of Arziak. 'And I myself have never heard a fluter play as well. My father once told me that he had a friend in his youth who was a master fluter too. I fancy he must have played much as you do.'

'It may well be so,' said Listener, 'for that man was my grandfather. He was known as the Gentle Fluter, and he taught me to play the flute.'

'Ah, then it wasn't mere chance that I thought of him when I heard you,' said Akka. 'Do you know that you have great power over people when you play your flute in that way?'

Listener glanced at her. Had she seen through him? Her eyes were turned on him as if she were trying to discover what went on inside his head. 'I do the best I can,' he said, avoiding a direct answer.

'I don't doubt that,' she remarked, 'but you ought to be aware of what your music may bring about. My father told some strange tales of that Gentle Fluter.'

'He was a clever man, to be sure,' said Listener, 'but he couldn't work magic.'

'Why, now you talk like my husband!' said Akka. 'You surprise me.'

'Why?' said Listener. 'Do you think anyone who can play a little music is a magician? My grandfather set me right once, and pretty sharply too, when I expected something of the sort from him.'

'No, no, that's not what I meant at all,' said Akka. 'But I fancy your grandfather was not a man to rely solely on his own skill.'

And she might be right there, thought Listener. But he also wondered where you might end, if you began doubting the reliability of your own reason. How were you to find your way if there was no landmark visible on the horizon at a measurable distance? It would be like riding over the boundless steppes without any path, or any end in view, and even there the eternally circling pattern of the heavenly bodies showed the way to a man who could read them, if he was ready to trust in the laws by which they moved. But suppose those points of light should leave their regular courses? And who was to say they hadn't done so long since, unnoticed? Listener realized that he was looking into Akka's eyes, with that play of colour in them which was so hard to describe, but was something between blue and green and violet, and in which he had been so often lost before.

'You're not quite as sure as you seem,' she said, smiling, and he felt that she was pleased with her observation. He turned his eyes away, and pretended to have to adjust something on his horse's bridle. These women of Urla's kin knew how to unsettle a man, he thought. When they looked at him, everything upon which he had been accustomed to rely seemed uncertain, and yet he did not feel lost, even if he did not know upon what the heart-warming trust he now felt was founded.

All things considered, it was a pleasant ride in Akka's company. The two menservants had dropped a little way behind them. Promezzo had sent them chiefly to protect his wife, Listener supposed; at least, each of them was armed with a short sword and a hunting bow. They were enjoying the ride like a day's holiday, talking idly and laughing, and hardly seeming to fear that something might happen to their mistress, although by now they had passed the iron smelters' huts and were riding up the steep track through the woods to the pass. Soon they had reached the top, and saw the tomb of the Raiding Riders ahead of them on the rocky terrain of the high plateau.

'If Arni's Folk should be coming over this pass in future, there'll be many a man among them who can greet a dead ancestor here,' said Listener.

Akka looked at him in surprise. 'How do you know what the monument is?' she asked. 'Were you ever here before?'

Listener realized he had almost given himself away, and bit his lip. 'I know the story of Urla,' he replied. 'Rikka told me.'

'I hope that Arni's Folk have not forgotten the story of Urla either,' said Akka.

'No, indeed they haven't, as I can show you,' said Listener. He took one of the silver coins out of his pouch and showed Akka the picture of Urla's head stamped on it. 'Arni's Folk pay for their needs in this coinage,' he said. 'The Rider on the other side is supposed to be your father.' Akka asked to take a closer look at the coin, and Listener made her a present of it.

When they reached Urla's cabin, the sun had passed its zenith. 'I hope you'll eat with us before you ride on,' said Akka. 'It isn't far from here to Arni's House, even if no one has gone that way for years.'

Listener knew better, but he said nothing. When they had dismounted and tied up their beasts, Akka opened the door of the hut and said to Listener, 'Come in and be my guest.'

Involuntarily, Listener looked for the falcon that had driven him into the hut some days before, but the sky was empty. This time, therefore, he entered in less of a hurry, and immediately found himself once more breathing in the fragrance of pinewood, and herbs, and all those things with which Urla spent her days. Akka asked him to sit at the round table and began to busy herself at the hearth. 'I can't offer you a banquet, with so little time to spare,' she said, 'but you shall not come hungry to the village of Arni's Folk.'

The two menservants had now arrived as well. Akka went out to them, asked them to perform some task or other, and then came back with a saddle-bag, from which she took various things to eat: a piece of meat, onions and other vegetables, cheese, bread and a jug of milk. By now there was a good fire on the hearth, and soon the smell of good savoury soup mingled with the fragrance of the room itself. Urla must have entertained her own guests in much this way. Akka said nothing of importance all this time, so that Listener wondered if, in the circumstances, she was holding to the custom of refraining from serious conversation with a guest before he had eaten his fill. When the soup was ready, she called in the two menservants, who wiped their hands on their trousers and seated themselves formally at the table. They ate their soup in silence and went straight out and back to their work again. Listener too rose, saying, 'I'd better ride on now if I'm to reach my journey's end in daylight.'

'I see you can hardly wait to reach these Folk of Arni's,' said Akka. 'Nothing but impatience in your eyes, as if you had a girl awaiting you there.' She smiled in a manner that was hard to interpret, and that made him even less sure where he stood with her than he was already. Did she know more about him than she admitted? If that were the case, then the cunning way he had played his cards seemed to have amused her. But perhaps she spoke like that only to embarrass him a little, in which she had obviously succeeded. He decided not to respond to her hint, and thanked her again for all her hospitality before he said goodbye.

She went outside the door with him, showing him the way to take to

Arni's House. 'The last part of the path is quite steep,' she said. 'You'll have to dismount there.' Listener did not show that he knew that already. 'Don't worry,' he said. 'I'm used to taking bad roads.'

'There are some bad roads, however, that you should not become too used to taking,' said Akka, and the way she looked at Listener brought the blood to his face. He mounted his horse quickly, raised his hand once more in farewell, and went trotting eastward over the mountain pasture.

Towards evening, he had the steep slope behind him, and saw the houses of Arni's Folk lying ahead. He had been unable to think of anything on the last stage of his journey but Narzia's green eyes reflecting the treasures that lay in his saddle-bag. As soon as he had reached level ground, he swung himself on his horse and galloped full speed to Arni's House. Here, fortunately, he recollected the polite customs of the place, which he must not neglect to observe in front of the people who had come out of doors to see who was riding so fast down the village street. Listener jumped off his horse and paid his respects to Arni's House with the usual low bow, a position in which he remained for some moments. Only when he felt that a proper amount of time had gone by did he straighten up and lead his horse to Honi's house. Taking off the saddle-bag, he gave it to one of the grooms, while he himself strode into the house bearing his treasures, to deliver his message to Arni's Deputy or his present to Narzia, depending on which of them crossed his path first.

He found them both in the living-room, sitting at the table and obviously in the midst of one of their discussions. When he saw who had come striding through the doorway, Honi jumped up with remarkable ability for a man of his girth. 'Have you run the whole way from Arziak, eh?' he asked. 'You look as if you brought good news.'

'And so I do,' said Listener, telling them the message Promezzo had given him. When he had delivered it, he unpacked the masterpieces wrought by the goldsmiths of Arziak and laid them one by one on the table. While Honi examined the precious things with pleasure, and not without a touch of greed, Listener saw nothing but Narzia's face. She did not seem particularly impressed, and glanced indifferently at the golden chains, rings and buckles, as if they were mere trash, scarcely worth a look. Wait until you see the falcon brooch, thought Listener. He had kept back that costly jewel to give her when they were alone together.

His opportunity was to arise even sooner than he had hoped. Honi tore himself away from gazing at the glittering, golden treasures and said, 'I had better summon the elders to meet tomorrow morning, for we mustn't keep Promezzo waiting too long for our answer. Pack these things up again, Listener; we won't leave them lying around here unguarded!' Then he rose, and went out.

Listener sat opposite Narzia in silence for a while, looking into her eyes. Then, unable to restrain himself any longer, he asked, 'Are you satisfied with me now?'

Narzia hesitated before she replied. Then she said, 'You have done all that Arni's Folk expected of you, and brought some pretty things back too. Were they all you found when you visited the master craftsmen of Arziak?'

Listener laughed triumphantly at that, saying, 'I knew none of those pieces was good enough – but I kept the best for you.' Then he took the golden falcon out of its leather wrapping and laid it in her hand. Narzia's eyes shone as she saw what the brooch represented. Listener looked at her admiringly, and thought: how alike they are, the golden bird with the emerald eye and my falcon maiden.

'Will you pin it on me?' asked Narzia, rising. Listener went to her and fastened the brooch over her left breast. His hand trembled as he felt the warmth of her body under her linen outer garment. Once again Narzia put her hand on his left cheek, but this time she also bent and kissed him on the other cheek. It was a quick kiss, just brushing his cheek, more of a fleeting caress of her lips, but it set Listener's heart beating wildly.

Before he could embrace her, however, she pushed him away again, saying, 'Sit down, Listener. I must talk to you.'

If he thought she was now going to discuss the date of their marriage with him, he was sadly mistaken. Wasting no words, she said directly, 'You will have to undertake a second journey for Arni's Folk if you are to get what you want, and this time it concerns a matter in which you yourself aren't entirely innocent. While you were with the Mountain Badgers, an envoy came from Khan Hunli, asking to speak to my father on a serious matter. To cut a long story short: somehow or other, Hunli found out that the man who sent him and his Riders chasing across the steppes was living here with us, and held in high honour too, and he did not like that at all. He was sending word to say that your deceitful trick had lost him twelve horses, and he wanted us to replace them.'

'Didn't I bring you back ten times their worth from Arziak?' asked Listener, but Narzia raised a hand to show she did not want to be interrupted, and added, 'Nor is that all. Hunli's message also said that if the Bearer of the Stone were so important a man, he should have courage enough to deliver the horses in person, and give the Khan satisfaction in one way or another; they might, for instance, play for this or for that, as is the custom of the Raiding Riders.'

Having uttered these remarks, Narzia fell silent, looking at Listener with her green eyes. He could well imagine what was meant by 'this or that'. It would not be the first time someone had had to play for his freedom or even his life in the Khan's tent. On the other hand, he could not refuse the challenge unless he wanted to be thought a coward. His reputation among Arni's Folk would be gone then, in any case, and he could put all thought of wooing Narzia out of his head. He saw in her eyes what she expected of him. 'So you think I should undertake this ride?' he said.

'Don't you?' asked Narzia, eyebrows raised in astonishment.

'Yes, of course,' Listener hastened to agree. 'I'm only wondering what game Hunli will want to play.'

'What do you suppose?' said Narzia. 'Chess, most likely. He won't want to compete in sports on horseback, not at his age, and it wouldn't be particularly honourable for you to bear arms against an old man in single combat either, even though he may well hold his own still in such conflicts. Can you play chess?'

'I know how to move the chessmen, but that's about all,' said Listener. 'He'll probably beat me after a couple of moves.'

'Something can be done about that,' said Narzia, unmoved.

'Are you planning to make me a master at the game of chess in a couple of days?' asked Listener. 'As far as I'm aware, only Arni could ever beat his brother.'

'You are right,' said Narzia, 'and Arni will help us, since we are his Folk. I think you should be able to ride in a couple of weeks' time.' And she would say no more that evening, but left him. Captivated by her springy walk and the smooth curve of her hips, he watched her until she had closed the door behind her.

These last few days, and particularly during the ride back over the mountains, he had thought how he would go to her and take her in his arms, and now it turned out that she was farther away than ever, for he had little hope of seeing this venture in Hunli's tent turn out well. He sat where he was for a while, staring into space and looking for some way out, but he couldn't think of any, and probably there was none either. Finally he pulled himself together, picked up his saddle-bag, and went to his bedroom, very downcast.

As he put away the things he had taken with him on the ride back in the cupboard on the wall where he kept his belongings, his hand fell upon the little flasks from his grandfather's cellar. He picked them up, one by one, in the vague hope that he might find some answer to his problems here, but the directions on the labels had nothing useful to say. 'Strength for an hour, sleep for three days' – that wouldn't help him now. He thought he would like to fall asleep at once and forget what awaited him out there in the steppes. 'One drop: sweet dreams for a night.' Yes, that was what he needed at the moment. He opened the little bottle and tipped it cautiously over his cupped hand, until a drop of dark, syrupy liquid fell into his palm. Then he closed the flask again and put it back in its place before he licked the shiny brown drop off his hand. One didn't know how quickly this mysterious elixir might work. It tasted sweet and bitter at once, seeming to fill his whole mouth, and it worked immediately. He just had time to fall on his bed, and then he began to dream:

The Sweet Dream

He was walking, or rather scrambling, through a thick wood, pushing his way through the undergrowth as huge ferns closed above his head, stroking his cheeks with their rough fronds. He did not know what he was doing here, but he had to keep going on through this wood, past whose tangled boughs scarcely a ray of light fell. He must have been on his journey for hours, or even days, he couldn't remember just how long, and nothing had changed all the way. But now the sweet fragrance of woodruff began to mingle with the sharp scent of the ferns. Something was going to happen. The wood grew lighter ahead of him, sunlight shining between the angular stems of the ferns, and then he came out of the undergrowth into the open, to find himself standing on a green carpet of delicately whorled sweet woodruff, sprinkled with tiny clusters of white flowers. The heady scent of the woodruff rose to his nostrils. He would have liked to lie down there and let that magical fragrance wash over him, but he sensed that he must go on, towards his journey's unknown end.

A few more paces brought him to a high hedge, an impenetrable tangle of privet and hawthorn, hornbeam and sloe, and he knew he must get through it to go where his heart was urging him. Yet he could not see the smallest opening in this hedge, no place where some woodland creature had made itself a way, no gap in the tangled bushes allowing so much as a glimpse of the other side. He pushed hard at the intertwining boughs, but only scratched his hands on the thorns, and stood there at a loss, with his arms caught in the branches.

As he stood trying to free them, he saw a robin that had built its nest in the twigs of the hedge right in front of his face. The robin did not seem in the least afraid of him, and was inspecting him curiously with its bright black eyes.

'I suppose you can't by any chance tell me how to get through this hedge?' asked Listener.

'Since you ask so politely,' said the robin, 'yes, I can. Come with me!' It hopped out of its nest and on to a twig, flew a little way along the hedge to the right, and then settled again, waiting for Listener. When he caught up with the robin, it called 'Come with me!' again, and flew a little farther, and so they went on for some time, until Listener asked how much longer this would last. But all the robin said was, 'Don't be so impatient, or you'll never get where you're going. Come with me!'

In this way they finally reached a place where the hedge consisted only of withered sloe bushes that had caught the frost in winter. The tangle of branches was covered with thorns as sharp as needles and almost a finger's length in size. 'You'll have to get through here,' said the robin. 'There's no other way.'

Cautiously, Listener put his hand into the thicket of thorns, and pricked it so badly that it bled in several places. 'How am I ever to get through if I can't even touch it without pricking myself?' he asked.

'You are too fearful,' said the robin. 'You'll never get where you're going while you think of what might happen.

> *Jump through the thorn,*
> *or all is forlorn.'*

And so saying, the robin flew away, and Listener could not call it back.

He examined the hedge once more, feeling sure he would tear the flesh from his bones if he tried jumping through it at this point. But if it cost him his life, he had to reach the other side. So he retreated a dozen paces from the thorny bushes, closed his eyes tight, took a run at the hedge, and jumped.

Next moment he felt as if flames were breaking over him. Colours exploded before his closed eyes, red globes bursting like fireworks into a rain of yellow, green and orange stars, unfolding into gigantic flowers of indescribable beauty that spread across the whole sky, slowly fading away at their outermost edges into muted shades of purple and violet, and at the same time a delicious warmth enveloped him, as if he had suddenly stepped out of the cool shade of leafy trees into a sun-drenched meadow.

And when he opened his eyes, feeling himself for any cuts and stabs, he was indeed lying in such a meadow. Remarkably, he had not so much as the slightest scratch, and even the wounds on his hand had healed. He stood up and looked at the hedge from this side. The thorny thicket of withered sloe bushes looked as impenetrable as ever, and showed not a trace of his passage through it. Finally he stopped puzzling over this curious phenomenon, and looked around, wondering what to do next.

His prospects were not hopeful. He was standing on a narrow strip of meadowland, the hedge behind him and a moat in front. The moat was much too wide for him to jump it, and on its far side stood a great wall of undressed stones, at least sixty feet high. He knew that he had to get over this wall. It would be a reckless undertaking to climb it, but he would try, if he could only get across the moat first.

Looking for a place where it might be jumped, he went a little way along its bank, but the moat was the same width everywhere, and it did not look shallow enough to be waded either. He could not see its bottom, even by the banks, although the water was so clear that he could make out the dark green backs of mighty carp swimming slowly by, deep down below. As Listener sat on the grass, wondering how to get over the moat, some ducks came flying across the sky and settled directly in front of him. The water foamed around their outstretched feet as they came down, and then they were rocking gently amidst countless rings of ripples spreading and intersecting on the surface of the water around them. They were wild ducks with brown plumage, among them a couple of drakes with bright steely blue wing feathers and delicate curly black plumes above their tails. Among them, however, there was one snow-white duck who swam slowly towards Listener, looking at him with so much interest that he plucked up his courage and asked her, 'Can you by any chance tell me if this water's very deep?'

'Since you ask so politely,' said the duck, 'yes, I can. This water is so deep that even we don't know if it has any bottom at all. I suppose you can't swim?'

'No,' said Listener. 'There are only narrow brooks and shallow little rivers in the place where I grew up.'

'And now you're wondering how to reach the other side,' said the duck. Her gentle quacking sounded like a suppressed chuckle.

'That's right,' said Listener, slightly annoyed. 'Do you know any way over?'

'Perhaps, if you have a little courage,' said the duck. 'Follow me!' So saying, she turned away and began swimming fast along the moat. After a while Listener asked, 'How much farther am I to follow you?' But the duck only said, 'Don't be so impatient, or you'll never get where you're going! Follow me!' And on she swam.

Finally they reached a place where round lily leaves floated on the water. The duck came waddling up on the bank and said, 'Here's the place. You need only jump from leaf to leaf, and you'll be over. There isn't any other way. But you mustn't take more than seven jumps, because there are only seven leaves that will carry you. With a bit of luck you'll find the right ones.'

Listener didn't think much of this proposition, considering that there were hundreds of lily leaves rocking on the water. Cautiously, he put his foot on a leaf that had unfurled close to the bank, but it did not offer him any support at all, and instantly went under. 'I shall probably drown miserably in this moat,' said Listener.

The duck shook her head disapprovingly and said, 'You're too fearful. You'll never get where you're going while you think of what might happen.

> *Jump from leaf to leaf*
> *and you won't come to grief.'*

And so saying, she took a short run and flew away, close above the surface of the water.

There stood Listener on the bank, trying to discover which of the water-lily leaves were the right ones, but they all looked the same. Finally he told himself that he must get over somehow, if it cost him his life. So he plucked up all his courage, took a run, and jumped.

He flew over the water, the wind whistling in his ears, his foot landed on a firm and springy surface, took off or was pushed off again, millions of waterdrops sprayed around him, shimmering in many colours in the sun, and he sprang through the sparkling curtain of drops to the next leaf, which received him on its springy surface and sent him on to the third; he sensed that it was not his own strength that sent him speeding over to the fourth leaf, but that the leaves themselves were playing with him as if he were a ball, thrown on by the fourth leaf to the fifth, which sent him on again to the sixth, and the opposite bank was still much too far away for a final jump, but the sixth leaf flung him powerfully on and through the shimmering spray of colour to the seventh, whose broad, round surface lay close to the bank, and it caught him as if in a hand.

He took the last jump to the grassy bank by himself. There was not much space there, for the wall rose right at the top of the slope. From where he now stood, it looked even higher than before, and quite impossible to climb. Listener attempted to force the toes of one foot into the crack between two stone blocks, but as soon as he tried pulling his other foot up to it, it slipped out, and he was back on the grass again. He tried several more times, at different places, and finally found one where the cracks between the stones were considerably broader and deeper, offering plenty of hand and footholds. Pressing close to the wall, he was soon almost halfway up, though he avoided looking down at the ground, for he was beginning to wonder what would happen if he fell from this height, possibly into the moat whose depths even the ducks didn't know. He also noticed that the cracks were getting narrower and narrower as he went up, until he could scarcely get his fingertips into them. Finally he had to admit to himself that he couldn't climb any farther without falling into the depths. His hand could find not the least hold now, for the stones in the upper part of the wall were so closely fitted together that you could scarcely have got a knife-blade between them.

So there he stood, high above the moat, fingertips clinging to their last tiny hold, toes crooked into the narrow cracks, looking up at the top of the wall as if he could pull himself up there by the power of his glance alone, or the strength of the longing that drove him on to overcome this obstacle. Then he saw a large dot swaying gently back and forth in the wind. This dot grew larger, came closer, turned out to have delicate, spindly legs, and finally he saw a fine specimen of a garden spider dangling right above his head. The spider stopped where it was and seemed to be observing him.

'It's all very well for you,' said Listener. 'You can spin your thread and climb up and down it just as you please. Can you by any chance show me how to get over this wall?'

The spider swung itself towards the wall on the end of its thread, and found a place to rest its scuttling legs in a crack between two stones. Then it turned to Listener. 'Since you ask so politely,' it said, 'yes, I'll show you, considering you're such a poor sort of creature and your legs are no good for climbing, and you can't spin a good strong thread either. So I'll spin you a thread of your own, and you can dangle on the end of it. At least you have two hands to hold on with.' And without waiting for any answer, the spider stuck its thread to a rough spot on the wall and scurried up to the top again. Listener stared after it, waiting, but there was no more sign of the spider. He felt the strength ebbing from his arms and legs, and his head was beginning to go round and round in circles. 'Spider!' he called. 'Come back down and help me, do!'

He heard the spider call, up above, 'Don't be so impatient, or you'll never get where you're going!' Next moment, however, it came down with a second thread, which it fastened on the wall next to the first, to keep it from drifting away on the strong wind that blew up here.

'Now, pull yourself up!' said the spider. Listener felt it was impossible for that shining thread, fine as a hair, to bear his weight. He cautiously tugged at the first thread the spider had spun, and it came away from the wall directly; when he tried to free it from his skin it crumbled in his fingers like dust. 'Is this thing supposed to bear me?' he asked. 'I can't even touch it without breaking it!'

'That was my thread you just broke, not yours!' said the spider crossly. 'You're too fearful. You'll never get where you're going while you think of what might happen.

> *Trust my thread's charm*
> *and you'll come to no harm!'*

And so saying, the spider left him to his fate, and scrambled rapidly up what remained of the first thread to the top of the wall and out of sight.

Listener felt that one way or another he couldn't hold out much longer. His knees were trembling, his toes were getting cramp, and the wind, which was growing stronger all the time, tugged at his clothes and threatened to blow him off the wall. Aware that he would be unable to help himself falling in a moment, he reached for the thread the spider had spun him and let all other hand and footholds go.

The wind immediately blew him away from the wall, so that he was hovering above the depths, light as a downy feather, held aloft only by the barely visible thread that connected him with the top of the wall, giving elastically and singing in the wind like the string of a fiddle: a sweet and airy melody that made his whole body swing, carrying him with it, and he let it bear him up like a kite in the wind, so that there was no more above or below, but earth and sky surrounded him and the leaves of the woods flickered in a thousand shades of green, until the sky came back into his field of vision, turning and turning in every hue from light blue to deep azure, shading into the deep violet of the unfathomed waters of the moat, a circle of colour with himself its centre, surrendered to the sweet song of that swinging string, he himself its instrument, for now he was singing with it, singing the song of the wind, and his voice filled the circling space, and in the song his longing to get over the wall increased, so that he pulled himself up, hand over hand, until he could grasp the stones at the top of the wall and seat himself astride the ridge.

So there he sat on those windy heights, looking down at a wonderful garden, so large that even from here he could not see the whole of it. Directly below him there were broad lawns surrounded by pale gravel paths, with groups of shrubs and tall trees of every kind growing beside them, covered with leaves right down to the ground, many of them reflected in the clear water of little pools and winding streams that had delicate bridges across them. On the far side of the lawns were beds of bright flowers, planted in fantastic ornamental shapes; archways had been built across some of the paths here, and cascades of red and yellow climbing roses scrambled over them, leading to arbours whose roofs were hidden by great pale blue clusters of luxuriant wistaria. Beyond this flower garden stood a maze of clipped box and yew hedges, with the white limbs of marble statues showing among them here and there, but this part of the garden was so far away that it was hard to make out any details. All the paths in the maze seemed to run their winding ways towards a central point hidden by high hedges. That was where he was going, as he now knew. But first he must get down to the ground from this wall, which towered above the tallest of the trees.

Fortunately, that looked considerably easier than getting up it. On the side facing the garden, the wall was overgrown with ivy, whose shoots, thick as a man's arm, had grown to its very top over the course of decades or perhaps even centuries, clinging to every crack and crevice with countless tiny tendrils. Yet he felt dizzy when he looked all that way down through the gleaming dark green leaves, and he could not pluck up the courage to leave his place of safety here.

'Scared again?' inquired a voice, and when he looked around for its

owner, he saw the spider sitting on the topmost ivy leaf. 'About time
you were on your way,' it observed. 'Don't you know you're expected?'

Hearing that, he plucked up his courage and let himself slip cautiously over the top of the wall, groping for a foothold. Then he grasped
one of the strong shoots that clung to the wall like a giant millipede,
and began climbing down. It was easier than he had dared to hope.
The lower he went, the more luxuriantly the ivy grew, so that he was
soon climbing down from stem to stem beneath a thick roof of foliage,
as if down a dimly lit shaft. At every step he came nearer the ground,
the words 'You're expected' thudded in his heart, making him hurry so
much that in the end he missed his footing and fell crashing through
the tangled tendrils and leaves. Luckily he was not very high above the
grass now, and broke no bones. As he sat at the foot of the wall, still
slightly dazed, he heard laughter in the ivy overhead, and it did not
sound at all like a spider, but like a woman laughing.

He stood up, brushed the dust and cobwebs off his clothes, and went
into the garden. From ground level, all he could now see were the
broad expanses of turf, the shrubs and the fine trees. As he approached
a group of towering cypresses like dark green flames flaring into the
sky, he saw spreading copper beeches come into view, their lowest
branches touching the ground; there were tall elms and planes, a great
weeping willow, its thin branches gracefully arching, and many other
strange trees and shrubs that he had never seen before in his life.
Taking great leaps and bounds, he ran over an arched bridge across a
stream bordered by reeds and rushes, and came to a pool of water-lilies
in full bloom, white and pale pink, and some with almost globular
bright yellow flowers.

After his hot climb down, he felt like bathing in this pool. He tore off
his clothes, threw them on the grass and ran into the water, splashing,
until it was up to his chest. He could go no deeper, but there was a
considerable expanse of water ahead of him, and as he strode through
it a foaming wave built up in front of his hairy chest, so that he felt like
a water spirit inspecting his domain. He smelled the water-lilies, and
tried to pick one, but the stem was so tough that he couldn't break it
off. So he splashed about in the shallow basin of the pool like a playful
child, tried to do a headstand, came up again, spluttering, spat the
water out of his mouth in a wide arc, like a statue in a fountain, and
watched, laughing, as a couple of alarmed frogs made off, swimming
strongly. When he had played long enough, he sat on one of the little
cairns of stones built like islands in the middle of the pool, let his legs

dangle in the water, and watched the fat carp with their moss-grown backs drift idly up to try nibbling his toes.

As he sat there day-dreaming, some ducks came swimming up from the other side of the pool. The white duck was among them again. She paddled slowly over to him, looked him up and down in all his hairy nakedness, and remarked, 'Happy playing the water-sprite here, are you? You'd better be on your way! Have you forgotten that you're expected?'

He had felt so cheerful splashing in the water that he really had forgotten, but now, like a rush of warmth to his heart, he remembered that he had an end to his journey in view, and he was indeed expected. With a great leap, he jumped off his rock, landed full length in the pool, sending great cascades spraying up around him, came up to the surface again spluttering and spitting out the water, rushed to the bank and ran on into the garden, without giving a thought to the clothes he had left behind. And as he ran over the turf he heard that laughter again behind him, sweet as the cooing of a dove, full-toned as a bronze bell ringing.

The bright green turf ended at a box hedge as high as his chest. Listener took a long run, jumped it, and landed in the midst of an eddying confusion of scents and colours. Flowers were crowded side by side in the beds, growing in many different patterns. Beside the browny yellow and purple of the wallflowers and stocks rose the splendid, deep red heads of peonies, with their sharp fragrance; there were drooping stems of pink lyreflowers, intoxicatingly fragrant blue and white hyacinths, and all was overlaid by the balmy scent of blue, purple and yellow flags, springing proudly from their tangled, snaky roots. Listener followed the winding paths between the beds, and found himself going in ever-narrowing spirals, until the path at last seemed to come to a dead end, but he simply leaped away from the confines of the spiral and ran on, past a delicate forest of tall fuchsias with red and white bell-shaped flowers, whose soundless ringing he seemed to hear, and whenever he thought he had found a path leading to his journey's end where it lay hidden among the tall, dark hedges, he kept going around a bend and back to vaulted walks with arches almost collapsing beneath the weight of the climbing roses in bloom they bore. On he went, seduced by the beguiling scents of jasmine covered with flowers like snow and of whorled yellow and ivory honeysuckle, by the intoxicating gold of laburnum and the velvety blue of clematis. Distracted from his purpose, led deeper and deeper into this magical maze, he let the magnificence of sky-blue delphinium and red foxgloves taller than a man overwhelm him, while the bitter-sweet fragrance of pale blue poppies washed over him too, whispering to him to cease hurrying so fast along these garden paths, give up his vain search for something beyond, and stay here thinking his own thoughts in the maze.

He was lying there, eyes closed, among the nodding poppy-heads, feeling their thin, silky petals fall on his face and breathing in their fragrance, when a voice addressed him. 'Going to dream your time away among these drowsy flowers, are you?' When he opened his eyes he saw the robin sitting there before him on the garden path. It scrutinized him mockingly, and added, 'You'd better be on your way! Have you forgotten that you're expected?' And the robin spread its wings, flew up and disappeared into a flowing curtain of wistaria in full bloom, with what appeared to Listener to be a dense, dark green wall of conifers hidden behind it. He jumped up, ran after the robin and pushed the curtain aside. Then he saw the way into the last part of the garden, a beautifully vaulted arch, and a straight path beyond it, with tall, smoothly clipped yew hedges on either side. He ran so fast through that shaded archway that he caught his foot in the twining wistaria tendrils and fell headlong to the ground. Luckily the path was covered with smooth, round pebbles, so that even naked as he was, he didn't graze his skin. And as he got to his feet again, he heard that laughter again behind the hedge, alluring, promising laughter, and the laughter drove him on his quest once more.

Even here, in this enclosure surrounded by dark hedges, it was not made easy for him to find his way to the centre where he longed to be. The path along which he had started led to a hedge, where it forked into two paths, one on either side of the hedge, and no sooner had he taken the right-hand path than it too forked. Taking the left-hand path this time, Listener found himself in a blind alley ending in a circular bay where the marble statue of a boy stood on a weathered pedestal. The child held a bow, with an arrow set to its string, and Listener wondered what he was aiming at, for the arrow was pointing the way he had just come. Are you showing me my way, he wondered, and followed the direction of the arrow to the crossing of the paths, where he immediately found himself faced with another decision, for he could choose between three branches here. There was no way he could get an overall view of the whole tangle of paths: he was always behind hedges too tall for him to see over them, with no view but that of the path where he stood. This time Listener chose the central path, and as he walked along it he thought he heard footsteps on the gravel the other side of the thick wall of greenery to his right. As soon as he stopped there was nothing to be heard, but when he went on again the gravel crunched on the other side of the hedge too, and there was a gurgling sound as well, like suppressed laughter. Listener stopped and tried to push the bushes aside with both arms, but he could not manage to see through the hedge. And yet he felt as if, just for a moment, he had touched a body, had touched warm, soft skin that immediately fled his grasp, and at the same time a bird flew up on the far side of the hedge, crossed his path, and disappeared beyond the next hedge. So there was nothing he could do but go on through the maze, and he gave up trying to go in any particular direction, but went at random down any of the branching paths he saw, so that soon he didn't know if he had already been at a given spot or not. At one point the path led to a round place surrounded by tall walls of box hedges again, and he thought he had come back to the boy with the bow and arrow, but the snow-white statue on the pedestal here was of an enchantingly lovely naked woman, standing on a shell lapped by waves, and holding out her hand to him. Admiring the flawless figure, he walked all around her, but she did not come to life, only pointed back to the way out of the round space, so Listener followed her directions, and went on, although he was beginning to tire of this game. When the path forked again soon afterwards, Listener leaned back, exhausted, against the springy wall of a yew hedge, and as he tried to think how he could ever get to his journey's end in this maze, he felt two hands groping through the branches behind his back, and taking him by the waist: two slender, white hands that lay on his own hairy skin for a moment, and were then quickly withdrawn, and once again he heard that dove-like coo of laughter that banished his weariness. 'Where are you?' he cried. 'Show me the way!' Once again it was only a bird that flew up and skimmed over the hedge and away, but it seemed to Listener as if he had been shown his way, and he went after the bird, which was just disappearing around a bend, and then rose in the air again, beating its wings, as if to show the way to go on. And when Listener had rounded the bend too, a few more paces brought him to a circular space surrounded by tall hedges, and he knew he had reached the centre of the garden. A fountain played in a stone basin, letting its water fall on two marble statues.

Listener stood there spellbound, looking at the figure of the woman holding her face up to the falling water. If he had admired the beauty of the statue he saw before, yet he had been aware it was a statue carved from cold, dead stone. But the woman standing in the cascading water of the fountain seemed full of life, and he would not have been surprised if she had moved her slender arms next moment, or turned her face to him, and his heart beat fast with expectation. He stood there for a long time, captivated by the beauty of the figure, before he became aware of the second statue too. This one, unmistakably, was a man – and yet not a man: the bearded head, covered with thick, curly hair, rose from a strong neck and broad, muscular shoulders, hair curled on his breast, and the farther down Listener's glance travelled, the more thickly was his body covered with a shaggy animal pelt that scarcely hid his goatish private parts, and hung down over his sharply angled legs, which ended in cloven hooves braced against the stone of the pedestal as if ready to spring. A vague memory passed through Listener's mind, as if he had seen something of the kind before, and he went up to this creature, a cross between man and animal, to look at him more closely, climbed into the basin amidst the playing water of the fountain, stood beside him and put an arm around his shoulders as if they were brothers. And before he knew it, he himself was the goat-legged faun, and he saw the woman turn her face to him, for she was not made of stone, but was alive and looking at him with dark eyes of a colour he could not describe, she came to him as he went to her, until they were in one another's arms, enveloped in the falling waters of the fountain that sparkled in the sun as it washed over them.

*   *   *

When he woke next morning, the dream had sunk almost below the level of his consciousness, and all he could remember was a wealth of colours, sounds, and intoxicating scents. He felt as if he had come back from a land of sweet harmony to which he could not now return, to a reality full of difficulty and danger, failed hopes and impossible wishes, a reality that oppressed him. That morning the assembly of the elders took place, and he did win suitable praise for the success of his journey – 'Arni was with you, Bearer of the Stone, guiding every step you took,' said a bald-headed ancient in a trembling voice – but he could not really enjoy this general approval, the more so as they scarcely seemed to notice his presence any more once the specimen pieces made by the goldsmiths of Arziak lay on the table. There was much touching of them, weighing up their value, reckoning of profit margins, and the men almost fell to quarrelling as to which of the traders should be permitted to ride to the Mountain Badgers and buy in a larger stock. Even the solemnity of speech usual at such gatherings suddenly seemed to forsake them. Listener sat there, taking no part, scarcely registered the decisions to which they finally came, and nodded silently when, for form's sake, he was asked if he was ready to take Khan Hunli the twelve horses.

Narzia hardly showed her face that day, or on the following days either. Listener once asked her when she was going to begin her chess lessons, but she only laughed and said that if he wanted to learn how to beat the Khan by his own efforts he would need a couple of years' practice. Not until nearly the end of that week did she tell him, at supper, that she wanted him to go to Arni's House with her when he had finished the milk he was drinking.

'About the chess?' he asked, and when Narzia nodded, he rose at once, leaving his milk, for he thought it was high time something was done about the matter.

The first thing he saw when he followed Narzia into Arni's House, and she had lit a candle on the table, was his stone lying shimmering in its golden dish.

'Am I to take the stone, and then Arni will help me?' he asked.

'No,' said Narzia. 'You mustn't rely only on dreams. I know of something that works better!' And she opened a chest in which all kinds of things Arni had once owned were kept, took out a long packet wrapped in a cloth, and went over to the table where the elders used to sit during assemblies.

'What's that?' asked Listener.

'You'll soon see,' said Narzia. She unwrapped the object, and Listener realized that it must be a chess set. He saw a box, its lid and base laid out in squares of different-coloured woods, so that when you opened it and put it on the table, its inside downwards, the two halves made a complete chess board. Narzia pushed back a concealed catch at the front of the box and opened it. It had two compartments containing the chessmen; one set was made of creamy ivory, the other of dark green jade.

'I've heard of a chess set like this before,' said Listener. 'Hunli played against Arni with such a set.'

'That must have been Hunli's set,' said Narzia. 'The brothers had identical chessmen, but Hunli would never use Arni's, particularly when they were playing against each other. I suppose he wasn't sure that Arni might not have cast a spell on his pieces.'

'Do you think Arni really did?' asked Listener.

'I don't know,' said Narzia. 'Maybe he didn't need to, but I'm going to cast one now.'

'You?' asked Listener, looking at her doubtfully.

Narzia smiled, mockingly, and said, 'Remember, my mother grew up in the Great Magician's house, and often sat at his feet; you can pick up a great deal in that way. Now, take the two queens out of the box and lay them side by side on the table. And then fetch what lies in the golden dish there, Bearer of the Stone!'

Listener did as he was told, and laid the stone at the heads of the two queens, as she directed him to do. 'I need something from yourself now,' said Narzia, and suddenly she had a slender but obviously extremely sharp knife in her hand. 'Give me your left arm!' She rolled up the sleeve of his shirt, and before he knew what she was about, cut deep into his flesh. Listener was scarcely aware of it, for as soon as her hand touched his skin he stood as if spellbound, looking into her face, which now truly showed the bold beauty of a falcon swooping on its prey, and he may well have thought at first that what he felt was the quick heat that her touch brought to his arm, but it turned out to be blood welling freely from the wound. Narzia dipped her finger in the red blood and drew a regular pentangle on the table top, around the chessmen and the stone. Then she told Listener to sit opposite her at the table, and said, 'It's ready now. You must keep quiet.'

She laid her hands flat on the worn wood, to right and left of the magic pentangle, spread her thumbs so that their tips touched, and told Listener to do the same, in such a way that the tips of his middle fingers could touch hers. Listener willingly obeyed her, and when the circle of their hands was closed, she began muttering something to herself under her breath in a strange language.

Listener had followed all these preparations, fascinated, but now that his part was to sit still, feeling the warmth of her fingertips, he looked into her green eyes, and soon realized that this was part of the magic too: very likely Narzia had omitted to mention it only because she was in no doubt that he would seek her gaze. At any rate, she kept her eyes unswervingly fixed upon him, so that there were now two links between them: the tangible contact of their fingers, through which secret currents seemed to flow from one to the other, and the no less exciting contact of their eyes. Narzia's eyes came closer and closer, soon filling his whole field of vision, and he went down into their green depths, down and then out again into a wan and colourless place where there was no ground underfoot, no horizon, no above and no below, and here, as if emerging slowly out of wavering mists, a face gradually formed, the wrinkled face of an old man with a thin, straggling beard and white braids of hair at his temples. Arni looked at him with his dark eyes, which were not grave at all, as Listener observed with some annoyance, but merry, even amused, and then he opened his mouth and began to laugh soundlessly, as if he found this whole performance extraordinarily comical.

After a while – how long, Listener could not have said – the image was extinguished as if a candle had been blown out, and he found himself sitting opposite Narzia at the table again. She took her hands away from his, which must mean that the spell had been cast. 'What did you see?' she asked eagerly.

'Arni,' said Listener, but he did not tell her how Arni had laughed.

'Good,' said Narzia, rising. 'Put the stone back in the dish! You will take the two chessmen with you. I'll give you a shirt with full sleeves, tied at the wrists, and you will carry the chessmen in those sleeves, one on the right and one on the left, but don't forget which side the white queen is hidden and which side the green. When you have cast lots for white or green before the game begins, all you have to do is exchange Arni's queen for your own from Hunli's set, and then it will really be Arni playing against the Khan; your hand will merely make the moves as he directs. And don't forget to put the proper queen back again afterwards!'

When he had taken the two chessmen, she wiped the bloody pentangle off the table with a cloth. 'You will ride tomorrow,' she said. 'Come here and let me bind up the wound in your arm!'

Listener had taken no notice at all of his cut, but he was happy to let Narzia swab the clotting blood away with a piece of linen, put an aromatic green leaf on the sore place, and wrap a narrow bandage around his arm. 'Does it hurt?' she asked, smiling. Listener shook his head and thanked her for tying it up. 'Is there anything in the tents of the Raiding Riders you would like me to bring you?' he asked.

Narzia thought for a moment, and then said, 'I know of only one thing there which I would dearly like to own. It is a finely woven silken rug, its border showing a train of mounted falconers in red on a green ground. It hangs above the cushions of Hunli's throne, on the wall of his tent, and is accounted one of his most precious possessions. I would like you to bring me that.'

Listener was alarmed to hear how much the Khan valued this rug,

but he promised he would try to bring it back for her. 'Then I'll wish
you a pleasant journey,' she said, and with a quick, unexpected
movement, she kissed him on the cheek, as if to avoid being taken in his
arms, and next moment she had left the room.

At least he need not ride alone this time, for he would have had his
work cut out to drive twelve horses ahead of him without any help.
Honi had given him four mounted men, each leading three horses on a
halter: tough, sturdy little horses of the steppes, such as the Raiding
Riders preferred. And these men, having once been Raiding Riders,
would surely know where to look for the Khan's camp. One of them,
Blorri by name, went to ride at their head when Listener told him that
he himself was not used to finding his own way in the steppes. As ever,
it was a mystery to Listener how these men got their bearings, when
there was nothing in sight but grass as far as the eye could see. He rode
up to join Blorri, and asked him, 'How do you find your way here? Do
you go by the position of the sun?'

'Among other things,' said Blorri, 'but that alone wouldn't be
enough, or we might ride past the camp just a couple of bowshots
away. Look over there.' He pointed to the horizon, and glanced expectantly at Listener, who, however, could see nothing but the play of
sunlight over the steppes, and said so.

'Look at the colours!' said Blorri.

Listener strained his eyes, and then said, 'Is the green just a little
darker over there ahead of us?'

'That's right,' said Blorri. 'It's a waterhole, and the grass around it is
juicier. We'll let our horses drink there and then ride on towards the
Wolf's Back.'

'Where is this Wolf's Back?' asked Listener. 'Can we see it yet?'

'Just a little farther to the left, on the horizon,' said Blorri.

Now that it had been pointed out, Listener could see it too: a barely
perceptible rise in the ground, breaking the otherwise perfectly straight
line between steppes and sky, and as they rode over the Wolf's Back
some time later, he also realized how this slight rise got that name: the
grass growing there was grey and shaggy like the hair of a wolf's pelt.
'The ground's dry here, so the grass dries up early,' said Blorri.

They rode for seven days, and during this time Listener discovered
that he was hardly able to perceive any of the inconspicuous landmarks
on those boundless plains unless they were pointed out to him. He had
grown up among hills, streams and woods, in a landscape full of obvious

variety, with marked differences in the lie of the land and the kind of plants that grew there, so he did not feel at ease in the steppes, and now he realized that it could be a disadvantage to be accustomed to noticing only those things that caught your eye at first glance. When it came to spotting almost imperceptible variations in what seemed total uniformity, he was as good as lost. The countryside that seemed so familiar and delightful to him had dulled his senses too. He tried to imagine how a dweller on the steppes must rejoice to see a slightly darker shade of green in the distance, or the scarcely measurable rise of the Wolf's Back, but he could not feel the same delight himself. The inexorable flatness of the steppes instilled fear into him: the boundless expanses of them, with no mountain or even a tree to lend them dimensions.

Towards evening of the seventh day some Riders came to meet them. 'There's the Khan's camp,' said Blorri, pointing ahead, though Listener could see nothing but the grass of the steppes shimmering in the evening sunlight. The troop of Riders came racing towards them at the gallop, as if about to ride them down, but Listener had experience of their habit of testing the nerves of new arrivals in this way, so he withstood the mock attack with fair composure. And sure enough, the Raiding Riders reined in their horses at the last moment, bringing them to a halt. Their leader called out a few words to Blorri, and then set himself at the head of the little troop to lead them to the camp.

After a while, Listener too could make out the black tents ahead of them on the plain, and he began wondering how Hunli would receive him. However, he need not have worried, for as he and the leaders of his horses dismounted outside the Khan's tent, Hunli came out and greeted him like an honoured guest. 'And when we met last time, Bearer of the Stone,' he remarked, 'I would have treated you more courteously had I known you were my brother's heir.' He spoke in friendly tones, but one could not miss hearing the reproof in these words, which also conveyed that Listener bore the whole blame for what had happened then. And perhaps it would indeed have been better if he'd trusted to his stone, thought Listener, but then he pulled himself together, saying, 'I am happy that you honour your brother Arni in me, Khan Hunli, and I thank you for your kind welcome. I have brought you replacements for the twelve horses you lost through my fault.'

Hunli nodded, satisfied, and said, 'I see you're not without discernment. However, it wasn't just the beasts I lost; there was a man too, who broke his neck trying to jump from his bolting horse. But we'll discuss that later. I should like to look at the horses now.'

He got Listener's companions to show him the twelve horses' paces, one by one, felt their fetlocks and looked in their mouths like a horse-dealer. Eventually he expressed himself satisfied, told some of his men to take the horses, and also gave orders for Blorri and his three men to be given a tent and whatever they might need. 'Good animals,' he told Listener. 'We will take it that the request I made of you and Arni's Folk has been fulfilled. Come into my tent and be my guest today, Bearer of the Stone!'

Listener did not fail to notice that Hunli was limiting his hospitality to that day, so as to have a free hand tomorrow. At least he could feel his life was safe till then.

As soon as he entered the tent behind the Khan, he saw the rug he was to bring Narzia, a shining, silken thing, longer than the height of a man, hanging between two tent-poles above the piled cushions of the throne upon which Hunli sat, before inviting Listener to sit at his side too. The Khan had observed Listener's admiring gaze, and said, 'You like that rug? It is very precious to me, for the Great Magician of the Falcon People gave it to me when I rode to Falkinor for Honi's wedding. The notion that Honi might someday set himself against me would never have entered my head at the time. However, it turned out that he'd chosen a wife who wasn't ready to follow the customs of the horde. She even wanted to have that rug back. Such women often estrange good men from their people – but she didn't get the rug!'

Now Listener understood why the rug was the only thing in the Raiding Riders' camp that Narzia wanted to own. He thought she felt more as if she belonged to the Falcon People than the folk among whom she had grown up, perhaps for the very reason that her foreign descent made her different from those around her. She was not someone to mind such a sense of difference; indeed, she wanted to be different, and was proud of it.

Meanwhile, some other men had come into the tent, and Hunli introduced Listener to them, first of all to his three sons Husski, Trusski and Belarni. The two older sons, who were both between thirty and forty years old, had their father's sharp features, and looked at Listener with hostility in their dark, stony eyes; Belarni was much younger, a boy of about sixteen, and he gave Listener a friendly smile on greeting him. Then the elders of the horde came up too, for the Khan had invited them to feast with him.

As soon as the last of them was seated, on cushions arranged in a circle on rugs laid before the Khan's throne, the food was brought in: a fat lamb, roasted on the spit, and seasoned with all kinds of bitter and aromatic herbs. Slaves handed all the guests flat cakes of bread, thin as leather and baked on hot stones, and then the Khan gave every man his piece of the lamb, starting with Listener, in whose honour the feast was being held, then proceeding to his sons, and after them the clan chieftains in order of age. The feast was eaten in silence, the guests being entertained by a man near the entrance to the tent who played a nasal melody on a shawm, accompanied by another man beating a small drum. The music sounded harsh and monotonous to Listener's ears, bringing to his mind's eye an image of the desolate steppes, where there was no colour but the grey-green of the whispering grass.

'I hope you like our music,' said Hunli. 'You'll understand that I prefer this instrument to your flute.' Listener understood only too well, and heard the undertone of warning in the Khan's voice. He would not allow the flute to be played again in his hearing.

When the men had eaten their fill, Hunli dismissed the musicians with a gesture, saying, 'And now we had better have a little talk, Bearer of the Stone. You have made good the loss of our horses. All that now remains is the matter of the man whose death you caused. What were you planning to offer me for that?'

Listener had not been prepared for such a question when he rode into the steppes. He saw the eyes of all present sitting in this circle directed at him, and felt that this question of Hunli's was a challenge to some kind of single combat, in which he might possibly have to fight for his own life. Trying to win time, he said, 'I didn't know of the man's death, Khan Hunli. Your message never mentioned it. Why did you keep it secret?'

'Meaning that if you'd known, you wouldn't have come?' asked the Khan, sharply, and he smiled like a man who has cornered his opponent in a game.

Yes, I might well have stayed at home, thought Listener, but naturally he did not say so, for he was not going to admit himself worsted so easily. Moreover, it annoyed him to see Hunli obviously preparing to play cat and mouse with him. 'What do you mean by that question?' he said. 'You didn't give me any chance to make a decision, so you've no right to ascribe one to me which would dishonour me in your people's eyes. I am here. What more do you want?'

'Satisfaction for the life of a man,' said Hunli. 'How do you mean to give it?'

Listener wondered what Raiding Riders usually offered one another for the life of a man. If the rule here was a life for a life, then the Khan might as well have killed him the moment he arrived, and not invited him into his tent as a guest first. Or did he only want to watch him squirm a little, before striking tomorrow? Listener felt fear rising in him, and to quell it, he said, 'I suppose you don't expect me to ask you to cut my throat.'

The Khan laughed. 'What good would that do me?' he inquired. 'For one thing, it would be extremely boring, and for another, I should still be a man short. Didn't they tell you the whole of my message? I rather expected you would fall in with the suggestion I made you.'

'You sent word that we might play for this or that, yes,' said Listener, relieved. Obviously the Khan had only been waiting for him to suggest a suitable game. Perhaps he was to suggest the stakes too.

'Did you think the Khan of the Raiding Riders would need to lure you here with a lie?' said Hunli impatiently. 'My brother doesn't seem to have told you much about our customs.'

'He didn't have much time for that,' said Listener. 'He was dying when I first saw him.'

'Ah, so then you're one of the Great Roarer's men after all,' said Hunli. 'Arni lost his life in the fight with them.'

'If you must know,' said Listener, 'my father is judge in Fraglund.'

'And you killed Arni and took his stone!' said Hunli, sounding almost pleased, for here at last was something that corresponded to his own notions. But Listener set him right at once.

'It isn't likely, in that case, that Arni would have told me the verse that goes with the stone,' he said. 'Do you know it?'

'I do,' said Hunli. 'Let's hear it!'

So Listener leaned over to Hunli, and whispered the verse in his ear:

> *Seek the light*
> *where the glow may fall;*
> *you have not sought aright,*
> *if you don't find it all.*

The Khan nodded. 'Yes, I see the stone's yours by right,' he said. 'Arni obviously gave it to you, even if, of all my brother's incomprehensible deeds, this is the hardest of all to understand. How could he make an enemy his heir?'

'I suppose he didn't take me for an enemy,' said Listener, 'since I gave him his last sip of water to drink.'

The Khan shook his head. 'Well, let anyone understand that who may!' he said. 'I can see you're another fool of Arni's kind.'

This jeer angered Listener, and as he had nothing more to lose anyway he said, 'Arni may have seemed a fool to you, but he could always beat you at chess!'

Hunli's face darkened with rage, and his hand went to the knife at his belt, but then he remembered that Listener was still his guest, and he let go of the gold-mounted hilt again. 'We could always see if you can do as much,' he said, malice in his tone.

'I've no objection,' said Listener, wondering in surprise by what strange and devious route he had come exactly where he wanted to be. He had told the Khan things he should really have kept quiet, thereby endangering his life, and yet he had achieved his ends.

'Then we will play chess tomorrow,' said the Khan, pleased. 'I hardly think Arni had time to teach you all his tricks and cunning dodges. Have you thought what you'll play for?'

Listener had wanted that question asked too. 'It's for you to name the stakes,' he said.

'I'm glad you recognize that,' said the Khan. 'Since I have lost a man, you will play for your freedom tomorrow. If you lose, you become my slave.'

Soon afterwards, the Khan dismissed his guests, inviting them to come back next day and watch the game that had been arranged. 'We will begin to play when the sun is at its height, Bearer of the Stone,' he said. 'You may move around the camp freely until then.'

When Listener left the tent, the clan chieftains rose from where they sat, as they would to honour an important guest, and this confirmed Listener in his feeling that he had not done badly in his conversation with the Khan. He strolled slowly through the camp to the tent that had been made ready for him to occupy alone. People cast him curious glances, but no one spoke to him.

There was a slave woman in his tent, busy preparing him a bed of rugs and shaggy sheepskins. As she chanced to step into the light of the oil lamp hanging from one of the tent-poles, Listener saw her face. Her pale blue eyes and receding chin reminded him of his grandfather's tale of the people who lived by the Brown River. She jumped in alarm when he gave her a friendly greeting. Presumably she wasn't used to having a free man take any notice of her unless he was looking for a woman to share his bed that night. 'Are you one of the Carphead people of the Brown River?' asked Listener.

'Yes, lord,' said the slave woman, pressing back against the side of the tent.

'You needn't be afraid of me,' said Listener. 'I may be in the slaves' huts with you and your companions tomorrow.'

At this the slave woman glanced up, looking at him with watery eyes. 'They say that you bear Arni's stone,' she said. 'Is it true?'

'He gave it to me,' said Listener, thinking of the stone lying far away in Arni's House.

'And they say you have a flute that was once played in our houses by the Brown River,' the woman went on.

'Yes, that's true too,' said Listener. 'Although the Khan isn't particularly keen to hear it.'

When he said that, the suggestion of a smile flitted over the woman's face. 'And with good reason!' she said.

'Well, he'll try to get his own back tomorrow, anyway,' said Listener.

Now the slave woman came closer, and said, 'Arni will stand by you, Bearer of the Stone. And the Great Carp we venerate will remember the friendship of Arni and the Gentle Fluter, just as those two men are not forgotten in our houses. Take this and wear it when you play tomorrow!' She took from around her neck a thong of woven rushes with a mirror carp's great scale strung on it, big as a leaf from a lime tree, pressed it into his hand, and scurried out of the tent.

Listener stood there for a while, looking at the shimmering scale, feeling its smooth and slightly rippling surface, and its sharp edges. It reminded him a little of the shell Arnilukka's mother had given her. The light of the oil lamp was refracted on the thin, translucent scale into streaks of colour, which changed shape and hue as soon as he moved it. He became so deeply absorbed in this game that those thoughts of tomorrow weighing on him melted away. The shimmering, horny scale was beautiful, though he doubted that it would be any use to him in his game with the Khan. After all, it was only an object to which the simple fisher folk of the Brown River happened to have attached their superstitions. At last he put the rough thong of rushes over his head, slipped the cool scale under his shirt so that he could feel it on his skin, and lay down on the bed.

Whether because the carp's scale watched over his slumbers, or just because he was so tired after his long ride over the steppes, Listener slept deeply and dreamlessly all that night until well into the morning, and did not wake until the slave woman who had made his bed the night before entered the tent with his breakfast, a bowl of sharp-tasting sour mare's milk, and a cake of the thin, flat bread.

'Thank you for your gift,' said Listener. 'It brought me deep sleep.'

'That is good,' said the woman. 'You'll need all your strength today. It is going to be hot. Don't forget the Great Carp's scale when you go to the Khan!' Listener opened his shirt and showed her the scale. She nodded, satisfied, and then left the tent.

When he had breakfasted, Listener went out and looked around the camp. It consisted of some seventy black felt tents, large and small, most with a smoke-hole at the top, between the protruding tent-poles. A row of low-built huts, their walls made of animal skins, their roofs made of grass, stood a little way off. A few pale-skinned, fair-haired women with the look of the Carphead people about their faces were busy there, preparing wool for spinning and scraping the insides of skins. So this was where the slaves lived. As Listener passed the women, some of them looked up and smiled at him. Did they know what he wore on his breast, underneath his shirt? It almost seemed so.

On the far side of the slaves' huts, a large paddock had been enclosed with posts and leather straps, and the horde's horses were grazing here, watched over by some men who also seemed to be of Carphead stock, short of stature, inclining to stoutness, slow and deliberate of movement. They too had that faded fair hair and receding chin, and most of them wore drooping moustaches that gave a melancholy expression to their faces. Listener discovered his own horse and those of his four companions in a pen of their own. One of the slaves, a grey-haired man with a remarkably unwrinkled, carp-like face, was grooming Snowfoot gently, talking quietly to the mare as he worked. Listener watched him for a while. He liked the kindliness expressed in all the man's movements. Finally he went over and patted his horse.

'That's a fine animal you have there, lord,' said the old man. 'Comes of a better breed than these shaggy little steppe horses.'

Listener thanked the man for looking after Snowfoot so well, and was going to give him a silver coin, but the old man refused to take the money, and seemed almost hurt at the idea of being paid for a service that had given him such pleasure. When Listener asked if there was anything else he could do for him, the old man said, 'I was a small child when Arni came to our house with a young fluter, and I heard him play that evening. I've never forgotten the sound of his flute. Is it true that you own that flute now, as they say?'

'Yes,' said Listener. 'The fluter was my grandfather, and left me his instrument when he died.'

'Good men have cast their shadows on you!' said the old groom. 'I would dearly like to hear you play the flute.'

'The Khan won't permit it,' said Listener. 'He doesn't care for the music of my flute.'

'I believe you,' said the old man, chuckling to himself. Obviously the slaves knew all about what had happened to Hunli and his Riders out in the steppes in early spring.

'I'd gladly do as you ask,' said Listener, 'but I don't know how I can, without arousing the Khan's anger.'

'Come here to the paddock this evening,' said the man. 'I'm on the night watch. The Khan is old and goes to his rest early.'

'I will come if I'm still a free man then,' said Listener.

At that the old man laughed, soundlessly, and said, 'Oh, you'll come, Fluter, or Bearer of the Stone, or whatever you're called. Don't forget who is protecting you.'

Listener returned to his tent towards noon. He took both chessmen out of his bags, hid them in the full sleeves of his shirt, the white queen on the right, the green queen on the left, and made sure they could not fall out of their own accord. Then he set off to meet his opponent.

The slave woman had been right: it was hot outside the tent now. The sun stood high in a sky of steely blue, and the air above the grass of the steppes shimmered with heat. Listener walked to the Khan's tent and went in. Hunli was sitting on the cushions of his throne, surrounded by his three sons and the elders who had already taken their seats around the sides of the tent. There was one cushion left unoccupied, opposite the throne, and the chessboard and chessmen stood ready between it and the Khan.

'Wanted to enjoy your life as a free man to the very last moment, did you?' said the Khan. 'I'm told you've already visited those Mud-biters whose huts you'll be sharing. But I suppose that won't bother you, Arni having been a guest of theirs too.'

Listener had determined not to yield to the Khan in anything. He looked him in the face, and said, 'I've nothing against the Carpheads. But you ought not to take a game as won, when we haven't even started to play.'

The Khan seemed unaccustomed to such a tone. He frowned, and said, 'Sit down, then. No more delay – let's begin!'

Listener seated himself on the cushion, saying, 'So I stake my freedom on this game, do I, Khan Hunli?'

'You know you do,' said Hunli. 'Are you afraid of losing now?'

'Not in the least,' said Listener. 'But you haven't yet told me what you yourself are staking.'

Such simple-mindedness made Hunli laugh. 'Don't let that trouble you!' said he. 'I can hardly suppose you see yourself winning anything in this game! But still, you shall not be able to say I didn't play fair. Since I have decided your stake, I'll let you decide mine. Name what you like, and it shall be yours if you beat me, though I have little fear of that.'

'Then you shall play for the rug that hangs above your throne,' said Listener.

On hearing this, some of the elders sprang up in indignation, protesting loudly, and the Khan himself looked as if he would be angry at first, but then he thought better of it, and said, forcing a smile, 'Everyone knows what the rug means to me. So I shall win all the more honour by putting it at stake. As you like it so much, I will sometimes order you to brush it when it's dusty.' And then he told one of the elders to cast the lots for choice of colour.

The grey-haired Raiding Rider picked one white and one green pawn off the chessboard, hid his hands behind his back for a moment, and then offered his clenched fists to the Khan. Hunli tapped his left fist, and drew green. Listener took it as a good sign that white was to be his, and with it the first move. Seeing that the white chessmen stood on the Khan's side of the board, he picked it up with both hands and turned it round so clumsily that the white pieces slid off and fell to the ground. As he bent to pick them up, he took Arni's white queen from his right sleeve, and put it on Hunli's board instead of its counterpart. Only then did he gather up the remaining chessmen from the rug below and replace them too. The Khan laughed a good deal at this mishap. 'Why, your chessmen fall over before I even have a chance to take them,' said he. 'Wouldn't you rather own yourself beaten at once?'

'Better for them to fall now than later,' said Listener, undisturbed, and he made his first move. Only when he let go of the pawn he had advanced towards Hunli's troops did he realize that he had made that move without thinking about it at all, and yet it seemed as if he had not moved the piece at random, but according to some plan, and as the game proceeded he felt ever more clearly that whenever it was his turn to move, he knew precisely what piece he must move to what square, although he could not have said what was to be achieved by it.

However that might be, it looked as if this method of play was leading straight to his downfall, for Hunli took one after another of his chessmen, and Listener could do very little by way of retaliation. Hunli's satisfaction increased with every white piece he removed from the board. 'Now do you see what you let yourself in for?' he said triumphantly, when a large number of Listener's chessmen stood lined up to one side of the board, while he had lost only three pawns himself.

'The game's not over yet,' said Listener, but he was beginning to doubt if Arni was really guiding his hand. Perhaps he only imagined it, and he was actually making moves at random, moves that brought him step by step closer to a life of slavery in the Raiding Riders' tents. He felt afraid, and at that moment Hunli threatened his king for the first time. But he managed to get the king to safety without much trouble, and so plucked up a little courage again. At this point, however, the Khan began an unnerving game of cat and mouse. Again and again, the white king was in danger, but every time, and against all expectation, Listener found a way of escape, and this happened so often that in the end Hunli said, with a certain respect, 'You're cleverer than you seemed at first. But you needn't entertain any hopes, not at this stage of the game.'

And indeed Listener had little cause to hope. By now his forces had dwindled to a handful of chessmen trying to hold their own against the green pieces, which far outnumbered them, and the way the white consistently did withstand the green seemed almost miraculous. It had become oppressively hot in the tent. Sweat stood out on the Khan's forehead, and the wrinkled skin of his face was flushed. Listener felt the heat himself, but with it a pleasantly refreshing sensation on his skin, as if he were bathing in running water on a hot summer's day, and it seemed to him that this cool sensation came from the scale lying on his chest. But wasn't it just a scrap of kitchen refuse from the Carpheads' huts? Listener began to wonder if something whose goodwill did not depend upon belief in its powers might not be helping him. But perhaps it was just that the touch of the scale's smooth surface gave the illusion of coolness. He had no time to think the matter over any more, for now Hunli, perhaps under the pressure of the ever-increasing heat, seemed anxious to end the game as soon as possible. Without stopping for much reflection, he took every opportunity that offered to threaten the white king again, or take more of Listener's pieces.

Finally, all the white pawns were gone, and besides his king and queen, Listener had only three other pieces left, with a dense phalanx still drawn up on Hunli's side of the board facing them.

Listener was very well aware of the dangerous situation into which his method of playing had led him, and he hesitated when his hand, as if of its own accord, picked up a bishop to move the piece two squares. But then he told himself it was too late now to continue the game by considering the moves for himself. If Arni had a hand in this, he must go on trusting him, even at the risk that Arni meant to punish him for his part in Narzia's magic; if he had merely imagined the whole thing he was finished anyway, and so he completed the move, although with doubt and fear. And his fears seemed to be confirmed only too soon, for with his next move Hunli took the bishop, saying, 'Your attention's slipping. Will you give in now?'

Listener shook his head. He still had a glimmer of hope until his king was taken. He moved his last knight into the attack with his next move, and this time he was almost expecting what indeed happened: the knight too fell victim to a counter-attack. Listener's hope went out like a spark that has glowed on for a while among the ashes until it can find nothing more to feed on. He looked at the board once more, and was already raising his hand to own himself beaten when suddenly, as if a veil had been lifted from his eyes, he recognized the plan that lay at the root of his game – or was it Arni's game? With his last two moves, and in his eagerness to sweep the white pieces off the board, Hunli had opened up two aisles between his own chessmen, both leading to the square next to the green king; one, going straight across the board, was commanded by Listener's white castle, and the other, passing diagonally through the green ranks from the left, was commanded by his queen. Listener could scarcely believe what lay there plainly to be seen, and tried to think of possible counter-moves Hunli might make. But there were none, and the only square to which Hunli's king could have moved for safety was occupied by one of his own green pieces.

Listener's hesitation was making Hunli impatient, and the heat was troubling him more and more as well. 'What are you mulling over all this time?' he said. 'Let's make an end of it and be done!'

'You are right,' said Listener, 'let's make an end of it.' He took his queen and set her beside the green king. Then he looked into Hunli's face, which was streaming with sweat, and said, 'You have lost, great Khan.'

'Won, you must mean, won,' the Khan corrected him, not troubling to look more closely at the board. He was so sure of victory that he laughed at what he took for Listener's slip of the tongue, and looked around the circle of his sons and the elders with satisfaction. Only then did he notice that none of them was joining in his laughter; instead, they were all staring at the chessboard as if unable to grasp what they saw there. And then, at last, he too saw how the pieces stood, and in an instant all the colour drained from his face. 'There's only one man can play like that,' he whispered. 'Arni always gave his opponent every advantage, and yet he still won.' He stared at his king, as if staring might yet save him, and then rage overcame him and he kicked the board, sending the chessmen rolling over the rug. Next moment he had himself in hand again, and said, in a carefully controlled voice, 'You are free, Bearer of the Stone, and the falconers' rug is yours. It would be discourteous to ask you to ride away so late in the afternoon, but you would do well to set out early in the morning with your companions.' Then he stood up and left the tent, walking stiffly.

Listener was thankful for the Khan's kick, which had sent the board flying. He could take this opportunity to retrieve the fallen chessmen, and change the two white queens back again. Then he bowed to the Khan's sons and the elders, and went out. The sun was already quite low, but it was still hot. When Listener looked around, he saw Hunli just turning into the path that led to the horses' paddock, and a moment later the Khan was racing out into the steppes on his shaggy stallion.

After those hours of extreme fear and strain in the stuffy tent, Listener breathed a great sigh of relief, but at the same time he felt overcome by such exhaustion that he could scarcely remain on his feet. He staggered to his tent, fell on his bed, and closed his eyes.

He lay there for some time, half asleep. Then he heard something moving aside the strips of felt that covered the entrance, opened his eyes, and saw the Khan's youngest son Belarni standing in the tent. The lad bowed, and said, 'Forgive me for disturbing your rest. I've brought you the rug you won in the game.'

Only now did Listener see that Belarni had a roll of something tied with string under his arm. He put it down beside the bed. Listener thanked him, and seeing that Belarni still stood where he was, looking rather irresolute, as if he had something else to say, he asked if he would like to stay and talk for a while.

'Yes, please,' said Belarni, 'and I have to admit the rug was only an excuse. I wanted a chance to talk to you.'

Listener liked the boy's frankness. He offered him a cushion to sit on, and asked Belarni to excuse him for lying on his bed. 'The game took a good deal out of me,' he said.

'Did you ever doubt you'd win?' asked Belarni, astonished. 'Didn't you know Arni was guiding your hand?'

Listener looked at the boy in surprise, and said, 'What makes you think that? I wasn't even sure of it myself.'

Belarni smiled. 'I recognized Arni's method of play at once,' he said. 'My father never learned to see through it, though. But you must have known from the outset that Arni never lets his friends down. If he made you his heir, he wouldn't let you end in the huts of my father's slaves.'

'Arni has been dead these five years,' said Listener.

Belarni shrugged his shoulders. 'What's that got to do with it?' he asked.

Listener found this boy more and more remarkable: talking to him as if to a friend, not caring what his father might say if he discovered. It was clear from Belarni's olive complexion, straight black hair and flat nose that he was of the Raiding Riders' stock, but he was like his father in nothing else. His broad brow gave him the look of a clever and level-headed young man, and his eyes did not have that opaque darkness as of polished stone, but were a dark, smoky grey, flecked with brown, and they were not hard, but thoughtful and sometimes amused.

'I think you were fond of your uncle Arni,' said Listener.

'Yes, I was,' said Belarni. 'It was so easy to talk to him, and he knew how to listen too. But above all, he was a free man.'

'What do you mean by that?' asked Listener. 'Surely all the Raiding Riders are free men!'

'Not the way I mean,' said Belarni. 'Our lives are hemmed in by countless customs that must be observed if you want to belong to the horde. For instance, if you have any pride in you, you don't talk to slaves, you only give them orders. You consider strangers enemies if they're not going to be useful to you in some way, and people won't think well of you unless you've killed as many men as possible and brought rich booty back. Do you call that freedom? Myself, I call it

constraint if I can't be friendly to other people in any way I want.'
Belarni had become quite heated as he spoke; his face was glowing,
and one could see that he had been thinking such thoughts for some
time, without being able to tell them to anyone. Listener could well
imagine the trouble in store for Belarni among his people, if he held
opinions like these.

'Your father would tell you,' he said, 'that those customs are
necessary to preserve the strength of the horde.'

'No need to remind me of that,' said Belarni. 'But who says we have
to live in such a way? Nobody but ourselves, surely! Is it decreed for all
time that the men of my people are to delight in murder and robbery?
I don't delight in it myself, anyway, and I don't want to lead a life I
hate.'

'That was what Honi thought, too, when he and his people left the
horde,' said Listener.

Belarni nodded agreement. 'That's really what I wanted to talk to
you about. Tell me how Arni's Folk live now.'

'I went there only this spring,' said Listener, 'and I've been away in
the mountains for some while since then. However, I did meet some of
their traders earlier, and talked to them, and I'll happily tell you what
I heard from those men, and then what I saw for myself later.' And he
described the courtesy of Arni's Folk, told of the traders' journeys,
showed Arni the silver coinage stamped with the pictures of Arni and
Urla, and told him how Arni's Folk honoured everything that was
connected in any way with Arni. 'Arni's House stands at the centre of
their settlement,' he said, 'and they keep all Arni's possessions there
and hold their assemblies in his living-room. Every word Arni ever
spoke is law to them, and they think every deed he did worthy of
imitation.'

Belarni seemed rather taken aback by all this. He shook his head,
and said, 'Perhaps you haven't lived with Arni's Folk long enough
to understand them properly. However, if it's really as you say, then
none of those men has really understood Arni. I was only a little
boy when he was killed, but old enough to realize that he didn't
want to make any laws or lay down any strict rules; he himself was
still searching. I remember he once told me, "Mark my words,
boy, if you ever think you see your life's goal clear ahead of you,
then you've probably lost your way." These Folk of Arni's are too
sure of what Arni had in mind for my liking. They seem to have made
him into a giver of good advice, to whom they can refer if necessary

when they want to further their own interests. They're obviously no more than good traders.'

Listener was rather struck by what the boy said, and wondered if he hadn't thought much the same himself. But then he dismissed the thought from his mind, since it cast doubt on everything he had hoped to achieve since he first entered Honi's house. Most likely all Belarni had said sprang merely from youthful enthusiasm. 'You were very small when your uncle died,' he said. 'Couldn't it be that you have created a picture in your memory which isn't quite the truth? Maybe you're only making Arni the embodiment of your own wishes.'

'No!' said Belarni fiercely. 'It's not like that! It's you and the rest of them making Arni into a puppet saying what *you* want. I had meant to ride back with you to Arni's Folk, but now I see I'd find no more than a different lack of freedom there. I must look for my own way.' And as he spoke, he stood up, and left the tent without a word of farewell.

Listener was sorry to have disappointed Belarni. He would have liked to ride back over the steppes to Arni's Folk with him. The boy would not have an easy life with the horde if he stuck to his opinions. He would have to learn that every community, of whatever kind, had to make rules by which people could live together if they were to preserve their unity, and the rules of Arni's Folk might be a little over-formal, but Listener was sure they were not so unreasonable.

When he noticed that it was beginning to get dark outside he rose and went out, to look for Blorri and tell him they must set off early next morning. He found him outside the tent allotted to him and his men, in conversation with a Raiding Rider who wore his hair in braids, and whom he had probably known before the Great Parting. 'So you actually beat Khan Hunli!' cried Blorri. 'The whole camp's talking of nothing else. They all swear Arni himself must have shown you how Hunli can be beaten.'

'Then you can thank Arni for it that we're getting away from here unscathed,' said Listener, and he told Blorri to have everything ready to ride at first light of dawn. After that he went back to his tent, took out his flute, and waited until night fell and all was still in the camp.

That time came at last, and Listener left the tent again. The starry sky was like a glittering bell above the steppes, divided by the palely shimmering band of the Milky Way. The black felt tents crouched side by side, like gigantic beasts asleep, and the air smelled of smoke. Listener felt like a spy creeping through an enemy camp. Cautiously, so as not to draw any attention to himself, he slipped from tent to tent, and when he turned into the alley leading to the paddock he could smell the horses. Next moment a shadow stepped out of the dark and approached him. Listener stopped, recognizing the slave who looked after the horses.

'Thank you for coming, lord,' said the old man. 'Arni guided your hand, and I think there was another who stood beside you too.'

'That may well be,' said Listener. 'The Khan was wet with sweat, but I hardly felt the heat at all.'

The old man laughed quietly. 'I knew you'd won when I saw Hunli fetch his horse and gallop out into the steppes,' he said. 'He must have been an angry man, and he didn't come back until nearly evening.'

'He won't forget his anger in a hurry, either,' said Listener. 'I and my companions must be gone from the camp before he wakes tomorrow morning.'

'Then you do me all the more honour, lord, coming here the night before you leave,' said the old man. 'Did you bring your flute?'

'Here it is,' said Listener, producing the flute. 'What would you like me to play?'

The old man thought for a while, and then said, 'I've come to love my horses in all the years I've lived here as a slave. Will you play me a song about horses?'

Listener nodded, and put the flute to his lips. He thought of the valley of Barlebogue, and the time Barlo had spent as a groom on Eldar's farm, and he began telling that tale with the notes of his flute, so that the old man heard how Barlo was forced into service at the castle whose master he really was, and how he found his only pleasure in the company of the noble horses that stood in the stables there.

As he played, he heard the snorting of the Raiding Riders' horses, and saw their shadows emerge from the darkness, trotting slowly closer. And when he had told his tale to its end, all the horses in the paddock were crowded together on that side of the enclosure, as if they too wanted to hear his song of their own kind.

'Thank you for that music, lord,' said the old man. 'Very comforting, it was, to a slave who spends his days with horses, and my beasts here liked it too, as you can see.'

'Then I'll play them another tune,' said Listener. While the horses were gathering, an idea had occurred to him: might not the angry Hunli pursue him once he and his companions had left the camp, and were riding unprotected over the steppes? And that was not all. Wasn't this an opportunity to put an end to the Riders' raiding for a while?

Belarni would be grateful to him for that, he felt sure. So he put his flute to his lips a second time, and now he was speaking to the horses. 'Hear me, little horses!' he played. 'Hear what my music tells you: when your riders mount and give you your heads, then gallop out into the steppes, gallop so that it's a joy for any man to ride you. Leap and race, fly like falcons, be gentle as lambs, do whatever your riders ask – but if they urge you on to attack peace-loving men, if you hear the war-cry of the horde, if your riders put arrows to their bowstrings and unsheathe their curved swords, then rear and turn and gallop away again as fast as your swift hooves will carry you! Gallop as far as you can, gallop until there is a good day's ride between you and the men your riders meant to attack! Remember that you are peaceful creatures, little horses, and give no help to any disturber of the peace!'

When he had played this music to its end, he went to the leather strap marking the boundary of the enclosure, and stroked the white noses of the horses who were putting their heads over it, snorting.

'I see you can talk to the animals too in your own way,' said the old man, 'though I am surprised these wild horses of the steppes like so peaceful a song as you played them. It sounded more like a ride for pleasure than raiding and battle.'

'Horses are peaceful creatures when they don't have Raiding Riders on their backs,' said Listener. 'Would you love your horses if they weren't?'

'Well, you may be right there,' said the old man. 'But I've kept you long enough. You'd better sleep now, to be fresh for your long ride in the morning. Take good care of that scale the girl of our people gave you. You may need help of such a kind again, who knows? You were friendly to the people of the Brown River who must live here on the dry steppes, and I have to thank you for that too.'

When Blorri woke Listener next morning it was still dark outside. Not until he left the tent did he see the sky growing lighter in the east. The horses stood there ready. Listener strapped the rolled rug to his saddle and mounted. The camp seemed dead. Everyone in it had been there to see them arrive, but not a soul showed his face now. 'I don't like this,' said Blorri. 'They don't usually let guests ride away without any farewells. I've not seen anyone today but the old slave who looks after the horses, and a Carphead girl who gave me a bundle of provisions for our journey: cakes of bread and dried meat. It strikes me you've won more friends among these slaves than among the Raiding Riders.'

'You must know Arni was once a guest of their folk by the Brown River,' said Listener. 'Come, let's be off! I don't want to stay here a minute longer.'

After three days, he felt reasonably sure that they were not being followed. Blorri, who had noticed the way Listener kept looking round, said once, 'Are you afraid Khan Hunli will try to seize your rightful winnings back? No, he'd lose face, and no one would ever play chess with him again. He must let you ride home unharmed. But after that, I'd be careful not to cross his path if I were you.'

Listener hoped Hunli really did observe this custom, but he still remembered the Khan's outbreak of rage too clearly to feel he could entirely rely on Blorri's reassurance. He wouldn't feel really safe until he had left the steppes behind him.

On this third day the heat was almost unbearable. The horses suffered from it more than anyone, and they had had nothing to drink since morning. 'We must reach the next waterhole even if we ride on into the night,' said Blorri, narrowing his eyes to peer at the shimmering horizon. The horses could hardly be persuaded even to trot, and plodded over the dry, rustling grass. Not until the sun was low in the west did Blorri spy a barely perceptible hollow on the horizon, only visible at all because the blood-red disk of the sun itself happened to be sinking at just that place in the haze. 'The waterhole's over there,' said Blorri, 'but it will be dark long before we reach it.'

They rode on towards the purple glow whose radiance gradually faded from the rim of the sky when the sun had sunk, until finally stars pierced the last faint brightness, and it was swallowed up in the darkness of the night. Listener let his horse trot on behind the leader, and hoped that Blorri would not lose his way; the other men were behind him. There was nothing to be heard but the rustle of hooves in the grass of the steppes, and then, suddenly, that sound too was stilled. Listener raised his head, and felt rather than saw that one of the horsemen had come up with him and was riding at his side, soundless, scarcely visible, a shadow blotting out the stars, a thin figure, bent low over the horse's back, yet in spite of the darkness its face was gradually illuminated by pale light: a wrinkled face, keen-featured, with colourless braids dangling at the temples.

'Well, are you proud of your deeds in Hunli's camp?' asked Arni. The question sounded as if there were nothing much to be proud of. Suddenly Listener felt cold rage against this old man, always out to deprive him of what little hard-won self-confidence he had. 'I did what

I set out to do,' he said. 'And more besides. Maybe you did help me, but this time I made sure you would first!'

He looked rebelliously into the shadowy rider's face, and he saw Arni put back his head and break into that soundless laughter again. 'What a donkey you are!' said Arni. 'Do you really believe that falcon girl can force me to anything with her conjuring tricks? If I hadn't wanted to help you, you'd be in one of the huts of my brother's slaves now. You were near enough coming to that.'

Listener felt furious. 'I suppose you let me think I was going to lose right to the end on purpose, did you?' he said, but that only made Arni laugh again. 'Didn't you deserve it, O mighty magician?' he said. 'And when I think what you did afterwards, with your flute, I'm almost sorry I did let you win in the end, after all.'

'What do you mean?' asked Listener, puzzled. 'Aren't you glad the horde won't be able to harm anyone for some time to come?'

'Not if the thing's done in that way,' said Arni, 'and you have yet to find out what will come of it.' He was not laughing now, but looked like a man who sees disaster ahead and can no longer prevent it.

'What have I done wrong this time?' asked Listener, but then he realized there was no one riding beside him any more, and he could hear the monotonous rustling of horses' hooves in the grass again. They reached the waterhole an hour later, let the horses drink, ate some of their provisions, and spent the rest of the night there.

There is no more to tell of the rest of their journey back, except that Listener's desire to unroll the falconers' rug at Narzia's feet grew with every passing day. He longed to see her step over its silken weft and then, at last, to take his green-eyed girl in his arms. He conjured up the picture in his mind's eye over and over again, but when the moment came, and he was in Honi's living-room, there was no opportunity for this moving scene to take place. First he had to tell Arni's Deputy how the Khan had received the horses, and Listener could not help sensing that Honi would have felt dishonoured if Hunli had had anything disparaging to say about the animals. 'I hope you did yourself credit with Khan Hunli in other ways too,' added Arni's Deputy, rather as if he feared Listener might have behaved in some improper fashion, thus damaging the reputation of Arni's Folk.

'I think so,' said Listener. 'We played chess together.' As he spoke, he looked at Narzia, who was sitting beside her father, and saw her triumphant smile. She seemed to know how the game had ended, though her father did not.

'Good, then he treated you as a man on an equal footing,' said Honi, pleased. 'It's no shame to lose at chess to Hunli.'

'Maybe not,' said Listener, with studied casualness, and thinking where he would be now if he had indeed lost. After a while, he added, 'Anyway, I won.'

'Won?' repeated Honi, with every appearance of astonishment. 'Won against Hunli? I can scarcely believe it!'

'It's true, however,' said Listener, 'or I wouldn't be here. I'd be in the huts of Arni's slaves instead.'

'High stakes!' said Honi, appreciatively. 'Now I see you are truly Arni's heir. No other man has ever been able to beat Hunli before. Arni's wisdom, may we all be granted it, was with you. And what did the Khan stake?'

'This rug,' said Listener, unrolling the precious thing.

'The rug with the mounted falconers!' cried Honi. 'Hunli must have been very sure of himself.'

'That was his mistake,' said Listener, trying to assume something of the pose of a careless victor. 'Will you allow me to give your daughter this rug?'

Honi smiled. 'You know well enough what would please her,' he said. 'I've no objection.'

So now, at last, Listener laid the rug at Narzia's feet, even if she could not step across it towards him, since she was sitting at the table. When he straightened up beside her she said, 'Come closer, so that I can thank you for your gift!' She put her hand on the back of his neck, drew his head down to her and kissed him on the mouth, quickly and rather lightly, with her lips closed, but all the same Listener thought his heart would stand still.

Honi laughed comfortably, and said, 'Sit down again, Listener! You mustn't think I haven't noticed the way you look at my daughter. I discussed the matter with Narzia while you were away.'

Listener looked expectantly from him to Narzia and back again, and when both remained silent, he said, 'Well, I suppose I don't need to tell you, Honi, that I want Narzia for my wife. When I came here I had done scarcely anything to earn the respect of Arni's Folk, but I hope I have made up for that a little now.' He looked Honi in the face again. Surely the man must speak up and agree to the marriage now! What more did he want? It would have been hard for anyone to perform such tasks better than he himself had done. Listener's good spirits began to ebb as irritation rose in him. Honi and the falcon maiden could hardly doubt his courage, now he had been to the Raiding Riders' camp and played chess with the Khan for his freedom. Did they expect still more? Or must he go through further solemn formalities of some sort, the kind of formalities by which these people set such store?

It seemed that Honi could read Listener's thoughts in his face, for he said, 'Don't misunderstand me, Bearer of the Stone. In all that you have now done, you've shown yourself worthy of the man who gave you his stone. However, there is an old custom among our people, one we still observe even after the Great Parting, for it strikes us as a good one: a man wooing the daughter of someone of a certain rank must perform three deeds of note, to show that he will bring no shame on his wife and her family.'

'Are you afraid I might bring shame on Narzia and yourself?' asked Listener angrily.

Honi tried to calm Listener's rising fury with a placatory gesture. 'Of course not,' he said. 'I know what you've done for Arni's Folk already. But one shouldn't break with a good old custom because observing it seems unnecessary in a particular case. Everyone would be able to refer to it later, as a precedent, and demand the same right. And it would bring you even more honour to submit to this custom, and undertake yet a third ride.'

Listener felt like saying he didn't care two hoots for the honour of it, but he could think of no arguments to set against Honi's logic, and so he saw the goal he had thought lay just within his reach unexpectedly retreat into the far distance again. 'And where am I to go this time?' he asked bitterly.

'To the Falcon People,' said Honi. 'At the time of the Parting of the Ways we took our little steppe horses with us and made use of them here. And we were able to satisfy the Khan with young beasts of that breed, but there's no selling them to other folk. So the Council of Elders has decided to acquire stud horses of a nobler breed, and I know none better than those swift horses the Falcon People keep. However, there's one difficulty: the Falcon People have always refused to sell any foreigner even a single stallion for breeding. But the Council thinks you would succeed, one way or another, in persuading them to make an exception for us.'

Listener could well imagine what he meant by 'one way or another'.

They wanted to make use of the power of his flute again, and they probably wanted to discover, into the bargain, if even the mighty Great Magician could be influenced in that way. It had all obviously been decided in advance, and he had no choice if he wanted to claim a place among Arni's Folk and win Honi's daughter for his bride. 'When am I to ride?' he asked, resigned.

'As soon as possible,' said Honi cheerfully. 'If you wait too long, you might be overtaken by the coming of winter on your way back, and if you have a valuable stallion with you he could come to harm. So rest for a week, and if you set out then, the leaves will just be changing colour as you turn home.'

It was plain that Honi had already discussed all these details with Narzia, and Listener could not help thinking that Honi's suggestions proceeded mainly from her. Considering her love for all connected with the Falcon People, this was only too probable. She hardly seemed to mind that he himself would be away on his journey for many weeks this time. No doubt her pride wouldn't allow her to take a wooer who couldn't boast of performing the usual three heroic tasks, and presumably he ought to be proud that such great things were expected of him, but he merely felt exhausted. He had a long ride behind him, he had been afraid, and a little lucky too, and now all he wanted was to take his green-eyed girl in his arms and feel her hold him close. But there was still a long way to go. 'I'm tired,' he said, and wished them both goodnight.

However, his disappointment would not let him sleep. Again and again, he saw himself riding over boundless plains with no end in sight. Yet again he felt fear, the fear that had never quite left him while he was delivered up, defenceless, to that wide horizon, and it grew and grew, filling all his mind. At last he felt there was no way of escape but into that realm of dreams of which he had only vague memories as a world full of colour and fragrance, enticement and fulfilment, utter security within the green walls of a garden. He reached for the little flask that promised such dreams, let another drop of the magical brew fall on his hand, and licked it up. But the flavour of the thick liquid seemed insipid, and he could not break through into that other world. Perhaps he had taken too small a quantity for the desired effect. Once more, he let the brown fluid drop into the palm of his hand, and this time it flung him back on his bed as soon as his tongue tasted its bitter sweetness, and next moment he began to dream:

The Black Dream

He was falling from above, down to the broad expanses of the garden, and for a moment he could see all that green domain, with its lawns and trees and waters, the intertwining flowers and the maze of dark green hedges with white marble limbs gleaming among them; he fell right into those eddying colours and scents, plunged through the spray of the fountain and felt all the sweetness of that union, compressed into the space of a single heartbeat, going through him like a knife, but he could not stop falling, and went on down and down into formless darkness. For a long time he felt nothing but that rushing fall as he was sucked deeper and deeper into the bottomless chasm of howling terror, and he still had a sense of falling when he came, quite suddenly, into a region of wan brightness whose source could not be any light, for even what was visible here seemed without light, merely a variety of darkness. He was in a space that hung askew while the whole of it went on plunging downwards, but it had bounds set to it, although its shape could not have been described, and the Grey One was sitting opposite him. He was aware that he knew this figure, though he could not think where he had met it, but he was acquainted with that grey, unmoving face that hung opposite him at an angle in this space, and spoke to him without any movement of its lips. 'So you've not disappointed my expectations,' said the Grey One, 'and you are slowly coming to see how the world works, though you can't yet quite free yourself of the notion that the heart in your breast is more than a pump to drive the blood through your veins. You could achieve far more if you would forget such childish dreams at last. Don't you feel your nature urging you on to win and exercise power over others? You can't escape that urge, and you will be one of life's losers as long as you struggle against it. Do you want to be one of the many who are dealt with as they please by those few who've understood the workings of the world? Devour or be devoured, that's all that counts. Even you can't change those laws.'

Then the space, together with the Grey One, tipped over to one side and disintegrated, still falling, into a disorderly teeming of jaws and claws, talons digging into horny skin that burst under them, fangs grasping twitching limbs, and Listener himself was whirling amongst this formless mass of bodies, was only a part of a monstrous body tearing itself to pieces in blind and furious frenzy. Fishlike creatures with cold, goggling eyes dug their teeth, sharp as needles, into the scaly skin of strange reptilian beings; others spread wings of membrane armed with claws and fought, jaws drooling; shaggy monsters rammed their horned heads together until their necks cracked and their bloodshot eyes started from their sockets; great serpents wound their streaked bodies together, smotheringly intertwined; and Listener himself attacked this slithering, slimy mass, dug his nails into twitching flesh, bit at the dangling extremities of limbs, ate himself a way through the dreadful turmoil, killed to survive, struck out around him, felt bones splinter and muscles slacken, kicked and hit until he had finally made himself some space. Mangled bits of bodies hovered in the insubstantial air, headless bodies, bodiless heads, driving apart as they were swept away, falling, into the emptiness of that region where there was no light, but he sensed that it had no horizon and went on for ever. As he fell on down alone into the never-ending depths, the victor, and thus released from the butchery of those nameless creatures, he became aware that the price of his victory was utter loneliness. To survive, he had destroyed all that moved around him, and now he was drifting on into nothing, like a mote of dust, and would drift on so for ever.

* * *

His awareness of being lost and falling, unable to stop, still weighed on him when he woke at dawn. Everything looked unreal in the pale twilight; the objects in his room seemed to consist of material too thin to be grasped. He felt unable to face any other human being, who might have more demands to make of him, and wanted nothing but to get to some safe place where no one would harm him. He rose quietly, dressed, staggering slightly, as if he had been drinking all night, and crept out of the house.

The buildings huddled together around Arni's House in the grey morning mist, looking empty and dead, and to the east, where the sky was light, the eye looked out over the endless distance of the steppes, their hazy expanses causing fear to rise in him again, hunting him before it towards the sheltering woods that grew to the north of the village, rising dark above its roofs. He ran, gasping for breath, until he felt safe under the roof of hanging branches and rustling tree-tops, among tall trunks and thick undergrowth that hid the view of that boundless plain. Only then did he drop to the moss, where he lay for a long time without moving; he did not feel the ants scurrying over his hands, or hear the birds greeting the dawning day with their song, or see the butterflies fluttering over the woodland grass; he was absorbed in himself, burrowing into last year's acrid dead leaves like a dying animal and clutching at the earth, as if that one firm support might suddenly be pulled from under him.

He did not know how long he had been lying like that when something tugged at his clothing. He raised his head, and saw a large he-goat standing over him. It had obviously taken his shirt for something to eat, and now leaped back in alarm, looking at him with its yellow eyes. However, when Listener made no move to attack it, or even rise to his feet, the goat lost interest in him, shook its great horns, and bent its head to graze a few plants from the ground. Only now did Listener see that the goat was not alone. It was followed by a herd of about a dozen she-goats, mothers with their udders hanging low, swaying back and forth at every step they took, and a few kids with horns just beginning to sprout from their heads too. Once the he-goat had decided the recumbent figure was not dangerous, the animals passed Listener by unconcerned, nibbling a tuft of grass here and there, or eating the leaves off some of the lower branches, even if they had to step over him to get at them.

Last of all a skinny little kid came staggering after the rest of the flock. It stopped beside Listener, blew warm breath into his ear, and began nibbling his earlobe. When he tried to push it away it caught his little finger, sucking as if it were a teat. 'Go and find your mother!' said Listener. 'You won't get anything from me.' But the kid was not to be shooed away. Perhaps it liked the taste of the salty sweat on his skin; at any rate, it stayed where it was and went on sucking to see if the finger might not, after all, give it some milk.

Listener was touched by the little animal's innocent faith in him, although he told himself it was following its urge to suck any warm, soft little thing that came into its mouth. Still, it seemed to trust him, with a kind of confidence not to be discouraged. He scratched the top of the little goat's head, patted its dark brown skin, and for the first time since his descent into that icy emptiness, he felt the warming presence of a living creature again.

Meanwhile, the flock had gone on. Listener could see the she-goats here and there among the tree-trunks and brushwood farther up the slope. 'A fine sort of mother you have!' he told the kid. 'Come along, let's go and look for her!' He picked the little creature up and began to climb the slope. This time it was his nose that risked becoming the substitute for an udder, but he soon reached the flock, and put his small charge down. However, he hadn't reckoned with the he-goat,

who did not care at all for the sight of this stranger with one of his own
young. He pawed the moss with his cloven hooves, lowered his horns,
and took a run at Listener, with a view to butting him and knocking
him down. Listener managed to jump aside just before the goat shot
past him and crashed into a tree-trunk. He didn't wait for the goat to
attack a second time, which it seemed perfectly ready to do, but went
running down the slope, taking great strides.

He did not stop until he reached the outskirts of the wood, where he
leaned against a trunk to get his breath back, and suddenly the whole
thing struck him as so comical that he began to laugh. He laughed at
the funny little kid whose world seemed to consist entirely of teats
dispensing milk, he laughed at the he-goat's rage over nothing at all,
and in his laughter he forgot what had really driven him into the
wood. Instead, he felt hungry, for he had left the house without any
breakfast, and by now the sun was a couple of hand's breadths above
the horizon. He set off homewards, keeping to the edge of the wood,
and came into the living-room just as his hosts were about to rise from
their morning meal.

'You seem to have been up early today,' said Honi. 'Where did you
go?'

'Oh, just walking in the woods a little, talking to the goats,' said
Listener.

'And what did you learn from them?' asked Honi.

'I learned that he-goats are short-tempered!' said Listener. 'I had to
run pretty fast!'

Honi laughed. 'I hope it gave you an appetite,' said he. 'You must
forgive me now; I've business on hand. No doubt Narzia will keep you
company.'

When Listener had had enough breakfast, Narzia remarked, 'I envy
you your ride to the Falcon People.' Listener did not see anything
particularly enviable about it, but thought he had better not say so.
Instead, he suggested, 'Come with me, then!'

The glance she gave him at that demand made his heart beat faster,
although he could not tell whether it was promise or rejection that lay
in her green eyes.

'You know that's not possible,' she said. 'In any case, you ride alone
on this occasion. It will do if you bring back one stallion of the Falkinor
breed, for a start. We'll try mating him with your mare, who seems to
have good blood herself.'

Listener was slightly annoyed to find his property being thus disposed of yet again, but felt in the end he should be proud to have his horse so commended.

'However, you will have to leave Snowfoot here in our stables this time,' Narzia continued.

This was too much for Listener. 'No, I can't do that!' he protested. 'We're long used to each other, she and I, and I need a horse I can rely on when I go on such a journey.'

'I'm afraid you'd have a hard time of it coming back, riding that mare and with a stud stallion on the halter!' said Narzia, smiling. 'No, we have a good strong gelding in the stables, rather higher in the shoulders than our steppe horses, and not so shaggy. He's just the mount you need. You can get to know him over the next few days.'

'I'd be glad if you'd go riding with me, then,' said Listener. 'I shall have to ride long enough alone.'

Narzia had no objection to that, so the two of them rode out together quite often during the days that followed. Listener had lent Narzia his mare, so that she need not trot along beside his tall gelding on one of the short little steppe horses. She proved a daring horsewoman, jumping hedges and ditches so boldly that Listener sometimes had difficulty in following her on his unfamiliar mount. After one such wild ride they went on a long way south, and came to the place where Listener had fallen into the hands of the Khan's Riders on his way to Arni's Folk. Listener spurred on his gelding until he caught up with Narzia, put his arm around her shoulders, and when she had slowed Snowfoot to a walk, he kissed her on the lips. Narzia brought her own mount to a halt and returned his kiss for a moment, but then she quickly freed herself, saying, 'Why this sudden onslaught?'

'The place is right for it,' said Listener, and told her how the Raiding Riders had caught him here. 'So you see,' he went on, 'good came of my sending the Khan and his Riders chasing out into the steppes after all. It helped me to the second deed I had to perform to win you, and it helped you to your falconers' rug. The Khan was an angry man to lose it.'

'I was afraid of that,' said Narzia. 'But I had to have the rug, for it was really meant for my mother. The Great Magician put it in the Khan's hands at my parents' wedding, because it is a custom of the Falcon People for the noblest of the bridal pair's companions to bear the richest gift away and lay it in the bride's new home. Hunli didn't know the custom, however; he thought the gift was meant for him, and was very angry when my father tried to make him understand whose it

really should be. My mother told me this, later, and afterwards I could
never see that rug hanging over the Khan's throne without wishing to
have it for my own.'

'So now it's a wedding gift again,' said Listener.

'You must perform the third deed before there's any wedding,' said
Narzia.

However, she could not discourage him now. He had just held his
falcon maiden in his arms and kissed her, and he felt so sure of success that he could see no great difficulty in his new task. 'Do you
doubt I'll do it?' he said. 'All that troubles me is to think of being
parted from you so long. And it seems almost too easy to get a horse
from the Falcon People. Isn't there anything else I can bring you
back too?'

'I do know of something,' said Narzia, 'but it won't be easy for you
to get it.'

'So that's just why you shall have it!' said Listener. 'What is this
thing?'

'A ring,' said Narzia. 'My mother told me of a golden ring that
would go well with the brooch you brought me back from the Mountain
Badgers. It bears a great emerald in a setting shaped like a falcon's
head. I would like you to bring me that ring.'

'And where will I find it?' asked Listener.

'On the Great Magician's hand,' Narzia said.

Realization dawned gradually; it was only when Listener had been
travelling downstream southwards for nearly a week that he became
fully aware of what he had let himself in for. He was not worried about
the stallion of the Falkinor breed, but getting the Great Magician's
ring was quite another matter. A man so skilled in magic arts would
not be duped as easily as the simple iron smelters and master craftsmen
of Arziak. Honi and the elders of Arni's Folk would be satisfied with
the stud horse, but not Narzia. He could not come before her without
the ring, he was sure of that, but rack his brains as he might, he could
think of no way to get it. Evening was coming on now, and the lower
the sun sank, the more hopeless did the enterprise upon which he had
ridden out seem to him.

Twilight was falling when he finally looked around for a place to
camp. He had been riding along the stream all day, and if Honi's
directions were correct, he would never leave the water until his
journey's end, for this stream, Honi said, would flow into one of the

sources of the Brown River after about seven days' ride, and then he must go on down the river. He could not expect to find any settlements until he reached the banks of that broad river where it teemed with fish, so he would have to go on sheltering in the bushes for the next few nights. Eventually he found a group of hazels whose thick leaves offered shelter from the wind that had come up from the steppes towards evening. He wrapped himself in his blanket, and ate a few morsels of the food Narzia had had packed up for him.

Searching his saddle-bag, his fingers touched the curve of the little flask which he had brought with him, just in case he happened to need 'strength for an hour' again. He took the bottle out, to look at the curly old-fashioned writing on its label again, and then he saw that in his packing he had picked up the wrong bottle, the one containing dreams, both good and bad. He remembered the last dream vaguely as a headlong descent into ever-increasing horror, and had refrained from trying the contents of the flask again, although every evening it was almost more than he could do to resist the temptation. But now longing arose in him again, longing for that garden into whose secret centre he had made his way past the tall hedges, and he yearned to find it once more, even if only for that single, painful moment before he fell into the Grey One's abyss. Perhaps it had been no accident that made him pick up this elixir; perhaps something over which he himself had no control had caused him to make sure he still had a chance of returning to that region of dreams, and now he was in no state to resist the compulsion. Once again, in the dwindling light, he read the words: 'Two drops: fall into the depths, again and again.' Again and again. No going back now. Greedily, he opened the flask and let the thick liquid trickle on to the palm of his hand, making sure that no more than two drops came out. He hardly felt himself lie back on his blanket, and immediately he began to dream:

The Second Black Dream

This time he unexpectedly found himself in the midst of the dark hedges once more, and he was about to set straight off in search of that place at their heart where the two figures stood in the spray of the fountain, but almost at once he stopped again, alarmed by the soundlessness of his own footsteps. The path looked as if it were covered with gravel, but not a stone crunched underfoot. Listener bent down and felt the ground. What lay on the path felt like gravel, no doubt of that, but the smooth little stones could not be shifted from the spot, as if some invisible power held them in place.

When he straightened up to go on he realized that everything in sight looked remarkably flat; the walls of the hedges to the right and left of the path, dwindling in perspective as they receded, seemed makeshift and artificial. And then he discovered the reason for this lack of depth: there were no shadows here. How could there be any shadows? Shadows are cast only where there is light, but a black sun stood in this colourless sky, a monstrous star of icy horror travelling above the frozen paths, and those paths were endless, and seemed to lead him round and round in circles. Once he stopped, thinking he saw a bird on a branch. Hoping to find something living in this desolate, lightless world at last, he approached it. He had not been wrong: a little bird did sit there, a bird like a robin, though grey all over, but it did not move, even though Listener came quite close. In the end he raised his hand and touched the bird, only to discover the truth of what he had secretly feared: this little creature was as stiff and motionless as the gravel beneath his feet. Even the branch on which it sat could not be moved, but resisted his touch with the brittle feel of glass.

And so Listener went on in circles, silently, casting no shadow. He must have passed the rigid bird dozens of times before he noticed a hole in the hedge. The path that lay beyond it looked just the same as the path he had been following before, but then it went round a bend, and unexpectedly led him to that round space with the fountain and the two figures.

For a moment Listener stood there, rooted to the spot, feeling his heart's blood welling up in a painful spasm of expectation at the thought of the fulfilment ahead, but then he took in the glazed rigidity of this scene too. The fountain's jet still rose from the middle of the basin, but every separate drop hung frozen in the air, and would never fall again on the two figures standing here, wrapped in a cloak of lustreless pearls. The blind marble eyes of the woman's statue stared into emptiness. Hoping the touch of his hand might bring her to life, he came closer, but nowhere could he push the network of hovering droplets aside, and the smooth marble skin remained out of reach, beyond his touch, dead.

The goat-legged faun on the other side had the Grey One's face. Listener's hair stood on end when he recognized that unmoving, expressionless countenance. He felt horror of the face, yet he approached the figure, as if irresistibly compelled, went round behind it, saw the tension of its marble neck close to his eyes, the curls of its stony hair, yet his glance seemed to pierce the cold stone, bored through the curve of the skull, and then he was seeing with the Grey One's eyes, saw the woman's figure frozen in a mindless contortion, an artificial smile on her stone lips that could utter no words and showed only the pretence of something living, thinking, loving, a pretence of something which did not really exist. And he looked out through that nothingness, as if through glass, down an endless aisle of lifeless hedges that ran on and on until they drew together in the endlessness, became a tiny point, and disappeared into nothing, and he fell out with it into nothing too, fell and fell, and nothing came any closer or went any farther away, and he remained there, falling and motionless, until morning came.

* * *

The morning was damp and grey. Swathes of mist hovered over the low land beside the stream, and through the mist he vaguely saw the outlines of a few alders and willows. Listener did not stop to eat anything, but mounted his gelding and urged him on along the stream. His brain was still going round and round with the dizziness of his fall. The mists did not begin to disperse until nearly noon, when the sun came through. So far, the landscape had not altered much: there were hills to the right, rising to higher mountainous country farther off, and the endless expanse of the steppes still reached away to his left. The view did not begin to change until nearly evening, when the mountains fell farther and farther back on the other side of the stream, and then, for the first time, Listener saw the headstream of the Brown River breaking out of a valley here in the hills and curving on southwards, its banks lightly wooded.

Before the stream reached the river valley, it was dammed by a fallen poplar tree on which all kinds of driftwood had been caught, and Listener saw trout in the pool that had formed here. Now he remembered that he had not eaten all day. Dismounting, he cut a hair from his gelding's tail and made a noose, just as he had done so often as a boy. Then he lay on his stomach in the grass and tried to slip the noose carefully over a trout lying close to the bank from behind, until he could catch it behind the fins and jerk it out of the water.

The excitement of the chase made him forget everything that had brought him to that place: he was a little boy again, trying to catch his first trout, his whole ambition being to succeed first time. Little by little, the noose made its way forward over the body of the fish as it moved gently in the slight current, and then at last it was in place. A jerk, and there lay the fish in the grass beside him, twitching. Listener killed it with the back of his knife, and then tried again, proud to have had such luck with his first catch. Obviously fishermen seldom came here, for the trout were not timid, and he soon had a second fish in his noose. He gutted both trout and carried them over to the wood where he had decided to spend the night. Kindling a fire with his flint and steel, he spitted the fish on slender willow wands, and roasted them over the embers. The aroma rose so pleasantly to his nostrils that he could hardly wait for the trout to be done. He ate them ravenously, and would have sworn they were the most delicious fish he ever tasted.

When he had eaten, he fetched his horse, which had been grazing over on the bank, brought it in under the trees and tied it up for the night. Then he went along the stream to the place where it joined the river, whose muddy brown waters came shooting turbulently down on the right. Sitting on the bank, he watched the swirling eddies that raced by, saw a piece of root washed free by the river somewhere up in the mountains drift past and followed the gnarled object's swaying progress with his eyes until it was out of sight. By now he felt tired. He went back to his camping place, wrapped himself in his blanket, and fell asleep at once.

He rode on for many days along the Brown River, and nothing in particular happened. Even the landscape did not change any more, except that the river rushing along past the overgrown bank to his right gradually became broader and broader, fed by the streams and little rivers from the distant mountains that were now no more than blue outlines on the horizon. In one way, Listener found a certain monotony in the fact that its tributaries always joined it on the other side, which was also a pity in that it gave him no more chance to exercise his skill in trout-fishing; but look at it another way, and the one-sided flow into the river of all the smaller streams had its advantages, since he need not bother with the constant crossing of watercourses. He had never much liked the steppes, but now he found the scarcity of water out on those endless plains quite useful, for it made his ride considerably easier. Night after night he found somewhere to camp in the bushes, but even the alders were so like each other that he was occasionally overcome by a feeling of having slept in this very place a night or so before. And when he rode on again in the morning he wondered if he had been getting anywhere at all. In the end, he wanted nothing so much as a change, whether some obstacle in his path or simply a movement on the horizon.

This last wish, against all expectation, was to be fulfilled. About noon of the next day, horsemen suddenly appeared beside the river a good way ahead of him: first three, then five, then a whole troop, galloping along full speed beside the wooded banks. Listener reined in his gelding. He had never seen anyone crouch down so boldly on low-built horses but the Raiding Riders galloping over the steppes. He could already hear the hollow drumming of hooves on the grassy ground, and when the sound of shrill, long-drawn-out cries reached his ears as well, he knew he was looking at part of Hunli's horde. Had the Khan learned that the man who won his falconers' rug at chess was now on his way southwards, and alone? There was no chance of fleeing from them now. His gelding might be a fast horse, but he would never get away from the racing horses of the steppes. Listener looked at the Riders. He could already see the braids flying about their temples. The only way of escape left to him was the river.

Listener wrenched his gelding round and urged it into the alders. Once on the bank, he leaped from the saddle and ran into the water, dragging the horse after him. The gelding tried to rear, but Listener hauled it on, and next moment he lost his own footing. Before the water closed over him, he let go of the horse's bridle and grasped the girth, and when he came up again, gasping for air, he could feel the gelding already swimming towards the middle of the river, where it met so swift a current that it was swept rapidly on downstream. Only now did Listener have time to look back at the bank. He saw the Riders race past beyond the alders and willows. Not one of them even tried to rein in his horse. Had they so much as noticed him? A few moments later, the horde had gone by without stopping at all.

Not until the swirling current threatened to sweep him away from his horse did Listener remember that he couldn't swim. It was lucky for him that this was plainly not the first time the gelding, at least, had been in deep water. The animal tossed its head back nervously now and then, but it could keep that head above water. After a while Listener felt his fingers growing stiff, and he tried to thrust his arm underneath the saddle, but the girth was buckled too tight, and the next eddy tore him away from his horse.

He felt himself going down. There was nothing before his eyes but the green glimmer of the water. He sank, holding his breath until his lungs felt as if they would burst, but suddenly the weight seemed taken off his chest, he felt himself borne up by smooth, broad backs, he sensed the gentle beat of fins beneath his shoulders. And before he lost consciousness, he heard singing down in the depths of the water, a full-toned song like the rising and falling resonance of a bell.

It was a voice that brought Listener back to his senses, a man's voice, high-pitched, uttering words he could not understand in a curious sing-song cadence. He opened his eyes, and saw the face of an elderly man close above him, a face with pale blue eyes, a drooping grey moustache, and the receding chin of the Carphead people. This man now turned his head aside and called to a second, whose face came into Listener's field of vision too: he was younger, with a moustache only just beginning to grow, like thin fair fluff on his upper lip. The two of them seemed glad that Listener was conscious again, and spoke to him in their own melodious tongue, rich in sibilants.

Listener was gradually beginning to feel his body again. He was lying on the grass, his drenched clothes clinging to his skin, and miserably cold. Hoping the men would understand him, he said, in the language of the Raiding Riders, 'I'm cold. Have you anything dry I could put on?'

Fortunately the elder of the two men understood him, although it was plain that he did not like to use that language. 'Only a blanket,' he said. 'We had to fetch your soul back from the fishes first.' Then he said something to his companion, and began to open Listener's clothing. Immediately, he started in surprise, and touched the carp's scale that Listener still wore around his neck. 'Who gave you that?' he asked.

'A slave woman in Khan Hunli's camp,' said Listener.

'Did you sleep with her?' asked the man.

Listener forced a smile. 'No,' he said. 'She wanted a great carp to protect me.'

'And you wouldn't be alive now but for that protection,' said the man. 'Are you one of Hunli's men?'

Listener shook his head. 'I jumped into the river with my horse for fear of his horde,' he added. 'Did you find my gelding too?'

'He was standing beside you when we found you on the bank,' said the man. He had stripped Listener naked now, and wrapped him in a coarse woollen blanket brought by his companion. 'The two of us will go for a little boat-ride,' he said, 'while Roshka here takes your horse home.' He jerked his head sideways, and Listener saw his gelding standing there in the sun, head hanging.

'You must be Carphead people, aren't you?' said Listener.

The man nodded. 'We're fishermen,' he said, 'and my name is Boshatzka.' Listener told him his own name, and tried to rise, but there was no strength in his legs, and they folded under him. 'Don't overdo it!' said Boshatzka. 'You must have been in the water quite a while. We saw the horde ourselves, about noon, racing past as if evil spirits were after them, and now it's nearly evening.' He signed to Roshka, and then the two men carried Listener to the bank and laid him in a fishing boat tied up in the bushes there. Boshatzka cast off, jumped in, picked up a paddle from the bottom of the boat, and propelled the swaying craft into the current that carried it on fast downstream.

The rocking of the boat made Listener drowsy. He pulled the blanket round his shoulders and shut his eyes. After a while, still half asleep, he felt the boat scraping over gravel somewhere and coming to rest. Boshatzka called out a few words, and next moment footsteps came tramping over wooden planks, Listener was picked up, carried a little way, a door was opened, warmth enveloped him, and when he finally opened his eyes he found himself lying on a bed of skins before an open fire over which a cauldron black with soot hung from an iron hook. A woman came over, threw some pieces of fish into the simmering water, and went away again. People were talking somewhere in the dimly lit room. Listener could make out Boshatzka's voice, plainly telling how and where he had found this man. Meanwhile, the aroma of fish soup began to mingle with the smoky smell of the wood fire. The woman came back and sprinkled a handful of herbs into the cauldron, took a carved ladle that hung from a hook on the wall by the hearth, stirred the soup and ladled some out into a wooden bowl. Then she knelt down on the floor beside Listener and began to feed him with a little wooden spoon.

The soup was delicious. Comforting warmth spread through his body with every mouthful he took. When at last he made a sign to the woman to convey that he had had enough, she called two men over, and they lifted him on to a bedstead near the fireplace. Meanwhile, the woman had gone out, and came back directly with a pile of sheets and blankets. She and another woman unwrapped Listener until he lay before them in all his hairy nakedness, a sight which surprised them both so much that they nudged one another and could not suppress a giggle. But they soon remembered their duties, spread a finely woven linen sheet over the recumbent man, and covered it with a soft woollen blanket which they tucked in around him. Listener felt warm and safe. The reflection of the fire, now burning low, flickered on the smoky beams of the ceiling above him. For a while he listened to the muted sing-song of the people talking, but since he did not understand their language his attention soon wandered, and the voices came to his ears only as a distant rushing sound like a lullaby.

When he woke again it was broad daylight. The sun was shining outside, casting a beam of light through the little skylight, which was covered with a thin skin of parchment, and on the rush-strewn floor. The woman who had looked after him the previous evening was standing by the hearth, putting pieces of wood on the flames beneath the steaming cauldron. As soon as Listener sat up she came over and put her hand on his forehead. Perhaps she wanted to see if he was feverish, for on finding his skin dry and cool, she poured water from the cauldron into a wooden tub and told Listener, by means of gestures, to rise and get into it.

The prospect of a warm bath seemed most inviting, and Listener waited with some impatience to be left alone. The woman, however, made no move to go out of the room, but stood there expectantly and repeated her demand, rather more forcefully this time. So Listener abandoned his modesty, threw off the sheet and blanket, and got cautiously off the bedstead, which stood at hip height, to see if his legs would carry him again. The woman took him solicitously by the arm, to support him as he climbed into the tub. Obviously the Carphead women thought nothing of washing naked men, for as soon as he was standing in the tingling hot water his hostess began soaping him all over, with practised movements, uttering cooing sounds of surprise as her fingertips stroked his thick body hair. As she washed his chest, she lifted the carp's scale reverently from the curly hair that grew there and put it to her forehead.

After the bath, she picked up a wooden bucket from the floor and poured a torrent of water over Listener's shoulders; it was so cold that he yelled with surprise. She laughed, as if it were a great joke, made Listener climb out of the tub, wrapped him in a warm linen cloth and rubbed him dry until his skin was red as a lobster. Then she brought him a clean shirt with fine embroidery around the collar, and set out his clothes, which had been hanging over a wooden frame by the fire to dry.

Listener felt wonderfully refreshed as he sat at the table a little later, fully dressed, spooning up the gruel the woman had put before him. While he ate, Boshatzka came into the room, wished him good morning, and sat down too. Listener thanked him for all his help, and asked just how the two fishermen had found him.

'First we saw your horse, standing on the bank,' said Boshatzka. 'It was snorting, and looking at something, and when we paddled closer we saw a man lying there too. It's not often the river washes a drowned man ashore, and I never before saw one cast up so high on the bank, lying on dry grass as you were. We thought at first the Raiding Riders had killed you as they passed by.'

'Do you know why Hunli's Riders were in such a hurry?' asked Listener. 'They galloped past like men possessed.'

'I can't tell why, myself,' said Boshatzka. 'Roshka and I had been paddling upstream all morning, and when we saw them race by so wildly about noon, coming from the direction of our village, we thought there'd been another raid. So we turned our boat and went back, and we picked you up on the way. But we didn't hear the strangest part of the story until we got back home. Our own people said Hunli's Riders had come out of the steppes in the morning, riding fast upstream this way. They probably meant to capture a few slave girls, as they so often do. And when they had almost reached the first houses they began to utter their usual war-cry. At that very moment their horses reared and turned and bolted away as if something had terrified them. None of us can explain it.'

Listener could have told him what had made the Raiding Riders' horses turn back, but he thought it better to keep his knowledge to himself, and merely said that such conduct seemed very strange to him too. At least he could now be sure that he had not played his tune to the horses of the steppes in vain. With that thought, he realized in alarm that he had no idea what had become of his saddle-bags. The gelding might have shed them as he swam, or the river could have washed away their contents, among them the flute with whose aid he hoped to perform his task in Falkinor. He asked Boshatzka if he knew where his bags were.

'Hanging out in the sun to dry,' said Boshatzka. 'We didn't venture to open them. I'll bring them in, and you can look and see if anything's lost.' He left the room, and soon came back with the saddle-bags.

Listener took them from him and carried them over to the hearth. The leather had absorbed a great deal of water, and as soon as he opened the fastenings a quantity of soaked bread met his eyes. His dried meat did not look very appetizing now, either. The clothes he had packed were wet and crumpled, but the little flask with the elixir of dreams was unharmed, and still tightly closed, and his flute was there as well. He cautiously drew it out of the sodden mass, and wiped it dry on a shirt. When he had cleaned the inside of the pipe as well, he put it to his lips and blew a couple of experimental notes.

Boshatzka had remained courteously in the background while Listener looked through his possessions. Now, however, he came over to the hearth, asking, 'Are you a minstrel, then?'

'A fluter, yes, as you see,' said Listener, and quickly he played a fisherman's song that had just come into his head.

Boshatzka was delighted. 'You know your trade, to be sure,' said he. 'I hope you'll do us the honour of being our guest a few days longer.'

'Alas, I can't,' said Listener, 'for you must know I'm on my way to Falkinor, where I have a commission to carry out.'

'Then stay another night, at least,' said Boshatzka, and Listener could not refuse this request, in gratitude for his rescue and the friendly welcome he had found here.

Boshatzka invited the whole village to a feast that evening. His cottage was too small for so many guests, and so he and Roshka set up tables and benches made of logs and planks of wood down on the banks of the river. Meanwhile his wife heated the baking oven that stood outside the house, kneaded dough and let it stand in the sun in round wicker baskets to rise, while she busied herself in the house with other preparations for the feast.

Towards evening the villagers came out, stood talking by the bank, and waited for Boshatzka to show his guest to the place of honour. Then they sat down on the benches themselves, and Boshatzka's wife at once dished up the products of her culinary skill. The mere fragrance of the freshly baked white bread she set out in baskets on the table made Listener's mouth water. All the delicacies, hot and cold, boiled and roasted that she served the guests came from the river, but they were far from uniform in flavour, and showed that Boshatzka's wife could do a great deal more than bath a naked man. There was salted sturgeon's roe, red boiled crayfish with fresh watercress, and well-seasoned fish soup, little fishes roasted on skewers, tench and pike cooked in seasoned vinegar, and finally carp in a sweet and sour brown sauce. Boshatzka poured his guests that sharp liquor of which the Gentle Fluter had once told Listener. Evening bird-song began to mingle with the sound of muted conversation and the quiet cracking of crayfish shells, and here and there ducks flew low over the river, or the water splashed as a fish jumped.

When the sun sank behind the undergrowth on the opposite bank, Listener thought the time had come for him to thank the Carpheads for their hospitality in his own way. As soon as he rose and brought out his flute, the talking died away; only a blackbird would not be still, and sang its evening song in the alders. Listener took up its tune, and for a while nature and art competed, but at last the gilded flute got the upper hand, outdoing the bird in cascades of runs and trills. Now that the field was his alone, Listener showed his skill in all kinds of songs and dances such as he thought these fisher folk might like, and once again he added transitional passages here and there, praising the noble nature of Arni's Folk, and putting the idea into the Carpheads' minds as he played that it would be a very useful thing to win the friendship of these peaceful traders. His flute seemed to produce these inserted passages of itself; his fingers moved as if under some compulsion, finding eloquent and persuasive themes, and yet in a strange way he felt detached, heard his own flute as if some stranger were playing it, and wondered what good Arni's Folk could get from these poor fishermen. Could there be a profitable trade in smoked fish, or that salted sturgeon's roe? His flute seemed to be thinking its own thoughts, and he let it, lent it his breath and hands, and observed its obvious effect in the faces of the Carpheads, who sat entranced, listening to playing such as they had never heard before.

It was almost dark when that strange, deep, bell-like echo came into his mind, the resonance he had heard when he sank into the waters of the Brown River, and his flute was already reproducing the sound that rose from the depths, together with the image of an ancient and gigantic carp making its way through green tendrils of waterweed, mouth rounded as it sang its song, the song of the Brown River, just as the Gentle Fluter had once heard it, a song praising the wonders of the flowing stream, the world of fish and waterfowl, bounded by alders and willows, giving and maintaining life, yet menacing too in its turbulent strength, and the menace of it sounded louder and louder in Listener's ears, until he realized that it was meant for him. 'Leave my children in peace!' roared the ancient carp. 'Do not play your cunning tricks on them, with their gentle natures! I saved you once for the sake of the sign you wear round your neck, for then I did not know your mind. But it will not help you a second time!' And at that very moment Listener felt the scale on his breast crumble into dust, as if it had fallen into the fire.

He stood there swaying, barely conscious, and did not come back to his senses until Boshatzka took his arm to support him. Then, at last, he took the flute from his lips, and sat down on the bench, breathing heavily. Through the appreciative murmurs of the villagers, he heard Boshatzka's voice as if it came from very far away. 'No one has played like that in our village,' Boshatzka was saying, 'not since Arni was our guest here many years ago, and had a young fluter with him. I've known people who heard him, but it's only now I understand what they told me: they said they had heard the Ancient One singing in the river. It was very beautiful, but I was afraid too.'

Listener nodded, dazed, and far too exhausted to say what he knew about that fluter. After a while, he said, 'I am very tired.'

By now the people had realized there would be no more music to hear, and they went home, while Boshatzka took his guest back to his own house.

That night Listener lay awake a long time. Through the snoring of his hosts, sleeping on benches by the wall at the other end of the room, and in the rushing of the river, he thought he could still hear the Ancient One's mighty voice, that eerie threat from the watery depths, and the longer he listened to it, the more he felt fear of the threat shake him, feeling himself delivered up to it and helpless. He put his head under the covers, but that voice of bronze only sounded all the louder in his ears, until there was nothing he could do but take refuge in dreams, of whatever kind they might be. He groped about him for his saddle-bag, took out the little flask, and in the faint light of the last embers on the hearth, he let two drops fall on his trembling hand. And he had scarcely tasted that heavy liquid on his tongue than he began to dream:

The Third Black Dream

He was sinking down in the gurgling current again, brown water washed over his eyes, and the brown of it grew darker and darker. He was being sucked into a whirlpool whose circling eddies drew him into the depths like a helplessly drifting fly; a gigantic mouth, surrounded

by barbs, snapped at him, soft, horny jaws nibbled and then spat him
out again: nasty, unpleasant vermin, not to the taste of the mouth's
owner. He was carried on into grey, rushing waters, past slimy and
colourless twining plants that came licking their way up from the
fathomless depths and soon surrounded him like the tentacles of the
monstrous jellyfish into whose glassy body he was inexorably sinking
down, and the closer he came to the creature's translucent bell-shaped
body, the more clearly did he see two figures beyond its streaked sides,
two pale and motionless figures, naked and lifeless, a woman with her
head thrown back, and a being half animal, half man, with shaggy
loins and the legs of a goat, straining towards her and yet unable, in his
rigidity, to reach her, and there was a third figure too, grey and
dressed with care, and this figure was moving. It circled around the
two chalk-white figures, gloating over their helpless, frozen yearning to
reach one another. The image was quite close now; Listener felt the
slippery membrane of the gelatinous bell beneath his hands, tough and
impenetrable, and now he saw what it was that gave the Grey One
such pleasure: the fluids in the hollow body of the jellyfish were gradually beginning to dissolve the pale figures, their limbs became thinner
and thinner, a finger dropped off the woman's hand and drifted slowly
away, the marble flesh was consumed, revealing hollow cheekbones
and bared teeth; the male figure's muscular shoulders dwindled, his
body snapped and collapsed like melting wax; for a while a few pieces
still drifted, mingling with the remains of the other figure, like flakes in
the turbid ooze contained in that flabby, hollow body, in whose centre
the Grey One now stood, his thin fingers grasping at the foam they left
as they dispersed. He caught a last remnant of it and showed it to
Listener on his outstretched hand: a few light little bubbles that burst
one by one, until nothing was left, nothing at all, for at that same
moment this image too was extinguished as Listener was drawn down
and down into the dark abyss, and felt no more but emptiness and
nameless fear.

* * *

He woke in the grey light of dawn, and found that he was clutching the
posts of the bedstead as if they might halt his fall, but the sensation of
that never-ending descent would not go away. He felt weak and
drained, and longed to be held tight so that the fall would end at last.
But the arms in which he hoped to be held were far away, beyond his
reach. He must get this journey over first. With difficulty, he sat up in

bed, then rose and dressed. He knew now that he must ride on that morning. He would let nothing more detain him until he had performed the third task too, and he would not baulk at anything to do it.

'You don't look well,' said Boshatzka, as he said goodbye. 'Are you sure you won't stay and rest a few days here?' But Listener shook his head, and said he had lost too much time already. Thanking the fisherman for all his help and hospitality, he rode downstream on his gelding.

He was many more days on his way between the river and the plains. A time came at last when he noticed that the dry steppes were no longer shimmering in the sun to the east; instead, there were green, lush meadows as far as the eye could see, broken here and there by groups of trees or little spinneys of bushes, their outlines overlapping as he rode by, so that the horizon was divided into constantly changing segments. The Brown River had become very wide here; the woods on the bank opposite were so far distant that they seemed only a dark, crinkled, mossy border to the wide, flowing expanse of water. And then, one morning, the angular outline of the Great House of Falkinor rose from the distant haze, far ahead of him.

Ever since he left the Carphead village, Listener had ridden along in a mood of dull indifference, lying down to sleep under some bush every evening, mounting his horse again next morning. The monotonous uniformity of his way, and the constant flowing of the river at his side, had deprived him of all sense of time, until finally he felt as if he had been riding this way aimlessly for years, or tens of years, and must ride on for ever, until the end of time. But when the house of the Great Magician appeared, he felt a marked change of mood. There was an end to his journey in sight, a place to which he must ride, and at the sight he remembered the task he would have to perform there, although for the time being he felt quite unable to plan any way to do it.

That afternoon, by which time the Great House was like a mighty block of stone towering above the plain, Listener saw a herd of horses grazing the pastures to the left of his path, and turned his own horse that way to look at the animals. Reaching their paddock, he dismounted, leaned against the wooden slats of the fence, and watched the slender-legged stallions grazing in groups, then, as if at some agreed signal, suddenly tossing their narrow heads and racing at a springy gallop through the paddock, rearing playfully, and trotting back to their pasture. He had never seen such noble horses before; every movement they made was full of indescribable grace, and yet one sensed the great power concealed in their easy gait.

As he stood leaning on the fence, feasting his eyes on the horses at play, a herdsman came over to him, a man of middle height and slight build, with the sharp and slightly hooked nose of the Falcon People, and gave him a friendly greeting. Listener replied in the language of the Raiding Riders, whereupon the herdsman looked at him in some surprise. 'Didn't take you for a Raiding Rider,' he remarked, 'even if your gelding's saddled and bridled in their fashion. From Khan Hunli's camp, are you?'

'No,' said Listener, 'but I spent a little while there. You must have been in the steppes yourself, if you know the language of the horde.'

'I was there once,' said the herdsman. 'I had a message to take from the Great Magician, and stayed a while waiting for the answer. But I like my own horses better than the shaggy beasts they ride there. Looks to me you feel the same way.'

Listener nodded. 'Are those your stud horses?' he asked.

'The best we have,' said the herdsman.

'Which would you recommend me to take home with me?' asked Listener.

The herdsman plainly thought this was a joke, and laughed. 'See that black horse over there, with the white star on his forehead?' he said. 'That's the one I'd take if I had my choice. But you'd better not come too near him if you value your life.'

'Thank you for your advice,' said Listener, in all seriousness. 'That black is the horse I'll have. What's his name?'

'Well, you're a joker, you are!' said the herdsman. 'If you can catch him, then you can keep him, as far as I'm concerned. He answers to the name of Morning Star, but you might as well try fetching down the morning star from the sky.'

'That remains to be seen,' said Listener, bringing out his flute, and he began to play. At the first notes, the stallion raised his head, pricked up his ears, and looked at the fence. He stood motionless for a while, listening to the alluring melody; then he shook his mane and came slowly trotting over. The herdsman seemed to regard him with great respect, for as soon as the animal was within about ten paces of him, he vaulted the fence to safety, and then watched in astonishment as the stallion came closer, stopped right in front of the flute-player, and bent his head as if in greeting. Listener went on playing for a while, and as soon as he took his flute from his lips, the black stallion nuzzled

Listener's face, laid his head on Listener's shoulder, and let the fluter scratch his mane and pat his neck. Then Listener climbed the fence and swung himself up on the stallion's back. The herdsman was so paralysed by terror that he was unable to hold this obvious madman back. Listener had put his flute to his lips again, and now he made Morning Star dance to his tune. The beautiful horse could be seen following every note of the flute, dancing now forward, now sideways, running in circles and stopping as soon as the melody ceased. At last Listener trotted the stallion back to the fence of the paddock, jumped off, and patted Morning Star's neck and flank once again. Then he turned to the herdsman, who was still standing outside the fence, in a state of utter confusion, and said, 'If you're a man of your word, this horse is mine now.'

'That – that's witchcraft!' stammered the herdsman.

'Whatever it may be,' said Listener calmly, 'you can't deny I not only caught the stallion, I rode him too.'

'I don't deny it, either,' said the herdsman, 'but I can't give you the horse. He belongs to the Great Magician, like all the stallions in this paddock. I'm only the herdsman.'

'Then you ought not to have offered me the stallion,' said Listener, pitilessly.

'I only said it as a joke,' wailed the herdsman, but Listener was not to be moved. 'What you meant by it is your business,' said he. 'I at least meant what I said seriously. You'll have to go to the Great Magician with me, and I'll ask if he means to keep his herdsman's promise.'

'You don't know what you're doing!' said the herdsman in alarm. 'I'd never dare come before the Great Magician with such a bold request!'

'Are you so afraid of your master?' asked Listener mockingly. 'If you won't go with me freely, then I'll have to make you.' And he reached for his flute again, and seemed about to put it to his lips. The herdsman turned white as a sheet, making a gesture to ward off the magic. 'I am in your hands, lord,' he said, his voice trembling. 'Don't play that flute, whatever you do. I'd rather come before the Great Magician and take my punishment. Only let me fetch my own horse to ride.'

'Then you can bring me a halter for the stallion, too,' said Listener.

A little later they were riding towards Falkinor. The stallion let Listener lead him by the halter and was quiet as a lamb, and so at last they trotted unhindered through the outer gate of the city and up the straight street towards the towering house of the Great Magician.

They were not stopped until they reached the gate in the inner wall. The herdsman said a few words to the man on guard, who opened the gate, indicating that they should dismount and lead their horses into the yard. Here the captain of the guard met them, asking something in the language of Falkinor. The herdsman bowed to him, and began on a long explanation, with many a gesture, pointing in turn to Listener and the black stallion. The captain listened, shaking his head, interrupted him after a while with an abrupt movement of his hand, and then, falling into the tongue of the Raiding Riders, asked Listener who he was, and what he was called. 'I am a fluter,' said Listener, and gave his name.

'This herdsman says you tamed the stallion whom even the grooms daren't approach, all in a moment, and rode him, and you did it by the magic power of your flute,' said the captain. 'Is that true?'

'It is,' said Listener. 'And did he tell you he told me that if I could do it, I could keep the stallion?'

At this the captain's face flushed red with anger. He shouted something at the herdsman, and when the latter confirmed what Listener said, the captain told Listener, 'This is a matter outside my competence. I'll have to hand you on to one of the court officials.' Beckoning to a couple of his men, he told them to put the three horses in the stables. Morning Star began to prance restlessly when one of the guards cautiously approached him, and reared as soon as the man tried to take his halter, but Listener was instantly able to soothe the horse again, and when he had whispered a few words into Morning Star's ear, the stallion obediently followed the guard.

The captain led Listener and the herdsman into the Great House, and said something to one of the servants waiting in the entrance hall, whereupon the servant hurried up a staircase and soon came down again, with a court official wearing a long robe of white silk: a thin old man, the pale parchment of his skin stretched tight over his jutting and angular cheekbones. The captain bowed to this dignitary, and briefly told him what the matter was. The official listened to him at first with face unmoved, like a man who is used to being bothered with minor matters, but in the end he too raised his eyebrows and shook his head in bewilderment.

'As I hear the tale,' he told Listener, 'it seems you wheedled the Great Magician's best stallion out of this simple herdsman. I suppose you'll hardly have the effrontery to press your claim!'

Listener was not going to let the man's condescending tone

discompose him. 'I don't call it effrontery to insist on the keeping of a promise once given,' he said. 'And there was no wheedling about it; I told this man quite clearly what I wanted. Is it my fault if he thought I was a braggart?'

'I imagine you were counting on his doing so,' said the official, coldly. 'In any event, the herdsman had as little right to give you the horse as I have, and I utterly refuse to trouble the Great Magician with so ridiculous an incident.'

Listener had already observed a certain uneasiness come into this otherwise supercilious personage's eyes when he put his hand to his flute, as if by chance, so now he took it right out, saying, 'We'll see if you persist in refusing. I think your will should be easier to break than the will of a wild stallion.' At this the official's previously haughty expression took on a distinct look of fear, and he raised both hands to ward the music off. 'Very well, I'll take you to one of the five Lesser Magicians,' he said. 'You can ask no more of me than that, for my authority reaches no farther.'

So saying, he climbed back up the steps down which he had come, leading Listener and the herdsman through a series of carpeted passages and anterooms, until he came to a door made of fragrantly resinous wood, its sole ornament the carved design of an ear surrounded by five circles. He stopped here, saying, 'You will meet the Master of Music beyond this door. I fancy he will be able to deal with the conjuring tricks of a rustic wandering minstrel. Do you still insist on what you call your rights?'

Listener himself began to have doubts about continuing his venture, and he wondered with what arts this musical Lesser Magician might surprise him. However, when he saw triumph dawning on the official's face, he shook off his fears and said, 'What are you waiting for? Tell him we're here, if you please!'

'As you like,' said the official, touching the carving of the ear on the door. A rising sequence of five clear, ringing, bell-like notes immediately sounded, and at the last note the two wings of the door opened, folding soundlessly back. 'May I?' inquired the official with courteous mockery, stepping into the room ahead of Listener and his companion and bowing low to a tall old man with bushy, snow-white hair, who wore a long robe of silk as yellow as sunlight. Listener bowed to this impressive figure too, and the herdsman almost collapsed under the awareness of his own insignificance.

Meanwhile, the official had begun acquainting the Master of Music with the facts of this difficult case. Listener could tell, from his disparaging gestures, that he was also trying to convey his own opinion of the matter, but the Lesser Magician did not seem to want to hear it, so the official, face wooden, briefly ended his account and was then dismissed.

As soon as the door had closed after him, the Master of Music turned to Listener, saying, 'So you're a fluter, I hear, and one who can do more than play a pretty tune. I should like to hear a specimen of your art. Are you prepared to play for me?'

'Willingly,' said Listener, not without some trepidation. 'What shall I play?'

'Let your flute tell me your own version of the story I have just heard from the court official's point of view,' said the Master of Music.

Flattered that the Magician felt confident he could do such a thing, Listener took out his instrument and began to play. He began by speaking of Arni's Folk and their peaceful life as traders and breeders of horses, mentioned his wooing of Honi's daughter, and told of the errand that brought him to Falkinor. All this was a kind of prelude to the story proper, the one he had been asked to tell. He gave all manner of comical accents to the tale of his conversation with the herdsman and the taming of the black stallion, for he had realized, from the laughter lines in the Lesser Magician's face, that he must be a man with a marked sense of humour, and he thought he would try to win him over in that way.

When he put his flute down, the Master of Music laughed, saying, 'Yes, I thought it would be something like that. This poor herdsman couldn't guess you meant what you said, as you very well knew. He has done nothing wrong, and may go back to his horses in peace.'

Greatly relieved, the herdsman took his leave with a low bow, and left the room. Listener, however, was not at all happy with this ruling. 'What about the stallion?' he asked.

'Ah, well, we'll discuss that later, for I can't decide the matter on my own,' said the Master of Music. 'But first I should like to talk about your music, for I have never before had a fluter quite like you as my guest.' And he offered Listener a chair and sat down opposite him. Listener now had a chance to look round the room. Musical instruments lay on shelves by the wall, on chests, on tables: flutes both large and small and other wind instruments, fiddles and dulcimers and a small harp. 'Do you play all these instruments?' he asked.

'As best I can,' said the Master of Music, in the casual tone of a man who has no need to boast of his abilities. 'Will you let me look at your flute?'

Listener handed it over, and the Magician examined it closely. 'While you were playing,' he remarked, 'I noticed that you build your tunes on a scale of seven notes, sometimes adding semi-tones between them. And I see the fingerholes of your flute are arranged accordingly. We employ only five keynotes in our own music.' Picking up the little harp from the table, he played the same sequence Listener had heard at the door, and developed from it a melody, then beginning to add rhythmic variations. His playing instantly held Listener enthralled: he forgot where he was, he scarcely saw the room and its contents, or even the Master of Music himself, he only heard the melody that unfolded as if by itself, according to a law dwelling within it. He felt as if he were watching a circling crystal that constantly showed new and different facets as it moved, and yet its perfect form remained unchanged. His perception of the music would allow his mind to stray nowhere else: he was alone with himself, within the enclosure the notes raised around him; he had no more will of his own to do or to change anything, for there was no need inside this dwelling of sound. And even when the melody had died away, no moment of sobering return to earth came; it could not come, for the music expressed sober equilibrium itself. It bent the hearer to no one else's will, but led him to himself, and when Listener became aware of that, he also saw that it had been the secret of his grandfather's playing, and he himself, with his own way of using the flute, had gone in the opposite direction. Ever since he had owned the flute, he had tried to influence his hearers and their minds in whatever way would serve his own good, and he supposed he would have to go on doing so if he wished for the fulfilment of his desires. The tunes the Master of Music had played on his harp were beautiful, indeed perfect in their own way, but they also struck him as being of no practical use. He would very much have liked to ask the Magician what point there was in his playing, but then he realized that the player of the harp had left the room.

Listener rose and looked at the instruments on the walls and the table, picked up a flute and tried it. This instrument too was limited to five keynotes by the arrangement of the finger holes. As soon as he tried to move to another key, his melody went wrong, and he realized that he could not make this flute do what he wanted. However, as long as he submitted himself to its own laws, he could build a structure of sound similar to the one the Magician had created with his harp. He tried that way of playing, caught himself up in a network of notes, but as soon as he succumbed to the temptation to alter the pattern on purpose, it all broke down again.

'You're too impatient,' said the Master of Music, behind him. 'You'll never find true perfection until you're ready to keep to the rules.'

Listener turned, and saw the Magician had come back, with another dignitary: a black-haired man of middle age in a brilliant red robe. They must both have been listening to him for some time. Listener put the flute down, rose, and said, 'Forgive me for offending your ears.'

The Magician shook his head, smiling. 'Oh, you didn't do that,' said he, 'for you are neither incompetent nor a man of ill will. Indeed, one can learn a good deal about you, hearing you try to make your own will felt. I would like to teach you a little of my art, but we haven't any time for that now. The Great Magician is waiting for you, and the Keeper of the Falcons will take you to him.'

When this personage too, highest of all in rank after the Great Magician himself, greeted him in very friendly tones, Listener began to see a certain comedy in the way he was passed on from one to another here in Falkinor: from the gatekeeper to the captain of the guard, from the captain to the court official, from him to the Master of Music, who was now consigning him to the care of the Keeper of the Falcons, to be taken by the latter to the Great Magician himself. He was going up and up on the ladder of the hierarchy, and at every upward rung these people became friendlier. If this went on, the lord of Falkinor would be embracing him like an old friend.

As he tried to picture such a thing, he realized that he was trembling at the knees. Only now did he actually take in what the Master of Music had said when he came back into the room, and he wondered if that amiable old man had not been sounding him out, after his own fashion. 'One can learn a good deal about you' – just what had his flute-playing given away? He had no time to think about it any further, for the Keeper of the Falcons was showing him to the door, while the musical Lesser Magician raised a hand in friendly farewell – or was the gesture one of mockery? Who knew?

But now he had to keep close behind the red-robed Keeper of the Falcons as he strode on fast down the dim corridor. Listener followed him up great flights of stairs, through suites of rooms, up more stairs, ever onward and upward in this towering labyrinth, sparsely lit by flickering oil lamps. The soft pile of carpets swallowed up the sound of their footsteps; sometimes the curious outline of some strange figure emerged from the shadows, or of a device whose purpose Listener could not tell, but he had no time to look more closely at these peculiar objects, for the red robe was already well ahead of him. The Great Magician seemed to be in great haste to meet his guest.

Listener was quite out of breath when he finally stood before that door of which he knew already, from Narzia's tale. The soft light of the two oil lamps barely illuminated its dark, bronze surface; only the falcon's head in the centre, polished by the touch of many hands, shone in the twilight before the Keeper of the Falcons lifted it, calling forth that deep, throbbing hum that made the air in the rooms and corridors vibrate. Then the door slid back, revealing a great room filled with the red light of the setting sun.

Listener had been prepared for the sudden dazzling brightness Narzia had mentioned, but the sun had already sunk into the haze on the horizon, hanging there like a gigantic red globe just above the purple outlines of distant hills. The view from such a height was so impressive that Listener stood there spellbound. Finally the Keeper of the Falcons took his elbow and propelled him through the doorway ahead of himself. Once they were in the room, he said, 'I have brought you that fluter called Listener, who rode your stallion Morning Star.'

Listener bowed in the general direction of the person to whom his companion had spoken, for he could not actually see much more than a shadow standing at the great west window. This shadow came soundlessly closer, took on shape and form, and then Listener was looking into the face of the Great Magician. It was a face whose features, despite their strangeness, struck him as curiously familiar: a thin face with a hooked and prominent nose, the white brows above it looking as if they were painted on the high, smooth forehead with a brush, the face of an old man with hair white as snow and cut short. But Listener was fascinated chiefly by the man's eyes, eyes as green as moss, unchanged by age.

'Welcome to Falkinor, Listener,' said the Great Magician, in a clear, metallic voice. 'I have been told such remarkable things about you that I should like to talk to you a little.' Then he thanked the Keeper of the Falcons for bringing his guest to him, and dismissed him.

If Listener had thought they were now about to discuss the matter of the stallion, he was wrong. The Great Magician put a friendly arm around his shoulders, led him to a comfortable chair by a table in front of the west window, and asked him to sit down. Then he seated himself opposite, and looked at his guest for a while in silence. Listener was surprised to see how simply the lord of Falkinor was clad. He wore a kind of black woollen habit, held in with a leather belt. His narrow, slender-boned hands were in curious contrast to that simple garment; they rested lightly on its coarse weave, and a great emerald in a golden setting made in the form of a falcon's head sparkled in the dwindling light upon the middle finger of his right hand. Listener found himself staring at the ring, and quickly turned his glance away, as if the Great Magician could guess the thoughts that came into his head when he saw the ring. And perhaps he could, for he said, 'You have come a long way to win Honi's daughter. She is obviously as lovely as her mother was.'

'Did you know her mother, then?' asked Listener.

The Great Magician smiled. 'Why, were you not aware?' he said. 'There was a time when I was known as Vendikar, Keeper of the Falcons. Should I not know my own daughter?'

Now Listener understood why the Great Magician's face had seemed so familiar to him, and he wondered if Narzia had known that it was her grandfather whose ring he was to bring her. In the circumstances, at least, the Great Magician would surely not refuse him the horse. However, just at the moment his thoughts seemed far from any discussion of the stallion; instead, he asked for news of his granddaughter, whom he had never seen, and Honi, of whose opposition to the Khan he had already heard something. 'I met this Arni at Honi's wedding,' he said. 'Even then, he kept aloof from his own people, and sought to talk with myself and the other Lesser Magicians. He held some peculiar views for a Raiding Rider. I once asked him if he would stay with us. The Master of the Stones had just died at the time, and we would happily have taken Arni into our circle. He asked for a little while to think it over, but in the end refused. He said he could not live outside the steppes for very long, and moreover, he had already made a firm decision to stay with the horde. I asked him if he hoped to alter the Raiding Riders' way of life, and he shrugged his shoulders and said, "Can one force a man to change his view of good and evil? All I know is what I myself would like to be." And when I remarked that every peaceable dog has a wolf for ancestor, he answered, "If you forbid an old wolf to go raiding, he will die or run mad." So I am all the more surprised by what you say concerning Arni's Folk.'

'Yet Arni's words and deeds did not die with him,' said Listener, and only the expression of slight surprise on the Great Magician's face made him realize that as he spoke, he had fallen into that solemn manner of speech in which such remarks were commonly uttered by Arni's Folk.

'I wonder if that was what Arni had in mind,' said the Great Magician.

'Honi's sure it was,' said Listener. 'They chose him as Arni's Deputy because no one can interpret Arni's words better.'

Listener's enthusiasm seemed to amuse the Great Magician. 'No need to extol Honi's capabilities to me,' he said, smiling. 'I knew him as a man clever in argument, and always keeping to practicable notions. He is neither a doubter nor a dreamer. If Honi undertakes to do something, then he knows exactly why. Perhaps Arni gave him a few ideas, but you may believe me when I say creating the community of Arni's Folk was Honi's work. And perhaps my daughter's too, a little. She died only just before the event you call the Great Parting, and I dare say she had her own opinion of the Raiding Riders' way of life.'

'I don't know anything about that,' said Listener. 'But if what you think is so, then Narzia has taken on her mother's role. Her father sets great store by what she says.'

'Then if you want her for your wife you had better make sure, in good time, that she sets great store by what *you* say,' said the Great Magician. 'Now, how did you actually come among Arni's Folk? Looking as you do, you can't be one of the horde yourself.'

'I am the Bearer of the Stone,' said Listener, with some pride, and he explained briefly how he had come by that honour. The Great Magician listened intently, and said at last, when he had finished his tale, 'Yes, in the circumstances, I see that Honi was obliged to bring you into his game. A man who calls upon Arni can't disregard his stone, even if he has to accept a genuine heir into the bargain.'

Listener found this view of things rather disconcerting. 'What do you mean by "into the bargain"?' he said, with a touch of pique in his voice. 'Honi has no objection to my wooing his daughter, after all!'

This argument made the Great Magician laugh. 'Precisely,' he said. 'I see the workings of Honi's mind in that very point! Either you will perish on one of these adventurous journeys, which are not without their dangers, and then you'll be out of his way, or if you survive then you will have shown yourself a capable man, who can be expected to be useful to the community in the future. Does that surprise you? You should accustom yourself to such notions if you mean to be an important personage among these people.'

'Are you telling me Narzia would play such a game too?' said Listener angrily. 'I don't believe it!'

'Well, that's your right,' said the Great Magician, and this seemed to end the discussion, so far as he was concerned. He picked up a silver bell standing on the table and rang it. The clear, penetrating sound had hardly died away before the deep bronze note of the door sounded in the room, and next moment the Keeper of the Falcons entered.

'I will ask you to take this young fluter home as your guest,' the Great Magician told him. 'He has been passed from one to another in my house long enough. He must be hungry, and tired too, with such a long ride behind him.'

Listener rose, bowed, and prepared to follow the red-robed Keeper, but the Great Magician detained him a moment. 'I would like to hear you play tomorrow,' he said. 'Come to me in the afternoon!' Listener nodded, and as he was turning to go the Great Magician added quite casually, as if it were a matter of no particular importance, 'And by the way, the horse is yours. Do as you think fit with him.'

As soon as the bronze door had closed behind him, Listener was overcome by such weariness that he was hardly able to follow the Keeper of the Falcons, who led him at his usual brisk pace through a tangled confusion of passages and suites of rooms until they reached those apartments in which he lived. Here a slender woman of uncertain age took charge of Listener. He did not know if she was his host's wife, or some kind of servant, but she set a meal before him, and he ate some of it, though he was half asleep already and could not really tell what it was. All he felt after that was someone helping him to undress, and he was asleep almost before he was in his bed, where he slept a deep and dreamless sleep all night and far into the next day.

At last sunlight awakened him. The window of the room in which he woke faced south, and judging from the height of the sun it must be nearly noon. Listener rose, washed in a basin of water that he found beside his bed, and dressed. Then he was not sure what to do next. It is always slightly awkward, waking in the house of strangers whose ways one doesn't know, and Listener could not now remember where the only door of this room led. As he stood indecisively at the window, looking out at the landscape of meadows and trees that stretched below, with the great curves of the Brown River flowing through the plain, its waters shining in the sunlight all the way to the horizon, he tried to recollect the events of the previous day. He vaguely remembered his conversation with the Great Magician, and knew that what the Magician said had irritated him in some way or other. But in the end he had given him the stallion, that Listener did remember. And today he was to play to the Great Magician. He got out his flute and practised for a while, without really knowing what he was going to play. As if of themselves, memories of the noble ideals of Arni's Folk came into the music, and as he listened to himself playing, it struck Listener that the Great Magician had expressed some doubt of those ideals yesterday evening. But then he remembered Narzia's green eyes, and swayed by her gaze and the whisperings of his flute he felt less inclined than ever to entertain such doubts himself. What did that old man know of Arni's Folk? He had never lived with them himself, he had only a few days' intimate knowledge of Honi, or rather of the young man Honi had been many years ago. And he didn't know his granddaughter at all. If he knew she had inherited his eyes, he would not speak of her as he had. Listener's thoughts were all bent on his falcon maiden now, and a vision rose before him in which he saw Narzia soaring in the sky on slender wings. Or was it himself hovering beneath the clouds, carried up on the wind? In the melody of his flute, he let the falcon rise until it disappeared into the blue of the sky, and then lowered the instrument.

'That was a fine tune,' said the Keeper of the Falcons, who had come into the room unnoticed. 'I saw my falcons fly as I heard you. I think you love those noble birds yourself.'

'One in particular,' said Listener.

'Is it your own?' asked the Keeper of the Falcons.

'Not yet,' said Listener, 'but I have half won it now.'

The Keeper of the Falcons smiled. 'It takes a great deal of patience to catch a falcon,' he said. 'And even more to tame it.'

'So I have found myself,' said Listener, beginning to wonder if his host guessed whom he really meant. But the Keeper dropped the subject, and invited him to come and eat.

The Great Magician sent for Listener late that afternoon. When they were alone together, he asked to see the flute, and examined it for a long time. He seemed particularly interested in the fivefold ring at the end of the gilded pipe, and passed his finger over its indentations, as if to feel something that his eyes could not make out. Finally he gave Listener back the flute, saying, 'Now play me something, whatever comes into your mind.'

Listener felt as if he had forgotten every tune he ever knew. However, he put the flute to his lips and left it to the instrument to guide his fingers. Once again, the flute began to speak of Arni's Folk, whose friendship could bring nothing but good to anyone who won it. They travelled the whole land with their packhorses, paying good silver for the wares offered them, peaceful men who had forgotten the war-cry of the horde, and always spoke courteously, ever concerned to follow the lofty teachings of Arni . . .

'No more of that!' said the Great Magician, interrupting Listener's playing with a brusque movement of his hand.

'Didn't my music please you?' asked Listener, dismayed.

'You're a good fluter, if that is what you want to hear,' said the Great Magician. 'But I've learned enough of these Folk of Arni's now. Tell me about the man who gave you this flute!' And when Listener opened his mouth, he raised a hand, adding, 'Not with words! Let your flute speak of him.'

This demand caught Listener entirely unprepared. He was aware that it was a long time since he had thought of his apprentice days with his grandfather. He began with the call of the blackbird who had been the Gentle Fluter's messenger, and those three notes awoke a memory of the green hills beyond the forests of Barlebogue. The Gentle Fluter came out of the bushes with his dancing step, playing that sweet and peaceful song with which he had calmed the furious Barlo, a tune that brought tears to the eyes. The low-built house where Listener had lived with the Gentle Fluter during the last days of his life nestled under the old lime trees in the hollow of the valley, flowers at its windows; once more he lay on his bed, saw the shadows of the leafy branches playing on the walls of his room in the moonlight, once again he heard his grandfather's life take shape in the music of the flute, a pattern woven of countless differing incidents, its separate parts yet remaining alive, each tiny and apparently insignificant gracenote able to give rise to new developments, spreading out in waves, until the little house was full of a world embracing all that had ever happened, or ever would happen, yet that overwhelming fullness did not burst its unassuming walls apart. Once again he saw himself standing by the bed where his grandfather lay on a white linen sheet, quiet and cheerful, the flute in his hands; he saw himself go through the empty rooms, look at the neatly ranged pots and pans on the kitchen shelves, raise the trapdoor and climb down into the dark cellar; he groped his way past shelves bearing jars of pickled cucumber, pushed aside his grandfather's herbal elixirs and felt for those dusty little flasks whose labels promised good and evil, strength and a change to stone, sweet dreams and the descent into a dark and bottomless pit where all longing petrified to frozen terror and dissolved into the emptiness of that which did not move, could not be heard, had no being, was nothing . . .

When Listener came back to his senses, he could still hear the painful echo of a single shrill note ringing in his ears. Before it died away, it must have been quivering in the air of the room who knew how long? The Great Magician was leaning back in his chair as if to ward it off, and his usually calm face showed a trace of horror. He had to pull himself together before he could speak, and then he said, 'That was not the way your master sent you, Listener. I knew the man they called the Gentle Fluter. Sit down here beside me, and I will tell you about him.

It was about thirty years ago your grandfather came to Falkinor. I had just been accepted into the circle of the five Lesser Magicians as Keeper of the Falcons. Previously, I had served in the mews, before ending up in charge there, for I had to learn all there is to know about birds of prey. I had made friends at this time with the overseer of the stables, a man called Ernebar. This Ernebar was a quiet and thoughtful man, never quick-tempered, most certainly never angry, and that was why the Great Magician had entrusted his horses to him.

I was all the more surprised, and so was everyone else employed about the place, when I happened to be standing outside the mews one morning and Ernebar came bursting out of the Great House in an obvious rage. He was stammering something meaningless, and foaming at the mouth, and before anyone could stop him he reached the stables, flung the gate open, untied the twenty-five stallions standing there, and drove them out into the yard, yelling wildly and cracking a whip. The horses raced about the walled yard like creatures possessed, rearing, kicking, running down anyone who stood in their path. Unfortunately the outer gate of the yard had just been opened, and before the guards could close it again the horses had discovered this way of escape and were making for it.

Our hearts all missed a beat when, at that very moment, a slender, slight-limbed man with curly grey hair came strolling calmly through the gate, playing a silver flute. He took no notice whatever of all the uproar, but walked straight towards the horses thundering towards him, his feet almost dancing; he seemed utterly absorbed in his playing. We could all see him lying there next moment trampled to pulp by the horses' hooves, but no such thing happened: as soon as the horses heard the melody of the flute they slowed to a walk, stopped, and snuffled at the paved ground as if disappointed to find no grass growing there. Finally the grooms ventured to approach the stallions, whereupon they all allowed themselves to be led back to their stables, perfectly docile, while the fluter saw to the mule he had left outside the gateway.

Meanwhile, Ernebar had been overpowered. He had struggled like a madman, and it took four men to restrain him, or he would have broken free again. A crowd of people were standing around, brought out of the house by all the noise, among them some of the court officials, and also Finistar, who had been Master of the Herbs and one of the five Lesser Magicians for some time. They were all talking at once, most of them claiming loudly that Ernebar was possessed by evil spirits. At this point the fluter made his way through the circle of onlookers, looked at Ernebar, who was still struggling with the four men, his face distorted into horrible grimaces, and then said, 'What's all this nonsense about evil spirits and the like? The man is sick. We must help him.'

When some of the people asked if he thought he could cure Ernebar, he said he would try. But then Finistar spoke up, saying if anyone in Falkinor had a right to heal the sick, then he did, for he was Master of the Herbs, and he was not going to let strangers meddle in his affairs. Moreover, he asked the fluter, what was his business here?

I was amazed, at the time, by the fluter's steadfast cheerfulness. We all of us knew Finistar's irascible nature, and were used to seeing him lose his temper easily, but the fluter had never set eyes on him before, and might well have taken offence. However, Finistar's unfriendly remarks ran off him like so much water. He said he had come to Falkinor because he had heard there were wise men to be found here. He saw that he had just met one of them, and was glad so experienced a master would be caring for this unfortunate man. He spoke with so friendly a smile that the angry Finistar was quite at a loss. Before he could think of a suitable answer, the fluter had bowed courteously and withdrawn from the circle of people.

I had already been impressed to see this unassuming, friendly man calm the horses, but I thought him even more remarkable after his conversation with Finistar. I followed him, spoke to him, and asked him to be my guest for as long as he liked. He accepted my invitation without more ado, and stayed in the Great House with me for a couple of weeks.

During that time, the following events occurred. Finistar had had the overseer of the stables, who was still hard to control, shut up in a room near the stables themselves, and he brewed all kinds of decoctions of herbs, which he gave his patient to drink. But Ernebar's condition did not improve. At times, to be sure, he sat apathetically in a corner of his room, brooding darkly, but then he would unexpectedly fall into a fit of madness again, his frenzy taking such dangerous forms that no one dared go into the room alone. The fluter inquired after the state of his health regularly, and when there was no change in it after a week, he shook his head in distress, and let it be seen that he was sorry he might not offer the Master of the Herbs a few modest pieces of advice to help with the treatment of this difficult case.

I was quite sure that Finistar would never permit it. However, Ernebar was my friend, and I would not leave anything that might help him untried. So I took the matter to the Great Magician, who had by now learned to value the company of the fluter, and liked his music so much that the then Master of Music once asked if he meant to be unfaithful to the beneficial powers of our own five-tone system. The question, however, was put only in jest, for he too liked the fluter, and they would often spend hours discussing problems of musical theory which were far beyond my understanding.

The Great Magician thought it over for a while, and then said, "It is a Magician's duty to be ready to learn all his life, and if Finistar won't see that, I think we must step in. If he doesn't succeed in curing the sick man tomorrow, let the fluter try his arts. I will be present myself, and you shall accompany me."

And so it was. Ernebar was calm that morning. He could be seen through a crack in the door crouching motionless in a corner of the bare room. Finistar had mixed another of his herbal brews, but he sent four strong men into the room first, to hold Ernebar down while he gave him the medicinal liquid. Then he hastily withdrew, and not a moment too soon, for as soon as the men had let go of the poor overseer, and bolted the door again, Ernebar began to rant and rave. Then the Gentle Fluter stepped forward, took up his instrument and began to play.

I find it hard to describe that music. It sounded as if the fluter were calling to someone hidden very far away, someone so frightened that he dared not come out of his hiding place. In his playing, the fluter exposed himself entirely, naked and unprotected, showing his empty hands and telling the listener to come out and have no more fear. And as he played, he made me a sign to unbolt the door. I looked inquiringly at the Great Magician, and at his nod I pushed back the bolt. The fluter played all the while the door was slowly opening, and then he handed me his instrument, went to Ernebar, who was now standing on the threshold, and took him in his arms like a child who has been afraid and needs comfort.

Ernebar looked like a man waking from a long sleep. At last he freed himself from the fluter's embrace, looked around him, confused, and asked what all this meant, and who the stranger was who had been holding him in his arms. The fluter told him he had not been very well, but he was over the worst of it now.

Finistar stood close to them, and the expression on his face showed that he was not particularly pleased with this turn of events. He was still holding the flask from which he had given the sick man his herbal brew, and the fluter now began to show an interest in that medicine. He asked the Master of the Herbs if he would allow him to look at the decoction. Finistar looked as if he were going to refuse angrily at first, but a glance from the Great Magician served to restrain him and remind him of his duties. He gave the fluter the flask, saying, if not in any very friendly tone, "A Magician must be ready to go on learning all his life."

The fluter examined the contents of the little flask, and sniffed it, and I had the impression that he shook his head, almost imperceptibly. Then he gave the flask back to Finistar, murmuring something that was plainly meant for his ears alone. I thought I caught the words "too strong", but I could have been mistaken; it seemed to me, however, if I remember correctly, that Finistar suddenly turned pale. If so, the fluter took no notice of it, but dropped the names of a few herbs that he would recommend for further treatment of the case. The fluter's knowledge of the effects of medicinal herbs utterly confused poor Finistar. He bowed nervously, and hurried away "to try them out", as he said. I think he was glad to be able to withdraw in good order. From that day on, Ernebar had no more fits of frenzy, although his demeanour was rather anxious ever afterwards, like that of a child who has been severely and unjustly beaten. Later on, for that reason, we had to abandon our plan of receiving him into the circle of Lesser Magicians as Master of the Horses. He died a few years ago.'

The Great Magician was silent for a while, as if seeking a suitable way of passing to another subject he wished to mention. 'So now you know,' he said at last, 'how I met your grandfather. But there is another reason why I told you that story. Finistar is still Master of the

Herbs in this house, and I see I must now question him in a matter that concerns you too.' He rang the little silver bell that stood on the table, and when the Keeper of the Falcons entered a moment later, asked him to fetch the Master of the Herbs.

Listener wondered what could be the connection between himself and this Finistar, but the Great Magician offered no further explanations. He looked thoughtfully into space and said not a word until the resonant note of the bronze door announced the arrival of the two men he expected.

Finistar was a tall, lean old man, with bushy white eyebrows, and the rather prominent eyes of a man who is easily angered. He wore a green silk robe, and had the air of a personage well aware of his own dignity. When the Great Magician had thanked the Keeper of the Falcons and dismissed him, Finistar bowed, and asked what the lord of Falkinor wanted.

'I want to talk to you about something which also concerns this young fluter,' said the Great Magician. 'Sit down with us, will you?'

Listener had risen respectfully to greet the Master of the Herbs with a bow, which Finistar returned only sketchily. They both sat down, and the Great Magician said, 'I must awaken a memory of long ago in you, Finistar, and one that you won't much welcome. Some thirty years since, we had another fluter as our guest in Falkinor, the man who gave you some help in curing Ernebar, the overseer of the stables. Do you remember?'

Finistar's face darkened. 'That's long ago indeed,' he said, hesitantly. 'Is there any reason for you to recall that stranger to my mind, after so long a time?'

'Yes, I am sure there is,' said the Great Magician. 'I would like, first, to talk to you about the day when that fluter rode away on his mule, some weeks after the healing of Ernebar. I recollect that you came down to the yard on purpose to see him off, and you gave him something to take on his journey. I was a little surprised at the time, for my impression had been that you did not particularly like the man. And now I am wondering just what it was you gave him.'

'How can I remember these trivial things after so many years?' said Finistar. But the Great Magician was not satisfied with this answer. 'I don't think they were trivial,' he said. 'I will give your memory a little help: they were small flasks such as you use for your herbal brews.'

'Oh, you mean that!' said Finistar. 'Yes, I had made him a draught that can be very useful to the traveller. It gives a weary man fresh strength, if only for an hour.'

'And lays him out for three days afterwards!' said Listener.

Finistar cast him a dark glance, and said, 'I did not suppose the fluter so stupid as to use that draught at the wrong time.'

'And you were quite right, too,' said the Great Magician. 'I fancy he was also wise enough not even to open the other flasks you gave him.'

'What other flasks?' asked Finistar, but the hunted expression in his eyes plainly showed that he knew what the Great Magician meant.

'If you will not admit to them,' said the Great Magician, 'then you are also admitting that you meant to harm that fluter. Shall I tell you what fate you intended for him? Black dreams of nothingness, or for his body to be turned to stone!'

'He knew what the flasks contained!' cried Finistar. 'I wrote the labels in his own language, on purpose! I am not to blame for anything.'

'You are a clever man, Finistar,' said the Great Magician, 'and I will tell you what was in your mind: at some time or other, everyone comes to the edge of such despair that he would reach for an elixir of that kind, and this fluter – so you said to yourself – will be no exception. How often have you wondered if he has yet met with the harm you meant him?'

Finistar bowed his head, and said no more, but the Great Magician had not finished. 'You underestimated the man, Finistar,' he said. 'He withstood the temptation. However, his grandson here found your flasks, and fell into the power of the black dreams instead.'

'I'll cure him,' said Finistar hastily, but the Great Magician shook his head. 'How can I trust you now?' he asked. 'I will see to the matter myself, for I too understand a little of such things.'

Finistar rose. 'Then I suppose you will allow me to leave,' he said.

'No!' said the Great Magician, incisively and sharply. He did not ask Finistar to be seated again, but went straight on. 'Out of all this, I find that another question arises: I cannot believe that you only wanted revenge for a humiliation inflicted upon you without any ill will by the fluter, in order to heal a sick man. I know now what it was the fluter said when he gave you back the flask whose contents the overseer of the stables had drunk. You had given Ernebar a strong poison to confuse his mind – and you gave it him before ever his sickness broke out.'

Now Finistar stood before the Great Magician slumped and broken, like a puppet with no will of its own. 'Nothing is hidden from you, lord,' he said quietly. 'I will tell you everything, before you thrust me out of the circle of the Lesser Magicians. Not long before those things of which we have been speaking happened, you were chosen Keeper of the Falcons, and I was one of those who spoke on your behalf. I say that not to win your favour now, but because it partly explains my conduct. I had always admired you, even when you were still Vendikar, Overseer of the Mews, for not only were you clever, you could also win people's liking with your friendly manner. I have always been a reserved man, at odds with myself, and thus, perhaps, impatient with others. And so I have never had any real friend. When you were raised to your new dignity, I determined to seek your friendship, yet though you had a kind word for everyone else, you were always cool to me. Ernebar could speak to you whenever he liked, although he was not one of our circle; I saw the pair of you daily walking arm in arm across the yard; when you rode out hawking he was at your side, and he mixed with your family like a close relation. Then I began to hate Ernebar, for I had come to believe that only he prevented you from paying me any attention, and so I decided to get him out of the way in this manner. It was not hard to give him the poison; he had no suspicions. I was afraid, at first, the fluter might have told the Great Magician what he had discovered. By the time I realized that he had held his peace, he was long gone, riding the country on his mule again, and the thought of the danger into which I had led him robbed me of sleep. Perhaps it will give you some satisfaction to know that since that time, I have lived a lonelier life than ever.'

The Great Magician shook his head. 'It gives me no satisfaction at all; it saddens me,' he said. 'I see now that I myself bear some responsibility for the wrong you did.' He rose, went over to the old man, and put an arm around his shoulders, and stood there for a while, looking at the floor, as if in search of some way out of a difficulty. Then he raised his head, saying, 'I am very sorry, but I can't let you hold your office any longer.'

'I know,' said Finistar, 'and I don't reproach you for that. When am I to leave your house, lord?'

'Not at all, if you would rather stay,' said the Great Magician at once. 'We shall have much to say to one another, in so far as you will allow me to make up a little for what I have left undone. And do not call me lord, for I am in your debt too.' So saying, he dismissed Finistar.

Listener had been following the two old men's conversation intently.

He felt drawn into a web of events that reached far beyond his own involvement in them, and his original dislike of Finistar had gradually turned to pity. The Great Magician looked thoughtfully at him, and after a while he said, 'So one fault grows from another, and if you inquire long enough you find your own in the end. One always plays some part in those events one witnesses. Now, bring me the flask that gives sweet and black dreams. After what I have now learned, I am all the more bound to keep you back from the brink of the abyss to which you have ventured.'

When Listener came back with the flask, the Great Magician had kindled a fire in the hearth by the wall of the room. He took the little flask that was the size of an apple from Listener's hand, and read the writing on the label, which was partly washed away by the waters of the Brown River, but could still be deciphered. 'Some time or other, you would have tasted the third drop too,' he said. 'Finistar knew very well where this brew would drive a man who had once drunk of it.'

He laid the little flask in the fire, took a poker from the wall and smashed it. The brown liquid sizzled, foaming over the burning logs, draining the flames of their colour; they faded to a pale violet, became transparent, and if the shimmering heat had not made the pattern of the tiles at the back of the hearth quiver you might have thought the fire had gone out. The strong fragrance of herbs given off by the bubbling liquid was pleasant at first, but soon became overpowering, smoke spread over the floor of the room like pale mist and began to rise, it rose and rose, and the room itself grew darker at the same time, although it was still broad daylight outside the window, but the light was thrust back by the blackness that inexorably spread, like thick mud, soon lapping around Listener's neck, and at last climbing above his eyes.

When Listener came back to his senses, he was lying full length on the rug by the hearth, and the fire had gone out. The Great Magician was leaning over him, putting a goblet to his mouth. Listener felt a cool, aromatic liquid on his lips, and drank thirstily. The dizziness which had been making his head go round instantly went away. 'Can you stand up?' asked the Great Magician. Listener tried, and against all his expectations, he was able to get to his feet at once. 'There, sit down at the table,' said the Great Magician, seating himself on the other chair. 'How do you feel?'

'Still a little dazed,' said Listener, attempting a wry smile.

'That will soon pass,' said the Great Magician. 'You will never again feel any desire to taste those drops, even if you still had them with you. But I cannot take the memory of your dreams from you, Listener. You will have to live with it from now on. Now, you had better go to sleep. I will ride out hawking with you tomorrow morning.'

Listener was woken by the Keeper of the Falcons at dawn. Still half asleep, he drank a mug of milk and ate a piece of bread, and then his host urged him to set out. 'We don't want to keep the Great Magician waiting,' he said, going to the stables with Listener. As Listener was saddling his gelding, the Great Magician himself came into the stables and stopped beside him. 'Won't you ride your stallion today?' he asked.

Listener had already thought of saddling the black horse, but had not ventured to do so, not knowing how the stallion's former owner would take it. Now that the Great Magician himself suggested it, Listener took the saddle off his gelding again, put it and the bridle on the black stallion, and led him out into the yard. The Keeper of the Falcons was already waiting there, along with a groom who had three falcons sitting on the crossbar of the perch he carried. Soon the little cavalcade was trotting out through the gateway.

While they were riding down the street past the houses of Falkinor they had to keep their horses reined in, even though people respectfully made way for them and bowed low to the Great Magician. Once in the open country, they broke into a fast trot. The black stallion stepped out so lightly that Listener felt he was hovering above the turf. No mount had ever carried him as gently, except his donkey Yalf in those years when he rode the land with Barlo. He felt lighter at heart and more carefree than he had for a long time, and wondered whether it was due to the noble horse, or the secret arts of the black-clad man trotting on before him. Listener was surprised to see the Great Magician still so upright in the saddle, despite his great age; he rode his white horse ahead of them all, setting the pace. After a while, he beckoned Listener to his side, and asked, 'Have you ever hunted with hawks before?'

'No,' said Listener. 'Only with bow and arrows.'

'Did you hunt birds?' asked the Great Magician.

'Seldom,' said Listener. 'Wolves, mostly. That's easier, I think.'

'More dangerous too, though, for the hunter,' said the Great Magician. 'Hawking is more like a game, though one must master its rules well. All you decide is the time at which the hunt begins, by flying your falcon at the right moment. In that hunt itself you take no part; you are only a spectator, trusting your luck to your falcon's skill. Or that's how many people see it. But it may be that your soul flies with the falcon, and goes hunting free of the body's limitations, and that that is what lends hawking its delights and its dignity.' And then he told Listener what to do when he took the falcon on his fist.

When they reached a wood on the banks of the Brown River, Listener remembered Narzia's tale. If she had passed on her father's account correctly, this must be the same poplar wood where Honi had hunted his white heron. As soon as they had reached the shade of the tall trees they dismounted, and the groom rammed the perch he was carrying into the ground. He held the hunters' gauntlets ready for them, and then each man took his falcon on his fist. The first flight was the Great Magician's. He waited until the groom had scared a couple of herons out of the trees, and then threw up his falcon. The powerful bird, its plumage flecked with white, rose quickly into the air, chose its prey from among the fleeing herons, swooped down, and both birds fell slowly to the ground, like a single four-winged creature, in a flurry of beating pinions and circling downy feathers.

Then it was Listener's turn. The Great Magician rode a little way upstream with him, while the groom beat the bushes along the bank in search of further prey. They heard him crashing through the undergrowth, and then he let out a yell; next moment three herons, beating their wings loudly, flew out of the tops of the trees. Listener took the hood off his falcon and flung it into the air, almost too fast, for the bird fluttered unsteadily overhead for a moment before getting its balance and beginning to make its way upwards. Listener's eyes followed it. He could feel, almost physically, how the widespread pinions were borne up on the air, carrying the falcon on towards its prey; a few moments later, it was hovering above the last of the herons, which were trying to describe a wide arc and get back to the safety of the trees on the bank, and then it fell steeply, swooping down. Listener felt his fingers tense as if he himself must sink his talons into the gleaming feathers, and then the falcon had seized its prey, and was spinning earthwards, united with it. Listener had been holding his breath, as if under great strain, and audibly let it out as the combat finished, and the heron lay on the grass beneath the falcon, twitching.

When the Keeper of the Falcons had tried his own luck, though his bird made no kill, they went back to their horses and sat on the grass.

The groom had already taken their falcons, put the birds back on their perch, and was now rewarding them with some morsels of meat. Then he fetched bread and cold roast fowl from the saddle-bag of his horse and laid it in front of the hunters.

As they ate, the Great Magician said to Listener, 'I watched you when your falcon flew. I think you understand now what I was saying about the delights of hawking.'

'Yes, I did feel them,' said Listener. 'Honi must have felt something similar when he came hawking here with your daughter. Narzia told me about that.'

'So he may have done,' said the Great Magician, 'though perhaps the circumstances were rather different.'

Indeed they were, thought Listener, wishing heartily he were hawking here with Narzia, and could take his prey in his arms as Honi had done.

When they had eaten, the Keeper of the Falcons rose, saying he would go a little way farther along the river with the groom and see if he could bring a heron down this time. Obviously his earlier failure nettled him, especially as the novice Listener had brought down prey at the first attempt. The Great Magician had no objection, and when the two men had disappeared around the next bend of the river, he asked Listener, 'Have you brought your flute with you?'

Listener took his instrument out, saying, 'I would never go very far from my flute.'

'Have you become so used to holding people spellbound with its voice?' said the Great Magician, smiling, looking at Listener with his green eyes. 'Try your art on me again!'

Listener no longer saw the old man's stern face, but only Narzia's green eyes; he let his flute speak of her, and in his song he once more dreamed the dream of his meeting with the falcon maiden in a forest clearing. The double transformation took place again, but when Listener was about to let his pinions carry him soaring to the clouds, a flash of green light met his eyes. Brought abruptly out of his dream song, Listener stared at the emerald sparkling in the sunlight on the Great Magician's hand, and a thought immediately came into his head: this was the moment when the power of his flute might move the Great Magician to give him the ring. No sooner had he thought of it than his flute took up the theme, its persuasive notes urging the owner of the ring to take the jewel from his finger and give it to the fluter, who could not win his falcon maiden without it.

But when Listener took the flute from his lips and looked up, he saw at first glance that the Great Magician had seen through his game. Experienced as he was in all magical arts, he was not to be led to do anything unawares. However, he was obviously not angry with Listener for making the attempt; instead, he seemed rather amused. 'So my granddaughter wants this ring!' he said, smiling, and made the emerald sparkle in the sun. 'You could have told me so straight out! But do you know the properties of the falcon ring?' And when Listener, rather ashamed of himself, shook his head, he went on, 'Then I will tell you. Before you decide whether to take her the ring, you ought to know the power that lies in it. The wearer of the ring is able to change men into animals, for a time or for ever. Doesn't it strike you as dangerous to give your future wife such power over you?'

Now Listener might almost have laughed to think how little this old magician knew of the desires of the young, for he had instantly realized what Narzia had in mind when she wished for the ring.

'May I ask you a question to do with the ring?' he asked, and when the Great Magician nodded, he went on, 'Can you tell me if your predecessor ever took it from his finger and lent it to someone else?'

The Great Magician looked at him in surprise. 'How do you know that?' he asked.

'I don't know it for sure,' said Listener. 'I only suspect he did.'

'Well, your suspicion is correct,' said the Great Magician. 'My daughter wore this ring on her finger for the space of a day. She had asked the Great Magician of the time to lend it to her when she rode out hawking with Honi for the last time, and my predecessor loved her so much that he could not refuse her request.'

'That's what I thought,' said Listener, satisfied, and he saw Narzia in his mind's eye, telling him about that last hawking expedition. When Honi had brought down his white heron, and came back to his senses a man again, he had held his falcon maiden in his arms and kissed her, and Narzia would come to his own arms when he had given her the ring. 'That's what I thought,' repeated Listener, 'and it makes me want to take Narzia this ring even more.'

'Then you shall have it,' said the Great Magician, taking the ring from his finger and putting it into Listener's hand. 'But never say, afterwards, I didn't warn you.'

* * *

A few days later Listener was riding upstream along the Brown River again, on his own. This time he had saddled his gelding and had the stallion on a leading rein; he did not want to tire the horse unnecessarily on the long journey home, wishing to present him to Arni's Folk in all his elegance and splendour.

The farther he rode, the clearer were the signs of approaching autumn. The grass along the wayside had withered long ago and turned to matted tufts of grey stalks; the leaves on the trees and bushes in the woods along the riverbanks were already showing touches of yellow and light red. It was becoming noticeably cooler, and from time to time a stiff wind drove showers of rain over the wide plain, but that was not the reason why Listener spurred on his horse. He kept imagining the scene of his arrival in the village of Arni's Folk, he saw its people gathering in the street, but he rode past, ignoring them, until he reached Honi's house, where he waited for Narzia to step out of the doorway and come to meet him. Nothing would stand between them then. He could scarcely wait for his imaginings to become reality, and when the path allowed, he often rode on until well into the night, to shorten the distance still parting him from his falcon maiden.

At this time of year the border between the grassy plain and the steppes was hard to distinguish, but one day Listener became aware that he had left the pastures of the Falcon People behind him. The endless grey steppes reached eastward under the pale, greenish sky, covered by streaky clouds; no trees or bushes grew on the steppes, there was nothing but distance and the blurred horizon, but although Listener usually felt uneasy at this sight, he now welcomed it as a sign that he was a little nearer his journey's end. He spent only one night with the Carpheads, and rode straight on early next morning, although his hosts begged him to stay at least a week. When he refused their request, Listener saw regret in the Carphead people's pale blue eyes, but his longing for Narzia was stronger and urged him on. And when at last the Brown River turned westward, and the mountains came closer instead, Listener knew he had only a few more days to ride, and could scarcely sleep when he lay in the shelter of a bush at night, wrapped in his blanket.

At last, after another week's journey, he saw the settlement of Arni's Folk ahead once more, just as he had first seen it through the trees and bushes when he was in flight from the Raiding Riders. This time, too, he was exhausted after his long ride, but even if he had now had with him the flask of liquor giving strength for an hour, he would not have been tempted to taste it, for he expected to enjoy his return to the full very soon now, and for more than an hour. There were many people in the village street as he rode past the log cabins towards Honi's house, and he was pleased and proud to observe the admiring glances they cast at the black stallion. He dismounted at Arni's House and bowed low, as was the custom, but he was too impatient to stay in that position long, let alone wait for Honi to station his massive body next to him and adopt the same respectfully submissive attitude, groaning slightly with the effort. So Listener soon straightened his back again, turning to the house of Arni's Deputy, where Narzia was waiting for him. Honi was just stepping out of the door, and came to meet him.

'So there you are!' he said, rubbing his hands. 'I didn't expect you back so soon. And I see you've been successful, too. That's a fine horse you've brought us, a really fine horse!'

'The best to be had in all Falkinor,' said Listener. 'He's the noblest of the Great Magician's stallions.'

'You've proved yourself very useful indeed,' said Honi. 'I think the assembly of elders will say so too, and then we can consider the third task accomplished. Come along in! I've no objection if there's a certain question you want to ask Narzia now.' And he called to a servant, telling him to lead both horses to the stables and tend them well.

Listener was slightly taken aback by this reception. Honi had certainly seemed pleased, had even brought himself to utter words of praise, but his homecoming should surely have been greeted rather differently, though he himself could not have said just how. With more solemnity? More heartfelt rejoicing? As the return of a bold warrior from battle, with tears of joy in the eyes of those who had remained behind, expressing something of the fears they had suffered for the hero's safety? Narzia might at least have come out of the house, he thought. For whose sake had he undertaken so long a journey? Certainly not for that stout and self-satisfied man, who had briefly patted the beautiful horse's slender neck with the air of a horse dealer who has just driven a good bargain, before the groom led it away by the halter.

Listener was surprised at himself. What did he really want? He had come back, he had passed his test, and nothing could part him from Narzia now. And yet he felt out of humour, in a way that was hard to overcome, as he followed the solid figure of Arni's Deputy towards the house.

Honi stopped outside the living-room door and told Listener, 'There's someone in there waiting for you.' He gave him a meaning nod, and then began to search among some objects lying on the lid of a chest, obviously to give the impression that he didn't intend to go into the room himself, but would wait to hear what had happened inside. Listener had often been alone with Narzia, but there was something almost indecent about the way her father was urging him to go to her now, and he did not like it. He's sending me in like a stallion chosen for his stud, he thought, and would rather have turned away. But then he could bear no more of the sly, expectant glances Honi was giving him, and so he opened the door.

Narzia was standing by the window. She turned as Listener came in. At first he could make out only the outline of her slim figure against the light, but then she came to meet him, and at every step she took her face became more clearly visible, until her green eyes broke through the shadows and looked at him. Her features seemed to him familiar, and yet not just as he remembered them. For a moment he felt as if he were facing the Great Magician, but then Narzia smiled, and she was herself again, his falcon maiden, of whom he had dreamed all these past weeks.

'Did you see the black stallion?' he asked.

'A handsome horse,' she said. 'Just as I imagined the horses of Falkinor.'

Why are we standing here talking about horses, Listener wondered, although he had begun it himself. He gulped nervously and then said, 'Your father thinks I have now performed my third task.'

'That may well be so, in the eyes of the elders,' said Narzia, looking at him expectantly.

'But not in yours,' said Listener. 'Exactly as I thought myself!' He put his hand in his pocket, brought out the emerald ring, and gave it to her. 'Your grandfather, who is now the Great Magician, sends you this.'

Narzia looked at the ring, and at that moment her eyes were so like the sparkling emerald set in the golden falcon's head that Listener wondered if the light of the stone itself was reflected in them. 'The falcon ring!' she cried. 'You really brought it!' She put the ring on her finger, threw her arms around Listener's neck and kissed him on the mouth, and now, all of a sudden, everything was just as he had dreamed after all. He stood there as if thunderstruck, and when it finally occurred to him to put his own arms round her she had already stepped back, and he hadn't even asked her that question at which Honi had hinted. Listener seized Narzia's hand, as if afraid the girl might escape him yet again, and said quickly, 'Will you be my wife now, Narzia?'

Narzia looked at him in some surprise, saying, 'Why, yes, that's all agreed, Listener. I expect the elders will have a few more wise words to say on the subject tomorrow, but they can have no objections now.' She smiled at him, and added, 'You had better get some sleep!'

Sensible advice, thought Listener, and also a promising allusion to the next night's pleasures, so that this time he was not disappointed when she left him alone again.

Next morning was swallowed up in a whirl of preparations. Maid-servants poured buckets of water over the stone flags in the hall of the house, and not a room was safe from their cleaning cloths. The clatter of pots and pans came from the kitchen, where they were boiling and baking and roasting until the house was full of all kinds of aromas, of fish and of meat, both sweet and sour. Listener stood in a bathtub full of hot water and was scrubbed from head to foot by two of the maids, elderly but still inclined to giggle, who ended up – whether as a joke or part of their duties Listener was not sure – by trying to brush his thick body hair. This was too much for him, and he turned them out of the room before rubbing himself dry and putting on the embroidered white shirt they had laid ready for him. The pattern around the collar and sleeves showed alternate cranes and falcons pursuing one another. Listener wondered if Narzia had embroidered the shirt herself. He couldn't really imagine her sitting quietly by the window, putting thousands of stitches into its fabric.

Then Honi came in, and said it was time to go to Arni's House. 'And bring that bag you wore around your neck,' he added. 'You shall wear Arni's stone on your breast today.'

The entire assembly of elders had gathered in Arni's House. Honi asked Listener to perform his office as Bearer of the Stone. Listener went over to the golden dish, and stood there for some time, looking at his stone where it lay shining in the curve of the metal. Finally he took it out and put it in the leather bag on his breast. Then Honi went to him, laid a hand on his shoulder, and said, 'This young man, named Listener, has given three proofs of his abilities, and I now ask you as his proxy whether you, our elders, will recognize these proofs. First, he rode to the Mountain Badgers, and opened up our traders' way to them. This first ride has already brought us great profit. Second,

Listener rode to the camp of the Raiding Riders to replace those horses Khan Hunli lost through him, and moreover he beat the Khan at chess, thus considerably increasing the repute of Arni's Folk. And third, he has ridden to Falkinor and brought us one of the Great Magician's stallions, although the Falcon People have never before let a foreigner have such a horse. Give me your opinion, then, and say if he has passed his three tests.'

The elders put their heads together as if to discuss the case, but it was plain that they were doing so only for form's sake. None of what Honi had just said was any news to them. So it was not long before the eldest of the elders rose and said, 'Plainly Arni is with the young man whom he named Bearer of his Stone. We confirm, in all due form, that Listener has passed his three tests.'

'If that is your opinion, then I have a second matter to mention, speaking again as his proxy,' said Honi. 'This young man Listener, who has passed his three tests, asks for the hand of my daughter Narzia. Give me your opinion, then, of his request.'

Yet again the elders put their heads together, and after a remarkably short time the eldest of the elders rose again and asked, 'Are you, Honi, ready to sanction this marriage?'

'I am,' said Honi, 'and I am glad to be able to welcome a man of such useful abilities into my family.'

'And what does your daughter say?' asked the spokesman.

'Ask her yourselves!' said Honi, going to the door and opening it. Listener saw that Narzia was standing there outside. She wore a white linen dress embroidered with the same pattern as his shirt. It was pinned together over her breast with the falcon brooch he had brought her back from the Mountain Badgers, and the Great Magician's ring sparkled on her hand. 'Come in!' Arni told her. 'The elders want to hear your opinion of this marriage.'

Narzia stepped through the doorway and stood before the assembly. When the eldest of the elders repeated his question, she looked at Listener and said, 'I am ready to be the wife of this man who is known as Listener, the Bearer of the Stone.'

Nobody's asking me about it, thought Listener, but then he remembered that Honi had been speaking as his proxy all this time. Well, he thought, he would get his own word in sometime, even if he must wait until evening.

As indeed he must, for now the less formal part of the wedding festivities followed. As soon as Narzia had declared her willingness,

Honi invited the elders to his house, where a feast awaited them in the big living-room, such a feast as Listener had never seen set before him in his life. The tables were tottering under the weight of the dishes they bore: poached fish of every size, staring glassy-eyed, with bunches of herbs in their mouths, like their last meal; roast ducks and pigeons, pheasants and partridges were piled high, drumsticks handily offered to the guests; and in the middle of the table a whole sheep, roasted on the spit, was offered up split open and filled with a rich brown sauce in which sprigs of sage and thyme swam, like mourning favours from the bereaved. To one side of the main tables, the manservant in charge of the feast presided over long lines of jugs from which he poured wine for the guests as soon as they were seated: red wine, white wine, and the dark yellow, heavy, spicy wine of the south that tasted almost like medicine given to a dying man to numb his pain.

The edge was soon taken off Listener's hunger, and then he sat there beside Narzia, impatient at first, later resigned to seeing the occasion run its inexorable course, nibbling a crust of bread or gnawing the back of a pheasant, fingers poking out those two small but especially tender pieces of meat to be found just above the leg joints. When night fell, Honi, swaying slightly, began to make an interminable speech, which was almost drowned out by the cracking of poultry and mutton bones and by the belching of the overfed guests, so that Listener heard it only as a distant murmur, but from the way Honi kept pointing to himself and Narzia, he concluded that his father-in-law was once more extolling the useful nature of their union. Finally, Honi sat down heavily in his chair again, and this seemed to be the signal for the bridal couple to leave. Narzia leaned over to Listener, saying softly, 'Come with me!'

They left the room almost unnoticed by the guests, and went up the stairs to Narzia's room side by side. 'Wait here!' said Narzia quietly, and hurried through the door without quite closing it after her. Listener stood in the passage outside, and saw candlelight flickering on the wall through the crack in the doorway. There was a rustle of linen, the soft sound of hair being brushed excited him, and his heart missed a beat at the gentle creak of the bedstead. He pushed the door open, and in the small circle of candlelight he saw Narzia lying on the low bed like a corpse on its bier, draped in a filmy garment that scarcely veiled her body. For a moment he saw himself again standing in Gisa's room, and heard her mocking laughter as she told him to take his clothes off. He did not need telling a second time. Quickly, he undressed, and in doing so discovered that he was still wearing the bag containing Arni's stone on his breast. Should he have put it back in its golden dish? In their haste to get at the wedding feast, none of the elders had thought of asking him to return it. But perhaps they meant him to wear it tonight. At any rate, he did not intend to take off his precious inheritance this time.

As he went towards the bed, he saw nothing but Narzia's green eyes, but as soon as he stepped into the candlelight those eyes widened, with a look of horror in them. 'No!' cried Narzia, and the expression in her distorted face was one of rejection and pure dread. 'Hairy as an animal!' she whispered tonelessly, and she was staring at the middle of his body. And then she screamed the same words, 'Hairy as an animal! You're like an animal!' She lay crouched in the bed, hugging her body with both arms, as if to protect it from the attack of that hairy monster, or perhaps realizing that she was unable to give any part of herself away, delivered into strange hands. Then she suddenly sat up, pointing her arm at Listener like a spear raised in self-defence. He saw the emerald flash on her outstretched finger in the candlelight, and heard her scream, piercingly, 'Then be one! Be an animal!'

The power of the ring struck him in the middle of his body like the blow of a heavy weapon. He felt the pain pass down from his loins through his legs and into his toes, almost flinging him to the ground. Staggering, he tottered backwards until he could feel the wall behind him, and then he stared at his wedge-shaped, cloven hooves, trying to find some firm foothold on the polished wooden floor to give the support required by his stiff legs, kneeless and bent backwards, if they were to carry his heavy body, covered from the hips downward by thick, shaggy hair. 'Be an animal!' he heard Narzia scream once more, but he also saw that so far her magic had only half worked. He was still a man where Arni's stone protected him. And fear that this part of himself might lose its human nature too finally set him in motion. With one sudden bound, he reached the door, clattered down the stairs on his clumsy hooves, stumbled, picked himself up, raced in leaps and bounds through the hall of the house and out into the yard. As he galloped across the paving stones, he heard a man's cry behind him. With one bound, he took cover behind the well in the yard, and looked back over its low breastwork. Two of the elders were standing by the doorway of the house, one of them vomiting while the other held his head, and the latter was saying, 'What was that? Something went by me!'

The other man raised his head, with difficulty, saying thickly, 'What was what? It'll have been an animal. A goat, maybe.' Then he cackled with laughter, and added, 'A he-goat got loose, looking for his mate!' The rest of his remarks were lost in the further retching that overcame him. Listener – or the creature that had once been Listener – waited no longer. An animal, he thought, but only half an animal. He raced out through the open gateway, and on past the darkened houses, out of the village, always going north, and he did not stop until he had reached the shelter of the leafy woodland trees.

Book Three

in whose first part a faun wanders the woods,
and the goats call him Stone-eye.
He is given a companion,
of whom he can make nothing at first.
A girl with eyes of a colour hard to describe reminds him
of a time he has forgotten, and when at last he remembers it
despair turns him to stone.
In the second part, a statue with the legs of a goat
is less lifeless than it seems,
and haunts the borders of time and space
waiting to be found.
In the first chapter of the third part
he finds himself again, Listener,
in Arnilukka's arms.
But in the two last chapters he discovers
that this is far from all.

Part One

How does a creature feel stalking the woods on cloven hooves, shaggy as a goat from the hips down, fallen out of his own human history? How does he think, or does he think at all? How far has his animal nature overtaken his brain? At first, perhaps, he thought and acted like the man Listener he had once been, but such a transformation will have certain effects in the end.

The beast-man galloping out into the night remembered little of his past but a flash of green lightning striking him in the middle of his body like a whiplash, changing him, driving him out of a house and past a vomiting man who took him for an animal, a he-goat looking for his mate. But I was just coming away from her, thought the goat-legged creature, although he could no longer remember what she looked like. Nothing remained to him but that green and agonizing flash; he had lost all the rest, and he did not try to remember it as he galloped down the village street, past the houses crouched in the darkness, houses where people who had made use of him ate out their secret burrows, like vermin, never to be exterminated, and he ran on until the air was free of the sweaty odour of their busy presence, and the smell of their fires burning was drowned by the bitter, wholesome scent of autumn leaves. He was going nowhere in particular; all that mattered was to put more distance between himself and the place where those people had settled. He had lost any wish to exercise power over them, along with the silver instrument he had used for that purpose, and if it had been in his hand now he would probably have thrown it away. However, the flute lay in a room indoors, a place where he could scarcely imagine himself living any more, and it would lie there a long time, until perhaps someone or other found it and took possession of it.

So he went on and on through the woods northwards, where there were no men who might mock his strange appearance. At first he kept looking down with a certain fascinated horror at the transformation he had undergone below the hips, revolted by the shaggy animal hair on his body and his misshapen, goatish legs; later he forced himself to pay no more attention to that part of his body. Whatever had happened to him, he was alive, and he went on and on through the endless ocean of the forest. The days were full of yellowing autumn leaves through which the rain fell, rustling and pattering, knocking acorns and beech-nuts off the branches; the forest floor smelled of the mushrooms coming up from the moist earth among the roots of oaks and beeches, or standing in fairy rings in the withering grass of the clearings. That autumn, he lived mainly on mushrooms, the bitter kernels of beechnuts, and the last of the blackberries that hung in dark clusters among red and purple leaves on the thorny brambles.

He met hardly any animals at this time. He made too much noise as he crashed through the undergrowth on his still unfamiliar hooves, treading on dry twigs at every step he took, or shuffling clumsily through fallen leaves. All he heard was the occasional cry of a jay now and then, calling 'Take care! Take care!' to warn the other forest creatures that a shaggy monster was coming their way.

At the time, he did not realize he had understood that warning cry. Everyone knows the meaning of the jay's call. But a little later, on a clear day when the sky was pale and greenish above the black branches of the trees, something happened to make him aware of it. As he crouched on a rootstock on the edge of a clearing, warming himself in the sun that stood just above the tree-tops, he took his eye-stone out of its bag and lost himself in the play of the circling colours, blue and green and violet, that spread from the centre of the smooth stone, breaking through the surface and lapping around him like water welling up from unfathomed depths, the water of a pool that kept spreading, its surface moved by ever-growing, rippling, intersecting rings, and among them, gradually, an image made of countless facets formed; at first he took it for the reflection of his own face, until it slowly took distinct shape and became the face of a woman looking at him, a face lapped by the water, a face that awakened the memory of a dream. He bent to grasp that vision, but as soon as his hand dipped into the pool the image dispersed in a shimmering spray of colour, and he had to wait a long time before the water was smooth and the face took shape once more. When at last it was looking calmly up at him again from the depths, the woman smiled and said, 'Always so im-patient! Don't you know yet that you can never have what you take, only what you're given? All things come to him who waits.'

'Who'll come to me now, misshapen as I am?' he said. 'They'll all run away from me.'

'Why, yes, as long as you trample through the bushes like a raging monster,' said the woman. 'You hate yourself; how would anyone else like you?'

'I hate having to live in the shape of a stinking goat,' he said, and it made him even angrier that on hearing this the woman began to laugh, although that deep-toned laughter, like the cooing of a dove, did not sound mocking, but as if she liked to look at the goatish monster he now was.

'Don't you care to see yourself as you are?' she said. 'You'll never learn to live if you despise that part of your body that looks so goatish now.'

'Live?' he said bitterly. 'What sort of a life can I lead like this?'

The woman laughed again, saying, 'What do you know about life? What you've learned hitherto is very far from all.'

He thought that what had happened to him was more than enough, and had not the slightest wish for any more such experiences, but before he could say so the image of the woman's face shattered into a thousand fragments, and he started in alarm at the flutter of wings brushing his skin. He felt a hard beak peck his finger, and when at last he managed to shake himself free of his vision, he saw a magpie fly across the clearing with something shining in its beak. A glance at his empty hands was enough to tell him the bird had stolen the last thing he still had.

He jumped up to run after the magpie, but as soon as he stepped out of the shelter of the trees he was suddenly overcome by unutterable fear of the open space of the clearing, which forced him back among the tree-trunks. He couldn't understand it, and tried once more, but it was as if he were running against a wall of glass; he almost fainted with terror as soon as he knew the open sky was above him, and the terror did not leave him until he was back in the shade of the wood.

By now the magpie had crossed the clearing, and he saw its bobbing flight as it disappeared into the branches of an oak. The nest where it kept its hoard of stolen goods must be there. He set off in haste through the bushes along the edge of the wood, never taking his eyes off the tree where the nest was, not caring if the brambles scratched him or the branches whipped into his face. He could not have said at the time what the stone meant to him, he only knew he must have it back at any price.

When at last he reached the tree, breathing heavily, and looked up at its trunk to see how best he could climb it, he realized he had more than one thief to deal with, for he heard the croaking of two birds. So there was an accomplice waiting in the nest. And it was at that moment he realized that he could understand what the two birds were saying to each other.

'The falcon told the truth,' croaked the first magpie. 'The goat-legged one had a pretty, shiny thing in his hands.'

'Can we keep it?' asked the other bird.

'No,' said the first, 'the falcon will come and fetch it.'

'When?' asked the second.

'This evening,' said the first.

'We could hide it,' said the second. 'A pretty, shiny thing. Too good for a falcon.'

'Too dangerous,' said the first. 'Do you want a falcon for an enemy?'

'Not much,' said the second. 'Did the goat-legged one notice?'

'Yes,' said the first. 'But he's a woodland creature, and couldn't follow me over the clearing. I dare say he's under our tree by now.'

At that the second bird cackled with laughter, saying, 'Let him stand there as long as he likes! He'll never climb up to our nest, not with those clumsy hooves of his!'

We'll see about that, thought the goat-legged creature, and he grasped the lowest branch, which grew from the trunk at about the level of his head. Carefully, he hauled himself up, trying to make as little noise as possible, so as not to alarm the birds. It did turn out difficult to balance on the branch with his smooth hooves, but he soon found out how to brace their horny sides against the crevices of the bark to get a firmer foothold. So he made his way up, little by little, and was just beginning to look for the nest when he heard the magpies talking again, not far above him.

'Is he still down there?' asked the first bird.

'Can't see him,' said the second. 'Perhaps he's gone away.'

'Then he didn't know what the shiny thing was worth,' said the first. 'The falcon thinks it's very valuable.'

'What's the falcon offering for it?' asked the second.

'Protection from her own kind,' said the first.

The second magpie laughed, nastily. Then it said, 'There's justice for you! Takes our find away, and kindly says she will let us live!'

'The falcon says she owns this shiny thing,' said the first bird.

'Do you believe a thief?' asked the second.

'No,' said the first, 'being a thief myself.'

This magpie is cleverer than I was, thought the goat-legged creature, and he hauled himself up to the next branch and shouted, 'Give me back what you took!'

The two birds fluttered up, screeching, circled his head and tried to peck at his eyes, but he fended them off with a violent sweep of his arm, seized his stone, which lay shimmering among all sorts of rubbish in the hollow of the nest, and put it in its bag. 'You were right,' he told the magpies, who had now settled rather higher up the tree, chattering angrily. 'This shiny thing is mine. The falcon took it away, but she won't get her talons on the stone again, and you can tell her that when she comes to fetch it this evening.'

'Not likely!' said the magpie who had stolen the stone. 'The falcon might be angry. Telling someone stronger than yourself bad news is unwise. We'll be the other side of the mountains by evening.'

And with that, the birds spread their wings and flew away westward through the tree-tops. He saw their white tail feathers now and then as they flew briefly up above the brown leaves, and then the magpies disappeared from sight.

Before he set about climbing down again, he looked into the nest where the magpies had hidden their stolen goods. It was in the crook of a branch, quite close to the trunk, and had been built of dry twigs thrown together in a rather slovenly way. There were a few more shiny things left in it, which he supposed were anyone's for the taking now that the birds had left their treasure chamber in such a hurry, never to return. Curiously, he poked about among these objects, and amidst various buttons and broken shards he discovered two which aroused his interest. One of them was the broken blade of a knife. He looked at the fragment of steel for a while, wondering if he wanted any more to do with such things, but then he decided to put the shiny thing in the bag with his stone; there was always the chance it might be useful to a creature walking the woods alone.

There was also a thin piece of flint, shaped like a shell where it had flaked away; the sun was reflected from its smooth surface. That was what must have made the magpies want to carry it home to their nest. However, not only did the stone cast back the light of the sun, it carried its warmth within it. You could make fire with flint and steel, he still remembered that; now he had both, and just at the right time, with winter about to set in. He should really be grateful to the falcon, he thought; without her greed, he would never have thought of climbing up to the magpies' nest. He put this find away in his bag too and climbed back down to the ground, discovering in the process that he knew just where to put his hooves this time.

He trotted the long way round through the woods to the other side of the clearing, sat in the sun again, and wondered whether to wait for the falcon who would come swooping down from the sky in the south that evening, to fetch the stone. It would be not unsatisfying to hear the bird screeching in vain for the thieving magpies, and watch her fly home again without what she had come for. But waiting wasn't really worth his while. And besides, it was possible this falcon had green eyes, and that was the last thing he wanted to see just now. Something that struck him as far more important was the way he had understood what the magpies were saying, and had indeed been able to speak to them himself without any difficulty. And as he absorbed this undoubted fact properly for the first time, he realized that he had understood the jay's warning cry as well. Had this anything to do with his partial transformation? Did the magic enable him to understand the language of the birds? Or perhaps of all the animal kingdom? That seemed if anything more likely, for he could see nothing at all birdlike about his present body.

From then on he tried to make a little less noise with his hooves, and listen to what the creatures of the wood were saying. He did not learn much new, apart from the fact that he could indeed understand the speech of all living creatures and not just the birds. Two squirrels, for instance, scurried up and down the trunk of an old beech tree, calling to each other, 'Quick, quick! Look for beechnuts, look for walnuts, look for pine cones! The winter's coming, the winter's coming!' Or he might hear a deer with two fawns grazing in a clearing, calling to them, 'Eat, eat! The winter will be long, the winter will be hard!' They all seemed to be in great haste to hoard provisions or fill their bellies for the last time before the snow fell, covering everything. Their conversations were not particularly interesting, but they did remind him that he must find winter quarters and stock up with provisions himself.

He decided to look for a place which would keep him at least partly dry, and spend the winter there. He remembered seeing a great rocky cliff fissured by crevices cutting its way through the woods rather higher up the slope, and set off at once to explore it for some overhanging ledge that might shelter him, or even a cave.

For the first time since his transformation he was not wandering aimlessly in the forest, but had something definite in mind, a purpose he was following, an intention he meant to carry out. He set hoof before hoof in the moss, going fast, peering ahead to see if the reddish tinge of the rock wall showed through the trees yet. At last the wood became less dense, and the trees themselves not so tall. Up here there were only saplings whose slim trunks had shot up now and then in isolation, among the thickets of hazel and dogwood. And here was the great cliff, towering up, steep and much too tall to climb, filling half the sky. When he had reached it he wondered whether to turn right or left. He had trotted along it before, both ways, but had never come to either end of it, or even been able to see any end in the distance ahead.

Finally he turned right, probably because the bushes grew more thickly in that direction, coming right up to the rock, although there were a few open, grassy clearings among them. He made his way along between the bushes and the cliff, investigating every crevice and peering into every cranny, but he could find none wide enough to offer him shelter.

Towards evening, when the sun was low over the trees, and he was about to give up his search, he discovered a hole at about hip-height, which seemed to lead farther into the rock. He crawled through this hole on his belly and found himself in a large cave, whose roof he could hardly make out at first in the faint light that penetrated the bushes across the entrance. When he was used to the darkness, he rose and began to explore his new home. The place seemed to be roughly the shape of an oval dome, and the ground was fairly level. Water splashed somewhere in the background.

Crossing the cave, he came upon a rocky barrier about the height of a man; the cave seemed to go on into the mountain beyond it. A stream flowed down the right-hand wall of this upper part and over the ledge of rock, to collect in a basin whence it obviously had some way of escape underground. He scooped up a handful of water and drank. It was icy cold, and tasted fresh and a little chalky. He could hardly have found anywhere more comfortable, he thought, and decided to explore the rest of the cave. It was easy enough to clamber up on the shelf of rock, and once on it he could just stand upright if he ducked his head slightly. The cave narrowed towards the back, but he could go about a dozen paces before the walls came so close that he dared venture no farther, although the fissure seemed to go on into the mountain. He went back, sat on the edge of the shelf of rock, and wondered how best to make himself at home. He would sleep here in the upper part of the cave, he thought, where he should be fairly safe from unwanted visitors.

Before it was quite dark, he crawled out again, collected a few armfuls of leaves and withered grass, and made himself a bed of them up on the shelf of rock. He also collected some dry wood and stacked it in the cave, for now it was time to try kindling a fire. He set to work with his flint and steel above a little heap of dry moss and grass, and the sparks leaped out from beneath his hands like tiny shooting stars. Soon his tinder began to smoulder, a thin thread of smoke rose, and blowing carefully, he managed to kindle a little flame, feeding it with strips of birch bark. Now all he had to do was put wood on his fire, thin twigs first and then a pyramid of branches the thickness of his arm. The flames ate their way greedily on, growing, spreading warmth; smoke billowed up, collected beneath the roof of the cave, and made its way out through a crack somewhere. Fascinated, he watched the play of the flames as they first sent a flickering bluish forerunner ahead over the crackling bark, then suddenly burst into blossoms of fire, their petals licking around the hissing wood. He waited until the branches collapsed, then put a couple of thicker chunks on the embers, and hauled himself up to his bedroom.

He lay awake for a little longer in the bitter fragrance of the beech leaves, mingled with the smoky smell of the fire, looking at the glowing logs and the little violet flames that scurried over them now and then. A gnarled branch stuck out of the wood on the fire, outlined against the crimson glow of the embers, a dark falcon spreading its wings to soar up from the falconer's hand and into the sky in search of prey. Yet it stayed caught in that attitude of tension, and from below pale horses with fluttering, transparent manes began storming up to it. However, before they reached it they reared, the purple of their tossing heads changed suddenly to bright orange, and a hiss was audible, like the sound of the distant cries with which the horses' riders urged them on. Then the attack collapsed, and there was only a faint glow creeping back to meet the embers below. The fire glowed on for a while, pulsating. Then the steeds shook their manes and began attacking again, though more feebly this time. The falcon seemed to reach upward, treading the hesitant riders down beneath its talons as they approached. With an explosive crack that made the drowsy watcher start up, a burst of flame arose, and then the pieces of wood shifted slightly and fell, burying the flames. In the darkness, the falcon was hardly visible now, but its attitude seemed yet prouder and more haughty than before, the attitude of a victor rising above his foes. Its entire outline became more clearly visible again, wings spread, arched neck bearing its narrow head and the sharply curved beak with a pair of green eyes staring out over it, lovely and terrible at once. However, this new brightness was only the sign of a further attack in preparation down below. Storming on again, the wild, flying manes licked up, bright red, and now the riders flung themselves upon their opponent from all sides, until a wreath of flames joined around the falcon and flared above its head. Now at last it seemed as if it would rise on its fiery pinions, to burst in glowing life amidst the crackling blaze that was devouring it, until it did burst apart with a crack and was consumed by the flames. With that, their mighty power was broken too. They burned on calm and steady for a while and then went out one by one, until there was nothing left but a few dots of red, like glow-worms crawling over the heap of ashes.

Hunger woke him in the morning. He lay where he was for a moment or so, staring at the fissured roof of the cave and trying to think. He had dry quarters now, he had a fire, but he had no food. He had lived from hand to mouth these last few weeks, and there had always been something to be found, a few late mushrooms, a handful of beechnuts. However, there would be no more of that once the first snow fell. It was high time for him to lay in provisions, if indeed it wasn't too late already.

Before he left the cave he fed the embers still smouldering beneath the ashes of his fire with a handful of twigs and put a few stout pieces of branch on top of them, to keep them from going out. It was cool and windy outside, but at least it wasn't raining. Now and then the clouds driving fast across the sky even let some sunlight through, although there was not much warmth left in the sun. The hazel bushes along the rock wall still bore some crumpled brown leaves on their wand-like branches, and the empty husks of nuts the wind had shaken down. Pushing the fallen leaves aside, he found the ground covered with nuts beneath them. When he had cracked a couple of handfuls between two stones to satisfy his hunger, he felt a sudden feverish urge to collect more, and began hectically scraping the nuts into piles, heaping them up just like the squirrels he had watched at their work. He soon found it too laborious to carry his harvest into the cave in handfuls, so he wove a deep basket of thin hazel wands, more like a shapeless bag by the time he had finished it, but it did its job if he covered the largest holes with grass.

He spent most of the day gathering nuts, and every time he tipped another basketful out at the back of his bedroom, he surveyed his growing stocks with pleasure. However, they would by no means last him a whole long winter in the mountains, so he went farther and farther from the cave, searching the ground beneath every hazel bush he saw.

One day, as evening came on, he set off home once more with another basket of nuts. As he trotted back, keeping between the bushes and the cliff itself, feeling tired, his back aching from his unwonted activity, he found a small flock of goats grazing in a grassy clearing close to the cave: about a dozen animals, including a powerful he-goat with great curving horns, who stood right in front of the thicket that covered the cave-mouth.

The nut-gatherer saw, with some alarm, that this formidable animal had obviously picked up his scent already, and was looking keenly his way. He tried to creep towards the entrance to the cave, still keeping between the bushes and the rock, but as soon as he was within about ten paces of it the he-goat lowered his head and charged him, ramming his horns into a bush just to one side so hard that its branches broke. A he-goat, as he vaguely remembered discovering before, was not to be trifled with when any stranger ventured near his flock. In any case, he thought it wise to have his hands free, so he cautiously backed off a little way, putting down his basket and wondering how best to shoo the creature away from the mouth of his cave. He searched the ground for a suitable stone to throw, and found one, but just as he was straightening up he heard a sudden rumbling from the cliff above. Next moment came the crack of stone as it broke away, and down came great boulders in a rock-fall. Leaping aside, he got into safety under an overhanging ledge, but the he-goat was less lucky. He took a great bound up the slope towards his flock, but a chunk of rock struck him and flung him to the ground. Farther downhill, the she-goats were galloping for dear life. They did not stop until they reached the tall trees, and then stood there bleating, looking anxiously back at their lord and master, who lay quite still.

The goat-legged creature waited until the last rocks had come rumbling down, and then emerged from his shelter and peered through the bushes, with concern, at the stricken animal lying on the edge of the little clearing. He would not have wished anything quite so drastic to happen, and he was sorry he had been going to throw stones to frighten the he-goat away. By now he had grown used to being unable to endure open spaces, so he did not even try to cross the grassy clearing, but made his way towards the goat through the shelter of the bushes, to see if he could help him.

A sharp-edged piece of rock had broken off the he-goat's right horn close to his head, and broken his left foreleg. The animal lay in the grass, stunned, looking at him with yellow eyes. As he leaned over the creature to look at his wounds, the he-goat tried to rise. 'It's all right,' he said, placing a hand on the shaggy shoulder. 'I won't hurt you or your flock.'

The he-goat bared his teeth and said, 'Did you do this, half-goat?'

'No,' he said. 'It was the mountain itself threw stones at you – and don't call me that!'

'Why not?' said the goat. 'I like you better the way you are now than when you tried to take the kid away. You were still one of those thin-legged men creatures then.'

'Ah, so it was you chased me through the wood!' he said, suddenly remembering that encounter again. 'I was only carrying the kid back to you, you fool! Tell your goats to stop bleating so loud! I'm not about to eat them. Now, let me see where you're hurt.'

He remembered that while he was collecting nuts among the hazel bushes he had seen some of those broad-leaved herbs that someone, he could no longer remember who, had once put on an injury of his own. He gathered a handful, broke off a couple of strong hazel shoots as well, and pulled up a tuft of long, tough grass blades. When he came back, the she-goats were already busy licking the blood from the stump of their leader's horn. However, as soon as the strange beast-man approached, they moved timidly aside, and watched from a safe distance as he crushed the leaves and put them on the wounds.

'A good smell,' said the he-goat. 'I know that herb. Good for the bellyache too.'

'Then it won't do your head any harm,' he said. 'Now let's look at your leg.' He set the broken bone as best he could, splinted it with the hazel shoots, and tied them in place with grass. 'Can you stand up now?' he asked.

The he-goat tried, stood tottering on three legs for a moment, and then collapsed again, at which his flock broke into loud bleating once more.

'Who's going to look after us now?' the beasts lamented. 'Who'll show us where to find food under the snow? The winter will kill us all!' And the he-goat stretched out all four legs, laid his head resignedly on the grass, and said, 'So it will. Even this nameless creature skilled in healing can't help that.'

'Yes, I can,' said the goat-legged creature, in a sudden moment of inspiration. 'I'll strike a bargain with you, One-horn.'

'Quick off the mark yourself, aren't you, when it comes to calling names?' said the he-goat. 'Who'd be any better off for such a bargain?'

'Both of us,' he said.

'Explain,' said the he-goat. 'What can you do for us?'

'I can help you keep the flock alive,' he said. 'I'm inviting you to live in my cave, warm yourselves by my fire, and drink from my spring. And I'll try to collect fodder for the flock before the snow falls. What do you say to that?'

'It sounds good,' said the he-goat. 'But what's in it for you? Do you want to mate with my goats?'

Seeing the angry glint in the he-goat's eyes, he made haste to assure him that he had no intention of trespassing upon any such rights of his. 'But in everything else, they are to obey me like yourself,' he added. 'In particular, I want the goats to let me have a little of their milk every day, to help me survive the winter too.'

'Ah, then you'll depend on us as well,' said the he-goat, pleased. 'I can agree to that, since three of the goats are carrying no young, so I'll strike this bargain with you for the flock's sake. You and I will both swear by whatever's dearest to us.' And he braced his sound foreleg on the ground, rose laboriously, and said to his flock, 'You heard what we were saying. From today I share my mastery of the flock with this nameless one, and you will give him your milk as long as he carries out his obligations. I swear it by my one remaining horn, and to keep me in mind of it, I will take the name he gave me. Your turn now, nameless one!'

He was not to remain nameless for long. He took his stone out of its bag, held it on the palm of his hand so that all the goats could see the ring of colour shining in the evening sunlight, and said, 'I swear by this stone eye that I will care for the flock as I have promised.'

The sight of the stone silenced even the young goats, who had been disturbing this solemn goatish ceremony with their loud bleating. The animals all looked at the shining, many-coloured thing, and then the goats lay down in the grass, one by one, as if they had no more cause to be uneasy. All suspicion had vanished from One-horn's yellow eyes as well. 'I trust this eye more than I trust you,' he said. 'You shall be called Stone-eye from now on, since today is a day for giving new names. Take the broken horn, so that all can see you are equal with me among us, and now take me to your cave!'

And so the goat-legged being came by a new name. He had quite forgotten that he ever bore another, and there was no one here who could have called him by it. From now on, in any case, he was no stranger to the goats, and they never tired of calling him by his name, Stone-eye, as if to keep reassuring themselves that he was a familiar figure. And there were plenty of occasions for that, for over the next few weeks Stone-eye had to do everything while One-horn lay in the cave, waiting for his broken leg to mend. Every morning, Stone-eye brought the he-goat fodder, then took his basket, led the goats out to pasture, and while the animals grazed he went collecting foodstuff of all kinds in the surrounding woods, hoping it would see the flock through the winter. He also had to keep a constant eye on them, for without the stern supervision of their lord and master the goats, self-willed creatures that they were, acted very giddily, losing their way among the trees and bushes, climbing steep rocks in the hope of finding particularly tasty herbs and then discovering that they couldn't get down again. Then it was a case of, 'Stone-eye, help me down!' or, 'Stone-eye, my kid's run off into the woods! Go and look for it!' or, 'Come quick, Stone-eye! There's a lynx crouching in the bushes!' The supposed lynx would turn out to be nothing but a stray wild-cat; however, the kid really had run half-way down the slope through the forest, and he had to rescue the goat from the heights too, if he didn't want another broken leg to treat.

In short, he was kept busy all day long, and in between times, to carry out the duties he had undertaken, he had to collect acorns and beechnuts, crab apples and rowanberries, anything that he thought a goat's stomach could digest. In return, he got his milk every evening, but by then he was almost too tired to drain the wooden bowl he had carved himself with his knife-blade for this purpose. However, the mountains of provisions he piled beside his bed rose daily, and he took ever-increasing pleasure in the sight before his eyes closed, while the goats shifted restlessly on their litter down in the cave below, staring wide-eyed at the glow of the unfamiliar fire that reminded them of the warmth of summer, although there was no sun in the sky.

One morning the sun did not seem to rise at all. Stone-eye was woken by the bleating of the goats as they pattered about in the dark down below. One of them trod in the smouldering embers under the ashes of the fire, sparks shot up, and for a moment he saw the animals chasing about the cave like shadows running purposelessly. 'Why aren't you asleep?' he asked. 'It isn't morning yet.'

'It must be day by now,' he heard One-horn say. 'We can feel it. But there's no sun.'

By now the firelight had died down again. Stone-eye made his way down into the lower cave, poked the embers, put a couple of branches on the fire and waited for them to burn up. The light of their flames calmed the goats a little. They were pressing around the he-goat, the reflection of the fire flickering in their eyes. Under the expectant eyes of his flock, Stone-eye felt obliged to do something, and he went to the mouth of the cave. The entrance looked dark ahead of him, and when he bent and tried to crawl out he discovered why. Instead of the open air, he met with an ice-cold wall. The mouth of the cave had been snowed up overnight.

For a moment he too had felt the darkness was uncanny, but now he couldn't help laughing at the timid goats. He crawled back, saying, 'Shall I give you daylight again?' Not waiting for any answer, he plucked a burning branch from the fire, swung it up above his head, laughing, so that the flames flared high, and called, 'Come back, sun! My goats want you!' Then he bent to crawl through the entrance and thrust the burning wood into the wall of snow, amidst much hissing. He soon poked a hole in the wall at the cave-mouth, and shovelled the rest of the snow aside with both hands, until he could crawl out into the snowy bushes, from which cascades of glittering crystals, fine as dust, came falling down on him, covering him with powdery whiteness. The world was without colour. Beneath the milky sky huddled bushes like clouds, reaching downhill to the foaming white waves of the forest trees. Winter had come.

By now the goats too were making their way out of the hole he had cleared at the mouth of the cave, and shook the snow off their coats. They gathered around Stone-eye as if he were the leader of their flock, staring admiringly at him with their shining amber eyes. At last one of them said, 'Oh, Stone-eye, you are very powerful if you can bring back the daylight. But now there's snow, and we won't be able to find food.'

'Come along,' was all Stone-eye said, and he marched ahead of them through the deep snow. He had expected something of this kind, and over the last few days had noted the position of a few grassy rises well exposed to the wind. Soon he found one that was swept almost clear of snow, and he pastured the goats here. When they got into difficulties they easily lost their heads, but as soon as they felt firm ground beneath the covering of snow they knew how to scrape the grass free with their sharp front hooves.

While the goats laboriously dug their fodder out of the snow, Stone-eye remained among the bushes, collected some dry wood, and made sure his little flock did not stray. For a while he watched a falcon circling in the sky, very high at first, so that it could hardly be made out in the haze, then coming down lower as if to look well at the flock, but at this time of the year the kids were too large for a falcon to do them any harm. Once the bird swooped down close above the bush from which Stone-eye was breaking a few dry branches, and then it flew away southwards, beyond the snowy tree-tops. Stone-eye ducked down, feeling exposed.

The goats could not eat their fill that day, for the withered yellow grass had no more goodness in it. When he led them back to the cave in the evening, and was going to milk his bowl full, they looked at him reproachfully, as if he had failed to do his duty. So he gave them some acorns and crab apples, and he found he had to do so every evening, however hard he worked trying to find suitable pasture.

At the same time, a change was taking place in him, one that he himself hardly noticed. When he joined the goats, his intention had been to make use of the animals and survive the winter with their help: he was a being who might have the legs of a goat as he walked the woods, but was still used to standing erect and looking down on four-footed creatures; he was an outcast who had unexpectedly come into possession of a flock, though he had negotiated as if on equal terms with the injured he-goat. But since the day they struck that bargain, a change had set in, showing itself, for instance, in the way he walked, bending low as he collected acorns or firewood from the forest floor, or as he moved among the bushes outside his cave, seeking shelter under their branches from the terrifying emptiness of the sky, in whose unfathomable depths a falcon might be hovering, watching him fixedly with green eyes.

This posture brought him closer to his goats. While at first they had seemed to him a group of animals whom it was hard to tell apart, except for the he-goat, he was now coming to learn the character of each individual goat, and could soon call them all by their names: there was gentle White-patch, for instance, with her comical tuft of light hairs between her horns, or moody Lame-foot, who had injured her right hind leg at some point, before he met the flock, and had trotted along with them ever since in a curious, limping way, now and then making use of her infirmity to kick out spitefully, as if by accident; or there was placid Full-udder, whom Stone-eye had come to value as being easily the best milker in the flock. A herdsman may learn to distinguish between his beasts in a similar way, but he stands upright beneath the sky, can see the whole flock at a glance, regarding them as his property, and moves out of the wind if the smell of the beasts is too much for him. Stone-eye, however, was becoming more of a member of the flock himself every day, a kind of leader, but one of them, surrounded by the odour of their bodies, and he was scarcely aware of his difference now, although occasionally he did feel the stirrings of a dim memory that he had once lived in houses, among men.

Then came the snowstorms. On the day the first storm broke, Stone-eye had been out among the hazel bushes with his goats, although the beasts could scrape out very few blades of grass from beneath the snow. They had been uneasy ever since morning, and he too felt a numbing emptiness behind his eyes; he moved restlessly through the bushes, and felt the approach of something that could not be held back. Then, looking up at the top of the rock wall, he saw a second wall looming above it, black with ragged grey edges, and a few minutes later the storm was coming down from the heights, sweeping the first sharp ice crystals before it.

Stone-eye whistled up the goats and drove them downhill to the cave. A moment ago the cliff had still been visible against the sky; now the swirling, driving snow had swallowed it up. He fought his way along the last of the path, leaning blindly into the icy current, which was an almost physical presence. Groping his way at last to the cave-mouth, already half drifted up, he hauled himself into the cave over the piles of snow.

His goats had made their way through the storm more easily than he could, and were there ahead of him. As he fed them, the entrance drifted up completely, cutting off the last remnants of daylight. There was nothing to be heard in the dark but the noise of the storm. Stone-eye blew up the fire, put wood on it to fend off the numbing cold, and then climbed up to his bed and burrowed into the litter there.

The storm's shrill piping penetrated his drowsiness like the rushing sound of a never-ending fall into a bottomless abyss; he was falling in formless voids of fear, and when at last he woke, cold and numb, he could still hear that same rush and hissing. At some point – whether it was day or night outside he had no idea – he climbed stiffly down to the animals pressing uneasily around the fire, which had burned low, gave them something to eat, and then clambered back up to his bed and tried to go on sleeping. But as soon as he stopped looking at the fixed point of the glowing fire and closed his eyes, that fall into blackness began again, as if the floor of the cave had opened up to swallow all living things. Ghostly visions slipped past him, pale and shaggy horses, their fluttering manes blown sideways in the storm, riders crouching low in their saddles, swinging whips and swords, racing through the emptiness, surrounding him in wild eddies, scattering in the four winds until they whirled through the cave like distant snowflakes, to approach again at amazing speed, one of them making straight towards him, coming close, face distorted with rage, straggling hair braided at the temples flying about it; the blade of a curved, drawn sword flashed, and then the rider swept right through him, like an icy current of air startling him into wakefulness.

The fire had disappeared under the ashes; there was no red, glowing point in the cave to which he could now hold fast, only the hissing roar, the deep, black darkness, and his uncertainty: did this cave still have walls, or had it, perhaps, extended into measureless space? He felt his limbs trembling, and could sense the cold coming up tangibly towards him, spreading like a smothering liquid that lapped heavily around him.

He was not aware what drove him to rise and make his way down to the fireplace, which still felt warm. He poked up the embers, put more wood on the fire, and waited for it to burn. In the light of the flames as they licked up, he saw his goats sleeping together by the fireside, brown bodies huddled together; he heard their gentle snuffling, saw the peaceful rise and fall of their breathing bodies, smelled their odour. Then he dropped to all fours, crept in among them, nestled against that warm, living flesh, and became one with the pulsating organism of the flock that took him in, warmed and nourished him. He slept a deep and dreamless sleep, waking now and then with a sense of safety and comfort to suck milk from an udder presented to him, then drowsed off once more and lost all sense of time, dreaming his way into the warm womb, pulsing with the heartbeat of the flock, where even the rushing of the storm died away and could be heard only as the distant, deep humming of a ground-note in a melodious chord, the resonant harmony of a passive world of security without desire, released from the pressures of time and space.

At some time – and he did not know if hours, days or even weeks had passed by – the roar of the storm ceased. The animals drew sluggishly apart; one goat nudged him with her nose, saying, 'Get up, Stone-eye! We're freezing. Make more fire!' Only now did he feel that he was lying naked in the darkness of the cave, outside the warm womb of the flock again, and the cold attacked him like a ravening wolf. So at last he moved his stiff limbs to get up, light the fire, put wood on it and warm himself along with the others. Then he shovelled the cave-mouth free until the light of the sun shone in through the bare branches of the bushes, led the flock out into the deep, dazzling snow, broke some branches for the beasts so that they could strip off buds and bark with their teeth, and spent the day thus, lying down to sleep with the goats at night. Later One-horn joined them. His leg was better now, but nothing of note happened to break the uniformity of these days. They were a flock passing the winter, and no more.

With all this, their stocks of provisions were gradually dwindling, and the goats began to feel hungry, but every day the sun rose a little higher above the forest, the patches of snow shrank, revealing the first clear places on the hillside. White and purple crocuses flowered there, and soon afterwards fresh, bright green grass-blades shot up among the brown and withered tufts.

And now One-horn began to claim back his position as leader. It was he who led the flock out to graze, and watched over it, and it was rather grudgingly that he said, one morning, 'You have kept your promise and seen the flock through the winter well, Stone-eye. But,' he added, 'you can leave them to me for the summer now, and take over again next winter. That strikes me as the best way for us to share the leadership, as agreed.'

'Do you want me to leave you?' asked Stone-eye, taken aback, for by now he could hardly imagine life without the flock.

'Take it as you please,' said the he-goat, whetting his mighty horn against the edge of a rock. 'I won't chase you off. But you might keep out of our way a bit now, and then my goats will know who their master is.'

So that was it: the he-goat was beginning to get jealous! Stone-eye could scarcely keep from grinning. Anyway, he had no objection to abdicating responsibility for the flock after his strenuous efforts of the winter, and enjoying a little leisure. 'I'll do that,' he said, 'but I'll stay with you a while longer, for I still have something to do here.'

And from now on he still slept with the flock night after night, enjoying the proximity of the peacefully breathing animals, but in the morning he let them go their own way, sat outside the cave under a hazel bush whose catkins were already dusty with pollen, and basked in the sun.

He had carried the broken goat's horn around with him all winter, as being to some extent proof of his status as leader of the flock, and while he sat there one spring day, playing with the horn, he wondered what else it might be good for. It lay comfortably in his hand, the grooves fitting as if naturally between his fingers, so that it was easy to hold. This made him think of turning it into a handle for his knife. It cost him some trouble, but at last he had the blade set firmly in the lower end of the horn, the point sticking a good way out. Then he whetted the knife on a stone until it was so sharp that he could mow down a tuft of grass and meet scarcely any resistance. Now he need only wait until the grass was ready to cut, for that was the plan he had in mind.

A few weeks later, when five of the goats had borne their kids, mowing time came. The soft, pink-tinged meadow grass was in bloom, with the white flowerheads of chervil and burnet saxifrage swaying in it; butterflies fluttered over it, and the air was full of the fragrance of mint and scented vernal grass. Once more, Stone-eye discovered that he was unable to go even a couple of paces away from the shelter of the bushes, and not only because of the falcon hovering high in the clouds above the clearing, as if it were spying down on him. He had to content himself with mowing the grass from the edge of the clearing, as far out as his knife could reach.

The flock came back from grazing that evening, and made as if to fall upon the freshly cut fodder. When Stone-eye shooed the she-goats out into the clearing, One-horn came up to him, head lowered menacingly, stood with his legs braced and inquired, 'Why did you drive my goats away? Are you going to eat all that yourself?'

Stone-eye laughed, and tried to explain that he planned to dry the grass and store it for later in the year. One-horn shook his head, baffled. 'I never before heard of a goat who bit off grass to let it lie,' he said. 'You're crazy!'

At this Stone-eye stuck his knife in the ground before him, so that the horn seemed to be growing erect out of the earth, and said, 'One-horn, by this horn I ask you whether you mean what you say when you tell me I'm to lead the flock again next winter.'

'Why such ceremony?' asked the he-goat. 'I won't break my word. But why talk about winter now? The woods have only just turned green, and the grass is juicy.'

'I see you can't think beyond today,' said Stone-eye. 'Very well: if you don't keep your goats away from the grass I've cut, I'll leave you to look after the flock next winter, and tell everyone that One-horn is quick to forget an oath he swears.'

One-horn did not want that, and so a couple of days later Stone-eye was able to bring in his hay and stack it in the upper part of the cave. He was busy with this task until darkness fell, when he dropped into the last of the hay and fell asleep at once, dazed by the heady scents of the herbs, which awakened a buried dream in him, the dream of a face bent over his, the face of a woman whose eyes were so close that they were like a dark sky above him, sparkling with stars of many colours, and this woman laughed softly as she looked at him, saying, 'Are you happy to live like a goat among goats? That was not really what Arni had in mind when he gave you the stone, and told you the verse that goes with it:

> *Seek the light*
> *where the glow may fall;*
> *you have not sought aright*
> *if you don't find it all.*'

When Stone-eye heard those words, he felt as if he were waking from long sleep in the very middle of his dream, or had been crawling endlessly through a dark cave and now, suddenly, saw a way out ahead of him, with the stars shining through it.

'Will I ever find it?' he asked.

'Not here with the goats,' said the woman, and as she spoke her face began to turn transparent, as it had by the spring on the borders of the Crooked Wood.

'Don't leave me alone again!' he said. 'I'm afraid to be alone.'

Her face could hardly be seen by now, but he heard her low voice say, 'Fear is a part of it too. Follow the light, and take care of your stone!'

Then her face went out, but her last words had sounded like a warning of some threatened danger. They were still ringing in his ears as he woke with a start, and at that very moment he felt something moving close to him in the hay, something tugging slightly at the thong on which he wore his little bag around his neck. He did not stir, tried to breathe quietly, like a sleeper, and waited. For a while nothing happened. Then something with a smooth, short-haired coat touched his neck, and busied itself about his bag. Without a sound, he slowly raised his hand, and then pounced. A slender little animal twisted in his grasp, squeaking, and instantly bit his finger. He yelped, but without loosening his grip, and grasped the animal's head in his other hand so that it couldn't bite again. 'I've a good mind to wring your neck for you,' he said furiously. 'Who are you, anyway? And what were you doing with my bag?'

Instead of answering, the creature uttered a few choked sounds; it is hard to talk when someone is holding your mouth shut, but at least the noises it was making sounded thoroughly submissive.

'Will you promise not to bite if I let go of your head?' asked Stone-eye. 'I'll take it that you mean yes if you stop wriggling like a snake.'

The animal went so limp that at first he thought he had killed it. But as soon as he removed the hand that had been holding the creature's mouth shut, it said, 'I'm a weasel, I go by the name of Needle-tooth, very much at your service!'

'I can do without that kind of service, thank you,' said Stone-eye, still keeping a cautious grip on the weasel with his other hand and licking the blood off his finger. 'Also, I'm still waiting for an answer to my second question.'

'I ask you a thousand pardons, Bearer of the Stone,' said the weasel. 'I thought it was only polite to introduce myself first.'

After months of hearing nothing but the simple talk of his goats, concerned only with the necessities of daily life, Stone-eye found the weasel's manner of speech rather surprising, and the name by which Needle-tooth had addressed him seemed even stranger, although it did arouse a vague memory, if one of which he could make no sense. 'Judging by the name you give me,' he said, 'you know what's in the bag I wear around my neck.'

'That's right,' said the weasel, 'and I can see now I never should have ventured to touch your property, O lord with the strong hands, in whose grip a humble creature like me is weak as water. Even in your sleep you are as watchful as a man who's had warning there's a thief about.'

'No need to reproach yourself,' said Stone-eye. 'I did have warning.'

'My most humble thanks for your magnanimity in trying to reassure me,' said the weasel, and Stone-eye thought he felt Needle-tooth try to bow politely in his grip as he went on, 'Is it permitted to ask who warned you?'

'A dream woman with eyes like the starry sky,' he said, wondering as he spoke what this weasel named Needle-tooth might make of such nocturnal visions. However, the weasel did not seem at all surprised, but said, in a rather resigned way, 'I suppose I should have known.

They say that stone once belonged to a wise old woman with great power over secret things.'

'Do they, though?' Stone-eye was trying to remember the story of his stone. He was sure he had once known it, but it would not come into his mind. What kind of old woman did the weasel mean? The woman he had seen in his dream had not seemed to him particularly old. Or at any rate, he had taken no notice of her age because she had been so extraordinarily beautiful that his heart still beat faster when he thought of her.

By now he had decided talking to Needle-tooth was worth his while. 'Listen,' he said, 'I should like a little more conversation with you. If you swear not to run away, and more particularly to leave my bag alone, I'll let go of you.'

'I swear it by the tails of my forefathers, used by kings to deck their coronation robes,' said Needle-tooth, which is the greatest and most sacred oath any weasel can swear. So Stone-eye let the animal slip out of his hand, whereupon Needle-tooth first stretched slightly, and then curled up beside his ear. For a while there was no sound but the weasel's washing of his coat. Then he said, 'Now I'm not in your power any more, I'll tell you something else. You've been good to me, though I didn't deserve it. If you will let me, I'll stay with you, for not only do you have a powerful protector in that stone of yours, you are kinder than the one who sent me to steal it from you.'

'And who was that?' asked Stone-eye, although he already guessed the answer.

'A green-eyed falcon, a female,' said the weasel, just as he had expected. 'I owed her a debt, for she sometimes left me a part of her prey, and I didn't want to seem discourteous, but now I see the falcon only wanted to make use of my modest skills to steal from you. She seems very anxious to have that stone you carry in the bag. In future I'll make sure you don't lose it one way or another in your sleep. Will you take me into your service?'

'By all means,' said Stone-eye, 'more particularly as I intend to leave these goats and cross the mountains.' This idea had only just come into his head as he talked to the weasel, but since One-horn had taken over command of the flock again, Stone-eye had come to feel himself superfluous. Perhaps that was his real reason for hay-making, to assert and ensure his position in the flock, but the animals had not understood the meaning of what he was doing. Now he also knew that the green-eyed falcon was aware of his hiding-place, and that greedy bird would surely try some other means of getting his stone. High time to move on, thought Stone-eye, and he added, 'Will you come with me, Needle-tooth?'

'With pleasure,' said the weasel. 'To be perfectly honest, your goats may be very estimable creatures, but they stink so horribly I wouldn't care to spend a second night in this cave.'

In the morning Stone-eye made himself a large bag to carry over his shoulder, woven of the goat's hair that lay around the cave in great tufts, filled it with the last of his hazelnuts, and set out. One-horn did not show any surprise at his sudden departure, and seemed relieved to be rid of his rival. 'You were very useful when I had my broken leg,' he said, 'but the way you've been acting recently makes no sense. Go as far as you like! We can manage very well without you now.'

'I'll be back before winter,' said Stone-eye, thinking to himself that One-horn might have shown a little more gratitude. However, the he-goat only repeated blankly, 'Before winter?' as if he scarcely knew the meaning of the word. 'Who cares for winter?'

'You will, when you're up to your belly in snow,' said Stone-eye, and with that he set off into the bushes. He had not seen the weasel again since waking that morning. Probably Needle-tooth had just been flattering him so as to get safely away. Or possibly he had merely dreamed the whole thing. However, when he had been trotting along beside the great cliff for some time, making northwards, he suddenly felt a little tug at the bag over his shoulder, and there was the weasel sitting on it, though he had not seen where the animal came from.

'So there you are again!' he said. 'I was beginning to think I'd only dreamed you.'

'I'm glad to know your finger doesn't hurt any more,' said the weasel.

'My finger?' asked Stone-eye, puzzled. Raising his hand, he saw the toothmarks on his index finger, and laughed. 'Well, at least that proves you weren't a dream!' he said. 'Where have you been hiding?'

'Far enough from the cave to be away from the smell of your goats,' said the weasel. 'I hope you don't mind my saying so, but the fact is, weasels are very sensitive that way.'

'That's all right,' said Stone-eye. 'I must get used to living without the smell of my flock myself now.'

That day he kept going along the foot of the cliff, through the bushes. Towards evening the land began to rise, and the forest came closer. Stone-eye felt safer as soon as he was under the tall beech and spruce trees. The weasel shot about the undergrowth like a streak of shiny brown lightning, and then would go a little more slowly until he had made a quick kill, whereupon he would jump back up to his place on the goat's-hair bag. Stone-eye could never hear him coming.

Meanwhile, the path was coming closer and closer to the top of the rock wall, which now stood only about twice the height of a man above the slope itself. The hillside became steep and stony, and finally Stone-eye reached the place where the last reddish rocks disappeared into the moss between the tall trunks of old fir trees. The ground here was springy with a brown carpet of needles, and rose only gently, to fall downhill again into a shallow valley where a narrow mountain stream ran fast and sparkling through leafy bushes. Stone-eye stopped here and looked around for a place to spend the night.

Beside the burn, he found a mossy hollow which was dry enough for him to sleep in it without catching a cold: a cold would be something of a nuisance on a journey of any length. 'Is this all right for you?' he asked his companion. The weasel lifted his nose, sniffing, and then nodded. 'A good place,' he said, took a single leap, and was gone into the bushes.

'All very well for you!' Stone-eye called after him. 'The woods don't provide *me* with anything to eat in springtime!'

A moment later he heard a shrill squeal in the undergrowth, suddenly cut short, followed by a brief sound of kicking and struggling, and then the weasel reappeared, dragging a dead rabbit, which he laid at Stone-eye's feet like a tribute. 'Will you do me the honour of accepting this rather skinny rabbit?' he inquired politely, and added, after a moment, 'Actually, there's more than enough hereabouts for you to eat.'

Stone-eye looked at the limp rabbit. There was a thin trickle of blood running over the soft fur of its neck. 'I could have talked to you only a few moments ago, rabbit,' he said almost to himself. 'I don't really feel much like eating you.'

'Don't you like rabbit meat?' asked the weasel. 'Or haven't you ever eaten it?'

'I think I used to, once,' said Stone-eye, 'but I didn't understand the rabbits' language then.'

'What's the difference?' asked the weasel. 'It was a rather stupid rabbit anyway, or I couldn't have caught it. You wouldn't have enjoyed a conversation with it much.'

Stone-eye had cracked a few nuts and was chewing energetically at them, for they were rather hard now. He spat out one which tasted rancid. However, he finally said, 'As you can see, I still have something to eat.'

The weasel cast the rejected nut a glance of slight distaste. 'What sort of food do you call that?' he inquired. 'Forgive me for asking, but how long are you planning to be on your travels?'

'Until autumn,' said Stone-eye.

'And how long will your stock of nuts last?'

Stone-eye put his hand in the bag and let the nuts run through his fingers. 'A week, maybe,' he said. 'If I go carefully with them, that is.'

'So in a week's time you'll have to eat a rabbit, or something similar,' said the weasel. 'Why not now?'

Stone-eye could not deny the logic of the weasel's argument. He stroked the rabbit's fur once more, feeling sorry for it, but then he said all at once, 'Yes, why not now?', took his knife out of the bag and began skinning the animal. He gutted it, and threw the entrails to the weasel, then collected dry wood, lit a fire, and when he had enough glowing embers he skewered the rabbit on a dry branch and began roasting it over them, turning it constantly until the juices dripped, hissing, on the charred wood. The aroma of roast meat made him ravenously hungry, and he tore the creature apart when it was only half cooked, ate and ate and did not stop eating until he had gnawed the last fibres of meat off the bones.

After that evening, Needle-tooth provided their daily meal, and Stone-eye nibbled a few of his nuts only when he felt hungry on the way. He had turned westward from his first camp, and was going higher and higher into the mountains, where the woods were not so dense, and the trees grew lower, and were more windblown. There were many places where the sky above could be seen, which Stone-eye did not like at all. He often felt that incomprehensible fear rise in him when he crossed small clearings, scurrying from tree to tree, to hide in the bushes again.

On one occasion, when he was making his way through the matted undergrowth beside a clearing once more, instead of crossing the open turf, so that branches whipped about the ears of the weasel perched on his bag, Needle-tooth looked up at him and asked, 'Are you afraid the falcon will see you here?'

'Maybe,' said Stone-eye, 'but I don't really know. I can't stand being under the open sky, anyway.'

'Then why are you climbing so high into the mountains?' inquired the weasel.

'Why am I climbing so high?' repeated Stone-eye, still moving on, and then he was silent for a while. At last he said, in a curiously empty voice, 'I don't really know that, either. All I know is that I must get over this wall and down on the other side.'

'What wall?' asked the weasel. 'I don't see any wall around here.' And when Stone-eye made no reply, but climbed silently and doggedly on, the weasel scuttled nervously up to his shoulder and squealed into his ear, 'Why don't you speak? Where's there a wall?'

Stone-eye jumped with alarm, stared blankly at the weasel, and asked, 'Who said anything about a wall? I want to get over the mountains. Do I have to keep on telling you my plans?'

He reached the top of the pass that day. Up here, above the low-growing, stunted bushes, the only large trees were a few isolated stone pines, thick with needles, dark green pyramids with mighty trunks, trees to which the stormy winds could do little harm. Stone-eye breathed in the sweet, resinous scent of their wood as he worked his way, bending low, through the tangled, tough branches of the dwarf mountain pines. He was almost paralysed by his fear, for the empty sky weighed down on the few branches swaying in the air above him. He felt like an ant in the grass, an ant upon which some monstrous boot might tread at any moment, and in the end he was crawling on all fours like an animal, but he never thought of turning back. And then the ground before him suddenly went steeply downhill. Stone-eye clutched a rocking branch that had grown into snake-like coils, his head emerged above the last boughs of the dwarf pines, and he was looking down over steeply descending tree-tops into a wide and shallow valley, through whose almost improbably green meadows a little river wound its way, reflecting the sunlight, while in the distance, where that incredible green faded into the haze, horses were out at pasture.

He lay there a long time in the hot, resinous fragrance of the pines, trying to pin down a memory that the sight of this broad green valley awoke in him. He felt as if he had seen all this before, if from another point of view, but he could not manage to connect it with any earlier experience. Hadn't there been a child with him? Or had he once dreamed of such a thing? He didn't know.

At this point the weasel, who had finally taken to making his own way uphill, arrived beside him and peered down into the valley. 'Happy now?' he inquired.

'Happy?' said Stone-eye, not sure what to make of the word. 'I must get down to that valley, that's all I know, but don't ask me why.'

During his laborious climb down the steep slope, he tried to keep in the shelter of the few scattered pines and mountain willows. Farther down, where the wooded ground sloped more gently towards the valley floor, there was a huge sycamore with dark green foliage; an alluring sight, and the goal for which he was making. When at last, breathing hard, he reached the shade of its broad crown, he realized that the stream running through the valley rose under this tree. The basin of the spring was surrounded by mossy rocks, and the water collected in a little pool before escaping to run down the grassy slopes between alders and birch trees, young limes and privet bushes.

He camped for the night here. The weasel liked the place too, went off and soon came back with a pigeon he had obviously caught drinking, so Stone-eye did not have to go to sleep hungry. His appetite satisfied, and feeling pleasantly tired after the steep climb down, he lay back in the soft woodland grass beside the spring, listening to the wind rustling in the leaves of the sycamore and the gurgling of the stream as it ran over the stones, and gazed drowsily into the dark. The alder bushes crouched out there like stout trolls wrapped up to their chins, and between them rose the pale, slender trunks of birches. When the wind moved in their branches, the birch trees moved too, like dancing girls standing in the grass, feet together, their bodies swaying gently to and fro. And then they moved their legs as well, their feet were no longer rooted to the spot, their pale bodies slipped in and out of the dark bushes, they spread and lifted their shimmering arms, took hands, moved apart again, and then began an eddying dance in which they all circled one another faster and faster, while soft chuckling and sudden bursts of laughter mingled with the rustling and pattering of their leaves.

Stone-eye sat up and saw the circle of dancing girls draw together in a foaming eddy of shimmering light, and then flow apart into separate figures again, will-o'-the-wisps hovering over the turf, and one of these figures was dancing straight towards him, was suddenly there in front of him, a living yet almost incorporeal whirlwind, with flying hair like water lapping around a face pale as birch bark, a face that was never just where he looked for it, as if it were everywhere and nowhere at once, its eyes looking at him from all sides, yet never lingering long enough for him to meet their gaze, or even decide if they were yellow as amber or green as moss, for next moment they were darker than the night in the shade of the trees again. Yet he wanted to fathom that darkness; he rose and tried clumsily to grasp the figure, followed her, stepping out of the shadow of the great tree. Then he heard that clear laughter again, and a voice cried, 'A faun! A faun! Sisters, come here! A faun!' Next moment he found himself surrounded by the eddying circle of dancing sisters; he stood stock still on the grass that was wet with dew, turned to try and get a proper view of one of the figures, but he wasn't quick enough, and kept losing sight of her. Then he reached out his arms, crying, 'Come here! Stay with me! Be my flock!'

On hearing that the sisters shook with laughter again, danced closer and closer around him, so that he was quite dizzy with looking at their turning, whirling circle, and amidst all the laughter he heard them call, 'Dance with us, dance, and then we will stay with you, faun!'

That was enough for him. With a wild, goatish leap he bounded into the midst of the girls, so that they scattered, squealing; he felt something real, corporeal touch his hairy skin, he ran after one of the sisters, who raced away before him, hair flying, and next moment there were three more, holding hands, dancing around him and coming so close that their lips nearly brushed his own mouth, and then they chased away, laughing, through the dark bushes, so that he had to run after them if he wasn't to lose sight of them, and next moment he was in the midst of the whole laughing troop, and let the sisters chase him for a change; they were behind him and beside him and everywhere, all at once, plucking at the shaggy hair around his goatish loins, though he could never catch one of them at it, however fast he whirled around.

Turning yet again on one hoof, he saw there was just one single figure left, running for the nearby bushes. He ran as fast as his goat's legs would carry him, was catching up, and almost stumbled and fell when the figure suddenly stopped just before she reached the shadowy alders, turned and looked at him. His heart rose into his throat as he took the last few steps that brought him up to her. He still could not make out the colour of her eyes, but he felt as if their gaze were breaking over him as he opened his arms and put them around her shoulders. For a brief moment he felt her soft, smooth body against his skin, and the touch on his mouth of lips that tasted of the birch trees' springtime sap, and then he was holding a fissured tree-trunk in his arms, its bark white and silky between the crevices of black, but cold and hard to his mouth.

Anyway, the girl had gone. Or else she had been transformed, and might be a kind of tree nymph that changed shape from time to time. He had sought a strange flock, this clumsy faun who still held a slender birch tree in his arms, believing she must turn soft and supple again for love of him. But no such thing happened; there was only the sound of the wind in the leaves now, and it sounded as if someone were laughing at him.

So there was nothing he could do but laugh as well. By way of farewell, he pressed a hearty kiss on the smooth, white bark, then crouched at the foot of the tree-trunk and looked around him. The birch trees stood tall and still among the dark bushes again, as if they had never left their places. His flock. Perhaps they had never really moved from the spot at all. You could dream strange dreams here in this valley, he thought as he rose and trotted slowly back to the sycamore, its crown looming like a monstrous black cloud before the night sky. Strange dreams. But he had liked the dream. He lay down in the grass again and tried to conjure up an image of the dancing sisters before his eyes closed.

Over the next few days he roamed the woods bordering the pastureland of the valley, sleeping near birch trees by night, always hoping to meet the dancing sisters again, but they never came back. Meanwhile, he was going farther and farther down the valley, and once, when he came close to the edge of the woods, he saw the horses grazing on the flat land of the valley floor: long-legged, strong-boned animals, moving slowly over the meadows as they grazed, tails flicking away the flies. Then he heard voices, and saw two herdsmen eating their breakfast of bread and cheese in the shade of a tree as they talked to each other. He had not heard men talking for as long as he could remember, and his first thought was to run away and hide in the thick forest, because their voices frightened him. They sounded sharper and louder than the voices of birds and beasts, and there was an opinionated, quarrelsome tone to them, although the two herdsmen seemed to be conversing in a perfectly friendly way.

He was about to slip away when he heard two words that struck him as familiar. One of the men had said something about 'Arni's Folk'. Stone-eye did not know what those words might mean, but it seemed to him that he had heard them before. 'Arni's Folk,' he said softly. 'Arni's Folk . . .' And as he listened to the sound of the syllables, he became more and more certain that he must once have had something to do with those people. He tried to remember, but as before, he soon came up against a barrier he could not cross. As soon as he tried to get over it, his thoughts tangled into an impenetrable thicket, allowing no glimpse of those earlier events which, he now felt sure, must lie beyond that threshold.

However, the herdsmen were speaking of such things as he might once have known himself, and this idea drove him to stalk cautiously closer to the place where they sat, and listen. By now he was well used to moving in the forest without a sound, and so he managed to reach a thick hawthorn bush by the edge of the wood, from where he could watch the two herdsmen without being seen. It was not particularly difficult, as the two men were sitting with their backs to the wood, looking out at their horses in the meadow. Stone-eye settled comfortably behind his bush and tried to follow the conversation. One of the herdsmen had so thick and curly a beard that you could see little of his face apart from his bulbous nose. The other man was still young and beardless, and spoke in a high, penetrating voice. It was he who had mentioned Arni's Folk, and now he said, 'Yes, that's right, when we drove the mares to the village of Arni's Folk we asked for Honi, the one they call Arni's Deputy. We were supposed to be handing the horses over to him, you see.'

'Did you get a sight of the black stallion who's to cover them?' asked the bearded man.

'Yes, but only later,' said the young man. 'And we never got to see Honi at all. They say he's very sick, and has handed all the business of the place over to his daughter. At least, that's what we heard from a man we asked in the village street, but from the way he spoke of it, you'd be almost inclined to think this daughter of Honi's, Narzia, didn't wait long for her father's permission before taking over.'

'Women in charge!' growled the older man. 'So that's what these strange new Raiding Riders have come to! I never liked them, nor their grovelling ways!'

The young man shrugged his shoulders. 'At least they know what's good for them, and they're polite enough about it!' he said. 'As for Honi's daughter Narzia, there was precious little grovelling about her! When she finally deigned to come out of the house and look at the mares she put some very apt questions, and when she looked at you with those green eyes of hers, why, you felt like a sparrow in her hand – you almost feared she'd keep you there along with the mares, and we none of us fancied that, not when we'd seen the way she treats her servants.'

'What servants are those?' asked the bearded man. 'I always thought

Arni's Folk didn't keep any slaves to serve them now, not since they cut off their braids.'

'So we thought too,' said the younger man. 'And strictly speaking that's right, there aren't any slaves there. It's just that they press their goods on the folk living in the settlements round about on credit, you see, and later, when the debtors can't pay, they have to work as servants for nothing. No, of course there aren't any slaves, Arni forbade that, but it comes to the same thing in the end. Anyway, I can tell you we were glad Narzia was satisfied with the mares!'

'A nasty lot, if you ask me,' said the bearded man. 'We never ought to have let ourselves in for dealing with those cunning traders. Why, even the goldsmiths of Arziak complain that Arni's Folk won't pay the right price these days, the way they promised they would at first. I tell you what: that fluter tricked us all!'

As Stone-eye listened to this conversation, blurred images came into his mind: the picture of a square surrounded by log cabins, one of them grey with age, but he could not remember where he had ever seen such a thing. And now, when the older man mentioned a fluter, the listener felt strangely stricken, as if someone were reproaching him, and he could not tell why. Nor had he much time to wonder at it, for the younger man was going on with his tale. 'I'm not surprised Arni's Folk pay less for our goldsmiths' pretty things these days,' he said. 'Why would they give good money for what they can get brought to them more cheaply?'

'Where from?' asked the older man. 'There aren't any goldsmiths anywhere around here, except in Arziak.'

'Ah, but you don't necessarily have to buy from the goldsmiths,' said the young man. 'I'll tell you how it goes, see? While we were with Arni's Folk, there was this horde of Raiding Riders came in from the steppes. We were just about to take off for the mountains as fast as we could, when we realized the villagers didn't seem scared, not a bit of it, but were looking out for their wild relations as if it was a friendly visit. And when we asked one of the men why he wasn't worried, he just smiled and said, "Anyone can tell you're simple mountain herdsmen! Didn't you hear how the Raiding Riders' horses have all gone peaceful on them? Try and get those horses to attack, and they'll turn tail and gallop away. Can't even use 'em for hunting. And a Raiding Rider without a horse is only half the warrior he was, a man there's no cause to fear." At first we couldn't believe it, but he seemed to be right, for the horde stopped a couple of bowshots away from the village, or thereabouts, and just three Riders came on, each of them leading a heavily laden packhorse, hands held up and out so anyone could see they had no tricks in mind. They were taken to Narzia's house, and of course I don't know just what went on there. But from all that happened afterwards, I can work out the general idea of it: now that the horde can't get enough by raiding to keep body and soul together, the people in their camp are starving. And they'd come to exchange the valuable jewellery they've stolen over the years, or maybe sometimes even bought, for corn and beans and meat. At any rate, the leather sacks the three Riders dragged into Narzia's house were pretty heavy, and so full you could see gold and silver chains bulging out of the tops of 'em. Later on, when the men came out again along with Narzia, that green-eyed witch, she told her men to load the packhorses up with provisions. Obviously Arni's Folk didn't trust their kin too well, for they wouldn't let more than three Riders into their village, so the three men had to take laden horses out to the horde a dozen times or more and fetch fresh beasts, before all they'd got was packed up, and I can tell you, the bargain didn't give them any pleasure! I was watching those three Riders, and they were gnawing their moustaches, and their thin faces were white with rage, and they looked straight through the grinning villagers as if they were no more than a few sheep standing by the roadside. I never had much time for Raiding Riders myself, but when I saw that, why, I almost felt sorry for 'em.'

'That's a nasty story you tell,' said the older man. 'Arni's Folk, of all people, ought to know what an angry Raiding Rider may do. The longer I think about it, the more your tale scares me.'

'I didn't feel too happy myself,' said the young man. 'But Narzia didn't seem worried. When the men rode away for the last time, she called something after them, sharpish, and one of the men turned and shouted back at her. It sounded like an oath. Then he spat and rode after the others. I asked one of Arni's Folk what Narzia wanted, and he told me she was asking for a golden brooch made like a Rider which was missing from the jewels, and if that piece wasn't brought next time, she wasn't letting them have so much as a handful of corn.'

'Then Narzia must be out of her mind!' said the older man. 'Why, I've heard of that brooch. Khan Hunli got it from Urla the Wise, that time she gave Arni the eye-stone whose whereabouts nobody really knows now. Arni's Folk may make a mystery out of it, but people do say it's gone missing.'

'The eye-stone!' cried Stone-eye, leaping up and clutching the bag around his neck. He had forgotten all his caution when he heard mention of the stone he carried with him, which linked him in some mysterious way to a life he had forgotten. 'What do you know about the eye-stone?' he asked, never noticing how he was yelling in his excitement. Only then did he see panic terror in the two herdsmen's eyes. They stared at him: a naked, hairy beast-man with a weasel perched on his shaggy hip, the little animal hissing at them more in fright than anger. They were all frightened, including Stone-eye, as soon as he realized that he had left his hiding place in a moment of agitation and let the two men see him. They stood facing each other for a while, quite still, as if any move might set some terrible event in motion. Then the herdsmen suddenly flung themselves down, touching the ground with their foreheads and stammering something to the effect that they begged the forest spirit to spare them. The elder of them, still bending low, crawled aside, groped for his knapsack without ever taking his eyes off the goat-legged creature, took out a flat cake of bread and a round little farmhouse cheese, and laid both at Stone-eye's feet, like an offering. Then the herdsmen crept back to the place where they had been sitting, on hands and knees. Only when they knew they had the stout tree-trunk between themselves and the terrifying beast-man did they grab their things and run for it across the pastures, as if a pack of wolves were after them.

Stone-eye was angry with himself for his thoughtlessness; but for that, he would probably have found out more about the eye-stone. He was sure now that that part of his life which was buried in his memory must lie hidden in the stone. He sat down in the grass, took the stone from its bag, and looked at it. Beneath the smooth surface, the sunlight was refracted into fine, cloudy filaments, and through them shone the green, blue and violet circles whose colour and extent changed as you moved the stone. He watched the play of circling colours, and waited for an image to emerge, as it had done before, maybe a face he knew, though without being able to say if he had ever met the woman whose face it was, and if so, where. But nothing of the kind happened. The stone was hiding its secret, although the goat-legged faun now thought he knew for certain that there was such a secret, and it must have something to do with himself. Once again, he had heard mention of an old woman who once possessed the stone. The herdsman had called her Urla. Stone-eye listened carefully to the sound of that name, which seemed to him familiar in the same way as the shimmering colours of his stone, and his anger faded the longer he looked into that soft glow, feeling the beauty of the colours warm and comfort his heart.

'That stone of yours is a very magical thing and no mistake!' said the weasel. 'It's even got you something to eat now.'

This remarkably prosaic observation brought Stone-eye back to a reality that seemed to him pale and commonplace, compared to that other reality into which he had looked through the stone eye, though without understanding it. Anyway, Needle-tooth's remark struck him as highly inappropriate. 'Can't think of anything more important than food, can you?' he inquired.

The weasel did not seem to notice the implied rebuke, and said equably, 'Food's always important if you want to stay alive.' Had he been able to do so, he would probably have shrugged his shoulders. 'I wasn't thinking of myself, either,' he went on. 'Personally, I don't care for that stuff the herdsman left in the grass, but I suppose you might like it.'

Now, at last, Stone-eye noticed the herdsman's offering. The sight of the bread's crisp brown crust aroused memories of a flavour he had not tasted for a very long time. He put the stone away, picked up the bread and broke it apart. When he smelled its sweet, floury aroma, he felt ravenously hungry, and he had devoured half the bread before it even occurred to him that he might eat a piece of cheese with it too.

Over the next few days Stone-eye kept coming back to the same spot, hoping to be able to overhear the herdsmen again, and thus learn more about the stone, or other mysteries connected with it, but he did not see the men a second time. Instead, he found a loaf of bread and something to eat with it left there every day: maybe a piece of bacon, a slice of dried meat, or another cheese. These offerings brought a little more variety to his diet, the more so as he was still accepting the weasel's prey, if only to avoid injuring his friend's feelings.

The rest of the time, the faun wandered the woods restlessly, always keeping close to the open valley floor. 'What is it you're really after here?' the weasel once asked, but he could not answer that question. The acorns were beginning to swell, the summer flowers were fading in the meadows, but Stone-eye stayed on in the valley, in a state of impatience, as if there were something for which he must wait.

While the weasel was off hunting one morning, and he was trotting aimlessly along the borders of the wood once more, keeping to the shelter of the bushes as usual, he saw a girl out in the middle of the valley, almost a child still, walking along beside the stream. He stopped and watched the slender figure moving through the tall meadow grass, now farther from him and now nearer as she followed the windings of the meandering stream.

At last the course of the stream led the girl straight to that place where Stone-eye crouched hidden in the undergrowth; her delicate, childlike features could be seen more and more clearly, and suddenly his gaze was caught by the girl's dark eyes as she looked towards the wood: eyes of a strange colour, a colour hard to describe, that seemed to look at him, and he knew at once that this was not the first time he had met those eyes, which appeared in a strange way to be both close and very far away. Now and then the girl leaned down and ran her hand through the water, and when she came to the place where the course of the stream turned back towards the middle of the valley, she sat down on the bank, dangled her legs in the current, and looked across the water to the woods. She stayed sitting there for a while, letting the water swirl around her ankles. And then the girl began to sing. Her low-pitched voice reminded him of the sound of a flute played in its lower register, and he understood every word of the song, as if he had been familiar with it for a very long time.

> *To the lake a girl did go*
> *every year,*
> *to the lake a girl did go*
> *with her cheeks as white as snow.*

> *Oh the Green Man he came out*
> *every year,*
> *oh the Green Man he came out*
> *and he kissed her on the mouth.*

> *The poor girl she wept sore*
> *every year,*
> *the poor girl she wept sore*
> *and she never came back more.*

> *To the lake did Agla go*
> *in that year,*
> *to the lake did Agla go*
> *in a dress as white as snow.*

Oh the Green Man he came out
in that year,
oh the Green Man he came out
and she kissed him on the mouth.

Oh fair Agla's laugh was light
in that year,
oh fair Agla's laugh was light
and the Green Man sang all night.

The listener in the bushes knew that this was the end of the song, yet the girl went on, adding one more verse:

The fluter played this song
last year,
the fluter played this song
but he did not stay here long.

And then the girl began to call out in a language that sounded different from the words humans generally use, but Stone-eye could understand that language too, and it seemed to him it must be the language of the fishes. 'Come here, my friends!' called the girl. 'Come swim to me, you trout and bream and sticklebacks!' And he saw the water crinkle as the shining silver bodies of the fish jumped, and splashed back into the stream, sending up spray. 'Listen,' cried the girl, 'listen to me!' Then the water was instantly calm again, but Stone-eye could see it turn dark at the girl's feet with the shadows of all the fish thronging close together. 'Listen!' said the girl again, and then she sang:

I seek a fluter,
one who can
talk to the wolves,
a minstrel man.

He rode with Barlo
to lend him aid,
and in the Marsh
for the Green Man played.

He sang me a song
to the Green Man dear,

the tale of Agla
who knew no fear.

To Arni's Folk
he went away,
and I have not seen him
since that day.

Oh ask the Green Man
where I can
find the fluter now,
the minstrel man.

When the girl had ended her chanting song, the water swirled up at her feet, and the shadowy shapes of the fish darted away, swift as a flight of arrows, over the bed of the stream.

The girl stood up, her strange eyes turned on the bushes where Stone-eye was hiding. At the very moment when he realized that he had risen erect, so as to see what was going on beside the stream, and had a clear view above the bushes, the girl suddenly flung up her arms, crying, 'Fluter!' He stood there rooted to the spot, watching the child leap lightly across the stream and run over the grass towards him. 'I saw you!' she called as she ran. 'You can stop hiding now! Come out, fluter!'

Then Stone-eye remembered that this was a game, a game where you had to find another person's hiding place. You looked away and counted to a given number, while the other player slipped off, found a place to hide and waited to be found. He clearly remembered the way the hidden player's heart beat as he crouched in hiding, when the seeker came close. His heart was thudding now, for he had been found, and the rules of the game said he must come out of hiding and give up. So he stepped out of the bushes, surrendering. But then the girl's eyes widened. She was very close now, and she stopped running so abruptly that she almost fell over. She stood there swaying slightly, pure horror on her face. 'No!' she cried, clapping her hands over her eyes, and then she whirled around, ran back over the grass, jumped the stream and raced back to the horses grazing a little way off. Once she reached them, she leaped on the back of a piebald pony, and urged the beast downstream at a gallop, over the valley floor and away.

Since recognizing the girl's eyes, Stone-eye had felt sure he knew the meaning of this game; he felt, indeed, that the game was his reason for coming to this shallow valley, and now he was baffled. Perhaps I came out of hiding too soon after all, he thought. I'm always over-impatient. He saw the slender figure racing over the meadows, far away now, and very tiny, and then it merged into the patches of brown that broke the regular green of the valley in the distance. They must be cottages and stables. 'I'll play better next time,' he said to himself, half aloud, and it seemed to him that there was nothing to keep him here now.

He set off on the homeward journey that same day, though he was in no particular hurry. He left the valley floor behind him, followed the watercourse upstream through light woodland, and eventually reached the spring beneath the sycamore again. The leaves of the birches were already turning colour, and shone yellow among the alder bushes, whose foliage was still dark green. 'Will you play with me again tonight?' said Stone-eye, as he wandered among their slender, white trunks, tenderly stroking the silky bark with his fingertips. He longed to hear the clear laughter of the dancing sisters, who felt no fear of his goatish form.

Meanwhile, Needle-tooth had gone off hunting, and before darkness fell he came back with a young black grouse, which made a delicious roast. When Stone-eye had eaten his fill, he lay down in the soft grass beside the stream and looked up above the fire, which was burning down, into the sprinkling of birch leaves that stood out pale in the moonlight against the dark, rounded shapes of the alders, waiting for the nimble sisters to come to life and dance with him.

As he waited, he must have fallen asleep, for when he was startled into wakefulness by a splashing sound close to his head the moon had set. The pale birch trunks beneath their dark cloud of leaves had not shifted from the spot, but something was moving on the edge of the pool where the spring rose. Stone-eye felt the weasel's slender body at his side braced like a steel spring, but he felt that whatever was approaching was no enemy, and laid a soothing hand on his friend's smooth coat, saying, 'No, let it be! You mustn't disturb the peace of this spring.'

'Thank you, my shaggy goatish friend,' said a soft voice with a slight gurgling sound to it. 'Then I can venture out of this pond.'

Stone-eye, who was sitting up now, heard rather than saw some kind of plump creature make its clumsy way out of the water. It crouched in the moss close to the place where he lay. In the faint starlight, he could make out little more than the gleam of warty skin glistening with moisture, and two golden eyes which seemed to be lit up from within. The newcomer was a toad of considerable size.

'You're not exactly the visitor I was expecting tonight,' he said.

The toad's gurgling chuckle told him that she knew very well whom he had hoped to play with that night. 'You picked the wrong time,' she said. 'Don't you see the sisters are wearing their yellow dresses now? They're light-minded creatures, the birch tree girls, too tired for such wild games at this season. They've gone to bed and will soon be dreaming of next spring. If it's company you're after, you'll have to make do with me, and I'm only here myself because you gave me such a pretty name.'

'What name was that? Have I ever met you before?' asked Stone-eye, racking his brains to think when it could have been.

'Keep on thinking and it'll come back to you,' said the toad, her beautiful eyes gazing expectantly at him.

Stone-eye did in fact feel as if this was a situation he had known once before: a gurgling stream under bushes by night, and the calm yet slightly mocking gaze in those eyes, which made one forget the shapeless toad's ugly form.

'Golden-eye,' he said, 'where have I met you before? It must have been before I forgot everything.'

'Well, at least you remember my name,' said the toad. 'That's something. Given time, a person who still knows names will find what goes with them. And maybe even himself in the end. What do they call *you* these days?'

'My goats call me Stone-eye,' said the goat-legged faun. 'Isn't that my real name?'

'You'll have to find out for yourself,' said the toad. 'Meanwhile, you should be glad it's Stone-eye. I can think of worse names people might have called you, for one reason or another. And at least you seem to have kept that jewel, even now you live a goatish life, which makes me think you won't end your days in the company of goats. I'd like to see the eye-stone again. Would you be kind enough to take it out and show me?'

'With pleasure,' said Stone-eye, opening the bag and taking out the stone. As soon as he had it on the palm of his hand, it began to shine. It was as if the golden glow of the toad's eyes were caught in the smooth curve of the stone, awakening the coloured rings to life. At first there was only a point of gold glowing deep in the heart of the stone, a germ

of light that grew and grew, spreading like rings of ripples in water
where a fish has just snapped at a fly. But what came up beneath the
shimmer of green and blue and violet was no fish, but a face, the face of
a girl looking at him, and the girl's eyes were of the same colours as the
stone, so that the goat-legged faun did not know if those rings of colour
were reflected in the girl's eyes, or the many shining colours arose from
those eyes themselves, and as he was still wondering the girl opened her
mouth and cried, 'Fluter! I saw you!'

'Who are you?' asked Stone-eye. 'Why did you run away from me?'

Then the image sank beneath the rippling circles, and the toad
uttered her gurgling chuckle again, as if she found the whole thing
rather comical. 'Well, are you surprised?' said she. 'The way you look
now, with your legs all goatish and shaggy, you gave the child a nasty
fright.'

'Why did she call me Fluter?' asked Stone-eye, putting his stone
away again.

'Perhaps you were a fluter once,' said the toad.

'Then she didn't mix me up with someone else?' asked Stone-eye,
intently.

'Could be,' said the toad, as if it didn't matter much.

'Why won't you give me a straight answer?' asked Stone-eye. 'This
is more important to me than anything in the world.'

'Glad to hear it,' said the toad, 'but you're not all that important
yourself, you know. And even if I told you, it wouldn't do you much
good just now.'

'I heard the girl singing to the fishes about this fluter,' said Stone-
eye. 'They were to tell someone called the Green Man. She wanted the
Green Man to look for the fluter.'

'I know,' said the toad. 'Why do you think I'm here, then? The
Green Man knows I know the fluter and so I'd be the first to find him.'

'And have you found him?' asked Stone-eye.

'What's the good of finding him if he isn't the fluter he used to be?'
said the toad. 'The way he looks now, he's not the one she's seeking.'

'Then the girl will never find him,' said Stone-eye, losing all hope.

'I didn't say that,' said the toad. 'But I fancy it'll be quite a time yet
before he's found.'

Such vague information was getting Stone-eye more and more
confused. Sometimes he felt as if they were talking about himself, and
then the toad would speak of this fluter as if he were a stranger. He
couldn't make head or tail of it. 'What am I to do now?' he asked.

'You didn't think very much of my advice once,' remarked the toad. 'At least *that* seems to have changed for the better! Well, for the time being, all you can do is go back over the mountains to your goats and let them see you through the winter. You might try looking around for a flute later. You heard her say she's in search of a man who can play one. So I'll wish you good speed, and thank you for showing me the stone again. Take good care of it!'

'You can leave that to me,' said the weasel, who had been lying curled up beside Stone-eye all this time.

'And you have a good bodyguard there!' said the toad. 'Goodbye, Stone-eye. Same to you, Needle-tooth, and kindly keep those sharp teeth of yours off my family!'

So saying, she hopped away into the bushes. There was a brief rustling in the dry leaves, and then all was still again.

'Funny friends you've got,' remarked Needle-tooth.

'Friends?' said Stone-eye. 'I don't really know. I may have met that toad before, but I can't remember. Let's get a little sleep now.' And with that he lay back in the grass again and closed his eyes. He heard the wind rustling in the tree-tops a little longer, a deep sound in the sycamore leaves and a clear one in the yellowing birches, and it sounded like the whisper of girls' voices, now soft and hesitant, then louder, as if a chorus of sisters were whispering together. Stone-eye listened to their voices, and gradually he came to think he understood what they were saying. 'That shaggy faun is here at our feet again. Did you know they're looking for him?' So I really am the one the Green Man was to seek, thought Stone-eye as he drowsed off, and the rustling faded away. Then the whispers rose again, and he heard one of the sisters say, 'Sleep well, faun! You're safe with us. Find out what happened, and then you will find your girl.' And Stone-eye saw before him that evanescent figure who had changed into a birch tree in his arms. He was going to ask just how he could find his way back into the past, but by then he had fallen asleep.

Next morning Stone-eye said goodbye to his birch trees. The sky was milky above their shimmering golden foliage, and a downwind, un-usually warm for the time of year, was blowing off the mountains, driving a few withered leaves before it. As he climbed the slope where the trees and bushes grew only sparsely, Stone-eye was overwhelmed again by that oppressive fear, but he had to endure it if he was to get back over the pass to his goats. Working his way step by step up the mountainside, clinging to the tough branches of the mountain willows, he tried to persuade himself that his sense of oppression was due to the sultry weather that made him sweat from every pore. Now and then a sudden gust of wind blew down on him, but there was no refreshment in it.

At last he reached the area of stunted bushes and tall stone pines, and crawled on beneath the dark branches, from which dry needles rained down on him. And now tall clouds, spreading fast, were towering in the sky, soon covering the pale sun, but making the air no cooler. 'We want to find shelter,' said Needle-tooth. 'There's a storm brewing.'

But Stone-eye did not wish to spend any longer than necessary in these sparsely wooded parts. He made his way on, hands sticky with resin, through the dense dwarf pines, stopping only for a few moments now and then to get his breath back under the thick boughs of one of the tall stone pines, and staring ahead of him, trying to see a way up to the top of the pass among the strewn boulders. He decided to climb up along a rocky channel where vegetation grew. It seemed to lead to the top of the pass, running between steep walls, but just as he had reached the spot where this last part of the climb began, the storm broke.

A bright white streak of lightning flashed down on the rocks from the lowering black clouds that had gathered above the pass, dazzling Stone-eye for the space of a dozen heartbeats, so that he could see nothing but the black, branching imprint of the flash. The roll of thunder that came crashing immediately after it made the ground shake as if the entire mountain were about to burst apart, and as it died away the scene was lit up with glaring light again, for lightning was now flashing down from the clouds on all sides, and the constant roar of the thunder brought Stone-eye down on the rocky ground among the gnarled roots of the mountain pines. As he clutched the earth, trembling, his face pressed to the dry, scratchy needles, he felt the weasel creep close to his ear. In between two rolls of thunder, Needle-tooth whispered, 'If you'll take my advice, I'd suggest you get under the ledge of rock over by that tall stone pine.'

Stone-eye raised his head, and saw a kind of cave at the foot of a cliff some twenty paces off. Its depths were lost in darkness. The first few heavy drops of rain were now falling, and it cost him an effort to decide to get to his feet in the middle of this raging storm and run to refuge, but he did it, leaping wildly through the harsh, springy shrubs and dashing the last few paces over bare ground to the mouth of the cave, driven by terror. Only when he knew there was a sheltering roof above him did he breathe again, and leaned panting against the cold rock wall. The weasel had got there before him. Needle-tooth was now sitting beside him, cleaning his coat.

Outside, the storm raged on. Lightning flash followed lightning flash, and the rumble of the thunder was amplified to a hollow booming echo under the rocky roof. And then the whole world seemed to explode with a deafening crash. For a moment, the tall stone pine just outside the cave stood in a halo of dazzling light, and then it went up in flames. The flames ate their way, hissing, through the dense needles on its branches, and a violent gust of wind sent the fire shooting up into the air like a banner, its drifting peak dissolving into a shower of sparks. The tall tree was all ablaze, the crash of its branches even drowning out the thunder, and the smoke, strongly laden with the sweet scent of resin, was driven in all directions by the wind.

Stone-eye stared at this tremendous spectacle, whose elemental power made him forget the storm itself, gazed at the giant tree of flames shooting up to the clouds, as if to set the sky itself on fire, a swaying pillar that burned and burned until the branches were consumed to the very top of the tree, and the gnarled trunk split with a thunderous crack, but even then the split wood of it burned on, as if the tree were to be destroyed to its roots. Then, after the last clap of thunder, the rain poured down, wiping out the whole picture in a moment, like a grey curtain drawn before the jagged mouth of the cave.

Stone-eye leaned back against the hard rock of the cave wall and breathed deeply, as if after some great exertion. As soon as he closed his eyes, he saw the pillar of fire blaze up again, and he did not know if he had been fascinated or horrified by the sight. He felt as if he had enjoyed the spectacle of a magnificent thing's destruction.

'That tree was beautiful even as it burned,' said a voice from the back of the cave.

Stone-eye whipped around, simultaneously bracing his hooves against the ground, ready to leap out of the confines of the cave. The speaker, whom he could scarcely make out in the darkness, must have noticed, for he said, 'You'll get rather wet if you run out, and I would be sorry too, for I'd like to talk to you a little, Stone-eye.'

The fact that this stranger, crouching like a rugged boulder in the shadows at the back of the cave, knew his name made Stone-eye uneasy, rather than causing him to trust the man. 'How do you know what I'm called?' he asked.

'Oh, they've started talking of you, this side and that of the mountains,' said the man. 'Goats, birch nymphs, horse-herds, all manner of other folk. Anyway, I've known you a long time.'

Stone-eye was going to ask how the man knew him, but suddenly the question struck him as superfluous. He felt the weasel at his side stretching, and asked, 'What do you think of this stranger, Needle-tooth?'

'His voice sounds all right,' said the weasel. 'Also, I'd rather stay here in the dry.'

'You have a sensible friend there, Stone-eye,' said the man. He rose, groaning slightly, and came slowly forward into the light: a thin, not very tall old man with a sparse white beard and a brown and wrinkled face. He walked with a slight stoop, as if he were always looking for something on the ground, and the stoop must have been caused by his way of life, since he wore a pointed hammer with a long handle hanging at his belt, and his worn leather bag left Stone-eye in no doubt.

'Oh, so you're a prospector,' he said, relieved, and almost a little disappointed.

The old man smiled, amused, and said, 'What did you expect, faun? One of the red-headed Bloodaxe People? An enchanter in a pointed hat? Or the Great Magician himself? You're likely to see prospectors in the mountains. I found shelter here a little sooner than you did when I saw the storm coming up, that's all. You were determined to get over the pass, but I had an idea we'd meet here in the end.'

'Did you want to meet me, then?' asked Stone-eye.

'People meet one another when the right time comes,' said the old man. 'May I sit down with you and your companion?'

The courtesy with which this prospector asked permission surprised Stone-eye. Despite his unassuming and almost fragile figure, the old man did not look at all like someone who had to ask if he wished to do something. However, he waited for Stone-eye to nod consent before sitting down by him. They sat there in silence for a while, side by side, looking out at the streaming curtain of rain that cut off this rocky chamber from the rest of the world, and the longer Stone-eye stared at that grey, streaked wall of water and spray, the more he felt as if he had been plucked out of the tangible world into some region beyond anywhere he could normally go, into a place where one was unexpectedly received, without having sought it, and which one could not leave of one's own volition either, not without falling through the wet and whirling curtain into a bottomless abyss.

After a while the old man turned to Stone-eye, saying, 'Well, we

ought to eat together before we talk. Be my guest, Stone-eye, and you
too, Needle-tooth.' He produced from his bag a flat cake of bread,
hard as a board, and also, surprisingly, a small piece of fresh meat, as if
he had provided in advance for the entertainment of a weasel. Besides
these, he brought out a flask made of turned, reddish pear-wood and
offered it to Stone-eye. 'Have a drop of red wine,' he said, 'to help the
dry bread down.' And Stone-eye thought it was a long time since he
had tasted anything so delicious. In his mouth the bread, seasoned
with fennel and coriander, mingled with the tart red wine to make a
dish of incomparable flavour, which he enjoyed to the very last as he
slowly chewed the hard bread, while the weasel helped himself to the
meat.

When he had eaten enough, and the old man had ended his own
meal with a last sip of wine, the latter said, 'And did you find what you
were looking for on your travels?'

This question surprised Stone-eye. Had he indeed been looking for
anything, or had he merely wandered the forests and mountains aimlessly? However, then it struck him that he must have had some end in
view when he undertook the torture of crossing the almost treeless pass,
and spent all summer on the very borders of the shallow valley. But
what? He had no idea. 'What do you think?' he asked. 'I mean, what
was I looking for?'

'Ah, that you'll have to find out for yourself,' said the old man. 'Is
there so little you want to know?'

'So little?' asked Stone-eye. 'No, I want to know too much. When I
came over the pass I had nothing much in mind but my flock of goats
the other side of the mountains. But this side, I sometimes felt as if the
herdsmen were talking of someone that might once have been me. And
then there was a girl who thought she knew me before she saw my
shaggy goatish form. I expect she was wrong, but I've been wondering
ever since if all that didn't have something to do with me after all.'

'And do you really only wonder?' asked the old man, looking him in
the face. His eyes were the colour of flecked, grey-green moss agate,
and seemed to shine from within in a curiously compelling way,
without any actual source of light to account for it. In this light Stone-
eye's experiences of the past few days stood out more clearly from the
murky cloudiness of his vague imaginings, began to take more distinct
shape, and gradually formed into a visible pattern where one element
fitted into another, scattered words came back into his mind, joined
with other words, and showed him connections that had been hidden

in obscurity before. He looked into the old man's eyes, still holding his question, and said, 'No – no, I don't really wonder. I know. But I can't remember the things they accused that fluter of doing, the fluter I suppose was once me.'

'What did they accuse him of?' asked the old man.

'Well, the herdsmen didn't speak very kindly of him,' said Stone-eye. 'They thought he had betrayed their people, in some kind of way.'

'And what about the girl?' asked the old man.

Stone-eye remembered the way the girl's strange eyes lit up when she saw him behind the bushes. 'The girl was glad when she thought she recognized the fluter,' he said. 'But then, when she saw me as I am, she was frightened and ran away.'

'Why?' asked the old man.

'Why?' repeated Stone-eye, trying to penetrate the dark veil that had descended over his past. 'I must have changed,' he said. 'One-horn once told me I used to be "one of those thin-legged men creatures". I'd quite forgotten that, but now I remember. He was lying on the ground, injured, and before he said that he called me "half-goat". I suppose he meant I once looked different. I must have had legs like those herdsmen. Or like the girl. That may be why I hate my goatish lower body so much.'

'You shouldn't despise that part of yourself,' said the old man. 'It still carries you around, and I think you'll have to trot through the woods on those hooves of yours for some while yet. But what about that girl, the child? Can't you remember her too?'

Stone-eye tried to conjure up a picture of the girl's face, and succeeded unexpectedly well. He saw it as clearly before him as if he had known it a long time, instead of encountering it once in that short meeting by the edge of the wood. Most distinctly of all, he remembered the way she had looked at him before horror came into her eyes. 'Her eyes,' he said. 'Those strange eyes. I couldn't describe them, but I do remember those eyes.'

'There, you see?' said the old man, smiling and pleased, as if everything were all right now. 'Go through that door, and you will find yourself.'

While Stone-eye was pondering this curious remark, the torrential rain which had been streaming down as violently as ever all the while suddenly slackened, a view of the landscape opened out again, as if a curtain had been drawn aside, a last few single, heavy drops fell splashing on the stones outside the cave, and then the clouds were blown apart too, driving away in the wind and revealing the clear sky. In the sunlight, the damp ground began to steam, the steep black pyramids of the stone pines rose into the blue-green sky above those hazy mists of vapour, and beyond the trees, clear as glass, towered the jagged outlines of the mountain peaks.

The old man rose, rubbed his stiff back and said, 'Well, we can set out again now. Good speed to you! And good hunting to you, Needle-tooth. My regards to your goats, faun!'

Stone-eye had not been prepared for this sudden parting. 'Can't you go part of the way with us?' he asked. But the old man shook his head. 'I must go down there,' he said, pointing to the valley out of which Stone-eye had climbed.

'I'm sorry,' said Stone-eye. 'When I talk to you, a great many things seem clearer, but I think there's much I still don't understand.'

'Well, bear that in mind,' said the old man, 'for what you have discovered is far from all. However, I'll give you a companion, someone for you to talk to now and then in winter. Your goats are good creatures, but where conversation's concerned they have one-track minds.' So saying, he left the cave and went over to the place where the tall stone pine had shot up towards the sky in flames. The heavy rain had put out the fire, and there was nothing left but blackened ruins, a few threads of smoke still rising from them. Stone-eye followed the old man, tasting the resinous smell of burning on his tongue as soon as he trod among the charred remains of the giant tree.

The old man stopped at the place where the mighty trunk had split right down to its roots, and poked about in the fallen heap of charred wood and ashes. At last he drew out a piece of wood that was longer than a man's arm, with a thick swelling at one end, took a knife from his bag, and began carefully cutting away its blackened crust.

'Still alive, then, old fellow,' he murmured. 'Far from dead and done for yet, I see.'

Stone-eye watched as the old man laid bare the bright, reddish wood with skilful strokes of the knife, and then shaved the narrower end into the point of a walking stick. 'Just to give the thing some practical use as well,' he remarked by way of explanation, though it explained very little to Stone-eye, but the old man did not seem concerned, and indeed Stone-eye got the impression that the person addressed was not himself but the wooden object upon which the old man was expending so much care. He now turned his attention to the other, thicker end of the stick murmuring, 'Don't worry, old fellow, I won't hurt you, I'm only going to peel your burnt skin away.' And he handled his knife with as much caution as if he risked cutting into living flesh.

At first Stone-eye could not see what shape the gnarled protuberance was taking under the old man's hands. The staff obviously ended in a crooked and knobbly root, of which only the outer bark was singed. The old man carefully cut away several scars left by the fire, shaved the wood a little more, and wiped its surface clean and smooth with a cloth he took out of his bag. Then he examined his work with satisfaction, and held it out to Stone-eye, saying, 'There he is. Try to make friends with him.'

Stone-eye took the staff, which immediately fitted into his hand, feeling warm and supple there, and looked at the intricate shape, its curious curve accentuated by the stripes of the wood's grain. The first thing to catch his eye was a dark stump standing out distinctly from the silky smooth surface, a place where the rootstock had probably branched before the fire, a smooth brown eye which seemed to be looking at him keenly and with a touch of mockery. As soon as he had recognized this as an eye, he could see the strange thing's head standing out from the tangled shape as well, with a broad, protuberant mouth, in shape somewhere between a duck's bill and the domed snout of a toad, and merging into the rounded head without any obvious point of division. The eye was in the middle of the face, a grotesquely distorted face which yet wore an expression of imperturbable calm, though slightly broken by a barely perceptible ironic quirk at the corners of the broad, firmly closed lips. And this head, undoubtedly one of much character, before whose gaze Stone-eye was overcome by something that almost felt like respect, indeed awe, was set on a body coiling around the upper end of the staff as if to meditate in peace there.

'Take a sniff at him – smell this gnarled old fellow,' said the old man. 'There's a resinous spot at the back of the head; you'll get the scent most strongly there.' And as Stone-eye bent his head and breathed in the sweet and resinous fragrance of the stone pine, the old man murmured:

> *Follow and find it,*
> *the scent of the living;*
> *but if you can't bind it,*
> *you've cause for misgiving;*
> *yet what's steadily minded*
> *shall still be reviving.*

Stone-eye took in these words, although they were spoken so softly it was more like a voice murmuring inside his head. He drank in the scent of the wood, sweet and bitter at once, awakening in him a boundless longing for life and to play some part in it, be received into it; he felt as if his body would burst with his unassuaged desire to feel and taste life, in whatever form it might be offered. At that moment, he could have embraced the whole world, and was on the point of beginning with this strange old prospector, but when he raised his head and looked up, the old man had disappeared. He thought he saw a fleeting movement far below among the stunted mountain pines, but then the dark green slope lay motionless again beneath the wide vault of the sky. And only now did he realize that he was standing under that open sky without feeling fear – or rather, had been standing thus, for a moment later the fear struck him with such force that he leaped for the shelter of the bushes, and flung himself, half fainting, into the branches of the low-growing mountain pines. He lay under them for a while, his heart beating as violently as if he had just escaped some great if unknown danger. When he could think clearly again he wondered how he had been able to stand out in the open, free of his fear. Had he been so fascinated by the old man's mysterious skill in carving? Or was it simply the old man's presence that kept his fear at bay? The first explanation seemed to him more reasonable, yet he was almost certain that the second was the right one, although he could not have said what reasons he had to suppose so.

'And I was just thinking the old man had cured you of your peculiar preference for shady places,' said the weasel, who had followed him, if not at such a headlong pace, and was now looking at him somewhat askance.

'You seem to think he could do anything!' said Stone-eye, and after a while he added, 'Well, and perhaps he could, but he probably had other things on his mind.'

'Like giving you another companion to take on your travels,' said the weasel, with a touch of jealousy audible in his emphasis on 'another', as Stone-eye noticed. 'Were you planning to spend the winter in the cave with my flock of goats, then?' he inquired.

The weasel wrinkled his nose, exposing his sharp teeth, and said, 'No, not even out of friendship for you, if you'll forgive my frankness. I take it that stick the old man gave you for company has a less sensitive nose, though I should think it'll be a pretty silent sort of companion.'

'At least it may come in useful for self-defence,' said Stone-eye, who had now risen as far as the low bushes would allow him, and was swinging the cudgel experimentally through the air.

'I doubt if that's why the old man was so careful to give it a face,' said Needle-tooth. 'That eye looks more peaceful than otherwise, if you ask me.'

That could hardly be denied, but Stone-eye felt little urge to go on discussing the hidden qualities of this strange wooden creature, whose calm, brown gaze he found unsettling rather than any encouragement to talk about it. So he said, 'We'd better be on our way. I don't want to spend the night up here.'

That day, first crawling under the swaying branches of the dwarf pines, and then, at last, walking more easily beneath a thicker roof of spruces, they crossed the pass and came down to the woods on the other side of the mountains. On the third day of their journey, they finally rounded the northern end of the great cliff, which was soon towering high above them again.

When the faun had been trotting down familiar pathways through the bushes for half a day, the weasel said, 'You'll soon be home, Stone-eye. I can smell your goats.'

Stone-eye's own sense of smell was not yet so keen, but after a while he too caught the goatish odour, and when a view down the slope opened up among the bushes, he saw the flock grazing down on the grassy hillside. By now their penetrating smell was so strong that Needle-tooth could not be persuaded to go a step closer. 'Just a moment,' he added, bounding off into the undergrowth. He was back almost at once, hauling a rabbit after him. 'One more roast for you,' he said. 'A goodbye present. I've enjoyed travelling the mountains with you, but this is where our ways part. I think I'll go a little farther south. You'll find me where the rock wall ends, if you happen to want me. Always pleased to be of service, even if your ways are a bit odd at times.'

'I'll be glad to remember that,' said Stone-eye, 'more particularly when I set off again next spring. Till then I'll be moving more or less as my goats do.' He thanked the weasel once more for all the excellent meat he had provided, and then, all at once, Needle-tooth was gone.

Stone-eye was about to step out of the hazel bushes and show himself to his goats when he realized that he had come at an awkward moment. One-horn was obviously busy carrying out his more enjoyable duties as leader of the flock. He was driving one of the she-goats before him, uphill and straight towards Stone-eye, and was not being very gentle with the lady of his choice, butting his one horn into her side and forcing her farther on, though this was only goatish love-play. Finally he brought her to a halt and mounted her just in front of the hidden observer. Stone-eye watched the proceedings with some excitement, and indeed, for a few moments he felt almost painfully at the mercy of his body's dual nature, both revolted and carried away by the physical power of the goats' mating; he felt his goat's legs tremble as a wave of the animals' acrid odour reached him. Then the he-goat had finished with his mate, who trotted straight back to the flock, obviously little moved by what had just happened to her.

This, thought Stone-eye, was the time to show himself to the flock's present leader. He stepped out of the bushes, saying, 'I'm glad to see you in such vigorous health, One-horn.'

The he-goat's head swung round as if he had unexpectedly scented an enemy, and he lowered his mighty horn threateningly. But then he recognized his co-leader, and relaxed his aggressive attitude slightly, although his voice sounded far from friendly as he said, 'You're back early, Stone-eye.'

'Too early, I suppose you mean,' said Stone-eye, a little disconcerted by this cool reception.

'Well, if that's how you take it, I won't contradict you,' remarked One-horn, his tone surly. 'I'm goat enough to look after my flock alone now.'

'So I saw,' said Stone-eye, smiling, but the he-goat did not care for such jokes.

'Are you making fun of me?' he inquired unpleasantly, lowering his horn again.

'Nothing's farther from my mind,' Stone-eye made haste to assure him, and after a while, he added, 'No; indeed, I admire you,' and wondered whether that was not in fact the truth.

'Then you can keep away from the flock a while longer,' said the he-goat. 'Sleep in your cave, if you like. We'll be out in the open at night as long as it's warm enough.'

'Very good of you,' said Stone-eye, but realizing that irony was entirely lost on the goat, he shrugged his shoulders and added only, 'I'll remember.' Then he turned and went on through the bushes to the mouth of the cave.

He found it in a state of some neglect. The wind had blown leaves and all kinds of other debris inside, spiders were scurrying over the floor, and farther in, the leaves of his old bedding were mouldering and had a stale smell, as of fungus. But the hay he had made in spring had kept dry at the back of the cave, and was sweetly fragrant. Stone-eye was busy for the rest of that day sweeping the stony floor with a besom of twigs, cleaning out the basin into which the spring fell, and gathering dry leaves for fresh bedding.

When he was at last sitting by his fire that evening, and the aroma of the roasting rabbit rose to his nostrils, he felt he was at home again. He ate slowly and deliberately, for he would have no such good suppers for some time to come. When he had finished, he sat on beside the embers for a while, looking at the stick the old man had carved for him. He turned it around in his hand, watching the play of light and shade on the broad planes of the face, whose dark eye seemed to be gazing imperturbably at him. 'And what am I to make of you, my silent friend?' he asked. 'Have you a name, I wonder?'

When he said that, it struck him that the wooden eye seemed to be observing him with awakening interest. He even fancied he saw the strange, gnarled creature give him an encouraging nod.

'Ah, so that's it, is it?' he said. 'Am I to guess your name?'

There was no answer, but now he was almost sure the staff had twitched in his hand. He might or he might not have imagined it – but at any rate, he felt a wish to play this game, and began thinking up names for this curious stick of his. 'Knot, maybe?' he said, looking intently at the wooden face. But nothing in it moved. 'Root, would it be?' However, that was evidently wrong too. Stone-eye began wondering if the old man might have given him any kind of hint. As he left, he had murmured a verse:

> *Follow and find it,*
> *the scent of the living . . .*

Stone-eye leaned over the gnarled end of the stick, and immediately breathed in the sweet, resinous aroma that rose from the wood, a delicious and magical fragrance, soft and exciting, strange and yet in some inexplicable way familiar, a scent that aroused visions of vanished dreams, the image of a face that had leaned over him in the darkness while the splash of a spring of water sounded through the night, eyes with the stars shining in their gaze, and that fragrance wafted around him as the woman's drifting hair fleetingly brushed his face. But he could not hold the vision fast, and it vanished like mist. However, the fragrance was still there, surrounding him like an embrace, the sweet fragrance of the resin of the stone pine. Was that, perhaps, the name he needed? 'Resin?' he asked. 'Is your name Resin?' But his words seemed to disperse the fragrance, the enchantment receded, and he was holding nothing but a piece of dead wood in his hand.

He let his guessing game be for that evening, covered the embers of the fire, and lay down to sleep. But in his dreams he saw that unmoving, wide-mouthed face, vigorous and larger than life-size, silently scrutinizing him with its smooth brown eye, an ancient creature coiled around itself, imperturbable in its calm, but not at all sleepy: wide awake and full of wisdom.

When Stone-eye remembered this dream on waking, he felt that he had a companion of whom something might yet be expected. But this morning he had no time to go on guessing at names; if he wanted to get his daily milk from the goats this winter, he must start gathering fodder for them. His hay alone would not feed the flock.

There is no need to describe in detail all that he brought home to the cave over the next few weeks, to be stacked beyond the place where he slept; suffice it to say that though there were almost no beechnuts that year, there was a rich harvest of hazelnuts – which was fortunate, for the hazelnuts were the only things he brought home that he liked to eat himself. He gathered great quantities of acorns as well, for the goats, and at last discovered a few crab apple trees, their branches weighed down to the ground by fruit. When evening came he fell on his bed, tired and stiff from all his bending, and slept a deep and dreamless sleep. He used his stick only to knock the apples from the higher branches.

Now and then he saw the flock grazing the grassy slopes below, on the borders of the timber forest, but he kept out of their way, so as not to trespass on the he-goat's preserves. The animals themselves kept away from the rocky cliff, and thus from the mouth of the cave; probably they still remembered the fright the rock-fall had given them. Now and then, when he unexpectedly smelled goat nearby, Stone-eye stood in the shelter of the bushes and peered out at the pasture where One-horn was driving one of the she-goats ahead of him. He remembered those winter nights when he had lain among the gently breathing bodies of those beasts, as if he too were a part of that living organism. Now that he was in hiding, a secret watcher, he became aware that he did not belong to the flock; he was shut out of the rhythm of their life, the rhythm that drove them to mate in the autumn season. Even if he didn't yet know who he really was, he had learnt one thing in his wanderings over the mountains and in the shallow valley: he was involved in events that had nothing to do with these goats.

After standing thus for a while, he would trot on through the undergrowth, plucking a few mushrooms from the moss here and there, or picking up a handful of nuts from the fallen leaves on the ground: a lonely wanderer in the woods, with no other aim but to provide for winter. The heavy, bitter scent of autumn hung among the silvery beech trunks, imparting a flavour of decaying foliage and rotting fungus to the mist that hovered above the meadows more often now in the mornings.

One day late in autumn, the sun broke through the clouds, and the sky was like a blue-green glass dome above the bare branches of the trees, swept clean by a brisk east wind that had blown the morning mists away. Stone-eye took his leisure that day. He had brought in enough provisions, and now wandered aimlessly through the woods, trying to eavesdrop on the birds, though without discovering anything particularly new. Around noon he stopped to look for a sheltered place near the edge of the woods, and found one under a mighty oak. He sat in the moss, leaned his back against the fissured bark of the oak tree, chewed a few hazelnuts and let the sun warm his skin. For a while he gazed up at the slope, where the feathery ears of countless slender blades of withering grass rose into the air, bending before the wind in swiftly rippling waves. Watching them, he fell asleep, drifting away himself on that sea of nodding grass blades, their empty ears shimmering silvery white in the sun, like foam driving on the waves that were washing the sleeper he knew not where, but he let himself drift with them, taking note of nothing but those softly whispering waters until, after a long while, he saw a bird hovering high in the sky, letting the wind bear it up on spreading pinions, tiny at first, as you might draw an angular little figure of a bird with a fine pen, but it soon dropped closer, increased in size, came diving down, and with it came fear cleaving through the glassy sky, for where the bird had passed there was a rift in the blue-green vault, a rift that quickly widened, and endless blackness flooded in through that flaw in the sky, a darkness that began to overcome all light, and next moment the bird's wings covered the sky from end to end, and its outstretched talons came down upon the sleeper, who saw the fixed stare of those flashing green eyes even as he raised his arms to protect himself in his sleep. He woke as the bird's sharp beak struck his neck.

At first he saw nothing but a flurry of brown feathers, and felt the hard pinions strike his raised arms. He struck out blindly, hit a body that fluttered aside and flew unsteadily away just above the dry grass, and then settled on a mouldering tree stump. Only now did Stone-eye see who had attacked him. It was a female falcon perching a few paces away, trying to smooth her ruffled feathers with her beak. Then she straightened up and looked at him with her green eyes.

Although Stone-eye could see now that this falcon was no larger than any other, fear still clutched at his heart. He felt horror of the bird that had passed into reality from his dreadful dream, or else from some past of his own which he could no longer remember. But now he knew that this was the same falcon that had watched him here last year.

'What do you want?' he asked.

'You know what I want,' said the falcon, 'and if you had not had a warning from somewhere or other, I would have it now.'

Stone-eye reached a hand to his neck where the falcon's beak had struck him, and felt the thong of the little bag beneath his fingers. 'The stone,' he said. 'You want the stone.'

'You stole it from us,' said the falcon.

'From whom?' asked Stone-eye. 'From the falcons?'

'From those I rule,' said the falcon.

Stone-eye tried to penetrate the wall cutting him off from the past, but he could not get much farther back than his meeting with the goats. All the same, he was sure the stone belonged to him. 'You are lying,' he said. 'It's my stone.'

'How do you think you know that?' said the falcon. 'You don't even know who you are.'

'But you seem to know,' said Stone-eye. 'Tell me!'

'Give me the stone first!' said the falcon. 'And then I'll tell you as much of your glorious past as you could wish to hear.'

Stone-eye thought this a tempting offer. He took the stone out of its bag, but still held it firmly in his closed fist, so that the falcon could not seize it suddenly. Between his fingers, he saw the rings of colour bloom in the light of the sinking sun: blue, violet and green. But this green was different from the hard, piercing green of the falcon's eyes; it had the silken shimmer of a summer meadow, and shone like young beech leaves in May when the sun falls through them from high above. As he gave himself up to the play of the colours the grip of fear was loosened, and now he knew he must not give away the stone for the uncertain prospect of what a greedy falcon might tell him. 'I know one thing for sure,' he said. 'I am the Bearer of the Stone.' For that, as he now remembered, was what Needle-tooth had called him.

This remark enraged the falcon. 'The weasel told you that nickname!' she screeched. 'But you don't know your real name, you shaggy goat! You know nothing of the power you could wield over others with your silver flute. You might have been sleeping in a silken bed and not with your stinking goats!'

Stone-eye looked at the stone, and its rings of colour spread around him like a shield off which the wrath of the falcon rebounded. The more the pulsating warmth of the stone penetrated him, the less did he think it worth hearing whatever this evil bird had to tell him, and moreover it was very doubtful whether she would tell the truth.

'Don't trouble yourself, falcon,' he said. 'I will be content for the time being to be known as Bearer of the Stone, or Stone-eye, as my goats call me. I feel it matters more to have this stone than to wield power over anyone; in fact, the way you put it sounds to me unpleasant, and I have a kind of feeling that wielding power is what brought me where I am now.'

'Does your stone say so?' asked the falcon.

'You see?' said Stone-eye, looking at the falcon. 'You admit yourself that the stone is mine!'

'Never mind if it's yours or not!' said the falcon angrily. 'Haven't you yet discovered that no one can possess this stone, as if it were any common object? It was only given to you in trust for us. So I have the right to demand it back.'

Stone-eye looked into the falcon's green eyes, and began to feel uncertain, but as soon as he lowered his gaze again, and felt himself drawn into the shimmering play of colours, his doubts fled. 'You may be right that the stone was only given me in trust,' he said, 'but I am sure it was not meant for the likes of you: it is a gift, not something one can ask for at will, and you won't get it from me.'

'Then you can stay a half-goat, trotting lonely through the woods!' screeched the falcon. 'You will be a stranger among the goats, and mankind will shrink from you, unless you can find a girl to love you, ugly as you are with your shaggy goatish legs!'

And the falcon uttered a harsh laugh, spread her wings and rose high into the sky, where she turned and flew away fast southwards.

Stone-eye watched her go, admiring the ease with which the slender bird rose aloft and let the wind carry her, free and apparently not bound by that sense of weight that causes other beings to set foot laboriously before foot on the ground, taking care not to stumble into the first hole they come across. You are lovely, falcon, he thought, you are very lovely, even when you are angry. And he determined to take great care of his stone in future.

Next day it rained. Stone-eye stayed in the cave, looking out through the entrance at the bare bushes, their branches black and glistening with moisture. There was nothing to be seen beyond them but straggling grass. Even in such weather, however, the goats were obviously not prepared to make for the cave; most likely they wouldn't come back until the first snow fell.

Stone-eye stayed crouching by his fire, trying to strike up a conversation with his stick again. He stared inquiringly at the timeless, ancient face of the wooden being carved there. 'It looks as if I must think of some different names for you, if I'm to get you to talk to me,' he said. 'Perhaps the names I thought up the other day were too short.' He tried to picture the gigantic tree with its blue-green cones at the top, fat and round as farmhouse doughnuts, and tried, 'Doughnut-treetop-cone?' But the smooth brown eye looked, if anything, less forthcoming than before. He thought again, and remembered how it had felt when the lower branches of the stone pine scratched his legs as he fled from the storm. 'Needly-leg-scratcher?' he suggested, but that was no more successful. Still following the same train of thought, it struck him that he had almost fallen over the gnarled roots of the pine as he ran, so he tried, 'Tumble-stumble-root?' At this, however, his silent companion looked rather disgusted. Evidently it did not care for this sort of humour. 'I'm sorry if I've insulted you,' Stone-eye told it, 'but you can see how hard it is to guess your real name. I don't suppose I shall think of anything better today.'

He put the stick aside, poked his fire a little, and thought about his conversation with the falcon. She could be no ordinary hawk, for she had said she ruled others, and it had not sounded as if she meant only falcons. Moreover, he must have had some dealings with the falcon at an earlier date. At least, the bird claimed to know something about his past, at a time when he had been called Bearer of the Stone. Stone-eye tried as hard as he could to dredge something up out of his memory, and as he did so he became more and more certain that he had seen the falcon once before, sitting on a tree stump in the middle of a meadow. He remembered now that this could not have been on a slope, as with yesterday's events, for his imagination showed him the picture of a flat, grassy clearing, surrounded by young trees with slender trunks, and the falcon had been closer to him too. Then the picture in his mind began to move, little by little the falcon's brown plumage fell away, and as the figure simultaneously grew in size it revealed the slim, white-limbed body of a girl looking at him with green eyes. Falcon maiden, he thought, and knew at once that this name too belonged to his past. So you have told me something about myself after all, falcon, he thought, but then the green eyes were suddenly directly in front of him, and he was overcome by fear again, for in the depths of those beautiful eyes he saw nothing but the lust for power, and he trembled as if he had already felt that power used on himself. Only when he laid his hand on his breast and made sure his stone was there did he breathe more steadily, and the fear ebbed away.

It poured with rain all day long, and towards evening Stone-eye heard the sound of the goats' hooves outside the cave. The he-goat put his mighty horn in through the entrance first, and looked round. Seeing Stone-eye sitting by the fire, he shook his wet beard, remarking, 'Filthy weather! Not a dry spot to be found. We'll sleep in the cave tonight.' Without waiting for any invitation, he made his way through the entrance, with the whole flock following him one by one.

'Warm yourselves first,' said Stone-eye, and soon the animals were lying around the fireplace, snuffling quietly, their wet coats steaming. Only the kids, who were not familiar either with the cave or with fire, hung back, shifting from leg to leg and bleating in alarm, until their mothers spoke to them gently and nudged them towards the warm glow.

That evening, Stone-eye filled his bowl with milk again for the first time, but he climbed up to his own bed to sleep. After this, the goats came back to the cave every evening at nightfall, and Stone-eye was glad to hear the animals' peaceful breathing at night and feel the warmth given off by their bodies. Soon after this the first snow fell, and that day One-horn said, 'You are leader of the flock now, for the rest of the winter. I can see you've made good provision.' And he munched a handful of hay with relish, the same hay whose harvesting he had quite failed to understand in the spring.

Now the days took on a calm monotony again, and after a while Stone-eye felt as if he had done nothing all his life but drive his goats to find pasture free from snow in the morning, and bring them back to the cave in the evening, give them a little extra food from his supplies, and milk them.

One evening, as he sat by the fire, turning his stick this way and that again, One-horn asked, 'What's that strange thing you brought back from your travels? You keep looking at it as if you'd like to talk to it.'

'And so I would,' said Stone-eye, 'but I don't know its name.'

'What, when you're so clever?' said One-horn. 'Try a name that suits its nature. That's how we goats give names, at least.'

Stone-eye liked the simplicity of this idea. When the goats were asleep, and he was lying in the higher part of the cave on his bedding, he took the stick in his hand and said, 'You're made of wood; yours is a wooden nature. Are you a Woodling, I wonder?'

The stick did not reply, but Stone-eye felt a slight twitch in the staff which encouraged him to follow this trail farther. 'The wood comes from a tree,' he went on, 'so yours is the nature of trees. Are you a Treekin?'

In the dim light that still came from the embers in the fireplace he thought he saw the eye in his dumb companion's broad face suddenly light up and look keenly at him, as if to say: go on, go on, you're nearly there! 'Well, you come from a particular tree,' Stone-eye continued. 'It was an ancient stone pine. Are you perhaps a Piney?'

'It took you plenty of guessing to find *that* out,' said the Piney. 'Not particularly bright, are you? Still, if the old man thought it worth giving me to you as your companion, I suppose he had something in mind for you.'

'You sound almost as if he'd done me a great favour,' said Stone-eye. 'You've not been especially useful so far.'

'What on earth do you expect in such a short time?' said the Piney, crossly. 'The old man won't have given you a Piney for knocking crab apples off the trees. Any ordinary cudgel will do that.'

'Well, he might have told me,' Stone-eye persisted. 'After all, he promised me a companion to talk to through the winter, but you haven't so much as opened your mouth all this long time!'

'Pineys speak only when addressed by their right name,' said the Piney. 'And what do you mean, all this long time? You must be very young and impatient if you call it any length of time worth mentioning.'

'I'm considerably older than you are,' said Stone-eye. 'The old man made you before my eyes.'

This claim brought the Piney to utter a dry and rather wooden laugh. 'Before your eyes?' he said. 'Have you any idea how old I am? Well, I'll tell you, and then I trust you'll feel a little more respect: I was three hundred and sixty-nine years old last spring, exactly the age at which a Piney may be sent out into the world. What you call a long time is scarcely a moment to me.'

Stone-eye found this hard to believe. 'But,' he said, 'I saw the old man pick up a piece of wood and –'

However, the Piney interrupted him. 'You saw!' he said. 'You saw – but you didn't understand at all! That piece of wood was the heart of the stone pine that you saw struck by lightning. The part that burned was only its outward shape, which has nothing to do with the matter. But the Piney that was freed then is still quite lively enough to tell a young know-all like you about Time! Who knows, perhaps that lightning struck because a Piney was needed, and you really ought to be a bit more grateful to think of such mighty events occurring for your benefit! And don't talk to me about Time! I had to stand up on that pass for three hundred and sixty-nine years to get any inkling of what the word means.'

After this long speech from the Piney, Stone-eye felt rather subdued. 'I beg your pardon,' he said. 'I wasn't to know. The old man didn't tell me any of that.'

'Very likely he thought you brighter than you are,' said the Piney. 'Do you have to be told everything? The likes of that old man do nothing by chance. If he's bothering about your affairs, that ought to make you think hard. Well, I've done enough talking for today.' And with that the Piney closed the conversation, leaving Stone-eye to try to make sense of it.

So the old prospector had given him a companion who knew the mysteries of time, if on rather too extended a scale for Stone-eye's own circumstances. With this thought, he became aware that he had, in fact, a very imperfect notion of the course of time, for the experience he could draw upon just now did not go much farther back than a year. He had lost all the rest, and if he wanted to find that part of his life again, it could be very useful to have a being like the Piney with him. He decided to ask his companion, when next he had the chance, how he could get back his memory of the time he had lost, and with that he fell asleep.

Sometimes time seemed to stand still. The snow fell outside, and the cold white wall at the mouth of the cave grew a little higher every day. The goats could find scarcely any grazing among the deep snow on the hillsides; they tore buds and bark off low-hanging branches with their teeth, and there were many days when they never left the cave. The stocks of firewood were getting low, and one morning Stone-eye had to go out looking for dry branches. He knew of an ancient, decaying beech near the edge of the wood, a tree that had fallen during the storms of autumn, and decided to go there for new supplies.

When he stepped out of the cave, he saw a flock of crows circling above the wood, and as he trudged knee-deep through the snow among the bushes, he heard the black birds' constant hoarse cries. Then he realized what was agitating them so much: a falcon was soaring just above them, obviously after prey. But if it thought it would have easy pickings among the crows, it was wrong. They suddenly closed together into a dense throng, turned and attacked the falcon, which only just managed to fly out of reach of their sharp beaks. Beating its wings rapidly, it soared up into the pale blue, frosty sky, and then flew away southwards.

At last Stone-eye reached the fallen tree, and began to break branches as thick as his arm from its shattered crown. By now the crows had settled in the bare branches of the tall trees, looking like over-ripe fruits blackened by the frost. Two of them were sitting in the boughs of an oak, directly above Stone-eye, and he began to listen to what they were saying.

'The impudence of it!' cawed one. 'Did you ever see such a bold falcon?'

'Don't you know Green-eye?' said the second bird. 'She's greedier than anyone.'

'Yes, I think I have heard caw of her,' said the first. 'But that was farther down south.'

'Well, she mostly goes hunting here along the great cliff now,' said the other. 'You're right, though. She nests near Arni's House. I've seen her myself, flying out of Narzia's window.'

'Does Narzia keep a hawk for hunting, then?' said the first crow. 'Why does she let the bird fly free?'

'It's not so certain the bird is her falcon,' said the second crow. 'In fact, some say it's Narzia herself, for she has the same green eyes as the falcon, greedy and cruel.'

'Yes, they are certainly alike there,' said the first. 'I hear that since her father died, Narzia's malice knows no bounds. She treats Arni's Folk like slaves, and if a man won't crawl to her, she breaks his will with evil magic. Do you know her dogs? Their coarse, thick coats look like the hair of Arni's Folk, and their eyes remind me of the eyes of certain humans who have disappeared. There's a smell of fear about Arni's House and the settlement.'

'Yes,' said the other crow, 'and it's come there since the bright eye vanished from the grey cabin, and the Bearer of the Stone with it. What I've heard is, Narzia goes flying out in the shape of that falcon, to hunt for him and get the stone away from him again.'

'Then he had better look out,' said the first crow, 'or she'll turn him into another of her dogs.'

'Perhaps she already has,' said the second.

'I think not,' said the first. 'Those dogs can't run away because she has broken their will. Perhaps that young man went home again with the stone. He wasn't one of Arni's Folk.'

'Do you know his name, and where he comes from?' asked the second.

'I do,' said the first, and at that moment a dry twig snapped beneath Stone-eye's hooves. The crows flew up in alarm, and went away over the tree-tops and out of sight.

Stone-eye cursed his clumsiness. He tried to follow the birds, but he very soon realized how pointless an undertaking it was. By the time he had made his laborious way through the deep snow, the crows would long since have flown away over the trees. He went back to the fallen tree and began pulling branches of a handy size out of the tangle of broken wood, and as he worked, he thought of what he had just heard. He had felt as if the mists veiling his memory were unexpectedly torn aside in places, and images had emerged, images he did not see as something strange, but recognized as familiar: log cabins on the borders of the woods, one of them, grey with age, standing like a shrine in the middle of the settlement, and he knew he had been in this place. He had heard names that brought back images of faces and people he knew: Arni's Folk were flat-nosed, with olive skins and thick black hair; he saw them going busily back and forth among the houses, leading laden pack animals. And the name of Narzia conjured up the face of a woman, or a girl: delicately boned, fair-skinned, with green eyes, a beautiful face that both excited and alarmed him. But what had happened to make him run away from the place, taking the stone he now wore on his breast? Beneath the thin skin of forgetfulness that still divided him from that memory, he felt horror rise, keeping him from pursuing it any farther. Still, now he knew the identity of the falcon to whom he had talked late in the autumn.

By now he had collected a bundle of dry branches, and he set off back to the cave. He returned to the place several times that day, and stacked up a good supply of firewood, but he saw no more of the crows. Meanwhile, the goats had scattered over the hillside, and were nibbling the twigs of the bushes, but they could get nothing like enough to satisfy them. When it was dark, they went back to the cave of their own accord, expecting more substantial nourishment. But Stone-eye himself could not get to sleep that night: he was still too excited by those inroads into his lost memory he had made that day.

When he had been lying on his bed for some time, looking up at the fissured roof of the cave, with the reflection of the firelight flickering over it, he picked up his staff, and said, 'Piney, you understand Time.'

Instead of answering, the Piney laughed his dry laugh. Then he said, 'Only someone without the faintest notion of Time could say a thing like that. Time is something which you understand less and less the more you learn about it. You can never be sure of it, you see. Watch Time and it will creep along at a snail's pace, but let something else distract you and it's off and away like a weasel. It's always there, but if you try to grasp it you find you're holding empty air, for it's gone again. Well, yes, I've had a bit of experience of Time, but I certainly can't say I understand it. What are you getting at? I observe that something's keeping you awake.'

'I found a few fragments of my lost time today,' said Stone-eye, and he told the Piney what he had overheard the crows saying. 'But they're only isolated pictures,' he finished. 'I don't know the connection between them.'

'And you want me to help you find it?' said the Piney. 'You'll have to do that for yourself. My time isn't the same as your time.'

'Did you never lose a piece of it?' asked Stone-eye.

The Piney thought for a while, and then said, 'Yes, as a matter of fact I once did. It must be about two hundred and fifty years ago. There was such a dry summer that my cones dried up before their time, growing no kernels, so that I couldn't bring any children into the world, which is a sad thing for us Pineys. Late that summer there was a violent storm, like the one the day we met, and I was struck by lightning then too. It went from the top of me right down my trunk to my roots, splitting the bark, but the rain came before I could burn. And I wasn't conscious of anything after that until next spring, and even later, when the wounds had closed again, it was some while before I knew what had happened to me.'

'But you must have found out somehow, or you couldn't tell me now,' said Stone-eye. 'How did you find your lost time again at last?'

'With the help of an ant,' said the Piney. 'It was in spring a few years later. I was in a melancholy mood at the time, hanging my branches; I was worried about my cones, because since the lightning struck I'd never been able to ripen any kernels. Well, that day this ant came crawling up to the top of my trunk, where it began nibbling at the resin oozing between the scales of the cones. And then I knew there'd been an ant up there before, looking for resin on my dry cones and nibbling at the dried crusts of it. It had suddenly crawled into a crack among the scales, and that was when the lightning struck and nearly killed me. When I remembered that, I felt the burning pain at last, and the fierce heat boiling the sap under my bark. And the pain brought me back my lost time.'

'Am I to go looking for such pain, then?' asked Stone-eye, and if it had not been so dark in the cave, one could have seen that he was not especially anxious to do so. The Piney noticed all the same, presumably from the reluctant way he spoke. 'No, no,' he said. 'What sane creature would do such a thing? No, you go and look for an ant. The pain will follow of its own accord.'

'What ant?' asked Stone-eye, confused. 'I don't remember any ant.'

'Dear heavens above, how slow on the uptake you are!' said the Piney. 'Why do you think I'm telling you this story? Look for the little things, pay attention to remarks that remind you of something! You were just telling me what you heard the crows say. They mentioned some house or other. Do you remember it?'

'Arni's House,' said Stone-eye. 'And the people who live there, in those log cabins, call themselves Arni's Folk.'

'Well, you must have lived with them once,' said the Piney. 'You're the young man who went off with the stone.'

'I know that, since I have the stone here,' said Stone-eye. 'But what was I running away from?'

'How should I know?' said the Piney. 'Perhaps it's all to do with this Narzia who seems to fly around these parts in the shape of a falcon at times. Do you know her?'

'I talked to the green-eyed falcon last autumn,' said Stone-eye. 'She said that if I would give her the stone, she would tell me who I am. I nearly did as she wanted.'

'You'd have driven a bad bargain,' said the Piney. 'You must find out who you are for yourself. It's no use whatever for anyone else to tell you. This Narzia seems to be mistress of many arts. Perhaps she wanted to turn you into one of her dogs.'

Throughout this conversation, Stone-eye had felt fear groping for his heart again, clutching it more and more strongly, and at these last words of the Piney's that fear seemed to close its grip with sudden force. 'No!' he cried. 'Be quiet! I don't want to hear any more.'

'Did I start it?' said the Piney. 'You're the one looking for your lost time. But I rather think you're running away from it, because you fear it. Well, you'll find your ant someday. We have time, plenty of time.'

And so indeed they did. The winter dragged slowly by. Sometimes snow-storms drifted up the mouth of the cave, so that it was dark by day as well as night, but this year Stone-eye did not go down and crawl in among the goats; instead, he slept on his own bedding as before. Perhaps he felt ashamed to go in with the goats under the Piney's eye, or perhaps the words of the falcon, when she said he would never be one of them, had so taken root in his mind that he feared the animals would not receive him into the warmth of the flock again, as they had last winter. Now and then he talked to the Piney, but he asked no more questions about the time he had lost, although he determined to pay more attention in future to little details and any remarks that came to his ears.

Then, one day, the snow began to melt. The streams of droplets that ran down over the cave-mouth by day, a sparkling curtain of shining jewels, still froze overnight to icicles like a mouthful of jagged teeth, but as soon as the sun was in the sky water dripped off them and quickly devoured them. When open grazing could be found outside, the goats left the cave in search of fodder. For a while they returned in the evening, to keep warm by the fire at night, but soon they were staying out the whole time. One-horn alone turned up once more, gave Stone-eye a gracious nod and said, 'You were useful enough again this winter, but now it's time I took over the flock myself. I must get my goats on the move before they bear their kids. If you can't find anything else to eat just yet, you can seek us out and drink milk like a suckling kid.'

Stone-eye thought this last remark was not particularly respectful, feeling he had earned rather more in the way of thanks for all the work he had undertaken for the goats' sake. However, as he was still dependent on their milk for the time being, he thanked One-horn for the offer, and had the cave to himself again. It would be some while yet before he could bring in the hay that would earn him his milk next winter.

After the goats had left he felt rather lost at night, missing the warm exhalations of the flock and the quiet snuffling of the resting creatures, and at first he made the fire up higher, so that he would feel something living near him as he slept. He felt more restless daily, as if something were driving him to go on his travels again, and when he went looking for the flock at evening he inspected the sprouting grass as he passed by, as if that would make it grow faster.

And then, one evening, he actually did feel something living near him, and indeed very near his throat: a good deal nearer than he liked. He was startled out of sleep by a shrill squealing, felt something small and furry scrabbling at his neck, and when he tried to brush his furry visitor away with his hand, something cold, smooth, and coiled touched him too. He sat up, and as he had put plenty of wood on the fire that night, he could see who had come calling. There was a snake coiled beside his bed, her scaly body shimmering in the firelight, and the snake had a mouse in her jaws. The mouse was squeaking miserably and kicking his legs about.

'Did you have to come hunting in my bed?' he asked the snake, annoyed to have his night's rest disturbed. 'I could have spared this little mouse a few of my nuts.'

When he said this, the snake made no move to swallow her prey; indeed, she bent her head backwards until she could deposit the furious little creature so that he was held tight in one of her coils, and then lifted her narrow head and said, in a soft and melodious voice, 'Forgive me for disturbing your sleep, Bearer of the Stone. My name is Rinkulla, and I arrived just in time to catch this miserable mouse trying to steal something better than nuts from you.'

Stone-eye saw, from the bright crescent moon shapes just above the snake's jaws, that he was speaking to a grass snake, and although he had never previously felt much liking for snakes, he watched the creature's graceful movements with admiration, and looked into her eyes, seeing many colours rising in the depths beneath their shining surface, as in an agate. 'What better thing could a mouse find here?' he asked, though from the name by which the snake had addressed him, he already guessed what the mouse had been after.

'None, or not for a mouse,' said Rinkulla.

'For a falcon, perhaps?' said Stone-eye.

'Let the mouse admit it himself,' said Rinkulla, letting the little

creature free of her coils. 'Very well,' she said, 'now tell the Bearer of
the Stone your story, but you had better stick to the truth if you value
your life. You know very well it's no use trying to escape me.'

The mouse was now crouched, trembling, between the snake and
Stone-eye's bed of dry leaves. He rapidly tried to smooth down his coat
with his forelegs, then made a humble obeisance, and said, 'Oh yes,
mighty Rinkulla, indeed I know I couldn't get away from you. And as
for you, Bearer of the Stone, I will tell you the whole truth of what I
meant to do, because I fear Rinkulla much more than I fear the falcon
you mentioned just now. It was indeed a falcon with green eyes who
told me to creep into your cave, gnaw through the thong around your
neck, and steal the bag in which you carry the stone that gives you
your name.'

'How could the green-eyed falcon order you to do such a thing?'
asked Stone-eye. 'Do you serve her?'

'Well, she had me in her clutches,' said the mouse, and it was plain
that this was not a very pleasant recollection.

'What did she offer you for the theft?' asked Stone-eye.

'To spare my life in future,' said the mouse.

Rinkulla's head swayed indignantly back and forth. 'And you believe
a falcon?' she inquired.

'Hope is sometimes enough for the likes of me,' said the mouse.

'Isn't your life always in danger one way or another?' said Rinkulla.
'You should be ashamed to do such a base deed for the sake of so
dubious a promise.'

These remarks did not seem to abash the mouse at all; indeed,
they infuriated him, in so far as one can speak of fury in so small an
animal. He rose on his hind paws, squeaking shrilly, 'Do you think I
don't know my life's always in danger, whether from falcons or
snakes? You want me to feel ashamed of trying to lessen that danger
or the fear of it a little, do you? It's all very well for you strong
ones. You can snap the likes of us up in passing, if you happen to
fancy a mouthful of mouse. Oh yes, it's easy for you to talk! Base
deeds, is it? You can despise them, you can afford to look down on
them! If you were to do such things they might well be base deeds,
seeing you're free to decide either way. But look at us, now – we
scurry through the leaves and grass, close to the ground and full of
fear, always feeling the threat of you breathing down our necks. You
want me to risk my life, do you, just so this hairy great monster here
can keep his toy? Well, you go and tell that falcon off for tempting

me to be so bold, but don't you preach at me! All right, now eat me up quick and let's get it over with!'

This was indeed a remarkable speech for a mouse to make, and obviously the snake herself was impressed, as well as Stone-eye, for she said, 'It would certainly be a pity to eat so brave a mouse! I must admit that you put me to shame. May I know your name, mouse?'

'Haven't got one yet,' said the mouse. 'With us mice, it's like this, see? You only get a name when you've done something special. So a lot of us die nameless, before we get a chance to do anything much. We die in the talons of a falcon, or the claws of a wild cat, or . . .' And here the mouse hesitated, and looked timorously at Rinkulla.

'Or?' said the snake, returning his glance with her agate eyes.

The mouse plucked up all his courage, and continued, 'Or the jaws of a snake.'

Rinkulla nodded her head, pleased, and said, 'You are indeed a brave mouse. And since you have now spoken not only in anger, but have overcome your fear, it is time you had a name. In future you shall be known as He-who-speaks-with-the-snake.' Then Rinkulla turned to Stone-eye and said, 'I think He-who-speaks-with-the-snake has earned a look at your stone. Let him learn that this matter is not to do with some silly toy, as he plainly believes.'

'You are right, wise Rinkulla,' said Stone-eye. 'And perhaps it will win me the friendship of this bold mouse too.' As he spoke, he was taking the stone out of its bag, and he laid it on the stony floor before the mouse. At first the jewel lay there in the dark like a black pebble, but then the fire in the cave flared up, and in the firelight the colours in the depths of the stone began to glow; they spread out in rings, rose and broke through the surface in throbbing waves of green, blue and violet light, surrounding the wondering mouse, and were reflected in Rinkulla's eyes so that it seemed three stones of the same kind were shining in the darkness of the cave. He-who-speaks-with-the-snake sat up quietly on his hind legs, looking into the play of colours. Within their shimmering light he seemed to grow, and no trace of trembling timidity was to be seen in him now; the gaze of his wide black eyes was clear, and his whiskers bristled boldly. Here, in short, was a mouse to be respected.

For a while, not one of them said a word. Then, at last, He-who-speaks-with-the-snake turned his eyes away from the jewel, looked at Stone-eye, and said, 'Now I know what a bad thing it would have been to steal this stone from you, but I have also learnt that you have forgiven me. Thank you for showing me the stone. All evil disappears in its light. I dare say I shall still tremble for my life now and then in future, but the fear that has always been with me and humiliated me daily has been taken away. By this stone, I swear that from this day on I will be your friend, just as you wished.'

All this was said with such dignity that it never occurred to Stone-eye to find the speech comical in the mouth of a mouse. As he put his stone back in its bag, he assured the mouse that there had been no need of any oath, and added that he was proud to have such a friend. Then he took a handful of nuts from his stock of provisions, and invited the mouse to eat some supper. The mouse accepted gratefully, remarking, 'Excitement always makes me hungry.'

Stone-eye cracked a few nuts himself. 'I am sorry I've nothing to offer you,' he said to Rinkulla.

'Oh, never mind that,' said the snake. 'I ate something only the day before yesterday. In any case, I didn't come down the stream and into your cave to go hunting here.'

'What were you looking for, then?'

'You,' said Rinkulla.

Stone-eye looked up in surprise. 'Me?' he said. 'But how did you even know I was here?'

'Oh, there's much talk of you among the water creatures,' said Rinkulla. 'Didn't you know? The Green Man had a search out for you last autumn.'

Then Stone-eye remembered the girl who had spoken to the fishes, and said, 'If I heard something correctly at the time, he was asked to find a fluter. A minstrel.'

'And aren't you a fluter and a minstrel?' asked Rinkulla, her agate eyes still on him.

'I don't know,' said Stone-eye. 'I spoke to Golden-eye about it, one autumn night over the other side of the mountains. But I was left not much wiser than before. She said something about a fluter, too.'

'You really don't know?' said Rinkulla, and in the firelight such colours now glowed in her eyes as if the shimmer of the stone were still reflected there.

Stone-eye searched his memory strenuously, but he could come up with nothing of the sort. 'I can't remember,' he said, 'but I suppose I must once have been this fluter. Did you come in search of me, then?'

'Oh no,' said Rinkulla. 'You were found long ago, and we know where you are. My task is only to take a look at you now and then, since my winter quarters are deep within this cave, and it was a good thing I happened to come visiting tonight.'

'Yes, very timely indeed,' said Stone-eye. 'Have you visited me often before?'

'A few times,' said Rinkulla, 'but there was no call to disturb you.'

'You'll have seen nothing but a half-goat snoring on his bedding of leaves,' said Stone-eye. 'No sign of any fluter or minstrel.'

'That was all I expected,' said Rinkulla. 'However, if you go out in the woods again in early summer, you might try cutting yourself a pipe to play. I know you have a knife.'

Stone-eye thanked Rinkulla for her kind advice, which she obviously took as a sign of farewell, for she bowed, saying, 'I have kept you from your sleep long enough tonight. I will see you again, somewhere near water. Take care of your stone!' And so saying, she slithered over to the stream that ran down inside the cave, and disappeared into the darkness.

The mouse had followed this conversation attentively, and remarked, 'It's a good thing I didn't know who protects you, or I'd never have ventured into your cave, and then I wouldn't have a name and I wouldn't have made friends with you. If you happen to need my services, there's a certain whistle which will always bring me to you.'

'So long as you're somewhere near!' said Stone-eye, smiling.

'Oh, not just then,' said the mouse. 'There are mice all over the place, and we pass on news very fast. Anyone who hears my whistle will let me know. Right, now listen!' And the mouse whistled three clear notes which were so familiar to Stone-eye that he could instantly whistle them himself.

'Excellent!' said the mouse. 'Well, goodnight, Bearer of the Stone, and thank you very much for the nuts.'

'Goodnight to you too, He-who-speaks-with-the-snake,' said Stone-eye. 'And beware of that falcon!'

'Same to you,' said the mouse, with a graceful bow, and he scurried away from the floor of the cave.

Stone-eye lay back on his bed, and whistled the three notes once more, by way of farewell. Immediately afterwards he heard his new friend reply, far off, but quite distinctly. And at that moment he remembered where he had heard that sound before. He had been sitting under a tree, with a blackbird sitting on a low branch in front of him, whistling the same sequence of notes that still rang in his ears now. He also knew that this was not just any blackbird, but a messenger from his grandfather the Gentle Fluter, to whom he was on his way through the great forests of Barlebogue. It was all clear and distinct in his memory: how he had met Gisa and lived in her castle, the whole story of Barlo who had lost his powers of speech through his fault, and who had then been given a new kind of language by the Gentle Fluter's arts, and after that, how he himself had gone riding the land with Barlo for three years. That was when he first heard the song about the Green Man, and the Green Man had twice come to their aid, until at last they defeated the wolves, along with a merry company of players, and drove Gisa out of the tall castle of Barlebogue.

'So I am the Gentle Fluter's grandson,' he whispered to himself. 'Did you hear that, Piney?'

The Piney beside him stirred, and said, 'Found your ant, have you?'

'My ant was a mouse,' said Stone-eye.

'Then now you know who you are,' said the Piney.

'Yes,' said Stone-eye. 'I can remember my grandfather, and my mother, his daughter, and my father, the Great Roarer. And I think I had another name in those days, but I don't remember it.'

'Were you a fluter then?' asked the Piney.

Stone-eye thought for a while. Then he shrugged his shoulders, and said, 'My grandfather was a fluter, and I rode the land for some time in the company of a fluter, and I had two proper human legs then, one either side of my saddle, but whether I was a fluter myself I can't remember, any more than I know how I come to have these goat's legs now.'

'Don't be so impatient,' said the Piney. 'You've found a part of your lost past, after all. Did you have your stone at that time?'

'Yes,' said Stone-eye. 'It all began with the stone. Arni, the brother of the Khan of the Raiding Riders, gave it to me when he was dying. He himself had it from an old woman who lived in the mountains.'

'I knew that woman,' said the Piney. 'In her younger days she once rested under my branches, for I was already a mighty tree then. She wore the stone on a chain around her neck, in a setting of silver wire. I knew it at once when I saw it with you. The woman's name was Urla, and she had very lovely eyes.'

'Now I begin to get a real idea of your age,' said Stone-eye. 'For Arni was married to a granddaughter of Urla's, and knew her only as a very old woman when he himself was young. And his daughter Akka had strands of white in her own hair when she told me the tale of Urla.'

The Piney laughed quietly at that. 'You humans, always in such a hurry to have children!' he said. 'I dare say that's what makes you so impatient, forever wanting everything at once. An impatient person shortens the time he has to live. Why, my youngest children were not a year old when the lightning struck me, and I am glad they were able to see their father, who is also their mother, chosen to be a Piney.'

'Their father and also their mother?' repeated Stone-eye, taken aback, but then he understood the Piney's meaning, and said, 'I was forgetting you're really a tree. Since I've been able to talk to you, I have felt you were a man.'

If the Piney could have shrugged his shoulders, he would probably have done so now. 'A man? What does that mean?' he said. 'And does it matter? You humans are very incomplete creatures, you know, with only half of life in any one of you.'

Stone-eye felt the old fellow spoke of humans in a rather arrogant way, which annoyed him. 'Well, you're just a piece of wood now!' he said. 'Even if you can talk. And you'll have no more children.'

If he had thought this would abash the Piney, he was wrong, for his wooden companion chuckled quietly and said, 'I've still enough life in me to give you some of it, my simple goatish friend!'

And with these last words, the Piney's voice had begun to change: it no longer sounded mocking, as one might have thought from the words themselves, but kindly and loving, as a mother speaks to comfort her child, and at the same moment Stone-eye caught the sweet, resinous fragrance rising from the purplish brown spot at the back of the Piney's head, enveloping him in the tender embrace with which the ripened blue scales of a cone, oozing resin, enclose the kernel. 'You have plenty of time,' said the stone pine's soft and motherly voice. 'You must just learn to wait. An impatient man will find everything slips away, but all things come to him who waits.'

Listening to the voice, breathing in the fragrance of the tree, Stone-eye felt the vigour of that ancient creature who had brought countless offspring into the world over the centuries pass into him, pervading his body with warmth. He lay back on his bed of leaves, closed his eyes, and at that moment, clearer and more distinctly than any vision, he saw the girl with the strange eyes running towards him again. Once more he came out from behind the bushes, but the girl was not afraid; instead, she ran on, laughing, and the closer she came the taller she seemed to grow, her childish features turned to the lovely face of a young woman, and she reached out her arms as she ran the last few paces towards him.

Soon after this the grass among the bushes was ready for cutting, so that Stone-eye was able to mow it and bring in the hay. This year, as before, One-horn watched his strange activities and shook his head, but at least he refrained from any mocking remarks. Obviously his mind retained some faint memory of the fact that this dry grass had turned out quite nourishing at a time which hardly bothered him now, when the grass was green and juicy. As soon as the hay harvest was in under the roof of the cave, Stone-eye was ready to leave. He put the remaining hazelnuts in his goat's-hair bag, hung it over his shoulder, took the Piney in his hand and set off, going south this time, for he hoped to meet his friend Needle-tooth.

He trotted along through the bushes at the foot of the cliff all day. Not until evening did the ground begin to rise, and the timber forest approached, so that Stone-eye was no longer forced to make his way from bush to bush, bending low, but could stride out freely in the shade of the tall pines.

The sun had already dipped down behind the rocky barrier when he heard a rustling and splashing which grew louder with every step he took, and rounding an angular projection of rock, he saw that the cliff came to an end here, enclosing a semi-circular hollow where alders and willows grew. A waterfall shot down from a cleft at the top of the cliff, foaming as it fell into a little lake, whose surface was kept in constant motion.

Stone-eye found a place to camp where the branches of the bushes hung out far over the water, put his few things down, and jumped into the lake to wash away the sweat of his long journey, and most of all, the goatish stink of the cave. Spluttering, he splashed about in the cold water, even ventured under the waterfall, was swept right down by the force of it, came up again spitting out water, and quickly made his way back to the roof of overhanging willow boughs. When he climbed back on land, shaking the water from his coat like a wet dog, he heard a shrill squeal. 'Is that any way to greet an old friend?' a high-pitched voice complained.

Stone-eye looked around, puzzled, and then he saw Needle-tooth sitting by his camping place. The weasel crossly wiped away some drops of water, adding, 'If there's one thing I can't stand, it's getting my coat wet.'

'Forgive my clumsiness,' said Stone-eye. 'I didn't see you. Anyway, it was for your sake I was taking a bath, to keep the smell of the goats from offending your sensitive nose. I hoped I'd meet you here.'

These remarks instantly mollified the ruffled weasel. They greeted one another as friends, and the weasel apologized with much courtesy for his cross remarks. 'Water's good to drink,' he said, 'but otherwise I prefer to keep away from it. It would be the greatest relief to my conscience if you would accept the young grouse that happened to cross my path just now.' And he dragged his prey out of the bushes and laid it at Stone-eye's feet.

A little later, they were sitting by the fire together, just as they did in the old days, each eating his supper in his own way: that is to say, Stone-eye had the breast and thighs of the grouse roasted on a spit, while the weasel ate the rest raw. And they told one another how things had gone since last they met. 'Poor hunting in the winter,' said Needle-tooth, 'and if you do happen to catch a white hare weak with hunger, or a half-frozen bird, it's not much more than skin and bones. That green-eyed falcon once snapped up a mouse from in front of my nose. It looks as if she's still around these parts. I was worried, because of your stone.'

'And you were right to be worried,' said Stone-eye, and told his friend whom the green-eyed falcon had enlisted to steal the stone this time, and who had come to his aid.

'I could have dealt with that mouse myself,' said Needle-tooth, not without a touch of jealousy in his voice, although it was not quite clear whether he minded about the service he could have done his friend or the prey that he had missed taking. At all events, he licked his whiskers with some relish, so that Stone-eye made haste to tell his tale to the end. 'And if you value my friendship,' he finished, 'then please leave mice alone while we're travelling together, or you might happen to eat my friend He-who-speaks-with-the-snake for breakfast.'

'I'll try to remember,' said Needle-tooth. 'I will spare grass snakes in future, too.'

'That sets my mind much at rest,' said Stone-eye, 'for I wouldn't like to lose your company.'

'You seem to think a lot of this grass snake,' said the weasel, slightly hurt.

'Rinkulla is no ordinary grass snake,' said Stone-eye, thinking of the fiery light of her agate eyes. 'She seems to know a good deal about my past life, the time I have forgotten.'

'Does the past matter so much to you?' asked Needle-tooth. 'Personally, I'm happy enough if I catch something nice and juicy every day!'

'That may well satisfy you,' said Stone-eye. 'As you know yourself, you are a weasel. But who am I? A half-goat? Or was I once a fluter, as some say?'

'Why ask me?' inquired the weasel. 'Make yourself a flute, and then you'll find out.'

'That's just what Rinkulla advised too,' said Stone-eye. 'I'll cut myself a willow pipe tomorrow.'

'Do that,' said the weasel. 'I like music.' And then they both lay down to sleep.

Next morning, therefore, Stone-eye took his knife with its goat's-horn handle out of the bag he carried over his shoulder, cut some willow twigs, and divided them into sections of different lengths. While he was busy carefully knocking the green and juicy bark with the handle of his knife, until he could push out the pale wood inside it, he felt as if he were a little boy again, sitting on the banks of the small river that ran through Fraglund, where an old shepherd had once taught him this art. He remembered just how to cut a short peg of wood and shave it flat on one side, so that there was an opening to blow through when you put it into the mouthpiece of the pipe. Then you made a notch in the pipe just where the peg ended inside it, and the instrument would play a note. He listened to the soft sound of the willow pipe mingling with the rushing of the waterfall, and in his imagination a melody he wanted to play grew from this one note. His fingers felt, as if of themselves, for holes that were not there, and only when the note continued unchanged did he realize his hands were remembering an art he himself had forgotten. They were obviously used to a different instrument, perhaps of the kind that his grandfather or mute Barlo had played; but at least he was now sure that he had once been able to play a flute. Meanwhile, he must make do with what the shepherd had taught him, so he made more pipes in the same way, each a little longer than its predecessor, tuned them to play together, and then, using a couple of thin willow withies, tied them in a row between two pieces of wood. He let the pipes pass quickly over his lips, from the longest to the shortest, and played a scale.

'Very nice,' said the weasel. 'So you must have been a fluter once.'

'That was only to try it out,' said Stone-eye, and then he played a tune that had just come into his head. It was the song the girl had sung last year before she called to the fishes: the song of Fair Agla and the Green Man. And now he knew where he had first heard it too, when he was riding the land with Barlo. As he played, following the words of the song in his mind, he suddenly realized that someone was actually singing them, and when he looked at the waterfall, from which he heard the high voice coming, he saw a woman sitting behind the bright, shimmering curtain of the cascading water, her long, greenish fair hair flowing down her body in constantly moving, streaming waves. He played until the water nymph had sung the last verse, and then took his pipes from his mouth. The water nymph laughed aloud, clear, rippling laughter, and then said, 'You haven't forgotten your songs yet, goat-legged fluter!'

'I've remembered this one, that's all,' said Stone-eye. 'I heard a girl sing it last year when I was the other side of the mountains.'

'I know,' said the water nymph. 'She's looking for a fluter.'

'Do you know the girl's name?' asked Stone-eye.

'You'll remember that at the right time too,' said the water nymph. 'When the girl has called you by your right name, you'll remember hers as well.'

'Where shall I find her?' asked Stone-eye at once, avidly.

The water nymph laughed again, and it sounded as if millions of water drops were falling on the rippling surface of the lake.

'Oh, you fool, so impatient!' she said. 'Do you want to frighten the child again?'

Stone-eye looked sadly down at his clumsy goat's hooves, and said, 'Then I suppose I shall never discover my name.' And after a while, he added, 'Can I see the girl, at least? She has such beautiful eyes.'

The water nymph looked kindly at him, and said, 'You will find her beyond the mountains in the shallow green valley again. But don't expect too much. One who is impatient makes the time of waiting longer.'

'Rinkulla said much the same,' replied Stone-eye.

'Then bear it in mind!' said the water nymph. 'Rinkulla is older and wiser than I am.' And then she laughed once more, cried, 'Thank you for the beautiful song!' slipped beneath the waterfall which sprayed its glittering waterdrops all over her, went under with such a splash that the water sprayed up, reaching the bank, and did not surface again.

The weasel shook himself crossly, remarking, 'I wasn't intending to take a bath. Does everyone around here have to keep splashing about?

I'm not staying near this lake any longer! I suppose you want to go back to that valley now?'

'Yes,' said Stone-eye. 'Even if I have to crawl over the pass under those low-growing pines.'

'Oh, as to that, don't worry,' said the weasel. 'I know a way where you can stay in the shade of the trees, though it means a bit of a climb.'

He led Stone-eye to a place where the wall of rock was split by a narrow cleft. Scurrying on ahead, he showed his friend how to work his way upwards, step by step. Halfway up, the path seemed to come to an end. Stone-eye searched the face of the rock above him, but there was no crevice or ledge, only the smooth and vertical precipice.

'What are you looking for up there?' asked Needle-tooth. 'This is the way.' And he slipped into a hole, worn smooth by water, just where the cleft ended. Crawling after him, Stone-eye found himself in a narrow passage leading diagonally upwards. Obviously a stream had once flowed along this channel, for the ground was loamy and covered with stones. At first he felt as if he were crawling on and on into the heart of the mountain, but after a while light came filtering down through a crack from above, and at the same time the rise became less steep, the channel grew wider, and next moment this strange path led out of the narrow passage and into the dense pine wood above.

'Now we just have to keep going west,' said the weasel.

They walked on for two days, through dark woods where the pine trees stood so close together that Stone-eye was glad of his shaggy coat that kept the branches from scratching him. Even at noon, there was only a green twilight here, and nothing but a few pale summer mushrooms grew on the forest floor, which was thick with brown, rotting needles. Few living creatures ever started up, and the weasel had his work cut out to provide for their evening meal. On the third day, the look of the trees began to change. Hitherto, the path had not been particularly steep, but it had been rising all the time, so that by now they must have reached a considerable height. The pines here were not so close together, or so tall. Their sturdy trunks were often forked, or distorted into grotesque shapes, and long grey strands of lichen drifted from them. They look like old, old men, Stone-eye thought, old men with pale, straggling hair and grey beards, and he had the feeling that he knew this wood, although he could not re-member when he might have been here before. Hadn't one of his companions then been afraid of these trees? If so, who? He mulled it over, but the answer would not come. At last the screech of a nutcracker aroused him from his thoughts. Looking up, he saw the brown-feathered bird rise from a tree-top, fly on a little way, and then disappear into the branches of a strangely twisted pine. And farther up the slope, where the trees grew even more sparsely, there was a view of a grassy summit with a flock of choughs circling over it.

'We'll climb up to the last of the trees,' said the weasel, 'and then I suppose we'll have to go along the outskirts of the wood, although the quicker way is over the summit there, but you won't want to take it.'

'I can't, even if I did want to,' said Stone-eye, striding on. The sight of the gently rolling mountain meadow seemed to him so familiar that he was now quite certain he had once been here before, and he hoped that something up there might jog his memory.

He had soon reached the last of the trees, and stopped under the broad branches of a tangled pine. Ahead of him, the dome of the mountain summit rose from the forest, covered with short grass where countless herbs and flowers bloomed: yellow, star-shaped arnica flowers, deep blue gentian, blood-red dianthus, and pale purple cushions of thyme whose scent rose under the hot, mid-day sun. A little way to his right, not far from the edge of the wood, an old rowan stood in the grass, and the choughs had settled in its branches, which were laden with clusters of white flowers. The birds must have scattered rowan berries year after year, for saplings with bright green, feathery leaves were coming up everywhere among the dark shapes of the last pines. One of these young rowans, hardly as tall as a man yet, had come up not far from the place where Stone-eye stood. He sat down on the trunk of a fallen pine and stared hard at it.

'Looking for something?' inquired the weasel.

'My lost time,' said Stone-eye. 'I know I've been here before; I'm sure of it. Something dreadful happened here, and it has to do with this rowan.'

'I don't believe that,' said the weasel. 'Rowans are good trees. Nothing bad can happen in their shade.'

'Maybe not,' said Stone-eye. 'My grandfather said the same. Yet I've been feeling cold with horror since we got here.'

'Then we'd better go on, fast, and get away from the place,' said the weasel.

'No,' said Stone-eye. 'If I stay here a while longer, I may remember what happened here.'

'I can't think what good you expect to come of that,' said the weasel, 'but far be it from me to prevent you. Personally, I'd be glad to forget an unpleasant experience! Well, I'll be off and see if I can find us any supper.' And with these words he scurried away, disappearing into the shade of the trees.

Stone-eye was afraid. He did not know what it was he feared, but that only made things worse. Then he remembered that at such times it was a help to look at the stone. He took it out of its bag and held it up to the sun on the palm of his hand. The iris-shaped rings shone and spread suddenly into a great explosion of colour, both beautiful and terrifying; the face that he had often seen emerge from the play of blue, green and violet circles came forward all at once, eyes wide, as if some danger threatened, and the woman cried, 'Take care!' And at that very moment something came shooting down from the glassy blue sky, the wind hummed in its feathery pinions, a shadow pounced, and then the stone was gone.

Stone-eye stared at his empty hand. His palm still felt the impact of a sharp beak. Then he looked up and saw a falcon rise above the mountain pasture, beating its wings fast. But the falcon was not alone in the sky. As soon as she passed over the old rowan, the choughs flew up from the branches, joined together in a flock, and mobbed her. She tried to gain height, but the choughs could fly just as skilfully, and had soon surrounded her. Singly, or in pairs, they shot down, their sharp beaks stabbing at the thief. At first the falcon managed to escape them, but she was increasingly hard-pressed, particularly as she could not use her beak, which held the stone.

Then Stone-eye saw the falcon struck for the first time, and she had difficulty in keeping on a steady course. Feathers came adrift and floated down, circling slowly, while the falcon escaped her pursuers yet again. Next moment the flock had surrounded her once more, and began the game anew. The falcon, realizing at last that her life was at stake, unexpectedly pounced on the choughs and struck one of them so hard that it fell to the ground, reeling, amidst a flurry of black feathers. But at the same time, and in the heat of battle, the falcon had dropped the stone from her beak. Stone-eye saw it fall, glittering, and disappear from sight somewhere farther up the mountain meadow.

The falcon made no attempt to get back the stone; she was fighting for her life now. Since she had nothing left to hinder her, she managed to clear a space around herself. Spiralling steeply, she rose into the sky and then flew away eastwards, so fast that the choughs abandoned their pursuit, circled the mountain summit for a while excitedly, and then came down and settled in the rowan tree again.

Stone-eye tried to memorize the spot where the stone must have fallen in the grass, but of course he was quite unable to run out of the shade of the trees and over the mountain meadow to look for his treasure. Very soon the weasel came back. He laid a grey rock partridge down by their camping place, and asked what the choughs were making so much noise about. Stone-eye told him what had happened, and asked him to go up the slope and look for the stone.

Although he had described the place where he thought it must lie in as much detail as possible, the weasel came back without it some time later. 'The stone may have rolled away somewhere else,' he said. 'It would take me weeks to search under every tuft of grass and behind every boulder on my own. Perhaps I'd better call in three or four of my cousins living hereabouts.'

'I have a better idea,' said Stone-eye, and he took his willow pipes out of his bag and blew a rising sequence of three notes, repeating it several times.

'What's the use of that?' inquired the weasel. 'Do you think it'll bring the stone running to you of its own accord?'

'Not the stone, no,' said Stone-eye, 'but I hope it will bring my friend He-who-speaks-with-the-snake and his people to my aid. You remember what you promised about mice?'

'Mice!' said the weasel, contemptuously. 'What good are mice?'

'Wait and see!' was all Stone-eye said.

And in fact they had to wait quite a long time. Although Stone-eye's horror of the place was if anything worse than before, they stayed there all that day, and nothing happened. Stone-eye plucked the partridge, they shared it for their supper when evening came, and then lay down to sleep.

At first light of dawn, Stone-eye was woken by a tug at his earlobe. When he felt for it, his hand touched something small and furry, and a little voice whispered, 'You called me, Bearer of the Stone, and I came as fast as I could.'

'Oh, it's you, He-who-speaks-with-the-snake,' said Stone-eye, in a normal speaking tone. However, the mouse hissed, 'Keep your voice down! There's a weasel lying in wait close to you!'

Stone-eye laughed out loud, and said, 'That's my friend Needle-tooth, and he's promised me to leave mice alone!'

The mouse seemed to doubt this, and whispered, 'But who'd believe a weasel?'

Here Needle-tooth joined in the conversation, asking, with some menace in his voice, 'Do you doubt my word, mouse?'

'Oh no, nothing farther from my mind!' the mouse made haste to assure him. 'Only the fact is, my previous dealings with weasels have been rather different.'

'I don't like mice,' said Needle-tooth curtly. 'If you've spoken with a snake, as they say you have, you won't be afraid of a weasel. Such a name as yours brings certain obligations with it.'

'You may be right,' said the mouse. 'And now I see why it isn't always easy to bear an honourable name.' Then he shook himself, and went on, with remarkable firmness of tone, 'But I'll show myself worthy of mine.' Turning to Stone-eye again, he asked how he could be of service. Stone-eye told him what had happened, finishing, 'I should think the only way to find the stone is to ask you to summon all the mice of these parts and search the summit of the mountain with them.'

'Easy!' said the mouse, letting out a couple of shrill squeaks. A few minutes later, there was a rustling sound all around them, dark little shadows came scurrying over the forest floor, the grass of the mountain meadow appeared to come to life, blades of grass abruptly started swaying, flowers rocked, and high-pitched squeaking whispers could be heard on all sides. 'I'll just go and lend my cousins a paw,' said the mouse, turning to go.

'Shall I come too?' asked Needle-tooth, but the mouse shook his head, saying, 'Definitely not! The sight of you might upset my relations.' And he scuttled away.

'All those mice make me nervous,' said Needle-tooth, when he was out of earshot. There was a gleam in his eyes, but he controlled himself, and lay where he was beside Stone-eye.

It was not long before they heard a shrill whistle from the slope of the mountainside. Hundreds of mice came streaming together from all directions, so that the meadow was grey with their coats where they met, and then they came scurrying down to Stone-eye's camp in a long procession, led by He-who-speaks-with-the-snake, who was rolling the eye-stone before him. He laid it at his friend's feet, saying, 'Here's your treasure. It was a pleasure to be of service. Anything else we can do for you?'

'You have done a very great deal for me already,' said Stone-eye. 'The stone is the most valuable thing I possess.' And he thanked them all heartily, finally saying, 'And now you'd better run home to your holes! I don't know how much longer Needle-tooth will be able to stand the sight of so many mice dancing about under his nose.'

This hint proved so effective that a few seconds later there was not a mouse to be seen anywhere around – except for Stone-eye's friend He-who-speaks-with-the-snake. The mouse would not deign even to look at the weasel, but bowed to Stone-eye and said, 'I cannot reconcile it with my name to leave you in such an undignified way, Bearer of the Stone. I don't want you thinking I'd run away from this weasel!'

Stone-eye bowed back, and replied, with equal gravity, 'I know how brave you are, He-who-speaks-with-the-snake, but I shall never think you a coward if you run from a stronger animal. Remember that, for our friendship's sake.'

'I will,' said the mouse, bowing once more, with great ceremony, and then he walked slowly away over the forest floor.

There was nothing to keep Stone-eye here now. He and Needle-tooth skirted the summit, staying just inside the woods, until they were on the other side of the mountain, and then they climbed down into the valley. That same evening they reached the last of the trees and looked out at the broad, flat meadows through which the stream wound its way. Yet again, there were a couple of dozen horses grazing a little farther down the valley, but no herdsmen could be seen. Perhaps they had gone home for supper, for smoke could be seen rising from one of the huts in the distance. It did not take Needle-tooth long to find meat for their own supper in these rich lowlands, and when they had eaten, they lay down in the bushes to sleep.

They spent the next few days wandering the woods of the valley. Stone-eye made sure he could always see the meadows through the trees, hoping to meet the girl again, as the water nymph had promised he would. But apart from a few horse-herds, who came now and then to tend their beasts, he could see no human beings at all. Sometimes he sat in a hidden place among the bushes, where he could have a view of the valley, playing his willow pipes. Needle-tooth liked the music, and was always courteous in his expressions of admiration, but that was not what Stone-eye was after.

Several weeks had passed like this, and one day he was among the alder bushes on the outskirts of the wood, sitting on a tree-stump and coaxing all manner of tunes from his pipes; he could not have said how he knew them. He was so caught up in the music that he forgot his surroundings, closed his eyes and listened to the sound of his instrument. Hearing something rustle in the bushes to one side, he put down the pipes and said without looking round, 'Have you brought something for supper, Needle-tooth?'

The rustling stopped, and there was no answer. Only now did he open his eyes and look at the place where he expected to find his friend. And then he saw the girl, standing quite close, among the alders. Her eyes were wide, as if with alarm, but she did not run away, did not move from the spot, only looked at him with those strange eyes of hers. They were both silent for a long while, and then the girl said, 'So you are the fluter, after all?'

Without a word, Stone-eye showed her his instrument, as if that would answer her question.

'You had a different flute before,' said the girl.

Stone-eye shrugged his shoulders, and said, 'I don't know what things were like before.'

'Why, you were happy then, and you knew a great many merry tales,' said the girl.

'I don't feel much like laughing now,' said Stone-eye, 'and I don't remember those stories any more.'

At that the girl began to weep. 'What happened to you, fluter?' she cried. 'What happened to make you look as you do?' And she buried her face in her hands.

'I don't know that, either,' said Stone-eye, and he stood up, wishing to comfort the girl in some way. But as soon as she heard him approaching on his goat's hooves, she dropped her hands from her face and flinched away. Stone-eye saw rising horror darken the indescribable colour of her eyes, he saw the girl look at his hairy body with disgust that she had difficulty in controlling, and when he was close, she screamed, 'Don't touch me!' And then she turned, forced her way through the bushes, and ran like the wind.

'I didn't mean to frighten you!' Stone-eye called after her, but she was out of earshot by now, running in the open, racing over the meadows, skirts flying, to the place where the horses were standing, her piebald pony among them. She leaped on its back and galloped down the valley towards the huts. Stone-eye watched her until she was out of sight. Then he sat down on the tree-stump once more. 'Did you see that, Piney?' he asked. 'She ran away from me again before I could find out anything.'

'What did you expect?' said the Piney. 'Girls of her age are rather timid, you know. Did you at least remember her name?'

'No,' said Stone-eye.

'Well, perhaps it'll come back to you next year,' said the Piney calmly, as if a year more or less hardly mattered. But Stone-eye was not ready to give up his present hopes yet. With Needle-tooth, he roamed the woods bordering the valley incessantly, and in the course of his wanderings came to a place where the stream rushed into a narrow ravine. Here he turned back, and watched the herdsmen's dwellings for days on end, but he never had another glimpse of the girl, so that at last he came to wonder if she were still in this valley at all. He had thrown away his willow pipes long ago, for the tubes of bark had distorted as they dried and would not give a true note any more. Meanwhile, the beech leaves were beginning to turn colour, the blackberries were ripening, and the woods smelled of mushrooms.

'If you're planning to spend the winter with those goats of yours again, it's time we set off on the way back,' said Needle-tooth one morning. By now Stone-eye had given up all hope of meeting the girl again, and only a crippling indecisiveness had kept him in the valley so long. He gave the weasel a silent nod, and then they climbed the path through the woods down which they had come to the valley in early summer.

They had not gone far when the weasel suddenly stopped, whispering, 'There's somebody coming towards us. Quick – into the bushes!'

Hastily, they found a place to hide, and as Stone-eye crouched motionless on the ground, listening, he heard a dry twig crack underfoot from time to time, and then the hollow sound of hoofbeats on the soft forest floor, and finally he heard voices. Two men, plainly, were riding down into the valley. They came rapidly closer, and could soon be seen among the tree-trunks. One was a tall, bearded man, who seemed to belong to the same people as the herdsmen; the other, however, attracted Stone-eye's attention at once. He was a short, elderly man, with a curiously flat face and a receding chin; a thin, white moustache drooped over the corners of his mouth, and there was a frightened look in his watery, pale blue eyes. He has a face like a fish, thought Stone-eye, as the men rode past his hiding place, and then he heard the bearded man say, 'No need to fear you won't be welcome here. We're always glad to see folk who understand horses.'

'I must know who that man is,' said Stone-eye, as soon as the men were out of earshot. 'We'll follow them.'

'Why, do you know him?' asked Needle-tooth. 'The fish-faced old man?'

'I think I may,' said Stone-eye. 'I don't know for certain. But I want to find out.'

Cautiously, therefore, they followed the two men, and saw them rein in their horses on the edge of the wood. 'There's the horses' pasture,' said the bearded man, 'and our people are over there with the beasts.' He called to the herdsmen, waving. Immediately three of them came hurrying across the meadows and greeted the bearded man, who, like his companion, had now dismounted.

'Who's this you've brought with you?' one of them asked.

'This is Vazzek, of the Carphead people,' said the bearded man. 'And if you can do with another horse-herd, he's your man.'

'Since when did the Carpheads know anything about horses?' asked one of the herdsmen, his expression clearly showing that he thought poorly of the Carphead people.

'That might be a long story,' said the bearded man, 'and if you want to hear it, friends, I think we'd better sit down.'

While the five men settled in a circle on the outskirts of the wood, Stone-eye crept closer and closer, so as not to miss a word of what was said. He found a good place behind a dense bush of privet, which gave him adequate cover without cutting off his own view. The old man with the fish-like face was sitting directly opposite him, and the bearded man beside him now cleared his throat and began the tale. 'It was like this: I had a message from the Ore Master to take to the village of Arni's Folk,' said he, 'and I was on my way back, you see, when I came upon this old man. He was lying unconscious by the roadside, and when I opened his garments to see if he was injured, I found his back cut to ribbons by a whiplash. I took him up on the horse in front of me and brought him back to Arziak, where my wife nursed him until he had recovered some of his strength. But he wouldn't stay. "They'll find me even here," he kept saying, and he asked to be taken to some place away from the main roads that folk travel. And since he said he had been working with horses for years, I thought he could come here and stay with you.'

'Where did he herd horses, then?' asked one of the men.

'Ah, now that I don't yet know myself,' said the bearded man. 'He wouldn't say anything about it before, but perhaps he'll tell us now he's in a place where he can feel safe.'

At this, the man Vazzek shook his head slowly, and said, 'I shall never feel safe anywhere now. But this place looks as if I could rest here for a while, and if you're willing to take me in, then you ought to know my story. In my youth, to be sure, I knew very little about horses, for I grew up in a fishing village far down the Brown River. One day the Raiding Riders came, and dragged me away into the steppes, along with many other young men and girls, and since then I've been one of the Khan's slaves. But I was lucky: they sent me to the horses' paddocks to help the grooms.

At first I didn't mind what happened to me. Day and night I thought of nothing but the rushing of the river, the cry of the grey herons in the trees on the banks, and the dark backs of the fish passing by, deep in the water where the Great Carp lives. In time, however, I came to find comfort in the affection of my horses. They liked me – perhaps because, in my grief, I treated them gently – and they would follow me like dogs. So in the end I discovered that I liked them too, those shaggy little horses of the steppes, with their soft and high-arched noses. And so the Raiding Riders gradually came to believe I knew a great deal about horses, and after many years, when I was beginning to go grey, the Khan put me in charge of the whole paddock.

This was the state of things when a young fluter came riding into the camp one day, not three years ago, bringing replacements for six horses that had died because of him. The way the men who were there at the time told the story, he had used the magic of his flute, and nothing more, to send the horses racing out into the steppes, forcing them to run until they dropped. That in itself seemed to me strange enough, but it was also said he owned Arni's stone, and Arni himself had named him his heir and Bearer of the Stone.

When I had heard all this about the young man, I was not surprised that he beat the Khan in a game of chess to which he had been challenged, winning a costly rug. Arni had been the only man who could ever beat his brother Hunli at chess, and wherever he might be now I was sure he had stood by the young man as he played.

All this aroused my interest in the fluter, and there was something else that occupied my mind too: in my young days, when I was still living in our village by the Brown River, I had heard a fluter who played in our village elder's house, and played in a way I never heard a fluter play before or since. They said of him that he could end any quarrel with the power of his music, and I believed it once I'd heard him play. When the young man came to me, to see how his horse was, I asked him if he knew that fluter, and I discovered he was the fluter's grandson and had inherited his instrument. The Khan, not surprisingly, had forbidden him to play that flute within the camp, but at my request the young man came to me at night, when it was dark, and played for me. I thought his mastery of the instrument no less than his grandfather's; while he played, all the horses gathered by the fence to listen, and finally he played them a tune of their own too. I was surprised, even then, to hear the gentle, peaceful melodies he thought suitable for the horde's war-horses, but being a peaceable soul myself I was glad of it, and thanked him, having no notion what the results of his playing would be.

I didn't begin wondering about it till later, long after the young fluter had ridden away. For it turned out that none of those horses would consent to carry their riders in any kind of attack. As soon as the warriors uttered their war-cries, the horses would turn tail in a body and run away, until there was no one in sight to be attacked. The Khan and his men could make nothing whatever of this, and they tried again and again, but their horses utterly refused to take part in any battle, and as the Riders weren't used to fighting on foot they were no longer able to attack villages or go on raids.

I had no objection to the horses' change of heart, knowing only too well what the Raiding Riders had done to my own people on the banks of the Brown River over the years. However, it was a serious matter for the Raiding Riders. Ever since anyone can remember, they have lived by raiding and robbing, and those who stayed with the horde at the time of the Great Parting did not want to go the same way as Arni's Folk.

But a wolf prevented from raiding will starve. Food was running short in the camp. We slaves were the first to feel it, and I began to wonder if what the fluter had done to the horses had been such a good thing after all. It came to the point where all the gold in the camp, and jewellery of any value, had to be collected to buy the necessities of life from Arni's Folk. The envoys Khan Hunli sent to them brought back provisions enough to last a year, but they were silent with fury at the humiliation they had suffered in driving that bargain. I was afraid when I saw their faces, fearing what their pent-up rage might lead them to do, and indeed I feared for my life.

So far nobody but myself knew the reason for the horses' strange behaviour, but Khan Hunli had had plenty of time to think it over, and gradually he began to put two and two together and guess what had happened. One day he came to me and said, "I suppose you're glad the horses I entrusted to you aren't fit for fighting any more? Was it you, I wonder, who bewitched them?"

I began to tremble under his gaze. "My lord, don't you see that I have as much to suffer as you and your own men?" I said.

"You might feel going hungry was worth it, to get your revenge," said the Khan. The way he played with his whip as he spoke increased my fear, and I began to curse that young fluter in my heart, for landing me in such trouble. Stammering with terror, I assured the Khan of my innocence again and again, but that only made him suspect me the more.

"The horses were in your care," he said at last, "and one way or another I intend to find out what you did to them."

I fell at his feet, for I knew only too well what he meant by "one way or another". But he pushed me aside, called two of his men and had me taken to his tent. There he told them to ram two spears into the ground, at some distance from each other, and hang me up between them by my thumbs. Then he stationed himself in front of me and asked if I had yet remembered how the horses came to lose their will to fight. It was a hot day when all this happened. Sweat was running down into my eyes, and my arms hurt so much that I bellowed aloud.

"I can't understand you," said the Khan. "Speak more clearly!"

Then I screamed, "Ask that fluter who played chess with you!"

On hearing this the Khan went white with rage. He had me untied and made me tell him just what the fluter had done to the horses that night. When I had finished, the Khan whispered, as if to himself, "I might have known it." Then he turned to me and said, "All this happened with your consent, slave, and you shall pay for it. But first you shall see how I deal with these ruined horses." What followed was one of the worst things I have ever known. The Khan assembled all men able to bear arms outside his tent, told them what he had just discovered, and then ordered them to draw their curved swords and kill all the horses on the spot, all but the one and two-year-olds, which had been born after the fluter came to us. They tied me to a post outside the paddock, and whenever I closed my eyes because I could bear the sight no longer, one of the Riders put a knife to my throat.

My poor horses had no idea what was going to happen to them. They ran happily to their masters, whinnying with pleasure and expecting to be patted on the neck. In went the Riders' swords instead, making the blood spurt out. You mustn't think the Riders enjoyed this butchery. They loved their horses, but they dared not go against their master's orders. I shall never forget the look on those men's faces, pale and bitter with helpless anger as they stared at their dying animals. Only two were spared, and I was yet to learn why the Khan wanted them.

When the slaughter was over, he cried, "And now at least we know what to live on until next spring! Gut the bodies and hang the horsemeat up on the tent-poles to dry!" Then he came over to me and said, "Did you enjoy that spectacle, slave? We will now deal with you as you have deserved. However, you needn't hope for a quick death."

He had my clothes torn off me and ordered two servants to whip me until there wasn't a shred of skin left whole on my back. The servants grieved for the horses too, so they did their work with care. At some point I lost consciousness and didn't come round until I was being thrown over the back of one of the remaining horses like a sack. A Rider mounted the other horse, took mine by the bridle, and rode out into the steppes with me.

The sun was still blazing down from the sky, although it was late in the afternoon by now. I opened my eyes occasionally, and at first I could still see the jagged outline of the tents across the endless expanse of grass, a little smaller and more blurred every time; later, there was nothing at all to be seen in the shimmering haze above the grey plains. When the sun was only a little way above the horizon, the Rider reined in his horse, took me by the feet and flung me head first into the grass. Then he rode away without a word.

So this was the slow death upon which Khan Hunli had decided. I knew that there were people who lived somewhere far to the west, where the setting sun hung glowing red above the whispering grass of the steppes, that there was water there, and shady trees, but all that was far away, beyond my reach; even a horseman would take days to get there. All the same, I tried to stand up and go westwards, but my strength failed me after the first few paces, so I lay there motionless, waiting for the cool of the night, and perhaps some dew I could lick from the sharp, dry grass-blades.

I don't know how long I lay like that. Now and then I lost consciousness and dozed until my thirst woke me again, but I couldn't find a trace of moisture on the dusty grasses. When I turned my head aside, I saw the stars wheeling slowly above me, icy points of light in the dark, moonless sky, as if measuring out the time I had left to live.

Then a shadow suddenly passed in front of the stars, partly hiding them. I hadn't noticed any movement, nor the sound of steps in the grass; the shadow had just suddenly appeared, and it stood motionless for a while near the place where I lay. And then a voice said, "Ah – I was searching for you, Vazzek."

I looked more closely at the shadow, and saw that a Rider had stopped beside me. At that moment the moon rose above the horizon, and in its cold light I saw white braids at the Rider's temples, and his features appeared out of the black of the night: the features of Khan Hunli, sitting his horse and looking down at me. I was extremely surprised to hear him speak my name, for that wasn't usually his way when addressing the slaves. I supposed he had come to kill me, and I didn't mind much now, having already resigned myself to dying there on the steppes. I was quite surprised to find I felt almost cheerful about it, and I said, "You've gone to a lot of trouble to see a slave die, Khan Hunli."

The Rider dismounted, bent over me, and said, "You're mixing me up with my brother, Vazzek. I've come to mend the harm the bearer of my stone has done, at least as far as you're concerned. None of this is your fault at all. However, I shall hardly be able to prevent what else may come of it."

When I realized it was Arni talking to me, I felt sure I had already crossed the boundary of death. "You do me great honour," I said, "welcoming me to your domain, when I was your brother's slave."

Arni laughed quietly to himself and said, "Why, does it surprise you, Vazzek? Those who've already taken all the honour they want need no more shown them. But you've never been one to trouble yourself much about such things." Then the old man lifted me from the ground, so easily that I was surprised at his strength, set me in front of his horse's saddle, and got up behind me. "Are you comfortable?" he asked. "We have a long, fast ride ahead of us."

"I never felt more comfortable in my life," I said, and it was the truth. Since the moment when he touched me I had felt no pain, and I leaned back in his arms like a child on his mother's breast. Then he urged on his horse, and we flew over the steppes so fast that the rustling grass beneath the horse's hooves shot by like the rushing current of a river. By now nothing surprised me, not the wheeling stars above me, or the fact that the night was nowhere near over when mountains appeared on the horizon ahead of us, shining pale in the moonlight, with the dark shapes of trees and bushes. Soon we began going uphill, leafy branches brushed my arms, and there was a smell of fresh grass and water in the air.

Soon afterwards Arni stopped his horse, dismounted and lifted me down. He went to a stream that ran gurgling through the bushes, fetched water in his cupped hands, and held it for me to drink. Then he laid me carefully on the soft grass by the wayside and said, "Sleep for a little, Vazzek. Someone will soon come past and find you." Before my eyes closed I was going to thank him, but he had vanished without a sound, just the way he came. And that was where this man found me.'

Stone-eye had listened to Vazzek's story with rising excitement, and he soon realized that it concerned him. But it is one thing to be told a tale of what you are said to have done at some past time, and quite another to remember it yourself, and the memory would not come back. He tried to picture the events in the Raiding Riders' camp, but he felt like a listener standing outside it all, while the teller of a tale tries to persuade him the dreadful story is all his fault. And he had no time to master his confusion just now, for the men were still in conversation. 'What do you think the Raiding Riders will do now they've lost all their horses?' asked the bearded man.

'You're forgetting the foals and colts,' said Vazzek. 'The two-year-olds are well enough grown to be broken in now.'

'But will those horses run away too when they're made to attack?' asked one of the herdsmen.

Vazzek shrugged his shoulders. 'I doubt it,' he said. 'But I go in fear of next spring. May I stay with you?'

'Stay as long as you like,' said the herdsman. 'We can probably learn a thing or two from a man who's tended Khan Hunli's horses. Only don't go letting that fluter near our own – for he tricked us, just as he tricked you.'

Vazzek raised his hands in protest. 'I never said he tricked me,' he said. 'I dare say he didn't stop to think what might come of that song he played the horses. He was a nice lad, really.'

'A nice lad!' said the herdsman indignantly. 'Apart from getting you a whipping that nearly cost you your life! Did he tell you in advance what he was thinking of doing to your horses?' And when Vazzek shook his head, the man went on, 'Well, there you are! It was exactly the same with us. When he came to Arziak the first time, he so bemused us with his playing that we gave ourselves up to Arni's Folk without a moment's thought. Only later did we discover Honi had sent him to soften us up. And now Arni's Folk are the only traders anywhere around, and our goldsmiths have to accept whatever prices they offer. You take my word for it, those smooth talkers may have cut their braids off, but they're still robbers like their cousins out in the steppes.'

'You shouldn't say a thing like that,' said Vazzek. 'Arni was a Raiding Rider too, and he didn't just take care of me, wherever he may have come from; he was a good friend to my people by the Brown River in the old days, and protected them from his own brother. Didn't Honi intend to follow Arni's example when he and many others left the horde and settled at Arni's House?'

'Well, that's what I thought myself, when first I heard that story,' said the bearded man. 'In fact I felt as if a dream I'd often had had come true, it seemed so amazing for Raiding Riders to turn peaceful! I don't know whether Honi really meant to go Arni's way at the time, but now his daughter's in charge, and I can tell you she's after nothing but her own good. I suppose there may still be some among Arni's Folk who remember how Arni himself acted. But I've heard say that many such folk have suddenly disappeared. There are nasty rumours going about near Arni's House.'

'So now do you see why I'm afraid?' asked Vazzek. 'If such a man's name can be so misused, there's trouble brewing, and you should all be on your guard.'

'And so I will be, Vazzek,' said the bearded man. 'But I must set off again now if I want to be home before midnight.'

As the bearded man was taking leave of the herdsmen, Vazzek unbuttoned his jerkin and took out a small object he wore on a thong around his neck. Lifting the thong over his head, he went over to the bearded man with a certain solemnity, and said, 'You will be closer than me to the trouble that's coming. Take this. It may protect you, especially if you're near water.'

'Near water?' asked the bearded man, at a loss, taking the thong. 'What is it?'

Stone-eye saw a thin, translucent object suddenly catch the sunlight, and at that moment he knew the answer even before he heard it.

'A scale from the Great Carp,' said Vazzek. 'The Great Carp will help anyone who carries it if he throws himself into the arms of the water. Wear it around your neck. I felt its cooling power even in the heat of the steppes when I lay exhausted in the sun. I shan't be needing it so much here, and the Great Old One helps his children even without that token.'

The bearded man looked at the scale for a little longer, and then put the thong over his head, embraced Vazzek in farewell, mounted his horse and rode away. The others waved, and then went over the meadows to their huts.

Stone-eye lay where he was behind the bushes, even when Vazzek and the herdsmen were out of sight. Nor did he watch them go; he was still seeing the scale shimmering in the sunlight. Or was it only a flickering flame reflected in it, the faint light of an oil lamp scarcely reaching the dark brown wool of the tent's walls, illuminating one side of the flat face of the slave woman standing before him, so that only half of it stood out from the darkness? He saw her eyes, pale as water, and remembered, and his memory spread like rings of ripples on the river when a carp's scales touch the surface. At first there was only the scale, then the tent and the slave woman, the Raiding Riders' camp, and the Khan, whom he had beaten at chess without knowing how. He saw the sweating face of Khan Hunli before him, heard him say, 'Only Arni could ever play like that!' and then Narzia's spell came up from oblivion too, and with it all that had happened since he came to Arni's Folk, including his journey to Arziak, and Promezzo, whose wife had the same eyes as that face which sometimes came into his dreams and spoke to him, and her daughter had looked at him, laughing, with those same eyes too, and she was the girl he had now met twice in this valley. But still he could not remember her name.

'What are you waiting for?' inquired the weasel. 'There's nobody left for you to hide from.'

With difficulty, Stone-eye managed to shake off these remembered images. He looked around him in confusion, as if he had quite forgotten where he was. 'Oh, Needle-tooth,' he said slowly, 'I wish I could hide from myself, now I've remembered some more of what I once did.'

'Have you found out if you were a fluter at last?' asked the weasel.

Stone-eye nodded, slowly. 'Yes,' he said. 'I was. But I played the wrong tunes.'

The weasel did not seem particularly impressed by this admission. 'Well, there you are,' he said. 'Now you see there's no point in digging up old bones! They don't feed you, they just make you feel sad. You'd better forget what's past – it's over and done with now.'

'No, that it is not,' said Stone-eye, 'as I know, now I've heard the tale that man Vazzek told. You go on ahead! I've a little more thinking to do.'

When he was alone, he took his stick, drove it into the ground, sat in front of it and said, 'Piney, I must talk to you!'

'Found another ant, have you?' asked the Piney.

'A carp's scale,' said Stone-eye.

'Then you've remembered all you'd forgotten now?' said the Piney.

Stone-eye shook his head. 'No, nothing like all,' he said. 'But what I do remember is not very pleasant.' And without glossing anything over, he told the Piney how he had tricked the people of Arziak and had cheated at chess in Hunli's tent. 'There's only one thing I don't understand,' he said at last. 'When I played that song to the horses, I really thought I had done a good thing, and now it seems to have been the worst of all. I destroyed every one of them, and I almost destroyed the man Vazzek as well. I am beginning to wonder what other consequences that tune may yet have.'

'A little late in the day to wonder!' said the Piney. 'You never seem to think beyond tomorrow, and all you ask is what will be of use to you.'

'Now you're being unfair,' said Stone-eye. 'That business of the horses was of use to everyone the Raiding Riders would have attacked during that time. Wasn't that a good thing to do?'

'So far as it goes, yes,' said the Piney, 'but not for the horde itself, and certainly not for Vazzek and the poor horses. You are to blame for what happened to them, and for all that may yet come of it.'

Stone-eye thought for a while, and then said, 'Is one to blame, then, if evil comes of what was well meant?'

'Meaning well is never enough,' said the Piney, 'not as long as you fail to think what Time may make of your good intentions.'

'Then one had better do nothing at all,' said Stone-eye bitterly. 'How am I to know what may happen if I throw a rabbit bone I've finished gnawing into the bushes behind me? Someone might come along, tread on it and die of blood poisoning. Why, you couldn't even crook your little finger without being to blame for something. You'd have to stand still as a statue and never move from the spot.'

'Exactly what I've done all my life,' said the Piney. 'However, I can see that's impossible for mankind. You're so made that you always have to be busy about something, instead of considering Time. No wonder you're forever making such a mess of the world.'

'It's all very well for you to talk,' said Stone-eye. 'You couldn't make a mess of anything while you stood up there on the pass.'

'For which I'm heartily thankful, now I've heard what you did with that flute of yours,' said the Piney. 'But even more important: all that time, I knew what I was there for – or rather, I should say, what I had been put there for. And that was quite enough for me. However, you obviously have no time to stop and wonder what's the point of all your chasing about. Or can you tell me what the point of it is?'

'Yes, of course,' said Stone-eye, and began to think. He was sure there was an answer to this simple question, but the more he thought about it, the harder it seemed to find a clear one.

'Well?' said the Piney.

Stone-eye shrugged his shoulders. 'It's not so easy to describe it,' he said.

'Excuses!' said the Piney. 'You just don't know, that's what.'

'Sometimes I did think I knew,' said Stone-eye. 'When Arni gave me his stone, I wanted to search for its secret, and I seemed to be near finding it several times. But I was always wrong, and now I'm rather inclined to think I was going farther and farther from what I sought, if indeed there's any end to that search.'

'Perhaps the secret runs away from you because you think of yourself too much,' said the Piney.

'Just as the girl has run away from me twice?' asked Stone-eye.

'Exactly!' said the Piney. 'Without help from others, you'd probably have reached a point where you saw nothing but yourself, and sought no other goal. You really do need someone to look after you, don't you?'

'Meaning yourself?' asked Stone-eye, who was beginning to lose his temper. What right did this piece of wood have to throw his mistakes and errors up at him so harshly? 'I thought you might comfort me,' he added, 'and instead you're only hurting.'

The Piney laughed. 'Dear me, you don't understand anything!' he said. 'Let me tell you a story. A carver chose a good piece of wood to make a spoon. When he set his knife to the wood, the wood cried out, and said to the knife, "Don't do that! You're hurting me!" For it didn't know the shape of a spoon was hidden inside it, and had no notion of the hand that guided the knife, still less of the carver's mind.'

'That's how you were made,' said Stone-eye.

'So I was,' said the Piney. 'And you have forgotten who made me. Do you think I'm speaking of myself when I say you need someone to look after you? Have you forgotten the stone you wear around your neck, that has kept you again and again from going entirely astray? Do you even know where it comes from?'

'From Arni,' said Stone-eye. 'Everyone knows that. Arni gave it to me when he was dying.'

'And who gave it to Arni?' asked the Piney.

'An old woman called Urla,' said Stone-eye.

'And who gave it to this old woman Urla?' asked the Piney.

'Her granddaughter Rikka once told me that,' said Stone-eye. 'I believe it was some prospector or other who gave it to Urla when she was a child.'

'Indeed?' said the Piney, in a tone which suggested he had resigned himself to the faun's slowness of wit. 'Some prospector or other!'

'You don't mean to say . . .' began Stone-eye, but he realized at once that there was no point in finishing his sentence. The Piney had lured him to a place beyond all measurable time, a domain where past, present and future mingled, and Stone-eye felt as if the firm ground were shifting beneath his feet. 'No!' he said. 'No!'

The Piney looked at him ironically. 'A little confused, are you, with your feeble notions of Time?' he said. 'I can tell it will take you some while yet to learn that your own time, along with the part of it you still don't remember, is very far from all.'

'And what good will that do me?' said Stone-eye. 'You speak as if I could break through the barriers of time. Don't you see I can't escape the prison of what I've done? What I started is spreading out there in the steppes like an illness, growing and proliferating, and I can't do anything to stop it now.'

'Not you, no,' said the Piney.

'Then who can?' asked Stone-eye, despairingly. 'That strange old prospector? He went on his way and left me alone with my fear of the open sky and of all I don't understand. And you're not much help with your clever remarks. I suppose one can't expect any more of a piece of wood.'

To this he got no answer. The Piney stood there, no more than a gnarled tangle of carving, so rigid and lifeless that Stone-eye was overcome by a feeling that he had been talking to nobody but himself all this time. Finally he pulled the stick out of the ground and set off.

After a while he was joined by the weasel, who had been hunting their supper. But Stone-eye was very silent as they walked in the woods, not only that evening but over the next few days. So they made their way gradually east again, until at last they reached the end of the great cliff.

'You weren't particularly talkative on the way home this time,' said the weasel, as they parted. 'Looks to me as if it wasn't worth digging up those old bones you'd buried after all, but I told you that before. Eat carrion and it makes you sick. Well, put it out of your mind, and I wish you a pleasant winter. Then you'll be cheerful again in spring and roam the woods with me.'

'Do you think nothing will ever change, then, and it will all go on just the same, year after year?' said Stone-eye.

The weasel looked at him blankly. 'What could change?' he asked. 'I suppose there'll be rabbits and grouse year after year!'

'And falcons,' said Stone-eye.

'Yes, and one of them's after you,' said the weasel, 'so don't forget it!'

'If only that were all,' said Stone-eye, but he thanked Needle-tooth for his kind advice, and for all his friendly services that summer, and then he trotted off alone again, through the bushes at the foot of the cliff, until he reached his cave.

At first it did indeed seem as if everything were to go on in just the same way for ever, or that was how it struck Stone-eye as he busied himself preparing for the third winter. He hauled baskets full of nuts, crab apples, beechmast and acorns through the bushes, and was aware that he had trotted along every one of the paths he trod before, and had made every such gesture thousands of times as, for instance, he pulled nuts from the withered leaves and put them in his basket. Nor did he see any way of changing this state of affairs. The goats, too, seemed used to seeing him appear when the leaves turned colour and the autumn wind shook acorns off the trees. To them, he was one of the natural events that came round with the changing seasons. They scarcely glanced up when he stopped on the outskirts of the wood to look at the flock grazing the already yellowing grass, so familiar did they find the sight of him.

But for his part, he found them more alien than ever before, even though he understood the trivialities which made up their scanty stock of conversational topics. The goats were content with the symmetry of their existence, alternating between spring and winter; they did not count the years as he did, and had never felt the wish to change anything. Even when they moved into the cave when the first snows fell, they did so as a matter of course, as if these had been their winter quarters from time immemorial, and on that day One-horn contented himself with a casual nod of the head by way of telling his partner that it was now his turn to look after the flock.

Stone-eye felt the rhythm of the flock determining his life more every day, but this time he resisted it. He left the cave with the goats in the morning and found them some suitable grazing, but while they dug the scanty fodder out of the snow with their front hooves he kept away from them, sat on a tree-stump somewhere on the outskirts of the wood, and wondered despairingly how he could alter his present situation. He also washed his body regularly in the snow, feeling distaste for the goatish smell that clung to his shaggy hair, and sometimes he annoyed a goat by milking her at an unwonted time because he happened to feel like a drink of milk.

In this way he managed to resist the herd instinct which came over him like an enchantment, particularly by night when the beasts thronged around the fire, or lay side by side, breathing peacefully. But simultaneously a sense of loneliness arose in him. Sometimes he tried to think of the girl who had twice run away from him, but the shallow green valley lay inaccessibly far away, and the girl was a frightened child, no companion for a shaggy faun who felt safe only in the thickets of the wood.

One day, the falcon reappeared in the sky. Stone-eye was sitting in his place on the edge of the wood, trying to persuade himself that the sun, low in the sky above the bare tree-tops, still gave a little warmth. Then he saw the falcon soaring up in the pale blue sky and circling above the snow-covered clearing. Although only the bird's dark outline could be made out from this distance, Stone-eye guessed it must be the green-eyed falcon, and as it came lower and lower down, flying close above him, he saw that his presentiment was correct. Narzia was visiting him again, and despite all he had learnt about her, he felt a sense of familiarity. He still could not remember exactly what he himself had had to do with the woman hiding beneath this falcon's feathers, and yet his heart beat fast, though he could not have said whether in fear or excitement, as if at an unexpected meeting with his beloved. Perhaps he had misunderstood all he had so far heard about this falcon maiden; perhaps it was only hatred or envy that led others to speak ill of the creature soaring so lightly above the clearing, mysterious and full of riddles which, once solved, promised untold gain.

The falcon soared up once more, came gliding down, followed by her black shadow flitting across the sparkling surface of the snow beneath, and then settled on a tree-stump, beating her wings. For a while her green eyes stared at Stone-eye's face. Then she opened her beak and said, in the clear voice of a human girl, 'You look lonely, faun. Won't your goats have any more to do with you?'

Stone-eye shook his head. 'The goats are the same as ever,' he said. 'I've had enough of their company, their silly chatter and their ruttish smell.'

'But it's still in your nostrils and on your mind,' said the falcon. 'That's what happens when one's alone. Are you still chasing your past?'

'It is catching up with me, step by step, like a pack of wolves eating at my soul,' said Stone-eye.

'You think too much,' said the falcon gently. 'When you're lonely, you start mulling things over, seeing the darker side of everything. You should forget the bad part, and remember only the good.'

'Then tell me what was good about my past,' said Stone-eye, 'for I can't remember anything of the kind.'

'That's a pity,' said the falcon. 'There would be plenty of pleasant things to tell you. Don't you remember the falcon maiden who was your promised wife?'

Stone-eye's heart leaped when he heard that. 'Are you speaking of yourself? Were you my promised wife? I can remember everything else, but nothing to do with you. Won't you help me remember?'

'You know the price,' said the falcon. 'Do you still mean to keep the stone for yourself?'

'The stone?' said Stone-eye. 'But what would I get for it? A few more of those memories that keep me awake at nights?'

The falcon laughed aloud, and said, 'I will show you a little of what you can expect. Look at me!'

Although the falcon was sitting still on the tree-stump, it seemed to Stone-eye as if her green eyes were coming closer and closer, growing larger and larger, until they entirely filled his field of vision. He plunged into those shimmering green depths, from which the delicately boned, fair-skinned face of a green-eyed girl arose, and next moment he found himself sitting by the girl's side at a table groaning under the weight of rich food. He tasted wine on his tongue, perceived, in an intoxicated haze, the heated faces of people laughing soundlessly and talking cheerfully to one another, and then he saw nothing but the green eyes of the girl as she slowly rose to her feet, giving him an almost imperceptible nod that told him to follow her. His heart contracted suddenly, so that the blood was rushing in his ears as he rose himself and went after the girl, who went gliding on before him along dark passages, in a flowing robe that disappeared around a corner and then came into sight again, and stopped. When he reached the girl, she was standing in a half-open doorway, and she raised her hand, telling him to wait there. Then she went into the room, leaving the door ajar. In the faint candlelight, he saw the billowing sheets of a bed, where the girl lay in a filmy shift that showed more of her lovely body than it hid. When he had hastily stripped off his clothes, and was stepping towards the bed, the girl looked at him, put out her hand, and said, 'Will you give me the stone now?'

His longing to cross the barriers of his loneliness, his desire to embrace that body, left him no choice. He reached blindly for the bag around his neck, took out the stone and laid it in Narzia's outstretched hand. Her fingers closed on the stone, and then he saw the flash of the emerald in the falcon ring. With that, the last veil over his memory was torn aside, and he knew what had happened before and what would happen now. Once more green lightning flung him back to the wall, once more he heard Narzia's voice scream, 'Be an animal!' and once more an icy pain shot through his body, the pain that had changed him to the shaggy goatish faun he now was.

When the pain had ebbed away, and Stone-eye was aware of his surroundings once more, he saw the falcon sitting on the tree-stump again, holding the stone in one of its claws. 'You have tricked me, Narzia,' he said. But the falcon only laughed. 'Tricked you? What do you mean?' she said in her clear voice. 'Haven't you learnt all that you'd forgotten? Don't you know now what to expect? Shall I tell you? A life as neither man nor animal, but something between the two, a stranger to the goats, a source of terror to human beings. Men will turn from you in horror, and women flee in disgust from your shaggy loins.'

'Why are you so cruel?' asked Stone-eye. 'My nakedness disgusted you even when I was still a man.'

'Yes,' said the falcon. 'You lustful goat, I only made what was already in you visible! Did you think I'd give up the strength of my magic to your desires? Was I to let your animal nature win power over me?'

'If you think me an animal, then let me be wholly an animal,' said Stone-eye. 'Why did you leave half your work undone?'

'Your stone kept me from completing it,' said the falcon. 'Now that it no longer hangs on your breast I could make you all animal, but I'll let you live as you are, half-goat, to remember what you might be, yet never will be again. For a woman must take you in her arms as you are now, to break my spell. See if you can find a girl who will do that!'

With which the falcon spread her wings, and soared up into the pale, wintry sky.

'You'll get no joy of the stone!' Stone-eye shouted up at her. 'Don't you know it brings misfortune to anyone who takes it by force or trickery?'

But the falcon did not listen to his warning. She described a circle above the clearing, and as she set off southwards over the bare tree-tops, Stone-eye saw the stone flash once more in her talons. Then the bird disappeared from sight.

Stone-eye spent the rest of that winter brooding miserably. He scarcely ever left the cave, and would often lie apathetically on the leaves of his bedding for days on end, searching the murky waters of his memory for something to which he could hold fast, something that might help him out of his hopeless situation. He now knew all that had happened during these last years, but that only made his torment the worse, for as he went over events again and again in his mind, he also saw how he had gone on and on in the wrong direction, misusing the gifts given to him. And so he had lost the flute, and now the stone too. The deeper he delved into his past, the farther any hope went from him.

Only his name was still forgotten, and he racked his brains day and night, wondering what he had once been called, babbling meaningless syllables to himself and listening to their sound, as if that would help him to find a magic formula which, if he could only utter it, would free him from this spell.

He spent his days in this way, and was haunted by bad dreams at night, dreams in which he saw again the girl's indescribable eyes, and she looked at him in horror and then turned and ran, while he ran after her, ran and ran over the dry, rustling grass of the steppes, beneath an empty, leaden sky whose weight pressed down more heavily on his shoulders with every step he took, until he could hardly manage to raise his feet from the ground, while the fleet-footed girl flew on over the steppes before him, quickly putting distance between them, becoming smaller and smaller until she was only a far-off, barely perceptible speck on the horizon. He tried desperately not to lose sight of that blurred speck, but then he was momentarily distracted by a shadow that he felt rather than saw beside him, and when he looked for the speck again, the far horizon was empty. But the shadow still lurked at his side, and he now felt that it had not just that moment appeared, but had been there for a long time. Perhaps for ever.

Since there was nothing to be seen in the distance now, he turned to the shadow, and saw a strange, grey gentleman standing by him, one he knew. As ever, he was dressed with great care, wore a fine suit of grey clothes, grey shoes and gloves, and not only his hair but his expressionless and utterly humourless face was grey as well.

'You are trying to run the wrong way, Stone-eye,' said the grey gentleman, his voice colourless, not a feature of his face moving. 'Don't you notice you're getting nowhere?'

'I did notice that, yes,' said Stone-eye, trying to look the Grey One in the eye. But where he had expected to see a grey iris, there was nothing but emptiness. He turned his glance away, so as not to be sucked through those holes into a fathomless abyss, and repeated, 'Yes, I noticed I was getting nowhere. But how else am I to reach the girl?'

'Are you to reach her?' said the Grey One. 'Aren't you just running after a dream, a vision? Turn and go the other way, with me, and you will see how easy it is.'

And sure enough, as soon as he had turned and began to put one foot in front of another, the leaden weight was lifted from his shoulders, and he could walk as lightly as if his own body weighed no more than a feather. He did not even feel his heart beating as he walked over the dry grass beside the Grey One. After a while he asked, 'Where are we going?'

'You'll soon see,' said the Grey One. 'And perhaps you will realize, at last, that you ought to have followed me before.'

He had not noticed when they left the desolate steppes behind them, but he found himself suddenly standing among the bushes at the foot of the cliff with his companion, and next moment they were in the cave itself. The goats lay sleeping around the fireplace, with the young animals in the middle of the circle, and the older ones and the he-goat on the outside.

'See how they lie there vegetating dully,' said the Grey One. 'Do you want to be like them? Or have you any remnant of intelligence left in you to raise you above such stupid beasts?'

'I depend upon these animals,' said Stone-eye.

'How can you say that?' The Grey One did not trouble to hide his contempt. 'Don't you mean that you make use of them? What are you, if you must ask these foolish eaters of grass for anything? Have you forgotten that you are destined to wield power? It's high time you remembered!'

'I have lost my flute,' said Stone-eye, and he felt the desire come over him to put his silver flute to his lips and bend his hearers to his will.

'You left it behind,' the Grey One corrected him. 'Go and fetch it back!'

'As I look now?' said Stone-eye.

'Are you embarrassed?' asked the Grey One, mockingly. 'Make yourself trousers if you're afraid people will laugh at you. Take your knife and kill a goat. Her skin will do to cover your shame.'

Next moment Stone-eye had his knife in his right hand, and was kneeling over one of the animals. As his fingers dug into her coat, he thought of nothing but that he must get back to the house in the village of Arni's Folk to fetch his flute. With the flute, he could do everything he wanted, and force anyone who withstood him to obey. Even the girl who was forever flying from him. 'I must have it,' he muttered to himself, 'I must have her,' and he was not sure if the flute or the girl was uppermost in his mind as he stabbed the quivering flesh through the shaggy hair, oblivious now of any connection between this bloody act of slaughter and his desire to have the power of the flute back again. All he knew was that the sacrifice had to be made. Something living must die, and the blood spurting over his hands would buy him back his power. He saw it run red from gaping wounds and stream down over the goat's skin, until it was all covered with blood, a crimson, slowly swirling tide of blood, rising and rising up to his neck, then up to his lips, and he screamed as a drowning man screams when he has lost all hope of help.

Only when he heard the shrill, broken echo that replied did he stop screaming. He found himself in impenetrable darkness, and felt the rustling leaves of his bedding under him. Close by, he heard the goats bleating in alarm. They must be pressing together directly below the ledge of rock where his bed lay, and seemed to be beside themselves with terror. 'Stone-eye!' bleated one. 'Why are you screaming so? Are you sick?'

He crawled to the edge of the rock beneath which the beasts were standing and tried to soothe them. 'It was a nightmare,' he said. 'I'm glad you woke me.' As he spoke, he reached down into the darkness whence the warmth of the animals rose to him and patted the first goat his fingers met. 'I'm sorry I alarmed you,' he said. 'Go back to sleep again.'

But the goats were not to be soothed so easily. He felt damp noses nuzzling his hand, and rough tongues licking the sweat of fear from his skin. Or was it the blood that had spurted over his fingers? The dream still had him in its grip, and he could feel the handle of the knife in the same hand that the goats were caressing with such concern. 'Don't worry,' he said, 'I won't hurt you.' But that only upset the animals even more.

'He's talking nonsense!' many of them cried, and others wailed, 'He's sick! His sweat tastes bitter!' They did not calm down until he rose and went down to them. He blew up the fire, and when the flames blazed up brightly he said, 'There, now do you see there's nothing wrong with me?'

The goats pressed around him, as if to convince themselves, and one of them asked, 'Then why do you say such crazy things? You're our protector! Why would you hurt us?'

'Why, indeed?' he said, and realized that he was addressing the question to himself. He was not at all sure there had not been some reason for driving the knife into one of these goats, although he could not imagine killing one of the gentle creatures now. He gave them a little fodder, for nothing is more soothing than food, and then climbed back to his sleeping place and lay down. Above him, the reflection of the dying fire flickered on the fissured roof of the cave, and it seemed to him as if the rocks were slowly descending to crush him. Only the Piney beside him seemed to notice none of this, but looked calmly with his one dark eye into endless space beyond the cave walls.

'I am afraid, Piney,' said Stone-eye. 'Afraid I shall never find my way out of this cramped hole in the rocks again.'

'Are you surprised?' said the Piney. 'Since you stopped wearing your stone, fear has been able to get at your heart unimpeded. Why did you take the stone off?'

'I haven't got it any more,' said Stone-eye. 'The falcon stole it.'

'Stole it?' inquired the Piney, in a tone that suggested he knew better.

'Well, Narzia tricked me out of it,' said Stone-eye.

'I can well imagine how she set about that,' said the Piney. 'But the stone will do her no good, and it'll come back to you sometime.'

'Sometime!' said Stone-eye bitterly. 'Like my flute, that I left with Arni's Folk.'

'Yes,' said the Piney, 'like your flute. Such things always come back to their real owners. You just have to wait for the right time to come.'

'What right time?' said Stone-eye. 'And when will it come? By your reckoning of time, ten, fifty or even a hundred years is nothing much. But what good will my flute do me if I'm an old man before I have it back? I want it now, at once!'

'Then go and get it!' said the Piney calmly. 'You know where you left it, don't you? Though if I were you, I'd wait for the snow to melt.'

Once he had sunk into the snow up to his waist next morning when trying at least to reach the outskirts of the forest, this last piece of advice struck Stone-eye as very sensible. But during the days that followed he made plans for breaking into Narzia's house unseen and finding his flute. It must certainly be done at night, so that no one could see what kind of shaggy woodland creature was haunting the place. Wait, Narzia, wait, he thought: I'll get my flute back, and then you'll all have to dance to my tune!

But the more often he imagined this nocturnal venture, the more dangers he saw in such an undertaking. What would happen if he unexpectedly met people, or if someone actually caught him trying to break into Narzia's house? He would probably be overpowered and publicly questioned. The thought of what would happen to him in such circumstances troubled him less than the idea of being exposed to all eyes in his naked and monstrous form, an idea which filled him with horror, so that sometimes he lost all heart for carrying out the plan, and lay brooding on his bed for days on end.

Then the thaw came. The goats left the cave again by day, and soon they took to staying out at night too. One evening, One-horn came back alone, to say, 'I'll see to the flock now. You've not taken all that much care of the beasts this winter anyway.'

Stone-eye looked moodily into the he-goat's yellow eyes, and said, 'Have any of you gone hungry?'

'No,' said One-horn, 'but that's the least of your part of our bargain. You've been throwing us our fodder like a stranger, and otherwise keeping aloof, as if you couldn't stand the smell of us. Your heart wasn't with your flock, and now I'm wondering if we can count on you at all next winter.'

'I don't know,' said Stone-eye. 'I don't know that myself. I shall always be a stranger in your flock, dreaming of another life.'

'Dreams that make you scream with fear,' said the he-goat. 'That's more than I can understand.'

'How should you?' said Stone-eye. 'You're all goat, and I'm only half of one. And I am also half a man, longing to live with men.'

'Looking as you do?' said One-horn. 'They'd run from you.'

'You think so?' said Stone-eye, with some malice. 'Wait and see how I stop them!'

The he-goat looked at him, shaking his head, and then said, 'I don't know what you have in mind, but the way you say that doesn't sound good.'

'You leave me to mind my own business,' said Stone-eye. 'I wish you good grazing this summer, which is all you need.'

'Isn't that enough?' said the he-goat.

When Stone-eye only shrugged his shoulders, the he-goat wished him a good journey and trotted out to his flock. Stone-eye lay back on his bed of leaves. He was almost glad that his conversation with the he-goat had made him decide to put his plan into action, and he spent a long time wondering how best to steal back the flute.

While he was thinking, night fell, and suddenly there was the Grey One again. Thin, colourless, he stood above Stone-eye's bed, his well-groomed grey head reaching to the roof of the cave. 'So you won't need a pair of trousers?' he said, and his voice did not show if he meant it mockingly, or was simply stating facts. In any case, he seemed to agree, for he went on, 'You are quite right, and there'd have been no point in it anyway. Once your flute has won you power again, no one will dare to wonder at the shape of your legs. Come along, let's set off for the settlement by Arni's House.'

Stone-eye was about to say that he hadn't really meant to start before morning, but then it struck him that he would reach his goal more easily in this man's company, and so he rose and followed the grey figure out of the cave. Outside, he instantly found himself in a translucent mist, illuminated from somewhere or other, although no source of light could be seen. Shadowy bushes slipped by, and the blurred outlines of tree-trunks, their crowns lost in the milky haze above. Stone-eye could not have said if he was walking or hovering above the ground that he could scarcely see, but anyway he had the impression that the huddled bushes, and then the tangled undergrowth, were passing at remarkable speed, although not so much as a branch touched his skin.

And so they went on downhill, first through woodland, then past trees growing more sparsely. Then, suddenly, a figure appeared among the trees: a man who, from the clothes he wore, seemed to be one of Arni's Folk. This man raised a hand, as if to beckon to Stone-eye, or else to wave him back into the woods – it was hard to say which for sure. Stone-eye was afraid and tried to hide behind a stout trunk. But suddenly the Grey One was close beside him, whispering, 'Why are you afraid of this man? Don't you see he's alone?'

He might be armed, thought Stone-eye, and before he could express that fear, the Grey One was handing him arrows and a stout hunting bow. 'Don't let that stop you!' he said. 'Think of your goal!'

Then Stone-eye knew what must be done now. He put an arrow to the bowstring, and aimed at the breast of the man who was slowly approaching, with the rolling gait of a Raiding Rider. Stone-eye bent the bow, and just as he let the arrow fly, he thought he recognized the man, and that thin, wrinkled face with the white braids at its temples.

The man had been only a few paces off. The arrow went through his chest, nailing him to the tree-trunk behind him. Stone-eye heard the dull thud of its point going into his heart, and next moment found himself close to the stricken man. He knew already that he had shot Arni, but now he saw it clearly: held up only by the arrow, the old Rider seemed to be hanging from the tree rather than standing by it. A thin trickle of blood ran down his leather jerkin where the arrow had entered his chest, but Arni seemed to feel no pain, for he smiled so that a thousand little wrinkles appeared around his eyes, and said, 'Well, the whole story began much like this, do you remember? Except that you've learnt to use a bow yourself since then.'

Stone-eye stared at the old man hanging from the tree in front of him, and felt horror rise in him, icy and inexorable. 'I didn't know who I was aiming at,' he said. 'I didn't want to hit you.'

'If you're going to shoot at people, you should expect to hit them,' said Arni. 'And if you set out to win power and use it, you should remember that someone else may suffer. Don't you know that yet?'

Before Stone-eye could think of an answer, the Grey One was suddenly between him and Arni. 'Let the old man die!' he said. 'Come on! We have better things to do than stand here arguing with a corpse.'

No sooner had he spoken those words than Arni suddenly stood erect, and pushed himself away from the tree with such force that the arrow came tearing out of the wood behind him. Arni walked right through the Grey One, as if he had not been there at all, and said, 'Which of us two is dead now, you grey ghost?'

Where the Grey One had been standing a moment ago, there was nothing but a pale and wavering mist, scattered and blown away next moment by a gust of wind. Arni flapped his hand briefly through the air, dispersing the last of it like a bad smell, and said, 'You should have taken better care of your stone, archer!' The arrow still stuck out of his chest, and blood was dripping from the wound.

'Have you brought me back the stone, Arni?' Stone-eye asked.

Arni laughed quietly, and then said, 'What do you want the stone for now? I thought you were off to get your flute back?' And he nodded to Stone-eye and walked slowly away through the trees with that rolling gait. It was as if he took what little light there was with him, for at once it turned so dark that Stone-eye couldn't even see the nearest tree-trunks any more. He was overwhelmed by fear of never finding his way out of this wood again. 'Wait for me!' he called after Arni. 'Don't leave me alone!'

'You're not alone,' said a voice, though it did not sound like Arni's, but higher and melodious, like the voice of a woman. Stone-eye felt something smooth and cool slide past his arm, and when he opened his eyes, he found himself back on his bed of leaves in the cave again. The fire had burnt down, there was a smell of wood-smoke, and it was so dark that he couldn't see his own hand before his face. But two agate-coloured eyes were shining in the darkness close beside him.

'Did you have a bad dream?' asked Rinkulla.

'I don't know if it was a bad dream, or what,' said Stone-eye, 'but I was very frightened.'

'Then it was as well I woke you, Bearer of the Stone.'

'Don't call me that any more,' said Stone-eye. 'I have lost the stone. But your eyes are so like it that I'm not frightened now. Why did you come?'

'I have a message for you,' said Rinkulla. 'Since the Green Man set the search for you afoot, he's kept an eye on all that concerns you, and now he has had word from the Carp in the Brown River of something you should know: the Raiding Riders have attacked the fishing folk of the Carphead people who live there. They were riding young, fast horses, as eager to attack as ever. Some of the fishermen managed to escape into the water, and so the Great Carp learned what was happening on the banks.'

'This is bad news,' said Stone-eye. Since the previous summer, he had feared some such thing, and now it had happened, and with it all hope was gone that the magic of his flute might have tamed the horses born after he played it. 'It does indeed concern me,' he continued, 'and the worst of it is that I can't do anything about it now.'

'That wasn't what the Great Carp thought,' said Rinkulla, 'and I fancy the Green Man didn't mean a mere warning, either, when he sent me to tell you.'

'Then what am I to do?' asked Stone-eye.

'I don't know that,' said Rinkulla. 'You'll have to find out for your-self.'

'Since I lost the stone, I've lost all heart too,' said Stone-eye sadly.

'I expect the Green Man had that in mind as well when he chose me as his messenger,' said Rinkulla. Her eyes were very close now, and Stone-eye went down into their circles of blue and green and violet, feeling the gentle glow of them warm his heart. In the dark, he thought he saw the face to which the eyes belonged; however, it was not the smooth, narrow head of a snake any more, but the face of a woman looking at him and saying, 'You are still the Bearer of the Stone, wherever it may be at the moment. Forget your fear; that is the door which lets the Grey One into your mind.'

'He was going to help me win back the power of my flute,' said Stone-eye.

'Power?' said the woman. 'Only those who are afraid want power. Your flute wasn't made for that.'

'Then I'm not to look for it?' asked Stone-eye.

'Why not?' asked the woman. 'The Grey One is nothing. He can only bring you to misuse what's good, he cannot destroy it. Don't do as your fear tells you, follow your heart!' Then the face disappeared, and he saw only Rinkulla's eyes in the dark. 'Now you have the whole message,' she said. 'You'd better start out soon. I can hear the cawing of the crows.' She bent her body and slid away to that place where the cave narrowed to no more than a crack. Stone-eye saw the shimmering of her eyes for a little longer, and then he was lying alone in the darkness again.

He could indeed hear crows cawing, and wondered what it might mean. Making his way down to the floor of the cave, he crawled out of the entrance. Outside, day was just beginning to dawn. A vast flock of black birds was circling in the grey sky above the tall tops of the beeches that grew near the edge of the wood. Their hoarse cries drowned out all other sounds, and when the flock flew over, describing a wide arc, and passed the top of the cliff, Stone-eye could make out what they were cawing:

> *Eat! Eat!*
> *Gather to eat!*
> *The Raiding Riders are on their way!*
> *The corpses taste sweet*
> *that the Riders slay.*

Plenty of meat!
Come before the break of day!
Gather to eat!
Eat! Eat!

The crows described another great circle over the cliff above the cave, as if inviting Stone-eye to their banquet, and then flew off southwards. Even when the flock was no more than a dark cloud hovering far away above the trees, Stone-eye could still hear their cawing. 'Eat! Eat!' the cry came echoing back to him, and he thought he could hear it long after the birds were out of sight.

He guessed where the crows were going: the settlement of Arni's Folk lay somewhere to the south, and he wondered if Hunli's Riders were now on their way to pay Narzia back for their humiliation, or whether the feast was already prepared for the black birds there. And now, too, he knew what he must do: go south and warn Arni's Folk. If he once had his flute in his hands again, he could force the Riders to turn round. He ran back into the cave, snatched up his goat's-hair bag and rapidly stuffed into it everything he thought he might need on the way: his knife, his flint and steel, and the remains of his hazelnuts. Then he took the stone-pine staff and went leaping down the slope and on through the forest southwards. As he made his way through the undergrowth, more and more flocks of crows passed above the tree-tops overhead, cawing their greedy song. He had cries of 'Eat! Eat!' ringing in his ears all day, and even when night had fallen and he crawled into the bushes exhausted, his limbs trembling.

He travelled like this for five days, urged on by the cawing of black carrion crows that drove him before them, until he saw them catch up and pass over him, above the branches of the beech trees, thickly set now with the buds of spring. When he crawled out of the place where he had been sleeping on the morning of the sixth day, he saw a light stand of birches ahead of him, tiny bright green leaves coming out on the fine web of their branches. And he looked out past the glimmer of their white trunks and down to an endless, grey-green, shimmering plain. He had reached the edge of the steppes at last, and a little way south, where the bushes grew out into the plain, a great flock of crows was circling around the smoke that rose to the pale morning sky. Arni's Folk were cooking their breakfast down there in their greyish-brown log cabins, dark shapes nestling among the birches and alders.

At first he heaved a sigh of relief. Obviously the Raiding Riders had not fallen upon the settlement yet. He had only to go down and warn Arni's Folk. With this thought, fear of appearing before the people's eyes in broad daylight in his goatish shape overcame him once more. The cawing of the crows came surging over to him now and then, as yet another flock arrived, and the cry of 'Eat! Eat!' rang in Stone-eye's ears. Were the people in those houses deaf? Couldn't they guess what that black and greedy army was waiting for? Apparently no one was bothered about the excited, swirling cloud of birds that darkened the sky above their roof-tops; nobody came out of doors, Stone-eye could not see people gathering anywhere. Then he realized that the crows whose cawing frayed his nerves wouldn't do his job for him. He must go down himself and call the people out of their houses.

He crept along the edge of the woods towards the settlement, going from tree to tree, until the cry of the hungry carrion birds in the air above him was like the roar of breaking waves. The crows saw him now, and groups of them came shooting through the trees, close above the goat-legged stranger, screeching as if to prevent him from spoiling the banquet they expected. Stone-eye flailed both arms over his head and ran blindly on through the birches. Then he heard a scream, looked up, and saw a girl carrying a bucket quite close to him. She would be a young maidservant, a girl of Arni's Folk, flat-nosed and black-haired, who had gone out in the morning to fetch water. Dark eyes wide with horror, she was staring at him. Her mouth was still open, as if to go on screaming soundlessly, but the only sound was the angry cawing of the crows which were now diving around the girl's head too. She stood like that for several moments, as if rooted to the spot. Then she flung the bucket at Stone-eye's feet, put out her hand in the gesture supposed to ward off evil spirits, and turned and ran away, her bare feet splashing down the dewy path.

'Stop!' Stone-eye called after her. 'Wait! I won't hurt you! I have something to tell you. The Raiding Riders . . .' But the girl had already vanished into one of the cabins. Then Stone-eye gave up hope of warning Arni's Folk. If the Raiding Riders hadn't come yet, he thought, they would probably not come today either, and he decided to carry out his original plan. If he waited for night, surely he could manage to get into Narzia's house somehow and find his flute. And then let Hunli's Riders come! They would be surprised by the reception awaiting them!

Stone-eye was now positively eager to play the part which was obviously to be his in this place, and as he trotted slowly uphill and into the woods, he imagined the impression it would make on everyone when he forced the attackers back into the steppes. He could see the whole picture before his eyes: the shaggy little horses rearing and racing back into that endless grey plain, pursued by the villagers' shouts of triumph. Arni's Folk would surely show themselves grateful for his aid. Once you have power, no one will dare to wonder at the shape of your legs . . . who had said something like that recently? He could not remember, and in the end he supposed he must have thought of it himself.

He put a considerable distance between himself and the village, so that no one else of Arni's Folk might run into him and spoil everything. He crouched under a tree on the edge of a clearing somewhere farther up the slope, warmed himself in the spring sun, cracked a few hazelnuts, and rested after his days of strenuous travel through the woods. As he leaned back against the trunk of the tree, eyes closed, he heard the birds singing in the branches above him: tits whistled, chaffinches sang their bridal songs, and now and then he heard a robin fluting away. Then a jay came screeching over the clearing, crying, 'Take care! Take care! The Raiding Riders are coming!'

'Let them come!' Stone-eye called up to him. 'You'll be surprised to see how fast they're off and away again!' And then he fell asleep.

When he woke, the sun was already low in the west behind the tree-trunks. There was a smell of burning in the air. To the south and farther down the slope, black smoke was rising to the sky. Stone-eye knew at once what had happened, yet he ran back to the village like one possessed, as if he could still prevent the disaster. When at last he was in the little birch wood from which he could see the village, it was obvious that he had slept right through the Raiding Riders' attack. All the log cabins were in flames; sluggish clouds of thick, heavy smoke rose above the bushes and drifted slowly upwards in the south wind, so that the sky grew dark as if a storm were about to break. But the violence was past its peak now. Only a few long-drawn-out, dying screams reached Stone-eye's ears, and now and then the shrill cries of Riders as they went looting. Not a crow was to be seen in the sky. They had begun to feast.

Stone-eye lay trembling on the ground in the sparse undergrowth among the birch trees, not daring to move. The stink of smoke lay heavily on his chest, and he coughed into last year's mouldering leaves to muffle the sound, afraid some prowling Rider might hear him. Eyes streaming, he stared through the wood at the blazing flames, trying to keep back the thought that he could have prevented all this if he had followed the maidservant into the village. He was still lying there when night fell, and nothing lit the darkness but the flicker of flames as they burned up once more. The horde would now be sitting around the village square while the Khan shared out the booty. Stone-eye heard the Riders' excited cries, and now and then a shout of joy as one of them received some particularly valuable item.

Then, suddenly, a strong gust of wind came sweeping down from the mountains, immediately followed by such a heavy downpour of rain that the image of the burning village was instantly extinguished. Stone-eye crawled farther into the dripping bushes and waited for morning to come. When at last the sky began to grow lighter in the east, above the steppes, the Riders whistled up their horses, and soon afterwards Stone-eye saw them take their beasts up the steep path leading to Arziak and past Urla's hut.

He waited until the last Rider had disappeared from sight up the mountainside. The rain had put out the fire, but occasional threads of smoke still rose from the burnt-out ruins. Cautiously, Stone-eye made his way to the village, listening to every sound. But there was nothing to be heard now except for the crash of a falling beam now and then, and the cawing of crows quarrelling over their food. He kept under the trees, for they grew right down to the houses, and indeed among them too, and so he crept into the village itself. A dead man lay in the doorway of the first log cabin, which was burnt right down to the joists of the floor. There was an arrow sticking out of his back. But this was not the house Stone-eye wanted to enter. Keeping in the shade of the alder bushes by the roadside, he reached the middle of the village. Arni's House, grey with age, was the only building still unharmed. Obviously Hunli had shrunk from destroying his brother's house with the rest. But the square around it was piled with the dead, and crows rose from them, cawing, to defend their meat against the intruder. However, he was not competing with them for that, but turned away from the dreadful sight, and approached Narzia's house from behind. The roof had fallen, charred beams stuck out into thin air, but the walls of that part of the house where his own room had been were still standing to above a man's height.

Before he had made up his mind which way to get in, he heard quick, running footsteps, and hid in the bushes. A half-grown girl in a pale linen skirt came running round the corner of the house, leaped nimbly over beams and fallen rafters, and disappeared among the alders as fast as she had come. Stone-eye heard her breaking swiftly through the bushes, and then she was gone, as if she had been a ghost. The whole thing happened so fast that he had scarcely been able to see anything but the girl's soot-stained skirts whirling around her calves, yet he had the feeling he had seen her somewhere before, a child who could run as fast as a deer in flight. And now he thought, too, that she had been holding something in her hand, as if it were loot she had snatched up, something slender and shining.

Stone-eye waited a little longer, and when all remained still, he set about entering the house. He climbed into the hall through a smoke-blackened window. The ceiling had half fallen in, and the acrid smell of burning was stifling. He forced his way through a mass of split and charred planks to his own room. The door had broken off its hinges, and hung into the room askew, but everything inside still seemed to be intact. The table and chairs stood in the middle of the room, the bed against the wall was unmade, its sheets thrown back, as if someone had leapt out of it in great haste. And the concealed wall cupboard behind the bed was open. This was where Stone-eye had kept his own possessions. He climbed on the bed and put his hand inside it. But the flute was not there any more. Instead, his fingers met with broken shards, to which some sticky liquid clung, and right at the back, in one corner, he felt a round object. Taking it out, he found he was holding a little flask the size of an apple, with a written label stuck on it. The writing was faded and barely legible. He went to the window and tried to make out the curling characters. The first lines seemed to be entirely lost, but he could still make out the last four:

> *In the stone be bound,*
> *held there by this token;*
> *if you are not found,*
> *you shall not be woken.*

Then Stone-eye knew what was left of all his things. Putting the little flask in his bag, he searched the rest of the room, without much hope, but he could not find his flute.

At last he gave up, and left his old room. A little farther on, he saw the door of the main room of the house standing open, but when he had looked inside, he gave up any idea of searching it more closely. The Raiding Riders had done that already, with great thoroughness. The table and chairs were overturned, the cupboards flung open and emptied, and inside an open chest lay the body of Honi's old steward, who must have continued in Narzia's service.

At the sight of the dead man, whom he had known well, Stone-eye wondered whether the Riders had killed Narzia too. If so, they would surely have looted the eye-stone as well. Her room lay upstairs, at the back of the house; perhaps she had fled there to jump out of the window and disappear into the bushes, like the girl he had seen just now. He decided to go and look, but that was not so easy.

The stairs to the upper floor still stood, but the ceiling of the passage leading to Narzia's room had completely fallen in. At last, however, he managed to get through to her doorway, and break its panels with a wooden post.

Faint light fell into the room through a few cracks in the ceiling, which had fallen slantwise on it. When Stone-eye was used to the dim light, he saw that the outer wall of this room had burnt down. The rafters of the ceiling there reached down to the ground. The fire had caught the panelling of the walls too, so that large parts of it had fallen away and lay everywhere, some of them still smouldering. The air was heavy with smoke. But Narzia was not here, either dead or alive.

Stone-eye clambered into the room through the hole in the door, pushed smouldering pieces of wood aside, gazed thoughtfully for a moment at the wide bed, which had collapsed under the falling beams, and then he saw the top of a small table, now smashed, lying on the floor in a corner under the rafters, where the window must once have been. Underneath charred pieces of wood and rubble, he saw something that glittered. The eye-stone, he thought, but when he had pushed the mess aside, he saw it was not his stone that lay there, but Narzia's falcon ring. He found something else as well: a delicate necklace of skilfully intertwined gold links, and when he looked more closely at this chain, he saw that each link was made in the shape of a falcon. He put both pieces in his goat's-hair bag, and poked around for a while longer in the debris, but he could not find his stone.

Giving up hope at last, he made his way out of the ruined house again. He left through the same window by which he had clambered in, and then sat down just below it, disheartened. Leaning his hairy back against the charred beams, he tried to escape the self-reproaches that were overwhelming his mind with increasing force. They wouldn't have listened to me if I'd followed the maidservant, he thought; they would probably have thrown stones and chased me out of the village before I could have said a word; perhaps the Raiding Riders were already so close that morning that no one could have escaped anyway – he thought all this, but at the same time he knew he ought to have tried to avert the disaster that had come upon Arni's Folk through his fault.

As he sat there brooding, a mighty mastiff came trotting out of the bushes and sniffed his hands. Stone-eye felt alarm at first, but as the dog seemed friendly, he patted its back, and said, 'So you hid in time, then?'

'Yes,' said the dog, 'and yesterday, for the first time, I was glad to be a dog and pass unnoticed. Are there any Riders left in the village?'

'Only the dead,' said Stone-eye, feeling the horror rise in him again. But the dog seemed to have expected no less. He turned his head and called, 'You can come out now! They've ridden away.'

And now six more dogs came out of the alder bushes, all as big and strong as the first, and lay on the ground around Stone-eye.

'What were you looking for in this house?' asked the first dog. 'Are you another raider and plunderer too?'

Stone-eye shook his head. 'I was only looking for what belongs to me,' he said. 'A flute and a stone.'

At that the dog looked intently at his face, and said, 'Oh, so it's you, fluter. I wouldn't have known you again, shaggy and bearded as you are. Have you found what you were after?'

'No,' said Stone-eye. 'Only these.' And he took Narzia's ring and necklace out of his bag.

When the dogs saw the jewels, they leaped up, yelping excitedly. 'He has the ring!' one of them cried, and another barked, 'We're saved!'

'How saved?' asked Stone-eye. 'What do these things mean to you?'

'Don't you know what kind of ring that is?' asked one of the dogs.

'Yes,' said Stone-eye, 'only too well, for Narzia used her power on me.'

'And on us,' said the dog, 'when she turned us into her dogs, one after another.'

'Then perhaps you know the properties of the necklace too,' said Stone-eye, 'for it looks to me very much like another of Narzia's magical things.'

One of the dogs pushed forward, and said, 'Yes, indeed I know; it was on account of that necklace that she turned me into a dog. Narzia pleased me, and I sometimes used to watch her in secret when she stood at the window of her room. So I saw her work her magic. When she laid the chain around her neck in such a way that she could close its clasp in front, over her breast, she turned into a falcon as soon as the catch went home, and flew out of the window. I just had time to hide when I saw it. Then, when the falcon came back, she had to creep through the chain head first, and she was a girl again. But when I had watched her work this second piece of magic, she saw me outside in the bushes and pointed her finger at me, and a flash of green lightning from her ring went through my body. And then I was one of her dogs, running around the house. If she isn't dead, then you hold her life in your hands with that chain, for it means she is flying through the air somewhere as a falcon. But you can turn us back into human beings with the ring. Put it on your finger, and try.'

'Gladly,' said Stone-eye. He put Narzia's falcon ring on his little finger, pointed to the dog who had told him all this, and said, 'Be a man!' And next moment, instead of the dog, there was a young man of Arni's Folk lying on the ground, apparently asleep. Then Stone-eye tried the ring on the other dogs, and very soon there were four men of various ages, two women and a girl of about seventeen, lying asleep on the grass around him. Stone-eye tried to wake them, for it had occurred to him that one of these people might be able to give him back his own human shape with the aid of the ring. But their sleep was so deep that he could not rouse them.

At last, then, he left them alone, sat under a birch tree a little way off and wondered what to do next. The Raiding Riders obviously intended to rob the goldsmiths' workshops of Arziak too. When he imagined similar slaughter being done by the horde there, he felt cold with horror. He thought of the girl with the eyes whose colour was so hard to describe. If she was at home with her parents, he would not be able to help her, for even if he could have caught up with the Riders, which was hardly likely, it would be utterly impossible for him to follow them along the path over the bare and rocky mountains, where there was not a tree for miles on end to offer him any shelter. He would have to take the long way round through the woods. However, there was still some hope that the girl might be in the Shallow Valley with the horses and their herdsmen, and he could give her warning there.

He jumped up, meaning to set out at once, but then it occurred to him that he must find something to eat first, for his provisions of nuts were almost finished. The storeroom beside the house was burnt out, and the Raiding Riders seemed to have been there before him and cleared the place, though hastily and without much care. Under a chest that had been left outside the door he found a quantity of broken flat cakes of bread, and one of the looters had lost a piece of smoked bacon in the bushes not far away. Stone-eye put all this in his bag, and then went round behind the house, where he saw that the sleepers had woken, and were engaged in excited conversation. As soon as they caught sight of him, they all let out cries of alarm, and flinched away.

'What's the matter?' asked Stone-eye. 'You were friendlier when you were dogs.'

One of them plucked up his courage, and said, 'We were seeing you with the eyes of animals then, but now it is hard for us to bear the sight of you. Please don't come any closer. The women among us have had to endure enough dreadful things already.' However, it was easy to see that he was just as much afraid himself. Little help could be expected from these people. So Stone-eye only said, 'I can't stay here anyway; I have a long way to go, and I must go fast.'

The seven people seemed much relieved to hear that, and the eldest of them said, 'Please don't misunderstand us. We are most grateful to you. Can't we do anything for you too?'

Stone-eye's hopes revived, and he said, 'Perhaps you could. If the magic powers of the ring worked on you, they might give me back my own human form. Will one of you try it?'

The old man raised his hands defensively, saying, 'Not me! I won't touch that accursed ring! It might change me back into a dog again.'

'Have you forgotten what this faun did for us?' the girl who had been a dog asked the old man. 'Throw the ring over!' she called to Stone-eye, though she avoided looking directly at him. She caught it neatly in the air, put it on her finger, pointed to Stone-eye and said, 'Be a man!' But nothing happened.

Stone-eye had feared as much, for he had been thinking all the time of the curse Narzia had laid on him. 'Thank you for trying, at least,' he said to the girl. 'I could have expected no more, unless you would take me in your arms like your lover as I am now.'

At that the girl did raise her eyes, and looked in horror at the hairy, goat-legged monster. She began to tremble. 'No!' she whispered. 'No! No, I can't!' And she threw the ring back to him, burying her face in her hands.

'No one could ask it of you,' said Stone-eye. 'What are you all going to do now?'

'First we must bury the dead,' said the old man. 'But we won't stay here any longer, for fear of Khan Hunli's Riders. They will come back some time or other and kill us too. We'll hide in the woods, though it will be a hard life for the women.'

'I have a better idea,' said Stone-eye, and he told them about the cave where he had spent three winters. He described the way to it, and went on, 'You'll find a flock of goats nearby, led by a he-goat with one horn. You can milk the goats, but be good to them. They are my flock.' Then he waved goodbye, and disappeared into the bushes.

Now he had to run through the woods again, but uphill this time, and that was even harder going. But he ran and ran, for he could not help thinking all the time of the girl with eyes of a colour that was hard to describe, and what might happen to her if she fell into the hands of the Raiding Riders. He had decided to go the way Needle-tooth had shown him last year. If he did not find the girl in the Shallow Valley, he could get to Arziak within a day taking the path through the Weird Wood, and see what might yet be done there.

With every day that he hurried up through the woods his hope of being able to change the inexorable course of events in any way ebbed, and at times he felt he was merely fleeing from the dreadful picture of the village of Arni's Folk imprinted on his mind: smoked ruins, and corpses everywhere among them, with the carrion crows quarrelling over their prey. Or else he was in flight from the thought that all this was only the consequence of that evening when he had tried to bend a whole people to his will with a little music on his flute. But then hungry flocks of crows passed overhead once more, cawing, in search of more to eat on the other side of the mountains, and he ran on again through the whipping undergrowth.

Towards evening on the fourth day, he finally reached the little lake at the southern end of the cliff, and let himself drop on the bank to drink, tired to death. He gulped up water like an animal, and then lay back under the hanging branches of the willows and tried to sleep, but his legs still twitched with the regular rhythm of his day's travelling, and as soon as he closed his eyes, he saw the dead around Arni's House once more, reminding him that even now the table might be laid for the black birds in the valley of Arziak.

As he dozed there, between sleep and waking, listening to the rush and roar of the waterfall, there was a rustling in the bushes beside him, and a voice said, 'You're early this year, Stone-eye. I didn't expect you yet, but I'm glad to see you. Going over to the Shallow Valley again, are you?'

'As fast as ever I can,' said Stone-eye, greeting the weasel. 'It's good to hear a friend's voice,' he added, 'when I've had nothing in my ears for days but the cawing of those greedy carrion crows.'

'Is it on their account you're in such a hurry?' said Needle-tooth. 'No need to fear the Raiding Riders here. I've heard they're out raiding again, but they went over the mountains farther south.'

'I know,' said Stone-eye. 'They took the shorter way.' And he told his friend all that had happened since last they met. When he mentioned the loss of the stone, Needle-tooth said, 'That's bad.'

'What happened afterwards is worse,' said Stone-eye. 'What good would the stone do me now?'

'How can you tell?' said Needle-tooth. 'What do you know about that stone? Not all, I'm sure, no, far from all. In any case, you ought to try to get it back.'

'How?' asked Stone-eye hopelessly. 'Anyway, I have something more important to do now.'

'Forgive me for contradicting you,' said the weasel, in his courteous way, 'but there are times when one doesn't know what's really important till later. What's more, you're forgetting you have friends, which distresses me.'

'Why, would you go looking for the stone?' asked Stone-eye. 'There are a thousand places where the falcon might have hidden it!'

'And there are thousands of mice,' said Needle-tooth. 'Why not call on your friend He-who-speaks-with-the-snake? He'll know how to find it.'

'You surprise me,' said Stone-eye. 'Your opinion of mice seems to have risen considerably. I suppose I can always try.' And he whistled the three notes the mouse had taught him as a signal. Then they sat together in silence for a while as night fell, listening. They heard the cascading of the waterfall, and a bird chirping now and then, but there was no answer from the mouse. 'Well, he won't be here just yet,' said the weasel at last. 'You'd better get some sleep now; you'll need to be well rested in the morning, if we're going to climb through the cleft. I'll see about finding us a good breakfast.'

The conversation with his friend had distracted Stone-eye's thoughts a little from the dreadful events of recent days, and so he fell asleep as soon as he turned on his side, and did not wake until the chaffinches were singing their morning song. The first thing he saw when he opened his eyes was the mouse, He-who-speaks-with-the-snake, sitting beside him in the grass, cleaning his long whiskers. He immediately interrupted this activity, said, 'Good morning, Bearer of the Stone!' and bowed politely. 'I've been here some time,' he added, 'but I didn't like to wake you. Your friend Needle-tooth told me you needed your rest.'

'You have obviously become accustomed to speaking with weasels too, my bold mouse,' said Stone-eye, greeting his friend.

'I owe it to my name, don't I?' said the mouse, puffing out his tiny chest. 'And any friend of yours is a friend of mine.'

'Needle-tooth will feel greatly honoured to have such a friend,' said Stone-eye. 'He thinks a lot of you, and indeed it was he who advised me to call on your aid.' And then he told the mouse about the stone. 'But this time it's not just a small mountain meadow you would have to search,' he ended his tale. 'The stone may be anywhere that a falcon can settle. I am not at all sure that I ought to put you in danger for the sake of that stone, for the falcon will keep a good eye on her treasure.'

At this the mouse rose to as full a height as he could manage and inquired, 'Do you want to insult a good friend?'

'Far from it,' Stone-eye hastened to assure him. 'It's just that I wouldn't like to lose you.'

'Oh, don't let that worry you,' said the mouse. 'A person who has spoken with snakes and weasels can deal with a falcon too. Where shall I bring you the stone?'

'I don't know,' said Stone-eye. 'I have a long way to go, and I can't say where I shall be in the immediate future. Look after the stone for me, if you should manage to get it away from the falcon. I would like you to keep it safe until I call you.'

The mouse bowed low, and said, 'My friendship with you has brought me a great name, but this is the highest honour I have ever been shown: to be Keeper of the Stone. I don't know how to thank you.'

'You will have to find it first,' said Stone-eye. 'But looking at you now, I am almost inclined to believe you can do it!'

Before the mouse could make any more fine speeches, the weasel came back from hunting, dragging a grouse after him. 'I think this'll do for our breakfast,' he said, laying his prey at Stone-eye's feet.

The mouse did his best to conceal his disgust. 'I hope you won't take it amiss,' said he to the weasel, 'if I leave this little bird for the two of you. It's rather small for three.'

'Extremely generous of you,' said Stone-eye, trying not to smile, so that He-who-speaks-with-the-snake would not lose face. 'Will you accept a few of my hazelnuts instead?'

'With the greatest of pleasure,' said the mouse. Stone-eye had soon kindled a fire, and he plucked and drew the bird, and turned it over the glowing embers on a wooden spit.

As they all three enjoyed their breakfast, the mouse asked Stone-eye, 'I know it's none of my business, but I'd very much like to know what this long way is you're going.'

Then Stone-eye realized that his amusement at the mouse's dignified bearing had briefly made him forget the purpose of his journey. The thought of what might by now have taken place in the valley of Arziak dropped like a stone into his heart, and he said, 'Terrible things happened in the village of Arni's Folk, and it was my fault. Now I'm at least trying to save a girl who lives the other side of the mountains from the Raiding Riders. I am glad you reminded me. I've sat here over breakfast too long. Come on, Needle-tooth! We must hurry, if it's not too late already.'

'A person in a hurry should stop and think of the quickest way to get what he wants,' said the weasel. 'Do you remember the water nymph we met here a year ago?'

'Of course,' said Stone-eye, preparing to go. 'But what use could she be to me now? Come along, do!'

'No, wait!' said the weasel. 'Didn't she know about that girl? Her messengers may travel faster than your feet.'

'That may be so,' said Stone-eye, 'but I don't know how to summon her. I don't even know her name.'

'Water nymphs come when you give them presents,' said the weasel. 'I thought you knew that.'

'How would I?' said Stone-eye. 'What did I give her last time, then?'

'The song you played on your pipes,' said the weasel.

Stone-eye shrugged his shoulders. 'I have no pipes now,' he said, 'and no time to make a set either.'

But the weasel was not to be discouraged. 'Haven't you anything else you could give her?' he asked.

Stone-eye shook his head. 'What kind of precious things do you think I carry about with me?' he said. 'See for yourself!' And he shook out the contents of his goat's-hair bag on the ground. Along with a quantity of hazelnuts, his flint and his knife, Narzia's ring rolled over the moss, and the falcon necklace slipped out after it, like a slender, sparkling snake.

'And you say you don't carry anything precious about with you?' inquired the weasel, reproachfully. 'Are you so fond of these shiny things that you can't bear to part with them?'

'Heaven forbid!' said Stone-eye. 'I had quite forgotten them. I'd be glad to be rid of this accursed magical stuff. It would be a sad day if Narzia ever got it into her clutches again.' And he picked up both jewels from the ground, went swiftly to the bank and threw them far out into the middle of the lake. 'Water nymph!' he called. 'Oh, water nymph, come to my aid!'

Ring and necklace dipped almost soundlessly beneath the surface of the water, which was kept constantly in motion by the falling stream, and it closed over them without so much as a splash, as if a mouth had swallowed the jewels up. Stone-eye saw a last flash of green in the depths, and then nothing happened for a while. There was only the cascade rushing down amidst spray, as usual. Then the centre of the lake suddenly rose, and up came the water nymph in a surge of water. She shook her green-tinged fair hair, spraying the bank with droplets, so that Needle-tooth leaped aside with a squeal of indignation. The water nymph laughed aloud and said, in her singing voice, 'One who calls on the water is likely to get wet! What do you want of me, Stone-eye? You must be greatly troubled to offer such precious and magical things.'

'Should I not be troubled, with Hunli's horde riding to Arziak?' said Stone-eye. 'I fear for the girl I met twice in the Shallow Valley.'

'And frightened twice, too!' said the water nymph, laughing again. 'Do you want to frighten her a third time?'

'No, no!' Stone-eye hastily assured her. 'I want to warn her, but I'm afraid it will be too late by the time I've gone the long way over the mountains. Can't you send her a message?'

'I can,' said the water nymph, 'though only if the girl comes close to a stream or pool. My friends can't find her in the steppes or the dry forest.' And then the water nymph raised her clear voice, and sang:

> *Hasten, friends, grant my wish!*
> *Seek the girl who knows the fish.*
> *You who swim in pool or stream,*
> *carp or trout, perch or bream –*
> *the Raiding Riders are on their way!*
> *Tell her to hide as fast as she may.*
> *Show her a place where she can run!*
> *Find her before this day is done.*

Even as she sang, the lake around her began to swarm with countless fishes: trout leaped glittering in the morning sunlight, and fell back into the water with a splash; pike came shooting up like dark arrows; even the portly carp beat the water with their tails and raised their round, bearded mouths above the surface. As soon as the song was over, the fish scattered in all directions, and disappeared into the green depths.

'That's all I can do for you,' said the water nymph. 'As for what happens on dry land, you'll have to see to that for yourself. But remember this, you impatient faun: things are not always what they seem at the time. If you don't give up hope, you will find what you are looking for. And thank you for the costly present.'

'Don't let any falcons see the jewels,' said Stone-eye. 'A falcon might try to rob you of them.'

At that the water nymph laughed again: ringing, splashing laughter that was like the sound of a thousand waterfalls cascading into the lake. 'Leave that to me!' she called, through her laughter. 'Any who want this falcon ring and necklace must come down to me in the deepest of the depths and fetch them up in person.'

'Will you tell me your name, so that I can call you if I ever need help again?' said Stone-eye.

'Call me by the name of Laianna,' said the water nymph, 'but it must be by a lake.'

And then she disappeared in a fountain of millions of sparkling water-drops, and vanished from sight.

Now the mouse took his leave as well, observing that he couldn't wait to get the eye-stone back from that green-eyed falcon, and he walked away with all the gravity appropriate to the dignity laid upon his small shoulders.

A little later, Needle-tooth and Stone-eye were climbing up the narrow cleft in the rock wall. They soon reached the way into the channel of the old stream bed, and crawled along it until they came out into daylight among the trees of the mountain woods.

As soon as Stone-eye felt reasonably firm ground under his hooves again, he broke into the rapid trot that had become second nature to him over the past few days. 'People in a hurry run past their prey without noticing it,' remarked the weasel breathlessly, as he ran leaping along beside him, but Stone-eye could not be persuaded to go any slower; the thought of what might have happened in Arziak drove him on, as if he could hardly wait to see these horrors with his own eyes.

Only when the pine wood became thicker and denser, so that at last daylight was only a dim green glow filtering down from above, was he forced to slacken his pace slightly, to avoid stumbling constantly over roots or running straight into the tree-trunks that emerged from the gloom. But even here he went as fast as he could, and ran on until evening came and it was so dark that he could hardly see his hand before his eyes. He was up again at first light of dawn, and so he reached the Weird Wood, this time, towards the evening of the second day.

It was still light when the two companions rounded the bare summit with the old, spreading rowan to one side of it. 'Hadn't we better spend the night here?' said the weasel. 'We can sleep in peace, undisturbed, under this good tree.' But Stone-eye was eager to go on, for the sight of the mountain meadow reminded him of all kinds of unpleasant memories which he preferred to forget. So they climbed down the rest of the path to the Shallow Valley as night was falling over the tree-tops. At last it was so dark that Stone-eye had to grope his way from tree to tree. He could tell when he finally reached the borders of the wood only from a certain change in the air, or perhaps from the way he had suddenly left behind the woodland sounds, with their quiet crackling and rustling. He looked towards the place where the herdsmen's huts must stand, but the darkness was broken by no distant lamp or lighted window. Were the people there already asleep? Stone-eye strained his ears, but no sound reached them through the night, neither the clink of any tool nor the snorting of horses.

'Something's not the same as last year,' said Needle-tooth, sniffing the night air. 'It smells different.'

'How?' asked Stone-eye, audibly drawing in air through his nostrils. 'I don't notice anything.'

'That's how you can stand to be with those goats of yours,' said Needle-tooth. 'It doesn't smell so much of horses, that's what. Smells a bit of fish, though.'

'Fish?' repeated Stone-eye. 'Well, perhaps that's because of the stream. There are plenty of fish in that stream.'

'Could be,' said the weasel, but he did not sound really convinced.

'And you can't smell the girl?' asked Stone-eye.

'I don't think so,' said the weasel. 'The smell of humans is a lot fainter this time, anyway.'

Stone-eye was ready to drop with weariness after his long and hasty journey, but what with all these mysterious observations of the weasel's, he felt he must know for certain the state of affairs here in the Shallow Valley. 'I'm sure you're as tired from our travels as I am,' he said to Needle-tooth. 'All the same, I will ask you to go over to those huts and see if there's anyone there, and if so, who.'

'I don't mind,' said the weasel, 'if you're in such a hurry.' And he scurried off.

All was still quiet out there in the valley. Once a dog barked, but it soon fell silent again. After some while, Needle-tooth came back and said, 'Now I know where the smell of fish comes from: there's no one in those huts but the old Carphead man, and he has only a few foals to look after. All the herdsmen have left, and all the horses fit to be ridden. Oh, and there's a dog there too, but he's probably even older than the Carphead, and hasn't a good tooth in his head.'

'What about the girl?' asked Stone-eye impatiently.

'Not there either,' said the weasel.

'Then I haven't much hope that she's alive,' said Stone-eye. He said not another word that night, and did not sleep either, but lay on his back on the grassy woodland floor and stared up at the impenetrable darkness, in which the quiet rustle of leaves could occasionally be heard. And he was on his feet at the first light of dawn once more.

'What are you going to do now?' asked the weasel.

'See what's happened to the Mountain Badgers in Arziak,' said Stone-eye. 'You can stay here if you're tired of running.'

'Do you think I'd let a friend down?' said Needle-tooth, sounding almost injured. 'Still, you might at least take time off for breakfast.'

'I've no appetite,' said Stone-eye. 'Later, perhaps. You can surely find us something edible as we go along.'

'He who sets off without breakfast has half lost already,' said the weasel, but Stone-eye pretended not to have heard this saying, worthy of note as it was, and began running up the slope again. He did not pause for a short rest until he was back near the summit of the mountain, for he could now feel the effects of a sleepless night on his limbs. The sun had only just risen, and was a blood-red globe hanging low in the eastern sky above the steppes. Stone-eye leaned against the trunk of a pine tree and stared at the glowing sun as it grew brighter, until he could look no longer. When he turned his eyes away, and glanced at the old rowan standing a little way off in the mountain meadow, at the edge of the Weird Wood, he thought he saw a rather large white bird asleep in its branches. He tried to look more closely at this curious phenomenon, but the greenish image of the rising sun imprinted on his eyes kept getting in the way, hiding it, and then the bird fluttered down from the branches, hovered or hopped fast over the top of the mountain, its pale wings flying out behind it like a scarf, and it was gone.

'Did you see that, Needle-tooth?' asked Stone-eye. 'What kind of bird was it?' However, the weasel was no longer at his side, but had gone off into the undergrowth hunting breakfast. When he came back a little later, with the pigeon he had caught, Stone-eye asked if he hadn't seen the big bird roosting in the branches of the rowan. But the weasel had been hunting in the opposite direction, and had not had a view of the tree. 'And anyway, I couldn't have harmed any creature sheltered by that rowan,' he added.

By now another great flock of crows was passing over the sky again, and if Stone-eye had had any appetite for breakfast the echoing caw of their summons to the feast would have spoiled it. 'We must go on, and fast!' he said. 'We can eat the pigeon later.' He put it in his bag, and trotted along the side of the mountain meadow to the Weird Wood, through which the way led down to the valley of Arziak.

As they were going downhill now, the two companions made fast progress, and about mid-day they reached a precipitous spur of rock from which the whole valley could be seen over the tree-tops of the woods that undulated steeply below. And then Stone-eye saw that he had come too late here, as well. Farther up the valley, where the Mountain Badgers' settlement stood, he saw countless pillars of black smoke slowly rising towards the mountains in the almost windless air, and then breaking up and drifting away eastwards in smoky ribbons. The country around Arziak was all ablaze, and isolated fires could be seen in the smaller valleys where the smelters had their huts. Stone-eye could picture the scene down there among the houses only too well; there would be piles of corpses lying in the streets and squares where the craftsmen and goldsmiths used to sell their wares, men, women and children, among them the Ore Master Promezzo, his wife Akka who had Urla's eyes, and their daughter, that girl upon whom he had set his hopes. He could imagine it all, but he did not want to see it; he had seen enough of the dead, and did not wish to have to look in the faces of those people who had once trusted him, and whom he had brought to their deaths; in particular he did not want to see the girl. He could not have endured the finality of her dead glance, and so he sat where he was, staring down into the valley and conjuring up dreadful pictures, though he could not know if they were near the truth or not.

'Aren't we going on?' asked the weasel.

Stone-eye shook his head and said, after a while, 'No point in it now.'

'Well, won't you at least roast the pigeon, then?' said the weasel, but Stone-eye flung him the blood-stained bird in silence, lay back and stared up at the pale blue spring sky, where occasional scraps of black smoke drifted slowly eastwards. He was still lying there when night fell, spreading above the woods, until nothing could be seen but an occasional fire flaring up again in the valley, and the stars in the unattainable vault of the sky. Stone-eye lay as if he had been hammered into the ground, exposed to the icy gaze of those immeasurably distant, impartial watchers, staring down at him like judges who have long since passed sentence, and he felt a nameless fear, as if he lay here only to await execution.

'So this is what you've come to,' said the Grey One. 'Lying here whimpering for mercy.' He was leaning against the trunk of a pine tree, looking down on Stone-eye, his face expressionless. 'Instead of minding your own business, you waste your time with Narzia's dogs, and then with that girl who was always running away from you. Why, you even threw the precious falcon ring and necklace to that water nymph, just to get a vague promise – and all for nothing, for nothing at all! Look down into the valley, and there you'll see the way to get on in the world. You must take what you want, you know. You won't get anything free. Come with me, and I'll show you!'

Stone-eye felt horror at the thought of going into the valley, but he had no power to withstand that order, and in a moment he was gliding down through the woods behind the grey figure, and then he was among the houses of Arziak. People came running out of every doorway to assemble in the market place, and though Stone-eye could tell, from their open mouths and distorted faces, that they were all shouting at the tops of their voices, there was not a sound to be heard. On the other side of the square, he saw the Ore Master's house, where the girl must live – the girl whom he was trying to find, though he did not know just why. He flung himself into the crowd, trying to part it like a swimmer parting the waves, but the people ran hither and thither in such aimless haste that he could hardly take a step forward. Then, suddenly, they all looked the way one would ride into the town from the mountains, and howled in fear, so far as could be told from their gesticulations, while the first Raiding Riders came galloping into the square, standing in their stirrups to shoot arrows at random into the frantically surging crowd. He saw several people hit: an arrow went into the throat of a fat man just in front of him, its head emerging through the back of his fleshy neck; he saw a woman with the baby she had been carrying through the crowd nailed to her breast by another arrow. And then the Riders were on them, drawing curved swords from their sheaths, cutting down any who crossed their path, and wherever their blades fell, broad red lips of flesh opened in a soundless scream. And each of these Riders took whatever seemed to him of value, here snatching a golden brooch from the shoulder of a stricken man even as he fell, there tearing the precious eardrop from a woman's ear.

Suddenly Stone-eye was aware that he too held a curved sword in his right hand. And now he forced his way through the throng to Promezzo's house, dealing out mighty blows in all directions, and seeing those he struck fall without a sound. When he leaped up the steps to the door, it opened and the girl came out. She was holding his flute, and put it to her lips, as if to usurp the power that belonged only to its rightful owner.

'Stop!' cried Stone-eye. 'That's my flute, and no one else shall play it!' And knowing that he might be rendered helpless next moment by the power the girl was preparing to wield, he raised his sword and brought it down on her head. When he had done that, he saw that the square where, a moment ago, the Riders had been cutting down the dense throng of the crowd, was now swept clear. There was nobody there but himself, still standing on the stone steps, and the girl lying before him, her face cut in half by a gaping wound, and incredible as it might seem, she said, with her cleft mouth, 'Now do you know how you ought to play your flute?' Then she fell backwards on the steps, staring at nothing with her empty eyes.

So then he took the flute from the dead girl's hands, and put it to his own lips, but he could not think of a single note to play. As he stared at the flute, he saw a shadow pass over the shining metal, and the reflection of the Grey One, distorted almost out of recognition, appeared on its smooth curve. 'Now do you see the real value of what you wanted to believe in?' said the Grey One. 'Do you realize at last how pointless it was to set your hopes on anyone like that girl? Did you think, perhaps, that love means more than the instinct which drives the he-goat to mount his mates? What's left of it all in the end? A little blood, a little rotting flesh, a little brain that's no more than a puddle of grey slop.'

He came round from behind Stone-eye's back and kicked the girl right down the steps, so that she fell, turning over and over, from step to step, on and on down an endless flight reaching into invisible depths, becoming smaller and smaller, until she could be discerned only as a dark and lifeless object, disappearing into the grey twilight of a bottomless abyss. Stone-eye stood dizzily alone on top of a grey pyramid that fell steeply away on all sides, motionless, spellbound by his howling fear that the yawning abyss would suck him down as well if he moved so much as a foot, and so he stood there until he felt his knees begin to tremble, and then he felt only the rush of his fall into endless nothing, and cried out without the slightest hope that anyone could hear him.

But for the moment, anyway, there was still someone around to do that. The weasel, startled by his scream, woke him and asked if he had had a bad dream.

'I don't know if it was a dream,' said Stone-eye. 'Perhaps it was a glimpse of something beyond those dreams I've been taking for reality.'

'And what's so dreadful about them, to make you scream like that?' said the weasel. 'Personally, I don't understand it. My dreams are only more of what I know by day. Sometimes I wake up feeling my legs tensed to spring on prey I've just seen in my dreams.'

'Yes,' said Stone-eye, 'and you're content with what you take for the reality of your life.'

'Why wouldn't I be?' asked the weasel, and added, after a pause, 'Why aren't you?'

'I see no reason for it,' said Stone-eye.

The weasel shook his head. 'Well, far be it from me to blame you,' he said, 'but I've noticed before that you're never content with what you are or what you have. I suppose it's human nature, and that's why I can't understand it.'

In spite of the polite tone in which the weasel made these observations, Stone-eye felt a great gulf of strangeness suddenly dividing him from that elegant beast of prey. Had the friendship between himself and Needle-tooth been only a pointless fancy of his dreams too? He could scarcely have said, now, what had united him with his companion, and indeed he even felt the dawning of something like irritation with the self-satisfied weasel, who seemed to feel all was well with his world, and was sitting here before him like a living reproach. It was more than he could bear just now. 'I don't take what you say ill,' he said. 'Very likely you're right about human nature too. And I want to thank you for your friendship, and for roaming the woods with me all this time. But now I will ask you to let me go my own way alone.'

Even as he spoke, he knew where he was going. He saw in his mind's eye the peaceful green pastures of the Shallow Valley, where he had twice met the girl. There, perhaps, he might manage to forget the picture of her corpse endlessly falling into nothingness before his eyes. And there he would be alone.

'What will you live on, if I'm not there to hunt for you?' asked the weasel, with concern.

'I won't be needing anything for a while,' said Stone-eye, preparing to go. The thought of food revolted him.

'You'll be hungry again sometime,' said the weasel. 'Wait and see if you aren't!'

'Can't you think of anything else at all?' said Stone-eye bitterly. He was now positively eager to escape the company of the beast of prey; he waved once more to Needle-tooth and strode quickly uphill towards his goal. When he reached the Weird Wood, night was already rising from the valleys below. In the end he was groping his way with his hands, fingers feeling the rough strands of lichen that hung like beards from the crooked pines, and catching his clumsy hooves in the tough roots, but he did not stop to rest until he had reached the last of the trees and saw the rounded shape of the mountain top ahead of him beneath the stars, a dark outline against the partly overcast night sky.

He did not want to stay very long here either, only to rest for a little after the effort of the steep climb up. As he looked for a suitable resting-place, he thought he saw movement a little way off to his right, among the tree-trunks, as if some large animal were stalking soundlessly towards him. Without any more distinct idea of what was there, he felt icy horror grip him. He tried to hide behind one of the lichen-hung trees, and then he saw the shadowy creature trotting closer over the mountain meadow, beside the trees: it was clearly visible now as a gigantic wolf, so emaciated as to be almost a skeleton. As it was running past him, it stopped suddenly, glowing yellow eyes looking his way. Then it uttered a deep, angry snarl, and leaped towards him.

Stone-eye ran blindly away, keeping to the edge of the wood, where there was no danger of stumbling over roots and tree-stumps. He heard the monstrous animal's panting breath coming closer and closer, and then, suddenly, a broad shadow loomed out of the darkness before him. He tried to jump over the obstacle, but caught his hoof on something and fell full length in the grass. 'Hold to the tree you set over me,' whispered a voice, and before he had really taken in the full import of these words he was grasping the smooth trunk of a young rowan, as thick as a man's arm, which stood directly before him. Then he heard the wolf howl angrily behind him, and thought he already felt its stinking breath on his neck.

After all that had happened over the last few days, he had thought he no longer cared for life, now that all hope seemed gone, but still he felt his body trembling with the fear of death, while his hands, wet with sweat, clung to the slender trunk of the rowan. So he lay there on the ground, waiting to perish horribly in the beast's jaws. However, the wolf did not leap on him, but began to circle him at a distance of a few paces. Every time it tried to break through that circle, it seemed to encounter an invisible wall, and then it raised its head and uttered a dreadful howl.

This went on for some time, until Stone-eye gradually realized that he was safe here. Without letting go of the little tree, he raised himself slightly and looked around him. Behind him lay the fallen trunk of a pine tree, the gnarled stumps of its branches sticking out in all directions. That was the obstacle over which he had fallen. The young rowan had grown from the place where the pine must once have been rooted. Someone had filled in the hole and planted the little tree, and then he suddenly knew what place this was, and who had saved him from the apparition of the wolf. 'Thank you for your help, Gisa,' he said. 'I killed you in this mountain meadow, and you have saved my life.' And when he got no answer, he added, after a while, 'Though I wonder if it was worth saving.'

As he listened to see if some answer might come after all, perhaps to contradict him, he felt the hanging leaves of the rowan brush him, like a soothing hand, in the gentle night breeze. And perhaps that was a kind of answer. He felt his body relax under their gentle touch, while the monstrous wolf still prowled outside the circle, and then he fell asleep.

When he woke, the morning sun was high in the sky, shining down on his face through the bright green canopy of the young rowan's leaves. He let go of the trunk, which he had still been clutching even in his sleep, and stood up. The wolf had disappeared, but three paces away, among primroses and gentians in the short mountain grass, Stone-eye found the bleached bones of a skeleton which might very well once have belonged to a mighty wolf.

This sight strengthened his feeling that he did not want to stay here any longer than necessary. He found his bag, which he had lost in his headlong flight, rounded the top of the mountain, and climbed down to the Shallow Valley on the other side.

As soon as he could see down through the trees to the valley floor, he looked over at the huts and the stables, but nothing had changed there. Then he went on up the valley until the wooded hills gradually drew closer together. Here the valley floor itself began to be sparsely wooded with alders, and Stone-eye was at last able to make his way to the stream to quench his thirst in their shelter. He scooped up some of the cold, clear water in his cupped hand, and then followed the stream until he reached its source under the huge sycamore among a light stand of birches. For the time being, he thought, he would stay here, where once, long ago, he had played with the birch tree girls. He sat on a rocky ledge above the spring, and looked back into the valley. Between the slender, shimmering white trunks of the birches, and the dark green of the alder bushes growing along the banks of the stream, he had a view of the pastures through which the stream wound its way, shining in the sun. The herdsmen's huts must lie somewhere in the hazy distance, but they could not be seen from here.

It seemed to him as if everything he had until recently considered important was suddenly very far distant, as if it had no more to do with him, and he wondered if there was really anything left to bind him to his life. 'You tell me, Piney!' he said to his wooden companion. 'Why did I spend three winters with the goats? Why did I roam this valley in the summers between them? What good came of it? A little longing, a little pain, a little disappointment, and now I realize there was not the slightest point in all that running about.'

'Running about is generally a pointless activity,' remarked the Piney. 'I've told you so before. Well, what are you planning to do now?'

'I don't know,' said Stone-eye. 'I've lost everything on which I set my hopes. I've given my stone away, for nothing or worse than nothing, some Raiding Rider is probably now trying to whistle up his horse with my flute, and if I ever had any friends, they lie dead among their houses, with the carrion crows eating them. And it was all my fault.'

'Well, if you see that, all hope's not lost,' said the Piney.

'Hope?' Stone-eye uttered the word as if the Piney were mocking him. 'I don't know what you mean by that. What could I hope for now?'

'Nothing you can imagine, anyway,' said the Piney. 'That was your trouble all along; you were forever trying to set things going in what you thought would be the best direction. I stood up on that pass for several hundred years, without any chance of setting things going, but I was never quite without hope in all that time.'

'I'm not a tree!' said Stone-eye, shrugging his shoulders, but after a while he added, 'Though I've reached a point when I could wish I were. I shall stay here for a while. Perhaps I'll be rooted to the spot, like the birch tree girls.'

He was hungry after all, he found, having gone such a long way, and as he searched for the last of the hazelnuts in his bag, his fingers chanced upon the round flask he had taken away from Narzia's house. He took it out, and tried to read the writing on the label yet again. Here in the bright spring sunlight, all the letters stood out distinctly once more:

> *When you stand at last*
> *by yourself dismayed,*
> *bitter though it taste,*
> *this will bring you aid.*
> *In the stone be bound,*
> *held there by this token;*
> *if you are not found,*
> *you shall not be woken.*

And all of a sudden it seemed to him that he held the answer to all his despair and hopelessness in his hands. Letting the nuts fall to the grass unheeded, he stood up and broke the seal of the flask. He wanted nothing now but to stand by this gushing spring and look out into the valley, for there was no place left where he might wish to go.

'Will you stay with me, Piney?' he asked. 'I may stand here for ever.'

'Of course,' said the Piney. 'You know that I was given to you as your companion.'

Then Stone-eye took the Piney firmly in his right hand, raised the flask to his mouth with his other hand, and drained it at one draught. The bitter liquid set his teeth on edge, and then he felt the magical potion brewed by the Master of Herbs spreading fast through his body. When he tried to change position slightly, he found he could no longer move his hooves; they had merged into the rock on which they stood. Slowly, his limbs turned to stone, the stone reached his heart and stopped it, rose to his shoulders, his chin, his mouth, his eyes, and closed about his head. The grey statue of a faun stood motionless above the spring, in the shade of the sycamore tree, and soon a robin settled on its head and sang.

Part Two

Green. He saw green all around him, every different shade and hue of green: bright green suffused with light, dark green, bluish green, brownish green. He did not see it with his eyes, which were fixed and stony in his skull; the sensation of green directly pervaded his awareness from every side, entirely filling it. Up above, shades of pale blue mingled with it, and down below the colours became deeper and richer, ranging to a brownish violet, and bright reflections flashed across them from time to time, lighting them up, and were then immediately extinguished. All these colours circled around him in a single shimmering eddy, in which nothing was constant, for the colours themselves were always changing: bright emerald green would darken to the blue shades of night, grew lighter again, was shot through by streaks of yellow and orange that withered to brown, and then a thousand hues of green flooded over it all once more. In this constant movement, no object could be distinguished, there was no fixed point in the glowing, swirling sensations of colour that streamed endlessly through his dim consciousness; this was not an event of whose beginning he knew anything, nor was it making towards any end; it was a condition outside time, a state of existence in a place that might be contracted into a single point of spraying colour, or then again might extend into a world of boundless space.

He had been here for an eternity, outside time, outside any distinct sense of space, when a speck of something brown appearing unexpectedly, and without any shape as yet, drew his attention to itself. Previously, he had done nothing but receive impressions, but now it was as if he were putting out an invisible feeler to grope into the formless play of colours. He found it hard to concentrate on the blurred speck, but it stayed where it was, was not swept away by the constantly renewed tide of colours, and gradually took on firm outlines, became a forked pattern of thin, dark brown lines, with swellings sprouting from their ends. That is a branch, he said to himself, wondering at the same time what the word meant. But he was about to discover, for this branch (whatever a branch might be) began to change. The swellings became fatter, and as the word bud occurred to him, the buds opened and let loose yellowish green tassels of delicate stems, bearing further tender buds at their ends, which instantly opened into apparitions of even more delicacy and brightness. Those must be flowers, he thought, and yellow dust drifted from the tiny hairs in the middle of the star-shaped flowers, which then closed again, and while the clusters of flowers drooped, crinkled green things broke from other buds on the branch, quickly unfolding into broad shapes hanging from thin stems, and made of something tender and green that stretched between darker veins and ended in five points, like the five fingers of a hand. Those are leaves, he thought, but what is a hand?

Now another change came over the faded flower clusters; their petals fell, drifting somewhere down below, and where the petals had been small growths emerged on either side of the centre, grew longer, and fluttered in a movement that passed through the whole cluster of similar shapes. I call those keys, he thought, but he was not sure what they were for. Then, however, he remembered: you carefully removed those keys, which were light as a feather, because where their thickened ends had been joined to the stems they could be divided into two halves, covered inside with a sticky juice. You stuck them on your nose (but where was a nose?) and everyone laughed. Who was everyone? Somehow or other, it had been funny. As he was wondering what that word meant, the keys loosened themselves from their stems one by one, hovering downwards in a turning, eddying flight, past other branches bearing leaves and bunches of keys, and more branches of different shapes came into his field of vision, while more and more of the keys came whirling down and sank to the ground on a shady surface cushioned with something velvety green, among countless others of their kind already lying there, and just beside the place where the key whose flight he had been following had fallen, he saw a mighty round pillar, its grey surface furrowed by deep cracks. He thought of the word trunk as he followed this tall thing upwards, to where it divided in every direction into more and more forked shapes, which became thinner and thinner, finally ending in branches with those bunches of keys hanging among their broad, hand-shaped leaves. That is a tree, he thought, and saw more of the keys flutter loose and come eddying down.

One of them reached the ground by the side of a transparent surface that sparkled with countless reflections, and was kept in constant motion by something gushing up from below, and now he could hear soft splashing and gurgling, and knew that this was a spring. Smooth pebbles shimmered on the sandy bottom: russet pebbles, brown pebbles, grey-blue pebbles, pebbles flecked with green. And the stuff that came up among them, filling the curved basin and flowing away, gurgling, through an opening in its side, was called water. He perceived this water as something cool and refreshing, and followed the course of the strings of tiny bubbles that rose from the bottom and broke into fine spray on the surface.

Then another movement by the side of the basin caught his attention. A small, furry creature with a long, thin tail had scurried up from somewhere, and was now crouching by the spring, cleaning his delicately spread whiskers with his forepaws. Then he dipped his pointed snout into the water and drank. I know you, he thought, you are a mouse. The mouse raised his head and looked up. 'I don't know if you can understand me, Stone-eye,' he said. 'You don't look as if there was much life left in you. But I'll give you my news all the same.'

What does the mouse mean, he thought, who is he talking to? And as he turned his whole attention to the little animal, the area of his field of vision suddenly widened. He was looking across endless woods spreading over gently undulating hills to a mountain range which, at that same moment, was suddenly below him, and then he plunged down, past a precipitous cliff into bushes and undergrowth, and slipped through a tiny hole and down a narrow passage into a cave, which was dark, though he could clearly see all that went on in it. There were countless mice crowding round the walls of the cave, their bright black eyes all looking at one who sat in the middle, and was speaking to them. 'Search everywhere a falcon can settle!' said this mouse. 'Go off and tell every one of our people you meet on your way! All mice are to look for the stone until it is found.'

After a while one of the mice stepped out of the circle and said, 'It could be dangerous to go looking for something that a falcon has taken. Why should we risk our lives for some old stone? You can't even eat a stone, can you?' And several of the assembled mice nodded to show they agreed with him.

The mouse in the middle rose as erect as he possibly could, and inquired, 'May I ask if you know who I am? I am He-who-speaks-with-the-snake, and that ought to be reason enough for you all to listen, and then do as I say. However, there's another thing too. This stone is not just any old stone. This stone is one of the greatest treasures in the whole world, perhaps the greatest of all. It has been passed on from one to another for a very long time, and each Bearer of the Stone has held it in as much honour as if his or her life depended on it. But it brings misfortune to anyone who steals it. So you needn't be afraid of the falcon; she's as good as done for already. What's more, isn't it a great honour for our people to have one of us chosen as Keeper of that jewel? Why, they'll be telling the tale for generation after generation in our holes.'

They all sat there in silence for a while, looking straight ahead of them and not seeming particularly eager to do as the mouse told them. But then a very old mouse rose, smoothed down her snow-white whiskers, and said, 'What cowards you all are! It's a good thing we mice give females a say in our councils, and not an unimportant say either, in my opinion. Well, let me tell you: if one of you has spoken with a snake, then I fancy you can deal with that falcon who's already brought her own downfall to her nest. I know we're more used to thinking of food than such notions as honour. But this matter is of more importance than the mere winning of a great name for someone. I can't tell you exactly what that stone means myself, but it is surely one of those secrets that help to preserve the life of all that exists. Believe you me, we females know more about such things than you males do! They say that a woman was the bearer of the stone, don't they? Well, you just do what the one called He-who-speaks-with-the-snake tells you!'

The mouse in the middle of the cave had been listening carefully, and now he went up to the older mouse, bowed low, and said, 'You put me to shame, Mother of our Council, and you have found better words than I ever could. Thank you!' And he bowed again, and then the other mice stood up, and each of them said which way he or she would go searching.

There was one young mouse who had been sitting silently in a corner throughout the council, listening. As he set off, he said, 'I'll try the top of the cliff.' He went along a narrow passage, came out into daylight under a hazel bush, and looked carefully all around him for safety's sake before he scurried purposefully uphill through bushes and tender shoots of woodland grass. Looking more closely, one could see that he was following a narrow pathway trodden by tiny mouse paws, winding its way around countless obstacles and patches of open ground offering no cover. At last the path led out of the shade of the tall trees into more open terrain, strewn with boulders and stones fallen from the rocky wall that towered to a vast height into the sky above the slope. The young mouse looked for a place in the shelter of a wild rose bush and sat down to watch the sky at his leisure.

Nothing of note seemed to happen for a long time. The air quivered with the chirping of grasshoppers, now and then the soft piping of a bird sounded in the woods, or the crack of a dry twig under the feet of some animal. The blue sky above the slope was empty, cut across by the jagged edge of the cliff. Then, suddenly, the small and furry figure of the young mouse tensed, and his previously rather sleepy gaze was turned intently on a dark dot that had appeared in the sky far away above the woods. It came quickly closer, could soon be seen to have spreading wings, and came down towards the tops of the trees. The young mouse retreated even farther beneath the thorny shoots of the rose bush, but his black eyes were following the flight of the bird, which was now clearly recognizable as a female falcon coming down over the slope at a moderate height. It looked almost as if the bird would ram her skull into the cliff, but at the last moment she slowed down, beating her wings, and settled on a rocky ledge below which a bush grew in a crevice, its sparse branches reaching out above the precipice. The bird stayed there for a while, busy with something among a tangled heap of dry twigs. Then she looked out across the slope, as if to make sure she was unobserved, and when she thought the coast was clear she rose into the air again, circled above the place once more, and flew swiftly away above the woods.

The young mouse waited for a little longer, looking up at the sky again and again. Finally he scrambled out of his hiding place and scurried over to the foot of the cliff, and that spot where the crevice at whose top the bush grew reached the bottom of the rock wall below. And then he began climbing up the crevice. He made his way cautiously on, step by step, slipped on a loose stone once and went sliding part of the way back with a shrill squeak, but then recovered himself and went on higher and higher. At last he reached the roots of the bush, wedged into the crevice and partly washed free by the rain, and after that it was child's play. He hauled himself up by his forepaws to the untidily built nest, crawled through the tangled twigs and grass of which it was made, and when he put his nose out through the dry twigs on top he saw a round stone lying in front of him, rings of colour shimmering under its smooth surface in the sunlight, as if in a living eye. The play of colour was reflected in his own eyes, the circles of blue, green and violet spread and slipped over his velvety fur, until he was entirely enveloped in their gentle glow. The young mouse sat there for a while without moving at all, except for a slight quivering of his whiskers.

At last he broke the spell, scrambled cautiously to the side of the nest, and sent a shrill whistle down the slope. Mice instantly came scurrying up from all sides, and gathered at the foot of the cliff.

'Have you found the stone?' one of them called, and the young mouse replied, 'Yes, it's up here, and so lovely you can scarcely take your eyes off it.'

'Never mind daydreaming, my boy!' said the other mouse. 'Are you going to stay there till the falcon comes back? Throw the stone down to us!'

But before the young mouse could follow this advice, the falcon appeared above the woods again, and came swooping down with a shrill cry. The mice on the slope at the foot of the cliff scattered, and next moment there was no trace of them, while the young mouse up at the top struggled to drag the stone down through the tangled nest. He had just managed to get the stone and then himself into safety in the crevice in the rock, behind the dense network of the bush's roots, when the falcon settled on her nest above him.

'Thief!' screamed the falcon. 'Where are you, thief? Where have you hidden my stone? I saw you! You must be here somewhere! Give me the stone before I wring your neck.'

The young mouse sat trembling in his hiding-place, and did not move. Then the falcon began furiously tearing her nest apart. Her talons swept the dry twigs down over the cliff, until there was not a stick left on the rocky ledge. And now she could see the young mouse crouching in the crevice, behind the fibrous roots, and clutching the stone to his breast with his forepaws.

'So there you are, you shabby little thief!' cried the falcon. 'Give me the stone!'

The young mouse was still trembling all over, but he raised his head, looked into the falcon's green eyes, and said, 'No!'

The falcon began tearing at the tough roots with her sharp beak, but she could not manage to get at the mouse wedged in his narrow crack in the rock. She battered at the place until her head was bleeding, but it was no use. At last she gave up, and stood there straddling the crevice. 'You will have to come out sometime,' she said. 'I can wait.'

'So can I,' said the young mouse, squeezing himself a little farther back into the crevice, for safety's sake.

'You are impudent, thief!' said the falcon, furiously. 'Just wait! I'll pay you out, you and all your kind!'

'Why go on at me?' inquired the young mouse. 'Aren't you a thief yourself? Didn't you steal the stone from its rightful owner?'

'What's that to do with you, my clever and talkative friend?' snapped the falcon. 'The stone is Arni's stone, and I keep it only because the luck of Arni's Folk depends on it.'

'You don't say!' replied the mouse. 'Arni's Folk haven't had much luck recently, from all I hear.'

The young mouse had spoken quite quietly, but his remark infuriated the falcon yet further. 'Glad of it, are you?' she screamed. 'I shall soon gather followers round me again, you wait and see!'

'Haven't you noticed that you're not in much luck yourself?' inquired the young mouse. 'They say the stone brings nothing but disaster to any who take it from its true Bearer. You ought to be glad I've removed it from you.'

'What do you know of these matters?' screeched the falcon. 'Haven't you stolen it yourself?'

'That's different,' said the young mouse. 'I'm only acting on behalf of its real owner.'

'Oh, so that's it!' screamed the falcon. 'So the goat-legged faun has made friends with mice as well as goats now! I suppose he couldn't find any better company than the smallest and weakest animals of all.'

On hearing this, the mouse rose erect, and even took a step forward, though making sure that he was still out of reach of the falcon's beak. He glanced at the glowing colours of the stone once more, and when he looked up again and met the falcon's eyes, without trembling at all this time, it was almost as if he had grown considerably larger. 'You may be right, falcon, and we mice are the smallest and weakest of all creatures,' he said. 'But it could be that a time will come when the smallest and weakest are given power over the strong and fierce who have always hunted them. We are glad, we little ones, of the warmth of our fellows, sleeping in our holes beside us, and in that community we find our strength.' He was speaking in a high, singsong voice, like someone talking in a dream. 'But as for you, falcon, you are alone, and you will be lonely all your life, and the sky will be empty around you as you circle above the forests. And it will be so because you did not heed the mystery of this stone.'

The falcon retreated, and for a moment it was almost as if she were afraid of this young mouse who had unexpectedly uttered such a solemn prophecy. But then she was overcome by tremendous rage, and she pecked at the fibrous roots, screeching, as if by killing the tiny mouse she could render his words unspoken. The young mouse now viewed the furious bird as a defeated enemy, and did not seem in the least afraid any more. But next moment something happened to shatter his composure entirely. He heard a scraping, rustling sound behind him, and when he turned round he saw the head of a snake slide up from the depths of the crevice. Pressing the stone to his grey, furry chest, he gazed, horrified, into the agate eyes of the biggest grass-snake he had ever seen in his life.

'Bravely and wisely spoken, my boy,' said the snake. 'Have you a name by which I can call you?' And when the mouse thus addressed remained rooted to the spot, unable to utter a word, she added, 'Surely you're not afraid of a snake, after showing so much courage in the face of a falcon? Do you want to be ashamed to face him who is known as He-who-speaks-with-the-snake?'

The young mouse pulled himself together, and said, stammering slightly, 'You're – you're Rinkulla.'

'I am,' said the snake. 'But you haven't answered my question about your name.'

The snake's information seemed to relieve the mouse's fears a little, although the sight of her obviously still made him nervous. He bowed politely, and said, 'Greetings, wise Rinkulla. Don't you see how young I am? I haven't won any name for myself as yet.'

'Then it's time you had one,' said the snake. 'I name you He-who-prophesies-to-the-falcon.' And so the young mouse received his name, wedged as he was in the rock between a furious falcon and a gigantic grass-snake.

'You do me more honour than I deserve, wise Rinkulla,' he said. 'I almost died of fright, looking at that falcon, and I'd never have found the courage to stand up to her if the stone hadn't strengthened my heart.'

'Modest too, O most excellent mouse!' said the snake. 'You have earned your name indeed, since you overcame your fear, which is a far braver thing than to feel no fear at all.'

At this the mouse bowed again, saying, 'I thank you for my name, Rinkulla, and I will try to prove myself worthy of it.'

'Fine, fine!' said the snake, swaying her head impatiently back and forth. 'Right, that's enough ceremony! Let us now remove ourselves from the vicinity of this deranged bird. She is making far too much noise for my liking.'

'How?' asked He-who-prophesies-to-the-falcon. 'I don't much want to get within reach of her claws.'

'You needn't,' said the snake. 'You're used to going along dark passages, aren't you? There are all kinds of ways through the rock here, ways that can't be seen from outside. Give me the stone. You'll be needing your paws for climbing.' And she opened her mouth and took the stone carefully in her sharp teeth. 'Come along!' she added, her speech somewhat impeded. 'I'll go ahead, and you only have to follow me.'

She turned her head, and went down into the crevice in the rock, and for a while there was nothing to be seen but the moving coils of the snake's scaly body wriggling up from below on one side of the crevice and disappearing between the rocks again on the other. It was as if there were no end to the snake at all, but at last the tip of her tail appeared, and then vanished again into the crevice, with a twitch, and as soon as she had entirely disappeared from sight the mouse followed her.

The narrow cleft sloped downwards. The mouse had only gone a little way when he heard the falcon screeching up above. 'Where are you, thieving mouse? Come out of hiding! I want to talk to you!' However, He-who-prophesies-to-the-falcon thought he had done quite enough talking to this one, and he followed the soft glow that faintly lit up the steep path ahead of him. It was hard to say if this glow came from the stone, or the snake's eyes, but in any case it showed him where to set his paws. For a while the path went straight down, and then it ran level for some way along a low corridor, which came out, after a while, into a wide cave. The walls of this cave were encrusted with tiny crystals glittering in all colours of the rainbow as the snake slithered past them. From somewhere up above, single drops fell at brief intervals into a pool, past which the snake was now gliding. Then the cave narrowed, and finally became a steep ravine worn away by the water overflowing from the pool, which ran down it into the depths. This did not bother the snake, but the mouse not only got his feet wet, he soon looked as if he had been fished out of the water, and he had trouble keeping his footing in the current. At last the slope became less steep, and the next moment the stream flowed out on the level ground of a cave, cascaded over a ledge, and gathered in a round basin below.

When he had scrambled down over this last ledge of rock with his slippery paws, the mouse bumped into the snake, who had coiled herself up on the floor of the cave and was waiting for him. The stone lay on the rocky ground in front of her. Reddish sunset light came in through an opening in the wall opposite, bringing only faint illumination to the high vault of the cave, but the stone caught even this last reflection of the sun, so that its play of colours glowed.

'Here we are,' said the snake. 'You can get out on the slope beneath the cliff over there. But I'd advise you to wait until it's quite dark, or that falcon might yet catch you.'

The mouse shook the water from his coat, raised his nose, snuffling, and said, 'It smells of goat in here.'

'No wonder,' said the snake. 'There's a flock of goats nearby, and they spend the winters here. The Bearer of the Stone himself lived in this cave for three winters, before the falcon tricked him out of his stone.'

'Will he come back here, do you think?' asked the mouse.

'Not very soon, I'm afraid,' said the snake.

After that they sat facing one another in silence until the very last of the daylight had faded. Then the snake said, 'You can whistle up your people now, He-who-prophesies-to-the-falcon.'

So the mouse took the stone, rolled it ahead of him to the cave mouth, went out into the dark and whistled. A few moments later mice came scurrying up from all sides, gathered around him in a circle, and gazed in wonder at the stone, which still glowed with a last remnant of coloured light. And before any of them could say a word, a snake's raised head emerged from the cave, above the young mouse, swaying back and forth and looking around. They all stood there, rooted to the spot. Then the snake opened her wide jaws, and said, 'Listen to me, for I am Rinkulla, with whom one of you has spoken before. This young mouse standing here grew up today and won his right name. From now on he is to be known as He-who-prophesies-to-the-falcon, for he looked that enchanted bird in her green eyes up on the cliff, and told her the truth about her life to her face. Now take the stone home, and guard it well until the Bearer of the Stone asks for it.'

At that all the mice bowed low, and the eldest of them said, 'Thank you, Rinkulla, for showing such honour to another of our people. You may be sure that He-who-speaks-with-the-snake will look after the stone well.' The snake inclined her head, and drew back into the cave, while the mice hurried to get the stone back to their own cave before dawn, exerting their united efforts.

When the stone was safely there at last, lying on a bed of fine mouse fur, guarded carefully by He-who-speaks-with-the-snake, who had taken up his duties as Keeper of the Stone at once, and when all the mice were sitting close together around the jewel, He-who-prophesies-to-the-falcon finally had time to tell his story. When he came to his meeting with Rinkulla, He-who-speaks-with-the-snake looked a little jealously at the young hero, since now he was not the only one who had spoken to her. However, his new dignity as Keeper of the Stone seemed enough to outweigh that, and when the young mouse had finished his tale, He-who-speaks-with-the-snake said, 'You have won your name by right, He-who-prophesies-to-the-falcon, and to your greater glory I will ask you to take the Bearer of the Stone the news that we have found it, and it is in my keeping.'

The young mouse bowed politely, and said, 'It looks as if I'll hardly have time to get my breath back in this affair. But these things must be, once one has attained such honours. Can you tell me how to find the Bearer of the Stone? I've never seen him in my life.'

'Oh, that's not hard,' said He-who-speaks-with-the-snake. 'Ask after someone who looks like a man from the waist up and a he-goat below. Anyone who's met him will know which way he went.'

So He-who-prophesies-to-the-falcon set out next morning, asking this person and that as he went along, and thus he came to the Weird Wood. Here, he was all but frightened to death when he came round the trunk of a pine tree thickly hung with lichen, and almost bumped into a weasel. He took a mighty leap into the undergrowth, but the weasel called out to him not to be frightened. 'I don't eat mice,' he added. 'I promised Stone-eye not to.'

At this, the mouse ventured out of the bushes again and asked the weasel if his name happened to be Needle-tooth, and upon the weasel's agreeing that it was, he delivered greetings from He-who-speaks-with-the-snake, politely introduced himself by his own name, and asked the weasel if he could tell him where to find Stone-eye.

'Have you found his stone?' asked the weasel.

'Yes,' said the mouse. 'I was lucky enough to come upon it in the falcon's nest.'

The weasel whistled appreciatively. 'You mice seem to be daring folk indeed, as anyone can tell from your fine, ringing names,' he said. 'You speak to snakes and falcons as if they were your own kind, and get a weasel to tell you the way!' And then he told the mouse how to find the spring at the head of the Shallow Valley. 'That's where he always went when he wanted to be alone,' he said.

The mouse thanked the weasel, who said, 'It was a great honour to meet you,' and then they parted. It was still a long way for a mouse's small legs to go over the mountain, down into the Shallow Valley, and then upstream to the birch wood and the mighty sycamore, but he did it within a few days, and then he delivered his message.

Now he saw the grey mouse sitting on the edge of the basin again, and thought how amazing were the deeds such a tiny creature could do. Much of what he had seen and heard among those mice had seemed familiar to him, and yet he had experienced it as an onlooker no longer concerned in these matters. However, it did strike him as odd to find so much fuss made about a stone; he wondered why that falcon had wanted it. The mouse now bowed with much ceremony, as if taking leave of someone of greatly superior rank. 'I hope', he added, 'that my words have reached your honourable if apparently stony ears,' and he bowed again, and scurried away among the pale trunks of the birch trees.

The watcher was not sure what all this meant. Compared to those events he had witnessed among the mice in that other world, the errand of the mouse who had just left, whatever it was, hardly seemed to matter. There was nothing to be seen beside the spring now except for the little sycamore keys, more of which came tumbling down as the wind shook the tree. Then a bird began to flute somewhere or other, fluting and fluting as if it would never stop. It was hard to imagine that so clear and elaborately constructed a melody, a tune of such sweetness, could proceed from a bird's little beak. But who else could be fluting here? No, it must be a bird singing its song somewhere down in the valley, and the song went on a long while.

At last the song of the fluting bird died away, and now there was nothing to be heard but the sound of the wind in the branches of the sycamore. The mouse had not reappeared, and was probably well on his way home now. Would the falcon try to get her revenge on him? He would certainly do well to be wary of the bird, and a strange bird she had been, with her emerald eyes, still lovely even in her mad rage. Evil and beautiful at once. And as he tried to picture the falcon again, he was in a room, with a broad bed that had an embroidered counterpane flung over it, and a carved chest by the wall, with a polished mirror above. There was a little table by the room's only window, which had a view of green bushes, alders, elder trees and birches, and a girl, or a young woman, stood beside this table, her green eyes looking at him. Or were they looking through him? It was obvious that she saw no one there, for when noises arose outside, the sound of hoofbeats and yelling cries, she hurried right past him through an open doorway, and on through another door into the room opposite. He saw her standing at the window there and looking down into a square across which horsemen were galloping wildly, men with braids of hair flying around their temples. There was a log cabin, grey with age, in the middle of the square, and the horsemen surrounded it, brandishing their curved swords and cutting down anyone who crossed their path.

The green-eyed girl uttered a stifled scream, and instantly pressed her hand to her mouth, as if she could thrust that betraying sound back in her throat. Then she turned, ran back to her room and closed the door. Her face was distorted with rage – or was it fear? She flung back the lid of the chest, hands flying, and snatched out some things, wrapped them in a cloth and prepared to climb out of the window. But one of the Riders came galloping round the corner, rode past beneath her window and flung a blazing torch at the roof. The green-eyed girl leaped back into the room, and now heavy blows were thundering against the door of the house. She looked around her like an animal in a trap. Then she hurried to the table by the window, and spread the cloth on it. There lay the things she had meant to take to safety: a ring with a great emerald sparkling in a setting shaped like a falcon's head, a golden necklace of delicate links, and the third thing was the stone. How did she come to have it? It was certainly the same stone the mice had taken from the falcon.

The green-eyed girl stood hesitating by the table, looking at these three things as if she could not decide what to do. Fire could be heard crackling in the attic above, smoke came seeping through the cracks between the rafters, sparks showered down, and the flames began eating their way through in several places. At the same time the door of the house fell in with a splintering crash under the Riders' blows. The green-eyed girl hesitated no longer. She snatched the necklace off the table, put it round her neck, and as she leaned over the table, fastening its clasp over her breast, her form suddenly shrank so quickly that it was hard to follow the progress of the change coming over her. Brown feathers covered her body where pale skin had been visible just now, and next moment a falcon was perched on the table, with the necklace lying around her, green eyes looking at the door. But it was still closed, although the looters could already be heard overturning furniture and breaking open chests in the house below.

By now the flames from the roof were burning inside the room, threatening to singe the falcon's feathers. She snatched up the stone in her beak and flew out of the window. From outside the house, he could see what a hold the fire had already gained (and he was not at all surprised to find himself now seeing that house from outside). The whole building was enveloped in flames, and it was surprising that the falcon had been able to escape into the open air at all. She flew swift as an arrow, close above the tops of the alders and birches, to an old oak whose gnarled trunk towered above all the other trees around it, and settled in a fork of its sturdy branches. Perhaps this was her observation post, for the whole village could be seen from here, and there was a view beyond it and out into the steppes. But the falcon had no time for observation now. She hid the stone in a hollow between the branches, rose into the air again, and flew hastily back. Perhaps she had intended to save the other precious things as well, but just as she reached the house the attic crashed in, smashing half the house wall and the window below which the jewels lay. The falcon uttered a piercing screech, and tried to find some other way into the house, but in vain: wherever she might have entered, bright flames came licking out. At last, wings singed, blackened with smoke and soot, she flew back to the oak tree and watched the village burn.

After a while, a large dog came though the bushes below, and stopped, growling, when he saw the falcon sitting in the oak. 'Well, Narzia?' he called up to the bird. 'Do you like to see your village burning and your people killed? You were able to save yourself, of course. I saw you fly out of your window, and you took Arni's stone with you. Perhaps none of this would have happened if you'd left it in its golden dish in Arni's House. But you're so set on magic that you wanted it for yourself, didn't you?'

'Hold your tongue, chatterer!' cried the falcon angrily. 'What do you understand of such things? The stone is worth more to me than those few people lying there among the houses!'

'What a selfish, cruel fool you are!' cried the dog. 'What you say only shows you've never understood what the stone means.' And he uttered a rough bark of laughter and then went on, 'I know at least this much of that stone – it brings misfortune to anyone who takes it unlawfully. You didn't have your magic necklace with you when you flew away – I saw that too. It will be roasting in the fire now, and once the house has burnt down, it will never be found. So now you see what the stone has brought on you: you will have to stay in your present shape, a lonely falcon in the air. You've met the same fate to which you condemned me and your other dogs!'

'And you yap like a dog too!' cried the falcon. 'See how far I rise above the likes of you!' Then she took the stone in her beak, spread her wings, and soared high into the sky, until the steppes, the woods and mountains lay far below her like a carpet speckled with grey and green, crinkling and moving slightly here and there. Somewhere between the light and the dark green, a trace of smoke arose, seeming scarcely more than a slight cloudiness, of no importance to the falcon, who flew swiftly north to her nest on the steep and precipitous cliff, lonely and inaccessible, where she carried her treasure to safety.

But the safety, as it had turned out, was a delusion, for all this must have happened before the mouse He-who-prophesies-to-the-falcon had climbed the cliff and taken the stone after all. Had the course of events gone wrong? Or robbed Time of its power? Perhaps there was no Time any more, as there seemed to be no limits set to space, to keep one from being here and many miles away at one and the same moment. He felt confused, like a spectator who has not yet managed to grasp the sense of a play, and yet wants to discover more of that sense, perhaps because, even without knowing it himself, he is seeking a point at which it will turn out that all these things concern himself.

For the time being, however, his feelings still seemed far from involved, and so he fastened on those details which occupied only the mind. For instance, there was that matter of the necklace, which seemed to him so mysterious that he thought it more important than much of the rest. He pictured again that swift transformation when the green-eyed girl had put the necklace around her throat and clasped it in front. How did she manage to return to human form? And above all, where did such magical things come from? Who had the art of making them? He would have liked to know that.

And there sat an incredibly thin, white-haired old man before him, wearing a kind of cassock of blue silk, busy fitting tiny golden links together into a chain. On closer examination, it could be seen that each of these delicate links of filigree was shaped like a falcon in flight, its claws attached to the next bird's wings. This was no ordinary craftsman, as was shown by more than his costly robe. The table where he sat was more like a goldsmith's workbench than anything else, but it was most exquisitely fitted up. It had a smoothly polished surface of black stone, set with squares of bright green; a cloth of black velvet was spread over this table, underneath the work in progress, and in the sunlight that fell through a wide window tiny tools of every kind lay sparkling and shining on the cloth, ready to hand. The room itself seemed to be of a curious shape, until one realized that it had five walls. There were glass cases along the walls, where precious jewels shone, and another glazed cupboard contained every kind of precious stone in its natural form: jagged crystals of violet, sunshine yellow and moss green, some that were clear and transparent as water, uncut emeralds, rubies and sapphires the size of walnuts, chunks of green-veined malachite, milky opals with countless shimmering lights of every shade flickering beneath the pale surface, and all manner of strangely branching tree-like shapes with a smooth and bright red surface.

Then a melodious note, like glass ringing, mingled with the slight clink of the tools; it seemed to proceed from a broad crystal dish standing on a pillar by the door. The old man looked up and said, in a cracked voice, 'Come in. I was expecting you.' And now he had raised his head, it could be clearly seen how frail this goldsmith looked: white, blotched skin was stretched over his cheekbones, and his sharp nose sprang from his face like the beak of a bird.

The door had now opened, and a strikingly tall man entered the room. He wore a scarlet robe that reached to his feet, was of middle age, and seemed to spend much of his time out of doors, for his face above his black beard was tanned brown by the sun. He was followed by a girl who could, at first sight, have been taken for the green-eyed falcon maiden, but when she approached the workbench at the red-robed man's side, and stepped out of the shadows into the sunlight flooding into the room, one saw that their faces were not the same, only similar, although both had the same green eyes.

'Greetings, Master of the Stones,' said the bearded man. 'Have you finished the chain?'

'You must forgive me, Vendikar,' said the old man, 'but no, the chain isn't yet completed; I am old, and my powers are failing. The links are all fitted together, falcon by falcon, but now the clasp must be set to the chain, and that is the hardest part of the work, since the falcon magic that is to serve your daughter will lie hidden in that clasp.'

'Then we won't disturb you any longer,' said the man addressed as Vendikar, turning to go, while his daughter lingered by the workbench, looking at the unfinished necklace.

'Does the chain please you?' asked the Master of the Stones.

'I never saw a lovelier,' said the girl. 'You are a great artist.'

'An old man, whose hands now tremble!' said the Master of the

Stones. 'Will you stay here while I fit the clasp? It is as well if the one who is to wear and use such a jewel puts her own power into it. Will you permit this, Vendikar?'

'You do my daughter great honour,' said Vendikar. With that, he left the room, and the heavy door closed quietly behind him.

'Take a chair and sit beside me, Belenika,' said the old man. 'I would like you near me while I do this work, for I'm afraid my own powers are no longer sufficient.'

'What do you mean?' asked the girl. 'Am I to help you?'

'No, I only want your presence,' said the old man.

Belenika took a stool from the back of the room and sat close to the Master. 'Is that the clasp?' she asked, pointing to a beautifully wrought piece lying beside the chain on the black cloth.

'It is,' said the old man. 'Look carefully at this clasp and tell me what you see.'

'Why, it has the shape of a falcon, like the other links in the chain,' said Belenika, 'but this one is a little bigger.'

'And what else do you see?' asked the Master.

Belenika looked more closely at the bird, which was perfectly imitated, down to every detail of a falcon's plumage, and then said, 'It is sitting on a gauntlet and wearing a hood with a plume of feathers, like a hawk taken out hunting.'

'Good,' said the Master. 'And now I will show you how to undo the chain.' He took the delicate piece off the table, turned the gauntlet slightly to the left on its own axis, and thus dislodged the falcon from its perch. 'If you want to clasp the necklace,' he went on, 'you must push the gauntlet between the two claws – thus – and turn it to the right, and the bird will be sitting firmly in place.' He gave her the clasp, and said, 'Now open it.'

Belenika took the falcon carefully in her fingertips and tried to twist the gauntlet, but she could not do it. 'I can't!' she said, after a while. The Master had been watching, with a smile. 'Excellent!' he said. 'Otherwise the clasp might come undone of itself. Now, press the thumb of the gauntlet slightly.'

Belenika touched the tiny projection with one finger, and now the gauntlet would turn. She laughed like a child who has performed a hard task. 'Is that all the magic?' she asked.

The Master shook his head. 'No,' said he, 'that's just ordinary goldsmith's work. The hardest part is still to come, but I will show you how it works. You know what the purpose of this necklace is?'

Belenika instantly looked grave, and said, 'Yes, my father has discussed it with me. But you must not think that is my only reason for marrying Honi. I do indeed love him, and I like his way of life. So at first, I did not want to undertake this task. It was the Great Magician who brought me to see the importance to Falkinor of knowing what the Raiding Riders do. He has promised me that no harm shall come to the Khan's people.'

'He should not have needed to tell you that,' the Master interrupted. 'You ought to know that Falkinor is a city of peace.'

'You are right,' said Belenika. 'And I also know now that what chiefly interests the Great Magician is to know what becomes of that strange brother of the Khan, the man they call Arni of the Stone, and I shall be happy to bring him such news, if your art will help me to do so.'

'It will,' said the Master. 'How could you fear that one of the Lesser Magicians of Falkinor would ever set his hand to work that would harm others? And this is the first thing you must impress upon your mind: the chain is meant only to serve the Great House of Falkinor, and all that is done for good does serve Falkinor. You must not use it for any other purpose.'

'Do you mean the magic won't work if it's used for other ends, or to do wrong?' asked Belenika.

'No,' said the Master, 'and this is the first and greatest danger I must mention to you. The magic is bound up with the handling of the clasp, and will always work. However, any who use it solely for their own ends, or indeed to harm others, will sooner or later destroy themselves. Think of that now, for the temptation will be greater than you may suppose.'

'I'll remember,' said Belenika. 'But you were going to show me how to release the power in the necklace.'

'Exactly as you fly a falcon,' said the Master. 'You must put the chain around your neck so that the falcons are flying to the left. Then, if you clasp it in front of you, over your breast, and push back the hood of the larger falcon so that its eyes are free, you will become a falcon yourself, one who can bring news to the Great Magician faster than any horseman – and most important, far more secretly.'

'Won't my husband notice, if I'm absent for some days?' asked Belenika, concerned.

'Honi will often be out with the Raiding Riders for long periods of time,' said the Master. 'Moreover, you will be able to fly much faster than an ordinary falcon, although only when your flight is in accordance with your service to the Great House of Falkinor. Should you use the chain for your own purposes, you will be no more than any common falcon after prey.'

Then, seeing Belenika try to move the falcon's hood, he put out his hand to stop her, and said, 'Wait! Here, too, one must make sure no such thing can happen by accident. You must press the plume of feathers on the hood lightly together with your fingertips. There, you see! And now it will move.'

'You've thought it out most carefully,' said Belenika. 'All I need to know now is how to return to my human form.'

'That's simple,' said the Master. 'You have only to put your falcon's head through the chain, this time so that the golden falcons are flying to the right, and then you will be Belenika again. But don't forget, the first thing you must then do is pull the hood back over the falcon's head! And most important of all, you must make sure that the chain doesn't go astray while you are away. You will be given a maidservant to accompany you, who knows about these matters, and will take care of it.'

'What happens if the chain does get lost while I'm away?' asked Belenika.

'That is the second risk you run,' said the Master. 'You would have to remain in the shape of a falcon.'

'And suppose I find it later?' asked Belenika. 'Surely I could become a woman again then?'

'That depends how long you have been a falcon,' said the Master, 'for this is the third risk, and one I cannot spare you. Although you could live in falcon's shape as long as you would have lived as a human woman, yet Belenika's own life will pass during that time as fast as the life of a falcon. The falcon will feel nothing of it, but just a single year spent in that shape would make you many years older once you returned to your own body. So be sure that your flights to Falkinor are made as fast as possible. Even those few days will cause you to age more quickly, but that is the price to be paid for the freedom of a falcon in the air.'

'It must be wonderful to fly over the steppes like a bird!' cried Belenika. 'I will happily give a part of my life for that!'

The Master looked at her, smiling. 'It seems to you easy to give a few weeks away!' he said. 'I began counting my own days long ago. But now I have one last thing to say. I have told you of the danger of this chain, so that you can now decide whether you will wear it. You may still step back from the task – and yet follow your Honi to the tents of the Raiding Riders!' he added, with a smile. Then he grew grave again, and continued, 'But if you are ready to serve the Great House of Falkinor in this way, you will forget all the warnings I have given you here, and do only what you think good and right. Do you feel capable of that?'

Belenika thought for a while, and then she raised her head and said, 'Yes, I'll undertake the task. I have at least learnt, in my short life, that one must not seek one's own good, but think what good or ill one's actions cause others.'

'I expected no other answer from Vendikar's daughter,' said the Master. 'Now, to work!' He took the clasp from Belenika's hand, unfastened its two parts, and fitted them to the ends of the chain. 'And now you must help me,' he said, 'for I am afraid it may be beyond my powers to force my will into that golden bird alone.'

He asked the girl to stand up, and himself rose with difficulty from the chair in which he sat working. Now he turned the falcon so that it was sitting on the gauntlet again, and the chain was clasped, and asked Belenika to put both hands around the clasp, while he placed his thin, skilful fingers around her hands.

'What do I do now?' asked Belenika.

'Nothing at all,' said the Master. 'But let me use your will, and the strength of your youth, and say no more for the moment.'

They stood side by side for a while, and nothing of note seemed to be happening: they were only a young girl and an old man with their intertwined hands around a golden chain, no more. But then a gradual transformation seemed to occur, barely perceptible at first, but quickly becoming more noticeable, so that soon it could not be overlooked. The old man's pale, emaciated face took on a pink tinge, his features became firmer, and at the same time his figure seemed to straighten and grow, as if decades of his life were visibly dropping away, while the colour drained from the girl's cheeks, until in the end she looked as if her frail figure were held upright only by the Master's strength. And then the Master began to speak, in a clear, strong voice:

> *Hear the spell,*
> *Falkinor's falcon:*
> *Who frees you shall*
> *in your likeness dwell.*
> *If used for good,*
> *all shall be well;*

> *if used for evil,*
> *ill I foretell.*

He had spoken these words so loudly that they set the crystal dish by the door quivering, and its humming note filled the room for some time. Only when that note died away did the Master loosen his hands from Belenika's. At that moment, all the strength went out of his body, his skin looked as pale and blotched as before, his cheeks fell in, he staggered, and seemed about to fall. Belenika was only just in time to catch him in her arms. She would have helped him into his chair, but he shook his head, saying in a voice that was already failing, 'No – hold me fast, Belenika, and let me die on my feet. It is good to be held in a girl's arms once more at such a moment.' And then his head dropped forward and his body slackened. When at last Belenika laid him back in his chair, his eyes were dim in death.

Obviously the making of such magical items was a risky business. That old Master of the Stones had paid with his life, anyway, and the handling of them seemed fraught with further dangers for the user. This struck him as hard to understand. How could one who wished to do good also allow the possibility of evil? Wasn't he incurring part of the blame for whatever wrong was done later with the aid of his arts? He remembered what that falcon maiden who was called Narzia had done to others. She had made use of the falcon ring as well as the necklace for her purposes, but by now he felt sure that the ring, similarly, contained both curse and blessing within its circle, and this was known even to the small and weak, like that young mouse He-who-prophesies-to-the-falcon.

How had the girl Narzia come by the necklace in the first place? Perhaps she's Belenika's daughter, he thought, and it did not seem at all strange to be witnessing, almost simultaneously, events which must really lie many years apart. He was far more concerned with the question of whether Narzia knew what dangers the misuse of such magic entailed. The longer he thought about it, however, the more clearly he realized that this was not what mattered in the long run, and at the same time he saw why it had been necessary for Belenika to forget all the Master's warnings. If a man shrank from doing wrong only because he knew it would mean his own ruin, what was that worth? He would do good not for its own sake, but merely from self-interest. And now he suddenly understood the old Master's wisdom.

He had not wished to enslave Belenika by forcing her to act rightly; instead, he gave her freedom to make her own decision as to how she would use the power of the magic necklace. The Master seemed to have thought very highly of her, to trust her so much. Or was he, too, subject to some law which did not let him limit another human being's freedom in such a way? But then he would have been acting under some kind of compulsion himself, and that did not seem to fit with his nature. The longer he thought about it, the more probable it seemed that the Lesser Magician had been unable to do other than believe well of all.

And had Belenika fulfilled his hopes? This question so occupied his mind that he instantly saw a falcon flying north, high above the steppes. The bird went swift as an arrow over the steel-blue evening sky, and there could be no doubt it was making for a definite goal, a place now visible in the distance of the steppes, which lay red in the light of the setting sun: a collection of dark tents, with countless horses grazing in a large paddock nearby. The falcon dropped lower, and flew over a group of Riders. One man looked up and followed its flight with his eyes. Then he spurred on his horse and rode towards the camp, followed by the others. Meanwhile, the falcon was flying low above the ground, entered the long shadows cast by the first tent, as if hiding from curious eyes, and flew on between the nearby tents until it reached one that was particularly large and richly furnished. It soared up again once more, on that side of the tent that lay in shadow, and slipped in through a small opening in the roof.

He was looking down from above at a small bedroom partitioned off with hanging rugs, where a maidservant sat working at a piece of embroidery. When she heard the fluttering of the falcon's wings over the tent, she looked up, laid down her sewing without any particular surprise, and picked up a silken cloth that was spread on the floor in the middle of the room. The golden chain lay under it, clasped in a circle. When the falcon flew in, the maidservant raised the chain slightly on one side, the falcon slipped its slender head beneath the links, and next moment a woman stood there instead, obviously Belenika, although she seemed considerably older than that girl who had sat beside the Master of the Stones at his work. Her fingers went to the clasp, she undid the necklace, and put it away in a little carved casket, which she locked carefully. She hung the key on a ribbon around her neck, hiding it beneath her dress. Then she turned to the maidservant, saying,

'Thank you for keeping watch for me as usual. You can go now – I shan't be needing you again today.'

The maidservant bowed in silence and left the room through an opening between the hangings. Belenika sat on a cushion at the side of the room, bent her head, and seemed to be thinking. There was a deep line between her brows, such as one sees in someone pondering a difficult question upon which much depends. She sat there for some time, while the little light that fell in through the opening in the roof of the tent faded. Then the hangings moved aside, and a girl came in. It was so dark in the tent now that her face could not be seen.

'So there you are, Mother,' said the girl. 'I never noticed you come back. Shall I bring you a light?'

'Yes, do,' said Belenika.

The girl put out her hand, unhooked an oil lamp from the chain by which it hung from the top of a tent-pole, and left the room. She soon came back with the lighted lamp and hung it in its place again. As she was busy about the lamp, its light fell on her features, and he saw that this was Narzia. She sat down beside her mother and looked hard at her face. 'It's strange,' she said, 'I came here looking for you just now, but there was no one in the place but your maid. And then I stayed in the tent to wait for you to return, but you didn't come back. And now here you are after all.'

'Perhaps you weren't paying attention,' said Belenika.

'Oh, but I was,' said Narzia. 'And now I think I know what way you slipped in.'

'Indeed?' said Belenika, and the deep line marked her forehead again.

'Yes,' said Narzia, eagerly. 'Well, I know you learned all kinds of magic arts at home in Falkinor. And this isn't the first time I've missed you, and then found you had suddenly appeared in this room somehow or other. Once, when I came in on such an occasion, you were busy putting a chain away in the little casket over there with your things. I managed to get a sight of the chain, and it was all made of little golden falcons. So then I remembered I'd seen a falcon flying around the tent another time when I was looking for you, and next moment here you were, with your maid. And now I think you're able to leave the camp in the shape of a falcon, with the help of this chain, and fly high in the air.'

Belenika let out a deep breath, and then said, 'Supposing that were so, then it would be better if you had seen nothing, Narzia. It is

dangerous to know such things, and even more dangerous to talk
about them. You had better keep such suppositions to yourself in
future. Don't mention them even to me.'

'Oh, Mother!' said Narzia. 'You can be sure I won't mention them
to anyone but you. But since I suspected what you did, I've kept
thinking how wonderful it must be to hover like a falcon, high among
the clouds, and see the steppes down below like a great carpet going on
and on all around. Won't you let me know that wonderful feeling
myself, just once? There's nothing in the world I want more!'

'No, I will not!' said Belenika, with unexpected brusqueness. 'You
don't know what you are talking about. The ideas you've taken into
your head give me quite enough to worry about, and by that I mean
especially the whole notion you have of such things. I won't deny that
they are possible, but you should know that magical objects of that
kind aren't made to give other people pleasure. They are not toys, and
it is a grave responsibility to have such an object entrusted to one.
Forget the whole thing, if you please! I never want to hear another
word about it!'

It was clear, however, that Narzia would be quite unable to forget
the matter. Her brow now showed the same deep line as her mother's,
and the two of them sat there in silence for a while. Then Belenika put
her hand on the girl's arm, but Narzia did not respond to the gesture
at all. And then a man's voice was heard behind the hanging rugs,
calling loudly and imperiously for Belenika, who rose, pushed back the
hangings, and left the bedroom.

'Oh, so there you are,' said the tall and rather portly man whom she
met in the next room. 'I must talk to you.' He stood in the darkness of
the tent, lit only dimly by a few oil lamps, and shook his head impatiently, so that the braids at his temples flew backwards. It was plain
that he had only just returned from a ride of some length, for his
leather clothing was grey with the dust of the steppes.

'You've been away many days, Honi,' said Belenika. 'Won't you
change your clothes first, and eat supper with me, and then we can
talk at our ease?' She was about to give orders to two maids busy with
something in a corner, but Honi stopped her, brusquely waving the
servants out of the tent. 'First I must ask you a question,' he said, as
soon as they were alone. 'Do you secretly keep a falcon – a hawk
trained for hunting?'

'What could make you think of that?' said Belenika.

'I didn't,' said Honi. 'The Khan's been asking; he saw such a falcon fly, and thought it came out of our tent. When he told me so I laughed, for surely I'd have noticed! But this evening, as we rode back to the camp, I saw a falcon myself. It was flying fast towards the camp, and disappeared among the tents, though I couldn't see just where it went. And the Khan, riding ahead of me, saw the same bird too. Shall I tell you what he thinks? It's his opinion that you keep this falcon to send secret messages to Falkinor. Are you a traitor to us, Belenika?'

'No,' said Belenika at once, 'I am not, whatever the Khan may think of me.'

'Good,' said Honi. 'I believe you. All the same, I suspect you learned secret arts of which I know nothing from your people at home.'

Belenika was going to interrupt him, but he stopped her with a gesture. 'I don't want to know about them, either,' he went on. 'Or not yet, anyway. But there's one more thing I have to tell you: the Khan will be keeping an eye on you and our tent in future. Be very careful in all you do! Will you promise me that?'

'I won't venture lightly into danger,' said Belenika. 'Is that all you wanted to say to me?'

'Not quite,' said Honi, 'but we can discuss the rest at more leisure.' He sat down on a cushioned bench by the side of the tent, and asked Belenika to sit beside him. 'Since Arni was shot from his saddle by the Great Roarer's men, I've been thinking about him a good deal,' he began.

'So have I,' said Belenika. 'I liked him better than his brother.'

'I know that,' said Honi. 'You always got on well with him; that's why I'm taking you into my confidence in this affair. There's a good deal of what Arni said and did that I didn't understand myself. But since he died, I've seen more and more clearly what an influence he had on the Khan and the horde. The men disagree more often now, and instead of settling their disputes Hunli eggs them on, as if it gave him pleasure to see them at odds. And once he no longer finds the game amusing, he punishes the gamecocks themselves with a cruelty that many of us now find unendurable. Over these last few weeks, I've been discussing this with certain men whom I can trust, and they are of my opinion.'

'If you have it in mind to take the dignity of Khan from Hunli, you will have to kill him,' said Belenika, 'for there's no other way he will give up his title.' It was plain to see that she did not like the idea at all, but Honi raised a pacifying hand, and said, 'No need for you to fear that. But we are thinking of leaving the horde, together with our families, and taking Arni as our pattern. Arni was always at odds with himself, living among us, because it went against the grain with him to attack or kill other folk for the sake of booty. Well, we mean to see if we can't live at peace with our neighbours.'

Belenika had been listening intently, and now she thought for a while. Then she said, 'You seem to have planned it all out in detail, and what you say sounds attractive. None the less, I doubt if it would be acting in Arni's spirit to destroy the unity of the horde. He, for one, stayed with them and at his brother's side, despite everything, and you have just said yourself that this was not without its advantages for the Raiding Riders. If you are united, then you should continue Arni's work here instead of leaving. Carry out your present plans, and there'll be hostility between you and the horde sooner or later. Would Arni have wanted that?'

Honi listened reluctantly to Belenika's objections, shaking his head, and then said, 'Who knows what Arni really wanted? Arni's dead, and we must seek our own way. Anyway, it's all as good as decided. I can't serve this Khan any longer.'

'Oh, so that's it?' said Belenika, with a touch of mockery as she looked into Honi's eyes. 'And I expect you've discussed who's to lead you in future? No doubt the others have already chosen you as their new Khan?'

'What can you mean?' protested Honi, awkwardly, but when his wife continued looking at him, he added, as if by the way, 'Well, a few of the men did hint at something of the kind, but what I said was, we shouldn't discuss such matters just yet.'

'Be that as it may,' said Belenika, 'you will be lord of those who wish to follow Arni, without knowing exactly what it was he really had in mind.'

Honi flared up. 'I've just told you –' he began, but stopped short at a glance from his wife, and then said, quietly, 'Can't you see how the task attracts me?'

'Yes, indeed,' said Belenika. 'I see that very well. Only I don't know if it's the right way to act, for I'm sure Arni wouldn't have done it.'

'Well, too late to talk about that now,' said Honi. 'I'm sorry our conversation has taken this turn. I really meant it to go another way, and mention something that occurred to me when the Khan spoke to me today about the falcon he suspects you keep.'

'What has your plan to do with that?' asked Belenika, surprised.

Honi looked at the floor in front of him for a while, as if seeking the right words for what he wanted to say. Then he said, 'If what you are up to in secret is what I think it is, then you could do me a great service. I don't know for sure how many will follow us away from the tents, but it will certainly be only a part of the horde. Well, I thought to myself it could be very useful to have the Great Magician of Falkinor on our side. I feel he would surely approve of our plans. It would merely be a matter of letting him know, and asking him to support us. Could you do that?'

'So you are putting me to the service of your cause,' said Belenika, and when Honi continued looking at her expectantly, she added, 'The question is not if I could, but if I should.'

'When you talk like that,' said Honi angrily, 'I begin to fear that the Khan's suspicions were right after all. You're my wife. Is there any other duty you set above your duty to me?'

'You are forcing me to a decision I would rather not make,' said Belenika. 'But if you ask me in that way, then I have no choice but to stand by you.' She rose, and went towards her own room, but Honi followed her and held her back. 'It will keep until morning,' he said. 'I've been away a long time, and was looking forward to lying with you tonight.'

At this Belenika smiled for the first time since their conversation began. 'Until dawn, then,' she said, 'and then you'll have to do without me for a while. Come!'

He saw the two of them, obviously at one in this matter at least, go into a nearby part of the tent, and wondered if Belenika had been wise to yield to this man Honi, who wanted to use her for his own ends. On the other hand, it seemed to him that from all he had learnt, the magicians of Falkinor would have no objection to Honi's plans. They were obviously a peace-loving people, although he could not yet understand the purpose behind their strange enchantments. He tried to recall what had happened in the room where the Master of the Stones worked, those events preceding the old man's sudden death. The Master had spoken of all kinds of dangers bound up with the use of the falcon necklace, and he wondered if Belenika were not upon the point of venturing into one such danger without knowing it. For if what the old man had then said was right, she had forgotten his warnings at the moment of declaring herself willing to assume the falcon magic. However, he was unable to tell whether she might have found a way, in her own mind, to see Honi's errand as compatible with her service to the Great House of Falkinor, or if she was going to perform it solely for love of her husband. Was that self-interest? After all, if Honi's plans came to fruition, she would be wife of the chieftain of these people, and that might be an alluring prospect. Though her original resistance had shown clearly enough that she was reluctant to do what Honi asked of her – but that, again, could only lead him to conclude that the flight she was obviously going to undertake was hard to reconcile with the part she played as the Great Magician's messenger. However one looked at the matter, it was not clear, and danger often lurks in lack of clarity, as was presently to be seen, for the sky above the camp was already turning pale, and soon afterwards a falcon rose from the top of one of the tents and began flying south. At that same moment a Rider galloped out of the shadow of the tents and tried to catch up with the falcon, which was only slowly gaining height, attempting in vain to get out of bowshot of its pursuer, for the Rider had a bow in his hand, and galloping at full stretch he put an arrow to its string. As soon as he was level with the falcon he abruptly reined in his horse, and loosed the arrow. It struck the falcon's shoulder and then fell tumbling to the ground, while the fluttering, wounded bird lost height at first before regaining control of itself. Beating its wings laboriously, it flew low over the grey grass of the steppes, describing a wide arc around the camp, and then slipped in among the tents on the opposite side, using the last of its strength to soar up to the opening in the roof of the tent through which it had only just emerged. While the bird struggled to keep its balance up among the tops of the tent-poles, Honi came out of the tent and walked away down the alley that ran through the camp.

Infinitely far below, the maidservant crouched before the outspread cloth on the rug that covered the floor. This time she looked up in alarm when she heard the flutter of wings above the tent. The falcon tumbled in, and was scarcely able to stop falling before it struck the ground. The maidservant uttered a muffled cry when she saw the blood-stained plumage. She swept the cloth aside, and put the chain round the falcon's neck herself, for it was obvious that the bird was no longer in any state to complete the enchantment by itself. And then Belenika lay there on the floor instead of the falcon. Her face was white and drawn with pain, and a bright red spot of blood began to spread on her linen dress, over the left breast, rapidly growing larger. The maidservant carefully undid the fastenings of the dress and stripped it off her mistress's shoulder. Then she saw the deep wound made by the arrow, with blood welling from it in a fast-pulsating rhythm.

As the maidservant snatched linen out of a chest and pressed it to the wound to stop the bleeding, Belenika opened her eyes and tried to speak, but only a gush of blood came from her mouth as she coughed convulsively. The maidservant took her beneath the shoulders, propped her up, and tried to wipe the blood from her face. However, Belenika pushed her hand away and said, with difficulty, 'The chain – lock it up!'

Obviously the maidservant knew how to handle the clasp, for she pushed the falcon's hood over its eyes, undid the necklace easily, and was going to lay it aside, but Belenika whispered once more, urgently, 'Lock it up!'

Then the maidservant laid Belenika back on the cushioned bench by the wall of the tent, put pillows under her head and shoulders, and took out the casket. She dropped the necklace into it, locked it with the key that hung around Belenika's neck, and then put the casket away again. As she turned back to tend her mistress's wound, Belenika shook her head, saying quietly, 'Let that be; no point in it. The casket – make sure – lay it in my grave! Promise me!'

The maidservant put her right hand on her heart and bowed low; perhaps that was her way of giving a promise. Was she dumb? He suspected she was, for apart from that cry of horror no sound had escaped her lips during all this time. She must know that there was no helping her mistress now, for she stayed there on the floor beside the bench where she lay, pressing the wad of linen to the wound and pushing back the tangled hair from Belenika's face.

Then quick footsteps were heard in the outer room of the tent, the hangings were pushed aside, and Honi strode in. 'The Khan has wounded your falcon with an arrow!' he cried, and only then did he see Belenika lying on the bench by the wall, saw her face, white as death, the blood on her lips, and the linen soaked with blood at her breast. He stood there in the middle of the room, staring down on her. 'But how did you . . .?' he stammered, and then the expression of his face showed his sudden understanding. He dropped on his knee beside his wife, saying tonelessly, 'You were the falcon yourself, Belenika.'

Belenika's green eyes looked at him, and she whispered, 'Did you really not know, Honi?'

Then that gasping cough shook her again. When the maidservant had wiped the blood from her mouth and chin, Belenika said, falteringly, 'It was my fault. I flew against my better judgement – a bad omen for your plan – stay with the horde –' These last words were barely audible. Her head fell back on the pillows, and she drew her last breath.

When Honi saw that she was dead, he cried out as if the arrow had struck himself. Leaping up, he roared, 'You shall pay for this, Khan Hunli! May you meet with misfortune, may your arrow never find its mark and your horse refuse to carry you! May you come off the loser in all your undertakings!'

Alarmed by this outburst of wrath, the maidservant had retreated to the wall of the tent. When Honi fell silent, standing there with his arms hanging helplessly, staring at his dead wife, she took the casket, laid it on Belenika's breast, and tried to tell Honi something by means of gestures. As he looked at her, uncomprehendingly, the hangings moved and Narzia came in.

'Why are you shouting so?' she asked. 'What's happened?' And then she saw her mother's bloodstained corpse. Her face instantly turned as white as the face of the dead. 'Who did this?' she whispered, and when her father still stood there, rooted to the spot, and did not answer, she took his arm and repeated her question. Then Honi noticed his daughter at last, looked at her and said tonelessly, 'The Khan shot a falcon this morning.'

Narzia looked at her dead mother, and asked, 'Did he know whom his arrow would strike?'

Honi shrugged his shoulders. 'I think he thought your mother kept a falcon to send secret messages to Falkinor,' he said. Then he noticed that the maidservant was still trying to tell him something to do with the casket. 'Do you know what the dumb woman wants?' he asked his daughter.

Narzia went over to the maidservant and looked closely at the eloquent movement of her hands as they laid the casket again and again on her dead mistress's breast, and then mimed the heaping of something over her corpse. 'I believe I know what she's asking you,' said Narzia. 'She wants you to bury this casket with my mother in her grave.'

'Do you understand the meaning of that?' asked Honi. 'What kind of a casket is it?'

Instead of replying, Narzia said to the maidservant, 'Go now and prepare everything in the next room to wash my mother's body and wrap her in a shroud. Don't come back until I call you!'

Reluctantly, the maidservant laid the casket back on the dead woman's breast, folded Belenika's hands over it, bowed to her, and went out. As soon as the hangings were still again behind her, Narzia turned to her father. 'This casket contains the secret of the falcon's flight,' she said. 'Obviously they told the dumb woman in Falkinor never to let it fall into strange hands. That's why she wants it buried with my mother.'

'Then so it shall be,' said Honi, with suppressed rage. 'This magic has done enough harm already.'

'Not the magic,' said Narzia, 'but the man who shot the arrow.'

'May he be accursed!' said Honi. 'I will make very sure he does not forget this deed. He shall meet with all misfortune, and what's more –' Here he stopped short, and looked his daughter in the eye. 'I trust you,' he went on, 'and I don't need, I imagine, to ask you to keep silent about what I tell you now: it's already decided that he will lose a great part of the horde anyway, since I am going to rise against him and ride away with all who will follow me.'

Narzia looked at the casket and said, after a while, 'If that is to be so, then it could be useful to you to have a falcon in your own service, to carry secret news.'

'What do you mean?' asked Honi, but following the glance of her eyes, still bent on the casket, he knew. 'Yourself?' he said. 'No! I don't want to lose you too.' And when Narzia tried further persuasion, he made a curiously vague gesture, which seemed more undecided than final, and said, 'Not another word on the subject! I am going out to the tents now to make it known that my wife has died suddenly of a fever – no more.'

When he had left the room, Narzia stood there for some time listening to his footsteps. As soon as she could be sure he was no longer in the tent, she stepped rapidly up to the bench where the dead woman lay, took the casket from her hands, and looked for the key under her bloodstained dress, her fingers flying. Her hands trembled so much that she could scarcely get the key into the lock, and it was almost as if that lifeless little object were reluctant to obey one not authorized to use it. But at last it slipped into the lock, and Narzia opened the casket, took out the falcon necklace and slipped it into the pocket of her skirt. Then she closed the casket again and left everything just as it had been before. 'Now let everyone think the magic lies six feet underground,' she said softly. 'But I will fly as a falcon on my own account.'

She rose, glanced once more at the dead woman, and then called in the maidservant.

*

Had the young mouse known of these events? It seemed to him most unlikely. Perhaps it was simply the case that small, weak creatures sensed the risks of such magical things, while anyone who used them for selfish ends was so stupefied by his own greed for power that he could no longer pick up the scent of danger. He-who-prophesies-to-the-falcon evidently had a right to that name.

A mouse was, in fact, just running along the side of the basin into which the spring gushed, and among the roots of the sycamore he met another mouse, rather a fat one, sitting there and nibbling at a hazelnut.

The fat mouse looked up from his meal and inquired, 'Still asleep, is he?'

'Don't know if you can call it sleeping,' said the other mouse. 'But there he still stands on his shaggy goat's legs, and never moves. Moss is starting to grow on his shoulders, the way it grows on a boulder. And yet whenever I look at him, I get the feeling he might climb down any moment and bathe his hooves in this pool. I tell you what: he may seem to be stone all the way through, but somehow or other I feel he's alive all the same.'

'Must be a funny sort of life,' said the fat mouse. 'Just standing there, rooted to the spot. Maybe you're only imagining it, so as not to get bored with all this waiting. If you ask me, we might just as well scurry around a bit and see if we can't find something a bit better than these dried-up nuts. He isn't about to run away from us, not him up there!'

'No,' said the other mouse. 'We're on duty! We've been given the job of keeping watch here until we're either relieved or the goat-legged one comes to life again, and if he does we're to tell him his stone's been found. I'd never forgive myself if I missed that moment.'

The fat mouse threw the empty nutshell away and shook his head dubiously. 'Ever since one of us went talking to that snake, and another of us tackling a falcon,' he remarked, 'we all suddenly act as if we mice could do anything! Personally, I'd as soon we didn't go showing off so! All it does is make the big, strong folk notice us, because they think that sort of thing's amusing, and if you've no more to show for yourself than a proud name you're liable to come to a swift and sticky end. Why, they say *he* was given big names once – him up there, I mean – and what's become of him now? Just a speechless statue, with the birds sitting on him and leaving their droppings about the place.'

'Never mind them!' said the other mouse.'The next rain will wash it all off his shoulders again. Who can harm a stone? You know, when I see him standing there, holding that strange stick, looking as if he'd set it to the ground any minute and walk off somewhere, he strikes me as somebody with plenty still to hope for ahead of him. No, he didn't come into the world to do nothing but crack hazelnuts, so I'm standing by him, and whenever it's my turn to be on duty I'm waiting right here till the day he comes to life again.'

'You're crazy,' said the fat mouse, starting on another nut.

'Life's crazy,' said the other mouse, 'and I like it that way. If you haven't happened to notice, why, you're missing the best of it all.' And then he settled among the sycamore roots and looked up at the branches where the yellowish green clusters of flowers were just unfolding, surrounded by thousands of wild bees, fruit-flies, and tiny blue butterflies.

Who were the mice talking about? They sounded as if he were there in front of them. And some time or other, there had been a mouse here before, with a message to do with a stone, and a falcon such as the bird sometimes to be seen circling in the sky, high above the crown of the sycamore tree.

As he wondered, he heard that bird fluting again, yet now he did begin to doubt if it was only a bird. The melody coming up from the valley was a tune that was both sad and full of hope, with the sweet tones of a flute echoing far and wide, silencing the birdsong, and it seemed to be coming closer and closer. Then the line of the tune died away, and a woman's voice began singing the same melody, a voice that was so clear and distinct he could make out every word.

> *He lives in the wood,*
> *don't know who.*
> *He lives in the wood,*
> *his skin is of stone,*
> *his mouth hard as bone,*
> *cold as death, you would*
> *say if you knew*
> *don't know who.*

Listening to the song, he tried to grasp the sense of it. The last line, with its expectant upward beat, sounded as if the singer had by no means given up hope of discovering the identity of this dweller in the wood, with his skin of stone, but was intent upon discovering the same person whom the mice had been discussing. He would have liked to see the singer who knew such sweet tunes, and as by now he was getting quite used to going instantly to the object of his thoughts, as an onlooker witnessing all kinds of incidents in which he was unable to participate himself, he directed his attention to that broad valley from which the voice had risen to him. But this time, no images would come. Although the sun shone in a cloudless spring sky, there seemed to be a milky mist over the valley floor, and his thoughts could not penetrate it. He tried as hard as he could, but the land beyond the birches and alders, now just putting out their first leaves, was beyond his reach, inaccessible to him, although it still seemed so close that you could hear a girl singing there.

Only when the birds in the trees and bushes around began to pipe and twitter again did he realize that the voice could no longer be heard. He felt suddenly abandoned, as if someone had just been there with him, and now was gone. However, the song that the voice had sung was still present, and seemed to him as familiar as if he had always known it. It aroused in his mind the idea of a pair of eyes, strange eyes, of a colour hard to describe; there was blue in them, but a bright shimmer of green as well, and down in their depths a dark violet that sometimes seemed near and then was infinitely far away. A face went with these eyes, a face which seemed young, but was framed in white hair, and the woman was standing right in front of him and smiling.

'But I'm not the one you are seeking,' she said. 'It's just that we all have the same eyes, you know!'

So whom was he seeking, he wondered. Was he in search of anything at all? Wasn't he merely a watcher, observing things and happenings that had nothing to do with him? But this time, he felt, they were in some way to do with him, and it made no difference that the face had suddenly become an old woman's. The eyes were still the same, and it all depended on those eyes.

'What do you want here, my boy?' asked the old woman. 'Aren't you the present bearer of my eye-stone? Come, sit at my table and be my guest!'

Only now was he aware that he stood inside a room. The walls were made of roughly hewn logs, like those of a simple log cabin, but the furnishings showed that this was the home of someone who united a love of beauty with appreciation of the practical. He saw a handsome wall cupboard and a big chest, and smelled the fragrance of herbs and dried fruits. And then he was sitting at the large, round table, whose thick top of sycamore wood had been scoured so often that the dark knots stood out as round protuberances.

The old woman brought him white sheep's milk cheese and flat cakes of bread on a wooden board, poured white wine from a brown earthenware jug into two goblets, and then sat down with him and told him to help himself. Later, he could not have said just how it was that he had sat at Urla's table, and eaten and drunk with her, but even afterwards he could still taste the sharp flavour of the cheese on his tongue, mingling agreeably with the tart, earthy wine, and he remembered that the bread was seasoned with caraway, fennel and coriander.

Urla seemed to know exactly when a guest had eaten enough, for when he had had all he wanted she did not press him to take more, but only poured him some wine. Then she said, 'Well, you have found your way to me from very far away, young man. Why were you looking for me?'

'Was I?' he asked. 'I was looking for a girl who sang down in the valley, but I couldn't find her. I found a pair of eyes instead, eyes like yours, but at first it didn't seem to be an old woman looking at me with those eyes.'

At that, Urla laughed, clear laughter like a girl's, and drank a sip of wine. 'No, I didn't think you were after an old woman,' she said. 'However, sometimes one reaches older kinsfolk by such ways. And now I suppose you're disappointed?'

He looked around the room that surrounded him protectively, and then gazed into the old woman's strangely familiar eyes, and said, 'No, indeed I am not. I feel at home with you.'

'Then rest, and tell me how things are with you,' said Urla.

'How things are with me?' he said, at a loss. 'I don't know. I see the sycamore, just coming into flower again, and I hear the splashing of the spring from which the birds drink. And sometimes the mice, too. They're always there, waiting for something, talking about strange things, particularly someone with goat's legs who has obviously lost a stone; they think a great deal of this stone. A falcon who is really a girl called Narzia got the stone from him by cunning, and one of the mice managed to take it away from this falcon again and get it to safety. I saw that happen myself. This mouse is now called He-who-prophesies-to-the-falcon, because he foretold that she would come to a bad end.'

'Excellent!' said Urla. 'I always thought highly of mice. But what about this goat-legged person of whom the mice talk?'

'They say he has turned to stone,' he said, 'and they're waiting for him to come back to life. But there's one of the mice, a fat one who must always be nibbling something, who thinks he's turned to stone for ever.'

'Nonsense!' said Urla. 'Never listen to those who have nothing better to think of than filling their bellies! Food is a good and important thing, at the right time and with the right people, but it's far from all in life. And have you ever seen him, this goat-legged one whom the mice discuss?'

'No,' he said, 'and that's the strange part of it. They speak as if he were there before them, yet I can't see him anywhere.'

'That's surprising, to be sure,' said Urla. 'What else do you know about the goat-legged one?'

'Only what the mice say,' he replied. 'That he once bore a great name, but now he can't even keep the birds from making a mess all over him. He seems to have lost his luck with the stone the falcon stole from him. Perhaps he counted on his great name too much. But plainly the mice are still his friends, and they are keeping his stone for him now.'

'Clever creatures, mice,' said Urla. 'Do you know where he got the stone himself?'

'From all I've heard so far, a certain Arni must once have had this stone before the goat-legged one. But first it belonged to an old woman.'

'You have learnt to listen very well,' said Urla. 'Who would this old woman have been?'

And now all he saw were her eyes, and suddenly he knew that the stone looked exactly like them, a glowing play of colours shining from within, blue, green and violet. 'It was you!' he said. 'Are you angry with the goat-legged one for losing the stone?'

'If I were, would I have invited him to my table?' said Urla. 'You speak of him as if he were a stranger. Didn't you hear me greet you as the bearer of my eye-stone?'

'Yes,' he said, 'but I thought you mistook me for someone else.'

Then the old woman took him in her arms and said, 'Oh, my boy, will you always refuse to be what you are? Look at yourself for once!'

Can one do that, he wondered in surprise, and looked down on a stony shape from whose moss-grown shoulders two rounded long things grew, hanging down to a shaggy, fissured region that was borne on two columns bent backwards, with cloven shapes at the ends of them. Cushions of moss surrounded the place where these supports grew from the rock beneath, and the whole figure was reflected in ripples in the moving water of the little pool where the mice used to drink. For a few moments the shining surface showed him the image of the figure's head, a face that was familiar to him, and that he now knew for his own. And then the stony slopes and protuberances came together into the shape of the goat-legged faun standing there with the mice waiting for him to come back to life. So that is myself, he thought; that is what I look like: a lump of stone on clumsy legs. Am I asleep, then? The mice say so, but I heard them say it, and even saw them in their home. He did not quite understand how he could stand above this spring, and yet witness events that took place somewhere beyond the alder and birch trees, and even, apparently, at a considerable distance from this spot. He had felt he was only a watcher, uninvolved, but now he realized that these events did indeed concern him, if he was the goat-legged one people were always mentioning. It was a strange feeling to be someone who existed, someone about whom he knew, pleasant and at the same time disturbing in that he didn't know just how he was involved in all these happenings.

He wondered if he would ever be able to find out, and as he wondered he came into a room that instantly seemed familiar to him. A large, long table stood in the middle of it, as if a number of guests were sometimes entertained here. All kinds of precious silver vessels stood on the high shelves along the walls: a little showy, he thought, but very impressive, and there was a fine, carved chest as long as a coffin by the wall. A rug woven of glowing colours was cast over it, yet he still had the impression of a coffin, as if a corpse would be found lying in the chest if anyone opened the lid. He saw that picture before him, the lid flung back and the corpse's legs hanging out, but when he tried to see the murdered man's face, the chest was closed and covered and standing by the wall again, and he had no time to puzzle out this curious phenomenon, for a door opened at one side of the room and Honi came in, followed by his green-eyed daughter. 'If he comes back this time, you will have to marry him,' said Honi. 'I hope you realize that.'

Honi seemed a little stouter than he remembered, and he no longer wore his hair in braids, but had cut it short above his ears. Narzia looked at him with raised eyebrows and shrugged her shoulders.

'Have you any objection?' she asked.

'None at all,' said her father. 'He has done very well in every way, and will be able to do us much more service with his flute. I merely had the impression you were in no great hurry to be married.'

'Oh?' said Narzia. 'Did you? Well, I shall be able to make up my mind when he comes back.'

'Make it up to what?' asked Honi.

'That we shall see,' said Narzia. 'For the time being, he's riding to Falkinor, and first we have to discover if he can perform his task.' She said this as if she doubted whether whoever they were discussing was likely to succeed.

'You ought not to underestimate that young man,' said Honi. 'I'll admit, I didn't expect much of him at the start. Who was he? A green youth, with a couple of gifts that fell into his lap without much need for any effort on his part. Arni can hardly have been in his right mind when he gave him the stone, and he simply inherited the flute from his grandfather. But one must say this for him: he can play it in a way that will bring him considerable power. You had better be careful, Narzia! He may come to be more than you can cope with, one of these days!'

'What, that boy?' Narzia laughed mockingly. 'Why, he's already so intoxicated by the power he thinks he holds in his hands, one can do what one likes with him, and he never even notices. He will always be running after his dreams, and one only need give him some such dreams to make him run where one likes.'

Honi looked at her, shaking his head, and said, 'I don't know what to make of you! You've always been a good daughter, and a great help to me since your mother died, but when I hear you talk like that I begain to feel afraid. Have you no fear that the magical things you use for your own advantage may turn against you someday? From all they say of the Gentle Fluter, he had other purposes in mind for his music than those for which the boy is now using it, on your advice. And I don't think Arni's stone was originally meant to lie in a golden dish, but on the heart of a living man or woman. I have followed your advice in these matters, but now I sometimes ask myself if it was the right thing to do.'

'You may leave that to me!' said Narzia, more sharply than was necessary. Suddenly her lips were set and hard, and the deep line she had inherited from her mother stood on her brow. 'You don't know enough about such things,' she added, rather more gently. 'If I hadn't taken the stone from the boy I couldn't have succeeded in bending his will indefinitely. I know exactly what I'm doing, and in any case, one can't go back when one has once decided to practise this kind of magic.' As she said that, he thought he saw a trace of fear in those green eyes, but she immediately pulled herself together, and added, 'If he brings me back what I've asked from Falkinor, my power over him and others will be all the greater, and then it won't matter if he lies beside me in bed at night.'

Honi smiled at this, and said, 'Only a girl who's never slept with a man can speak like that! Well, I'm all the more in favour of the marriage now. It may be that you'll be taught a magic stronger than your wish for power.'

As Honi chuckled comfortably to himself, Narzia turned away to hide the quick colour that shot into her cheeks at these words. 'No!' she cried. 'No, never!'

By now he was so used to being an invisible witness of such incidents that he took fright when Narzia suddenly looked straight at him, and just as he was thinking that it was mere chance she happened to be looking that way, he suddenly realized that she actually did see him. 'There!' she whispered. 'There he is! Naked and hairy as an animal!' She was trembling all over.

Honi swung round, and he too looked that way, but obviously the apparition was not meant for him, for he said, 'Who do you mean? I see nothing but the cupboard in the corner.'

'He's there, though,' said Narzia, her voice expressionless. 'Grey as a dead man, staring at me with his stony eyes.' She put out her hand in the gesture used to ward off evil spirits, crying, 'Go! I never summoned you!' But he himself had no idea how he had come into this room, and was equally unable to obey her injunction. At least, Narzia still seemed to see an image of his goat-legged figure, for she put her hands over her eyes. Then her father took her in his arms, and at that moment the picture of the room was suddenly extinguished, as if a candle had been blown out.

He was so confused that it was a moment before he could find his bearings. There was a pale gleam of light, wavering in the darkness. Then he recognized the trembling reflection of the moon in the rippling water of the pool where the spring gushed out, he heard the wind in the branches of the sycamore, and knew where he was again; he supposed he had been standing here all the time on his stony goat's legs. He was dismayed to find that Narzia had seen him. Urla had seen him too, but she had been neither alarmed nor particularly surprised, and had treated him like a guest to be invited in and entertained. And finally she had taken him in her arms. But Narzia had been overcome by sheer horror at the sight of him, the goat-legged creature. What had so frightened her? Had that moment given her some inkling of what she was bringing upon herself with the kind of magic she practised? He had understood that the young man whom she was discussing with her father was himself, for he had owned the stone. But he had obviously also owned a flute, whose music seemed to have strange powers, and Narzia was making use of those powers too in her own greedy way. No doubt the flute was another magical thing that might be used for either good or evil. From all he had just heard, he had not played the flute in the way for which it had been made. How had this Gentle Fluter mentioned by Honi played it? He wished he could hear him, give himself up to the sound of that flute-playing, and as he thought so, the trembling reflection of the moon was wiped away, and there was grey twilight over a lake with a belt of reeds around it, a blurred shape in the milky morning mists. A landing-stage of narrow planks nailed to rough wooden posts projected a little way out from the bank. A boat was tied up to the end of this landing-stage, resting quietly on the water. Ducks could be heard quacking somewhere in the mists.

Then muffled footsteps disturbed them, and they flew away, noisily beating their wings. A shadowy figure emerged from the reeds fringing the lake, came slowly closer, and turned out to be a bearded man carrying a limp leather sack over his shoulder. He stopped on the bank of the lake and peered out at the water, whose dully shining surface was swallowed up in the mist a little farther out. Then he turned and gave a quiet whistle. Immediately a second shadow came hurrying up, and proved to be a ragged woman carrying a small child on her hip. The man beckoned her over and said softly, 'See those posts out in the lake? That's where the fishermen have made their creels fast. We'll soon have breakfast now. Sit on the landing-stage while I get it!'

As the woman crouched on the planks, sighing slightly, and spoke softly to the child, the man untied the boat and poled it out to the posts sticking a little above the surface just where it seemed to merge with the mist. He leaned over the side, groped beneath the water, and soon brought up a creel of densely woven willow. Putting his hand through the hole where the fish swam in, he plunged his arm in up to the shoulder, and one by one drew out three fat eels which wriggled in his grasp like black, wetly shining snakes as he held them up to show the woman his catch. He put the eels in his leather sack, and emptied three more creels in the same way. Then he threw the creels back overboard, with a splash, and poled the boat back to the landing-stage.

'Why did you take the whole catch?' asked the woman. 'They

wouldn't have missed two or three eels, and we'd have been fed – but now the fishermen will be angry and come looking for the thief.'

The man laughed unpleasantly and said, 'Perhaps I want them to notice it – those fat fishermen who sit comfortably here on the bank, waiting for the Green Man to drive the catch into their nets, while the likes of us get nothing to eat. And we can smoke the eels over the fire. Then we'll have food to live on for a little while.'

'All the same, it's not right,' said the woman.

The man turned on her angrily, growling, 'Right, not right – whose rights do you mean, then? The fishermen's rights? Or the rights of beggars and vagrants? Is it right for your child to go hungry?'

The woman was about to answer him, but then her child began to cry. She rocked it in her arms, chanting a rhyme in a soothing, sing-song voice:

> *Don't cry, babykin,*
> *and I will make some soupykin,*
> *if it's too hot for babykin,*
> *I'll blow on it a bittykin,*
> *and you shall have a fishykin,*
> *in your little dishykin,*
> *all for pretty babykin.*

Then she added, in her normal voice, 'Even if it's only eel soup.'

By now the man had collected some dry reeds and a few pieces of driftwood. He took a pot with a handle out of his sack and filled it with water. With practised gestures, he made a couple of pieces of wood into a framework from which he hung the pot over a little heap of rushes. In a few moments, he had a fire going, and soon the flames were crackling under the pot. Next the man picked up an eel and showed it to the woman again. 'A fine, fat fellow, eh?' he called. He killed the eel with a blow from the back of his knife, slit it open, threw the guts into the lake and cut the eel up into pieces which he threw in the pot. 'Let me have some salt!' he asked the woman.

'Oh, just a little!' she said. 'We haven't much left.' She took a small leather bag out of her pocket, dipped her fingertips in and sprinkled a few grains on the palm of the man's hand. He added them to the soup, which was beginning to bubble and steam. As he was doing so, however, he froze and listened intently. 'Someone's coming!' he whispered. 'Hide in the rushes, and mind the child doesn't cry! It may be only a man on his own, come to look at his creels first thing in the morning. If so, I can deal with him.' As he spoke, he pulled out his knife and slapped the palm of his other hand with the blade.

The woman jumped up, clasping the child, and a few paces took her into hiding in the rushes. The man followed her part of the way, but then stood waiting among the first of the reeds.

Now the footsteps could be heard quite clearly. Someone was coming that way from the land, taking no trouble to tread quietly. He was whistling, and his feet squelched over the damp ground. Then his figure could be seen, vaguely outlined in the mist; it strolled closer, became more distinct, and suddenly stopped. It was now plain that the newcomer standing here, sniffing the air, was a young man in heavy fisherman's boots. 'So who's been lighting a fire here?' he said, half under his breath. Then all carelessness left his manner. With a stride or so, he came to the fire with the steaming pot over it; no doubt he had smelt the soup bubbling there, for he called, 'I'll show you how to cook my eels, I will!' and peered all around him for the thief, who, however, now sure that he had only one man to deal with, came slowly closer, saying almost casually, 'Right, show me, greenhorn! Still wet behind the ears, aren't you?' He was holding his knife in the hollow of his hand, the tip pointing forward.

At that the fisherman snatched his own knife from his belt, and next moment the two of them were at grips, each trying to stab the other. The young fisherman seemed stronger than the bearded man, but the latter handled his weapon better. 'Never slit anything but eels, have you?' he growled as he easily fended off the young man's clumsy lunge with his left forearm. The young man stepped backwards, stumbled over the wooden framework, and fell full length into the fire, sending the sparks flying. The pot tipped over, pouring hot broth over the fallen man's legs. He let out a yell and tried to scramble to his feet, but the bearded man was on him, saying, 'Did Mummy's boy get burnt, then? Just wait a moment and nothing'll hurt you any more!' He struck out, and if the young man had not thrown himself aside it would have been a mortal blow, but as it was the blade only pierced his shoulder, and before the bearded man could withdraw it again, the young man had a grip on his wrist, and they began wrestling once more.

All the same, the fisherman could not have withstood the vagrant much longer if his yell had not summoned other men busy nearby. Suddenly they emerged from all sides in the mist, striding up in their heavy boots, and tore the combatants apart. 'Why are you fighting this fellow, Bargash?' one asked.

The young man pressed his hand to the wound in his shoulder, from which blood was running down over his linen smock, and said, gasping, 'He robbed my creels, and when I called him to account for it, he went for me with that knife.'

'This is a serious matter, then,' said the other man. 'We'll take him to Rulosh. Rulosh will pass judgement on him.' And turning to the men holding the bearded vagrant, he said, 'Bind him, so he can't do any more harm.'

The vagrant struggled, cursing, and tried to shake the men off, but they forced his arms behind his back and tied his wrists with a rope. Then someone found the leather sack. 'Hey, Bargash, here are your eels!' he called.

'Except the one he was going to make into soup,' said Bargash, angrily.

The vagrant laughed, taunting him. 'And make it into soup I did! Wasn't it hot enough for you?'

One of the men struck him in the mouth with the flat of his hand. 'You'll soon be done with mocking,' he said. 'Thief and murderer!'

By now the mist was lifting, so that one could look far out over the lake, and see the opposite bank as a blurred grey line. Wooded mountains appeared to lie behind the drifting wisps, their dark slopes only to be guessed at here and there in the haze.

The fishermen surrounded the bearded man and set off for home with him. They had to drag rather than lead him along, for he was still struggling, and braced his legs in the soft ground, trying to break free, but he could do nothing against so many. So the group moved slowly along a well-trodden path a little above the belt of reeds by the bank. After a while the reed-thatched rooftops of the fishing village appeared, standing among fruit trees. A few children, sensing that something unusual was up, came running out of the houses to meet them. When they saw the bound man being dragged along by men of their own village, however, they fell back, glancing timidly at the ragged vagrant.

So they reached the village. The prisoner was still cursing the fishermen roundly, and they gave him back as good as they got. The noise brought some women out of doors too. One of them, grey-haired and past her youth, came running and flung herself at young Bargash, whose shoulder was still dripping blood. 'What's happened?' she cried. 'You're bleeding! Come in and let me see to it!' However, Bargash shook off her hand. 'Let it be, mother!' he said. 'It's not much, just a

scratch. First we have to take this man to Rulosh for judgement.
Rulosh must see what the fellow did for himself.'

The woman, setting up a wail, was going to object to this plan, but
Bargash simply left her and walked on. It was clear, from his furious
expression, that he was bent first and foremost on seeing the man who
had wounded him punished.

The group finally stopped outside a house much like the rest, but a
little larger and better kept. One of the men – he seemed to be the oldest,
and thus the one who felt in duty bound to take the lead – knocked at the
door and then stepped back and waited. In a moment it was opened,
and a sturdy, rather short-legged man of about sixty came out. He wore
his white hair cut short, like a close-fitting cap on his round skull. 'What
do you want?' he asked. 'We could hear you shouting all the way down
the village street! And who's this you're dragging along?'

The fisherman who had knocked on the door replied, 'You must
pass judgement on him, Rulosh. He robbed Bargash's creels, and what's
more, he attacked him and wounded him with a knife, and if we'd not
come up I reckon he'd have killed him.'

'You can be sure of that!' growled the bound man.

Rulosh looked him coldly in the face with a pair of grey eyes, and
said, 'You may come to be sorry you spoke those words.' Then he
turned to the fishermen, saying, 'Well, come indoors and we'll deal
with the matter. Was anybody else there who can give evidence?'

'No, just us,' said the old fisherman. 'Bargash is the main witness, of
course.'

'What about your wound?' Rulosh asked the young man, but he
shook his head, saying, 'It can wait.'

'Good,' said Rulosh. 'Come in, then.' He went ahead of them into
the dimly lit hall, where he opened a door leading into a low-ceilinged
but large room, containing a massive table of smooth-scoured sycamore
wood. Rulosh seated himself in a large armchair at the head of the
table, and told the others to sit down on the rush-seated stools that
stood around it.

'Set the man opposite me,' he said, 'and two of you had better stay
near him, in case he gives any more trouble.'

'Wise of you,' said the bearded man, 'since I mean to give you all the
trouble I can, you stinking, croaking frogs!'

'You've a strange way of defending yourself,' said Rulosh.

'I use nothing but my knife to defend myself,' said the bearded man.
'But your people have taken that away from me.'

'And not without good reason, it would seem,' said Rulosh. 'Which brings me to the point. Tell me what happened, Bargash!'

The young fisherman stood up, and said, 'The tale's soon told. I was going to look at my creels, and when I reached the bank I smelled smoke. So then I went down to the landing-stage and found a fire there, with a pot of eel soup boiling over it, and before I knew it that fellow came out of the reeds and attacked me with his knife. I'd have got the better of him if I hadn't stumbled over the fire.'

This made the bearded man laugh. 'I'd like to see you get the better of me, greenhorn!' he said. 'Give me back my knife, and then let him show what he can do!'

Rulosh was beginning to lose his temper with this obstreperous fellow who showed so little respect for the law. 'Hold your tongue!' he said sharply. 'This is not the time or place to see who's handier with a knife; we do justice here. Be quiet, and don't speak till you're spoken to!'

He leaned back, took a deep breath, and then asked, more calmly, 'And can you others bear out what Bargash says? You speak, Haulesh!'

The old fisherman who had already appointed himself spokesman stood up and said, 'Well, we weren't there when the thing began, seeing as we were still up on the path above the bank. Then we heard a shout from over where Bargash has his moorings, and we came down and saw him lying on the ground, and this man stabbing him with a knife. So we dragged the man off Bargash and took his knife away. And then we found his leather sack beside the fire, too, with a dozen live eels in it.'

'Theft of fish and attempted murder,' said Rulosh, turning back to the bearded man. 'You've already informed me, by way of greeting, that you wanted to kill Bargash. What have you to say in your defence?'

'I say I don't care two hoots for all your talk!' said the bearded man. 'I look for what I need and take it where I find it, and any who tries to stop me will feel my knife. That's how I've lived, and how I'll live in future, though you lot sitting here on your fat behinds mightn't understand it. The Green Man sends fish swimming straight into your nets, you hardly need to take any trouble, but if a man like me ever tries to help himself you screech blue murder and talk about your rights! Who gave you rights over these fishing grounds? Your people took them, some time or other, the way I took a few eels today.'

'If you'd come into the village we would have given you something to eat,' said Rulosh, but that only infuriated the bearded man even more.

'A couple of stinking fishheads, and I must beg for them first!' he said. 'That's not the way I see my life. I'll help myself, by force if I must. And you won't stop me!' With a sudden, unexpected movement, he tore himself free and made for the door, but before he could get it open with his bound hands the men were upon him, and dragged him back to the table. 'He's like a wild beast – best killed out of hand!' said one of them.

'And you're worse than beasts!' shouted the bearded man. 'No animal stops another hunting in the forest or eating what it likes. But you weave a fine net of laws to spread over what you call your property, and if a man won't go along with your customs you send him packing – you'd rather he starved than let him through the net. Go on then, and do as you like!'

'Is that all you have to say?' asked Rulosh. The bearded man shrugged his shoulders and made no answer. Then Rulosh stood up, saying, 'As there is obviously no more evidence to be given, I will now deliver my judgement. First, this man stole a dozen eels from Bargash's creels.'

'Thirteen,' said Bargash. 'One was in the soup already.'

'Very well, thirteen,' said Rulosh, 'but we could have come to some agreement, I think, over the theft. Second, however, this man attacked one of our villagers and tried to kill him. Moreover, he has boasted in this very room that he would do the same another time, in similar circumstances. He is indeed like a wild beast, a danger to all who cross his path.'

'Then throw me into your lake to fatten your eels even more!' shouted the bearded man.

Rulosh looked at him unmoved, and said, 'No, not the lake. The lake is for life, not death. And it might displease the Green Man if we sullied his domain in such a way. We shall take you into the marshes.'

'Ah, so that's how you do it,' said the bearded man, with curious calm. 'When?'

'Now,' said Rulosh. He rose, and so did the other fishermen. The two who were guarding the bearded man dragged him through the doorway and the dim entrance hall and out into the open. Women and a few children were standing among the houses outside, some way off, staring. When the men set out along the path leading away from the lake and inland, a boy with a breaking voice shouted, 'They're taking him into the marshes!' And the little crowd stood silent, watching the small procession leave the village along a narrow path that was obviously seldom used.

At first sour meadowland spread to right and left of the path, with clumps of bulrushes growing among the grass. Later, the land was overgrown with grey-green heather, interspersed with patches flecked white with the fluffy seeds of cotton grass. A boggy pool gleamed brown and oily here and there. Parts of the path were now reinforced with logs laid across them, and brown, marshland water gurgled between these logs when the fishermen trod over them in their heavy boots.

By now the mist had fully lifted, the sun was high in the blue sky, and the sharp scent of moorland herbs rose in its warmth. They went on until the village was long out of sight. Only the lake still lay behind them like a pale blue streak on the horizon, between the marshes and the blue-green woods that rose beyond its waters. Rulosh suddenly stopped and said, 'Here!' The almost circular surface of a marshy pool gleamed among the bulrushes, a little to one side of the path. Its clouded waters were nearly black, as if it went down to immeasurable depths.

'Bind his legs too,' said Rulosh.

'Afraid I may yet run away from you?' inquired the bearded man. He no longer spoke so loud or so violently, but almost casually, as if it were already all over. But his face was pale, and there was a flicker of fear in his eyes.

'No, there's no fear of that,' said Rulosh, 'but it will be quicker this way.'

As two of the fishermen tied the bearded man's feet with a cord, another looked back down the path along which they had come. 'There's someone coming after us,' he said.

Rulosh looked the same way, shading his eyes with his hand to see better. 'Yes; a man I don't know,' he said after a while. 'And obviously in a hurry to catch up with us.'

'Well, there we are,' said one of the men who had been binding the bearded man's legs. 'Shall we . . .?'

'No, wait!' said Rulosh. 'I want to find out why this man's following us first.'

They were now all looking at the man who came hurrying along the path through the marshes, with rapid, almost dancing footsteps. He was rather small, his figure slender, and when he was close enough for his face to be seen he waved to them, not urgently or officiously, but in an almost cheerful way, as one waves to a friend from a distance when meeting him in some strange place. He was slightly out of breath by the time he reached the group of men and stopped. The first thing he did was to glance at the bound man. 'Ah,' he said, 'I see I'm just in time!'

'What do you mean?' asked Rulosh sternly. 'I have passed my sentence, and you won't force me to repeal it, whatever this man may mean to you.'

At that, this curious character actually began to laugh so much that his gold-rimmed eyeglasses danced about. 'Force you?' he cried. 'Me? Good heavens above, how could a man like me force you to do anything? Do I look as if I could?'

He certainly did not look as if he had ever tried any such thing. His cheerful face with its red apple cheeks radiated sheer goodwill, and his eyes seemed as guileless as a child's, although his hair was white. Seeing the distrust in Rulosh's face, he became rather graver, and said, 'Do forgive me for laughing. I know you are concerned with a very serious matter. As for what this man means to me, I'll tell you: he's a human being.'

'So are all of us,' said Rulosh, rather at a loss.

'Precisely!' said the cheerful man, as if that explained everything.

Rulosh plainly realized he was getting nowhere this way. He looked keenly at the stranger. 'Who are you, anyway?' he asked.

'They call me the Gentle Fluter,' said the man, adding, 'No need to introduce yourself. I know you're Rulosh, judge in the village down there. And I call it very creditable of you to compel yourself to watch your sentence carried out. It makes one think twice, another time, of what punishment's dealt out to a poor fellow such as this.'

Rulosh looked at him in some surprise. 'How do you know I have to compel myself to watch?' he asked, adding almost defiantly, 'Perhaps I like to see such things.'

'Don't make yourself out worse than you are,' said the Gentle Fluter. 'Your eyes give you the lie.'

'Very well, you're right,' said Rulosh, lowering his glance. But then he raised his head again, shaking it, and said, 'However, this man is such a danger to everyone that he must die. He has—'

The fluter interrupted him with a gesture, saying, 'No need to tell me what he's done. I know all about it. And I won't stop you dealing with him as you've decided is fit. But first you ought to grant me one thing.'

'That depends what it is,' said Rulosh, cautiously. 'Tell me what you want.'

'Nothing much,' said the Gentle Fluter. 'Only to play this man a little music on my flute.'

The bearded man had been following this conversation with bafflement. 'What's all this nonsense?' he asked roughly. 'Make an end of it and throw me in the water! Music! As if I felt like hearing dance tunes now!'

'Don't you?' asked the Gentle Fluter. 'You surprise me. You used to like to dance, didn't you? And wasn't life good then? Don't you want to know, once more, that you are alive and can feel joy?'

'Joy?' said the bearded man. 'I doubt if your flute could get me to feel that, here by this pond in the marshes!' But his voice sounded almost as if he were saying: will you bet you can't do it? That, in any event, was how the fluter took it. 'Have you any objection?' he asked Rulosh.

Rulosh shrugged his shoulders. 'No,' he said, 'but keep it short.'

Then the small man took a silver flute out of his pocket, put it to his lips and began to play. In the face of this desolate landscape, and the bound man beside the dark pool in the marshes, the first few notes came as a shock: the fluter began with a cheerful tune, the kind of merry, lilting dance in which a man whirls his partner round and round, her skirts flying. At first the men looked askance at the fluter playing such unseemly music here; however, he was not at all disturbed, but mingled even merrier trills and runs with his melody, as if they were exactly right for this time and place. It wasn't that he actually got the men dancing, and probably he didn't intend to, but their faces relaxed, the stern determination faded from their eyes, and they no longer stood there stiffly, each man in isolation, but were like a group outside a tavern, wondering whether to go in for another drink or straight home. The bound man himself seemed to be one of the group; he even smiled as he watched the flute-player, admiring the dexterity of his fingers.

Now the fluter gradually let this merry dance die away, and began weaving other and gentler tunes into his playing, linking them skilfully, so that you felt two people were talking, giving question and answer, as the originally contrasting melodies took on sequences of notes from one another, building them into their own patterns, until one seemed the reflection of the other, although both were still different, and themselves. And so the fluter erected a structure of musical sound around the men gathered there, one that enclosed them like a warm room in which people talked together with the sole aim of understanding one another, and these melodies were so sweet that one by one the men felt tears come into their eyes, and were not at all ashamed, nor was the bearded man the last to whom this happened.

They stood there for some while after the fluter had finished playing. The bearded man had never taken his eyes off the player of the flute all this time. Now he cleared his throat, as if to get his voice back, and said, 'It's a long time since anyone spoke to me like that flute of yours.'

'Not your wife?' asked the Gentle Fluter.

The bound man looked at him in alarm, and said, 'What do you know about my wife?' Then he pulled himself together, and added, 'Yes, she could. Only there's not been much opportunity for that, not with the life we've led lately. Did you meet her?'

'Yes,' said the Gentle Fluter. 'You needn't worry about her. I met her by the lake, washing the child, and then she went back to the fishing village with me after she'd told me what happened. When I set off for the marshes she was drinking good warm soup, and your child was well fed and sleeping.'

Rulosh, who had been listening to this exchange, now looked at the bearded man as if he were seeing him for the first time. 'I didn't know you had a wife and child,' he said. 'Why didn't you tell me?'

'You didn't ask, Rulosh,' said the bearded man, 'and I don't suppose I'd have told you anyway, the way I felt in that room of yours.'

'That may well be,' said Rulosh. 'All the same, I ought to have asked you. What's more, it now strikes me that I conducted your trial a good deal too hastily. I don't even know what you're called.'

'If that's the case,' the Gentle Fluter told him, 'you will have to hold the trial again. I suppose it's your custom here, as elsewhere, to ask the accused his name?'

'You are perfectly right,' said Rulosh, ashamed. 'We were all rather angry over what had happened, but still, a judge must not be influenced by anger.'

'I gave you reason enough,' said the bearded man. 'And so you don't need to ask me any more, I'll tell you my name directly: it's Barnulf.'

'And a good name for you too,' said Rulosh. 'It sounds like a bear's name, and you look like a bear, and can be as angry as one of them roused from his winter sleep!'

When he said that, the other men looked at Barnulf too, and grinned.

The Gentle Fluter seemed pleased with this new turn events had taken. 'How would it be,' he asked, 'if you untied Barnulf now? After all, he's not been legally sentenced, and he seems to me a peaceable sort of man anyway.'

The fishermen looked inquiringly at Rulosh, and when he nodded, one of them set about untying the prisoner's bonds. The cord was too valuable for him simply to cut it through. When Barnulf was free, he rubbed his wrists to get the circulation going, and then went over to Bargash. 'Can you forgive me for what I did?' he asked. 'Now I look at you properly, I'm doubly sorry, for you seem a nice young fellow.'

'And I like you better myself than I did this morning, Barnulf,' said Bargash, with a smile. 'No need to trouble yourself about this scratch of mine. One can get as much in any brawl – and after all, I have my eels back.'

'Except for one,' said Barnulf.

'Well, I got a taste of that one, anyway,' said Bargash, and everyone laughed, for by now they knew that the whole potful had spilled over him.

Rulosh was the first to recover his gravity. 'I suppose you've all forgotten just why we came out to the marshes?' he remarked.

'I haven't,' said Barnulf. 'I put myself in your hands, because I trust you now.'

Rulosh looked at him a little dubiously, as if he still found all this hard to grasp, but then he said, 'Well, let's go home and hold the trial again. Justice must be done, after all.' Turning to the Gentle Fluter, he added, 'I'd like to have you beside me at the trial. You make it easy for a man to see things the right way.'

So they turned back, and none of the fishermen looked at all as if he were guarding a prisoner on the way home. It was an entirely amicable sight to see the men walk in twos or threes, without any particular haste, along the narrow path through the marshes and towards the distant lake, whose smooth surface now shone brightly beneath the sun at its zenith.

How did that fluter do it, the watcher wondered, as he saw the little procession walking back to the village in such friendship. Did he cast a spell on them with his flute, so that they forgot what they had determined to do? Did he force them to his will like that?

'What on earth are you thinking of?' the Gentle Fluter asked him, looking straight into his eyes, as if to exclude any possible doubt that he knew just who had asked the question. 'Am I one of those magicians who make others do things they don't really want to do at all? The flute isn't all that important, either. It just gives me a little help in saying things that are hard to express with words. Anyway, I like to play music. You must look at it like this: anger came over them all like a sickness, confusing their minds, and it was that anger which made them do what they wouldn't have done in their right minds – neither Barnulf nor the fishermen and their judge Rulosh. All I did was free their minds from anger with my music, and let them feel I trusted the good in them. Couldn't you hear that? You ought to have learnt to listen by now!'

'What was that you said?' asked Rulosh. 'Forgive me, I was thinking, and didn't hear you properly.'

'Never mind,' said the Gentle Fluter, smiling. 'It wasn't meant for you, anyway. What were you thinking of?'

'Hard to say, and it sounds rather strange in a judge's mouth too: but I was wondering how I'm to sit in judgement on Barnulf now, for I suddenly feel he's a friend, someone I like.'

'What's so strange in that?' asked the Gentle Fluter. 'How can a man be a good judge if he doesn't like the people before him? Wouldn't that make the justice he deals out a hollow mockery? You'll be able to reach the right verdict now – you see if you don't!'

'The fact is,' said Rulosh, 'he seems to me quite a different man, now I've watched his face as he listened to your playing. That's what makes it so hard.'

'A different man?' repeated the Gentle Fluter. 'Isn't it, rather, that you've only just seen the man he is? How did you think of him when you were passing sentence?'

'I said he was like a wild beast,' said Rulosh, and only then did he see that the fluter had made his point. 'Yes: I judged him as if he were a wolf from the forest, to be struck down without scruple,' he said. 'Now I see that I'm a poor sort of judge. I'd like to put his trial in your hands.'

'No, that you will not!' said the Gentle Fluter firmly. 'You are the judge; you can't shrug off your office like a coat you no longer care for. Who would trust you, later, if you don't trust yourself any more?

Question Barnulf and the witnesses a second time, and then give your verdict!'

By now they were close enough to the village for the children, who were busy ducking a screaming boy in a muddy puddle on the wet meadowland beyond the houses, to interrupt their macabre game and look at the path. One lad noticed that Barnulf was coming back with the fishermen, and called out his discovery to the others, and then they all ran back to the village shouting their news. So there were women out of doors again as the men reached the village, Barnulf's wife among them. When she saw her husband she ran to him, and threw her arms around his neck.

'How's the boy?' asked Barnulf.

'Fed, and sleeping,' said his wife. 'You're back, you're back! So the old man kept the promise he gave me.'

'What did he promise you, then?' asked Rulosh, looking suspiciously at the Gentle Fluter.

The woman let go of her husband and looked awkwardly at the judge.

'Well?' said Rulosh sternly. 'Did he promise to bring your husband back unharmed?'

'No, sir,' said the woman. 'No, he didn't say that.'

'What did he say, then?' asked Rulosh.

'Well, I hope you won't hold it against him,' said the woman. 'He promised to make you and your men see sense, and my own man too.'

Rulosh looked at her in surprise. Then his glance went to the Gentle Fluter, standing equably beside him, as if none of this concerned him at all. At that, Rulosh slapped him on the back and began to roar with laughter. 'And so he did!' he cried. 'So he did!' Then he sobered up again, and added, 'But your husband's not free yet. We're going to my justice chamber, to hold the trial again.'

The woman bowed her head, saying, 'Yes, I know you must, since Barnulf injured one of you. Can I come to the trial with my husband?'

'You not only can, you must!' said Rulosh. 'Not that you need say anything that might harm your husband, but it may be that you can help me deliver the right verdict on this case, all the same.'

'I'll gladly try,' said the woman. 'And first, I think you ought to give Barnulf something to eat, for he hasn't even had any breakfast today, and what's more, a man with something inside him doesn't lose his temper so easily.'

'You are a wise woman!' said Rulosh, laughing. 'Come along, and we'll see that your husband gets his breakfast at long last.'

Back at his house, Rulosh led all who had come with him not into the justice chamber, but into a room opposite, where there was a cauldron of fish soup bubbling over a fire. Its aroma wafted towards them, warm and fragrant, as they came in. 'I think we'd better all fortify ourselves with this first,' said Rulosh, inviting the company to sit at a large round wooden table. A maidservant ladled out the soup, bringing everyone a helping in a turned wooden bowl, and then she cut up a loaf of bread as big as a millstone, put the slices in a shallow basket, and set it on the middle of the table so that all could help themselves.

'Eat up!' said Rulosh. 'None of us should come to this trial in anger.'

They spooned up the soup in silence, broke the bread, and finally wiped out their dishes with it, a sure sign that they had enjoyed the soup. Even Barnulf's wife, who had already tasted the fisher folk's hospitality not long ago, had eaten too, as if it were a matter of importance for all to share the meal in common. When the last man put down his spoon, Rulosh rose and said, 'I hope you've all had enough. Well, if you're ready, then we'll go over into the other room and bring this case to an end.'

So they all pushed back their chairs, rose, and followed him across the hall into the justice chamber. Rulosh set a chair beside his own for the Gentle Fluter, and all the rest sat where they had been sitting that morning, while the two men who had been guarding Barnulf each found a spare stool. But Barnulf's wife remained standing beside her husband.

'You can sit at the table with us,' Rulosh told her. 'There's no charge brought against you.'

'I'd rather stand beside my husband,' said the woman.

'Well, there's no objection to that,' said Rulosh, 'and you seem to me a woman who knows her own mind very well. Yet I don't even know your name, and I won't be blamed for ignorance of the names of those in my court again. Will you tell me what you're called?'

'My name is Eiren,' said the woman.

'A lovely name,' said Rulosh. 'I should very much like to know why people like you two are wandering the countryside, living by such means as robbing a fisherman's creels. Can you tell me what brought you to this, Barnulf?'

'It's a long story,' said Barnulf, 'but I see I shall have to tell it, if you're to understand that not everyone can sit at home in peace and comfort like you folk here.'

When he said that, his wife put her hand on his shoulder, as if to warn him to be circumspect. He looked at her, smiling, and said, 'All right, I'm not going to get worked up, just tell them our story.' And he turned back to Rulosh, and went on. 'I was once a shepherd in the upper valley of Barlebogue, like my father before me. I had a house there, with a kitchen garden outside it, and I made a good living from my flock. Eiren here is from the same village, the daughter of a farmer who knows a lot about horse-breeding, as many do in Barlebogue. We married about three years ago, and lived happily together, and when Eiren had a son we called him Barlo, after the Count who was once judge in our valley, and was famous far and wide as a wise and just man. His son Fredebar took over the office of judge after his death, and that wasn't quite the same. He was known to be very clever, but he took less notice of what went on in the villages. And especially after his wife died, he began to let things drift, and sat in his tall castle of Barlebogue, making merry with his grand friends, and drinking more than is good for a man who has to be responsible for others.

Well, this made no great difference to us at first; in a little village on the edge of the forest, things generally sort themselves out if you stick to the old ways, and no one much minds if the great lords leave you in peace. It's only when something has effects reaching beyond the village that you may find the order of things outside has fallen into decay, without anyone's knowing it.

That's what happened the day after a night when a pack of wolves fell on my fold and killed all my sheep. I'd heard the dog bark, but by the time I was out of bed and had snatched up a staff and run out to the flock, there wasn't one of them left alive. You may say I was too careless. But we never saw such a pack of wolves in our valley before. There must have been some fifty wolves, all attacking the flock at once, and I never saw hide nor hair of any of them. Or not then, anyway.

When I went through the fold next morning to count the dead beasts and see if I could at least save a couple of skins, a troop of men in wolfskin coats came out of the forest, led by a young woman. This woman, who was very beautiful and had eyes of such a blue as I'd never seen before, except in those sapphires that are found in our streams, asked me what had happened, and when I told her, she said her men were wolf-hunters and offered us their help. As neither I nor the village farmers were in any position to employ so many men, we took them to Barlebogue Castle, so that Fredebar could see to the matter. We knew this much: he couldn't call on men of his own to deal with that pack of wolves, for his friends knew how to hunt nothing but hares and deer.

I remember I didn't like those wolf-hunters from the first. None of them ever laughed, and they looked at us with their yellow eyes as if we and not the wolves were to be their prey. At the time, however, I was beside myself with the death of my sheep, and could think of nothing but doing away with those wolves; I didn't mind who did the job. Fredebar was glad to see men who'd take such dangerous work off his hands, and invited them to his table. He was having another of his banquets, with much drinking and rich food. He invited the hunters' lady to sit beside him, where his wife once used to sit, made eyes at her and drank to her as if they were lovers already. I didn't like to see that. You must know that though she'd been sick a long time, his wife had done more for us in the villages than he did in all the time he was lord of Barlebogue, and when I saw him dallying like that with a strange woman, I lost my temper and left the hall and the castle without a word.

That was my good luck, because dreadful things happened in the castle as soon as darkness fell. Just what they were I can't tell you; nobody survived that night except for the young woman who called herself Gisa, and her wolf-hunters. There are many who think that as soon as the sun sank those men changed into the very wolves who attacked my sheep, and the wolves turned and killed Fredebar, his friends, and everyone else in the castle, and by now I've come to believe it must have been so myself.

Next morning, anyway, Gisa was mistress of Barlebogue. Her yellow-eyed retainers in their wolfskins went out to even the most remote villages, to be her overseers, and got us all into her power. Nobody dared venture out of doors by night, for you'd hear the wolves howling until sunrise, and not one of those uncanny hunters ever did anything about it. Yes, I reckon it's really true, they do turn into wolves by night, and don't go back to human form until the sun casts its first rays.

So every soul in the valley of Barlebogue has lived in fear since then, and not just by night, either. Those wolfskin-clad retainers of Gisa's took young men from the villages, just as they thought fit, and made them work on the deposits of gems in the rivers, and later in the mines up in the mountains, for Gisa was never satisfied in her desire for sapphires and other precious stones. Some fellows from our village were taken too, and it didn't trouble Gisa's men if they had families to feed, or parents to support. But worse than all this was the fear that had taken hold of everyone. Soon nobody dared help a neighbour who'd come to grief in some such way, because that might attract the attention of Gisa's retainers, and then you'd be the next to be dragged off.

Having no sheep of my own left, I went to work for my father-in-law as a labourer, to earn us the necessities of life. Well, one of the yellow-eyed men came to his farm one day, watched me at work in silence for a while, and then he put his hand on my shoulder, saying, 'Come along! Gisa can do with strong men.' I told him I had a wife and child to keep, but he took no notice, just drove me out of the farmyard ahead of him. My father-in-law and his men stood there helpless, and none of them dared lift a finger to help me. That day I made up my mind to live like a wolf myself in future. It seemed the only way to get by in life.

The yellow-eyed man was so sure of himself and our fear of him that he hadn't even looked to see what I was carrying, so he never noticed I had a knife in my pocket. When our way passed close to the forest, I bent as if to tie my shoe, and waited until the yellow-eyed man was beside me. Then I leaped up, drove the knife into his breast, and dragged the corpse into the bushes. After that I ran home as fast as I could, fetched Eiren and the baby, and fled into the forest with them. We made what progress we could by day, hiding as soon as we heard any noise, and in the evening we'd climb a tree and spend the night there, while the wolves prowled in the undergrowth below, howling. We lived on berries, mushrooms, beechnuts and acorns during those weeks, because luckily all this happened in autumn.

When we finally made our way out of the forest, we dragged ourselves to a village, dirty and ragged as we were, and we were going to ask for shelter for the night and something to eat, but the folk there chased us out of doors, calling us thieves and vagabonds, and set the dogs on us. Since then, I've taken what we needed to keep us alive. But I told you that this morning.'

'You did,' said Rulosh, 'but I can understand it better now. So that's how you came to be robbing Bargash's creels. Did you help him, Eiren?'

'No,' said Barnulf's wife. 'But I watched, and I didn't stop him, because my child was hungry.'

'Why don't you tell him what you said to me, Eiren?' asked Barnulf.

'What I said doesn't matter now,' Eiren replied, but Rulosh seemed to disagree. 'It's for me to decide what matters at this trial,' he said. 'Well, what did your wife say to you, Barnulf?'

'She blamed me for emptying all the creels, instead of just taking two or three eels out of them,' said Barnulf. 'Eiren was never really able to get accustomed to the life we had to lead, and she always thought it wrong when I stole chickens from the farmers' henhouses or broke into their storerooms.'

The Gentle Fluter had been listening attentively to all that was said, without joining in himself. But now he raised his head and said, 'May I ask Barnulf something, Rulosh?' When Rulosh nodded, he went on, 'Did it trouble you, Barnulf, to know Eiren didn't agree with what you were doing?'

Barnulf thought for a while, and then said, 'That's a hard question to answer. You know I'd determined to live the life of a wolf, but I suppose it would have troubled me more if Eiren had had no objection. I loved her even more for the way she reproached me – perhaps because in that way she kept alive some part of the life we used to lead together.'

'You put that very well,' said the Gentle Fluter.

When Rulosh saw the fluter lean back, apparently with no more questions to ask, he said, 'Well, now we can close the case of the theft of the fish. How high do you put your losses, Bargash?'

Thus addressed, Bargash stood up and said, 'That one eel's not worth mentioning, and as for the others, I got them back. I don't want any compensation.' Then he sat down again.

'That concludes the matter, then,' said Rulosh. 'However, we now have to look at Barnulf's attack with the knife, which seems to me less easy to settle. What was in your mind, Barnulf, when you went for Bargash?'

'I was thinking,' said Barnulf, 'that a man who wants to dispute my prey with me must prove he's the stronger first.'

'Like a wolf,' said Rulosh.

'Yes, like a wolf,' said Barnulf. 'I learned that from Gisa's retainers.'

Here the Gentle Fluter made a sign to show that he would like to ask another question, and Rulosh nodded. The fluter turned to Barnulf and said, 'You told us just now that you didn't like those yellow-eyed men from the first. So how is it that you took to their own wolfish ways?'

'If there's no one left to get a man his rights, he must see to getting them himself,' said Barnulf. 'At least, that's what I thought at the time. But if you think it gave me any pleasure, you're wrong. I've not liked myself much ever since.'

'Just as I suspected,' said the Gentle Fluter. 'You thought that in a world ruled by wolves you had no choice but to be a wolf yourself. But that went against the grain, for you're a man, taking pleasure in love and not in hatred. So you also felt those yellow-eyed men making you into something you didn't want to be. Shouldn't you have known, too, that such wolfishness might make anyone who suffered at your hands into a wolf instead of a man himself?'

'You're right,' said Barnulf, 'but I didn't think of that, not until you played your flute out there in the marshes. You can't drive wolves from the world by becoming wolfish yourself. I'd forgotten there's a power among mankind that's stronger than the wolves' law of eat or be eaten.'

'A good discovery,' remarked the Gentle Fluter. 'I've no more questions now.'

So Rulosh spoke again, and asked Barnulf, 'Does that mean that you'll keep your knife undrawn on any such future occasions?'

'Yes,' said Barnulf. 'That seems to me the only way to keep the wolves' ways from spreading.'

'Good,' said Rulosh. 'But it doesn't quite settle the matter. I want to see the damage you did with your knife. Let Bargash come forward and show the wound Barnulf gave him.'

The young fisherman rose, opened his shirt and stripped it off. There was a gaping cut across his right shoulder; the wound had stopped bleeding, but it looked bad enough. Rulosh examined it closely, and then said, 'Right, you can put your shirt on again, Bargash. Let your mother lay healing herbs on the cut, and bandage it up. Now I will deliver my verdict: this man called Barnulf shall serve you for no wages until the last scab has fallen off your wound. And then he shall work to pay off the expense of bed and board for himself and his family. After that, Barnulf is free either to go on his way, or stay with us and work as a fisherman for a decent wage. He knows how to empty a creel already! Do you accept this sentence, Barnulf?'

'Much more happily than the one you pronounced this morning!' said Barnulf, smiling. 'And I already know that I'd like to stay here with you, at least as long as Gisa's mistress of Barlebogue. I'm tired of roaming the country.'

'I'm very glad to hear it,' said Rulosh. 'Well, Bargash, now I must ask if you agree to my decision, for you'll have to take the three of them into your house.'

'I've no objection at all,' said Bargash. 'There's room enough there, and my old mother will be glad to have someone to lend a hand about the place. And after all I've heard now, I'd rather have Barnulf as my friend than my enemy.'

'You think he could hit harder than you were previously willing to admit, eh?' said Rulosh. 'And of course, he seems to have the recipe for a particularly well-seasoned fish soup!' In the general laughter that followed, he added, 'The trial's over!' and brought his fist down on the table, although it was not quite clear if this was his way of closing judicial proceedings or expressing his own satisfaction.

The men rose, and left the room one by one. Bargash went over to Barnulf and Eiren, and asked them to follow him home. At last no one was left but Rulosh and the Gentle Fluter, standing side by side and watching the former enemies go peaceably out of the door together. 'You should be a judge yourself, fluter,' said Rulosh. 'Your questions showed me what mattered in the case.'

The fluter raised his hands in a deprecating gesture. 'That's no kind of job for me,' he said. 'My verdicts would seem too strange for most people's liking. And now, let me sit outside your house in the sun for a while, before evening falls.'

So he left the justice chamber too, and sat on a bench outside the door of the house. The children were still playing in the village street, but as soon as they saw the fluter they came running up, stopped a little way away from him, and looked curiously at the old man who had managed to change the village judge's mind. And word seemed to have gone round of the way he had done it, for one of the little girls called out, 'Play us something, fluter!'

The Gentle Fluter took out his silver instrument. 'What shall I play?' he asked.

'Do you know the Song of Fair Agla?' asked the girl.

'I heard it once, many years ago, when I was in these parts,' said the fluter. 'But you'll have to help me; I don't know if I remember it all. Can you sing it?'

'That's easy!' said the girl, coming over and sitting down beside him on the bench.

'Then let's try the song,' said the fluter. He played a few notes, and then took the flute from his lips and asked, 'Is that how it begins?'

'Of course!' said the girl. 'Every child in the village knows that! Are we starting properly now?'

The Gentle Fluter nodded, put the flute to his mouth again and began to play, while the girl sang the words of the song in a clear if slightly wavering voice.

> *To the lake a girl did go*
> *every year,*
> *to the lake a girl did go*
> *with her cheeks as white as snow.*
>
> *Oh the Green Man he came out*
> *every year,*
> *oh the Green Man he came out*
> *and he kissed her on the mouth.*
>
> *The poor girl she wept sore*
> *every year,*
> *the poor girl she wept sore*
> *and she never came back more.*
>
> *To the lake did Agla go*
> *in that year,*
> *to the lake did Agla go*
> *in a dress as white as snow.*
>
> *Oh the Green Man he came out*
> *in that year,*
> *oh the Green Man he came out*
> *and she kissed him on the mouth.*
>
> *Oh fair Agla's laugh was light*
> *in that year,*
> *oh fair Agla's laugh was light*
> *and the Green Man sang all night.*

As he listened to the girl's song, he remembered hearing it before, not only by this lake, but on a later occasion too. He saw another girl sitting by a pool, singing the same song, while the fish raised their heads from the water at her feet as if they could understand every word. Then, just for a moment, the girl glanced at him, and he saw her eyes, eyes of a colour that was hard to describe, and that were as familiar to him as if he had known them for ever.

As soon as the song was over, that remembered picture was gone, and he was back with the little girl from the fishing village sitting by the fluter, her legs dangling. The other children had come closer as he played, and were now crowding around the two of them. Right at the front stood a thin, rather pale boy, his clothes smeared with mud as if he had been dragged through a ditch. He was looking at the fluter, wide-eyed. 'I wish I could play like that!' he said.

The other children laughed at him. One boy called, mockingly, 'Little Hurlush wants to be a fluter – and he squeaks like a mouse when we put him in the water!'

The Gentle Fluter looked keenly at the speaker. 'Oh, so it was little Hurlush here you were ducking in that pool not so long ago?' he said. 'Why?'

'We were playing executions,' said the boy. 'Somebody's got to be the condemned man.'

'And you do best to choose the weakest, who can't defend himself,' said the Gentle Fluter. 'Perhaps you ought to be chosen yourself, next time.' The merriment had gone from his eyes entirely. 'I suggest you ask Rulosh what he thinks of such games,' he added. Then he turned to little Hurlush, to whose eyes the others' mockery had brought tears, and said, 'Come here and sit down beside me, Hurlush.'

The boy went over and sat on the fluter's other side, still staring at him as if he were some fabulous animal. 'Do you really want to learn to play the flute, Hurlush?' asked the Gentle Fluter, and when the boy merely nodded, silently, he took a little wooden flute out of his pocket and put it in his hand. 'Then you shall have your first lesson here and now,' he said, and he showed the boy how to place his fingers over the holes of the flute. 'Now, watch carefully,' he said. 'This is how the blackbird sings.' And he played a rising three-note sequence on his silver instrument. 'Now you try it,' he said, and the boy played the blackbird's call without a single mistake.

'You will become a great master!' said the fluter, and his voice left no one in any doubt that he meant his words seriously. They seemed to make an impression on the other children; at any rate, they were no longer mocking little Hurlush, but looking at him in quite a different way. Not that the thin little boy noticed; he tried the blackbird's call once more, and played it so well that one was tempted to look round for the bird who sang so sweetly.

'Excellent!' said the Gentle Fluter. 'And now for a real song. It's about someone turned to stone, standing in the forest somewhere, waiting to be found and brought back to life. But one like you will be able to tell the subject of the song from its tune. I'll play it to you first, and tell you the words later.'

At the very first notes, it seemed to the watcher as if someone were singing the words of the song to that music; the voice was that of a girl or a woman, with a different, deeper, clearer sound than the voice of the child who had just sung the Song of Fair Agla, and anyway the little fisher girl was sitting silent beside the fluter, watching his fingers glide over the silver flute. But when he tried to see if perhaps she was really singing after all, both the barefooted child and the fluter had vanished from sight, and so had Rulosh's house with its reed thatch, and the broad surface of the lake, which just now had stretched to the distant wooded mountain range on the opposite bank, glowing red in the setting sun. Instead, he was surrounded by shimmering green in an endless variety of shades, its pattern constantly and confusingly changing; the broad leaves of the sycamore fluttered in the evening breeze, and beyond them the foliage of birches and alders quivered. Before he had quite found his bearings again, the girl was singing the second verse of the song:

> *He stands in the moss,*
> *don't know where.*
> *He stands in the moss,*
> *never shifts from that place,*
> *and his motionless face*
> *shows no pain, no loss,*
> *no joy and no care;*
> *don't know where.*

The voice now sounded much nearer than the first time he had heard it, as if the singer were hiding behind the nearest alder bushes, and she seemed to be coming yet closer with every line of the song. He felt as if the lilting notes were breaking through the stony skin of his body and penetrating his breast of stone itself to reach his heart, which lay there somewhere, silent and motionless, like a heavy pebble. He gave himself up to the sound of that voice, wishing for nothing but to feel the sweet quivering of the air release his heart from the stone and set it beating, for he now remembered that there were certain sensations which shook the heart thus. But this was only his imagining of what had been in the past, and nothing like it happened. If only I could see the singer, he thought, putting out all the power of his will towards the voice, trying to penetrate the shimmering green wall of leaves, but the singer remained hidden, no one came out of the bushes, and now the song had long since died away.

For a while he heard nothing but the rustling of the wind in the leaves, and he watched the little air bubbles rise in the pool at his feet. The mice were squeaking somewhere among the sycamore roots; he heard one of them inquire, 'Hear that song, did you? It might have been made for the goat-legged one. Do you think the girl's looking for him?'

'No idea!' said the other mouse. 'What's it got to do with us? It wouldn't do the girl much good to see this chunk of stone standing by the spring here. Even that couldn't bring him to life, could it? Or did you ever see a stone suddenly move and walk away on its own two feet?' The speaker must have been the fat mouse; there was no mistaking his self-satisfied and complacent manner of speech.

This wasn't good enough for the other mouse, who said, 'Why, do you suppose nothing exists but what you've seen for yourself? If there are songs being sung about this goat-legged stone statue, then he isn't yet lost from memory, and if that girl is looking for him, we ought to tell her where to find him.'

The fat mouse chuckled unctuously and remarked, 'Girls don't like mice! Why, the singer would pick up her skirts and run away screaming at the sight of you!'

However, the other mouse was not to be discouraged. 'It's worth a try,' he said, and he scurried through the swaying grass and disappeared among the alder bushes.

'Trying to make himself important,' squeaked the fat mouse, in an ill-tempered way, and then he could be heard gnawing at something.

For a while nothing happened. Then the mouse came running back, calling from afar, 'I saw the girl!'

'Fancy that!' said the fat mouse. 'Did she stop to listen to you?'

'No,' the other mouse admitted. 'She was walking away across the meadows, and I couldn't catch up, because she mounted her horse and rode off down the valley.'

'And what's so special about that, to make you come running back in such a state of excitement?' inquired the fat mouse.

'Her eyes!' cried his companion. 'I got a sight of her eyes when she turned and looked back. They're the same strange colour as the stone that belongs to the goat-legged one.'

'That doesn't do him any good either,' remarked the fat mouse. 'What's the use of his stone, now he's standing around here, a great block of stone himself?'

'You'll see!' said the other mouse. 'One day –' But the fat mouse interrupted him, saying 'Oh, you and your wonderful tales of mysterious stones and so forth! You've made it up, that's what it is!'

He had been listening to the conversation of the two mice, and now indeed he wondered what use the stone really was to him. He had once owned it, that much was certain. And previously it had been in the possession of that Arni who had assumed such a remarkable role among the Raiding Riders. Was his strange behaviour the stone's doing? Belenika had liked Arni, and thought highly of him. Her husband seemed to have been more bent upon making use of Arni's memory, but there must have been something noteworthy about that brother of Khan Hunli's who had made him his heir, and it suddenly seemed to him very important to find out the man's secret.

He was looking out into the wide meadows of the valley, through the branches of the birch trees, but were these still the same birch trees, their foliage shimmering dully in the pale morning sun? The shapes of the trees and bushes to right and left of a narrow path suddenly struck him as different, and anyway, there hadn't been any path in that spot just now. Then he heard hoofbeats, and next moment a little troop of Raiding Riders trotted up in pairs, bows and arrows ready in their hands. The Riders were observing all other precautions too, stopping at frequent intervals and looking all around them: they were obviously an advance guard sent ahead to explore the road.

The last two Riders were a curious pair: one was a thin old man, the braids hanging from his temples already white as snow. He sat his shaggy horse with his shoulders sagging, and was the only man not to carry a bow. There was a thin, stringy beard around his lips, moving comically when the old man spoke. His companion, a boy of about twelve, sat upright in the saddle, and seemed as much at one with his horse as if he had learnt to ride before he could walk. He was talking eagerly to the old man, and was just saying, 'What I don't understand, Uncle Arni, is why you're out on this raid at all. My father ordered me to ride with the horde, and I can't go against Khan Hunli's will. Or not yet, anyway. But you can do as you like, and ride wherever you want, and yet you joined the expedition even though I know you don't like falling on villages to plunder them, or attacking people who've never hurt you.'

'Perhaps one shouldn't even attack people who see one as an enemy to be opposed,' remarked Arni.

'What's the good of that?' asked the boy. 'If you acted that way, why, anyone who didn't like the look of your braids might strike you down!'

'How do you know?' asked Arni. 'Have you ever tried?'

The boy laughed. 'Now you're making fun of me!' he said. 'The first attempt would probably cost me my life.'

'You say probably,' said Arni, 'so you don't know for certain. I was being perfectly serious. If everyone were to strike down any man he takes for an enemy, without any more ado, then he'd never know if that man really was hostile, or perhaps just afraid, or had the wrong idea about the person he was encountering.'

The boy thought for a while, and then said, 'I honestly don't know if I'd have the courage to try it.'

The old man nodded. 'You put your finger on the difficult part,' he said. 'People will go on killing each other as long as nobody finds the courage to make that attempt.'

'If you think so,' said the boy, 'then I still don't understand why you came with us.'

'Oh, that's simple, Belarni,' said Arni. 'Could I have prevented this raid by staying at home?'

'No,' said Belarni. 'My father decided on the raid, and not even you could have kept him from it.'

'There, you see?' said Arni. 'What are you to do, if you can't stop what you don't like happening? Stay at home and act as if it were none of your business? What good does that do anyone?'

'What good does your coming with us do anyone, then?' asked the boy.

'You can never tell, beforehand,' said Arni.

'Are you going to stop the horde attacking a village?' asked the boy.

Arni shook his head. 'That's not what it's all about,' he said. 'It's never about anything but individuals, and so you can't foresee what will be required of you. I'd most likely have ridden anyway, but when I heard that Hunli was sending you out on the raid for the first time, that in itself was reason enough.'

The boy looked at him indignantly. 'Did you think I'd be afraid without you, or I couldn't be let out with the horde without someone to keep an eye on me?'

Arni laughed softly. 'Most certainly not,' he said. 'More likely, you're not afraid enough. But I thought you might like to have a friend with you.'

Before the boy could answer, the Riders at the head of the procession reined in their horses, waiting for the others to come up. 'The path forks here,' said the leader of the advance party, a thin, grey-haired man with a scarred face. 'You've been in these parts before, Arni. Can you tell me which way we'd do better to take?'

'It depends what you mean by that,' said Arni. 'Personally, I'd take the left-hand path. It leads through a quiet valley with excellent fishing waters, a good place to camp. How do you fancy fried trout? My mouth waters when I think of the fragrance of those sizzling fish!'

'And where does the other path lead?' asked the leader, unimpressed by this enticing prospect.

'Through a wooded ravine and straight towards Fraglund,' said Arni, 'and you can be sure the Great Roarer and his men will be lying in wait for us somewhere along it. Don't ask me where, though; there are dozens of suitable spots.'

'We go right, then,' said the leader. 'We didn't ride all this way to catch trout.' He spurred his horse on, and rode along the right-hand path, followed by his men. Arni shrugged his shoulders. 'A pity,' he said. 'I should really enjoy some fried trout.'

'Then ride left,' said the boy.

'And which way will you ride?' asked Arni.

'Right, of course,' said the boy. 'I must stay with the horde.'

'No trout, then,' said Arni equably, guiding his horse on after the other Riders, who were now trotting along the path some way ahead of them.

As they rode first through bushes, and then through undulating meadowland, Arni put his hand to a bag at his belt and took out his stone. He held it in his fingertips and let it glow in the mid-day sun.

'Why are you doing that?' asked Belarni.

'It's a habit of mine,' said Arni. 'When I find a decision difficult to make, I look at my stone.'

'And does the stone tell you what to do?' asked the boy. Spellbound, he was watching the pulsating play of colours, blue, green and violet, that shone out of the old man's thin, knotted fingers, making them look almost transparent.

'No, it's not as easy as that,' said Arni. He held the stone so that Belarni could get a good look at it, and went on, 'Well, I ask you, does a stone talk? What kind of a man would I be if I never did anything but what a stone told me? I should be a slave with no will of my own, able to do only what his master orders. Would you like to live in such a way?'

'Well, no,' said Belarni. 'Still, it would be nice to get some advice now and then, when you don't know just what to do. I always thought it was this stone made you the person you are. At least, they say it was only after Urla gave you the stone that you became so different from my father.'

'And that's not quite right, either,' said Arni. 'I chose the stone for myself that day because I liked it better than the golden Rider with his curved sword that your father wanted. Urla herself said that I had made the choice because I had always been different from my brother. However, I didn't know that, then, which was why I disputed the succession to the title of Khan with your father. The stone showed me that I had to go another way. It helped me to be as I really wished to be, without caring what others thought of me.'

'Is it true that this stone is the same colour as Urla's eyes?' asked Belarni.

'Yes,' said Arni. 'And not only like Urla's eyes, but like the eyes of my wife, who was a granddaughter of Urla's. When I look at it, I feel as if I were looking into the eyes of the person I loved most, and so it's not hard for me to do what I really know already to be right.'

'So that's the secret of your stone,' said Belarni, and it could be seen from his face that he had expected some less simple explanation. Noticing this, Arni said, smiling, 'All important things are quite simple once you've grasped the idea of them. The difficult part is the way you must go to get there.'

Meanwhile, the path was winding its gentle way around tall hills where bushes grew, hazels and alder, and later on, young beeches and pines, and soon they were riding beside a brook that ran through a deep ravine between steep and thickly wooded slopes. The Riders stayed close together here, their weapons poised to shoot, peering intently in all directions, for it would be easy to set an ambush anywhere here.

The watcher saw the men crouching in the undergrowth, their bows bent, before the Raiding Riders noticed them, and involuntarily he uttered a warning cry. The Riders did not seem to hear him, but let their horses walk on; Arni, however, snatched the bridle of Belarni's horse at that same moment, but it could have been a coincidence, for the path was steep, and full of loose stones washed up by the brook at high water. Then the first arrows came hissing out of the bushes, and two of the horsemen were hit and fell from their saddles. The leader let out a yell, whereupon the Riders shot a hail of arrows into the undergrowth around them, turned their horses and galloped back.

In the confusion of their retreat, Arni and the boy had come to the head of the party, and so Arni was the first to see the marksman standing upright in the bushes close to the path to halt the fleeing men. As he rode, Arni seized the boy, snatching him off his horse with extraordinary strength, so that he came over on to his own mount, face downwards on the crupper. Belarni grabbed at the saddle, pulled himself upright, sat astride the horse behind his uncle, and with all this, he had not yet noticed the danger. Arni saw the arrow leap from the bowstring; he would only have had to bend to avoid it, but instead he sat up very straight in his saddle, spreading out his arms, intent at all costs on halting the arrow which went deep into his breast with a dull thump a split second later. For a moment Arni seemed to be frozen, then he gave his horse a mighty blow, so that it reared up, whinnying, and as he himself slipped out of the saddle and fell crashing into the undergrowth, the horse raced away with the boy like a creature possessed, and out of the ravine ahead of all the others.

So that was how Arni had died. Had he guessed what would happen when he looked at his stone on the way to that place? He must have lain in the bushes for a while, still alive, at least until that moment when he handed on the stone. At this thought, the watcher suddenly realized that he was part of this picture himself, and had been crouching in the undergrowth somewhere among the marksmen until the short battle was over. He tried to go over what he had just seen in his mind again, and discover the one who must once have been himself in the thickets covering the slopes on either side of the path, but none of the faces he remembered were like the swaying reflection in the moving surface of the pool at his feet. He tried in vain to discover some likeness between one of those fleetingly glimpsed shapes and that blurred figure of which he could only ever make out a few outlines in the water, among the sparkling reflections of the light: a goat's leg braced against the rock, the shaggy curve of the hips, a hand grasping a kind of cudgel that ended in a thick and complicated knob above the closed fist. For a moment, that gnarled shape, a wooden brown, was distinctly reflected above the pebbles at the bottom, and showed a curiously distorted face; a dark eye looked up at him inquiringly, almost challengingly, as if he ought to know who was looking at him. And then he remembered. 'Why, you're the Piney,' he said in his thoughts.

'Who else?' said the Piney, a little crossly. 'I've not exactly had much in the way of bright conversation from you since you took to standing here.'

'Did it seem a long time?' he asked.

'A long time?' The Piney gave a wooden chuckle. 'What on earth do you take me for? I came to feel I was a full-grown tree again, rooted in firm ground, which is the best feeling in the world for the likes of us. I was just a bit disappointed your stock of conversational material had obviously dried up, that's all. I hope at least your limited notions of Time have become a little broader now?'

'I don't know that you could call it that,' he said. 'It seems more as if Time's all mixed up. I see things that happened long ago, played out before my eyes, and things that happened later come before the earlier ones, and I almost met myself just now. It's as if there were no Before or After at all, just an All-at-once.'

'Well, that's a remarkable insight, for a human being who generally thinks he can hold Time fast, or even measure it,' said the Piney. 'I'm inclined to think some good has come of your standing above this pool for a while. And you only had to look in the water to understand what you still think strange. See it this way: a little ripple coming from the spot where a dry twig fell into the water just now sends part of your face running across the surface. Your reflection was here a moment ago, and now it runs on and appears somewhere else, emerges and disappears again. But did you move? You can't; you are made of stone. The way it all went over the water was nothing but a reflection. And that's how it is when you look at nothing but what appears visibly, runs by and passes away again. That's what you humans call Time, never noticing that you're overlooking the important part, which was always there from the first and never passes away.'

'Is all life nothing but such a delusion, then?' he said. 'You take away all hope that I may ever come out of this stony trance and be the man I once was.'

'What a simpleton you are!' said the Piney. 'Life's no delusion! Your only delusion is what it really means. Haven't you had plenty of opportunity to see what efforts are being made on your behalf? That ought to give you reason to hope. It strikes me one of those mice down there is a good deal cleverer than you. Though as for his companion,

we'll say no more about him. Stop and think, do! Then you'll understand!'

With this, the Piney had obviously said enough for one occasion,
and no sound came from the mice, either, although they were usually
to be heard whispering or gnawing something among the roots of the
sycamore. From somewhere or other, there came a hoarse and croaking
screech that he had never heard before. What creature could it be that
screeched with such an ugly sound? It sounded more like a large bird
than anything else. And when the cry cut shrilly through the air once
more, somewhere to the left, beyond the alder bushes, he began looking
out for whatever uttered it.

Where the dark green of the alders had hidden the landscape beyond
them, a moment ago, he now had a view of an extensive, carefully laid
out and well tended garden, surrounded by tall hedges clipped into an
angular shape. The regular network of gravel paths was bordered by
box bushes, some clipped into globes and some into pyramids, and
between them lay beds of flowers in bright, glowing colours: borders of
velvety blue blooms surrounded little woods of fuchsias in flower, rose
bushes filled the spaces between low box hedges, and all this was
arranged in a way that wove the pattern and ornaments together as if
in a rug. At the intersections of the paths, and beside them, beneath
arches of climbing roses, stood stone figures: armed men with helmets
on their heads, holding weapons in their hands, naked female figures of
perfectly regular beauty, and all kinds of strange animals – winged
horses, stags spouting water in the midst of the oval basins of fountains,
mighty lionesses with women's heads resting outstretched on their
pedestals, and seeming to stare out into endless space.

Paths from all directions led, like rays, to a large and richly constructed building, a castle with finely designed gables ornamented with
scrolls, flights of steps, balconies, turrets and shining rows of windows.

On a balustrade that divided the castle moat from the garden on
either side of the entrance, there stood a row of figures of fierce-looking
dwarves, with such large, shapeless heads as to give the impression of a
tribe of giants whose limbs had suddenly shrunk to such deformity.

And strangely dressed people were walking along all these paths, not
appearing to be about any business, but just stopping now and then to
look at one of the figures, or admire the flowers. The men wore trousers
of unusual length, falling loosely to their shoes; they had not buttoned
up their jackets, obviously to show a narrow scarf made of coloured
material with its points hanging down in front. Many of them carried a

small, shining object slung on a leather strap, which they raised to
their eyes now and then, pointing it at one of the statues or the castle,
as if it would help them to see things better. If the men had covered
their legs, the women's skirts were so short that their own legs could be
seen almost to the knee, and even the older women were not ashamed
to show themselves like that. Among all these people strolling slowly
along, children went running down the pathways, taking no notice of
all the fine sights, but playing Tag and Catch, as children do everywhere. Only the very smallest, who couldn't walk yet, were pushed by
their mothers in carts with high wheels.

When the hoarse cry rang out again, it was not hard to discover the
creature who screeched so harshly. A large bird sat on the pedestal of
one of the stone figures, a bird with a tail hanging down to the ground
and decorated with large eyes of blue, green and violet that shimmered
at the end of its feathers. There must have been more than a dozen of
those eyes, and their attraction was so strong that he might almost have
failed to notice the bird's tiny head, set on a slender neck, if it had not
borne a swaying coronet of delicate feathers.

But then his glance fell on the statue at whose feet the bird sat, and
he thought he saw himself as he stood on the rock above the pool where
the spring rose, for this statue was the exact likeness of the goat-legged
faun he now was. It stood in the edge of the basin of a fountain in
whose midst a jet of water played, and the figure of an enchantingly
beautiful, naked woman stood on a similar pedestal on the opposite
side of the fountain, reaching out her slender arms towards the shaggy
faun as if to run straight towards him through the spray, while the faun
himself had already braced his clumsy hooves on the ground to leap
into the foaming water of the basin. Have I found the secret centre of
the garden again at last, he wondered, and was not sure where this
notion came from, for it had flashed into his memory as if out of some
forgotten dream.

As he was puzzling these things out, the bird flapped away into the
bushes, and an old woman came along the path, with a little girl
holding her hand. She passed the faun and sat down on a bench
standing to one side of the basin. The little girl ran all around the
fountain, looking at both statues. She was particularly intrigued by the
unwieldy figure of the faun, and even climbed on the pedestal to stroke
the shaggy coat covering his loins with a careful hand. The old woman
looked at the girl, smiling, and let her alone. At last the child jumped
down to the gravel again and sat beside the old woman. 'What's that

funny man, Grandmother?' she asked. 'He has legs like a great big goat, but he's a man from the waist up. He looks as if he were going to run straight to that lady who wants to bathe in the fountain.'

'Yes, that's what he really does want to do,' said the old woman, 'but he's a curious sort of fellow, you see, always wanting whatever he sees, there and then, so there'll be some difficulties in his way before he can get over what looks like such a short distance. He's called a faun, and the naked girl over there is a nymph: the nymph of a spring. Such nymphs used to live wherever a spring came up out of the ground, and they made sure its waters stayed fresh and clear. Many people say this one was called Marica, but that's not known for certain now, for the tale of the two of them has been passed down from one storyteller to another over many hundreds of years, and so names and events have become a little confused. You can imagine what happens when someone makes such a story go in what he thinks will be the best way. In any case, those two are supposed to have fallen in love at first sight, but then they lost track of each other again. While the faun roamed the woods, looking for his nymph, they say he kept meeting other girls, and he liked them too. A faun is glad of such distractions, you see – and anyway, that's why he kept on going astray.'

'So did he never find this Marica, or whatever her name was?' asked the girl.

'Oh yes, he did,' said her grandmother, 'but what the books say about it is so contradictory that I can't believe it.'

'How do you know about it yourself, then?' asked the little girl, moving closer to her grandmother in the expectation of a story.

'From my grandmother,' said the old woman, 'who told me she had heard the story told by her great-grandmother, who in her turn had it from an old woman in her family. I can't say over how many generations it's been handed down in this way, but it must be very old. As the story goes, there was once a boy who went out to battle with the other men of his village, but he carried no weapons, and after the fight he tried to help the men his own side had wounded. One of the dying, an old man called Arni, gave this young man a precious stone, like a living eye glowing with three colours, blue, green and violet. He believed, you see, that anyone who acted as this boy had done was destined to be Bearer of his Stone.

Well, when that battle was over, the boy went out into the world to discover the uses of the stone, and they say he kept dreaming of a girl he must seek. On the way he met his grandfather, whom he'd never seen before. And from him he learned to play the flute, for this grandfather had a silver flute whose sound was able to move men's minds to do good, if it was played in the right way. The boy inherited this flute too when his grandfather died, but then he went the same way as that faun in the story: he was a curious fellow too, always wanting everything for himself. So he went astray as well, and lost his stone, and the flute, and fell into the hands of a wicked enchantress who turned him into another such faun. However, in the end he saw, for good or ill, all that he had done wrong. But that realization was so dreadful that he turned to stone, and stood above a spring for a long time, just like the statue there. However, it was lucky for him that he had sought out that particular place, because the girl found him there at last. Perhaps she was a kind of nymph too, but her name wasn't Marica.'

'What was it?' asked the little girl.

'I knew, once,' said her grandmother, 'but I've forgotten. Maybe I'll remember sometime, and then I'll tell you.'

'You talk about them as if it was all true, and not just a story,' said the little girl.

Her grandmother raised one hand. 'Why shouldn't stories be true?' she asked. 'Why do you think that tale's been handed down in our family from generation to generation? After all, we're descended from the pair of them!' And as she said that she looked up, and he saw her eyes, eyes of a colour hard to describe, between blue, green and violet, looking at him as if the old woman could see him. 'Yes, that's the fact of it!' she said once more, and now he could hardly say if it was an old woman he did not know or Urla herself who had told the little girl that story.

The little girl looked at the two statues again, and he could see that the child had indeed inherited the same eyes. 'Will those two here by the fountain ever find each other again?' she asked.

'Why not?' said the old woman. 'There's a song I learned from my grandmother too, and it suits the stone faun very well. Listen, now, and perhaps you can pass it on to your own granddaughter when you're an old woman yourself:

> *He lives in the wood,*
> *don't know who.*
> *He lives in the wood,*
> *his skin is of stone,*

his mouth hard as bone,
cold as death, you would
say if you knew
don't know who.

As the old woman sang, in her quavering old voice, he felt as if a flute, very far away, was accompanying her song with a sweet and silvery sound that gave it strength and coherence, and when she began the second verse, her voice sounded deeper and clearer:

He stands in the moss,
don't know where.
He stands in the moss,
never shifts from that place,
and his motionless face
shows no pain, no loss,
no joy and no care;
don't know where.

From line to line, the song became richer in tone and more distinct, as if the singer herself were coming closer step by step, although the old woman still sat there on the bench beside the fountain, with the little girl beside her. But the more closely he looked, the more blurred did their outlines seem, their figures became transparent, as did the shapes of the bench and the clipped yews behind it, until it all merged with the irregular green background of the alders and birches. However, the song did not die away as the image vanished, but was quite close now.

He waits by the spring,
don't know when.
He waits by the spring,
for the spell to be broken;
he waits to be woken
by one who will bring
new life to him then.
Don't know when.

And with those last words, an alder bush moved, was parted and pushed aside by an arm, and a young woman stepped out through its swaying branches, holding a silver flute in her hands. At first glance, he saw the young woman's eyes; indeed, he saw nothing but those eyes, which resembled the eyes of the old storyteller, or Urla's eyes when she welcomed him to her hut.

The woman looked anxiously up at the branches of the tree, as if some danger lurked there, and then walked swiftly along the course of the stream, stopping only when she reached the pool where the spring rose, to bend and scoop up water in her cupped hand. He saw her lean down and dip her hand in the pool, and at the same time he could see the rippling, melting reflection that rose to meet her from the depths; the face in the shimmering water became more distinct, seemed to hover beneath the surface close enough to touch, and when their hands met, the eyes of that watery creature met his own. He felt as if the stone in his breast were melting in the warmth of those eyes, whose dark colours spread like quiet rings of ripples within him. Then the woman who had been leaning over the water raised her head and looked straight into his face. 'So there you are, stone faun! I've found you at last!' she said, and rose and came slowly along the side of the pool towards him. For a moment, she stopped under the rocky ledge where his cloven hooves rested, and then, with a quick movement, she had clambered up beside him, and her hand was stroking the rough, fissured, shaggy surface of his coat. He sensed her tender fingers on his loins, and felt them burrowing through his coat to the skin and gently scratching him, and at that soft touch the rigidity left his limbs, his unfeeling skin lost its hardness and felt sensations that ran through his body with an awakening thrill, and the heart in his breast began to beat like a hammer shattering the last remnants of his stoniness.

He stood motionless as long as he could, giving himself up to the tender touch of her hand, but then he could not restrain his desire to move any longer. He raised his arm, touched the woman's shoulder, and pressed closer, to feel the warmth of her living body. At that she took fright. She cried out, leaped down to the grass, and with a few bounds she had disappeared into the bushes.

He looked the way she had gone for a long while, but the branches of the alders did not move again. So then he stepped down from his pedestal, sat by the side of the pool, scooped up water and drank like a man who has reached a well after a long journey in the steppes.

Part Three

Chapter One

When he woke, he was lying in the grass near the pool where the spring rose, and he saw the intricate branches of the sycamore above him, with blue sky shining down through its foliage here and there. He must have slept long and deeply, for he remembered that it had still been daylight when he lay down there, and now the sun was high in the sky again. He remembered that he had suddenly felt infinitely weary, as if he had not slept for longer than he could remember; nor indeed had he, although he had been standing motionless on his pedestal above the pool. Events had passed constantly before him, holding his attention, filling his thoughts: images and incidents which he remembered as well as if he had been there himself, although that was quite impossible and could not be so, for now he also remembered the whole of his life up to the moment when he was turned to stone. He knew everything he had partly forgotten, and then gradually remembered again, and finally lost once more, so that he haunted time and space as a watcher, uninvolved and yet most deeply concerned with all these events, until the woman found him again at last.

When he tried to recall that brief meeting to his memory, he realized that he could remember her only by her eyes, eyes of a colour that was hard to describe and that he knew well, eyes familiar to him from countless dreams and stories. He knew, too, that he had met a girl several times here in this valley, and she had looked at him with alarm and even horror in eyes such as those before she ran away. But that girl had been much younger, the daughter of Promezzo the Ore Master and his wife Akka, although he still could not remember her own name. The woman who had found him here and woken him must have been taller than that child, in any case; for he now remembered that when she stood beside him, she had been able to look into his face. He could still feel her body beside him, and it had not been a child's slender body, but that of a grown woman. So she couldn't be the same person as the girl, he thought. But then who was she? And why had she run away, although she had stroked him so tenderly? Perhaps she was still somewhere nearby?

As soon as this thought came into his mind, he jumped up and set off in search of her, running to the alder bushes on his ungainly goat's legs, parting the branches with his arms, and looking out into the wide, flat valley. He saw the stream winding its way through the gently sloping meadows, which were yellow with dandelions and buttercups in flower, but there was not a soul in sight, only a slight trail leading down the valley and losing itself somewhere in the green of the meadows.

One step out of the shade of the bush into those meadows taught him that as soon as he felt the open sky above him, he was still overcome by a sudden attack of the old overwhelming fear, which forced him back into the shelter of the branches. He seated himself under the thick foliage of an alder and looked down into the valley. The herdsmen's huts must lie somewhere in that distant haze, and he wondered if the young woman lived there.

As he was still wondering what woman of Urla's family had met him here, a mouse approached him with measured step, bowed politely and said, 'I am wonderfully pleased to see you so lively, Stone-eye, and not at all stony any more, so far as I can see. Allow me to offer you the heartfelt greetings of an elderly mouse of our people, known to us by the title of Keeper of the Stone. He wishes me to tell you that your precious jewel is safe with us, and awaits your orders as to when and where we give it back to you.'

Stone-eye remained seated, so as not to rise too high above the messenger who was sitting far below him in the grass anyway, and looking up at him. 'Thank you for your news,' he said. 'As a matter of fact, I knew one of you had managed to outwit the falcon. Please carry my greetings and thanks to He-who-speaks-with-the-snake, who, as I also know, is keeping my stone for me, and ask him to bring it to me here, because I am planning to stay in this place a little longer.'

The mouse seemed surprised by these remarks. 'I thought I'd be the first to give you the news,' he said, rather disappointed. 'But you're obviously a little out of date. That venerable leader of our council, He-who-speaks-with-the-snake, went home to our ancestors some time ago, at a great old age, never having let your stone out of his sight for the rest of his life.'

'That's very sad to hear,' said Stone-eye. 'I have lost a brave and helpful friend in him. Who is keeping the stone for me now?'

'His successor was He-who-prophesies-to-the-falcon,' said the mouse, and it was plain that he was proud of being able to count folk with such resounding names among his people.

'A name that suits him well,' said Stone-eye. 'He was the one who stood up to the falcon and got the stone away from her.'

This information totally confused the poor mouse. 'Who told you all this before I did?' he asked. 'You only came to life again yesterday, and you've been asleep ever since!'

'I was there when he did it,' said Stone-eye, but realizing that such a revelation was quite beyond the mouse's understanding, he added, 'Never mind! I wasn't quite as lifeless as I seemed, you see, and I learned all kinds of things during that time. But there's one thing I still have to ask you: what do you know about the woman who woke me from my stony trance? If I understand you correctly, you saw it happen.'

'I certainly did!' said the mouse, and seemed to swell visibly with pride at having news to tell after all. 'I've been waiting for that day a long time, even though people kept on mocking me.'

'The fat mouse, you mean?' said Stone-eye, laughing. 'Where is he, by the way?'

'Asleep,' said the mouse, who had given up wondering how the faun knew all these things. 'Had too much to eat yesterday, I wouldn't be surprised. But I can tell you about the woman all right. She often came up from the valley, playing her flute, and sometimes she sang a song with words about you when you were standing here turned to stone by the spring. I'd have liked to tell her where to find the person she was looking for, but she was usually on horseback again by the time I reached her. Once I did manage to come face to face with her, but she didn't understand me, even though she isn't scared of mice, the way people always say women and girls are. She stroked my fur and gave me a little of her bread before she rode away. And later on, I met a toad down by the stream, who told me the woman could talk to the fishes, and this toad passed my news on to them, and I suppose that's how she'll have discovered where to find you. At least, she's never been up here by the stream before. It's as if she were afraid of the thick bushes.'

'And then she ran away again,' said Stone-eye, sadly. 'No wonder, either, ugly as I look with shaggy goat's hair all over me.'

'Well, admittedly she'll have been a little frightened,' said the mouse, with the air of a man of experience, 'but you mustn't take that the wrong way. She'll soon think better of it. Do you suppose she'd forget you so soon, when she's been looking for you all this time, singing her song about you?'

'Are you just trying to cheer me up, or do you mean it?' asked Stone-eye, eager to hear something more of the same kind, and he did not feel it was at all comical to be seeking comfort from a mouse.

'Oh yes, that woman will be back, as sure as I'm standing here before you,' said the mouse, firmly.

'I'd be only too happy to believe it,' said Stone-eye. 'Can you tell me your name, so that I know what good friend has been speaking to me?'

The mouse bowed his head. 'Well, I've never done anything notable yet,' he said, 'so I haven't any name.'

Stone-eye thought this surprising, in a mouse of such tenacity. Evidently none of his people had yet noticed that quality. Something like admiration could be seen even in the eye of the Piney, who was lying on the grass beside the grey-coated little creature. Stone-eye picked him up. 'What do you think of that, Piney?' he asked. 'It's obviously harder to get a name among mice than men.'

'Are you surprised?' said the Piney, with a sardonic twist to the corners of his mouth. 'You should know what can happen to a man who gets a fine name too early, if anyone does. But this bold mouse has certainly earned one now. I know a name for him, too.'

'If you say so, then the time for it has certainly come,' said Stone-eye, 'for we may be very sure you've never done anything in too much of a hurry. So give my friend his name, and then I can address him by it.'

At this the Piney looked at the mouse with his shiny, brown wooden eye, and said, 'You display a quality, young fellow, which I value highly, and indeed it is quite remarkable. I'll name you accordingly. You shall be known, in future, as He-who-never-gives-up-hope.'

The mouse thus named certainly blushed with pride and embarrassment at this, but of course it couldn't be seen through his thick, velvety fur. He bowed low and said, 'I thank you, Ancient One, for this honour, and will endeavour to be true to my name.'

'Yes, well, that's all right,' said the Piney. 'No need to make any fine speeches. I've seen what sort you are, and this goat-legged fellow here might well follow your example, although one might have thought he'd have learnt how to wait by now.'

'Then I'll be off, and make haste so that he needn't wait too long for his stone,' said the mouse, and he bowed and scurried away.

No sooner had he disappeared into the undergrowth than a fat mouse came ambling slowly through the grass, looked around him, blinking sleepily, and finally spotted the faun sitting under the bushes. 'Hullo, what are you doing here?' he asked, in some confusion. 'I must still be dreaming, that's what it is! You ought to be standing above the spring!'

'Ought I?' said Stone-eye, smiling. 'Why?'

'Because you're only a stone statue!' said the mouse, rubbing his eyes.

'Do I look like a stone statue?' inquired Stone-eye. 'You seem to have missed a few recent events since lying down to sleep off your dinner yesterday.'

'Good gracious me!' cried the fat mouse. 'You mean you really did come back to life after all? I must hurry to tell the Keeper of the Stone! Oh, what an honour it will be for me! What an honour!'

'No need to be in too much of a hurry,' said Stone-eye. 'He-who-never-gives-up-hope is on his way already, and with your figure, I doubt if you'll be able to catch up with him.'

'He-who-never-gives-up-hope? Who's that?' asked the fat mouse, baffled.

'You ought to know better than anyone,' said Stone-eye. 'I mean the mouse who was keeping watch with you here. You weren't around when he got his name.'

'That officious fool!' said the fat mouse, crossly. 'Well, I must say, he might at least have woken me! Now I'll have to run after him and get a stitch in my side!' With which he turned to go, bounding ponderously away.

'Yes, do try running!' Stone-eye called after him. 'It will be very good for you.'

And then he sat under the alder again, quite still, looking out into the valley to see if he might, after all, see some trace of the woman somewhere in the hazy distance. He had stuck the Piney into the ground in front of him, his chin propped on the gnarled knob. And as he did so, although he was not aware of it at first, the sweet, resinous fragrance of the rootstock rose to his nostrils, alluring and full of promise, a fragrance that aroused a longing for meeting and touching, embraces and passion. He felt that fragrance enveloping all his senses, and as he gave himself up entirely to the sensation, closing his eyes, he thought he heard a quiet laugh, the warm, deep laughter of the mother pine, whose life-giving magic surrounded him as the juicy and resinous cones surround the nut, and in that maternal embrace his hope for the fulfilment of his wishes and longings grew with a power that almost burst his heart in two.

He could not have said how long he had been sitting there, given up to the mysterious power of that ancient and manifold mother, when he heard the sound of the flute: a melody in which all that he himself felt took on form and shape, and the music, soaring towards him in long phrases, came closer and closer until it filled all his senses and made them tremble. Then he raised his head and opened his eyes. The young woman who had Urla's eyes was standing a few paces away from him, just taking the silver flute from her lips, and smiling. Farther down the valley, he saw her horse under the rosy evening sky, grazing as it walked slowly over the meadow. 'Are you back?' he asked. 'Why did you run away yesterday?'

'I don't quite know myself,' she said. 'I think it frightened me when your coat wasn't stone any more, and you moved. But I had to bring you your flute. It is yours, isn't it?' And so saying, she offered him the instrument.

He took it in his hand and looked at it, examining its flawless curve, and the tiny writing engraved around the lower end of the pipe. 'Yes,' he said, 'it's my flute, just as I inherited it from my grandfather. Where did you find it?'

'I'll tell you later,' she said. 'Don't you want to see if you can still play it?' So he put the flute to his lips, without any clear idea of a tune in his head, but his fingers found the right holes as if by themselves, slipped over the silver pipe, and began to form notes and put them together, themes that began where the young woman had just left off, developing into answers to those melodies that had moved his mind so powerfully, and as he played, he saw nothing but those eyes that had accompanied him ever since he first had Arni's stone; he was submerged in the pulsating light of the coloured rings of blue, green and violet, and found all those images that had ever kept his hope for this moment alive: that fleeting apparition that had been near him once on the frozen path along the banks of the ice-covered river, and had spoken to him until her eyes drifted away with the grey clouds; the face of the woman who had leaned over him with the background of the stars behind her, while he felt his head in her lap, at the spring by the borders of the Crooked Wood, and who had kissed him so that he would not quite forget where he was going. And while those images rose from his memory, he realized that without the longing these mysterious encounters had awoken in him, he would have gone utterly astray, and reached that frontier at which one is cast out into emptiness and nothing; and the terror of the fear that had come over him at such moments of realization took shape in his music too, threatening to tear the melodious phrases shrilly apart, but the bridge of notes stood firm, arch joining arch, making a way to those eyes whose play of colour now encompassed the whole horizon of the world, and with the disappearance of daylight and the coming of night the music grew fuller and deeper, voices took up the singing of the flute, and continued it long after Listener had put the instrument down again.

And now he saw them again, the birch tree girls who had woken from sleep at nightfall, and were dancing lightly over the grass. They cast each other parts of the tune as if playing ball, only a few of them at first, their clear, almost incorporeal voices scarcely to be distinguished from the splash of the spring and the whisper of the wind in the leaves, but soon more and more voices joined in, woven into a song of such sweetness that the birds around woke and added their own trills and sweet whistling calls to the melody. Listener stood there as if in a dream, surrounded by that music, which fell from the sky like a rain of stars, and brought the flowers into blossom in the young grass growing on the ground: in the dark, anemones unfolded the shimmering cups of their petals, cowslips rang their golden bells, hyacinths and butterfly orchids exhaled their magical fragrance. Listener found himself encircled by the birch tree girls dancing their round, until the lilt of their song took hold of him too; forgetting his ungainly goat's legs, he was going to join that dancing circle, but they wouldn't let him in, and flew by so fast that he could scarcely tell one figure from another. A hand stroked his shaggy loins, a laughing mouth slipped by, but nothing could be held fast, until suddenly that pair of eyes he had been seeking ever since he began his journey was there before him again, and while the dance rose to a wild eddying, those eyes stayed with him, gates wide open to a land he did not know, and he said, 'Your eyes are like the stone I've lost, but even lovelier.'

And as he ventured to take his first steps through the gates of those eyes into the endless depths of that land, he heard the woman looking at him through them continue the dancing song of the birch tree girls:

> *She stands in the wood*
> *on this night.*
> *She stands in the wood,*

> *with the faun who has woken,*
> *whose spell has been broken,*
> *and long though he stood,*
> *yet all shall be right*
> *on this night.*

Her voice rose clear and warm above the fleeting voices of the birch tree girls, and he felt as if the sound of it touched his heart. 'Your voice is like the sound of the flute you've brought me back, but even lovelier,' he said. And no sooner had he spoken than he felt the woman put her arms around his neck and pull him down to her, as she sang:

> *She sits in the moss*
> *on this night.*
> *She sits in the moss*
> *to hear the sweet sound*
> *of the flute, her arms round*
> *him, for after long loss,*
> *their eyes shall be bright*
> *on this night.*

He felt the woman's body lying beside him, her fragrant hair falling over his face, and that fragrance too was familiar to him. 'Your hair smells as sweet as the resin of the stone pine, the ancient mother of a thousand trees, but even more intoxicating,' he said.

And the woman sang once more:

> *She lies by the spring*
> *on this night.*
> *She lies by the spring*
> *with her love, who became*
> *that faun, Listener by name.*
> *May his own heart take wing*
> *and his laughter be light*
> *on this night.*

Then he knew her, and smiled. 'Arnilukka!' he said. 'Arnilukka!'

At some time in the night, Listener woke up and saw the pale trunks of the birch trees standing around them like slender sentinels in the darkness. A few stars twinkled down through the network of branches in leaf, and he felt as light as if he had only just lost the stony weight of his body. He picked up his flute, trying to find a tune to express that sense of hovering above the ground, and as he joined note to note, Arnilukka stirred at his side, and what he was playing fell into the shape of words and lines of verse, which ran like this:

> *Light as a bird,*
> *hovering*
> *hold me fast*
> *or I shall fly*
> *up and up*
> *into the sky.*

Then she took him in her arms once more and held him fast, as if she were afraid of losing him again.

'I still don't understand one thing,' said Listener, after a while. 'When I saw you last year, you were just a child, and now you're a grown woman.'

'Last year?' said Arnilukka. 'Don't you know how much time has passed, then? It was in the summer of the Great Raid that I met you here in the valley, and ran away from you, and that's nearly ten years ago.'

'Then I was a stone faun for nine years,' said Listener.

Arnilukka laughed. 'You're still a faun,' she said.

'Doesn't it frighten you?' asked Listener.

'Not any more,' said Arnilukka, holding him close. And so they lay side by side until morning, and when the sky grew lighter above the woods Listener got up to go and drink at the spring. Only when he felt the damp grass beneath the soles of his bare feet did he realize that he was no longer walking on cloven hooves. 'Arnilukka!' he cried. 'Wake up! I'm not a faun any more! The spell's broken!'

Arnilukka opened her eyes and looked at him, smiling. 'Just as I was getting fond of your goat's legs, too!' she said. 'But how is it that you've returned to human form?'

'Through you,' he said, and he told her what spell Narzia had cast on him.

'I suppose she thought she was doing you a bad turn,' said Arnilukka. 'I can see how that might be: she herself didn't care for the faun already present in your hairy body, and couldn't imagine anyone loving you in that shape. But I'm glad that you're so hairy you still look a little like a faun. It means I shall never forget you as you were when I found you.'

'You sound almost as if you were sorry I had real legs again, and can go among human beings without frightening them,' he said.

Arnilukka laughed. 'You'd better not go among human beings as I see you now, naked and hairy!' she said. 'I'll ride to the herdsmen's huts and bring you some clothes to wear. The faun in you is only for me to see! And I'd like to breakfast with you here, too.' She rose, put on her linen dress, and called up her horse, who was standing a little way off in the meadow, looking their way. He tossed his head, whinnying, and came to his mistress at a quick trot.

'I'll be back as soon as I can,' said Arnilukka. 'Wait for me here!' She sounded almost as if she were afraid Listener might suddenly disappear after all the magical transformations he had already undergone. Kissing him swiftly on the mouth, she mounted her horse and rode away down the valley and over the pastures at a fast gallop.

Listener lay down on the grass under the alder bushes again, watching her until she had disappeared from sight, and wondering if he had reached his journey's end. Didn't it all lie clear before him now? He would live in a house with Arnilukka somewhere, she would bear him children, and at last they would grow old together.

As he painted this picture of their future life, he heard a shrill cry high above. He looked up through the branches of the alders, and saw a falcon circling up in the sky. Then the bird suddenly plunged steeply down, as if spotting prey, but stopped just above the ground, wings fluttering, and flew up to perch on an alder branch. She sat there staring at Listener with her green eyes for quite a long time. Then she said, in her soft and girlish voice, 'So you found someone to hold you in her arms after all, Listener.'

'Yes,' he said. 'Your magic has no more power over me.'

The falcon laughed, mockingly. 'Well, you have your handsome legs again,' she said. 'And I suppose you plan to go down into the valley with that woman, and live there like anyone else.'

'What's to stop me?' asked Listener, but there had been a note in the falcon's voice which sent a shiver down his spine.

'You can always try,' said the falcon. She uttered one more screech of laughter, spread her wings and rose into the morning sky until she was almost out of sight, when she turned and went quickly east.

Listener stared at the empty sky and brooded over the falcon's words. What did they mean? Did the falcon know something hidden from himself? Suddenly he was afraid Arnilukka might not come back. He looked down into the valley until his eyes were smarting, and still there was no sign of her. He crouched there under the bushes for a long time, his fear growing with every heartbeat. Perhaps he had only dreamed all that had happened last night? He looked around, to see if there were any traces of the girl to be seen, and found his flute lying in the grass. Picking it up to make sure that there was no deception about that, he felt the cool, smooth curve beneath his fingers, and read the writing that ran, in close-packed lines, around the lower end of the pipe:

Follow my song,
whither you will,
yet force is wrong;
use none, or the song
will bring you ill.

He had a better idea what that meant now, and he wondered if he had yet reaped all the harvest of his misuse of the flute, or if what had happened to him was merely the preliminary to something even worse. Only now did it strike him that the flute had lost its gilding, which had hidden the words from sight, and he felt almost as if this gave grounds for hope.

Preoccupied as he was with his flute, he had entirely forgotten to look out for Arnilukka, so that she was quite close before he caught the muffled sound of her horse's hooves. She came quickly riding up, slipped out of the saddle, and took a pack off the horse's back.

'There, put something on!' she said. 'And I will see to breakfast.' She threw him a bundle of clothes, and set to work cutting bread, putting a pot of honey on the grass, and unwrapping a sheep's milk cheese from a damp cloth, while he struggled with a pair of close-fitting linen trousers and got a shirt over his head. Arnilukka watched him, laughing. 'Now you look as if you were never a faun at all!' she said. 'But I know better. Be my guest! Sit down and eat with me!'

As he ate, he thought that Urla had invited him to her table with almost the same words, but he said nothing about that, not knowing how to explain it to Arnilukka. So he kept silent, only looking up now and again, enjoying the sight of her hands' graceful movements.

When he had eaten enough, and Arnilukka, who had eaten heartily too, was putting away the remains of their breakfast in a basket, he asked, 'How did the flute come to lose the gilding your father gave it?'

'It was in a fire,' said Arnilukka, 'and the gilding cracked and melted in the heat. But the fire couldn't hurt your flute itself.'

'Where did you find it?' he asked.

'Where the fire had burnt,' she said.

'And when was that?' he asked her.

'Nine years ago,' said she, 'when the Riders' Great Raid swept through the village of Arni's Folk.'

'And that was my fault,' said Listener. 'I hate the thought of it, but now I must know what happened, both then and later. Will you tell me?'

'Yes,' said Arnilukka. 'Come here and lay your head in my lap. It's a long story, and will be easier to bear if you feel the warmth of a living person beside you.

It began in the autumn before the year in which all these things happened, when I rode over the mountains with my father to the settlement of Arni's Folk. I didn't know what kind of business my father had with Narzia, but I knew she had sent him a friendly invitation to bring his daughter, who, she had heard, had always so liked to visit Arni's House. At first my father didn't want to take me, but I pleaded until he gave in, because I longed to see the wide steppes again, after so long. I remember how I shouted for joy when we passed a ridge of rock and saw the grey, shimmering plains stretching to the distant horizon down below. I stood there for a long time, drinking in the sight, until at last my father urged me to hurry, because the sun was already low in the west over the mountain peaks. So we reached the village that evening, just before darkness fell.

My father rode into the yard of Narzia's house with me. As we dismounted, a groom came to take our horses, but my father told me to go to the stables with the man, while he spoke to Narzia inside the house. So I took my own pony's bridle and followed the groom, who was leading my father's horse to the stables, where we rubbed the animals down, and the groom gave them some oats. Then he took me round the stables and showed me Narzia's horses. He was particularly proud of a long-legged, black stallion of the Falkinor breed, and there were already five foals sired by that horse.

While we were looking at the foals, a man came into the stables and told me to go to the house: his mistress wanted to see me. So I went with him, and he led me into a large room where my father and Narzia were sitting opposite each other at a table. They must have been arguing, for I could see at once that my father was furious. Narzia greeted me in a friendly enough manner, but her eyes were hard as the eyes of a falcon fixing on its prey. "They have told me", she said, "that you have a special liking for this place, here on the edge of the steppes. Is that true?"

"Yes," I said, and I told her how pleased I had always been to go and visit my grandfather Arni. "I know nothing better than riding over the steppes, where there's nothing but grass and sky as far as the eye can see," I said.

"You see?" Narzia told my father. "She herself would like to stay."

My father glared at her and said, "Leave the child out of this!"

"Why?" asked Narzia, with a cold smile. "Do you think I'll voluntarily relinquish a pawn that's to my advantage in this game?" Then she turned to me again and asked, "Would you like to stay at Arni's House?"

I didn't know what to say. The thought of being able to ride out in the steppes every day seemed tempting, but at the same time, I was beginning to guess that Narzia wanted to use me for her own ends in some way. So I said, cautiously, "If my father says I can."

"Well?" said Narzia, looking at my father. "Won't you give her your permission?" And when my father only shook his head in silence, she went on, "Shame on you, Promezzo, denying her this pleasure! I shall keep the child here in any case, as you know quite well. Perhaps that will stop you dealing with other traders in future. Remember how you once granted us sole rights to trade in your goldsmiths' work. I shall make sure you keep your word."

"You must pay us higher prices if we're to live by that alone," said my father, but Narzia only laughed and said, "Your people will simply have to do more work, and then you'll make more money." '

'So she took you hostage,' said Listener. 'That sounds like her.'

'Yes,' said Arnilukka, 'she did, and she knew very well that my father would not do anything that might harm me. So he rode back alone next morning. When he said goodbye to me, and none of Arni's Folk happened to be nearby, he told me, in whispers, of a secret path over the mountains, one unknown to Arni's Folk. "If you can escape," he said, "you must start northwards through the woods, and go on for three days before turning west until you reach the great cliff." And he also told me a way to get up to the woods above the Shallow Valley.

"I feel afraid in the woods," I said, but he took me in his arms and told me, "Your mother and I will be afraid, too, as long as you're obliged to live here with that green-eyed witch. Don't forget that!"

After that I lived in Narzia's house. She gave me a little room at the back. There was a bed against the wall, and a little table with turned legs, two stools, and a chest by the wall opposite the door, but I owned almost nothing to put in the chest, except for the clothes on my back.'

'I had that room while I lived with Arni's Folk,' said Listener.

'I know you did,' said Arnilukka. 'When I was in bed at night, I found the door to a little wall cupboard in the panelling over it.'

'And that was where you found my flute,' said Listener.

'Yes,' said Arnilukka, 'and there were two little earthenware bottles too, but I didn't know what was in them, so I left them alone. However, I recognized the flute at once, and when I knew there was nobody in the house, I tried to play it. Narzia's steward almost caught me in the act once. I heard him coming along the passage, and I was just in time to hide the flute under my bedclothes when he came into the room, looking around inquiringly, and finally asked me what that fluting had been. "A blackbird outside the window," I said. He was an old man, rather hard of hearing, but I wasn't quite sure he believed me, so I decided not to keep the flute in my room any more, but hide it somewhere else in the house where no one would find it. I thought the attic would be a good place, and I went up there and put the flute in a crack between two beams. It fitted exactly. I was determined not to leave it in that house when I went back to Arziak.

But there was no prospect of my doing that just yet, for I wasn't allowed a step outside the house on my own. If I wanted to go riding, Narzia sent one of her men with me, and he kept by my side, while her dogs prowled round the house at night, and they were such large, strange dogs that I wouldn't have dared go out.

At first Narzia often summoned me and asked me to tell her things about Arziak – about the goldsmiths' workshops, for instance, or the mines, or she would ask me if strangers ever came to the village. From the way in which she inquired after this or that, apparently casually, I soon noticed that she hoped I would tell her things which my father had kept from her, and so I told her nothing but what she must know already. I soon came to feel like an old woman always telling the same old stories. As time went by, she noticed it herself, and didn't summon me so often, but after that I never got permission to go riding again, on all sorts of pretexts.

Later, when the snow had fallen, she came to my room one morning and told me I was going hunting with her. "Your horse is saddled and ready in the yard," she said. I was glad to get out of doors again at last; I quickly put on the furs I'd been given to wear in the winter and ran out. Narzia was already on horseback, and there was a hunting bow hanging by the pommel of her saddle, along with a quiver of arrows.

"Are we riding alone?" I asked. Narzia laughed, and said, "We need no one to keep watch when you go riding with me. Show me how you can ride, then!" She dug her heels into her horse's side and galloped out of the gateway, with me after her. We raced each other for a while, keeping close to the edge of the steppes with bushes and birch trees to our left, and the endless gleaming snow of the plains to our right. Once I almost managed to catch up with her, but then she leaned over her horse's neck, and whispered something in his ear, and next moment he seemed to be flying across the crusted snow as if he had wings.

She stopped and dismounted when she reached a log cabin on the outskirts of the woods. When I rode up, she said, "We'll leave our horses behind, or the sound of their hooves might alarm the game." So we led the horses to a stable at the back of the cabin, rubbed them down with straw and threw blankets over them. Narzia took her bow and arrows, and then we went cautiously on along by the wood. After a while Narzia stopped and whispered, "There's a deer in the bushes ahead. Wait here until I get to the other side of it, and then drive it towards me."

She ran lightly over the snow, rounded the spinney that reached out into the steppes at this point like a tongue, and disappeared behind the trees and bushes. I was alone for the first time since I had been living with Arni's Folk. I thought this was my chance to escape, the chance for which I'd been waiting so long. Without stopping to think any further, I plunged into the bushes, their branches whipping about my ears, and towards the wooded slope that rose darkly to the sky behind the bare branches of the birch trees. I ran and ran, and then it was lighter ahead of me again, and I found, to my alarm, that I still had to cross another open snowfield dividing the spinney from the wooded mountains.

As soon as I was in the open, I saw Narzia, standing farther to the right at the end of the peninsula of bushes, as if she had been waiting for me there. She did not pursue me when I ran on over the crunching snow, but I felt the gaze of her green eyes on the back of my neck. And then, all of a sudden, I was a mouse, still running for my life, but the safety of the wood lay infinitely far away on the horizon, and behind me I heard the cry of a falcon whose shadow came gliding past above me. I tried to swerve aside, but the falcon swooped down and seized me in its claws.

When I came back to my senses, I was lying on the snow with Narzia standing over me. "The deer escaped," she said. "You ran the wrong way." She was looking down at me like a huntswoman looking at her prey, and when I saw her eyes I realized she knew just what I had meant to do, and I understood the double meaning of her words. "Get up!" she said. "We'll ride home now."

At the time I didn't realize what had actually happened. It was only later, when winter was coming to an end, that I learned Narzia's secret. There was a young maidservant in the house who was always kind to me. When I was lying in bed the evening after that strange hunt, sobbing into my pillows because I could still feel the falcon above me, holding me in its claws, she came quietly into my room, sat down beside me and caressed me. "Weep it all out, my dear," she said. "Has that green-eyed witch harmed you, then?" So I told her what had happened, and it did me good to tell someone how I still felt like a helpless mouse, even here in my bed. The maidservant – Lingli was her name – took me in her arms and tried to comfort me as if I were her own child. "There, my dear, you're not a mouse!" she said. "Look at your hands and their pretty little fingers, and your arms and legs! Does a mouse look like that?"

"But I was a mouse!" I sobbed. "And the falcon nearly killed me. Can you explain that?"

"Yes," said the maid, "I can, though I wish with all my heart I'd never discovered anything about it." And then she told me that Narzia not only had the magical power of flying in the sky, in the shape of a falcon, she could turn other people into animals too.'

'As I know only too well,' said Listener, 'for she tried her arts on me, though they only half worked.'

'So that's what happened to you,' said Arnilukka. 'Then I needn't tell you any more about that. It was she who turned you into my faun!' She laughed, and ran her hand through his hair. Then she grew graver again, saying, 'But worse happened to poor Lingli. After that night, when she stayed in my room so that I wouldn't be afraid, she often came there to me, and we became such friends that I asked her if she knew any way I could escape. "That's difficult, my dear," she said. "Narzia has eyes everywhere, and you never know if she isn't sitting in a tree in a falcon's shape herself." But she promised to look out for an opportunity for me.

Meanwhile the winter passed, the snow melted, and on the borders of the wood the coltsfoot was coming into flower further every day.

Then Lingli came to me one evening and asked, "Do you still want to run away?" And when I just nodded, silently, she went on, "Then you must do it tonight! The traders who have been travelling far away came back this afternoon. Narzia was very pleased with the business they'd done, and she is having a great celebration with them in the main room. Most of them are drunk already – they brought wine back with them."

Now that my chance had come, I felt very frightened of the dark woods. "Couldn't we at least wait until it's light?" I asked. "What, so that Narzia can see you better?" said Lingli. "No, if you want to go, you must go now." "I'm so frightened," I said. Lingli put her hands on my shoulders, looked at me for a long time, and then said, "Would you take me with you? I'd feel less frightened anywhere in the world than I do in this house." It took a great weight off my mind to think I needn't go out into the night alone, and I hugged Lingli with relief.

"I've taken something for us to eat on the way, so that we won't go hungry," said Lingli, showing me a bundle tied up in a cloth. I put on my furs, for the nights were still cold, and then we slipped past the door of the big room where the drunken men were shouting and singing, scurried out of the house, and ran towards the woods in the shelter of the bushes.

We were already among the trunks of the first tall pine trees when we found Narzia standing there before us, as if she had sprung out of the ground. We didn't see where she came from. "Do you like my house so little that you'd run off without a word of farewell, Arnilukka?" she asked. "And I see you've turned one of my maids against me too! Do you know what I do to servants who cross me? You don't? Then I'll show you!" She reached out her hand, a green stone flashed on it in the moonlight, and next moment there was a large dog beside me instead of the maidservant, a dog that howled aloud and crawled over the ground to its mistress. "Yes, I prefer you this way, Lingli!" said Narzia. But when the dog pushed against her, wagging its tail as if begging her to break the spell again, she kicked it aside, saying, "Run away and join the others prowling round the house at night!" Then she looked at me. "And what shall we do with you?" she said. "Would you care to feel what it's like to be a mouse hunted by a falcon again? The falcon's claws might strike a little deeper this time, though!"

I stood transfixed where she had caught us, trembling all over, unable to utter a word. Narzia looked mockingly at me for a while, and then said, "Or did you have enough of that last time? Off you go home, then!" She turned back to the settlement without once looking round, and I followed as if she were pulling me after her on an invisible cord.

I didn't sleep a wink that night. It was only when I heard Narzia's dogs prowling in the bushes outside, snarling, that I truly understood what Lingli had told me about this house. I trembled at the mere thought of meeting Narzia again next morning, and wondered whether the other dogs had once been servants who opposed their mistress too. This struck me as so likely that I suddenly lost all fear of them; I suppose I thought that anyone whom Narzia had treated in such a way must be my friend. That night, in any case, I decided to help Lingli as best I could.

At first light of dawn, I opened my window, which I had always kept closed at night before, for fear of the dogs, and climbed out of the house. The dogs were nowhere to be seen, although at this time of day they were usually still prowling around the house. So I ran to the bushes behind the house and called softly for Lingli. All remained still for a while, but then something came running out of the woods, the dead leaves on the ground rustled slightly as it passed, and next moment a huge dog, a bitch, came leaping straight towards me. Was this Lingli? I didn't know, but I stood my ground, although the sight of that uncanny creature made me tremble again.

The bitch stopped in front of me, stepping from foot to foot, pushed her wet nose against my dangling hand, then ran a little way towards the wood, looked round, and seeing me still standing in the same place she turned back and tried to make me come over to the tall trees by gently butting me with her head. At last I understood that I was to go with her, and I went on ahead into the thick undergrowth. The other dogs were lying there, all together, six more of them in all, watching the houses intently.

When the bitch lay down too, I sat down beside her myself and stroked her coat. We sat there together for quite a long time, and I didn't know what to do next. Once, when I tried standing up, the dogs growled, and the bitch whom I took to be Lingli laid her head in my lap to make me stay where I was. For all that, the dogs lay perfectly still, although they were wide awake. Their tension gradually communicated itself to me, and in the end I felt as if a storm might break at any moment, although there wasn't a cloud in the sky, only a vast flock of crows, circling above the houses, whose cawing made the atmosphere of the morning even stranger.

By now the sun was high above the village, and I was just wondering what Narzia would do on finding I was gone, when I suddenly heard hoofbeats coming from the steppes, like the sound of a great troop of Riders approaching, and next moment a yelling cry went up. Now I guessed what the dogs had scented, and realized why Lingli had led me into the wood. I was sure, now, that she was the dog lying beside me and licking my hand.

What happened next was like a dreadful nightmare. I saw the Raiding Riders gallop into the settlement, their braids flying; I saw them everywhere among the houses, I heard them breaking down doors, with the sound of hollow blows and the crash of splintering wood, and then came the death cries of Arni's Folk, long, drawn-out, shrill screams that suddenly broke off short. I saw a few people run out of doors and down the roads until arrows struck them in the back, and then I saw them stop, swaying on their feet, and then fall and lie twitching on the ground until at last they stopped moving. Meanwhile the Riders were dragging chests and coffers out of doors, flinging all kinds of household goods out of the smashed and broken windows, and yelling as they showed one another their booty. Then the first torches sailed up to the rooftops, and a little later the whole settlement was in flames, including Narzia's house, the closest to us.

I thought of your flute hidden up between the beams in the attic, and I was very sorry I'd left it behind. As I was still staring in horror at the black smoke and flickering flames rising from the roof, I saw a window open beneath it, and then something emerged from the rising fumes. A falcon flew over us, wings beating fast, and disappeared into the tree-tops. And I knew that Narzia had saved herself while the Raiding Riders killed her people. It was nearly evening now. There were no more screams to be heard; no sound carried over to us but the monotonous songs of the Riders, sitting together somewhere among the burning houses. Clouds had come up in the sky, and that night there was a heavy rainstorm that put out the flames. All this time, I lay there with the dogs, getting soaked to the skin, but Lingli, or the dog who had once been Lingli, pressed close to me and warmed me with her body. The Riders left when it was nearly morning. To my horror, I saw them lead their horses along the path over the mountains to Arziak, so I realized that even now, when there was no one keeping watch on me any more, I must take that secret path through the forest if I wanted to get home, supposing I had any home left by the time I reached it. But first I would at least try to save your flute.

The dogs didn't stop me rising and going back to the settlement now. I was careful to keep in the shelter of the bushes, but I soon realized there wasn't a living soul in the place any more. The dead lay in every alleyway, and I forced myself not to look when I had to run past them. I shall never in my life be able to forget what I saw, all the same.

Narzia's house was about half burnt down, and most of the roof timbers had fallen in. The smell of smoke almost took my breath away, but I still managed to climb up over the broken beams to that part of the attic which hadn't collapsed, and made my way to the place where I'd hidden your flute. A single beam had withstood the flames here. It may be chance that an oak beam was used at this place – perhaps because there was no other wood to hand at the time – whereas most of the timber of the roof was pine. But I wonder now if it was also chance that I had hidden the flute under that very beam. At any rate, the beam had protected it. The uprights between which I had put it were charred, and the flute itself was still hot when I took it out. It looked different, too. The gilding had peeled away and melted into tiny little balls. But the silver pipe itself had suffered no harm and shone without flaw as I wiped it on my soot-smeared skirt.

As soon as I was sure that the flute was undamaged, I made my way down through the rubble of the fire, ran out of the gate and around the house and back to the wood.'

'I saw you there,' said Listener.

'You?' said Arnilukka. 'How could you?'

'I was standing behind the house, just about to climb in through a window and look for my flute myself,' he said.

Arnilukka stared at him in surprise. 'Were you really there that day?' she cried. And then she suddenly laughed, and said, 'Well, perhaps it was a good thing I didn't see you. I might well have fallen down dead of fright! Did you recognize me?'

'No,' said Listener, 'although you did seem somehow familiar. But all I saw was a thin child in a sooty skirt running to the wood. You'd disappeared before I could see who it was.'

'Well, then I found I was alone,' Arnilukka continued her tale. 'I called for Lingli, called and called, but there was no sign of her. I still wonder what became of her, and if she's still roaming the burnt ruins of the village of Arni's Folk with the other dogs.'

'No,' said Listener, 'no, she isn't.' And he told Arnilukka how he had met the dogs, and turned them back into human beings with the help of Narzia's ring. 'If they took my advice, they'll be living in a cave under the great cliff,' he said, and after thinking for a while, he added, 'It's strange: look at it the right way, and Narzia saved that girl's life when she changed her into a dog. The evil things she does seem to turn out well, quite contrary to her intentions. She hid Arni's stone for herself too, and but for that the mice couldn't have got it away from her again and kept it for me. And she changed me into a faun so that you could find me.'

'Am I to be grateful to her for that?' said Arnilukka. 'No; I'm more inclined to think life's so fashioned that it can make use even of evil deeds, weaving them into the pattern of the growing, expanding weft of all that lives.'

'Your grandfather Arni might have said that,' said Listener.

'It was he who taught me such ideas of life when I was a child,' said Arnilukka. 'But it's very hard to keep those thoughts in mind when you're running through a dark wood with fear hunting you, and frightened to death by every twig that cracks in the undergrowth. That was how I felt as I made my way through the woods alone. I can't tell you how many days the journey took me; that time is buried in my memory like a single dreadful dream of darkness, fear and mortal terror. I don't know how often I lost my way and went round in circles, until I recognized a clearing or a tree I'd passed before. Sometimes I dug sprouting acorns and beechnuts out of the fallen leaves to take the edge off my hunger, but the hunger wasn't as bad as the fear that kept leaping out on me again from every dark place in the undergrowth. You know that I never liked going through woods, but now I kept seeing dead men lying in the shadows even when my eyes were open, staring at me with their own sightless eyes. Once I lay down, wishing only to die. And then something happened which I do remember very well: suddenly there was a toad sitting beside my head, saying, "Why do you want to die when you're so close to the living water?" Only then did I see that I was lying by a stream that ran through the woods over mossy stones. "I can't find a way out of this forest," I said. "Do you know one?"

"If you could think straight you'd find it for yourself," said the toad. "Go on up the stream to a little lake, and just beyond it you'll find the entrance to the old way through the great cliff."

And this toad looked at me in so friendly a manner, with her beautiful golden eyes, that I plucked up courage again, but as soon as I was walking through the forest alone once more, the fear overwhelmed me.

I can hardly have been in my right mind when I finally reached the great cliff and crawled along the old bed of the stream – a dark, narrow tunnel, that seemed to have no end, and even once I was up it my path went on through endless forest. Then I woke one morning and realized I had been sleeping in the Weird Wood. I was frozen with horror, and at first I hardly dared to move, seeing those wolves lurking behind every twisted tree, though I knew they were really dead. But such knowledge isn't much good when fear has gripped your heart as if it were a fluttering bird and is squeezing it tight. At some point, when it was a little lighter, I ran uphill like a hunted thing, got entangled in the drifting lichen on the pines, stumbled over roots that came crawling out of the ground everywhere like snakes, and at last I reached the meadow on top of the mountain. I could breathe a little more freely there. I spent the next night in the branches of the old rowan; I felt safe in that tree.'

'The big bird,' said Listener.

'What bird?' asked Arnilukka, and she looked at him in surprise.

'When I was up there myself, at the same time,' said Listener, 'I saw a large white bird come fluttering down from the branches in the morning and scurry across the meadow. It must have been you. But I was so full of my own despair that I thought no more of it.'

'Then we kept just missing each other,' said Arnilukka.

'Yes,' said Listener, 'and it's strange that we were so close at the time, when we felt so utterly alone.'

'I probably wouldn't have noticed you even if you'd crossed my path,' said Arnilukka. 'All I could see were the dreadful pictures my fear showed me. That day, then, I went the last of the way through the woods and eventually came down into the Shallow Valley. I went a little farther into the meadows, until I reached a few foals grazing there, and then I lost consciousness. Vazzek found me there towards evening, when he came to drive the horses home to their stable. Later, he told me that I lay sick with a fever for weeks, talking deliriously. But at last the bird of death, as he put it, departed from my bed, and I could get up, and later I helped him with the horses, because he was all alone at the time. Somewhere in my mind, however, the fear I felt then still lurks, and if I so much as step into a wood it breaks out again, driving me back into the open. Indeed, it was not easy for me to go this short distance to the spring past the alders and birches, although the sky shows everywhere through their branches, and the view of the valley isn't hidden by undergrowth or thickets. My fishes told me where to find you, but I would never have come this way of my own free will.'

'You owe that message to a mouse who was on watch here, and would let nothing shake his belief that I was still alive, and wouldn't stand like a block of stone above the spring for ever. That's why he is now called He-who-never-gives-up-hope.' Yet even as he told Arnilukka this, he felt a premonition, vague but dreadful, rising in him at her last words. 'Your fear overcomes you if you have no clear view,' he said, 'just as mine always overcame me as soon as I was out in the open under the sky. But surely that was only a part of the enchantment from which you've freed me.' He was hoping desperately that this was really the case, and Arnilukka seemed to assume that it must be, for she cried, 'Then come out into the open with me now!' She rose, took his hand, pulled him up from the ground, and was going to run out with him into the meadows that shone in the sunlight, bright green and sprinkled with the colours of countless flowers. But as soon as he stepped out of the shade of the bushes, fear struck him like a clenched fist, almost flinging him to the ground. Letting go of Arnilukka's hand, he rushed back into the bushes and lay trembling among them. So that's what made the falcon laugh, he thought. I have my human form back again, but the worst part of the spell is still unbroken, and Narzia knew it.

He looked out at Arnilukka standing in the bright sunlight and gazing back at him in alarm, and he knew that this would never change. Wherever they were, one or other of them would always be afraid.

At last Arnilukka came back to him. There were tears in her eyes as she saw him lying so helpless on the ground. 'Come!' she said. 'Get up! We'll find some way, and anyway you can't stay here. Let's go down the valley to the herdsmen's huts, along the side of the wood; I can walk in the grass and you can stay among the bushes, and we'll be so close to each other that we can touch hands whenever we like.'

She called up her horse, and they set off. Sometimes they held hands until a hazel or cornel cherry bush parted them, and when they met again, a few paces farther on, they fell into one another's arms, laughing, as if they had not met for weeks. Arnilukka seemed to think this a delightful game, and Listener let her merriment infect him, but still each of these partings gave him a sharp pang, and it seemed almost a miracle when Arnilukka actually did appear again beyond the bushes, happily reaching out her hand to him.

So they made their way slowly, and with many delays, on down the valley until the herdsmen's huts lay before them. Horses grazed beyond the huts, farther down the valley. As they crossed a path leading from the stables to a log cabin that could be seen a few dozen paces farther off, in the wood and among tall pines, Arnilukka stopped and said, 'Now we must really part, for I see that you can't cross the meadow to the huts. You will have to live in the woodcutters' cabin over there for the time being, and I can't come to you there. I'll send Vazzek over with what you need for the night, and I shall be waiting for you here by the edge of the wood tomorrow morning.'

They embraced as if their farewell was for ever, and would no doubt have stood there for hours if the horse hadn't snorted and tugged at the bridle. 'My mare wants her stable,' said Arnilukka. She gave Listener one more kiss, swung herself into the saddle, and rode over to the buildings at a fast trot.

He watched until she had disappeared beyond the stables, and then went slowly into the wood and towards the log cabin. Its door was not locked, and he passed through a narrow porch into a low-ceilinged room smelling of the smoke of the countless wood fires that had burned on the enclosed hearth. The wall behind it was lined with slates to protect the logs of the structure from the heat, and these slates were blackened with smoke right up to the ceiling. A good solid table and a few stools stood in the middle of the room, and there was a shelf by the wall holding pans and all kinds of kitchen utensils, and a chest, and a broad bed where several men would have room to sleep at once.

Listener fetched an armful of billets from a woodpile he had seen outside the door, cut some chips, and kindled a fire with his flint and steel. As soon as the crackling flames began eating into the wood he felt very much at home in the cabin. Smoke gathered below the ceiling and made its way out through an opening. Listener sat by the fire and watched the flames flicker over the pale wood until it turned rapidly darker, and crevices in it burst open, their edges glowing red. It was a strange feeling to sit in a room indoors again, after all the years he had spent in the open air. Even a fire burned differently here; out of doors, any breath of air blew the flames aside. He tried to imagine what course his life might take now, but he could not seem to form any plan of it: everything remained vague and blurred. He felt like a man in unfamiliar country, unsure which way to take.

He was still sitting there, musing aimlessly, when he heard the outer door open, and next moment Vazzek came into the room. The old Carphead had changed very little over the last few years, though his snow-white hair was thinner than before, and his eyes paler and more watery. He was carrying a bundle which he set down on the bed before turning to Listener. 'I thought it was you, fluter,' he said, 'though Arnilukka didn't say much when she sent me over. It's a long time since we last met, outside Khan Hunli's paddock.'

'I've already heard that you had much to suffer on my account, Vazzek,' said Listener. 'Can you forgive me for acting so thoughtlessly then? I meant well, but I never thought of the consequences.' He rose and took a step or so towards the old man, who had been spreading woollen blankets on the bed, and was now putting some provisions away on the shelf: flat cakes of bread and a piece of bacon, a wineskin, and a few other items of food. Vazzek arranged all this carefully before turning and looking at Listener with a smile. 'I know that,' said he. 'Why, I'm not angry with you!' He offered his hand, held Listener's own in his clasp for some time, and studied him from head to foot. 'You were scarcely more than a boy at the time,' he said. 'And anyway, that's all long ago now.'

Listener invited him to sit by the fire for a while, and when the old man willingly drew up a stool and sat astride it, Listener took two goblets from the shelf, poured wine, and sat down with him.

'I did see you once again, later,' he said, 'although you didn't notice me.' And he told the old man how he had witnessed his arrival in the Shallow Valley.

'Ah, so that's why you weren't surprised to see me here,' said Vazzek. 'Yes, those were bad times. Frightened as I was, I could have crept down a mousehole to hide.'

'And I was to blame for what they did to you,' said Listener.

'Blame?' said Vazzek, shaking his head slowly. 'Why, who's to blame when such things happen? I'll tell you all the folk who might be to blame for the Great Raid nine years ago. First, the Raiding Riders, who've always attacked dwellers on the borders of the steppes, robbing them and dragging them off into slavery, as they once did with me and my people by the Brown River. The Riders knew no other way of life; that was how the horde had lived as long as anyone could remember. And we looked on their raids as a fierce storm, against which there's no defending oneself. Are we to blame for putting up no resistance, if only to make the Riders aware of the wrong they were doing us? Well, then Arni came along, and showed a few of those who didn't think him completely crazy that there was another way to live. And when he died, others tried to imitate him, though I won't ask whether or not they understood him properly. At first, even a man like Honi may have meant it sincerely, though then again, he may have had other reasons for acting as he did. But he soon came to see he could win power in that way, and his daughter surely far outdid him there! However, the story of Arni's Folk begins with Arni himself. Does that mean he's to blame for all that came of it? And then, last of all, you came along with your fine idea for making the Riders' horses useless, and now you think you were to blame for everything that happened. Back then, when I discovered the magical trick you'd played, I thought it wasn't such a bad notion – though only until I suffered for it myself. Perhaps I'm a little to blame too, for not preventing you from playing that song to the horses. That's what Khan Hunli thought, anyway, and I fancy he wasn't entirely wrong, because I knew very well he'd forbidden you to play your flute in the horde's camp. In his own way, he had a very good notion of what even a Raiding Rider may not do, so in spite of all the humiliations Narzia heaped on him, he refrained, in his own lifetime, from doing any harm to those who named themselves after his brother; he had promised Urla to leave Arni in peace. However, he died the winter before the Great Raid – or to be exact, he had a stroke during a fit of rage at Narzia's arrogance, and his eldest son Husski, who became Khan after him, didn't feel bound by the same promise. So there again, Narzia herself may be to blame for the killing of all her people. Look at things that way, and you can come to think it doesn't make so very much difference who was involved in bringing about this or that disaster, because then everyone would be to blame.'

Listener thought for a while, and then said, 'Hearing you talk so, one might conclude that everyone could do as he liked, anything that came into his mind, because he would be to blame whatever happened.'

'And it's not as easy as that either,' said Vazzek, smiling. 'I'll tell you a story I heard from a fisherman in our village when I was a boy. There were two brothers called Oleg and Boleg, whose father was mortally sick. He had sent for a wise woman skilled in magic, and she told him there was an island farther up the river, where magic mistletoe grew on the branches of huge balsam poplar trees. The berries of this mistletoe could heal any sickness, and he would not recover unless someone brought him that medicine. However, the thing must be done with great caution, because an Elf Queen lived on the island, and she took it very ill if anyone harmed her beautiful trees.

So the sick man summoned his son Oleg, told him what the wise woman had said, and asked him to pick a branch of the magic mistletoe and bring it home to cure him. Oleg took his axe, got into his boat, and rowed upstream. He rowed for three days, and then the river divided into two arms ahead of him. There was an island between the two arms of the river, where he saw huge balsam poplar trees with their branches reaching out over the water. He came ashore on the bank, made his boat fast, took his axe, and went all over that island until at last he found a poplar with a great bush of mistletoe on its topmost branch.

Oleg tried to climb the tree, but the trunk had no branches until it was taller than the height of three men, and it was so thick that three men couldn't have spanned it. He looked up to the mistletoe bush swaying in the wind high above him, and he couldn't reach it unless he chopped the tree down to get at the mistletoe. He sat down under the tree and wondered what to do. His father had told him he would anger the Elf Queen if he did anything to injure the tree, but Oleg was determined not to go home without the mistletoe. If I bring my father a branch of that mistletoe, he thought, he'll be so grateful that he'll make me his sole heir. And when he looked up once more, and saw how large and full of branches the mistletoe bush was, another idea occurred to him: he could win much renown and great power if he owned such a bush, which must have hundreds of berries on it. All who were sick and near death would send to ask for one of the berries, so that each of those berries could be worth more than ten times its weight in gold to him.

Without any more delay, Oleg took his axe and began cutting a notch in the trunk. The tree was very thick, of course, but poplar is a soft wood, so the notch quickly grew deeper, and after a while the tree began to creak and sway, and it fell crashing into the bushes on the bank. Oleg thought he heard a cry as the poplar fell; however, he took no notice of that, but ran to the place where the top of the tree had come down, along with the mistletoe bush. He soon found it, but as he was about to cut the bush away with his knife, he saw that the branch had struck an otter as it fell, and the otter was now lying underneath it, whimpering.

The otter looked at Oleg with its round eyes and said, "Please get me out from under this branch, and give me one of the mistletoe berries to eat, and then I shall be cured." Oleg laughed. "What will you give me for it?" he asked. "My friendship," said the otter. "I can't buy anything with that," said Oleg, "and what's more, the Elf Queen may catch me if

I hang about here any longer." So he cut off the mistletoe bush and went back to his boat. But before he could get there the Elf Queen was suddenly standing in his way. Her eyes were flashing with anger, and when she raised her hand Oleg was rooted to the spot and couldn't move. "You have killed one of my finest trees," she said, "and so you shall stand here for ever like a tree, unless someone comes to plead for you." And so saying, she left him there.

Well, Oleg's father waited in vain for his son to come home. His sickness grew worse, and when a week had passed, and he felt his end was near, he summoned Boleg and said, "I have no hope now that your brother will return. He must have fallen into the Elf Queen's power. Will you go out to get me one of those mistletoe branches?" And he went on to tell him of the risks the venture entailed.

Boleg saw that his father would die if he did not get such help, so in his turn he took his axe, got into his boat, and rowed upstream for three days until he came to the island. He came ashore, made his boat fast, and went all over the island until he came to a tall balsam poplar tree, with a mistletoe bush on its topmost branch. This tree too was impossible to climb, so Boleg sat down at the foot of its trunk and wondered what to do. If I don't bring home a mistletoe branch, he thought, my father will die. If I want to help him I shall have to chop this tree down, even at the risk of arousing the Elf Queen's anger. And when he looked up and saw how large that mistletoe bush was, another idea occurred to him: he would be able to help a great many other people with its berries too. So he made the decision to fell the tree.

Without any more delay, he took his axe and began to cut a notch in the trunk. He cut deeper and deeper into the soft, pale wood, and after a while the tree began to creak and to sway, and it fell crashing into the bushes on the bank. Boleg felt as if the tree had cried out as it fell, and he was dismayed. However, it was down now, so Boleg went along its shattered trunk until he reached the branch bearing the mistletoe, and he was just about to cut the bush off with his knife when he saw that the branch had struck a beaver, and the beaver was now lying underneath it, whimpering.

The beaver looked at Boleg and said, "Please get me out from under this branch, and give me one of those berries to eat, and then I shall be cured."

When Boleg saw what he had done without ever meaning to, he set to work with all his might, and he managed to lift the branch against the whole weight of the tree, just enough for the beaver to crawl out. Then Boleg picked a berry of the magic mistletoe and tucked it behind the beaver's long teeth. The beaver chewed the berry a bit, and then it sat up, shook itself, and said, "Right, you'd better hurry back to your boat now, because the Elf Queen will be very angry when she finds that you've chopped down one of her fine trees."

"Are you sure you're quite all right?" asked Boleg.

"I am," said the beaver, "and thank you very much for helping me. But you'd better not waste any more time, or you'll regret it." And the beaver went to the bank, dived into the water and swam away.

So Boleg cut off the mistletoe bush and went along the bank to his boat. But before he could get there, the Elf Queen was suddenly standing in his way. Her eyes were sparkling with anger, and when she raised her hand Boleg too was rooted to the spot and couldn't move.

"You have killed one of my finest trees, like your brother before you," she said, "and so you shall stand here for ever like a tree, unless someone comes to plead for you."

So saying, she turned to go, but before she had taken three steps there was a sound of rushing water, and the beaver came splashing up on the bank. It shook the water from its coat and said, "Elf Queen, I plead with you to let Boleg go."

"Do you know what he's done?" said the Elf Queen. "He has felled one of my finest poplars, like his brother Oleg before him, and it will take more than a hundred years for another such tree to grow."

"I know all about that," said the beaver. "I was under the tree when it fell. However, Boleg proved merciful. He freed me and gave me one of the mistletoe berries to cure me."

"Then you are right to plead for him," said the Elf Queen. She stretched her hand out, and immediately Boleg could move again. He thanked the Elf Queen, and thanked the beaver too, for pleading for him, and then he was about to pick up the mistletoe bush, which he had dropped in his fright. Seeing this, the Elf Queen asked him why he needed the mistletoe.

"My father is mortally sick," said Boleg, "and he asked me to bring him a branch of mistletoe from this island to cure him."

"And did he tell you that I punish anyone who harms my trees?" said the Elf Queen.

"He did," said Boleg. "But there was no other way of getting at the mistletoe, and I love my father so much that I was ready to take the risk."

"Fair enough," said the Elf Queen. "But why take the whole bush, when all you need is one little twig with a single berry on it?"

"I thought," said Boleg, "that I could help others with the magic mistletoe. There are sick and dying people all over the world."

"I know that," said the Elf Queen. "But anyone who wants such a mistletoe berry must go to the trouble of fetching it himself, just as you have fetched one for your father. So break a little branch off, but leave the bush behind!"

"If that's the case, then I'm content," said Boleg, bending and breaking off a twig with a single, milky white berry among its leaves. When he had done that, he went up to the Elf Queen and said, "I have bowed to your will in this, for you are the mistress of this island, but now I plead with you to set my brother Oleg free too."

"Do you know what he's done?" asked the Elf Queen.

"The same as I did," said Boleg. "You said so yourself."

"The same, yet not the same," said the Elf Queen. "When I came to the tree Oleg killed, I found an otter underneath its branches, and the otter was dead. Perhaps that otter asked for help too, and Oleg wouldn't give it any."

"May not the otter have died at once?" asked Boleg. "Then my brother couldn't have helped it."

"That may or may not be so," said the Elf Queen. "However, he has two lives on his conscience now: the lives of the tree and the otter."

"When he cut the tree down, he couldn't know that it would kill the otter," said Boleg. "I plead with you again: set him free, for I can't face my father without my brother."

So the Elf Queen told him to follow her, and soon he saw Oleg standing in the bushes, rigid and motionless. He was still holding his mistletoe bush. As soon as the Elf Queen had stretched out her hand, the spell on Oleg was broken. When he recognized his brother, and saw that he was carrying a mistletoe branch, he cried, "Let's have a race, and see who can row home faster!" For he knew he was the better oarsman, and he was thinking of what he might hope to get from his father with his mistletoe bush. However, the Elf Queen stopped him with an imperious wave of her hand, saying, "Wait! You must leave that mistletoe bush here. Your brother has a branch, and that's enough."

Oleg looked at her angrily and said, "My father sent me out first. Am I to come home empty-handed?"

The Elf Queen looked hard into his eyes and said, "What do you really care for, Oleg? To see your father cured, or to be the one who brings him that cure? Put the bush down! Or do you want to stand here for ever? I set you free only because your brother was ready to plead for you."

So Oleg angrily threw his mistletoe away, saying, "Come along, Boleg! Let's row home!" And he turned and went to his boat. Boleg thanked the Elf Queen once again, and she said to him, "I hope you won't regret asking for your brother's freedom."

"How could I regret sparing my father such a grief?" said Boleg, and then he followed his brother.

Oleg had been tying his brother's boat to his own, and when he saw Boleg coming he said, "We'll go together in my boat. Then one of us can row, and the other can rest, and so we'll get home faster." Boleg thought this was a good idea, so they went downstream, which was much quicker than rowing against the current. Oleg let his brother row first, and after a while, observing that Boleg was tiring, he said, "Rest now! You've had to row for the last three days, while I was able to rest." Boleg had no objection. He lay down in the bows of the boat, and soon fell asleep.

Oleg was careful not to wake him, and kept the boat going quietly downstream with the current until he could see his father's house. Then he steered the boat to the landing-stage, took the mistletoe branch from his brother's hand, climbed out very cautiously, made the empty boat they had been towing fast to the landing-stage, and pushed the other boat, in which his brother was sleeping, out into the river again.

So he was the first to reach his father and give him the mistletoe branch. As soon as his father had eaten the berry, his health visibly improved, so much so that he was able to get up that very day and eat a hearty meal. "You have saved my life," he told Oleg. "When I lay sick in bed, and the two of you were on your way to the Elf Queen's island, I made up my mind to make whichever of you brought me the mistletoe branch my heir. So now that's settled."

Oleg could scarcely hide his delight in the success of his plan, and when his father asked if he hadn't met his brother on the river Oleg said no, he hadn't seen him anywhere. And Boleg was known to be no very good oarsman, so he might have gone the wrong way.

"Let's hope he comes home safe and sound," said their father, and from then on he went down to the landing-stage several times a day, to keep a look-out for Boleg.

Meanwhile, Boleg drifted on downstream in the boat, still asleep.

However, there were dangerous rapids ahead that way, and as soon as the boat came near them, it went on faster and faster. In his exhaustion, however, Boleg was sleeping so soundly that he never even heard the roar of the waterfalls become louder and louder as he came closer, and he didn't wake up until his boat was being tossed about among the rocks and capsized. Before he was fully aware what was happening, the raging current flung him against a boulder so violently that he lost consciousness, and was swept helplessly on, until as evening fell the rapids came to an end, the river grew calmer, and cast him up on an island.

He lay there all night, battered and bruised, half regaining consciousness now and then, but unable to move a muscle. When he came to his senses again towards morning, as day was dawning, he heard something come splashing up out of the water nearby, and when he opened his eyes he saw two beavers sitting beside him, looking at him.

"This man seems to be in a bad way," said one of them.

"He must have been in the rapids," said the other.

"Then he lives farther upstream," said the first. "Do you know him? You used to have your lodge up there."

The second beaver took another careful look, and then said, "Isn't this Boleg, who helped our cousin out from under the fallen tree on the Elf Queen's island?"

"I don't know anything about that," said the first beaver. "When did it happen?"

"Only yesterday," said the second beaver. "Didn't you hear the sand martins twittering about it?"

"They're always twittering," said the first beaver. "Who takes any notice of them?"

"I do, for one," said the second. "And a good thing too. You stay here with Boleg while I set off for the Elf Queen's island to fetch him a mistletoe branch."

So saying, the beaver slipped into the water and swam away upstream.

Well, Boleg lay there on the bank, with his legs in the water, and the sun rose higher and higher, blazing down on him, but the beaver who had stayed with him had set to work. It gnawed the thin alder stems around him with such skill that they dipped to form a shady roof above Boleg's head, and it dug a channel from the bank to his head, so that he could drink. That was all the beaver could do for him. So days and nights went by – Boleg wasn't counting – until the other beaver came back with a mistletoe branch in its teeth. No sooner did Boleg taste the sour berry than he felt the strength return to his body, and his wounds instantly healed. He thanked the beavers, swam to land, and set off home along the bank.

Meanwhile, Oleg had gone back to work as usual, and the day after his return he went out fishing on the river. He cast his lines, threw a net into the water, and then lay down in the boat to get a little sleep. As he lay there dozing, he heard something come swimming up and busy itself about his boat. He was so sleepy that he could scarcely open his eyes, but he saw a dark face with round eyes peer over the side for a moment, though he was too lazy to get up and look more closely. It could have been an inquisitive otter, he thought, and then he heard someone in the water saying, "Isn't this Oleg, who let our cousin die on the Elf Queen's island?" "It is," said another voice, "and he'll catch no more fish here." Next moment Oleg felt a tug at his net, and saw his lines twitching. He sat up, cursing, but all he pulled into the boat was a torn net, and his lines had been bitten through. And so it went on, day after day, although he provided himself with a cudgel to pay the otters out. They would suddenly come shooting up from somewhere in the depths, and before he knew it they had spoiled his mended net and his lines again.

So it went on for a while, until one evening Oleg's father said, "You've not had much luck fishing recently."

"It's the otters," said Oleg, "they're stealing my catch, but I'll soon show them!"

That evening Boleg came home, ragged, dirty and without his boat. His father took him in his arms, saying, "Thanks be, you're back again! Where have you been?" Boleg looked at his brother. "I got into the rapids, and lost my boat," he said.

"You see, Father?" said Oleg. "I told you so! He went downstream and couldn't hold his own against the current. It wouldn't have happened to a good oarsman."

Boleg was going to give him the answer he deserved, and say how he had reached those rapids, but when he saw that his father was still marked by the sickness from which he had just recovered, he said nothing, to keep from upsetting him.

"Well, we can't all be good at the same things," said their father. "As we have only the one boat now, Oleg will go out fishing as usual, and you, Boleg, will take your bow and arrows and lie in wait for the otters who steal his catch."

This put Boleg in a difficult position. He knew very well what the otters had against Oleg, and he remembered how angry the Elf Queen had been at the death of one of their kind. On the other hand, he and his father depended on Oleg's catch. There was scarcely anything to eat in the house, and sooner or later they would find themselves starving.

So he was sitting by the river one day, troubled in his mind, when two otters came swimming up, climbed on to the bank, and began scuffling playfully with each other like a couple of kittens. He enjoyed the sight of the otters' nimble games, and after a while he said, "But I really ought to shoot you!"

One of the otters looked at him and said, "Why would you want to do a thing like that, when you helped the beaver on the Elf Queen's island?"

"I don't want to," said Boleg, "but I shall have to if you keep on spoiling my brother's fishing."

"It's his own fault," said the otter.

"I know," said Boleg, "but if you carry on like this much longer we shall all starve: my father, and Oleg, and myself."

"Doesn't your father know what happened on the Elf Queen's island, then, and how your brother behaved?" asked the otter.

Boleg shook his head. "I couldn't tell him," he said. "I wanted to spare him that grief."

"Then you're to blame yourself, for letting things come to this," said the otter. "You'll have to tell your father the whole story if you're to straighten yourselves out again. You can't expect us to forget what your brother did to our cousin."

So that evening, when both sons were sitting indoors with their father, Boleg plucked up courage and told his father all that had happened. Oleg listened in silence, and when Boleg had finished his tale, he said, "He envies me my inheritance, Father. That's why he is telling you such a parcel of lies."

"Is it a parcel of lies?" asked his father, looking keenly at Oleg. Then he rose and said, "I have listened to your story carefully, Boleg. Now I want you both to come down to the landing-stage, where I shall soon find out which of you spoke the truth."

He went ahead of them, and when all three were down on the landing-stage, he pulled in the boat and examined it carefully. Then he stood up again, saying, "Oleg, how is it that you've been using your brother's boat since you came home, although you said you never even met him on the way to the Elf Queen's island?" And when Oleg couldn't answer, but stared defiantly at the ground, his father said, "I have only one son now! Come back into the house with me, Boleg!" But with the first step he took, he clutched at his heart, collapsed, and was dead the next moment.

Now ask yourself, fluter: who was to blame for that man's death? Oleg, who gave him his life with the mistletoe branch, or Boleg, who killed him with the truth?'

Listener thought for a long time, and then said, 'Boleg caused his father's death, yes, but he always acted with the best of intentions. How can he be blamed for that?'

'You see?' said Vazzek. 'When you ask who's to blame, you shouldn't suppose it's just a matter of cause and effect. If it were, then we might as well all cut our throats and be done with it, since nobody could escape such blame. You must follow the story back to its beginning to find the root of the evil. What did the brothers do first?'

'They both cut down a tree, although they knew it was against the Elf Queen's will,' said Listener.

'But though two people may do the same thing, it may not mean the same,' said Vazzek. 'The more important question is: why did they do it?'

'To get at the mistletoe bush,' said Listener.

'And why did they want to do that?' asked Vazzek.

'They both wanted to bring their father a berry of the magic mistletoe,' said Listener.

'Why?' Vazzek pressed him.

'Boleg wanted to save his father's life,' said Listener.

'What about Oleg?' asked Vazzek.

'Why, he was thinking chiefly of his inheritance and the power he might win with the mistletoe bush,' said Listener.

'Yes, there you have it!' said Vazzek. 'But don't ask me what made him think that way! The evil starts when someone's bent on winning power at any price. At first there's just the idea of it, but then that idea eats its way on beneath the surface, hollowing out the ground, until someone unsuspectingly steps through it and falls to the bottom. And many people killed each other in that way at the time of the Great Raid, without really knowing why. No one but Khan Belarni was able to put an end to that.'

'Khan Belarni?' asked Listener. 'But how did Hunli's youngest son come to be chosen Khan?'

'Don't you know?' said Vazzek, surprised. 'Where in the world have you been these last few years? And Belarni is only the Khan's foster-son. When he was a baby, his father died in battle trying to protect the Khan, and in such circumstances the man whose life was saved takes the orphaned child into his tent and gives him all the rights of a child of his own.'

'All I know,' said Listener, 'is that Hunli died the winter before the Great Raid, and his eldest son Husski became Khan.'

'That's right,' said Vazzek, 'and Husski was bent on paying Arni's Folk back for the humiliation he had had to suffer at their hands. He led the horde himself on that raid, and when he had settled his account with Narzia, he went on with the Riders to the valley of Arziak. Soon the iron smelters' huts in the higher valleys were in flames, but that gave warning to the people of Arziak itself, and the Ore Master had time to gather those men who could bear arms before the Riders reached the town. That very night men came over to the Shallow Valley to fetch all horses fit to be ridden back across the mountains. I stayed here alone, with a few foals. As for what happened next, I learned about that only much later, when it was all over, since the Raiding Riders didn't get to this valley. But I found Arnilukka one day, lying near the foals. The child was almost out of her mind with fear, but at least I was glad to have another human being here again.

Well, Promezzo rode out to meet the horde with his own men, and there was a bitter battle in which many lost their lives. Husski was among the dead himself, and his Riders chose his brother Trusski as Khan on that same day. Promezzo managed to defend the town of Arziak, but he couldn't protect the farms out in the country, and had to watch the Raiding Riders plunder them and burn them down. Then they disappeared into the woods.

Most people thought at the time that the worst was now over, but a few days later the horde attacked a village down the valley. When Promezzo at last got there with his men, he found nothing but corpses and smoking ruins: not a trace of the murderers who had burned the place down. The same thing happened a couple more times, and this guerrilla warfare went on for weeks, until Promezzo managed to lure the horde into a trap. He had been able to work out which village was next in line to be attacked, and one night he secretly took up quarters there along with his fighting force. At dawn the horde broke out of the woods and galloped towards the village, but Promezzo held his men back, waiting until the Riders were among the houses. Then he gave the signal to attack. About half the Raiding Riders, along with their Khan, Trusski, lost their lives in that slaughter, but Promezzo was struck by an arrow himself, and died on the evening of that day, after the remains of the horde had managed to withdraw into the woods again.

After that, no more was heard of them for a few days. Promezzo's wife Akka had little time for mourning. She took up the reins in Arziak without more ado, had the dead buried, and helped the farmers whose farms had been burnt down. When eventually, for form's sake, she was chosen Ore Mistress, it was only confirmation of a state of affairs that already existed.

So things stood when something remarkable happened. One of the herdsmen working with me here saw it, and told me about it. It began when three Raiding Riders came trotting slowly down to Arziak from the woods one morning. As they came closer, it could be seen that they were unarmed. None the less, the people probably wouldn't have let them ride through the streets unscathed if Akka, who had been told immediately, hadn't given orders to leave the three Riders alone. So they came to the house of the Ore Mistress, who was standing in the doorway to meet the three as they dismounted. One of them stepped forward, bowed, and said his name was Belarni, and he had been chosen Khan by the remnant of the Raiding Riders who had escaped Promezzo's ambush. And when Akka asked what he wanted, Belarni said he had come to make peace.'

'I know this Belarni,' said Listener, 'so I'm not surprised to hear he wanted to put an end to the killing. He thought a great deal of his uncle Arni, and indeed he understood his mind at the time rather better than those who called themselves Arni's Folk.'

'I know he often rode out with Arni,' said Vazzek, 'and he was one of the few in the camp who had a kind word for a slave like myself, too. But the people of Arziak thought it very strange for a Khan of the Raiding Riders to be asking for peace. Anyway, Akka invited him and his companions into her house, and talked with them for a long time. I can't tell you the details of what was said; all I know is that soon the whole population of Arziak had assembled outside the house, and were waiting to hear what would come of this discussion.

At last Belarni and Akka came out, and the herdsman who told me the tale later said you could see at once that they were on friendly terms. Many people didn't like that, and called out asking if Akka had already forgotten how her husband died, but Akka did not reply to that, and said she had known Belarni as a child, when he got on better with her own father Arni than his foster-father Hunli, and so she trusted him, and she asked all the people gathered there to listen quietly to what Khan Belarni had to say.

At that Belarni stepped forward and made a speech which was so much discussed at the time that I can repeat it from memory, though I didn't hear it myself. "People of Arziak," said Belarni, "you are surprised to see a Khan of the Raiding Riders standing here beside your Ore Mistress Akka in friendship, asking for peace. I can well understand your suspicion, for people of our tribe have come to you before, having cut off their braids, making themselves out to be peaceful neighbours and partners in trade, but you discovered later that all they wanted was to wield power over you in a different way. They may have called themselves after my uncle Arni, but Arni was dead by then, and unable to tell them that they were misusing his words and thoughts. When the horde was in difficulties, Narzia humiliated our envoys, and tried to extend her rule to the steppes themselves. I learned one thing from that: anyone who ever tastes such power will want more and more of it, and won't rest until he controls everything. But as people wish to be free, this means he is inviting the wrath of all who won't bow to his yoke, and that wrath grew among the horde daily, like an underground fire, ready to burst out some day to devastating effect. You know what I'm talking about, and I know too, since I had to ride with the horde, though I would rather have stayed at home. But I learned from Arni that it does no one any good in such circumstances if you look away and pretend it's nothing to do with you.

So when the houses of Arni's Folk were burning, and their inhabitants all lay dead in the streets, whether guilty of any of this or not, that stench of smoke and blood intoxicated the horde, driving it on over the mountains. Many of the Riders thought you were friends of Arni's Folk who should be punished too, and it was little use telling them they were wrong. Nobody listens to the voice of reason in such a frenzy of slaughter and revenge. I felt horror as we rode over the mountains, and I don't know if anyone but myself saw the monument you once set up for those Riders who died up there in the snowstorm many years ago, after attacking your valley.

You know what happened after that: Hunli's two sons were killed in battle, and so many Riders with them that I doubt if the horde can ever recover from that blow. Many of your own men died as well, in particular your Ore Master Promezzo. So the elders of the horde tried to persuade me not to ride here, fearing for my life, but I set my hopes on the fact that Promezzo's widow Akka is one of Arni's daughters, and Arni was a man of peace, not vengeance.

And now I will tell you what we have been discussing. It has turned out that those who laid down their arms and cut off their braids in Arni's name were on the wrong path, still concerned only with their own wellbeing and the subjugation of others. Akka and I have both come to realize that this can be prevented only if, in future, we live not apart, but together like friends in the villages and settlements, with all of us contributing to the common good as best we can. You know how to dig ore and make it into tools or jewellery; we know how to breed horses and cattle. No doubt it will be some time before we get used to each other, but that strangeness will grow less with every day we work together, and every night we spend under the same roof."

This was the speech Belarni made outside the Ore Mistress's house, and when he had finished, Akka took him in her arms before all eyes and kissed him on both cheeks. The same day, the council of Arziak agreed to the proposal, and then Belarni and his companions rode back into the woods to fetch the rest of the horde. Hardly a man of those Riders was uninjured, and many of them had to be nursed back to health in the houses of Arziak before Belarni could ride back over the mountains with them to break camp in the steppes. Even then, some men of Arziak rode with him, and in a few weeks' time they all came back, along with the old people, women and children, their cattle and all their other possessions. Some of the Riders went on living in their tents for a while, but by now they're all used to dwelling in houses. And most of the herdsmen who live in these huts come from the steppes too, and hardly remember how I used to tend their horses as a slave.'

'So I have the death of Arnilukka's father on my conscience too,' said Listener. He had scarcely been able to think of anything else since Vazzek told him about the Ore Master's death, and he was wondering how he could ever look Arnilukka in the face again. It was not hard for Vazzek to guess his thoughts. 'Now don't go reckoning up your share of blame again!' he said. 'If you can pluck up courage to talk to Arnilukka about it, the dead man won't stand between you.' So saying, he drained his goblet, stood up, and wished Listener a good night.

*

Listener lay awake for a long time on the unfamiliar bed, trying to think of words in which he might be able to tell Arnilukka of his share in the guilt of her father's death, but his thoughts were overwhelmed again and again by that tide of feelings that had swept over him the night before, when he held the vision of so many years in his arms, went down into those eyes, of a colour that was hard to describe, and sank in the surging sea of blue, green and violet that caught him as if in soft arms and released him from the last of his stoniness. In the end, he hardly knew if it had been just a dream, or reality, and when he went up the valley again with Arnilukka next morning, keeping to the borders of the wood, he still thought he was dreaming, and found himself looking to see if her feet trod down the grass, or if she hovered just above it like a supernatural being.

It was obvious that she was not hovering, but running happy and carefree over the meadows, reaching her hand to him through the bushes now and then, so that he could touch and hold it. And the grasp of that hand was entirely firm and real as well. At one such moment, Listener did not let Arnilukka's hand go again, but said, 'Wait. I must talk to you while this bush stands between us, or I'll never find the words for what I want to say.' Then he told her how he had enchanted the Raiding Riders' horses with his flute, so bringing about the Great Raid. 'And in that way,' he finished, 'I am to blame for your father's death.'

Arnilukka was silent for a long time, but then she suddenly made her way past the bush and took him in her arms. 'Oh, Listener, does what you once did matter now?' she said. 'I want you just as you are, with your mistakes and faults and weaknesses.' She kissed him, and added, 'Anyway, it's all so long ago, and the people who killed my father now live in Arziak as our friends. But it was a good thing you told me, a good thing for you, and I wouldn't have wanted to hear it from anyone else myself.'

They stood there together for some time, until at last Listener said, 'Stay here with me!' And even as he spoke he saw Arnilukka's eyes stray, as she realized with sudden dismay that she was standing in the dim shade of the bush, shut in with branches bearing thick foliage as if she were in a cage. Her eyes darkened with fear, and she said, 'I can't!' and fled out into the meadow. Only when she felt open space around her again did she turn, with a sigh of relief, reaching out her arms to Listener and crying, 'Come here to me!' He tried, but his first step into the open brought the great weight of the infinitely deep, blue sky down on his shoulders, almost crushing him. 'I can't!' he said, and fled back into the shade of the bushes.

'What will come of this?' asked Arnilukka, in such a tone of voice that Listener did not know if she had been asking him the question, or only talking to herself, and his own answer sounded more as if he were thinking aloud. 'We've found and recognized each other,' he said, 'and that in itself is more than I ever dared hope for. Now we must try to live with it, some way or other.'

'How?' asked Arnilukka.

'I don't know,' said Listener. 'All I know is that I shall never feel quite lost again, now you have found me. I don't want to think beyond that today. Come up to the birch trees by the spring! There's a place between light and shade there, where we can both stay without feeling too much fear.'

They went that way daily. Luckily there was not much rain that spring, so that they could lie together in the soft, dry grass, constantly reassuring themselves of each other's tangible presence. One day, as they sat embracing in the flickering play of sunlight falling through the leaves of one of the last birch trees, right on the edge of the meadow-land, an old mouse came out of the bushes, stepped towards them with much dignity, and bowed low. Although his whiskers had turned white as snow over the years, Listener recognized him at once. 'I am delighted to see you in good health, He-who-prophesies-to-the-falcon,' he said, and he formally introduced Arnilukka to the mouse.

Not only did He-who-prophesies-to-the-falcon feel greatly honoured in being thus addressed by name, he was very much surprised too. 'How do you know who I am?' he inquired. 'As far as I know, we've never met before!'

Only then did Listener remember in what circumstances he had been able to see the mouse do his heroic deed, but it was hard to explain, so at last he said, 'I saw you escape the falcon with my stone in a dream, and I must say that I admired your courage immensely.'

Such praise was sweet music to the mouse's ears. 'Too kind!' he said modestly, bowing again. 'Too kind! I'd have been done for without wise Rinkulla.'

'That in no way detracts from your merit,' said Listener. 'But for your daring, the stone would not have been saved. I hear that you have been its Keeper of recent years.'

'I have,' said the mouse, 'and that's why I'm here. It hasn't been easy for us to carry the stone so far, through the woods and over the mountains, and I was afraid you might be getting tired of waiting. But I'm relieved to see you have someone with you to help you pass the time.' He looked hard at Arnilukka's eyes, and added, 'Though it looks as though the stone's already come back to you, in a different way, and our trouble was all for nothing!'

Noticing the disappointment in the mouse's expression, Listener said, 'Why, I can hardly wait to compare Arni's stone with Arnilukka's eyes. Where is it?'

At this He-who-prophesies-to-the-falcon turned, gave a shrill whistle, and immediately a long procession of mice came tripping out of the bushes, two by two, carrying a finely woven net of thin grass-blades between them. They put their burden down at Listener's feet, and the old mouse opened the delicate tissue. There lay the stone in the sunlight, its glowing play of colours rising so strongly from the depths that the reflection of blue, green and violet was mirrored in the tiny black eyes of the wondering mice.

'Arni's stone!' cried Arnilukka. 'They've brought you Arni's stone!'

'Of course,' said Listener. 'It's mine. That's what we were talking about!' And only then did he realize that he still understood the language of the animals, though he was no longer a faun.

'I can talk to the fishes, but not to mice as you can,' said Arnilukka.

'And not just mice, but all the other beasts and birds as well,' said Listener. 'That part of my enchantment still remains with me too, but I would gladly give it to be able to come out into the open with you.'

But even as he spoke, looking sadly down at the stone, he felt the pulsing light of the coloured rings warm his heart and drive away his rising melancholy; he sensed the ancient promise that rose from the depths of the crystal, and found its fulfilment in Arnilukka's eyes, and he knew that this endless moment in which time stood still, or seemed not to exist at all, could not be taken away from him, and made up in advance for everything that might yet happen, so that not wishing to keep the joy he felt to himself he said, 'This is a day for celebration, and you shall all be our guests!'

The party that followed was a memorable one for all of them gathered there on the outskirts of the birch wood. Arnilukka unpacked the basket she had brought with her that morning, and it was almost as if she had known what guests she would be entertaining that day. There was a bag full of sweet nut kernels, last year's dried apples, pears and plums, crisp bread as fragrant as if it had only just come out of the oven, firm white sheep's milk cheese, and a bottle of perry. The mice gathered in a circle, rapidly washed their whiskers, and then Arnilukka laid these delicacies before them, with a shallow dish of perry in the midst. They all ate heartily, and the mice became visibly merrier the more often they dipped their pointed little snouts into the sparkling perry. Before long one of them sat up on his hindquarters and began to sing; it was a kind of heroic epic in praise of He-who-never-gives-up-hope, describing that young mouse's constant attendance at his post, which provoked the mockery of his stout and sceptical companion, until the day when his waiting was rewarded. The song had innumerable verses, and the singer was free with his mockery of the fat mouse who had slept through it all, describing every scene so dramatically that he was frequently interrupted by the laughter of the other mice. He came to the climax of his story in the last three verses:

> *Pot-belly dozed off, feeling dead on his feet,*
> *and lay snoring and dreaming of good things to eat.*
> *So he slept and he slept and he slept, and what's more,*
> *he never did see what the brave youngster saw!*

> *For up came the nymph, rising out of the spring,*
> *to caress the stone faun with her hand and to bring*
> *life back to the statue that, cold as December,*
> *had stood by the water since mice can remember.*

> *Oh, the greedy old mouse learned a lesson that day:*
> *Always hope, never mind what the mockers may say!*
> *And the young mouse who stuck to his post rose to fame*
> *and proved himself worthy to win a great name.*

As the singer rendered this ballad, Listener translated every word of it for Arnilukka's benefit, and when the song was over she asked if the mouse with the noble name was among their guests. In fact, Listener had already spotted He-who-never-gives-up-hope, and now he placed him on the palm of his hand and introduced him to Arnilukka. 'He wanted to show you where to find me,' he told her, 'but you couldn't understand him.'

'I remember that,' said Arnilukka. 'He had such pretty, soft fur. Didn't he pass on the news to my fishes? I must thank him properly for that.' And she took the mouse in her cupped hands, where he sat as if in a warm cavern, and kissed him on the tip of his tiny nose. The other mice thought this extremely entertaining, and one of them called out,

'You've earned another name now! Shouldn't we call you He-whom-the-nymph-kisses?'

This was all slightly embarrassing to He-who-never-gives-up-hope, and he crept so far into the hollow of Arnilukka's hands that he could hardly be seen. But when she put him down among the other mice again, it was obvious that he was proud of this distinction.

So the party went merrily on, until He-who-prophesies-to-the-falcon said it was time to leave. He thanked his hosts, in the name of all the mice, and when saying goodbye to Listener he added, 'Take good care of your stone! The green-eyed falcon is still circling in the sky. I hear she's promised all the birds and beasts fabulous things if they can only find a certain golden chain. Do you know anything about that?'

'Yes, I do,' said Listener, 'and the chain lies in a place where no one can get at it.'

'Not even you?' asked the mouse.

'Hardly,' said Listener. 'And what would I want with the chain?'

'Well, you never can tell,' said the mouse. 'I know that falcon, and I have a kind of feeling her story's not over yet.'

'You may well be right there,' said Listener, thinking of that part of the spell that still bound him. But he said nothing about it, for it was not likely that He-who-prophesies-to-the-falcon could help him in this matter. So he thanked the mouse once more for keeping his stone so long, and then the mice set out, some of them a little unsteadily, but endeavouring to march off in two straight lines in a reasonably dignified fashion, at least until they were out of sight.

That day, Arnilukka told Listener she had heard news from Arziak of the people Narzia had turned into dogs: they had been found in the cave under the great cliff. 'The morning after you told me about them,' she said, 'I sent my mother a message, asking her to have a search made. They've lived there all these years, fearing the Raiding Riders might yet track them down. There are twelve of them now; two of the men took wives who bore them children there in the cave. Lingli herself is the mother of three little girls. They are all living in a village farther down the valley now, along with their flock of goats.'

*   *   *

Listener and Arnilukka lived all that summer as if they were on an island outside the world. They wished for nothing but to be together, and soon acquired unerring skill in finding those places where neither would feel too much oppression: a light stand of hazels on the edge of the pastures, or a spot among the alders where the stream wound its way into woodland. However, the place they liked best was still the sunlit birch spinney up by the spring. And as they sat under a birch tree one hot day late in the summer, leaning back against its white, silky bark, Arnilukka said, 'Listener, I'm expecting a child.'

Once he had grasped the sense of Arnilukka's words, his first feeling was that the news disturbed that timeless state of suspension in which he was living, and he realized that he had been taking each day as it came without any thought of the future, as if life must go on like this for all eternity, and any change was the last thing he could envisage. It was not until he saw the joy in Arnilukka's eyes that he realized she had been speaking of his own child too: a new being in whose still unborn body both their own lives were indissolubly united. 'We are going to have a child!' he said.

'Yes,' said Arnilukka. 'And it will be born in winter.'

'Excellent!' he said. 'Why not winter?' And he embraced her.

Only a few weeks later did he begin to understand what she had been trying to tell him. Autumn came to the valley, with cold winds that swept the withering leaves from the trees, and the days when he and Arnilukka could resort to one of their own places were few and far between. When the rain drummed down on the roof of his cabin he must stay alone, for Arnilukka was unable to go through the woods to him, just as he was unable to cross the meadows to the herdsmen's huts.

And now he began to wonder about the winter. He spent nights on end trying to work out some way in which he could live with Arnilukka. A house on the edge of the woods would be the thing, he thought; the door must open exactly between light and shade, so that they could go out and wander along the border between woodland and meadows together. By now he knew every plant along their usual path, every blackberry bush, every root, every unevenness in the ground, and suddenly he realized that he would never see anything for the rest of his life but that path if he was going to live with Arnilukka.

Once he had formed this idea in his head, he could not shake it off again, and he began to wonder if this were the point of all the dreams and visions that had accompanied him until the evening when at last he held Arnilukka in his arms. Although the mere thought of that meeting made him feel it was unendurable to lie here alone in the old woodcutters' cabin, parted from her, he was also overcome by a feeling of having gone up a blind alley from which he could find no way out.

All summer long, she had been the only human being to whom he had spoken, for whom he had played his flute, and he had passed the time he spent alone waiting for his next meeting with her. In his mind's eye, he saw the little house where his grandparents used to live. He had seen, then, how close they were to each other, and yet the Gentle Fluter had much more on his mind than spending every moment in his wife's company, while she herself probably wouldn't have had it otherwise, for all her forthright remarks. As his thoughts dwelt on his grandparents' house, and in so doing entered his grandfather's workshop, where the flutes were made and he himself had learnt the turner's craft, he felt the urge to hollow out a piece of wood as he had then, and turn the smooth curves of a flute. I must do something, he thought, or I shall begin to turn round in circles myself.

When he stepped outside the cabin next morning, there was a clear, turquoise autumn sky above the branches of the trees, which were almost bare now. Just the weather for a walk to the spring, he thought, going quickly along the path towards the meadows, which lay grey-green in the sunlight. He saw Arnilukka standing by the edge of the wood long before he reached her. It was now plain to see that she was carrying a child, but he thought that made her lovelier than ever. He told her so when he met and embraced her, and she thanked him with a smile, but he saw that her eyes were grave.

'What is it?' he asked. 'Are you sad?'

Arnilukka left this question unanswered. 'Come along,' she said. 'Let's go up to the spring once more.'

He wondered why she said 'once more', but she was already a little way ahead, so he said nothing, but made his way swiftly through the bushes until he was beside her again. Yet again they played their game, trying to clasp hands through the bushes, and it was the more easily played now that they could see one another through the bare branches. But Listener also saw how hard Arnilukka found it, each time, to loosen that clasp again.

In the spinney above the spring, the ground was covered with the bright yellow leaves of the birch trees, and the shadow of their thin, drooping branches lay over the yellow leaves like a delicate web. The two of them sat side by side for a long time in silence, looking down at the fading grass in the meadows, sprinkled with the pale violet of autumn crocus.

'I must talk to you,' said Arnilukka at last.

'Is that so difficult?' said Listener. 'Why, we can always talk to each other!'

'Yes,' replied Arnilukka, 'but it's hard to know how to start this time.' She put her hand on his, and then went on. 'I can't bring my child into the world here, in the herdsmen's huts, where there's no woman to help me. And if I stay here any longer, I shan't be able to ride back the more difficult way through the ravine.'

'The path through the Weird Wood would be easier,' said Listener, but even as he spoke he saw pure horror rise in Arnilukka's eyes.

'No!' she almost screamed, and after a while she went on, more quietly, 'You know I can't bear to go that way. I will set out for Arziak tomorrow morning, with one of the herdsmen, and spend the winter there.'

Listener felt numb. 'Tomorrow?' he said, but he knew he had guessed as much all the time, though he would not admit it to himself. 'Then I shan't see you all winter.'

'Does that matter so much?' asked Arnilukka. 'All that matters is that we met. My mother once told me about my great-great-grandmother Urla, the first to own your stone. She was a young woman with a small child when the Raiding Riders killed her husband, and left her in despair. Yet she was such a happy woman all her life that she could pass on some of the love she had known to any who entered her cottage.'

'Yes, I know,' said Listener. 'I was her guest myself when I stood like a stone above the spring.'

Arnilukka did not seem much surprised by this information, but only said, 'Then I'm almost sure you'll learn to understand this. It would be bad if you were to spend the winter here in melancholy brooding. Bad for me, because I should sense it, and bad for you too. That kind of grief's like a greedy worm eating away your heart until you feel nothing any more. And I wanted to talk to you about that, too. What will you do when I'm not here?'

'I've already thought of that,' said Listener, and he told her about his grandfather's workshop. 'Now, could you get me a few of the drills and knives I need for a turner's lathe from one of your smiths in Arziak? I can build the rest of it myself if you'll send me the carpenter's tools I'll require as well. There's plenty of wood here. I fancy the notion of making a few flutes. And perhaps there'll be someone I can teach to play them.' Then he told her what tools he would need, growing eager as he talked, and he tore off a piece of birch bark, took a sharp stone and scratched the outlines of the implements he wanted. When he looked up again to explain his drawings to Arnilukka, he saw that the secret grief had gone from her eyes. She got him to describe the turning of a flute, and finally asked him to play her his silver instrument once more.

He had had that in his own mind all this while, for sequences of notes had come into his head, music to express his grief at their parting, but when he began to play, still looking into Arnilukka's eyes, a touch of merriment unexpectedly mingled with the melody, and soon got the upper hand, sweeping away the last echo of his sadness in a cheerful succession of runs, trills and leaps. Arnilukka's eyes danced with sparkling blue, green and violet as she sat before him listening, her arms around her knees. When he had finished his tune, she kissed him on the mouth and said, 'I shall hear that music all winter, and be glad of it.'

Next morning they met by the border of the wood once more. Listener felt as if the parting were already behind him, and he could think of nothing else that seemed right to say to Arnilukka. And then the man came with her horse. Listener helped her into the saddle and she rode away with her companion down the valley, without once looking back.

For the next few days, Listener was busy choosing the wood he wanted for his purposes from the stacks behind his cabin. He set aside some long ash-tree trunks for the lathe, and he also found two beautifully grained billets of sycamore wood, bearing no branches, well seasoned and just right for the making of flutes. He had found a hatchet in the cabin, and began roughly trimming pieces of sycamore cut to an arm's length.

A week later, as he sat on the chopping block outside his cabin, examining a piece of ash from which he meant to cut the axle of the spindle for his lathe, to make sure it had no flaws, the young man who had escorted Arnilukka came along the path through the wood from the herdsmen's huts to his cabin, leading a packhorse. He heaved a heavy bundle off the pack-saddle and put it down by the door. 'And I'm to bring you greetings from the young mistress,' he said. 'We had no trouble going through the ravine, and she got all you wanted from a smith next day. I brought the stuff through the Weird Wood yesterday.' Listener thanked him, and asked if Arnilukka had said anything else.

'Yes, she did,' said the herdsman, 'but let anyone understand it who can! I'm to tell you there's a great shortage of flutes in Arziak. Do you know what she means by that?'

'Of course!' said Listener, amused. 'For instance, have you got a flute yourself?'

'Why, no,' said the herdsman, bewildered. And now Listener looked at him more closely for the first time. He was little more than a boy, and had obviously been born in one of the Raiding Riders' tents. However, he wore his coarse black hair cut short, like the people of Arziak. What had principally attracted Listener's attention, though, was the youth's voice: he spoke in a way that sounded as if he were intent on making every sentence into a melody. There was hidden music in all his words, only waiting to unfold more freely; that, at least, was how his manner of speech struck Listener, and it gave him an idea. 'Would you like one, then?' he asked.

'A flute?' asked the boy. 'What would I do with a flute?'

'What do you suppose?' said Listener. 'Play it, of course!'

'The way you play your silver one?' asked the boy. 'I could never do that!' But it was plain that the notion was beginning to interest him.

'I'll teach you if you like,' said Listener.

'When?' asked the boy eagerly. 'I could spare a little time this afternoon.'

Listener laughed. 'I'm afraid it can't be done as soon as that,' he said, and explained what he was planning to do with the tools packed up in the bundle.

'Can you make the lathe all by yourself?' asked the boy.

'I hope so,' said Listener, 'but the work would go faster if you'd lend a hand.'

'I'd like to,' said the boy, 'but I must ask Vazzek's permission first.'

'You let me have a word with him,' said Listener. 'I'm sure he won't object, if I ask him. What's your name, by the way?'

'Derli,' said the boy.

'A melodious name for a fluter,' said Listener. 'Right, when you see Vazzek, tell him there's something I'd like to discuss with him.'

And so it was that Listener had an assistant over the next few weeks as he set to work in earnest to build himself a lathe. Vazzek had raised no objections, far from it. The lad wasn't much use in the stables anyway, he said; as soon as you took your eyes off him, he'd be found sitting dreaming in some corner, or busy with some nonsense, and it was high time he learned to put his mind seriously to something. So Listener had the youth entirely at his disposal, and as it turned out, Derli soon came to enjoy his new task. Whether it was the prospect of having his own flute, and the teaching that Listener had promised him, or whether he just liked carpentry better than mucking out stables, he proved to be handy and skilful, and so they made fast progress with the building of the lathe.

And one day it was ready. Listener hollowed out the first piece of sycamore wood, showed Derli how to shape it roughly with a hand-held knife, and then fixed it in the spindle of the lathe. 'And now we'll shape the outside of it,' he told Derli, who was watching intently. As soon as Listener worked the treadle with his foot, the piece of rough wood began to turn, thin spiral shavings peeled away under the knife-blade, and left a finely grooved curve behind. Gradually the slender body of the instrument became smooth, and the wavy grain of the wood stood out more clearly. When Listener disengaged the blade for the last time and let the lathe run down, Derli asked, 'Is that my flute?'

'It's not ready yet,' said Listener. 'The hardest part of the work lies ahead: we must get it to make a sound.' He took the smooth pipe out of the lathe, cut a deep notch diagonally in the wood beneath the thickened head, and drove a short peg into the opening of the pipe, leaving only a narrow crack to blow through.

'That's more or less what you do with willow pipes,' said Derli.

Listener looked at him in surprise. 'Why, you do know something of the art of it after all!' he said. 'I knew you'd make a fluter. Who showed you that?'

'The young mistress, Arnilukka,' said Derli, 'but it's a long time ago. I was just a child, and we'd only been living in Arziak about a year. I didn't feel at home to start with – I was afraid, in among those tall mountain slopes, and all the trees. The only thing I liked was seeing so much water; water's precious out in the steppes. So when I was sitting by the stream one day, as I often did, longing for the wide spaces of the plains, I heard someone playing a pipe. I followed the sound, and saw Arnilukka sitting under a willow tree, playing a set of pipes of different lengths, and the fish were all jumping about in the water at her feet, sending up drops into the sunlight in sparkling rainbow colours. I listened to her playing to the fishes for a while, and then she saw me, and showed me how to make a set of pipes like hers. The tunes I played on them were a great comfort at the time, but it's a long while since I tried it.'

'That's the kind of thing one should never forget,' said Listener, and he saw Arnilukka sitting under the willow tree, a little girl with eyes of a colour hard to describe, talking to the fish as if they were human beings and playing them her tunes. 'It's good to have a flute when you're alone. Now, see what yours sounds like!' He handed over the instrument, Derli put it to his lips, and when he breathed into it a deep, warm note sounded, swelled gradually, and did not die away until the boy ran out of breath.

'It sounds good,' said Derli, 'but it has only the one note.'

'Only wait!' said Listener. 'It has many more notes, but we must free them from the wood by boring each a hole. It all depends on setting them at the correct intervals, and luckily I have a pattern for that.' He fetched his silver flute, laid it beside the wooden pipe, and marked the places for the finger-holes with a piece of charcoal. 'Now we know where the notes are sleeping,' he said, 'and next we'll wake them.'

He took a thin drill and turned it carefully at that place in the wood where he had made the lowest mark. When the hole was smooth, he gave Derli back the flute, saying, 'If you cover that hole with the little finger of your right hand, you'll hear the first note again, but take the finger away and another will sound.'

Derli followed his instructions, and the first, deep note was instantly followed by a second and slightly higher one.

'Compare that with the same note on my flute here,' said Listener, and he played the two notes. 'Well, what do you think?'

'The second note on my flute is just a little lower,' said Derli at once.

'You have a fine ear,' Listener told him. 'You will be a master fluter; I'm sure of it now. Yes, we must make the hole just a little larger, so that the note can come out properly.' And when he had done that, and tried again, both flutes played exactly in tune. In the same way, he drilled seven holes in all, tried them and adjusted them until the two instruments would play without the slightest deviation from each other. Finally, Listener oiled the flute well to keep the wood from drying out, and then set it aside. 'You've already learnt the fingering in testing the flute,' he said. 'We can begin teaching you to play tomorrow.'

This promising start was followed by weeks of busy activity. During the day, Listener sat at his lathe, while Derli watched him intently, sometimes trying his hand at the craft himself. He proved very skilful at it, but showed a particular gift for choosing suitable pieces of wood. 'Take this one,' he would say. 'It sounds good.' And he would knock the wood with his knuckles. After a while, once Listener saw how carefully, indeed almost lovingly Derli went about the work, he left him to bore out the wood from the middle of the pipes. In the evening, he taught the youth the art of flute-playing, just like his grandfather when once he taught Barlo. Meanwhile, winter came to the Shallow Valley, the meadows were knee-deep in snow, and frost made the tree-trunks crack, but there was plenty of wood for fires, and Vazzek had made sure that the two of them had stocks of provisions in the wood-cutters' cabin.

At night, however, Listener could not get away from those thoughts he tried to escape by day in flinging himself so eagerly into the making of flutes. He would lie awake on his wooden bed, wondering what would happen when winter was over. He clung with all his might to the hope that Arnilukka would return to the Shallow Valley, if only to bring him her child. But what then? How would they live here if they had no choice but to wander beside the border of the trees, up or down the valley, until they could no longer endure the cage whose bars kept them forever going round in circles? What kind of hope was it that led to hopelessness when one took the second step?

'Wake up, will you, Piney?' he said one night, finding himself back at this point again and unable to get any farther. 'You claim to know something about hope. Can you tell me what I may hope for?'

The Piney was lying at the head of the bed, as usual. The flickering firelight passed over his gnarled face, lending a look of constant change to his expression, so that it was impossible to say if his shiny, dark brown eye were looking at Listener attentively or with irony. 'No need to wake me up,' he remarked. 'Did you ever see me close my eye in sleep? As for all that drivel about hope, it just goes to show you don't know what you're talking about.'

'I know what I'm talking about very well, my wooden-headed old friend,' said Listener. 'I rack my brains, night after night, thinking how all my hopes depend on Arnilukka, and yet I can't think of any way to keep her with me.'

'Well, should you?' inquired the Piney. 'That shows what a peculiar notion of hope you've got! Keep her, indeed! If it were only a matter of wanting to have and hold something, I wouldn't go on about it so. I mean, once you've got all you want, you've reached the pinnacle of hopelessness! Don't you see that yet? When I still stood up on the pass among the other stone pines, we told a tale of a tree who always wanted everything for himself. First he didn't like the way it turned cold and dark at night. "I want the sun," he said, so he got the sun. The sun stopped right over him, blazing down until his branches were so dry they were cracking, and their needles turned brown and dry as tinder. When he'd had enough, he said, "Sun, I can't stand you any longer. I want the rain." So up came a big black cloud, stopped above him, and let a positive torrent of rain fall on him. He liked it at first, but when the rain refused to stop, he didn't fancy that so much either. "I'm getting wet right under my bark," he said. "If this goes on, my needles will begin to rot. I want the wind, to come and dry me with his breath." And immediately a whirlwind began blowing around him, bending his branches. They were tugged this way and that, until he was aching in every fibre, and he felt quite dizzy with that wind, which was practically uprooting him from the ground. He began to moan and groan and said, "I can't stand this any longer! As soon as I get what I want, it starts killing me. I don't want anything at all." At that the wind stopped blowing, and the tree stood there again like all the other trees on the pass, and when the sun came out and shone down on him he said, "Thank you, Sun, for giving me a little of your warmth!" and when it rained he was content with that too, and said, "Thank you, Rain, for giving me a little of your cool water!" and when the wind blew the tree was glad to hear it rushing through his branches, and said, "Thank you, Wind, for giving me a little of your breath." And he told the other trees, "It's good to know that there's sun and rain and wind. One can live every day in hopes of getting a little of each of them, and if not today, one may get it tomorrow." And such was the case with this tree.'

'Yes, well, that's a tale for trees, who have goodness only knows how many hundred years to live,' said Listener. 'What's more, people used to tell me similar stories when I was a child and wanted something I couldn't have, and I soon tired of listening to them. Can you tell me, I wonder, what was the point of my stone's leading me to my love by so many devious ways? I'd hoped I had reached my journey's end, and could stay with Arnilukka, but now it seems there is scarcely anywhere we can live together.'

'You did find a place where the two of you could be happy,' pointed out the Piney. 'But that's the way you humans are: you can't bear to stay in the same place the whole time. That's how you came to go so many devious ways, as you call them, and turned yourself into a woodland creature that can't stand to be out under the open sky.'

'I have Narzia and no one else to thank for that,' said Listener, but under the Piney's placid gaze he ended the sentence with less conviction than he had begun it, as that ancient wooden gnome instantly noticed.

'You see?' said the Piney. 'Don't believe it yourself, do you? So why say it? You were following neither your stone nor the commandment written on your flute at the time. And now you're surprised to find where you ended up. Still, as I say, that's how it is with you humans: as soon as you start moving about you take devious ways and go astray.'

Listener knew only too well that the Piney was right, and that knowledge merely increased his desperation. 'If what you say is true,' he said, 'then I wonder why we live at all, since there's no hope for us.'

The Piney laughed his wooden laugh. 'You,' he said, 'are a fool! Here I go, talking and talking, and you fail to understand any of it. Haven't you had proof in this valley, time and again, that you're loved? Would you have come this far at all otherwise? That should be reason enough for hope to last you all your life. Ever since you first saw those eyes you can't even describe, you should have felt it, but most of the time you were busy grabbing something. Think of all you've been given in the little bit of life you have behind you! And you pocketed the lot as if it were yours by right. Maybe you ought to start giving things away sometime, and then you might see what you still have to hope for. You've made a start, I'll admit, with that lad you're teaching to play the flute, and I thought you'd finally seen what it's all about. But your sort need everything hammered home before you'll see what was in front of your eyes all along.' With which the Piney had said enough for one night. He shut his wide mouth so firmly that Listener didn't dare to ask any more questions. However, he had plenty to think about that night, and indeed in the weeks that followed.

The days were lengthening again now, and catkins were appearing on the hazel bushes, waiting for sunny weather to let the wind disperse their yellow pollen. There was a sizeable pile of finished flutes on the shelf in Listener's living-room already, and Derli was having difficulty finding any more suitable wood in the woodpiles.

'Plenty of wood for turning,' he said one morning, 'but nothing that'll do for making flutes.'

'Then I'll make something else,' said Listener. He had already devised a plan, for he wanted to give Arnilukka a present when she came back to the Shallow Valley with her baby. At the beginning of the winter he had felt as if she were going farther away from him with every lengthening night, but now that the sun rose a little higher above the woods every day at noon, and the buds were swelling and shining glossily, she was coming closer every day. She would not come while there was still snow on the ground, but icicles were already dripping from the eaves, and masses of snow went slipping off branches in the wood. 'We'll make a cradle,' he said. 'I shall need a few stout planks for the bottom and the rockers, and then we'll make a lattice of turned bars, so that my child can lie safely inside them.'

'I know the wood for that,' said Derli. 'There's the trunk of a wild cherry tree on the woodpile behind the cabin, beautiful red-grained wood, just the thing for a cradle.'

As the snow gradually melted outside, the two of them set to work on their new task, and when the cradle was ready, and spring had not yet come, Listener began to ornament the ends of the turned bars, which he had assembled in a delicate ladder-like formation, with all kinds of carvings. There was a whole flock of goats grazing along the sides, led by a he-goat with a single but enormous horn, and a donkey reared up boldly opposite the he-goat. At the foot of the cradle, a weasel raised his slender head; there was a toad squatting to the weasel's right, and a grass-snake came crawling from the bars on his left, while three mice peered through the bars over the cradle's head. And so Listener told the child he had never yet seen his own story, little by little, saying at last, 'And first and foremost, I entrust my child to you three mice, He-who-speaks-with-the-snake, He-who-prophesies-to-the-falcon, and He-who-never-gives-up-hope, for none of you ever doubted that life is stronger than any evil magic.'

He had scarcely left his workbench for days, and was now at work on his carving all night too. When he put down his knife that morning and went outside the door, he saw that the last of the snow had melted. The air was cool and clear, and tasted of pollen, and the yellow stars of coltsfoot were in flower along the path. Then Listener heard footsteps, and saw a man coming towards him from the herdsmen's huts. At first he could make out nothing but his outline against the bright background: the tall, lean figure of a young man, treading the woodland path with quick and slightly impatient steps. Listener waited outside his door, and did not recognize the newcomer until he stood before him and raised his head.

'Good morning, Belarni,' said Listener. 'It's a long time since we met. When did you reach the Shallow Valley?'

'Yesterday evening,' Belarni said. 'I rode up through the ravine with Arnilukka.'

When Listener heard that, his heart seemed to miss a beat. He had tried to picture this moment again and again over the past few weeks, longing for it to come, imagining what it would be like when Arnilukka stood by the edge of the wood waiting for him again. He had not dared to think beyond that. But now, with dismay, he realized that the meeting also meant some decision about the future must be made. 'How is she?' he asked.

'Well,' said Belarni. 'She's brought her daughter, and is waiting for us just beyond the wood.' And seeing Listener put out a groping hand behind him, and then sink down on the chopping block that stood there, he added, 'Don't you want to come with me?'

'Indeed I do,' said Listener. 'Of course. Give me a moment. I've been working all night. I wasn't expecting her here just yet.'

Belarni seemed slightly surprised, but did not say so; instead, he leaned back against the logs of the cabin wall and stood there silent for a while. Listener looked surreptitiously at him, trying to see in Belarni's face the boy who had brought him Hunli's falcon rug long ago in the camp of the Raiding Riders, but it was difficult to find any remaining trace of boyish softness in the lean, taut features of this young man, who had been burdened with great responsibility over-early in life, and whose face was already marked by strong lines above the corners of his mouth. 'We argued, if you remember, when you came to my tent to question me about Arni's Folk,' said Listener.

Belarni looked at him as if he scarcely remembered the circumstances of that meeting. 'Yes,' he said, 'I think I was angry to see a man like Honi presume to make himself out Arni's successor. If I left you in anger, you must forgive me; I was only a child then.'

Listener shook his head slowly. 'There's nothing to forgive,' he said. 'Your opinion of Arni's Folk was quite right, and if I had listened to you a good many people might be living to this day.'

'Maybe, and maybe not,' said Belarni. 'Who can tell, after the event? I've taught myself not to brood on what's done and can't be altered. And I probably wouldn't have had much time for brooding these last few years. Moreover, you didn't get away unscathed yourself, as I hear.'

Listener looked keenly at him. How had Belarni heard that? Had Arnilukka told him? If she had, why didn't he say so? It seemed to be a source of some embarrassment to Belarni to have mentioned it at all. 'Well, that's in the past,' said Listener after a while, 'and now I have recovered some hope again.'

'I know,' said Belarni, and he abruptly added, 'I'd like to ask you to stay my friend, whatever else may happen.'

What should happen, Listener wondered, surprised by this curious phrasing. He gave Belarni his hand, saying, 'I'll gladly promise you that. Now, let's not keep Arnilukka waiting any longer. I'll just fetch something from my cabin, and then we will go to her.'

When he came out of the cabin again, he had the cradle on his shoulders, and so the two of them walked along the path together in silence. At every step they took, the view of the valley beyond the trees widened out, and then Listener saw Arnilukka standing out in the meadow, in the light of the morning sun. She was holding her baby in her arms, and came to meet them as soon as they approached the borders of the wood. They met in the shade of the last trees, stopped and looked at one another for a while, silently. Listener had quite forgotten that Belarni was beside him; he saw no one but Arnilukka, and she seemed to him a thousand times lovelier than he remembered her. The smile on her lips and the look in her eyes took his breath away. But at last he felt the weight of the cradle on his shoulders, and he put it down carefully on the grass, saying, 'I've brought you something, Arnilukka.'

She laughed. 'And I've brought you something too, Listener!' she said, holding out her baby. 'It's a girl.'

He took the baby carefully in his arms, and was almost startled when he looked at her, though he should have been prepared for the sight: she was gazing up at him with eyes like Arnilukka's, and the eyes of all the other women of Urla's kin whom he had known. 'Have you given her a name yet?' he asked.

'I wanted to wait until I could discuss it with you,' said Arnilukka, 'but I've had my own secret name for her from the first.'

Listener looked thoughtfully at the baby, and then said, 'Urla. You called her Urla.'

'Yes,' said Arnilukka, smiling. 'You've guessed. If you don't mind, we'll call her after her ancestress.'

As Listener went on gazing at those eyes, so young and yet so ancient in the baby's tiny face, Belarni, standing beside him, cleared his throat and said, 'I'll just go and see to the horses.' He made an awkwardly apologetic gesture, and walked off over the meadow, a little stiffly, towards the herdsmen's huts. Listener watched him go. 'Belarni is a sensitive man,' he said. 'I like him a great deal, but I'm grateful to him for leaving us alone now.'

'I'm glad you like him,' said Arnilukka, 'for I want to tell you some things about him.' She indicated a fallen trunk on the edge of the wood with a nod of her head. 'We can sit down there, and let our child lie in her beautiful new cradle for the first time.'

Listener cushioned the hard wooden floor of the cradle with dry leaves, Arnilukka spread the shawl in which she had been carrying the baby on top, and then she laid little Urla in the cradle. 'Come and sit down,' she said, and as soon as Listener was sitting on the fissured oak tree trunk with her, she began her tale without more ado.

'You know,' she said, 'how I came to this valley at the time of the Great Raid, and old Vazzek nursed me back to health. Later on, when the fighting in Arziak was over, two men came back to the Shallow Valley one day with the surviving horses, and when they discovered me living here with Vazzek they said my mother was deeply concerned about me. One of them rode straight back to give her the news that I was safe and well, and he soon returned to the herdsmen's huts with my mother herself. As soon as I was quite better, she and I rode through the ravine to Arziak. She had prepared me to find my father gone, but I didn't fully realize he was dead until I was living in our house again, with everything in it that reminded me of him. I would often look into the living-room to ask him something and only then, when I didn't find him, would I remember that I should never again see him alive.

However, I sometimes found Belarni in that room. My mother had taken him into her own house. At first I regarded him only as one of the Riders who had killed my father, and I didn't see how my mother could bear to have him under her roof. I refused to speak to him, and gave him nothing but angry looks if he tried to talk to me. I was so full of my grief and anger at that time that I never even noticed how exhausted Belarni was himself. He spent many hours on horseback daily, riding up and down the valley and making sure that his men and their families all had a roof over their heads, negotiating with the farmers from the villages, to see to it that the beasts had fodder and the people had food, or settling quarrels when former Raiding Riders got into disputes with the valley people. And besides all this, he gave my mother all the help he could.

One day I was sitting in my father's chair in the living-room again, weeping, when he came in, walked straight up to me, sat down beside me and put an arm around my shoulders. I was so surprised that I sat there perfectly rigid, not daring to move. "You know," he said, "since we're living under the same roof we might just as well talk as avoid each other like deadly enemies. Don't you see I am as sorry as you are for what happened here? I've been trying for weeks to do what I can to make it possible for people to live in this valley again, but I've come to the end of my own endurance, and I can't bear you to think of me as your enemy any more, when I'm not. No one can alter what happened now, but if we all let grief and anger eat our hearts away as you're doing, nothing will improve either. Shout at me if you want to, hit me, but do please take the weight of your resentment off my back."

When he had said that, and a few other things too, I looked into his face with full awareness for the first time, and then I did see his exhaustion and the despair in his eyes, whereupon I put my arms round his neck and wept my heart out, while he held me and rocked me gently like the child I still was.

After that I would talk to Belarni, and it was then I began to have dreams, dreams I didn't mention to anyone for a long time. At first I couldn't make much sense of them, although I felt they were in some way connected. Chiefly, however, they seemed to me much more real than anything I'd ever dreamed before. For instance, I saw a young man riding along a path by a river in winter. I clearly remember the broken sheets of ice caught in the bushes on the bank. The young man dismounted after a while, let his donkey roam as it liked, and walked slowly and apparently aimlessly on. I could see that young man close before me, and I could even see through his jerkin and discover something glowing inside a bag he wore on his breast. Then that bag too suddenly became clear as the finest of glass, showing me that the young man had Arni's stone. How can he wander along so sadly and aimlessly, I thought, when he has that jewel? For nobody knew where it was at the time. I wish he would come to me, I thought. I had liked him the moment I set eyes on him. And then I spoke, to encourage him, because I had the impression that he didn't yet quite understand what he possessed in that stone. I didn't know if he could hear me or not, so I put out my hand, but as soon as I touched him, the vision in the dream went out like a light.

And another time, when I was a little older, I saw the young man lying by a spring among bushes at night, and I knew he had set off along a path that would lead him the wrong way. Don't ask me how I knew; I could tell, that's all. And I saw the despair into which he would fall, although there was no way I could stop him choosing that path. Then I took him in my arms, so that he might remember that comfort when despair overcame him, but he melted away from me like smoke, and I couldn't see him any more, though I heard the sound of the spring for a little while longer.

Later on, I had a very short dream. I saw the young man again, though he seemed rather different this time. He was sitting on a tree stump at the edge of a clearing, staring at Arni's stone, which he had in his hand. Next moment a shadow passed over the stone, extinguishing its light all at once, and I saw a bird swoop down from the sky, its talons reaching for the stone. Then I cried out, to warn the young man, and next moment the vision disappeared.'

'Did you know that all these things really happened, and I could feel you near me every time?' asked Listener.

'I hoped you did,' said Arnilukka, 'and I was sure my dreams were showing me a part of reality. It was then I first told Belarni about them. I had become so friendly with him by now that he, for his part, often discussed what was on his mind with me. I couldn't quite understand a good deal of it, but I felt it did him good to talk to someone, or to have someone to listen to him. I had been afraid he would laugh at me when I told him my dreams, but he just listened, and thought for a while, and then said, "It looks as if someone is on his way to you without knowing it. Indeed, I think I know who he is."

"Tell me, then!" I cried, but Belarni shook his head. "If your dreams don't tell you, then you're not supposed to know yet," he said. "That young man will have to make his own way onward alone until he knows where it is he's going. But it will help him to feel your thoughts put out to meet him." And after that I lived ever more intensely with the young man in my thoughts and dreams. I had long felt that he reminded me of someone, but I didn't know who it was until I first came back to the Shallow Valley and ran away from you. At first I thought I was seeing the young man from my dreams, and then I recognized the face of the fluter who had ridden through the Weird Wood with me, and I knew they were one and the same. But the sight of your shaggy coat and your nakedness put such fear into me that I thought some wood-spirit was deluding me, and as you know, I did no better the second time either.

And then I had a dreadful dream, in which I saw the faun with the face of the young man, or of the fluter, standing on a rock above a spring. His eyes were empty as the eyes of a dead man. He was raising a flask to his lips, and I knew at that moment that he was about to do something terrible. I wanted to stop him, but I couldn't move a muscle. I had to stand and watch him drain that little round flask, and drop it. And then it was as if a kind of greyness rose inexorably all around his limbs, from his goat's legs upwards, spreading quickly, dulling his skin to the colour of stone. This was the last such dream I had, but then, one night, I heard that song about the stone man standing in the wood, waiting for someone to find him. I heard it again and again, and soon knew it by heart, and that was when I took your flute out of my chest and learned to play the song on it.

Belarni was listening once when I sang the song, and he looked at me in a strange way, thoughtfully and sadly, and said, "You'll never be able to think of anyone else until you find and waken that stone man."

"Ought I not to, then?" I asked, but he only shrugged his shoulders and muttered something to the effect that there was nothing he could do to change matters. That was when I realized that he loved me, and was trying to hide his love for the sake of the young man, because he believed I must find him.

And so I did, and all last summer that I spent here in the Shallow Valley with you, I scarcely thought of Belarni at all. When I came home late in the autumn, and everyone could see the condition I was in, he was not at all surprised, but seemed to have been expecting some such thing, quite unlike my mother, who had a good many questions to ask me. Some of them were the same questions I'd asked myself, but had put aside again. Now, however, I had to answer them, and in doing so I came to realize that I had no idea at all what was to happen next.

Belarni soon saw that I was not as happy as a young woman ought to be after such a summer, and in the end he asked me what the matter was. So I told him the way things were with us, and how there was hardly a place to be found where both of us could be together without fear. He tried to comfort me, but he had no practical suggestions either. Then I went into labour, and at first, after the baby was born, I tried not to think about the future. However, spring came closer and closer, and with every passing day I saw more clearly that I couldn't spend my whole life walking the borders of that terror behind which your own world begins. Can you understand that, Listener?'

He nodded slowly. 'I've thought about it a great deal myself in the long winter nights,' he said, 'but I never found any solution.'

'There probably isn't one,' said Arnilukka. 'And so I told Belarni in the end. That evening he asked me if I would be his wife.'

'Do you love him, then?' asked Listener. His own voice sounded like a stranger's to him, and as he spoke he prepared to feel the pain which would surely fall on him, but did not strike just yet. Arnilukka looked at him for a long time, and then she said, 'Yes, I love Belarni, though not in the same way as I love you. What's more, he needs me. I think he needs me more than you do now.'

'Then you have already decided,' said Listener, feeling the pain come closer and closer.

'No,' said Arnilukka. He saw her trying to control herself, but then she lost her carefully preserved composure, and almost screamed, 'Can't you see how such a decision rends my heart?' She fell silent for a while and then said, rather more calmly, 'With you – with you it's love against all reason, overpoweringly beautiful, but very close to the bottomless abyss of fear, and never resting. With Belarni it's stead-fastness, love like a strongly built house in which one can live all one's life. I don't know how to decide. You must tell me.'

'You know already,' said Listener, and now the pain was there, striking its terrible blow. He tried to withstand it. Then he reached for the little bag over his heart, took out the stone, and laid it on the breast of the baby girl Urla in her cradle. 'You have the eyes,' he told her.

> *Seek the light*
> *where the glow may fall;*
> *you have not sought aright,*
> *if you don't find it all.*

Arnilukka looked at him, bewildered, and asked, 'But how will you live without the stone?'

'I don't need it any more,' said Listener. 'It was only a symbol of what you gave me, and that's a part of me now. I thought, for a long time, that you yourself were my journey's end, but now it looks as if you were only to show me where that end lies. And with such things as this stone, I think owning them is less important than giving them away at the right time. So now Urla has the stone back. Will Belarni be good to our child?'

'He loves her already,' said Arnilukka, and rose to stop Urla putting the sparkling stone in her mouth.

'Keep it for her until she's big enough to look for its secret,' said Listener. They stood there side by side in silence for a while, looking at the baby as her tiny hands grasped the carved figures around the cradle. Then they embraced, and stood there a long time, pressed as close together as if they had only one body between them. And only then did Listener become aware, to his amazement, that the pain had disappeared at the moment when he gave away Arni's stone.

When Belarni came back from the herdsmen's huts, they were standing by the cradle again, playing with the baby.

'What will you do now?' Arnilukka asked.

'Travel in the forests for a while, and see if a fluter's needed anywhere,' said Listener. 'Can you leave me two horses? One to ride, and a pack-horse.'

'Vazzek will give you everything you need,' said Arnilukka.

Next morning Arnilukka and Belarni rode back to Arziak with the baby. Listener stood by the edge of the wood, watching them go until they were out of sight. Then he went back into his workshop, and with Derli's help, he began to make a second lathe, one that could be easily dismantled and reassembled. In the evenings he taught the young man more of the art of playing the flute, although his mind was not entirely on the matter.

When summer came, Listener gave the young man the old lathe, some of the tools that went with it, and three of the flutes they had made that winter. 'And now,' he said, 'it's time you went back to Arziak, to show the people there what you have learnt.'

Next morning, he fastened the parts of his new lathe to the pack-horse's saddle, along with his tools and a leather sack containing the rest of the flutes, and rode away down the valley through the woods.

Chapter Two

On the evening when the story that is to be told here began, Listener was sitting under the lintel of his doorway, looking up at the ridge of the high mountains, whose jagged, towering peaks were still tinged with red from the last rays of the setting sun, while the glaciers lower down lay grey in the shadows. When first the Bloodaxe People brought him here to their village, he had shuddered at the sight of this bleak landscape, cleft by crevasses and rockslides, with only a few malformed shrubs growing here and there on the long scree slopes. It was now nearly twelve years since the day when the red-headed ruffians had captured him somewhere in the wild forest, but his heart still trembled when he thought of that ride into the mountains. They had tied him on his horse with long straps, and didn't even look round when he cried out in terror as soon as the path led out of the woods and into the open country of the high mountain meadows, with the deep blue sky weighing down upon them like a sheet of steel. They had gone on talking in their guttural, harsh language as he slumped half-fainting in his saddle, eyes closed. In the village, they had shut him up in a small log cabin which was obviously intended for such purposes, and only here, in the dim room, where a little light filtered in through two narrow slits of windows, did he partly come round again. They've no need to bar the door, he had thought at the time, for he was sure he would never leave this room of his own free will and expose himself to the agony of that sky, which seemed to hang above the mountain peaks close enough to touch.

When one of the men came back later, indicating that Listener was to follow him somewhere, he simply refused, and the man soon realized that he would have to drag his prisoner out of the hut by force if he wanted to get him into the open. Finally he gave it up, shaking his head, went away, barring the door again behind him, and soon returned with another red-haired man of middle age, who towered above him by a full head, although he himself was by no means short. Judging by the golden buckle on this second man's belt, and the brooch set with red stones pinned to his shirt, he must be a leader of some kind. He also turned out to be something of a linguist, for he asked Listener if he came from Arziak, in the tongue of the valleys.

'How can you tell?' asked Listener.

'From your horse's harness,' said the man. 'I know every kind of harness for thirty days' ride around; there's hardly a place of any size within that area from which I haven't had a prisoner to hold to ransom.'

'Then you're the chieftain here?' said Listener. 'I once heard tell of a man called Skullcleaver, but that can't be you; his story lies some time in the past.'

'Skullcleaver?' said the man, with a great booming laugh. 'Nobody here talks of him any more, I can tell you! He lost face after some crazy old man beat him at the board game. He took to quarrelling with anyone and everyone, and got himself killed in some such argument. I've been chieftain here since. What's your name?'

Listener told him, thinking that it must have been this hulking brute himself who had killed Skullcleaver. However, the memory of it did not appear to trouble the giant, but rather gave him considerable satisfaction. Looking at his scarred face, Listener asked, 'What do I call you?'

'My name's Axewielder,' said the chieftain, 'and you can guess how I got it.' The thought of whatever incident which had won him his name also appeared to afford him great pleasure, for he laughed again so loud that the low beams of the ceiling shook, and then added, 'You're a strange sort of fellow, you are. Screaming your head off on the way, I hear, and now you dare refuse to come before me. What's the matter with you, then?'

'It's a long story,' said Listener.

Axewielder was immediately interested. 'I like stories!' said he. 'Sit down and tell it!' He waved the other red-haired man out of the room as if he were a troublesome chicken, then dropped on the settle by the wall, making its timbers creak, and indicated that Listener was to sit beside him. 'Right,' he said. 'I'm listening.'

So Listener told him how a witch had cast a spell on him, and now he could not bear to be out under the open sky. The chieftain seemed to find this a fascinating tale. He listened intently, asked about certain details from time to time, and slapped his mighty thigh with wonderment. At last he said, 'A fine spell, that! And so useful, too! No need to lock up a man with a spell like that cast on him, not here where there's no trees; he can't run away, and that's that. I wouldn't mind employing this witch myself. Where will I find her?'

'Everywhere, yet nowhere,' said Listener, unable to help laughing himself at the readiness with which Axewielder had instantly seen the practical side of his tale of enchantment. 'She was caught in her own toils, and now she's a falcon flying somewhere in the sky.'

'Pity, that,' said Axewielder, with genuine regret. 'Still, at least we don't need to set a guard on you any more. Got anyone to pay your ransom, then, have you?'

Listener thought for a little while. Arnilukka would probably move heaven and earth to ransom him, but she was the very last person to whom he wanted to appeal now. As for his parents, he didn't even know if they were still alive, and in any case they had not been rich. Barlo? He had heard nothing of Barlo for years. He shook his head. 'I'm a poor catch for you,' he said. 'I'm only a wandering fluter with no real home; who would pay ransom for me?'

'Another useless mouth, then,' said Axewielder. 'Maybe we'd do well to get rid of you quick.' And Listener no longer felt like laughing, for Axewielder said this in as matter-of-fact a way as if he were wondering whether to fatten a calf a little more or slaughter it at once. However, the chieftain obviously still hesitated to decide the matter so swiftly. 'What's that stuff you brought on your pack-horse?' he inquired.

'A turner's lathe,' said Listener. 'I make flutes as well as playing them, and I can make all kinds of other wooden things too.'

'Pieces for the board game?' asked Axewielder.

'Of course,' said Listener. 'Pieces of any shape, whatever you fancy. The last thing I made was a cradle with turned and carved bars for my daughter.'

The chieftain's head came up as if he had suddenly found a fresh trail. 'Your daughter, eh? Then you've got a wife somewhere who could pay for you!'

'No,' said Listener. 'My daughter's mother married another man.'

'I might have known it!' Axewielder's fist came down on the settle, and he bellowed with laughter. 'Somebody snapped her up under your nose, did he? A feeble sort of fellow you are!' Then he sobered down, and said, 'Very well, so you're a turner. That's something. You'll work for me here, and when we have a feast, then you'll sit in the doorway if you can't stand to be outside, and play us your flute. For that, I'll let you live and give you food.' He said this as if he were doing his prisoner a great favour, and indeed Listener was thankful enough to be spared closer acquaintance with one of these people's knife-edged battleaxes.

He had lived here with the Bloodaxe People in this cabin since that day, making pieces for the board game out of stone-pine wood or goat's horn, and all kinds of toys for children, and now and then he played his flute for the villagers' wild festivals. It had certainly crossed his mind to bring his art to bear on the dancers and make them let him go, but he remembered only too well what came of it when he last used the magic of the flute for his own ends. In any case, where could he have gone in these rocky highlands, where the nearest woodland was far away, beyond his reach? So he had stayed, and in time he learned the rough speech of the Bloodaxe People, so that after a while he could talk a little to the old woman who brought him food. Her name was Keevit, which meant 'mountain chough' in her own language, and with her hooked, prominent nose she actually did look rather like those black, yellow-billed birds who circled around the mountain peaks in easy flight by day, and sometimes came down to the village.

And then there was Snowfinch, Keevit's grandson. Listener had first noticed the fair-haired, thin-faced boy when he was sitting in his doorway at one of the festivals, playing the flute. He had been living some years in the mountain village by then, and had become used to the fact that nobody really listened to his music much. That was what made him notice the flaxen-headed boy. While the other lads leaped about among the dancers, or scuffled with each other somewhere on the edge of the hurlyburly, this flaxen-haired child stood a few paces away from him in the village square, listening. He hardly seemed to notice the others jostle or mock him because he wouldn't take part in their fights, but gave himself up to the music so whole-heartedly that he could ignore the noise and bustle all around. Even when Listener sometimes played his flute just for himself, he could be sure that the boy would soon appear as if he had sprung out of the ground, and would stay until there was no more music to be heard.

He didn't know who the boy was at first, and found out only when Keevit addressed him one day, as he ate the buckwheat groats with bacon she had brought him. 'That grandson of mine,' she said, 'Snowfinch, that's his name, well, he's crazy about your flute. When he hears you start to play, he'll drop everything and run over here so as not to miss a note of it.'

'Is he a thin, fair-haired boy?' asked Listener.

'That's right,' said she. 'He's a bit weakly, you see; he's got a lot to put up with from those red-headed louts in the village here. I often worry, I can tell you, wondering what's to become of him. I reckon he'll never grow to be a great brawling splitter of skulls like the men around here, and I wondered, couldn't he learn to be a fluter? What do you think?'

Listener had nothing against this notion, and thus he had acquired a pupil whose zeal surpassed even Derli's. Snowfinch positively soaked up the music, and it soon turned out that his fingers found the holes on the wooden flute Listener had given him from his stock almost of their own accord.

Listener had gone slowly in teaching the boy, for he had all the time in the world, but in the few years since they began, Snowfinch had achieved a mastery of the instrument which would long since have made him a minstrel much sought after anywhere else. In this village, however, he was regarded as crazy, a lad who was no use for any proper kind of work. He had shot up, and was a lanky, thin young fellow who hardly knew what to do with his awkward arms unless he had a flute in his hands.

On that evening, then, which we mentioned at the start of this story, Listener had been giving his pupil a lesson, teaching him a few refinements, such as how to calm an angry man or put heart into a timid one with the music of the flute. And then he had sent Snowfinch home, meaning to sit in his doorway alone for a while and watch the sun set. By now he was so familiar with the strange landscape that had terrified him at first that he could not only bear the sight of it, but had even come to sense some of its wild beauty.

As he sat there, watching the sharply defined line between the crimson sunset glow on the rocks and the dull grey of the stone beneath move slowly upwards, a little flock of mountain choughs came flying across a small scree-filled hollow that had long been in shadow, and settled on the roof of his cabin. There was nothing unusual about this, for Keevit often threw a few breadcrumbs or other scraps of food out into the square for them, and they would peck up the best. She had done that today before going home, and soon a couple of the choughs came flying down from the rooftop to see what pickings might be had.

As soon as the rising shadow had swallowed up the last mountain peak, and only the sky above it was still barred with dull red and deep violet, Listener turned his attention to the choughs, who were inspecting the scraps on the stony ground with their heads on one side. They were in no great hurry; there was plenty of food about for them in summer.

'Can't say I much fancy what the folk here eat,' remarked one of the birds. Listener noticed that this one had a tiny white feather above his beak, which gave him a rather perky appearance.

'Yes, well,' said the other chough, 'I've eaten better suppers myself; still, it's only polite to peck about a bit, or the old lady will be disappointed if she sees none of it gone tomorrow. And where were you last winter, White-feather, to get yourself such grand ideas?'

'Round about Arziak,' said the bird thus addressed. 'Since the people there took in what was left of the Raiding Riders, they've been able to go about their work in peace again, and make a good profit trading with their fine jewellery for themselves. You can tell that, just from what they put on their tables! A bird's got no need to go hungry there in winter, I can tell you. Why, you get to eat fine white bread, and scraps of roast meat too, and other such delicious morsels!'

'Hm, I must remember that,' said the other chough. 'I found myself other winter quarters when all that trouble was going on in the valley. So the folk there are all living happy and content again?'

'Well, most of them,' said White-feather. 'Not Mistress Arnilukka, though, who's forgotten how to laugh, and her husband Belarni's not the merriest of men either. They both fret about their eldest daughter, that's what it is.'

Here the other choughs came flying down from the rooftop, and gathered around White-feather. 'What about the daughter?' they all called at once. 'Do you know a story, then? Tell us, tell us!'

Listener was no less eager than the choughs to hear what White-feather had to say. He dared not move a muscle, for fear of scaring the birds away, and then White-feather began his tale.

'As to this daughter of theirs,' he began, 'well, there's something strange about her. She's very beautiful, with nutbrown hair and eyes of a colour I can hardly describe. And she's very friendly to one and all, and clever at everything she does. But she can't talk as humans do. You can imagine what a grief it is to her parents, never able to exchange a word with their own child.'

'Is the cause of her trouble known?' asked one of the choughs. White-feather observed a moment of silence, to heighten the suspense, and then went on, 'Well, not to the parents anyway, or they wouldn't have gone trying to get the girl to talk by any means they can think of.'

'But you know! You've found out!' cried the second chough, and the others all called louder than ever, 'Tell us, tell us!'

White-feather looked around, to make sure everyone was listening properly, and then said, 'That's right, I found out, though I can't say I understood all I heard. There's some kind of magic behind it: I learned that much when I was on my way back to the mountains in spring. I was flying over that shallow green valley where the folk of Arziak graze their horses. There's a spring rises at the upper end of the valley, and I drank at it before settling in that great sycamore that spreads its branches over the spring, for a little rest. So as I was sitting there, a shadow came gliding through the young leaves, and when I looked up, I saw a falcon circling in the sky. Well, I kept quiet under the leaves, so as not to be spotted, but a mouse down in the grass wasn't so careful. Before he knew it, the falcon, a female, was on him, shooting down like an arrow, and seized him in her talons, though she didn't kill him at once.

This mouse was squeaking his head off, terrified, and then he calmed down and said, "All right, you've caught me, so hurry up and let's get it over and done with!"

However, the falcon was taking her time, maybe just because this mouse turned out a brave one and wasn't begging to be spared. She didn't seem to like that. "Why in such a hurry?" she said. "I've plenty of time, and it's boring, flying alone in the sky. I'd like a little conversation with you. How about a riddle game? If you win, I'll let you go."

She still had the mouse firmly beneath her claw, but he wasn't to be dismayed. He raised his head and looked the falcon in the face. It was then I saw the falcon had green eyes. The mouse seemed to notice that too, and he said, "One of my people had words with you before. Well, I don't mind being another to have the privilege of showing you that mice don't lose their heads in the clutches of the likes of you!"

This infuriated the falcon, but as she had offered to play the riddle game she couldn't withdraw now, so she said, "You'll soon change that high-and-mighty tune when you hear my three riddles. Here's the first: a robber, yet no robber; a son, yet no son; a father, yet no father. Who is he?"

At this the mouse actually began to chuckle. "Simple!" he said. "If you don't know any better riddles than that, my life's safe. You mean Belarni. He's a Raiding Rider, yet he never went out after loot; he is called the son of Hunli, but he is not Hunli's son; he is like a father to Arnilukka's daughter, but he's not her father."

The falcon screeched angrily. "How do you know all that, you cunning little thing?" she snapped.

"Wings aren't the only way to get around, you know," said the mouse. "And I've a liking for stories, so I listen carefully when anyone tells one. How does your second riddle go, then?"

"You'll never guess this one!" said the falcon. "Listen: the father talks to goats, the mother talks to fish, no wonder their child is mute. Can you tell me the answer?"

"Nothing easier!" said the mouse cheerfully. "You mean the girl Urla, who can't talk like other human beings, though her mother can speak to the fishes. Is it, I wonder, anything to do with the fact that Urla's father still had the legs of a goat when he lay with Arnilukka?"

The falcon screeched with rage to find that she had given away more than she meant to, and was about to put an end to that mouse. However, the mouse squeaked, "Do you want people saying you were too cowardly to play the riddle game to its end? Ask me the third riddle, and then you can kill me if I don't know the answer!"

"That will give me the greatest of pleasure," said the falcon, "and you'd better be quick about answering, because my patience is running very short. Listen:

> *The one gives him a shaggy coat,*
> *the other takes my feathers and beak,*
> *both one and the other must be found*
> *to bring the silent child to speak.*

What are they? Quick!"

"Ring and chain!" cried the mouse at once, and looking at the falcon, it was easy to see that he had the right answer. She ruffled up her feathers and raised her curved beak to finish off the mouse, but she hadn't reckoned with me. I wasn't going to leave so bold a mouse in the lurch, so I flew up off my branch with a loud cry, and shot past so close to the falcon that I touched the feathers on her head. She was so startled that she let the mouse go, and I was just able to see him disappear into the bushes. By the time the falcon realized who'd been interfering, I was high in the sky and flying north to the mountains as fast as I could go, because I didn't plan on getting into any fight. So now see if you can work out the way to break the spell on the girl.'

'Ring and chain? Ring and chain?' cried the other choughs. 'What kind of ring? What kind of chain?'

'No idea,' said White-feather, but Listener, who had heard it all, knew very well what chain and ring were meant. However, he also knew that those jewels now lay somewhere in the depths of the lake, below the great cliff, where no one would ever be able to find them. No one? He was still pondering that question, long after the choughs had flown away, and it would not let him go as he lay sleepless in bed that night. He alone knew where to look for the chain and the ring, and so he alone could help his child. The weasel had been with him when he threw both jewels into the lake, but Needle-tooth must have gone to his ancestors long ago, as he himself would have put it. Gradually, a plan took shape in Listener's mind, and when day began to dawn outside, he had come to a decision, and dozed off briefly until Keevit came and woke him with his breakfast of bread and milk.

Composedly, he spooned up the softened pieces of bread, drank the remaining goat's milk from the wooden bowl he had made himself, wiped his mouth with the back of his hand, and asked the old woman, who was tidying the room, 'Can you send Snowfinch over here this morning? I've something to discuss with him, concerning the feast the day after tomorrow. Axewielder shall have some particularly good music this time, played on two flutes!'

'As if he ever listened to it!' said Keevit, but she promised to tell the boy he was wanted. She hadn't long left the cabin before Snowfinch came running. 'Grandmother said I can play at the feast with you!' he cried before he was even through the doorway. 'Is it true?'

'Certainly,' said Listener. 'You shall show the whole village what you've learnt, the day after tomorrow. But that's not so very important, compared with the matter I really want to discuss. Do you intend to spend your whole life in this village?'

Snowfinch looked at him in dismay. 'Are you sending me away?' he asked. 'As long as you're here I want to stay too, to learn yet more of your art!'

'That's not the point,' said Listener. 'Would you be prepared to come with me if I were to escape?'

'At once, if need be!' said Snowfinch, going quite red with his eagerness. 'But – but you can't go out in the open at all, even if you wanted to! Everyone in the village knows that.'

'I mean to ride away in the same manner as I arrived,' said Listener, 'but I shall need your help if I'm to do it.'

'When are we to go?' asked Snowfinch.

'The day after tomorrow, after the feast and at night, when they're all dead drunk in their homes,' said Listener. 'We shall be well away and in the forest by the time they've slept it off and find we're gone.' And then he told the boy his plan.

*   *   *

The feast was to celebrate a successful raid from which Axewielder and his men had returned a few days before. They had taken no prisoners, but as well as all kinds of other useful items, they had brought back some skins of heavy, red wine, although the chieftain kept these back at the beginning of the feast. First they drank mead, and the men danced their wild, stamping dances. They stood in a circle, holding one another's belts, bent their knees all together, leaped up again, and then the circle slowly began to turn while the women stood around, clapping their hands in time. Faster and faster went the closed chain of dancing men, until they suddenly stopped with a loud yell, though still stamping on the spot. Now, however, they let go of one another's belts and all clapped the rousing rhythm as two of the dancers leaped towards each other in the middle of the circle. They had snatched their axes from their belts and were whirling them above their heads, suddenly lunging at one another every now and then. This manoeuvre, however, obviously followed a set of strict rules, for the handles of the weapons always met, with a crack, while the axes sprang back into their circling movement and then made for each other once again, at a different angle on each occasion, as in a carefully rehearsed military exercise in which every possible blow of the adversary's must be parried. At last the two dancers locked their axes together and whirled faster and faster around the central point thus created, until you could scarcely tell their two heads apart, so fast did the dance go, while the tempo of the clapping rose to a frenzy, and finally ended with another high-pitched yell, whose sound came echoing back over and over again from the mountains. At this moment, the two dancers in the middle disengaged their axes, and the vigour of their movement flung them backwards with such force that the men in the circle had difficulty in catching them. There were roars of laughter when several men fell over one another, and then the group of dancers dispersed.

Only now did Axewielder have the wineskins brought, and he presided over the pouring of wine for the exhausted dancers himself. As soon as every man had a goblet of wine in his hand, the noise died down. Listener, who had been sitting in the doorway of his cabin with Snowfinch, watching the wild dance, rose, picked up his flute, and said, 'Well, now's our time to play them a tune.'

Raising his flute to his lips, he began alone. A few of the revellers had still been laughing or shouting as they drank to one another, but they soon fell silent now. Listener had taken up the rhythm of the dance that had just finished, and made it into a catchy tune. The effect

was as if what had gone before were only the accompaniment to a song
which now began in good earnest, its rising and falling phrases giving
true meaning to the dance that still had the men's feet moving to its
beat. They all looked Listener's way as he brought the tune to an end
in a bold, rising phrase, took his flute from his lips for a moment, and
whispered to Snowfinch, 'Now you!'

The boy took up the melody on his deeper-toned wooden flute.
Many of the revellers were humming it now, like a song, and after the
first few bars Listener began to wind an accompaniment of swift trills
and runs around this song on his silver instrument, its sound rising to
the evening sky like birdsong. When Snowfinch had brought the second
verse of the song to a close, they both began the third verse together,
and now many powerful voices were joining in. As soon as Listener
could tell that the singers were sure of their melody, he signed to the
boy, and then both flutes dropped the theme itself to surround it with
an eddying spray of trills.

When they had finished playing, there was loud applause; such
music had never been heard in the village before. Snowfinch was
obviously pleased to get public recognition for the first time in his life,
and in so resounding a manner too. 'Shall we play them another
piece?' he asked, reaching for his flute again, but Listener held him
back. 'Let them drink a little more first,' he said, 'and then we'll give
them a lullaby.'

They sat down in the doorway again, and Axewielder himself came
over with the wineskin. 'You've earned a sip too,' said he. 'We can run
to a couple of goblets for you and the lad here.' Snowfinch jumped up
and fetched two wooden drinking vessels from the cabin, and the
chieftain filled them to the brim. 'I didn't know I had two such fluters
in the village,' he remarked. 'You are worth the feeding after all. Good
music, that! I liked it. You may drink my health!'

He stood there until they had tasted the wine, as if to make sure they
appreciated his gift, and never noticed that neither drank more than a
small sip, for by the time they put their goblets down again he had
turned away and was going back to his men.

That evening the mountain choughs came to Listener's cabin again,
but seeing so many people out in the square they stayed sitting on the
roof, except for White-feather, who fluttered down to see what Keevit
had thrown them this time. Watching the bird, Listener had an idea.
'That was an interesting story you told the day before yesterday,' he
said.

The chough was so startled to be thus addressed that he fluttered a little way up in the air again, but then his curiosity won the day, and he came back down to the ground, settling at a safe distance. 'Where did you learn our language?' he asked.

'It's too long a story to tell you now,' said Listener. 'Perhaps it will do if I say I was mentioned in one of the falcon's riddles. And the point is that I know where to look for the ring and the chain.'

On hearing this, the chough hopped a little closer and looked at him keenly. 'Then you must have been the faun said to be Urla's father.'

'I was,' said Listener.

'If that's so, then you'd better set out to help your daughter,' said White-feather.

'I should like to, very much,' said Listener, 'but it's not so easy to set out anywhere when you're a prisoner of the Bloodaxe People. Would you and your friends help me?'

'Glad to, if we can,' said White-feather at once, 'if only for the mute girl's sake. What do you want us to do?'

So Listener told the bird how he was planning to escape with Snowfinch that night. 'Will you be able to find us once we're in the forest?' he asked.

'Nothing easier,' said White-feather. 'Up in the sky, we see birds fly up from the trees when humans are passing down below.'

'Then follow us until I call you,' said Listener. He crumbled a piece of bread, and now the other choughs ventured down from the roof themselves to peck up their supper.

By now the noise out in the square had risen again. Most of the revellers were too drunk to walk straight at all, and some had already been felled by the wine, and lay babbling under the settles.

'And now to play them a gentle lullaby,' said Listener, picking up his flute. He began with a soft note that swelled louder and louder, until its quivering sound seemed to fill the whole hollow of the valley, silencing the last of the brawlers. When there was not another voice to be heard, Listener let the note die slowly away again, and took it as the point of departure for a gentle, swaying melody, such as mothers sing by their babies' cradles. Snowfinch had understood the nature of the song at once, and accompanied it with sweet, soft harmonies, and so they repeated that regular and soothing sequence again and again, first Listener and then Snowfinch taking the leading part. And as they played, night fell slowly over the mountains to the east, spreading across the sky until it reached the peaks on the opposite side of the valley. In the dark, a few figures could be seen staggering towards their cabins, while others stayed where they were, snoring among the upturned settles on the ground. The double song of the flutes hovered quietly over the sleeping village a little longer, grew fainter and fainter, and at last died away with a long-drawn-out and barely audible note.

Listener put down his flute. 'And now to work, Snowfinch,' he said. First he took his lathe apart, and the boy carried the pieces out of the cabin. He came back to fetch the rest of the tools, the bag of flutes, and Listener's few other possessions. 'Now I'll get your horse,' he said, leaving the cabin for the last time. Soon afterwards he brought the horse to the door, leading it by its halter.

Listener did not hear him until the last minute, for Snowfinch had wrapped rags around the horse's hooves. 'Bring it right to the door, so that it's under the porch,' he said, and when the boy had done as he asked, he climbed into the saddle. 'Now, tie my feet firmly together under the horse's belly,' he said. Snowfinch had brought a leather strap for that purpose, and when he had bound Listener's feet, Listener told him to tie his hands behind his back as well. 'And now the gag,' he said. 'But tie a cloth tightly over it, so that I can't push it out. And see that we ride fast! I want to get this first part of the journey behind me as soon as possible.'

When Snowfinch had conscientiously carried out all these directions, he took the horse by the bridle and led it out into the open. As soon as Listener no longer had a roof above his head, fear came crashing down from the black night sky on his heart like a great boulder, and he could not have refrained from screaming aloud if the gag had not been in his mouth. Snowfinch rounded the hut and began to hurry up the slope, still leading the horse, while Listener began to curse the notion that had led him to expose himself to such torture. He was just able to see Snowfinch turn aside behind a tall rock, in whose shelter he had hidden two more horses; one was a pack-horse, its saddle piled high, and the boy quickly mounted the second, took the bridles of both the other animals, and rode away southward with them at a brisk trot.

Afterwards, Listener could not have said how long they rode in the dark, between steep walls of rock. His fear rained blows on him ever more violently, constricting his chest as if some invisible hand were squeezing his heart in its grip. Now and then he lost consciousness until his horse stumbled and brought him round, delivering him up once more to the torment of the naked sky, sprinkled with icily sparkling stars. At last he felt the way begin to lead more steeply downwards, the shapes of a few windblown mountain pines flitted past to left and right of them, became groups of trees drawing closer and closer together, and then the path went down into the forest. On this last part of the way, Listener's sense of oppression had become noticeably less, and when he felt the thick roof of the tree-tops over him again, he nodded to his companion, and brought his horse to a halt by the pressure of his thighs.

The boy dismounted and quickly freed him from his gag and bonds. Listener was breathing heavily, as if after some immense exertion, and despite the cool night air his face was streaming with sweat. 'That was the worst of it,' he said, once he had his breath back. 'But for the bonds and the gag I wouldn't even have got as far as the other two horses, and I'd have woken the entire village with my yelling. Now do you see why all that was necessary?'

'I'd never have thought it would take you as badly as that,' said Snowfinch. 'It must be a strong spell the witch cast on you.'

'We must deal with her, none the less,' said Listener. 'Now, to horse, and down into the woods as fast as we can go! I see the sky growing light behind the mountains in the east.' As day slowly dawned, they rode on as fast as the rough mountain track would allow, still going downhill. After a while, Listener heard the mountain choughs calling in the sky above the tree-tops. White-feather came flying down through the swaying branches of the pines and settled on his shoulder. 'Here we are,' he said. 'Now what do we do?'

'I'd like the flock to keep close,' said Listener, 'but you yourself had better stay with me. I might not be able to call loud enough when I need you.'

So they trotted on, without stopping to rest, until early in the afternoon. When they came to a spring surrounded by dense bushes, Listener reined in his horse and said, 'They won't catch up with us very easily now. Let's rest here.' They both dismounted. Snowfinch opened the bundle of provisions they had brought for the journey, and took out a flat cake of hard bread and a piece of streaky bacon seasoned with garlic and juniper. Observing that there was something to eat, the choughs came fluttering down from the trees and had their share. So the two fugitives sat peacefully side by side for a while, munching the hard bread, and discussing what way to go now. Then Listener called to White-feather, and asked, 'If you flew up above the trees again, would you be able to see if Axewielder and his men are after us?'

'Of course,' said the chough. He flew up above the trees and circled there for a while. Fluttering down again, he called, 'You'd better set off again, fast! They're so close we'll soon be able to hear them.'

Listener leaped up, and Snowfinch, who could understand none of this conversation, realized there was danger and got the horses ready. 'And now you can help us,' Listener told White-feather. 'You said one can tell where people are in the forest from the way the birds fly up. Axewielder will know that too, for it's his trade to pursue travellers. You must lay him a false trail. We will ride to the right of the mountain projecting there ahead of us, going south-east and down into the valley, but I want you to keep to the left, going south-west, and set up a lot of noise. Keep coming down into the trees until our pursuers are close to you, and then fly on as if someone had scared you out of the branches. And call as loud as you can!'

'That's a good plan,' said White-feather. 'You can count on us to lead them a merry dance!'

Listener thanked the birds, and watched the flock fly back northwards above the trees. But the hollow thud of horses' hoofbeats could already be heard on the soft pine needles of the forest floor. It was too late to ride away now. Listener and Snowfinch drew their horses into the bushes behind the spring and waited. A little way up the path, the horsemen stopped, and one of them said, 'Now to decide whether we search to right or left of that rocky promontory.'

As they were arguing about the way to take, the choughs could be heard screeching farther up the path. They circled in the sky, and then flew back south-west. 'There's someone in the woods there!' one of the horsemen cried. 'That'll be them!' And they urged on their horses with shrill cries, riding fast after the choughs. Some time later, the high calling of the birds was heard again, but farther away, and then all was quiet among the trees.

So they had shaken off their pursuers. Listener had a rough idea of the way they ought to go, but they made only slow progress down the wooded mountainside, broken up as it was by countless little mountain streams and valleys. They often had to go a long way round, and dismount to lead their horses down steep slopes. Fortunately, Snowfinch had brought plenty of provisions. 'Did you plunder your grandmother's larder?' asked Listener, when they had found a good camping place by the banks of a mountain stream that evening, and the boy brought out a whole side of bacon, strips of dried meat, a goat's milk cheese, and two more of the hard, aromatically seasoned cakes of bread.

'No, no!' said Snowfinch. 'There's a plank loose in the floor of the chieftain's storehouse; I've known about it for some time. And the place is so full of stuff, Axewielder will scarcely notice anything's gone. He can spare it more easily than my grandmother.'

So Listener was able to enjoy the meal without any pangs of conscience, particularly as his own provisions of twelve years ago must have found their way to the chieftain's storehouse. Afterwards, he sat on the bank of the stream, bathing his hot feet in the cold mountain water. He saw a shoal of trout under an overhanging rock, not at all disturbed by his presence; indeed, one of them even swam over with a flick of its fins and inspected each of his toes separately. It would be easy to catch trout here, he thought, but this notion soon gave way to another image that emerged from his memory: he saw Arnilukka as a little girl, sitting on the banks of a pool under a willow tree and talking to the fish. He had not been able to understand what she said at the time, but it was otherwise now. He watched the trout, so close to his feet in the stream, and it seemed to be looking up at him as if waiting for something. He crumbled a piece of bread and scattered the crumbs in the water. The trout snapped at them instantly, and then put its head up above the fast-moving surface of the stream and looked directly at him. It was obviously after something other than breadcrumbs. He had never tried talking to fish yet, but there is a first time for everything, so he asked, 'Do you know Arnilukka?'

The fish shot out of the water with a single flap of its tail, was suspended in the air for a moment, amidst a cascade of sparkling colour, and then fell back into the stream with a splash. Listener took this to be some kind of affirmative, and went on, 'Then please send her a message from Listener: I am on my way to help our mute child.' The trout raised its head above the water again, and opened its round mouth, but the voice that he heard at the same time did not seem to proceed from any outside source, sounding instead within his own mind, and it said:

> *You're far astray in your pursuit!*
> *The girl you speak of is not mute.*
> *Her human speech waits to be woken*
> *once the evil spell is broken.*
> *Yet many a woodland creature may*
> *understand what she can say.*

'Mute or not,' said Listener, 'the fact is that she can't talk to her parents, and if I am to break that spell on her, I need the ring and the chain I threw into the lake beneath the great cliff. How am I ever to find them again?'

No sooner had he asked than the voice sounded again:

Where you spent three winters go:
find the shaft and climb below.
Yet the golden chain and ring
will not avail you anything.
Use of them, if use is made,
must be with the falcon's aid.

'That will be a dangerous business,' said Listener. 'This falcon is the last creature on earth to whom I would wish to entrust those magical things. However, it seems I must look for the falcon too. I suppose you can't tell me where to find her?' But the voice had an answer to that as well:

Where the spring begins to run,
where the birch trees in the sun
come the Shallow Valley nigh,
you will see her in the sky.
Give the jewels, give the gold,
and then be wary, wise and bold.

'You are a clever trout,' said Listener, 'and a wise one too. Thank you for your help. Now I am better informed of the way I have to go.'

* * *

The two horsemen now bore more towards the east, but it was another week before the woods through which they rode seemed familiar to Listener. That evening, they reached the spring at the upper end of the Shallow Valley, and let the great sycamore tree lull them to sleep with its rustling leaves. Listener was not looking for the falcon; he would do that on his way back, if he had something to offer her. Next morning, they rode uphill through the forest again, and three days later they reached the cleft in the rock by which one could climb down into the great cliff itself. Listener left Snowfinch there with the horses, and took nothing with him but his flute. 'Wait for me here three days,' he said, 'and if I'm not back by then, ride down to the herdsmen's huts. I'll meet you there sometime.'

'But what shall I do if you don't come back at all?' asked Snowfinch.

'I will, never fear,' said Listener. And he started to climb down.

He was alone again now, and he felt almost as he had when he was a faun roaming the woods on his own. Climbing down through the cleft in the rock had been harder then, however, with his ungainly goat's legs and his hooves. It was not long before he reached firm ground at the bottom, and looked for a way through the willows beyond which the surface of the lake shone. He sat on the bank for a while, wondering whether to call on the water nymph to whom he had given Narzia's jewels. The air was full of the rushing of the waterfall, the high notes of the water wagtails' calls sounding in it now and again. Listening to this music, he took out his flute, and composed a melody to its accompaniment which ought surely to have pleased the water nymph, but there was no sign of her. At last he gave up hope of recovering his gift in so easy a way. The trout had probably known it wouldn't work, since its verses mentioned neither a lake nor a water nymph.

> *Where you spent three winters go:*
> *find the shaft and climb below.*

That could only mean the cave where he had lived with his goats. He could not remember any shaft leading from it, but no doubt he would find some such thing when he got there. So he put his flute in his pocket and set off along the foot of the great cliff.

The entrance to the cave was so drifted up with dead leaves that he could hardly have found it if he hadn't remembered the place so well. Clearing the leaves away, he crawled into the dark chamber. At first he could scarcely see anything, but gradually his eyes became used to the dim light, and then he could make out wooden furnishings along the right-hand wall of the cave. This was where the people who were once Narzia's dogs had lived: roughly made tables, benches and bedsteads stood ranged there, some of them broken. The inhabitants of the cave would have taken everything else when they were brought to Arziak. But where could the shaft be? There was no other way into the main part of the cave; he could not see so much as a crack.

Before searching further, Listener gathered dry wood from the remains of the furniture and lit a fire in the middle of the cave. Then, a burning branch in his hand, he climbed up to what had once been his sleeping-place.

He had remembered that up here the cave seemed to lead farther back, just where the rocky walls came closer together and the stream ran out of a crevice. He had never tried to go on through the narrow cleft himself when he lived here, but if there was a shaft to be found at all, then it must be here.

At first the space was so narrow that Listener could only just wriggle through it, and here and there he had to crawl on the ground along the slippery bed of the stream. Then the path divided. To the right, the stream came shooting down the channel it had hollowed out for itself, and to the left there was another crevice in the rock, a dry one, leading on over fallen boulders. Listener decided to explore this path, and after some difficult clambering, he found himself in a smaller cave. The pale stone of its walls showed streaks of azure blue and malachite green in the flickering light of his torch, and at the far end of the cave a narrow passage led steeply down. This must be the shaft the trout had meant. Before he could start to climb down it, however, a hiss close to his ear made him swing round in alarm. At first all he saw was a pair of agate eyes shining in the torchlight; then he saw the snake lying coiled in a niche in the rock, head raised.

'So here you are at last, Listener,' said the snake.

Now he knew who had been waiting for him here. 'You gave me quite a fright, Rinkulla,' he said, shining his torch into the snake's nesting-place. 'But I'm very glad indeed to see you in this place.'

Rinkulla flinched away from the crackling flame and said sharply, 'Yes, well, put that light out. The creatures who live down here don't like fire.'

'But I can't climb down into that hole in the dark,' said Listener, apprehensively.

'Yes, you can,' said Rinkulla. 'You'll have to, if you want to find what you're looking for. Put the torch out, or you'll never get it!'

So Listener obeyed, and trod out the flame. The acrid smoke took his breath away, and for a moment he thought he would stifle to death down here. Then, gradually, the air cleared, but now it was pitch dark.

He dared not move for fear of falling down some bottomless abyss. The image of the flame going out hovered before his eyes for a little longer, and then there was nothing but shapeless blackness all around him. 'I shall never get anywhere like this, though,' he said hopelessly, crouching on the ground. He could not even have said where the snake was, or if she was still there at all. But then he heard the light scraping of her scaly skin on the rough stone, and that at least was something to cling to in this impenetrable darkness.

'Wait, wait!' said Rinkulla. 'You'll soon find your way.' And when he looked in the direction from which her words came, he thought he saw two barely perceptible lighter spots in the dark, and the longer he looked that way, the more clearly defined did those spots of light become, until he realized that they were Rinkulla's eyes. 'Won't you come with me when I climb down?' he asked. 'The light of your eyes would be enough for me.'

'No,' said the snake. 'You must go that way alone. If you really want to find anything here, another light would only distract you. Think of your name, and trust to your hearing, and don't forget what you're looking for!'

As Rinkulla spoke these last words, the pale glow of her eyes had been fading, and her voice grew softer too, as if it came from farther away. He could still hear the scraping of her scaly skin for a little while as she slid away, and then he was alone in the darkness.

At first he was near panic. Silent blackness surrounded him like a threat before which he felt helpless. He sat there motionless for a long time, listening, and just as he was wondering if he had gone deaf in this cave, shut off as it was from the whole world outside, a barely audible sound did come to his ears, perhaps of a waterdrop falling from some rocky ledge on to a slab of stone. After a long interval, in which he almost gave up hope again, a second drop fell, and soon after that a third. The clear note seemed to rise from somewhere below, and surely told him where the shaft must be.

Feeling his way over the rough floor of the cave, Listener began slowly crawling in the direction from which the sound had come. He felt as if he had travelled an endless distance when at last his fingers felt empty space immediately before him. Cool air blew up from below into his face, and when the sound broke the silence again, it was quite distinct now, almost within reach. At this Listener plucked up courage and began to make his way cautiously down the steep passage, feet first. He had to grope for every foothold with his toes, and test its stability before he ventured to put his weight on it and go a little farther. Once, a piece of stone broke away beneath his foot and went bouncing down to the depths. His progress was painfully slow, yet perspiration soon broke out on his forehead.

At one point he stopped to rest for a moment on a ledge, and was just about to continue his downward climb, when he heard a quiet whispering coming up to him from below, with the slight current of air. He stopped moving at once, and listened, but all was still again. Only when he had gone a little farther down did he hear that whispering again, rather more distinctly this time. It sounded like someone talking softly and monotonously to himself, but Listener could not make out the words. At the same time, peering down, he saw something yellowish shining far below. Now that he had a goal before his eyes – and indeed, there was soon a faint glow bright enough to help him make out a few handholds and footholds – he made faster progress, and with every step farther down that he climbed, the voice became clearer.

'So here's a nice, fat, round nugget of gold,' it was saying, 'and here's another to go with it, and I'll just fetch that one over there too.' Listener heard a quiet dragging, groaning sound, as if some heavy body were on the move, and then the whispering came again. 'There you are, my lovely shiny golden nugget, let's just put you with the others, then; come along, my love, my precious jewel.'

Listener was now directly above the place where the downward slope seemed to reach a larger space, from which the light shone up. Cautiously and silently, he let himself down the last of the shaft and found himself looking into a vaulted cave, dimly lit by the glow of lumps of shining golden metal which studded all the walls like currants in a cake. More of them were heaped up on the ground at the back of the cave. As Listener was still wondering where the voice he had heard might come from, he saw a kind of shapeless mass, which he had taken for a boulder, crawling slowly over the uneven ground. It began heaving itself on top of the piles of fist-sized golden nuggets.

'Is somebody coming to steal my gold?' asked the voice. 'Let me cover you nicely, my dears, we won't let anyone see you, won't let anyone touch you, won't let anyone take you away!' And only as the shining nuggets disappeared gradually beneath the shapeless body did Listener begin to get some idea of the size of the creature crawling over its treasure like a monstrous snail, until it was entirely hidden from sight. But no sooner was the thing still than it began whispering again. 'Oh, such a lovely nugget of gold in the wall over there, and I can't go and get it, I mustn't leave my treasure.'

This creature, whose shape could hardly be made out in the gloom, horrified Listener, but if he wanted to go farther into the depths, he must cross the cave to reach the mouth of a passage which yawned in the wall opposite; there was no other way. So he took his courage in both hands and said, 'I don't want your gold. Please will you just let me pass through your cave?'

'Doesn't want gold?' the creature whispered. 'This little fellow doesn't want gold? Is he lying, the little fellow? Just let him dare come in here! Oh, he'll be sorry he did! Oh, he'll be sorry, with me lying on him and squashing him flat! Oh, just let him try it!'

'I won't take anything,' said Listener. 'What I seek is hidden even deeper in this mountain.'

'What does he seek, then, the little fellow?' asked the creature. 'Let him tell me what he wants, then!'

'A ring and a chain,' said Listener.

'So he wants the golden ring, does he? So he wants the golden chain?' said the creature. 'So he does want gold!'

'Not for myself,' said Listener, but the creature hissed angrily and said, 'Lying again, is he, the little fellow? Why would anyone take a thing if not for himself? He's a thief, a thief, and I'll smother him.'

Listener realized he was getting nowhere. The creature seemed so possessed by its greed for gold that it could think of nothing else. If only he could free its thoughts of that obsession, he thought, and then his flute came into his mind. He took it out of his pocket, put it to his lips, and as he played the first few notes he heard the creature whisper, 'What's the little fellow doing, then, with that pretty, shiny thing? It speaks another language, it hurts, hurts me inside. Mustn't do that! Mustn't!' The creature had almost screamed these last few words; however, Listener took no notice, but went on playing, his music groping for the heart of this creature, always supposing it had one.

He tried to think his way into the life of the thing that crouched over its golden bed near the way out of the cave, barely visible in its monstrosity, moaning quietly. How long had it guarded its hoard here, shut away from the world? Had it always lived in this place, or had it once crawled into these depths by chance, and was then unable to part from the sparkling gold? Perhaps it had once been a creature of a different sort, before the glittering treasures confused its mind? Was there not a distant memory, in the words it had spoken to the dead nuggets of gold, of feelings that now lay buried under the greed for shining metal that dominated its whole being? 'My dears,' it had said, and 'My love,' as you might speak to a living thing you treasured, and so he tried to lay bare, with the music of his flute, the heart where some faint memory of such feelings might still live. And as his music felt its way closer and closer, the creature's moaning gradually changed to whimpering and weeping, until at last it was sobbing, 'What's he doing to me, this little fellow, what's he doing with his shiny magic thing? Showing me pictures, long ago, before I lived here in the cave.

There was love. There was tenderness. Come here, little fellow, and let me feel your warm hand, let me feel the tenderness again!'

Listener saw the creature slithering slowly off its bed and coming closer. Terror of this dreadful being seized him, but he knew he must go through with what he had begun. Putting the flute in his pocket, he went towards the creature until he could smell its musty odour, and its formless, monstrously towering mass was quite close. It bent something like a head down to him, saying, 'He'll have a little love to spare for poor Mollo, the little fellow, won't he?'

And at that Listener felt pity; he put out his hand and touched the creature that called itself Mollo. Mollo sighed with pleasure, and purred almost like a cat as Listener stroked the smooth, dry skin, and after he had stroked it for a while, Mollo said, 'Now the little fellow can take a couple of lovely round gold nuggets,' and crawled aside to let him get at the treasure.

Involuntarily, Listener stepped up to those heaped nuggets, and felt tempted to take the shining things in his hand. If one could pick up the whole treasure and drag it out into the daylight, he thought, how magnificently it would shine! One could be a great man with such riches, one could buy a whole kingdom.

'Aren't they lovely, my dear nuggets?' Mollo whispered. 'Wouldn't you like to burrow into them, right into the pile, and stop thinking of anything else? I meant it all for me, but you can take a little, just a little.'

Hearing this, Listener felt the same greed overcome him as had held Mollo spellbound here in the dark cave. He was appalled. With difficulty, he tore his eyes away from the golden gleam that had almost made him forget why he was down here. 'No,' he said. 'I don't want gold, Mollo. Let me go on farther down.'

Mollo shook that formless head, saying, 'Oh, he's clever, this little fellow. He might have been sorry, so he might, the little fellow, if he'd taken any of the gold. Who knows if Mollo could bear to see someone take any of his gold? Go away, little fellow, go away while you can!'

Listener did not wait for a second invitation. He slipped through the other way out and into a cleft leading on over almost level ground, and soon the last of the glow from Mollo's golden cave died away behind him, so that he had to grope his way into the dark again. Once, the path seemed to end in a smooth wall, but after a long and difficult search Listener found a crevice through which he could squeeze. He had to clamber over boulders barring his way, and then crawled on his stomach along a low tunnel where he could hardly raise his head, and this narrow place opened out into a large chamber from whose walls every sound echoed and re-echoed. Listener stood up to cross this cave, but his first step was on loose, sliding stones that carried him into an abyss, down which he fell faster and faster, surrounded by sliding, clattering shingle. He felt his feet hit rocky ground, and lay there for a while half-fainting with fright, while more pieces of stone showered down around him. Finally he scrambled to his feet, and found that he was in a narrow passage high enough for him to stand upright.

When the stones sliding down after him had at last come to rest, he could hear a muttering that seemed to come from the far end of the passage. He groped his way slowly on along the wall, and going round a bend, he saw a hint of light far ahead of him. Cautiously proceeding towards this faint light, he could make the muttering out more clearly. A few words rose above the monotonous murmur: 'Crystal . . . surface . . . angle . . . symmetry.' He could catch no more of it yet. When he had reached the next bend in the passage, he found himself looking through a smooth, round opening into a cavern full of cold, colourless light. A few steps took him to the end of the passage, and now he could see where the light was coming from.

In the middle of the large cave countless crystals, sparkling white, hovered as if hanging from invisible strings, circling one another in constant movement, and beside them was a strange, spider-like figure: a tiny thin body with immensely long, thin limbs and a pear-shaped head, its bald skull huge and shapeless above the crumpled face, and this little creature was dancing jerkily around the hovering crystals, muttering the whole time. 'Got it all in order now,' it was saying, 'all the crystals at the right angles to each other. All surfaces parallel, every sector reflecting the next, all the circles co-ordinated – no, wait! Must adjust the ecliptic here, it's out of order there, mustn't be like that!' And the little creature was leaping towards the circling crystals, reaching out its pale, spidery arms, to grasp at something in that magical pattern, but two of the crystals struck each other with a clear note like glass, and staggered out of their orbits. 'Such disorder, such disorder!' muttered the little thing. 'Got to start all over again now, got to work it all out, got to adjust everything, got to regulate it all!' His thin fingers snatched the errant crystals out of the dance of the others, then put them back most carefully in their right places, and gave them a little nudge to set them circling peacefully again.

Listener had been watching these strange manoeuvres with astonishment, and in so doing had seen a second circular opening in the wall opposite, through which one could leave the cave on its far side. For a while he did not venture to disturb the little creature as it hopped busily back and forth, but since it kept on fiddling with its toys and muttering the whole time, he came to the conclusion that he could wait here for ever before this spider-legged personage would stop for a rest. 'Forgive me for disturbing your game,' he said, 'but will you allow me to cross your cave? I have to go on farther down.'

The little creature whisked round as if a snake had bitten it. 'Game?' it snapped. 'Disturb? Why, the whole world will fall apart if you say another word! Do you know what hard work it is, keeping the world going? A game, you call it! It's no game, I can tell you, watching over the stars in their courses, looking after the equilibrium of the circling heavenly bodies, harmonizing their paths. Order, I tell you! We must have order!' Then he chuckled triumphantly, and continued, 'But I'm the Principal, I've got the power to create order and keep it! I can adjust it all, and don't you dare disturb me at my work!'

Another deranged creature, thought Listener, and he was about to step through the entrance and cross the cave even without permission, but he collided with an invisible wall that would not let him by.

'Aha, so you thought you needn't trouble with the Principal?' chuckled the little thing. 'Surprised, eh? There, now do you see the Principal has power to use forces, forces you can't perceive?' And turning back to the circling crystals, he murmured, 'Got to have order, got to have order, everything moving to my will. Oh dear, oh dear, it's going wrong again!' His thin arm went in among the hovering crystals, and once more he was unable to prevent the ensuing disorder. Several of the crystals touched each other, producing clear ringing notes of different tones, so that it sounded like delicate, glassy music.

Listener wondered if he might move this creature too by the sound of his flute. He took it out, and as more and more of the crystals clashed and were thrown off course, he took up the sequence of their notes and formed it into a melody. Is this rigid, glassy order supposed to be an image of the world, he wondered: is this eternal circling in tracks that are always the same, and out of which one can never break into new and unforeseen movement, meant to show life? No, impossible. Life is like a flower growing, unfolding its leaves, bearing blossom and fruit: and as that came into his mind, he remembered the music he had heard on the night his grandfather died, those sequences of notes flowering in every colour, from whose expansive phrases something new was always rising, fitting itself into the context of the whole without giving up its own identity, and he played that song as he remembered it, yet none the less it became new and different, for such a song cannot be repeated. As this music filled the cavern with its sound, the crystals formed new patterns, swerved aside from their pre-ordained orbits, and seemed to range freely in space, yet none of them disturbed the movement of any other, until at last each seemed to be impelled by its own ever-changing force, although the interplay of the whole was not lost: a living pattern of incomparable beauty, its figures changing, constantly bringing forth new forms.

The Principal hopped around this sparkling pattern with increasing agitation, saying crossly, 'Stop that stupid fluting! You're getting it all out of order! Can't you see how my stars are going astray? They'll crash any moment, they'll crash! Oh, such disorder, such disorder! The world will end!' And he tried to intervene and save what he thought ought to be saved, but the crystals escaped his grasp, yet took the hasty movements of his thin, spidery fingers into the play of their own dance, without in any way impairing the harmony of the whole.

At last the little creature realized that none of this was the result of his own activities, and he stood there for a while speechless and astonished beneath those sparkling, twinkling crystals. 'I don't understand,' he muttered. 'It's all flying about the place, but there's order there, and I don't know its rules. I thought out so many laws, and now they don't hold good! It's more than I can understand! How do you do it, fluter? You must show me! Let me be your pupil! You're the truly great master who can keep the world going. Come in, come in! You're welcome! Teach me your wisdom!'

And now no invisible power kept Listener from entering the cave, where he stopped, wondering, before the hovering crystals. It was beautiful to watch them at close quarters as they went their way, forming ever new and surprising figures, like variations on a tune. 'You must play!' said the little creature, who was now leaping around him, bowing deferentially. 'Play your flute before it all goes out of order again! You are the master now, guiding the whole world with your will.'

And for a moment it did seem to Listener as if this were really the entire universe hovering brightly in the darkness of the cave before him, and he felt a desire to enjoy more of the power his flute gave him, putting on such a show for himself as the world could not equal, for it was the whole world itself his power would move. He would do it better, too, than this Principal who was urging him on with busy little gestures. 'Stay here!' murmured the spidery dwarf. 'Once you're lost in the dance of the stars, you'll never want anything else.'

Never want anything else . . . but he had indeed wanted something else before he entered this cavern. Something other than to give himself up to the compulsion of these chiming crystals. And Listener saw the temptation to which he had nearly succumbed. 'I'll leave you your toy,' he said. 'I do indeed want something else, and it lies hidden yet deeper in the mountain.'

He leaped through the opening in the opposite wall of the cave and strode on fast, for as long as he could make out the fissured floor of the passage in the dwindling light of the crystals, while he heard the Principal behind him, wailing, 'My stars – they're all out of order again, and I don't know the rules the fluter gave them, I don't know what way they're to go! How am I to get them in order now? How am I to do it?' And then the muttering died away, and Listener was alone in the dark again.

As he felt his way slowly on along the wall, which was covered with curiously smooth furrows, he felt moisture beneath his fingers, and there were puddles of water into which he unexpectedly stepped here and there on the uneven ground. Water dripped constantly from the roof above, and over to the side he heard the gurgle of streams running down through channels between cracks in the rock and disappearing far below. Then the path itself went down, and the water level rose. Soon he was up to his waist in a river that was fed by more and more streams. He felt the smooth surface of stalactites beneath his fingers; they came down to the surface of the water, barring his path, but he broke his way past them and, though drenched to the skin, came to a place where his passage through the rock seemed to end at a steeply rising wall. There was no place to get by on either side of it, so he set about climbing the wall, which was covered with a calcareous deposit as smooth as ice.

He slipped and fell back into the water a couple of times, but at last he managed to climb higher, until he reached a ledge beyond which the passage seemed to continue. When he got his head over this ledge, he saw greenish reflections of light flickering on the roof above, and after he had crawled a little farther, he found he was looking down on a great underground lake like a vast, glowing, green jewel that filled a cavern from whose roof countless stalactites hung: tapering cones, gently rippling curtains that looked as if they had been fluttering in the wind before they froze to milky stone. The emerald light seemed to come up from the depths of the lake, and grew darker towards the water's edge in ever deeper shades of green, until it reached the hue of an almost black tourmaline.

He was still lying on the rock above, gazing at this sight in wonder, when the water boiled up and three green-haired water nymphs rose from its depths. They slid like dolphins through the foaming waves, smooth breasts and softly rounded hips caught the light, and as the water nymphs circled one another in play, they began to sing a wordless song that was thrown echoing back from the walls of the cave, and whose sweet, alluring melody aroused a longing in Listener to plunge through the spraying water to the nymphs down below, and caress their gleaming skin. But he had not forgotten what he was looking for, and so he straightened up and cried, 'Listen, lovely water nymphs! Can you tell me where to find a golden ring made in the shape of a falcon, and a necklace after the same fashion? Do you know those jewels?'

The three nymphs laughed, the sound of their laughter echoed back from the walls, and one of them called, 'You will never find those! They lie so deep on the bed of this lake that you'd be drowned before ever you were halfway down to them, you poor little human being!' And the three shook with laughter again.

'Couldn't you bring them up to me?' asked Listener, climbing a little lower.

'How could we do a thing like that?' called the three water nymphs. 'No greedy human hands can get at what's safe in this lake.' And they began to sing again, paying no more attention to their uninvited audience. Their song made Listener think that his flute might help him once more. He drew it out of his pocket, blew the water out of it, and began to accompany the water nymphs' song with melodies that might make them more inclined to do as he asked. But the longer he listened to the sound of their high, birdlike voices, the more strongly he felt a desire to join the green-haired nymphs' dance in the emerald water, catch one of those supple creatures and hold her in his arms, and that desire even won power over his playing of the flute, until the nymphs called, 'Come down to the lake, Listener! Come down and stay with us, and play us your music.'

And Listener could not withstand that invitation. He leaped down the last few ledges of rock, sat on the bank, and played yet sweeter variations on the song of the nymphs, who swam closer and closer to him, drawn, as he thought, by the power of his flute. They were beside him now, clasping his feet, their wet hands touching his face, and at last one of them said, 'Come into the water, fluter! Come and be one of us.'

So Listener put down his flute, and they drew him into the cold waves to play with him. As soon as he was in the lake, however, Listener realized, to his horror, that the water did not bear him up but was dragging him irresistibly down, closing above his head. As he thrashed about wildly, amidst the laughter of the water nymphs, he remembered the name of the nymph who had come to his aid once before. 'Laianna!' he cried. 'Laianna, help me!' And then he sank again, never to come up, as he thought, going down and down. He was barely conscious when he felt someone take him by the hand and draw him up again.

He lay on the bank for some time, panting and gasping and spitting out the water he had swallowed. Then, slowly, he came back to his senses, and saw that it was indeed Laianna who had pulled him out of the lake. She was sitting beside him, smiling. 'Better not meddle with water nymphs like that!' said she. 'Some of our kind are rather foolish, and don't remember that humans can't last long in the water. I sent them away, in case the sight of them confused your mind again. But they told me why you're here. Are you sorry now that you gave me the chain and the ring?'

'No,' said Listener. 'I would rather they both lay on the bottom of this lake for ever. But from all I've heard, nothing can be done for my daughter without the aid of those magic things.' And he told her what he knew.

'So you only want to borrow the falcon jewels?' asked Laianna.

'Yes,' said Listener. 'You shall have them back, for they're yours.'

'But suppose the falcon won't let them go again?' asked Laianna.

Listener shrugged his shoulders. 'Then I shall have to try getting the jewels away from her once more,' he said.

'I hope you know what you're about,' said the water nymph. 'This is a dangerous venture, but you shall have the magic jewels, though you must leave a pledge here with me.'

'What kind of pledge?' asked Listener. 'I didn't bring much with me when I climbed down here.'

'You brought enough,' said Laianna. 'You have something with you that far outweighs the worth of Narzia's jewels, and that's your flute.'

Listener was dismayed. If he did not get the jewels back, he would lose his flute into the bargain. But then he thought of his daughter, and nodded. He picked up the flute, which was still lying where he had left it when the nymphs lured him into the water, and put it in Laianna's hands. 'Will you get me the ring and the chain now?' he asked.

'I can't do that,' said Laianna. 'Don't you remember what I told you when you gave them to me? Anyone who wants them must fetch them up from the depths himself.'

At this Listener despaired. 'How can I?' he asked. 'I nearly drowned down there just now.'

But Laianna smiled. 'You'll find you can swim underwater like a fish,' she said. She pulled out one of her long, greenish fair hairs, and tied it around Listener's bare upper arm. 'As long as you have this hair on you,' she said, 'you will be like one of us, able to breathe under water. You must dive right down to the bottom. When there is a green sun above you, you'll find what you are looking for, and you must swim towards that sun. Good luck, Listener, and remember your flute!'

Having nearly drowned a moment ago, Listener much disliked the thought of entrusting himself to the water again, but he had no choice. So he let himself slip into the shimmering green of the lake, and sank straight down. Rocks passed him by, pale and jagged stalactites ranged on them like the teeth of some mighty monster sucking him down into its vast jaws. He went deeper and deeper, still holding his breath, less from lack of faith in Laianna than because his body would not let him breathe as long as the water surrounded him. He had red circles before his eyes and was on the point of fainting before he gave up and, against all reason, forced himself to take a breath. What streamed into his lungs was as cool and refreshing as the clear air one breathes resting on a mountain peak after a long climb. At once he felt familiar with the element in which he found himself. His movements accommodated themselves to the slight current drawing him down, and now he really was swimming like a fish, head first, on towards the emerald glow that shone up to him ever more brightly.

As he approached the bottom of the lake, he entered a fantastic landscape. There were rolling hills here, and winding valleys, their surfaces covered by a turf of sparkling crystals in whose mirror surfaces the green light broke a thousandfold. He swam over them at his leisure, discovering that there was much more to be found here, and of more value too, than Narzia's magic jewels. A pendant of silkily glowing pearls the size of walnuts lay in a nest of crystals clear as glass; a golden crown set with jewels stood on the stump of a broken stalagmite, with a sword of very ancient design below it, its ivory hilt bearing a ruby as big as an egg as the pommel. Golden vessels stood on a level slab with an iridescent surface: goblets, dishes and ewers, all richly chased with ornamentation which showed men in strange garments riding out hunting, some with falcons on their fists, others with bows and arrows; at the bottom of one shallow dish, girls danced in fluttering robes, and dolphins and every other kind of water creature played on the curved side of a double-handled beaker.

Quite at his ease now, Listener looked at all these treasures, wondering what mighty folk they might have been who sacrificed part of their riches to get the water nymphs' goodwill. Their gifts had obviously been held in honour, for they were carefully ranged in this subterranean treasury, whose extent seemed to be much larger than that of the lake through which he had come down to it. Now and then the rocky walls drew closer together, and then the cavern widened out again to reveal further halls in which yet more precious things shone in the green light which was always the same, casting no shadows, and Listener passed on above them, feeling as if he were dreaming of hovering weightlessly, a dream that would never end, leading him on and on into more caverns.

He did not know how long he had been swimming when the intensity of the light suddenly increased. Involuntarily, he looked up, and saw an emerald sun above him, its circular outline standing out distinctly in the water. Then he knew he had reached the place where Narzia's magic jewels must lie. The undulating floor of the cavern was covered at this point with glittering moss composed of tiny crystals, forming plump cushions, and Listener saw the necklace lying on one of those rounded cushions, spread out in a circle, with the ring inside it. He hovered above them for a while, admiring the beautiful workmanship of the gold, and the sparkling stone which seemed to catch all the light that flooded down from above. Then he picked up the jewels, put them in his pocket, and swam up towards the green sun.

The circular, glowing, green surface above grew wider the closer he came to it, and then he saw that it was an opening in the roof of the cavern, covered by water suffused with light. He was so eager to discover what lay up there that he struck out fast as he came through the opening, and in so doing brushed the rough rock wall with his arm. Laianna's hair broke, and next moment he felt as if he were stifling with the sudden compression of his lungs. He kicked out wildly, swallowed water, and was only just conscious when he felt his head come out above the surface. Greedily, he gasped for air, saw a rocky bank directly ahead of him, struggled through the water, felt firm ground beneath his feet, and dragged himself up on land. He lay there for a while, panting and gasping for air, until gradually his heart slowed to a calmer beat.

When he rose and looked around him, he found himself on the bank of that lake into which he had thrown the jewels many years before. The red-tinged wall of the great cliff towered above him, and the afternoon sun was in the sky. He rested for a little longer, and then climbed up through the cleft in the rock and crawled on along the old stream bed, until he came out in the open up in the woods. Even as he worked his way through the narrow channel, he had heard the sound of a flute above him, and when he clambered out of the cleft he saw Snowfinch sitting at the foot of a towering pine, playing his instrument. The boy broke off in the middle of a phrase as soon as he saw him, leaped up and ran to meet him. 'Here you are at last!' he cried. 'I was just going to pack up our things and ride down to the herdsmen's huts.'

'Why so soon?' asked Listener. 'I told you to wait three days.'

'The three days were up this morning,' said the boy, 'and the sun will soon be sinking. Didn't you know?'

'There's no measurable time where I've been,' said Listener. 'I couldn't have told you if I was there half a day or a couple of weeks. But now you tell me I've been away more than three days, I believe you! It's a long time since I felt so hungry.'

The first thing they did, therefore, was to sit down and eat some of the provisions Snowfinch had brought, and when he had packed up what remained of them, he asked, 'Did you find what you went to get?'

'Yes,' said Listener, putting his hand in his pocket, and he brought out Narzia's magic jewels. Snowfinch looked at the precious necklace and the ring with the sparkling emerald. 'Did you just take these things?' he asked.

'No,' said Listener. 'I had to leave my flute behind as a pledge. If a fluter should be needed in the near future, you'll have to play instead of me.'

They spent the next three days riding back through the woods to the spring under the sycamore, and when they got there Listener said, 'Now to see if the falcon is in these parts.' And the trout's information proved correct here too: as soon as Listener had gone a little way down the valley through the alder bushes, and began to look up at the sky, he saw a falcon circling far above. It was flying much too high to be called down, but Listener knew that this particular falcon could see a mouse on the ground even from such a height. So he took the ring out of his pocket and flashed the stone in the sun.

No sooner had he done so than the falcon seemed to stop in midflight for a moment, and then she fell from the sky like a stone. She settled on an alder branch just above Listener's head. 'That's my ring!' she cried. 'Give it to me!'

'Gently, gently!' said Listener, putting the ring on his little finger. 'This magic thing is in my hands at the moment, and I shall think twice before I even let you near it. The ring alone wouldn't do you much good, either. I know that much.'

'So you have the chain too,' said the falcon. 'Have you got it there? Show me!'

'With pleasure!' said Listener, taking the necklace out of his pocket and letting its links shine in the sunlight. 'I have both those magic jewels, and I'm open to offers, if you'd like to tell me what you'd give for them.'

'You're a thief!' cried the bird. 'Those things are mine!'

'You of all people shouldn't take that tone!' said Listener. 'I found them both, in a house that had burned down, and brought them away with me. Moreover, you can see that I'm ready to discuss the matter with you. Well, what do you suggest?'

The falcon stared angrily at him with her green eyes, and she was silent for a while. At last she said, 'If you give me the jewels, I could free you from the fear that attacks you when you stand out under the open sky.'

This offer did indeed strike Listener as tempting. He thought how wonderful it would be to walk freely through fields and meadows again, or climb high in the mountains until the last trees were left in the valley below, and walk on over the short grass of the mountain meadows with the scent of thyme rising from them. And as he was thinking of all this, the falcon added, 'There'd be nothing then to stop you living with that woman who found you here as a faun, and who's afraid to walk in woods.'

'It's too late for that,' said Listener. 'She married another man long ago.'

'Does it matter, if you want her?' said the falcon.

'Yes,' said Listener. 'It most certainly does matter. But that reminds me of something. The daughter this woman bore me has been mute since birth, I hear, and I suspect that's to do with the effect of your spell, by which I was still bound when the child was conceived. Perhaps she inherited the last of my animal nature in that way. Now, I'll make you a proposition: you shall have the ring and the necklace if you will restore my daughter Urla's powers of speech. Can you do that?'

'Of course I can,' said the falcon, 'but only with the help of those two jewels. You'll have to give them to me first.'

'I see there's no avoiding it,' said Listener. 'It may be foolish of me to trust you in this, but perhaps there's still some trace of mercy slumbering in your heart. Very well: I will send a message to Arziak, telling Arnilukka and her daughter to ride here to the herdsmen's huts. And then I will wait in the woodcutters' cabin until they come. Their arrival won't escape your keen eyes, and we will meet next morning on the edge of the wood, between the herdsmen's huts and the cabin. Will you come there?'

'You may be sure I will,' said the falcon, and then she spread her wings and soared high into the sky.

That day they rode on down the valley to the woodcutters' cabin, and Listener sent the boy over to the herdsmen's huts. 'Find Vazzek, or whatever man now fills his post, and ask him to come to me here,' he said.

He found the woodcutters' cabin unlocked, opened the door and went through the little porch into the living-room. Little had changed here since he left twelve years ago, except that the lathe was gone. Derli had probably taken it back to Arziak to put in a workshop of his own there. Listener went outside again, unharnessed the horses, and led them out to graze. Then he went back to the cabin and carried the saddles and saddle-bags in.

He had just opened a window, and lit a fire on the hearth to rid the room of its musty smell, when he heard the outer door opening. Next moment a tall, grey-bearded man came in, with Snowfinch behind him, carrying a bundle wrapped in blankets on his back. The man stopped in the doorway, looked at Listener and said, 'So it really is you! I couldn't believe what the lad said at first. Nothing's been heard of you here for years.'

'You know me, then?' asked Listener.

'Well, I heard you a couple of times,' said the man, 'but you won't remember me, for we never talked together.'

'Oh, I remember you very well,' said Listener. 'You're the man who brought old Vazzek to the valley.'

'That's right,' said the man, surprised, 'but how can you tell? You weren't here at the time.'

'I was, in fact,' said Listener, 'although you couldn't see me, because I was hiding in the bushes. However, I don't know your name.'

'It's Ruzzo, and I'm in charge of the grazing here, since Vazzek died three years ago,' said the man. 'Well, the boy said you want to speak to me. What's it about?'

'No need to discuss it on our feet,' said Listener, and he invited Ruzzo to sit beside the fire with him. By now Snowfinch had put the bundle down on the bedstead; he undid the blankets to reveal a linen bag full of all kinds of provisions, which he set on the table: flat cakes of bread, a large piece of dried meat, a round cheese, and a wineskin made of goat's leather.

Ruzzo had been watching. 'Well, if there's much to discuss, we might as well drink a little wine too,' he said. 'Fetch us a couple of beakers off that shelf, lad, and get one for yourself as well.'

Snowfinch put three wooden beakers on the table, opened the wineskin and poured the wine, and then sat down with the other two.

'I'm sorry to hear old Vazzek's dead,' said Listener. 'I would have liked to see him once again.'

'I can well understand that,' said Ruzzo. 'He was an easy man to talk to, besides being good with horses. He told me a good deal about yourself, which led me to change my mind about you. For the fact is, we didn't have much good to say of a certain fluter here in Arziak at one time.'

'You had every reason not to,' said Listener, 'more particularly Vazzek himself. And yet it was he who helped me deal with my own sense of guilt.'

'As for me, he saved my life,' said Ruzzo. 'That time I brought him to the Shallow Valley, he gave me a fish-scale as a parting gift. I hung it around my neck, not thinking much of the matter, but I wore it under my shirt afterwards, more as a memento of a friend than anything. I thought more of it when the Raiding Riders came ravaging Arziak. I rode with the Ore Master's men at the time, and when we'd beaten off the first attack on the town, he assigned me to a small troop of horsemen who were to keep watch and see if the Raiding Riders showed up again anywhere in the valley. At first you might have thought the earth had swallowed them up. We rode up and down the valley for days, without spotting so much as a horse's tail. And then, once we felt secure and hardly feared an attack any more, they were suddenly upon us. They broke out of the wood just ahead, fifty or sixty Riders, and we were only six men in all. We rode our horses down towards the valley at a gallop; two of us were shot from the saddle, the three ahead of me made their way over a ford across the river, which is quite broad just there, but my horse shied and threw me.

As I lay on the ground, hearing the Riders thundering down upon me with their shrill cries, I remembered what Vazzek had said about that scale. So I scrambled up, ran the short distance to the river as arrows began to hiss past me, and flung myself into the water. I knew that place; I'd been fishing there. There's a deep pool above the ford, which always has trout in it. So I let myself sink in under the bushes that hang over the steep bank, went right down to the bottom, held my breath and waited.

Next moment I heard the Riders searching the bushes on the bank above me. They were probably watching the surface of the water too. I knew I was done for if I came up, and I would soon run out of air, but I'd decided to stay down there as long as I could stand it. And after a while I realized that I'd gone long beyond the time a human being can spend under water, and yet I felt no lack of air. I saw fish in the pool around me, looking at me quite fearlessly with their round eyes, as much as to say: wait a little longer, the danger will soon be over. And so it turned out. The Riders fumbled around in the bushes on the bank for a few more minutes, and then I heard a cry, and next moment the ground was trembling under their horses' hooves as they rode fast away.

So that was how I escaped alive, with the help of the Great Old One, as Vazzek used to call the mysterious provider of those scales. I worked under him here later, and I wouldn't have missed that time for the world. I never learned as much from anyone in my life as I did from that old Carphead, and not just about horses either. But here I go, talking and talking, never letting you get a word in yourself. You had something to tell me, didn't you?'

And Ruzzo drank a sip of wine, and looked expectantly at Listener, who now told him what he had learnt about Arnilukka's mute daughter, and how he meant to break that spell. 'Can you send a messenger to Arnilukka, to bring her and her daughter back here?' he asked, at the end of his tale.

'I'll ride to Arziak myself, first thing tomorrow morning!' said Ruzzo. 'That's news I'd like to carry in person. You can expect us back about evening of the day after tomorrow, for the Mistress won't stop to think twice when she hears what it's about!'

All this time, Snowfinch had been sitting there, listening enthralled to Ruzzo's tale, and now he said, 'Can I ask you something, Ruzzo?'

'Ask away, lad!' said the horse-master. 'Today's a day for the giving of every kind of information.'

'Listener told me about a boy called Derli who learned the flute from him in this cabin,' said Snowfinch. 'What became of him?'

'Derli?' said Ruzzo. 'Ah, he's a man of importance now! They call him the Merry Fluter, and he's not a boy any more, not by a long chalk, but he hasn't taken a wife yet, though all the girls in the valley of Arziak are running after him, making eyes at him. No wonder he can't decide. But there's no wedding or fair in these parts where he doesn't play until the dancers run out of breath. Yes, he certainly made sure the folk could be merry again, after all the dreadful things that happened, and that's more than can be said of many a good man. You've a fine future before you, lad, if you go on learning from Listener here. Was that what you wanted to know?'

Snowfinch looked down at the table-top for a while, and then raised his head again and said, 'Well, I think there are different ways to play the flute. A merry fluter, like Derli, will have been just what the people of the valley needed, so he did what was right for him to do, in his own way. But it's another kind of fluter I'd like to be.'

'What kind?' asked Ruzzo.

'I don't know yet,' said Snowfinch.

Listener was surprised by the boy's remarks. Snowfinch had put into words something that he himself had vaguely felt, and yet had never been able to express. There seemed to be even more than he had guessed in this lanky scion of the Bloodaxe People.

Soon afterwards Ruzzo left, to prepare for his ride next morning. Listener could not sleep that night. He lay on the bedstead beside the peacefully breathing boy, wondering what the falcon, or more exactly, what Narzia would do once she had the magic jewels in her clutches. She might well turn all who were present into animals, or rise back into the air in her falcon's shape, leaving the child as mute as ever. He believed her fully capable of any of this, but he saw no way of avoiding that danger. 'What am I to do, Piney?' he asked, picking up his stick. 'Whatever way I look at it, we shall all be helpless in Narzia's power once I've given her the chain and the ring, and I have no flute now to keep her from doing her worst.'

'Then why enter upon any of this at all?' inquired the Piney. 'First you take it into your head to go saving people again, then you get frightened when things turn serious. What do you really want, then?'

'To help my daughter,' said Listener. 'That's all.'

'And what about Arnilukka?' asked the Piney. 'I suppose you'd like to see her again, wouldn't you?'

'Of course,' said Listener. 'But I have no false hopes of such a meeting now.'

'False hopes?' inquired the Piney, with some surprise. 'And what do you mean by that? I'll tell you something: you don't mean hope at all, for if you did, it'd reach beyond the little length of time you humans live. But you don't want to go losing true hope, oh dear me, no!'

Despite the Piney's ironic tone, these words comforted Listener, as if it were the mother pine rather than the Piney himself speaking. 'Well, I'll try to keep true and false hope apart, then,' he said. 'For just as you say, false hope is no hope at all.'

'Ah, but will you be able to remember the subtle difference when you see Arnilukka in person?' asked the Piney.

And Listener felt his heart beat faster at the mere thought of it. 'I don't know,' he said. 'Perhaps you'll be good enough to remind me.'

'So long as you ask me,' said the Piney. 'You know perfectly well I speak only when I'm spoken to.'

'I rather think you have other ways of attracting my attention,' said Listener. 'You are not, it seems to me, entirely helpless in the matter.'

The Piney gave his wooden chuckle and said, 'Not so very sure of yourself, are you? However, none of your kind ever are, if they'd be honest about it. As long as you think only of little Urla, it should all go the way you plan. And perhaps you shouldn't rely on yourself too much; you can always hope you won't be left to manage alone, so long as you'll at least try to stand by your resolution.'

Once again, Listener breathed in the sweet, resinous fragrance of the ancient tree creature, making him feel as if the motherly pine were taking him in her arms like a child uncertain which way to turn. 'Sleep now, Listener,' she said softly, in the voice that sounded so different from the creaking, sarcastic voice of the Piney. 'Go to sleep, and have a little faith. The likes of us have always been able to deal with the clumsy sort of magic Narzia practises.'

*

Listener spent most of the next two days on the outskirts of the woods, watching the horses that wandered over the pastures, grazing and lifting their heads now and then to glance his way. And whenever he looked at the sky, he saw the falcon circling very high up, beneath the clouds. Late on the afternoon of the second day, several riders came up the valley; Listener saw them coming a long way off, and the falcon too sank lower to hover over them. After a while Listener could see that the party was made up of two men, a woman and a child, on their way to the herdsmen's huts, and then he knew that Arnilukka had come.

A little later she came out of the log cabins again and crossed the meadows towards him. The closer she came, the lovelier she seemed, and when at last she stood before him the remembered image he had carried about with him faded beside the beauty of this woman gazing at him with eyes of a colour that was hard to describe.

'Where have you been all this time, Listener?' she asked.

So he told her about his years with the Bloodaxe People, and how he had heard that Urla was mute. 'Snowfinch helped me to escape,' he said.

'I'd heard already that you were on your travels,' said Arnilukka.

'From your fishes?' asked Listener, and when Arnilukka nodded, he said, 'You have trusty messengers there. It was wrong of me, I think, to run away from you, though I never meant to go so far. I often thought of you up in the mountains. Perhaps we oughtn't to lose sight of each other so entirely, even though you have another man for your husband.'

'Belarni rode to the herdsmen's huts with me,' said Arnilukka, 'but he thought I should see you alone first. You know, I suppose, that he is your good friend?'

'I do,' said Listener. 'I've forgotten that as little as I forgot the colour of your eyes, although I've not been able to picture your face very well recently. But your eyes were with me, as if I were still wearing Arni's stone on my breast.'

'Oh, Listener,' said Arnilukka, taking him in her arms, 'so here we are, and I am very glad you've come back now.'

And Listener lost himself in the bewildering play of colour in her eyes, while the intoxicating scent of her hair left him almost fainting. Then, however, he was rudely brought out of this happy oblivion and back to reality: he felt a sharp blow on his foot. The Piney had indeed got his word in, for in Arnilukka's embrace Listener had dropped his stick, and the gnarled head fell and struck his toes. 'Yes, very well, Piney!' he murmured. 'I take your point.' And freeing himself from her arms, he said, 'Sit down here by the edge of the wood with me, Arnilukka, and tell me about little Urla. Is she really as mute as they say?'

Arnilukka sat down, gazed at the grass in silence for a while, and then said, 'If you mean she can't speak like a human being, then yes, she's mute. But she often babbles to herself, strange sounds that sometimes might make you think she was speaking a language no one can understand. She seems to grasp the meaning of much that's said to her, but I can never be sure if she really knows the words, or picks up what one's trying to tell her in some other way. She is sweet, and friendly, and clever at everything she does, but I have no idea what she is thinking or what goes on in her mind.'

'How does she get on with animals?' asked Listener.

Arnilukka looked at him in surprise. 'It's strange you should ask that,' she said. 'Urla loves to be with animals, and has more confidence with them than I ever saw in a child before. If an animal is sick, she always knows what ails it, and her clever little hands will show you what needs to be done for it.'

Listener nodded; this was much as he had suspected. Then he asked Arnilukka if Ruzzo had told her how he meant to help the child.

'Yes, he has,' said Arnilukka, 'and on the way here I thought and thought, wondering whether we ought to take this step. It may be dangerous for us all, particularly Urla herself.'

'I know,' said Listener, 'yet I can't help hoping that there may still be something even in a witch like Narzia to move her to do good. But if the possible price seems too high to you, then you'd better ride back to Arziak with Urla. I will do nothing against your will.'

'No,' said Arnilukka. 'We must take the risk. If we don't, surely we'll lose all hope that good is stronger than evil in this world. And how could we live then?'

So they agreed on the place and time where they would meet next morning, and then Arnilukka turned back to the herdsmen's cottages. Listener watched her walk slowly over the meadows, and could no longer understand his old decision to keep out of her way. He was surprised to realize how little he now minded her going to Belarni. What mattered more was his joy in knowing she was real, and not just a vision in a dream he had invented for himself. She was alive, she was here, and she trusted him, and all this filled him with joy as he walked back to the woodcutters' cabin through the trees, having made sure that the falcon was still hovering low above the valley floor.

* * *

Next morning Listener was standing with Snowfinch on the border of the wood at sunrise, looking out at the herdsmen's huts. A little later, he saw Belarni come out of doors with Arnilukka, each of them holding one of little Urla's hands, and so they all three came towards him.

Listener had eyes for no one but the girl now. She was about the same age as Arnilukka when he first met her in Arziak, and she had her mother's eyes. She wore Arni's stone around her neck, in a delicate setting of silver wire. Urla looked straight at Listener as she came closer, and when they were face to face she said, 'You're the man who made my cradle.'

'Yes, so I am,' he said, and only on seeing the surprised faces of Arnilukka and Belarni did he realize that Urla had spoken to him in a language that sounded more like the speech of the goats than anything else. At that he laughed. 'The child's not mute,' he said. 'You don't understand the language she speaks, that's all.'

'You thought that might be it, yesterday,' said Arnilukka.

'Yes,' he said, 'but I couldn't be sure then.'

However, before they could say anything more, Urla was speaking again. 'And I know all the stories about you,' she said. 'Your animals told me: the funny donkey Yalf, and One-horn the goat with his flock, and Golden-eye and Needle-tooth and Rinkulla the snake, and the three mice with the long names I'm always mixing up. Even when I was still in my cradle they told me stories, but my two brothers had the cradle after me. They couldn't understand what the creatures said. Anyway, I've got the cradle back in my own room now, so I can talk to your animals. I like the mice best.'

'I'm not surprised,' said Listener. 'Those brave mice gave me more help than anyone. But now let me greet Belarni.'

He was going to offer his hand, but Belarni embraced him as he would a friend, saying, 'I'm glad you're back too, Listener. Now I see you talking to Urla I feel sure you'll succeed in what you mean to do.'

He still wore braids at his temples, and seeing Listener glance at them, he added, 'Yes, those of us who lived in the steppes didn't cut off our braids like Arni's Folk. We don't want anyone thinking it's enough to alter your outward appearance when you want to change your whole life.'

As they were talking, Listener had seen the falcon swooping low above the meadows, and now she settled on a tree-stump by the borders of the wood. 'Well,' said the bird, 'so now you must give me back my property, if the child's to learn to speak like other human beings.'

Hearing this voice they could not understand, and yet which did not sound like the cry of a falcon, Arnilukka and Belarni took the girl between them as if to protect her from the enchanted creature.

'Those two don't much like this, do they?' said the falcon mockingly. 'Now give me the jewels, Listener! Or have you thought better of it?'

'No,' said Listener. 'I count on you to keep your word.' He took the few paces to the tree-stump, and laid the chain and the ring on the dark and weathered wood.

Then everything happened very fast: the falcon bent her slender head to the chain, and next moment Narzia stood there instead, putting the ring on her finger. The falcon necklace lay golden and sparkling round her slender throat, and she looked as young as on the day Listener last saw her. She went slowly over to little Urla, and stopped in front of her. 'That's a pretty thing you have around your neck,' she said in honeyed tones, putting out her hand to the stone. And then, her voice suddenly sharp, she said, 'Give it to me, if you don't want to stay mute!'

'That wasn't in the bargain!' said Listener.

'Bargain or no bargain,' said Narzia, 'you ought to have thought of it before, you fool! Now I have my falcon ring on my finger again, you had better be wary of crossing me. You should know better than anyone how it feels when my magic power strikes.'

Urla was still looking into the green eyes of the young woman who had appeared so suddenly. She could scarcely have understood what Narzia was saying, but she had a very good idea of what this woman wanted. With a quick movement, she put the chain bearing Arni's stone over her head and laid the jewel in Narzia's hand. 'I'll give you the stone,' she said, in her own strange language. 'Don't you know it's unlucky to take it by force? You must get it as a present, and then it will bring you luck.'

It was obvious that Narzia had not understood what the girl was saying. She looked greedily at the stone and said, 'You're a clever child to give me this glittering thing of your own free will. It would have been the worse for you if you'd refused me.' And she looked at Listener in triumph. 'So you've lost the game after all! There's nothing to keep me here now.' She was undoing the chain of Arni's stone, to put it around her own neck. Belarni, who had watched this scene with growing anger, was about to step forward and prevent her, but Listener

restrained him, shaking his head. He was wishing desperately that he
had his flute to hand now. At this moment, he would have been ready
to bring all possible pressure to bear on the green-eyed witch, but
wishing was no good: the flute lay beyond his reach and in Laianna's
care, deep on the bottom of the lake.

Narzia had now clasped the chain at the nape of her neck, and
the eye-stone shone on her breast. And at that very moment, the
expression on her face changed. Listener saw it at once. It was like
the face of someone waking from a hateful dream. The look of
scornful triumph was wiped away. Her features relaxed, making her
seem to him more beautiful now than he had ever seen her, and she
looked at the girl as if she were seeing her for the first time. 'Come
here, Urla!' she said, in quite another voice. 'Come here and let me
thank you for the stone. I feel as if a band of enchantment around my
heart had burst!'

She took the child in her arms, and holding her close, she put the
hand wearing the falcon ring to Urla's lips and whispered, 'Speak like
a human being, little Urla!' As she spoke, her face seemed to age
visibly. Her hands were trembling like an old woman's as she took the
chain bearing Arni's stone from her own neck again and put it around
the girl's. 'I want to give something away for once in my life,' she
whispered. 'I give you back the stone, and I know very well you will
follow its light.'

Her body was now so frail and decrepit that Urla had to hold her to
keep her from collapsing. Her green eyes were still as clear as the
emerald in the ring, but their expression was utterly changed as she
looked at Listener and said, 'Play me something on your flute, while I
can still hear!'

And now indeed Listener had reason to be sorry he did not have his
flute with him, but as he stood there hesitating, not knowing what to
do, Snowfinch put his own instrument to his lips and began to play. He
started with a soft, deep note, almost a kind of humming, like the wind
blowing through the grass on the steppes, and the volume of that note
gradually increased until it was strong as the storm wind bowing the
blades of grass to the ground; then the note faded away, but other
notes rose one by one from that formless plain, gradually coming together in a monotonous tune such as used to be played in the tents of
the Raiding Riders. Quiet and meditative at first, the sequence of
notes heightened its rhythm, became faster and faster, until Listener
saw the shaggy little horses galloping over the endless grey expanses of

the grass, saw the thundering hooves, the tracks they left behind, the earth flying up, and he saw yet more as the boy played on: harsh, dissonant sounds broke from the melody, but each time these apparently irreconcilable tones gave rise to a new kind of harmony, its beauty heightened by the almost unbearable tension of the beginning, and now images gradually formed in Listener's mind, and he saw Narzia changing him into that hybrid being, the faun, to preserve him for his meeting with Arnilukka; he saw her show him the way to his flint and steel by means of the magpies, so that he could keep warm by a fire in winter, and he saw her send him the weasel and the mouse, who had become his friends; all the people she had turned into dogs had lived and been saved from the Great Raid; she had even set out her magic jewels ready for him, so that he could return them to her and she could give little Urla the gift of human speech. All these things that had seemed so wrong at their beginning had mysteriously turned out for the best, as he truly understood only now, and looking into Narzia's eyes, he saw that she too understood as she listened to Snowfinch's playing, variation upon variation of that sequence in which apparent disorder came to the point at which it crystallized into a newly unfolding order.

Urla had laid Narzia's failing body in the soft woodland grass under the bushes; the only living things about the dying woman now were her eyes, glowing like emeralds in her death's-head skull, and as Snowfinch played melody after melody, she looked at Listener in sudden dismay and whispered, 'Your fear! I haven't taken it away yet. You shall stand under the open sky again.' With a last, painful effort, she raised her right hand, upon which the falcon ring still sparkled, and murmured faintly, 'Be . . .' And then her hand dropped again, and all that was left of her body crumbled within a moment or so to grey dust, leaving nothing behind but the chain and the ring.

At last Snowfinch took the flute from his lips. He stood there for a moment, arms dangling, as if listening to the last dying notes, and then said, almost apologetically, 'You did bring me in case a fluter was needed.'

'I did,' said Listener, 'and I couldn't have done half as well myself. I am glad now that I had to leave the water nymph my flute as a pledge, but one never understands these things until later.'

'I learned all I know from you,' said Snowfinch, but Listener shook his head. 'That kind of learning means nothing much,' he said. 'What matters is knowing when and why to play, and you've found out that for yourself. Nor does it make much difference if the flute itself is wooden or silver.'

'But you must take the magic jewels back so that you can redeem your flute,' said the boy.

'Yes, and first and foremost because they're not mine but Laianna's,' said Listener. 'I must give them back to her.' When he picked up the necklace and the ring, a little more dust trickled from their intricate ornamentation and blew away in the wind. The rest had already fallen into the grass and weeds.

Little Urla had been standing with her parents all this while, talking to them as if to make up for everything she had never been able to say before. 'And that woman with the green eyes,' she was saying now, 'she must have been enchanted too, because she wasn't anything like as bad as she seemed at first.'

'You broke that spell yourself when you gave her the stone,' said Listener. 'You did the one thing that had to be done, at just the right moment, and but for you we might all be mice scurrying in the grass now.'

Urla laughed. 'That sounds funny!' she said. 'I like mice. But she wouldn't have bewitched me. I know she wouldn't.'

That made them all laugh, and Belarni said, 'I don't think the people of Arziak would have been best pleased to see your mother and myself come back from this expedition looking like a couple of mice.'

Urla laughed harder than ever, and when she had her breath back, she said, 'I could have kept you both in the pockets of my skirt, one mouse on the right and the other mouse on the left, so as not to get you mixed up, and when the Great Assembly came round I'd have put you on the table. "This is the Ore Mistress," I'd have said, "and this is the Khan. Everyone be quiet so you can hear them squeaking to you!"'

Smiling, Listener had heard her out, but he was taken aback by her last words. 'Are you Ore Mistress now, Arnilukka?' he asked.

'Why, yes,' she said. 'My mother died five years ago. And I would very much like to ask you into our room in the herdsmen's huts over there, to tell you all the news of Arziak, but I don't know if Narzia was in time to free you from her spell. Will you try it and see if you can come with us?'

From the moment when Narzia's powerless hand dropped to her side Listener had indeed been wondering whether she had managed to complete her lifting of the spell, even if inaudibly, but keeping to the shelter of the trees had become so much a habit with him that it was a great effort to step out of their shade and into the open. As he stood there hesitating, little Urla took his hand, saying, 'You must try! Come on!' She pulled him out into the meadow, and Listener was ready for his fear to crash down on him like a falling boulder. But the blow did not fall. He felt nothing but a slight sense of uneasiness, which might just as well be the result of his having avoided open country for so long.

'You see?' said Urla, laughing. 'It's all right!' She let go of his hand to run back to her mother, and as she did so an iron ring seemed to press around his heart. His fear was back, if not so overpoweringly as to render him unconscious. Summoning up all his strength, he stood where he was, and realized that he could bear it, though a cold sweat stood out on his forehead. 'She only half did it,' he said, with difficulty, and with a touch of grim humour he added, 'It looks as if all magic only half works on me! Give me your hand, Urla. It's easier if you're with me.' And so it was: as soon as he was holding her warm little hand the oppression went away, and the sense of uneasiness that remained with him seemed hardly worth mentioning.

So they all crossed the meadows to the herdsmen's huts together, and when he had a roof over his head again, Listener could breathe freely once more. It was the same room in which he and Arnilukka had sat when she was a child. He remembered her sitting here on the settle in the corner, while he played her merry tunes to make her forget the fear the two wolves had instilled in her. Now she was mistress of the place, and she brought bread, cheese, and a piece of smoked bacon, set a goblet on the table for everyone, and finally a pitcher of wine. Only then did she sit down and invite them to help themselves. 'Be my guest, Listener!' she said. 'And you too, Snowfinch, who can play the flute so well. Sit down and eat!'

Arnilukka observed the old customs too; Listener remembered that dream of his while he was a stone faun, in which he had been Urla's guest. She had addressed him as Arnilukka did now, and it was only natural and fitting that no matters of importance were discussed during the meal. Urla went on with her mouse stories as they ate, and never tired of inventing new fancies in which her parents featured as mice. 'And I'd have had to feed you,' she said, 'because you couldn't have reached up to the table.' With which she popped a morsel into both their mouths. They all played the mouse game, delighted that Urla could talk like a human being, and it was a very pleasant meal.

When they had had enough, and could eat no more for all

Arnilukka's urging, she took the dishes away, poured more wine, and sat down beside Belarni again.

'You have two sons, if I understood Urla correctly,' said Listener. 'She mentioned them when she was telling me about her cradle.'

'That's right,' said Belarni. 'Azzo is ten years old now, and Arnizzo will be seven this month. And they're not by any means the only children in the valley of Arziak to unite the dark eyes of the Riders of the Steppes with the fair or brown hair of the Mountain Badgers.'

'Riders of the Steppes?' said Listener. 'Is that what you call yourselves now?'

'Those who grew up in tents on the grassy plains do, anyway,' said Belarni. 'But many such distinctions have become blurred over the past twenty years. Although there are still some folk who stand aloof and prefer to "keep their blood pure", as they put it. On the one hand, there's the goldsmiths' guild; its members refuse to let any descendant of the Riders into their houses, let alone their families. They've unearthed an old, almost forgotten law which forbids them to employ a former thief or even a member of his family, or enter into marriage with such people. And there may once have been good sense in that law, for anyone who constantly has valuable items in his house must be careful not to let any suspicious character in. But I think it wrong to use the law against people of the steppes who are not after plunder now, but want to live peacefully with the Mountain Badgers. A law loses its point if it's used as nothing but a form of words to be invoked by those with other purposes in mind.'

'And what purposes do the goldsmiths have in mind?' asked Listener.

'They think themselves rather better than other folk,' said Belarni, 'and, as they put it, don't want their blood mingling with that of ordinary Raiding Riders. Yes, you heard correctly: they are the only ones who still call us by that old name. However, then again there's a group of families from the tents of the horde who keep themselves to themselves as well: they tend to be the kin of former chieftains. Even their children won't fit into the community. The young men often go riding over the mountains together, to spend a few weeks living in tents out on the steppes and exercise on horseback. It's more of a sport than anything, for the time being, but I did hear that they're said to have stolen horses from some village on the outskirts of the steppes. We couldn't discover the culprits, but I am concerned about it, all the same.'

And his concern was plain to see. Deep lines cut into his lean face, and his shoulders were slightly stooped, as if he habitually had a heavy burden to bear. Arnilukka laid her hand on his arm, saying, 'Don't forget these are only a few people, compared to the many who live content and happy together in Arziak. It was a lucky thing you sent us Derli, Listener. There's music to be heard all over the valley now, and nothing makes people feel they know each other sooner than dancing and singing together. We missed that in the first years after the Great Raid.'

'Your mother must have had a hard task then,' said Listener.

'She did,' said Arnilukka. 'It was only when she died so suddenly that we realized how it had undermined her strength. But everyone had the greatest respect for her. To the Mountain Badgers, moreover, she was Promezzo's widow, and as Urla's great-granddaughter she was from one of the old goldsmiths' families herself; the Riders of the Steppes saw her as a niece of their old Khan, and for any who couldn't get used to having a woman in authority there was always Belarni, whose people still regarded him as their Khan. And our marriage was a sign of the final uniting of our two peoples. Those few folk Belarni mentioned will see sense too someday.'

'I hope so,' said Belarni, 'but still their obstinacy makes me uneasy. When I came to that agreement with your mother, it seemed like the fulfilment of a dream I'd entertained since I was a boy. Why must there always be people who cling to their old notions and won't see that it's better to live together in friendship than keep apart? Can't they be made to do what one sees is right?'

'No, they can't,' said Listener, 'as you should know better than anyone, having ridden with Arni so often! At least, it was always his view that one can't make other people's decisions for them.'

'Then I'll never see the perfect fulfilment of my dream,' said Belarni.

'Well, that's the way of dreams,' replied Listener. He noticed Arnilukka glancing at him as he said that, and under her eyes he became fully aware, for the first time, that he had been speaking of himself, and he went on, 'Still, it would be wrong to forget such dreams, for they're a sign that perfection does exist, even if it seems out of reach.'

Hitherto, Snowfinch had taken no part in this conversation, but had sat staring thoughtfully at the table in front of him. Now he raised his head and said, 'But wouldn't it be unbearable to reach such perfection? What would there be left to do then? Wouldn't we freeze, motionless, for fear of destroying the state of perfection? When I begin to play my flute, I have an idea of the perfect melody I'd like to invent. But there's a limit to the movement my fingers can make, my breath runs out at the vital moment, and the instrument itself, good as it is, resists me. However, that's where I find the charm of playing: groping towards the perfect melody I know I'll never reach within the limits set to my music. And anyway, I don't think perfection is fixed and final, but something that keeps developing. At least, I can imagine it only as something living, and all living things grow and change.'

'Well, you know how to give a man hope, Snowfinch,' said Belarni, 'which to my mind is worth even more than the cheerfulness the Merry Fluter has brought to our valley. What are you planning to do now, Listener? Will you stay with us?'

'For the time being, yes,' said Listener, 'if you'll let me live in the woodcutters' cabin again. But first I must take the water nymph's falcon jewels back to her.'

'And when you come back,' said little Urla, 'you must play me all the tunes you played my mother on your flute.'

'I promise I will,' said Listener. 'Now, will you take me back to my cabin? I can stand being in the open quite well if you're with me.'

Next morning, Listener and Snowfinch saddled their horses to set out for the great cliff. Listener noticed that the boy was packing all his own things, and taking a good stock of provisions. 'We shan't be away as long as all that, Snowfinch,' he pointed out.

'You won't, no,' agreed Snowfinch, 'but I thought I'd look around the world a little. After all, I don't know about anywhere much but my own people's mountain village, and now this valley. You once told me of the fishermen by the Brown River, who seldom see a minstrel, though they're so fond of music. I'd like to visit those Carpheads, and then perhaps I'll ride on down the river to Falkinor. I'd like to meet the Master of Music, who can make that strange music out of five tones, and I can take the opportunity of telling the magicians what became of Narzia's magic jewels.'

'I see you have your plans all made!' said Listener. He was sorry to be losing the boy, but after the flute-playing he had heard from him that day, he knew there was not much more he could teach him. So he added, 'And you're right to want to stand on your own feet. But I hope you'll come with me as far as the lake below the cliff?'

'Gladly,' said Snowfinch. 'We'll have to take a path along which I can ride to the lake, though; I'll hardly be able to squeeze my horse through the cleft in the great cliff.'

So this time they rode from the sycamore spring and eastwards on into the mountains, leading their horses up to the pass where the Piney had stood when he was still a tree. Climbing the slope where only distorted trees and bushes grew, Listener felt that oppressive sense of fear, and would have liked to crawl up it under the swaying branches of the dwarf pines again, but as he had to hold his horse's bridle he had no choice but to walk on upright under the blue sky, and the closeness of the warm, living animal that snuffled at his hand now and then helped him to bear the burden of that sky.

Since it was now evening, they stayed overnight in the cave where Listener had once taken refuge from the storm. When they had eaten, he told the boy that story, and then picked up his stick and said, 'So here we are back where we once set out together, Piney. It's nearly twenty-three years ago.'

'What's twenty-three years?' said the Piney. 'Nothing much seems to have changed here. My children have grown a little, brought a few more children of their own into the world, that's all. Still, it's good to see them again.'

The sweet, resinous scent of the stone pines came wafting down from the pass that was still bathed in reddish sunset light, filling the cave more all the time.

'It smells good here!' said Snowfinch. 'Like home.'

'If the boy likes the smell so much,' said the Piney, 'he can look around for a piece of me. I'll be glad to give him one. There must be plenty of the charred wood still lying about out there. Of course, you only get a real Piney when there's been a transformation like mine, but a good piece of resinous wood is not to be despised. Its scent will remind him of this day long after he's grown old.'

So Listener and the boy went out again to the place where the lightning had struck long ago, and Snowfinch picked a good stout, handy piece of wood from the rootstock out of the ground where the soil was still mingled with black ashes. Back in the cave, Listener shaved away its charred bark with his knife, and laid bare a shape that might have been the Piney's little brother. A brownish-purple, shining eye even came into view on the coiled shape of the rootstock, looking calmly at the boy for whom the gift was destined. Finally Listener polished the result of his labours on his trousers, and put it in

Snowfinch's hand. 'My Piney gives you this to take on your way,' he
said. 'Its fragrance will comfort you when you're alone.'

The Piney viewed the gnarled object with satisfaction. 'Why, it's
almost as if I had a twin,' he remarked.

Next day, they led their horses down the other side of the pass and into
the woods, and rode on until they came to the northern end of the
great cliff. Now they had only to keep in its shadow. On the afternoon
of the third day, they heard the rushing of the waterfall, and a little
later, as they rounded the end of the cliff, they saw the ever-moving
surface of the lake shining in the sunlight. They tied up their horses
under a willow tree, and then Listener took the falcon jewels out of his
pocket and went down to the bank. 'Laianna!' he called. 'Laianna,
I've come to bring you back the ring and the chain.'

Then he threw them both far out into the lake.

He saw the glittering jewels dip under the rippling surface, and
watched them sink until they became blurred against the dark green
depths below. Next moment the water in the middle of the lake began
to seethe, and Laianna rose in a wave of foaming spray, with the silver
flute in her hand. 'So you're back, Listener!' she called. 'Did you
manage to outwit Narzia so soon?'

'No,' said Listener. 'It was the child herself who broke Narzia's
spell.'

At that the water nymph laughed so much that the water sprayed
up all around her. 'What's the use of all your cleverness against such
magic as that, you hairy great man?' she cried. 'Why, a little girl has
more power than you! Will you play to me once more before you go?'

'By all means, if you'll give me my flute,' said Listener. 'But I'd
advise you to ask this boy, Snowfinch, to play for you instead. He is a
fluter beyond compare.'

'I'll believe it, if you say so,' said Laianna. 'Play me something, then,
Snowfinch.' And she swam over and put the flute on the bank.

Snowfinch looked questioningly at Listener, who said, 'If Laianna
asks you, it would be most discourteous not to grant her wish.'

So Snowfinch picked up the flute and began to play. It was a song
that began with a sparkling cascade of notes falling like the drops of
the waterfall on the lake, and then Snowfinch told, in his own way,
how Narzia had been freed from her own evil magic, and then had
loosened little Urla's tongue. And the song contained all that Snowfinch
had said to Belarni that evening in the living-room of the herdsmen's

cottage, for again and again a series of notes apparently thrown up by chance turned unexpectedly into the foundations of a new and almost perfect melody, whose beauty consisted in the very fact that you began to grasp the point of it only when the whole closed into a unity. And the water too belonged to the world Snowfinch was building with his notes, for the sparkle and spray of it was present in the music all the time.

So Snowfinch played to Laianna, and when he took the flute from his mouth, she said, 'I will never forget that song, Snowfinch. You have shown me that my own world runs like a rushing river through that world where you humans live, and both belong together. I am happier than I have felt for a long time!' And she leaped out of the water, like a beautiful, slender fish, so that her greenish fair hair flew about her head, and then dropped back with a mighty splash into her element and dived into the depths.

The two of them on the bank wiped the water from their faces, and laughed at this damp farewell. Snowfinch rubbed the drops of water off the silver flute with the sleeve of his shirt, and was about to hand it to Listener, but Listener shook his head. 'No, keep it,' he said. 'I have had it long enough, but you have shown me at last how I really ought to have played it. You'll play it better than I did. And never forget the words engraved on the end of it.

> *Follow my song*
> *whither you will,*
> *yet force is wrong;*
> *use none, or the song*
> *will bring you ill.'*

And he added the rest of what had to be said when the flute was handed on.

They slept under the willow by the lake that night, and the rushing of the waterfall mingled with their dreams, sounding to Snowfinch like a forerunner of the Brown River, along whose banks he meant to ride downstream, and to Listener like the sound, made up of the harmony of countless droplets, of the rush of time that seemed to be slipping by him faster and faster. Next morning, Snowfinch rode on down through the woods, while Listener set off on his way back to the Shallow Valley.

Chapter Three

I

With the passing of time, Listener's life became like a worn, washed-out shirt. Only his hearing had become keener, in a way that surprised himself, since the day he gave his flute away. It was almost as if the instrument, put in his hands too soon, had prevented his learning to listen as befitted his name, even during the time he had been obliged to live without it, for his thoughts and wishes then had been directed all the more strongly to its silver sound, which he had lost.

Now that he was riding alone through the forest north of Barlebogue and into the mountains where Gisa had made her people mine gems, the air around him was filled with thousands of different sounds, to which he listened as if they were a story of which he would never hear either the beginning or the end, only the part that was told along his way. Below his path the mountain torrent shot steeply down, foaming over boulders worn smooth by the water, and above its rushing Listener thought he heard the faint ringing of the sapphires and rubies that the water carried along, to be deposited farther downstream in the pool near Barlebogue Castle. The wind rushed through the tops of the tall pines too, but this rushing was a different sound, almost like the deep, humming voices of giants standing motionless here above the path, looking down on the white-haired old man riding his horse at walking pace up the stony track. 'Do you know him?' one of them growled. 'Yes,' another hummed back. 'He rode here before, and went hunting game in the forest with that cold-eyed Gisa. He's aged in the few years since then.' 'Shall I drop a cone on his head?' growled the first. 'You might have done that at the time,' replied the second, 'and then perhaps he'd have woken from the spell that wolfish witch cast on him and run away from her in time to avoid the trial of Barlo, and turn all that came of that another way. He was given so many gifts, and might have made a great name for himself. But look at him now: don't you see how wearily his shoulders droop? Let him ride on!'

Then the wind that had been blowing from the pass in great gusts died down, and the giants fell silent. But now a jay spotted the horseman, cried, 'Take care! Take care!' and next moment a secret hurrying began in the bushes. A doe called to her young, a wild boar broke through the undergrowth, grunting, stood in the middle of the path for a moment and stared at the horseman. 'Oh, only you,' he grunted, and strolled slowly back into the forest. The bluetits had not been disturbed, but hopped about on the branches above the path, their voices sounding clear as the blows of tiny silver hammers as they stared down curiously at the rider. 'No danger!' they called. 'No danger! Can't you see? Only an old man on a tired horse!'

That was himself, yes. An old man on a tired horse, and he wondered what had really been his purpose in coming back to this valley, where he had helped to drive Gisa and her wolves from the castle over half a century before. After he finally settled in the Shallow Valley, twenty-seven years ago, he had travelled around a good deal, though less frequently of recent years, but he always came back to the woodcutters' cabin, in which he had set up his lathe again so that he could sell his flutes in the villages round about, and play the people a few songs. He lived on what he earned in this way, and Arnilukka and Belarni, or his daughter Urla, used sometimes to come to see him and talk to him in the Shallow Valley, and those had always been great occasions, when the eyes of both women, of that colour hard to describe, had been with him even in his dreams when he lay in bed at night. And indeed he had been quite content with this life, until a strange restlessness came over him a few weeks ago. Had he wanted to see his first travelling companion once more, before his failing powers prevented him from undertaking such a long journey? Or was it the wish to find his early youth, which had seemed to come closer and closer to him of late? He could not have said what really made him take that journey. However it might be, one morning in early summer he had packed up the provisions he would need, put a few flutes in his saddle-bag, and then set off, passing the sycamore spring and going on south through the woods at the upper end of the valley of Arziak and up into the mountains between Arziak and Barlebogue. He had asked the herdsmen there where he could find a pass over the mountain range that did not rise above the tree-line, for he still feared the open sky, especially when he was travelling alone.

After a few days, and several rather cold nights, some of which he spent in herdsmen's huts and others in those bark-roofed shelters which the woodcutters put up for temporary accommodation, he rode down

into the valley of Barlebogue. He had already caught sight, now and
then, of its green hollow lying ahead of him down below, the castle
rising on its hill in the middle of the valley, but when he at last reached
the place where his path led out of the trees, into the meadowland
that fell in gentle undulations to the valley floor, he had not dared to
trot on into the open, but turned his horse right to ride along the edge
of the forest. A little farther down the valley and close to the forest, he
remembered, he should find Eldar's farm, where they had stayed before
the driving out of Gisa.

He recognized the property at once when he saw it lying below his
path. There was an orchard behind the great stable, going all the way
to the borders of the wood, and so it had not been too much of an effort
for him to ride into the farm. He had seen an old man with short white
hair sitting on the bench by the farmhouse door, and wondered who
this might be. He couldn't be Eldar, who must have died long ago.
Judging by the man's broad shoulders, which still looked powerful, he
could be Eldar's son Bragar, just out of Gisa's mines when Listener last
saw him, and when the old man rose from the bench, as Listener
himself clambered stiffly off his horse, and turned out to be a sturdy
and rather short-legged figure, he was sure of it.

'Good evening, Bragar,' he said. 'Have you a bed for me tonight?
I've not slept very comfortably in the mountains.'

'There's always room for a guest,' the old man said, looking at him
keenly. 'Have you been in our valley before, then, that you know my
name?'

'Don't you remember how we fell upon Gisa's wolves?' he said. 'I
rode here then, with Barlo.'

At this the old man, who was indeed Bragar, recognized him and
called for his son to take their guest's horse to the stable, while he
himself went into the house with Bragar. After the meal served by
Bragar's daughter-in-law, he learned how things were in Barlebogue.
Barlo himself, now advanced in years, still sat as judge in the castle,
though he generally contented himself with letting his opinion of a case
be known by means of brief gestures, and left the rest of its conduct to
his eldest son.

As he listened to Bragar telling him this, and much more, he had
felt an ever stronger impression that since he left, nothing much had
changed in Barlebogue, apart from the fact that the people he knew
were older now. Barlo's reputation as a judge seemed to lag in no way
behind that of his grandfather, of the same name, and so life ran its

ordered way here, much as it had in those years when old Barlo rode the land.

When Bragar discovered the effort it cost his guest to ride through open country, he sent his son to the castle with news, and next morning Barlo came riding to Bragar's farm himself. He was surely a frequent guest here, since Bragar was his brother-in-law, yet in the greetings of the two old men some of the familiarity generally found between such close relations was lacking. There was a feeling that the visitor was welcome, but one to be treated with considerable respect, a man who had, so to speak, come down to the level of these people. Not that Barlo was cool, or haughty, but the weight of his office could be felt in him: the law that he incorporated, and that had plainly marked his whole bearing. He still had the flute on which he had learned to speak again, and had raised it to his lips in greeting, with a measured movement that awoke the expectation of something significant to come. 'Listener!' he played. 'I rejoice to be able to embrace you once more!' It sounded a little formal, and he had not actually embraced him, but laid both hands on his shoulders, and scrutinized him keenly from that distance, like a father whose runaway son has unexpectedly turned up.

Remembering this again on his homeward journey, Listener realized that he had instantly felt like Barlo's serving-boy again. This might be partly because the judge still towered above him by a head, but it had not been only the difference of physical size that put him in his sub-ordinate place. The feeling had, if anything, been heightened in the course of the morning. 'Tell me how you have fared!' said Barlo, with his flute, motioning him to a seat at the table as if he were master of the house himself, while Bragar came up from the cellar with a pitcher to pour them perry. The farmer did not sit down with them until Barlo invited him to do so.

There had certainly been enough for him to tell, and no need to rack his brains for tales, and as he spoke of Arni's Folk, his ride to Falkinor, and his years spent as a woodland faun and a prisoner of the Bloodaxe People, Barlo could not keep from shaking his head now and then, and when he put an occasional question, the tone of his flute expressed some slight surprise. What he was hearing did not seem to suit the orderly way in which, as a judge, he viewed the world, and when finally, with a note on the flute that sounded almost like a lament, he said, 'What a life! Have you never really settled anywhere?' it seemed a positive reproof, as if the wanderer had purposely avoided any con-stancy in his disorderly life. Was this the same Barlo with whom he had ridden for three years, having all kinds of adventures? As he thought of it, it seemed to him that even at the time, Barlo had undertaken the journey with some reluctance; he had known from the start where his goal lay, and all the rest had seemed to him no more than a troublesome diversion. When he recalled those days, however, he thought the path they had taken and all their meetings along the way had been what mattered to himself, unwillingly as he had set out upon that path at first. Why, in the end he had been almost sorry to achieve their ends, so that Barlo could take up the office of judge in Barlebogue. Although that might well have been because Barlo's goal was not the same as his, and now he came to think of it, he himself had always pursued things of a temporary if not an actually dubious nature, and in that pursuit hadn't even managed to settle anywhere, or not as Barlo would understand it; this was easy to see, for when he described the old woodcutters' cabin in the Shallow Valley, where he kept his lathe and to which he always returned in winter, he felt, under Barlo's pitying gaze, almost like a restless vagrant, crawling into shelter anywhere when the roads were impassable under snow and ice.

'But you still had Arni's stone then, and later you had your grandfather's silver flute,' Barlo said. 'Didn't they help you to see your way clear ahead?'

And what could he say to that? He found it hard to give Barlo a real explanation of the fact that he had given both away again, and the information seemed to puzzle Barlo a great deal. He had seemed like a man determined not to understand such behaviour, because that might shake the foundations of his own attitude to life.

'Barlo, have you quite forgotten the merry jesters who helped us win the castle back?' he asked after a while. But even this reminder did not help him to break through the judge's stern dignity. 'My office leaves me little time for jesting,' he had said, and when, next moment, he invited Listener to stay here with him in Barlebogue, it sounded like an attempt to bring the life of a man once entrusted to him as a servant into order and security at long last, and the judge was obviously sorry to have the invitation refused. When they parted, Listener had given Barlo one of the flutes he had made himself, and then the judge did embrace him after all, and rode back up the grassy slope to the castle, and even from behind you could tell it was a man of importance riding there, still upright in his saddle despite his white hairs.

That had been his meeting with Barlo. If he had been looking for anything in particular in the valley of Barlebogue, all he had found was the knowledge that he would not have cared to live in that well-ordered world, where everything had its place. He had spent a few more days resting with Bragar, sitting on the bench outside the house with the old man, playing a flute now and then, and listening to the stories the farmer told of Barlo's legendary judgements. Then he had packed his things and set off back up the valley towards the mountains, well stocked up with all kinds of good provisions pressed upon him by Bragar's daughter-in-law.

'Well, Fair-mane, can you tell me why we set out on that hard ride across the mountains?' he inquired of his horse.

'To see a worthy judge sitting in the saddle like his own monument,' said the horse, and they both began to laugh so much that Fair-mane had to stop because he was out of breath, not being in his first youth either. They whinnied and laughed so much that the sound re-echoed from the rocks, and that laughter dispersed the last remnant of the depression from which he had suffered increasingly during his visit to Bragar's farm. He had felt strangely useless, in the face of these people's activity. Ah, Barlo, he thought now, when he had finished laughing, you've become an amazingly impressive man, but I'm too old to be your serving boy now! Up here in the fresh air of the heights, he felt free again, and began looking forward to the ride through the mountains.

The path ran a little way along the side of the mountain here, above the torrential stream. The pines grew farther apart, bearing ragged beards of grey lichen, but they still gave enough shade to keep him from the terror of the open sky. Golden yellow arnica bloomed in the patches of grass between the trees, and pale blue harebells, and the scent of sage and wild thyme wafted towards him. Then he came to a cliff at whose foot the stony path led on through bushes. Below the path, a scree slope overgrown with grass and mountain flowers went down to the stream, and beyond the next curve Listener could see where it began: the entrance to a shaft driven into the mountain gaped in the rock wall ahead.

Since it was time to rest anyway, Listener dismounted. 'You'll find plenty of good herbs to nibble here, Fair-mane,' he said, sitting down under a pine by the side of the path, and investigating the provisions Bragar's daughter-in-law had packed up for him. He ate heartily, and then climbed the short distance down the slope to the burn to drink. As he bent to catch the water that shot down over shining pebbles in the hollow of his hand, he saw, on the bed of the stream, a piece of stone with red crystals sparkling on its surface. He plucked it out of the water and looked at it more closely. Several walnut-sized red garnets were set in the silver-grey, slaty stone, like raisins kneaded into heavy dough;

their edges had been slightly worn by the pebbles of the stream. So this was where the miners had worked to get gems for Gisa's treasuries. As Listener slowly climbed back to the path, he took his find with him, not because the value of the garnets mattered to him, but because he liked to see the translucent crystals stand out of the grey schist. In themselves, they would hardly have caught a prospector's eye, but their background enhanced their beauty, and one could see the beauty of the multiple layers and almost woodlike construction of the mother stone itself by contrast with the crystals it enclosed; what he liked was the association of the unusual and the ordinary. He looked at that beautiful structure for a while, wondering if there were any more such stones to be found inside the shaft in the mountain.

As he was in no hurry, he went a little way into the shaft, and stumbling over some pieces of wood in the dark, he found a whole pile of pinewood torches by whose light the miners might have searched the rock for precious stones. The miners had probably left everything as it was when Barlo's message reached them, and never went back to the place where they had been forced to labour. Listener lit one of the long torches, fragrant with resin, tucked a few more into his belt, and went on into the shaft.

The miners had been working their way along a fault in the rock whose crevices still bore traces of their hammers and chisels. They had obviously been cutting crystals out of a softer, gritty stone at this point. Remains of these crystals still sparkled in the torchlight in many places, but there were none worth mentioning left to be found.

Round a bend which cut off the last gleams of daylight, the shaft widened into a cavernous space of such size that the men could hardly have hacked it out of the rock themselves. More probably, they had come upon a natural cave, and the remains of crystal encrustation still shone on its walls. When Listener crossed the cavern to the other side, where it began to narrow again, he found the place where the miners must have been alerted by Barlo's message, for here at the back of the cave untouched areas of crystals still shone on the walls: sharp yellow citrines stuck out of the rock, dark violet pyramids of amethyst stood close together in a hollow, and farther back yet, where the passage became a narrow cleft, he saw the glow of wine-red garnets such as those that had lured him into the shaft.

He supposed that after Gisa was driven away, no one in the valley had felt like coming back here to break any of these precious gems out of the rock for himself. The memory of the evil that Gisa's greed for such shining things had brought to Barlebogue would still have been too strong. Listener himself felt no desire to do further damage to this hidden treasure-chamber, but only enjoyed the beauty of it, the regular shapes of the crystals and the mysterious glow of their colours.

As his glance swept over the magnificence of the rock wall, a faint shimmer of a colour that was hard to describe led him deeper yet into the cleft. Raising his torch, he forced himself through a crevice that was barely passable and into a narrow place where he could only just stand upright, and there, shining before him, he saw what might have been the twin of Arni's stone. This eye lay embedded in a hollow of streaked, red and grey agate, and the coloured rings rose from its translucent depths, blue and green and violet, unfolding their mysterious life in the torchlight. It was hard to realize that something so full of life could have grown there, hidden in the darkness of the mountains, back in the distant past, but there it was, warming his heart with its glow. And as he gazed into that eye, he saw the faces that had looked back at him with eyes of its own colour: the faces of ancient Urla, her granddaughters Rikka and Akka, the face of Arnilukka and the face of her own daughter Urla, a grown woman long ago, the mother of three sons and a baby daughter. But in the end it was Arnilukka's face that took precedence over the rest, and she seemed to be calling something to him from afar. 'Come back, Listener!' he thought he heard her say. 'Come back, we need you!'

He did not know how long he had been standing in this narrow cleft before the flame of his pinewood torch burned down to the point at which it singed his hand. He flung the torch to the ground so violently that it went out, and he was in the dark. As he was groping around to get his bearings, he heard tapping footsteps from the entrance, and then light fell into the cavern as a man with a torch came round the corner of the shaft. He was short, and slightly stooped, and held the pinewood torch in front of him to light his way. He came slowly closer, crossed the cavern, made straight for the cleft through which Listener was watching him, and did not raise the torch until he stood directly before him. In the light of the steadily burning flame, Listener saw the wrinkled face of the old prospector who had given him the Piney years ago, and before he had recovered from his surprise at finding the old man still going about his work, the prospector said, 'Ah, I see you found the eye-stone just at the right time.'

'The right time?' asked Listener. 'What do you mean?'

'Didn't you discover anything as you stood here in the cleft, while your light was still burning?' asked the old man.

'I did think Arnilukka was trying to call out to me,' said Listener. 'Can it be that I'm really needed?'

'Are you surprised?' said the old man. 'Every human being's needed; the trouble is, not everyone realizes it.'

'Then I'll set off at once,' said Listener, pushing his way through the crevice in the rock. He stopped beside the prospector, and seeing the sharp hammer in the old man's hand, he asked, 'Are you going to cut the eye-stone out?'

The old man shook his head. 'Not for the world!' he said. 'Look at it once more! Beautiful, isn't it, lying there in its agate bowl?'

And when Listener looked back through the crevice, every corner of the little chamber was filled with the pulsing light of the eye-stone breaking again and again over the crystalline walls, a living torrent of blue, green and violet, and as the reflection of that light fell on his face he knew for certain that there were people who needed him and were awaiting him.

'I am going to close this crevice now,' said the old man. 'It was just for you, today.' He raised his hammer and struck the rock directly above the crevice. Listener was wondering how he thought he could close an opening of that size with such a small, delicate tool, when a mighty boulder came thundering down and covered the entrance to that miracle of light and colour. Listener had jumped back in alarm, but the old man still stood in the same place, although the stone door had come down not a hand's breadth from his feet. Only now did he turn, slowly, and say, 'You've time to eat a morsel with me first.'

They went back through the cavern and along the shaft together, and sat out in the sun under the pine in whose shade Listener had been resting. Although he had made a hearty meal already, he did not refuse the prospector's invitation. The old man took a dry cake of bread out of his leather bag, two turned wooden beakers and a small wineskin. Breaking the bread in two, he filled the beakers and said, 'Be my guest, Listener. May you enjoy the meal!'

Listener dipped the hard crust in the wine and chewed it slowly, the better to enjoy the delicious flavour of the bread, seasoned with caraway, fennel and coriander, and the sharp red wine. They ate in silence, and when the old man had swept up the last crumbs and scattered them on the path for the birds, Listener said, 'Until now, I thought there was only one stone of that kind.'

'Does it matter?' asked the old man. 'That stone you used to wear on your breast once lay hidden somewhere in the mountain too, in a place where no light could awaken its play of colour, just a part of the rock and no more. What happened to it later is more important: for instance, the way Urla gave it to the man she loved, and when her husband had been killed she remembered the stone and protected the Khan's son from the snowstorm with her own body; or the way Arni, trying to fathom the secret of the stone, visited people he had once despised and asked their hospitality, and in the end gave his life for Belarni's. All that was bound up with the stone, and that's the significance of it. Did you think it was one of those magical things that work without human agency? That would be mere foolish witchcraft. No, the secret of the stone lies in all the tales told about it.'

'But it did call me when I was alone in the crevice with it just now,' said Listener.

'Of course it did,' said the old man, 'but by calling the people who need you into your mind. You were well on the way to thinking no one needed an old flute-maker like yourself any more.'

'Then I'll hurry back to Arziak,' said Listener. 'Can you go a little of the way with me?'

'Not this time,' said the prospector. 'I am going down to Barlebogue to visit an old man who has scarcely had a chance to forget he's needed, all his life.' And he waved to Listener, and went on his way. Listener called up his horse, and when he looked round once more, the prospector was nowhere to be seen.

'Now, bestir yourself a little, Fair-mane!' he said, once he had mounted. 'We're needed!' And the idea suddenly seemed to make both himself and his horse years younger. He was amazed to find how easy the ride over the mountains seemed, when it had been so laborious going the other way.

He did not stay long in the Shallow Valley, slept just one night in his cabin, and rode straight on to Arziak next morning, through the Weird Wood. He had already found himself a route running through woods as far as possible to take on his rare visits to Arnilukka, but the last part of the way, down a sloping meadow towards the houses, still gave him a considerable sense of uneasiness, and he urged Fair-mane on to a faster pace, trotting rapidly through the streets to the Ore Mistress's house, and making haste to get beneath a roof again. So he was rather breathless when he entered the living-room, where he found Arnilukka and Belarni.

Arnilukka jumped up as soon as she saw him and ran to meet him. 'Oh, I'm glad you're here, Listener!' she cried. 'I didn't know you were back from your journey, or I'd have sent you a message.'

'I got your message,' said Listener, 'though I was still the other side of the mountains at the time.'

Belarni had come around the table too. 'It always amazes me how the pair of you communicate,' he said. 'For days, we've wanted nothing so much as to see you come back, Listener, and now here you are.'

'Looking as if you'd run the whole way,' added Arnilukka. 'Sit down with us and eat something first! We can talk later.'

Despite her snow-white hair, she was still in vigorous health. She firmly sat him down in a comfortable chair, went out and soon came back with all kinds of good things: smoked ham, cheese, a pot of honey, crusty new bread and a jug of wine. 'Be our guest, Listener!' she said, when she had set it all ready, and she filled the goblets and sat down again.

During the meal, Listener kept looking at Arnilukka. Her face was coming to resemble her great-grandmother Urla's more and more, and seemed to him more beautiful than ever. Strange, he thought, how little age can touch a face one loves, and when Arnilukka spoke to him and their eyes met, his heart beat faster.

Belarni had eaten little, merely taking a sip of wine now and then. The shape of his skull could almost be seen beneath the brown, furrowed skin of his thin face, between the white braids at his temples. His cares had grown no less, and indeed were greater now; the parties of the Goldsmiths and the Riders of the Steppes, who had set their faces against fraternizing between the two peoples, had by no means merged into the community over the last few years, but were more bitterly opposed than ever, so that there were often clashes between them in the open street. Listener had rarely ridden to Arziak, but the horse-herds and their horsemaster Ruzzo had plenty of tales to tell. What the young sons of the Riders of the Steppes had begun as a game had long since become deadly earnest, he had heard. They were now a group of men of around forty who had formed a Riders' League along with young men of their families, and the members of this League often disappeared with their horses, reappearing some days later, and never saying where they had been. But when travelling traders told tales of attacks on villages in remote valleys, one could put two and two together. These cares of Belarni's were nothing new to Listener, and that very fact meant that they could not be the reason why his presence was required in Arziak. What use is an old man like myself in such matters, he wondered, indicating that he had eaten enough. Now, at last, he would hear what the matter was.

Belarni had obviously been waiting for this moment, for he now said, 'No doubt you want to know why we've been wishing so heartily for your return, Listener.'

'Is it more trouble over those quarrels between the Goldsmiths' clans and that horde of Riders?' asked Listener. 'I don't know what good I could be to you there.'

'It's not just that,' said Belarni. 'You know that Azzo has always been inclined to support the Goldsmiths. Since his mother comes from one of their oldest families, they didn't quibble at his origins, and were glad enough to have the Ore Mistress's son frequenting their houses, even if his father's a Rider of the Steppes. Well, he's been courting the daughter of the Elder of the Guild for some time, but nothing's come of it yet, although he's long been of an age when a man should have a wife and children. It rather looks to me as though those old-established clans don't want to take their useful connection so far as to welcome the son of a Rider into the family. But if you try discussing the matter, Azzo gets so angry there's no saying anything to him.

On the other hand, Arnizzo always kept well clear of such quarrels, but I'm sorry to say that's changed now that the Merry Fluter has gone right over to the Squires, as the Riders of that League have taken to calling themselves. Recently, Derli's played nothing but songs in mockery of the "Paunches-of-Gold", as he calls the Goldsmiths; indeed, he's actually stirring the young men up to deprive the old families of the Mountain Badgers of their rights here, by force if necessary. Arnizzo made friends with Derli when he first began playing the flute here in the valley, and I was glad to see it. I dare say he thought he'd imitate his great-grandfather Arni, who had a fluter for a friend himself. With all I have to do, however, I failed to notice how much the boy had fallen under the Merry Fluter's influence. I realize only now, when he's joined the Squires, obviously because of that same influence. And now you know how I hope you can help me: Derli was your pupil, and if anyone has any influence on the man himself, then you have.'

Listener thought for a while, drinking a sip of wine now and then, and then he said, 'I don't know if I'm in any position to help. I haven't seen Derli for years, though I've heard a good deal about him. He never visited me in the Shallow Valley when I came back from the Bloodaxe People, and I can explain that only by supposing he's been avoiding me because he's in search of his own way to play the flute, and would rather keep clear of my influence. I don't like what you tell me either, but perhaps one shouldn't take it too seriously. Young people often go strange ways before they find themselves.'

Belarni shook his head and gestured impatiently. 'Arnizzo's not so young that he need meddle in such nonsense,' he said. 'And shouldn't I take it seriously when my two sons come to blows the moment they set eyes on each other? Arnilukka and I are not the only ones to be troubled. Your daughter Urla has tried to make peace between them, several times, though she has enough to do with her own four children.'

He was interrupted by a knock at the door, and the steward of the house came in: an elderly, grey-haired man, obviously one of the original people of Arziak, judging by his face and his manner of dress. He asked if he might trouble Belarni a moment, and when Belarni nodded, the steward told him it had come to his ears that the Squires were about to band together again, and maybe it might be as well, said the man, to do something about it before there was a clash.

'There, you see?' said Belarni to Listener. 'And presumably Arnizzo will be riding at their head, along with the Merry Fluter!' With which he and the steward left the room together.

Ever since Belarni had mentioned Urla, Listener had been thinking of her daughter. 'I don't mean to distract you from your concern,' he told Arnilukka, 'but I should like to know how Urla is. She hasn't been to the Shallow Valley since she had her fourth child over a year ago. I only know that she has a daughter now, as well as her three sons.'

'A daughter with Urla's eyes!' said Arnilukka, smiling, and not saying whether she meant the old or the young Urla. 'She called the baby Rikka, after her great-aunt, who was married to a blacksmith too.'

'Those eyes called me back to you,' said Listener, and he told her what had happened to him up in the mountains. As he talked, he could not take his gaze from her eyes, which still seemed to him as young as on the day he first looked into them. 'But here I go talking,' he said at last, 'when I really want to hear about our daughter. Was the birth so difficult that Urla couldn't come to the Shallow Valley to show me the child?'

'It was,' said Arnilukka. 'She was very weak for a long while afterwards, and has gradually recovered only these last few months. Luckily she has a good maidservant to help her keep the household going.

There are always guests to be entertained in a smithy: folk who want their horses shod, and say they'll wait while it's done, or others placing orders for a weapon or an implement. You know how it is: they have to discuss how this or that's to be, and you can't leave a customer sitting without a bite to eat and something to drink. She likes the life, for she loves to have people around her, but of course she has her hands full. And with all that, she still finds time to concern herself with her brothers' quarrels. She can't bear brothers to be opposed in such a way.'

'She bears Arni's stone,' said Listener, which seemed to him an adequate explanation.

At this moment Belarni came back into the room. 'I was going to stop Arnizzo, but he'd already ridden out,' he said. 'And Azzo's been out of the house since morning. Well, all I can do now is send the Elder of the Goldsmiths a message recommending him to keep his people off the streets, for fear of riots. Though whether that will be any use I rather doubt.'

As he was speaking, the sound of horses' hooves could be heard approaching out in the square. 'There they are,' said Belarni, going to the window. Listener rose and followed him, and saw the Squires riding up. He well remembered the sight of a horde of Raiding Riders, braids flying, galloping over the grey grass in their worn leather clothing and on their shaggy little horses, but what he saw here was very different from the untamed wildness of those hunters of the steppes. The riders in this cavalcade all sat high-bred horses that danced nervously at every step, and their clothing might bear witness to their origins, but was made of the finest light-tanned leather, almost overloaded with coloured embroidery, one fantastically ornamented design seeming to vie with the next. The sheaths of their curved swords were richly wrought as well. The Squires had even woven coloured ribbons into the braids at their temples; obviously these were designed to show that they belonged to a particular family, because there was one group with green ribbons, whose members must be brothers, so far as one could tell from the similarity of their features, and the same was the case with the men who wore blue or red ribbons in their braids. As the riders trotted closer, it could also be seen that the embroidery on their clothes favoured certain patterns according to their membership of one family or other. Some wore designs of horses, others of vultures, others again of wolves or the great cats. It was a fine sight to see this horde – or this decoratively refined version of a horde – come trotting up, led by a tall young fellow with a great spear from whose tip there waved a mighty horsetail, decked with ribbons of every colour, and one of the two riders immediately behind him must be Derli, now known as the Merry Fluter.

Listener would scarcely have known him again if he had not been carrying a handsomely turned flute. He had become a rather corpulent man, with a mocking smile lurking around the corners of his mouth. He had woven ribbons of every colour into the already slightly grizzled braids at his temples, which in Listener's opinion made him look a fool, although the men with whom he was riding seemed to take him perfectly seriously, in particular the thin, dark-skinned rider beside him, in whom Listener recognized Belarni's younger son only after some hesitation. He remembered Arnizzo as a rather quiet boy, who rarely laughed and tended to stay in the background when his elder brother and sister got up to some nonsense or other, but now he seemed quite changed as he laughed with almost exaggerated exuberance at Derli's jokes, and tried to imitate his friend's mocking smile.

Until that moment, this colourful scene had struck Listener as a festive parade of cheerful young men, but now Derli called something out, pointing to the far side of the square, where a group of men had appeared, all of them – like the Squires themselves – somewhere between twenty and forty years old, and immediately an almost unbearable tension seemed to settle over the space between the houses. People who had been standing out of doors talking to each other a moment ago said hasty goodbyes, parted rapidly, and most of them vanished into their homes. Only a few remained on their doorsteps, ready enough to gape at whatever spectacle was brewing, but ready too to get behind a bolted door at speed.

By now the men of the other group had stepped out into the square. They were on foot, but in their magnificent garments they offered no less colourful a picture than the horde of Riders. The most striking feature, at first glance, was that each wore a heavy golden chain around his shoulders over a coloured cloth doublet, and all kinds of other golden ornaments dangled from their clothing as well. The belts on which they wore their long daggers were also made of gold, and precious stones sparkled in the hilts of the daggers themselves. Their membership of their Guild showed in the way they had smartened up those leather caps that goldsmiths wear at work, to keep back their hair, into a particularly magnificent form of headdress denoting their social standing. Cunningly wrought brooches set with blood-red garnets and other gemstones shone on these caps, they sprouted bunches of heron's plumes like strange flowers, and as these members of the Goldsmiths' Guild walked with measured tread towards the Squires, Listener felt the mocking designation of Paunches-of-Gold was not perhaps so wide of the mark, since it was clear that many of these rich citizens' sons were disinclined to deny themselves the pleasures of the table.

Belarni's son Azzo himself, one of the leaders of the group, was rather broadly built, though in no way stout, but merely powerful. Azzo had never let the braids at his temples grow, but his rather flat-nosed face clearly showed his origins, if he did not look as much like a Raiding Rider as his brother. There was no laughter among the Goldsmiths; they seemed more bent on displaying a dignified demeanour, like men well aware of their own importance.

Belarni had watched this parade with growing anger. A knotted vein, thick as cord, stood out on his temple as he struck the window sill with his fist, saying, 'Will these hotheads never see sense?'

Arnilukka, who had joined them at the window some time ago sighed and said, 'You'll have to try and keep them apart, Belarni!'

'Easier to keep cats and dogs from each other's throats!' growled Belarni, striding out of the room. Next moment Listener saw him crossing the square towards the Goldsmiths, who all bowed with much formality when he stopped beside them, but showed little interest in what he was saying.

Meanwhile, the Squires had dismounted and tied their horses to the fences. Listener heard Arnizzo call out, 'Play us a song, Merry Fluter!'

Plainly Derli had only been waiting for this moment. He put his flute to his lips and began a leaping melody, which sounded to Listener both impudent and hostile. There was a discordant note of illwill running beneath the hectic merriment of the tune which made him feel uncomfortable, indeed almost afraid. However, the Squires seemed to like this kind of music, and they were obviously familiar with the words of the song, for they immediately gathered around the fluter, and one of them began singing the verse in a high, shrill voice, while the others yelled out the refrain in chorus:

> *Who's fat as lard, both breast and belly?*
> *Paunch-of-Gold!*
> *Who's as wobbly as a great big jelly?*
> *Paunch-of-Gold!*

Who can't sit his poor old nag,
because his jewellery makes it sag?
    Paunch-of-Gold, Paunch-of-Gold!
    Now it can be told!

As soon as the Goldsmiths' sons heard this song, with which they appeared to be familiar, they simply left Belarni standing there and came striding slowly on, but something like pent-up rage showed in their deliberate tread now, and also, perhaps, in the way they moved closer together and in a certain stiffness of their bearing. The game seemed to amuse the Squires immensely, and after a sharp little introduction played by the fluter, one of them began to sing the next verse:

Who stalks proudly through the muck?
    Paunch-of-Gold!
Who can't move because his feet get stuck?
    Paunch-of-Gold!
Yet who still wants to be the first
to speak in Assembly and to quench his thirst?
    Paunch-of-Gold, Paunch-of-Gold!
    Now it can be told!

'And what do you idle Raiding Riders live on, then?' shouted a fat-faced young dandy dressed with especial magnificence. 'Those who don't work like us should have no say in Arziak! Arziak's no place for thieving rabble!'

The Squires seemed in no way insulted, but fairly shook with laughter at the indignation of the portly young Goldsmith. 'It'd take more than three men to heave him into the saddle!' cried one, whinnying with laughter. 'And then the poor horse would collapse! Go on, Derli! The song's not finished yet!' And one of them struck up the next verse:

Who'll we milk like our own fat cow?
    Paunch-of-Gold!
Who'll provide plenty of plunder now?
    Paunch-of-Gold!
If we take his jewels, he may
all the more easily ride away!
    Paunch-of-Gold, Paunch-of-Gold!
    Now it can be told!

At this Azzo, who by now was standing close to the Squires, along with his friends of the Guild, turned to his father and cried, 'There – hear for yourself what this idle lot are planning to do! It's those plunderers you should be warning to keep the peace, not us! We won't stand here listening to their mockery any longer!' And the expressions on his companions' faces had darkened too as they began to finger the costly belts from which their daggers hung.

So far, Belarni was the only person who had made any attempt to keep the opposing factions apart. As he now made his way through the Goldsmiths, to prevent the Squires from uttering any further taunts, Listener saw his own daughter Urla come out of the smithy at the far end of the square. As soon as she saw what was going on, she called out something to her husband, who appeared in the doorway behind her, and then ran quickly over the flagstones. The other lookers-on remained standing in their doorways, watching impassively, obviously of the opinion that lesser folk had better keep out of the way when the more powerful came to blows. Only the blacksmith followed his wife, though more slowly, and it looked as if it were not mere chance that he was holding his heavy, long-handled hammer in his hand. But before Belarni could do anything, and before Urla had quite reached the men, Arnizzo cried, 'Go on, Derli, play! I know another verse of the song!' And he planted himself, legs wide, in front of his brother, who was a dozen paces or so away from him, and sang in a shrill voice that was almost cracking:

> *Who's got a Rider knocking on his door?*
> *Paunch-of-Gold!*
> *Who won't give the Rider his daughter any more?*
> *Paunch-of-Gold!*
> *Who won't let the Rider into bed,*
> *beside his darling to lay his head?*
> *Paunch-of-Gold, Paunch-of-Gold!*
> *Now it can be told!*

As the Squires bellowed rather than sang this last refrain, with much hilarity, Listener looked at the face of Belarni's elder son, who had suddenly gone white to his very lips, and what else he saw there instantly made him forget his stance as a mere observer. Pushing himself off from the window ledge, he strode across the room and was almost running before he was out of the entrance hall and through the open door, which showed him a scene the sight of which left him standing paralysed in the doorway. All that now and almost simultaneously happened seemed to unfold incredibly slowly, and yet there was no stopping it. Urla had reached the crowd of men. Skirts flying, she ran between the two groups towards Arnizzo, whose jeering song she must have been able to hear. Belarni was still impeded by the Goldsmiths, who stood there as if rooted to the ground, and was trying in vain to reach Azzo; Azzo himself had already plucked his dagger from its sheath, and before anyone could stop him, he flung it at his brother. At that moment Urla at last reached Arnizzo and grasped his shoulders with both hands, as if to shake some sense into him. Azzo's dagger buried itself in her back up to the hilt. Her hands clutched convulsively, and then she slid slowly from her brother's breast to the ground, and was unconscious by the time her husband caught up with her. He stood in the space between the two factions, staring at the scene before him, unable to grasp what had happened.

For a while everyone stood there frozen. Then Arnizzo bent down to his sister. He too seemed unable to understand, as yet, what that sparkling thing between her shoulderblades might mean, and he put out a hand to the hilt with its gleaming rubies, but at that moment the smith let out a great roar, raised his hammer in the air, and leaped towards his wife's supposed murderer. And now, at last, the other witnesses of this bloody deed came to life. Several men of both factions surrounded the blacksmith at once as he hit out frantically around him, got the hammer away, and spoke to him insistently. Listener himself found he could move at last, and this time he was driven out into the shadowless square by a fear stronger than that oppression that weighed down on him from the open sky. He ran to his daughter where she lay on the ground, reaching her at the same time as Belarni and Arnilukka, who had run out of the house after him. It was she who at last took the dagger and pulled it from the wound. Then she sat down in the dust of the square and cradled Urla in her lap.

Urla had closed her eyes, and her face was so bloodless that Listener thought there was no life left in his daughter at all. But then she opened her eyes once more, and their colour, which was so hard to describe, seemed to glow with twice its usual strength in her chalk-white face. She looked at all of them standing around her one by one, and when her gaze fell on Arnizzo she said, haltingly, 'Where's Azzo?'

Belarni understood at once, and beckoned his elder son over with an imperious gesture which Azzo unhesitatingly obeyed. When he stood with his brother before the dying woman, she looked at them both, a look they would surely never forget in their lives, and said, 'Be like brothers at last!' Then her glance went to her husband, who had now been brought to her side. His face still wore an expression of uncomprehending horror. Quite unexpectedly, Urla smiled, and shook her head slightly, as if the big man were making far too much fuss about what had just happened. Then she groped for Arni's stone at her breast, where it hung in its silver network, and said, 'Keep it for Rikka!' And when she had settled that as well, she curled up like a child in her mother's lap, and died.

II

After the burial of Urla, Listener had decided to stay in Arziak for a while, though less because of any feeling that he should stand by Arnilukka in her grief, for she was remarkably composed, than on account of Belarni's perplexity, which was in no way due to any continued enmity between his two sons. After the events leading to Urla's death, neither had remained with their former friends, but had simply turned away from them, gone home and stayed there. During meals they sat silently at table, scarcely daring to raise their eyes, and only picked at their food. It could be seen that they both felt guilty of their sister's death, and that in a way which made them doubt everything they had ever done, while at the same time this led to a new kind of understanding between them; they did not avoid each other, but were often to be seen together, although they hardly appeared to exchange a word.

Belarni's perplexity had roots that went deeper, as he showed one evening when he asked Listener to sit with him a while longer after Arnilukka had cleared away the supper, and the brothers had gone out. Belarni stared at the table in front of him for a while, and then said quietly, as if he were continuing a conversation begun long before, 'Now what have I done wrong? Can you tell me that, Listener? Should I have forced the two boys not to mix with those people? Or indeed, should I have refused to allow the Squires and Goldsmiths to set themselves apart and make themselves out great gentlemen from the very first? I am not made like Khan Hunli, who bent everyone to his will. Until now, I always hoped it would be enough to show people how they should live together, and for the rest, leave them free to find their own way of doing it.'

'That's not the way to put the question,' said Listener. 'Hunli himself couldn't prevent Honi from opposing his will and leaving, with a large part of the horde.'

'And that was where all this evil had its beginning,' said Belarni.

'No,' said Listener. 'The beginning of the evil doesn't lie in such events as the Parting of the Ways, but in the thoughts and desires of individual human beings who want power over others, and as we humans are so made that we easily fall prey to the temptations of power, I suppose that evil can never be entirely rooted out of the world.'

'It's easy for you to talk,' said Belarni. 'A fluter like yourself can keep out of all these quarrels and go his own way. But I'm responsible for the people of Arziak, and all that happens here rests on my shoulders. Including Urla's death. And my dream of seeing the people of this valley, at least, live peacefully together is running away beneath my hands.' He laid his empty hands before him on the table, palms upwards, as if to show what remained of his dream.

Seeing Belarni sitting there so helplessly, Listener could not help thinking of Barlo, under whose well-ordered jurisdiction the people of Barlebogue did live peacefully together, and he wondered about the source of that depression that had increasingly overcome him in the valley where the judge's rule held sway. 'Belarni,' he said, 'I think I should tell you about my visit to Barlebogue. Barlo, with whom I rode for three years when I was a boy, is still judge of the whole valley, sitting in his castle, and under his rule everything there goes its well-ordered way. I think there's hardly a man or woman in all Barlebogue who doesn't ask, when beginning anything: what would Barlo say about this? I don't want you to suppose he's a tyrant who oppresses the people. Far from it: he is an entirely just man, whose wise decisions the people all up and down that valley can tell you off by heart. There's peace and harmony everywhere, and anyone who so much as begins to break out of that ordered way of life is aware from the start that he'll soon have to answer for it to the judge. And yet all the time I was there, I felt as if I couldn't breathe freely. I had the constant impression that the great Barlo was looking over my shoulder to see if I was behaving as I should, and you know, for an old vagrant like me that came to seem so unbearable that I set off for home quite soon. Since then I've asked myself again and again what it was that really troubled me, and over these past days it's gradually come clear: the folk there are all like Barlo's children. They rely on him to know what's just and what is unjust, and so they're never even tempted to make a decision on their own initiative. Barlo is responsible. Yes, that peace and order of which you dream reigns there, but I ask you: is it the right way for people to live?'

'If I understand what you're saying correctly,' said Belarni, 'to make my dream come true would mean depriving everyone else of their rights?'

'Not necessarily,' said Listener. 'Only if you were to make it impossible for them to decide in favour of your dream for themselves.'

'But that,' said Belarni, 'means that my dream can never be fully realized. You said yourself that people will always fall prey to the temptation of their own greed for power.'

'And that's where the secret lies,' said Listener. 'If there were no evil in this world, then no one would have the freedom to decide for the good of his own accord. In that way, you could say evil is always the servant of good. You can't alter the world at a single stroke. Individual people always come first. That's what Arni told you, just before he was killed.'

Belarni looked up in surprise. 'Now how do you know that? When he said it, we were on our own, riding behind the others.'

'Arni's death was one of the events I witnessed while I was a stone faun,' said Listener. 'And even he couldn't prevent that battle, in which there were other dead men besides himself, but he did save your life.'

'Not just that,' said Belarni. 'At the time, I thought I'd finally understood the dream he dreamed, but now I see I've always been very far wide of the mark. Urla understood the point of it better than I did, and so at least my two sons are like brothers to one another now. And yet there'll have to be a judicial hearing of the case of Urla's killing.'

Listener looked at Belarni in dismay. 'You can't sit in judgement on your own sons!' he said.

'No,' said Belarni, 'indeed I can't, and it's difficult to think of a suitable man to do it at all; there are so many who might be accused of being partisan. For instance, the Elder of the Goldsmiths is out of the question, because Azzo was on the side of the members of his Guild when he threw the dagger; nor can anyone from the old families of the Riders of the Steppes be judge, because the attack was on Arnizzo and thus on one of the Squires. And the Master of the Blacksmiths might be biased, because Urla was the wife of one of his own Guild. Can you tell me who should hear this case? I'd already wondered if I might ask Barlo to do it. You've told me yourself of his great reputation as a judge.'

'I know of no more experienced man,' said Listener, surprised to hear with how little enthusiasm that came out, but he told himself this must be the result of his personal feelings about the lord of Barlebogue. In any case, Belarni did not seem to detect any reserva;ions in this reply, and he sent a messenger over the mountains that same day. The man must have made the difficult journey at great speed, for he came back a week later with the news that Barlo had died a few days before. The whole valley was in deep mourning, he said, and he had spoken to grown men with tears running down their cheeks as if they had lost their own fathers.

The news gave Listener fresh cause to wonder at himself, for as well as his sincere sorrow at the death of his former master and travelling companion, he felt something like relief, and this relief was less because he thus avoided any danger of being made to feel like Barlo's serving-boy again than because he had felt increasingly doubtful, all that week, whether the noble judge of Barlebogue could manage to apply his own adamant standards of justice to such a case, a case of truly alarming complexity, in such a way as to reach the true heart and meaning of the matter. Be that as it might, Barlo's flute was silent now, and another judge must be found.

'If old Vazzek were still alive,' said Listener to Belarni, 'I would have advised you to turn to the wise old Carphead. He knew more about such matters as guilt than anyone. But there is a man whom I know to have learnt a great deal from him. In your place, I'd ask Ruzzo the horsemaster to judge the case. He took no part at all in the events themselves, and he is a man with no prejudice against either of the parties concerned.'

So it was that Ruzzo rode over from the Shallow Valley to do justice in Arziak. The trial was conducted in public, and held the day after Ruzzo arrived, in the square outside the Ore Mistress's house and thus on the very spot where the murder had been done. All who had taken part in those incidents in any way, or who at least had witnessed them, were obliged to attend, and in fact the whole population gathered in the square, with the exception of small children and a few sick people who were too weak to drag themselves to the place of justice.

Ruzzo seated himself on the judge's chair, which Belarni had had carried out, and called the names of those whom he would wish to have at hand in the case. It turned out that the two factions were keeping well apart on this day. Listener saw the Goldsmiths' Guild standing all together to Ruzzo's right, while the Squires, along with their families, had gathered to his left. Derli was among them. But it could also now be seen how much these two groups were in the minority, as compared to the rest of the people of Arziak, crowding together in the middle, though that might be partly because some of the Squires, and some of the Goldsmiths' sons as well, had left off their magnificent clothing for today, as if to avoid the danger of being held in any way responsible for the violent deed. Azzo and Arnizzo, who as those chiefly concerned stood directly before the judge, showed no allegiance to either group in their clothing, but they had other good reasons for that. Listener stood in the shelter of the doorway, so as not to expose himself to the fear he felt in the open square, and from that vantage point he watched Ruzzo open the trial.

'You threw the dagger, Azzo,' said the horsemaster. 'What did you have in mind at the time?'

'I must have been crazy,' said Azzo. 'All my life, I shall never forget that it was my fault Urla died, although I didn't mean to hit her.'

'Whom did you mean to hit, then?' asked Ruzzo.

Azzo turned even paler than he was already, but then said, in a steady voice, 'My brother Arnizzo.'

'So you aimed at your brother, and hit your sister,' said Ruzzo. 'Would it have been any better if your dagger had hit the mark at which you aimed it?'

'No,' said Azzo. 'It would have been just as bad.'

'Have you anything to say in your own defence?' asked Ruzzo.

At this question, Azzo merely bowed his head and said nothing. But now Arnizzo spoke up, saying, 'My brother had reason enough to be furious with me. I made him look ridiculous in front of everyone.'

'So you admit that you provoked the deed?' said Ruzzo.

'Yes,' said Arnizzo, 'and in a way that will have made him too angry to know what he was doing.'

On hearing this, Derli thrust his way forward. 'Are you out of your mind, Arnizzo?' he cried. 'If your brother can't take a joke, well, that's his problem, but it's no reason to go throwing knives about the place!' And those few Squires that he had gathered around him showed their agreement, asking loudly who had actually drawn the dagger, and was the victim going to be made out guilty? This seemed about to set off further uproar, for the Goldsmiths' sons, or at least those who had come to the trial in all their magnificent gear, were roused to shake their fists and begin calling the Squires agitators and cut-throats.

Ruzzo raised his eyebrows and listened to this for a few moments, but it then turned out that he had a powerful voice at his disposal if need be, against whose great boom the strife that was breaking out sounded like fishwives quarrelling. 'Are you about to break the peace even before the seat of justice?' he thundered, as if he had a couple of unruly horse-herds before him, and when the other spectators, who had not previously held to either of the factions, preferring to withdraw into their own homes, suddenly began to feel their own strength and angrily warned the bawling men to hold their tongues, the noise soon died down, and everyone could hear Ruzzo when he went on again, voice calm. 'You intervened in this trial unasked, Derli, but since you have spoken up, perhaps you can tell me why you don't like to see Arnizzo taking part of the guilt upon himself. Could it be that you yourself were not quite uninvolved in the quarrel that led to Urla's death?'

And now everyone was looking at the fluter, but this merely seemed to strengthen Derli in the opinion that this was his chance to take the stage. Visibly ruffling himself up, he inquired, 'Since when has it been a crime to play a merry song in this valley? Nobody's ever objected before, apart from those spoilsport Paunches-of-Gold! We Squires are not that sort!' And so saying, his glance swept round the little group of Squires with their beribboned braids, looking for approval. 'We like a little fun now and then, and I just play the music for it!'

'And have the Squires dancing to your tune,' said Ruzzo. 'Yes; I've heard that there's always trouble in the streets when the music of your flute begins to play.'

'Going to judge cases of talebearing too, are you?' asked Derli, impudently.

'No,' said Ruzzo. 'But it could be that another may teach you the way to play a flute, if you carry on like this.' Derli laughed mockingly, and seemed about to answer back again, but Ruzzo silenced him with an abrupt gesture, and went on, 'It is hard to weigh up the separate shares men bear in the blame for this matter. It all has its origin in the way you Squires, and you of the Goldsmiths' Guild, began to stand aloof from the community, make yourselves out great lords, and set about outdoing each other with your trinkets and your clothing and your highflown speeches. No sooner do the Squires come out in the street than the Goldsmiths must band together as well to steal a march on them. And this fluter, whom I myself don't find so very amusing, makes sure it doesn't stop at mere parading, but eggs you on until you come to blows. That's what happened to you, Arnizzo, but you're old enough to know where a joke ends. You've admitted yourself that you gave your brother great provocation, and it would have been your own doing if his dagger had struck you. And that means that you bear a part of the blame for the death of your sister, who died in your place. However, that makes your own share in the guilt only a little less, Azzo, particularly as you are the elder. You would have done better to help your father keep the peace in Arziak, instead of going around with these gilded popinjays here. However, you were the one who drew the weapon, and even if it was done in anger, it was done with the intention of killing your brother. The fact that you accidentally killed your sister may be punishment enough in itself for you, but a killing of this kind must be punished according to the law. Therefore, as the custom is, I banish you from Arziak and all other places in this valley for the space of three years. Your father shall give you a horse, and provisions for seven days, so that you can leave Arziak and hire yourself out as a servant in some remote place. The same sentence should really be pronounced on you, Arnizzo, but I don't want to deprive your parents entirely of their children. So I impose on you the task in pursuit of which your sister died: you shall see to the keeping of the peace in Arziak. You know better than anyone now where such quarrels can lead. And it seems to me time you remembered the man after whom you were named. You've brought little honour to Arni's name as yet. Do you both accept this verdict?'

When the brothers had answered in the affirmative, Ruzzo brought the trial to an end, and rose from his chair. As the people still stood discussing what had happened, Derli gathered his remaining adherents around him, and began to play one of his provocative songs. That fluter has understood nothing at all, thought Listener, hearing the impudent piece in which his former pupil mocked both trial and verdict. And perhaps because of the very fact that he himself had taught Derli to play the flute, he was overcome by boundless anger with this now quite middle-aged fellow who thought so much of his own art, and in that surge of anger he suddenly thought he saw the point of Ruzzo's remark to the effect that someone else might teach the mocker to play the flute. Taking his own instrument out of his pocket, he began to play a melody of his own, countering Derli's mocking song, as if they were taking part in some musical competition.

Derli was so surprised that his rhythm wavered. Such a thing never seemed to have happened to him before. He cast Listener a venomous look, and then went on with his bold song, rather more insistently this time, while his friends sang the words at the top of their voices:

> *Who cares for Badger folk that wake*
> *to labour every morn?*
> *A Rider free his loot will take*
> *and laugh the fools to scorn!*
> *They dig and delve to get their ore,*
> *forge many a golden chain,*
> *but let a Rider armed for war*
> *tickle them up, they'll cry full sore,*
> *and beg him to be off again!*
> *Yes, that is very plain!*

Listener could scarcely make his little wooden flute heard through the yelling of the Squires as they bellowed this ditty, although his rival tune did succeed in making the song falter slightly, but as soon as the verse was over, he played straight on, and now he showed his art in his ability to make the content of his song quite clear, although nobody was singing the words. In his fury, he raised his playing to a volume which he himself would never have thought possible, and what the people understood his song to be saying was as follows:

> *Who minds this boastful fluting fake*
> *to whom your eyes are drawn?*
> *A man whose reason is awake*
> *will laugh the fool to scorn!*
> *His envy makes him mock the more,*
> *he'd like a golden chain!*
> *His head is weak, his songs are poor,*
> *his manners those of any boor*
> *who's only bent on giving pain.*
> *Yes, that is very plain!*

He could never have dreamed that this verse would go down so well. The square echoed with roars of laughter, and the Goldsmiths seemed to suppose that they now had a fluter on their own side. They applauded him loudly, urging him to give them more such verses. However, his playing had obviously turned most of the ordinary people against Derli and his few Squires, and many bent to pick up stones and chase the wearers of beribboned braids from the square. Listener, whose anger had blown over by now, looked with dismay at the milling crowd of onlookers, some laughing, some ready for new deeds of violence, and he met the eyes of an old and slightly stooping man whom he had not noticed before. He was dressed in the worn clothing of a prospector, and stood there motionless in the middle of the shouting, bawling throng, looking at Listener in a way that implied anything but approval. Seeing that Listener had recognized him, he shook his head slightly, turned and walked away as if he were alone in the square and not wedged among such a crowd. A moment later, Listener had lost sight of him. When he looked around for Derli, he was relieved to find that that not very merry fluter had made off, together with his followers. Now the crowd began to disperse at last, and Listener waited for his hosts and their family in the doorway.

The first thing Belarni did was to provide his elder son with all that the judge had allowed him, and when the horse stood saddled in the yard, he embraced Azzo without many words. Arnilukka, too, took her son in her arms, and then asked him if he knew where he would go.

'I've heard a great deal about the peaceful, gentle natures of the Carphead people who live by the Brown River,' said Azzo. 'Perhaps they need a man to work at fishing for them there.'

'That would be a good place for you,' said Arnilukka, and she kissed Azzo before she let him go.

Then Azzo faced his brother, arms dangling helplessly, as if he dared not touch the man at whose breast he had flung his dagger. 'Your task will be harder than mine, Arnizzo,' he said. 'And I must learn to control my violent temper now. Can you forgive me?'

Instead of answering, Arnizzo, too, took his brother in his arms, and begged him to forget the mocking song he had sung about him.

'As to that,' said Azzo, with a rather wry smile, 'I'm glad enough I must be away from Arziak for a while.' He was obviously referring less to the song itself than to the subject of it.

Last of all, Azzo said goodbye to Listener, saying, 'Perhaps you'll manage to bring your former pupil to reason. It looks as if you let him leave off learning too soon.' Then he mounted his horse and rode out of the yard gate.

Listener lay awake a long time that night, wondering how he could put an end to Derli's game. It was obvious that even the trial had not brought the fluter to his senses, and indeed it seemed as if the dwindling of his influence had made him more impudent than ever. Only now did Listener really understand why Belarni had wanted him here: not just for his skill as a fluter, but because he was responsible for the playing of his pupil, whose instruction he had never completed. At the time, he had had nothing in his head but to remove himself from Arnilukka as fast as possible; he had not given a thought to what would become of the pupil he was leaving behind. That decision had turned out wrong in many ways, and its consequences now faced him like a tangle which looked as if it could never be unravelled. He felt another access of that anger which had driven him to cut the tough knot by force after the trial. He now knew that the less than merry fluter could be driven from Arziak by such means. But what would that achieve? He would go and play even worse songs somewhere else.

'What's to be done, Piney?' he said, at his wits' end. 'I see little hope of disposing of Derli in any way that will put an end to his mocking songs once and for all.'

'Ought you to be disposing of him?' inquired the Piney. 'You speak as though you'd given up all hope that your pupil might yet learn something new. In which case I suppose the best thing would be to kill him out of hand, that being the only way to dispose of a person once and for all.'

'You surely don't mean that!' said Listener, dismayed.

'Of course I mean it, from your point of view,' said the Piney. 'I'm only trying to think your own remarks out to the end. "Dispose of," you say, and "once and for all"! That's the way to strike a man down with words. But is it the way to make up for what you left undone as a teacher? While there's life there's hope. You of all people ought to know that.'

'And how do you think I can go on teaching him?' asked Listener.

'Well, not by using his own songs as a stick to beat him with, anyway,' said the Piney. 'Don't you see, that makes you his pupil instead? I know a better teacher for you than that.'

'Who?' asked Listener.

'That mouse,' said the Piney. 'He-who-never-gives-up-hope.' And not another word was to be had from him after that.

It soon turned out that Derli had no intention of giving up his provocative flute-playing. His adherents were certainly considerably fewer than before, for the death of Urla, who had been deeply respected by everyone in Arziak, and loved by most, had given many of them a salutary shock, nor had Derli's behaviour at the trial been such as to consolidate his position in Arziak. However, there are always people who obviously need such an insolent attitude to strengthen their own self-confidence, so that a number of the Squires still rode the streets with Derli, in their colourful finery, and there were also some of the Goldsmiths' sons who took this as a challenge to go out in their jewels and golden chains, and show the people that they were still around, and well able to stand up for themselves.

Arnizzo, therefore, had plenty to do. As soon as he heard that some such matter was afoot, he would be off to try keeping the brawlers apart. It was not easy for him, since the Squires with whom he used to ride treated him as a defector, indeed a traitor, and Derli began to play mocking songs about the weakling who feared the mere flash of a curved sword. 'But what can you expect?' he asked his cronies. 'The man's not a pure-blooded Rider. His mother may be Arni's grand-daughter, but then Arni was another such crazy dreamer who didn't like the sight of blood.' And Arnizzo was not much more successful with the Goldsmiths' sons, since he did not belong to them at all. 'His brother showed us what these men of mixed blood are like,' they would say. 'When it comes to the point, they'll pocket their pride and leave us in the lurch.'

Remarkably enough, however, Arnizzo did succeed in keeping them from ever actually coming to blows. This might be because the mere sight of him was enough to remind those finely dressed fellows how Urla took the dagger meant for him in her own back, but it was probably also to do with the fact that most people no longer hid in their houses while Squires and Goldsmiths were about the streets. There were a number of men who stayed put, casually enough, and holding axes or heavy hammers in their hands as if by chance. They just stood there, appearing to take no notice of the young gentlemen with their beribboned braids or massive jewellery, but their presence helped to ensure that the trouble went no further than jeering and a little flute-playing. Arnizzo had not encouraged them to do any such thing, or enlisted them into any kind of auxiliary troop; they obviously did it of their own accord, let anyone think what he liked of it.

Meanwhile, Listener would sit on the steps under Arnilukka's porch, playing the flute to himself. At first, after what they had heard him play after the trial, people came running as soon as he appeared with his flute, no doubt expecting some new show, but many soon turned away, disappointed, among them some of the Goldsmiths' Guild, who had thought Derli was about to be taught another lesson. Listener played quite ordinary songs, simple melodies he had learned from mountain shepherds, or from fisher-girls beside the lake, sad songs and merry ones, although there was not much merriment in his own heart. But in time he came to enjoy his fluting again, particularly when Arnilukka came out on the porch to listen. 'Now you are playing as you did long ago, when you first came to this house,' she said. 'And I thought you'd forgotten all your old songs.'

'So many terrible things have happened since then,' said Listener. 'How could I have played such songs?'

'Well, that's why you're a fluter,' said Arnilukka. 'When others are near losing hope, you must remind them how good life is in spite of everything.'

He looked up at her and saw how her eyes, of that colour which was hard to describe, were still darkened by grief for her daughter, and yet still, or perhaps for that very reason, they seemed to him most beautiful and full of life, and his heart was warm with joy to have such a woman standing beside him speaking to him in such a way. It sounded like the affirmation of his own thoughts when Arnilukka said, 'Yes, Listener, indeed you should play such songs, even though our child is now dead. Play me the Song of Fair Agla, who laughed when the Green Man came to drag her down into the lake.'

So he played her that song, and played it again and again over the next few days, as well as many other songs he now remembered. He still had a circle of hearers, and indeed it was growing ever larger: it was made up of children. As soon as his flute sounded in the square they came gathering round him; some sat down on the steps beside him and asked for this or that melody that they'd heard him play before. As time went by, he taught them the words, and soon the children could be heard singing Listener's songs all over Arziak. Now and then a few adults too stopped beside him to listen, and once a man said, 'We haven't heard anyone play like this for a long time, not since the Merry Fluter joined the Squires.'

So Listener's music came to be heard all over Arziak, although he never went so much as a step from the porch of the house. Few had any objection to it, but Derli was furious when he heard a child singing one of those songs. He would interrupt with shrill notes on his own flute, but as he couldn't be playing the flute all the time, and more particularly couldn't play it everywhere, he was unable to get the better of Listener's music, which made him even more furious than before.

One day, when Listener was sitting on the porch surrounded by a circle of children, playing them a new song, Derli came riding through the square with his friends, and set up such a loud, discordant fluting that Listener took his own instrument from his lips and inquired, 'Can't you go somewhere else, if you have to make such a noise? You certainly never learned from me what you're playing now. Or does it bother you if we sit here and sing our songs?'

'Yes,' said Derli, 'it does. Your childish nonsense bothers me a good deal! A man can't go anywhere without having his ears insulted by such stuff. Why, there's a childish voice croaking your sing-song somewhere or other even at night, when one wants to sleep.'

'I make my own kind of music, and you make yours,' said Listener. 'What's the matter with that? You can hear half a dozen minstrels at Draglope fair, and they don't intrude on one another's pitches. Surely there's room for two fluters in Arziak.'

'No,' said Derli. 'There's room for only one, and that one has been myself, so I've the right to challenge you to a contest. We'll soon see who's the better fluter, and the loser can clear out.'

'I see,' said Listener. 'And when is this remarkable event to take place?'

'Oh, I'll give you a little time for preparation,' said Derli, condescendingly. 'Let's say here in this square, in three days' time.'

'I'll think it over,' said Listener. 'You'll have to wait and see if I go along with your suggestion.'

After supper, he told Belarni about Derli's challenge. 'What do you think?' he asked. 'Should I accept it?'

Belarni shook his head slightly. 'Such a challenge is a serious matter,' he said, 'and this one in particular. If you don't take it up, Derli's reputation and thus his influence in Arziak will rise. We don't want that. Are you afraid of defeat?'

Listener laughed briefly, but grew grave again next moment, saying, 'That's not what makes me hesitate. But I am indeed afraid: afraid I may lose my temper again when I hear his provocative songs.'

'That might not be such a bad thing!' said Belarni, grinning, but here Arnilukka, who had been sitting with them in silence, joined in. 'Sometimes the old Raiding Rider in you shows through, Belarni!' she said. 'It would do no one any good if he enraged Derli even more.' She added, looking at Listener, 'I'll be near you if you enter upon that contest.'

Listener looked into her eyes. 'That will be as if I still wore Arni's stone on my breast. I'll accept the challenge.'

He made no such preparations as Derli had suggested, but continued to sit on the steps outside the house, playing his songs, surrounded by children who watched him with shining eyes and joined in many of his melodies with their fresh, slightly shrill young voices. He was sitting like this on the evening before the contest, watching his hearers, who were spellbound by his songs, singing quite unselfconsciously themselves as evening came on, and suddenly he felt he had a magical power to induce any mood he pleased in these children, who were barefoot and slightly dirty from the day's wild games. They gave themselves up unresistingly to the tones of his flute, and he remembered that troop of children he had once lured beyond the walls of Draglope with his tunes, making them dance to his playing until the pursuers came riding up and broke the spell. Once again he saw the empty eyes of the children he had lured away into flat, exposed country, saw their helpless little figures sink exhausted into the dust of the wayside, and felt the fear that had seized him then, causing him to turn his horse abruptly and gallop away in headlong flight from those dulled faces in which feverish enthusiasm had just been shining.

The tune his fingers had been playing all this while slipped away from him in the midst of a rising phrase, the children's singing hesitated and became confused, though one tousle-headed little girl did manage to sing the verse to the end in her thin, piping voice. 'Go home now,' Listener told them. 'I'm tired.'

He could not rid himself of that image of the children of Draglope he had enticed away, not as he sat silent over his supper, scarcely saying a word, nor most certainly when he lay in bed at last, staring at the pattern of the carved beams in the ceiling above, which could hardly be distinguished in the dark.

'Well, now do you see what you are about, with these children?' asked the Grey One. His colourless face hung somewhere in the darkness, looking down on him.

'Aren't they my friends? Don't they love my music?' said Listener, making a feeble attempt to preserve what he had felt until now when the small singers took up the tunes of his flute, and he himself was carried along by the chorus of their thin and wavering voices.

'Friendship! Love!' said the Grey One, looking as if he were spitting out the rotten core of an over-ripe fruit into which he had bitten for the sweetness its outside promised. 'What kind of words are those? Let a man come along tomorrow who plays in a different way, and knows his craft as well as you do, and they'll hang on every note he plays and sing his songs as if spellbound. You're always dreaming of what doesn't exist at all. Everyone tries to get power over others in his own way, some with the sword, some with gold, you with your flute. What's the difference? You're only deceiving yourself if you call the way those dirty urchins bawl your songs friendship or even love.'

'Well, someone will indeed come along tomorrow who plays in a different way,' said Listener, 'and I must compete with him.'

'And do you want this Derli to win?' asked the Grey One.

'No,' said Listener.

'There, you see?' said the Grey One. 'I like you better when you say that. At heart, you know very well how to deal with that Merry Fluter. Why, he never even learned all you could teach him! Will you, the master, let your raw pupil get the better of you? You mark my words, you can play him into the ground if you'll only make up your mind at long last to use your flute in the one right way.'

And with that the Grey One's face faded. Listener thought he could make out his vague shape for a little longer, but then he realized that he was staring at a face carved on a beam, which stood out more clearly as the dim light of dawn crept in.

He felt weary and worn from lack of sleep when he went out on the porch after breakfast, and looked at the great square, where people had already come to listen to the contest. The late summer sun was only a little way above the shingled roofs, in a deep blue sky, yet it burned down with such fierce heat that a thought shot through Listener's mind: there'll be a thunderstorm this evening. At the moment, however, there was not a cloud in sight, although the swallows were dipping low as they shot past the white plasterwork of the house walls.

Meanwhile, the square filled up more and more; men and women stood in groups, discussing the chances of the two fluters who were to play against each other, and the children ran around, chasing each other or dancing in a ring to one of Listener's songs, as if to put him in the right mood for the contest. However, he could not feel very much at ease. Were those little figures down there, he wondered, really no more than puppets with no will of their own, puppets he had made dance to his tunes?

He had no time to muse on this question any further, for Derli came riding into the square with his friends, their coloured ribbons threaded into their braids. Altogether there were about a dozen Squires parading in front of the spectators on their nervously prancing steeds, before they dismounted and tied up their horses to a fence. Then Derli walked into the middle of the square, with a slightly mincing step, turned to his adversary and called, 'I have challenged this fluter named Listener to a contest, which will show us at last who's to have the right to play the flute in Arziak where and when he will. All of you assembled here shall judge the contest, and whichever of us manages to gather most hearers around him by the end shall be the winner. Are you ready, Listener?'

Listener had seated himself on the steps, as usual, and Arnilukka stood under the porch beside him, while Belarni and Arnizzo were leaning against the wall of the house a little way off. In answer to Derli's question, Listener slowly rose to his feet and said, 'I'll be glad to begin at last. It's going to be hot work today.'

'You may be sure it is!' said Derli, taking this to refer to more than the weather. 'I challenged you, so you have the right to play first.'

Listener glanced at Arnilukka, plunging again into the mysterious power of her eyes, and while he felt entirely caught up once more in the shimmering colour of those ripples of blue, green and violet, he put his flute to his lips and played the Song of Fair Agla. He began with the simple melody the fisher-girl had sung him long ago, but from the second verse on he began to stray from the melody, just as the image which came ever more clearly before his eyes moved him: it showed the lake, spreading in front of the distant blue haze of the wooded slopes, shimmering as it reflected the sun in its gently moving surface: it showed the banks bordered by reeds, the leaves along their stems hanging down at an angle, and closing into a thick, dark green belt, with an opening through them to the water, where a landing-stage of planks ran out into the lake on weed-grown posts, and in the shadow of the wooden landing-stage tiny fish scurried over the pebbles on the bottom, their scales shining like mother-of-pearl at every move they made. Then the sky which had been so bright grew dark, night fell, and a procession of wailing women in black robes approached from the land, among them a few men too, their faces set, driving a girl who was also dressed in black before them. He saw the face of that girl, chalk-white like his daughter's when she lay dying in Arnilukka's lap, but the eyes of this girl were fixed in horror, and her cheeks wet with tears, and then the men pushed the girl into the lake, farther and deeper in, until only her head and her breast were above the surface, which was moving now, and not only with the disturbance of the men's bodies, but it began to bubble up from below, until the surface was seething over a wide area, and out of this surging turbulence rose the Green Man's mighty head, wreathed in barbels like those of a fish, and his flabby, webbed hands seized the screaming girl and drew her down to the bottom. The water soon grew calm, and there were only a few ripples around the place where they had both disappeared.

The lake lay quiet again, glowing rosily under the sun, now low in the sky. Far out, a boat could be seen, with fishermen in it busy hauling in their nets, and the outline of their boat, and all the movements they made, were reflected in the water below. They put out their oars and rowed to land, and as the boat and its reflection crawled slowly like a crab towards the bank, the blood-red sun touched the lake, cast one last long, glowing ray over the water, and then dipped inexorably below the horizon.

And now that procession of wailing, black-robed women was coming down to the lake again, and so were the men, but this time they had no need to drive their sacrifice before them; ahead of them all a girl in a snow-white dress danced her way down to the water, and the girl's face was merry, her brown eyes shone with delight, and as she ran into the water she laughed aloud and sang:

> *Green Man*
> *grant our wish,*
> *from your deep lake give us fish.*
> *Lie not in the water*
> *sorrowing for your daughter;*
> *lord of fish to north and south,*
> *kiss Fair Agla on the mouth.*

Then the water began to boil and bubble again, the bewhiskered, wetly shining head of the Green Man rose from the waves once more, but the girl did not scream; instead she took the straggling hair of the water-sprite's head in her hands, to left and to right, and kissed him full on the mouth. At that the Green Man let her go again, and took a mighty leap high above the lake, and when he splashed back into the water a great fountain shot up to the sky as if the whole wide lake were exploding. And as Fair Agla laughed and laughed, the Green Man swam far out, singing:

> *Agla*
> *lovely child,*

long I was by grief beguiled.
Now your laughter's gladness
drives away my sadness:
after all the loss and pain
life comes from the lake again.

Agla
in their need
all your children I will feed.
They shall find, in the lake,
all the fish they can take.
Your sweet love, your dear kiss,
make me sing with joy and bliss.

And so he sang on, far into the night, although the words of his song could no longer be distinguished because he had swum so far out, and also, no doubt, because he was now singing of the beauty of his green and watery world, which only creatures of the deeps can fully understand. And with this melody, drifting out strangely into waters past understanding, Listener finished playing and put down his flute.

His hearers, particularly those who had never heard him play anything but his little songs, had not been prepared for music of such artistry. They had listened, enthralled, to the ballad, living through the tale of the lovely fisher-girl from its grim, sad beginning to the happy laughter of its end. Many had to wipe their eyes, and it was hard to tell if they were wiping away tears of emotion or of the laughter that had arisen at the Green Man's mighty splash into the water. They had all gathered around Listener, applauding; only Derli with his cronies remained out in the square. It must have fretted him a good deal, for he did not even wait for the shouts of approval to die away, but broke right into them with his own music.

The very first notes sounded to Listener impudent and unruly, but his initial dislike of the tune was mingled with a certain appreciation, almost admiration, of the way the fluter picked up themes from the Song of Fair Agla and turned them to mockery, so that what had seemed grave before was now comical, and the happy part of his own tale became something slyly underhand. The other listeners seemed to feel the same. Some frowned and shook their heads to hear him mock emotions that had brought tears to their eyes just a moment ago, but there were plenty of others who couldn't help grinning at the Merry

Fluter's version, and went closer to him, so as not to miss any part of his song.

By now Derli had finished the introductory passage, and he took his flute from his lips to sing the words, in his high and rather unctuous voice:

No doubt you liked that pretty story:
the maid in sacrificial glory –
a sight to touch the heart!
A little joy, a little pain:
such tales, I hardly need explain
appear to use no art.
And many a child they help to go
happy to bed, and lull to sleep.
But you're not children now, I know.
You've done with childish toys, and so
I doubt if I shall make you weep
by saying this tale is sleep!

So now I'll sing another song –
which could as well be right as wrong –
of how it might have been.
For that old fluter sitting here,
you mark my words, he wasn't there!
Such things he's never seen.
They say this fluter used to be
a faun who once would range
the woods with goats, and now if he
can't sleep at night, then tales, you see,
he must invent to make a change:
and surely this one's strange!

As for the pretty fisher-maid,
I think it fairly may be said
she liked (and it's no crime)
some merriment: no child was she
of sadness, but in jollity
she wished to spend her time.
Alas, no fisher to her mind
she saw, nor any likely lad!

Poor as they were, how could she find
a man with pockets nicely lined,
and jewels to make her glad?
Dear me, this tale is sad!

A Count lived not so far away:
a lusty fellow, so they say,
although his ways weren't steady.
His castle was in easy reach
of the great lake, and on the beach
he kept a boat all ready.
And when he saw a fisher-maid
put out, he'd start to row.
'My pretty dear, my love,' he said
'with you and none but you I'll wed!'
So with him she would go.
Ah, what a tale of woe!

For once the Count had got his will,
and of that girl he'd had his fill,
he'd take her out a-fishing
at night, when no one was about,
and from the boat he'd push her out.
So much for all her wishing
to be his wife! 'Farewell,' he'd say,
'my pretty one, for now instead
of you with others I will play!
Be off, my dear, and swim away.'
So very soon she would be dead –
Oh, what a tale of dread!

Our fisher-maid had got her eye
upon this Count: the reason why
was not to be his wife.
He took her to his castle, where
for many a day the happy pair
enjoyed a merry life.
But when at last he tired of her,
She said, 'Go fishing? What, at night?
No thank you very much, dear sir!

Out of this castle I won't stir!
Not while the stars are shining bright.'
His was a piteous plight!

So then she plagued him night and day
and still refused to go away
until he gave her gold,
silver and gems, and what was more
his fishing rights away she bore,
as hers to have and hold.
And once she had this handsome fee
she rowed away for many a mile,
to live a life of joy and glee.
A clever maid, you will agree!
And if you've listened all this while,
I hope my tale has made you smile.

As Derli played and sang his version of the ballad, the atmosphere had become oppressively hot, and black storm-clouds were towering up in the sky to the west. However, the people scarcely noticed, but gathered around the fluter, who soon had to add little interludes to his performance, not so much in order to prepare the next verse as to occupy the time until the roars of laughter died down enough for him to make himself heard again. Even Listener found himself unexpectedly moved to laughter by the Merry Fluter's comical song, until he realized exactly what he was laughing at, when he was doubly angry, and not entirely because this mocking fluter was holding his own song up to ridicule, or because he himself had known the fisher-folk and remembered their merry brown eyes, which were said to be like Fair Agla's own. No, what made him angry was the way Derli set about destroying and removing the enchantment from all that gave life its meaning: sadness and joy, trust and love, it was all washed away by loud laughter, leaving nothing but wickedness, cunning and greed, and the sly fluter had put it all so humorously as to dupe even Listener himself. He should indeed be shown how to play the flute, that grinning fool, he thought, as the red wheels of anger turned in his brain. Leaping up, he put his own flute to his mouth, but with the first note that he whistled rather than blew, to make it ring out above the square, there came the sound of another flute, a note that carried far and caused him to lower his own instrument again.

At first no one could tell where the sound of this other flute came from, until a tall, rather lanky minstrel with pale fair hair came past the houses at the far end of the square, walking slowly towards the people who were thronging around Derli. He played a silver flute, but as for the music itself, it could scarcely be described. Listener felt as he had long ago after his breathless, frantic flight through the thick forests of Barlebogue, when the dumb man was riding around him, cudgel in hand, and then, suddenly, the Gentle Fluter stepped out of the bushes playing that silver flute. His anger was swept away, and he recollected, in astonishment, that he had just been involved in a contest that now seemed quite pointless, compared to the music of this fluter, who set no store at all by a great show of his art, let alone by outplaying anyone else. New sequences of notes kept unfolding like flowers, and when the structure seemed complete, it would turn out that the whole was only a bud from which new forms broke forth, promising yet more and still unguessed-at variety. What the fluter played was a song of life itself, cheerfulness and gravity, sorrow and joy, despair and hope, love and hate, all inextricably woven into a single web, so that one felt like both laughing and crying at the beauty of that music, and it restored Listener's belief that he had not just imagined any of those things, but that they were realities which he was only now, gradually, beginning to understand.

At last the fluter ended his tune, in such a way that one felt the music was far from all that might yet be heard, and only a faint shadow of what he would really have wished to play. Almost all the people in the square were now clustered around him, even the last of Derli's Squires. Only Derli himself still stood aside, but more like a man who dared not come any closer, and every trace of insolence had gone from his bearing.

Listener too had held back, but for other reasons. He had forgotten all his fear and anger, and felt light as a bird. Arnilukka was still standing beside him. Now she said, 'Snowfinch has come back. Just at the right time, too!'

'Yes,' said Listener. 'What fools we've been!' And they looked into one another's eyes, and laughed heartily, as they hadn't laughed for a long while. Then, at last, the storm broke with a great flash of lightning, followed immediately by a clap of thunder. The crowd quickly scattered, running to their houses as the first drops fell. Only Derli took his time. He was still standing in the square, irresolute, as the rain began pouring down, and then he came over to the Ore Mistress's house. He stopped in front of Arnilukka, under the porch, and said, 'I'd quite forgotten what it was like when you first taught me to play those pipes under the willow by the river, when I was a little boy, and frightened of the narrow valleys and dark woods. But I remember now. I hope I shall never forget again.'

Arnilukka looked into his eyes, and smiled. 'One must remember such things for oneself,' she said. 'It's not much use if anyone else reminds you.'

By now, all Listener recalled of Derli's song was the humorous way he had put it. 'You won't give up being a Merry Fluter, I hope?' he said.

At that Derli laughed. 'So you liked it a little yourself, did you? No, it would go against the grain with me to play in any other way, but I fancy it's time I started to earn my name, for it seems to me my songs haven't been as merry as all that. Your other pupil has brought you more honour. I hope you'll stay in Arziak a while, so that I can complete my apprenticeship at last.'

'So far as such things can ever be completed, I will be happy to help where I can,' said Listener.

III

And now, having completed one task, Listener had taken on another, but such is the way of the world: one's tasks are never done. Surprisingly, Derli now wanted to hear all the little songs he had despised so much before. He particularly liked the merry ones, and was soon able to perform them so comically that the children began running after him.

Snowfinch stayed in Arziak too, although he seldom played the flute, and then used his wooden instrument for little improvisations which sounded like patterns picked out of that intricate tapestry of notes which he had displayed on his arrival. His music was very different from the Merry Fluter's, but the two seemed to get on well, and to value one another's qualities.

As the three fluters sat together one evening with Belarni and Arnilukka, Snowfinch told the tale of his travels. It turned out that it was not by chance he had come back to Arziak. At first he had spent some while, as he intended, with the fishermen by the Brown River. After that he had ridden on down the river to Falkinor, where he had stayed as a guest in the Great House with the Master of Music, learning a great many things from him, such as the art of taking five tones and building them into a gateway through which one entered an endlessly varied world, a world of which one could know nothing by one's own powers. 'Extraordinary things you find there,' he said. 'And dreadful abysses open up, but then you find powers slumbering which will help you to fill the emptiness of such an abyss to the brim with sounds and images, giving some slight notion of what life's really about.'

'When I was there in my youth,' said Listener, 'I could never master those five-tone melodies.'

'That needn't surprise you,' said Snowfinch, smiling. 'You were only in the Great House of Falkinor for a short time, and moreover, you went on a particular mission which took your mind off the real thing. I spent nine years there, and it was only in the last year that I succeeded in playing such a tune of five tones.'

'Did you tell them what became of Narzia's falcon jewels?' asked Listener.

'Yes, indeed,' said Snowfinch. 'I told the Great Magician at the very start, when he received me. He was the second successor of the man who held that office when you were there, but he knew all about the ring and the chain, although none of the magicians you met was still alive. I am to thank you, in his name, for using those things in the right way, and then disposing of them so well. And he asked me to give you a message if I ever saw you again. "Tell him," he said to me, "that if a man goes astray, that doesn't mean he may not still be on the right path." At the time, I thought this message sounded like nonsense, but afterwards I began to see the point of it.'

'Then I may still hope to understand it myself someday,' said Listener, 'for all I know now is that I have taken the wrong path.'

Snowfinch let it rest at that, and told how he had gone on southwards later, and had all kinds of strange experiences which, however, are not part of this story. 'And last year,' he said, 'I rode north again. I spent the winter with the fishermen by the Brown River, and then I stayed on with them until well into the summer. One day a man came riding into the village, asking if they needed anyone to help with the fishing. From the first, I didn't think he looked like a fisherman, for he sat in the saddle like a man who's had to do with horses since his childhood. At first, judging by his looks, I thought he was a Raiding Rider, although he wore no braids and wasn't dressed like a Rider, but such things are easily changed. He wouldn't say where he came from, or why he was travelling alone, but the fisher-folk took him in and gave him work. It was only when I'd been playing my flute a little one evening that he came to me and told me his name. That was how I met your son Azzo, and when he told me what had happened in Arziak, it seemed to me that a fluter might be needed here, so I set off the very next day.'

Later, when Listener was in bed, he kept thinking of Snowfinch's tale, and in particular of the message sent by the Great Magician, who had probably never met him. What did the Magician know about him? Just what his predecessor might have passed on, the tale of a boy who wanted to try the powers of his flute, and looked as if he might be going astray? Had that been enough for him to send such a message to an old man who had once been that boy? Or had they known in advance, in the Great House of Falkinor, what devious ways the boy was going to take? And what did the second part of the message mean? Listener saw too clearly how he should have acted otherwise, throughout his life, to retain any notion that he was going the right way. He had not even managed to bring his own merry pupil to see reason. That was Snowfinch's doing, when he made the long journey from the Brown River and over the mountains to Arziak, obviously in great haste. Which surely showed that Snowfinch had not believed he, Listener, had the power to perform that task!

Indeed, he had come to seem to himself increasingly superfluous recently. His two pupils treated him, to be sure, with that friendly respect which a master shows his old teacher, under whose guidance he took his first steps in his art, but he didn't know what more they might learn from him. They kept surprising him with new ideas of their own, thus unintentionally showing, each in his own way, such independent mastery that he was left to play the part of an admiring listener, not that of a teacher who could lead them to any higher achievement.

'What do you suppose I'm doing here, Piney?' he asked his stick. 'Those young fellows can get along very well without me.'

At this, the Piney gave his wooden chuckle and said, 'Making you envious of their flute-playing, are they?'

'I don't know if you could call what I feel envy,' said Listener. 'But I feel like an old village musician, shown what he might have done with his instrument by a couple of wandering minstrels. However, my fingers are too stiff now, and I feel the limits of my own imagination more clearly all the time. Those two have caught up with me, and passed me, and I'm left hopelessly behind.'

'Hopelessly?' said the Piney, and his creaking voice showed how deeply he disliked that word. 'Have you forgotten that they were your pupils, and would never have become such masters without your help?'

'What did I teach them?' said Listener. 'A few trills and exercises! What really matters – the boldness of imagination, the wit of their thoughts – they got all that from themselves.'

'But they could never have expressed it if you hadn't taught them the hard discipline of playing,' said the Piney. 'Shouldn't you be pleased that each, in his way, has become a great artist?'

'Of course I'm pleased,' said Listener, 'but I am sad, too, that I can't keep pace with them any more. My merits as a teacher don't seem much to speak of.'

At this the Piney became quite seriously cross. His wooden body creaked as if he were trying to draw himself up, and he said, 'Does everything have to be hammered home into your stupid brain bit by bit? What earthly use is a teacher whose pupils don't outdistance him? That's exactly what he should be hoping for – for them to come a little closer to that perfect music he never could play himself, that nobody in this world ever will play, because then he wouldn't know what else to do with his life. You should be pleased you set those two young fellows on their way, instead of staring at what you couldn't do yourself! Really, you humans are a trial! Always carrying on because you think it's up to you to go out and get things for yourselves – things you can only have as a gift!'

* * *

However, Listener's restlessness was driving him on, if not so far as before. But he felt the urge to return to the Shallow Valley, and work at his lathe a little in the cabin in the woods. Before he set out, though, he wanted to see his granddaughter Rikka, to whom Urla had left her stone, and he asked Arnilukka to go to the smithy with him, to help him master the fear he felt under the open sky.

So Arnilukka led the old fluter over the great square, and what with the touch of her hand and the sight of her eyes, he almost forgot the oppression that settled on his heart again as soon as he ventured into the open. He thought how his daughter Urla had died here, and it now seemed to him that she had fulfilled the promise of the stone in doing so, for everything that happened afterwards at that place had turned out to be an answer to the desire for peace and love she had expressed to her quarrelling brothers here.

The blacksmith came to his door to meet them, and Listener saw that he was wearing Arni's stone in its silver setting around his neck. Noticing his glance, the smith said, almost apologetically, 'I couldn't think of any better place to keep it safe for Rikka. And since I've had it on my breast, I've felt almost as if Urla were still with us.' He smiled as he said that, and Listener looked with amazement at the huge man who had made for Arnizzo like a madman to strike him down, and whose voice now sounded so gentle. 'Come in and be my guests,' said the blacksmith. 'The boys are playing outside somewhere, but Rikka's asleep in the cradle where her mother once lay.'

He invited them to eat first, and while a maidservant brought in the food, he himself poured wine, and then sat down with his guests. As they ate they talked, according to the custom, of unimportant things, yet one could never tell whether one might not, unforeseen, break through the thin skin of superficiality and venture into regions which were not unimportant at all. For instance, the blacksmith asked Listener to tell him about the turning of flutes. 'A curious thing, that,' he said, after hearing Listener's explanation. 'You cut a piece of living wood in the forest, and let it dry out, till it looks as if there's no more life in it, and you trim it with a hatchet and bore out its inside, and turn the outside on your lathe, and then you pierce that thin, almost fragile pipe with holes all over the place, you harm it every way you can, so that there's nothing left of its own natural form, and only then will the wood make music and come to new and different life.'

'It's the same with iron, surely?' said Listener. 'The iron was formed inside the mountain once, too, but the ore has to be got out with picks and hammers, and smashed to pieces, and melted down in the heat of a fire until none of its natural shape is left. But when you heat the pure metal again you can make it into any new shape, and only then, in its new form, will it show its hidden beauty, or perhaps its usefulness as a tool for work in the fields.'

'Or for killing,' said the blacksmith. 'Everything we make can be used for good or for evil. I forged Azzo the blade that killed Urla myself. I have made no weapons since, but other things instead. If you've had enough, I'll show you something.'

He led them to his workshop, and when he opened the door the clear ringing of the hammer which they had heard throughout their meal was suddenly twice as loud. A journeyman stood at the anvil, half naked under his wide leather apron, beating a flattened piece of red-hot iron. A fire burned by the wall beside him, blown up by a boy with a pair of bellows, and a spindle-shaped, white-hot iron bar lay among the glowing red coals.

The blacksmith led his two guests to the far end of the room, went to his battered workbench, and picked up an object that had been lying there among a few small hammers and files. In the dim light, Listener could not at first see what this strangely shaped thing was, but when the smith took it closer to the fire, its outline became clearer, and Listener recognized the simple shapes, reduced to their bare essentials, as those of two people, a man and a woman, standing close together and embracing. Listener admired the tenderness the smith had managed to express in his recalcitrant medium, and the smith said, 'When I walked over the square again after Urla died, Azzo's dagger was still lying there. Nobody wanted to touch it. So I picked it up and brought it back here. I threw away the finery on the hilt; it would only have reminded me how the sparkling thing stuck out of Urla's back. But I made this out of the blade that had been in her heart.'

Listener could think of nothing to say when the smith laid the iron down on his bench again. Should he praise his host's skill, or the beauty of the couple forged in iron, or simply say he liked it? Any of that would have sounded foolish and inappropriate to his own ears. And Arnilukka was silent too, but she knew a better way of expressing what she felt, and embraced the big man, who seemed like a child being comforted by his mother, although she scarcely reached his chin.

When they had left the workshop, and closed the door behind them, they heard the child laughing amidst the now muffled ringing of the hammer blows. 'Rikka's awake,' said the blacksmith. 'And you really came to see her, not me.'

'Both of you,' said Arnilukka, opening another door that led to a room at the back of the house. The window looked out on a sunny garden: branches laden to breaking point with red-cheeked apples and yellow pears hung above blue and purple asters in flower. Rikka was sitting in her cradle, which rocked slightly, her little hands grasping the carved animals on the bars. 'One-horn!' she said, trying to make a fierce face, for the he-goat did indeed look rather grim. 'Yalf!' she cried, seizing the leaping donkey on the other side of the cradle, and crowing with laughter.

'I don't know who taught her those animals' names,' said the smith. 'Maybe Urla told her about them, though Rikka's really too young to understand such stories.'

But it was plain that she did know a great deal about them, for she turned to the three mice at the head of the cradle, pointed to them one by one and said, 'Speaks snake, prophesies falcon, gives hope!' And Listener saw, to his surprise, that she knew exactly which mouse bore which name.

He pulled up a stool, sat down by the cradle, and looked into the eyes of the laughing child, eyes in which blue, green and violet mingled in a way that was hard to describe. 'Why, you know them all apart!' he said. 'That's right: the third mouse, He-who-never-gives-up-hope, was the youngest of them. All three of them were brave, but that one could do something which comes hard to young folk: he could wait. Some people never learn that at all. But this mouse could do it, and the reason he could was because he believed in something crazy. He believed a stone could come alive. Think of that: a hard, lifeless stone, quite a big one too. People laughed at that mouse, and said he was crazy himself. But he didn't let that bother him. He sat there day after day, week after week, year after year, watching that stone and waiting. And still nothing happened, but he didn't give up hope, he wondered how the stone could be brought to life. It needs love, he thought; if people love each other, something new comes alive. He liked that stone, but it was too big for him to take it in his own mousy arms. So he started looking for someone to love the stone in the right way.

And then he met a young woman with eyes like your own. As soon as he looked into her eyes he knew she was the right person, but it wasn't easy for a little mouse to start a conversation with this woman, who was so much bigger than he was. Not that she was frightened of him, oh no! Only stupid people are frightened of mice and fail to see how pretty they are. But at first she didn't notice him at all as he ran through the tall grass after her. However, still that mouse never gave up hope.

Then, one day, she did see him. She bent down to him, stroked his soft, velvety fur, and gave him a few breadcrumbs. But she couldn't understand what the mouse was telling her in his high little voice, and in the end she left him there in the grass and went away.

So now what was he to do? Many would have gone home and stopped bothering. But our mouse wasn't that sort. He still didn't give up hope. He began asking people for news of the woman, and so he discovered that though she might not be able to talk to mice, she could talk to the fishes. The person who told him that was a rather fat old toad with beautiful golden eyes, and as toads like to be near water, and go splashing about in ponds, they know a little of the language of the fish, so the mouse asked the toad to pass his message on to them. And that was how the young woman finally heard about the stone.

Now it turned out that she had been searching for that stone a long while herself. When she heard where it was, she ran to find it, and when she saw it, she took it in her arms, warmed it and loved it. And then the stone came to life at last, and moved, raised its arms and put them round the woman. As for the mouse who had waited so long for that moment, he was happy, and after that he was called He-who-never-gives-up-hope. So you see, that's how it was. The mouse didn't make a great fuss about it, he just said: well, it wasn't that difficult. You only have to believe that love can bring anything to life, however dead it seems.'

Little Rikka had been lying in her cradle quite still all this while, looking at Listener with her eyes of that colour which was so hard to describe. When he fell silent, she said, 'Gives hope!' but no doubt that was imitation of the sound of the words, rather than proof that she understood their meaning. Who was I really telling that story for, Listener wondered: for this child? For the blacksmith, who is grieving for the death of his wife? For Arnilukka, the girl in the story? Or for myself? He could not say. But who knew if a child might not, after all, grasp something of the sense of such a tale?

* * *

Listener set off to ride back to the Shallow Valley a few days later. He led his horse while Arnilukka went with him to the borders of the woodland, holding his other hand to make it easier for him to go under the open, deep blue sky. It was clear, sunny autumn weather. The branches of the fruit trees on the grassy slope they were climbing were bent under their weight of apples and pears, and purple fruit hung in dark clusters among the leaves of the plum trees. Walking along, Arnilukka picked a red-tinged apple from the bough, took a bite and then gave it to Listener. As he bit it in his turn, the juice ran over his lips and filled his mouth, sweet and sharp at once. So they went together in silence to the hazel bushes beyond which the silvery grey trunks of the beeches rose. The beechnuts were not quite ripe yet, so they left the fringed clusters hanging there and embraced one another in farewell. 'I'll come over with little Rikka to see you in spring,' said Arnilukka.

'I shall not leave the Shallow Valley again,' said Listener, and it sounded so final to his own ears that he wondered if he had merely meant to tell Arnilukka she would find him there, or if there was something else behind the words. He looked into her eyes as if he could find the answer there, and went down once more into their mysterious, unfathomed play of blue, green and violet, which lapped around him like life itself. Then they kissed, and Listener mounted, not without some difficulty, while Arnilukka held his horse's bridle. This time she stood by the edge of the wood to watch him go. When he turned to look back, he could see her for some time standing in the emerald green of the sunlit meadow, until the trees of the wood, growing closer together, cut off his view.

He rode down the valley through the beeches until he could take the path to the Weird Wood. Soon he came up to the pines, with their thick layer of fallen needles underfoot to muffle his horse's hoofbeats. The wood smelled of mushrooms, and he saw them too, growing in the moss between the rough, brown tree-trunks, some bright yellow, some velvety brown, and mushrooms of every other shade as well. He did not trouble to dismount. There would be plenty more mushrooms growing in the woods of the Shallow Valley.

After he had been riding for some while along the path, which rose more and more steeply, he saw a man walking ahead of him among the lichen-hung trunks: a small and slightly stooping man, obviously going his way. Only when he was quite close did this man turn to look at the rider, and Listener recognized the prospector whom he had met several times before. He let his horse catch up with the old man, and was about to dismount to greet him, but the prospector shook his head and said, 'Stay in your saddle, Listener. You're not as young as you were, and the climb might be a strain on you.'

Listener was, in fact, relieved not to have to go this last and steepest part of the way on foot. He reached his hand down to the old man, who still seemed surprisingly hale and hearty, and said, 'I'm very glad to see you again. It looks as if we're going in the same direction.'

'Yes,' said the old man, 'and I'll gladly go part of the way with you this time, if you'll let your horse walk slowly enough.'

'Fair-mane won't mind that,' said Listener. 'He's not in his first youth either.'

So they went along side by side for a while, the old man on foot, Listener on horseback, and then the prospector said, 'Well, how have you been since last we talked? Were you able to fulfil the hopes they had of you in Arziak?'

Listener looked at the old man's wrinkled face and said, after a while, 'I don't know. I was too late to prevent the disaster that was brewing there, and I'm not sure if I could have stopped it if I'd arrived sooner. The quarrel between her brothers cost my daughter Urla her life, but her death reconciled the two of them.'

'She wore the stone,' said the old man, as if that explained it.

'Yes,' said Listener, 'and now I feel as if I killed her myself by giving her that gift; for I do at least know that the stone encouraged her to come between her brothers and stop one of them killing the other.'

'What you say about the stone is true,' said the old man. 'It made her sure that love was stronger than hate. And wasn't she right?'

'If you look at it that way, she was,' said Listener, 'but now she's not alive any more.'

'What do you mean by that?' asked the old man. 'You sound as if you had no idea what life means. Didn't you tell your little grand-daughter yourself, or maybe it was her father you were telling, that story of the lifeless stone which came alive when someone loved it?'

'How do you know?' asked Listener, and receiving no answer, went on, 'Anyway, it was just a story about things that actually happened to me.'

'I know,' said the old man. 'But what does that prove? You don't seem to have seen the point of your own story.' He paused for a moment to get his breath back, and then said, 'Didn't they need you as a fluter in Arziak, then?'

Listener nodded. 'Belarni had some such thing in mind when he wished for me there,' he said. 'But there was nothing much I could do apart from playing the children a song or so on my flute.'

'Is that nothing much?' said the old man. 'At least you stopped the children picking up Derli's mocking songs, and you made him ex-tremely unsure of himself too.'

'He didn't strike me as unsure of himself,' said Listener. 'Just angry.'

'You people are always angry when you're unsure of yourselves,' said the old man, smiling. 'No, Derli suddenly realized there was something missing from his songs, and he was too gifted a fluter not to hear that it was exactly the thing your little songs contained; that's what made him so unsure.'

'What was this thing, then?' asked Listener.

'You should know!' said the old man. 'It was to be heard in your music as long as you didn't lose your own temper: belief in the good, belief that no one can render it powerless. Even Narzia, with all her witchcraft, couldn't stop everything turning out well in the end.'

'Snowfinch knew that,' said Listener.

'Yes, well, he plays your silver flute,' said the old man, and once again it sounded like an explanation.

By now they had reached the Weird Wood. Pines grew to right and left of the path, broken by the wind, grotesquely distorted, but always reaching to the sky again, thickly hung with tangled grey beards of lichen.

'What are you planning to do now?' asked the prospector.

'Oh, turn a little wood on my lathe,' said Listener. 'There's plenty of wood here for making things.'

'As long as a man's occupied with something, he has hope,' said the old man, 'and you have your Piney too.'

They stopped among the last of the trees and looked out at the gentle swell of the grassy summit that rose before them in an almost green sky.

'Well, I'm going over the mountain now,' said the old man.

'That's a pity,' said Listener. 'I must stay under the trees.'

'Then rest under the rowan there a while,' said the old man. 'It's a good place.' And he waved to him once more, and then went slowly up the slope of the mountain meadow. The evening sun shone down on his back from the south-east, clear and bright, and by the time the old prospector had disappeared over the summit he looked like a great blazing golden flame.

Then it suddenly went dark, although the sun was still in the sky. Listener clung to his horse's back, swaying, and felt that the darkness was not outside him, but came from somewhere behind his own eyes. He just managed to get Fair-mane over to the old rowan, hardly minding that he had to ride a little way in the open before reaching shelter in the shade of the tree, with its countless bunches of bright red berries. He slipped out of his saddle and lay at the foot of the tree-trunk for some time, almost unconscious.

It was cold and dark when he opened his eyes again. And there was the Grey One, standing over him, looking at him with his empty eyes.

'I thought one was safe from the likes of you in this place,' said Listener.

'What do you take me for?' said the Grey One. 'Am I a troll from the Crooked Wood, or some such bugbear? I am everywhere, because I am that Nothing into which you're about to fall.' And when Listener went on looking at him, silently, he continued, 'What's become of your life now? You've lost all you had, and here you lie in the grass, a feeble old man with empty hands.'

On hearing the Grey One speak like that, Listener was overcome by tremendous anger. He rose, only to his knees at first, but then, with the help of the Piney, he managed to rise to his full height, so that he was eye to eye with the Grey One. 'You have no idea what I still have!' he shouted in the Grey One's face. 'I have it all in here!' And he struck his breast. 'The living light of the eye-stone, the sound of my flute – I still have it all!'

'Anything else?' said the Grey One, drily. 'None of that's worth more than an empty nutshell, you dreamer! Show it to me! Show me, if you can!'

'I can show you one thing, my colourless friend!' cried Listener, and suddenly he felt quite cheerful, for he actually did have something in his hands. 'My Piney here, that's what I'll show you!' And he took the stick by its thinner end, swung it up above his head, and brought it down with all the force of which his worn-out body was still capable between the grey phantom's empty eyes.

He ought to have known he would be striking at nothing. The impetus of the blow almost knocked him off his feet. As he watched the shape of the Grey One drift away like pale smoke, a stabbing pain went through his chest as if someone had run a dagger into his heart. He stood there upright a moment longer, and then collapsed.

When he opened his eyes again it was light. A broad, shining, golden sky stretched above the branches of the rowan tree, with a magnificent bright sun in it, but a sun at which he could look without being dazzled, a play of colour of indescribable variety, lovely as a living eye looking down on him and warming his heart with its light.

Listener lay there for a long time, glad of the sun. Then he rose, took his Piney in his hand, and came out from under the branches of the rowan. He hardly noticed that he could stand under that sky without any sense of oppression at all. He saw the gently rising summit of the mountain ahead of him, and felt a wish to climb to the top and admire the view. After a few steps, it occurred to him that he ought not to take anything at all on his way. There could be nothing better, he thought, than to walk empty-handed beneath this sky, so he drove the Piney into the meadow and went on up the slope.

Half-way up he looked back, and there was his Piney just putting out a few branches. Bunches of dark green needles emerged, the young tree grew with amazing power, shooting upwards until it towered hugely above the meadow, a copy of the tree it once had been, and the blue-green cones were already swelling in its crown, ripening and dropping their seeds, from which more stone pines shot up and grew to be mighty trees, and a sweet, resinous scent wafted from that splendid wood and rejoiced his heart. As he was still marvelling at the tall wood, he heard the sound of a flute, music that was lovelier than anything he had ever heard before. He listened to that indescribable melody, and then he saw who was playing it, for the Gentle Fluter stepped out of the wood from among the dark pyramids of the stone pines, his delicate hands playing an invisible instrument as he came towards Listener with his almost dancing step.

'So there you are at last,' he said, reaching him, yet while he spoke the wonderful music went on uninterrupted.

'How do you do that?' asked Listener. 'Your fingers move in the air as if you were holding a flute, and the music doesn't stop even when you talk!'

'Oh, there's nothing special about it,' said the Gentle Fluter. 'You'll learn quite soon. You only have to imagine music here and it begins to play. It's just an old habit of mine to keep moving my fingers too. Come over the mountain with me! We've been waiting for you. People such as you are needed here.'

'Needed?' repeated Listener. 'What use is a weak old man like me?' But even as he spoke he realized he was talking nonsense, for he felt so carefree and light-hearted that he could easily have run up the steep slope.

'There, you see?' said the Gentle Fluter. 'This is where it really all begins. What went before was only a faint dream of the beginning,

not all,

no,

very far from all.'

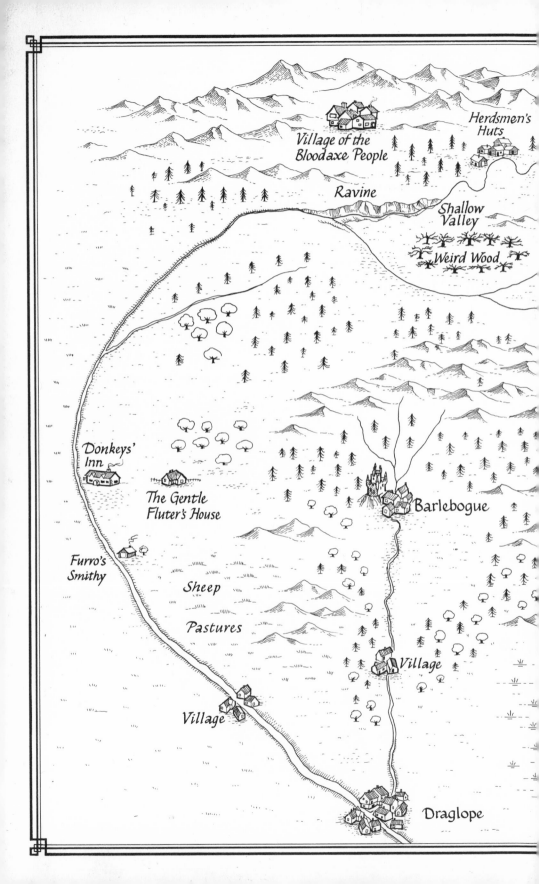